HERMAN MELVILLE

HERMAN MELVILLE

REDBURN
His First Voyage

WHITE-JACKET
or The World in a Man-of-War

MOBY-DICK
or, The Whale

THE LIBRARY OF AMERICA

The paper used in this publication meets the
minimum requirements of the American National Standard
for Information Sciences—Permanence of Paper for
Printed Library Materials, ANSI z39.48–1984.

Distributed to the trade in the United States
and Canada by the Viking Press.

Library of Congress Catalog Card Number: 82-18677
For Cataloging in Publication Data, see end of *Notes* section.
ISBN: 0-940450-09-7

Sixth Printing
The Library of America—9

Manufactured in the United States of America

G. THOMAS TANSELLE
WROTE THE NOTES AND CHRONOLOGY
AND SELECTED THE TEXTS
FOR THIS VOLUME

This volume prints the texts of Redburn, White-Jacket, and Moby-Dick from The Northwestern-Newberry Edition of The Writings of Herman Melville edited by Harrison Hayford, Hershel Parker, and G. Thomas Tanselle and published by Northwestern University Press and The Newberry Library, with the permission of the publishers.

Grateful acknowledgement is made to the National Endowment for the Humanities and the Ford Foundation for their generous financial support of this series.

Contents

REDBURN

His First Voyage

Being the Sailor-boy Confessions and Reminiscences of
the Son-of-a-Gentleman, in the Merchant Service

TO MY YOUNGER BROTHER
Thomas Melville
Now a Sailor on a Voyage to China
THIS VOLUME IS INSCRIBED

Contents

Chapter 1

WELLINGBOROUGH, as you are going to sea, suppose you take this shooting-jacket of mine along; it's just the thing—take it, it will save the expense of another. You see, it's quite warm; fine long skirts, stout horn buttons, and plenty of pockets."

Out of the goodness and simplicity of his heart, thus spoke my elder brother to me, upon the eve of my departure for the seaport.

"And, Wellingborough," he added, "since we are both short of money, and you want an outfit, and I have none to give, you may as well take my fowling-piece along, and sell it in New York for what you can get.—Nay, take it; it's of no use to me now; I can't find it in powder any more."

I was then but a boy. Some time previous my mother had removed from New York to a pleasant village on the Hudson River, where we lived in a small house, in a quiet way. Sad disappointments in several plans which I had sketched for my future life; the necessity of doing something for myself, united to a naturally roving disposition, had now conspired within me, to send me to sea as a sailor.

For months previous I had been poring over old New York papers, delightedly perusing the long columns of ship advertisements, all of which possessed a strange, romantic charm to me. Over and over again I devoured such announcements as the following:

FOR BREMEN.
*The coppered and copper-fastened brig Leda, having nearly
completed her cargo, will sail for the above port on Tuesday
the twentieth of May.
For freight or passage apply on board at Coenties Slip.*

To my young inland imagination every word in an advertisement like this, suggested volumes of thought.

A brig! The very word summoned up the idea of a black, sea-worn craft, with high, cozy bulwarks, and rakish masts and yards.

Coppered and copper-fastened! That fairly smelt of the salt water! How different such vessels must be from the wooden, one-masted, green-and-white-painted sloops, that glided up and down the river before our house on the bank.

Nearly completed her cargo! How momentous the announcement; suggesting ideas, too, of musty bales, and cases of silks and satins, and filling me with contempt for the vile deck-loads of hay and lumber, with which my river experience was familiar.

Will sail on Tuesday the 20th of May—and the newspaper bore date the fifth of the month! Fifteen whole days beforehand; think of that; what an important voyage it must be, that the time of sailing was fixed upon so long beforehand; the river sloops were not used to make such prospective announcements.

For freight or passage apply on board! Think of going on board a coppered and copper-fastened brig, and taking passage for Bremen! And who could be going to Bremen? No one but foreigners, doubtless; men of dark complexions and jet-black whiskers, who talked French.

Coenties Slip. Plenty more brigs and any quantity of ships must be lying there. Coenties Slip must be somewhere near ranges of grim-looking warehouses, with rusty iron doors and shutters, and tiled roofs; and old anchors and chain-cable piled on the walk. Old-fashioned coffee-houses, also, must abound in that neighborhood, with sunburnt sea-captains going in and out, smoking cigars, and talking about Havanna, London, and Calcutta.

All these my imaginations were wonderfully assisted by certain shadowy reminiscences of wharves, and warehouses, and shipping, with which a residence in a seaport during early childhood had supplied me.

Particularly, I remembered standing with my father on the wharf when a large ship was getting under way, and rounding the head of the pier. I remembered the *yo heave ho!* of the sailors, as they just showed their woolen caps above the high bulwarks. I remembered how I thought of their crossing the great ocean; and that that very ship, and those very sailors, so near to me then, would after a time be actually in Europe.

Added to these reminiscences my father, now dead, had several times crossed the Atlantic on business affairs, for he had been an importer in Broad-street. And of winter evenings in New York, by the well-remembered sea-coal fire in old Greenwich-street, he used to tell my brother and me of the monstrous waves at sea, mountain high; of the masts bending like twigs; and all about Havre, and Liverpool, and about going up into the ball of St. Paul's in London. Indeed, during my early life, most of my thoughts of the sea were connected with the land; but with fine old lands, full of mossy cathedrals and churches, and long, narrow, crooked streets without side-walks, and lined with strange houses. And especially I tried hard to think how such places must look of rainy days and Saturday afternoons; and whether indeed they did have rainy days and Saturdays there, just as we did here; and whether the boys went to school there, and studied geography, and wore their shirt collars turned over, and tied with a black ribbon; and whether their papas allowed them to wear boots, instead of shoes, which I so much disliked, for boots looked so manly.

As I grew older my thoughts took a larger flight, and I frequently fell into long reveries about distant voyages and travels, and thought how fine it would be, to be able to talk about remote and barbarous countries; with what reverence and wonder people would regard me, if I had just returned from the coast of Africa or New Zealand; how dark and romantic my sunburnt cheeks would look; how I would bring home with me foreign clothes of a rich fabric and princely make, and wear them up and down the streets, and how grocers' boys would turn back their heads to look at me, as I went by. For I very well remembered staring at a man myself, who was pointed out to me by my aunt one Sunday in Church, as the person who had been in Stony Arabia, and passed through strange adventures there, all of which with my own eyes I had read in the book which he wrote, an arid-looking book in a pale yellow cover.

"See what big eyes he has," whispered my aunt, "they got so big, because when he was almost dead with famishing in the desert, he all at once caught sight of a date tree, with the ripe fruit hanging on it."

Upon this, I stared at him till I thought his eyes were really of an uncommon size, and stuck out from his head like those of a lobster. I am sure my own eyes must have magnified as I stared. When church was out, I wanted my aunt to take me along and follow the traveler home. But she said the constables would take us up, if we did; and so I never saw this wonderful Arabian traveler again. But he long haunted me; and several times I dreamt of him, and thought his great eyes were grown still larger and rounder; and once I had a vision of the date tree.

In course of time, my thoughts became more and more prone to dwell upon foreign things; and in a thousand ways I sought to gratify my tastes. We had several pieces of furniture in the house, which had been brought from Europe. These I examined again and again, wondering where the wood grew; whether the workmen who made them still survived, and what they could be doing with themselves now.

Then we had several oil-paintings and rare old engravings of my father's, which he himself had bought in Paris, hanging up in the dining-room.

Two of these were sea-pieces. One represented a fat-looking, smoky fishing-boat, with three whiskerandoes in red caps, and their trowsers legs rolled up, hauling in a seine. There was high French-like land in one corner, and a tumbledown gray lighthouse surmounting it. The waves were toasted brown, and the whole picture looked mellow and old. I used to think a piece of it might taste good.

The other represented three old-fashioned French men-of-war with high castles, like pagodas, on the bow and stern, such as you see in Froissart; and snug little turrets on top of the mast, full of little men, with something undefinable in their hands. All three were sailing through a bright-blue sea, blue as Sicily skies; and they were leaning over on their sides at a fearful angle; and they must have been going very fast, for the white spray was about the bows like a snow-storm.

Then, we had two large green French portfolios of colored prints, more than I could lift at that age. Every Saturday my brothers and sisters used to get them out of the corner where they were kept, and spreading them on the floor, gaze at them with never-failing delight.

They were of all sorts. Some were pictures of Versailles, its masquerades, its drawing-rooms, its fountains, and courts, and gardens, with long lines of thick foliage cut into fantastic doors and windows, and towers and pinnacles. Others were rural scenes, full of fine skies, pensive cows standing up to the knees in water, and shepherd-boys and cottages in the distance, half concealed in vineyards and vines.

And others were pictures of natural history, representing rhinoceroses and elephants and spotted tigers; and above all there was a picture of a great whale, as big as a ship, stuck full of harpoons, and three boats sailing after it as fast as they could fly.

Then, too, we had a large library-case, that stood in the hall; an old brown library-case, tall as a small house; it had a sort of basement, with large doors, and a lock and key; and higher up, there were glass doors, through which might be seen long rows of old books, that had been printed in Paris, and London, and Leipsic. There was a fine library edition of the Spectator, in six large volumes with gilded backs; and many a time I gazed at the word "*London*" on the title-page. And there was a copy of D'Alembert in French, and I wondered what a great man I would be, if by foreign travel I should ever be able to read straight along without stopping, out of that book, which now was a riddle to every one in the house but my father, whom I so much liked to hear talk French, as he sometimes did to a servant we had.

That servant, too, I used to gaze at with wonder; for in answer to my incredulous cross-questions, he had over and over again assured me, that he had really been born in Paris. But this I never entirely believed; for it seemed so hard to comprehend, how a man who had been born in a foreign country, could be dwelling with me in our house in America.

As years passed on, this continual dwelling upon foreign associations, bred in me a vague prophetic thought, that I was fated, one day or other, to be a great voyager; and that just as my father used to entertain strange gentlemen over their wine after dinner, I would hereafter be telling my own adventures to an eager auditory. And I have no doubt that this presentiment had something to do with bringing about my subsequent rovings.

But that which perhaps more than any thing else, converted my vague dreamings and longings into a definite purpose of seeking my fortune on the sea, was an old-fashioned glass ship, about eighteen inches long, and of French manufacture, which my father, some thirty years before, had brought home from Hamburgh as a present to a great-uncle of mine: Senator Wellingborough, who had died a member of Congress in the days of the old Constitution, and after whom I had the honor of being named. Upon the decease of the Senator, the ship was returned to the donor.

It was kept in a square glass case, which was regularly dusted by one of my sisters every morning, and stood on a little claw-footed Dutch tea-table in one corner of the sitting-room. This ship, after being the admiration of my father's visitors in the capital, became the wonder and delight of all the people of the village where we now resided, many of whom used to call upon my mother, for no other purpose than to see the ship. And well did it repay the long and curious examinations which they were accustomed to give it.

In the first place, every bit of it was glass, and that was a great wonder of itself; because the masts, yards, and ropes were made to resemble exactly the corresponding parts of a real vessel that could go to sea. She carried two tiers of black guns all along her two decks; and often I used to try to peep in at the portholes, to see what else was inside; but the holes were so small, and it looked so very dark indoors, that I could discover little or nothing; though, when I was very little, I made no doubt, that if I could but once pry open the hull, and break the glass all to pieces, I would infallibly light upon something wonderful, perhaps some gold guineas, of which I have always been in want, ever since I could remember. And often I used to feel a sort of insane desire to be the death of the glass ship, case, and all, in order to come at the plunder; and one day, throwing out some hint of the kind to my sisters, they ran to my mother in a great clamor; and after that, the ship was placed on the mantle-piece for a time, beyond my reach, and until I should recover my reason.

I do not know how to account for this temporary madness

of mine, unless it was, that I had been reading in a story-book about Captain Kidd's ship, that lay somewhere at the bottom of the Hudson near the Highlands, full of gold as it could be; and that a company of men were trying to dive down and get the treasure out of the hold, which no one had ever thought of doing before, though there she had lain for almost a hundred years.

Not to speak of the tall masts, and yards, and rigging of this famous ship, among whose mazes of spun-glass I used to rove in imagination, till I grew dizzy at the main-truck, I will only make mention of the people on board of her. They, too, were all of glass, as beautiful little glass sailors as any body ever saw, with hats and shoes on, just like living men, and curious blue jackets with a sort of ruffle round the bottom. Four or five of these sailors were very nimble little chaps, and were mounting up the rigging with very long strides; but for all that, they never gained a single inch in the year, as I can take my oath.

Another sailor was sitting astride of the spanker-boom, with his arms over his head, but I never could find out what that was for; a second was in the fore-top, with a coil of glass rigging over his shoulder; the cook, with a glass ax, was split-ting wood near the fore-hatch; the steward, in a glass apron, was hurrying toward the cabin with a plate of glass pudding; and a glass dog, with a red mouth, was barking at him; while the captain in a glass cap was smoking a glass cigar on the quarter-deck. He was leaning against the bulwark, with one hand to his head; perhaps he was unwell, for he looked very glassy out of the eyes.

The name of this curious ship was *La Reine*, or The Queen, which was painted on her stern where any one might read it, among a crowd of glass dolphins and sea-horses carved there in a sort of semicircle.

And this Queen rode undisputed mistress of a green glassy sea, some of whose waves were breaking over her bow in a wild way, I can tell you, and I used to be giving her up for lost and foundered every moment, till I grew older, and per-ceived that she was not in the slightest danger in the world.

A good deal of dust, and fuzzy stuff like down, had in the course of many years worked through the joints of the case, in which the ship was kept, so as to cover all the sea with a light dash of white, which if any thing improved the general effect, for it looked like the foam and froth raised by the terrible gale the good Queen was battling against.

So much for *La Reine*. We have her yet in the house, but many of her glass spars and ropes are now sadly shattered and broken,—but I will not have her mended; and her figurehead, a gallant warrior in a cocked-hat, lies pitching head-foremost down into the trough of a calamitous sea under the bows—but I will not have him put on his legs again, till I get on my own; for between him and me there is a secret sympathy; and my sisters tell me, even yet, that he fell from his perch the very day I left home to go to sea on this *my first voyage*.

Chapter 2

REDBURN'S DEPARTURE FROM HOME

IT WAS WITH A HEAVY HEART and full eyes, that my poor mother parted with me; perhaps she thought me an erring and a willful boy, and perhaps I was; but if I was, it had been a hardhearted world, and hard times that had made me so. I had learned to think much and bitterly before my time; all my young mounting dreams of glory had left me; and at that early age, I was as unambitious as a man of sixty.

Yes, I will go to sea; cut my kind uncles and aunts, and sympathizing patrons, and leave no heavy hearts but those in my own home, and take none along but the one which aches in my bosom. Cold, bitter cold as December, and bleak as its blasts, seemed the world then to me; there is no misanthrope like a boy disappointed; and such was I, with the warm soul of me flogged out by adversity. But these thoughts are bitter enough even now, for they have not yet gone quite away; and they must be uncongenial enough to the reader; so no more of that, and let me go on with my story.

"Yes, I will write you, dear mother, as soon as I can," murmured I, as she charged me for the hundredth time, not to fail to inform her of my safe arrival in New York.

"And now Mary, Martha, and Jane, kiss me all round, dear sisters, and then I am off. I'll be back in four months—it will be autumn then, and we'll go into the woods after nuts, and I'll tell you all about Europe. Good-by! good-by!"

So I broke loose from their arms, and not daring to look behind, ran away as fast as I could, till I got to the corner where my brother was waiting. He accompanied me part of the way to the place, where the steamboat was to leave for New York; instilling into me much sage advice above his age, for he was but eight years my senior, and warning me again and again to take care of myself; and I solemnly promised I would; for what cast-away will not promise to take care of himself, when he sees that unless he himself does, no one else will.

We walked on in silence till I saw that his strength was giving out,—he was in ill health then,—and with a mute grasp of the hand, and a loud thump at the heart, we parted.

It was early on a raw, cold, damp morning toward the end of spring, and the world was before me; stretching away a long muddy road, lined with comfortable houses, whose inmates were taking their sunrise naps, heedless of the wayfarer passing. The cold drops of drizzle trickled down my leather cap, and mingled with a few hot tears on my cheeks.

I had the whole road to myself, for no one was yet stirring, and I walked on, with a slouching, dogged gait. The gray shooting-jacket was on my back, and from the end of my brother's rifle hung a small bundle of my clothes. My fingers worked moodily at the stock and trigger, and I thought that this indeed was the way to begin life, with a gun in your hand!

Talk not of the bitterness of middle-age and after life; a boy can feel all that, and much more, when upon his young soul the mildew has fallen; and the fruit, which with others is only blasted after ripeness, with him is nipped in the first blossom and bud. And never again can such blights be made good; they strike in too deep, and leave such a scar that the air of Paradise might not erase it. And it is a hard and cruel thing thus in early youth to taste beforehand the pangs which should be reserved for the stout time of manhood, when the gristle has become bone, and we stand up and fight out our lives, as a thing tried before and foreseen; for then we are veterans used to sieges and battles, and not green recruits, recoiling at the first shock of the encounter.

At last gaining the boat we pushed off, and away we steamed down the Hudson. There were few passengers on board, the day was so unpleasant; and they were mostly congregated in the after cabin round the stoves. After breakfast, some of them went to reading; others took a nap on the settees; and others sat in silent circles, speculating, no doubt, as to who each other might be.

They were certainly a cheerless set, and to me they all looked stony-eyed and heartless. I could not help it, I almost hated them; and to avoid them, went on deck, but a storm of sleet drove me below. At last I bethought me, that I had not procured a ticket, and going to the captain's office to pay my passage and get one, was horror-struck to find, that the price of passage had been suddenly raised that day, owing to the other boats not running; so that I had not enough money to pay for my fare. I had supposed it would be but a dollar, and only a dollar did I have, whereas it was two. What was to be done? The boat was off, and there was no backing out; so I determined to say nothing to any body, and grimly wait until called upon for my fare.

The long weary day wore on till afternoon; one incessant storm raged on deck; but after dinner the few passengers, waked up with their roast-beef and mutton, became a little more sociable. Not with me, for the scent and savor of poverty was upon me, and they all cast toward me their evil eyes and cold suspicious glances, as I sat apart, though among them. I felt that desperation and recklessness of poverty which only a pauper knows. There was a mighty patch upon one leg of my trowsers, neatly sewed on, for it had been executed by my mother, but still very obvious and incontrovertible to the eye. This patch I had hitherto studiously endeavored to hide with the ample skirts of my shooting jacket; but now I stretched out my leg boldly, and thrust the patch under their noses, and looked at them so, that they soon looked away, boy though I was. Perhaps the gun that I clenched frightened them into respect; or there might have been something ugly in my eye; or my teeth were white, and my jaws were set. For several hours, I sat gazing at a jovial party seated round a mahogany table, with some crackers and cheese, and wine and cigars. Their faces were flushed with the good dinner they had eaten; and mine felt pale and wan with a long fast. If I had presumed to offer to make one of their party; if I had told them of my circumstances, and solicited something to refresh me, I very well knew from the peculiar hollow ring of their laughter, they would have had the waiters put me out of the cabin, for a beggar, who had no business to be warming himself at their stove. And for that insult, though only a conceit, I sat and gazed at them, putting up no petitions for their prosperity. My whole soul was soured within me, and when at last the captain's clerk, a slender young man, dressed in the height of fashion, with a gold

watch chain and broach, came round collecting the tickets, I
buttoned up my coat to the throat, clutched my gun, put on
my leather cap, and pulling it well down, stood up like a sentry before him. He held out his hand, deeming any remark
superfluous, as his object in pausing before me must be obvious. But I stood motionless and silent, and in a moment he
saw how it was with me. I ought to have spoken and told
him the case, in plain, civil terms, and offered my dollar, and
then waited the event. But I felt too wicked for that. He did
not wait a great while, but spoke first himself; and in a gruff
voice, very unlike his urbane accents when accosting the wine
and cigar party, demanded my ticket. I replied that I had
none. He then demanded the money; and upon my answering that I had not enough, in a loud angry voice that attracted
all eyes, he ordered me out of the cabin into the storm. The
devil in me then mounted up from my soul, and spread over
my frame, till it tingled at my finger ends; and I muttered out
my resolution to stay where I was, in such a manner, that the
ticket man faltered back.

"There's a dollar for you," I added, offering it.

"I want two," said he.

"Take that or nothing," I answered; "it is all I have."

I thought he would strike me. But, accepting the money,
he contented himself with saying something about sportsmen
going on shooting expeditions, without having money to pay
their expenses; and hinted that such chaps might better lay
aside their fowling pieces, and assume the buck and saw. He
then passed on, and left every eye fastened upon me.

I stood their gazing some time, but at last could stand it
no more. I pushed my seat right up before the most insolent
gazer, a short fat man, with a plethora of cravat round his
neck, and fixing my gaze on his, gave him more gazes than
he sent. This somewhat embarrassed him, and he looked
round for some one to take hold of me; but no one coming,
he pretended to be very busy counting the gilded wooden
beams overhead. I then turned to the next gazer, and clicking
my gun-lock, deliberately presented the piece at him.

Upon this, he overset his seat in his eagerness to get beyond my range, for I had him point blank, full in the left eye;
and several persons starting to their feet, exclaimed that I

must be crazy. So I was at that time; for otherwise I know not how to account for my demoniac feelings, of which I was afterward heartily ashamed, as I ought to have been, indeed; and much more than that.

I then turned on my heel, and shouldering my fowling-piece and bundle, marched on deck, and walked there through the dreary storm, till I was wet through, and the boat touched the wharf at New York.

Such is boyhood.

Chapter 3

He Arrives in Town

FROM THE BOAT'S BOW, I jumped ashore, before she was secured, and following my brother's directions, proceeded across the town toward St. John's Park, to the house of a college friend of his, for whom I had a letter.

It was a long walk; and I stepped in at a sort of grocery to get a drink of water, where some six or eight rough looking fellows were playing dominoes upon the counter, seated upon cheese boxes. They winked, and asked what sort of sport I had had gunning on such a rainy day, but I only gulped down my water and stalked off.

Dripping like a seal, I at last grounded arms at the doorway of my brother's friend, rang the bell and inquired for him.

"What do you want?" said the servant, eying me as if I were a housebreaker.

"I want to see your lord and master; show me into the parlor."

Upon this my host himself happened to make his appearance, and seeing who I was, opened his hand and heart to me at once, and drew me to his fireside; he had received a letter from my brother, and had expected me that day.

The family were at tea; the fragrant herb filled the room with its aroma; the brown toast was odoriferous; and every thing pleasant and charming. After a temporary warming, I was shown to a room, where I changed my wet dress, and returning to the table, found that the interval had been well improved by my hostess; a meal for a traveler was spread, and I laid into it sturdily. Every mouthful pushed the devil that had been tormenting me all day farther and farther out of me, till at last I entirely ejected him with three successive bowls of Bohea.

Magic of kind words, and kind deeds, and good tea! That night I went to bed thinking the world pretty tolerable, after all; and I could hardly believe that I had really acted that morning as I had, for I was naturally of an easy and forbearing disposition; though when such a disposition is temporarily roused, it is perhaps worse than a cannibal's.

Next day, my brother's friend, whom I choose to call Mr. Jones, accompanied me down to the docks among the shipping, in order to get me a place. After a good deal of searching, we lighted upon a ship for Liverpool, and found the captain in the cabin; which was a very handsome one, lined with mahogany and maple; and the steward, an elegant looking mulatto in a gorgeous turban, was setting out on a sort of sideboard some dinner service which looked like silver, but it was only Britannia ware highly polished.

As soon as I clapped my eye on the captain, I thought to myself he was just the captain to suit me. He was a fine looking man, about forty, splendidly dressed, with very black whiskers, and very white teeth, and what I took to be a free, frank look out of a large hazel eye. I liked him amazingly. He was promenading up and down the cabin, humming some brisk air to himself when we entered.

"Good morning, sir," said my friend.

"Good morning, good morning, sir," said the captain. "Steward, chairs for the gentlemen."

"Oh! never mind, sir," said Mr. Jones, rather taken aback by his extreme civility. "I merely called to see whether you want a fine young lad to go to sea with you. Here he is; he has long wanted to be a sailor; and his friends have at last concluded to let him go for one voyage, and see how he likes it."

"Ah! indeed!" said the captain, blandly, and looking where I stood. "He's a fine fellow; I like him. So you want to be a sailor, my boy, do you?" added he, affectionately patting my head. "It's a hard life, though; a hard life."

But when I looked round at his comfortable, and almost luxurious cabin, and then at his handsome care-free face, I thought he was only trying to frighten me, and I answered, "Well, sir, I am ready to try it."

"I hope he's a country lad, sir," said the captain to my friend, "these city boys are sometimes hard cases."

"Oh! yes, he's from the country," was the reply, "and of a highly respectable family; his great-uncle died a Senator."

"But his great-uncle don't want to go to sea too?" said the captain, looking funny.

"Oh! no, oh, no!—Ha! ha!"

"Ha! ha!" echoed the captain.

A fine funny gentleman, thought I, not much fancying, however, his levity concerning my great-uncle, he'll be cracking his jokes the whole voyage; and so I afterward said to one of the riggers on board; but he bade me look out, that he did not crack my head.

"Well, my lad," said the captain, "I suppose you know we havn't any pastures and cows on board; you can't get any milk at sea, you know."

"Oh! I know all about that, sir; my father has crossed the ocean, if I havn't."

"Yes," cried my friend, "his father, a gentleman of one of the first families in America, crossed the Atlantic several times on important business."

"Embassador extraordinary?" said the captain, looking funny again.

"Oh! no, he was a wealthy merchant."

"Ah! indeed!" said the captain, looking grave and bland again, "then this fine lad is the son of a gentleman?"

"Certainly," said my friend, "and he's only going to sea for the humor of it; they want to send him on his travels with a tutor, but he *will* go to sea as a sailor."

The fact was, that my young friend (for he was only about twenty-five) was not a very wise man; and this was a huge fib, which out of the kindness of his heart, he told in my behalf, for the purpose of creating a profound respect for me in the eyes of my future lord.

Upon being apprized, that I had willfully forborne taking the grand tour with a tutor, in order to put my hand in a tar-bucket, the handsome captain looked ten times more funny than ever; and said that *he* himself would be my tutor, and take me on my travels, and pay for the privilege.

"Ah!" said my friend, "that reminds me of business. Pray, captain, how much do you generally pay a handsome young fellow like this?"

"Well," said the captain, looking grave and profound, "we are not so particular about beauty, and we never give more than three dollars to a green lad like Wellingborough here, that's your name, my boy? Wellingborough Redburn!— Upon my soul, a fine sounding name."

"Why, captain," said Mr. Jones, quickly interrupting him, "that won't pay for his clothing."

"But you know his highly respectable and wealthy relations will doubtless see to all that," replied the captain, with his funny look again.

"Oh! yes, I forgot that," said Mr. Jones, looking rather foolish. "His friends will of course see to that."

"Of course," said the captain smiling.

"Of course," repeated Mr. Jones, looking ruefully at the patch on my pantaloons, which just then I endeavored to hide with the skirt of my shooting-jacket.

"You are quite a sportsman I see," said the captain, eying the great buttons on my coat, upon each of which was a carved fox.

Upon this my benevolent friend thought that here was a grand opportunity to befriend me.

"Yes, he's quite a sportsman," said he, "he's got a very valuable fowling-piece at home, perhaps you would like to purchase it, captain, to shoot gulls with at sea? It's cheap."

"Oh! no, he had better leave it with his relations," said the captain, "so that he can go hunting again when he returns from England."

"Yes, perhaps that *would* be better, after all," said my friend, pretending to fall into a profound musing, involving all sides of the matter in hand. "Well, then, captain, you can only give the boy three dollars a month, you say?"

"Only three dollars a month," said the captain.

"And I believe," said my friend, "that you generally give something in advance, do you not?"

"Yes, that is sometimes the custom at the shipping offices," said the captain, with a bow, "but in this case, as the boy has rich relations, there will be no need of that, you know."

And thus, by his ill-advised, but well-meaning hints concerning the respectability of my paternity, and the immense wealth of my relations, did this really honest-hearted but foolish friend of mine, prevent me from getting three dollars in advance, which I greatly needed. However, I said nothing, though I thought the more; and particularly, how that it would have been much better for me, to have gone on board alone, accosted the captain on my own account, and told him the plain truth. Poor people make a very poor business of it when they try to seem rich.

The arrangement being concluded, we bade the captain good-morning; and as we were about leaving the cabin, he smiled again, and said, "Well, Redburn, my boy, you won't get home-sick before you sail, because that will make you very sea-sick when you get to sea."

And with that he smiled very pleasantly, and bowed two or three times, and told the steward to open the cabin-door, which the steward did with a peculiar sort of grin on his face, and a slanting glance at my shooting-jacket.

And so we left.

Chapter 4

How He Disposed of His Fowling-Piece

NEXT DAY I WENT ALONE to the shipping office to sign the articles, and there I met a great crowd of sailors, who as soon as they found what I was after, began to tip the wink all round, and I overheard a fellow in a great flapping sou'-wester cap say to another old tar in a shaggy monkey-jacket, "Twig his coat, d'ye see the buttons, that chap ain't going to sea in a merchantman, he's going to shoot whales. I say, maty—look here—how d'ye sell them big buttons, by the pound?"

"Give us one for a saucer, will ye?" said another.

"Let the youngster alone," said a third. "Come here, my little boy, has your ma put up some sweetmeats for ye to take to sea?"

They are all witty dogs, thought I to myself, trying to make the best of the matter, for I saw it would not do to resent what they said; they can't mean any harm, though they are certainly very impudent; so I tried to laugh off their banter, but as soon as ever I could, I put down my name and beat a retreat.

On the morrow, the ship was advertised to sail. So the rest of that day I spent in preparations. After in vain trying to sell my fowling-piece for a fair price to chance customers, I was walking up Chatham-street with it, when a curly-headed little man with a dark oily face, and a hooked nose, like the pictures of Judas Iscariot, called to me from a strange-looking shop, with three gilded balls hanging over it.

With a peculiar accent, as if he had been over-eating himself with Indian-pudding or some other plushy compound, this curly headed little man very civilly invited me into his shop; and making a polite bow, and bidding me many unnecessary good mornings, and remarking upon the fine weather, begged me to let him look at my fowling-piece. I handed it to him in an instant, glad of the chance of disposing of it, and told him that was just what I wanted.

"Ah!" said he, with his Indian-pudding accent again, which I will not try to mimic, and abating his look of eagerness, "I thought it was a better article, it's very old."

"No," said I, starting in surprise, "it's not been used more than three times; what will you give for it?"

"We dont *buy* any thing here," said he, suddenly looking very indifferent, "this is a place where people *pawn* things."

Pawn being a word I had never heard before, I asked him what it meant; when he replied, that when people wanted any money, they came to him with their fowling-pieces, and got one third its value, and then left the fowling-piece there, until they were able to pay back the money.

What a benevolent little old man, this must be, thought I, and how very obliging.

"And pray," said I, "how much will you let me have for my gun, by way of a pawn?"

"Well, I suppose it's worth six dollars, and seeing you're a boy, I'll let you have three dollars upon it."

"No," exclaimed I, seizing the fowling piece, "it's worth five times that, I'll go somewhere else."

"Good morning, then," said he, "I hope you'll do better," and he bowed me out as if he expected to see me again pretty soon.

I had not gone very far, when I came across three more balls hanging over a shop. In I went, and saw a long counter, with a sort of picket-fence, running all along from end to end, and three little holes, with three little old men standing inside of them, like prisoners looking out of a jail. Back of the counter were all sorts of things, piled up and labeled. Hats, and caps, and coats, and guns, and swords, and canes, and chests, and planes, and books, and writing-desks, and every thing else. And in a glass case were lots of watches, and seals, chains, and rings, and breastpins, and all kinds of trinkets. At one of the little holes, earnestly talking with one of the hook-nosed men, was a thin woman in a faded silk gown and shawl, holding a pale little girl by the hand. As I drew near, she spoke lower in a whisper; and the man shook his head, and looked cross and rude; and then some more words were exchanged over a miniature, and some money was passed through the hole, and the woman and child shrank out of the door.

I won't sell my gun to that man, thought I; and I passed on to the next hole; and while waiting there to be served, an elderly man in a high-waisted surtout, thrust a silver snuff-box through; and a young man in a calico shirt and a shiny coat with a velvet collar presented a silver watch; and a sheepish boy in a cloak took out a frying-pan; and another little boy had a Bible; and all these things were thrust through to the hook-nosed man, who seemed ready to hook any thing that came along; so I had no doubt he would gladly hook my gun, for the long picketed counter seemed like a great seine, that caught every variety of fish.

At last I saw a chance, and crowded in for the hole; and in order to be beforehand with a big man who just then came in, I pushed my gun violently through the hole; upon which the hook-nosed man cried out, thinking I was going to shoot him. But at last he took the gun, turned it end for end, clicked the trigger three times, and then said, "one dollar."

"What about one dollar?" said I.

"That's all I'll give," he replied.

"Well, what do you want?" and he turned to the next person. This was a young man in a seedy red cravat and a pimply face, that looked as if it was going to seed likewise, who, with a mysterious tapping of his vest-pocket and other hints, made a great show of having something confidential to communicate.

But the hook-nosed man spoke out very loud, and said, "None of that; take it out. Got a stolen watch? We don't deal in them things here."

Upon this the young man flushed all over, and looked round to see who had heard the pawnbroker; then he took something very small out of his pocket, and keeping it hidden under his palm, pushed it into the hole.

"Where did you get this ring?" said the pawnbroker.

"I want to pawn it," whispered the other, blushing all over again.

"What's your name?" said the pawnbroker, speaking very loud.

"How much will you give?" whispered the other in reply, leaning over, and looking as if he wanted to hush up the pawnbroker.

At last the sum was agreed upon, when the man behind the counter took a little ticket, and tying the ring to it began to write on the ticket; all at once he asked the young man where he lived, a question which embarrassed him very much; but at last he stammered out a certain number in Broadway.

"That's the City Hotel: you don't live there," said the man, cruelly glancing at the shabby coat before him.

"Oh! well," stammered the other blushing scarlet, "I thought this was only a sort of form to go through; I don't like to tell where I do live, for I ain't in the habit of going to pawnbrokers."

"You stole that ring, you know you did," roared out the hook-nosed man, incensed at this slur upon his calling, and now seemingly bent on damaging the young man's character for life. "I'm a good mind to call a constable; we don't take stolen goods here, I tell you."

All eyes were now fixed suspiciously upon this martyrized young man; who looked ready to drop into the earth; and a poor woman in a night-cap, with some baby-clothes in her hand, looked fearfully at the pawnbroker, as if dreading to encounter such a terrible pattern of integrity. At last the young man slunk off with his money, and looking out of the window, I saw him go round the corner so sharply that he knocked his elbow against the wall.

I waited a little longer, and saw several more served; and having remarked that the hook-nosed men invariably fixed their own price upon every thing, and if that was refused told the person to be off with himself; I concluded that it would be of no use to try and get more from them than they had offered; especially when I saw that they had a great many fowling-pieces hanging up, and did not have particular occasion for mine; and more than that, they must be very well off and rich, to treat people so cavalierly.

My best plan then seemed to be, to go right back to the curly-headed pawnbroker, and take up with my first offer. But when I went back, the curly-headed man was very busy about something else, and kept me waiting a long time; at last I got a chance and told him I would take the three dollars he had offered.

"Ought to have taken it when you could get it," he replied. "I won't give but two dollars and a half for it now."

In vain I expostulated; he was not to be moved, so I pocketed the money and departed.

Chapter 5

He Purchases His Sea-Wardrobe, and on a
Dismal Rainy Day Picks Up His Board and
Lodging along the Wharves

THE FIRST THING I now did was to buy a little stationery,
and keep my promise to my mother, by writing her; and
I also wrote to my brother, informing him of the voyage I
purposed making, and indulging in some romantic and misanthropic views of life, such as many boys in my circumstances, are accustomed to do.

The rest of the two dollars and a half I laid out that very
morning in buying a red woolen shirt near Catharine Market,
a tarpaulin hat, which I got at an out-door stand near Peck
Slip, a belt and jack-knife, and two or three trifles. After these
purchases, I had only one penny left, so I walked out to the
end of the pier, and threw the penny into the water. The
reason why I did this, was because I somehow felt almost
desperate again, and didn't care what became of me. But if
the penny had been a dollar, I would have kept it.

I went home to dinner at Mr. Jones', and they welcomed
me very kindly, and Mrs. Jones kept my plate full all the time
during dinner, so that I had no chance to empty it. She
seemed to see that I felt bad, and thought plenty of pudding
might help me. At any rate, I never felt so bad yet, but I
could eat a good dinner. And once, years afterward, when I
expected to be killed every day, I remember my appetite was
very keen, and I said to myself, "Eat away, Wellingborough,
while you can, for this may be the last supper you will have."

After dinner I went into my room, locked the door carefully, and hung a towel over the knob, so that no one could
peep through the keyhole, and then went to trying on my red
woolen shirt before the glass, to see what sort of a looking
sailor I was going to make. As soon as I got into the shirt I
began to feel a sort of warm and red about the face, which I
found was owing to the reflection of the dyed wool upon my
skin. After that, I took a pair of scissors and went to cutting

30

my hair, which was very long. I thought every little would help, in making me a light hand to run aloft.

Next morning I bade my kind host and hostess good-by, and left the house with my bundle, feeling somewhat misanthropical and desperate again.

Before I reached the ship, it began to rain hard; and as soon as I arrived at the wharf, it was plain that there would be no getting to sea that day.

This was a great disappointment to me, for I did not want to return to Mr. Jones' again after bidding them good-by; it would be so awkward. So I concluded to go on board ship for the present.

When I reached the deck, I saw no one but a large man in a large dripping pea-jacket, who was calking down the main-hatches.

"What do you want, Pillgarlic?" said he.

"I've shipped to sail in this ship," I replied, assuming a little dignity, to chastise his familiarity.

"What for? a tailor?" said he, looking at my shooting jacket.

I answered that I was going as a "boy;" for so I was technically put down on the articles.

"Well," said he, "have you got your traps aboard?"

I told him I didn't know there were any rats in the ship, and hadn't brought any "trap."

At this he laughed out with a great guffaw, and said there must be hay-seed in my hair.

This made me mad; but thinking he must be one of the sailors who was going in the ship, I thought it wouldn't be wise to make an enemy of him, so only asked him where the men slept in the vessel, for I wanted to put my clothes away.

"*Where's* your clothes?" said he.

"Here in my bundle," said I, holding it up.

"Well if that's all you've got," he cried, "you'd better chuck it overboard. But go forward, go forward to the forecastle; that's the place you'll live in aboard here."

And with that he directed me to a sort of hole in the deck in the bow of the ship; but looking down, and seeing how dark it was, I asked him for a light.

"Strike your eyes together and make one," said he, "we

don't have any lights here." So I groped my way down into the forecastle, which smelt so bad of old ropes and tar, that it almost made me sick. After waiting patiently, I began to see a little; and looking round, at last perceived I was in a smoky looking place, with twelve wooden boxes stuck round the sides. In some of these boxes were large chests, which I at once supposed to belong to the sailors, who must have taken that method of appropriating their "bunks," as I afterward found these boxes were called. And so it turned out.

After examining them for a while, I selected an empty one, and put my bundle right in the middle of it, so that there might be no mistake about my claim to the place, particularly as the bundle was so small.

This done, I was glad to get on deck; and learning to a certainty that the ship would not sail till the next day, I resolved to go ashore, and walk about till dark, and then return and sleep out the night in the forecastle. So I walked about all over, till I was weary, and went into a mean liquor shop to rest; for having my tarpaulin on, and not looking very gentlemanly, I was afraid to go into any better place, for fear of being driven out. Here I sat till I began to feel very hungry; and seeing some doughnuts on the counter, I began to think what a fool I had been, to throw away my last penny; for the doughnuts were but a penny apiece, and they looked very plump, and fat, and round. I never saw doughnuts look so enticing before; especially when a negro came in, and ate one before my eyes. At last I thought I would fill up a little by drinking a glass of water; having read somewhere that this was a good plan to follow in a case like the present. I did not feel thirsty, but only hungry; so had much ado to get down the water; for it tasted warm; and the tumbler had an ugly flavor; the negro had been drinking some spirits out of it just before.

I marched off again, every once in a while stopping to take in some more water, and being very careful not to step into the same shop twice, till night came on, and I found myself soaked through, for it had been raining more or less all day. As I went to the ship, I could not help thinking how lonesome it would be, to spend the whole night in that damp and dark forecastle, without light or fire, and nothing to lie on but the bare boards of my bunk. However, to drown all such thoughts, I gulped down another glass of water, though I was wet enough outside and in by this time; and trying to put on a bold look, as if I had just been eating a hearty meal, I stepped aboard the ship.

The man in the big pea-jacket was not to be seen; but on going forward I unexpectedly found a young lad there, about my own age; and as soon as he opened his mouth I knew he was not an American. He talked such a curious language though, half English and half gibberish, that I knew not what to make of him; and was a little astonished, when he told me he was an English boy, from Lancashire.

It seemed, he had come over from Liverpool in this very ship on her last voyage, as a steerage passenger; but finding that he would have to work very hard to get along in America, and getting home-sick into the bargain, he had arranged with the captain to work his passage back.

I was glad to have some company, and tried to get him conversing; but found he was the most stupid and ignorant boy I had ever met with. I asked him something about the river Thames; when he said that he hadn't traveled any in America and didn't know any thing about the rivers here. And when I told him the river Thames was in England, he showed no surprise or shame at his ignorance, but only looked ten times more stupid than before.

At last we went below into the forecastle, and both getting into the same bunk, stretched ourselves out on the planks, and I tried my best to get asleep. But though my companion soon began to snore very loud, for me, I could not forget myself, owing to the horrid smell of the place, my being so wet, cold, and hungry, and besides all that, I felt damp and clammy about the heart. I lay turning over and over, listening to the Lancashire boy's snoring, till at last I felt so, that I had to go on deck; and there I walked till morning, which I thought would never come.

As soon as I thought the groceries on the wharf would be open I left the ship and went to make my breakfast of another glass of water. But this made me very qualmish; and soon I felt sick as death; my head was dizzy; and I went staggering along the walk, almost blind. At last I dropt on a heap of chain-cable, and shutting my eyes hard, did my best to rally myself, in which I succeeded, at last, enough to get up and walk off. Then I thought that I had done wrong in not returning to my friend's house the day before; and would have walked there now, as it was, only it was at least three miles up town; too far for me to walk in such a state, and I had no sixpence to ride in an omnibus.

Chapter 6

He is Initiated in the Business of Cleaning Out the Pig-Pen, and Slushing Down the Top-Mast

B Y THE TIME I got back to the ship, every thing was in an uproar. The pea-jacket man was there, ordering about a good many men in the rigging, and people were bringing off chickens, and pigs, and beef, and vegetables from the shore. Soon after, another man, in a striped calico shirt, a short blue jacket and beaver hat, made his appearance, and went to ordering about the man in the big pea-jacket; and at last the captain came up the side, and began to order about both of them.

These two men turned out to be the first and second mates of the ship.

Thinking to make friends with the second mate, I took out an old tortoise-shell snuff-box of my father's, in which I had put a piece of Cavendish tobacco, to look sailor-like, and offered the box to him very politely. He stared at me a moment, and then exclaimed, "Do you think we take snuff aboard here, youngster? no, no, no time for snuff-taking at sea; don't let the 'old man' see that snuff-box; take my advice and pitch it overboard as quick as you can."

I told him it was not snuff, but tobacco; when he said, he had plenty of tobacco of his own, and never carried any such nonsense about him as a tobacco-box. With that, he went off about his business, and left me feeling foolish enough. But I had reason to be glad he had acted thus, for if he had not, I think I should have offered my box to the chief mate, who in that case, from what I afterward learned of him, would have knocked me down, or done something else equally uncivil.

As I was standing looking round me, the chief mate approached in a great hurry about something, and seeing me in his way, cried out, "Ashore with you, you young loafer! There's no stealings here; sail away, I tell you, with that shooting-jacket!"

Upon this I retreated, saying that I was going out in the
ship as a sailor.

"A sailor!" he cried, "a barber's clerk, you mean; *you* going
out in the ship? what, in that jacket? Hang me, I hope the
old man hasn't been shipping any more greenhorns like
you—he'll make a shipwreck of it if he has. But this is the
way nowadays; to save a few dollars in seamen's wages, they
think nothing of shipping a parcel of farmers and clodhoppers
and baby-boys. What's your name, Pillgarlic?"

"Redburn," said I.

"A pretty handle to a man, that; scorch you to take hold of
it; havn't you got any other?"

"Wellingborough," said I.

"Worse yet. Who had the baptizing of ye? Why didn't they
call you Jack, or Jill, or something short and handy. But I'll
baptize you over again. D'ye hear, sir, henceforth your name
is *Buttons*. And now do you go, Buttons, and clean out that
pig-pen in the long-boat; it has not been cleaned out since
last voyage. And bear a hand about it, d'ye hear; there's them
pigs there waiting to be put in; come, be off about it, now."

Was this then the beginning of my sea-career? set to cleaning out a pig-pen, the very first thing?

But I thought it best to say nothing; I had bound myself
to obey orders, and it was too late to retreat. So I only asked
for a shovel, or spade, or something else to work with.

"We don't dig gardens here," was the reply; "dig it out
with your teeth!"

After looking round, I found a stick and went to scraping
out the pen, which was awkward work enough, for another
boat called the "jolly-boat," was capsized right over the long-
boat, which brought them almost close together. These two
boats were in the middle of the deck. I managed to crawl
inside of the long-boat; and after barking my shins against
the seats, and bumping my head a good many times, I got
along to the stern, where the pig-pen was.

While I was hard at work a drunken sailor peeped in, and
cried out to his comrades, "Look here, my lads, what sort of
a pig do you call this? Hallo! inside there! what are you 'bout
there? trying to stow yourself away to steal a passage to

Liverpool? Out of that! out of that, I say." But just then the
mate came along and ordered this drunken rascal ashore.

The pig-pen being cleaned out, I was set to work picking
up some shavings, which lay about the deck; for there had
been carpenters at work on board. The mate ordered me to
throw these shavings into the long-boat at a particular place
between two of the seats. But as I found it hard work to push
the shavings through in that place, and as it looked wet there,
I thought it would be better for the shavings as well as myself, to thrust them where there was a larger opening and a
dry spot. While I was thus employed, the mate observing me,
exclaimed with an oath, "Didn't I tell you to put those shavings somewhere else? Do what I tell you, now, Buttons, or
mind your eye!"

Stifling my indignation at his rudeness, which by this time
I found was my only plan, I replied that that was not so good
a place for the shavings as that which I myself had selected,
and asked him to tell me *why* he wanted me to put them in
the place he designated. Upon this, he flew into a terrible
rage, and without explanation reiterated his order like a clap
of thunder.

This was my first lesson in the discipline of the sea, and I
never forgot it. From that time I learned that sea-officers
never gave reasons for any thing they order to be done. It is
enough that they command it, so that the motto is, "*Obey
orders, though you break owners.*"

I now began to feel very faint and sick again, and longed
for the ship to be leaving the dock; for then I made no doubt
we would soon be having something to eat. But as yet, I saw
none of the sailors on board, and as for the men at work in
the rigging, I found out that they were "*riggers*," that is, men
living ashore, who worked by the day in getting ships ready
for sea; and this I found out to my cost, for yielding to the
kind blandishment of one of these *riggers*, I had swapped
away my jack-knife with him for a much poorer one of his
own, thinking to secure a sailor friend for the voyage.

At last I watched my chance, and while people's backs were
turned, I seized a carrot from several bunches lying on deck,
and clapping it under the skirts of my shooting-jacket, went

forward to eat it; for I had often eaten raw carrots, which taste something like chestnuts. This carrot refreshed me a good deal, though at the expense of a little pain in my stomach. Hardly had I disposed of it, when I heard the chief mate's voice crying out for "Buttons." I ran after him, and received an order to go aloft and "slush down the main-top mast."

This was all Greek to me, and after receiving the order, I stood staring about me, wondering what it was that was to be done. But the mate had turned on his heel, and made no explanations. At length I followed after him, and asked what I must do.

"Didn't I tell you to slush down the main-top mast?" he shouted.

"You did," said I, "but I don't know what that means."

"Green as grass! a regular cabbage-head!" he exclaimed to himself. "A fine time I'll have with such a greenhorn aboard. Look you, youngster. Look up to that long pole there—d'ye see it? that piece of a tree there, you timber-head—well—take this bucket here, and go up the rigging—that rope-ladder there—do you understand?—and dab this slush all over the mast, and look out for your head if one drop falls on deck. Be off now, Buttons."

The eventful hour had arrived; for the first time in my life I was to ascend a ship's mast. Had I been well and hearty, perhaps I should have felt a little shaky at the thought; but as I was then, weak and faint, the bare thought appalled me.

But there was no hanging back; it would look like cowardice, and I could not bring myself to confess that I was suffering for want of food; so rallying again, I took up the bucket.

It was a heavy bucket, with strong iron hoops, and might have held perhaps two gallons. But it was only half full now of a sort of thick lobbered gravy, which I afterward learned was boiled out of the salt beef used by the sailors. Upon getting into the rigging, I found it was no easy job to carry this heavy bucket up with me. The rope handle of it was so slippery with grease, that although I twisted it several times about my wrist, it would be still twirling round and round, and slipping off. Spite of this, however, I managed to mount as far as the "top," the clumsy bucket half the time straddling and swinging about between my legs, and in momentary danger of capsizing. Arrived at the "top," I came to a dead halt, and looked up. How to surmount that overhanging impediment completely posed me for the time. But at last, with much straining, I contrived to place my bucket in the "top;" and then, trusting to Providence, swung myself up after it. The rest of the road was comparatively easy; though whenever I incautiously looked down toward the deck, my head spun round so from weakness, that I was obliged to shut my eyes to recover myself. I do not remember much more. I only recollect my safe return to the deck.

In a short time the bustle of the ship increased; the trunks of cabin passengers arrived, and the chests and boxes of the steerage passengers, besides baskets of wine and fruit for the captain.

At last we cast loose, and swinging out into the stream, came to anchor, and hoisted the signal for sailing. Every thing, it seemed, was on board but the crew; who in a few hours after, came off, one by one, in Whitehall boats, their chests in the bow, and themselves lying back in the stern like lords; and showing very plainly the complacency they felt in keeping the whole ship waiting for their lordships.

"Ay, ay," muttered the chief mate, as they rolled out of their boats and swaggered on deck, "it's your turn now, but it will be mine before long. Yaw about while you may, my hearties, I'll do the yawing after the anchor's up."

Several of the sailors were very drunk, and one of them was lifted on board insensible by his landlord, who carried him down below and dumped him into a bunk. And two other sailors, as soon as they made their appearance, immediately went below to sleep off the fumes of their drink.

At last, all the crew being on board, word was passed to go to dinner fore and aft, an order that made my heart jump with delight, for now my long fast would be broken. But though the sailors, surfeited with eating and drinking ashore, did not then touch the salt beef and potatoes which the black cook handed down into the forecastle; and though this left the whole allowance to me; to my surprise, I found that I could eat little or nothing; for now I only felt deadly faint, but not hungry.

Chapter 7

He Gets to Sea, and Feels Very Bad

EVERY THING at last being in readiness, the pilot came on board, and all hands were called to up anchor. While I worked at my bar, I could not help observing how haggard the men looked, and how much they suffered from this violent exercise, after the terrific dissipation in which they had been indulging ashore. But I soon learnt that sailors breathe nothing about such things, but strive their best to appear all alive and hearty, though it comes very hard for many of them.

The anchor being secured, a steam tug-boat with a strong name, the Hercules, took hold of us; and away we went past the long line of shipping, and wharves, and warehouses; and rounded the green south point of the island where the Battery is, and passed Governor's Island, and pointed right out for the Narrows.

My heart was like lead, and I felt bad enough, Heaven knows; but then, there was plenty of work to be done, which kept my thoughts from becoming too much for me.

And I tried to think all the time, that I was going to England, and that, before many months, I should have actually been there and home again, telling my adventures to my brothers and sisters; and with what delight they would listen, and how they would look up to me then, and reverence my sayings; and how that even my elder brother would be forced to treat me with great consideration, as having crossed the Atlantic Ocean, which he had never done, and there was no probability he ever would.

With such thoughts as these I endeavored to shake off my heavy-heartedness; but it would not do at all; for this was only the first day of the voyage, and many weeks, nay, several whole months must elapse before the voyage was ended; and who could tell what might happen to me; for when I looked up at the high, giddy masts, and thought how often I must be going up and down them, I thought sure enough that some luckless day or other, I would certainly fall overboard

and be drowned. And then, I thought of lying down at the
bottom of the sea, stark alone, with the great waves rolling
over me, and no one in the wide world knowing that I was
there. And I thought how much better and sweeter it must
be, to be buried under the pleasant hedge that bounded the
sunny south side of our village grave-yard, where every Sunday I had used to walk after church in the afternoon; and I
almost wished I was there now; yes, dead and buried in that
church-yard. All the time my eyes were filled with tears, and
I kept holding my breath, to choke down the sobs, for indeed
I could not help feeling as I did, and no doubt any boy in the
world would have felt just as I did then.

As the steamer carried us further and further down the bay,
and we passed ships lying at anchor, with men gazing at us
and waving their hats; and small boats with ladies in them
waving their handkerchiefs; and passed the green shore of
Staten Island, and caught sight of so many beautiful cottages
all overrun with vines, and planted on the beautiful fresh
mossy hill-sides; oh! then I would have given any thing if
instead of sailing *out* of the bay, we were only coming *into*
it; if we had crossed the ocean and returned, gone over and
come back; and my heart leaped up in me like something alive
when I thought of really entering that bay at the end of the
voyage. But that was so far distant, that it seemed it could
never be. No, never, never more would I see New York again.

And what shocked me more than any thing else, was to
hear some of the sailors, while they were at work coiling away
the hawsers, talking about the boarding-houses they were
going to, when they came back; and how that some friends
of theirs had promised to be on the wharf when the ship
returned, to take them and their chests right up to Franklin-
square where they lived; and how that they would have a
good dinner ready, and plenty of cigars and spirits out on the
balcony. I say this kind of talking shocked me, for they did
not seem to consider, as I did, that before any thing like that
could happen, we must cross the great Atlantic Ocean, cross
over from America to Europe and back again, many thousand
miles of foaming ocean.

At that time I did not know what to make of these sailors;
but this much I thought, that when they were boys, they

could never have gone to the Sunday School; for they swore so, it made my ears tingle, and used words that I never could hear without a dreadful loathing.

And are these the men, I thought to myself, that I must live with so long? these the men I am to eat with, and sleep with all the time? And besides, I now began to see, that they were not going to be very kind to me; but I will tell all about that when the proper time comes.

Now you must not think, that because all these things were passing through my mind, that I had nothing to do but sit still and think; no, no, I was hard at work: for as long as the steamer had hold of us, we were very busy coiling away ropes and cables, and putting the decks in order; which were littered all over with odds and ends of things that had to be put away.

At last we got as far as the Narrows, which every body knows is the entrance to New York Harbor from sea; and it may well be called the Narrows, for when you go in or out, it seems like going in or out of a door-way; and when you go out of these Narrows on a long voyage like this of mine, it seems like going out into the broad highway, where not a soul is to be seen. For far away and away, stretches the great Atlantic Ocean; and all you can see beyond is where the sky comes down to the water. It looks lonely and desolate enough, and I could hardly believe, as I gazed around me, that there could be any land beyond, or any place like Europe or England or Liverpool in the great wide world. It seemed too strange, and wonderful, and altogether incredible, that there could really be cities and towns and villages and green fields and hedges and farm-yards and orchards, away over that wide blank of sea, and away beyond the place where the sky came down to the water. And to think of steering right out among those waves, and leaving the bright land behind, and the dark night coming on, too, seemed wild and foolhardy; and I looked with a sort of fear at the sailors standing by me, who could be so thoughtless at such a time. But then I remembered, how many times my own father had said he had crossed the ocean; and I had never dreamed of such a thing as doubting him; for I always thought him a marvelous being, infinitely purer and greater than I was, who could not by any possibility do wrong, or say an untruth. Yet now, how could I credit it, that he, my own father, whom I so well remembered, had ever sailed out of these Narrows, and sailed right through the sky and water line, and gone to England, and France, Liverpool, and Marseilles. It was too wonderful to believe.

Now, on the right hand side of the Narrows as you go out, the land is quite high; and on the top of a fine cliff is a great castle or fort, all in ruins, and with the trees growing round it. It was built by Governor Tompkins in the time of the last war with England, but was never used, I believe, and so they left it to decay. I had visited the place once when we lived in New York, as long ago almost as I could remember, with my father, and an uncle of mine, an old sea-captain, with white hair, who used to sail to a place called Archangel in Russia, and who used to tell me that he was with Captain Langsdorff, when Captain Langsdorff crossed over by land from the sea of Okotsk in Asia to St. Petersburgh, drawn by large dogs in a sled. I mention this of my uncle, because he was the very first sea-captain I had ever seen, and his white hair and fine handsome florid face made so strong an impression upon me, that I have never forgotten him, though I only saw him during this one visit of his to New York, for he was lost in the White Sea some years after.

But I meant to speak about the fort. It was a beautiful place, as I remembered it, and very wonderful and romantic, too, as it appeared to me, when I went there with my uncle. On the side away from the water was a green grove of trees, very thick and shady; and through this grove, in a sort of twilight you came to an arch in the wall of the fort, dark as night; and going in, you groped about in long vaults, twisting and turning on every side, till at last you caught a peep of green grass and sunlight, and all at once came out in an open space in the middle of the castle. And there you would see cows quietly grazing, or ruminating under the shade of young trees, and perhaps a calf frisking about, and trying to catch its own tail; and sheep clambering among the mossy ruins, and cropping the little tufts of grass sprouting out of the sides of the embrasures for cannon. And once I saw a black goat with a long beard, and crumpled horns, standing with his fore-feet lifted high up on the topmost parapet, and looking to sea, as if he were watching for a ship that was bringing over his cousin. I can see him even now, and though I have changed since then, the black goat looks just the same as ever; and so I suppose he would, if I live to be as old as Methusaleh, and have as great a memory as he must have had. Yes, the fort was a beautiful, quiet, charming spot. I should like to build a little cottage in the middle of it, and live there all my life. It was noon-day when I was there, in the month of June, and there was little wind to stir the trees, and every thing looked as if it was waiting for something, and the sky overhead was blue as my mother's eye, and I was so glad and happy then. But I must not think of those delightful days, before my father became a bankrupt, and died, and we removed from the city; for when I think of those days, something rises up in my throat and almost strangles me.

Now, as we sailed through the Narrows, I caught sight of that beautiful fort on the cliff, and could not help contrasting my situation now, with what it was when with my father and uncle I went there so long ago. Then I never thought of working for my living, and never knew that there were hard hearts in the world; and knew so little of money, that when I bought a stick of candy, and laid down a sixpence, I thought the confectioner returned five cents, only that I might have money to buy something else, and not because the pennies were my change, and therefore mine by good rights. How different my idea of money now!

Then I was a schoolboy, and thought of going to college in time; and had vague thoughts of becoming a great orator like Patrick Henry, whose speeches I used to speak on the stage; but now, I was a poor friendless boy, far away from my home, and voluntarily in the way of becoming a miserable sailor for life. And what made it more bitter to me, was to think of how well off were my cousins, who were happy and rich, and lived at home with my uncles and aunts, with no thought of going to sea for a living. I tried to think that it was all a dream, that I was not where I was, not on board of a ship, but that I was at home again in the city, with my father alive, and my mother bright and happy as she used to be. But it would not do. I was indeed where I was, and here was the ship, and there was the fort. So, after casting a last look at some boys who were standing on the parapet, gazing off to sea, I turned away heavily, and resolved not to look at the land any more.

About sunset we got fairly "outside," and well may it so be called; for I felt thrust out of the world. Then the breeze began to blow, and the sails were loosed, and hoisted; and after a while, the steamboat left us, and for the first time I felt the ship roll, a strange feeling enough, as if it were a great barrel in the water. Shortly after, I observed a swift little schooner running across our bows, and re-crossing again and again; and while I was wondering what she could be, she suddenly lowered her sails, and two men took hold of a little boat on her deck, and launched it overboard as if it had been a chip. Then I noticed that our pilot, a red-faced man in a rough blue coat, who to my astonishment had all this time been giving orders instead of the captain; I noticed that he began to button up his coat to the throat, like a prudent person about leaving a house at night in a lonely square, to go home; and he left the giving orders to the chief mate, and stood apart talking with the captain, and put his hand into his pocket, and gave him some newspapers.

And in a few minutes, when we had stopped our headway, and allowed the little boat to come alongside, he shook hands with the captain and officers and bade them good-by, without saying a syllable of farewell to me and the sailors; and so he went laughing over the side, and got into the boat, and they pulled him off to the schooner, and then the schooner made sail and glided under our stern, her men standing up and waving their hats, and cheering; and that was the last we saw of America.

Chapter 8

He Is Put into the Larboard Watch; Gets
Sea-Sick; and Relates Some Other of His
Experiences

It was now getting dark, when all at once the sailors were ordered on the quarter-deck, and of course I went along with them.

What is to come now, thought I; but I soon found out. It seemed we were going to be divided into watches. The chief mate began by selecting a stout good-looking sailor for his watch; and then the second mate's turn came to choose, and he also chose a stout good-looking sailor. But it was not me;—no; and I noticed, as they went on choosing, one after the other in regular rotation, that both of the mates never so much as looked at me, but kept going round among the rest, peering into their faces, for it was dusk, and telling them not to hide themselves away so in their jackets. But the sailors, especially the stout good-looking ones, seemed to make a point of lounging as much out of the way as possible, and slouching their hats over their eyes; and although it may only be a fancy of mine, I certainly thought that they affected a sort of lordly indifference as to whose watch they were going to be in; and did not think it worth while to look any way anxious about the matter. And the very men who, a few minutes before, had showed the most alacrity and promptitude in jumping into the rigging and running aloft at the word of command, now lounged against the bulwarks the most lazily; as if they were quite sure, that by this time the officers must know who the best men were, and they valued themselves well enough to be willing to put the officers to the trouble of searching them out; for if they were worth having, they were worth seeking.

At last they were all chosen but me; and it was the chief mate's next turn to choose; though there could be little choosing in my case, since I was a thirteener, and must,

whether or no, go over to the next column, like the odd figure you carry along when you do a sum in addition.

"Well, Buttons," said the chief mate, "I thought I'd got rid
of you. And as it is, Mr. Rigs," he added, speaking to the
second mate, "I guess you had better take him into your
watch;—there, I'll let you have him, and then you'll be one
stronger than me."

"No, I thank you," said Mr. Rigs.

"You had better," said the chief mate—"see, he's not a bad
looking chap—he's a little green, to be sure, but you were so
once yourself, you know, Rigs."

"No, I thank you," said the second mate again. "Take him
yourself—he's yours by good rights—I don't want him."
And so they put me in the chief mate's division, that is the
larboard watch.

While this scene was going on, I felt shabby enough; there
I stood, just like a silly sheep, over whom two butchers are
bargaining. Nothing that had yet happened so forcibly reminded me of where I was, and what I had come to. I was
very glad when they sent us forward again.

As we were going forward, the second mate called one of
the sailors by name:—"You, Bill?" and Bill answered, "Sir?"
just as if the second mate was a born gentleman. It surprised
me not a little, to see a man in such a shabby, shaggy old
jacket addressed so respectfully; but I had been quite as much
surprised when I heard the chief mate call him *Mr.* Rigs during the scene on the quarter-deck; as if this *Mr. Rigs* was a
great merchant living in a marble house in Lafayette Place.
But I was not very long in finding out, that at sea all officers
are *Misters*, and would take it for an insult if any seaman presumed to omit calling them so. And it is also one of their
rights and privileges to be called *sir* when addressed—*Yes,
sir; No, sir; Ay, ay, sir:* and they are as particular about being
sirred as so many knights and baronets; though their titles are
not hereditary, as is the case with the Sir Johns and Sir Josh-
uas in England. But so far as the second mate is concerned,
his titles are the only dignities he enjoys; for, upon the whole,
he leads a puppyish life indeed. He is not deemed company
at any time for the captain, though the chief mate occasionally

is, at least deck-company, though not in the cabin; and besides this, the second mate has to breakfast, lunch, dine, and sup off the leavings of the cabin table, and even the steward, who is accountable to nobody but the captain, sometimes treats him cavalierly; and he has to run aloft when topsails are reefed; and put his hand a good way down into the tar-bucket; and keep the key of the boatswain's locker, and fetch and carry balls of marline and seizing-stuff for the sailors when at work in the rigging; besides doing many other things, which a true-born baronet of any spirit would rather die and give up his title than stand.

Having been divided into watches we were sent to supper; but I could not eat any thing except a little biscuit, though I should have liked to have some good tea; but as I had no pot to get it in, and was rather nervous about asking the rough sailors to let me drink out of theirs; I was obliged to go without a sip. I thought of going to the black cook and begging a tin cup; but he looked so cross and ugly then, that the sight of him almost frightened the idea out of me.

When supper was over, for they never talk about going to *tea* aboard of a ship, the watch to which I belonged was called on deck; and we were told it was for us to stand the first night watch, that is, from eight o'clock till midnight.

I now began to feel unsettled and ill at ease about the stomach, as if matters were all topsy-turvy there; and felt strange and giddy about the head; and so I made no doubt that this was the beginning of that dreadful thing, the sea-sickness. Feeling worse and worse, I told one of the sailors how it was with me, and begged him to make my excuses very civilly to the chief mate, for I thought I would go below and spend the night in my bunk. But he only laughed at me, and said something about my mother not being aware of my being out; which enraged me not a little, that a man whom I had heard swear so terribly, should dare to take such a holy name into his mouth. It seemed a sort of blasphemy, and it seemed like dragging out the best and most cherished secrets of my soul, for at that time the name of mother was the center of all my heart's finest feelings, which ere that, I had learned to keep secret, deep down in my being.

But I did not outwardly resent the sailor's words, for that would have only made the matter worse.

Now this man was a Greenlander by birth, with a very white skin where the sun had not burnt it, and handsome blue eyes placed wide apart in his head, and a broad good-humored face, and plenty of curly flaxen hair. He was not very tall, but exceedingly stout-built, though active; and his back was as broad as a shield, and it was a great way between his shoulders. He seemed to be a sort of lady's sailor, for in his broken English he was always talking about the nice ladies of his acquaintance in Stockholm and Copenhagen and a place he called the Hook, which at first I fancied must be the place where lived the hook-nosed men that caught fowling-pieces and every other article that came along. He was dressed very tastefully, too, as if he knew he was a good-looking fel-low. He had on a new blue woolen Havre frock, with a new silk handkerchief round his neck, passed through one of the vertebral bones of a shark, highly polished and carved. His trowsers were of clear white duck, and he sported a handsome pair of pumps, and a tarpaulin hat bright as a looking-glass, with a long black ribbon streaming behind, and getting en-tangled every now and then in the rigging; and he had gold anchors in his ears, and a silver ring on one of his fingers, which was very much worn and bent from pulling ropes and other work on board ship. I thought he might better have left his jewelry at home.

It was a long time before I could believe that this man was really from Greenland, though he looked strange enough to me, then, to have come from the moon; and he was full of stories about that distant country; how they passed the win-ters there; and how bitter cold it was; and how he used to go to bed and sleep twelve hours, and get up again and run about, and go to bed again, and get up again—there was no telling how many times, and all in one night; for in the winter time in his country, he said, the nights were so many weeks long, that a Greenland baby was sometimes three months old, before it could properly be said to be a day old.

I had seen mention made of such things before, in books of voyages; but that was only reading about them, just as you read the Arabian Nights, which no one ever believes; for somehow, when I read about these wonderful countries, I never used really to believe what I read, but only thought it very strange, and a good deal too strange to be altogether true; though I never thought the men who wrote the book meant to tell lies. But I don't know exactly how to explain what I mean; but this much I will say, that I never believed in Greenland till I saw this Greenlander. And at first, hearing him talk about Greenland, only made me still more incredulous. For what business had a man from Greenland to be in my company? Why was he not at home among the icebergs; and how could he stand a warm summer's sun, and not be melted away? Besides, instead of icicles, there were ear-rings hanging from his ears; and he did not wear bear-skins, and keep his hands in a huge muff; things, which I could not help connecting with Greenland and all Greenlanders.

But I was telling about my being sea-sick and wanting to retire for the night. This Greenlander seeing I was ill, volunteered to turn doctor and cure me; so going down into the forecastle, he came back with a brown jug, like a molasses jug, and a little tin cannikin, and as soon as the brown jug got near my nose, I needed no telling what was in it, for it smelt like a still-house, and sure enough proved to be full of Jamaica spirits.

"Now, Buttons," said he, "one little dose of this will be better for you than a whole night's sleep; there, take that now, and then eat seven or eight biscuits, and you'll feel as strong as the mainmast."

But I felt very little like doing as I was bid, for I had some scruples about drinking spirits; and to tell the plain truth, for I am not ashamed of it, I was a member of a society in the village where my mother lived, called the Juvenile Total Abstinence Association, of which my friend, Tom Legare, was president, secretary, and treasurer, and kept the funds in a little purse that his cousin knit for him. There was three and sixpence on hand, I believe, the last time he brought in his accounts, on a May day, when we had a meeting in a grove on the river-bank. Tom was a very honest treasurer, and never spent the Society's money for peanuts; and besides all, was a fine, generous boy, whom I much loved. But I must not talk about Tom now.

When the Greenlander came to me with his jug of medicine, I thanked him as well as I could; for just then I was
leaning with my mouth over the side, feeling ready to die;
but I managed to tell him I was under a solemn obligation
never to drink spirits upon any consideration whatever;
though, as I had a sort of presentiment that the spirits would
now, for once in my life, do me good, I began to feel sorry,
that when I signed the pledge of abstinence, I had not taken
care to insert a little clause, allowing me to drink spirits in
case of sea-sickness. And I would advise temperance people
to attend to this matter in future; and then if they come to
go to sea, there will be no need of breaking their pledges,
which I am truly sorry to say was the case with me. And a
hard thing it was, too, thus to break a vow before unbroken;
especially as the Jamaica tasted any thing but agreeable, and
indeed burnt my mouth so, that I did not relish my meals for
some time after. Even when I had become quite well and
strong again, I wondered how the sailors could really like
such stuff; but many of them had a jug of it, besides the
Greenlander, which they brought along to sea with them, *to
taper off with*, as they called it. But this tapering off did not
last very long, for the Jamaica was all gone on the second day,
and the jugs were tossed overboard. I wonder where they are
now?

But to tell the truth, I found, in spite of its sharp taste, the
spirits I drank was just the thing I needed; but I suppose, if
I could have had a cup of nice hot coffee, it would have done
quite as well, and perhaps much better. But that was not to
be had at that time of night, or, indeed, at any other time;
for the thing they called *coffee*, which was given to us every
morning at breakfast, was the most curious tasting drink I
ever drank, and tasted as little like coffee, as it did like lem-
onade; though, to be sure, it was generally as cold as lemon-
ade, and I used to think the cook had an ice-house, and dropt
ice into his coffee. But what was more curious still, was the
different quality and taste of it on different mornings. Sometimes it tasted fishy, as if it was a decoction of Dutch herrings; and then it would taste very salt, as if some *old horse*,
or sea-beef, had been boiled in it; and then again it would
taste a sort of cheesy, as if the captain had sent his cheese-

parings forward to make our coffee of; and yet another time it would have such a very bad flavor, that I was almost ready to think some old stocking-heels had been boiled in it. What under heaven it was made of, that it had so many different bad flavors, always remained a mystery; for when at work at his vocation, our old cook used to keep himself close shut up in his caboose, a little cook-house, and never told any of his secrets.

Though a very serious character, as I shall hereafter show, he was for all that, and perhaps for that identical reason, a very suspicious looking sort of a cook, that I don't believe would ever succeed in getting the cooking at Delmonico's in New York. It was well for him that he was a black cook, for I have no doubt his color kept us from seeing his dirty face; I never saw him wash but once, and that was at one of his own soup pots one dark night when he thought no one saw him. What induced him to be washing his face then, I never could find out; but I suppose he must have suddenly waked up, after dreaming about some real estate on his cheeks. As for his coffee, notwithstanding the disagreeableness of its flavor, I always used to have a strange curiosity every morning, to see what new taste it was going to have; and though, sure enough, I never missed making a new discovery, and adding another taste to my palate, I never found that there was any change in the badness of the beverage, which always seemed the same in that respect as before.

It may well be believed, then, that now when I was sea-sick, a cup of such coffee as our old cook made would have done me no good, if indeed it would not have come near making an end of me. And bad as it was, and since it was not to be had at that time of night, as I said before, I think I was excusable in taking something else in place of it, as I did; and under the circumstances, it would be unhandsome of them, if my fellow-members of the Temperance Society should re-proach me for breaking my bond, which I would not have done except in case of necessity. But the evil effect of breaking one's bond upon any occasion whatever, was witnessed in the present case; for it insidiously opened the way to subsequent breaches of it, which though very slight, yet carried no apology with them.

Chapter 9

THE LATTER PART of this first long watch that we stood
was very pleasant, so far as the weather was concerned.
From being rather cloudy, it became a soft moonlight; and
the stars peeped out, plain enough to count one by
one; and there was a fine steady breeze; and it was not very
cold; and we were going through the water almost as smooth
as a sled sliding down hill. And what was still better, the wind
held so steady, that there was little running aloft, little pulling
ropes, and scarcely any thing disagreeable of that kind.

The chief mate kept walking up and down the quarter-
deck, with a lighted long-nine cigar in his mouth by way of a
torch; and spoke but few words to us the whole watch. He
must have had a good deal of thinking to attend to, which in
truth is the case with most seamen the first night out of port,
especially when they have thrown away their money in foolish
dissipation, and got very sick into the bargain. For when
ashore, many of these sea-officers are as wild and reckless in
their way, as the sailors they command.

While I stood watching the red cigar-end promenading up
and down, the mate suddenly stopped and gave an order, and
the men sprang to obey it. It was not much, only something
about hoisting one of the sails a little higher up on the mast.
The men took hold of the rope, and began pulling upon it;
the foremost man of all setting up a song with no words to
it, only a strange musical rise and fall of notes. In the dark
night, and far out upon the lonely sea, it sounded wild
enough, and made me feel as I had sometimes felt, when in a
twilight room a cousin of mine, with black eyes, used to play
some old German airs on the piano. I almost looked round
for goblins, and felt just a little bit afraid. But I soon got used
to this singing; for the sailors never touched a rope without
it. Sometimes, when no one happened to strike up, and the
pulling, whatever it might be, did not seem to be getting for-

ward very well, the mate would always say, *"Come, men, can't any of you sing? Sing now, and raise the dead."* And then some one of them would begin, and if every man's arms were as much relieved as mine by the song, and he could pull as much better as I did, with such a cheering accompaniment, I am sure the song was well worth the breath expended on it. It is a great thing in a sailor to know how to sing well, for he gets a great name by it from the officers, and a good deal of popularity among his shipmates. Some sea-captains, before shipping a man, always ask him whether he can sing out at a rope.

During the greater part of the watch, the sailors sat on the windlass and told long stories of their adventures by sea and land, and talked about Gibraltar, and Canton, and Valparaiso, and Bombay, just as you and I would about Peck Slip and the Bowery. Every man of them almost was a volume of Voyages and Travels round the World. And what most struck me was that like books of voyages they often contradicted each other, and would fall into long and violent disputes about who was keeping the Foul Anchor tavern in Portsmouth at such a time; or whether the King of Canton lived or did not live in Persia; or whether the bar-maid of a particular house in Hamburg had black eyes or blue eyes; with many other mooted points of that sort.

At last one of them went below and brought up a box of cigars from his chest, for some sailors always provide little delicacies of that kind, to break off the first shock of the salt water after laying idle ashore; and also by way of *tapering off*, as I mentioned a little while ago. But I wondered that they never carried any pies and tarts to sea with them, instead of spirits and cigars.

Ned, for that was the man's name, split open the box with a blow of his fist, and then handed it round along the windlass, just like a waiter at a party, every one helping himself. But I was a member of an Anti-Smoking Society that had been organized in our village by the Principal of the Sunday School there, in conjunction with the Temperance Association. So I did not smoke any then, though I did afterward upon the voyage, I am sorry to say. Notwithstanding I declined; with a good deal of unnecessary swearing, Ned assured me that the cigars were real genuine Havannas; for he had been in Havanna, he said, and had them made there under his own eye. According to his account, he was very particular about his cigars and other things, and never made any importations, for they were unsafe; but always made a voyage himself direct to the place where any foreign thing was to be had that he wanted. He went to Havre for his woolen shirts, to Panama for his hats, to China for his silk handkerchiefs, and direct to Calcutta for his cheroots; and as a great joker in the watch used to say, no doubt he would at last have occasion to go to Russia for his halter; the wit of which saying was presumed to be in the fact, that the Russian hemp is the best; though that is not wit which needs explaining.

By dint of the spirits which, besides stimulating my fainting strength, united with the cool air of the sea to give me an appetite for our hard biscuit; and also by dint of walking briskly up and down the deck before the windlass, I had now recovered in good part from my sickness, and finding the sailors all very pleasant and sociable, at least among themselves, and seated smoking together like old cronies, and nothing on earth to do but sit the watch out, I began to think that they were a pretty good set of fellows after all, barring their swearing and another ugly way of talking they had; and I thought I had misconceived their true characters; for at the outset I had deemed them such a parcel of wicked hard-hearted rascals that it would be a severe affliction to associate with them.

Yes, I now began to look on them with a sort of incipient love; but more with an eye of pity and compassion, as men of naturally gentle and kind dispositions, whom only hardships, and neglect, and ill-usage had made outcasts from good society; and not as villains who loved wickedness for the sake of it, and would persist in wickedness, even in Paradise, if they ever got there. And I called to mind a sermon I had once heard in a church in behalf of sailors, when the preacher called them strayed lambs from the fold, and compared them to poor lost children, babes in the wood, orphans without fathers or mothers.

And I remembered reading in a magazine, called the Sailors' Magazine, with a sea-blue cover, and a ship painted on the back, about pious seamen who never swore, and paid over all their wages to the poor heathen in India; and how that when they were too old to go to sea, these pious old sailors found a delightful home for life in the Hospital, where they had nothing to do, but prepare themselves for their latter end. And I wondered whether there were any such good sailors among my ship-mates; and observing that one of them laid on deck apart from the rest, I thought to be sure he must be one of them: so I did not disturb his devotions: but I was afterward shocked at discovering that he was only fast asleep, with one of the brown jugs by his side.

I forgot to mention by the way, that every once in a while, the men went into one corner, where the chief mate could not see them, to take a "swig at the halyards," as they called it; and this swigging at the halyards it was, that enabled them "to taper off" handsomely, and no doubt it was this, too, that had something to do with making them so pleasant and so-ciable that night, for they were seldom so pleasant and socia-ble afterward, and never treated me so kindly as they did then. Yet this might have been owing to my being something of a stranger to them, then; and our being just out of port. But that very night they turned about, and taught me a bitter lesson; but all in good time.

I have said, that seeing how agreeable they were getting, and how friendly their manner was, I began to feel a sort of compassion for them, grounded on their sad conditions as amiable outcasts; and feeling so warm an interest in them, and being full of pity, and being truly desirous of benefiting them to the best of my poor powers, for I knew they were but poor indeed, I made bold to ask one of them, whether he was ever in the habit of going to church, when he was ashore, or dropping in at the Floating Chapel I had seen lying off the dock in the East River at New York; and whether he would think it too much of a liberty, if I asked him, if he had any good books in his chest. He stared a little at first, but marking what good language I used, seeing my civil bearing toward him, he seemed for a moment to be filled with a certain in-voluntary respect for me, and answered, that he had been to church once, some ten or twelve years before, in London, and on a week-day had helped to move the Floating Chapel round the Battery, from the North River; and that was the only time he had seen it. For his books, he said he did not know what

I meant by good books; but if I wanted the Newgate Calendar, and Pirate's Own, he could lend them to me.

When I heard this poor sailor talk in this manner, showing so plainly his ignorance and absence of proper views of religion, I pitied him more and more, and contrasting my own situation with his, I was grateful that I was different from him; and I thought how pleasant it was, to feel wiser and better than he could feel; though I was willing to confess to myself, that it was not altogether my own good endeavors, so much as my education, which I had received from others, that had made me the upright and sensible boy I at that time thought myself to be. And it was now, that I began to feel a good degree of complacency and satisfaction in surveying my own character; for, before this, I had previously associated with persons of a very discreet life, so that there was little opportunity to magnify myself, by comparing myself with my neighbors.

Thinking that my superiority to him in a moral way might sit uneasily upon this sailor, I thought it would soften the matter down by giving him a chance to show his own superiority to me, in a minor thing; for I was far from being vain and conceited.

Having observed that at certain intervals a little bell was rung on the quarter-deck by the man at the wheel; and that as soon as it was heard, some one of the sailors forward struck a large bell which hung on the forecastle; and having observed that how many times soever the man astern rang his bell, the man forward struck his—tit for tat,—I inquired of this Floating Chapel sailor, what all this ringing meant; and whether, as the big bell hung right over the scuttle that went down to the place where the watch below were sleeping, such a ringing every little while would not tend to disturb them and beget unpleasant dreams; and in asking these questions I was particular to address him in a civil and condescending way, so as to show him very plainly that I did not deem myself one whit better than he was, that is, taking all things together, and not going into particulars. But to my great surprise and mortification, he in the rudest kind of manner laughed aloud in my face, and called me a "Jimmy Dux," though that was not my real name, and he must have known it; and also the "son of a farmer," though as I have previously related, my father was a great merchant and French importer in Broad-street in New York. And then he began to laugh and joke about me, with the other sailors, till they all got round me, and if I had not felt so terribly angry, I should certainly have felt very much like a fool. But my being so angry prevented me from feeling foolish, which is very lucky for people in a passion.

Chapter 10

WHILE THE SCENE last described was going on, we were all startled by a horrid groaning noise down in the forecastle; and all at once some one came rushing up the scuttle in his shirt, clutching something in his hand, and trembling and shrieking in the most frightful manner, so that I thought one of the sailors must be murdered below.

But it all passed in a moment; and while we stood aghast at the sight, and almost before we knew what it was, the shrieking man jumped over the bows into the sea, and we saw him no more. Then there was a great uproar; the sailors came running up on deck; and the chief mate ran forward, and learning what had happened, began to yell out his orders about the sails and yards; and we all went to pulling and hauling the ropes, till at last the ship lay almost still on the water. Then they lowered a boat, which kept pulling round the ship for more than an hour, but they never caught sight of the man. It seemed that he was one of the sailors who had been brought aboard dead drunk, and tumbled into his bunk by his landlord; and there he had lain till now. He must have suddenly waked up, I suppose, raging mad with the delirium tremens, as the chief mate called it, and finding himself in a strange silent place, and knowing not how he had got there, he had rushed on deck, and so, in a fit of frenzy, put an end to himself.

This event, happening at the dead of night, had a wonderfully solemn and almost awful effect upon me. I would have given the whole world, and the sun and moon, and all the stars in heaven, if they had been mine, had I been safe back at Mr. Jones', or still better, in my home on the Hudson River. I thought it an ill-omened voyage, and railed at the folly which had sent me to sea, sore against the advice of my best friends, that is to say, my mother and sisters.

Alas! poor Wellingborough, thought I, you will never see your home any more. And in this melancholy mood I went below, when the watch had expired, which happened soon after. But to my terror, I found that the suicide had been occupying the very bunk which I had appropriated to myself, and there was no other place for me to sleep in. The thought of lying down there now, seemed too horrible to me, and what made it worse, was the way in which the sailors spoke of my being frightened. And they took this opportunity to tell me what a hard and wicked life I had entered upon, and how that such things happened frequently at sea, and they were used to it. But I did not believe this; for when the suicide came rushing and shrieking up the scuttle, they looked as frightened as I did; and besides that, and what makes their being frightened still plainer, is the fact, that if they had had any presence of mind, they could have prevented his plunging overboard, since he brushed right by them. However, they lay in their bunks smoking, and kept talking on some time in this strain, and advising me as soon as ever I got home to pin my ears back, so as not to hold the wind, and sail straight away into the interior of the country, and never stop until deep in the bush, far off from the least running brook, never mind how shallow, and out of sight of even the smallest puddle of rain-water.

This kind of talking brought the tears into my eyes, for it was so true and real, and the sailors who spoke it seemed so false-hearted and insincere; but for all that, in spite of the sickness at my heart, it made me mad, and stung me to the quick, that they should speak of me as a poor trembling coward, who could never be brought to endure the hardships of a sailor's life; for I felt myself trembling, and knew that I was but a coward then, well enough, without their telling me of it. And they did not say I was cowardly, because they perceived it in me, but because they merely supposed I must be, judging, no doubt, from their own secret thoughts about themselves; for I felt sure that the suicide frightened them very badly. And at last, being provoked to desperation by their taunts, I told them so to their faces; but I might better have kept silent; for they now all united to abuse me. They asked me what business I, a boy like me, had to go to sea, and take the bread out of the mouth of honest sailors, and fill a good seaman's place; and asked me whether I ever dreamed of becoming a captain, since I was a gentleman with white hands; and if I ever *should* be, they would like nothing better than to ship aboard my vessel and stir up a mutiny. And one of them, whose name was Jackson, of whom I shall have a good deal more to say by-and-by, said, I had better steer clear of him ever after, for if ever I crossed his path, or got into his way, he would be the death of me, and if ever I stumbled about in the rigging near *him*, he would make nothing of pitching me overboard; and that he swore too, with an oath. At first, all this nearly stunned me, it was so unforeseen; and then I could not believe that they meant what they said, or that they could be so cruel and black-hearted. But how could I help seeing, that the men who could thus talk to a poor, friendless boy, on the very first night of his voyage to sea, must be capable of almost any enormity. I loathed, detested, and hated them with all that was left of my bursting heart and soul, and I thought myself the most forlorn and miserable wretch that ever breathed. May I never be a man, thought I, if to be a boy is to be such a wretch. And I wailed and wept, and my heart cracked within me, but all the time I defied them through my teeth, and dared them to do their worst.

At last they ceased talking and fell fast asleep, leaving me awake, seated on a chest with my face bent over my knees between my hands. And there I sat, till at length the dull beating against the ship's bows, and the silence around, soothed me down, and I fell asleep as I sat.

Chapter II

He Helps Wash the Decks, and Then Goes to Breakfast

THE NEXT THING I knew, was the loud thumping of a handspike on deck as the watch was called again. It was now four o'clock in the morning, and when we got on deck the first signs of day were shining in the east. The men were very sleepy, and sat down on the windlass without speaking, and some of them nodded and nodded, till at last they fell off like little boys in church during a drowsy sermon. At last it was broad day, and an order was given to wash down the decks. A great tub was dragged into the waist, and then one of the men went over into the chains, and slipped in behind a band fastened to the shrouds, and leaning over, began to swing a bucket into the sea by a long rope; and in that way with much expertness and sleight of hand, he managed to fill the tub in a very short time. Then the water began to splash about all over the decks, and I began to think I should surely get my feet wet, and catch my death of cold. So I went to the chief mate, and told him I thought I would just step below, till this miserable wetting was over; for I did not have any water-proof boots, and an aunt of mine had died of consumption. But he only roared out for me to get a broom and go to scrubbing, or he would prove a worse consumption to me than ever got hold of my poor aunt. So I scrubbed away fore and aft, till my back was almost broke, for the brooms had uncommon short handles, and we were told to scrub hard.

At length the scrubbing being over, the mate began heaving buckets of water about, to wash every thing clean, by way of finishing off. He must have thought this fine sport, just as captains of fire engines love to point the tube of their hose; for he kept me running after him with full buckets of water, and sometimes chased a little chip all over the deck, with a continued flood, till at last he sent it flying out of a scupper-hole into the sea; when if he had only given me permission, I could have picked it up in a trice, and dropped it overboard without saying one word, and without wasting so much water. But he said there was plenty of water in the ocean, and to spare; which was true enough, but then I who had to trot after him with the buckets, had no more legs and arms than I wanted for my own use.

I thought this washing down the decks was the most foolish thing in the world, and besides that it was the most uncomfortable. It was worse than my mother's house-cleanings at home, which I used to abominate so.

At eight o'clock the bell was struck, and we went to breakfast. And now some of the worst of my troubles began. For not having had any friend to tell me what I would want at sea, I had not provided myself, as I should have done, with a good many things that a sailor needs; and for my own part, it had never entered my mind, that sailors had no table to sit down to, no cloth, or napkins, or tumblers, and had to provide every thing themselves. But so it was.

The first thing they did was this. Every sailor went to the cook-house with his tin pot, and got it filled with coffee; but of course, having no pot, there was no coffee for me. And after that, a sort of little tub called a "kid," was passed down into the forecastle, filled with something they called "burgoo." This was like mush, made of Indian corn meal and water. With the "kid," a little tin cannikin was passed down with molasses. Then the Jackson that I spoke of before, put the kid between his knees, and began to pour in the molasses, just like an old landlord mixing punch for a party. He scooped out a little hole in the middle of the mush, to hold the molasses; so it looked for all the world like a little black pool in the Dismal Swamp of Virginia.

Then they all formed a circle round the kid; and one after the other, with great regularity, dipped their spoons into the mush, and after stirring them round a little in the molasses-pool, they swallowed down their mouthfuls, and smacked their lips over it, as if it tasted very good; which I have no doubt it did; but not having any spoon, I wasn't sure.

I sat some time watching these proceedings, and wondering how polite they were to each other; for, though there were a great many spoons to only one dish, they never got

entangled. At last, seeing that the mush was getting thinner
and thinner, and that it was getting low water, or rather low
molasses in the little pool, I ran on deck, and after searching
about, returned with a bit of stick; and thinking I had as
good a right as any one else to the mush and molasses, I
worked my way into the circle, intending to make one of the
party. So I shoved in my stick, and after twirling it about,
was just managing to carry a little *burgoo* toward my mouth,
which had been for some time standing ready open to receive
it, when one of the sailors perceiving what I was about,
knocked the stick out of my hands, and asked me where I
learned my manners; Was that the way gentlemen eat in my
country? Did they eat their victuals with splinters of wood,
and couldn't that wealthy gentleman my father afford to buy
his gentlemanly son a spoon?

All the rest joined in, and pronounced me an ill-bred,
coarse, and unmannerly youngster, who, if permitted to go
on with such behavior as that, would corrupt the whole crew,
and make them no better than swine.

As I felt conscious that a stick was indeed a thing very un-
suitable to eat with, I did not say much to this, though it
vexed me enough; but remembering that I had seen one of
the steerage passengers with a pan and spoon in his hand
eating his breakfast on the fore hatch, I now ran on deck
again, and to my great joy succeeded in borrowing his spoon,
for he had got through his meal, and down I came again,
though at the eleventh hour, and offered myself once more as
a candidate.

But alas! there was little more of the Dismal Swamp left,
and when I reached over to the opposite end of the kid, I
received a rap on the knuckles from a spoon, and was told
that I must help myself from my own side, for that was the
rule. But *my* side was scraped clean, so I got no *burgoo* that
morning.

But I made it up by eating some salt beef and biscuit,
which I found to be the invariable accompaniment of every
meal; the sailors sitting cross-legged on their chests in a circle,
and breaking the hard biscuit, very sociably, over each other's
heads, which was very convenient indeed, but gave me the
headache, at least for the first four or five days till I got used

to it; and then I did not care much about it, only it kept my hair full of crumbs; and I had forgot to bring a fine comb and brush, so I used to shake my hair out to windward over the bulwarks every evening.

Chapter 12

He Gives Some Account of One of His Ship-mates Called Jackson

WHILE WE SAT eating our beef and biscuit, two of the men got into a dispute, about who had been sea-faring the longest; when Jackson, who had mixed the *burgoo*, called upon them in a loud voice to cease their clamor, for he would decide the matter for them. Of this sailor, I shall have something more to say, as I get on with my narrative; so, I will here try to describe him a little.

Did you ever see a man, with his hair shaved off, and just recovered from the yellow fever? Well, just such a looking man was this sailor. He was as yellow as gamboge, had no more whisker on his cheek, than I have on my elbows. His hair had fallen out, and left him very bald, except in the nape of his neck, and just behind the ears, where it was stuck over with short little tufts, and looked like a worn-out shoe-brush. His nose had broken down in the middle, and he squinted with one eye, and did not look very straight out of the other. He dressed a good deal like a Bowery boy; for he despised the ordinary sailor-rig; wearing a pair of great over-all blue trowsers, fastened with suspenders, and three red woolen shirts, one over the other; for he was subject to the rheumatism, and was not in good health, he said; and he had a large white wool hat, with a broad rolling brim. He was a native of New York city, and had a good deal to say about *high-binders*, and *rowdies*, whom he denounced as only good for the gallows; but I thought he looked a good deal like a *high-binder* himself.

His name, as I have said, was Jackson; and he told us, he was a near relation of General Jackson of New Orleans, and swore terribly, if any one ventured to question what he asserted on that head. In fact he was a great bully, and being the best seaman on board, and very overbearing every way, all the men were afraid of him, and durst not contradict him, or cross his path in any thing. And what made this more wonderful was, that he was the weakest man, bodily, of the whole crew; and I have no doubt that young and small as I was then, compared to what I am now, I could have thrown him down. But he had such an over-awing way with him; such a deal of brass and impudence, such an unflinching face, and withal was such a hideous looking mortal, that Satan himself would have run from him. And besides all this, it was quite plain, that he was by nature a marvelously clever, cunning man, though without education; and understood human nature to a kink, and well knew whom he had to deal with; and then, one glance of his squinting eye, was as good as a knock-down, for it was the most deep, subtle, infernal looking eye, that I ever saw lodged in a human head. I believe, that by good rights it must have belonged to a wolf, or starved tiger; at any rate, I would defy any oculist, to turn out a glass eye, half so cold, and snaky, and deadly. It was a horrible thing; and I would give much to forget that I have ever seen it; for it haunts me to this day.

It was impossible to tell how old this Jackson was; for he had no beard, and no wrinkles, except small crows-feet about the eyes. He might have seen thirty, or perhaps fifty years. But according to his own account, he had been to sea ever since he was eight years old, when he first went as a cabin-boy in an Indiaman, and ran away at Calcutta. And according to his own account, too, he had passed through every kind of dissipation and abandonment in the worst parts of the world. He had served in Portuguese slavers on the coast of Africa; and with a diabolical relish used to tell of the *middle-passage*, where the slaves were stowed, heel and point, like logs, and the suffocated and dead were unmanacled, and weeded out from the living every morning, before washing down the decks; how he had been in a slaving schooner, which being chased by an English cruiser off Cape Verde, received three shots in her hull, which raked through and through a whole file of slaves, that were chained.

He would tell of lying in Batavia during a fever, when his ship lost a man every few days, and how they went reeling ashore with the body, and got still more intoxicated by way of precaution against the plague. He would talk of finding a cobra-di-capello, or hooded snake, under his pillow in India, when he slept ashore there. He would talk of sailors being poisoned at Canton with drugged "*shampoo*," for the sake of their money; and of the Malay ruffians, who stopped ships in the straits of Gaspar, and always saved the captain for the last, so as to make him point out where the most valuable goods were stored.

His whole talk was of this kind; full of piracies, plagues and poisonings. And often he narrated many passages in his own individual career, which were almost incredible, from the consideration that few men could have plunged into such infamous vices, and clung to them so long, without paying the death-penalty.

But in truth, he carried about with him the traces of these things, and the mark of a fearful end nigh at hand; like that of King Antiochus of Syria, who died a worse death, history says, than if he had been stung out of the world by wasps and hornets.

Nothing was left of this Jackson but the foul lees and dregs of a man; he was thin as a shadow; nothing but skin and bones; and sometimes used to complain, that it hurt him to sit on the hard chests. And I sometimes fancied, it was the consciousness of his miserable, broken-down condition, and the prospect of soon dying like a dog, in consequence of his sins, that made this poor wretch always eye me with such malevolence as he did. For I was young and handsome, at least my mother so thought me, and as soon as I became a little used to the sea, and shook off my low spirits somewhat, I began to have my old color in my cheeks, and, spite of misfortune, to appear well and hearty; whereas *he* was being consumed by an incurable malady, that was eating up his vitals, and was more fit for a hospital than a ship.

As I am sometimes by nature inclined to indulge in unauthorized surmisings about the thoughts going on with regard to me, in the people I meet; especially if I have reason to think they dislike me; I will not put it down for a certainty that what I suspected concerning this Jackson relative to his thoughts of me, was really the truth. But only state my honest opinion, and how it struck me at the time; and even now, I think I was not wrong. And indeed, unless it was so, how could I account to myself, for the shudder that would run through me, when I caught this man gazing at me, as I often did; for he was apt to be dumb at times, and would sit with his eyes fixed, and his teeth set, like a man in the moody madness.

I well remember the first time I saw him, and how I was startled at his eye, which was even then fixed upon me. He was standing at the ship's helm, being the first man that got there, when a steersman was called for by the pilot; for this Jackson was always on the alert for easy duties, and used to plead his delicate health as the reason for assuming them, as he did; though I used to think, that for a man in poor health, he was very swift on the legs; at least when a good place was to be jumped to; though that might only have been a sort of spasmodic exertion under strong inducements, which every one knows the greatest invalids will sometimes show.

And though the sailors were always very bitter against any thing like *sogering*, as they called it; that is, any thing that savored of a desire to get rid of downright hard work; yet, I observed that, though this Jackson was a notorious old *soger* the whole voyage (I mean, in all things not perilous to do, from which he was far from hanging back), and in truth was a great veteran that way, and one who must have passed unhurt through many campaigns; yet, they never presumed to call him to account in any way; or to let him so much as think, what they thought of his conduct. But I often heard them call him many hard names behind his back; and sometimes, too, when, perhaps, they had just been tenderly inquiring after his health before his face. They all stood in mortal fear of him; and cringed and fawned about him like so many spaniels; and used to rub his back, after he was undressed and lying in his bunk; and used to run up on deck to the cookhouse, to warm some cold coffee for him; and used to fill his pipe, and give him chews of tobacco, and mend his jackets and trowsers; and used to watch, and tend, and nurse him every way. And all the time, he would sit scowling on them, and found fault with what they did; and I noticed, that those who did the most for him, and cringed the most before him, were the very ones he most abused; while two or three who held more aloof, he treated with a little consideration.

It is not for me to say, what it was that made a whole ship's company submit so to the whims of one poor miserable man like Jackson. I only know that so it was; but I have no doubt, that if he had had a blue eye in his head, or had had a different face from what he did have, they would not have stood in such awe of him. And it astonished me, to see that one of the seamen, a remarkably robust and good-humored young man from Belfast in Ireland, was a person of no mark or influence among the crew; but on the contrary was hooted at, and trampled upon, and made a butt and laughing-stock; and more than all, was continually being abused and snubbed by Jackson, who seemed to hate him cordially, because of his great strength and fine person, and particularly because of his red cheeks.

But then, this Belfast man, although he had shipped for an *able-seaman*, was not much of a sailor; and that always lowers a man in the eyes of a ship's company; I mean, when he ships for an *able-seaman*, but is not able to do the duty of one. For sailors are of three classes— *able-seamen*, *ordinary-seamen*, and *boys*; and they receive different wages according to their rank. Generally, a ship's company of twelve men will only have five or six able seamen, who if they prove to understand their duty every way (and that is no small matter either, as I shall hereafter show, perhaps), are looked up to, and thought much of by the ordinary-seamen and boys, who reverence their very pea-jackets, and lay up their sayings in their hearts.

But you must not think from this, that persons called *boys* aboard merchant-ships are all youngsters, though to be sure, I myself was called a *boy*, and a boy I was. No. In merchant-ships, a *boy* means a green-hand, a landsman on his first voyage. And never mind if he is old enough to be a grandfather, he is still called a *boy*; and boys' work is put upon him.

But I am straying off from what I was going to say about Jackson's putting an end to the dispute between the two sailors in the forecastle after breakfast. After they had been disputing some time about who had been to sea the longest, Jackson told them to stop talking; and then bade one of them open his mouth; for, said he, I can tell a sailor's age just like a horse's—by his teeth. So the man laughed, and opened his mouth; and Jackson made him step out under the scuttle, where the light came down from deck; and then made him throw his head back, while he looked into it, and probed a little with his jack-knife, like a baboon peering into a junk-bottle. I trembled for the poor fellow, just as if I had seen him under the hands of a crazy barber, making signs to cut his throat, and he all the while sitting stock still, with the lather on, to be shaved. For I watched Jackson's eye and saw it snapping, and a sort of going in and out, very quick, as if it were something like a forked tongue; and somehow, I felt as if he were longing to kill the man; but at last he grew more composed, and after concluding his examination, said, that the first man was the oldest sailor, for the ends of his teeth were the evenest and most worn down; which, he said, arose from eating so much hard sea-biscuit; and this was the reason he could tell a sailor's age like a horse's.

At this, every body made merry, and looked at each other, as much as to say— *come, boys, let's laugh*; and they did laugh; and declared it was a rare joke.

This was always the way with them. They made a point of shouting out, whenever Jackson said any thing with a grin; that being the sign to them that he himself thought it funny; though I heard many good jokes from others pass off without a smile; and once Jackson himself (for, to tell the truth, he sometimes had a comical way with him, that is, when his back did not ache) told a truly funny story, but with a grave face; when, not knowing how he meant it, whether for a laugh or otherwise, they all sat still, waiting what to do, and looking perplexed enough; till at last Jackson roared out upon them for a parcel of fools and idiots; and told them to their beards, how it was; that he had purposely put on his grave face, to see whether they would not look grave, too; even when he was telling something that ought to split their sides. And with that, he flouted, and jeered at them, and laughed them all to scorn; and broke out in such a rage, that his lips began to glue together at the corners with a fine white foam.

He seemed to be full of hatred and gall against every thing and every body in the world; as if all the world was one person, and had done him some dreadful harm, that was rankling and festering in his heart. Sometimes I thought he was really crazy; and often felt so frightened at him, that I thought of going to the captain about it, and telling him Jackson ought

to be confined, lest he should do some terrible thing at last.
But upon second thoughts, I always gave it up; for the captain would only have called me a fool, and sent me forward
again.

But you must not think that all the sailors were alike in
abasing themselves before this man. No: there were three or
four who used to stand up sometimes against him; and when
he was absent at the wheel, would plot against him among
the other sailors, and tell them what a shame and ignominy it
was, that such a poor miserable wretch should be such a tyrant over much better men than himself. And they begged
and conjured them as men, to put up with it no longer, but
the very next time, that Jackson presumed to play the dictator, that they should all withstand him, and let him know his
place. Two or three times nearly all hands agreed to it, with
the exception of those who used to slink off during such discussions; and swore that they would not any more submit to
be ruled by Jackson. But when the time came to make good
their oaths, they were mum again, and let every thing go on
the old way; so that those who had put them up to it, had to
bear all the brunt of Jackson's wrath by themselves. And
though these last would stick up a little at first, and even mutter something about a fight to Jackson; yet in the end, finding
themselves unbefriended by the rest, they would gradually become silent, and leave the field to the tyrant, who would then
fly out worse than ever, and dare them to do their worst, and
jeer at them for white-livered poltroons, who did not have a
mouthful of heart in them. At such times, there were no
bounds to his contempt; and indeed, all the time he seemed
to have even more contempt than hatred, for every body and
every thing.

As for me, I was but a boy; and at any time aboard ship, a
boy is expected to keep quiet, do what he is bid, never presume to interfere, and seldom to talk, unless spoken to. For
merchant sailors have a great idea of their dignity, and superiority to *greenhorns* and *landsmen*, who know nothing about
a ship; and they seem to think, that an *able seaman* is a great
man; at least a much greater man than a little boy. And the
able seamen in the Highlander had such grand notions about
their seamanship, that I almost thought that able seamen re-

ceived diplomas, like those given at colleges; and were made a sort of *A.M.'s, or Masters of Arts.*

But though I kept thus quiet, and had very little to say, and well knew that my best plan was to get along peaceably with every body, and indeed endure a good deal before showing fight, yet I could not avoid Jackson's evil eye, nor escape his bitter enmity. And his being my foe, set many of the rest against me; or at least they were afraid to speak out for me before Jackson; so that at last I found myself a sort of Ishmael in the ship, without a single friend or companion; and I began to feel a hatred growing up in me against the whole crew—so much so, that I prayed against it, that it might not master my heart completely, and so make a fiend of me, something like Jackson.

Chapter 13

THE SECOND DAY out of port, the decks being washed down and breakfast over, the watch was called, and the mate set us to work.

It was a very bright day. The sky and water were both of the same deep hue; and the air felt warm and sunny; so that we threw off our jackets. I could hardly believe that I was sailing in the same ship I had been in during the night, when every thing had been so lonely and dim; and I could hardly imagine that this was the same ocean, now so beautiful and blue, that during part of the night-watch had rolled along so black and forbidding.

There were little traces of sunny clouds all over the heavens; and little fleeces of foam all over the sea; and the ship made a strange, musical noise under her bows, as she glided along, with her sails all still. It seemed a pity to go to work at such a time; and if we could only have sat on the windlass again; or if they would have let me go out on the bowsprit, and lay down between the *man-ropes* there, and look over at the fish in the water, and think of home, I should have been almost happy for a time.

I had now completely got over my sea-sickness, and felt very well; at least in my body, though my heart was far from feeling right; so that I could now look around me, and make observations.

And truly, though we were at sea, there was much to behold and wonder at; to me, who was on my first voyage. What most amazed me was the sight of the great ocean itself, for we were out of sight of land. All round us, on both sides of the ship, ahead and astern, nothing was to be seen but water—water—water; not a single glimpse of green shore, not the smallest island, or speck of moss any where. Never did I realize till now what the ocean was: how grand and majestic, how solitary, and boundless, and beautiful and blue;

for that day it gave no tokens of squalls or hurricanes, such as I had heard my father tell of; nor could I imagine, how any thing that seemed so playful and placid, could be lashed into rage, and troubled into rolling avalanches of foam, and great cascades of waves, such as I saw in the end.

As I looked at it so mild and sunny, I could not help calling to mind my little brother's face, when he was sleeping an infant in the cradle. It had just such a happy, careless, inno-cent look; and every happy little wave seemed gamboling about like a thoughtless little kid in a pasture; and seemed to look up in your face as it passed, as if it wanted to be patted and caressed. They seemed all live things with hearts in them, that could feel; and I almost felt grieved, as we sailed in among them, scattering them under our broad bows in sun-flakes, and riding over them like a great elephant among lambs.

But what seemed perhaps the most strange to me of all, was a certain wonderful rising and falling of the sea; I do not mean the waves themselves, but a sort of wide heaving and swelling and sinking all over the ocean. It was something I can not very well describe; but I know very well what it was, and how it affected me. It made me almost dizzy to look at it; and yet I could not keep my eyes off it, it seemed so pass-ing strange and wonderful.

I felt as if in a dream all the time; and when I could shut the ship out, almost thought I was in some new, fairy world, and expected to hear myself called to, out of the clear blue air, or from the depths of the deep blue sea. But I did not have much leisure to indulge in such thoughts; for the men were now getting some *stun'-sails* ready to hoist aloft, as the wind was getting fairer and fairer for us; and these stun'-sails are light canvas which are spread at such times, away out be-yond the ends of the yards, where they overhang the wide water, like the wings of a great bird.

For my own part, I could do but little to help the rest, not knowing the name of any thing, or the proper way to go about aught. Besides, I felt very dreamy, as I said before; and did not exactly know where, or what I was; every thing was so strange and new.

While the stun'-sails were lying all tumbled upon the deck,

and the sailors were fastening them to the booms, getting them ready to hoist, the mate ordered me to do a great many simple things, none of which could I comprehend, owing to the queer words he used; and then, seeing me stand quite perplexed and confounded, he would roar out at me, and call me all manner of names, and the sailors would laugh and wink to each other, but durst not go farther than that, for fear of the mate, who in his own presence would not let any body laugh at me but himself.

However, I tried to wake up as much as I could, and keep from dreaming with my eyes open; and being, at bottom, a smart, apt lad, at last I managed to learn a thing or two, so that I did not appear so much like a fool as at first.

People who have never gone to sea for the first time as sailors, can not imagine how puzzling and confounding it is. It must be like going into a barbarous country, where they speak a strange dialect, and dress in strange clothes, and live in strange houses. For sailors have their own names, even for things that are familiar ashore; and if you call a thing by its shore name, you are laughed at for an ignoramus and a land-lubber. This first day I speak of, the mate having ordered me to draw some water, I asked him where I was to get the pail; when I thought I had committed some dreadful crime; for he flew into a great passion, and said they never had any *pails* at sea, and then I learned that they were always called *buckets*. And once I was talking about sticking a little wooden peg into a bucket to stop a leak, when he flew out again, and said there were no *pegs* at sea, only *plugs*. And just so it was with every thing else.

But besides all this, there is such an infinite number of to-tally new names of new things to learn, that at first it seemed impossible for me to master them all. If you have ever seen a ship, you must have remarked what a thicket of ropes there are; and how they all seemed mixed and entangled together like a great skein of yarn. Now the very smallest of these ropes has its own proper name, and many of them are very lengthy, like the names of young royal princes, such as the *starboard-main-top-gallant-bow-line*, or the *larboard-fore-top-sail-clue-line*.

I think it would not be a bad plan to have a grand new

naming of a ship's ropes, as I have read, they once had a simplifying of the classes of plants in Botany. It is really wonderful how many names there are in the world. There is no counting the names, that surgeons and anatomists give to the various parts of the human body; which, indeed, is something like a ship; its bones being the stiff standing-rigging, and the sinews the small running ropes, that manage all the motions.

I wonder whether mankind could not get along without all these names, which keep increasing every day, and hour, and moment; till at last the very air will be full of them; and even in a great plain, men will be breathing each other's breath, owing to the vast multitude of words they use, that consume all the air, just as lamp-burners do gas. But people seem to have a great love for names; for to know a great many names, seems to look like knowing a good many things; though I should not be surprised, if there were a great many more names, than things in the world. But I must quit this rambling, and return to my story.

At last we hoisted the stun'-sails up to the top-sail yards; and as soon as the vessel felt them, she gave a sort of bound like a horse, and the breeze blowing more and more, she went plunging along, shaking off the foam from her bows, like foam from a bridle-bit. Every mast and timber seemed to have a pulse in it that was beating with life and joy; and I felt a wild exulting in my own heart, and felt as if I would be glad to bound along so round the world.

Then was I first conscious of a wonderful thing in me, that responded to all the wild commotion of the outer world; and went reeling on and on with the planets in their orbits, and was lost in one delirious throb at the center of the All. A wild bubbling and bursting was at my heart, as if a hidden spring had just gushed out there; and my blood ran tingling along my frame, like mountain brooks in spring freshets.

Yes! yes! give me this glorious ocean life, this salt-sea life, this briny, foamy life, when the sea neighs and snorts, and you breathe the very breath that the great whales respire! Let me roll around the globe, let me rock upon the sea; let me race and pant out my life, with an eternal breeze astern, and an endless sea before!

But how soon these raptures abated, when after a brief idle

interval, we were again set to work, and I had a vile commission to clean out the chicken coops, and make up the beds of
the pigs in the long-boat.

Miserable dog's life is this of the sea! commanded like a
slave, and set to work like an ass! vulgar and brutal men lording it over me, as if I were an African in Alabama. Yes, yes,
blow on, ye breezes, and make a speedy end to this abominable voyage!

Chapter 14

HE CONTEMPLATES MAKING A SOCIAL CALL ON THE CAPTAIN IN HIS CABIN

WHAT REMINDED ME most forcibly of my ignominious condition, was the widely altered manner of the captain toward me. I had thought him a fine, funny gentleman, full of mirth and good humor, and good will to seamen, and one who could not fail to appreciate the difference between me and the rude sailors among whom I was thrown. Indeed, I had made no doubt that he would in some special manner take me under his protection, and prove a kind friend and benefactor to me; as I had heard that some sea-captains are fathers to their crew; and so they are; but such fathers as Solomon's precepts tend to make—severe and chastising fathers, fathers whose sense of duty overcomes the sense of love, and who every day, in some sort, play the part of Brutus, who ordered his son away to execution, as I have read in our old family Plutarch.

Yes, I thought that Captain Riga, for Riga was his name, would be attentive and considerate to me, and strive to cheer me up, and comfort me in my lonesomeness. I did not even deem it at all impossible that he would invite me down into the cabin of a pleasant night, to ask me questions concerning my parents, and prospects in life; besides obtaining from me some anecdotes touching my great-uncle, the illustrious senator; or give me a slate and pencil, and teach me problems in navigation; or perhaps engage me at a game of chess. I even though he might invite me to dinner on a sunny Sunday, and help me plentifully to the nice cabin fare, as knowing how distasteful the salt beef and pork, and hard biscuit of the forecastle must at first be to a boy like me, who had always lived ashore, and at home.

And I could not help regarding him with peculiar emotions, almost of tenderness and love, as the last visible link in the chain of associations which bound me to my home. For, while yet in port, I had seen him and Mr. Jones, my brother's friend, standing together and conversing; so that from the captain to my brother there was but one intermediate step; and my brother and mother and sisters were one.

And this reminds me how often I used to pass by the places on deck, where I remembered Mr. Jones had stood when we first visited the ship lying at the wharf; and how I tried to convince myself that it was indeed true, that he had stood there, though now the ship was so far away on the wide Atlantic Ocean, and he perhaps was walking down Wall-street, or sitting reading the newspaper in his counting room, while poor I was so differently employed.

When two or three days had passed without the captain's speaking to me in any way, or sending word into the forecastle that he wished me to drop into the cabin to pay my respects, I began to think whether I should not make the first advances, and whether indeed he did not expect it of me, since I was but a boy, and he a man; and perhaps that might have been the reason why he had not spoken to me yet, deeming it more proper and respectful for me to address him first. I thought he might be offended, too, especially if he were a proud man, with tender feelings. So one evening, a little before sundown, in the second dog-watch, when there was no more work to be done, I concluded to call and see him.

After drawing a bucket of water, and having a good washing, to get off some of the chicken-coop stains, I went down into the forecastle to dress myself as neatly as I could. I put on a white shirt in place of my red one, and got into a pair of cloth trowsers instead of my duck ones, and put on my new pumps, and then carefully brushing my shooting-jacket, I put that on over all, so that upon the whole, I made quite a genteel figure, at least for a forecastle, though I would not have looked so well in a drawing-room.

When the sailors saw me thus employed, they did not know what to make of it, and wanted to know whether I was dressing to go ashore; I told them no, for we were then out of sight of land; but that I was going to pay my respects to the captain. Upon which they all laughed and shouted, as if I were a simpleton; though there seemed nothing so very simple in going to make an evening call upon a friend. When some of them tried to dissuade me, saying I was green and raw; but Jackson, who sat looking on, cried out, with a hideous grin, "Let him go, let him go, men—he's a nice boy. Let him go; the captain has some nuts and raisins for him." And so he was going on, when one of his violent fits of coughing seized him, and he almost choked.

As I was about leaving the forecastle, I happened to look at my hands, and seeing them stained all over of a deep yellow, for that morning the mate had set me to tarring some strips of canvas for the rigging, I thought it would never do to present myself before a gentleman that way; so for want of kids, I slipped on a pair of woolen mittens, which my mother had knit for me to carry to sea. As I was putting them on, Jackson asked me whether he shouldn't call a carriage; and another bade me not forget to present his best respects to the skipper. I left them all tittering, and coming on deck was passing the cook-house, when the old cook called after me, saying I had forgot my cane.

But I did not heed their impudence, and was walking straight toward the cabin-door on the quarter-deck, when the chief mate met me. I touched my hat, and was passing him, when, after staring at me till I thought his eyes would burst out, he all at once caught me by the collar, and with a voice of thunder, wanted to know what I meant by playing such tricks aboard a ship that he was mate of? I told him to let go of me, or I would complain to my friend the captain, whom I intended to visit that evening. Upon this he gave me such a whirl round, that I thought the Gulf Stream was in my head; and then shoved me forward, roaring out I know not what. Meanwhile the sailors were all standing round the windlass looking aft, mightily tickled.

Seeing I could not effect my object that night, I thought it best to defer it for the present; and returning among the sailors, Jackson asked me how I had found the captain, and whether the next time I went, I would not take a friend along and introduce him.

The upshot of this business was, that before I went to sleep that night, I felt well satisfied that it was not customary for sailors to call on the captain in the cabin; and I began to have

an inkling of the fact, that I had acted like a fool; but it all
arose from my ignorance of sea usages.

And here I may as well state, that I never saw the inside of
the cabin during the whole interval that elapsed from our sailing till our return to New York; though I often used to get a
peep at it through a little pane of glass, set in the house on
deck, just before the helm, where a watch was kept hanging
for the helmsman to strike the half hours by, with his little
bell in the binnacle, where the compass was. And it used to
be the great amusement of the sailors to look in through the
pane of glass, when they stood at the wheel, and watch the
proceedings in the cabin; especially when the steward was setting the table for dinner, or the captain was lounging over a
decanter of wine on a little mahogany stand, or playing the
game called *solitaire*, at cards, of an evening; for at times he
was all alone with his dignity; though, as will ere long be
shown, he generally had one pleasant companion, whose society he did not dislike.

The day following my attempt to drop in at the cabin,
I happened to be making fast a rope on the quarter-deck,
when the captain suddenly made his appearance, promenading up and down, and smoking a cigar. He looked very
good-humored and amiable, and it being just after his
dinner, I thought that this, to be sure, was just the chance I
wanted.

I waited a little while, thinking he would speak to me
himself; but as he did not, I went up to him, and began by
saying it was a very pleasant day, and hoped he was very
well. I never saw a man fly into such a rage; I thought he
was going to knock me down; but after standing speechless
awhile, he all at once plucked his cap from his head and
threw it at me. I don't know what impelled me, but I ran
to the lee-scuppers where it fell, picked it up, and gave it
to him with a bow; when the mate came running up, and
thrust me forward again; and after he had got me as far as
the windlass, he wanted to know whether I was crazy or
not; for if I was, he would put me in irons right off, and
have done with it.

But I assured him I was in my right mind, and knew perfectly well that I had been treated in the most rude and un-

gentlemanly manner both by him and Captain Riga. Upon this, he rapped out a great oath, and told me if I ever repeated what I had done that evening, or ever again presumed so much as to lift my hat to the captain, he would tie me into the rigging, and keep me there until I learned better manners. "You are very green," said he, "but I'll ripen you." Indeed this chief mate seemed to have the keeping of the dignity of the captain; who, in some sort, seemed too dignified personally to protect his own dignity.

I thought this strange enough, to be reprimanded, and charged with rudeness for an act of common civility. However, seeing how matters stood, I resolved to let the captain alone for the future, particularly as he had shown himself so deficient in the ordinary breeding of a gentleman. And I could hardly credit it, that this was the same man who had been so very civil, and polite, and witty, when Mr. Jones and I called upon him in port.

But this astonishment of mine was much increased, when some days after, a storm came upon us, and the captain rushed out of the cabin in his nightcap, and nothing else but his shirt on; and leaping up on the poop, began to jump up and down, and curse and swear, and call the men aloft all manner of hard names, just like a common loafer in the street.

Besides all this, too, I noticed that while we were at sea, he wore nothing but old shabby clothes, very different from the glossy suit I had seen him in at our first interview, and after that on the steps of the City Hotel, where he always boarded when in New York. Now, he wore nothing but old-fashioned snuff-colored coats, with high collars and short waists; and faded, short-legged pantaloons, very tight about the knees; and vests, that did not conceal his waistbands, owing to their being so short, just like a little boy's. And his hats were all caved in, and battered, as if they had been knocked about in a cellar; and his boots were sadly patched. Indeed, I began to think that he was but a shabby fellow after all; particularly as his whiskers lost their gloss, and he went days together without shaving; and his hair, by a sort of miracle, began to grow of a pepper and salt color, which might have been owing, though, to his discontinuing the use of some kind of dye while at sea.

I put him down as a sort of imposter; and while ashore, a
gentleman on false pretenses; for no gentleman would have
treated another gentleman as he did me.

Yes, Captain Riga, thought I, you are no gentleman, and
you know it!

Chapter 15

The Melancholy State of His Wardrobe

And now that I have been speaking of the captain's old clothes, I may as well speak of mine.

It was very early in the month of June that we sailed; and I had greatly rejoiced that it was that time of the year; for it would be warm and pleasant upon the ocean, I thought; and my voyage would be like a summer excursion to the sea shore, for the benefit of the salt water, and a change of scene and society.

So I had not given myself much concern about what I should wear; and deemed it wholly unnecessary to provide myself with a great outfit of pilot-cloth jackets, and trowsers, and Guernsey frocks, and oil-skin suits, and sea-boots, and many other things, which old seamen carry in their chests. But one reason was, that I did not have the money to buy them with, even if I had wanted to. So in addition to the clothes I had brought from home, I had only bought a red shirt, a tarpaulin hat, and a belt and knife, as I have previously related, which gave me a sea outfit, something like the Texian rangers', whose uniform, they say, consists of a shirt collar and a pair of spurs.

But I was not many days at sea, when I found that my shore clothing, or "*long togs*," as the sailors call them, were but ill adapted to the life I now led. When I went aloft, at my yard-arm gymnastics, my pantaloons were all the time ripping and splitting in every direction, particularly about the seat, owing to their not being cut sailor-fashion, with low waistbands, and to wear without suspenders. So that I was often placed in most unpleasant predicaments, straddling the rigging, sometimes in plain sight of the cabin, with my table linen exposed in the most inelegant and ungentlemanly manner possible.

And worse than all, my best pair of pantaloons, and the pair I most prided myself upon, was a very conspicuous and remarkable looking pair.

I had had them made to order by our village tailor, a little fat man, very thin in the legs, and who used to say he imported the latest fashions direct from Paris; though all the fashion plates in his shop were very dirty with fly-marks.

Well, this tailor made the pantaloons I speak of, and while he had them in hand, I used to call and see him two or three times a day to try them on, and hurry him forward; for he was an old man with large round spectacles, and could not see very well, and had no one to help him but a sick wife, with five grandchildren to take care of; and besides that, he was such a great snuff-taker, that it interfered with his business; for he took several pinches for every stitch, and would sit snuffling and blowing his nose over my pantaloons, till I used to get disgusted with him. Now, this old tailor had shown me the pattern, after which he intended to make my pantaloons; but I improved upon it, and bade him have a slit on the outside of each leg, at the foot, to button up with a row of six brass bell buttons; for a grown-up cousin of mine, who was a great sportsman, used to wear a beautiful pair of pantaloons, made precisely in that way.

And these were the very pair I now had at sea; the sailors made a great deal of fun of them, and were all the time calling on each other to "*twig*" them; and they would ask me to lend them a button or two, by way of a joke; and then they would ask me if I was not a soldier. Showing very plainly that they had no idea that my pantaloons were a very genteel pair, made in the height of the sporting fashion, and copied from my cousin's, who was a young man of fortune and drove a tilbury.

When my pantaloons ripped and tore, as I have said, I did my best to mend and patch them; but not being much of a sempstress, the more I patched the more they parted; because I put my patches on, without heeding the joints of the legs, which only irritated my poor pants the more, and put them out of temper.

Nor must I forget my boots, which were almost new when I left home. They had been my Sunday boots, and fitted me to a charm. I never had had a pair of boots that I liked better; I used to turn my toes out when I walked in them, unless it was night time, when no one could see me, and I had something else to think of; and I used to keep looking at them during church; so that I lost a good deal of the sermon. In a word, they were a beautiful pair of boots. But all this only unfitted them the more for sea-service; as I soon discovered. They had very high heels, which were all the time tripping me in the rigging, and several times came near pitching me overboard; and the salt water made them shrink in such a manner, that they pinched me terribly about the instep; and I was obliged to gash them cruelly, which went to my very heart. The legs were quite long, coming a good way up toward my knees, and the edges were mounted with red morocco. The sailors used to call them my "*gaff-topsail-boots.*" And sometimes they used to call me "Boots," and sometimes "Buttons," on account of the ornaments on my pantaloons and shooting-jacket.

At last, I took their advice, and "*razeed*" them, as they phrased it. That is, I amputated the legs, and shaved off the heels to the bare soles; which, however, did not much improve them, for it made my feet feel flat as flounders, and besides, brought me down in the world, and made me slip and slide about the decks, as I used to at home, when I wore straps on the ice.

As for my tarpaulin hat, it was a very cheap one; and therefore proved a real sham and shave; it leaked like an old shingle roof; and in a rain storm, kept my hair wet and disagreeable. Besides, from lying down on deck in it, during the night watches, it got bruised and battered, and lost all its beauty; so that it was unprofitable every way.

But I had almost forgotten my shooting-jacket, which was made of moleskin. Every day, it grew smaller and smaller, particularly after a rain, until at last I thought it would completely exhale, and leave nothing but the bare seams, by way of a skeleton, on my back. It became unspeakably unpleasant, when we got into rather cold weather, crossing the Banks of Newfoundland, when the only way I had to keep warm during the night, was to pull on my waistcoat and my roundabout, and then clap the shooting-jacket over all. This made it pinch me under the arms, and it vexed, irritated, and tormented me every way; and used to incommode my arms seriously when I was pulling the ropes; so much so, that the mate asked me once if I had the cramp.

I may as well here glance at some trials and tribulations of a similar kind. I had no mattress, or bed-clothes, of any sort; for the thought of them had never entered my mind before going to sea; so that I was obliged to sleep on the bare boards of my bunk; and when the ship pitched violently, and almost stood upon end, I must have looked like an Indian baby tied to a plank, and hung up against a tree like a crucifix.

I have already mentioned my total want of table-tools; never dreaming, that, in this respect, going to sea as a sailor was something like going to a boarding-school, where you must furnish your own spoon and knife, fork, and napkin. But at length, I was so happy as to barter with a steerage passenger a silk handkerchief of mine for a half-gallon iron pot, with hooks to it, to hang on a grate; and this pot I used to present at the cook-house for my allowance of coffee and tea. It gave me a good deal of trouble, though, to keep it clean, being much disposed to rust; and the hooks sometimes scratched my face when I was drinking; and it was unusually large and heavy; so that my breakfasts were deprived of all ease and satisfaction, and became a toil and a labor to me. And I was forced to use the same pot for my bean-soup, three times a week, which imparted to it a bad flavor for coffee.

I can not tell how I really suffered in many ways for my improvidence and heedlessness, in going to sea so ill provided with every thing calculated to make my situation at all comfortable, or even tolerable. In time, my wretched "long togs" began to drop off my back, and I looked like a Sam Patch, shambling round the deck in my rags and the wreck of my gaff-topsail-boots. I often thought what my friends at home would have said, if they could but get one peep at me. But I hugged myself in my miserable shooting-jacket, when I considered that that degradation and shame never could overtake me; yet, I thought it a galling mockery, when I remembered that my sisters had promised to tell all inquiring friends, that Wellingborough had gone "*abroad*;" just as if I was visiting Europe on a tour with my tutor, as poor simple Mr. Jones had hinted to the captain.

Still, in spite of the melancholy which sometimes overtook me, there were several little incidents that made me forget myself in the contemplation of the strange and to me most wonderful sights of the sea.

And perhaps nothing struck into me such a feeling of wild romance, as a view of the first vessel we spoke. It was of a clear sunny afternoon, and she came bearing down upon us, a most beautiful sight, with all her sails spread wide. She came very near, and passed under our stern; and as she leaned over to the breeze, showed her decks fore and aft; and I saw the strange sailors grouped upon the forecastle, and the cook looking out of his cook-house with a ladle in his hand, and the captain in a green jacket sitting on the taffrail with a speaking-trumpet.

And here, had this vessel come out of the infinite blue ocean, with all these human beings on board, and the smoke tranquilly mounting up into the sea-air from the cook's funnel as if it were a chimney in a city; and every thing looking so cool, and calm, and of-course, in the midst of what to me, at least, seemed a superlative marvel.

Hoisted at her mizzen-peak was a red flag, with a turreted white castle in the middle, which looked foreign enough, and made me stare all the harder.

Our captain, who had put on another hat and coat, and was lounging in an elegant attitude on the poop, now put his high polished brass trumpet to his mouth, and said in a very rude voice for conversation, *"Where from?"*

To which the other captain rejoined with some outlandish Dutch gibberish, of which we could only make out, that the ship belonged to Hamburg, as her flag denoted.

Hamburg! Bless my soul! and here I am on the great Atlantic Ocean, actually beholding a ship from Holland! It was passing strange. In my intervals of leisure from other duties, I followed the strange ship till she was quite a little speck in the distance.

I could not but be struck with the manner of the two sea-captains during their brief interview. Seated at their ease on their respective "poops" toward the stern of their ships, while the sailors were obeying their behests; they touched hats to each other, exchanged compliments, and drove on, with all the indifference of two Arab horsemen accosting each other on an airing in the Desert. To them, I suppose, the great Atlantic Ocean was a puddle.

Chapter 16

I MUST NOW RUN BACK a little, and tell of my first going
aloft at sea.

It happened on the second night out of port, during the
middle watch, when the sea was quite calm, and the breeze
was mild.

The order was given to loose the *main-skysail*, which is the
fifth and highest sail from deck. It was a very small sail, and
from the forecastle looked no bigger than a cambric pocket-
handkerchief. But I have heard that some ships carry still
smaller sails, above the skysail; called *moon-sails*, and *sky-
scrapers*, and *cloud-rakers*. But I shall not believe in them till I
see them; a *skysail* seems high enough in all conscience; and
the idea of any thing higher than that, seems preposterous.
Besides, it looks almost like tempting heaven, to brush the
very firmament so, and almost put the eyes of the stars out;
when a flaw of wind, too, might very soon take the conceit
out of these cloud-defying *cloud-rakers*.

Now, when the order was passed to loose the skysail, an
old Dutch sailor came up to me, and said, "Buttons, my boy,
it's high time you be doing something; and it's boy's business, Buttons, to loose de royals, and not old men's business,
like me. Now, d'ye see dat leetle fellow way up dare? *dare*,
just behind dem stars dare: well, tumble up, now, Buttons, I
zay, and looze him; way you go, Buttons."

All the rest joining in, and seeming unanimous in the opinion, that it was high time for me to be stirring myself, and
doing *boy's business*, as they called it, I made no more ado,
but jumped into the rigging. Up I went, not daring to look
down, but keeping my eyes glued, as it were, to the shrouds,
as I ascended.

It was a long road up those stairs, and I began to pant and
breathe hard, before I was half way. But I kept at it till I got
to the *Jacob's Ladder*; and they may well call it so, for it took

me almost into the clouds; and at last, to my own amazement, I found myself hanging on the skysail-yard, holding on might and main to the mast; and curling my feet round the rigging, as if they were another pair of hands.

For a few moments I stood awe-stricken and mute. I could not see far out upon the ocean, owing to the darkness of the night; and from my lofty perch, the sea looked like a great, black gulf, hemmed in, all round, by beetling black cliffs. I seemed all alone; treading the midnight clouds; and every second, expected to find myself falling—falling—falling, as I have felt when the nightmare has been on me.

I could but just perceive the ship below me, like a long narrow plank in the water; and it did not seem to belong at all to the yard, over which I was hanging. A gull, or some sort of sea-fowl, was flying round the truck over my head, within a few yards of my face; and it almost frightened me to hear it; it seemed so much like a spirit, at such a lofty and solitary height.

Though there was a pretty smooth sea, and little wind; yet, at this extreme elevation, the ship's motion was very great; so that when the ship rolled one way, I felt something as a fly must feel, walking the ceiling; and when it rolled the other way, I felt as if I was hanging along a slanting pine-tree.

But presently I heard a distant, hoarse noise from below; and though I could not make out any thing intelligible, I knew it was the mate hurrying me. So in a nervous, trembling desperation, I went to casting off the *gaskets*, or lines tying up the sail; and when all was ready, sung out as I had been told, to *"hoist away!"* And hoist they did, and me too along with the yard and sail; for I had no time to get off, they were so unexpectedly quick about it. It seemed like magic; there I was, going up higher and higher; the yard rising under me, as if it were alive, and no soul in sight. Without knowing it at the time, I was in a good deal of danger, but it was so dark that I could not see well enough to feel afraid—at least on that account; though I felt frightened enough in a promiscuous way. I only held on hard, and made good the saying of old sailors, that the last person to fall overboard from the rigging is a landsman, because he grips the ropes so fiercely; whereas old tars are less careful, and sometimes pay the penalty.

After this feat, I got down rapidly on deck, and received something like a compliment from Max the Dutchman.

This man was perhaps the best natured man among the crew; at any rate, he treated me better than the rest did; and for that reason he deserves some mention.

Max was an old bachelor of a sailor, very precise about his wardrobe, and prided himself greatly upon his seamanship, and entertained some straight-laced, old-fashioned notions about the duties of boys at sea. His hair, whiskers, and cheeks were of a fiery red; and as he wore a red shirt, he was altogether the most combustible looking man I ever saw.

Nor did his appearance belie him; for his temper was very inflammable; and at a word, he would explode in a shower of hard words and imprecations. It was Max that several times set on foot those conspiracies against Jackson, which I have spoken of before; but he ended by paying him a grumbling homage, full of resentful reservations.

Max sometimes manifested some little interest in my welfare; and often discoursed concerning the sorry figure I would cut in my tatters when we got to Liverpool, and the discredit it would bring on the American Merchant Service; for like all European seamen in American ships, Max prided himself not a little upon his naturalization as a Yankee, and if he could, would have been very glad to have passed himself off for a born native.

But notwithstanding his grief at the prospect of my reflecting discredit upon his adopted country, he never offered to better my wardrobe, by loaning me any thing from his own well-stored chest. Like many other well-wishers, he contented him with sympathy. Max also betrayed some anxiety to know whether I knew how to dance; lest, when the ship's company went ashore, I should disgrace them by exposing my awkwardness in some of the sailor saloons. But I relieved his anxiety on that head.

He was a great scold, and fault-finder, and often took me to task about my short-comings; but herein, he was not alone; for every one had a finger, or a thumb, and sometimes both hands, in my unfortunate pie.

Chapter 17

IT WAS ON A SUNDAY we made the Banks of Newfoundland; a drizzling, foggy, clammy Sunday. You could hardly see the water, owing to the mist and vapor upon it; and every thing was so flat and calm, I almost thought we must have somehow got back to New York, and were lying at the foot of Wall-street again in a rainy twilight. The decks were dripping with wet, so that in the dense fog, it seemed as if we were standing on the roof of a house in a shower.

It was a most miserable Sunday; and several of the sailors had twinges of the rheumatism, and pulled on their monkey-jackets. As for Jackson, he was all the time rubbing his back and snarling like a dog.

I tried to recall all my pleasant, sunny Sundays ashore; and tried to imagine what they were doing at home; and whether our old family friend, Mr. Bridenstoke, would drop in, with his silver-mounted tasseled cane, between churches, as he used to; and whether he would inquire about myself.

But it would not do. I could hardly realize that it was Sunday at all. Every thing went on pretty much the same as before. There was no church to go to; no place to take a walk in; no friend to call upon. I began to think it must be a sort of second Saturday; a foggy Saturday, when school-boys stay at home reading Robinson Crusoe.

The only man who seemed to be taking his ease that day, was our black cook; who according to the invariable custom at sea, always went by the name of *the doctor*.

And *doctors*, cooks certainly are, the very best medicos in the world; for what pestilent pills and potions of the Faculty are half so serviceable to man, and health-and-strength-giving, as roasted lamb and green peas, say, in spring; and roast beef and cranberry sauce in winter? Will a dose of calomel and jalap do you as much good? Will a bolus build up a fainting man? Is there any satisfaction in dining off a powder? But these doctors of the frying-pan sometimes kill men off by a surfeit; or give them the headache, at least. Well, what then? No matter. For if with their most goodly and ten times jolly medicines, they now and then fill our nights with tribulations, and abridge our days, what of the social homicides perpetrated by the Faculty? And when you die by a pill-doctor's hands, it is never with a sweet relish in your mouth, as though you died by a frying-pan-doctor; but your last breath villainously savors of ipecac and rhubarb. Then, what charges they make for the abominable lunches they serve out so stingily! One of their bills for boluses would keep you in good dinners a twelvemonth.

Now, our doctor was a serious old fellow, much given to metaphysics, and used to talk about original sin. All that Sunday morning, he sat over his boiling pots, reading out of a book which was very much soiled and covered with grease spots: for he kept it stuck into a little leather strap, nailed to the keg where he kept the fat skimmed off the water in which the salt beef was cooked. I could hardly believe my eyes when I found this book was the Bible.

I loved to peep in upon him, when he was thus absorbed; for his smoky studio or study was a strange-looking place enough; not more than five feet square, and about as many high; a mere box to hold the stove, the pipe of which stuck out of the roof.

Within, it was hung round with pots and pans; and on one side was a little looking-glass, where he used to shave; and on a small shelf were his shaving tools, and a comb and brush. Fronting the stove, and very close to it, was a sort of narrow shelf, where he used to sit with his legs spread out very wide, to keep them from scorching; and there, with his book in one hand, and a pewter spoon in the other, he sat all that Sunday morning, stirring up his pots, and studying away at the same time; seldom taking his eye off the page. Reading must have been very hard work for him; for he muttered to himself quite loud as he read; and big drops of sweat would stand upon his brow, and roll off, till they hissed on the hot stove before him.

But on the day I speak of, it was no wonder that he got perplexed, for he was reading a mysterious passage in the Book of Chronicles. Being aware that I knew how to read, he called me as I was passing his premises, and read the passage over, demanding an explanation. I told him it was a mystery that no one could explain; not even a parson. But this did not satisfy him, and I left him poring over it still.

He must have been a member of one of those negro churches, which are to be found in New York. For when we lay at the wharf, I remembered that a committee of three reverend looking old darkies, who, besides their natural canonicals, wore quaker-cut black coats, and broad-brimmed black hats, and white neck-cloths; these colored gentlemen called upon him, and remained conversing with him at his cookhouse door for more than an hour; and before they went away they stepped inside, and the sliding doors were closed; and then we heard some one reading aloud and preaching; and after that a psalm was sung and a benediction given; when the door opened again, and the congregation came out in a great perspiration; owing, I suppose, to the chapel being so small, and there being only one seat besides the stove.

But notwithstanding his religious studies and meditations, this old fellow used to use some bad language occasionally; particularly of cold, wet, stormy mornings, when he had to get up before daylight and make his fire; with the sea breaking over the bows, and now and then dashing into his stove.

So, under the circumstances, you could not blame him much, if he did rip a little, for it would have tried old Job's temper, to be set to work making a fire in the water.

Without being at all neat about his premises, this old cook was very particular about them; he had a warm love and affection for his cook-house. In fair weather, he spread the skirt of an old jacket before the door, by way of a mat; and screwed a small ring-bolt into the door for a knocker; and wrote his name, "Mr. Thompson," over it, with a bit of red chalk.

The men said he lived round the corner of *Forecastle-square*, opposite the *Liberty Pole*; because his cook-house was right behind the foremast, and very near the quarters occupied by themselves.

Sailors have a great fancy for naming things that way on shipboard. When a man is hung at sea, which is always done from one of the lower yard-arms, they say he "*takes a walk up Ladder-lane, and down Hemp-street.*"

Mr. Thompson was a great crony of the steward's, who, being a handsome, dandy mulatto, that had once been a barber in West-Broadway, went by the name of Lavender. I have mentioned the gorgeous turban he wore when Mr. Jones and I visited the captain in the cabin. He never wore that turban at sea, though; but sported an uncommon head of frizzled hair, just like the large, round brush, used for washing windows, called a *Pope's Head*.

He kept it well perfumed with Cologne water, of which he had a large supply, the relics of his West-Broadway stock in trade. His clothes, being mostly cast-off suits of the captain of a London liner, whom he had sailed with upon many previous voyages, were all in the height of the exploded fashions, and of every kind of color and cut. He had claret-colored suits, and snuff-colored suits, and red velvet vests, and buff and brimstone pantaloons, and several full suits of black, which, with his dark-colored face, made him look quite clerical; like a serious young colored gentleman of Barbadoes, about to take orders.

He wore an uncommon large pursy ring on his fore-finger, with something he called a real diamond in it; though it was very dim, and looked more like a glass eye than any thing else. He was very proud of his ring, and was always calling your attention to something, and pointing at it with his ornamented finger.

He was a sentimental sort of a darky, and read the "*Three Spaniards*," and "*Charlotte Temple*," and carried a lock of frizzled hair in his vest pocket, which he frequently volunteered to show to people, with his handkerchief to his eyes.

Every fine evening, about sunset, these two, the cook and steward, used to sit on the little shelf in the cook-house, leaning up against each other like the Siamese twins, to keep from falling off, for the shelf was very short; and there they would stay till after dark, smoking their pipes, and gossiping about the events that had happened during the day in the cabin.

And sometimes Mr. Thompson would take down his Bible, and read a chapter for the edification of Lavender, whom he knew to be a sad profligate and gay deceiver ashore; addicted to every youthful indiscretion. He would read over to him the story of Joseph and Potiphar's wife; and hold Joseph up to him as a young man of excellent principles, whom he ought to imitate, and not be guilty of his indiscretion any more. And Lavender would look serious, and say that he knew it was all true—he was a wicked youth, he knew it— he had broken a good many hearts, and many eyes were weeping for him even then, both in New York, and Liverpool, and London, and Havre. But how could he help it? He hadn't made his handsome face, and fine head of hair, and graceful figure. It was not *he*, but the others, that were to blame; for his bewitching person turned all heads and subdued all hearts, wherever he went. And then he would look very serious and penitent, and go up to the little glass, and pass his hands through his hair, and see how his whiskers were coming on.

Chapter 18

HE ENDEAVORS TO IMPROVE HIS MIND; AND TELLS OF ONE BLUNT AND HIS DREAM-BOOK

O N THE SUNDAY AFTERNOON I spoke of, it was my watch below, and I thought I would spend it profitably, in improving my mind.

My bunk was an upper one; and right over the head of it was a *bull's-eye*, or circular piece of thick ground glass, inserted into the deck to give light. It was a dull, dubious light, though; and I often found myself looking up anxiously to see whether the bull's eye had not suddenly been put out; for whenever any one trod on it, in walking the deck, it was momentarily quenched; and what was still worse, sometimes a coil of rope would be thrown down on it, and stay there till I dressed myself and went up to remove it—a kind of interruption to my studies which annoyed me very much, when diligently occupied in reading.

However, I was glad of any light at all, down in that gloomy hole, where we burrowed like rabbits in a warren; and it was the happiest time I had, when all my messmates were asleep, and I could lie on my back, during a forenoon watch below, and read in comparative quiet and seclusion.

I had already read two books loaned to me by Max, to whose share they had fallen, in dividing the effects of the sailor who had jumped overboard. One was an account of Shipwrecks and Disasters at Sea, and the other was a large black volume, with *Delirium Tremens* in great gilt letters on the back. This proved to be a popular treatise on the subject of that disease; and I remembered seeing several copies in the sailor book-stalls about Fulton Market, and along South-street, in New York.

But this Sunday I got out a book, from which I expected to reap great profit and sound instruction. It had been presented to me by Mr. Jones, who had quite a library, and took down this book from a top shelf, where it lay very dusty. When he gave it to me, he said, that although I was going to sea, I must not forget the importance of a good education; and that there was hardly any situation in life, however humble and depressed, or dark and gloomy, but one might find leisure in it to store his mind, and build himself up in the exact sciences. And he added, that though it *did* look rather unfavorable for my future prospects, to be going to sea as a common sailor so early in life; yet, it would no doubt turn out for my benefit in the end; and, at any rate, if I would only take good care of myself, would give me a sound constitution, if nothing more; and *that* was not to be undervalued, for how many very rich men would give all their bonds and mortgages for my boyish robustness.

He added, that I need not expect any light, trivial work, that was merely entertaining, and nothing more; but here I would find entertainment and edification beautifully and harmoniously combined; and though, at first, I might possibly find it dull, yet, if I perused the book thoroughly, it would soon discover hidden charms and unforeseen attractions; besides teaching me, perhaps, the true way to retrieve the poverty of my family, and again make them all well to do in the world.

Saying this, he handed it to me, and I blew the dust off, and looked at the back: "*Smith's Wealth of Nations*." This not satisfying me, I glanced at the title page, and found it was an "*Enquiry into the Nature and Causes*" of the alleged wealth of nations. But happening to look further down, I caught sight of "*Aberdeen*," where the book was printed; and thinking that any thing from Scotland, a foreign country, must prove some way or other pleasing to me, I thanked Mr. Jones very kindly, and promised to peruse the volume carefully.

So, now, lying in my bunk, I began the book methodically, at page number one, resolved not to permit a few flying glimpses into it, taken previously, to prevent me from making regular approaches to the gist and body of the book, where I fancied lay something like the philosopher's stone, a secret talisman, which would transmute even pitch and tar to silver and gold.

Pleasant, though vague visions of future opulence floated before me, as I commenced the first chapter, entitled "*Of the causes of improvement in the productive power of labor*." Dry as crackers and cheese, to be sure; and the chapter itself was not much better. But this was only getting initiated; and if I read on, the grand secret would be opened to me. So I read on and on, about "*wages and profits of labor*," without getting any profits myself for my pains in perusing it.

Dryer and dryer; the very leaves smelt of saw-dust; till at last I drank some water, and went at it again. But soon I had to give it up for lost work; and thought that the old backgammon board, we had at home, lettered on the back, "*The History of Rome*," was quite as full of matter, and a great deal more entertaining. I wondered whether Mr. Jones had ever read the volume himself; and could not help remembering, that he had to get on a chair when he reached it down from its dusty shelf; *that* certainly looked suspicious.

The best reading was on the fly leaves; and, on turning them over, I lighted upon some half effaced pencil-marks to the following effect: "*Jonathan Jones, from his particular friend Daniel Dods, 1798.*" So it must have originally belonged to Mr. Jones' father; and I wondered whether *he* had ever read it; or, indeed, whether any body had ever read it, even the author himself; but then authors, they say, never read their own books; writing them, being enough in all conscience.

At length I fell asleep, with the volume in my hand; and never slept so sound before; after that, I used to wrap my jacket round it, and use it for a pillow; for which purpose it answered very well; only I sometimes waked up feeling dull and stupid; but of course the book could not have been the cause of that.

And now I am talking of books, I must tell of Jack Blunt the sailor, and his Dream Book.

Jackson, who seemed to know every thing about all parts of the world, used to tell Jack in reproach, that he was an *Irish Cockney.* By which I understood, that he was an Irishman born, but had graduated in London, somewhere about Radcliffe Highway; but he had no sort of brogue that I could hear.

He was a curious looking fellow, about twenty-five years old, as I should judge; but to look at his back, you would have taken him for a little old man. His arms and legs were very large, round, short, and stumpy; so that when he had on his great monkey-jacket, and sou'west cap flapping in his face, and his sea boots drawn up to his knees, he looked like a fat porpoise, standing on end. He had a round face, too, like a walrus; and with about the same expression, half human and half indescribable. He was, upon the whole, a good-natured fellow, and a little given to looking at sea-life romantically; singing songs about susceptible mermaids who fell in love with handsome young oyster boys and gallant fishermen. And he had a sad story about a man-of-war's-man who broke his heart at Portsmouth during the late war, and threw away his life recklessly at one of the quarter-deck carronades, in the battle between the Guerriere and Constitution; and another incomprehensible story about a sort of fairy sea-queen, who used to be dunning a sea-captain all the time for his auto-graph to boil in some eel soup, for a spell against the scurvy.

He believed in all kinds of witch-work and magic; and had some wild Irish words he used to mutter over during a calm for a fair wind.

And he frequently related his interviews in Liverpool with a fortune-teller, an old negro woman by the name of De Squak, whose house was much frequented by sailors; and how she had two black cats, with remarkably green eyes, and nightcaps on their heads, solemnly seated on a claw-footed table near the old goblin; when she felt his pulse, to tell what was going to befall him.

This Blunt had a large head of hair, very thick and bushy; but from some cause or other, it was rapidly turning gray; and in its transition state made him look as if he wore a shako of badger skin.

The phenomenon of gray hairs on a young head, had per-plexed and confounded this Blunt to such a degree that he at last came to the conclusion it must be the result of the black art, wrought upon him by an enemy; and that enemy, he opined, was an old sailor landlord in Marseilles, whom he had once seriously offended, by knocking him down in a fray.

So while in New York, finding his hair growing grayer and grayer, and all his friends, the ladies and others, laughing at him, and calling him an old man with one foot in the grave, he slipt out one night to an apothecary's, stated his case, and wanted to know what could be done for him.

The apothecary immediately gave him a pint bottle of something he called "*Trafalgar Oil* for restoring the hair," *price one dollar*; and told him that after he had used that bottle, and it did not have the desired effect, he must try bottle No. 2, called "*Balm of Paradise, or the Elixir of the Battle of Copenhagen.*" These high-sounding naval names delighted Blunt, and he had no doubt there must be virtue in them.

I saw both bottles; and on one of them was an engraving, representing a young man, presumed to be gray-headed, standing in his night-dress in the middle of his chamber, and with closed eyes applying the Elixir to his head, with both hands; while on the bed adjacent stood a large bottle, conspicuously labeled, "*Balm of Paradise.*" It seemed from the text, that this gray-headed young man was so smitten with his hair-oil, and was so thoroughly persuaded of its virtues, that he had got out of bed, even in his sleep; groped into his closet, seized the precious bottle, applied its contents, and then to bed again, getting up in the morning without knowing any thing about it. Which, indeed, was a most mysterious occurrence; and it was still more mysterious, how the engraver came to know an event, of which the actor himself was ignorant, and where there were no bystanders.

Three times in the twenty-four hours, Blunt, while at sea, regularly rubbed in his liniments; but though the first bottle was soon exhausted by his copious applications, and the second half gone, he still stuck to it, that by the time we got to Liverpool, his exertions would be crowned with success. And he was not a little delighted, that this gradual change would be operating while we were at sea; so as not to expose him to the invidious observations of people ashore; on the same principle that dandies go into the country when they purpose raising whiskers. He would often ask his shipmates, whether they noticed any change yet; and if so, how much of a change? And to tell the truth, there was a very great change indeed; for the constant soaking of his hair with oil, operating in conjunction with the neglect of his toilet, and want of a brush and comb, had matted his locks together like a wild horse's mane, and imparted to it a blackish and extremely glossy hue.

Besides his collection of hair-oils, Blunt had also provided himself with several boxes of pills, which he had purchased from a sailor doctor in New York, who by placards stuck on the posts along the wharves, advertised to remain standing at the northeast corner of Catharine Market, every Monday and Friday, between the hours of ten and twelve in the morning, to receive calls from patients, distribute medicines, and give advice gratis.

Whether Blunt thought he had the dyspepsia or not, I can not say; but at breakfast, he always took three pills with his coffee; something as they do in Iowa, when the bilious fever prevails; where, at the boarding-houses, they put a vial of blue pills into the castor, along with the pepper and mustard, and next door to another vial of toothpicks. But they are very ill-bred and unpolished in the western country.

Several times, too, Blunt treated himself to a flowing bumper of *horse salts* (Glauber salts); for like many other sea-men, he never went to sea without a good supply of that luxury. He would frequently, also, take this medicine in a wet jacket, and then go on deck into a rain storm. But this is nothing to other sailors, who at sea will doctor themselves with calomel off Cape Horn, and still remain on duty. And in this connection, some really frightful stories might be told; but I forbear.

For a landsman to take salts as this Blunt did, it would perhaps be the death of him; but at sea the salt air and the salt water prevent you from catching cold so readily as on land; and for my own part, on board this very ship, being so illy-provided with clothes, I frequently turned into my bunk soaking wet, and turned out again piping hot, and smoking like a roasted sirloin; and yet was never the worse for it; for then, I bore a charmed life of youth and health, and was dagger-proof to bodily ill.

But it is time to tell of the Dream Book. Snugly hidden in one corner of his chest, Blunt had an extraordinary looking pamphlet, with a red cover, marked all over with astrological signs and ciphers, and purporting to be a full and complete treatise on the art of Divination; so that the most simple sailor could teach it to himself.

It also purported to be the selfsame system, by aid of which Napoleon Bonaparte had risen in the world from being a corporal to an emperor. Hence it was entitled the *Bonaparte Dream Book*; for the magic of it lay in the interpretation of dreams, and their application to the foreseeing of future events; so that all preparatory measures might be taken beforehand; which would be exceedingly convenient, and satisfactory every way, if true. The problems were to be cast by means of figures, in some perplexed and difficult way, which, however, was facilitated by a set of tables in the end of the pamphlet, something like the Logarithm Tables at the end of Bowditch's Navigator.

Now, Blunt revered, adored, and worshiped this *Bonaparte Dream Book* of his; and was fully persuaded that between those red covers, and in his own dreams, lay all the secrets of futurity. Every morning before taking his pills, and applying his hair-oils, he would steal out of his bunk before the rest of the watch were awake; take out his pamphlet, and a bit of chalk; and then straddling his chest, begin scratching his oily head to remember his fugitive dreams; marking down strokes on his chest-lid, as if he were casting up his daily accounts.

Though often perplexed and lost in mazes concerning the cabalistic figures in the book, and the chapter of directions to beginners; for he could with difficulty read at all; yet, in the end, if not interrupted, he somehow managed to arrive at a conclusion satisfactory to him. So that, as he generally wore a good-humored expression, no doubt he must have thought, that all his future affairs were working together for the best.

But one night he started us all up in a fright, by springing from his bunk, his eyes ready to start out of his head, and crying, in a husky voice—"Boys! boys! get the benches ready! Quick, quick!"

"What benches?" growled Max—"What's the matter?"

"Benches! benches!" screamed Blunt, without heeding him, "cut down the forests, bear a hand, boys; the Day of Judgment's coming!"

But the next moment, he got quietly into his bunk, and laid still, muttering to himself, he had only been rambling in his sleep.

I did not know exactly what he had meant by his *benches*; till, shortly after, I overheard two of the sailors debating, whether mankind would stand or sit at the Last Day.

Chapter 19

A Narrow Escape

T HIS DREAM BOOK of Blunt's reminds me of a narrow escape we had, early one morning.

It was the larboard watch's turn to remain below from midnight till four o'clock; and having turned in and slept, Blunt suddenly turned out again about three o'clock, with a wonderful dream in his head; which he was desirous of at once having interpreted.

So he goes to his chest, gets out his tools, and falls to ciphering on the lid. When, all at once, a terrible cry was heard, that routed him and all the rest of us up, and sent the whole ship's company flying on deck in the dark. We did not know what it was; but somehow, among sailors at sea, they seem to know when real danger of any kind is at hand, even in their sleep.

When we got on deck, we saw the mate standing on the bowsprit, and crying out *Luff! Luff!* to some one in the dark water before the ship. In that direction, we could just see a light, and then, the great black hull of a strange vessel, that was coming down on us obliquely; and so near, that we heard the flap of her topsails as they shook in the wind, the trampling of feet on the deck, and the same cry of *Luff! Luff!* that our own mate was raising.

In a minute more, I caught my breath, as I heard a snap and a crash, like the fall of a tree, and suddenly, one of our flying-jib guys jerked out the bolt near the cat-head; and presently, we heard our jib-boom thumping against our bows.

Meantime, the strange ship, scraping by us thus, shot off into the darkness, and we saw her no more. But she, also, must have been injured; for when it grew light, we found pieces of strange rigging mixed with ours. We repaired the damage, and replaced the broken spar with another jib-boom we had; for all ships carry spare spars against emergencies.

The cause of this accident, which came near being the death of all on board, was nothing but the drowsiness of the

look-out men on the forecastles of both ships. The sailor who
had the look-out on our vessel was terribly reprimanded by
the mate.

No doubt, many ships that are never heard of after leaving
port, meet their fate in this way; and it may be, that sometimes two vessels coming together, jib-boom-and-jib-boom,
with a sudden shock in the middle watch of the night, mutually destroy each other; and like fighting elks, sink down
into the ocean, with their antlers locked in death.

While I was at Liverpool, a fine ship that lay near us in the
docks, having got her cargo on board, went to sea, bound for
India, with a good breeze; and all her crew felt sure of a
prosperous voyage. But in about seven days after, she came
back, a most distressing object to behold. All her starboard
side was torn and splintered; her starboard anchor was gone;
and a great part of the starboard bulwarks; while every one
of the lower yard-arms had been broken, in the same direction; so that she now carried small and unsightly *jury-yards*.

When I looked at this vessel, with the whole of one side
thus shattered, but the other still in fine trim; and when I
remembered her gay and gallant appearance, when she left the
same harbor into which she now entered so forlorn; I could
not help thinking of a young man I had known at home, who
had left his cottage one morning in high spirits, and was
brought back at noon with his right side paralyzed from head
to foot.

It seems that this vessel had been run against by a strange
ship, crowding all sail before a fresh breeze; and the stranger
had rushed past her starboard side, reducing her to the sad
state in which she now was.

Sailors can not be too wakeful and cautious, when keeping
their night look-outs; though, as I well know, they too often
suffer themselves to become negligent, and nod. And this is
not so wonderful, after all; for though every seaman has heard
of those accidents at sea; and many of them, perhaps, have
been in ships that have suffered from them; yet, when you
find yourself sailing along on the ocean at night, without having seen a sail for weeks and weeks, it is hard for you to
realize that any are near. Then, if they *are* near, it seems almost incredible that on the broad, boundless sea, which

washes Greenland at one end of the world, and the Falkland Islands at the other, that any one vessel upon such a vast highway, should come into close contact with another. But the likelihood of great calamities occurring, seldom obtrudes upon the minds of ignorant men, such as sailors generally are; for the things which wise people know, anticipate, and guard against, the ignorant can only become acquainted with, by meeting them face to face. And even when experience has taught them, the lesson only serves for that day; inasmuch as the foolish in prosperity are infidels to the possibility of adversity; they see the sun in heaven, and believe it to be far too bright ever to set.

And even, as suddenly as the bravest and fleetest ships, while careering in pride of canvas over the sea, have been struck, as by lightning, and quenched out of sight; even so, do some lordly men, with all their plans and prospects gallantly trimmed to the fair, rushing breeze of life, and with no thought of death and disaster, suddenly encounter a shock unforeseen, and go down, foundering, into death.

Chapter 20

IN A FOG HE IS SET TO WORK AS A BELL-TOLLER,
AND BEHOLDS A HERD OF OCEAN-ELEPHANTS

WHAT IS THIS that we sail through? What palpable obscure? What smoke and reek, as if the whole steaming world were revolving on its axis, as a spit?

It is a Newfoundland Fog; and we are yet crossing the Grand Banks, wrapt in a mist, that no London in the Novemberest November ever equaled. The chronometer pronounced it noon; but do you call this midnight or mid-day? So dense is the fog, that though we have a fair wind, we shorten sail for fear of accidents; and not only that, but here am I, poor Wellingborough, mounted aloft on a sort of belfry, the top of the "*Sampson-Post,*" a lofty tower of timber, so called; and tolling the ship's bell, as if for a funeral.

This is intended to proclaim our approach, and warn all strangers from our track.

Dreary sound! toll, toll, toll, through the dismal mist and fog.

The bell is green with verdigris, and damp with dew; and the little cord attached to the clapper, by which I toll it, now and then slides through my fingers, slippery with wet. Here I am, in my slouched black hat, like the "*bull that could pull,*" announcing the decease of the lamented Cock-Robin.

A better device than the bell, however, was once pitched upon by an ingenious sea-captain, of whom I have heard. He had a litter of young porkers on board; and while sailing through the fog, he stationed men at both ends of the pen with long poles, wherewith they incessantly stirred up and irritated the porkers, who split the air with their squeals; and no doubt saved the ship, as the geese saved the Capitol.

The most strange and unheard-of noises came out of the fog at times: a vast sound of sighing and sobbing. What could it be? This would be followed by a spout, and a gush, and a cascading commotion, as if some fountain had suddenly jetted out of the ocean.

Seated on my Sampson-Post, I stared more and more, and suspended my duty as a sexton. But presently some one cried out—*"There she blows! whales! whales close alongside!"*

A whale! Think of it! whales close to *me*, Wellingborough;—would my own brother believe it? I dropt the clapper as if it were red-hot, and rushed to the side; and there, dimly floating, lay four or five long, black snaky-looking shapes, only a few inches out of the water.

Can these be whales? Monstrous whales, such as I had heard of? I thought they would look like mountains on the sea; hills and valleys of flesh! regular krakens, that made it high tide, and inundated continents, when they descended to feed!

It was a bitter disappointment, from which I was long in recovering. I lost all respect for whales; and began to be a little dubious about the story of Jonah; for how could Jonah reside in such an insignificant tenement; how could he have had elbow-room there? But perhaps, thought I, the whale, which according to Rabbinical traditions was a female one, might have expanded to receive him like an anaconda, when it swallows an elk and leaves the antlers sticking out of its mouth.

Nevertheless, from that day, whales greatly fell in my estimation.

But it is always thus. If you read of St. Peter's, they say, and then go and visit it, ten to one, you account it a dwarf compared to your high-raised ideal. And, doubtless, Jonah himself must have been disappointed when he looked up to the domed midriff surmounting the whale's belly, and surveyed the ribbed pillars around him. A pretty large belly, to be sure, thought he, but not so big as it might have been.

On the next day, the fog lifted; and by noon, we found ourselves sailing through fleets of fishermen at anchor. They were very small craft; and when I beheld them, I perceived the force of that sailor saying, intended to illustrate restricted quarters, or being *on the limits. It is like a fisherman's walk*, say they, *three steps and overboard.*

Lying right in the track of the multitudinous ships crossing the ocean between England and America, these little vessels are sometimes run down, and obliterated from the face of the waters; the cry of the sailors ceasing with the last whirl of the whirlpool that closes over their craft. Their sad fate is frequently the result of their own remissness in keeping a good look-out by day, and not having their lamps trimmed, like the wise virgins, by night.

As I shall not make mention of the Grand Banks on our homeward-bound passage, I may as well here relate, that on our return, we approached them in the night; and by way of making sure of our whereabouts, the deep-sea-lead was heaved. The line attached is generally upward of three hundred fathoms in length; and the lead itself, weighing some forty or fifty pounds, has a hole in the lower end, in which, previous to sounding, some tallow is thrust, that it may bring up the soil at the bottom, for the captain to inspect. This is called "*arming*" the lead.

We "hove" our deep-sea-line by night, and the operation was very interesting, at least to me. In the first place, the vessel's headway was stopt; then, coiled away in a tub, like a whale-rope, the line was placed toward the after part of the quarter-deck; and one of the sailors carried the lead outside of the ship, away along to the end of the jib-boom, and at the word of command, far ahead and overboard it went, with a plunge; scraping by the side, till it came to the stern, when the line ran out of the tub like light.

When we came to haul it up, I was astonished at the force necessary to perform the work. The whole watch pulled at the line, which was rove through a block in the mizen-rigging, as if we were hauling up a fat porpoise. When the lead came in sight, I was all eagerness to examine the tallow, and get a peep at a specimen of the bottom of the sea; but the sailors did not seem to be much interested by it, calling me a fool for wanting to preserve a few grains of the sand.

I had almost forgotten to make mention of the Gulf Stream, in which we found ourselves previous to crossing the Banks. The fact of our being in it was proved by the captain in person, who superintended the drawing of a bucket of salt water, in which he dipped his thermometer. In the absence of the Gulf-weed, this is the general test; for the temperature of this current is eight degrees higher than that of the ocean, and the temperature of the ocean is twenty degrees higher than that of the Grand Banks. And it is to this remarkable difference of temperature, for which there can be no equilibrium, that many seamen impute the fogs on the coast of Nova Scotia and Newfoundland; but why there should always be such ugly weather in the Gulf, is something that I do not know has ever been accounted for.

It is curious to dip one's finger in a bucket full of the Gulf Stream, and find it so warm; as if the Gulf of Mexico, from whence this current comes, were a great caldron or boiler, on purpose to keep warm the North Atlantic, which is traversed by it for a distance of two thousand miles, as some large halls in winter are by hot air tubes. Its mean breadth being about two hundred leagues, it comprises an area larger than that of the whole Mediterranean, and may be deemed a sort of Mississippi of hot water flowing through the ocean; off the coast of Florida, running at the rate of one mile and a half an hour.

Chapter 21

A Whaleman and a Man-of-War's-Man

THE SIGHT OF THE WHALES mentioned in the preceding chapter was the bringing out of Larry, one of our crew, who hitherto had been quite silent and reserved, as if from some conscious inferiority, though he had shipped as an *ordinary seaman*, and, for aught I could see, performed his duty very well.

When the men fell into a dispute concerning what kind of whales they were which we saw, Larry stood by attentively, and after garnering in their ignorance, all at once broke out, and astonished every body by his intimate acquaintance with the monsters.

"They ar'n't sperm whales," said Larry, "their spouts ar'n't bushy enough; they ar'n't Sulphur-bottoms, or they wouldn't stay up so long; they ar'n't Hump-backs, for they ar'n't got any humps; they ar'n't Fin-backs, for you won't catch a Fin-back so near a ship; they ar'n't Greenland whales, for we ar'n't off the coast of Greenland; and they ar'n't right whales, for it wouldn't be right to say so. I tell ye, men, them's Crinkum-crankum whales."

"And what are them?" said a sailor.

"Why, them is whales that can't be cotched."

Now, as it turned out that this Larry had been bred to the sea in a whaler, and had sailed out of Nantucket many times; no one but Jackson ventured to dispute his opinion; and even Jackson did not press him very hard. And ever after, Larry's judgment was relied upon concerning all strange fish that happened to float by us during the voyage; for whalemen are far more familiar with the wonders of the deep than any other class of seamen.

This was Larry's first voyage in the merchant service, and that was the reason why, hitherto, he had been so reserved; since he well knew that merchant seamen generally affect a certain superiority to "*blubber-boilers*," as they contemptuously style those who hunt the leviathan. But Larry turned out to be such an inoffensive fellow, and so well understood his business aboard ship, and was so ready to jump to an order, that he was exempted from the taunts which he might otherwise have encountered.

He was a somewhat singular man, who wore his hat slanting forward over the bridge of his nose, with his eyes cast down, and seemed always examining your boots, when speaking to you. I loved to hear him talk about the wild places in the Indian Ocean, and on the coast of Madagascar, where he had frequently touched during his whaling voyages. And this familiarity with the life of nature led by the people in that remote part of the world, had furnished Larry with a sentimental distaste for civilized society. When opportunity offered, he never omitted extolling the delights of the free and easy Indian Ocean.

"Why," said Larry, talking through his nose, as usual, "in *Madagasky* there, they don't wear any togs at all, nothing but a bowline round the midships; they don't have no dinners, but keeps a dinin' all day off fat pigs and dogs; they don't go to bed any where, but keeps a noddin' all the time; and they gets drunk, too, from some first rate arrack they make from cocoa-nuts; and smokes plenty of 'baccy, too, I tell ye. Fine country, that! Blast Ameriky, I say!"

To tell the truth, this Larry dealt in some illiberal insinuations against civilization.

"And what's the use of bein' *snivelized*?" said he to me one night during our watch on deck; "snivelized chaps only learns the way to take on 'bout life, and snivel. You don't see any Methodist chaps feelin' dreadful about their souls; you don't see any darned beggars and pesky constables in *Madagasky*, I tell ye; and none o' them kings there gets their big toes pinched by the gout. Blast Ameriky, I say."

Indeed, this Larry was rather cutting in his innuendoes.

"Are *you* now, Buttons, any better off for bein' snivelized?" coming close up to me and eying the wreck of my gaff-topsail-boots very steadfastly. "No; you ar'n't a bit—but you're a good deal *worse* for it, Buttons. I tell ye, ye wouldn't have been to sea here, leadin' this dog's life, if you hadn't been snivelized—that's the cause why, now. Snivelization has been the ruin on ye; and it's spiled me complete; I might have been a great man in Madagasky; it's too darned bad! Blast Ameriky, I say." And in bitter grief at the social blight upon his whole past, present, and future, Larry turned away, pulling his hat still lower down over the bridge of his nose.

In strong contrast to Larry, was a young man-of-war's man we had, who went by the name of "*Gun-Deck*," from his always talking of sailor life in the navy. He was a little fellow with a small face and a prodigious mop of brown hair; who always dressed in man-of-war style, with a wide, braided collar to his frock, and Turkish trowsers. But he particularly prided himself upon his feet, which were quite small; and when we washed down decks of a morning, never mind how chilly it might be, he always took off his boots, and went paddling about like a duck, turning out his pretty toes to show his charming feet.

He had served in the armed steamers during the Seminole War in Florida, and had a good deal to say about sailing up the rivers there, through the everglades, and popping off Indians on the banks. I remember his telling a story about a party being discovered at quite a distance from them; but one of the savages was made very conspicuous by a pewter plate, which he wore round his neck, and which glittered in the sun. This plate proved his death; for, according to *Gun-Deck*, he himself shot it through the middle, and the ball entered the wearer's heart. It was a rat-killing war, he said.

Gun-Deck had touched at Cadiz: had been to Gibraltar; and ashore at Marseilles. He had sunned himself in the Bay of Naples: eaten figs and oranges in Messina; and cheerfully lost one of his hearts at Malta, among the ladies there. And about all these things, he talked like a romantic man-of-war's man, who had seen the civilized world, and loved it; found it good, and a comfortable place to live in. So he and Larry never could agree in their respective views of civilization, and of savagery, of the Mediterranean and *Madagasky*.

Chapter 22

The Highlander Passes a Wreck

W E WERE STILL on the Banks, when a terrific storm came down upon us, the like of which I had never before beheld, or imagined. The rain poured down in sheets and cascades; the scupper holes could hardly carry it off the decks; and in bracing the yards we waded about almost up to our knees; every thing floating about, like chips in a dock.

This violent rain was the precursor of a hard squall, for which we duly prepared, taking in our canvas to double-reefed-top-sails.

The tornado came rushing along at last, like a troop of wild horse before the flaming rush of a burning prairie. But after bowing and cringing to it awhile, the good Highlander was put off before it; and with her nose in the water, went wallowing on, ploughing milk-white waves, and leaving a streak of illuminated foam in her wake.

It was an awful scene. It made me catch my breath as I gazed. I could hardly stand on my feet, so violent was the motion of the ship. But while I reeled to and fro, the sailors only laughed at me; and bade me look out that the ship did not fall overboard; and advised me to get a handspike, and hold it down hard in the weather-scuppers, to steady her wild motions. But I was now getting a little too wise for this foolish kind of talk; though all through the voyage, they never gave it over.

This storm past, we had fair weather until we got into the Irish Sea.

The morning following the storm, when the sea and sky had become blue again, the man aloft sung out that there was a wreck on the lee-beam. We bore away for it, all hands looking eagerly toward it, and the captain in the mizzen-top with his spy-glass. Presently, we slowly passed alongside of it.

It was a dismantled, water-logged schooner, a most dismal sight, that must have been drifting about for several long weeks. The bulwarks were pretty much gone; and here and there the bare *stanchions*, or posts, were left standing, splitting in two the waves which broke clear over the deck, lying almost even with the sea. The foremast was snapt off less than four feet from its base; and the shattered and splintered remnant looked like the stump of a pine tree thrown over in the woods. Every time she rolled in the trough of the sea, her open main-hatchway yawned into view; but was as quickly filled, and submerged again, with a rushing, gurgling sound, as the water ran into it with the lee-roll.

At the head of the stump of the mainmast, about ten feet above the deck, something like a sleeve seemed nailed; it was supposed to be the relic of a jacket, which must have been fastened there by the crew for a signal, and been frayed out and blown away by the wind.

Lashed, and leaning over sideways against the taffrail, were three dark, green, grassy objects, that slowly swayed with every roll, but otherwise were motionless. I saw the captain's glass directed toward them, and heard him say at last, "They must have been dead a long time." These were sailors, who long ago had lashed themselves to the taffrail for safety; but must have famished.

Full of the awful interest of the scene, I surely thought the captain would lower a boat to bury the bodies, and find out something about the schooner. But we did not stop at all; passing on our course, without so much as learning the schooner's name, though every one supposed her to be a New Brunswick lumberman.

On the part of the sailors, no surprise was shown that our captain did not send off a boat to the wreck; but the steerage passengers were indignant at what they called his barbarity. For me, I could not but feel amazed and shocked at his indifference; but my subsequent sea experiences have shown me, that such conduct as this is very common, though not, of course, when human life can be saved.

So away we sailed, and left her; drifting, drifting on; a garden spot for barnacles, and a playhouse for the sharks.

"Look there," said Jackson, hanging over the rail and coughing—"look there; that's a sailor's coffin. Ha! ha! Buttons," turning round to me—"how do you like that, Buttons? Wouldn't you like to take a sail with them 'ere dead men? Wouldn't it be nice?" And then he tried to laugh, but only coughed again.

"Don't laugh at dem poor fellows," said Max, looking grave; "do' you see dar bodies, dar souls are farder off dan de Cape of Dood Hope."

"Dood Hope, Dood Hope," shrieked Jackson, with a horrid grin, mimicking the Dutchman, "dare is no dood hope for dem, old boy; dey are drowned and d . . . . d, as you and I will be, Red Max, one of dese dark nights."

"No, no," said Blunt, "all sailors are saved; they have plenty of squalls here below, but fair weather aloft."

"And did you get that out of your silly Dream Book, you Greek?" howled Jackson through a cough. "Don't talk of heaven to me—it's a lie—I know it—and they are all fools that believe in it. Do you think, you Greek, that there's any heaven for *you*? Will they let *you* in there, with that tarry hand, and that oily head of hair? Avast! when some shark gulps you down his hatchway one of these days, you'll find, that by dying, you'll only go from one gale of wind to another; mind that, you Irish cockney! Yes, you'll be bolted down like one of your own pills: and I should like to see the whole ship swallowed down in the Norway maelstrom, like a box on 'em. That would be a dose of salts for ye!" And so saying, he went off, holding his hands to his chest, and coughing, as if his last hour was come.

Every day this Jackson seemed to grow worse and worse, both in body and mind. He seldom spoke, but to contradict, deride, or curse; and all the time, though his face grew thinner and thinner, his eyes seemed to kindle more and more, as if he were going to die out at last, and leave them burning like tapers before a corpse.

Though he had never attended churches, and knew nothing about Christianity; no more than a Malay pirate; and though he could not read a word, yet he was spontaneously an atheist and an infidel; and during the long night watches, would enter into arguments, to prove that there was nothing to be believed; nothing to be loved, and nothing worth living for; but every thing to be hated, in the wide world. He was a horrid desperado; and like a wild Indian, whom he resembled in his tawny skin and high cheek bones, he seemed to run a muck at heaven and earth. He was a Cain afloat; branded on his yellow brow with some inscrutable curse; and going about corrupting and searing every heart that beat near him.

But there seemed even more woe than wickedness about the man; and his wickedness seemed to spring from his woe; and for all his hideousness, there was that in his eye at times, that was ineffably pitiable and touching; and though there were moments when I almost hated this Jackson, yet I have pitied no man as I have pitied him.

Chapter 23

AN UNACCOUNTABLE CABIN-PASSENGER, AND A
MYSTERIOUS YOUNG LADY

AS YET, I have said nothing special about the passengers we carried out. But before making what little mention I shall of them, you must know that the Highlander was not a Liverpool liner, or packet-ship, plying in connection with a sisterhood of packets, at stated intervals, between the two ports. No: she was only what is called a *regular trader* to Liverpool; sailing upon no fixed days, and acting very much as she pleased, being bound by no obligations of any kind: though in all her voyages, ever having New York or Liverpool for her destination. Merchant vessels which are neither liners nor regular traders, among sailors come under the general head of *transient ships*; which implies that they are here to-day, and somewhere else to-morrow, like Mullins's dog.

But I had no reason to regret that the Highlander was not a liner; for aboard of those liners, from all I could gather from those who had sailed in them, the crew have terrible hard work, owing to their carrying such a press of sail, in order to make as rapid passages as possible, and sustain the ship's reputation for speed. Hence it is, that although they are the very best of sea-going craft, and built in the best possible manner, and with the very best materials, yet, a few years of scudding before the wind, as they do, seriously impairs their constitutions—like robust young men, who live too fast in their teens—and they are soon sold out for a song; generally to the people of Nantucket, New Bedford, and Sag Harbor, who repair and fit them out for the whaling business.

Thus, the ship that once carried over gay parties of ladies and gentlemen, as tourists, to Liverpool or London, now carries a crew of harpooneers round Cape Horn into the Pacific. And the mahogany and bird's-eye maple cabin, which once held rosewood card-tables and brilliant coffee-urns, and in which many a bottle of champagne, and many a bright eye sparkled, *now* accommodates a bluff Quaker captain from

Martha's Vineyard; who, perhaps, while lying with his ship in the Bay of Islands, in New Zealand, entertains a party of naked chiefs and savages at dinner, in place of the packet-captain doing the honors to the literati, theatrical stars, foreign princes, and gentlemen of leisure and fortune, who generally talked gossip, politics, and nonsense across the table, in transatlantic trips. The broad quarter-deck, too, where these gentry promenaded, is now often choked up by the enormous head of the sperm-whale, and vast masses of unctuous blubber; and every where reeks with oil during the prosecution of the fishery. *Sic transit gloria mundi!* Thus departs the pride and glory of packet-ships! It is like a broken down importer of French silks embarking in the soap-boiling business.

So, not being a liner, the Highlander of course did not have very ample accommodations for cabin passengers. I believe there were not more than five or six state-rooms, with two or three berths in each. At any rate, on this particular voyage she only carried out one regular cabin-passenger; that is, a person previously unacquainted with the captain, who paid his fare down, and came on board soberly, and in a business-like manner with his baggage.

He was an extremely little man, that solitary cabin-passenger—the passenger who came on board in a business-like manner with his baggage; never spoke to any one, and the captain seldom spoke to him.

Perhaps he was a deputy from the Deaf and Dumb Institution in New York, going over to London to address the public in pantomime at Exeter Hall concerning the signs of the times.

He was always in a brown study; sometimes sitting on the quarter-deck with arms folded, and head hanging upon his chest. Then he would rise, and gaze out to windward, as if he had suddenly discovered a friend. But looking disappointed, would retire slowly into his state-room, where you could see him through the little window, in an irregular sitting position, with the back part of him inserted into his berth, and his head, arms, and legs hanging out, buried in profound meditation, with his forefinger aside of his nose. He never was seen reading; never took a hand at cards; never smoked;

never drank wine; never conversed; and never staid to the dessert at dinner-time.

He seemed the true microcosm, or little world to himself: standing in no need of levying contributions upon the surrounding universe. Conjecture was lost in speculating as to who he was, and what was his business. The sailors, who are always curious with regard to such matters, and criticise cabin-passengers more than cabin-passengers are perhaps aware at the time, completely exhausted themselves in suppositions, some of which were characteristically curious.

One of the crew said he was a mysterious bearer of secret dispatches to the English court; others opined that he was a traveling surgeon and bonesetter, but for what reason they thought so, I never could learn; and others declared that he must either be an unprincipled bigamist, flying from his last wife and several small children; or a scoundrelly forger, bank-robber, or general burglar, who was returning to his beloved country with his ill-gotten booty. One observing sailor was of opinion that he was an English murderer, overwhelmed with speechless remorse, and returning home to make a full confession and be hanged.

But it was a little singular, that among all their sage and sometimes confident opinings, not one charitable one was made; no! they were all sadly to the prejudice of his moral and religious character. But this is the way all the world over. Miserable man! could you have had an inkling of what they thought of you, I know not what you would have done.

However, not knowing any thing about these surmisings and suspicions, this mysterious cabin-passenger went on his way, calm, cool, and collected; never troubled any body, and nobody troubled him. Sometimes, of a moonlight night, he glided about the deck, like the ghost of a hospital attendant; flitting from mast to mast; now hovering round the skylight, now vibrating in the vicinity of the binnacle. Blunt, the Dream Book tar, swore he was a magician; and took an extra dose of salts, by way of precaution against his spells.

When we were but a few days from port, a comical adventure befell this cabin-passenger. There is an old custom, still in vogue among some merchant sailors, of tying fast in the rigging any lubberly landsman of a passenger who may be detected taking excursions aloft, however moderate the flight of the awkward fowl. This is called *"making a spread eagle"* of the man; and before he is liberated, a promise is exacted, that before arriving in port, he shall furnish the ship's company with money enough for a treat all round.

Now this being one of the perquisites of sailors, they are always on the keen look-out for an opportunity of levying such contributions upon incautious strangers; though they never attempt it in presence of the captain; as for the mates, they purposely avert their eyes, and are earnestly engaged about something else, whenever they get an inkling of this proceeding going on. But, with only one poor fellow of a cabin-passenger on board of the Highlander, and *he* such a quiet, unobtrusive, unadventurous wight, there seemed little chance for levying contributions.

One remarkably pleasant morning, however, what should be seen, half way up the mizzen rigging, but the figure of our cabin-passenger, holding on with might and main by all four limbs, and with his head fearfully turned round, gazing off to the horizon. He looked as if he had the nightmare; and in some sudden and unaccountable fit of insanity, he must have been impelled to the taking up of that perilous position.

"Good heavens!" said the mate, who was a bit of a wag, "you will surely fall, sir! Steward, spread a mattress on deck, under the gentleman!"

But no sooner was our Greenland sailor's attention called to the sight, than snatching up some rope-yarn, he ran softly up behind the passenger, and without speaking a word, began binding him hand and foot. The stranger was more dumb than ever with amazement; at last violently remonstrated; but in vain; for as his fearfulness of falling made him keep his hands glued to the ropes, and so prevented him from any effectual resistance, he was soon made a handsome *spread-eagle* of, to the great satisfaction of the crew.

It was now discovered for the first, that this singular passenger stammered and stuttered very badly, which, perhaps, was the cause of his reservedness.

"Wha-wha-what i-i-is this f-f-for?"

"Spread-eagle, sir," said the Greenlander, thinking that those few words would at once make the matter plain.

"Wha-wha-what that me-me-mean?"

"Treats all round, sir," said the Greenlander, wondering at the other's obtusity, who, however, had never so much as heard of the thing before.

At last, upon his reluctant acquiescence in the demands of the sailor, and handing him two half-crown pieces, the unfortunate passenger was suffered to descend.

The last I ever saw of this man was his getting into a cab at Prince's Dock Gates in Liverpool, and driving off alone to parts unknown. He had nothing but a valise with him, and an umbrella; but his pockets looked stuffed out; perhaps he used them for carpet-bags.

I must now give some account of another and still more mysterious, though very different, sort of an occupant of the cabin, of whom I have previously hinted. What say you to a charming young girl?—just the girl to sing the Dashing White Sergeant; a martial, military-looking girl; her father must have been a general. Her hair was auburn; her eyes were blue; her cheeks were white and red; and Captain Riga was her most devoted.

To the curious questions of the sailors concerning who she was, the steward used to answer, that she was the daughter of one of the Liverpool dock-masters, who, for the benefit of her health and the improvement of her mind, had sent her out to America in the Highlander, under the captain's charge, who was his particular friend; and that now the young lady was returning home from her tour.

And truly the captain proved an attentive father to her, and often promenaded with her hanging on his arm, past the forlorn bearer of secret dispatches, who would look up now and then out of his reveries, and cast a furtive glance of wonder, as if he thought the captain was audacious.

Considering his beautiful ward, I thought the captain behaved ungallantly, to say the least, in availing himself of the opportunity of her charming society, to wear out his remaining old clothes; for no gentleman ever pretends to save his best coat when a lady is in the case; indeed, he generally thirsts for a chance to abase it, by converting it into a pontoon over a puddle, like Sir Walter Raleigh, that the ladies may not soil the soles of their dainty slippers. But this Captain Riga was no Raleigh, and hardly any sort of a true gentleman whatever, as I have formerly declared. Yet, perhaps, he might have worn his old clothes in this instance, for the express purpose of proving, by his disdain for the toilet, that he was nothing but the young lady's guardian; for many guardians do not care one fig how shabby they look.

But for all this, the passage out was one long paternal sort of a shabby flirtation between this hoydenish nymph and the ill-dressed captain. And surely, if her good mother, were she living, could have seen this young lady, she would have given her an endless lecture for her conduct, and a copy of Mrs. Ellis's Daughters of England to read and digest.

I shall say no more of this anonymous nymph; only, that when we arrived at Liverpool, she issued from her cabin in a richly embroidered silk dress, and lace hat and vail, and a sort of Chinese umbrella or parasol, which one of the sailors declared "spandangalous;" and the captain followed after in his best broadcloth and beaver, with a gold-headed cane; and away they went in a carriage, and that was the last of her; I hope she is well and happy now; but I have some misgivings.

It now remains to speak of the steerage passengers. There were not more than twenty or thirty of them, mostly mechanics, returning home, after a prosperous stay in America, to escort their wives and families back. These were the only occupants of the steerage that I ever knew of; till early one morning, in the gray dawn, when we made Cape Clear, the south point of Ireland, the apparition of a tall Irishman, in a shabby shirt of bed-ticking, emerged from the fore hatchway, and stood leaning on the rail, looking landward with a fixed, reminiscent expression, and diligently scratching its back with both hands. We all started at the sight, for no one had ever seen the apparition before; and when we remembered that it must have been burrowing all the passage down in its bunk, the only probable reason of its so manipulating its back became shockingly obvious.

I had almost forgotten another passenger of ours, a little boy not four feet high, an English lad, who, when we were about forty-eight hours from New York, suddenly appeared on deck, asking for something to eat.

It seems he was the son of a carpenter, a widower, with

this only child, who had gone out to America in the High-lander some six months previous, where he fell to drinking, and soon died, leaving the boy a friendless orphan in a foreign land.

For several weeks the boy wandered about the wharves, picking up a precarious livelihood by sucking molasses out of the casks discharged from West India ships, and occasionally regaling himself upon stray oranges and lemons found floating in the docks. He passed his nights sometimes in a stall in the markets, sometimes in an empty hogshead on the piers, sometimes in a doorway, and once in the watch-house, from which he escaped the next morning, running, as he told me, right between the door-keeper's legs, when he was taking another vagrant to task for repeatedly throwing himself upon the public charities.

At last, while straying along the docks, he chanced to catch sight of the Highlander, and immediately recognized her as the very ship which brought him and his father out from England. He at once resolved to return in her; and, accosting the captain, stated his case, and begged a passage. The captain refused to give it; but, nothing daunted, the heroic little fellow resolved to conceal himself on board previous to the ship's sailing; which he did, stowing himself away in the *between-decks*; and moreover, as he told us, in a narrow space between two large casks of water, from which he now and then thrust out his head for air. And once a steerage passenger rose in the night and poked in and rattled about a stick where he was, thinking him an uncommon large rat, who was after stealing a passage across the Atlantic. There are plenty of passengers of that kind continually plying between Liverpool and New York.

As soon as he divulged the fact of his being on board, which he took care should not happen till he thought the ship must be out of sight of land; the captain had him called aft, and after giving him a thorough shaking, and threatening to toss him overboard as a tit-bit for *John Shark*, he told the mate to send him forward among the sailors, and let him live there. The sailors received him with open arms; but before caressing him much, they gave him a thorough washing in the lee-scuppers, when he turned out to be quite a handsome lad, though thin and pale with the hardships he had suffered. However, by good nursing and plenty to eat, he soon improved and grew fat; and before many days was as fine a looking little fellow, as you might pick out of Queen Victoria's nursery.

The sailors took the warmest interest in him. One made him a little hat with a long ribbon; another a little jacket; a third a comical little pair of man-of-war's-man's trowsers; so that in the end, he looked like a juvenile boatswain's-mate. Then the cook furnished him with a little tin pot and pan; and the steward made him a present of a pewter tea-spoon; and a steerage passenger gave him a jack-knife. And thus provided, he used to sit at meal times half way up on the forecastle ladder, making a great racket with his pot and pan, and merry as a cricket. He was an uncommonly fine, cheerful, clever, arch little fellow, only six years old, and it was a thousand pities that he should be abandoned, as he was. Who can say, whether he is fated to be a convict in New South Wales, or a member of Parliament for Liverpool? When we got to that port, by the way, a purse was made up for him; the captain, officers, and the mysterious cabin passenger contributing their best wishes, and the sailors and poor steerage passengers something like fifteen dollars in cash and tobacco. But I had almost forgot to add that the daughter of the dock-master gave him a fine lace pocket-handkerchief and a card-case to remember her by; very valuable, but somewhat inappropriate presents. Thus supplied, the little hero went ashore by himself; and I lost sight of him in the vast crowds thronging the docks of Liverpool.

I must here mention, as some relief to the impression which Jackson's character must have made upon the reader, that in several ways he at first befriended this boy; but the boy always shrunk from him; till, at last, stung by his conduct, Jackson spoke to him no more; and seemed to hate him, harmless as he was, along with all the rest of the world.

As for the Lancashire lad, he was a stupid sort of fellow, as I have before hinted. So little interest was taken in him, that he was permitted to go ashore at last, without a good-by from any person but one.

Chapter 24

B UT WE HAVE not got to Liverpool yet; though, as there
is little more to be said concerning the passage out, the
Highlander may as well make sail and get there as soon as
possible. The brief interval will perhaps be profitably employed in relating what progress I made in learning the duties
of a sailor.

After my heroic feat in loosing the main-skysail, the mate
entertained good hopes of my becoming a rare mariner. In
the fullness of his heart, he ordered me to turn over the superintendence of the chicken-coop to the Lancashire boy;
which I did, very willingly. After that, I took care to show
the utmost alacrity in running aloft, which by this time became mere fun for me; and nothing delighted me more than
to sit on one of the topsail-yards, for hours together, helping
Max or the Greenlander as they worked at the rigging.

At sea, the sailors are continually engaged in "*parcelling*,"
"*serving*," and in a thousand ways ornamenting and repairing
the numberless shrouds and stays; mending sails, or turning
one side of the deck into a rope-walk, where they manufacture a clumsy sort of twine, called *spun-yarn*. This is spun
with a winch; and many an hour the Lancashire boy had to
play the part of an engine, and contribute the motive power.
For material, they use odds and ends of old rigging called
"*junk*," the yarns of which are picked to pieces, and then
twisted into new combinations, something as most books are
manufactured.

This "junk" is bought at the junk shops along the wharves;
outlandish looking dens, generally subterranean, full of old
iron, old shrouds, spars, rusty blocks, and superannuated
tackles; and kept by villainous looking old men, in tarred
trowsers, and with yellow beards like oakum. They look
like wreckers; and the scattered goods they expose for sale,

involuntarily remind one of the sea-beach, covered with keels and cordage, swept ashore in a gale.

Yes, I was now as nimble as a monkey in the rigging, and at the cry of *"tumble up there, my hearties, and take in sail,"* I was among the first ground-and-lofty tumblers, that sprang aloft at the word.

But the first time we reefed top-sails of a dark night, and I found myself hanging over the yard with eleven others, the ship plunging and rearing like a mad horse, till I felt like being jerked off the spar; then, indeed, I thought of a feather-bed at home, and hung on with tooth and nail; with no chance for snoring. But a few repetitions, soon made me used to it; and before long, I tied my reef-point as quickly and expertly as the best of them; never making what they call a *"granny-knot,"* and slipt down on deck by the bare stays, in-stead of the shrouds. It is surprising, how soon a boy over-comes his timidity about going aloft. For my own part, my nerves became as steady as the earth's diameter, and I felt as fearless on the royal yard, as Sam Patch on the cliff of Niag-ara. To my amazement, also, I found, that running up the rigging at sea, especially during a squall, was much easier than while lying in port. For as you always go up on the windward side, and the ship leans over, it makes more of a *stairs* of the rigging; whereas, in harbor, it is almost straight up and down.

Besides, the pitching and rolling only imparts a pleasant sort of vitality to the vessel; so that the difference in being aloft in a ship at sea, and a ship in harbor, is pretty much the same, as riding a real live horse and a wooden one. And even if the live charger should pitch you over his head, *that* would be much more satisfactory, than an inglorious fall from the other.

I took great delight in furling the top-gallant sails and roy-als in a hard blow; which duty required two hands on the yard.

There was a wild delirium about it; a fine rushing of the blood about the heart; and a glad thrilling and throbbing of the whole system, to find yourself tossed up at every pitch into the clouds of a stormy sky, and hovering like a judgment angel between heaven and earth; both hands free, with one foot in the rigging, and one somewhere behind you in the air. The sail would fill out like a balloon, with a report like a small cannon, and then collapse and sink away into a handful. And the feeling of mastering the rebellious canvas, and tying it down like a slave to the spar, and binding it over and over with the *gasket*, had a touch of pride and power in it, such as young King Richard must have felt, when he trampled down the insurgents of Wat Tyler.

As for steering, they never would let me go to the helm, except during a calm, when I and the figure-head on the bow were about equally employed.

By the way, that figure-head was a passenger I forgot to make mention of before.

He was a gallant six-footer of a Highlander "*in full fig*," with bright tartans, bare knees, barred leggings, and blue bonnet and the most vermilion of cheeks. He was game to his wooden marrow, and stood up to it through thick and thin; one foot a little advanced, and his right arm stretched forward, daring on the waves. In a gale of wind it was glorious to watch him standing at his post like a hero, and plunging up and down the watery Highlands and Lowlands, as the ship went foaming on her way. He was a veteran with many wounds of many sea-fights; and when he got to Liverpool a figure-head-builder there, amputated his left leg, and gave him another wooden one, which I am sorry to say, did not fit him very well, for ever after he looked as if he limped. Then this figure-head-surgeon gave him another nose, and touched up one eye, and repaired a rent in his tartans. After that the painter came and made his toilet all over again; giving him a new suit throughout, with a plaid of a beautiful pattern.

I do not know what has become of Donald now, but I hope he is safe and snug with a handsome pension in the "Sailors'-Snug-Harbor" on Staten Island.

The reason why they gave me such a slender chance of learning to steer was this. I was quite young and raw, and steering a ship is a great art, upon which much depends; especially the making a short passage; for if the helmsman be a clumsy, careless fellow, or ignorant of his duty, he keeps the ship going about in a melancholy state of indecision as to its precise destination; so that on a voyage to Liverpool, it may be pointing one while for Gibraltar, then for Rotterdam, and now for John o' Groat's; all of which is worse than wasted time. Whereas, a true steersman keeps her to her work night and day; and tries to make a bee-line from port to port.

Then, in a sudden squall, inattention, or want of quickness at the helm, might make the ship "*lurch to*"—or "*bring her by the lee.*" And what those things are, the cabin passengers would never find out, when they found themselves going down, down, down, and bidding good-by forever to the moon and stars.

And they little think, many of them, fine gentlemen and ladies that they are, what an important personage, and how much to be had in reverence, is the rough fellow in the pea-jacket, whom they see standing at the wheel, now cocking his eye aloft, and then peeping at the compass, or looking out to windward.

Why, that fellow has all your lives and eternities in his hand; and with one small and almost imperceptible motion of a spoke, in a gale of wind, might give a vast deal of work to surrogates and lawyers, in proving last wills and testaments.

Ay, you may well stare at him now. He does not look much like a man who might play into the hands of an heir-at-law, does he? Yet such is the case. Watch him close, therefore; take him down into your state-room occasionally after a stormy watch, and make a friend of him. A glass of cordial will do it.

And if you or your heirs are interested with the under-writers, then also have an eye on him. And if you remark, that of the crew, all the men who come to the helm are care-less, or inefficient; and if you observe the captain scolding them often, and crying out: "*Luff, you rascal; she's falling off!*" or, "*Keep her steady, you scoundrel, you're boxing the compass!*" then hurry down to your state-room, and if you have not yet made a will, get out your stationery and go at it; and when it is done, seal it up in a bottle, like Columbus' log, and it may possibly drift ashore, when you are drowned in the next gale of wind.

Chapter 25

QUARTER-DECK FURNITURE

THOUGH, for reasons hinted at above, they would not let me steer, I contented myself with learning the compass, a graphic fac-simile of which I drew on a blank leaf of the "*Wealth of Nations*," and studied it every morning, like the multiplication table.

I liked to peep in at the binnacle, and watch the needle; and I wondered how it was that it pointed north, rather than south or west; for I do not know that any reason can be given why it points in the precise direction it does. One would think, too, that, as since the beginning of the world almost, the tide of emigration has been setting west, the needle would point that way; whereas, it is forever pointing its fixed forefinger toward the Pole, where there are few inducements to attract a sailor, unless it be plenty of ice for mint-juleps.

Our binnacle, by the way, the place that holds a ship's compasses, deserves a word of mention. It was a little house, about the bigness of a common bird-cage, with sliding panel doors, and two drawing-rooms within, and constantly perched upon a stand, right in front of the helm. It had two chimney stacks to carry off the smoke of the lamp that burned in it by night. It was painted green, and on two sides had Venetian blinds; and on one side two glazed sashes; so that it looked like a cool little summer retreat, a snug bit of an arbor at the end of a shady garden lane. Had I been the captain, I would have planted vines in boxes, and placed them so as to overrun this binnacle; or I would have put canary-birds within; and so made an aviary of it. It is surprising what a different air may be imparted to the meanest thing by the dainty hand of taste.

Nor must I omit the helm itself, which was one of a new construction, and a particular favorite of the captain. It was a complex system of cogs and wheels and spindles, all of polished brass, and looked something like a printing-press, or power-loom. The sailors, however, did not like it much,

owing to the casualties that happened to their imprudent fingers, by catching in among the cogs and other intricate contrivances. Then, sometimes in a calm, when the sudden swells
would lift the ship, the helm would fetch a lurch, and send
the helmsman revolving round like Ixion, often seriously
hurting him; a sort of breaking on the wheel.

The *harness-cask*, also, a sort of sea side-board, or rather
meat-safe, in which a week's allowance of salt pork and beef
is kept, deserves being chronicled. It formed part of the standing furniture of the quarter-deck. Of an oval shape, it was
banded round with hoops all silver-gilt, with gilded bands
secured with gilded screws, and a gilded padlock, richly
chased. This formed the captain's smoking-seat, where he
would perch himself of an afternoon, a tasseled Chinese cap
upon his head, and a fragrant Havanna between his white and
canine-looking teeth. He took much solid comfort, Captain
Riga.

Then the magnificent *capstan*! The pride and glory of the
whole ship's company, the constant care and dandled darling
of the cook, whose duty it was to keep it polished like a tea-
pot; and it was an object of distant admiration to the steerage
passengers. Like a parlor center-table, it stood full in the middle of the quarter-deck, radiant with brazen stars, and variegated with diamond-shaped veneerings of mahogany and
satin wood. This was the captain's lounge, and the chief
mate's secretary, in the bar-holes keeping paper and pencil for
memorandums.

I might proceed and speak of the *booby-hatch*, used as a sort
of settee by the officers, and the *fife-rail* round the mainmast,
inclosing a little park of canvas, painted green, where a small
white dog with a blue ribbon round his neck, belonging to
the dock-master's daughter, used to take his morning walks,
and air himself in this small edition of the New York Bowling-Green.

Chapter 26

A Sailor a Jack of All Trades

As I began to learn my sailor duties, and show activity in running aloft, the men, I observed, treated me with a little more consideration, though not at all relaxing in a certain air of professional superiority. For the mere knowing of the names of the ropes, and familiarizing yourself with their places, so that you can lay hold of them in the darkest night; and the loosing and furling of the canvas, and reefing topsails, and hauling braces; all this, though of course forming an indispensable part of a seaman's vocation, and the business in which he is principally engaged; yet these are things which a beginner of ordinary capacity soon masters, and which are far inferior to many other matters familiar to an "*able seaman*."

What did I know, for instance, about *striking a top-gallant-mast*, and sending it down on deck in a gale of wind? Could I have *turned in a dead-eye*, or in the approved nautical style have *clapt a seizing on the main-stay*? What did I know of "*passing a gammoning*," "*reeving a Burton*," "*strapping a shoe-block*," "*clearing a foul hawse*," and innumerable other intricacies?

The business of a thorough-bred sailor is a special calling, as much of a regular trade as a carpenter's or lock-smith's. Indeed, it requires considerably more adroitness, and far more versatility of talent.

In the English merchant service boys serve a long apprenticeship to the sea, of seven years. Most of them first enter the Newcastle colliers, where they see a great deal of severe coasting service. In an old copy of the Letters of Junius, belonging to my father, I remember reading, that coal to supply the city of London could be dug at Blackheath, and sold for one half the price that the people of London then paid for it; but the Government would not suffer the mines to be opened, as it would destroy the great nursery for British seamen.

A thorough sailor must understand much of other avocations. He must be a bit of an embroiderer, to work fanciful collars of hempen lace about the shrouds; he must be something of a weaver, to weave mats of rope-yarns for lashings to the boats; he must have a touch of millinery, so as to tie graceful bows and knots, such as *Matthew Walker's roses*, and *Turk's heads*; he must be a bit of a musician, in order to sing out at the halyards; he must be a sort of jeweler, to set dead-eyes in the standing rigging; he must be a carpenter, to enable him to make a jury-mast out of a yard in case of emergency; he must be a sempstress, to darn and mend the sails; a rope-maker, to twist *marline* and *Spanish foxes*; a blacksmith, to make hooks and thimbles for the blocks: in short, he must be a sort of Jack of all trades, in order to master his own. And this, perhaps, in a greater or less degree, is pretty much the case with all things else; for you know nothing till you know all; which is the reason we never know any thing.

A sailor, also, in working at the rigging, uses special tools peculiar to his calling—*fids*, *serving-mallets*, *toggles*, *prickers*, *marlingspikes*, *palms*, *heavers*, and many more. The smaller sort he generally carries with him from ship to ship in a sort of canvas reticule.

The estimation in which a ship's crew hold the knowledge of such accomplishments as these, is expressed in the phrase they apply to one who is a clever practitioner. To distinguish such a mariner from those who merely "*hand, reef, and steer*," that is, run aloft, furl sails, haul ropes, and stand at the wheel, they say he is "*a sailor-man*;" which means that he not only knows how to reef a topsail, but is an artist in the rigging.

Now, alas! I had no chance given me to become initiated in this art and mystery; no further, at least, than by looking on, and watching how that these things might be done as well as others. The reason was, that I had only shipped for this one voyage in the Highlander, a short voyage too; and it was not worth while to teach *me* any thing, the fruit of which instructions could be only reaped by the next ship I might belong to. All they wanted of me was the good-will of my muscles, and the use of my backbone—comparatively small though it was at that time—by way of a lever, for the above-mentioned artists to employ when wanted. Accordingly, when any embroidery was going on in the rigging, I was set

to the most inglorious avocations; as in the merchant service
it is a religious maxim to keep the hands always employed at
something or other, never mind what, during their watch on
deck.

Often furnished with a club-hammer, they swung me over
the bows in a bowline, to pound the rust off the anchor; a
most monotonous, and to me a most uncongenial and irksome business. There was a remarkable fatality attending the
various hammers I carried over with me. Somehow they
would drop out of my hands into the sea. But the supply of
reserved hammers seemed unlimited: also the blessings and
benedictions I received from the chief mate for my clumsi-
ness.

At other times, they set me to picking oakum, like a convict, which hempen business disagreeably obtruded thoughts
of halters and the gallows; or whittling belaying-pins, like a
Down-Easter.

However, I endeavored to bear it all like a young philosopher, and whiled away the tedious hours by gazing through
a port-hole while my hands were plying, and repeating Lord
Byron's Address to the Ocean, which I had often spouted on
the stage at the High School at home.

Yes, I got used to all these matters, and took most things
coolly, in the spirit of Seneca and the stoics.

All but the "*turning out*," or rising from your berth when
the watch was called at night— *that* I never fancied. It was a
sort of acquaintance, which the more I cultivated, the more I
shrunk from; a thankless, miserable business, truly.

Consider that after walking the deck for four full hours,
you go below to sleep: and while thus innocently employed
in reposing your wearied limbs, you are started up—it seems
but the next instant after closing your lids—and hurried on
deck again, into the same disagreeably dark and, perhaps,
stormy night, from which you descended into the forecastle.

The previous interval of slumber was almost wholly lost to
me; at least the golden opportunity could not be appreciated:
for though it is usually deemed a comfortable thing to be
asleep, yet at the time no one is conscious that he is so enjoying himself. Therefore I made a little private arrangement
with the Lancashire lad, who was in the other watch, just to

step below occasionally, and shake me, and whisper in my ear—"*Watch below, Buttons; watch below*"—which pleasantly reminded me of the delightful fact. Then I would turn over on my side, and take another nap; and in this manner I enjoyed several complete watches in my bunk to the other sailors' one. I recommend the plan to all landsmen contemplating a voyage to sea.

But notwithstanding all these contrivances, the dreadful sequel could not be avoided. Eight bells would at last be struck, and the men on deck, exhilarated by the prospect of changing places with us, would call the watch in a most provokingly mirthful and facetious style.

As thus:—

"Starboard watch, ahoy! eight bells there, below! Tumble up, my lively hearties; steamboat alongside waiting for your trunks: bear a hand, bear a hand with your knee-buckles, my sweet and pleasant fellows! fine shower-bath here on deck. Hurrah, hurrah! your ice-cream is getting cold!"

Whereupon some of the old croakers who were getting into their trowsers would reply with—"Oh, stop your gabble, will you? don't be in such a hurry, now. You feel sweet, don't you?" with other exclamations, some of which were full of fury.

And it was not a little curious to remark, that at the expiration of the ensuing watch, the tables would be turned; and we on deck became the wits and jokers, and those below the grizzly bears and growlers.

Chapter 27

He Gets a Peep at Ireland, and at Last Arrives at Liverpool

THE HIGHLANDER was not a grayhound, not a very fast sailer; and so, the passage, which some of the packet ships make in fifteen or sixteen days, employed us about thirty.

At last, one morning I came on deck, and they told me that Ireland was in sight.

Ireland in sight! A foreign country actually visible! I peered hard, but could see nothing but a bluish, cloud-like spot to the northeast. Was that Ireland? Why, there was nothing remarkable about that; nothing startling. If *that's* the way a foreign country looks, I might as well have staid at home.

Now what, exactly, I had fancied the shore would look like, I can not say; but I had a vague idea that it would be something strange and wonderful. However, there it was; and as the light increased and the ship sailed nearer and nearer, the land began to magnify, and I gazed at it with increasing interest.

Ireland! I thought of Robert Emmet, and that last speech of his before Lord Norbury; I thought of Tommy Moore, and his amatory verses; I thought of Curran, Grattan, Plunket, and O'Connell; I thought of my uncle's ostler, Patrick Flinnigan; and I thought of the shipwreck of the gallant Albion, tost to pieces on the very shore now in sight; and I thought I should very much like to leave the ship and visit Dublin and the Giant's Causeway.

Presently a fishing-boat drew near, and I rushed to get a view of it; but it was a very ordinary looking boat, bobbing up and down, as any other boat would have done; yet, when I considered that the solitary man in it was actually a born native of the land in sight; that in all probability he had never been in America, and knew nothing about my friends at home, I began to think that he looked somewhat strange.

He was a very fluent fellow, and as soon as we were within

hailing distance, cried out—"Ah, my fine sailors, from Ameriky, ain't ye, my beautiful sailors?" And concluded by calling
upon us to stop and heave a rope. Thinking he might have
something important to communicate, the mate accordingly
backed the main yard, and a rope being thrown, the stranger
kept hauling in upon it, and coiling it down, crying, "pay
out! pay out, my honeys; ah! but you're noble fellows!" Till
at last the mate asked him why he did not come alongside,
adding, "Haven't you enough rope yet?"

"Sure and I have," replied the fisherman, "and it's time for
Pat to cut and run!" and so saying, his knife severed the rope,
and with a Kilkenny grin, he sprang to his tiller, put his little
craft before the wind, and bowled away from us, with some
fifteen fathoms of our tow-line.

"And may the Old Boy hurry after you, and hang you in
your stolen hemp, you Irish blackguard!" cried the mate,
shaking his fist at the receding boat, after recovering from his
first fit of amazement.

Here, then, was a beautiful introduction to the eastern
hemisphere; fairly robbed before striking soundings. This
trick upon experienced travelers certainly beat all I had ever
heard about the wooden nutmegs and bass-wood pumpkin
seeds of Connecticut. And I thought if there were any more
Hibernians like our friend Pat, the Yankee peddlers might as
well give it up.

The next land we saw was Wales. It was high noon, and a
long line of purple mountains lay like banks of clouds against
the east.

Could this be really Wales?—Wales?—and I thought of
the Prince of Wales.

And did a real queen with a diadem reign over that very
land I was looking at, with the identical eyes in my own
head?—And then I thought of a grandfather of mine, who
had fought against the ancestor of this queen at Bunker's
Hill.

But, after all, the general effect of these mountains was
mortifyingly like the general effect of the Kaatskill Mountains
on the Hudson River.

With a light breeze, we sailed on till next day, when we
made Holyhead and Anglesea. Then it fell almost calm, and

what little wind we had, was ahead; so we kept tacking to and fro, just gliding through the water, and always hovering in sight of a snow-white tower in the distance, which might have been a fort, or a light-house. I lost myself in conjectures as to what sort of people might be tenanting that lonely edifice, and whether they knew any thing about us.

The third day, with a good wind over the taffrail, we arrived so near our destination, that we took a pilot at dusk.

He, and every thing connected with him were very different from our New York pilot. In the first place, the pilot boat that brought him was a plethoric looking sloop-rigged boat, with flat bows, that went wheezing through the water; quite in contrast to the little gull of a schooner, that bade us adieu off Sandy Hook.

Aboard of her were ten or twelve other pilots, fellows with shaggy brows, and muffled in shaggy coats, who sat grouped together on deck like a fire-side of bears, wintering in Aroostook. They must have had fine sociable times, though, together; cruising about the Irish Sea in quest of Liverpool-bound vessels; smoking cigars, drinking brandy-and-water, and spinning yarns; till at last, one by one, they are all scattered on board of different ships, and meet again by the side of a blazing sea-coal fire in some Liverpool tap-room, and prepare for another yachting.

Now, when this English pilot boarded us, I stared at him as if he had been some wild animal just escaped from the Zoological Gardens; for here was a real live Englishman, just from England. Nevertheless, as he soon fell to ordering us here and there, and swearing vociferously in a language quite familiar to me; I began to think him very common-place, and considerable of a bore after all.

After running till about midnight, we "*hove-to*" near the mouth of the Mersey; and next morning, before day-break, took the first of the flood; and with a fair wind, stood into the river; which, at its mouth, is quite an arm of the sea. Presently, in the misty twilight, we passed immense buoys, and caught sight of distant objects on shore, vague and shadowy shapes, like Ossian's ghosts.

As I stood leaning over the side, and trying to summon up some image of Liverpool, to see how the reality would an-

swer to my conceit; and while the fog, and mist, and gray
dawn were investing every thing with a mysterious interest, I
was startled by the doleful, dismal sound of a great bell,
whose slow intermitting tolling seemed in unison with the
solemn roll of the billows. I thought I had never heard so
boding a sound; a sound that seemed to speak of judgment
and the resurrection, like belfry-mouthed Paul of Tarsus.

It was not in the direction of the shore; but seemed to
come out of the vaults of the sea, and out of the mist and
fog.

Who was dead, and what could it be?

I soon learned from my ship-mates, that this was the famous *Bell-Buoy*, which is precisely what its name implies; and
tolls fast or slow, according to the agitation of the waves. In
a calm, it is dumb; in a moderate breeze, it tolls gently; but
in a gale, it is an alarum like the tocsin, warning all mariners
to flee. But it seemed fuller of dirges for the past, than of
monitions for the future; and no one can give ear to it, without thinking of the sailors who sleep far beneath it at the
bottom of the deep.

As we sailed ahead the river contracted. The day came, and
soon, passing two lofty land-marks on the Lancashire shore,
we rapidly drew near the town, and at last, came to anchor in
the stream.

Looking shoreward, I beheld lofty ranges of dingy warehouses, which seemed very deficient in the elements of the
marvelous; and bore a most unexpected resemblance to the
ware-houses along South-street in New York. There was
nothing strange; nothing extraordinary about them. There
they stood; a row of calm and collected ware-houses; very
good and substantial edifices, doubtless, and admirably
adapted to the ends had in view by the builders; but plain,
matter-of-fact ware-houses, nevertheless, and that was all that
could be said of them.

To be sure, I did not expect that every house in Liverpool
must be a Leaning Tower of Pisa, or a Strasbourg Cathedral;
but yet, these edifices I must confess, were a sad and bitter
disappointment to me.

But it was different with Larry the whaleman; who to my
surprise, looking about him delighted, exclaimed, "Why, this

'ere is a considerable place—I'm *dummed* if it ain't quite a place.—Why, them 'ere houses is considerable houses. It beats the coast of Afriky, all hollow; nothing like this in *Madagasky*, I tell you;—I'm *dummed*, boys, if Liverpool ain't a city!"

Upon this occasion, indeed, Larry altogether forgot his hostility to civilization. Having been so long accustomed to associate foreign lands with the savage places of the Indian Ocean, he had been under the impression, that Liverpool must be a town of bamboos, situated in some swamp, and whose inhabitants turned their attention principally to the cultivation of log-wood and curing of flying-fish. For that any great commercial city existed three thousand miles from home, was a thing, of which Larry had never before had a "*realizing sense.*" He was accordingly astonished and delighted; and began to feel a sort of consideration for the country which could boast so extensive a town. Instead of holding Queen Victoria on a par with the Queen of Madagascar, as he had been accustomed to do; he ever after alluded to that lady with feeling and respect.

As for the other seamen, the sight of a foreign country seemed to kindle no enthusiasm in them at all: no emotion in the least. They looked round them with great presence of mind, and acted precisely as you or I would, if, after a morning's absence round the corner, we found ourselves returning home. Nearly all of them had made frequent voyages to Liverpool.

Not long after anchoring, several boats came off; and from one of them stept a neatly-dressed and very respectable-looking woman, some thirty years of age, I should think, carrying a bundle. Coming forward among the sailors, she inquired for Max the Dutchman, who immediately was forthcoming, and saluted her by the mellifluous appellation of *Sally*.

Now during the passage, Max in discoursing to me of Liverpool, had often assured me, that that city had the honor of containing a spouse of his; and that in all probability, I would have the pleasure of seeing her. But having heard a good many stories about the bigamies of seamen, and their having wives and sweethearts in every port, the round world over; and having been an eye-witness to a nuptial parting between

this very Max and a lady in New York; I put down this relation of his, for what I thought it might reasonably be worth.
What was my astonishment, therefore, to see this really decent, civil woman coming with a neat parcel of Max's shore
clothes, all washed, plaited, and ironed, and ready to put on
at a moment's warning.

They stood apart a few moments giving loose to those
transports of pleasure, which always take place, I suppose, between man and wife after long separations.

At last, after many earnest inquiries as to how he had behaved himself in New York; and concerning the state of his
wardrobe; and going down into the forecastle, and inspecting
it in person, Sally departed; having exchanged her bundle of
clean clothes for a bundle of soiled ones, and this was precisely what the New York wife had done for Max, not thirty
days previous.

So long as we laid in port, Sally visited the Highlander
daily; and approved herself a neat and expeditious getter-up
of duck frocks and trowsers, a capital tailoress, and as far
as I could see, a very well-behaved, discreet, and reputable
woman.

But from all I had seen of her, I should suppose Meg, the
New York wife, to have been equally well-behaved, discreet,
and reputable; and equally devoted to the keeping in good
order Max's wardrobe.

And when we left England at last, Sally bade Max good-
by, just as Meg had done; and when we arrived at New York,
Meg greeted Max precisely as Sally had greeted him in Liverpool. Indeed, a pair of more amiable wives never belonged
to one man; they never quarreled, or had so much as a difference of any kind; the whole broad Atlantic being between
them; and Max was equally polite and civil to both. For many
years, he had been going Liverpool and New York voyages,
plying between wife and wife with great regularity, and sure
of receiving a hearty domestic welcome on either side of the
ocean.

Thinking this conduct of his, however, altogether wrong
and every way immoral, I once ventured to express to him my
opinion on the subject. But I never did so again. He turned
round on me, very savagely; and after rating me soundly for

meddling in concerns not my own, concluded by asking me triumphantly, whether *old King Sol*, as he called the son of David, did not have a whole frigate-full of wives; and that being the case, whether he, a poor sailor, did not have just as good a right to have two? "What was not wrong then, is right now," said Max; "so, mind your eye, Buttons, or I'll crack your pepper-box for you!"

Chapter 28

He Goes to Supper at the Sign of the Baltimore Clipper

IN THE AFTERNOON our pilot was all alive with his orders; we hove up the anchor, and after a deal of pulling, and hauling, and jamming against other ships, we wedged our way through a lock at high tide; and about dark, succeeded in working up to a berth in *Prince's Dock*. The hawsers and tow-lines being then coiled away, the crew were told to go ashore, select their boarding-house, and sit down to supper.

Here it must be mentioned, that owing to the strict but necessary regulations of the Liverpool docks, no fires of any kind are allowed on board the vessels within them; and hence, though the sailors are supposed to sleep in the forecastle, yet they must get their meals ashore, or live upon cold potatoes. To a ship, the American merchantmen adopt the former plan; the owners, of course, paying the landlord's bill; which, in a large crew remaining at Liverpool more than six weeks, as we of the Highlander did, forms no inconsiderable item in the expenses of the voyage. Other ships, however—the economical Dutch and Danish, for instance, and sometimes the prudent Scotch—feed their luckless tars in dock, with precisely the same fare which they give them at sea; taking their salt junk ashore to be cooked, which, indeed, is but scurvy sort of treatment, since it is very apt to induce the scurvy. A parsimonious proceeding like this is regarded with immeasurable disdain by the crews of the New York vessels, who, if their captains treated them after that fashion, would soon bolt and run.

It was quite dark, when we all sprang ashore; and, for the first time, I felt dusty particles of the renowned British soil penetrating into my eyes and lungs. As for *stepping* on it, that was out of the question, in the well-paved and flagged condition of the streets; and I did not have an opportunity to do so till some time afterward, when I got out into the country;

and then, indeed, I saw England, and snuffed its immortal loam—but not till then.

Jackson led the van; and after stopping at a tavern, took us up this street, and down that, till at last he brought us to a narrow lane, filled with boarding-houses, spirit-vaults, and sailors. Here we stopped before the sign of a Baltimore Clipper, flanked on one side by a gilded bunch of grapes and a bottle, and on the other by the British Unicorn and American Eagle, lying down by each other, like the lion and lamb in the millennium.—A very judicious and tasty device, showing a delicate apprehension of the propriety of conciliating American sailors in an English boarding-house; and yet in no way derogating from the honor and dignity of England, but placing the two nations, indeed, upon a footing of perfect equality.

Near the unicorn was a very small animal, which at first I took for a young unicorn; but it looked more like a yearling lion. It was holding up one paw, as if it had a splinter in it; and on its head was a sort of basket-hilted, low-crowned hat, without a rim. I asked a sailor standing by, what this animal meant, when, looking at me with a grin, he answered, "Why, youngster, don't you know what that means? It's a young jackass, limping off with a kedgeree pot of rice out of the cuddy."

Though it was an English boarding-house, it was kept by a broken-down American mariner, one Danby, a dissolute, idle fellow, who had married a buxom English wife, and now lived upon her industry; for the lady, and not the sailor, proved to be the head of the establishment.

She was a hale, good-looking woman, about forty years old, and among the seamen went by the name of "*Handsome Mary.*" But though, from the dissipated character of her spouse, Mary had become the business personage of the house, bought the marketing, overlooked the tables, and conducted all the more important arrangements, yet she was by no means an Amazon to her husband, if she *did* play a masculine part in other matters. No; and the more is the pity, poor Mary seemed too much attached to Danby, to seek to rule him as a termagant. Often she went about her household concerns with the tears in her eyes, when, after a fit of intoxication, this brutal husband of hers had been beating her. The sailors took her part, and many a time volunteered to give him a thorough thrashing before her eyes; but Mary would beg them not to do so, as Danby would, no doubt, be a better boy next time.

But there seemed no likelihood of this, so long as that abominable bar of his stood upon the premises. As you entered the passage, it stared upon you on one side, ready to entrap all guests.

It was a grotesque, old-fashioned, castellated sort of a sentry-box, made of a smoky-colored wood, and with a grating in front, that lifted up like a portcullis. And here would this Danby sit all the day long; and when customers grew thin, would patronize his own ale himself, pouring down mug after mug, as if he took himself for one of his own quarter-casks.

Sometimes an old crony of his, one Bob Still, would come in; and then they would occupy the sentry-box together, and swill their beer in concert. This pot-friend of Danby was portly as a dray-horse, and had a round, sleek, oily head, twinkling eyes, and moist red cheeks. He was a lusty troller of ale-songs; and, with his mug in his hand, would lean his waddling bulk partly out of the sentry-box, singing:

> "No frost, no snow, no wind, I trow,
>   Can hurt me if I wold,
>   I am so wrapt, and thoroughly lapt
>   In jolly good ale and old,—
>   I stuff my skin so full within,
>   Of jolly good ale and old."

Or this,—

> "Your wines and brandies I detest,
>   Here's richer juice from barley press'd.
>   It is the quintessence of malt,
>   And they that drink it want no salt.
>   Come, then, quick come, and take this beer,
>   And water henceforth you'll forswear."

Alas! Handsome Mary. What avail all thy private tears and remonstrances with the incorrigible Danby, so long as that brewery of a toper, Bob Still, daily eclipses thy threshhold with the vast diameter of his paunch, and enthrones himself in the sentry-box, holding divided rule with thy spouse?

The more he drinks, the fatter and rounder waxes Bob; and the songs pour out as the ale pours in, on the well-known principle, that the air in a vessel is displaced and expelled, as the liquid rises higher and higher in it.

But as for Danby, the miserable Yankee grows sour on good cheer, and dries up the thinner for every drop of fat ale he imbibes. It is plain and demonstrable, that much ale is not good for Yankees, and operates differently upon them from what it does upon a Briton: ale must be drank in a fog and a drizzle.

Entering the sign of the Clipper, Jackson ushered us into a small room on one side, and shortly after, Handsome Mary waited upon us with a courtesy, and received the compliments of several old guests among our crew. She then disappeared to provide our supper. While my shipmates were now engaged in tippling, and talking with numerous old acquaintances of theirs in the neighborhood, who thronged about the door, I remained alone in the little room, meditating profoundly upon the fact, that I was now seated upon an English bench, under an English roof, in an English tavern, forming an integral part of the English empire. It was a staggering fact, but none the less true.

I examined the place attentively; it was a long, narrow, little room, with one small arched window with red curtains, looking out upon a smoky, untidy yard, bounded by a dingy brick-wall, the top of which was horrible with pieces of broken old bottles, stuck into mortar.

A dull lamp swung overhead, placed in a wooden ship suspended from the ceiling. The walls were covered with a paper, representing an endless succession of vessels of all nations continually circumnavigating the apartment. By way of a pictorial mainsail to one of these ships, a map was hung against it, representing in faded colors the flags of all nations. From the street came a confused uproar of ballad-singers, bawling women, babies, and drunken sailors.

And this is England?

But where are the old abbeys, and the York Minsters, and

the lord mayors, and coronations, and the May-poles, and fox-hunters, and Derby races, and the dukes and duchesses, and the Count d'Orsays, which, from all my reading, I had been in the habit of associating with England? Not the most distant glimpse of them was to be seen.

Alas! Wellingborough, thought I, I fear you stand but a poor chance to see the sights. You are nothing but a poor sailor boy; and the Queen is not going to send a deputation of noblemen to invite you to St. James's.

It was then, I began to see, that my prospects of seeing the world as a sailor were, after all, but very doubtful; for sailors only go *round* the world, without going *into* it; and their reminiscences of travel are only a dim recollection of a chain of tap-rooms surrounding the globe, parallel with the Equator. They but touch the perimeter of the circle; hover about the edges of terra-firma; and only land upon wharves and pier-heads. They would dream as little of traveling inland to see Kenilworth, or Blenheim Castle, as they would of sending a card overland to the Pope, when they touched at Naples.

From these reveries I was soon roused, by a servant girl hurrying from room to room, in shrill tones exclaiming, "Supper, supper ready."

Mounting a rickety staircase, we entered a room on the second floor. Three tall brass candlesticks shed a smoky light upon smoky walls, of what had once been sea-blue, covered with sailor-scrawls of foul anchors, lovers' sonnets, and ocean ditties. On one side, nailed against the wainscot in a row, were the four knaves of cards, each Jack putting his best foot foremost as usual. What these signified I never heard.

But such ample cheer! Such a groaning table! Such a superabundance of solids and substantials! Was it possible that sailors fared thus?—the sailors, who at sea live upon salt beef and biscuit?

First and foremost, was a mighty pewter dish, big as Achilles' shield, sustaining a pyramid of smoking sausages. This stood at one end; midway was a similar dish, heavily laden with farmers' slices of head-cheese; and at the opposite end, a congregation of beef-steaks, piled tier over tier. Scattered at intervals between, were side dishes of boiled potatoes, eggs by the score, bread, and pickles; and on a stand adjoining, was an ample reserve of every thing on the supper table.

We fell to with all our hearts; wrapt ourselves in hot jackets of beef-steaks; curtailed the sausages with great celerity; and sitting down before the head-cheese, soon razed it to its foundations.

Toward the close of the entertainment, I suggested to Peggy, one of the girls who had waited upon us, that a cup of tea would be a nice thing to take; and I would thank her for one. She replied that it was too late for tea; but she would get me a cup of *"swipes"* if I wanted it.

Not knowing what *"swipes"* might be, I thought I would run the risk and try it; but it proved a miserable beverage, with a musty, sour flavor, as if it had been a decoction of spoiled pickles. I never patronized *swipes* again; but gave it a wide berth; though, at dinner afterward, it was furnished to an unlimited extent, and drunk by most of my shipmates, who pronounced it good.

But Bob Still would not have pronounced it so; for this *swipes*, as I learned, was a sort of cheap substitute for beer; or a bastard kind of beer; or the washings and rinsings of old beer-barrels. But I do not remember now what they said it was, precisely. I only know, that *swipes* was my abomination. As for the taste of it, I can only describe it as answering to the name itself; which is certainly significant of something vile. But it is drunk in large quantities by the poor people about Liverpool, which, perhaps, in some degree, accounts for their poverty.

Chapter 29

THE SHIP REMAINED in Prince's Dock over six weeks; but as I do not mean to present a diary of my stay there, I shall here simply record the general tenor of the life led by our crew during that interval; and will then proceed to note down, at random, my own wanderings about town, and impressions of things as they are recalled to me now, after the lapse of so many years.

But first, I must mention that we saw little of the captain during our stay in the dock. Sometimes, cane in hand, he sauntered down of a pleasant morning from the *Arms Hotel*, I believe it was, where he boarded; and after lounging about the ship, giving orders to his Prime Minister and Grand Vizier, the chief mate, he would saunter back to his drawing-rooms.

From the glimpse of a play-bill, which I detected peeping out of his pocket, I inferred that he patronized the theaters; and from the flush of his cheeks, that he patronized the fine old Port wine, for which Liverpool is famous.

Occasionally, however, he spent his nights on board; and mad, roystering nights they were, such as rare Ben Jonson would have delighted in. For company over the cabin-table, he would have four or five whiskered sea-captains, who kept the steward drawing corks and filling glasses all the time. And once, the whole company were found under the table at four o'clock in the morning, and were put to bed and tucked in by the two mates. Upon this occasion, I agreed with our woolly Doctor of Divinity, the black cook, that they should have been ashamed of themselves; but there is no shame in some sea-captains, who only blush after the third bottle.

During the many visits of Captain Riga to the ship, he always said something courteous to a gentlemanly, friendless custom-house officer, who staid on board of us nearly all the time we lay in the dock.

And weary days they must have been to this friendless custom-house officer; trying to kill time in the cabin with a newspaper; and rapping on the transom with his knuckles. He was kept on board to prevent smuggling; but he used to smuggle himself ashore very often, when, according to law, he should have been at his post on board ship. But no wonder; he seemed to be a man of fine feelings, altogether above his situation; a most inglorious one, indeed; worse than driving geese to water.

And now, to proceed with the crew.

At daylight, all hands were called, and the decks were washed down; then we had an hour to go ashore to breakfast; after which we worked at the rigging, or picked oakum, or were set to some employment or other, never mind how trivial, till twelve o'clock, when we went to dinner. At half-past one we resumed work; and finally *knocked off* at four o'clock in the afternoon, unless something particular was in hand. And after four o'clock, we could go where we pleased, and were not required to be on board again till next morning at daylight.

As we had nothing to do with the cargo, of course, our duties were light enough; and the chief mate was often put to it to devise some employment for us.

We had no watches to stand, a ship-keeper, hired from shore, relieving us from that; and all the while the men's wages ran on, as at sea. Sundays we had to ourselves.

Thus, it will be seen, that the life led by sailors of American ships in Liverpool, is an exceedingly easy one, and abounding in leisure. They live ashore on the fat of the land; and after a little wholesome exercise in the morning, have the rest of the day to themselves.

Nevertheless, these Liverpool voyages, likewise those to London and Havre, are the least profitable that an improvident seaman can take. Because, in New York he receives his month's advance; in Liverpool, another; both of which, in most cases, quickly disappear; so that by the time his voyage terminates, he generally has but little coming to him; sometimes not a cent. Whereas, upon a long voyage, say to India or China, his wages accumulate; he has more inducements to economize, and far fewer motives to extravagance; and when he is paid off at last, he goes away jingling a quart measure of dollars.

Besides, of all sea-ports in the world, Liverpool, perhaps, most abounds in all the variety of land-sharks, land-rats, and other vermin, which make the hapless mariner their prey. In the shape of landlords, bar-keepers, clothiers, crimps, and boarding-house loungers, the land-sharks devour him, limb by limb; while the land-rats and mice constantly nibble at his purse.

Other perils he runs, also, far worse; from the denizens of notorious Corinthian haunts in the vicinity of the docks, which in depravity are not to be matched by any thing this side of the pit that is bottomless.

And yet, sailors love this Liverpool; and upon long voyages to distant parts of the globe, will be continually dilating upon its charms and attractions, and extolling it above all other sea-ports in the world. For in Liverpool they find their Paradise—not the well known street of that name—and one of them told me he would be content to lie in Prince's Dock till he *hove up anchor* for the world to come.

Much is said of ameliorating the condition of sailors; but it must ever prove a most difficult endeavor, so long as the antidote is given before the bane is removed.

Consider, that, with the majority of them, the very fact of their being sailors, argues a certain recklessness and sensualism of character, ignorance, and depravity; consider that they are generally friendless and alone in the world; or if they have friends and relatives, they are almost constantly beyond the reach of their good influences; consider that after the rigorous discipline, hardships, dangers, and privations of a voyage, they are set adrift in a foreign port, and exposed to a thousand enticements, which, under the circumstances, would be hard even for virtue itself to withstand, unless virtue went about on crutches; consider that by their very vocation they are shunned by the better classes of people, and cut off from all access to respectable and improving society; consider all this, and the reflecting mind must very soon perceive that the case of sailors, as a class, is not a very promising one.

Indeed, the bad things of their condition come under the head of those chronic evils which can only be ameliorated, it would seem, by ameliorating the moral organization of all civilization.

Though old seventy-fours and old frigates are converted into chapels, and launched into the docks; though the "Boatswain's Mate" and other clever religious tracts in the nautical dialect are distributed among them; though clergymen harangue them from the pier-heads: and chaplains in the navy read sermons to them on the gun-deck; though evangelical boarding-houses are provided for them; though the parsimony of ship-owners has seconded the really sincere and pious efforts of Temperance Societies, to take away from seamen their old rations of grog while at sea:—notwithstanding all these things, and many more, the relative condition of the great bulk of sailors to the rest of mankind, seems to remain pretty much where it was, a century ago.

It is too much the custom, perhaps, to regard as a special advance, that unavoidable, and merely participative progress, which any one class makes in sharing the general movement of the race. Thus, because the sailor, who to-day steers the Hibernia or Unicorn steam-ship across the Atlantic, is a somewhat different man from the exaggerated sailors of Smollett, and the men who fought with Nelson at Copenhagen, and survived to riot themselves away at North Corner in Plymouth;—because the modern tar is not quite so gross as heretofore, and has shaken off some of his shaggy jackets, and docked his Lord Rodney queue:—therefore, in the estimation of some observers, he has begun to see the evils of his condition, and has voluntarily improved. But upon a closer scrutiny, it will be seen that he has but drifted along with that great tide, which, perhaps, has two flows for one ebb; he has made no individual advance of his own.

There are classes of men in the world, who bear the same relation to society at large, that the wheels do to a coach: and are just as indispensable. But however easy and delectable the springs upon which the insiders pleasantly vibrate: however sumptuous the hammer-cloth, and glossy the door-panels; yet, for all this, the wheels must still revolve in dusty, or muddy revolutions. No contrivance, no sagacity can lift *them* out of the mire; for upon something the coach must be bottomed; on something the insiders must roll.

Now, sailors form one of these wheels: they go and come round the globe; they are the true importers, and exporters of spices and silks; of fruits and wines and marbles; they carry missionaries, embassadors, opera-singers, armies, merchants, tourists, scholars to their destination: they are a bridge of boats across the Atlantic; they are the *primum mobile* of all commerce; and, in short, were they to emigrate in a body to man the navies of the moon, almost every thing would stop here on earth except its revolution on its axis, and the orators in the American Congress.

And yet, what are sailors? What in your heart do you think of that fellow staggering along the dock? Do you not give him a wide berth, shun him, and account him but little above the brutes that perish? Will you throw open your parlors to him; invite him to dinner? or give him a season ticket to your pew in church?—No. You will do no such thing; but at a distance, you will perhaps subscribe a dollar or two for the building of a hospital, to accommodate sailors already broken down; or for the distribution of excellent books among tars who can not read. And the very mode and manner in which such charities are made, bespeak, more than words, the low estimation in which sailors are held. It is useless to gainsay it; they are deemed almost the refuse and offscourings of the earth; and the romantic view of them is principally had through romances.

But can sailors, one of the wheels of this world, be wholly lifted up from the mire? There seems not much chance for it, in the old systems and programmes of the future, however well-intentioned and sincere; for with such systems, the thought of lifting them up seems almost as hopeless as that of growing the grape in Nova Zembla.

But we must not altogether despair for the sailor; nor need those who toil for his good be at bottom disheartened. For Time must prove his friend in the end; and though sometimes he would almost seem as a neglected step-son of heaven, permitted to run on and riot out his days with no hand to restrain him, while others are watched over and tenderly cared for; yet we feel and we know that God is the true Father of all, and that none of his children are without the pale of his care.

AMONG the odd volumes in my father's library, was a collection of old European and English guide-books, which he had bought on his travels, a great many years ago. In my childhood, I went through many courses of studying them, and never tired of gazing at the numerous quaint embellishments and plates, and staring at the strange title-pages, some of which I thought resembled the mustached faces of foreigners.

Among others was a Parisian-looking, faded, pink-covered pamphlet, the rouge here and there effaced upon its now thin and attenuated cheeks, entitled, "*Voyage Descriptif et Philosophique de L'Ancien et du Nouveau Paris: Miroir Fidèle*;" also a time-darkened, mossy old book, in marbleized binding, much resembling verd-antique, entitled, "*Itinéraire Instructif de Rome, ou Description Générale des Monumens Antiques et Modernes et des Ouvrages les plus Remarquables de Peinture, de Sculpture, et de Architecture de cette Célébre Ville*;" on the russet title-page is a vignette representing a barren rock, partly shaded by a scrub-oak (a forlorn bit of landscape), and under the lee of the rock and the shade of the tree, maternally reclines the houseless foster-mother of Romulus and Remus, giving suck to the illustrious twins; a pair of naked little cherubs sprawling on the ground, with locked arms, eagerly engaged at their absorbing occupation; a large cactus-leaf or diaper hangs from a bough, and the wolf looks a good deal like one of the no-horn breed of barn-yard cows; the work is published "*Avec privilege du Souverain Pontife.*" There was also a velvet-bound old volume, in brass clasps, entitled, "*The Conductor through Holland*," with a plate of the Stadt House; also a venerable "*Picture of London*," abounding in representations of St. Paul's, the Monument, Temple-Bar, Hyde-Park-Corner, the Horse Guards, the Admiralty, Charing-Cross, and Vauxhall Bridge. Also, a bulky book, in a dusty-looking yellow cover, reminding one of the paneled doors of a mail-coach, and bearing an elaborate title-page, full of printer's flourishes, in emulation of the cracks of a four-in-hand whip, entitled, in part, "*The Great Roads, both direct and cross, throughout England and Wales, from an actual Admeasurement by order of His Majesty's Postmaster-General: This work describes the Cities, Market and Borough and Corporate Towns, and those at which the Assizes are held, and gives the time of the Mails' arrival and departure from each: Describes the Inns in the Metropolis from which the stages go, and the Inns in the country which supply post-horses and carriages: Describes the Noblemen and Gentlemen's Seats situate near the Road, with Maps of the Environs of London, Bath, Brighton, and Margate.*" It is dedicated "*To the Right Honorable the Earls of Chesterfield and Leicester, by their Lordships' Most Obliged, Obedient, and Obsequious Servant, John Cary,* 1798." Also a green pamphlet, with a motto from Virgil, and an intricate coat of arms on the cover, looking like a diagram of the Labyrinth of Crete, entitled, "*A Description of York, its Antiquities and Public Buildings, particularly the Cathedral; compiled with great pains from the most authentic records.*" Also a small scholastic-looking volume, in a classic vellum binding, and with a frontispiece bringing together at one view the towers and turrets of King's College and the magnificent Cathedral of Ely, though geographically sixteen miles apart, entitled, "*The Cambridge Guide: its Colleges, Halls, Libraries, and Museums, with the Ceremonies of the Town and University, and some account of Ely Cathedral.*" Also a pamphlet, with a japaned sort of cover, stamped with a disorderly higgledy-piggledy group of pagoda-looking structures, claiming to be an accurate representation of the "*North or Grand Front of Blenheim,*" and entitled, "*A Description of Blenheim, the Seat of His Grace the Duke of Marlborough; containing a full account of the Paintings, Tapestry, and Furniture: a Picturesque Tour of the Gardens and Parks, and a General Description of the Famous China Gallery, &c.; with an Essay on Landscape Gardening: and embellished with a View of the Palace, and a New and Elegant Plan of the Great Park.*" And lastly, and to the purpose, there was a volume called "THE PICTURE OF LIVERPOOL."

It was a curious and remarkable book; and from the many fond associations connected with it, I should like to immortalize it, if I could.

But let me get it down from its shrine, and paint it, if I may, from the life.

As I now linger over the volume, to and fro turning the pages so dear to my boyhood,—the very pages which, years and years ago, my father turned over amid the very scenes that are here described; what a soft, pleasing sadness steals over me, and how I melt into the past and forgotten!

Dear book! I will sell my Shakspeare, and even sacrifice my old quarto Hogarth, before I will part with you. Yes, I will go to the hammer myself, ere I send you to be knocked down in the auctioneer's shambles. I will, my beloved,—old family relic that you are;—till you drop leaf from leaf, and letter from letter, you shall have a snug shelf somewhere, though I have no bench for myself.

In size, it is what the booksellers call an 18*mo*; it is bound in green morocco, which from my earliest recollection has been spotted and tarnished with time; the corners are marked with triangular patches of red, like little cocked hats; and some unknown Goth has inflicted an incurable wound upon the back. There is no lettering outside; so that he who lounges past my humble shelves, seldom dreams of opening the anonymous little book in green. There it stands; day after day, week after week, year after year; and no one but myself regards it. But I make up for all neglects, with my own abounding love for it.

But let us open the volume.

What are these scrawls in the fly-leaves? what incorrigible pupil of a writing-master has been here? what crayon sketcher of wild animals and falling air-castles? Ah, no!—these are all part and parcel of the precious book, which go to make up the sum of its treasure to me.

Some of the scrawls are my own; and as poets do with their juvenile sonnets, I might write under this horse, "*Drawn at the age of three years*," and under this autograph, "*Executed at the age of eight*."

Others are the handiwork of my brothers, and sisters, and cousins; and the hands that sketched some of them are now moldered away.

But what does this anchor here? this ship? and this sea-ditty of Dibdin's? The book must have fallen into the hands of some tarry captain of a forecastle. No: that anchor, ship, and Dibdin's ditty are mine; this hand drew them; and on this very voyage to Liverpool. But not so fast; I did not mean to tell that yet.

Full in the midst of these pencil scrawlings, completely surrounded indeed, stands in indelible, though faded ink, and in my father's hand-writing, the following:—

WALTER REDBURN.
Riddough's Royal Hotel,
Liverpool, March 20th, 1808.

Turning over that leaf, I come upon some half-effaced miscellaneous memoranda in pencil, characteristic of a methodical mind, and therefore indubitably my father's, which he must have made at various times during his stay in Liverpool. These are full of a strange, subdued, old, midsummer interest to me: and though, from the numerous effacements, it is much like cross-reading to make them out; yet, I must here copy a few at random:—

	£	s.	d.
Guide-Book		3	6
Dinner at the Star and Garter......		10	
Trip to Preston (distance 31m.)......	2	6	3
Gratuities		4	
Hack		4	6
Thomson's Seasons		5	
Library		1	
Boat on the river		6	
Port wine and cigars.....................		4	

And on the opposite page, I can just decipher the following:

> *Dine with Mr. Roscoe on Monday.*
> *Call upon Mr. Morille same day.*
> *Leave card at Colonel Digby's on Tuesday.*
> *Theatre Friday night—Richard III. and new farce.*
> *Present letter at Miss L——'s on Tuesday.*
> *Call on Sampson & Wilt, Friday.*
> *Get my draft on London cashed.*

Write home by the Princess.
Letter bag at Sampson and Wilt's.

Turning over the next leaf, I unfold a map, which in the midst of the British Arms, in one corner displays in sturdy text, that this is *"A Plan of the Town of Liverpool."* But there seems little plan in the confined and crooked looking marks for the streets, and the docks irregularly scattered along the bank of the Mersey, which flows along, a peaceful stream of shaded line engraving.

On the northeast corner of the map, lies a level Sahara of yellowish white: a desert, which still bears marks of my zeal in endeavoring to populate it with all manner of uncouth monsters in crayons. The space designated by that spot is now, doubtless, completely built up in Liverpool.

Traced with a pen, I discover a number of dotted lines, radiating in all directions from the foot of Lord-street, where stands marked *"Riddough's Hotel,"* the house my father stopped at.

These marks delineate his various excursions in the town; and I follow the lines on, through street and lane; and across broad squares; and penetrate with them into the narrowest courts.

By these marks, I perceive that my father forgot not his religion in a foreign land; but attended St. John's Church near the Hay-market, and other places of public worship: I see that he visited the News Room in Duke-street, the Lyceum in Bold-street, and the Theater Royal; and that he called to pay his respects to the eminent Mr. Roscoe, the historian, poet, and banker.

Reverentially folding this map, I pass a plate of the Town Hall, and come upon the Title Page, which, in the middle, is ornamented with a piece of landscape, representing a loosely clad lady in sandals, pensively seated upon a bleak rock on the sea shore, supporting her head with one hand, and with the other, exhibiting to the stranger an oval sort of salver, bearing the figure of a strange bird, with this motto elastically stretched for a border—*"Deus nobis hæc otia fecit."*

The bird forms part of the city arms, and is an imaginary representation of a now extinct fowl, called the *"Liver,"* said

to have inhabited a "*pool*," which antiquarians assert once covered a good part of the ground where Liverpool now stands;
and from that bird, and this pool, Liverpool derives its name.

At a distance from the pensive lady in sandals, is a ship
under full sail; and on the beach is the figure of a small man,
vainly essaying to roll over a huge bale of goods.

Equally divided at the top and bottom of this design, is the
following title complete; but I fear the printer will not be able
to give a fac-simile: —

The
Picture
of
Liverpool:
or,
Stranger's Guide
and
Gentleman's Pocket Companion
FOR THE TOWN.
Embellished
With Engravings
By the Most Accomplished and Eminent Artists.
Liverpool:
Printed in Swift's Court,
And sold by Woodward and Alderson, 56 Castle St.
1803.

A brief and reverential preface, as if the writer were all the
time bowing, informs the reader of the flattering reception
accorded to previous editions of the work; and quotes "*testi-
monies of respect which had lately appeared in various quarters—
the British Critic, Review, and the seventh volume of the Beauties
of England and Wales*"—and concludes by expressing the
hope, that this new, revised, and illustrated edition might
"*render it less unworthy of the public notice, and less unworthy
also of the subject it is intended to illustrate.*"

A very nice, dapper, and respectful little preface, the time
and place of writing which is solemnly recorded at the end—
Hope Place, 1st Sept. 1803.

But how much fuller my satisfaction, as I fondly linger over
this circumstantial paragraph, if the writer had recorded the

precise hour of the day, and by what time-piece; and if he had but mentioned his age, occupation, and name.

But all is now lost; I know not who he was; and this estimable author must needs share the oblivious fate of all literary incognitos.

He must have possessed the grandest and most elevated ideas of true fame, since he scorned to be perpetuated by a solitary initial. Could I find him out now, sleeping neglected in some churchyard, I would buy him a head-stone, and record upon it naught but his title-page, deeming that his noblest epitaph.

After the preface, the book opens with an extract from a prologue written by the excellent Dr. Aiken, the brother of Mrs. Barbauld, upon the opening of the Theater Royal, Liverpool, in 1772: —

> "Where Mersey's stream, long winding o'er the plain,
> Pours his full tribute to the circling main,
> A band of fishers chose their humble seat;
> Contented labor blessed the fair retreat,
> Inured to hardship, patient, bold, and rude,
> They braved the billows for precarious food:
> Their straggling huts were ranged along the shore,
> Their nets and little boats their only store."

Indeed, throughout, the work abounds with quaint poetical quotations, and old-fashioned classical allusions to the Æneid and Falconer's Shipwreck.

And the anonymous author must have been not only a scholar and a gentleman, but a man of gentle disinterestedness, combined with true city patriotism; for in his "*Survey of the Town*" are nine thickly printed pages of a neglected poem by a neglected Liverpool poet.

By way of apologizing for what might seem an obtrusion upon the public of so long an episode, he courteously and feelingly introduces it by saying, that "*the poem has now for several years been scarce, and is at present but little known; and hence a very small portion of it will no doubt be highly acceptable to the cultivated reader; especially as this noble epic is written with great felicity of expression and the sweetest delicacy of feeling.*"

Once, but once only, an uncharitable thought crossed my mind, that the author of the Guide-Book might have been the author of the epic. But that was years ago; and I have never since permitted so uncharitable a reflection to insinuate itself into my mind.

This epic, from the specimen before me, is composed in the old stately style, and rolls along commanding as a coach and four. It sings of Liverpool and the Mersey; its docks, and ships, and warehouses, and bales, and anchors; and after descanting upon the abject times, when "*his noble waves, inglorious, Mersey rolled,*" the poet breaks forth like all Parnassus with: —

> "*Now o'er the wondering world her name resounds,*
> *From northern climes to India's distant bounds —*
> *Where'er his shores the broad Atlantic waves;*
> *Where'er the Baltic rolls his wintry waves;*
> *Where'er the honored flood extends his tide,*
> *That clasps Sicilia like a favored bride.*
> *Greenland for her its bulky whale resigns,*
> *And temperate Gallia rears her generous vines:*
> *'Midst warm Iberia citron orchards blow,*
> *And the ripe fruitage bends the laboring bough;*
> *In every clime her prosperous fleets are known,*
> *She makes the wealth of every clime her own.*"

It also contains a delicately-curtained allusion to Mr. Roscoe:—

> "*And here R*s*o*, with genius all his own,*
> *New tracks explores, and all before unknown.*"

Indeed, both the anonymous author of the Guide-Book, and the gifted bard of the Mersey, seem to have nourished the warmest appreciation of the fact, that to their beloved town Roscoe imparted a reputation which gracefully embellished its notoriety as a mere place of commerce. He is called the modern Guicciardini of the modern Florence, and his histories, translations, and Italian Lives, are spoken of with classical admiration.

The first chapter begins in a methodical, business-like way, by informing the impatient reader of the precise latitude and longitude of Liverpool; so that, at the outset, there may be no misunderstanding on that head. It then goes on to give an account of the history and antiquities of the town, beginning with a record in the *Doomsday-Book* of William the Conqueror.

Here, it must be sincerely confessed, however, that notwithstanding his numerous other merits, my favorite author betrays a want of the uttermost antiquarian and penetrating spirit, which would have scorned to stop in its researches at the reign of the Norman monarch, but would have pushed on resolutely through the dark ages, up to Moses, the man of Uz, and Adam; and finally established the fact beyond a doubt, that the soil of Liverpool was created with the creation.

But, perhaps, one of the most curious passages in the chapter of antiquarian research, is the pious author's moralizing reflections upon an interesting fact he records: to wit, that in A.D. 1571, the inhabitants sent a memorial to Queen Elizabeth, praying relief under a subsidy, wherein they style themselves "*her majesty's poor decayed town of Liverpool.*"

As I now fix my gaze upon this faded and dilapidated old guide-book, bearing every token of the ravages of near half a century, and read how this piece of antiquity enlarges like a modern upon previous antiquities, I am forcibly reminded that the world is indeed growing old. And when I turn to the second chapter, "*On the increase of the town, and number of inhabitants,*" and then skim over page after page throughout the volume, all filled with allusions to the immense grandeur of a place, which, since then, has more than quadrupled in population, opulence, and splendor, and whose present inhabitants must look back upon the period here spoken of with a swelling feeling of immeasurable superiority and pride, I am filled with a comical sadness at the vanity of all human exaltation. For the cope-stone of to-day is the corner-stone of to-morrow; and as St. Peter's church was built in great part of the ruins of old Rome, so in all our erections, however imposing, we but form quarries and supply ignoble materials for the grander domes of posterity.

And even as this old guide-book boasts of the, to us, insignificant Liverpool of fifty years ago, the New York guide-books are now vaunting of the magnitude of a town, whose future inhabitants, multitudinous as the pebbles on the beach, and girdled in with high walls and towers, flanking endless avenues of opulence and taste, will regard all our Broadways and Bowerys as but the paltry nucleus to their Nineveh. From far up the Hudson, beyond Harlem River, where the young saplings are now growing, that will overarch their lordly mansions with broad boughs, centuries old; they may send forth explorers to penetrate into the then obscure and smoky alleys of the Fifth Avenue and Fourteenth-street; and going still farther south, may exhume the present Doric Custom-house, and quote it as a proof that their high and mighty metropolis enjoyed a Hellenic antiquity.

As I am extremely loth to omit giving a specimen of the dignified style of this "*Picture of Liverpool*," so different from the brief, pert, and unclerkly hand-books to Niagara and Buffalo of the present day, I shall now insert the chapter of antiquarian researches; especially as it is entertaining in itself, and affords much valuable, and perhaps rare information, which the reader may need, concerning the famous town, to which I made *my first voyage*. And I think that with regard to a matter, concerning which I myself am wholly ignorant, it is far better to quote my old friend verbatim, than to mince his substantial baron-of-beef of information into a flimsy ragout of my own; and so, pass it off as original. Yes, I will render unto my honored guide-book its due.

But how can the printer's art so dim and mellow down the pages into a soft sunset yellow; and to the reader's eye, shed over the type all the pleasant associations which the original carries to me!

No! by my father's sacred memory, and all sacred privacies of fond family reminiscences, I will not! I will *not* quote thee, old Morocco, before the cold face of the marble-hearted world; for your antiquities would only be skipped and dishonored by shallow-minded readers; and for me, I should be charged with swelling out my volume by plagiarizing from a guide-book—the most vulgar and ignominious of thefts!

Chapter 31

WHEN I LEFT HOME, I took the green morocco guide-book along, supposing that from the great number of ships going to Liverpool, I would most probably ship on board of one of them, as the event itself proved.

Great was my boyish delight at the prospect of visiting a place, the infallible clew to all whose intricacies I held in my hand.

On the passage out I studied its pages a good deal. In the first place, I grounded myself thoroughly in the history and antiquities of the town, as set forth in the chapter I intended to quote. Then I mastered the columns of statistics, touching the advance of population; and pored over them, as I used to do over my multiplication-table. For I was determined to make the whole subject my own; and not be content with a mere smattering of the thing, as is too much the custom with most students of guide-books. Then I perused one by one the elaborate descriptions of public edifices, and scrupulously compared the text with the corresponding engraving, to see whether they corroborated each other. For be it known that, including the map, there were no less than seventeen plates in the work. And by often examining them, I had so impressed every column and cornice in my mind, that I had no doubt of recognizing the originals in a moment.

In short, when I considered that my own father had used this very guide-book, and that thereby it had been thoroughly tested, and its fidelity proved beyond a peradventure; I could not but think that I was building myself up in an unerring knowledge of Liverpool; especially as I had familiarized my-self with the map, and could turn sharp corners on it, with marvelous confidence and celerity.

In imagination, as I lay in my berth on ship-board, I used to take pleasant afternoon rambles through the town; down St. James-street and up Great George's, stopping at various places of interest and attraction. I began to think I had been born in Liverpool, so familiar seemed all the features of the map. And though some of the streets there depicted were thickly involved, endlessly angular and crooked, like the map of Boston, in Massachusetts, yet, I made no doubt, that I could march through them in the darkest night, and even run for the most distant dock upon a pressing emergency.

Dear delusion!

It never occurred to my boyish thoughts, that though a guide-book, fifty years old, might have done good service in its day, yet it would prove but a miserable cicerone to a modern. I little imagined that the Liverpool my father saw, was another Liverpool from that to which I, his son Wellingborough was sailing. No; these things never obtruded; so accustomed had I been to associate my old morocco guide-book with the town it described, that the bare thought of there being any discrepancy, never entered my mind.

While we lay in the Mersey, before entering the dock, I got out my guide-book to see how the map would compare with the identical place itself. But they bore not the slightest resemblance. However, thinks I, this is owing to my taking a horizontal view, instead of a bird's-eye survey. So, never mind old guide-book, *you*, at least, are all right.

But my faith received a severe shock that same evening, when the crew went ashore to supper, as I have previously related.

The men stopped at a curious old tavern, near the Prince's Dock's walls; and having my guide-book in my pocket, I drew it forth to compare notes, when I found, that precisely upon the spot where I and my shipmates were standing, and a cherry-cheeked bar-maid was filling their glasses, my infallible old Morocco, in that very place, located a fort; adding, that it was well worth the intelligent stranger's while to visit it for the purpose of beholding the guard relieved in the evening.

This was a staggerer; for how could a tavern be mistaken for a castle? and this was about the hour mentioned for the guard to turn out; yet not a red coat was to be seen. But for all this, I could not, for one small discrepancy, condemn the old family servant who had so faithfully served my own father before me; and when I learned that this tavern went by the name of "*The Old Fort Tavern*;" and when I was told that many of the old stones were yet in the walls, I almost completely exonerated my guide-book from the half-insinuated charge of misleading me.

The next day was Sunday, and I had it all to myself; and now, thought I, my guide-book and I shall have a famous ramble up street and down lane, even unto the furthest limits of this Liverpool.

I rose bright and early; from head to foot performed my ablutions "with Eastern scrupulosity," and I arrayed myself in my red shirt and shooting-jacket, and the sportsman's pantaloons; and crowned my entire man with the tarpaulin; so that from this curious combination of clothing, and particularly from my red shirt, I must have looked like a very strange compound indeed: three parts sportsman, and two soldier, to one of the sailor.

My shipmates, of course, made merry at my appearance; but I heeded them not; and after breakfast, jumped ashore, full of brilliant anticipations.

My gait was erect, and I was rather tall of my age; and that may have been the reason why, as I was rapidly walking along the dock, a drunken sailor passing, exclaimed, *"Eyes right! quick step there!"*

Another fellow stopped me to know whether I was going fox-hunting; and one of the dock-police, stationed at the gates, after peeping out upon me from his sentry box, a snug little den, furnished with benches and newspapers, and hung round with storm jackets and oiled capes, issued forth in a great hurry, crossed my path as I was emerging into the street, and commanded me to *halt!* I obeyed; when scanning my appearance pertinaciously, he desired to know where I got that tarpaulin hat, not being able to account for the phenomenon of its roofing the head of a broken-down fox-hunter. But I pointed to my ship, which lay at no great distance; when remarking from my voice that I was a Yankee, this faithful functionary permitted me to pass.

It must be known that the police stationed at the gates of the docks are extremely observant of strangers going out; as many thefts are perpetrated on board the ships; and if they chance to see any thing suspicious, they probe into it without mercy. Thus, the old men who buy "*shakings*," and rubbish from vessels, must turn their bags wrong side out before the police, ere they are allowed to go outside the walls. And often they will search a suspicious looking fellow's clothes, even if he be a very thin man, with attenuated and almost imperceptible pockets.

But where was I going?

I will tell. My intention was in the first place, to visit Riddough's Hotel, where my father had stopped, more than thirty years before: and then, with the map in my hand, follow him through all the town, according to the dotted lines in the diagram. For thus would I be performing a filial pilgrimage to spots which would be hallowed in my eyes.

At last, when I found myself going down Old Hall-street toward Lord-street, where the hotel was situated, according to my authority; and when, taking out my map, I found that Old Hall-street was marked there, through its whole extent with my father's pen; a thousand fond, affectionate emotions rushed around my heart.

Yes, in this very street, thought I, nay, on this very flagging my father walked. Then I almost wept, when I looked down on my sorry apparel, and marked how the people regarded me; the men staring at so grotesque a young stranger, and the old ladies, in beaver hats and ruffles, crossing the walk a little to shun me.

How differently my father must have appeared; perhaps in a blue coat, buff vest, and Hessian boots. And little did he think, that a son of his would ever visit Liverpool as a poor friendless sailor-boy. But I was not born then: no, when he walked this flagging, I was not so much as thought of; I was not included in the census of the universe. My own father did not know me then; and had never seen, or heard, or so much as dreamed of me. And that thought had a touch of sadness to me; for if it had certainly been, that my own parent, at one time, never cast a thought upon me, how might it be with me hereafter? Poor, poor Wellingborough! thought I, miserable boy! you are indeed friendless and forlorn. Here you wander a stranger in a strange town, and the very thought of your father's having been here before you, but carries with it the reflection that, he then knew you not, nor cared for you one whit.

But dispelling these dismal reflections as well as I could, I pushed on my way, till I got to Chapel-street, which I crossed; and then, going under a cloister-like arch of stone, whose gloom and narrowness delighted me, and filled my Yankee soul with romantic thoughts of old Abbeys and Minsters, I emerged into the fine quadrangle of the Merchants' Exchange.

There, leaning against the colonnade, I took out my map, and traced my father right across Chapel-street, and actually through the very arch at my back, into the paved square where I stood.

So vivid was now the impression of his having been here, and so narrow the passage from which he had emerged, that I felt like running on, and overtaking him round the Town Hall adjoining, at the head of Castle-street. But I soon checked myself, when remembering that he had gone whither no son's search could find him in this world. And then I thought of all that must have happened to him since he paced through that arch. What trials and troubles he had encountered; how he had been shaken by many storms of adversity, and at last died a bankrupt. I looked at my own sorry garb, and had much ado to keep from tears.

But I rallied, and gazed round at the sculptured stonework, and turned to my guide-book, and looked at the print of the spot. It was correct to a pillar; but wanted the central ornament of the quadrangle. This, however, was but a slight subsequent erection, which ought not to militate against the general character of my friend for comprehensiveness.

The ornament in question is a group of statuary in bronze, elevated upon a marble pedestal and basement, representing Lord Nelson expiring in the arms of Victory. One foot rests on a rolling foe, and the other on a cannon. Victory is dropping a wreath on the dying admiral's brow; while Death, under the similitude of a hideous skeleton, is insinuating his bony hand under the hero's robe, and groping after his heart. A very striking design, and true to the imagination; I never could look at Death without a shudder.

At uniform intervals round the base of the pedestal, four

naked figures in chains, somewhat larger than life, are seated
in various attitudes of humiliation and despair. One has his
leg recklessly thrown over his knee, and his head bowed over,
as if he had given up all hope of ever feeling better. Another
has his head buried in despondency, and no doubt looks
mournfully out of his eyes, but as his face was averted at the
time, I could not catch the expression. These woe-begone figures of captives are emblematic of Nelson's principal victories;
but I never could look at their swarthy limbs and manacles,
without being involuntarily reminded of four African slaves
in the market-place.

And my thoughts would revert to Virginia and Carolina;
and also to the historical fact, that the African slave-trade
once constituted the principal commerce of Liverpool; and
that the prosperity of the town was once supposed to have
been indissolubly linked to its prosecution. And I remembered that my father had often spoken to gentlemen visiting
our house in New York, of the unhappiness that the discussion of the abolition of this trade had occasioned in Liverpool; that the struggle between sordid interest and humanity
had made sad havoc at the fire-sides of the merchants; estranged sons from sires; and even separated husband from
wife. And my thoughts reverted to my father's friend, the
good and great Roscoe, the intrepid enemy of the trade; who
in every way exerted his fine talents toward its suppression;
writing a poem ("*the Wrongs of Africa*"), several pamphlets;
and in his place in Parliament, he delivered a speech against
it, which, as coming from a member for Liverpool, was supposed to have turned many votes, and had no small share in
the triumph of sound policy and humanity that ensued.

How this group of statuary affected me, may be inferred
from the fact, that I never went through Chapel-street without going through the little arch to look at it again. And
there, night or day, I was sure to find Lord Nelson still falling
back; Victory's wreath still hovering over his sword-point;
and Death grim and grasping as ever; while the four bronze
captives still lamented their captivity.

Now, as I lingered about the railing of the statuary, on the
Sunday I have mentioned, I noticed several persons going in
and out of an apartment, opening from the basement under

the colonnade; and, advancing, I perceived that this was a news-room, full of files of papers. My love of literature prompted me to open the door and step in; but a glance at my soiled shooting-jacket prompted a dignified looking personage to step up and shut the door in my face. I deliberated a minute what I should do to him; and at last resolutely determined to let him alone, and pass on; which I did; going down Castle-street (so called from a castle which once stood there, said my guide-book), and turning down into Lord.

Arrived at the foot of the latter street, I in vain looked round for the hotel. How serious a disappointment was this may well be imagined, when it is considered that I was all eagerness to behold the very house at which my father stopped; where he slept and dined, smoked his cigar, opened his letters, and read the papers. I inquired of some gentlemen and ladies where the missing hotel was; but they only stared and passed on; until I met a mechanic, apparently, who very civilly stopped to hear my questions and give me an answer.

"Riddough's Hotel?" said he, "upon my word, I think I have heard of such a place; let me see—yes, yes—that was the hotel where my father broke his arm, helping to pull down the walls. My lad, you surely can't be inquiring for Riddough's Hotel! What do you want to find there?"

"Oh! nothing," I replied, "I am much obliged for your information"—and away I walked.

Then, indeed, a new light broke in upon me concerning my guide-book; and all my previous dim suspicions were almost confirmed. It was nearly half a century behind the age! and no more fit to guide me about the town, than the map of Pompeii.

It was a sad, a solemn, and a most melancholy thought. The book on which I had so much relied; the book in the old morocco cover; the book with the cocked-hat corners; the book full of fine old family associations; the book with seventeen plates, executed in the highest style of art; this precious book was next to useless. Yes, the thing that had guided the father, could not guide the son. And I sat down on a shop step, and gave loose to meditation.

Here, now, oh, Wellingborough, thought I, learn a lesson, and never forget it. This world, my boy, is a moving world;

its Riddough's Hotels are forever being pulled down; it never stands still; and its sands are forever shifting. This very harbor of Liverpool is gradually filling up, they say; and who knows what your son (if you ever have one) may behold, when he comes to visit Liverpool, as long after you as you come after his grandfather. And, Wellingborough, as your father's guide-book is no guide for you, neither would yours (could you afford to buy a modern one to-day) be a true guide to those who come after you. Guide-books, Wellingborough, are the least reliable books in all literature; and nearly all literature, in one sense, is made up of guide-books. Old ones tell us the ways our fathers went, through the thoroughfares and courts of old; but how few of those former places can their posterity trace, amid avenues of modern erections; to how few is the old guide-book now a clew! Every age makes its own guide-books, and the old ones are used for waste paper. But there is one Holy Guide-Book, Wellingborough, that will never lead you astray, if you but follow it aright; and some noble monuments that remain, though the pyramids crumble.

But though I rose from the door-step a sadder and a wiser boy, and though my guide-book had been stripped of its reputation for infallibility, I did not treat with contumely or disdain, those sacred pages which had once been a beacon to my sire.

No.—Poor old guide-book, thought I, tenderly stroking its back, and smoothing the dog-ears with reverence; I will not use you with despite, old Morocco! and you will yet prove a trusty conductor through many old streets in the old parts of this town; even if you are at fault, now and then, concerning a Riddough's Hotel, or some other forgotten thing of the past.

As I fondly glanced over the leaves, like one who loves more than he chides, my eye lighted upon a passage concerning "*The Old Dock*," which much aroused my curiosity. I determined to see the place without delay: and walking on, in what I presumed to be the right direction, at last found myself before a spacious and splendid pile of sculptured brown stone; and entering the porch, perceived from incontrovertible tokens that it must be the Custom-house. After admiring it awhile, I took out my guide-book again; and what was my amazement at discovering that, according to its authority, I was entirely mistaken with regard to this Custom-house; for precisely where I stood, "*The Old Dock*" must be standing. And reading on concerning it, I met with this very apposite passage:— "*The first idea that strikes the stranger in coming to this dock, is the singularity of so great a number of ships afloat in the very heart of the town, without discovering any connection with the sea.*"

Here, now, was a poser! Old Morocco confessed that there was a good deal of "singularity" about the thing; nor did he pretend to deny that it was, without question, amazing, that this fabulous dock should seem to have no *connection with the sea!* However, the same author went on to say, that the "*astonished stranger must suspend his wonder for awhile, and turn to the left.*" But, right or left, no place answering to the description was to be seen.

This was too confounding altogether, and not to be easily accounted for, even by making ordinary allowances for the growth and general improvement of the town in the course of years. So, guide-book in hand, I accosted a policeman standing by, and begged him to tell me whether he was acquainted with any place in that neighborhood called the "*Old Dock.*" The man looked at me wonderingly at first, and then seeing I was apparently sane, and quite civil into the bargain, he whipped his well-polished boot with his rattan, pulled up his silver-laced coat-collar, and initiated me into a knowledge of the following facts.

It seems that in this place originally stood the "*pool,*" from which the town borrows a part of its name, and which originally wound round the greater part of the old settlements; that this pool was made into the "Old Dock," for the benefit of the shipping; but that, years ago, it had been filled up, and furnished the site for the Custom-house before me.

I now eyed the spot with a feeling somewhat akin to the Eastern traveler standing on the brink of the Dead Sea. For here the doom of Gomorrah seemed reversed, and a lake had been converted into substantial stone and mortar.

Well, well, Wellingborough, thought I, you had better put the book into your pocket, and carry it home to the Society

of Antiquaries; it is several thousand leagues and odd furlongs behind the march of improvement. Smell its old morocco binding, Wellingborough; does it not smell somewhat
mummyish? Does it not remind you of Cheops and the Catacombs? I tell you it was written before the lost books of
Livy, and is cousin-german to that irrecoverably departed volume, entitled, "*The Wars of the Lord*," quoted by Moses in
the Pentateuch. Put it up, Wellingborough, put it up, my
dear friend; and hereafter follow your nose throughout Liverpool; it will stick to you through thick and thin: and be
your ship's mainmast and St. George's spire your landmarks.

No!—And again I rubbed its back softly, and gently adjusted a loose leaf: No, no, I'll not give you up yet. Forth,
old Morocco! and lead me in sight of the venerable Abbey of
Birkenhead; and let these eager eyes behold the mansion once
occupied by the old earls of Derby!

For the book discoursed of both places, and told how the
Abbey was on the Cheshire shore, full in view from a point
on the Lancashire side, covered over with ivy, and brilliant
with moss! And how the house of the noble Derbys' was now
a common jail of the town; and how that circumstance was
full of suggestions, and pregnant with wisdom!

But, alas! I never saw the Abbey; at least none was in sight
from the water: and as for the house of the earls, I never saw
that.

Ah me, and ten times alas! am I to visit old England in
vain? in the land of Thomas-a-Becket and stout John of
Gaunt, not to catch the least glimpse of priory or castle? Is
there nothing in all the British empire but these smoky ranges
of old shops and warehouses? is Liverpool but a brick-kiln?
Why, no buildings here look so ancient as the old gable-
pointed mansion of my maternal grandfather at home, whose
bricks were brought from Holland long before the revolu-
tionary war! 'Tis a deceit—a gull—a sham—a hoax! This
boasted England is no older than the State of New York: if it
is, show me the proofs—point out the vouchers. Where's the
tower of Julius Cæsar? Where's the Roman wall? Show me
Stonehenge!

But, Wellingborough, I remonstrated with myself, you are
only in Liverpool; the old monuments lie to the north, south,

east, and west of you; you are but a sailor-boy, and you can not expect to be a great tourist, and visit the antiquities, in that preposterous shooting-jacket of yours. Indeed, you can not, my boy.

True, true—that's it. I am not the traveler my father was. I am only a common-carrier across the Atlantic.

After a weary day's walk, I at last arrived at the sign of the Baltimore Clipper to supper; and Handsome Mary poured me out a brimmer of tea, in which, for the time, I drowned all my melancholy.

Chapter 32

THE DOCKS

FOR MORE THAN SIX WEEKS, the ship Highlander lay in Prince's Dock; and during that time, besides making observations upon things immediately around me, I made sundry excursions to the neighboring docks, for I never tired of admiring them.

Previous to this, having only seen the miserable wooden wharves, and slip-shod, shambling piers of New York, the sight of these mighty docks filled my young mind with wonder and delight. In New York, to be sure, I could not but be struck with the long line of shipping, and tangled thicket of masts along the East River; yet, my admiration had been much abated by those irregular, unsightly wharves, which, I am sure, are a reproach and disgrace to the city that tolerates them.

Whereas, in Liverpool, I beheld long China walls of masonry; vast piers of stone; and a succession of granite-rimmed docks, completely inclosed, and many of them communicating, which almost recalled to mind the great American chain of lakes: Ontario, Erie, St. Clair, Huron, Michigan, and Superior. The extent and solidity of these structures, seemed equal to what I had read of the old Pyramids of Egypt.

Liverpool may justly claim to have originated the model of the Wet Dock,* so called, of the present day; and every thing that is connected with its design, construction, regulation, and improvement. Even London was induced to copy after Liverpool, and Havre followed her example. In magnitude, cost, and durability, the docks of Liverpool, even at the present day surpass all others in the world.

*This term—*Wet Dock*—did not originate, (as has been erroneously opined by the otherwise learned Bardoldi); from the fact, that persons falling into one, never escaped without a soaking; but it is simply used, in order to distinguish these docks from the *Dry-Dock*, where the bottoms of ships are repaired.

The first dock built by the town was the "*Old Dock*," alluded to in my Sunday stroll with my guide-book. This was erected in 1710, since which period has gradually arisen that long line of dock-masonry, now flanking the Liverpool side of the Mersey.

For miles you may walk along that river-side, passing dock after dock, like a chain of immense fortresses:—Prince's, George's, Salt-House, Clarence, Brunswick, Trafalgar, King's, Queen's, and many more.

In a spirit of patriotic gratitude to those naval heroes, who by their valor did so much to protect the commerce of Britain, in which Liverpool held so large a stake; the town, long since, bestowed upon its more modern streets, certain illustrious names, that Broadway might be proud of:—Duncan, Nelson, Rodney, St. Vincent, Nile.

But it is a pity, I think, that they had not bestowed these noble names upon their noble docks; so that they might have been as a rank and file of most fit monuments to perpetuate the names of the heroes, in connection with the commerce they defended.

And how much better would such stirring monuments be; full of life and commotion; than hermit obelisks of Luxor, and idle towers of stone; which, useless to the world in themselves, vainly hope to eternize a name, by having it carved, solitary and alone, in their granite. Such monuments are cenotaphs indeed; founded far away from the true body of the fame of the hero; who, if he be truly a hero, must still be linked with the living interests of his race; for the true fame is something free, easy, social, and companionable. They are but tomb-stones, that commemorate his death, but celebrate not his life. It is well enough that over the inglorious and thrice miserable grave of a Dives, some vast marble column should be reared, recording the fact of his having lived and died; for such records are indispensable to preserve his shrunken memory among men; though that memory must soon crumble away with the marble, and mix with the stagnant oblivion of the mob. But to build such a pompous vanity over the remains of a hero, is a slur upon his fame, and an insult to his ghost. And more enduring monuments are built in the closet with the letters of the alphabet, than even Cheops himself could have founded, with all Egypt and Nubia for his quarry.

Among the few docks mentioned above, occur the names of the *King's* and *Queen's*. At the time, they often reminded me of the two principal streets in the village I came from in America, which streets once rejoiced in the same royal appellations. But they had been christened previous to the Declaration of Independence; and some years after, in a fever of freedom, they were abolished, at an enthusiastic town-meeting, where King George and his lady were solemnly declared unworthy of being immortalized by the village of L——. A country antiquary once told me, that a committee of two barbers were deputed to write and inform the distracted old gentleman of the fact.

As the description of any one of these Liverpool docks will pretty much answer for all, I will here endeavor to give some account of Prince's Dock, where the Highlander rested after her passage across the Atlantic.

This dock, of comparatively recent construction, is perhaps the largest of all, and is well known to American sailors, from the fact, that it is mostly frequented by the American shipping. Here lie the noble New York packets, which at home are found at the foot of Wall-street; and here lie the Mobile and Savannah cotton ships and traders.

This dock was built like the others, mostly upon the bed of the river, the earth and rock having been laboriously scooped out, and solidified again as materials for the quays and piers.

From the river, Prince's Dock is protected by a long pier of masonry, surmounted by a massive wall; and on the side next the town, it is bounded by similar walls, one of which runs along a thoroughfare. The whole space thus inclosed forms an oblong, and may, at a guess, be presumed to comprise about fifteen or twenty acres; but as I had not the rod of a surveyor when I took it in, I will not be certain.

The area of the dock itself, exclusive of the inclosed quays surrounding it, may be estimated at, say, ten acres. Access to the interior from the streets is had through several gateways; so that, upon their being closed, the whole dock is shut up like a house. From the river, the entrance is through a water-

gate, and ingress to ships is only to be had, when the level of
the dock coincides with that of the river; that is, about the
time of high tide, as the level of the dock is always at that
mark. So that when it is low tide in the river, the keels of the
ships inclosed by the quays are elevated more than twenty feet
above those of the vessels in the stream. This, of course, produces a striking effect to a stranger, to see hundreds of immense ships floating high aloft in the heart of a mass of
masonry.

Prince's Dock is generally so filled with shipping, that the
entrance of a new-comer is apt to occasion a universal stir
among all the older occupants. The dock-masters, whose authority is declared by tin signs worn conspicuously over their
hats, mount the poops and forecastles of the various vessels,
and hail the surrounding strangers in all directions:—*"Highlander ahoy! Cast off your bow-line, and sheer alongside the Neptune!"*—*"Neptune ahoy! get out a stern-line, and sheer alongside the Trident!"*—*"Trident ahoy! get out a bow-line, and drop
astern of the Undaunted!"* And so it runs round like a shock
of electricity; touch one, and you touch all. This kind of work
irritates and exasperates the sailors to the last degree; but it is
only one of the unavoidable inconveniences of inclosed docks,
which are outweighed by innumerable advantages.

Just without the water-gate, is a basin, always connecting
with the open river, through a narrow entrance between pier-
heads. This basin forms a sort of ante-chamber to the dock
itself, where vessels lie waiting their turn to enter. During a
storm, the necessity of this basin is obvious; for it would be
impossible to "*dock*" a ship under full headway from a voyage
across the ocean. From the turbulent waves, she first glides
into the ante-chamber between the pier-heads, and from
thence into the docks.

Concerning the cost of the docks, I can only state, that the
King's Dock, comprehending but a comparatively small area,
was completed at an expense of some £20,000.

Our old ship-keeper, a Liverpool man by birth, who had
long followed the seas, related a curious story concerning this
dock. One of the ships which carried over troops from England to Ireland in King William's war, in 1688, entered the
King's Dock on the first day of its being opened in 1788, after

an interval of just one century. She was a dark little brig, called the *Port-a-Ferry*. And probably, as her timbers must have been frequently renewed in the course of a hundred years, the name alone could have been all that was left of her at the time.

A paved area, very wide, is included within the walls; and along the edge of the quays are ranges of iron sheds, intended as a temporary shelter for the goods unladed from the shipping. Nothing can exceed the bustle and activity displayed along these quays during the day; bales, crates, boxes, and cases are being tumbled about by thousands of laborers; trucks are coming and going; dock-masters are shouting; sailors of all nations are singing out at their ropes; and all this commotion is greatly increased by the resoundings from the lofty walls that hem in the din.

Chapter 33

S URROUNDED by its broad belt of masonry, each Liverpool dock is a walled town, full of life and commotion; or rather, it is a small archipelago, an epitome of the world, where all the nations of Christendom, and even those of Heathendom, are represented. For, in itself, each ship is an island, a floating colony of the tribe to which it belongs.

Here are brought together the remotest limits of the earth; and in the collective spars and timbers of these ships, all the forests of the globe are represented, as in a grand parliament of masts. Canada and New Zealand send their pines; America her live oak; India her teak; Norway her spruce; and the Right Honorable Mahogany, member for Honduras and Campeachy, is seen at his post by the wheel. Here, under the beneficent sway of the Genius of Commerce, all climes and countries embrace; and yard-arm touches yard-arm in brotherly love.

A Liverpool dock is a grand caravansary inn, and hotel, on the spacious and liberal plan of the *Astor House*. Here ships are lodged at a moderate charge, and payment is not demanded till the time of departure. Here they are comfortably housed and provided for; sheltered from all weathers and secured from all calamities. For I can hardly credit a story I have heard, that sometimes, in heavy gales, ships lying in the very middle of the docks have lost their top-gallant-masts. Whatever the toils and hardships encountered on the voyage, whether they come from Iceland or the coast of New Guinea, here their sufferings are ended, and they take their ease in their watery inn.

I know not how many hours I spent in gazing at the shipping in Prince's Dock, and speculating concerning their past voyages and future prospects in life. Some had just arrived from the most distant ports, worn, battered, and disabled; others were all a-taunt-o—spruce, gay, and brilliant, in readiness for sea.

Every day the Highlander had some new neighbor. A black brig from Glasgow, with its crew of sober Scotch caps, and its staid, thrifty-looking skipper, would be replaced by a jovial French hermaphrodite, its forecastle echoing with songs, and its quarter-deck elastic from much dancing.

On the other side, perhaps, a magnificent New York Liner, huge as a seventy-four, and suggesting the idea of a Mivart's or Delmonico's afloat, would give way to a Sidney emigrant ship, receiving on board its live freight of shepherds from the Grampians, ere long to be tending their flocks on the hills and downs of New Holland.

I was particularly pleased and tickled, with a multitude of little salt-droghers, rigged like sloops, and not much bigger than a pilot-boat, but with broad bows painted black, and carrying red sails, which looked as if they had been pickled and stained in a tan-yard. These little fellows were continually coming in with their cargoes for ships bound to America; and lying, five or six together, alongside of those lofty Yankee hulls, resembled a parcel of red ants about the carcass of a black buffalo.

When loaded, these comical little craft are about level with the water; and frequently, when blowing fresh in the river, I have seen them flying through the foam with nothing visible but the mast and sail, and a man at the tiller; their entire cargo being snugly secured under hatches.

It was diverting to observe the self-importance of the skipper of any of these diminutive vessels. He would give himself all the airs of an admiral on a three-decker's poop; and no doubt, thought quite as much of himself. And why not? What could Cæsar want more? Though his craft was none of the largest, it was subject to *him*; and though his crew might only consist of himself; yet, if he governed it well, he achieved a triumph, which the moralists of all ages have set above the victories of Alexander.

These craft have each a little cabin, the prettiest, charming-est, most delightful little dog-hole in the world; not much bigger than an old fashioned alcove for a bed. It is lighted by little round glasses placed in the deck; so that to the insider, the ceiling is like a small firmament twinkling with astral radiations. For tall men, nevertheless, the place is but ill-adapted; a sitting, or recumbent position being indispensable to an occupancy of the premises. Yet small, low, and narrow as the cabin is, somehow, it affords accommodations to the skipper and his family. Often, I used to watch the tidy good-wife, seated at the open little scuttle, like a woman at a cottage door, engaged in knitting socks for her husband; or perhaps, cutting his hair, as he kneeled before her. And once, while marveling how a couple like this found room to turn in, below; I was amazed by a noisy irruption of cherry-cheeked young tars from the scuttle, whence they came rolling forth, like so many curly spaniels from a kennel.

Upon one occasion, I had the curiosity to go on board a salt-drogher, and fall into conversation with its skipper, a bachelor, who kept house all alone. I found him a very sociable, comfortable old fellow, who had an eye to having things cozy around him. It was in the evening; and he invited me down into his sanctum to supper; and there we sat together like a couple in a box at an oyster-cellar.

"He, he," he chuckled, kneeling down before a fat, moist, little cask of beer, and holding a cocked-hat pitcher to the faucet—"You see, Jack, I keep every thing down here; and nice times I have by myself. Just before going to bed, it ain't bad to take a nightcap, you know; eh! Jack?—here now, smack your lips over that, my boy—have a pipe?—but stop, let's to supper first."

So he went to a little locker, a fixture against the side, and groping in it awhile, and addressing it with—*"What cheer here, what cheer?"* at last produced a loaf, a small cheese, a bit of ham, and a jar of butter. And then placing a board on his lap, spread the table, the pitcher of beer in the center.

"Why that's but a two legged table," said I, "let's make it four."

So we divided the burthen, and supped merrily together on our knees.

He was an old ruby of a fellow, his cheeks toasted brown; and it did my soul good, to see the froth of the beer bubbling at his mouth, and sparkling on his nut-brown beard. He looked so like a great mug of ale, that I almost felt like taking him by the neck and pouring him out.

"Now Jack," said he, when supper was over, "now Jack, my boy, do you smoke?—Well then, load away." And he handed me a seal-skin pouch of tobacco and a pipe. We sat smoking together in this little sea-cabinet of his, till it began to look much like a state-room in Tophet; and notwithstanding my host's rubicund nose, I could hardly see him for the fog.

"He, he, my boy," then said he—"I don't never have any bugs here, I tell ye: I smokes 'em all out every night before going to bed."

"And where may you sleep?" said I, looking round, and seeing no sign of a bed.

"Sleep?" says he, "why I sleep in my jacket, that's the best counterpane; and I use my head for a pillow. He-he, funny, ain't it?"

"Very funny," says I.

"Have some more ale?" says he; "plenty more."

"No more, thank you," says I; "I guess I'll go;" for what with the tobacco-smoke and the ale, I began to feel like breathing fresh air. Besides, my conscience smote me for thus freely indulging in the pleasures of the table.

"Now, don't go," said he; "don't go, my boy; don't go out into the damp; take an old Christian's advice," laying his hand on my shoulder; "it won't do. You see, by going out now, you'll shake off the ale, and get broad awake again; but if you stay here, you'll soon be dropping off for a nice little nap."

But notwithstanding these inducements, I shook my host's hand and departed.

There was hardly any thing I witnessed in the docks that interested me more than the German emigrants who come on board the large New York ships several days before their sailing, to make every thing comfortable ere starting. Old men, tottering with age, and little infants in arms; laughing girls in bright-buttoned bodices, and astute, middle-aged men with pictured pipes in their mouths, would be seen mingling together in crowds of five, six, and seven or eight hundred in one ship.

Every evening these countrymen of Luther and Melancthon gathered on the forecastle to sing and pray. And it was exalting to listen to their fine ringing anthems, reverberating among the crowded shipping, and rebounding from the lofty walls of the docks. Shut your eyes, and you would think you were in a cathedral.

They keep up this custom at sea; and every night, in the dog-watch, sing the songs of Zion to the roll of the great ocean-organ: a pious custom of a devout race, who thus send over their hallelujahs before them, as they hie to the land of the stranger.

And among these sober Germans, my country counts the most orderly and valuable of her foreign population. It is they who have swelled the census of her Northwestern States; and transferring their ploughs from the hills of Transylvania to the prairies of Wisconsin; and sowing the wheat of the Rhine on the banks of the Ohio, raise the grain, that, a hundred fold increased, may return to their kinsmen in Europe.

There is something in the contemplation of the mode in which America has been settled, that, in a noble breast, should forever extinguish the prejudices of national dislikes.

Settled by the people of all nations, all nations may claim her for their own. You can not spill a drop of American blood without spilling the blood of the whole world. Be he Englishman, Frenchman, German, Dane, or Scot; the European who scoffs at an American, calls his own brother *Raca*, and stands in danger of the judgment. We are not a narrow tribe of men, with a bigoted Hebrew nationality—whose blood has been debased in the attempt to ennoble it, by maintaining an exclusive succession among ourselves. No: our blood is as the flood of the Amazon, made up of a thousand noble currents all pouring into one. We are not a nation, so much as a world; for unless we may claim all the world for our sire, like Melchisedec, we are without father or mother.

For who was our father and our mother? Or can we point to any Romulus and Remus for our founders? Our ancestry is lost in the universal paternity; and Cæsar and Alfred, St. Paul and Luther, and Homer and Shakspeare are as much ours as Washington, who is as much the world's as our own. We are the heirs of all time, and with all nations we divide our inheritance. On this Western Hemisphere all tribes and people are forming into one federated whole; and there is a future which shall see the estranged children of Adam restored as to the old hearth-stone in Eden.

The other world beyond this, which was longed for by the devout before Columbus' time, was found in the New; and the deep-sea-lead, that first struck these soundings, brought up the soil of Earth's Paradise. Not a Paradise then, or now; but to be made so, at God's good pleasure, and in the fullness and mellowness of time. The seed is sown, and the harvest must come; and our children's children, on the world's jubilee morning, shall all go with their sickles to the reaping. Then shall the curse of Babel be revoked, a new Pentecost come, and the language they shall speak shall be the language of Britain. Frenchmen, and Danes, and Scots; and the dwellers on the shores of the Mediterranean, and in the regions round about; Italians, and Indians, and Moors; there shall appear unto them cloven tongues as of fire.

Chapter 34

THE IRRAWADDY

AMONG THE VARIOUS SHIPS lying in Prince's Dock, none interested me more than the Irrawaddy, of Bombay, a "*country ship*," which is the name bestowed by Europeans upon the large native vessels of India. Forty years ago, these merchantmen were nearly the largest in the world; and they still exceed the generality. They are built of the celebrated teak wood, the oak of the East, or in Eastern phrase, "*the King of the Oaks.*"

The Irrawaddy had just arrived from Hindostan, with a cargo of cotton. She was manned by forty or fifty Lascars, the native seamen of India, who seemed to be immediately governed by a countryman of theirs of a higher caste. While his inferiors went about in strips of white linen, this dignitary was arrayed in a red army-coat, brilliant with gold lace, a cocked hat, and drawn sword. But the general effect was quite spoiled by his bare feet.

In discharging the cargo, his business seemed to consist in flagellating the crew with the flat of his saber, an exercise in which long practice had made him exceedingly expert. The poor fellows jumped away with the tackle-rope, elastic as cats.

One Sunday, I went aboard of the Irrawaddy, when this oriental usher accosted me at the gangway, with his sword at my throat. I gently pushed it aside, making a sign expressive of the pacific character of my motives in paying a visit to the ship. Whereupon he very considerately let me pass.

I thought I was in Pegu, so strangely woody was the smell of the dark-colored timbers, whose odor was heightened by the rigging of *kayar*, or cocoa-nut fiber.

The Lascars were on the forecastle-deck. Among them were Malays, Mahrattas, Burmese, Siamese, and Cingalese. They were seated round "kids" full of rice, from which, according to their invariable custom, they helped themselves with one hand, the other being reserved for quite another purpose. They were chattering like magpies in Hindostanee, but I found that several of them could also speak very good English. They were a small-limbed, wiry, tawny set; and I was informed made excellent seamen, though ill adapted to stand the hardships of northern voyaging.

They told me that seven of their number had died on the passage from Bombay; two or three after crossing the tropic of Cancer, and the rest met their fate in the Channel, where the ship had been tost about in violent seas, attended with cold rains, peculiar to that vicinity. Two more had been lost overboard from the flying-jib-boom.

I was condoling with a young English cabin-boy on board, upon the loss of these poor fellows, when he said it was their own fault; they would never wear monkey-jackets, but clung to their thin India robes, even in the bitterest weather. He talked about them much as a farmer would about the loss of so many sheep by the murrain.

The captain of the vessel was an Englishman, as were also the three mates, master, and boatswain. These officers lived astern in the cabin, where every Sunday they read the Church of England's prayers, while the heathen at the other end of the ship were left to their false gods and idols. And thus, with Christianity on the quarter-deck, and paganism on the forecastle, the Irrawaddy ploughed the sea.

As if to symbolize this state of things, the "*fancy piece*" astern comprised, among numerous other carved decorations, a cross and a miter; while forward, on the bows, was a sort of devil for a figure-head—a dragon-shaped creature, with a fiery red mouth, and a switchy-looking tail.

After her cargo was discharged, which was done "to the sound of flutes and soft recorders"—something as work is done in the navy to the music of the boatswain's pipe—the Lascars were set to "*stripping the ship*;" that is, to sending down all her spars and ropes.

At this time, she lay alongside of us, and the Babel on board almost drowned our own voices. In nothing but their girdles, the Lascars hopped about aloft, chattering like so many monkeys; but, nevertheless, showing much dexterity and seamanship in their manner of doing their work.

Every Sunday, crowds of well-dressed people came down to the dock to see this singular ship: many of them perched themselves in the shrouds of the neighboring craft, much to the wrath of Captain Riga, who left strict orders with our old ship-keeper, to drive all strangers out of the Highlander's rigging. It was amusing at these times, to watch the old women with umbrellas, who stood on the quay staring at the Lascars, even when they desired to be private. These inquisitive old ladies seemed to regard the strange sailors as a species of wild animal, whom they might gaze at with as much impunity, as at leopards in the Zoological Gardens.

One night I was returning to the ship, when just as I was passing through the Dock Gate, I noticed a white figure squatting against the wall outside. It proved to be one of the Lascars who was smoking, as the regulations of the docks prohibit his indulging this luxury on board his vessel. Struck with the curious fashion of his pipe, and the odor from it, I inquired what he was smoking; he replied "*Joggerry*," which is a species of weed, used in place of tobacco.

Finding that he spoke good English, and was quite communicative, like most smokers, I sat down by *Dallabdoolmans*, as he called himself, and we fell into conversation. So instructive was his discourse, that when we parted, I had considerably added to my stock of knowledge. Indeed, it is a God-send to fall in with a fellow like this. He knows things you never dreamed of; his experiences are like a man from the moon—wholly strange, a new revelation. If you want to learn romance, or gain an insight into things quaint, curious, and marvelous, drop your books of travel, and take a stroll along the docks of a great commercial port. Ten to one, you will encounter Crusoe himself among the crowds of mariners from all parts of the globe.

But this is no place for making mention of all the subjects upon which I and my Lascar friend mostly discoursed; I will only try to give his account of the *teak-wood* and *kayar rope*, concerning which things I was curious, and sought information.

The "*sagoon*," as he called the tree which produces the teak, grows in its greatest excellence among the mountains of Malabar, whence large quantities are sent to Bombay for ship-building. He also spoke of another kind of wood, the "*sissoo*," which supplies most of the "*shin-logs*," or "*knees*," and crooked timbers in the *country ships*. The sagoon grows to an immense size; sometimes there is fifty feet of trunk, three feet through, before a single bough is put forth. Its leaves are very large; and to convey some idea of them, my Lascar likened them to elephants' ears. He said a purple dye was extracted from them, for the purpose of staining cottons and silks. The wood is specifically heavier than water; it is easily worked, and extremely strong and durable. But its chief merit lies in resisting the action of the salt water, and the attacks of insects; which resistance is caused by its containing a resinous oil called "*poonja*."

To my surprise, he informed me that the Irrawaddy was wholly built by the native shipwrights of India, who, he modestly asserted, surpassed the European artisans.

The rigging, also, was of native manufacture. As the *kayar*, of which it is composed, is now getting into use both in England and America, as well for ropes and rigging as for mats and rugs, my Lascar friend's account of it, joined to my own observations, may not be uninteresting.

In India, it is prepared very much in the same way as in Polynesia. The cocoa-nut is gathered while the husk is still green, and but partially ripe; and this husk is removed by striking the nut forcibly, with both hands, upon a sharp-pointed stake, planted uprightly in the ground. In this way a boy will strip nearly fifteen hundred in a day. But the *kayar* is not made from the husk, as might be supposed, but from the rind of the nut; which, after being long soaked in water, is beaten with mallets, and rubbed together into fibers. After this being dried in the sun, you may spin it, just like hemp, or any similar substance. The fiber thus produced makes very strong and durable ropes, extremely well adapted, from their lightness and durability, for the running rigging of a ship; while the same causes, united with its great strength and buoyancy, render it very suitable for large cables and hawsers.

But the elasticity of the *kayar* ill fits it for the shrouds and standing-rigging of a ship, which require to be comparatively firm. Hence, as the Irrawaddy's shrouds were all of this substance, the Lascar told me, they were continually setting up or slacking off her standing-rigging, according as the weather was cold or warm. And the loss of a foretop-mast, between the tropics, in a squall, he attributed to this circumstance.

After a stay of about two weeks, the Irrawaddy had her heavy Indian spars replaced with Canadian pine, and her *kayar* shrouds with hempen ones. She then mustered her pagans, and hoisted sail for London.

Chapter 35

GALLIOTS, COAST-OF-GUINEA-MAN, AND FLOATING CHAPEL

A NOTHER very curious craft often seen in the Liverpool docks, is the Dutch galliot, an old-fashioned looking gentleman, with hollow waist, high prow and stern, and which, seen lying among crowds of tight Yankee traders, and pert French brigantines, always reminded me of a cocked hat among modish beavers.

The construction of the galliot has not altered for centuries; and the northern European nations, Danes and Dutch, still sail the salt seas in this flat-bottomed salt-cellar of a ship; although, in addition to these, they have vessels of a more modern kind.

They seldom paint the galliot; but scrape and varnish all its planks and spars, so that all over it resembles the "*bright side*," or polished *streak*, usually banding round an American ship.

Some of them are kept scrupulously neat and clean, and remind one of a well-scrubbed wooden platter, or an old oak table, upon which much wax and elbow vigor has been expended. Before the wind, they sail well; but on a bowline, owing to their broad hulls and flat bottoms, they make leeway at a sad rate.

Every day, some strange vessel entered Prince's Dock; and hardly would I gaze my fill at some outlandish craft from Surat or the Levant, ere a still more outlandish one would absorb my attention.

Among others, I remember, was a little brig from the Coast of Guinea. In appearance, she was the ideal of a slaver; low, black, clipper-built about the bows, and her decks in a state of most piratical disorder.

She carried a long, rusty gun, on a swivel, amid-ships; and that gun was a curiosity in itself. It must have been some old veteran, condemned by the government, and sold for any thing it would fetch. It was an antique, covered with half-effaced inscriptions, crowns, anchors, eagles; and it had two

handles near the trunnions, like those of a tureen. The knob
on the breech was fashioned into a dolphin's head; and by a
comical conceit, the touch-hole formed the orifice of a human
ear; and a stout tympanum it must have had, to have withstood the concussions it had heard.

The brig, heavily loaded, lay between two large ships in
ballast; so that its deck was at least twenty feet below those
of its neighbors. Thus shut in, its hatchways looked like the
entrance to deep vaults or mines; especially as her men were
wheeling out of her hold some kind of ore, which might have
been gold ore, so scrupulous were they in evening the bushel
measures, in which they transferred it to the quay; and so
particular was the captain, a dark-skinned whiskerando, in a
Maltese cap and tassel, in standing over the sailors, with his
pencil and memorandum-book in hand.

The crew were a bucaniering looking set; with hairy chests,
purple shirts, and arms wildly tattooed. The mate had a
wooden leg, and hobbled about with a crooked cane like a
spiral staircase. There was a deal of swearing on board of this
craft, which was rendered the more reprehensible when she
came to moor alongside the Floating Chapel.

This was the hull of an old sloop-of-war, which had been
converted into a mariner's church. A house had been built
upon it, and a steeple took the place of a mast. There was a
little balcony near the base of the steeple, some twenty feet
from the water; where, on week-days, I used to see an old
pensioner of a tar, sitting on a camp-stool, reading his Bible.
On Sundays he hoisted the Bethel flag, and like the *muezzin*
or cryer of prayers on the top of a Turkish mosque, would
call the strolling sailors to their devotions; not officially, but
on his own account; conjuring them not to make fools of
themselves, but muster round the pulpit, as they did about
the capstan on a man-of-war. This old worthy was the sexton.
I attended the chapel several times, and found there a very
orderly but small congregation. The first time I went, the
chaplain was discoursing of future punishments, and making
allusions to the Tartarean Lake; which, coupled with the
pitchy smell of the old hull, summoned up the most forcible
image of the thing which I ever experienced.

The floating chapels which are to be found in some of the

docks, form one of the means which have been tried to induce the seamen visiting Liverpool to turn their thoughts toward serious things. But as very few of them ever think of entering these chapels, though they might pass them twenty times in the day, some of the clergy, of a Sunday, address them in the open air, from the corners of the quays, or wherever they can procure an audience.

Whenever, in my Sunday strolls, I caught sight of one of these congregations, I always made a point of joining it; and would find myself surrounded by a motley crowd of seamen from all quarters of the globe, and women, and lumpers, and dock laborers of all sorts. Frequently the clergyman would be standing upon an old cask, arrayed in full canonicals, as a divine of the Church of England. Never have I heard religious discourses better adapted to an audience of men, who, like sailors, are chiefly, if not only, to be moved by the plainest of precepts, and demonstrations of the misery of sin, as conclusive and undeniable as those of Euclid. No mere rhetoric avails with such men; fine periods are vanity. You can not touch them with tropes. They need to be pressed home by plain facts.

And such was generally the mode in which they were addressed by the clergy in question: who, taking familiar themes for their discourses, which were leveled right at the wants of their auditors, always succeeded in fastening their attention. In particular, the two great vices to which sailors are most addicted, and which they practice to the ruin of both body and soul; these things, were the most enlarged upon. And several times on the docks, I have seen a robed clergyman addressing a large audience of women collected from the notorious lanes and alleys in the neighborhood.

Is not this as it ought to be? since the true calling of the reverend clergy is like their divine Master's;—not to bring the righteous, but sinners to repentance. Did some of them leave the converted and comfortable congregations, before whom they have ministered year after year; and plunge at once, like St. Paul, into the infected centers and hearts of vice: *then* indeed, would they find a strong enemy to cope with; and a victory gained over *him*, would entitle them to a conqueror's wreath. Better to save one sinner from an obvious vice that is destroying him, than to indoctrinate ten thousand saints. And as from every corner, in Catholic towns, the shrines of Holy Mary and the Child Jesus perpetually remind the commonest wayfarer of his heaven; even so should Protestant pulpits be founded in the market-places, and at street corners, where the men of God might be heard by all of His children.

Chapter 36

THE OLD CHURCH OF ST. NICHOLAS, AND THE
DEAD-HOUSE

THE FLOATING CHAPEL recalls to mind the "*Old Church*," well known to the seamen of many generations, who have visited Liverpool. It stands very near the docks, a venerable mass of brown stone, and by the town's people is called the Church of St. Nicholas. I believe it is the best preserved piece of antiquity in all Liverpool.

Before the town rose to any importance, it was the only place of worship on that side of the Mersey; and under the adjoining Parish of Walton was a *chapel-of-ease*; though from the straight backed pews, there could have been but little comfort taken in it.

In old times, there stood in front of the church a statue of St. Nicholas, the patron of mariners; to which all pious sailors made offerings, to induce his saintship to grant them short and prosperous voyages. In the tower is a fine chime of bells; and I well remember my delight at first hearing them on the first Sunday morning after our arrival in the dock. It seemed to carry an admonition with it; something like the premonition conveyed to young Whittington by Bow Bells. "*Welling-borough! Wellingborough! you must not forget to go to church, Wellingborough! Don't forget, Wellingborough! Wellingborough! don't forget!*"

Thirty or forty years ago, these bells were rung upon the arrival of every Liverpool ship from a foreign voyage. How forcibly does this illustrate the increase of the commerce of the town! Were the same custom now observed, the bells would seldom have a chance to cease.

What seemed the most remarkable about this venerable old church, and what seemed the most barbarous, and grated upon the veneration with which I regarded this time-hallowed structure, was the condition of the grave-yard sur-rounding it. From its close vicinity to the haunts of the swarms of laborers about the docks, it is crossed and recrossed by thoroughfares in all directions; and the tomb-stones, not being erect, but horizontal (indeed, they form a complete flagging to the spot), multitudes are constantly walking over the dead; their heels erasing the death's-heads and cross-bones, the last mementos of the departed. At noon, when the lumpers employed in loading and unloading the shipping, retire for an hour to snatch a dinner, many of them resort to the grave-yard; and seating themselves upon a tomb-stone use the adjoining one for a table. Often, I saw men stretched out in a drunken sleep upon these slabs; and once, removing a fellow's arm, read the following inscription, which, in a manner, was true to the life, if not to the death: —

> HERE LYETH YE BODY OF
> TOBIAS DRINKER.

For two memorable circumstances connected with this church, I am indebted to my excellent friend, Morocco, who tells me that in 1588 the Earl of Derby, coming to his resi-dence, and waiting for a passage to the Isle of Man, the cor-poration erected and adorned a sumptuous stall in the church for his reception. And moreover, that in the time of Crom-well's wars, when the place was taken by that mad nephew of King Charles, Prince Rupert, he converted the old church into a military prison and stable; when, no doubt, another "*sumptuous stall*" was erected for the benefit of the steed of some noble cavalry officer.

In the basement of the church is a Dead House, like the Morgue in Paris, where the bodies of the drowned are ex-posed until claimed by their friends, or till buried at the pub-lic charge.

From the multitudes employed about the shipping, this dead-house has always more or less occupants. Whenever I passed up Chapel-street, I used to see a crowd gazing through the grim iron grating of the door, upon the faces of the drowned within. And once, when the door was opened, I saw a sailor stretched out, stark and stiff, with the sleeve of his frock rolled up, and showing his name and date of birth tat-tooed upon his arm. It was a sight full of suggestions; he seemed his own head-stone.

I was told that standing rewards are offered for the recovery of persons falling into the docks; so much, if restored to life, and a less amount if irrecoverably drowned. Lured by this, several horrid old men and women are constantly prying about the docks, searching after bodies. I observed them principally early in the morning, when they issued from their dens, on the same principle that the rag-rakers, and rubbish-pickers in the streets, sally out bright and early; for then, the night-harvest has ripened.

There seems to be no calamity overtaking man, that can not be rendered merchantable. Undertakers, sextons, tomb-makers, and hearse-drivers, get their living from the dead; and in times of plague most thrive. And these miserable old men and women hunted after corpses to keep from going to the church-yard themselves; for they were the most wretched of starvelings.

Chapter 37

What Redburn Saw in Launcelott's-Hey

THE DEAD-HOUSE reminds me of other sad things; for in the vicinity of the docks are many very painful sights.

In going to our boarding-house, the sign of the Baltimore Clipper, I generally passed through a narrow street called "Launcelott's-Hey," lined with dingy, prison-like cotton warehouses. In this street, or rather alley, you seldom see any one but a truck-man, or some solitary old warehouse-keeper, haunting his smoky den like a ghost.

Once, passing through this place, I heard a feeble wail, which seemed to come out of the earth. It was but a strip of crooked side-walk where I stood; the dingy wall was on every side, converting the mid-day into twilight; and not a soul was in sight. I started, and could almost have run, when I heard that dismal sound. It seemed the low, hopeless, endless wail of some one forever lost. At last I advanced to an opening which communicated downward with deep tiers of cellars beneath a crumbling old warehouse; and there, some fifteen feet below the walk, crouching in nameless squalor, with her head bowed over, was the figure of what had been a woman. Her blue arms folded to her livid bosom two shrunken things like children, that leaned toward her, one on each side. At first, I knew not whether they were alive or dead. They made no sign; they did not move or stir; but from the vault came that soul-sickening wail.

I made a noise with my foot, which, in the silence, echoed far and near; but there was no response. Louder still; when one of the children lifted its head, and cast upward a faint glance; then closed its eyes, and lay motionless. The woman also, now gazed up, and perceived me; but let fall her eye again. They were dumb and next to dead with want. How they had crawled into that den, I could not tell; but there they had crawled to die. At that moment I never thought of relieving them; for death was so stamped in their glazed and unimploring eyes, that I almost regarded them as already no more. I stood looking down on them, while my whole soul swelled within me; and I asked myself, What right had any body in the wide world to smile and be glad, when sights like this were to be seen? It was enough to turn the heart to gall; and make a man-hater of a Howard. For who were these ghosts that I saw? Were they not human beings? A woman and two girls? With eyes, and lips, and ears like any queen? with hearts which, though they did not bound with blood, yet beat with a dull, dead ache that was their life.

At last, I walked on toward an open lot in the alley, hoping to meet there some ragged old women, whom I had daily noticed groping amid foul rubbish for little particles of dirty cotton, which they washed out and sold for a trifle.

I found them; and accosting one, I asked if she knew of the persons I had just left. She replied, that she did not; nor did she want to. I then asked another, a miserable, toothless old woman, with a tattered strip of coarse baling stuff round her body. Looking at me for an instant, she resumed her raking in the rubbish, and said that she knew who it was that I spoke of; but that she had no time to attend to beggars and their brats. Accosting still another, who seemed to know my errand, I asked if there was no place to which the woman could be taken. "Yes," she replied, "to the church-yard." I said she was alive, and not dead.

"Then she'll never die," was the rejoinder. "She's been down there these three days, with nothing to eat;—that I know myself."

"She desarves it," said an old hag, who was just placing on her crooked shoulders her bag of pickings, and who was turning to totter off, "that Betsey Jennings desarves it—was she ever married? tell me that."

Leaving Launcelott's-Hey, I turned into a more frequented street; and soon meeting a policeman, told him of the condition of the woman and the girls.

"It's none of my business, Jack," said he. "I don't belong to that street."

"Who does then?"

"I don't know. But what business is it of yours? Are you not a Yankee?"

"Yes," said I, "but come, I will help you remove that woman, if you say so."

"There, now, Jack, go on board your ship, and stick to it; and leave these matters to the town."

I accosted two more policemen, but with no better success; they would not even go with me to the place. The truth was, it was out of the way, in a silent, secluded spot; and the misery of the three outcasts, hiding away in the ground, did not obtrude upon any one.

Returning to them, I again stamped to attract their attention; but this time, none of the three looked up, or even stirred. While I yet stood irresolute, a voice called to me from a high, iron-shuttered window in a loft over the way; and asked what I was about. I beckoned to the man, a sort of porter, to come down, which he did; when I pointed down into the vault.

"Well," said he, "what of it?"

"Can't we get them out?" said I, "haven't you some place in your warehouse where you can put them? have you nothing for them to eat?"

"You're crazy, boy," said he; "do you suppose, that Parkins and Wood want their warehouse turned into a hospital?"

I then went to my boarding-house, and told Handsome Mary of what I had seen; asking her if she could not do something to get the woman and girls removed; or if she could not do that, let me have some food for them. But though a kind person in the main, Mary replied that she gave away enough to beggars in her own street (which was true enough) without looking after the whole neighborhood.

Going into the kitchen, I accosted the cook, a little shriveled-up old Welshwoman, with a saucy tongue, whom the sailors called *Brandy-Nan*; and begged her to give me some cold victuals, if she had nothing better, to take to the vault. But she broke out in a storm of swearing at the miserable occupants of the vault, and refused. I then stepped into the room where our dinner was being spread; and waiting till the girl had gone out, I snatched some bread and cheese from a stand, and thrusting it into the bosom of my frock, left the house. Hurrying to the lane, I dropped the food down into the vault. One of the girls caught at it convulsively, but fell back, apparently fainting; the sister pushed the other's arm aside, and took the bread in her hand; but with a weak uncertain grasp like an infant's. She placed it to her mouth; but letting it fall again, murmured faintly something like "water." The woman did not stir; her head was bowed over, just as I had first seen her.

Seeing how it was, I ran down toward the docks to a mean little sailor tavern, and begged for a pitcher; but the cross old man who kept it refused, unless I would pay for it. But I had no money. So as my boarding-house was some way off, and it would be lost time to run to the ship for my big iron pot; under the impulse of the moment, I hurried to one of the Boodle Hydrants, which I remembered having seen running near the scene of a still smoldering fire in an old rag house; and taking off a new tarpaulin hat, which had been loaned me that day, filled it with water.

With this, I returned to Launcelott's-Hey; and with considerable difficulty, like getting down into a well, I contrived to descend with it into the vault; where there was hardly space enough left to let me stand. The two girls drank out of the hat together; looking up at me with an unalterable, idiotic expression, that almost made me faint. The woman spoke not a word, and did not stir. While the girls were breaking and eating the bread, I tried to lift the woman's head; but, feeble as she was, she seemed bent upon holding it down. Observing her arms still clasped upon her bosom, and that something seemed hidden under the rags there, a thought crossed my mind, which impelled me forcibly to withdraw her hands for a moment; when I caught a glimpse of a meager little babe, the lower part of its body thrust into an old bonnet. Its face was dazzlingly white, even in its squalor; but the closed eyes looked like balls of indigo. It must have been dead some hours.

The woman refusing to speak, eat, or drink, I asked one of the girls who they were, and where they lived; but she only stared vacantly, muttering something that could not be understood.

The air of the place was now getting too much for me; but I stood deliberating a moment, whether it was possible for me to drag them out of the vault. But if I did, what then?

They would only perish in the street, and here they were at least protected from the rain; and more than that, might die in seclusion.

I crawled up into the street, and looking down upon them again, almost repented that I had brought them any food; for it would only tend to prolong their misery, without hope of any permanent relief: for die they must very soon; they were too far gone for any medicine to help them. I hardly know whether I ought to confess another thing that occurred to me as I stood there; but it was this—I felt an almost irresistible impulse to do them the last mercy, of in some way putting an end to their horrible lives; and I should almost have done so, I think, had I not been deterred by thoughts of the law. For I well knew that the law, which would let them perish of themselves without giving them one cup of water, would spend a thousand pounds, if necessary, in convicting him who should so much as offer to relieve them from their miserable existence.

The next day, and the next, I passed the vault three times, and still met the same sight. The girls leaning up against the woman on each side, and the woman with her arms still folding the babe, and her head bowed. The first evening I did not see the bread that I had dropped down in the morning; but the second evening, the bread I had dropped that morning remained untouched. On the third morning the smell that came from the vault was such, that I accosted the same policeman I had accosted before, who was patrolling the same street, and told him that the persons I had spoken to him about were dead, and he had better have them removed. He looked as if he did not believe me, and added, that it was not his street.

When I arrived at the docks on my way to the ship, I entered the guard-house within the walls, and asked for one of the captains, to whom I told the story; but, from what he said, was led to infer that the Dock Police was distinct from that of the town, and this was not the right place to lodge my information.

I could do no more that morning, being obliged to repair to the ship; but at twelve o'clock, when I went to dinner, I hurried into Launcelott's-Hey, when I found that the vault was empty. In place of the woman and children, a heap of quick-lime was glistening.

I could not learn who had taken them away, or whither they had gone; but my prayer was answered—they were dead, departed, and at peace.

But again I looked down into the vault, and in fancy beheld the pale, shrunken forms still crouching there. Ah! what are our creeds, and how do we hope to be saved? Tell me, oh Bible, that story of Lazarus again, that I may find comfort in my heart for the poor and forlorn. Surrounded as we are by the wants and woes of our fellow-men, and yet given to follow our own pleasures, regardless of their pains, are we not like people sitting up with a corpse, and making merry in the house of the dead?

Chapter 38

THE DOCK-WALL BEGGARS

I MIGHT RELATE other things which befell me during the six weeks and more that I remained in Liverpool, often visiting the cellars, sinks, and hovels of the wretched lanes and courts near the river. But to tell of them, would only be to tell over again the story just told; so I return to the docks.

The old women described as picking dirty fragments of cotton in the empty lot, belong to the same class of beings who at all hours of the day are to be seen within the dock walls, raking over and over the heaps of rubbish carried ashore from the holds of the shipping.

As it is against the law to throw the least thing overboard, even a rope yarn; and as this law is very different from similar laws in New-York, inasmuch as it is rigidly enforced by the dock-masters; and, moreover, as after discharging a ship's cargo, a great deal of dirt and worthless dunnage remains in the hold, the amount of rubbish accumulated in the appointed receptacles for depositing it within the walls is extremely large, and is constantly receiving new accessions from every vessel that unlades at the quays.

Standing over these noisome heaps, you will see scores of tattered wretches, armed with old rakes and picking-irons, turning over the dirt, and making as much of a rope-yarn as if it were a skein of silk. Their findings, nevertheless, are but small; for as it is one of the immemorial perquisites of the second mate of a merchant ship to collect, and sell on his own account, all the condemned "old junk" of the vessel to which he belongs, he generally takes good heed that in the buckets of rubbish carried ashore, there shall be as few rope-yarns as possible.

In the same way, the cook preserves all the odds and ends of pork-rinds and beef-fat, which he sells at considerable profit; upon a six months' voyage frequently realizing thirty or forty dollars from the sale, and in large ships, even more than that. It may easily be imagined, then, how desperately driven to it must these rubbish-pickers be, to ransack heaps of refuse which have been previously gleaned.

Nor must I omit to make mention of the singular beggary practiced in the streets frequented by sailors; and particularly to record the remarkable army of paupers that beset the docks at particular hours of the day.

At twelve o'clock the crews of hundreds and hundreds of ships issue in crowds from the dock gates to go to their dinner in the town. This hour is seized upon by multitudes of beggars to plant themselves against the outside of the walls, while others stand upon the curbstone to excite the charity of the seamen. The first time that I passed through this long lane of pauperism, it seemed hard to believe that such an array of misery could be furnished by any town in the world.

Every variety of want and suffering here met the eye, and every vice showed here its victims. Nor were the marvelous and almost incredible shifts and stratagems of the professional beggars, wanting to finish this picture of all that is dishonorable to civilization and humanity.

Old women, rather mummies, drying up with slow starving and age; young girls, incurably sick, who ought to have been in the hospital; sturdy men, with the gallows in their eyes, and a whining lie in their mouths; young boys, hollow-eyed and decrepit; and puny mothers, holding up puny babes in the glare of the sun, formed the main features of the scene.

But these were diversified by instances of peculiar suffering, vice, or art in attracting charity, which, to me at least, who had never seen such things before, seemed to the last degree uncommon and monstrous.

I remember one cripple, a young man rather decently clad, who sat huddled up against the wall, holding a painted board on his knees. It was a picture intending to represent the man himself caught in the machinery of some factory, and whirled about among spindles and cogs, with his limbs mangled and bloody. This person said nothing, but sat silently exhibiting his board. Next him, leaning upright against the wall, was a tall, pallid man, with a white bandage round his brow, and his face cadaverous as a corpse. He, too, said nothing; but with one finger silently pointed down to the square of flagging at his feet, which was nicely swept, and stained blue, and bore this inscription in chalk:—

> *"I have had no food for three days;*
> *My wife and children are dying."*

Further on lay a man with one sleeve of his ragged coat removed, showing an unsightly sore; and above it a label with some writing.

In some places, for the distance of many rods, the whole line of flagging immediately at the base of the wall, would be completely covered with inscriptions, the beggars standing over them in silence.

But as you passed along these horrible records, in an hour's time destined to be obliterated by the feet of thousands and thousands of wayfarers, you were not left unassailed by the clamorous petitions of the more urgent applicants for charity. They beset you on every hand; catching you by the coat; hanging on, and following you along; and, *for Heaven's sake*, and *for God's sake*, and *for Christ's sake*, beseeching of you but *one ha'penny*. If you so much as glanced your eye on one of them, even for an instant, it was perceived like lightning, and the person never left your side until you turned into another street, or satisfied his demands. Thus, at least, it was with the sailors; though I observed that the beggars treated the town's people differently.

I can not say that the seamen did much to relieve the destitution which three times every day was presented to their view. Perhaps habit had made them callous; but the truth might have been that very few of them had much money to give. Yet the beggars must have had some inducement to infest the dock walls as they did.

As an example of the caprice of sailors, and their sympathy with suffering among members of their own calling, I must mention the case of an old man, who every day, and all day long, through sunshine and rain, occupied a particular corner, where crowds of tars were always passing. He was an uncommonly large, plethoric man, with a wooden leg, and dressed in the nautical garb; his face was red and round; he was continually merry; and with his wooden stump thrust forth, so as almost to trip up the careless wayfarer, he sat upon a great pile of monkey jackets, with a little depression in them between his knees, to receive the coppers thrown him. And plenty of pennies were tost into his poor-box by the sailors, who always exchanged a pleasant word with the old man, and passed on, generally regardless of the neighboring beggars.

The first morning I went ashore with my shipmates, some of them greeted him as an old acquaintance; for that corner he had occupied for many long years. He was an old man-of-war's man, who had lost his leg at the battle of Trafalgar; and singular to tell, he now exhibited his wooden one as a genuine specimen of the oak timbers of Nelson's ship, the Victory.

Among the paupers were several who wore old sailor hats and jackets, and claimed to be destitute tars; and on the strength of these pretensions demanded help from their brethren; but Jack would see through their disguise in a moment, and turn away, with no benediction.

As I daily passed through this lane of beggars, who thronged the docks as the Hebrew cripples did the Pool of Bethesda, and as I thought of my utter inability in any way to help them, I could not but offer up a prayer, that some angel might descend, and turn the waters of the docks into an elixir, that would heal all their woes, and make them, man and woman, healthy and whole as their ancestors, Adam and Eve, in the garden.

Adam and Eve! If indeed ye are yet alive and in heaven, may it be no part of your immortality to look down upon the world ye have left. For as all these sufferers and cripples are as much your family as young Abel, so, to you, the sight of the world's woes would be a parental torment indeed.

Chapter 39

THE BOOBLE-ALLEYS OF THE TOWN

THE SAME SIGHTS that are to be met with along the dock walls at noon, in a less degree, though diversified with other scenes, are continually encountered in the narrow streets where the sailor boarding-houses are kept.

In the evening, especially when the sailors are gathered in great numbers, these streets present a most singular spectacle, the entire population of the vicinity being seemingly turned into them. Hand-organs, fiddles, and cymbals, plied by strolling musicians, mix with the songs of the seamen, the babble of women and children, and the groaning and whining of beggars. From the various boarding-houses, each distinguished by gilded emblems outside—an anchor, a crown, a ship, a windlass, or a dolphin—proceeds the noise of revelry and dancing; and from the open casements lean young girls and old women, chattering and laughing with the crowds in the middle of the street. Every moment strange greetings are exchanged between old sailors who chance to stumble upon a shipmate, last seen in Calcutta or Savannah; and the invariable courtesy that takes place upon these occasions, is to go to the next spirit-vault, and drink each other's health.

There are particular paupers who frequent particular sections of these streets, and who, I was told, resented the intrusion of mendicants from other parts of the town.

Chief among them was a white-haired old man, stone-blind; who was led up and down through the long tumult by a woman holding a little saucer to receive contributions. This old man sang, or rather chanted, certain words in a peculiarly long-drawn, guttural manner, throwing back his head, and turning up his sightless eyeballs to the sky. His chant was a lamentation upon his infirmity; and at the time it produced the same effect upon me, that my first reading of Milton's Invocation to the Sun did, years afterward. I can not recall it all; but it was something like this, drawn out in an endless groan—

"Here goes the blind old man; blind, blind, blind; no more will he see sun nor moon—no more see sun nor moon!" And thus would he pass through the middle of the street; the woman going on in advance, holding his hand, and dragging him through all obstructions; now and then leaving him standing, while she went among the crowd soliciting coppers.

But one of the most curious features of the scene is the number of sailor ballad-singers, who, after singing their verses, hand you a printed copy, and beg you to buy. One of these persons, dressed like a man-of-war's-man, I observed every day standing at a corner in the middle of the street. He had a full, noble voice, like a church-organ; and his notes rose high above the surrounding din. But the remarkable thing about this ballad-singer was one of his arms, which, while singing, he somehow swung vertically round and round in the air, as if it revolved on a pivot. The feat was naturally unaccountable; and he performed it with the view of attracting sympathy; since he said that in falling from a frigate's mast-head to the deck, he had met with an injury, which had resulted in making his wonderful arm what it was.

I made the acquaintance of this man, and found him no common character. He was full of marvelous adventures, and abounded in terrific stories of pirates and sea murders, and all sorts of nautical enormities. He was a monomaniac upon these subjects; he was a Newgate Calendar of the robberies and assassinations of the day, happening in the sailor quarters of the town; and most of his ballads were upon kindred subjects. He composed many of his own verses, and had them printed for sale on his own account. To show how expeditious he was at this business, it may be mentioned, that one evening on leaving the dock to go to supper, I perceived a crowd gathered about the *Old Fort Tavern*; and mingling with the rest, I learned that a woman of the town had just been killed at the bar by a drunken Spanish sailor from Cadiz. The murderer was carried off by the police before my eyes, and the very next morning the ballad-singer with the miraculous arm, was singing the tragedy in front of the boarding-houses, and handing round printed copies of the song, which, of course, were eagerly bought up by the seamen.

This passing allusion to the murder will convey some idea

of the events which take place in the lowest and most abandoned neighborhoods frequented by sailors in Liverpool. The pestilent lanes and alleys which, in their vocabulary, go by the names of Rotten-row, Gibraltar-place, and Booble-alley, are putrid with vice and crime; to which, perhaps, the round globe does not furnish a parallel. The sooty and begrimed bricks of the very houses have a reeking, Sodom-like, and murderous look; and well may the shroud of coal-smoke, which hangs over this part of the town, more than any other, attempt to hide the enormities here practiced. These are the haunts from which sailors sometimes disappear forever; or issue in the morning, robbed naked, from the broken doorways. These are the haunts in which cursing, gambling, pickpocketing, and common iniquities, are virtues too lofty for the infected gorgons and hydras to practice. Propriety forbids that I should enter into details; but kidnappers, burkers, and resurrectionists are almost saints and angels to them. They seem leagued together, a company of miscreant misanthropes, bent upon doing all the malice to mankind in their power. With sulphur and brimstone they ought to be burned out of their arches like vermin.

Chapter 40

PLACARDS, BRASS-JEWELERS, TRUCK-HORSES, AND STEAMERS

A S I WISH to group together what fell under my observation concerning the Liverpool docks, and the scenes roundabout, I will try to throw into this chapter various minor things that I recall.

The advertisements of pauperism chalked upon the flagging round the dock walls, are singularly accompanied by a multitude of quite different announcements, placarded upon the walls themselves. They are principally notices of the approaching departure of "*superior, fast-sailing, coppered and copper-fastened ships*," for the United States, Canada, New South Wales, and other places. Interspersed with these, are the advertisements of Jewish clothesmen, informing the judicious seaman where he can procure of the best and the cheapest; together with ambiguous medical announcements of the tribe of quacks and empirics who prey upon all seafaring men. Not content with thus publicly giving notice of their whereabouts, these indefatigable Sangrados and pretended Samaritans hire a parcel of shabby workhouse-looking knaves, whose business consists in haunting the dock walls about meal times, and silently thrusting mysterious little billets—duodecimo editions of the larger advertisements—into the astonished hands of the tars.

They do this, with such a mysterious hang-dog wink; such a sidelong air; such a villainous assumption of your necessities; that, at first, you are almost tempted to knock them down for their pains.

Conspicuous among the notices on the walls, are huge Italic inducements to all seamen disgusted with the merchant service, to accept a round bounty, and embark in her Majesty's navy.

In the British armed marine, in time of peace, they do not ship men for the general service, as in the American navy; but for particular ships, going upon particular cruises. Thus, the frigate Thetis may be announced as about to sail under the command of that fine old sailor, and noble father to his crew, *Lord George Flagstaff.*

Similar announcements may be seen upon the walls concerning enlistments in the army. And never did auctioneer dilate with more rapture upon the charms of some country-seat put up for sale, than the authors of these placards do, upon the beauty and salubrity of the distant climes, for which the regiments wanting recruits are about to sail. Bright lawns, vine-clad hills, endless meadows of verdure, here make up the landscape; and adventurous young gentlemen, fond of travel, are informed, that here is a chance for them to see the world at their leisure, and be paid for enjoying themselves into the bargain. The regiments for India are promised plantations among valleys of palms; while to those destined for New Holland, a novel sphere of life and activity is opened; and the companies bound to Canada and Nova Scotia are lured by tales of summer suns, that ripen grapes in December. No word of war is breathed; hushed is the clang of arms in these announcements; and the sanguine recruit is almost tempted to expect that pruning-hooks, instead of swords, will be the weapons he will wield.

Alas! is not this the cruel stratagem of Bruce at Bannockburn, who decoyed to his war-pits by covering them over with green boughs? For instead of a farm at the blue base of the Himalayas, the Indian recruit encounters the keen saber of the Sikh; and instead of basking in sunny bowers, the Canadian soldier stands a shivering sentry upon the bleak ramparts of Quebec, a lofty mark for the bitter blasts from Baffin's Bay and Labrador. There, as his eye sweeps down the St. Lawrence, whose every billow is bound for the main that laves the shore of Old England; as he thinks of his long term of enlistment, which sells him to the army as Doctor Faust sold himself to the devil; how the poor fellow must groan in his grief, and call to mind the church-yard stile, and his Mary.

These army announcements are well fitted to draw recruits in Liverpool. Among the vast number of emigrants, who daily arrive from all parts of Britain to embark for the United States or the colonies, there are many young men, who, upon arriving at Liverpool, find themselves next to penniless; or, at least, with only enough money to carry them over the sea, without providing for future contingencies. How easily and naturally, then, may such youths be induced to enter upon the military life, which promises them a free passage to the most distant and flourishing colonies, and certain pay for doing nothing; besides holding out hopes of vineyards and farms, to be verified in the fullness of time. For in a money-less youth, the decision to leave home at all, and embark upon a long voyage to reside in a remote clime, is a piece of adventurousness only one remove from the spirit that prompts the army recruit to enlist.

I never passed these advertisements, surrounded by crowds of gaping emigrants, without thinking of rat-traps.

Besides the mysterious agents of the quacks, who privily thrust their little notes into your hands, folded up like a powder; there are another set of rascals prowling about the docks, chiefly at dusk; who make strange motions to you, and beckon you to one side, as if they had some state secret to disclose, intimately connected with the weal of the commonwealth. They nudge you with an elbow full of indefinite hints and intimations; they glitter upon you an eye like a Jew's or a pawnbroker's; they dog you like Italian assassins. But if the blue coat of a policeman chances to approach, how quickly they strive to look completely indifferent, as to the surrounding universe; how they saunter off, as if lazily wending their way to an affectionate wife and family.

The first time one of these mysterious personages accosted me, I fancied him crazy, and hurried forward to avoid him. But arm in arm with my shadow, he followed after; till amazed at his conduct, I turned round and paused.

He was a little, shabby, old man, with a forlorn looking coat and hat; and his hand was fumbling in his vest pocket, as if to take out a card with his address. Seeing me stand still, he made a sign toward a dark angle of the wall, near which we were; when taking him for a cunning foot-pad, I again wheeled about, and swiftly passed on. But though I did not look round, I *felt* him following me still; so once more I stopped. The fellow now assumed so mystic and admonitory an air, that I began to fancy he came to me on some warning errand; that perhaps a plot had been laid to blow up the

Liverpool docks, and he was some Monteagle bent upon accomplishing my flight. I was determined to see what he was. With all my eyes about me, I followed him into the arch of a warehouse; when he gazed round furtively, and silently showing me a ring, whispered, "You may have it for a shilling; it's pure gold—I found it in the gutter—hush! don't speak! give me the money, and it's yours."

"My friend," said I, "I don't trade in these articles; I don't want your ring."

"Don't you? Then take that," he whispered, in an intense hushed passion; and I fell flat from a blow on the chest, while this infamous jeweler made away with himself out of sight. This business transaction was conducted with a counting-house promptitude that astonished me.

After that, I shunned these scoundrels like the leprosy: and the next time I was pertinaciously followed, I stopped, and in a loud voice, pointed out the man to the passers by; upon which he absconded; rapidly turning up into sight a pair of obliquely worn and battered boot-heels. I could not help thinking that these sort of fellows, so given to running away upon emergencies, must furnish a good deal of work to the shoemakers; as they might, also, to the growers of hemp and gallows-joiners.

Belonging to a somewhat similar fraternity with these irritable merchants of brass jewelry just mentioned, are the peddlers of Sheffield razors, mostly boys, who are hourly driven out of the dock gates by the police; nevertheless, they contrive to saunter back, and board the vessels, going among the sailors and privately exhibiting their wares. Incited by the extreme cheapness of one of the razors, and the gilding on the case containing it, a shipmate of mine purchased it on the spot for a commercial equivalent of the price, in tobacco. On the following Sunday, he used that razor; and the result was a pair of tormented and tomahawked cheeks, that almost required a surgeon to dress them. In old times, by the way, it was not a bad thought, that suggested the propriety of a barber's practicing surgery in connection with the chin-harrowing vocation.

Another class of knaves, who practice upon the sailors in Liverpool, are the pawnbrokers, inhabiting little rookeries among the narrow lanes adjoining the dock. I was astonished at the multitude of gilded balls in these streets, emblematic of their calling. They were generally next neighbors to the gilded grapes over the spirit-vaults; and no doubt, mutually to facilitate business operations, some of these establishments have connecting doors inside, so as to play their customers into each other's hands. I often saw sailors in a state of intoxication rushing from a spirit-vault into a pawnbroker's; stripping off their boots, hats, jackets, and neckerchiefs, and sometimes even their pantaloons on the spot, and offering to pawn them for a song. Of course such applications were never refused.

But though on shore, at Liverpool, poor Jack finds more sharks than at sea, he himself is by no means exempt from practices, that do not savor of a rigid morality; at least according to law. In tobacco smuggling he is an adept: and when cool and collected, often manages to evade the Customs completely, and land goodly packages of the weed, which owing to the immense duties upon it in England, commands a very high price.

As soon as we came to anchor in the river, before reaching the dock, three Custom-house underlings boarded us, and coming down into the forecastle, ordered the men to produce all the tobacco they had. Accordingly several pounds were brought forth.

"Is that all?" asked the officers.

"All," said the men.

"We will see," returned the others.

And without more ado, they emptied the chests right and left; tossed over the bunks and made a thorough search of the premises; but discovered nothing. The sailors were then given to understand, that while the ship lay in dock, the tobacco must remain in the cabin, under custody of the chief mate, who every morning would dole out to them one plug per head, as a security against their carrying it ashore.

"Very good," said the men.

But several of them had secret places in the ship, from whence they daily drew pound after pound of tobacco, which they smuggled ashore in the manner following.

When the crew went to meals, each man carried at least one

plug in his pocket; *that* he had a right to; and as many more were hidden about his person as he dared. Among the great crowds pouring out of the dock-gates at such hours, of course these smugglers stood little chance of detection; although vigilant looking policemen were always standing by. And though these "*Charlies*" might suppose there were tobacco smugglers passing; yet to hit the right man among such a throng, would be as hard, as to harpoon a speckled porpoise, one of ten thousand darting under a ship's bows.

Our forecastle was often visited by foreign sailors, who knowing we came from America, were anxious to purchase tobacco at a cheap rate; for in Liverpool it is about an American penny per pipe-full. Along the docks they sell an English pennyworth, put up in a little roll like confectioners' mottoes, with poetical lines, or instructive little moral precepts printed in red on the back.

Among all the sights of the docks, the noble truck-horses are not the least striking to a stranger. They are large and powerful brutes, with such sleek and glossy coats, that they look as if brushed and put on by a valet every morning. They march with a slow and stately step, lifting their ponderous hoofs like royal Siam elephants. Thou shalt not lay stripes upon these Roman citizens; for their docility is such, they are guided without rein or lash; they go or come, halt or march on, at a whisper. So grave, dignified, gentlemanly, and courteous did these fine truck-horses look—so full of calm intelligence and sagacity, that often I endeavored to get into conversation with them, as they stood in contemplative attitudes while their loads were preparing. But all I could get from them was the mere recognition of a friendly neigh; though I would stake much upon it that, could I have spoken in their language, I would have derived from them a good deal of valuable information touching the docks, where they passed the whole of their dignified lives.

There are unknown worlds of knowledge in brutes; and whenever you mark a horse, or a dog, with a peculiarly mild, calm, deep-seated eye, be sure he is an Aristotle or a Kant, tranquilly speculating upon the mysteries in man. No philosophers so thoroughly comprehend us as dogs and horses. They see through us at a glance. And after all, what is a horse, but a species of four-footed dumb man, in a leathern overall, who happens to live upon oats, and toils for his masters, half-requited or abused, like the biped hewers of wood and drawers of water? But there is a touch of divinity even in brutes, and a special halo about a horse, that should forever exempt him from indignities. As for those majestic, magisterial truck-horses of the docks, I would as soon think of striking a judge on the bench, as to lay violent hand upon their holy hides.

It is wonderful what loads their majesties will condescend to draw. The truck is a large square platform, on four low wheels; and upon this the lumpers pile bale after bale of cotton, as if they were filling a large warehouse, and yet a procession of three of these horses will tranquilly walk away with the whole.

The truckmen themselves are almost as singular a race as their animals. Like the Judiciary in England, they wear gowns,—not of the same cut and color though,—which reach below their knees; and from the racket they make on the pavements with their hob-nailed brogans, you would think they patronized the same shoemaker with their horses. I never could get any thing out of these truckmen. They are a reserved, sober-sided set, who, with all possible solemnity, march at the head of their animals; now and then gently advising them to sheer to the right or the left, in order to avoid some passing vehicle. Then spending so much of their lives in the high-bred company of their horses, seems to have mended their manners and improved their taste, besides imparting to them something of the dignity of their animals; but it has also given to them a sort of refined and uncomplaining aversion to human society.

There are many strange stories told of the truck-horse. Among others is the following: There was a parrot, that from having long been suspended in its cage from a low window fronting a dock, had learned to converse pretty fluently in the language of the stevedores and truckmen. One day a truckman left his vehicle standing on the quay, with its back to the water. It was noon, when an interval of silence falls upon the docks; and Poll, seeing herself face to face with the horse, and having a mind for a chat, cried out to him, *"Back! back! back!"*

Backward went the horse, precipitating himself and truck into the water.

Brunswick Dock, to the west of Prince's, is one of the most interesting to be seen. Here lie the various black steamers (so unlike the American boats, since they have to navigate the boisterous Narrow Seas) plying to all parts of the three kingdoms. Here you see vast quantities of produce, imported from starving Ireland; here you see the decks turned into pens for oxen and sheep; and often, side by side with these inclosures, Irish deck-passengers, thick as they can stand, seemingly penned in just like the cattle. It was the beginning of July when the Highlander arrived in port; and the Irish laborers were daily coming over by thousands, to help harvest the English crops.

One morning, going into the town, I heard a tramp, as of a drove of buffaloes, behind me; and turning round, beheld the entire middle of the street filled by a great crowd of these men, who had just emerged from Brunswick Dock gates, arrayed in long-tailed coats of hoddin-gray, corduroy knee-breeches, and shod with shoes that raised a mighty dust. Flourishing their Donnybrook shillelahs, they looked like an irruption of barbarians. They were marching straight out of town into the country; and perhaps out of consideration for the finances of the corporation, took the middle of the street, to save the side-walks.

"Sing Langolee, and the Lakes of Killarney," cried one fellow, tossing his stick into the air, as he danced in his brogans at the head of the rabble. And so they went! capering on, merry as pipers.

When I thought of the multitudes of Irish that annually land on the shores of the United States and Canada, and, to my surprise, witnessed the additional multitudes embarking from Liverpool to New Holland; and when, added to all this, I daily saw these hordes of laborers, descending, thick as locusts, upon the English corn-fields; I could not help marveling at the fertility of an island, which, though her crop of potatoes may fail, never yet failed in bringing her annual crop of men into the world.

Chapter 41

REDBURN ROVES ABOUT HITHER
AND THITHER

I DO NOT KNOW that any other traveler would think it worth while to mention such a thing; but the fact is, that during the summer months in Liverpool, the days are exceedingly lengthy; and the first evening I found myself walking in the twilight after nine o'clock, I tried to recall my astronomical knowledge, in order to account satisfactorily for so curious a phenomenon. But the days in summer, and the nights in winter, are just as long in Liverpool as at Cape Horn; for the latitude of the two places very nearly corresponds.

These Liverpool days, however, were a famous thing for me; who, thereby, was enabled after my day's work aboard the Highlander, to ramble about the town for several hours. After I had visited all the noted places I could discover, of those marked down upon my father's map; I began to extend my rovings indefinitely; forming myself into a committee of one, to investigate all accessible parts of the town; though so many years have elapsed, ere I have thought of bringing in my report.

This was a great delight to me: for wherever I have been in the world, I have always taken a vast deal of lonely satisfaction in wandering about, up and down, among out-of-the-way streets and alleys, and speculating upon the strangers I have met. Thus, in Liverpool I used to pace along endless streets of dwelling-houses, looking at the names on the doors, admiring the pretty faces in the windows, and invoking a passing blessing upon the chubby children on the door-steps. I was stared at myself, to be sure: but what of that? We must give and take on such occasions. In truth, I and my shooting-jacket produced quite a sensation in Liverpool: and I have no doubt, that many a father of a family went home to his children with a curious story, about a wandering phenomenon they had encountered, traversing the side-walks that day. In the words of the old song, "*I cared for nobody, no not I, and nobody cared for me.*" I stared my fill with impunity, and took all stares myself in good part.

Once I was standing in a large square, gaping at a splendid chariot drawn up at a portico. The glossy horses quivered with good-living, and so did the sumptuous calves of the gold-laced coachman and footmen in attendance. I was particularly struck with the red cheeks of these men: and the many evidences they furnished of their enjoying this life with a wonderful relish.

While thus standing, I all at once perceived, that the objects of my curiosity, were making me an object of their own; and that they were gazing at me, as if I were some unauthorized intruder upon the British soil. Truly, they had reason: for when I now think of the figure I must have cut in those days, I only marvel that, in my many strolls, my passport was not a thousand times demanded.

Nevertheless, I was only a forlorn looking mortal among tens of thousands of rags and tatters. For in some parts of the town, inhabited by laborers, and poor people generally; I used to crowd my way through masses of squalid men, women, and children, who at this evening hour, in those quarters of Liverpool, seem to empty themselves into the street, and live there for the time. I had never seen any thing like it in New York.

Often, I witnessed some curious, and many very sad scenes; and especially I remembered encountering a pale, ragged man, rushing along frantically, and striving to throw off his wife and children, who clung to his arms and legs; and, in God's name, conjured him not to desert them. He seemed bent upon rushing down to the water, and drowning himself, in some despair, and craziness of wretchedness. In these haunts, beggary went on before me wherever I walked, and dogged me unceasingly at the heels. Poverty, poverty, poverty, in almost endless vistas: and want and woe staggered arm in arm along these miserable streets.

And here, I must not omit one thing, that struck me at the time. It was the absence of negroes; who in the large towns in the "free states" of America, almost always form a considerable portion of the destitute. But in these streets, not a negro was to be seen. All were whites; and with the exception of the Irish, were natives of the soil: even Englishmen; as much Englishmen, as the dukes in the House of Lords. This conveyed a strange feeling: and more than any thing else, reminded me that I was not in my own land. For *there*, such a being as a native beggar is almost unknown; and to be a born American citizen seems a guarantee against pauperism; and this, perhaps, springs from the virtue of a vote.

Speaking of negroes, recalls the looks of interest with which negro-sailors are regarded when they walk the Liverpool streets. In Liverpool indeed the negro steps with a prouder pace, and lifts his head like a man; for here, no such exaggerated feeling exists in respect to him, as in America. Three or four times, I encountered our black steward, dressed very handsomely, and walking arm in arm with a good-looking English woman. In New York, such a couple would have been mobbed in three minutes; and the steward would have been lucky to escape with whole limbs. Owing to the friendly reception extended to them, and the unwonted immunities they enjoy in Liverpool, the black cooks and stewards of American ships are very much attached to the place and like to make voyages to it.

Being so young and inexperienced then, and unconsciously swayed in some degree by those local and social prejudices, that are the marring of most men, and from which, for the mass, there seems no possible escape; at first I was surprised that a colored man should be treated as he is in this town; but a little reflection showed that, after all, it was but recognizing his claims to humanity and normal equality; so that, in some things, we Americans leave to other countries the carrying out of the principle that stands at the head of our Declaration of Independence.

During my evening strolls in the wealthier quarters, I was subject to a continual mortification. It was the humiliating fact, wholly unforeseen by me, that upon the whole, and barring the poverty and beggary, Liverpool, away from the docks, was very much such a place as New York. There were the same sort of streets pretty much; the same rows of houses with stone steps; the same kind of sidewalks and curbs; and the same elbowing, heartless-looking crowd as ever.

I came across the Leeds Canal, one afternoon; but, upon my word, no one could have told it from the Erie Canal at Albany. I went into St. John's Market on a Saturday night; and though it was strange enough to see that great roof supported by so many pillars, yet the most discriminating observer would not have been able to detect any difference between the articles exposed for sale, and the articles exhibited in Fulton Market, New York.

I walked down Lord-street, peering into the jewelers' shops; but I thought I was walking down a block in Broadway. I began to think that all this talk about travel was a humbug; and that he who lives in a nut-shell, lives in an epitome of the universe, and has but little to see beyond him.

It is true, that I often thought of London's being only seven or eight hours' travel by railroad from where I was; and that *there*, surely, must be a world of wonders waiting my eyes: but more of London anon.

Sundays were the days upon which I made my longest explorations. I rose bright and early, with my whole plan of operations in my head. First walking into some dock hitherto unexamined, and then to breakfast. Then a walk through the more fashionable streets, to see the people going to church; and then I myself went to church, selecting the goodliest edifice, and the tallest Kentuckian of a spire I could find.

For I am an admirer of church architecture; and though, perhaps, the sums spent in erecting magnificent cathedrals might better go to the founding of charities, yet since these structures are built, those who disapprove of them in one sense, may as well have the benefit of them in another.

It is a most Christian thing, and a matter most sweet to dwell upon and simmer over in solitude, that any poor sinner may go to church wherever he pleases; and that even St. Peter's in Rome is open to him, as to a cardinal; that St. Paul's in London is not shut against him; and that the Broadway Tabernacle, in New York, opens all her broad aisles to him, and will not even have doors and thresholds to her pews, the better to allure him by an unbounded invitation. I say, this consideration of the hospitality and democracy in churches, is a most Christian and charming thought. It speaks whole volumes of folios, and Vatican libraries, for Christianity; it is more eloquent, and goes farther home than all the sermons of Massillon, Jeremy Taylor, Wesley, and Archbishop Tillotson.

Nothing daunted, therefore, by thinking of my being a stranger in the land; nothing daunted by the architectural superiority and costliness of any Liverpool church; or by the streams of silk dresses and fine broadcloth coats flowing into the aisles; I used humbly to present myself before the sexton, as a candidate for admission. He would stare a little, perhaps (one of them once hesitated), but in the end, what could he do but show me into a pew; not the most commodious of pews, to be sure; nor commandingly located; nor within very plain sight or hearing of the pulpit. No; it was remarkable, that there was always some confounded pillar or obstinate angle of the wall in the way; and I used to think, that the sextons of Liverpool must have held a secret meeting on my account, and resolved to apportion me the most inconvenient pew in the churches under their charge. However, they always gave me a seat of some sort or other; sometimes even on an oaken bench in the open air of the aisle, where I would sit, dividing the attention of the congregation between myself and the clergyman. The whole congregation seemed to know that I was a foreigner of distinction.

It was sweet to hear the service read, the organ roll, the sermon preached—just as the same things were going on three thousand five hundred miles off, at home! But then, the prayer in behalf of her majesty the Queen, somewhat threw me aback. Nevertheless, I joined in that prayer, and invoked for the lady the best wishes of a poor Yankee.

How I loved to sit in the holy hush of those brown old monastic aisles, thinking of Harry the Eighth, and the Reformation! How I loved to go a roving with my eye, all along the sculptured walls and buttresses; winding in among the intricacies of the pendent ceiling, and wriggling my fancied way like a wood-worm. I could have sat there all the morning long, through noon, unto night. But at last the benediction would come; and appropriating my share of it, I would slowly move away, thinking how I should like to go home with some of the portly old gentlemen, with high-polished boots and Malacca canes, and take a seat at their cosy and comfortable dinner-tables. But, alas! there was no dinner for me except at the sign of the Baltimore Clipper.

Yet the Sunday dinners that Handsome Mary served up were not to be scorned. The roast beef of Old England abounded; and so did the immortal plum-puddings, and the unspeakably capital gooseberry pies. But to finish off with that abominable "*swipes*" almost spoiled all the rest: not that I myself patronized "*swipes*," but my shipmates did; and every cup I saw them drink, I could not choose but taste in imagination, and even then the flavor was bad.

On Sundays, at dinner-time, as, indeed, on every other day, it was curious to watch the proceedings at the sign of the Clipper. The servant girls were running about, mustering the various crews, whose dinners were spread, each in a separate apartment; and who were collectively known by the names of their ships.

"Where are the *Arethusas*?—Here's their beef been smoking this half-hour."—"Fly, Betty, my dear, here come the *Splendids*."—"Run, Molly, my love; get the salt-cellars for the *Highlanders*."—"You Peggy, where's the *Siddons'* pickle-pot?"—"I say, Judy, are you never coming with that pudding for the *Lord Nelsons*?"

On week days, we did not fare quite so well as on Sundays; and once we came to dinner, and found two enormous bullock hearts smoking at each end of the Highlanders' table. Jackson was indignant at the outrage.

He always sat at the head of the table; and this time he squared himself on his bench, and erecting his knife and fork like flag-staffs, so as to include the two hearts between them, he called out for Danby, the boarding-house keeper; for although his wife Mary was in fact at the head of the establishment, yet Danby himself always came in for the fault-findings.

Danby obsequiously appeared, and stood in the door-way, well knowing the philippics that were coming. But he was not prepared for the peroration of Jackson's address to him; which consisted of the two bullock hearts, snatched bodily off the dish, and flung at his head, by way of a recapitulation of the preceding arguments. The company then broke up in disgust, and dined elsewhere.

Though I almost invariably attended church on Sunday

mornings, yet the rest of the day I spent on my travels; and it was on one of these afternoon strolls, that on passing through St. George's-square, I found myself among a large crowd, gathered near the base of George the Fourth's equestrian statue.

The people were mostly mechanics and artisans in their holiday clothes; but mixed with them were a good many soldiers, in lean, lank, and dinnerless undresses, and sporting attenuated rattans. These troops belonged to the various regiments then in town. Police officers, also, were conspicuous in their uniforms. At first perfect silence and decorum prevailed.

Addressing this orderly throng was a pale, hollow-eyed young man, in a snuff-colored surtout, who looked worn with much watching, or much toil, or too little food. His features were good, his whole air was respectable, and there was no mistaking the fact, that he was strongly in earnest in what he was saying.

In his hand was a soiled, inflammatory-looking pamphlet, from which he frequently read; following up the quotations with nervous appeals to his hearers, a rolling of his eyes, and sometimes the most frantic gestures. I was not long within hearing of him, before I became aware that this youth was a Chartist.

Presently the crowd increased, and some commotion was raised, when I noticed the police officers augmenting in number; and by and by, they began to glide through the crowd, politely hinting at the propriety of dispersing. The first persons thus accosted were the soldiers, who accordingly sauntered off, switching their rattans, and admiring their high-polished shoes. It was plain that the Charter did not hang very heavy round their hearts. For the rest, they also gradually broke up; and at last I saw the speaker himself depart.

I do not know why, but I thought he must be some despairing elder son, supporting by hard toil his mother and sisters; for of such many political desperadoes are made.

That same Sunday afternoon, I strolled toward the outskirts of the town, and attracted by the sight of two great Pompey's pillars, in the shape of black steeples, apparently rising directly from the soil, I approached them with much curiosity. But looking over a low parapet connecting them, what was my surprise to behold at my feet a smoky hollow in the ground, with rocky walls, and dark holes at one end, carrying out of view several lines of iron railways; while far beyond, straight out toward the open country, ran an endless railroad. Over the place, a handsome Moorish arch of stone was flung; and gradually, as I gazed upon it, and at the little side arches at the bottom of the hollow, there came over me an undefinable feeling, that I had previously seen the whole thing before. Yet how could that be? Certainly, I had never been in Liverpool before: but then, that Moorish arch! surely I remembered that very well. It was not till several months after reaching home in America, that my perplexity upon this matter was cleared away. In glancing over an old number of the Penny Magazine, there I saw a picture of the place to the life; and remembered having seen the same print years previous. It was a representation of the spot where the Manchester railroad enters the outskirts of the town.

Chapter 42

His Adventure with the Cross Old Gentleman

MY ADVENTURE in the News-Room in the Exchange, which I have related in a previous chapter, reminds me of another, at the Lyceum, some days after, which may as well be put down here, before I forget it.

I was strolling down Bold-street, I think it was, when I was struck by the sight of a brown stone building, very large and handsome. The windows were open, and there, nicely seated, with their comfortable legs crossed over their comfortable knees, I beheld several sedate, happy-looking old gentlemen reading the magazines and papers, and one had a fine gilded volume in his hand.

Yes, this must be the Lyceum, thought I; let me see. So I whipped out my guide-book, and opened it at the proper plate; and sure enough, the building before me corresponded stone for stone. I stood awhile on the opposite side of the street, gazing at my picture, and then at its original; and often dwelling upon the pleasant gentlemen sitting at the open windows; till at last, I felt an uncontrollable impulse to step in for a moment, and run over the news.

I'm a poor, friendless sailor-boy, thought I, and they can not object; especially as I am from a foreign land, and strangers ought to be treated with courtesy. I turned the matter over again, as I walked across the way; and with just a small tapping of a misgiving at my heart, I at last scraped my feet clean against the curb-stone, and taking off my hat while I was yet in the open air, slowly sauntered in.

But I had not got far into that large and lofty room, filled with many agreeable sights, when a crabbed old gentleman lifted up his eye from the *London Times*, which words I saw boldly printed on the back of the large sheet in his hand, and looking at me as if I were a strange dog with a muddy hide, that had stolen out of the gutter into this fine apartment, he shook his silver-headed cane at me fiercely, till the spectacles fell off his nose. Almost at the same moment, up stepped a terribly cross man, who looked as if he had a mustard plaster on his back, that was continually exasperating him; who throwing down some papers which he had been filing, took me by my innocent shoulders, and then, putting his foot against the broad part of my pantaloons, wheeled me right out into the street, and dropped me on the walk, without so much as offering an apology for the affront. I sprang after him, but in vain; the door was closed upon me.

These Englishmen have no manners, that's plain, thought I; and I trudged on down the street in a reverie.

Chapter 43

He Takes a Delightful Ramble into the Country; and Makes the Acquaintance of Three Adorable Charmers

WHO THAT DWELLS in America has not heard of the bright fields and green hedges of England, and longed to behold them? Even so had it been with me; and now that I was actually in England, I resolved not to go away without having a good, long look at the open fields.

On a Sunday morning I started, with a lunch in my pocket. It was a beautiful day in July; the air was sweet with the breath of buds and flowers, and there was a green splendor in the landscape that ravished me. Soon I gained an elevation commanding a wide sweep of view; and meadow and mead, and woodland and hedge, were all around me.

Ay, ay! this was old England, indeed! I had found it at last—there it was in the country! Hovering over the scene was a soft, dewy air, that seemed faintly tinged with the green of the grass; and I thought, as I breathed my breath, that perhaps I might be inhaling the very particles once respired by Rosamond the Fair.

On I trudged along the London road—smooth as an entry floor—and every white cottage I passed, embosomed in honey-suckles, seemed alive in the landscape.

But the day wore on; and at length the sun grew hot; and the long road became dusty. I thought that some shady place, in some shady field, would be very pleasant to repose in. So, coming to a charming little dale, undulating down to a hollow, arched over with foliage, I crossed over toward it; but paused by the road-side at a frightful announcement, nailed against an old tree, used as a gate-post—

☞ "MAN-TRAPS AND SPRING-GUNS!"

In America I had never heard of the like. What could it mean? They were not surely *cannibals*, that dwelt down in that beautiful little dale, and lived by catching men, like weasels and beavers in Canada!

"A man-trap!" It must be so. The announcement could bear but one meaning—that there was something near by, intended to catch human beings; some species of mechanism, that would suddenly fasten upon the unwary rover, and hold him by the leg like a dog; or, perhaps, devour him on the spot.

Incredible! In a Christian land, too! Did that sweet lady, Queen Victoria, permit such diabolical practices? Had her gracious majesty ever passed by this way, and seen the announcement?

And who put it there?

The proprietor, probably.

And what right had he to do so?

Why, he owned the soil.

And where are his title-deeds?

In his strong-box, I suppose.

Thus I stood wrapt in cogitations.

You are a pretty fellow, Wellingborough, thought I to myself; you are a mighty traveler, indeed:—stopped on your travels by a *man-trap*! Do you think Mungo Park was so served in Africa? Do you think Ledyard was so entreated in Siberia? Upon my word, you will go home not very much wiser than when you set out; and the only excuse you can give, for not having seen more sights, will be *man-traps— man-traps, my masters!* that frightened you!

And then, in my indignation, I fell back upon first principles. What right has this man to the soil he thus guards with dragons? What excessive effrontery, to lay sole claim to a solid piece of this planet, right down to the earth's axis, and, perhaps, straight through to the antipodes! For a moment I thought I would test his traps, and enter the forbidden Eden. But the grass grew so thickly, and seemed so full of sly things, that at last I thought best to pace off.

Next, I came to a hawthorn lane, leading down very prettily to a nice little church; a mossy little church; a beautiful little church; just such a church as I had always dreamed to be in England. The porch was viny as an arbor; the ivy was climbing about the tower; and the bees were humming about the hoary old head-stones along the walls.

Any man-traps here? thought I—any spring-guns?

No.

So I walked on, and entered the church, where I soon found a seat. No Indian, red as a deer, could have startled the simple people more. They gazed and they gazed; but as I was all attention to the sermon, and conducted myself with perfect propriety, they did not expel me, as at first I almost imagined they might.

Service over, I made my way through crowds of children, who stood staring at the marvelous stranger, and resumed my stroll along the London Road.

My next stop was at an inn, where under a tree sat a party of rustics, drinking ale at a table.

"Good day," said I.

"Good day; from Liverpool?"

"I guess so."

"For London?"

"No; not this time. I merely come to see the country."

At this, they gazed at each other; and I, at myself; having doubts whether I might not look something like a horse-thief.

"Take a seat," said the landlord, a fat fellow, with his wife's apron on, I thought.

"Thank you."

And then, little by little, we got into a long talk: in the course of which, I told who I was, and where I was from. I found these rustics a good-natured, jolly set; and I have no doubt they found me quite a sociable youth. They treated me to ale; and I treated them to stories about America, concerning which, they manifested the utmost curiosity. One of them, however, was somewhat astonished that I had not made the acquaintance of a brother of his, who had resided somewhere on the banks of the Mississippi for several years past; but among twenty millions of people, I had never happened to meet him, at least to my knowledge.

At last, leaving this party, I pursued my way, exhilarated by the lively conversation in which I had shared, and the pleasant sympathies exchanged: and perhaps, also, by the ale I had drunk:—fine old ale; yes, English ale, ale brewed in England! And I trod English soil; and breathed English air; and every blade of grass was an Englishman born. Smoky old

Liverpool, with all its pitch and tar was now far behind; nothing in sight but open meadows and fields.

Come, Wellingborough, why not push on for London?— Hurra! what say you? let's have a peep at St. Paul's! Don't you want to see the queen? Have you no longing to behold the duke? Think of Westminster Abbey, and the Tunnel under the Thames! Think of Hyde Park, and the ladies!

But then, thought I again, with my hands wildly groping in my two vacuums of pockets—who's to pay the bill?—You can't beg your way, Wellingborough; that would never do; for you are your father's son, Wellingborough; and you must not disgrace your family in a foreign land; you must not turn pauper.

Ah! Ah! it was indeed too true; there was no St. Paul's or Westminster Abbey for me; that was flat.

Well, well, up heart, you'll see it one of these days.

But think of it! here I am on the very road that leads to the Thames—think of *that*!—here I am—ay, treading in the wheel-tracks of coaches that are bound for the metropolis!— It was too bad; too bitterly bad. But I shoved my old hat over my brows, and walked on; till at last I came to a green bank, deliciously shaded by a fine old tree with broad branching arms, that stretched themselves over the road, like a hen gathering her brood under her wings. Down on the green grass I threw myself and there lay my head, like a last year's nut. People passed by, on foot and in carriages, and little thought that the sad youth under the tree was the great-nephew of a late senator in the American Congress.

Presently, I started to my feet, as I heard a gruff voice behind me from the field, crying out—"What are you doing there, you young rascal?—run away from the work'us, have ye? Tramp, or I'll set Blucher on ye!"

And who was Blucher? A cut-throat looking dog, with his black bull-muzzle thrust through a gap in the hedge. And his master? A sturdy farmer, with an alarming cudgel in his hand.

"Come, are you going to start?" he cried.

"Presently," said I, making off with great dispatch. When I had got a few yards into the middle of the highroad (which belonged as much to me as it did to the queen herself), I turned round, like a man on his own premises, and said—

"Stranger! if you ever visit America, just call at our house, and you'll always find there a dinner and a bed. Don't fail."

I then walked on toward Liverpool, full of sad thoughts concerning the cold charities of the world, and the infamous reception given to hapless young travelers, in broken-down shooting-jackets.

On, on I went, along the skirts of forbidden green fields; until reaching a cottage, before which I stood rooted.

So sweet a place I had never seen: no palace in Persia could be pleasanter; there were flowers in the garden; and six red cheeks, like six moss-roses, hanging from the casement. At the embowered door-way, sat an old man, confidentially communing with his pipe: while a little child, sprawling on the ground, was playing with his shoe-strings. A hale matron, but with rather a prim expression, was reading a journal by his side: and three charmers, three Peris, three Houris! were leaning out of the window close by.

Ah! Wellingborough, don't you wish you could step in?

With a heavy heart at this cheerful sight, I was turning to go, when—is it possible? the old man called me back, and invited me in.

"Come, come," said he, "you look as if you had walked far; come, take a bowl of milk. Matilda, my dear" (how my heart jumped) "go fetch some from the dairy." And the white-handed angel did meekly obey, and handed me— *me*, the vagabond, a bowl of bubbling milk, which I could hardly drink down, for gazing at the dew on her lips.

As I live, I could have married that charmer on the spot!

She was by far the most beautiful rosebud I had yet seen in England. But I endeavored to dissemble my ardent admiration; and in order to do away at once with any unfavorable impressions arising from the close scrutiny of my miserable shooting-jacket, which was now taking place, I declared myself a Yankee sailor from Liverpool, who was spending a Sunday in the country.

"And have you been to church to-day, young man?" said the old lady, looking daggers.

"Good madam, I have; the little church down yonder, you know—a most excellent sermon—I am much the better for it."

I wanted to mollify this severe looking old lady; for even my short experience of old ladies had convinced me that they are the hereditary enemies of all strange young men.

I soon turned the conversation toward America, a theme which I knew would be interesting, and upon which I could be fluent and agreeable. I strove to talk in Addisonian English, and ere long could see very plainly that my polished phrases were making a surprising impression, though that miserable shooting-jacket of mine was a perpetual drawback to my claims to gentility.

Spite of all my blandishments, however, the old lady stood her post like a sentry; and to my inexpressible chagrin, kept the three charmers in the back ground, though the old man frequently called upon them to advance. This fine specimen of an old Englishman seemed to be quite as free from ungenerous suspicions as his vinegary spouse was full of them. But I still lingered, snatching furtive glances at the young ladies, and vehemently talking to the old man about Illinois, and the river Ohio, and the fine farms in the Genesee country, where, in harvest time, the laborers went into the wheat fields a thousand strong.

Stick to it, Wellingborough, thought I; don't give the old lady time to think; stick to it, my boy, and an invitation to tea will reward you. At last it came, and the old lady abated her frowns.

It was the most delightful of meals; the three charmers sat all on one side, and I opposite, between the old man and his wife. The middle charmer poured out the souchong, and handed me the buttered muffins; and such buttered muffins never were spread on the other side of the Atlantic. The butter had an aromatic flavor; by Jove, it was perfectly delicious.

And there they sat—the charmers, I mean—eating these buttered muffins in plain sight. I wished I was a buttered muffin myself. Every minute they grew handsomer and handsomer; and I could not help thinking what a fine thing it would be to carry home a beautiful English wife! how my friends would stare! a lady from England!

I might have been mistaken; but certainly I thought that Matilda, the one who had handed me the milk, sometimes looked rather benevolently in the direction where I sat. She certainly *did* look at my jacket; and I am constrained to think at my face. Could it be possible she had fallen in love at first sight? Oh, rapture! But oh, misery! that was out of the question; for what a looking suitor was Wellingborough?

At length, the old lady glanced toward the door, and made some observations about its being yet a long walk to town. She handed me the buttered muffins, too, as if performing a final act of hospitality; and in other fidgety ways vaguely hinted her desire that I should decamp.

Slowly I rose, and murmured my thanks, and bowed, and tried to be off; but as quickly I turned, and bowed, and thanked, and lingered again and again. Oh, charmers! oh, Peris! thought I, must I go? Yes, Wellingborough, you must; so I made one desperate congée, and darted through the door.

I have never seen them since: no, nor heard of them; but to this day I live a bachelor on account of those ravishing charmers!

As the long twilight was waning deeper and deeper into night, I entered the town; and, plodding my solitary way to the same old docks, I passed through the gates, and scrambled my way among tarry smells, across the tiers of ships between the quay and the Highlander. My only resource was my bunk; in I turned, and, wearied with my long stroll, was soon fast asleep, dreaming of red cheeks and roses.

Chapter 44

Redburn Introduces Master Harry Bolton
to the Favorable Consideration of
the Reader

İT WAS THE DAY following my Sunday stroll into the country, and when I had been in England four weeks or more, that I made the acquaintance of a handsome, accomplished, but unfortunate youth, young Harry Bolton. He was one of those small, but perfectly formed beings, with curling hair, and silken muscles, who seem to have been born in cocoons. His complexion was a mantling brunette, feminine as a girl's; his feet were small; his hands were white; and his eyes were large, black, and womanly; and, poetry aside, his voice was as the sound of a harp.

But where, among the tarry docks, and smoky sailor-lanes and by-ways of a seaport, did I, a battered Yankee boy, encounter this courtly youth?

Several evenings I had noticed him in our street of boarding-houses, standing in the doorways, and silently regarding the animated scenes without. His beauty, dress, and manner struck me as so out of place in such a street, that I could not possibly divine what had transplanted this delicate exotic from the conservatories of some Regent-street to the untidy potato-patches of Liverpool.

At last I suddenly encountered him at the sign of the Baltimore Clipper. He was speaking to one of my shipmates concerning America; and from something that dropped, I was led to imagine that he contemplated a voyage to my country. Charmed with his appearance, and all eagerness to enjoy the society of this incontrovertible son of a gentleman—a kind of pleasure so long debarred me—I smoothed down the skirts of my jacket, and at once accosted him; declaring who I was, and that nothing would afford me greater delight than to be of the least service, in imparting any information concerning America that he needed.

He glanced from my face to my jacket, and from my jacket

to my face, and at length, with a pleased but somewhat puzzled expression, begged me to accompany him on a walk.

We rambled about St. George's Pier until nearly midnight;
but before we parted, with uncommon frankness, he told me
many strange things respecting his history.

According to his own account, Harry Bolton was a native
of Bury St. Edmunds, a borough in Suffolk, not very far from
London, where he was early left an orphan, under the charge
of an only aunt. Between his aunt and himself, his mother
had divided her fortune; and young Harry thus fell heir to a
portion of about five thousand pounds.

Being of a roving mind, as he approached his majority he
grew restless of the retirement of a country place; especially
as he had no profession or business of any kind to engage his
attention.

In vain did Bury, with all its fine old monastic attractions,
lure him to abide on the beautiful banks of her Larke, and
under the shadow of her stately and storied old Saxon tower.

By all my rare old historic associations, breathed Bury; by
my Abbey-gate, that bears to this day the arms of Edward the
Confessor; by my carved roof of the old church of St. Mary's,
which escaped the low rage of the bigoted Puritans; by the
royal ashes of Mary Tudor, that sleep in my midst; by my
Norman ruins, and by all the old abbots of Bury, do not, oh
Harry! abandon me. Where will you find shadier walks than
under my lime-trees? where lovelier gardens than those within
the old walls of my monastery, approached through my lordly
Gate? Or if, oh Harry! indifferent to my historic mosses, and
caring not for my annual verdure, thou must needs be lured
by other tassels, and wouldst fain, like the Prodigal, squander
thy patrimony, then, go not away from old Bury to do it. For
here, on Angel-Hill, are my coffee and card-rooms, and billiard saloons, where you may lounge away your mornings,
and empty your glass and your purse as you list.

In vain. Bury was no place for the adventurous Harry, who
must needs hie to London, where in one winter, in the company of gambling sportsmen and dandies, he lost his last
sovereign.

What now was to be done? His friends made interest for
him in the requisite quarters, and Harry was soon embarked

for Bombay, as a midshipman in the East India service; in which office he was known as a "*guinea-pig*," a humorous appellation then bestowed upon the middies of the Company. And considering the perversity of his behavior, his delicate form, and soft complexion, and that gold guineas had been his bane, this appellation was not altogether, in poor Harry's case, inapplicable.

He made one voyage, and returned; another, and returned; and then threw up his warrant in disgust. A few weeks' dissipation in London, and again his purse was almost drained; when, like many prodigals, scorning to return home to his aunt, and amend—though she had often written him the kindest of letters to that effect—Harry resolved to precipitate himself upon the New World, and there carve out a fresh fortune.

With this object in view, he packed his trunks, and took the first train for Liverpool. Arrived in that town, he at once betook himself to the docks, to examine the American shipping, when a new crotchet entered his brain, born of his old sea reminiscences. It was to assume duck trowsers and tarpaulin, and gallantly cross the Atlantic as a sailor. There was a dash of romance in it; a taking abandonment; and a scorn of fine coats, which exactly harmonized with his reckless contempt, at the time, for all past conventionalities.

Thus determined, he exchanged his trunk for a mahogany chest; sold some of his superfluities; and moved his quarters to the sign of the Gold Anchor in Union-street.

After making his acquaintance, and learning his intentions, I was all anxiety that Harry should accompany me home in the Highlander, a desire to which he warmly responded.

Nor was I without strong hopes that he would succeed in an application to the captain; inasmuch as during our stay in the docks, three of our crew had left us, and their places would remain unsupplied till just upon the eve of our departure.

And here, it may as well be related, that owing to the heavy charges to which the American ships long staying in Liverpool are subjected, from the obligation to continue the wages of their seamen, when they have little or no work to employ them, and from the necessity of boarding them ashore, like lords, at their leisure, captains interested in the ownership of their vessels, are not at all indisposed to let their sailors abscond, if they please, and thus forfeit their money; for they well know that, when wanted, a new crew is easily to be procured, through the crimps of the port.

Though he spake English with fluency, and from his long service in the vessels of New York, was almost an American to behold, yet Captain Riga was in fact a Russian by birth, though this was a fact that he strove to conceal. And though extravagant in his personal expenses, and even indulging in luxurious habits, costly as Oriental dissipation, yet Captain Riga was a niggard to others; as, indeed, was evinced in the magnificent stipend of three dollars, with which he requited my own valuable services. Therefore, as it was agreed between Harry and me, that he should offer to ship as a "*boy*," at the same rate of compensation with myself, I made no doubt that, incited by the cheapness of the bargain, Captain Riga would gladly close with him; and thus, instead of paying sixteen dollars a month to a thorough-going tar, who would consume all his rations, buy up my young blade of Bury, at the rate of half a dollar a week; with the cheering prospect, that by the end of the voyage, his fastidious palate would be the means of leaving a handsome balance of salt beef and pork in the *harness-cask*.

With part of the money obtained by the sale of a few of his velvet vests, Harry, by my advice, now rigged himself in a Guernsey frock and man-of-war trowsers; and thus equipped, he made his appearance, one fine morning, on the quarterdeck of the Highlander, gallantly doffing his virgin tarpaulin before the redoubtable Riga.

No sooner were his wishes made known, than I perceived in the captain's face that same bland, benevolent, and bewitchingly merry expression, that had so charmed, but deceived me, when, with Mr. Jones, I had first accosted him in the cabin.

Alas, Harry! thought I,—as I stood upon the forecastle looking astern where they stood,—that "*gallant, gay deceiver*" shall not altogether cajole you, if Wellingborough can help it. Rather than that should be the case, indeed, I would forfeit the pleasure of your society across the Atlantic.

At this interesting interview the captain expressed a sympathetic concern touching the sad necessities, which he took upon himself to presume must have driven Harry to sea; he confessed to a warm interest in his future welfare; and did not hesitate to declare that, in going to America, under such circumstances, to seek his fortune, he was acting a manly and spirited part; and that the voyage thither, as a sailor, would be an invigorating preparative to the landing upon a shore, where he must battle out his fortune with Fate.

He engaged him at once; but was sorry to say, that he could not provide him a home on board till the day previous to the sailing of the ship; and during the interval, he could not honor any drafts upon the strength of his wages.

However, glad enough to conclude the agreement upon any terms at all, my young blade of Bury expressed his satisfaction; and full of admiration at so urbane and gentlemanly a sea-captain, he came forward to receive my congratulations.

"Harry," said I, "be not deceived by the fascinating Riga— that gay Lothario of all inexperienced, sea-going youths, from the capital or the country; he has a Janus-face, Harry; and you will not know him when he gets you out of sight of land, and mounts his cast-off coats and trowsers. For *then* he is another personage altogether, and adjusts his character to the shabbiness of his integuments. No more condolings and sympathy then; no more blarney; he will hold you a little better than his boots, and would no more think of addressing you than of invoking wooden Donald, the figure-head on our bows."

And I further admonished my friend concerning our crew, particularly of the diabolical Jackson, and warned him to be cautious and wary. I told him, that unless he was somewhat accustomed to the rigging, and could furl a royal in a squall, he would be sure to subject himself to a sort of treatment from the sailors, in the last degree ignominious to any mortal who had ever crossed his legs under mahogany.

And I played the inquisitor, in cross-questioning Harry respecting the precise degree in which he was a practical sailor;—whether he had a giddy head; whether his arms could bear the weight of his body; whether, with but one hand on a shroud, a hundred feet aloft in a tempest, he felt he could look right to windward and beard it.

To all this, and much more, Harry rejoined with the most off-hand and confident air; saying that in his "*guinea-pig*" days, he had often climbed the masts and handled the sails in a gentlemanly and amateur way; so he made no doubt that he would very soon prove an expert tumbler in the Highlander's rigging.

His levity of manner, and sanguine assurance, coupled with the constant sight of his most unseamanlike person—more suited to the Queen's drawing-room than a ship's forecastle—bred many misgivings in my mind. But after all, every one in this world has his own fate intrusted to himself; and though we may warn, and forewarn, and give sage advice, and indulge in many apprehensions touching our friends; yet our friends, for the most part, will "*gang their ain gate;*" and the most we can do is, to hope for the best. Still, I suggested to Harry, whether he had not best cross the sea as a steerage passenger, since he could procure enough money for that; but no, he was bent upon going as a sailor.

I now had a comrade in my afternoon strolls, and Sunday excursions; and as Harry was a generous fellow, he shared with me his purse and his heart. He sold off several more of his fine vests and trowsers, his silver-keyed flute and enameled guitar; and a portion of the money thus furnished was pleasantly spent in refreshing ourselves at the road-side inns in the vicinity of the town.

Reclining side by side in some agreeable nook, we exchanged our experiences of the past. Harry enlarged upon the fascinations of a London life; described the curricle he used to drive in Hyde Park; gave me the measurement of Madame Vestris' ankle; alluded to his first introduction at a club to the madcap Marquis of Waterford; told over the sums he had lost upon the turf on a Derby day; and made various but enigmatical allusions to a certain Lady Georgiana Theresa, the noble daughter of an anonymous earl.

Even in conversation, Harry was a prodigal; squandering his aristocratic narrations with a careless hand; and, perhaps, sometimes spending funds of reminiscences not his own.

As for me, I had only my poor old uncle the senator to fall

back upon; and I used him upon all emergencies, like the knight in the game of chess; making him hop about, and stand stifly up to the encounter, against all my fine comrade's array of dukes, lords, curricles, and countesses.

In these long talks of ours, I frequently expressed the earnest desire I cherished, to make a visit to London; and related how strongly tempted I had been one Sunday, to walk the whole way, without a penny in my pocket. To this, Harry rejoined, that nothing would delight him more, than to show me the capital; and he even meaningly but mysteriously hinted at the possibility of his doing so, before many days had passed. But this seemed so idle a thought, that I only imputed it to my friend's good-natured, rattling disposition, which sometimes prompted him to out with any thing, that he thought would be agreeable. Besides, would this fine blade of Bury be seen, by his aristocratic acquaintances, walking down Oxford-street, say, arm in arm with the sleeve of my shooting-jacket? The thing was preposterous; and I began to think, that Harry, after all, was a little bit disposed to impose upon my Yankee credulity.

Luckily, my Bury blade had no acquaintance in Liverpool, where, indeed, he was as much in a foreign land, as if he were already on the shores of Lake Erie; so that he strolled about with me in perfect abandonment; reckless of the cut of my shooting-jacket; and not caring one whit who might stare at so singular a couple.

But once, crossing a square, faced on one side by a fashionable hotel, he made a rapid turn with me round a corner; and never stopped, till the square was a good block in our rear. The cause of this sudden retreat, was a remarkably elegant coat and pantaloons, standing upright on the hotel steps, and containing a young buck, tapping his teeth with an ivory-headed riding-whip.

"Who was he, Harry?" said I.

"My old chum, Lord Lovely," said Harry, with a careless air, "and Heaven only knows what brings Lovely from London."

"A lord?" said I, starting; "then I must look at him again;" for lords are very scarce in Liverpool.

Unmindful of my companion's remonstrances, I ran back

to the corner; and slowly promenaded past the upright coat
and pantaloons on the steps.

It was not much of a lord to behold; very thin and limber
about the legs, with small feet like a doll's, and a small, glossy
head like a seal's. I had seen just such looking lords standing
in sentimental attitudes in front of Palmo's in Broadway.

However, he and I being mutual friends of Harry's, I
thought something of accosting him, and taking counsel concerning what was best to be done for the young prodigal's
welfare; but upon second thoughts I thought best not to intrude; especially, as just then my lord Lovely stepped to the
open window of a flashing carriage which drew up; and
throwing himself into an interesting posture, with the sole of
one boot vertically exposed, so as to show the stamp on it—
a coronet—fell into a sparkling conversation with a magnificent white satin hat, surmounted by a regal marabout feather,
inside.

I doubted not, this lady was nothing short of a peeress; and
thought it would be one of the pleasantest and most charming things in the world, just to seat myself beside her, and
order the coachman to take us a drive into the country.

But, as upon further consideration, I imagined that the
peeress might decline the honor of my company, since I had
no formal card of introduction; I marched on, and rejoined
my companion, whom I at once endeavored to draw out,
touching Lord Lovely; but he only made mysterious answers;
and turned off the conversation, by allusions to his visits to
Ickworth in Suffolk, the magnificent seat of the Most Noble
Marquis of Bristol, who had repeatedly assured Harry that he
might consider Ickworth his home.

Now, all these accounts of marquises and Ickworths, and
Harry's having been hand in glove with so many lords and
ladies, began to breed some suspicions concerning the rigid
morality of my friend, as a teller of the truth. But, after all,
thought I to myself, who can prove that Harry has fibbed?
Certainly, his manners are polished, he has a mighty easy address; and there is nothing altogether impossible about his
having consorted with the master of Ickworth, and the
daughter of the anonymous earl. And what right has a poor
Yankee, like me, to insinuate the slightest suspicion against

what he says? What little money he has, he spends freely; he can not be a polite blackleg, for I am no pigeon to pluck; so *that* is out of the question;—perish such a thought, concerning my own bosom friend!

But though I drowned all my suspicions as well as I could, and ever cherished toward Harry a heart, loving and true; yet, spite of all this, I never could entirely digest some of his imperial reminiscences of high life. I was very sorry for this; as at times it made me feel ill at ease in his company; and made me hold back my whole soul from him; when, in its loneliness, it was yearning to throw itself into the unbounded bosom of some immaculate friend.

Chapter 45

Harry Bolton Kidnaps Redburn, and Carries Him Off to London

IT MIGHT HAVE BEEN a week after our glimpse of Lord Lovely, that Harry, who had been expecting a letter, which, he told me, might possibly alter his plans; one afternoon came bounding on board the ship, and sprang down the hatchway into the *between-decks*, where, in perfect solitude, I was engaged picking oakum; at which business the mate had set me, for want of any thing better.

"Hey for London, Wellingborough!" he cried. "Off to-morrow! first train—be there the same night—come! I have money to rig you all out—drop that hangman's stuff there, and away! Pah! how it smells here! Come; up you jump!"

I trembled with amazement and delight.

London? it could not be!—and Harry—how kind of him! he was then indeed what he seemed. But instantly I thought of all the circumstances of the case, and was eager to know what it was that had induced this sudden departure.

In reply my friend told me, that he had received a remittance, and had hopes of recovering a considerable sum, lost in some way that he chose to conceal.

"But how am I to leave the ship, Harry?" said I; "they will not let me go, will they? You had better leave me behind, after all; I don't care very much about going; and besides, I have no money to share the expenses."

This I said, only pretending indifference, for my heart was jumping all the time.

"Tut! my Yankee bantam," said Harry; "look here!" and he showed me a handful of gold.

"But they are *yours*, and not *mine*, Harry," said I.

"Yours *and* mine, my sweet fellow," exclaimed Harry. "Come, sink the ship, and let's go!"

"But you don't consider, if I quit the ship, they'll be sending a constable after me, won't they?"

"What! and do you think, then, they value your services so

highly? Ha! ha!—Up, up, Wellingborough: I can't wait."

True enough. I well knew that Captain Riga would not trouble himself much, if I *did* take French leave of him. So, without further thought of the matter, I told Harry to wait a few moments, till the ship's bell struck four; at which time I used to go to supper, and be free for the rest of the day.

The bell struck; and off we went. As we hurried across the quay, and along the dock walls, I asked Harry all about his intentions. He said, that go to London he must, and to Bury St. Edmund's; but that whether he should for any time remain at either place, he could not now tell; and it was by no means impossible, that in less than a week's time we would be back again in Liverpool, and ready for sea. But all he said was enveloped in a mystery that I did not much like; and I hardly know whether I have repeated correctly what he said at the time.

Arrived at the *Golden Anchor*, where Harry put up, he at once led me to his room, and began turning over the contents of his chest, to see what clothing he might have, that would fit me.

Though he was some years my senior, we were about the same size—if any thing, I was larger than he; so, with a little stretching, a shirt, vest, and pantaloons were soon found to suit. As for a coat and hat, those Harry ran out and bought without delay; returning with a loose, stylish sack-coat, and a sort of foraging cap, very neat, genteel, and unpretending.

My friend himself soon doffed his Guernsey frock, and stood before me, arrayed in a perfectly plain suit, which he had bought on purpose that very morning. I asked him why he had gone to that unnecessary expense, when he had plenty of other clothes in his chest. But he only winked, and looked knowing. This, again, I did not like. But I strove to drown ugly thoughts.

Till quite dark, we sat talking together; when, locking his chest, and charging his landlady to look after it well, till he called, or sent for it; Harry seized my arm, and we sallied into the street.

Pursuing our way through crowds of frolicking sailors and fiddlers, we turned into a street leading to the Exchange. There, under the shadow of the colonnade, Harry told me to stop, while he left me, and went to finish his toilet. Wondering what he meant, I stood to one side; and presently was joined by a stranger in whiskers and mustache.

"It's *me*," said the stranger; and who was *me* but Harry, who had thus metamorphosed himself? I asked him the reason; and in a faltering voice, which I tried to make humorous, expressed a hope that he was not going to turn gentleman forger.

He laughed, and assured me that it was only a precaution against being recognized by his own particular friends in London, that he had adopted this mode of disguising himself.

"And why afraid of your friends?" asked I, in astonishment, "and we are not in London yet."

"Pshaw! what a Yankee you are, Wellingborough. Can't you see very plainly that I have a plan in my head? And this disguise is only for a short time, you know. But I'll tell you all by and by."

I acquiesced, though not feeling at ease; and we walked on, till we came to a public house, in the vicinity of the place at which the cars are taken.

We stopped there that night, and next day were off, whirled along through boundless landscapes of villages, and meadows, and parks: and over arching viaducts, and through wonderful tunnels; till, half delirious with excitement, I found myself dropped down in the evening among gas-lights, under a great roof in Euston Square.

London at last, and in the West-End!

Chapter 46

A Mysterious Night in London

"No time to lose," said Harry, "come along."

He called a cab: in an under tone mentioned the number of a house in some street to the driver; we jumped in, and were off.

As we rattled over the boisterous pavements, past splendid squares, churches, and shops, our cabman turning corners like a skater on the ice, and all the roar of London in my ears, and no end to the walls of brick and mortar; I thought New York a hamlet, and Liverpool a coal-hole, and myself somebody else: so unreal seemed every thing about me. My head was spinning round like a top, and my eyes ached with much gazing; particularly about the corners, owing to my darting them so rapidly, first this side, and then that, so as not to miss any thing; though, in truth, I missed much.

"Stop," cried Harry, after a long while, putting his head out of the window, all at once—"stop! do you hear, you deaf man? you have passed the house—No. 40 I told you—that's it—the high steps there, with the purple light!"

The cabman being paid, Harry adjusting his whiskers and mustache, and bidding me assume a lounging look, pushed his hat a little to one side, and then locking arms, we sauntered into the house; myself feeling not a little abashed; it was so long since I had been in any courtly society.

It was some semi-public place of opulent entertainment; and far surpassed any thing of the kind I had ever seen before.

The floor was tesselated with snow-white, and russet-hued marbles; and echoed to the tread, as if all the Paris catacombs were underneath. I started with misgivings at that hollow, boding sound, which seemed sighing with a subterraneous despair, through all the magnificent spectacle around me; mocking it, where most it glared.

The walls were painted so as to deceive the eye with interminable colonnades; and groups of columns of the finest Scagliola work of variegated marbles—emerald-green and

gold, St. Pons veined with silver, Sienna with porphyry—
supported a resplendent fresco ceiling, arched like a bower,
and thickly clustering with mimic grapes. Through all the
East of this foliage, you spied in a crimson dawn, Guido's
ever youthful Apollo, driving forth the horses of the sun.
From sculptured stalactites of vine-boughs, here and there
pendent hung galaxies of gas lights, whose vivid glare was
softened by pale, cream-colored, porcelain spheres, shedding
over the place a serene, silver flood; as if every porcelain
sphere were a moon; and this superb apartment was the
moon-lit garden of Portia at Belmont; and the gentle lovers,
Lorenzo and Jessica, lurked somewhere among the vines.

At numerous Moorish looking tables, supported by Cary-
atides of turbaned slaves, sat knots of gentlemanly men, with
cut decanters and taper-waisted glasses, journals and cigars,
before them.

To and fro ran obsequious waiters, with spotless napkins
thrown over their arms, and making a profound salaam, and
hemming deferentially, whenever they uttered a word.

At the further end of this brilliant apartment, was a rich
mahogony turret-like structure, partly built into the wall, and
communicating with rooms in the rear. Behind, was a very
handsome florid old man, with snow-white hair and whiskers,
and in a snow-white jacket—he looked like an almond tree
in blossom—who seemed to be standing, a polite sentry over
the scene before him; and it was he, who mostly ordered
about the waiters; and with a silent salute, received the silver
of the guests.

Our entrance excited little or no notice; for every body
present seemed exceedingly animated about concerns of their
own; and a large group was gathered around one tall, military
looking gentleman, who was reading some India war-news
from the Times, and commenting on it, in a very loud voice,
condemning, in toto, the entire campaign.

We seated ourselves apart from this group, and Harry, rapping on the table, called for wine; mentioning some curious
foreign name.

The decanter, filled with a pale yellow wine, being placed
before us, and my comrade having drunk a few glasses; he

whispered me to remain where I was, while he withdrew for a moment.

I saw him advance to the turret-like place, and exchange a confidential word with the almond tree there, who immediately looked very much surprised,—I thought, a little disconcerted,—and then disappeared with him.

While my friend was gone, I occupied myself with looking around me, and striving to appear as indifferent as possible, and as much used to all this splendor as if I had been born in it. But, to tell the truth, my head was almost dizzy with the strangeness of the sight, and the thought that I was really in London. What would my brother have said? What would Tom Legare, the treasurer of the Juvenile Temperance Society, have thought?

But I almost began to fancy I had no friends and relatives living in a little village three thousand five hundred miles off, in America; for it was hard to unite such a humble reminiscence with the splendid animation of the London-like scene around me.

And in the delirium of the moment, I began to indulge in foolish golden visions of the counts and countesses to whom Harry might introduce me; and every instant I expected to hear the waiters addressing some gentleman as "*My Lord*," or "*Your Grace*." But if there were really any lords present, the waiters omitted their titles, at least in my hearing.

Mixed with these thoughts were confused visions of St. Paul's and the Strand, which I determined to visit the very next morning, before breakfast, or perish in the attempt. And I even longed for Harry's return, that we might immediately sally out into the street, and see some of the sights, before the shops were all closed for the night.

While I thus sat alone, I observed one of the waiters eying me a little impertinently, as I thought, and as if he saw something queer about me. So I tried to assume a careless and lordly air, and by way of helping the thing, threw one leg over the other, like a young Prince Esterhazy; but all the time I felt my face burning with embarrassment, and for the time, I must have looked very guilty of something. But spite of this, I kept looking boldly out of my eyes, and straight

through my blushes, and observed that every now and then
little parties were made up among the gentlemen, and they
retired into the rear of the house, as if going to a private
apartment. And I overheard one of them drop the word
Rouge; but he could not have used rouge, for his face was
exceedingly pale. Another said something about *Loo*.

At last Harry came back, his face rather flushed.

"Come along, Redburn," said he.

So making no doubt we were off for a ramble, perhaps to
Apsley House, in the Park, to get a sly peep at the old Duke
before he retired for the night, for Harry had told me the
Duke always went to bed early, I sprang up to follow him;
but what was my disappointment and surprise, when he only
led me into the passage, toward a staircase lighted by three
marble Graces, unitedly holding a broad candelabra, like an
elk's antlers, over the landing.

We rambled up the long, winding slope of those aristocratic stairs, every step of which, covered with Turkey rugs,
looked gorgeous as the hammer-cloth of the Lord Mayor's
coach; and Harry hied straight to a rosewood door, which,
on magical hinges, sprang softly open to his touch.

As we entered the room, methought I was slowly sinking
in some reluctant, sedgy sea; so thick and elastic the Persian
carpeting, mimicking parterres of tulips, and roses, and jon-
quils, like a bower in Babylon.

Long lounges lay carelessly disposed, whose fine damask
was interwoven, like the Gobelin tapestry, with pictorial tales
of tilt and tourney. And oriental ottomans, whose cunning
warp and woof were wrought into plaited serpents, undulating beneath beds of leaves, from which, here and there, they
flashed out sudden splendors of green scales and gold.

In the broad bay windows, as the hollows of King Charles'
oaks, were Laocoon-like chairs, in the antique taste, draped
with heavy fringes of bullion and silk.

The walls, covered with a sort of tartan-French paper, variegated with bars of velvet, were hung round with mytholog-
ical oil-paintings, suspended by tasseled cords of twisted silver
and blue.

They were such pictures as the high-priests, for a bribe,
showed to Alexander in the innermost shrine of the white

temple in the Libyan oasis: such pictures as the pontiff of the sun strove to hide from Cortez, when, sword in hand, he burst open the sanctorum of the pyramid-fane at Cholula: such pictures as you may still see, perhaps, in the central alcove of the excavated mansion of Pansa, in Pompeii—in that part of it called by Varro *the hollow of the house*: such pictures as Martial and Suetonius mention as being found in the private cabinet of the Emperor Tiberius: such pictures as are delineated on the bronze medals, to this day dug up on the ancient island of Capreæ: such pictures as you might have beheld in an arched recess, leading from the left hand of the secret side-gallery of the temple of Aphrodite in Corinth.

In the principal pier was a marble bracket, sculptured in the semblance of a dragon's crest, and supporting a bust, most wonderful to behold. It was that of a bald-headed old man, with a mysteriously-wicked expression, and imposing silence by one thin finger over his lips. His marble mouth seemed tremulous with secrets.

"Sit down, Wellingborough," said Harry; "don't be frightened, we are at home.—Ring the bell, will you? But stop;"—and advancing to the mysterious bust, he whispered something in its ear.

"He's a knowing mute, Wellingborough," he said; "who stays in this one place all the time, while he is yet running of errands. But mind you don't breathe any secrets in his ear."

In obedience to a summons so singularly conveyed, to my amazement a servant almost instantly appeared, standing transfixed in the attitude of a bow.

"Cigars," said Harry. When they came, he drew up a small table into the middle of the room, and lighting his cigar, bade me follow his example, and make myself happy.

Almost transported with such princely quarters, so undreamed of before, while leading my dog's life in the filthy forecastle of the Highlander, I twirled round a chair, and seated myself opposite my friend.

But all the time, I felt ill at heart; and was filled with an under current of dismal forebodings. But I strove to dispel them; and turning to my companion, exclaimed, "And pray, do you live here, Harry, in this Palace of Aladdin?"

"Upon my soul," he cried, "you have hit it:—you must

have been here before! Aladdin's Palace! Why, Wellingborough, it goes by that very name."

Then he laughed strangely: and for the first time, I thought he had been quaffing too freely: yet, though he looked wildly from his eyes, his general carriage was firm.

"Who are you looking at so hard, Wellingborough?" said he.

"I am afraid, Harry," said I, "that when you left me just now, you must have been drinking something stronger than wine."

"Hear him now," said Harry, turning round, as if addressing the bald-headed bust on the bracket,—"a parson 'pon honor!—But remark you, Wellingborough, my boy, I must leave you again, and for a considerably longer time than before:—I may not be back again to-night."

"What?" said I.

"Be still," he cried, "hear me, I know the old duke here, and—"

"Who? not the Duke of Wellington," said I, wondering whether Harry was really going to include *him* too, in his long list of confidential friends and acquaints.

"Pooh!" cried Harry, "I mean the white-whiskered old man you saw below; they call him *the Duke*:— *he* keeps the house. I say, I know him well, and he knows *me*; and he knows what brings me here, also. Well; we have arranged every thing about you; you are to stay in this room, and sleep here to-night, and—and—" continued he, speaking low—"you must guard this letter—" slipping a sealed one into my hand— "and, if I am not back by morning, you must post right on to Bury, and leave the letter there;—here, take this paper— it's all set down here in black and white—where you are to go, and what you are to do. And after that's done—mind, this is all in case I don't return—then you may do what you please: stay here in London awhile, or go back to Liverpool. And here's enough to pay all your expenses."

All this was a thunder stroke. I thought Harry was crazy. I held the purse in my motionless hand, and stared at him, till the tears almost started from my eyes.

"What's the matter, Redburn?" he cried, with a wild sort of laugh—"you are not afraid of me, are you?—No, no! I believe in you, my boy, or you would not hold that purse in your hand; no, nor that letter."

"What in heaven's name do you mean?" at last I exclaimed, "you don't really intend to desert me in this strange place, do you, Harry?" and I snatched him by the hand.

"Pooh, pooh," he cried, "let me go. I tell you, it's all right: do as I say: that's all. Promise me now, will you? Swear it!— no, no," he added, vehemently, as I conjured him to tell me more—"no, I won't: I have nothing more to tell you—not a word. Will you swear?"

"But one sentence more for your own sake, Harry: hear me!"

"Not a syllable! Will you swear?—you will not? then here, give me that purse:—there—there—take that—and that— and that;—that will pay your fare back to Liverpool; good-by to you: you are not my friend," and he wheeled round his back.

I know not what flashed through my mind, but something suddenly impelled me; and grasping his hand, I swore to him what he demanded.

Immediately he ran to the bust, whispered a word, and the white-whiskered old man appeared: whom he clapped on the shoulder, and then introduced me as his friend—young Lord Stormont; and bade the almond tree look well to the comforts of his lordship, while he—Harry—was gone.

The almond tree blandly bowed, and grimaced, with a peculiar expression, that I hated on the spot. After a few words more, he withdrew. Harry then shook my hand heartily, and without giving me a chance to say one word, seized his cap, and darted out of the room, saying, "Leave not this room to-night; and remember the letter, and Bury!"

I fell into a chair, and gazed round at the strange-looking walls and mysterious pictures, and up to the chandelier at the ceiling; then rose, and opened the door, and looked down the lighted passage; but only heard the hum from the roomful below, scattered voices, and a hushed ivory rattling from the closed apartments adjoining. I stepped back into the room, and a terrible revulsion came over me; I would have given the world had I been safe back in Liverpool, fast asleep in my old bunk in Prince's Dock.

I shuddered at every footfall, and almost thought it must be some assassin pursuing me. The whole place seemed infected; and a strange thought came over me, that in the very damasks around, some eastern plague had been imported. And was that pale yellow wine, that I drank below, drugged? thought I. This must be some house whose foundations take hold on the pit. But these fearful reveries only enchanted me fast to my chair; so that, though I then wished to rush forth from the house, my limbs seemed manacled.

While thus chained to my seat, something seemed suddenly flung open; a confused sound of imprecations, mixed with the ivory rattling, louder than before, burst upon my ear, and through the partly open door of the room where I was, I caught sight of a tall, frantic man, with clenched hands, wildly darting through the passage, toward the stairs.

And all the while, Harry ran through my soul—in and out, at every door, that burst open to his vehement rush.

At that moment my whole acquaintance with him passed like lightning through my mind, till I asked myself why he had come here, to London, to do this thing?—why would not Liverpool have answered? and what did he want of me? But, every way, his conduct was unaccountable. From the hour he had accosted me on board the ship, his manner seemed gradually changed; and from the moment we had sprung into the cab, he had seemed almost another person from what he had seemed before.

But what could I do? He was gone, that was certain;— would he ever come back? But he might still be somewhere in the house; and with a shudder, I thought of that ivory rattling, and was almost ready to dart forth, search every room, and save him. But that would be madness, and I had sworn not to do so. There seemed nothing left, but to await his return. Yet, if he did not return, what then? I took out the purse, and counted over the money, and looked at the letter and paper of memoranda.

Though I vividly remember it all, I will not give the superscription of the letter, nor the contents of the paper. But after I had looked at them attentively, and considered that Harry could have no conceivable object in deceiving me, I thought to myself, Yes, he's in earnest; and here I am—yes, even in

London! And here in this room will I stay, come what will. I will implicitly follow his directions, and so see out the last of this thing.

But spite of these thoughts, and spite of the metropolitan magnificence around me, I was mysteriously alive to a dreadful feeling, which I had never before felt, except when penetrating into the lowest and most squalid haunts of sailor iniquity in Liverpool. All the mirrors and marbles around me seemed crawling over with lizards; and I thought to myself, that though gilded and golden, the serpent of vice is a serpent still.

It was now grown very late; and faint with excitement, I threw myself upon a lounge; but for some time tossed about restless, in a sort of night-mare. Every few moments, spite of my oath, I was upon the point of starting up, and rushing into the street, to inquire where I was; but remembering Harry's injunctions, and my own ignorance of the town, and that it was now so late, I again tried to be composed.

At last, I feel asleep, dreaming about Harry fighting a duel of dice-boxes with the military-looking man below; and the next thing I knew, was the glare of a light before my eyes, and Harry himself, very pale, stood before me.

"The letter and paper," he cried.

I fumbled in my pockets, and handed them to him.

"There! there! there! thus I tear you," he cried, wrenching the letter to pieces with both hands like a madman, and stamping upon the fragments. "I am off for America; the game is up."

"For God's sake explain," said I, now utterly bewildered, and frightened. "Tell me, Harry, what is it? You have not been gambling?"

"Ha, ha," he deliriously laughed. "Gambling? red and white, you mean?—cards?—dice?—the bones?—Ha, ha!—Gambling? gambling?" he ground out between his teeth—"what two devilish, stiletto-sounding syllables they are!"

"Wellingborough," he added, marching up to me slowly, but with his eyes blazing into mine—"Wellingborough"—and fumbling in his breast-pocket, he drew forth a dirk—"Here, Wellingborough, take it—take it, I say—are you stupid?—there, there"—and he pushed it into my hands. "Keep it away from me—keep it out of my sight—I don't want it near me, while I feel as I do. They serve suicides scurvily here, Wellingborough; they don't bury them decently. See that bell-rope! By Heaven, it's an invitation to hang myself"—and seizing it by the gilded handle at the end, he twitched it down from the wall.

"In God's name, what ails you?" I cried.

"Nothing, oh nothing," said Harry, now assuming a treacherous, tropical calmness—"nothing, Redburn; nothing in the world. I'm the serenest of men."

"But give me that dirk," he suddenly cried—"let me have it, I say. Oh! I don't mean to murder myself—I'm past that now—give it me"—and snatching it from my hand, he flung down an empty purse, and with a terrific stab, nailed it fast with the dirk to the table.

"There now," he cried, "there's something for the old duke to see to-morrow morning; that's about all that's left of me—that's my skeleton, Wellingborough. But come, don't be down-hearted; there's a little more gold yet in Golconda; I have a guinea or two left. Don't stare so, my boy; we shall be in Liverpool to-morrow night; we start in the morning"—and turning his back, he began to whistle very fiercely.

"And this, then," said I, "is your showing me London, is it, Harry? I did not think this; but tell me your secret, whatever it is, and I will not regret not seeing the town."

He turned round upon me like lightning, and cried, "Redburn! you must swear another oath, and instantly."

"And why?" said I, in alarm, "what more would you have me swear?"

"Never to question me again about this infernal trip to London!" he shouted, with the foam at his lips—"never to breathe it! swear!"

"I certainly shall not trouble you, Harry, with questions, if you do not desire it," said I, "but there's no need of swearing."

"Swear it, I say, as you love me, Redburn," he added, imploringly.

"Well, then, I solemnly do. Now lie down, and let us forget ourselves as soon as we can; for me, you have made me the most miserable dog alive."

"And what am I?" cried Harry; "but pardon me, Redburn, I did not mean to offend; if you knew all—but no, no!—never mind, never mind!" And he ran to the bust, and whispered in its ear. A waiter came.

"Brandy," whispered Harry, with clenched teeth.

"Are you not going to sleep, then?" said I, more and more alarmed at his wildness, and fearful of the effects of his drinking still more, in such a mood.

"No sleep for me! sleep if *you* can—*I* mean to sit up with a decanter!—let me see"—looking at the ormolu clock on the mantel—"it's only two hours to morning."

The waiter, looking very sleepy, and with a green shade on his brow, appeared with the decanter and glasses on a salver, and was told to leave it and depart.

Seeing that Harry was not to be moved, I once more threw myself on the lounge. I did not sleep; but, like a somnambulist, only dozed now and then; starting from my dreams; while Harry sat, with his hat on, at the table; the brandy before him; from which he occasionally poured into his glass. Instead of exciting him, however, to my amazement, the spirits seemed to soothe him down; and, ere long, he was comparatively calm.

At last, just as I had fallen into a deep sleep, I was wakened by his shaking me, and saying our cab was at the door.

"Look! it is broad day," said he, brushing aside the heavy hangings of the window.

We left the room; and passing through the now silent and deserted hall of pillars, which, at this hour, reeked as with blended roses and cigar-stumps decayed; a dumb waiter, rubbing his eyes, flung open the street door; we sprung into the cab; and soon found ourselves whirled along northward by railroad, toward Prince's Dock and the Highlander.

Chapter 47

HOMEWARD-BOUND

ONCE MORE in Liverpool; and wending my way through the same old streets to the sign of the Golden Anchor; I could scarcely credit the events of the last thirty-six hours.

So unforeseen had been our departure in the first place; so rapid our journey; so unaccountable the conduct of Harry; and so sudden our return; that all united to overwhelm me. That I had been at all in London seemed impossible; and that I had been there, and come away little the wiser, was almost distracting to one who, like me, had so longed to behold that metropolis of marvels.

I looked hard at Harry as he walked in silence at my side; I stared at the houses we passed; I thought of the cab, the gas-lighted hall in the Palace of Aladdin, the pictures, the letter, the oath, the dirk; the mysterious place where all these mysteries had occurred; and then, was almost ready to conclude, that the pale yellow wine had been drugged.

As for Harry, stuffing his false whiskers and mustache into his pocket, he now led the way to the boarding-house; and saluting the landlady, was shown to his room; where we immediately shifted our clothes, appearing once more in our sailor habiliments.

"Well, what do you propose to do now, Harry?" said I, with a heavy heart.

"Why, visit your Yankee land in the Highlander, of course—what else?" he replied.

"And is it to be a visit, or a long stay?" asked I.

"That's as it may turn out," said Harry; "but I have now more than ever resolved upon the sea. There is nothing like the sea for a fellow like me, Redburn; a desperate man can not get any further than the wharf, you know; and the next step must be a long jump. But come, let's see what they have to eat here, and then for a cigar and a stroll. I feel better already. Never say die, is my motto."

We went to supper; after that, sallied out; and walking

along the quay of Prince's Dock, heard that the ship Highlander had that morning been advertised to sail in two days'
time.

"Good!" exclaimed Harry; and I was glad enough myself.

Although I had now been absent from the ship full forty-
eight hours, and intended to return to her, yet I did not
anticipate being called to any severe account for it from the
officers; for several of our men had absented themselves
longer than I had, and upon their return, little or nothing was
said to them. Indeed, in some cases, the mate seemed to know
nothing about it. During the whole time we lay in Liverpool,
the discipline of the ship was altogether relaxed; and I could
hardly believe they were the same officers who were so dicta-
torial at sea. The reason of this was, that we had nothing
important to do; and although the captain might now legally
refuse to receive me on board, yet I was not afraid of that, as
I was as stout a lad for my years, and worked as cheap, as any
one he could engage to take my place on the homeward
passage.

Next morning we made our appearance on board before
the rest of the crew; and the mate perceiving me, said with
an oath, "Well, sir, you have thought best to return then,
have you? Captain Riga and I were flattering ourselves that
you had made a run of it for good."

Then, thought I, the captain, who seems to affect to know
nothing of the proceedings of the sailors, has been aware of
my absence.

"But turn to, sir, turn to," added the mate; "here! aloft
there, and free that pennant; it's foul of the back-stay—
jump!"

The captain coming on board soon after, looked very benevolently at Harry; but, as usual, pretended not to take the
slightest notice of myself.

We were all now very busy in getting things ready for sea.
The cargo had been already stowed in the hold by the stevedores and lumpers from shore; but it became the crew's business to clear away the *between-decks*, extending from the cabin
bulkhead to the forecastle, for the reception of about five
hundred emigrants, some of whose boxes were already litter-
ing the decks.

To provide for their wants, a far larger supply of water was needed than upon the outward-bound passage. Accordingly, besides the usual number of casks on deck, rows of immense tierces were lashed amid-ships, all along the *between-decks*, forming a sort of aisle on each side, furnishing access to four rows of bunks,—three tiers, one above another,—against the ship's sides; two tiers being placed over the tierces of water in the middle. These bunks were rapidly knocked together with coarse planks. They looked more like dog-kennels than any thing else; especially as the place was so gloomy and dark; no light coming down except through the fore and after hatchways, both of which were covered with little houses called "*booby-hatches.*" Upon the main-hatches, which were well calked and covered over with heavy tarpaulins, the "*passengers'-galley* " was solidly lashed down.

This *galley* was a large open stove, or iron range—made expressly for emigrant ships, wholly unprotected from the weather, and where alone the emigrants are permitted to cook their food while at sea.

After two days' work, every thing was in readiness; most of the emigrants on board; and in the evening we worked the ship close into the outlet of Prince's Dock, with the bow against the water-gate, to go out with the tide in the morning.

In the morning, the bustle and confusion about us was indescribable. Added to the ordinary clamor of the docks, was the hurrying to and fro of our five hundred emigrants, the last of whom, with their baggage, were now coming on board; the appearance of the cabin passengers, following porters with their trunks; the loud orders of the dock-masters, ordering the various ships behind us to preserve their order of going out; the leave-takings, and good-by's, and God-bless-you's, between the emigrants and their friends; and the cheers of the surrounding ships.

At this time we lay in such a way, that no one could board us except by the bowsprit, which overhung the quay. Staggering along that bowsprit, now came a one-eyed *crimp*, leading a drunken tar by the collar, who had been shipped to sail with us the day previous. It has been stated before, that two or three of our men had left us for good, while in port. When

the crimp had got this man and another safely lodged in a
bunk below, he returned on shore; and going to a miserable
cab, pulled out still another apparently drunken fellow, who
proved completely helpless. However, the ship now swinging
her broadside more toward the quay, this stupefied sailor,
with a Scotch cap pulled down over his closed eyes, only revealing a sallow Portuguese complexion, was lowered on
board by a rope under his arms, and passed forward by the
crew, who put him likewise into a bunk in the forecastle, the
crimp himself carefully tucking him in, and bidding the by-
standers not to disturb him till the ship was away from the
land.

This done, the confusion increased, as we now glided out
of the dock. Hats and handkerchiefs were waved; hurrahs
were exchanged; and tears were shed; and the last thing I
saw, as we shot into the stream, was a policeman collaring a
boy, and walking him off to the guard-house.

A steam-tug, the *Goliath*, now took us by the arm, and
gallanted us down the river past the fort.

The scene was most striking.

Owing to a strong breeze, which had been blowing up the
river for four days past, holding wind-bound in the various
docks a multitude of ships for all parts of the world; there
was now under weigh, a vast fleet of merchantmen, all steering broad out to sea. The white sails glistened in the clear
morning air like a great Eastern encampment of sultans; and
from many a forecastle, came the deep mellow old song *Ho-
o-he-yo, cheerily men!* as the crews catted their anchors.

The wind was fair; the weather mild; the sea most smooth;
and the poor emigrants were in high spirits at so auspicious
a beginning of their voyage. They were reclining all over the
decks, talking of soon seeing America, and relating how the
agent had told them, that twenty days would be an uncommonly long voyage.

Here it must be mentioned, that owing to the great number of ships sailing to the Yankee ports from Liverpool, the
competition among them in obtaining emigrant passengers,
who as a cargo are much more remunerative than crates and
bales, is exceedingly great; so much so, that some of the
agents they employ, do not scruple to deceive the poor appli-

cants for passage, with all manner of fables concerning the short space of time, in which their ships make the run across the ocean.

This often induces the emigrants to provide a much smaller stock of provisions than they otherwise would; the effect of which sometimes proves to be in the last degree lamentable; as will be seen further on. And though benevolent societies have been long organized in Liverpool, for the purpose of keeping offices, where the emigrants can obtain reliable information and advice, concerning their best mode of embarkation, and other matters interesting to them; and though the English authorities have imposed a law, providing that every captain of an emigrant ship bound for any port of America shall see to it, that each passenger is provided with rations of food for sixty days; yet, all this has not deterred mercenary ship-masters and unprincipled agents from practicing the grossest deception; nor exempted the emigrants themselves from the very sufferings intended to be averted.

No sooner had we fairly gained the expanse of the Irish Sea, and, one by one, lost sight of our thousand consorts, than the weather changed into the most miserably cold, wet, and cheerless days and nights imaginable. The wind was tempestuous, and dead in our teeth; and the hearts of the emigrants fell. Nearly all of them had now hied below, to escape the uncomfortable and perilous decks: and from the two "*booby-hatches*" came the steady hum of a subterranean wailing and weeping. That irresistible wrestler, sea-sickness, had overthrown the stoutest of their number, and the women and children were embracing and sobbing in all the agonies of the poor emigrant's first storm at sea.

Bad enough is it at such times with ladies and gentlemen in the cabin, who have nice little state-rooms; and plenty of privacy; and stewards to run for them at a word, and put pillows under their heads, and tenderly inquire how they are getting along, and mix them a posset: and even then, in the abandonment of this soul and body subduing malady, such ladies and gentlemen will often give up life itself as unendurable, and put up the most pressing petitions for a speedy annihilation; all of which, however, only arises from their intense anxiety to preserve their valuable lives.

How, then, with the friendless emigrants, stowed away like bales of cotton, and packed like slaves in a slave-ship; confined in a place that, during storm time, must be closed against both light and air; who can do no cooking, nor warm so much as a cup of water; for the drenching seas would instantly flood their fire in their exposed galley on deck? How, then, with these men, and women, and children, to whom a first voyage, under the most advantageous circumstances, must come just as hard as to the Honorable De Lancey Fitz Clarence, lady, daughter, and seventeen servants.

Nor is this all: for in some of these ships, as in the case of the Highlander, the emigrant passengers are cut off from the most indispensable conveniences of a civilized dwelling. This forces them in storm time to such extremities, that no wonder fevers and plagues are the result. We had not been at sea one week, when to hold your head down the fore hatchway was like holding it down a suddenly opened cess-pool.

But still more than this. Such is the aristocracy maintained on board some of these ships, that the most arbitrary measures are enforced, to prevent the emigrants from intruding upon the most holy precincts of the quarter-deck, the only completely open space on ship-board. Consequently—even in fine weather—when they come up from below, they are crowded in the waist of the ship, and jammed among the boats, casks, and spars; abused by the seamen, and sometimes cuffed by the officers, for unavoidably standing in the way of working the vessel.

The cabin-passengers of the Highlander numbered some fifteen in all; and to protect this detachment of gentility from the barbarian incursions of the "*wild Irish*" emigrants, ropes were passed athwart-ships, by the main-mast, from side to side: which defined the boundary line between those who had paid three pounds passage-money, from those who had paid twenty guineas. And the cabin-passengers themselves were the most urgent in having this regulation maintained.

Lucky would it be for the pretensions of some parvenus,

whose souls are deposited at their banker's, and whose bodies but serve to carry about purses, knit of poor men's heart-strings, if thus easily they could precisely define, ashore, the difference between them and the rest of humanity.

But, I, Redburn, am a poor fellow, who have hardly ever known what it is to have five silver dollars in my pocket at one time; so, no doubt, this circumstance has something to do with my slight and harmless indignation at these things.

Chapter 48

A Living Corpse

I<small>T WAS DESTINED</small> that our departure from the English strand, should be marked by a tragical event, akin to the sudden end of the suicide, which had so strongly impressed me on quitting the American shore.

Of the three newly shipped men, who in a state of intoxication had been brought on board at the dock gates, two were able to be engaged at their duties, in four or five hours after quitting the pier. But the third man yet lay in his bunk, in the self-same posture in which his limbs had been adjusted by the crimp, who had deposited him there.

His name was down on the ship's papers as Miguel Saveda, and for Miguel Saveda the chief mate at last came forward, shouting down the forecastle-scuttle, and commanding his instant presence on deck. But the sailors answered for their new comrade; giving the mate to understand that Miguel was still fast locked in his trance, and could not obey him; when, muttering his usual imprecation, the mate retired to the quarter-deck.

This was in the first dog-watch, from four to six in the evening. At about three bells, in the next watch, Max the Dutchman, who, like most old seamen, was something of a physician in cases of drunkenness, recommended that Miguel's clothing should be removed, in order that he should lie more comfortably. But Jackson, who would seldom let any thing be done in the forecastle that was not proposed by himself, capriciously forbade this proceeding.

So the sailor still lay out of sight in his bunk, which was in the extreme angle of the forecastle, behind the *bowsprit-bitts*—two stout timbers rooted in the ship's keel. An hour or two afterward, some of the men observed a strange odor in the forecastle, which was attributed to the presence of some dead rat among the hollow spaces in the side planks; for some days before, the forecastle had been smoked out, to extirpate the vermin overrunning her. At midnight, the larboard watch, to which I belonged, turned out; and instantly as every man waked, he exclaimed at the now intolerable smell, supposed to be heightened by the shaking up of the bilge-water, from the ship's rolling.

"Blast that rat!" cried the Greenlander.

"He's blasted already," said Jackson, who in his drawers had crossed over to the bunk of Miguel. "It's a water-rat, shipmates, that's dead; and here he is"—and with that, he dragged forth the sailor's arm, exclaiming, "Dead as a timber-head!"

Upon this the men rushed toward the bunk, Max with the light, which he held to the man's face.

"No, he's not dead," he cried, as the yellow flame wavered for a moment at the seaman's motionless mouth. But hardly had the words escaped, when, to the silent horror of all, two threads of greenish fire, like a forked tongue, darted out between the lips; and in a moment, the cadaverous face was crawled over by a swarm of worm-like flames.

The lamp dropped from the hand of Max, and went out; while covered all over with spires and sparkles of flame, that faintly crackled in the silence, the uncovered parts of the body burned before us, precisely like a phosphorescent shark in a midnight sea.

The eyes were open and fixed; the mouth was curled like a scroll, and every lean feature firm as in life; while the whole face, now wound in curls of soft blue flame, wore an aspect of grim defiance, and eternal death. Prometheus, blasted by fire on the rock.

One arm, its red shirt-sleeve rolled up, exposed the man's name, tattooed in vermilion, near the hollow of the middle joint; and as if there was something peculiar in the painted flesh, every vibrating letter burned so white, that you might read the flaming name in the flickering ground of blue.

"Where's that d—d Miguel?" was now shouted down among us from the scuttle by the mate, who had just come on deck, and was determined to have every man up that belonged to his watch.

"He's gone to the harbor where they never weigh anchor," coughed Jackson. "Come you down, sir, and look."

Thinking that Jackson intended to beard him, the mate

sprang down in a rage; but recoiled at the burning body as if he had been shot by a bullet. "My God!" he cried, and stood holding fast to the ladder.

"Take hold of it," said Jackson, at last, to the Greenlander; "it must go overboard. Don't stand shaking there, like a dog; take hold of it, I say! But stop"—and smothering it all in the blankets, he pulled it partly out of the bunk.

A few minutes more, and it fell with a bubble among the phosphorescent sparkles of the damp night sea, leaving a corruscating wake as it sank.

This event thrilled me through and through with unspeakable horror; nor did the conversation of the watch during the next four hours on deck, at all serve to soothe me.

But what most astonished me, and seemed most incredible, was the infernal opinion of Jackson, that the man had been actually dead when brought on board the ship; and that knowingly, and merely for the sake of the month's advance, paid into his hand upon the strength of the bill he presented, the body-snatching crimp had knowingly shipped a corpse on board of the Highlander, under the pretense of its being a live body in a drunken trance. And I heard Jackson say, that he had known of such things having been done before. But that a really dead body ever burned in that manner, I can not even yet believe. But the sailors seemed familiar with such things; or at least with the stories of such things having happened to others.

For me, who at that age had never so much as happened to hear of a case like this, of animal combustion, in the horrid mood that came over me, I almost thought the burning body was a premonition of the hell of the Calvinists, and that Miguel's earthly end was a foretaste of his eternal condemnation.

Immediately after the burial, an iron pot of red coals was placed in the bunk, and in it two handfuls of coffee were roasted. This done, the bunk was nailed up, and was never opened again during the voyage; and strict orders were given to the crew not to divulge what had taken place to the emigrants: but to this, they needed no commands.

After the event, no one sailor but Jackson would stay alone in the forecastle, by night or by noon; and no more would they laugh or sing, or in any way make merry there, but kept all their pleasantries for the watches on deck. All but Jackson: who, while the rest would be sitting silently smoking on their chests, or in their bunks, would look toward the fatal spot, and cough, and laugh, and invoke the dead man with incredible scoffs and jeers. He froze my blood, and made my soul stand still.

Chapter 49

CARLO

THERE WAS on board our ship, among the emigrant passengers, a rich-cheeked, chestnut-haired Italian boy, arrayed in a faded, olive-hued velvet jacket, and tattered trowsers rolled up to his knee. He was not above fifteen years of age; but in the twilight pensiveness of his full morning eyes, there seemed to sleep experiences so sad and various, that his days must have seemed to him years. It was not an eye like Harry's, tho' Harry's was large and womanly. It shone with a soft and spiritual radiance, like a moist star in a tropic sky; and spoke of humility, deep-seated thoughtfulness, yet a careless endurance of all the ills of life.

The head was if any thing small; and heaped with thick clusters of tendril curls, half overhanging the brows and delicate ears, it somehow reminded you of a classic vase, piled up with Falernian foliage.

From the knee downward, the naked leg was beautiful to behold as any lady's arm; so soft and rounded, with infantile ease and grace. His whole figure was free, fine, and indolent; he was such a boy as might have ripened into life in a Neapolitan vineyard; such a boy as gipsies steal in infancy; such a boy as Murillo often painted, when he went among the poor and outcast, for subjects wherewith to captivate the eyes of rank and wealth; such a boy, as only Andalusian beggars are, full of poetry, gushing from every rent.

Carlo was his name; a poor and friendless son of earth, who had no sire; and on life's ocean was swept along, as spoon-drift in a gale.

Some months previous, he had landed in Prince's Dock, with his hand-organ, from a Messina vessel; and had walked the streets of Liverpool, playing the sunny airs of southern climes, among the northern fog and drizzle. And now, having laid by enough to pay his passage over the Atlantic, he had again embarked, to seek his fortunes in America.

From the first, Harry took to the boy.

"Carlo," said Harry, "how did you succeed in England?"

He was reclining upon an old sail spread on the long-boat; and throwing back his soiled but tasseled cap, and caressing one leg like a child, he looked up, and said in his broken English—that seemed like mixing the potent wine of Oporto with some delicious syrup:—said he, "Ah! I succeed very well!—for I have tunes for the young and the old, the gay and the sad. I have marches for military young men, and love-airs for the ladies, and solemn sounds for the aged. I never draw a crowd, but I know from their faces what airs will best please them; I never stop before a house, but I judge from its portico for what tune they will soonest toss me some silver. And I ever play sad airs to the merry, and merry airs to the sad; and most always the rich best fancy the sad, and the poor the merry."

"But do you not sometimes meet with cross and crabbed old men," said Harry, "who would much rather have your room than your music?"

"Yes, sometimes," said Carlo, playing with his foot, "sometimes I do."

"And then, knowing the value of quiet to unquiet men, I suppose you never leave them under a shilling?"

"No," continued the boy, "I love my organ as I do myself, for it is my only friend, poor organ! it sings to me when I am sad, and cheers me; and I never play before a house, on purpose to be paid for leaving off, not I; would I, poor organ?"—looking down the hatchway where it was. "No, that I never have done, and never will do, though I starve; for when people drive me away, I do not think my organ is to blame, but they themselves are to blame; for such people's musical pipes are cracked, and grown rusted, that no more music can be breathed into their souls."

"No, Carlo; no music like yours, perhaps," said Harry, with a laugh.

"Ah! there's the mistake. Though my organ is as full of melody, as a hive is of bees; yet no organ can make music in unmusical breasts; no more than my native winds can, when they breathe upon a harp without chords."

Next day was a serene and delightful one; and in the evening when the vessel was just rippling along impelled by a gentle yet steady breeze, and the poor emigrants, relieved from their late sufferings, were gathered on deck; Carlo suddenly started up from his lazy reclinings; went below, and, assisted by the emigrants, returned with his organ.

Now, music is a holy thing, and its instruments, however humble, are to be loved and revered. Whatever has made, or does make, or may make music, should be held sacred as the golden bridle-bit of the Shah of Persia's horse, and the golden hammer, with which his hoofs are shod. Musical instruments should be like the silver tongs, with which the high-priests tended the Jewish altars—never to be touched by a hand profane. Who would bruise the poorest reed of Pan, though plucked from a beggar's hedge, would insult the melodious god himself.

And there is no humble thing with music in it, not a fife, not a negro-fiddle, that is not to be reverenced as much as the grandest architectural organ that ever rolled its flood-tide of harmony down a cathedral nave. For even a Jew's-harp may be so played, as to awaken all the fairies that are in us, and make them dance in our souls, as on a moon-lit sward of violets.

But what subtle power is this, residing in but a bit of steel, which might have made a tenpenny nail, that so enters, without knocking, into our inmost beings, and shows us all hidden things?

Not in a spirit of foolish speculation altogether, in no merely transcendental mood, did the glorious Greek of old fancy the human soul to be essentially a harmony. And if we grant that theory of Paracelsus and Campanella, that every man has four souls within him; then can we account for those banded sounds with silver links, those quartettes of melody, that sometimes sit and sing within us, as if our souls were baronial halls, and our music were made by the hoarest old harpers of Wales.

But look! here is poor Carlo's organ; and while the silent crowd surrounds him, there he stands, looking mildly but inquiringly about him; his right hand pulling and twitching the ivory knobs at one end of his instrument.

Behold the organ!

Surely, if much virtue lurk in the old fiddles of Cremona,

and if their melody be in proportion to their antiquity, what divine ravishments may we not anticipate from this venerable, embrowned old organ, which might almost have played the Dead March in Saul, when King Saul himself was buried.

A fine old organ! carved into fantastic old towers, and turrets, and belfries; its architecture seems somewhat of the Gothic, monastic order; in front, it looks like the West-Front of York Minster.

What sculptured arches, leading into mysterious intricacies!—what mullioned windows, that seem as if they must look into chapels flooded with devotional sunsets!—what flying buttresses, and gable-ends, and niches with saints!—But stop! 'tis a Moorish iniquity; for here, as I live, is a Saracenic arch; which, for aught I know, may lead into some interior Alhambra.

Ay, it does; for as Carlo now turns his hand, I hear the gush of the Fountain of Lions, as he plays some thronged Italian air—a mixed and liquid sea of sound, that dashes its spray in my face.

Play on, play on, Italian boy! what though the notes be broken, here's that within that mends them. Turn hither your pensive, morning eyes; and while I list to the organs twain—one yours, one mine—let me gaze fathoms down into thy fathomless eye;—'tis good as gazing down into the great South Sea, and seeing the dazzling rays of the dolphins there.

Play on, play on! for to every note come trooping, now, triumphant standards, armies marching—all the pomp of sound. Methinks I am Xerxes, the nucleus of the martial neigh of all the Persian studs. Like gilded damask-flies, thick clustering on some lofty bough, my satraps swarm around me.

But now the pageant passes, and I droop; while Carlo taps his ivory knobs, and plays some flute-like saraband—soft, dulcet, dropping sounds, like silver oars in bubbling brooks. And now a clanging, martial air, as if ten thousand brazen trumpets, forged from spurs and sword-hilts, called North, and South, and East, to rush to West!

Again—what blasted heath is this?—what goblin sounds of Macbeth's witches?—Beethoven's Spirit Waltz! the muster-call of sprites and specters. Now come, hands joined, Me-

dusa, Hecate, she of Endor, and all the Blocksberg's, demons
dire.

Once more the ivory knobs are tapped; and long-drawn,
golden sounds are heard—some ode to Cleopatra; slowly
loom, and solemnly expand, vast, rounding orbs of beauty;
and before me float innumerable queens, deep dipped in silver
gauzes.

All this could Carlo do—make, unmake me; build me up;
to pieces take me; and join me limb to limb. He is the architect of domes of sound, and bowers of song.

And all is done with that old organ! Reverenced, then, be
all street organs; more melody is at the beck of my Italian
boy, than lurks in squadrons of Parisian orchestras.

But look! Carlo has that to feast the eye as well as ear; and
the same wondrous magic in me, magnifies them into grandeur; though every figure greatly needs the artist's repairing
hand, and sadly needs a dusting.

His York Minster's West-Front opens; and like the gates
of Milton's heaven, it turns on golden hinges.

What have we here? The inner palace of the Great Mogul?
Grouped and gilded columns, in confidential clusters; fixed
fountains; canopies and lounges; and lords and dames in silk
and spangles.

The organ plays a stately march; and presto! wide open
arches; and out come, two and two, with nodding plumes, in
crimson turbans, a troop of martial men; with jingling scim-
eters, they pace the hall; salute, pass on, and disappear.

Now, ground and lofty tumblers; jet black Nubian slaves.
They fling themselves on poles; stand on their heads; and
downward vanish.

And now a dance and masquerade of figures, reeling from
the side-doors, among the knights and dames. Some sultan
leads a sultaness; some emperor, a queen; and jeweled sword-
hilts of carpet knights fling back the glances tossed by co-
quettes of countesses.

On this, the curtain drops; and there the poor old organ
stands, begrimed, and black, and rickety.

Now, tell me, Carlo, if at street corners, for a single penny,
I may thus transport myself in dreams Elysian, who so rich as
I? Not he who owns a million.

And Carlo! ill betide the voice that ever greets thee, my Italian boy, with aught but kindness; cursed the slave who ever drives thy wondrous box of sights and sounds forth from a lordling's door!

Chapter 50

HARRY BOLTON AT SEA

As YET I have said nothing about how my friend, Harry, got along as a sailor.

Poor Harry! a feeling of sadness, never to be comforted, comes over me, even now when I think of you. For this voyage that you went, but carried you part of the way to that ocean grave, which has buried you up with your secrets, and whither no mourning pilgrimage can be made.

But why this gloom at the thought of the dead? And why should we not be glad? Is it, that we ever think of them as departed from all joy? Is it, that we believe that indeed they are dead? They revisit us not, the departed; their voices no more ring in the air; summer may come, but it is winter with them; and even in our own limbs we feel not the sap that every spring renews the green life of the trees.

But Harry! you live over again, as I recall your image before me. I see you, plain and palpable as in life; and can make your existence obvious to others. Is he, then, dead, of whom this may be said?

But Harry! you are mixed with a thousand strange forms, the centaurs of fancy; half real and human, half wild and grotesque. Divine imaginings, like gods, come down to the groves of our Thessalies, and there, in the embrace of wild, dryad reminiscences, beget the beings that astonish the world.

But Harry! though your image now roams in my Thessaly groves, it is the same as of old; and among the droves of mixed beings and centaurs, you show like a zebra, banding with elks.

And indeed, in his striped Guernsey frock, dark glossy skin and hair, Harry Bolton, mingling with the Highlander's crew, looked not unlike the soft, silken quadruped-creole, that, pursued by wild Bushmen, bounds through Caffrarian woods.

How they hunted you, Harry, my zebra! those ocean barbarians, those unimpressible, uncivilized sailors of ours! How they pursued you from bowsprit to mainmast, and started you out of your every retreat!

Before the day of our sailing, it was known to the seamen that the girlish youth, whom they daily saw near the sign of the Clipper in Union-street, would form one of their homeward-bound crew. Accordingly, they cast upon him many a critical glance; but were not long in concluding that Harry would prove no very great accession to their strength; that the hoist of so tender an arm would not tell many hundredweight on the maintop-sail halyards. Therefore they disliked him before they became acquainted with him; and such dislikes, as every one knows, are the most inveterate, and liable to increase. But even sailors are not blind to the sacredness that hallows a stranger; and for a time, abstaining from rudeness, they only maintained toward my friend a cold and unsympathizing civility.

As for Harry, at first the novelty of the scene filled up his mind; and the thought of being bound for a distant land, carried with it, as with every one, a buoyant feeling of undefinable expectation. And though his money was now gone again, all but a sovereign or two, yet that troubled him but little, in the first flush of being at sea.

But I was surprised, that one who had certainly seen much of life, should evince such an incredible ignorance of what was wholly inadmissible in a person situated as he was. But perhaps his familiarity with lofty life, only the less qualified him for understanding the other extreme. Will you believe me, this Bury blade once came on deck in a brocaded dressing-gown, embroidered slippers, and tasseled smoking-cap, to stand his morning watch.

As soon as I beheld him thus arrayed, a suspicion, which had previously crossed my mind, again recurred, and I almost vowed to myself that, spite his protestations, Harry Bolton never could have been at sea before, even as a *Guinea-pig* in an Indiaman; for the slightest acquaintance with the sea-life and sailors, should have prevented him, it would seem, from enacting this folly.

"Who's that Chinese mandarin?" cried the mate, who had made voyages to Canton. "Look you, my fine fellow, douse that mainsail now, and furl it in a trice."

"Sir?" said Harry, starting back. "Is not this the morning watch, and is not mine a morning gown?"

But though, in my refined friend's estimation, nothing could be more appropriate; in the mate's, it was the most monstrous of incongruities; and the offensive gown and cap were removed.

"It is too bad!" exclaimed Harry to me; "I meant to lounge away the watch in that gown until coffee time;—and I suppose your Hottentot of a mate won't permit a gentleman to smoke his Turkish pipe of a morning; but by gad, I'll wear straps to my pantaloons to spite him!"

Oh! that was the rock on which you split, poor Harry! Incensed at the want of polite refinement in the mates and crew, Harry, in a pet and pique, only determined to provoke them the more; and the storm of indignation he raised very soon overwhelmed him.

The sailors took a special spite to his chest, a large mahogany one, which he had had made to order at a furniture warehouse. It was ornamented with brass screw-heads, and other devices; and was well filled with those articles of the wardrobe in which Harry had sported through a London season; for the various vests and pantaloons he had sold in Liverpool, when in want of money, had not materially lessened his extensive stock.

It was curious to listen to the various hints and opinings thrown out by the sailors at the occasional glimpses they had of this collection of silks, velvets, broadcloths, and satins. I do not know exactly what they thought Harry had been; but they seemed unanimous in believing that, by abandoning his country, Harry had left more room for the gamblers. Jackson even asked him to lift up the lower hem of his trowsers, to test the color of his calves.

It is a noteworthy circumstance, that whenever a slender made youth, of easy manners and polite address, happens to form one of a ship's company, the sailors almost invariably impute his sea-going to an irresistible necessity of decamping from terra-firma in order to evade the constables.

These white-fingered gentry must be light-fingered too, they say to themselves, or they would not be after putting their hands into our tar. What else can bring them to sea?

Cogent and conclusive this; and thus Harry, from the very beginning, was put down for a very equivocal character.

Sometimes, however, they only made sport of his appearance; especially one evening, when his monkey jacket being wet through, he was obliged to mount one of his swallow-tailed coats. They said he carried two mizen-peaks at his stern; declared he was a broken-down quill-driver, or a footman to a Portuguese running barber, or some old maid's tobacco-boy. As for the captain, it had become all the same to Harry as if there were no gentlemanly and complaisant Captain Riga on board. For to his no small astonishment,—but just as I had predicted,—Captain Riga never noticed him now, but left the business of indoctrinating him into the little experiences of a greenhorn's career solely in the hands of his officers and crew.

But the worst was to come. For the first few days, whenever there was any running aloft to be done, I noticed that Harry was indefatigable in coiling away the slack of the rigging about decks; ignoring the fact that his shipmates were springing into the shrouds. And when all hands of the watch would be engaged *clewing up a t'-gallant-sail*, that is, pulling the proper ropes on deck that wrapped the sail up on the yard aloft, Harry would always manage to get near the *belaying-pin*, so that when the time came for two of us to spring into the rigging, he would be inordinately fidgety in making fast the *clew-lines*, and would be so absorbed in that occupation, and would so elaborate the hitchings round the pin, that it was quite impossible for him, after doing so much, to mount over the bulwarks before his comrades had got there. However, after securing the clew-lines beyond a possibility of their getting loose, Harry would always make a feint of starting in a prodigious hurry for the shrouds; but suddenly looking up, and seeing others in advance, would retreat, apparently quite chagrined that he had been cut off from the opportunity of signalizing his activity.

At this I was surprised, and spoke to my friend; when the alarming fact was confessed, that he had made a private trial of it, and it never would do: *he could not go aloft*; his nerves would not hear of it.

"Then, Harry," said I, "better you had never been born.

Do you know what it is that you are coming to? Did you not tell me that you made no doubt you would acquit yourself well in the rigging? Did you not say that you had been two voyages to Bombay? Harry, you were mad to ship. But you only imagine it: try again; and my word for it, you will very soon find yourself as much at home among the spars as a bird in a tree."

But he could not be induced to try it over again; the fact was, *his nerves could not stand it*; in the course of his courtly career, he had drunk too much strong Mocha coffee and gunpowder tea, and had smoked altogether too many Havannas.

At last, as I had repeatedly warned him, the mate singled him out one morning, and commanded him to mount to the main-truck, and unreeve the short signal halyards.

"Sir?" said Harry, aghast.

"Away you go!" said the mate, snatching a whip's end.

"Don't strike me!" screamed Harry, drawing himself up.

"Take that, and along with you," cried the mate, laying the rope once across his back, but lightly.

"By heaven!" cried Harry, wincing—not with the blow, but the insult: and then making a dash at the mate, who, holding out his long arm, kept him lazily at bay, and laughed at him, till, had I not feared a broken head, I should infallibly have pitched my boy's bulk into the officer.

"Captain Riga!" cried Harry.

"Don't call upon *him*," said the mate; "he's asleep, and won't wake up till we strike Yankee soundings again. Up you go!" he added, flourishing the rope's end.

Harry looked round among the grinning tars with a glance of terrible indignation and agony; and then settling his eye on me, and seeing there no hope, but even an admonition of obedience, as his only resource, he made one bound into the rigging, and was up at the main-top in a trice. I thought a few more springs would take him to the truck, and was a little fearful that in his desperation he might then jump overboard; for I had heard of delirious greenhorns doing such things at sea, and being lost forever. But no; he stopped short, and looked down from the top. Fatal glance! it unstrung his every fiber; and I saw him reel, and clutch the shrouds, till the mate shouted out for him not to squeeze the tar out of the ropes.

"Up you go, sir."

But Harry said nothing.

"You Max," cried the mate to the Dutch sailor, "spring after him, and help him; you understand?"

Max went up the rigging hand over hand, and brought his red head with a bump against the base of Harry's back. Needs must when the devil drives; and higher and higher, with Max bumping him at every step, went my unfortunate friend. At last he gained the royal yard, and the thin signal halyards— hardly bigger than common twine—were flying in the wind.

"Unreeve!" cried the mate.

I saw Harry's arm stretched out—his legs seemed shaking in the rigging, even to us, down on deck; and at last, thank heaven! the deed was done.

He came down pale as death, with bloodshot eyes, and every limb quivering. From that moment he never put foot in rattlin; never mounted above the bulwarks; and for the residue of the voyage, at least, became an altered person.

At the time, he went to the mate—since he could not get speech of the captain—and conjured him to intercede with Riga, that his name might be stricken off from the list of the ship's company, so that he might make the voyage as a steerage passenger; for which privilege, he bound himself to pay, as soon as he could dispose of some things of his in New York, over and above the ordinary passage-money. But the mate gave him a blunt denial; and a look of wonder at his effrontery. Once a sailor on board a ship, and *always* a sailor for that voyage, at least; for within so brief a period, no officer can bear to associate on terms of any thing like equality with a person whom he has ordered about at his pleasure.

Harry then told the mate solemnly, that he might do what he pleased, but go aloft again he *could* not, and *would* not. He would do any thing else but that.

This affair sealed Harry's fate on board of the Highlander; the crew now reckoned him fair play for their worst jibes and jeers, and he led a miserable life indeed.

Few landsmen can imagine the depressing and self-humiliating effect of finding one's self, for the first time, at the beck of illiterate sea-tyrants, with no opportunity of exhibiting any trait about you, but your ignorance of every thing connected with the sea-life that you lead, and the duties you are constantly called upon to perform. In such a sphere, and under such circumstances, Isaac Newton and Lord Bacon would be sea-clowns and bumpkins; and Napoleon Bonaparte be cuffed and kicked without remorse. In more than one instance I have seen the truth of this; and Harry, poor Harry, proved no exception. And from the circumstances which exempted me from experiencing the bitterest of these evils, I only the more felt for one who, from a strange constitutional nervousness, before unknown even to himself, was become as a hunted hare to the merciless crew.

But how was it that Harry Bolton, who spite of his effeminacy of appearance, had evinced, in our London trip, such unmistakable flashes of a spirit not easily tamed—how was it, that he could now yield himself up to the almost passive reception of contumely and contempt? Perhaps his spirit, for the time, had been broken. But I will not undertake to explain; we are curious creatures, as every one knows; and there are passages in the lives of all men, so out of keeping with the common tenor of their ways, and so seemingly contradictory of themselves, that only He who made us can expound them.

Chapter 51

THE EMIGRANTS

AFTER THE FIRST miserable weather we experienced at sea, we had intervals of foul and fair, mostly the former, however, attended with head winds; till at last, after a three days' fog and rain, the sun rose cheerily one morning, and showed us Cape Clear. Thank heaven, we were out of the weather emphatically called "*Channel weather*," and the last we should see of the eastern hemisphere was now in plain sight, and all the rest was broad ocean.

Land ho! was cried, as the dark purple headland grew out of the north. At the cry, the Irish emigrants came rushing up the hatchway, thinking America itself was at hand.

"Where is it?" cried one of them, running out a little way on the bowsprit. "Is *that* it?"

"Aye, it doesn't look much like *ould* Ireland, does it?" said Jackson.

"Not a bit, honey:—and how long before we get there? to-night?"

Nothing could exceed the disappointment and grief of the emigrants, when they were at last informed, that the land to the north was their own native island, which, after leaving three or four weeks previous in a steamboat for Liverpool, was now close to them again; and that, after newly voyaging so many days from the Mersey, the Highlander was only bringing them in view of the original home whence they started.

They were the most simple people I had ever seen. They seemed to have no adequate idea of distances; and to them, America must have seemed as a place just over a river. Every morning some of them came on deck, to see how much nearer we were: and one old man would stand for hours together, looking straight off from the bows, as if he expected to see New York city every minute, when, perhaps, we were yet two thousand miles distant, and steering, moreover, against a head wind.

The only thing that ever diverted this poor old man from his earnest search for land, was the occasional appearance of porpoises under the bows; when he would cry out at the top of his voice—"Look, look, ye divils! look at the great pigs of the s'a!"

At last, the emigrants began to think, that the ship had played them false; and that she was bound for the East Indies, or some other remote place; and one night, Jackson set a report going among them, that Riga purposed taking them to Barbary, and selling them all for slaves; but though some of the old women almost believed it, and a great weeping ensued among the children, yet the men knew better than to believe such a ridiculous tale.

Of all the emigrants, my Italian boy Carlo, seemed most at his ease. He would lie all day in a dreamy mood, sunning himself in the long boat, and gazing out on the sea. At night, he would bring up his organ, and play for several hours; much to the delight of his fellow voyagers, who blessed him and his organ again and again; and paid him for his music by furnishing him his meals. Sometimes, the steward would come forward, when it happened to be very much of a moonlight, with a message from the cabin, for Carlo to repair to the quarter-deck, and entertain the gentlemen and ladies.

There was a fiddler on board, as will presently be seen; and sometimes, by urgent entreaties, he was induced to unite his music with Carlo's, for the benefit of the cabin occupants; but this was only twice or thrice: for this fiddler deemed himself considerably elevated above the other steerage-passengers; and did not much fancy the idea of fiddling to strangers; and thus wear out his elbow, while persons, entirely unknown to him, and in whose welfare he felt not the slightest interest, were curveting about in famous high spirits. So for the most part, the gentlemen and ladies were fain to dance as well as they could to my little Italian's organ.

It was the most accommodating organ in the world; for it could play any tune that was called for; Carlo pulling in and out the ivory knobs at one side, and so manufacturing melody at pleasure.

True, some censorious gentlemen cabin-passengers protested, that such or such an air, was not precisely according to Handel or Mozart; and some ladies, whom I overheard talking about throwing their nosegays to Malibran at Covent Garden, assured the attentive Captain Riga, that Carlo's organ was a most wretched affair, and made a horrible din.

"Yes, ladies," said the captain, bowing, "by your leave, I think Carlo's organ must have lost its mother, for it squeals like a pig running after its dam."

Harry was incensed at these criticisms; and yet these cabin-people were all ready enough to dance to poor Carlo's music.

"Carlo"—said I, one night, as he was marching forward from the quarter-deck, after one of these sea-quadrilles, which took place during my watch on deck:—"Carlo"—said I, "what do the gentlemen and ladies give you for playing?"

"Look!"—and he showed me three copper medals of Britannia and her shield—three English pennies.

Now, whenever we discover a dislike in us, toward any one, we should ever be a little suspicious of ourselves. It may be, therefore, that the natural antipathy, with which almost all seamen and steerage-passengers, regard the inmates of the cabin, was one cause at least, of my not feeling very charitably disposed toward them, myself.

Yes: that might have been; but nevertheless, I will let nature have her own way for once; and here declare roundly, that, however it was, I cherished a feeling toward these cabin-passengers, akin to contempt. Not because they happened to be cabin-passengers: not at all: but only because they seemed the most finical, miserly, mean men and women, that ever stepped over the Atlantic.

One of them was an old fellow in a robust looking coat, with broad skirts; he had a nose like a bottle of port-wine; and would stand for a whole hour, with his legs straddling apart, and his hands deep down in his breeches pockets, as if he had two mints at work there, coining guineas. He was an abominable looking old fellow, with cold, fat, jelly-like eyes; and avarice, heartlessness, and sensuality stamped all over him. He seemed all the time going through some process of mental arithmetic; doing sums with dollars and cents: his very mouth, wrinkled and drawn up at the corners, looked like a purse. When he dies, his skull ought to be turned into a savings' box, with the till-hole between his teeth.

Another of the cabin inmates, was a middle-aged Londoner, in a comical Cockney-cut coat, with a pair of semicircular tails: so that he looked as if he were sitting in a swing. He wore a spotted neckerchief; a short, little, fiery-red vest; and striped pants, very thin in the calf, but very full about the waist. There was nothing describable about him but his dress; for he had such a meaningless face, I can not remember it; though I have a vague impression, that it looked at the time, as if its owner was laboring under the mumps.

Then there were two or three buckish looking young fellows, among the rest; who were all the time playing at cards on the poop, under the lee of the *spanker*; or smoking cigars on the taffrail; or sat quizzing the emigrant women with opera-glasses, leveled through the windows of the upper cabin. These sparks frequently called for the steward to help them to brandy and water, and talked about going on to Washington, to see Niagara Falls.

There was also an old gentleman, who had brought with him three or four heavy files of the *London Times*, and other papers; and he spent all his hours in reading them, on the shady side of the deck, with one leg crossed over the other; and without crossed legs, he never read at all. That was indispensable to the proper understanding of what he studied. He growled terribly, when disturbed by the sailors, who now and then were obliged to move him to get at the ropes.

As for the ladies, I have nothing to say concerning them; for ladies are like creeds; if you can not speak well of them, say nothing.

Chapter 52

THE EMIGRANTS' KITCHEN

I HAVE MADE some mention of the "galley," or great stove for the steerage passengers, which was planted over the main hatches.

During the outward-bound passage, there were so few occupants of the steerage, that they had abundant room to do their cooking at this galley. But it was otherwise now; for we had four or five hundred in the steerage; and all their cooking was to be done by one fire; a pretty large one, to be sure, but, nevertheless, small enough, considering the number to be accommodated, and the fact that the fire was only to be kindled at certain hours.

For the emigrants in these ships are under a sort of martial-law; and in all their affairs are regulated by the despotic ordinances of the captain. And though it is evident, that to a certain extent this is necessary, and even indispensable; yet, as at sea no appeal lies beyond the captain, he too often makes unscrupulous use of his power. And as for going to law with him at the end of the voyage, you might as well go to law with the Czar of Russia.

At making the fire, the emigrants take turns; as it is often very disagreeable work, owing to the pitching of the ship, and the heaving of the spray over the uncovered "galley." Whenever I had the morning watch, from four to eight, I was sure to see some poor fellow crawling up from below about daybreak, and go to groping over the deck after bits of rope-yarn, or tarred canvas, for kindling-stuff. And no sooner would the fire be fairly made, than up came the old women, and men, and children; each armed with an iron pot or saucepan; and invariably a great tumult ensued, as to whose turn to cook came next; sometimes the more quarrelsome would fight, and upset each other's pots and pans.

Once, an English lad came up with a little coffee-pot, which he managed to crowd in between two pans. This done, he went below. Soon after a great strapping Irishman, in knee-breeches and bare calves, made his appearance; and eying the row of things on the fire, asked whose coffee-pot that was; upon being told, he removed it, and put his own in its place; saying something about that individual place belonging to him; and with that, he turned aside.

Not long after, the boy came along again; and seeing his pot removed, made a violent exclamation, and replaced it; which the Irishman no sooner perceived, than he rushed at him, with his fists doubled. The boy snatched up the boiling coffee, and spirted its contents all about the fellow's bare legs; which incontinently began to dance involuntary hornpipes and fandangoes, as a preliminary to giving chase to the boy, who by this time, however, had decamped.

Many similar scenes occurred every day; nor did a single day pass, but scores of the poor people got no chance whatever to do their cooking.

This was bad enough; but it was a still more miserable thing, to see these poor emigrants wrangling and fighting together for the want of the most ordinary accommodations. But thus it is, that the very hardships to which such beings are subjected, instead of uniting them, only tends, by imbittering their tempers, to set them against each other; and thus they themselves drive the strongest rivet into the chain, by which their social superiors hold them subject.

It was with a most reluctant hand, that every evening in the second dog-watch, at the mate's command, I would march up to the fire, and giving notice to the assembled crowd, that the time was come to extinguish it, would dash it out with my bucket of salt water; though many, who had long waited for a chance to cook, had now to go away disappointed.

The staple food of the Irish emigrants was oatmeal and water, boiled into what is sometimes called *mush*; by the Dutch is known as *supaan*; by sailors *burgoo*; by the New Englanders *hasty-pudding*; in which hasty-pudding, by the way, the poet Barlow found the materials for a sort of epic.

Some of the steerage passengers, however, were provided with sea-biscuit, and other perennial food, that was eatable all the year round, fire or no fire.

There were several, moreover, who seemed better to do in the world than the rest; who were well furnished with hams, cheese, Bologna sausages, Dutch herrings, alewives, and other delicacies adapted to the contingencies of a voyager in the steerage.

There was a little old Englishman on board, who had been a grocer ashore, whose greasy trunks seemed all pantries; and he was constantly using himself for a cupboard, by transferring their contents into his own interior. He was a little light of head, I always thought. He particularly doated on his long strings of sausages; and would sometimes take them out, and play with them, wreathing them round him, like an Indian juggler with charmed snakes. What with this diversion, and eating his cheese, and helping himself from an inexhaustible junk bottle, and smoking his pipe, and meditating, this crack-pated grocer made time jog along with him at a tolerably easy pace.

But by far the most considerable man in the steerage, in point of pecuniary circumstances at least, was a slender little pale-faced English tailor, who it seemed had engaged a passage for himself and wife in some imaginary section of the ship, called the *second cabin*, which was feigned to combine the comforts of the first cabin with the cheapness of the steerage. But it turned out that this second cabin was comprised in the after part of the steerage itself, with nothing intervening but a name. So to his no small disgust, he found himself herding with the rabble; and his complaints to the captain were unheeded.

This luckless tailor was tormented the whole voyage by his wife, who was young and handsome; just such a beauty as farmers'-boys fall in love with; she had bright eyes, and red cheeks, and looked plump and happy.

She was a sad coquette; and did not turn away, as she was bound to do, from the dandy glances of the cabin bucks, who ogled her through their double-barreled opera-glasses. This enraged the tailor past telling; he would remonstrate with his wife, and scold her; and lay his matrimonial commands upon her, to go below instantly, out of sight. But the lady was not to be tyrannized over; and so she told him. Meantime, the bucks would be still framing her in their lenses, mightily enjoying the fun. The last resource of the poor tailor would be, to start up, and make a dash at the rogues, with clenched fists;

but upon getting as far as the mainmast, the mate would accost him from over the rope that divided them, and beg leave to communicate the fact, that he could come no further.

This unfortunate tailor was also a fiddler; and when fairly baited into desperation, would rush for his instrument, and try to get rid of his wrath by playing the most savage, remorseless airs he could think of.

While thus employed, perhaps his wife would accost him—

"Billy, my dear;" and lay her soft hand on his shoulder.

But Billy, he only fiddled the harder.

"Billy, my love!"

The bow went faster and faster.

"Come, now, Billy, my dear little fellow, let's make it all up;" and she bent over his knees, looking bewitchingly up at him, with her irresistible eyes.

Down went fiddle and bow; and the couple would sit together for an hour or two, as pleasant and affectionate as possible.

But the next day, the chances were, that the old feud would be renewed, which was certain to be the case at the first glimpse of an opera-glass from the cabin.

Chapter 53

The Horatii and Curiatii

WITH A SLIGHT ALTERATION, I might begin this chapter after the manner of Livy, in the 24th section of his first book: — *"It happened, that in each family were three twin brothers, between whom there was little disparity in point of age or of strength."*

Among the steerage passengers of the Highlander, were two women from Armagh, in Ireland, widows and sisters, who had each three twin sons, born, as they said, on the same day.

They were ten years old. Each three of these six cousins were as like as the mutually reflected figures in a kaleidoscope; and like the forms seen in a kaleidoscope, together, as well as separately, they seemed to form a complete figure. But, though besides this fraternal likeness, all six boys bore a strong cousin-german resemblance to each other; yet, the O'Briens were in disposition quite the reverse of the O'Regans. The former were a timid, silent trio, who used to revolve around their mother's waist, and seldom quit the maternal orbit; whereas, the O'Regans were "broths of boys," full of mischief and fun, and given to all manner of devilment, like the tails of the comets.

Early every morning, Mrs. O'Regan emerged from the steerage, driving her spirited twins before her, like a riotous herd of young steers; and made her way to the capacious deck-tub, full of salt water, pumped up from the sea, for the purpose of washing down the ship. Three splashes, and the three boys were ducking and diving together in the brine; their mother engaged in *shampooing* them, though it was haphazard sort of work enough; a rub here, and a scrub there, as she could manage to fasten on a stray limb.

"Pat, ye divil, hould still while I wash ye. Ah! but it's you, Teddy, you rogue. Arrah, now, Mike, ye spalpeen, don't be mixing your legs up with Pat's."

The little rascals, leaping and scrambling with delight, enjoyed the sport mightily; while this indefatigable, but merry matron, manipulated them all over, as if it were a matter of conscience.

Meanwhile, Mrs. O'Brien would be standing on the boat-swain's locker—or rope and tar-pot pantry in the vessel's bows—with a large old quarto Bible, black with age, laid before her between the knight-heads, and reading aloud to her three meek little lambs.

The sailors took much pleasure in the deck-tub perfor-mances of the O'Regans, and greatly admired them always for their archness and activity; but the tranquil O'Briens they did not fancy so much. More especially they disliked the grave matron herself; hooded in rusty black; and they had a bitter grudge against her book. To that, and the incantations mut-tered over it, they ascribed the head winds that haunted us; and Blunt, our Irish cockney, really believed that Mrs. O'Brien purposely came on deck every morning, in order to secure a foul wind for the next ensuing twenty-four hours.

At last, upon her coming forward one morning, Max the Dutchman accosted her, saying he was sorry for it, but if she went between the knight-heads again with her book, the crew would throw it overboard for her.

Now, although contrasted in character, there existed a great warmth of affection between the two families of twins, which upon this occasion was curiously manifested.

Notwithstanding the rebuke and threat of the sailor, the widow silently occupied her old place; and with her children clustering round her, began her low, muttered reading, stand-ing right in the extreme bows of the ship, and slightly leaning over them, as if addressing the multitudinous waves from a floating pulpit. Presently Max came behind her, snatched the book from her hands, and threw it overboard. The widow gave a wail, and her boys set up a cry. Their cousins, then ducking in the water close by, at once saw the cause of the cry; and springing from the tub, like so many dogs, seized Max by the legs, biting and striking at him: which, the before timid little O'Briens no sooner perceived, than they, too, threw themselves on the enemy, and the amazed seaman found himself baited like a bull by all six boys.

And here it gives me joy to record one good thing on the

part of the mate. He saw the fray, and its beginning; and rushing forward, told Max that he would harm the boys at his peril; while he cheered them on, as if rejoiced at their giving the fellow such a tussle. At last Max, sorely scratched, bit, pinched, and every way aggravated, though of course without a serious bruise, cried out "enough!" and the assailants were ordered to quit him; but though the three O'Briens obeyed, the three O'Regans hung on to him like leeches, and had to be dragged off.

"There now, you rascal," cried the mate, "throw overboard another Bible, and I'll send you after it without a bowline."

This event gave additional celebrity to the twins throughout the vessel. That morning all six were invited to the quarter-deck, and reviewed by the cabin-passengers, the ladies manifesting particular interest in them, as they always do concerning twins, which some of them show in public parks and gardens, by stopping to look at them, and questioning their nurses.

"And were you all born at one time?" asked an old lady, letting her eye run in wonder along the even file of white heads.

"Indeed, an' we were," said Teddy; "wasn't we, mother?"

Many more questions were asked and answered, when a collection was taken up for their benefit among these magnanimous cabin-passengers, which resulted in starting all six boys in the world with a penny apiece.

I never could look at these little fellows without an inexplicable feeling coming over me; and though there was nothing so very remarkable or unprecedented about them, except the singular coincidence of two sisters simultaneously making the world such a generous present; yet, the mere fact of their being twins always seemed curious; in fact, to me at least, all twins are prodigies; and still I hardly know why this should be; for all of us in our own persons furnish numerous examples of the same phenomenon. Are not our thumbs twins? A regular Castor and Pollux? And all of our fingers? Are not our arms, hands, legs, feet, eyes, ears, all twins; born at one birth, and as much alike as they possibly can be?

Can it be, that the Greek grammarians invented their dual number for the particular benefit of twins?

Chapter 54

IT HAS BEEN mentioned how advantageously my shipmates disposed of their tobacco in Liverpool; but it is to be related how those nefarious commercial speculations of theirs reduced them to sad extremities in the end.

True to their improvident character, and seduced by the high prices paid for the weed in England, they had there sold off by far the greater portion of what tobacco they had; even inducing the mate to surrender the portion he had secured under lock and key by command of the Custom-house officers. So that when the crew were about two weeks out, on the homeward-bound passage, it became sorrowfully evident that tobacco was at a premium.

Now, one of the favorite pursuits of sailors during a dog-watch below at sea is cards; and though they do not understand whist, cribbage, and games of that kidney, yet they are adepts at what is called "*High-low-Jack-and-the-game*," which name, indeed, has a Jackish and nautical flavor. Their stakes are generally so many plugs of tobacco, which, like rouleaux of guineas, are piled on their chests when they play. Judge, then, the wicked zest with which the Highlander's crew now shuffled and dealt the pack; and how the interest curiously and invertedly increased, as the stakes necessarily became less and less; and finally resolved themselves into "*chaws*."

So absorbed, at last, did they become at this business, that some of them, after being hard at work during a night-watch on deck, would rob themselves of rest below, in order to have a brush at the cards. And as it is very difficult sleeping in the presence of gamblers; especially if they chance to be sailors, whose conversation at all times is apt to be boisterous; these fellows would often be driven out of the forecastle by those who desired to rest. They were obliged to repair on deck, and make a card-table of it; and invariably, in such cases, there was a great deal of contention, a great many ungentlemanly charges of nigging and cheating; and, now and then, a few parenthetical blows were exchanged.

But this was not so much to be wondered at, seeing they could see but very little, being provided with no light but that of a midnight sky; and the cards, from long wear and rough usage, having become exceedingly torn and tarry, so much so, that several members of the four suits might have seceded from their respective clans, and formed into a fifth tribe, under the name of "*Tar-spots.*"

Every day the tobacco grew scarcer and scarcer; till at last it became necessary to adopt the greatest possible economy in its use. The modicum constituting an ordinary "*chaw*," was made to last a whole day; and at night, permission being had from the cook, this self-same "chaw" was placed in the oven of the stove, and there dried; so as to do duty in a pipe.

In the end not a plug was to be had; and deprived of a solace and a stimulus, on which sailors so much rely while at sea, the crew became absent, moody, and sadly tormented with the hypos. They were something like opium-smokers, suddenly cut off from their drug. They would sit on their chests, forlorn and moping; with a steadfast sadness, eying the forecastle lamp, at which they had lighted so many a pleasant pipe. With touching eloquence they recalled those happier evenings—the time of smoke and vapor; when, after a whole day's delectable "*chawing*," they beguiled themselves with their genial, and most companionable puffs.

One night, when they seemed more than usually cast down and disconsolate, Blunt, the Irish cockney, started up suddenly with an idea in his head—"Boys, let's search under the bunks!"

Bless you, Blunt! what a happy conceit!

Forthwith, the chests were dragged out; the dark places explored; and two sticks of *nail-rod* tobacco, and several old "*chaws*," thrown aside by sailors on some previous voyage, were their cheering reward. They were impartially divided by Jackson, who, upon this occasion, acquitted himself to the satisfaction of all.

Their mode of dividing this tobacco was the rather curious one generally adopted by sailors, when the highest possible degree of impartiality is desirable. I will describe it, recom-

mending its earnest consideration to all heirs, who may hereafter divide an inheritance; for if they adopted this nautical
method, that universally slanderous aphorism of Lavater
would be forever rendered nugatory—*"Expect not to understand any man till you have divided with him an inheritance."*

The *nail-rods* they cut as evenly as possible into as many
parts as there were men to be supplied; and this operation
having been performed in the presence of all, Jackson, placing
the tobacco before him, his face to the wall, and back to the
company, struck one of the bits of weed with his knife, crying
out, "Whose is this?" Whereupon a respondent, previously
pitched upon, replied, at a venture, from the opposite corner
of the forecastle, "Blunt's;" and to Blunt it went; and so on,
in like manner, till all were served.

I put it to you, lawyers—shade of Blackstone, I invoke
you—if a more impartial procedure could be imagined than
this?

But the nail-rods and last-voyage *"chaws"* were soon gone,
and then, after a short interval of comparative gayety, the
men again drooped, and relapsed into gloom.

They soon hit upon an ingenious device, however—but
not altogether new among seamen—to allay the severity of
the depression under which they languished. Ropes were unstranded, and the yarns picked apart; and, cut up into small
bits, were used as a substitute for the weed. Old ropes were
preferred; especially those which had long lain in the hold,
and had contracted an epicurean dampness, making still richer
their ancient, cheese-like flavor.

In the middle of most large ropes, there is a straight, central part, round which the exterior strands are twisted. When
in picking oakum, upon various occasions, I have chanced,
among the old junk used at such times, to light upon a fragment of this species of rope, I have ever taken, I know not
what kind of strange, nutty delight in untwisting it slowly,
and gradually coming upon its deftly hidden and aromatic
"heart;" for so this central piece is denominated.

It is generally of a rich, tawny, Indian hue, somewhat inclined to luster; is exceedingly agreeable to the touch; diffuses
a pungent odor, as of an old dusty bottle of Port, newly
opened above ground; and, altogether, is an object which no

man, who enjoys his dinners, could refrain from hanging over, and caressing.

Nor is this delectable morsel of *old junk* wanting in many interesting, mournful, and tragic suggestions. Who can say in what gales it may have been; in what remote seas it may have sailed? How many stout masts of seventy-fours and frigates it may have staid in the tempest? How deep it may have lain, as a hawser, at the bottom of strange harbors? What outlandish fish may have nibbled at it in the water, and what uncatalogued sea-fowl may have pecked at it, when forming part of a lofty stay or a shroud?

Now, this particular part of the rope, this nice little "cut" it was, that among the sailors was the most eagerly sought after. And getting hold of a foot or two of old cable, they would cut into it lovingly, to see whether it had any "*tenderloin*."

For my own part, nevertheless, I can not say that this titbit was at all an agreeable one in the mouth; however pleasant to the sight of an antiquary, or to the nose of an epicure in nautical fragrancies. Indeed, though possibly I might have been mistaken, I thought it had rather an astringent, acrid taste; probably induced by the tar, with which the flavor of all ropes is more or less vitiated. But the sailors seemed to like it, and at any rate nibbled at it with great gusto. They converted one pocket of their trowsers into a junk-shop, and when solicited by a shipmate for a "chaw," would produce a small coil of rope.

Another device adopted to alleviate their hardships, was the substitution of dried tea-leaves, in place of tobacco, for their pipes. No one has ever supped in a forecastle at sea, without having been struck by the prodigious residuum of tea-leaves, or cabbage stalks, in his tin-pot of bohea. There was no lack of material to supply every pipe-bowl among us.

I had almost forgotten to relate the most noteworthy thing in this matter; namely, that notwithstanding the general scarcity of the genuine weed, Jackson was provided with a supply; nor did it give out, until very shortly previous to our arrival in port.

In the lowest depths of despair at the loss of their precious solace, when the sailors would be seated inconsolable as the

Babylonish captives, Jackson would sit cross-legged in his
bunk, which was an upper one, and enveloped in a cloud of
tobacco smoke, would look down upon the mourners below,
with a sardonic grin at their forlornness.

He recalled to mind their folly in selling for filthy lucre,
their supplies of the weed; he painted their stupidity; he enlarged upon the sufferings they had brought upon themselves; he exaggerated those sufferings, and every way
derided, reproached, twitted, and hooted at them. No one
dared to return his scurrilous animadversions, nor did any
presume to ask him to relieve their necessities out of his fullness. On the contrary, as has been just related, they divided
with him the *nail-rods* they found.

The extraordinary dominion of this one miserable Jackson,
over twelve or fourteen strong, healthy tars, is a riddle, whose
solution must be left to the philosophers.

Chapter 55

THE CLOSING ALLUSION to Jackson in the chapter preceding, reminds me of a circumstance—which, perhaps, should have been mentioned before—that after we had been at sea about ten days, he pronounced himself too unwell to do duty, and accordingly went below to his bunk. And here, with the exception of a few brief intervals of sunning himself in fine weather, he remained on his back, or seated cross-legged, during the remainder of the homeward-bound passage.

Brooding there, in his infernal gloom, though nothing but a castaway sailor in canvas trowsers, this man was still a picture, worthy to be painted by the dark, moody hand of Salvator. In any of that master's lowering sea-pieces, representing the desolate crags of Calabria, with a midnight ship-wreck in the distance, this Jackson's would have been the face to paint for the doomed vessel's figure-head, seamed and blasted by lightning.

Though the more sneaking and cowardly of my shipmates whispered among themselves, that Jackson, sure of his wages, whether on duty or off, was only feigning indisposition, nevertheless it was plain that, from his excesses in Liverpool, the malady which had long fastened its fangs in his flesh, was now gnawing into his vitals.

His cheek became thinner and yellower, and the bones projected like those of a skull. His snaky eyes rolled in red sockets; nor could he lift his hand without a violent tremor; while his racking cough many a time startled us from sleep. Yet still in his tremulous grasp he swayed his scepter, and ruled us all like a tyrant to the last.

The weaker and weaker he grew, the more outrageous became his treatment of the crew. The prospect of the speedy and unshunable death now before him, seemed to exasperate his misanthropic soul into madness; and as if he had indeed sold it to Satan, he seemed determined to die with a curse between his teeth.

I can never think of him, even now, reclining in his bunk, and with short breaths panting out his maledictions, but I am reminded of that misanthrope upon the throne of the world—the diabolical Tiberius at Capreæ; who even in his self-exile, imbittered by bodily pangs, and unspeakable mental terrors only known to the damned on earth, yet did not give over his blasphemies, but endeavored to drag down with him to his own perdition, all who came within the evil spell of his power. And though Tiberius came in the succession of the Cæsars, and though unmatchable Tacitus has embalmed his carrion, yet do I account this Yankee Jackson full as dignified a personage as he, and as well meriting his lofty gallows in history; even though he was a nameless vagabond without an epitaph, and none, but I, narrate what he was. For there is no dignity in wickedness, whether in purple or rags; and hell is a democracy of devils, where all are equals. There, Nero howls side by side with his own malefactors. If Napoleon were truly but a martial murderer, I pay him no more homage than I would a felon. Though Milton's Satan dilutes our abhorrence with admiration, it is only because he is not a genuine being, but something altered from a genuine original. We gather not from the four gospels alone, any high-raised fancies concerning this Satan; we only know him from thence as the personification of the essence of evil, which, who but pickpockets and burglars will admire? But this takes not from the merit of our high-priest of poetry; it only enhances it, that with such unmitigated evil for his material, he should build up his most goodly structure.

But in historically canonizing on earth the condemned below, and lifting up and lauding the illustrious damned, we do but make ensamples of wickedness; and call upon ambition to do some great iniquity, and be sure of fame.

Chapter 56

Under the Lee of the Long-Boat, Redburn and Harry Hold Confidential Communion

A SWEET THING is a song; and though the Hebrew captives hung their harps on the willows, that they could not sing the melodies of Palestine before the haughty beards of the Babylonians; yet, to themselves, those melodies of other times and a distant land were sweet as the June dew on Hermon.

And poor Harry was as the Hebrews. He, too, had been carried away captive, though his chief captor and foe was himself; and he, too, many a night, was called upon to sing for those who through the day had insulted and derided him.

His voice was just the voice to proceed from a small, silken person like his; it was gentle and liquid, and meandered and tinkled through the words of a song, like a musical brook that winds and wantons by pied and pansied margins.

"I can't sing to-night"—sadly said Harry to the Dutchman, who with his watchmates requested him to while away the middle watch with his melody—"I can't sing to-night. But, Wellingborough," he whispered,—and I stooped my ear,— "come *you* with me under the lee of the long-boat, and there I'll hum you an air."

It was *The Banks of the Blue Moselle.*

Poor, poor Harry! and a thousand times friendless and forlorn! To be singing that thing, which was only meant to be warbled by falling fountains in gardens, or in elegant alcoves in drawing-rooms,—to be singing it here—*here*, as I live, under the tarry lee of our long-boat.

But he sang, and sang, as I watched the waves, and peopled them all with sprites, and cried "*chassez!*" "*hands across!*" to the multitudinous quadrilles, all danced on the moonlit, musical floor.

But though it went so hard with my friend to sing his songs to this ruffian crew, whom he hated, even in his dreams, till the foam flew from his mouth while he slept; yet at last I prevailed upon him to master his feelings, and make them subservient to his interests. For so delighted, even with the rudest minstrelsy, are sailors, that I well knew Harry possessed a spell over them, which, for the time at least, they could not resist; and it might induce them to treat with more deference the being who was capable of yielding them such delight. Carlo's organ they did not so much care for; but the voice of my Bury blade was an accordeon in their ears.

So one night, on the windlass, he sat and sang; and from the ribald jests so common to sailors, the men slid into silence at every verse. Hushed, and more hushed they grew, till at last Harry sat among them like Orpheus among the charmed leopards and tigers. Harmless now the fangs with which they were wont to tear my zebra, and backward curled in velvet paws; and fixed their once glaring eyes in fascinated and fascinating brilliancy. Ay, still and hissingly all, for a time, they relinquished their prey.

Now, during the voyage, the treatment of the crew threw Harry more and more upon myself for companionship; and few can keep constant company with another, without revealing some, at least, of their secrets; for all of us yearn for sympathy, even if we do not for love; and to be intellectually alone is a thing only tolerable to genius, whose cherisher and inspirer is solitude.

But though my friend became more communicative concerning his past career than ever he had been before, yet he did not make plain many things in his hitherto but partly divulged history, which I was very curious to know; and especially he never made the remotest allusion to aught connected with our trip to London; while the oath of secrecy by which he had bound me held my curiosity on that point a captive. However, as it was, Harry made many very interesting disclosures; and if he did not gratify me more in that respect, he atoned for it in a measure, by dwelling upon the future, and the prospects, such as they were, which the future held out to him.

He confessed that he had no money but a few shillings left from the expenses of our return from London; that only by selling some more of his clothing, could he pay for his first week's board in New York; and that he was altogether without any regular profession or business, upon which, by his own exertions, he could securely rely for support. And yet, he told me that he was determined never again to return to England; and that somewhere in America he must work out his temporal felicity.

"I have forgotten England," he said, "and never more mean to think of it; so tell me, Wellingborough, what am I to do in America?"

It was a puzzling question, and full of grief to me, who, young though I was, had been well rubbed, curried, and ground down to fine powder in the hopper of an evil fortune, and who therefore could sympathize with one in similar circumstances. For though we may look grave and behave kindly and considerately to a friend in calamity; yet, if we have never actually experienced something like the woe that weighs him down, we can not with the best grace proffer our sympathy. And perhaps there is no true sympathy but between equals; and it may be, that we should distrust that man's sincerity, who stoops to condole with us.

So Harry and I, two friendless wanderers, beguiled many a long watch by talking over our common affairs. But inefficient, as a benefactor, as I certainly was; still, being an American, and returning to my home; even as he was a stranger, and hurrying from his; therefore, I stood toward him in the attitude of the prospective doer of the honors of my country; I accounted him the nation's guest. Hence, I esteemed it more befitting, that I should rather talk with him, than he with me: that *his* prospects and plans should engage our attention, in preference to my own.

Now, seeing that Harry was so brave a songster, and could sing such bewitching airs: I suggested whether his musical talents could not be turned to account. The thought struck him most favorably—"Gad, my boy, you have hit it, you have," and then he went on to mention, that in some places in England, it was customary for two or three young men of highly respectable families, of undoubted antiquity, but unfortunately in lamentably decayed circumstances, and threadbare coats;—it was customary for two or three young gentlemen, so situated, to obtain their livelihood by their voices: coining their silvery songs into silvery shillings.

They wandered from door to door, and rang the bell—*Are the ladies and gentlemen in?* Seeing them at least gentlemanly looking, if not sumptuously appareled, the servant generally admitted them at once; and when the people entered to greet them, their spokesman would rise with a gentle bow, and a smile, and say, *We come, ladies and gentlemen, to sing you a song: we are singers, at your service.* And so, without waiting reply, forth they burst into song; and having most mellifluous voices, enchanted and transported all auditors; so much so, that at the conclusion of the entertainment, they very seldom failed to be well recompensed, and departed with an invitation to return again, and make the occupants of that dwelling once more delighted and happy.

"Could not something of this kind, now, be done in New York?" said Harry, "or are there no parlors with ladies in them, there?" he anxiously added.

Again I assured him, as I had often done before, that New York was a civilized and enlightened town; with a large population, fine streets, fine houses, nay, plenty of omnibuses; and that for the most part, he would almost think himself in England; so similar to England, in essentials, was this outlandish America that haunted him.

I could not but be struck—and had I not been, from my birth, as it were, a cosmopolite—I had been amazed at his skepticism with regard to the civilization of my native land. A greater patriot than myself might have resented his insinuations. He seemed to think that we Yankees lived in wigwams, and wore bear-skins. After all, Harry was a spice of a Cockney, and had shut up his Christendom in London.

Having then assured him, that I could see no reason, why he should not play the troubadour in New York, as well as elsewhere; he suddenly popped upon me the question, whether I would not join him in the enterprise; as it would be quite out of the question to go alone on such a business.

Said I, "My dear Bury, I have no more voice for a ditty, than a dumb man has for an oration. Sing? Such Macadamized lungs have I, that I think myself well off, that I can talk; let alone nightingaling."

So that plan was quashed; and by-and-by Harry began to give up the idea of singing himself into a livelihood.

"No, I won't sing for my mutton," said he—"what would Lady Georgiana say?"

"If I could see her ladyship once, I might tell you, Harry," returned I, who did not exactly doubt him, but felt ill at ease for my bosom friend's conscience, when he alluded to his various noble and right honorable friends and relations.

"But surely, Bury, my friend, you must write a clerkly hand, among your other accomplishments; and *that* at least, will be sure to help you."

"I *do* write a hand," he gladly rejoined—"there, look at the implement!—do you not think, that such a hand as *that* might dot an *i*, or cross a *t*, with a touching grace and tenderness?"

Indeed, but it did betoken a most excellent penmanship. It was small; and the fingers were long and thin; the knuckles softly rounded; the nails hemispherical at the base; and the smooth palm furnishing few characters for an Egyptian fortune-teller to read. It was not as the sturdy farmer's hand of Cincinnatus, who followed the plough and guided the state; but it was as the perfumed hand of Petronius Arbiter, that elegant young buck of a Roman, who once cut great Seneca dead in the forum.

His hand alone, would have entitled my Bury blade to the suffrages of that Eastern potentate, who complimented Lord Byron upon his feline fingers, declaring that they furnished indubitable evidence of his noble birth. And so it did: for Lord Byron was as all the rest of us—the son of a *man*. And so are the dainty-handed, and wee-footed half-cast paupers in Lima; who, if their hands and feet were entitled to consideration, would constitute the oligarchy of all Peru.

Folly and foolishness! to think that a gentleman is known by his finger-nails, like Nebuchadnezzar, when his grew long in the pasture: or that the badge of nobility is to be found in the smallness of the foot, when even a fish has no foot at all!

Dandies! amputate yourselves, if you will; but know, and be assured, oh, democrats, that, like a pyramid, a great man stands on a broad base. It is only the brittle porcelain pagoda, that tottles on a toe.

But though Harry's hand was lady-like looking, and had once been white as the queen's cambric handkerchief, and free from a stain as the reputation of Diana; yet, his late pulling and hauling of halyards and clew-lines, and his occasional dabbling in tar-pots and slush-shoes, had somewhat subtracted from its original daintiness.

Often he ruefully eyed it.

Oh! hand! thought Harry, ah, hand! what have you come to? Is it seemly, that you should be polluted with pitch, when you once handed countesses to their coaches? Is *this* the hand I kissed to the divine Georgiana? with which I pledged Lady Blessington, and ratified my bond to Lord Lovely? *This* the hand that Georgiana clasped to her bosom, when she vowed she was mine?—Out of sight, recreant and apostate!—deep down—disappear in this foul monkey-jacket pocket where I thrust you!

After many long conversations, it was at last pretty well decided, that upon our arrival at New York, some means should be taken among my few friends there, to get Harry a place in a mercantile house, where he might flourish his pen, and gently exercise his delicate digits, by traversing some soft foolscap; in the same way that slim, pallid ladies are gently drawn through a park for an airing.

Chapter 57

ALMOST A FAMINE

"MAMMY! mammy! come and see the sailors eating out of little troughs, just like our pigs at home." Thus exclaimed one of the steerage children, who at dinner-time was peeping down into the forecastle, where the crew were assembled, helping themselves from the "kids," which, indeed, resemble hog-troughs not a little.

"Pigs, is it?" coughed Jackson, from his bunk, where he sat presiding over the banquet, but not partaking, like a devil who had lost his appetite by chewing sulphur.—"Pigs, is it?—and the day is close by, ye spalpeens, when you'll want to be after taking a sup at our troughs!"

This malicious prophecy proved true.

As day followed day without glimpse of shore or reef, and head winds drove the ship back, as hounds a deer; the improvidence and shortsightedness of the passengers in the steerage, with regard to their outfits for the voyage, began to be followed by the inevitable results.

Many of them at last went aft to the mate, saying that they had nothing to eat, their provisions were expended, and they must be supplied from the ship's stores, or starve.

This was told to the captain, who was obliged to issue a ukase from the cabin, that every steerage passenger, whose destitution was demonstrable, should be given one sea-biscuit and two potatoes a day; a sort of substitute for a muffin and a brace of poached eggs.

But this scanty ration was quite insufficient to satisfy their hunger: hardly enough to satisfy the necessities of a healthy adult. The consequence was, that all day long, and all through the night, scores of the emigrants went about the decks, seeking what they might devour. They plundered the chicken-coop; and disguising the fowls, cooked them at the public galley. They made inroads upon the pig-pen in the boat, and carried off a promising young shoat: *him* they devoured raw, not venturing to make an incognito of his carcass; they prowled about the cook's caboose, till he threatened them with a ladle of scalding water; they way-laid the steward on his regular excursions from the cook to the cabin; they hung round the forecastle, to rob the bread-barge; they beset the sailors, like beggars in the streets, craving a mouthful in the name of the Church.

At length, to such excesses were they driven, that the Grand Russian, Captain Riga, issued another ukase, and to this effect: Whatsoever emigrant is found guilty of stealing, the same shall be tied into the rigging and flogged.

Upon this, there were secret movements in the steerage, which almost alarmed me for the safety of the ship; but nothing serious took place, after all; and they even acquiesced in, or did not resent, a singular punishment which the captain caused to be inflicted upon a culprit of their clan, as a substitute for a flogging. For no doubt he thought that such rigorous discipline as *that* might exasperate five hundred emigrants into an insurrection.

A head was fitted to one of the large deck-tubs—the half of a cask; and into this head a hole was cut; also, two smaller holes in the bottom of the tub. The head—divided in the middle, across the diameter of the orifice—was now fitted round the culprit's neck; and he was forthwith coopered up into the tub, which rested on his shoulders, while his legs protruded through the holes in the bottom.

It was a burden to carry; but the man could walk with it; and so ridiculous was his appearance, that spite of the indignity, he himself laughed with the rest at the figure he cut.

"Now, Pat, my boy," said the mate, "fill that big wooden belly of yours, if you can."

Compassionating his situation, our old "doctor" used to give him alms of food, placing it upon the cask-head before him; till at last, when the time for deliverance came, Pat protested against mercy, and would fain have continued playing Diogenes in the tub for the rest of this starving voyage.

Chapter 58

Though the Highlander Puts into No Harbor
As Yet; She Here and There Leaves Many of
Her Passengers Behind

Although fast-sailing ships, blest with prosperous breezes, have frequently made the run across the Atlantic in eighteen days; yet, it is not uncommon for other vessels to be forty, or fifty, and even sixty, seventy, eighty, and ninety days, in making the same passage. Though in the latter cases, some signal calamity or incapacity must occasion so great a detention. It is also true, that generally the passage out from America is shorter than the return; which is to be ascribed to the prevalence of westerly winds.

We had been outside of Cape Clear upward of twenty days, still harassed by head-winds, though with pleasant weather upon the whole, when we were visited by a succession of rain storms, which lasted the greater part of a week.

During this interval, the emigrants were obliged to remain below; but this was nothing strange to some of them; who, not recovering, while at sea, from their first attack of sea-sickness, seldom or never made their appearance on deck, during the entire passage.

During the week, now in question, fire was only once made in the public galley. This occasioned a good deal of domestic work to be done in the steerage, which otherwise would have been done in the open air. When the lulls of the rain-storms would intervene, some unusually cleanly emigrant would climb to the deck, with a bucket of slops, to toss into the sea. No experience seemed sufficient to instruct some of these ignorant people in the simplest, and most elemental principles of ocean-life. Spite of all lectures on the subject, several would continue to shun the leeward side of the vessel, with their slops. One morning, when it was blowing very fresh, a simple fellow pitched over a gallon or two of something to windward. Instantly it flew back in his face; and also, in the face of the chief mate, who happened to be standing by at the time. The offender was collared, and shaken on the spot; and ironically commanded, never, for the future, to throw any thing to windward at sea, but fine ashes and scalding hot water.

During the frequent *hard blows* we experienced, the hatchways on the steerage were, at intervals, hermetically closed; sealing down in their noisome den, those scores of human beings. It was something to be marveled at, that the shocking fate, which, but a short time ago, overtook the poor passengers in a Liverpool steamer in the Channel, during similar stormy weather, and under similar treatment, did not overtake some of the emigrants of the Highlander.

Nevertheless, it was, beyond question, this noisome confinement in so close, unventilated, and crowded a den: joined to the deprivation of sufficient food, from which many were suffering; which, helped by their personal uncleanliness, brought on a malignant fever.

The first report was, that two persons were affected. No sooner was it known, than the mate promptly repaired to the medicine-chest in the cabin: and with the remedies deemed suitable, descended into the steerage. But the medicines proved of no avail; the invalids rapidly grew worse; and two more of the emigrants became infected.

Upon this, the captain himself went to see them; and returning, sought out a certain alleged physician among the cabin-passengers; begging him to wait upon the sufferers; hinting that, thereby, he might prevent the disease from extending into the cabin itself. But this person denied being a physician; and from fear of contagion—though he did not confess that to be the motive—refused even to enter the steerage.

The cases increased: the utmost alarm spread through the ship: and scenes ensued, over which, for the most part, a vail must be drawn; for such is the fastidiousness of some readers, that, many times, they must lose the most striking incidents in a narrative like mine.

Many of the panic-stricken emigrants would fain now have domiciled on deck; but being so scantily clothed, the wretched weather—wet, cold, and tempestuous—drove the best part of them again below. Yet any other human beings, perhaps, would rather have faced the most outrageous storm, than continued to breathe the pestilent air of the steerage. But some of these poor people must have been so used to the most abasing calamities, that the atmosphere of a lazar-house almost seemed their natural air.

The first four cases happened to be in adjoining bunks; and the emigrants who slept in the farther part of the steerage, threw up a barricade in front of those bunks; so as to cut off communication. But this was no sooner reported to the captain, than he ordered it to be thrown down; since it could be of no possible benefit; but would only make still worse, what was already direful enough.

It was not till after a good deal of mingled threatening and coaxing, that the mate succeeded in getting the sailors below, to accomplish the captain's order.

The sight that greeted us, upon entering, was wretched indeed. It was like entering a crowded jail. From the rows of rude bunks, hundreds of meager, begrimed faces were turned upon us; while seated upon the chests, were scores of unshaven men, smoking tea-leaves, and creating a suffocating vapor. But this vapor was better than the native air of the place, which from almost unbelievable causes, was foetid in the extreme. In every corner, the females were huddled together, weeping and lamenting; children were asking bread from their mothers, who had none to give; and old men, seated upon the floor, were leaning back against the heads of the water-casks, with closed eyes and fetching their breath with a gasp.

At one end of the place was seen the barricade, hiding the invalids; while—notwithstanding the crowd—in front of it was a clear area, which the fear of contagion had left open.

"That bulkhead must come down," cried the mate, in a voice that rose above the din. "Take hold of it, boys."

But hardly had we touched the chests composing it, when a crowd of pale-faced, infuriated men rushed up; and with terrific howls, swore they would slay us, if we did not desist.

"Haul it down!" roared the mate.

But the sailors fell back, murmuring something about merchant seamen having no pensions in case of being maimed, and they had not shipped to fight fifty to one. Further efforts were made by the mate, who at last had recourse to entreaty; but it would not do; and we were obliged to depart, without achieving our object.

About four o'clock that morning, the first four died. They were all men; and the scenes which ensued were frantic in the extreme. Certainly, the bottomless profound of the sea, over which we were sailing, concealed nothing more frightful.

Orders were at once passed to bury the dead. But this was unnecessary. By their own countrymen, they were torn from the clasp of their wives, rolled in their own bedding, with ballast-stones, and with hurried rites, were dropped into the ocean.

At this time, ten more men had caught the disease; and with a degree of devotion worthy all praise, the mate attended them with his medicines; but the captain did not again go down to them.

It was all-important now that the steerage should be purified; and had it not been for the rains and squalls, which would have made it madness to turn such a number of women and children upon the wet and unsheltered decks, the steerage passengers would have been ordered above, and their den have been given a thorough cleansing. But, for the present, this was out of the question. The sailors peremptorily refused to go among the defilements to remove them; and so besotted were the greater part of the emigrants themselves, that though the necessity of the case was forcibly painted to them, they would not lift a hand to assist in what seemed their own salvation.

The panic in the cabin was now very great; and for fear of contagion to themselves, the cabin passengers would fain have made a prisoner of the captain, to prevent him from going forward beyond the mainmast. Their clamors at last induced him to tell the two mates, that for the present they must sleep and take their meals elsewhere than in their old quarters, which communicated with the cabin.

On land, a pestilence is fearful enough; but there, many can flee from an infected city; whereas, in a ship, you are locked and bolted in the very hospital itself. Nor is there any possibility of escape from it; and in so small and crowded a place, no precaution can effectually guard against contagion.

Horrible as the sights of the steerage now were, the cabin, perhaps, presented a scene equally despairing. Many, who had seldom prayed before, now implored the merciful heavens, night and day, for fair winds and fine weather. Trunks were opened for Bibles; and at last, even prayer-meetings were held over the very table across which the loud jest had been so often heard.

Strange, though almost universal, that the seemingly nearer prospect of that death which any body at any time may die, should produce these spasmodic devotions, when an everlasting Asiatic Cholera is forever thinning our ranks; and die by death we all must at last.

On the second day, seven died, one of whom was the little tailor: on the third, four; on the fourth, six, of whom one was the Greenland sailor, and another, a woman in the cabin, whose death, however, was afterward supposed to have been purely induced by her fears. These last deaths brought the panic to its height; and sailors, officers, cabin-passengers, and emigrants—all looked upon each other like lepers. All but the only true leper among us—the mariner Jackson, who seemed elated with the thought, that for *him*—already in the deadly clutches of another disease—no danger was to be apprehended from a fever which only swept off the comparatively healthy. Thus, in the midst of the despair of the healthful, this incurable invalid was not cast down; not, at least, by the same considerations that appalled the rest.

And still, beneath a gray, gloomy sky, the doomed craft beat on; now on this tack, now on that; battling against hostile blasts, and drenched in rain and spray; scarcely making an inch of progress toward her port.

On the sixth morning, the weather merged into a gale, to which we stripped our ship to a storm-stay-sail. In ten hours' time, the waves ran in mountains; and the Highlander rose and fell like some vast buoy on the water. Shrieks and lamentations were driven to leeward, and drowned in the roar of the wind among the cordage; while we gave to the gale the blackened bodies of five more of the dead.

But as the dying departed, the places of two of them were filled in the rolls of humanity, by the birth of two infants, whom the plague, panic, and gale had hurried into the world before their time. The first cry of one of these infants, was almost simultaneous with the splash of its father's body in the sea. Thus we come and we go. But, surrounded by death, both mothers and babes survived.

At midnight, the wind went down; leaving a long, rolling sea; and, for the first time in a week, a clear, starry sky.

In the first morning-watch, I sat with Harry on the wind-lass, watching the billows; which, seen in the night, seemed real hills, upon which fortresses might have been built; and real valleys, in which villages, and groves, and gardens, might have nestled. It was like a landscape in Switzerland; for down into those dark, purple glens, often tumbled the white foam of the wave-crests, like avalanches; while the seething and boiling that ensued, seemed the swallowing up of human beings.

By afternoon of the next day this heavy sea subsided; and we bore down on the waves, with all our canvas set; stun'-sails alow and aloft; and our best steersman at the helm; the captain himself at his elbow;—bowling along, with a fair, cheering breeze over the taffrail.

The decks were cleared, and swabbed bone-dry; and then, all the emigrants who were not invalids, poured themselves out on deck, snuffing the delightful air, spreading their damp bedding in the sun, and regaling themselves with the gener-ous charity of the captain, who of late had seen fit to increase their allowance of food. A detachment of them now joined a band of the crew, who proceeding into the steerage, with buckets and brooms, gave it a thorough cleansing, sending on deck, I know not how many bucketsful of defilements. It was more like cleaning out a stable, than a retreat for men and women. This day we buried three; the next day one, and then the pestilence left us, with seven convalescent; who, placed near the opening of the hatchway, soon rallied under the skill-ful treatment, and even tender care of the mate.

But even under this favorable turn of affairs, much appre-hension was still entertained, lest in crossing the Grand Banks of Newfoundland, the fogs, so generally encountered there, might bring on a return of the fever. But, to the joy of all hands, our fair wind still held on; and we made a rapid run across these dreaded shoals, and southward steered for New York.

Our days were now fair and mild, and though the wind abated, yet we still ran our course over a pleasant sea. The steerage-passengers—at least by far the greater number—wore a still, subdued aspect, though a little cheered by the genial air, and the hopeful thought of soon reaching their port. But those who had lost fathers, husbands, wives, or children, needed no crape, to reveal to others, who they were. Hard and bitter indeed was their lot; for with the poor and desolate, grief is no indulgence of mere sentiment, however sincere, but a gnawing reality, that eats into their vital beings; they have no kind condolers, and bland physicians, and troops of sympathizing friends; and they must toil, though to-morrow be the burial, and their pall-bearers throw down the hammer to lift up the coffin.

How, then, with these emigrants, who, three thousand miles from home, suddenly found themselves deprived of brothers and husbands, with but a few pounds, or perhaps but a few shillings, to buy food in a strange land?

As for the passengers in the cabin, who now so jocund as they? drawing nigh, with their long purses and goodly portmanteaus to the promised land, without fear of fate. One and all were generous and gay, the jelly-eyed old gentleman, before spoken of, gave a shilling to the steward.

The lady who had died, was an elderly person, an American, returning from a visit to an only brother in London. She had no friend or relative on board, hence, as there is little mourning for a stranger dying among strangers, her memory had been buried with her body.

But the thing most worthy of note among these now light-hearted people in feathers, was the gay way in which some of them bantered others, upon the panic into which nearly all had been thrown.

And since, if the extremest fear of a crowd in a panic of peril, proves grounded on causes sufficient, they must then indeed come to perish;—therefore it is, that at such times they must make up their minds either to die, or else survive to be taunted by their fellow-men with their fear. For except

in extraordinary instances of exposure, there are few living
men, who, at bottom, are not very slow to admit that any
other living men have ever been very much nearer death than
themselves. Accordingly, *craven* is the phrase too often applied to any one who, with however good reason, has been
appalled at the prospect of sudden death, and yet lived to
escape it. Though, should he have perished in conformity
with his fears, not a syllable of *craven* would you hear. This
is the language of one, who more than once has beheld the
scenes, whence these principles have been deduced. The subject invites much subtle speculation; for in every being's ideas
of death, and his behavior when it suddenly menaces him, lies
the best index to his life and his faith. Though the Christian
era had not then begun, Socrates died the death of the Christian; and though Hume was not a Christian in theory, yet he,
too, died the death of the Christian,—humble, composed,
without bravado; and though the most skeptical of philosophical skeptics, yet full of that firm, creedless faith, that embraces the spheres. Seneca died dictating to posterity;
Petronius lightly discoursing of essences and love-songs; and
Addison, calling upon Christendom to behold how calmly a
Christian could die; but not even the last of these three, perhaps, died the best death of the Christian.

The cabin passenger who had used to read prayers while
the rest kneeled against the transoms and settees, was one of
the merry young sparks, who had occasioned such agonies of
jealousy to the poor tailor, now no more. In his rakish vest,
and dangling watch-chain, this same youth, with all the awfulness of fear, had led the earnest petitions of his companions; supplicating mercy, where before he had never solicited
the slightest favor. More than once had he been seen thus
engaged by the observant steersman at the helm: who looked
through the little glass in the cabin bulk-head.

But this youth was an April man; the storm had departed;
and now he shone in the sun, none braver than he.

One of his jovial companions ironically advised him to enter into holy orders upon his arrival in New York.

"Why so?" said the other, "have I such an orotund voice?"

"No;" profanely returned his friend—"but you are a coward—just the man to be a parson, and pray."

However this narrative of the circumstances attending the
fever among the emigrants on the Highlander may appear;
and though these things happened so long ago; yet just such
events, nevertheless, are perhaps taking place today. But the
only account you obtain of such events, is generally contained
in a newspaper paragraph, under the shipping-head. *There* is
the obituary of the destitute dead, who die on the sea. They
die, like the billows that break on the shore, and no more are
heard or seen. But in the events, thus merely initialized in the
catalogue of passing occurrences, and but glanced at by the
readers of news, who are more taken up with paragraphs of
fuller flavor; what a world of life and death, what a world of
humanity and its woes, lies shrunk into a three-worded sentence!

You see no plague-ship driving through a stormy sea; you
hear no groans of despair; you see no corpses thrown over
the bulwarks; you mark not the wringing hands and torn hair
of widows and orphans:—all is a blank. And one of these
blanks I have but filled up, in recounting the details of the
Highlander's calamity.

Besides that natural tendency, which hurries into oblivion
the last woes of the poor; other causes combine to suppress
the detailed circumstances of disasters like these. Such things,
if widely known, operate unfavorably to the ship, and make
her a bad name; and to avoid detention at quarantine, a captain will state the case in the most palliating light, and strive
to hush it up, as much as he can.

In no better place than this, perhaps, can a few words be
said, concerning emigrant ships in general.

Let us waive that agitated national topic, as to whether
such multitudes of foreign poor should be landed on our
American shores; let us waive it, with the one only thought,
that if they can get here, they have God's right to come;
though they bring all Ireland and her miseries with them. For
the whole world is the patrimony of the whole world; there
is no telling who does not own a stone in the Great Wall of
China. But we waive all this; and will only consider, how best
the emigrants can come hither, since come they do, and come
they must and will.

Of late, a law has been passed in Congress, restricting ships to a certain number of emigrants, according to a certain rate. If this law were enforced, much good might be done; and so also might much good be done, were the English law likewise enforced, concerning the fixed supply of food for every emigrant embarking from Liverpool. But it is hardly to be believed, that either of these laws is observed.

But in all respects, no legislation, even nominally, reaches the hard lot of the emigrant. What ordinance makes it obligatory upon the captain of a ship, to supply the steerage-passengers with decent lodgings, and give them light and air in that foul den, where they are immured, during a long voyage across the Atlantic? What ordinance necessitates him to place the *galley*, or steerage-passengers' stove, in a dry place of shelter, where the emigrants can do their cooking during a storm, or wet weather? What ordinance obliges him to give them more room on deck, and let them have an occasional run fore and aft?—There is no law concerning these things. And if there was, who but some Howard in office would see it enforced? and how seldom is there a Howard in office!

We talk of the Turks, and abhor the cannibals; but may not some of *them*, go to heaven, before some of *us*? We may have civilized bodies and yet barbarous souls. We are blind to the real sights of this world; deaf to its voice; and dead to its death. And not till we know, that one grief outweighs ten thousand joys, will we become what Christianity is striving to make us.

Chapter 59

THE LAST END OF JACKSON

"OFF CAPE COD!" said the steward, coming forward from the quarter-deck, where the captain had just been taking his noon observation; sweeping the vast horizon with his quadrant, like a dandy circumnavigating the dress-circle of an amphitheater with his glass.

Off Cape Cod! and in the shore-bloom that came to us—even from that desert of sand-hillocks—methought I could almost distinguish the fragrance of the rose-bush my sisters and I had planted, in our far inland garden at home. Delicious odors are those of our mother Earth; which like a flower-pot set with a thousand shrubs, greets the eager voyager from afar.

The breeze was stiff, and so drove us along that we turned over two broad, blue furrows from our bows, as we plowed the watery prairie. By night it was a reef-topsail-breeze; but so impatient was the captain to make his port before a shift of wind overtook us, that even yet we carried a main-topgallant-sail, though the light mast sprung like a switch.

In the second dog-watch, however, the breeze became such, that at last the order was given to douse the top-gallant-sail, and clap a reef into all three top-sails.

While the men were settling away the halyards on deck, and before they had begun to haul out the reef-tackles, to the surprise of several, Jackson came up from the forecastle, and, for the first time in four weeks or more, took hold of a rope.

Like most seamen, who during the greater part of a voyage, have been off duty from sickness, he was, perhaps, desirous, just previous to entering port, of reminding the captain of his existence, and also that he expected his wages; but, alas! his wages proved the wages of sin.

At no time could he better signalize his disposition to work, than upon an occasion like the present; which generally attracts every soul on deck, from the captain to the child in the steerage.

His aspect was damp and death-like; the blue hollows of his eyes were like vaults full of snakes; and issuing so unexpectedly from his dark tomb in the forecastle, he looked like a man raised from the dead.

Before the sailors had made fast the reef-tackle, Jackson was tottering up the rigging; thus getting the start of them, and securing his place at the extreme weather-end of the topsail-yard—which in reefing is accounted the post of honor. For it was one of the characteristics of this man, that though when on duty he would shy away from mere dull work in a calm, yet in tempest-time he always claimed the van, and would yield it to none; and this, perhaps, was one cause of his unbounded dominion over the men.

Soon, we were all strung along the main-topsail-yard; the ship rearing and plunging under us, like a runaway steed; each man griping his reef-point, and sideways leaning, dragging the sail over toward Jackson, whose business it was to confine the reef corner to the yard.

His hat and shoes were off; and he rode the yard-arm end, leaning backward to the gale, and pulling at the earing-rope, like a bridle. At all times, this is a moment of frantic exertion with sailors, whose spirits seem then to partake of the commotion of the elements, as they hang in the gale, between heaven and earth; and *then* it is, too, that they are the most profane.

"Haul out to windward!" coughed Jackson, with a blasphemous cry, and he threw himself back with a violent strain upon the bridle in his hand. But the wild words were hardly out of his mouth, when his hands dropped to his side, and the bellying sail was spattered with a torrent of blood from his lungs.

As the man next him stretched out his arm to save, Jackson fell headlong from the yard, and with a long seethe, plunged like a diver into the sea.

It was when the ship had rolled to windward, which, with the long projection of the yard-arm over the side, made him strike far out upon the water. His fall was seen by the whole upward-gazing crowd on deck, some of whom were spotted with the blood that trickled from the sail, while they raised a spontaneous cry, so shrill and wild, that a blind man might have known something deadly had happened.

Clutching our reef-points, we hung over the stick, and gazed down to the one white, bubbling spot, which had closed over the head of our shipmate; but the next minute it was brewed into the common yeast of the waves, and Jackson never arose. We waited a few minutes, expecting an order to descend, haul back the fore-yard, and man the boat; but instead of that, the next sound that greeted us was, "Bear a hand, and reef away, men!" from the mate.

Indeed, upon reflection, it would have been idle to attempt to save Jackson; for besides that he must have been dead, ere he struck the sea—and if he had not been dead then, the first immersion must have driven his soul from his lacerated lungs—our jolly-boat would have taken full fifteen minutes to launch into the waves.

And here it should be said, that the thoughtless security in which too many sea-captains indulge, would, in case of some sudden disaster befalling the Highlander, have let us all drop into our graves.

Like most merchant ships, we had but two boats: the long-boat and the jolly-boat. The long-boat, by far the largest and stoutest of the two, was permanently bolted down to the deck, by iron bars attached to its sides. It was almost as much of a fixture as the vessel's keel. It was filled with pigs, fowls, firewood, and coals. Over this the jolly-boat was capsized without a *thole-pin* in the gunwales; its bottom bleaching and cracking in the sun.

Judge, then, what promise of salvation for us, had we ship-wrecked; yet in this state, one merchant ship out of three, keeps its boats. To be sure, no vessel full of emigrants, by any possible precautions, could in case of a fatal disaster at sea, hope to save the tenth part of the souls on board; yet provision should certainly be made for a handful of survivors, to carry home the tidings of her loss; for even in the worst of the calamities that befell patient Job, some *one* at least of his servants escaped to report it.

In a way that I never could fully account for, the sailors, in my hearing at least, and Harry's, never made the slightest allusion to the departed Jackson. One and all they seemed tacitly to unite in hushing up his memory among them. Whether it was, that the severity of the bondage under which this man held every one of them, did really corrode in their secret hearts, that they thought to repress the recollection of a thing so degrading, I can not determine; but certain it was, that *his* death was *their* deliverance; which they celebrated by an elevation of spirits, unknown before. Doubtless, this was to be in part imputed, however, to their now drawing near to their port.

Chapter 60

HOME AT LAST

NEXT DAY was Sunday; and the mid-day sun shone upon a glassy sea.

After the uproar of the breeze and the gale, this profound, pervading calm seemed suited to the tranquil spirit of a day, which, in godly towns, makes quiet vistas of the most tumultuous thoroughfares.

The ship lay gently rolling in the soft, subdued ocean swell; while all around were faint white spots; and nearer to, broad, milky patches, betokening the vicinity of scores of ships, all bound to one common port, and tranced in one common calm. Here the long, devious wakes from Europe, Africa, India, and Peru converged to a line, which braided them all in one.

Full before us quivered and danced, in the noon-day heat and mid-air, the green heights of New Jersey; and by an optical delusion, the blue sea seemed to flow under them.

The sailors whistled and whistled for a wind; the impatient cabin-passengers were arrayed in their best; and the emigrants clustered around the bows, with eyes intent upon the long-sought land.

But leaning over, in a reverie, against the side, my Carlo gazed down into the calm, violet sea, as if it were an eye that answered his own; and turning to Harry, said, "This America's skies must be down in the sea; for, looking down in this water, I behold what, in Italy, we also behold overhead. Ah! after all, I find my Italy somewhere, wherever I go. I even found it in rainy Liverpool."

Presently, up came a dainty breeze, wafting to us a white wing from the shore—the pilot-boat! Soon a monkey-jacket mounted the side, and was beset by the captain and cabin people for news. And out of bottomless pockets came bundles of newspapers, which were eagerly caught by the throng.

The captain now abdicated in the pilot's favor, who proved to be a tiger of a fellow, keeping us hard at work, pulling and hauling the braces, and trimming the ship, to catch the least *cat's-paw* of wind.

When, among sea-worn people, a strange man from shore suddenly stands among them, with the smell of the land in his beard, it conveys a realization of the vicinity of the green grass, that not even the distant sight of the shore itself can transcend.

The steerage was now as a bedlam; trunks and chests were locked and tied round with ropes; and a general washing and rinsing of faces and hands was beheld. While this was going on, forth came an order from the quarter-deck, for every bed, blanket, bolster, and bundle of straw in the steerage to be committed to the deep.—A command that was received by the emigrants with dismay, and then with wrath. But they were assured, that this was indispensable to the getting rid of an otherwise long detention of some weeks at the quarantine. They therefore reluctantly complied; and overboard went pallet and pillow. Following them, went old pots and pans, bottles and baskets. So, all around, the sea was strewn with stuffed bed-ticks, that limberly floated on the waves— couches for all mermaids who were not fastidious. Numberless things of this sort, tossed overboard from emigrant ships nearing the harbor of New York, drift in through the Narrows, and are deposited on the shores of Staten Island; along whose eastern beach I have often walked, and speculated upon the broken jugs, torn pillows, and dilapidated baskets at my feet.

A second order was now passed for the emigrants to muster their forces, and give the steerage a final, thorough cleaning with sand and water. And to this they were incited by the same warning which had induced them to make an offering to Neptune of their bedding. The place was then fumigated, and dried with pans of coals from the galley; so that by evening, no stranger would have imagined, from her appearance, that the Highlander had made otherwise than a tidy and prosperous voyage. Thus, some sea-captains take good heed that benevolent citizens shall not get a glimpse of the true condition of the steerage while at sea.

That night it again fell calm; but next morning, though the wind was somewhat against us, we set sail for the Narrows;

and making short tacks, at last ran through, almost bringing
our jib-boom over one of the forts.

An early shower had refreshed the woods and fields, that
glowed with a glorious green; and to our salted lungs, the
land breeze was spiced with aromas. The steerage passengers
almost neighed with delight, like horses brought back to
spring pastures; and every eye and ear in the Highlander was
full of the glad sights and sounds of the shore.

No more did we think of the gale and the plague; nor turn
our eyes upward to the stains of blood, still visible on the
topsail, whence Jackson had fallen; but we fixed our gaze on
the orchards and meads, and like thirsty men, drank in all their
dew.

On the Staten Island side, a white staff displayed a pale
yellow flag, denoting the habitation of the quarantine officer;
for as if to symbolize the yellow fever itself, and strike a panic
and premonition of the black vomit into every beholder, all
quarantines all over the world, taint the air with the stream-
ings of their fever-flag.

But though the long rows of white-washed hospitals on the
hill side were now in plain sight, and though scores of ships
were here lying at anchor, yet no boat came off to us; and to
our surprise and delight, on we sailed, past a spot which every
one had dreaded. How it was that they thus let us pass without boarding us, we never could learn.

Now rose the city from out the bay, and one by one, her
spires pierced the blue; while thick and more thick, ships,
brigs, schooners, and sail boats, thronged around. We saw the
Hartz Forest of masts and black rigging stretching along the
East River; and northward, up the stately old Hudson, covered with white sloop-sails like fleets of swans, we caught a
far glimpse of the purple Palisades.

Oh! he who has never been afar, let him once go from
home, to know what home is. For as you draw nigh again to
your old native river, he seems to pour through you with all
his tides, and in your enthusiasm, you swear to build altars
like mile-stones, along both his sacred banks.

Like the Czar of all the Russias, and Siberia to boot, Captain
Riga, telescope in hand, stood on the poop, pointing out to the
passengers, Governor's Island, Castle Garden, and the Battery.

"And *that*," said he, pointing out a vast black hull which, like a shark, showed tiers of teeth, "*that*, ladies, is a line-of-battle-ship, the North Carolina."

"Oh, dear!"—and "Oh my!"—ejaculated the ladies; and—"Lord, save us," responded an old gentleman, who was a member of the Peace Society.

Hurra! hurra! and ten thousand times hurra! down goes our old anchor, fathoms down into the free and independent Yankee mud, one handful of which was now worth a broad manor in England.

The Whitehall boats were around us, and soon, our cabin passengers were all off, gay as crickets, and bound for a late dinner at the Astor House; where, no doubt, they fired off a salute of champagne corks in honor of their own arrival. Only a very few of the steerage passengers, however, could afford to pay the high price the watermen demanded for carrying them ashore; so most of them remained with us till morning. But nothing could restrain our Italian boy, Carlo, who, promising the watermen to pay them with his music, was triumphantly rowed ashore, seated in the stern of the boat, his organ before him, and something like "Hail Columbia!" his tune. We gave him three rapturous cheers, and we never saw Carlo again.

Harry and I passed the greater part of the night walking the deck, and gazing at the thousand lights of the city.

At sunrise, we *warped* into a berth at the foot of Wall-street, and knotted our old ship, stem and stern, to the pier. But that knotting of *her*, was the unknotting of the bonds of the sailors, among whom, it is a maxim, that the ship once fast to the wharf, they are free. So with a rush and a shout, they bounded ashore, followed by the tumultuous crowd of emigrants, whose friends, day-laborers and house-maids, stood ready to embrace them.

But in silent gratitude at the end of a voyage, almost equally uncongenial to both of us, and so bitter to one, Harry and I sat on a chest in the forecastle. And now, the ship that we had loathed, grew lovely in our eyes, which lingered over every familiar old timber; for the scene of suffering is a scene of joy when the suffering is past; and the silent reminiscence of hardships departed, is sweeter than the presence of delight.

Chapter 61

THERE WE SAT in that tarry old den, the only inhabitants of the deserted old ship, but the mate and the rats.

At last, Harry went to his chest, and drawing out a few shillings, proposed that we should go ashore, and return with a supper, to eat in the forecastle. Little else that was eatable being for sale in the paltry shops along the wharves, we bought several pies, some doughnuts, and a bottle of ginger-pop, and thus supplied we made merry. For to us, whose very mouths were become pickled and puckered, with the continual flavor of briny beef, those pies and doughnuts were most delicious. And as for the ginger-pop, why, that ginger-pop was divine! I have reverenced ginger-pop ever since.

We kept late hours that night; for, delightful certainty! placed beyond all doubt—like royal landsmen, we were masters of the watches of the night, and no *starb-o-leens ahoy!* would annoy us again.

"All night in! think of *that*, Harry, my friend!"

"Ay, Wellingborough, it's enough to keep me awake forever, to think I may now sleep as long as I please."

We turned out bright and early, and then prepared for the shore, first stripping to the waist, for a toilet.

"I shall never get these confounded tar-stains out of my fingers," cried Harry, rubbing them hard with a bit of oakum, steeped in strong suds. "No! they will *not* come out, and I'm ruined for life. Look at my hand once, Wellingborough!"

It was indeed a sad sight. Every finger nail, like mine, was dyed of a rich, russet hue; looking something like bits of fine tortoise shell.

"Never mind, Harry," said I—"You know the ladies of the east steep the tips of their fingers in some golden dye."

"And by Plutus," cried Harry—"I'd steep mine up to the arm-pits in gold; since you talk about *that*. But never mind, I'll swear I'm just from Persia, my boy."

We now arrayed ourselves in our best, and sallied ashore;

and, at once, I piloted Harry to the sign of a Turkey Cock in Fulton-street, kept by one Sweeny, a place famous for cheap Souchong, and capital buckwheat cakes.

"Well gentlemen, what will you have?"—said a waiter, as we seated ourselves at a table.

"*Gentlemen!*" whispered Harry to me—"*gentlemen!*—hear him!—I say now, Redburn, they didn't talk to us that way on board the old Highlander. By heaven, I begin to feel my straps again:—Coffee and hot rolls," he added aloud, crossing his legs like a lord, "and fellow—come back—bring us a venison-steak."

"Havn't got it, gentlemen."

"Ham and eggs," suggested I, whose mouth was watering at the recollection of that particular dish, which I had tasted at the sign of the Turkey Cock before. So ham and eggs it was; and royal coffee, and imperial toast.

But the butter!

"Harry, did you ever taste such butter as this before?"

"Don't say a word,"—said Harry, spreading his tenth slice of toast. "I'm going to turn dairyman, and keep within the blessed savor of butter, so long as I live."

We made a breakfast, never to be forgotten; paid our bill with a flourish, and sallied into the street, like two goodly galleons of gold, bound from Acapulco to Old Spain.

"Now," said Harry, "lead on; and let's see something of these United States of yours. I'm ready to pace from Maine to Florida; ford the Great Lakes; and jump the River Ohio, if it comes in the way. Here, take my arm;—lead on."

Such was the miraculous change, that had now come over him. It reminded me of his manner, when we had started for London, from the sign of the Golden Anchor, in Liverpool.

He was, indeed, in most wonderful spirits; at which I could not help marveling; considering the cavity in his pockets; and that he was a stranger in the land.

By noon he had selected his boarding-house, a private establishment, where they did not charge much for their board, and where the landlady's butcher's bill was not very large.

Here, at last, I left him to get his chest from the ship; while I turned up town to see my old friend Mr. Jones, and learn what had happened during my absence.

With one hand, Mr. Jones shook mine most cordially; and with the other, gave me some letters, which I eagerly devoured. Their purport compelled my departure homeward; and I at once sought out Harry to inform him.

Strange, but even the few hours' absence which had intervened; during which, Harry had been left to himself, to stare at strange streets, and strange faces, had wrought a marked change in his countenance. He was a creature of the suddenest impulses. Left to himself, the strange streets seemed now to have reminded him of his friendless condition; and I found him with a very sad eye; and his right hand groping in his pocket.

"Where am I going to dine, this day week?"—he slowly said. "What's to be done, Wellingborough?"

And when I told him that the next afternoon I must leave him; he looked downhearted enough. But I cheered him as well as I could; though needing a little cheering myself; even though I *had* got home again. But no more about that.

Now, there was a young man of my acquaintance in the city, much my senior, by the name of Goodwell; and a good natured fellow he was; who had of late been engaged as a clerk in a large forwarding house in South-street; and it occurred to me, that he was just the man to befriend Harry, and procure him a place. So I mentioned the thing to my comrade; and we called upon Goodwell.

I saw that he was impressed by the handsome exterior of my friend; and in private, making known the case, he faithfully promised to do his best for him; though the times, he said, were quite dull.

That evening, Goodwell, Harry, and I, perambulated the streets, three abreast:—Goodwell spending his money freely at the oyster-saloons; Harry full of allusions to the London Club-houses: and myself contributing a small quota to the general entertainment.

Next morning, we proceeded to business.

Now, I did not expect to draw much of a salary from the ship; so as to retire for life on the profits of *my first voyage*; but nevertheless, I thought that a dollar or two might be coming. For dollars are valuable things; and should not be overlooked, when they are owing. Therefore, as the second morning after our arrival, had been set apart for paying off the crew, Harry and I made our appearance on ship-board, with the rest. We were told to enter the cabin; and once again I found myself, after an interval of four months, and more, surrounded by its mahogany and maple.

Seated in a sumptuous arm-chair, behind a lustrous, inlaid desk, sat Captain Riga, arrayed in his City Hotel suit, looking magisterial as the Lord High Admiral of England. Hat in hand, the sailors stood deferentially in a semicircle before him, while the captain held the ship-papers in his hand, and one by one called their names; and in mellow bank notes— beautiful sight!—paid them their wages.

Most of them had less than ten, a few twenty, and two, thirty dollars coming to them; while the old cook, whose piety proved profitable in restraining him from the expensive excesses of most seafaring men, and who had taken no pay in advance, had the goodly round sum of seventy dollars as his due.

Seven ten dollar bills! each of which, as I calculated at the time, was worth precisely one hundred dimes, which were equal to one thousand cents, which were again subdivisible into fractions. So that he now stepped into a fortune of seventy thousand American "*mills*." Only seventy dollars, after all; but then, it has always seemed to me, that stating amounts in sounding fractional sums, conveys a much fuller notion of their magnitude, than by disguising their immensity in such aggregations of value, as doubloons, sovereigns, and dollars. Who would not rather be worth 125,000 francs in Paris, than only £5000 in London, though the intrinsic value of the two sums, in round numbers, is pretty much the same.

With a scrape of the foot, and such a bow as only a negro can make, the old cook marched off with his fortune; and I have no doubt at once invested it in a grand, underground oyster-cellar.

The other sailors, after counting their cash very carefully, and seeing all was right, and not a bank-note was dog-eared, in which case they would have demanded another: for they are not to be taken in and cheated, your sailors, and they know their rights, too; at least, when they are at liberty, after the voyage is concluded:—the sailors also salaamed, and withdrew, leaving Harry and me face to face with the Pay-master-general of the Forces.

We stood awhile, looking as polite as possible, and expect-ing every moment to hear our names called, but not a word did we hear; while the captain, throwing aside his accounts, lighted a very fragrant cigar, took up the morning paper—I think it was the Herald—threw his leg over one arm of the chair, and plunged into the latest intelligence from all parts of the world.

I looked at Harry, and he looked at me; and then we both looked at this incomprehensible captain.

At last Harry hemmed, and I scraped my foot to increase the disturbance.

The Paymaster-general looked up.

"Well, where do you come from? Who are *you*, pray? and what do you want? Steward, show these young gentlemen out."

"I want my money," said Harry.

"My wages are due," said I.

The captain laughed. Oh! he was exceedingly merry; and taking a long inspiration of smoke, removed his cigar, and sat sideways looking at us, letting the vapor slowly wriggle and spiralize out of his mouth.

"Upon my soul, young gentlemen, you astonish me. Are your names down in the City Directory? Have you any letters of introduction, young gentlemen?"

"Captain Riga!" cried Harry, enraged at his impudence— "I tell you what it is, Captain Riga; this won't do—where's the rhino?"

"Captain Riga," added I, "do you not remember, that about four months ago, my friend Mr. Jones and myself had an interview with you in this very cabin; when it was agreed that I was to go out in your ship, and receive three dollars per month for my services? Well, Captain Riga, I have gone out with you, and returned; and now, sir, I'll thank you for my pay."

"Ah, yes, I remember," said the captain. "*Mr. Jones!* Ha! ha! I remember Mr. Jones: a very gentlemanly gentleman; and stop—*you*, too, are the son of a wealthy French importer; and—let me think—was not your great-uncle a barber?"

"No!" thundered I.

"Well, well, young gentleman, really I beg your pardon. Steward, chairs for the young gentlemen—be seated, young gentlemen. And now, let me see," turning over his accounts—"Hum, hum!—yes, here it is: Wellingborough Redburn, at three dollars a month. Say four months, that's twelve dollars; less three dollars advanced in Liverpool—that makes it nine dollars; less three hammers and two scrapers lost overboard—that brings it to four dollars and a quarter. I owe you four dollars and a quarter, I believe, young gentleman?"

"So it seems, sir," said I, with staring eyes.

"And now let me see what you owe me, and then we'll be able to square the yards, Monsieur Redburn."

Owe *him!* thought I—what do I owe him but a grudge, but I concealed my resentment; and presently he said, "By running away from the ship in Liverpool, you forfeited your wages, which amount to twelve dollars; and as there has been advanced to you, in money, hammers, and scrapers, seven dollars and seventy-five cents, you are therefore indebted to me in precisely that sum. Now, young gentleman, I'll thank you for the money;" and he extended his open palm across the desk.

"Shall I pitch into him?" whispered Harry.

I was thunderstruck at this most unforeseen announcement of the state of my account with Captain Riga; and I began to understand why it was that he had till now ignored my absence from the ship, when Harry and I were in London. But a single minute's consideration showed that I could not help myself; so, telling him that he was at liberty to begin his suit, for I was a bankrupt, and could not pay him, I turned to go.

Now, here was this man actually turning a poor lad adrift without a copper, after he had been slaving aboard his ship for more than four mortal months. But Captain Riga was a bachelor of expensive habits, and had run up large wine bills at the City Hotel. He could not afford to be munificent. Peace to his dinners.

"Mr. Bolton, I believe," said the captain, now blandly bowing toward Harry. "Mr. Bolton, *you* also shipped for three dollars per month: and you had one month's advance in Liverpool; and from dock to dock we have been about a month and a half; so I owe you just one dollar and a half, Mr. Bolton; and here it is;" handing him six two-shilling pieces.

"And this," said Harry, throwing himself into a tragical attitude, "*this* is the reward of my long and faithful services!"

Then, disdainfully flinging the silver on the desk, he exclaimed, "There, Captain Riga, you may keep your tin! It has been in *your* purse, and it would give me the itch to retain it. Good morning, sir."

"Good morning, young gentlemen; pray, call again," said the captain, coolly bagging the coins. His politeness, while in port, was invincible.

Quitting the cabin, I remonstrated with Harry upon his recklessness in disdaining his wages, small though they were; I begged to remind him of his situation; and hinted that every penny he could get might prove precious to him. But he only cried *Pshaw!* and that was the last of it.

Going forward, we found the sailors congregated on the forecastle-deck, engaged in some earnest discussion; while several carts on the wharf, loaded with their chests, were just in the act of driving off, destined for the boarding-houses up-town. By the looks of our shipmates, I saw very plainly that they must have some mischief under weigh; and so it turned out.

Now, though Captain Riga had not been guilty of any particular outrage against the sailors; yet, by a thousand small meannesses—such as indirectly causing their allowance of bread and beef to be diminished, without betraying any appearance of having any inclination that way, and without speaking to the sailors on the subject—by this, and kindred actions, I say, he had contracted the cordial dislike of the whole ship's company; and long since they had bestowed upon him a name unmentionably expressive of their contempt.

The voyage was now concluded; and it appeared that the subject being debated by the assembly on the forecastle was, how best they might give a united and valedictory expression of the sentiments they entertained toward their late lord and master. Some emphatic symbol of those sentiments was desired; some unmistakable token, which should forcibly impress Captain Riga with the justest possible notion of their feelings.

It was like a meeting of the members of some mercantile company, upon the eve of a prosperous dissolution of the concern; when the subordinates, actuated by the purest gratitude toward their president, or chief, proceed to vote him a silver pitcher, in token of their respect. It was something like this, I repeat—but with a material difference, as will be seen.

At last, the precise manner in which the thing should be done being agreed upon, Blunt, the "Irish cockney," was deputed to summon the captain. He knocked at the cabin-door, and politely requested the steward to inform Captain Riga, that some gentlemen were on the pier-head, earnestly seeking him; whereupon he joined his comrades.

In a few moments the captain sallied from the cabin, and found the *gentlemen* alluded to, strung along the top of the bulwarks, on the side next to the wharf. Upon his appearance, the row suddenly wheeled about, presenting their backs; and making a motion, which was a polite salute to every thing before them, but an abominable insult to all who happened to be in their rear, they gave three cheers, and at one bound, cleared the ship.

True to his imperturbable politeness while in port, Captain Riga only lifted his hat, smiled very blandly, and slowly returned into his cabin.

Wishing to see the last movements of this remarkable crew, who were so clever ashore and so craven afloat, Harry and I followed them along the wharf, till they stopped at a sailor retreat, poetically denominated "The Flashes." And here they all came to anchor before the bar; and the landlord, a lantern-jawed landlord, bestirred himself behind it, among his villainous old bottles and decanters. He well knew, from their looks, that his customers were "flush," and would spend their money freely, as, indeed, is the case with most seamen, recently paid off.

It was a touching scene.

"Well, maties," said one of them, at last—"I spose we shan't see each other again:—come, let's splice the mainbrace all round, and drink to *the last voyage!*"

Upon this, the landlord danced down his glasses, on the bar, uncorked his decanters, and deferentially pushed them over toward the sailors, as much as to say—*"Honorable gentlemen, it is not for me to allowance your liquor; —help yourselves, your honors."*

And so they did; each glass a bumper; and standing in a row, tossed them all off; shook hands all round, three times three; and then disappeared in couples, through the several doorways; for *"The Flashes"* was on a corner.

If to every one, life be made up of farewells and greetings, and a *"Good-by, God bless you,"* is heard for every *"How d'ye do, welcome, my boy"*—then, of all men, sailors shake the most hands, and wave the most hats. They are here and then they are there; ever shifting themselves, they shift among the shifting: and like rootless sea-weed, are tossed to and fro.

As, after shaking our hands, our shipmates departed, Harry and I stood on the corner awhile, till we saw the last man disappear.

"They are gone," said I.

"Thank heaven!" said Harry.

Chapter 62

THE LAST THAT WAS EVER HEARD OF
HARRY BOLTON

THAT SAME AFTERNOON, I took my comrade down to the
Battery; and we sat on one of the benches, under the
summer shade of the trees.

It was a quiet, beautiful scene; full of promenading ladies
and gentlemen; and through the foliage, so fresh and bright,
we looked out over the bay, varied with glancing ships; and
then, we looked down to our boots; and thought what a fine
world it would be, if we only had a little money to enjoy it.
But that's the everlasting rub—oh, who can cure an empty
pocket?

"I have no doubt, Goodwell will take care of you, Harry,"
said I, "he's a fine, good-hearted fellow; and will do his best
for you, I know."

"No doubt of it," said Harry, looking hopeless.

"And I need not tell you, Harry, how sorry I am to leave
you so soon."

"And I am sorry enough myself," said Harry, looking very
sincere.

"But I will be soon back again, I doubt not," said I.

"Perhaps so," said Harry, shaking his head. "How far is it
off?"

"Only a hundred and eighty miles," said I.

"A hundred and eighty miles!" said Harry, drawing the
words out like an endless ribbon. "Why, I couldn't walk that
in a month."

"Now, my dear friend," said I, "Take my advice, and while
I am gone, keep up a stout heart; never despair, and all will
be well."

But notwithstanding all I could say to encourage him,
Harry felt so bad, that nothing would do, but a rush to a
neighboring bar, where we both gulped down a glass of
ginger-pop; after which we felt better.

He accompanied me to the steamboat, that was to carry me

homeward; he stuck close to my side, till she was about to put off; then, standing on the wharf, he shook me by the hand, till we almost counteracted the play of the paddles; and at last, with a mutual jerk at the arm-pits, we parted. I never saw Harry again.

I pass over the reception I met with at home; how I plunged into embraces, long and loving:—I pass over this; and will conclude *my first voyage* by relating all I know of what overtook Harry Bolton.

Circumstances beyond my control, detained me at home for several weeks; during which, I wrote to my friend, without receiving an answer.

I then wrote to young Goodwell, who returned me the following letter, now spread before me.

"Dear Redburn: —Your poor friend, Harry, I can not find any where. After you left, he called upon me several times, and we walked out together; and my interest in him increased every day. But you don't know how dull are the times here, and what multitudes of young men, well qualified, are seeking employment in counting-houses. I did my best; but could not get Harry a place. However, I cheered him. But he grew more and more melancholy, and at last told me, that he had sold all his clothes but those on his back to pay his board. I offered to loan him a few dollars, but he would not receive them. I called upon him two or three times after this, but he was not in; at last, his landlady told me that he had permanently left her house the very day before. Upon my questioning her closely, as to where he had gone, she answered, that she did not know, but from certain hints that had dropped from our poor friend, she feared he had gone on a whaling voyage. I at once went to the offices in South-street, where men are shipped for the Nantucket whalers, and made inquiries among them; but without success. And this, I am heartily grieved to say, is all I know of our friend. I can not believe that his melancholy could bring him to the insanity of throwing himself away in a whaler; and I still think, that he must be somewhere in the city. You must come down yourself, and help me seek him out."

This letter gave me a dreadful shock. Remembering our adventure in London, and his conduct there; remembering how liable he was to yield to the most sudden, crazy, and

contrary impulses; and that, as a friendless, penniless foreigner in New York, he must have had the most terrible in-
citements to committing violence upon himself; I shuddered
to think, that even now, while I thought of him, he might no
more be living. So strong was this impression at the time,
that I quickly glanced over the papers to see if there were any
accounts of suicides, or drowned persons floating in the harbor of New York.

I now made all the haste I could to the seaport, but though
I sought him all over, no tidings whatever could be heard.

To relieve my anxiety, Goodwell endeavored to assure me,
that Harry must indeed have departed on a whaling voyage.
But remembering his bitter experience on board of the Highlander, and more than all, his nervousness about going aloft,
it seemed next to impossible.

At last I was forced to give him up.

* * *

Years after this, I found myself a sailor in the Pacific, on
board of a whaler. One day at sea, we spoke another whaler,
and the boat's crew that boarded our vessel, came forward
among us to have a little sea-chat, as is always customary
upon such occasions.

Among the strangers was an Englishman, who had shipped
in his vessel at Callao, for the cruise. In the course of conversation, he made allusion to the fact, that he had now been in
the Pacific several years, and that the good craft Huntress of
Nantucket had had the honor of originally bringing him
round upon that side of the globe. I asked him why he had
abandoned her; he answered that she was the most unlucky
of ships.

"We had hardly been out three months," said he, "when
on the Brazil banks we lost a boat's crew, chasing a whale
after sundown; and next day lost a poor little fellow, a countryman of mine, who had never entered the boats; he fell over
the side, and was jammed between the ship, and a whale,
while we were cutting the fish in. Poor fellow, he had a hard
time of it, from the beginning; he was a gentleman's son, and
when you could coax him to it, he sang like a bird."

"What was his name?" said I, trembling with expectation;

"what kind of eyes did he have? what was the color of his hair?"

"Harry Bolton was not your brother?" cried the stranger, starting.

Harry Bolton! it was even he!

But yet, I, Wellingborough Redburn, chance to survive, after having passed through far more perilous scenes than any narrated in this, *My First Voyage*—which here I end.

THE END

WHITE-JACKET

or
The World in a Man-of-War

CONCEIVE HIM *now in a man-of-war; with his letters of mart, well armed, victualed, and appointed, and see how he acquits himself.*

FULLER'S "Good Sea-Captain."

Note

IN THE YEAR 1843 I shipped as "ordinary seaman" on board of a United States frigate, then lying in a harbor of the Pacific Ocean. After remaining in this frigate for more than a year, I was discharged from the service upon the vessel's arrival home. My man-of-war experiences and observations are incorporated in the present volume.

NEW YORK, *March, 1850.*

Contents

Chapter 1

THE JACKET

I T WAS NOT a *very* white jacket, but white enough, in all conscience, as the sequel will show.

The way I came by it was this.

When our frigate lay in Callao, on the coast of Peru—her last harbor in the Pacific—I found myself without a *grego*, or sailor's surtout; and as, toward the end of a three years' cruise, no pea-jackets could be had from the purser's steward; and being bound for Cape Horn, some sort of a substitute was indispensable; I employed myself, for several days, in manufacturing an outlandish garment of my own devising, to shelter me from the boisterous weather we were so soon to encounter.

It was nothing more than a white duck frock, or rather shirt; which, laying on deck, I folded double at the bosom, and by then making a continuation of the slit there, opened it lengthwise—much as you would cut a leaf in the last new novel. The gash being made, a metamorphosis took place, transcending any related by Ovid. For, presto! the shirt was a coat!—a strange-looking coat, to be sure; of a Quakerish amplitude about the skirts; with an infirm, tumble-down collar; and a clumsy fullness about the wristbands; and white, yea, white as a shroud. And my shroud it afterward came very near proving, as he who reads further will find.

But, bless me, my friend, what sort of a summer jacket is this, in which to weather Cape Horn? A very tasty, and beautiful white linen garment it may have seemed; but then, people almost universally sport their linen next to their skin.

Very true; and that thought very early occurred to me; for no idea had I of scudding round Cape Horn in my shirt; for *that* would have been almost scudding under bare poles, indeed.

So, with many odds and ends of patches—old socks, old trowser-legs, and the like—I bedarned and bequilted the inside of my jacket, till it became, all over, stiff and padded, as

King James's cotton-stuffed and dagger-proof doublet; and no buckram or steel hauberk stood up more stoutly.

So far, very good; but pray, tell me, White-Jacket, how do you propose keeping out the rain and the wet in this quilted *grego* of yours? You don't call this wad of old patches a Mackintosh, do you?—You don't pretend to say that worsted is water-proof?

No, my dear friend; and that was the deuce of it. Water-proof it was not, no more than a sponge. Indeed, with such recklessness had I bequilted my jacket, that in a rain-storm I became a universal absorber; swabbing bone-dry the very bulwarks I leaned against. Of a damp day, my heartless shipmates even used to stand up against me, so powerful was the capillary attraction between this luckless jacket of mine and all drops of moisture. I dripped like a turkey a' roasting; and long after the rain storms were over, and the sun showed his face, I still stalked a Scotch mist; and when it was fair weather with others, alas! it was foul weather with me.

Me? Ah me! Soaked and heavy, what a burden was that jacket to carry about, especially when I was sent up aloft; dragging myself up, step by step, as if I were weighing the anchor. Small time then, to strip, and wring it out in a rain, when no hanging back or delay was permitted. No, no; up you go: fat or lean: Lambert or Edson: never mind how much avoirdupoise you might weigh. And thus, in my own proper person, did many showers of rain reascend toward the skies, in accordance with the natural laws.

But here be it known, that I had been terribly disappointed in carrying out my original plan concerning this jacket. It had been my intention to make it thoroughly impervious, by giving it a coating of paint. But bitter fate ever overtakes us unfortunates. So much paint had been stolen by the sailors, in daubing their overhaul trowsers and tarpaulins, that by the time I—an honest man—had completed my quiltings, the paint-pots were banned, and put under strict lock and key.

Said old Brush, the captain of the *paint-room*—"Look ye, White-Jacket," said he, "ye can't have any paint."

Such, then, was my jacket: a well-patched, padded, and porous one; and in a dark night, gleaming white, as the White Lady of Avenel!

Chapter 2

Homeward-Bound

"ALL HANDS UP ANCHOR! Man the capstan!"

"High die! my lads, we're homeward bound!"

Homeward bound!—harmonious sound! Were you ever homeward bound?—No?—Quick! take the wings of the morning, or the sails of a ship, and fly to the uttermost parts of the earth. There, tarry a year or two; and then let the gruffest of Boatswains, his lungs all goose-skin, shout forth those magical words, and you'll swear "the harp of Orpheus were not more enchanting."

All was ready; boats hoisted in, stun' sail gear rove, messenger passed, capstan-bars in their places, accommodation-ladder below; and in glorious spirits, we sat down to dinner. In the ward-room, the lieutenants were passing round their oldest Port, and pledging their friends; in the steerage, the *middies* were busy raising loans to liquidate the demands of their laundress, or else—in the navy phrase—preparing to pay their creditors *with a flying fore-topsail*. On the poop, the captain was looking to windward; and in his grand, inaccessible cabin, the high and mighty commodore sat silent and stately, as the statue of Jupiter in Dodona.

We were all arrayed in our best, and our bravest; like strips of blue sky, lay the pure blue collars of our frocks upon our shoulders; and our pumps were so springy and playful, that we danced up and down as we dined.

It was on the gun-deck that our dinners were spread; all along between the guns; and there, as we cross-legged sat, you would have thought a hundred farm-yards and meadows were nigh. Such a cackling of ducks, chickens, and ganders; such a lowing of oxen, and bleating of lambkins, penned up here and there along the deck, to provide sea repasts for the officers. More rural than naval were the sounds; continually reminding each mother's son of the old paternal homestead in the green old clime; the old arching elms; the hill where we gambolled; and down by the barley banks of the stream where we bathed.

"All hands up anchor!"

When that order was given, how we sprang to the bars, and heaved round that capstan; every man a Goliath, every tendon a hawser!—round and round—round, round it spun like a sphere, keeping time with our feet to the time of the fifer, till the cable was straight up and down, and the ship with her nose in the water.

"Heave and pall! unship your bars, and make sail!"

It was done:—bar-men, nipper-men, tierers, veerers, idlers and all, scrambled up the ladder to the braces and halyards; while like monkeys in Palm-trees, the sail-loosers ran out on those broad boughs, our yards; and down fell the sails like white clouds from the ether—top-sails, top-gallants, and royals; and away we ran with the halyards, till every sheet was distended.

"Once more to the bars!"

"Heave, my hearties, heave hard!"

With a jerk and a yerk, we broke ground; and up to our bows came several thousand pounds of old iron, in the shape of our ponderous anchor.

Where was White-Jacket then?

White-Jacket was where he belonged. It was White-Jacket that loosed that main-royal, so far up aloft there, it looks like a white albatross' wing. It was White-Jacket that was taken for an albatross himself, as he flew out on the giddy yard-arm!

Chapter 3

HAVING just designated the place where White-Jacket belonged, it must needs be related how White-Jacket came to belong there.

Every one knows that in merchantmen the seamen are divided into watches—starboard and larboard—taking their turn at the ship's duty by night. This plan is followed in all men-of-war. But in all men-of-war, besides this division, there are others, rendered indispensable from the great number of men, and the necessity of precision and discipline. Not only are particular bands assigned to the three *tops*, but in getting under weigh, or any other proceeding requiring all hands, particular men of these bands are assigned to each yard of the tops. Thus, when the order is given to loose the main-royal, White-Jacket flies to obey it; and no one but him.

And not only are particular bands stationed on the three decks of the ship at such times, but particular men of those bands are also assigned to particular duties. Also, in tacking ship, reefing top-sails, or "coming to," every man of a frigate's five-hundred-strong, knows his own special place, and is infallibly found there. He sees nothing else, attends to nothing else, and will stay there till grim death or an epaulette orders him away. Yet there are times when, through the negligence of the officers, some exceptions are found to this rule. A rather serious circumstance growing out of such a case will be related in some future chapter.

Were it not for these regulations a man-of-war's crew would be nothing but a mob, more ungovernable stripping the canvass in a gale than Lord George Gordon's tearing down the lofty house of Lord Mansfield.

But this is not all. Besides White-Jacket's office as looser of the main-royal, when all hands were called to make sail; and besides his special offices, in tacking ship, coming to anchor, &c.; he permanently belonged to the Starboard Watch, one of the two primary, grand divisions of the ship's company. And in this watch he was a main-top-man; that is, was stationed in the main-top, with a number of other seamen, always in readiness to execute any orders pertaining to the main-mast, from above the main-yard. For, including the main-yard, and below it to the deck, the main-mast belongs to another detachment.

Now the fore, main, and mizen-top-men of each watch—Starboard and Larboard—are at sea respectively subdivided into Quarter Watches; which regularly relieve each other in the tops to which they may belong; while, collectively, they relieve the whole Larboard Watch of top-men.

Besides these topmen, who are always made up of active sailors, there are Sheet-Anchor-men—old veterans all—whose place is on the forecastle; the fore-yard, anchors, and all the sails on the bowsprit being under their care.

They are an old weather-beaten set, culled from the most experienced seamen on board. These are the fellows that sing you *"The Bay of Biscay Oh!"* and *"Here a sheer hulk lies poor Tom Bowling!"* *"Cease, rude Boreas, blustering railer!"* who, when ashore, at an eating-house, call for a bowl of tar and a biscuit. These are the fellows, who spin interminable yarns about Decatur, Hull, and Bainbridge; and carry about their persons bits of "Old Ironsides," as Catholics do the wood of the true cross. These are the fellows, that some officers never pretend to damn, however much they may anathematize others. These are the fellows, that it does your soul good to look at;—hearty old members of the Old Guard; grim sea grenadiers, who, in tempest time, have lost many a tarpaulin overboard. These are the fellows, whose society some of the youngster midshipmen much affect; from whom they learn their best seamanship; and to whom they look up as veterans; if so be, that they have any reverence in their souls, which is not the case with all midshipmen.

Then, there is the *After-guard*, stationed on the Quarter-deck; who, under the Quarter-Masters and Quarter-Gunners, attend to the main-sail and spanker, and help haul the main-brace, and other ropes in the stern of the vessel.

The duties assigned to the After-Guard's-Men being comparatively light and easy, and but little seamanship being expected from them, they are composed chiefly of landsmen; the least robust, least hardy, and least sailor-like of the crew; and being stationed on the Quarter-deck, they are generally selected with some eye to their personal appearance. Hence, they are mostly slender young fellows, of a genteel figure and gentlemanly address; not weighing much on a rope, but weighing considerably in the estimation of all foreign ladies who may chance to visit the ship. They lounge away the most part of their time, in reading novels and romances; talking over their lover affairs ashore; and comparing notes concerning the melancholy and sentimental career which drove them—poor young gentlemen—into the hard-hearted navy. Indeed, many of them show tokens of having moved in very respectable society. They always maintain a tidy exterior; and express an abhorrence of the tar-bucket, into which they are seldom or never called to dip their digits. And pluming themselves upon the cut of their trowsers, and the glossiness of their tarpaulins, from the rest of the ship's company, they acquire the name of "*sea-dandies*" and "*silk-sock-gentry.*"

Then, there are the *Waisters*, always stationed on the gun-deck. These haul aft the fore and main-sheets, besides being subject to ignoble duties; attending to the drainage and sewerage below hatches. These fellows are all Jimmy Duxes— sorry chaps, who never put foot in ratlin, or venture above the bulwarks. Inveterate "*sons of farmers*," with the hay-seed yet in their hair, they are consigned to the congenial superintendence of the chicken-coops, pig-pens, and potato-lockers. These are generally placed amidships, on the gun-deck of a frigate, between the fore and main hatches; and comprise so extensive an area, that it much resembles the market-place of a small town. The melodious sounds thence issuing, continually draw tears from the eyes of the Waisters; reminding them of their old paternal pig-pens and potato-patches. They are the tag-rag and bob-tail of the crew; and he who is good for nothing else is good enough for a *Waister*.

Three decks down—spar-deck, gun-deck, and berth-deck —and we come to a parcel of Troglodites or "*holders*," who burrow, like rabbits in warrens, among the water-tanks, casks, and cables. Like Cornwall miners, wash off the soot from their skins, and they are all pale as ghosts. Unless upon rare occasions, they seldom come on deck to sun themselves. They may circumnavigate the world fifty times, and they see about as much of it as Jonah did in the whale's belly. They are a lazy, lumpish, torpid set; and when going ashore after a long cruise, come out into the day, like terrapins from their caves, or bears in the spring, from tree-trunks. No one ever knows the names of these fellows; after a three years' voyage, they still remain strangers to you. In time of tempests, when all hands are called to save ship, they issue forth into the gale, like the mysterious old men of Paris, during the massacre of the Three Days of September; every one marvels who they are, and whence they come; they disappear as mysteriously; and are seen no more, until another general commotion.

Such are the principal divisions into which a man-of-war's crew is divided; but the inferior allotments of duties are endless, and would require a German commentator to chronicle.

We say nothing here of Boatswain's mates, Gunner's mates, Carpenter's mates, Sail-maker's mates, Armorer's mates, Master-at-Arms, Ship's corporals, Cockswains, Quarter-masters, Quarter-gunners, Captains of the Forecastle, Captains of the Fore-top, Captains of the Main-top, Captains of the Mizentop, Captains of the After-Guard, Captains of the Main-Hold, Captains of the Fore-Hold, Captains of the Head, Coopers, Painters, Tinkers, Commodore's Steward, Captain's Steward, Ward-Room Steward, Steerage Steward, Commodore's cook, Captain's cook, Officers' cook, Cooks of the range, Mess-cooks, hammock-boys, messenger boys, cot-boys, loblolly-boys, and numberless others, whose functions are fixed and peculiar.

It is from this endless subdivision of duties in a man-of-war, that, upon first entering one, a sailor has need of a good memory, and the more of an Arithmetician he is, the better.

White-Jacket, for one, was a long time rapt in calculations, concerning the various "numbers" allotted him by the *First Luff*, otherwise known as the First Lieutenant. In the first place, White-Jacket was given the *number of his mess*; then, his *ship's number*, or the number to which he must answer when the watch-roll is called; then, the number of his hammock; then, the number of the gun to which he was assigned; besides a variety of other numbers; all of which would have

taken Jedediah Buxton himself some time to arrange in battalions, previous to adding up. All these numbers, moreover,
must be well remembered, or woe betide you.

Consider, now, a merchant-sailor altogether unused to the
tumult of a man-of-war, for the first time stepping on board,
and given all these numbers to recollect. Already, before hearing them, his head is half stunned with the unaccustomed
sounds ringing in his ears; which ears seem to him like belfries full of tocsins. On the gun-deck, a thousand scythed
chariots seem passing; he hears the tread of armed marines;
the clash of cutlasses and curses. The Boatswain's mates whistle round him, like hawks screaming in a gale, and the strange
noises under decks, are like volcanic rumblings in a mountain.
He dodges sudden sounds, as a raw recruit falling bombs.

Well-nigh useless to him, now, all previous circumnavigations of this terraqueous globe; of no account his arctic, antarctic, or equinoctial experiences; his gales off Beachy Head,
or his dismastings off Hatteras. He must begin anew; he
knows nothing; Greek and Hebrew could not help him, for
the language he must learn has neither grammar nor lexicon.

Mark him, as he advances along the files of old ocean-war-
riors; mark his debased attitude, his deprecating gestures, his
Sawney stare, like a Scotchman in London in King James's
time; his—*"cry your mercy, noble seignors!"* He is wholly non-
plused, and confounded. And when, to crown all, the First
Lieutenant, whose business it is to welcome all new-comers,
and assign them their quarters; when this officer—none of
the most bland or amiable either—gives him number after
number to recollect—246—139—478—351—the poor fellow
feels like decamping.

Study, then, your mathematics, and cultivate all your memories, oh ye! who think of cruising in men-of-war.

Chapter 4

JACK CHASE

THE FIRST NIGHT out of port was a clear, moonlight one; the frigate gliding through the water, with all her batteries.

It was my Quarter Watch in the top; and there I reclined on the best possible terms with my top-mates. Whatever the other seamen might have been, these were a noble set of tars, and well worthy an introduction to the reader.

First and foremost was Jack Chase, our noble First Captain of the Top. He was a Briton, and a true-blue; tall and well-knit, with a clear open eye, a fine broad brow, and an abounding nut-brown beard. No man ever had a better heart or a bolder. He was loved by the seamen and admired by the officers; and even when the Captain spoke to him, it was with a slight air of respect. Jack was a frank and charming man.

No one could be better company in forecastle or saloon; no man told such stories, sang such songs, or with greater alacrity sprang to his duty. Indeed, there was only one thing wanting about him; and that was, a finger of his left hand, which finger he had lost at the great battle of Navarino.

He had a high conceit of his profession as a seaman; and being deeply versed in all things pertaining to a man-of-war, was universally regarded as an oracle. The main-top, over which he presided, was a sort of oracle of Delphi; to which, many pilgrims ascended, to have their perplexities or differences settled.

There was such an abounding air of good sense and good feeling about the man, that he who could not love him, would thereby pronounce himself a knave. I thanked my sweet stars, that kind fortune had placed me near him, though under him, in the frigate; and from the outset Jack and I were fast friends.

Wherever you may be now rolling over the blue billows, dear Jack! take my best love along with you; and God bless you, wherever you go!

Jack was a gentleman. What though his hand was hard, so was not his heart, too often the case with soft palms. His manners were easy and free; none of the boisterousness, so common to tars; and he had a polite, courteous way of saluting you, if it were only to borrow your knife. Jack had read all the verses of Byron, and all the romances of Scott. He talked of Rob Roy, Don Juan, and Pelham; Macbeth and Ulysses; but, above all things, was an ardent admirer of Camoens. Parts of the Lusiad, he could recite in the original. Where he had obtained his wonderful accomplishments, it is not for me, his humble subordinate, to say. Enough, that those accomplishments were so various; the languages he could converse in, so numerous; that he more than furnished an example of that saying of Charles the Fifth — *he who speaks five languages is as good as five men*. But Jack, he was better than a hundred common mortals; Jack was a whole phalanx, an entire army; Jack was a thousand strong; Jack would have done honor to the Queen of England's drawing-room; Jack must have been a by-blow of some British Admiral of the Blue. A finer specimen of the island race of Englishmen could not have been picked out of Westminster Abbey of a coronation day.

His whole demeanor was in strong contrast to that of one of the Captains of the fore-top. This man, though a good seaman, furnished an example of those insufferable Britons, who, while preferring other countries to their own as places of residence; still, overflow with all the pompousness of national and individual vanity combined. "When I was on board the Audacious"—for a long time, was almost the invariable exordium to the fore-top Captain's most cursory remarks. It is often the custom of men-of-war's-men, when they deem any thing to be going on wrong aboard ship, to refer to *last cruise*, when of course every thing was done *ship-shape and Bristol fashion*. And by referring to the *Audacious*—an expressive name by the way—the fore-top Captain meant a ship in the English navy, in which he had had the honor of serving. So continual were his allusions to this craft with the amiable name, that at last, the *Audacious* was voted a bore by his shipmates. And one hot afternoon, during a calm, when the fore-top Captain, like many others, was standing still and yawning on the spar-deck; Jack Chase, his own countryman, came up to him, and pointing at his open mouth, politely inquired, whether that was the way they caught *flies* in Her Britannic Majesty's ship, the *Audacious*? After that, we heard no more of the craft.

Now, the tops of a frigate are quite spacious and cosy. They are railed in behind so as to form a kind of balcony, very pleasant of a tropical night. From twenty to thirty loungers may agreeably recline there, cushioning themselves on old sails and jackets. We had rare times in that top. We accounted ourselves the best seamen in the ship; and from our airy perch, literally looked down upon the landlopers below, sneaking about the deck, among the guns. In a large degree, we nourished that feeling of "*esprit de corps*," always pervading, more or less, the various sections of a man-of-war's crew. We main-top-men were brothers, one and all; and we loaned ourselves to each other with all the freedom in the world.

Nevertheless, I had not long been a member of this fraternity of fine fellows, ere I discovered that Jack Chase, our captain, was—like all prime favorites and oracles among men—a little bit of a dictator; not peremptorily, or annoyingly so, but amusingly intent on egotistically mending our manners and improving our taste, so that we might reflect credit upon our tutor.

He made us all wear our hats at a particular angle—instructed us in the tie of our neck handkerchiefs; and protested against our wearing vulgar *dungeree* trowsers; besides giving us lessons in seamanship; and solemnly conjuring us, forever to eschew the company of any sailor we suspected of having served in a whaler. Against all whalers, indeed, he cherished the unmitigated detestation of a true man-of-war's man. Poor Tubbs can testify to that.

Tubbs was in the After-Guard; a long, lank Vineyarder, eternally talking of line-tubs, Nantucket, sperm oil, stove boats, and Japan. Nothing could silence him; and his comparisons were ever invidious.

Now, with all his soul, Jack abominated this Tubbs. He said he was vulgar, an upstart—Devil take him, he's been in a whaler. But like many men, who have been where *you* haven't been; or seen what *you* haven't seen; Tubbs, on account of his whaling experiences, absolutely affected to look down upon Jack, even as Jack did upon him; and this it was that so enraged our noble captain.

One night, with a peculiar meaning in his eye, he sent me down on deck to invite Tubbs up aloft for a chat. Flattered by so marked an honor—for we were somewhat fastidious, and did not extend such invitations to every body—Tubbs quickly mounted the rigging, looking rather abashed at finding himself in the august presence of the assembled Quarter-Watch of main-top-men. Jack's courteous manner, however, very soon relieved his embarrassment; but it is no use to be courteous to *some* men in this world. Tubbs belonged to that category. No sooner did the bumpkin feel himself at ease, than he lanched out, as usual, into tremendous laudations of whalemen; declaring that whalemen alone deserved the name of sailors. Jack stood it some time; but when Tubbs came down upon men-of-war, and particularly upon main-top-men, his sense of propriety was so outraged, that he lanched into Tubbs like a forty-two pounder.

"Why, you limb of Nantucket! you train-oil man! you sea-tallow strainer! you bobber after carrion! do *you* pretend to vilify a man-of-war? Why, you lean rogue, you, a man-of-war is to whalemen, as a metropolis to shire-towns, and sequestered hamlets. *Here's* the place for life and commotion; *here's* the place to be gentlemanly and jolly. And what did you know, you bumpkin! before you came on board this *Andrew Miller*? What knew you of gun-deck, or orlop, mustering round the capstan, beating to quarters, and piping to dinner? Did you ever roll to *grog* on board your greasy ballyhoo of blazes? Did you ever winter at Mahon? Did you ever '*lash and carry*?' Why, what are even a merchant-seaman's sorry yarns of voyages to China after tea-caddies, and voyages to the West Indies after sugar puncheons, and voyages to the Shetlands after seal-skins—what are even these yarns, you Tubbs you! to high life in a man-of-war? Why, you dead-eye! I have sailed with lords and marquises for captains; and the King of the Two Sicilies has passed me, as I here stood up at my gun. Bah! you are full of the fore-peak and the forecastle; you are only familiar with Burtons and Billy-tackles; your ambition never mounted above pig-killing! which, in my poor opinion, is the proper phrase for whaling! Topmates! has not this Tubbs here been but a misuser of good oak planks, and a vile desecrator of the thrice holy sea? turning his ship, my hearties! into a fat-kettle, and the ocean into a whale-pen? Begone! you graceless, godless knave! pitch him over the top there, White-Jacket!"

But there was no necessity for my exertions. Poor Tubbs, astounded at these fulminations, was already rapidly descending by the rigging.

This outburst on the part of my noble friend Jack made me shake all over, spite of my padded surtout; and caused me to offer up devout thanksgivings, that in no evil hour had I divulged the fact of having myself served in a whaler; for having previously marked the prevailing prejudice of men-of-war's-men to that much-maligned class of mariners, I had wisely held my peace concerning stove boats on the coast of Japan.

Chapter 5

JACK CHASE ON A SPANISH QUARTER-DECK

HERE, I must frankly tell a story about Jack, which, as touching his honor and integrity, I am sure, will not work against him, in any charitable man's estimation. On this present cruise of the frigate Neversink, Jack had deserted; and after a certain interval, had been captured.

But with what purpose had he deserted? To avoid naval discipline? to riot in some abandoned sea-port? for love of some worthless signorita? Not at all. He abandoned the frigate from far higher and nobler, nay, glorious motives. Though bowing to naval discipline afloat; yet ashore, he was a stickler for the Rights of Man, and the liberties of the world. He went to draw a partisan blade in the civil commotions of Peru; and befriend, heart and soul, what he deemed the cause of the Right.

At the time, his disappearance excited the utmost astonishment among the officers, who had little suspected him of any such conduct as deserting.

"What? Jack, my great man of the main-top, gone!" cried the Captain: "I'll not believe it."

"Jack Chase cut and run!" cried a sentimental middy. "It must have been all for love, then; the signoritas have turned his head."

"Jack Chase not to be found?" cried a growling old sheet-anchor-man, one of your malicious prophets of past events: "I thought so; I know'd it; I could have sworn it—just the chap to make sail on the sly. I always s'pected him."

Months passed away, and nothing was heard of Jack; till at last, the frigate came to anchor on the coast, alongside of a Peruvian sloop of war.

Bravely clad in the Peruvian uniform, and with a fine, mixed martial and naval step, a tall, striking figure of a long-bearded officer was descried, promenading the Quarter-deck of the stranger; and superintending the salutes, which are exchanged between national vessels on these occasions.

This fine officer touched his laced hat most courteously to our Captain, who, after returning the compliment, stared at him, rather impolitely, through his spy-glass.

"By Heaven!" he cried at last—"it is he—he can't disguise his walk—that's his beard; I'd know him in Cochin China.— Man the first cutter there! Lieutenant Blink, go on board that sloop of war, and fetch me yon officer."

All hands were aghast—What? when a piping-hot peace was between the United States and Peru, to send an armed body on board a Peruvian sloop of war, and seize one of its officers, in broad daylight?—Monstrous infraction of the Law of Nations! What would Vattel say?

But Captain Claret must be obeyed. So off went the cutter, every man armed to the teeth, the lieutenant commanding having secret instructions, and the midshipmen attending looking ominously wise, though, in truth, they could not tell what was coming.

Gaining the sloop of war, the lieutenant was received with the customary honors; but by this time the tall, bearded officer had disappeared from the Quarter-deck. The Lieutenant now inquired for the Peruvian Captain; and being shown into the cabin, made known to him, that on board his vessel was a person belonging to the United States Ship Neversink; and his orders were, to have that person delivered up instanter.

The foreign captain curled his mustache in astonishment and indignation; he hinted something about beating to quarters, and chastising this piece of Yankee insolence.

But resting one gloved hand upon the table, and playing with his sword-knot, the Lieutenant, with a bland firmness, repeated his demand. At last, the whole case being so plainly made out, and the person in question being so accurately described, even to a mole on his cheek, there remained nothing but immediate compliance.

So the fine-looking, bearded officer, who had so courteously doffed his chapeau to our Captain, but disappeared upon the arrival of the Lieutenant, was summoned into the cabin, before his superior, who addressed him thus:—

"Don John, this gentleman declares, that of right you belong to the frigate Neversink. Is it so?"

"It is even so, Don Sereno," said Jack Chase, proudly folding his gold-laced coat-sleeves across his chest—"and as there is no resisting the frigate, I comply.—Lieutenant Blink, I am ready. Adieu! Don Sereno, and Madre de Dios protect you! You have been a most gentlemanly friend and captain to me. I hope you will yet thrash your beggarly foes."

With that he turned; and entering the cutter, was pulled back to the frigate, and stepped up to Captain Claret, where that gentleman stood on the quarter-deck.

"Your servant, my fine Don," said the Captain, ironically lifting his chapeau, but regarding Jack at the same time with a look of intense displeasure.

"Your most devoted and penitent Captain of the Main-top, sir; and one who, in his very humility of contrition is yet proud to call Captain Claret his commander," said Jack, making a glorious bow, and then tragically flinging overboard his Peruvian sword.

"Reinstate him at once," shouted Captain Claret—"and now, sir, to your duty; and discharge that well to the end of the cruise, and you will hear no more of your having run away."

So Jack went forward among crowds of admiring tars, who swore by his nut-brown beard, which had amazingly lengthened and spread during his absence. They divided his laced hat and coat among them; and on their shoulders, carried him in triumph along the gun-deck.

Chapter 6

THE QUARTER-DECK OFFICERS, WARRANT OFFICERS,
AND BERTH-DECK UNDERLINGS OF A MAN-OF-WAR;
WHERE THEY LIVE IN THE SHIP; HOW THEY LIVE;
THEIR SOCIAL STANDING ON SHIP-BOARD; AND WHAT
SORT OF GENTLEMEN THEY ARE

SOME ACCOUNT has been given of the various divisions
into which our crew was divided; so it may be well to
say something of the officers; who they are, and what are
their functions.

Our ship, be it known, was the flag-ship; that is, we
sported a *broad pennant*, or *bougee*, at the main, in token that
we carried a Commodore—the highest rank of officers recognized in the American navy. The bougee is not to be confounded with the *long pennant* or *coach-whip*, a tapering,
serpentine streamer worn by all men-of-war.

Owing to certain vague, republican scruples, about creating
great officers of the navy, America has thus far had no admirals; though, as her ships of war increase, they may become
indispensable. This will assuredly be the case, should she ever
have occasion to employ large fleets; when she must adopt
something like the English plan, and introduce three or four
grades of flag-officers, above a Commodore—Admirals, Vice-
Admirals, and Rear-Admirals of Squadrons; distinguished by
the colors of their flags,—red, white, and blue, corresponding to the centre, van, and rear. These rank respectively with
Generals, Lieutenant Generals, and Major Generals in the
army; just as a Commodore takes rank with a Brigadier General. So that the same prejudice which prevents the American
Government from creating Admirals should have precluded
the creation of all army officers above a Brigadier.

An American Commodore, like an English Commodore, or
the French *Chef d'Escadre*, is but a senior Captain, temporarily commanding a small number of ships, detached for any
special purpose. He has no permanent rank, recognized by
Government, above his captaincy; though once employed as

a Commodore, usage and courtesy unite in continuing the title.

Our Commodore was a gallant old man, who had seen service in his time. When a lieutenant, he served in the Late War with England; and in the gun-boat actions on the Lakes near New Orleans, just previous to the grand land engagements, received a musket-ball in his shoulder; which, with the two balls in his eyes, he carries about with him to this day.

Often, when I looked at the venerable old warrior, doubled up from the effect of his wound, I thought what a curious, as well as painful sensation, it must be, to have one's shoulder a lead-mine; though, sooth to say, so many of us civilized mortals convert our mouths into Golcondas.

On account of this wound in his shoulder, our Commodore had a body-servant's pay allowed him, in addition to his regular salary. I can not say a great deal, personally, of the Commodore; he never sought my company at all; never extended any gentlemanly courtesies.

But though I can not say much of him personally, I can mention something of him in his general character, as a flag-officer. In the first place, then, I have serious doubts, whether, for the most part, he was not dumb; for, in my hearing, he seldom or never uttered a word. And not only did he seem dumb himself, but his presence possessed the strange power of making other people dumb for the time. His appearance on the Quarter-deck seemed to give every officer the lock-jaw.

Another phenomenon about him was the strange manner in which every one shunned him. At the first sign of those epaulets of his on the weather side of the poop, the officers there congregated invariably shrunk over to leeward, and left him alone. Perhaps he had an evil eye; may be he was the Wandering Jew afloat. The real reason probably was, that, like all high functionaries, he deemed it indispensable religiously to sustain his dignity; one of the most troublesome things in the world, and one calling for the greatest self-denial. And the constant watch, and many-sided guardedness, which this sustaining of a Commodore's dignity requires, plainly enough shows that, apart from the common dignity of manhood, Commodores, in general, possess no real dignity at all. True, it is expedient for crowned heads, generalissimos,

Lord-high-admirals, and Commodores, to carry themselves straight, and beware of the spinal complaint; but it is not the less veritable, that it is a piece of assumption, exceedingly uncomfortable to themselves, and ridiculous to an enlightened generation.

Now, how many rare good fellows there were among us main-top-men, who, invited into his cabin over a social bottle or two, would have rejoiced our old Commodore's heart, and caused that ancient wound of his to heal up at once.

Come, come, Commodore, don't look so sour, old boy; step up aloft here into the *top*, and we'll spin you a sociable yarn.

Truly, I thought myself much happier in that white jacket of mine, than our old Commodore in his dignified epaulets.

One thing, perhaps, that more than any thing else helped to make our Commodore so melancholy and forlorn, was the fact of his having so little to do. For as the frigate had a captain; of course, so far as *she* was concerned, our Commodore was a supernumerary. What abundance of leisure he must have had, during a three years' cruise! how indefinitely he might have been improving his mind!

But as every one knows that idleness is the hardest work in the world, so our Commodore was specially provided with a gentleman to assist him. This gentleman was called the *Commodore's secretary*. He was a remarkably urbane and polished man; with a very graceful exterior, and looked much like an Embassador Extraordinary from Versailles. He messed with the Lieutenants in the Ward-room, where he had a stateroom, elegantly furnished as the private cabinet of Pelham. His cot-boy used to entertain the sailors with all manner of stories about the silver-keyed flutes and flageolets, fine oil paintings, morocco bound volumes, Chinese chess-men, gold shirt-buttons, enameled pencil cases, extraordinary fine French boots with soles no thicker than a sheet of scented note-paper, embroidered vests, incense-burning sealing-wax, alabaster statuettes of Venus and Adonis, tortoise-shell snuffboxes, inlaid toilet-cases, ivory-handled hair-brushes and mother-of-pearl combs, and a hundred other luxurious appendages scattered about this magnificent secretary's state-room.

I was a long time in finding out what this secretary's duties comprised. But it seemed, he wrote the Commodore's dispatches for Washington, and also was his general amanuensis. Nor was this a very light duty, at times; for some Commodores, though they do not *say* a great deal on board ship, yet they have a vast deal to write. Very often, the regimental orderly, stationed at our Commodore's cabin-door, would touch his hat to the First Lieutenant, and with a mysterious air hand him a note. I always thought these notes must contain most important matters of state; until one day, seeing a slip of wet, torn paper in a scupper-hole, I read the following:

"Sir, you will give the people pickles to-day with their fresh meat.
"To Lieutenant Bridewell.
"By command of the Commodore.
"ADOLPHUS DASHMAN, Priv. Sec."

This was a new revelation; for, from his almost immutable reserve, I had supposed that the Commodore never meddled immediately with the concerns of the ship, but left all that to the captain. But the longer we live, the more we learn of Commodores.

Turn we now to the second officer in rank, almost supreme, however, in the internal affairs of his ship. Captain Claret was a large, portly man, a Harry the Eighth afloat, bluff and hearty; and as kingly in his cabin as Harry on his throne. For a ship is a bit of terra firma cut off from the main; it is a state in itself; and the captain is its king.

It is no limited monarchy, where the sturdy Commons have a right to petition, and snarl if they please; but almost a despotism, like the Grand Turk's. The captain's word is law; he never speaks but in the imperative mood. When he stands on his Quarter-deck at sea, he absolutely commands as far as eye can reach. Only the moon and stars are beyond his jurisdiction. He is lord and master of the sun.

It is not twelve o'clock till he says so. For when the sailing-master, whose duty it is to take the regular observation at noon, touches his hat, and reports twelve o'clock to the officer of the deck; that functionary orders a midshipman to repair to the captain's cabin, and humbly inform him of the respectful suggestion of the sailing-master.

"Twelve o'clock reported, sir," says the middy.

"*Make* it so," replies the captain.

And the bell is struck eight by the messenger-boy, and twelve o'clock it is.

As in the case of the Commodore, when the captain visits the deck, his subordinate officers generally beat a retreat to the other side; and, as a general rule, would no more think of addressing him, except concerning the ship, than a lackey would think of hailing the Czar of Russia on his throne, and inviting him to tea. Perhaps no mortal man has more reason to feel such an intense sense of his own personal consequence, as the captain of a man-of-war at sea.

Next in rank comes the First or Senior Lieutenant, the chief executive officer. I have no reason to love the particular gentleman who filled that post aboard of our frigate, for it was he who refused my petition for as much black paint as would render water-proof that white jacket of mine. All my soakings and drenchings lie at his state-room door. I hardly think I shall ever forgive him; every twinge of the rheumatism, which I still occasionally feel, is directly referable to him. The Immortals have a reputation for clemency; and *they* may pardon him; but he must not dun me to be merciful. But my personal feelings toward the man shall not prevent me from here doing him justice. In most things, he was an excellent seaman; prompt, loud, and to the point; and as such, was well fitted for his station. The First Lieutenancy of a frigate demands a good disciplinarian, and, every way, an energetic man. By the captain he is held responsible for every thing; by that magnate, indeed, he is supposed to be omnipresent; down in the hold, and up aloft, at one and the same time.

He presides at the head of the Ward-room officers' table, who are so called from their messing together in a part of the ship thus designated. In a frigate it comprises the after part of the berth-deck. Sometimes it goes by the name of the Gunroom, but oftener is called the Ward-room. Within, this Ward-room much resembles a long, wide corridor in a large hotel; numerous doors opening on both hands to the private apartments of the officers. The first time I had a look at it, the Chaplain was seated at the table in the centre, playing chess with the Lieutenant of Marines. It was mid-day, but the place was lighted by lamps.

Besides the First Lieutenant, the Ward-room officers include the junior lieutenants, in a frigate six or seven in number, the Sailing-master, Purser, Chaplain, Surgeon, Marine officers, and Midshipmen's Schoolmaster, or "the Professor." They generally form a very agreeable club of good fellows; from their diversity of character, admirably calculated to form an agreeable social whole. The Lieutenants discuss sea-fights, and tell anecdotes of Lord Nelson and Lady Hamilton; the Marine officers talk of storming fortresses, and the siege of Gibraltar; the Purser steadies this wild conversation by occasional allusions to the rule of three; the Professor is always charged with a scholarly reflection, or an apt line from the classics, generally Ovid; the Surgeon's stories of the amputation-table judiciously serve to suggest the mortality of the whole party as men; while the good chaplain stands ready at all times to give them pious counsel and consolation.

Of course these gentlemen all associate on a footing of perfect social equality.

Next in order come the Warrant or Forward officers, consisting of the Boatswain, Gunner, Carpenter, and Sail-maker. Though these worthies sport long coats and wear the anchor-button; yet, in the estimation of the ward-room officers, they are not, technically speaking, rated gentlemen. The First Lieutenant, Chaplain, or Surgeon, for example, would never dream of inviting them to dinner. In sea parlance, "they come in at the hawse holes;" they have hard hands; and the carpenter and sail-maker practically understand the duties which they are called upon to superintend. They mess by themselves. Invariably four in number, they never have need to play whist with a dummy.

In this part of the category now come the "reefers," otherwise "middies" or midshipmen. These boys are sent to sea, for the purpose of making commodores; and in order to become commodores, many of them deem it indispensable forthwith to commence chewing tobacco, drinking brandy and water, and swearing at the sailors. As they are only placed on board a sea-going ship to go to school and learn the duty of a Lieutenant; and until qualified to act as such, have few

or no special functions to attend to; they are little more, while
midshipmen, than supernumeraries on board. Hence, in a
crowded frigate, they are so everlastingly crossing the path of
both men and officers, that in the navy it has become a proverb, that a useless fellow is "*as much in the way as a reefer*."

In a gale of wind, when all hands are called and the deck
swarms with men, the little "middies" running about distracted and having nothing particular to do, make it up in
vociferous swearing; exploding all about under foot like tor-
pedoes. Some of them are terrible little boys, cocking their
caps at alarming angles, and looking fierce as young roosters.
They are generally great consumers of Macassar oil and the
Balm of Columbia; they thirst and rage after whiskers; and
sometimes, applying their ointments, lay themselves out in
the sun, to promote the fertility of their chins.

As the only way to learn to command, is to learn to obey,
the usage of a ship of war is such that the midshipmen are
constantly being ordered about by the Lieutenants; though,
without having assigned them their particular destinations,
they are always going somewhere, and never arriving. In
some things, they almost have a harder time of it than the
seamen themselves. They are messengers and errand-boys to
their superiors.

"Mr. Pert," cries an officer of the deck, hailing a young
gentleman forward. Mr. Pert advances, touches his hat, and
remains in an attitude of deferential suspense. "Go and tell
the boatswain I want him." And with this perilous errand,
the middy hurries away, looking proud as a king.

The middies live by themselves in the steerage, where,
nowadays, they dine off a table, spread with a cloth. They
have a castor at dinner; they have some other little boys (selected from the ship's company) to wait upon them; they
sometimes drink coffee out of china. But for all these, their
modern refinements, in some instances the affairs of their club
go sadly to rack and ruin. The china is broken; the japanned
coffee-pot dented like a pewter mug in an ale-house; the
pronged forks resemble tooth-picks (for which they are sometimes used); the table-knives are hacked into hand-saws; and
the cloth goes to the sail-maker to be patched. Indeed, they
are something like collegiate freshmen and sophomores, liv-

ing in the college buildings, especially so far as the noise they make in their quarters is concerned. The steerage buzzes, hums, and swarms like a hive; or like an infant-school of a hot day, when the schoolmistress falls asleep with a fly on her nose.

In frigates, the ward-room—the retreat of the Lieutenants—immediately adjoining the steerage, is on the same deck with it. Frequently, when the middies, waking early of a morning, as most youngsters do, would be kicking up their heels in their hammocks, or running about with double-reefed night-gowns, playing *tag* among the "clews;" the Senior Lieutenant would burst among them with a—"Young gentlemen, I am astonished. You must stop this sky-larking. Mr. Pert, what are you doing at the table there, without your pantaloons? To your hammock, sir. Let me see no more of this. If you disturb the ward-room again, young gentlemen, you shall hear of it." And so saying, this hoary-headed Senior Lieutenant would retire to his cot in his state-room, like the father of a numerous family after getting up in his dressing-gown and slippers, to quiet a daybreak tumult in his populous nursery.

Having now descended from Commodore to Middy, we come lastly to a set of nondescripts, forming also a "mess" by themselves, apart from the seamen. Into this mess, the usage of a man-of-war thrusts various subordinates—including the master-at-arms, purser's steward, ship's corporals, marine sergeants, and ship's yeomen, forming the first aristocracy above the sailors.

The master-at-arms is a sort of high constable and school-master, wearing citizen's clothes, and known by his official rattan. He it is whom all sailors hate. His is the universal duty of a universal informer and hunter-up of delinquents. On the berth-deck he reigns supreme; spying out all grease-spots made by the various cooks of the seamen's messes, and driving the laggards up the hatches, when all hands are called. It is indispensable that he should be a very Vidocq in vigilance. But as it is a heartless, so is it a thankless office. Of dark nights, most masters-at-arms keep themselves in readiness to dodge forty-two pound balls, dropped down the hatchways near them.

The ship's corporals are this worthy's deputies and ushers.

The marine sergeants are generally tall fellows with unyielding spines and stiff upper lips, and very exclusive in their tastes and predilections.

The ship's yeoman is a gentleman who has a sort of counting-room in a tar-cellar down in the fore-hold. More will be said of him anon.

Except the officers above enumerated, there are none who mess apart from the seamen. The "*petty officers*," so called; that is, the Boatswain's, Gunner's, Carpenter's, and Sailmaker's mates, the Captains of the Tops, of the Forecastle, and of the After-Guard, and of the Fore and Main holds, and the Quarter-Masters, all mess in common with the crew, and in the American navy are only distinguished from the common seamen by their slightly additional pay. But in the English navy they wear crowns and anchors worked on the sleeves of their jackets, by way of badges of office. In the French navy they are known by strips of worsted worn in the same place, like those designating the Sergeants and Corporals in the army.

Thus it will be seen, that the dinner-table is the criterion of rank in our man-of-war world. The Commodore dines alone, because he is the only man of his rank in the ship. So too with the Captain; and the Ward-room officers, warrant officers, midshipmen, the master-at-arms' mess, and the common seamen;—all of them, respectively, dine together, because they are, respectively, on a footing of equality.

For the same reason, the Commodore has his own steward and cook, who wait upon nobody but him; also his own stove, where nothing is cooked but for his meals. So, too, with the Captain. The ward-room officers, also, have their own steward and cook; also, the midshipmen. The cooking for these two classes is done at a distinct part of the great galley—the forward end—a place called "the range." This is a wide grate, several feet long.

Chapter 7

BREAKFAST, DINNER, AND SUPPER

NOT ONLY is the dinner-table a criterion of rank on board a man-of-war, but also the dinner hour. He who dines latest is the greatest man; and he who dines earliest is accounted the least. In a flag-ship, the Commodore generally dines about four or five o'clock; the Captain about three; the Lieutenants about two; while *the people** (by which phrase the common seamen are specially designated in the nomenclature of the quarter-deck) sit down to their salt beef exactly at noon.

Thus it will be seen, that while the two estates of sea-kings and sea-lords dine at rather patrician hours—and thereby, in the long run, impair their digestive functions—the sea-commoners, or *the people*, keep up their constitutions, by keeping up the good old-fashioned, Elizabethan, Franklin-warranted dinner hour of twelve.

Twelve o'clock! It is the natural centre, key-stone, and very heart of the day. At that hour, the sun has arrived at the top of his hill; and as he seems to hang poised there a while, before coming down on the other side, it is but reasonable to suppose that he is then stopping to dine; setting an eminent example to all mankind. The rest of the day is called *afternoon*; the very sound of which fine old Saxon word conveys a feeling of the lee bulwarks and a nap; a summer sea—soft breezes creeping over it; dreamy dolphins gliding in the distance. *Afternoon!* the word implies, that it is an after-piece, coming after the grand drama of the day; something to be taken leisurely and lazily. But how can this be, if you dine at five? For, after all, though Paradise Lost be a noble poem, and we men-of-war's men, no doubt, largely partake in the immortality of the immortals; yet, let us candidly confess it, shipmates, that, upon the whole, our dinners are the most momentous affairs of these lives we lead beneath the moon.

*In the same nomenclature, they are also especially designated as "the men."

What were a day without a dinner? a dinnerless day! such a day had better be a night.

Again: twelve o'clock is the natural hour for us men-of-war's men to dine, because at that hour the very time-pieces we have invented arrive at their terminus; they can get no further than twelve; when straightway they continue their old rounds again. Doubtless, Adam and Eve dined at twelve; and the Patriarch Abraham in the midst of his cattle; and old Job with his noon mowers and reapers, in that grand plantation of Uz; and old Noah himself, in the Ark, must have gone to dinner at precisely *eight bells* (noon), with all his floating families and farm-yards.

But though this antediluvian dinner hour is rejected by modern Commodores and Captains, it still lingers among "*the people*" under their command. Many sensible things banished from high life find an asylum among the mob.

Some Commodores are very particular in seeing to it, that no man on board the ship dare to dine after his (the Commodore's) own dessert is cleared away.—Not even the Captain. It is said, on good authority, that a Captain once ventured to dine at five, when the Commodore's hour was four. Next day, as the story goes, that Captain received a private note; and in consequence of that note, dined for the future at half past three.

Though in respect of the dinner hour on board a man-of-war, *the people* have no reason to complain; yet they have just cause, almost for mutiny, in the outrageous hours assigned for their breakfast and supper.

Eight o'clock for breakfast; twelve for dinner; four for supper; and no meals but these; no lunches and no cold snacks. Owing to this arrangement (and partly to one watch going to their meals before the other, at sea), all the meals of the twenty-four hours are crowded into a space of less than eight! Sixteen mortal hours elapse between supper and breakfast; including, to one watch, eight hours on deck! This is barbarous; any physician will tell you so. Think of it! Before the Commodore has dined, you have supped. And in high latitudes, in summer-time, you have taken your last meal for the day, and five hours, or more, daylight to spare!

Mr. Secretary of the Navy, in the name of *the people*, you

should interpose in this matter. Many a time have I, a main-top-man, found myself actually faint of a tempestuous morning watch, when all my energies were demanded—owing to this miserable, unphilosophical mode of allotting the government meals at sea. We beg of you, Mr. Secretary, not to be swayed in this matter by the Honorable Board of Commodores, who will no doubt tell you that eight, twelve, and four are the proper hours for *the people* to take their meals; inasmuch, as at these hours the watches are relieved. For, though this arrangement makes a neater and cleaner thing of it for the officers, and looks very nice and superfine on paper; yet, it is plainly detrimental to health; and in time of war is attended with still more serious consequences to the whole nation at large. If the necessary researches were made, it would perhaps be found that in those instances where men-of-war adopting the above-mentioned hours for meals have encountered an enemy at night, they have pretty generally been beaten; that is, in those cases where the enemies' meal times were reasonable; which is only to be accounted for by the fact that *the people* of the beaten vessels were fighting on an empty stomach instead of a full one.

Chapter 8

Selvagee contrasted with Mad-Jack

Having glanced at the grand divisions of a man of-war, let us now descend to specialties; and, particularly, to two of the junior lieutenants; lords and noblemen; members of that House of Peers, the gun-room. There were several young lieutenants on board; but from these two—representing the extremes of character to be found in their department—the nature of the other officers of their grade in the Neversink must be derived.

One of these two quarter-deck lords went among the sailors by a name of their own devising—Selvagee. Of course, it was intended to be characteristic; and even so it was.

In frigates, and all large ships of war, when getting under weigh, a large rope, called a *messenger*, is used to carry the strain of the cable to the capstan; so that the anchor may be weighed, without the muddy, ponderous cable itself going round the capstan. As the cable enters the hawse-hole, therefore, something must be constantly used, to keep this traveling chain attached to this traveling *messenger*; something that may be rapidly wound round both, so as to bind them together. The article used is called a *selvagee*. And what could be better adapted to the purpose? It is a slender, tapering, unstranded piece of rope; prepared with much solicitude; peculiarly flexible; and wreathes and serpentines round the cable and messenger like an elegantly-modeled garter-snake round the twisted stalks of a vine. Indeed, *Selvagee* is the exact type and symbol of a tall, genteel, limber, spiralizing exquisite. So much for the derivation of the name which the sailors applied to the Lieutenant.

From what sea-alcove, from what mermaid's milliner's shop, hast thou emerged, Selvagee! with that dainty waist and languid cheek? What heartless step-dame drove thee forth, to waste thy fragrance on the salt sea-air?

Was it *you*, Selvagee! that, outward-bound, off Cape Horn, looked at Hermit Island through an Opera-glass? Was it *you*, who thought of proposing to the Captain, that when the sails were furled in a gale, a few drops of lavender should be dropped in their "bunts," so that when the canvass was set again, your nostrils might not be offended by its musty smell? I do not *say* it was you, Selvagee; I but deferentially inquire.

In plain prose, Selvagee was one of those officers whom the sight of a trim-fitting naval coat had captivated in the days of his youth. He fancied, that if a sea-officer dressed well, and conversed genteelly, he would abundantly uphold the honor of his flag, and immortalize the tailor that made him. On that rock many young gentlemen split. For upon a frigate's quarter-deck, it is not enough to sport a coat fashioned by a Stultz; it is not enough to be well braced with straps and suspenders; it is not enough to have sweet reminiscences of Lauras and Matildas. It is a right down life of hard wear and tear, and the man who is not, in a good degree, fitted to become a common sailor will never make an officer. Take that to heart, all ye naval aspirants. Thrust your arms up to the elbow in pitch, and see how you like it, ere you solicit a warrant. Prepare for white squalls, living gales and Typhoons; read accounts of shipwrecks and horrible disasters; peruse the Narratives of Byron and Bligh; familiarize yourselves with the story of the English frigate Alceste, and the French frigate Medusa. Though you may go ashore, now and then, at Cadiz and Palermo; for every day so spent among oranges and ladies, you will have whole months of rains and gales.

And even thus did Selvagee prove it. But with all the intrepid effeminacy of your true dandy, he still continued his Cologne-water baths, and sported his lace-bordered handkerchiefs in the very teeth of a tempest. Alas, Selvagee! there was no getting the lavender out of you.

But Selvagee was no fool. Theoretically he understood his profession; but the mere theory of seamanship forms but the thousandth part of what makes a seaman. You can not save a ship by working out a problem in the cabin; the deck is the field of action.

Well aware of his deficiency in some things, Selvagee never took the trumpet—which is the badge of the deck officer for the time—without a tremulous movement of the lip, and an earnest, inquiring eye to the windward. He encouraged those old Tritons, the Quarter-masters, to discourse with him concerning the likelihood of a squall; and often followed their advice as to taking in, or making sail. The smallest favors in that way were thankfully received. Sometimes, when all the North looked unusually lowering, by many conversational blandishments, he would endeavor to prolong his predecessor's stay on deck, after that officer's watch had expired. But in fine, steady weather, when the Captain would emerge from his cabin, Selvagee might be seen, pacing the poop with long, bold, indefatigable strides, and casting his eye up aloft with the most ostentatious fidelity.

But vain these pretences; he could not deceive. Selvagee! you know very well, that if it comes on to blow pretty hard, the First Lieutenant will be sure to interfere with his paternal authority. Every man and every boy in the frigate knows, Selvagee, that you are no Neptune.

How unenviable his situation! His brother officers do not insult him, to be sure; but sometimes their looks are as daggers. The sailors do not laugh at him outright; but of dark nights they jeer, when they hearken to that mantua-maker's voice ordering *a strong pull at the main brace,* or *hands by the halyards!* Sometimes, by way of being terrific, and making the men jump, Selvagee raps out an oath; but the soft bomb stuffed with confectioner's kisses seems to burst like a crushed rose-bud diffusing its odors. Selvagee! Selvagee! take a main-top-man's advice; and this cruise over, never more tempt the sea.

With this gentleman of cravats and curling irons, how strongly contrasts the man who was born in a gale! For in some time of tempest—off Cape Horn or Hatteras—*Mad Jack* must have entered the world—such things have been—not with a silver spoon, but with a speaking-trumpet in his mouth; wrapped up in a caul, as in a main-sail—for a charmed life against shipwrecks he bears—and crying, *Luff! luff, you may!—steady!—port! World ho!—here I am!*

Mad Jack is in his saddle on the sea. *That* is his home; he would not care much, if another Flood came and overflowed the dry land; for what would it do but float his good ship higher and higher and carry his proud nation's flag round the globe, over the very capitals of all hostile states! Then would masts surmount spires; and all mankind, like the Chinese boatmen in Canton River, live in flotillas and fleets, and find their food in the sea.

Mad Jack was expressly created and labelled for a tar. Five feet nine is his mark, in his socks; and not weighing over eleven stone before dinner. Like so many ship's shrouds, his muscles and tendons are all set true, trim, and taut; he is braced up fore and aft, like a ship on the wind. His broad chest is a bulk-head, that dams off the gale; and his nose is an aquiline, that divides it in two, like a keel. His loud, lusty lungs are two belfries, full of all manner of chimes; but you only hear his deepest bray, in the height of some tempest—like the great bell of St. Paul's, which only sounds when the King or the Devil is dead.

Look at him there, where he stands on the poop—one foot on the rail, and one hand on a shroud—his head thrown back, and his trumpet like an elephant's trunk thrown up in the air. Is he going to shoot dead with sound, those fellows on the main-topsail-yard?

Mad Jack was a bit of a tyrant—they *say* all good officers are—but the sailors loved him all round; and would much rather stand fifty watches with him, than one with a rose-water sailor.

But Mad Jack, alas! has one fearful failing. He drinks. And so do we all. But Mad Jack, *he* only drinks brandy. The vice was inveterate; surely, like Ferdinand, Count Fathom, he must have been suckled at a puncheon. Very often, this bad habit got him into very serious scrapes. Twice was he put off duty by the Commodore; and once he came near being broken for his frolics. So far as his efficiency as a sea-officer was concerned, on shore at least, Jack might *bouse away* as much as he pleased; but afloat it will not do at all.

Now, if he only followed the wise example set by those ships of the desert, the camels; and while in port, drank for the thirst past, the thirst present, and the thirst to come—so that he might cross the ocean sober; Mad Jack would get along pretty well. Still better, if he would but eschew brandy altogether; and only drink of the limpid white-wine of the rills and the brooks.

Chapter 9

Of the Pockets that were in the Jacket

I MUST MAKE some further mention of that white jacket of mine.

And here be it known—by way of introduction to what is to follow—that to a common sailor, the living on board a man-of-war is like living in a market; where you dress on the door-steps, and sleep in the cellar. No privacy can you have; hardly one moment's seclusion. It is almost a physical impossibility, that you can ever be alone. You dine at a vast *table d'hôte*; sleep in commons, and make your toilet where and when you can. There is no calling for a mutton chop and a pint of claret by yourself; no selecting of chambers for the night; no hanging of pantaloons over the back of a chair; no ringing your bell of a rainy morning, to take your coffee in bed. It is something like life in a large manufactory. The bell strikes to dinner, and hungry or not, you must dine.

Your clothes are stowed in a large canvas bag, generally painted black, which you can get out of the "rack" only once in the twenty-four hours; and then, during a time of the utmost confusion; among five hundred other bags, with five hundred other sailors diving into each, in the midst of the twilight of the berth deck. In some measure to obviate this inconvenience, many sailors divide their wardrobes between their hammocks and their bags; stowing a few frocks and trowsers in the former; so that they can shift at night, if they wish, when the hammocks are piped down. But they gain very little by this.

You have no place whatever but your bag or hammock, in which to put any thing in a man-of-war. If you lay any thing down, and turn your back for a moment, ten to one it is gone.

Now, in sketching the preliminary plan, and laying out the foundation of that memorable white jacket of mine, I had had an earnest eye to all these inconveniences, and resolved to avoid them. I proposed, that not only should my jacket keep me warm, but that it should also be so constructed as to contain a shirt or two, a pair of trowsers, and divers knick-knacks—sewing utensils, books, biscuits, and the like. With this object, I had accordingly provided it with a great variety of pockets, pantries, clothes-presses, and cupboards.

The principal apartments, two in number, were placed in the skirts, with a wide, hospitable entrance from the inside; two more, of smaller capacity, were planted in each breast, with folding-doors communicating, so that in case of emergency, to accommodate any bulky articles, the two pockets in each breast could be thrown into one. There were, also, several unseen recesses behind the arras; insomuch, that my jacket, like an old castle, was full of winding stairs, and mysterious closets, crypts, and cabinets; and like a confidential writing-desk, abounded in snug little out-of-the-way lairs and hiding-places, for the storage of valuables.

Superadded to these, were four capacious pockets on the outside; one pair to slip books into when suddenly started from my studies to the main-royal-yard; and the other pair, for permanent mittens, to thrust my hands into of a cold night-watch. This last contrivance was regarded as needless by one of my top-mates, who showed me a pattern for sea-mittens, which he said was much better than mine.

It must be known, that sailors, even in the bleakest weather, only cover their hands when unemployed; they never wear mittens aloft; since aloft, they literally carry their lives in their hands, and want nothing between their grasp of the hemp, and the hemp itself.—Therefore, it is desirable, that whatever things they cover their hands with, should be capable of being slipped on and off in a moment. Nay, it is desirable, that they should be of such a nature, that in a dark night, when you are in a great hurry—say, going to the helm—they may be jumped into, indiscriminately; and not be like a pair of right-and-left kids; neither of which will admit any hand, but the particular one meant for it.

My top-mate's contrivance was this—he ought to have got out a patent for it—each of his mittens was provided with two thumbs, one on each side; the convenience of which needs no comment. But though for clumsy seamen, whose fingers are all thumbs, this description of mitten might do very well, White-Jacket did not so much fancy it. For when your hand was once in the bag of the mitten, the empty thumb-hole sometimes dangled at your palm, confounding your ideas of where your real thumb might be; or else, being carefully grasped in the hand, was continually suggesting the insane notion, that you were all the while having hold of some one else's thumb.

No; I told my good top-mate to go away with his four thumbs, I would have nothing to do with them; two thumbs were enough for any man.

For some time after completing my jacket, and getting the furniture and household stores in it; I thought that nothing could exceed it, for convenience. Seldom now did I have occasion to go to my bag, and be jostled by the crowd who were making their wardrobe in a heap. If I wanted any thing in the way of clothing, thread, needles, or literature, the chances were that my invaluable jacket contained it. Yes: I fairly hugged myself, and reveled in my jacket; till alas! a long rain put me out of conceit of it. I, and all my pantries and their contents, were soaked through and through, and my pocket-edition of Shakspeare was reduced to an omelet.

However, availing myself of a fine sunny day that followed, I emptied myself out in the main-top, and spread all my goods and chattels to dry. But spite of the bright sun, that day proved a black one. The scoundrels on deck detected me in the act of discharging my saturated cargo; they now knew that the white jacket was used for a store-house. The consequence was that, my goods being well dried and again stored away in my pockets, the very next night, when it was my quarter watch on deck, and not in the top (where they were all honest men), I noticed a parcel of fellows skulking about after me, wherever I went. To a man, they were pickpockets, and bent upon pillaging me. In vain I kept clapping my pockets like nervous old gentlemen in a crowd; that same night I found myself minus several valuable articles. So, in the end, I masoned up my lockers and pantries; and save the two used for mittens, the white jacket ever after was pocketless.

Chapter 10

FROM POCKETS TO PICKPOCKETS

A S THE LATTER PART of the preceding chapter may seem strange to those landsmen, who have been habituated to indulge in high-raised, romantic notions of the man-of-war's man's character; it may not be amiss, to set down here certain facts on this head, which may serve to place the thing in its true light.

From the wild life they lead, and various other causes (needless to mention), sailors, as a class, entertain the most liberal notions concerning morality and the Decalogue; or rather, they take their own views of such matters, caring little for the theological or ethical definitions of others concerning what may be criminal, or wrong.

Their ideas are much swayed by circumstances. They will covertly abstract a thing from one, whom they dislike; and insist upon it, that, in such a case, stealing is no robbing. Or, where the theft involves something funny, as in the case of the white jacket, they only steal for the sake of the joke; but this much is to be observed nevertheless, i.e., that they never spoil the joke by returning the stolen article.

It is a good joke, for instance, and one often perpetrated on board ship, to stand talking to a man in a dark night watch, and all the while be cutting the buttons from his coat. But once off, those buttons never grow on again. There is no spontaneous vegetation in buttons.

Perhaps it is a thing unavoidable, but the truth is that, among the crew of a man-of-war, scores of desperadoes are too often found, who stop not at the largest enormities. A species of highway robbery is not unknown to them. A *gang* will be informed, that such a fellow has three or four gold pieces in the monkey-bag, so called, or purse, which many tars wear round their necks, tucked out of sight. Upon this, they deliberately lay their plans; and in due time, proceed to carry them into execution. The man they have marked is perhaps strolling along the benighted berth-deck to his mess-chest; when, of a sudden, the foot-pads dash out from their hiding-place, throw him down, and while two or three gag him, and hold him fast, another cuts the bag from his neck, and makes away with it, followed by his comrades. This was more than once done in the Neversink.

At other times, hearing that a sailor has something valuable secreted in his hammock, they will rip it open from underneath while he sleeps, and reduce the conjecture to a certainty.

To enumerate all the minor pilferings on board a man-of-war would be endless. With some highly commendable exceptions, they rob from one another, and rob back again, till, in the matter of small things, a community of goods seems almost established; and at last, as a whole, they become relatively honest, by nearly every man becoming the reverse. It is in vain that the officers, by threats of condign punishment, endeavor to instill more virtuous principles into their crew; so thick is the mob, that not one thief in a thousand is detected.

Chapter II

THE PURSUIT OF POETRY UNDER DIFFICULTIES

THE FEELING of insecurity concerning one's possessions in the Neversink, which the things just narrated begat in the minds of honest men, was curiously exemplified in the case of my poor friend Lemsford, a gentlemanly young member of the After-Guard. I had very early made the acquaintance of Lemsford. It is curious, how unerringly a man pitches upon a spirit, any way akin to his own, even in the most miscellaneous mob.

Lemsford was a poet; so thoroughly inspired with the divine afflatus, that not even all the tar and tumult of a man-of-war could drive it out of him.

As may readily be imagined, the business of writing verse is a very different thing on the gun-deck of a frigate, from what the gentle and sequestered Wordsworth found it at placid Rydal Mount in Westmoreland. In a frigate, you can not sit down and meander off your sonnets, when the full heart prompts; but only, when more important duties permit: such as bracing round the yards, or reefing top-sails fore and aft. Nevertheless, every fragment of time at his command was religiously devoted by Lemsford to the Nine. At the most unseasonable hours, you would behold him, seated apart, in some corner among the guns—a shot-box before him, pen in hand, and eyes "*in a fine frenzy rolling.*"

"What's that 'ere born nat'ral about?"—"He's got a fit, hain't he?" were exclamations often made by the less learned of his shipmates. Some deemed him a conjurer; others a lunatic; and the knowing ones said, that he must be a crazy Methodist. But well knowing by experience the truth of the saying, that *poetry is its own exceeding great reward*, Lemsford wrote on; dashing off whole epics, sonnets, ballads, and acrostics, with a facility which, under the circumstances, amazed me. Often he read over his effusions to me; and well worth the hearing they were. He had wit, imagination, feeling, and humor in abundance; and out of the very ridicule with which some persons regarded him, he made rare metrical sport, which we two together enjoyed by ourselves; or shared with certain select friends.

Still, the taunts and jeers so often leveled at my fine friend the poet, would now and then rouse him into rage; and at such times the haughty scorn he would hurl on his foes, was proof positive of his possession of that one attribute, irritability, almost universally ascribed to the votaries of Parnassus and the Nine.

My noble Captain, Jack Chase, rather patronized Lemsford, and he would stoutly take his part against scores of adversaries. Frequently, inviting him up aloft into his top, he would beg him to recite some of his verses; to which he would pay the most heedful attention, like Mecænas listening to Virgil, with a book of the Æneid in his hand. Taking the liberty of a well-wisher, he would sometimes gently criticise the piece, suggesting a few immaterial alterations. And upon my word, noble Jack, with his native-born good sense, taste, and humanity, was not ill qualified to play the true part of a *Quarterly Review*;—which is, to give quarter at last, however severe the critique.

Now Lemsford's great care, anxiety, and endless source of tribulation was the preservation of his manuscripts. He had a little box, about the size of a small dressing-case, and secured with a lock, in which he kept his papers and stationery. This box, of course, he could not keep in his bag or hammock, for, in either case, he would only be able to get at it once in the twenty-four hours. It was necessary to have it accessible at all times. So when not using it, he was obliged to hide it out of sight, where he could. And of all places in the world, a ship of war, above her *hold*, least abounds in secret nooks. Almost every inch is occupied; almost every inch is in plain sight; and almost every inch is continually being visited and explored. Added to all this, was the deadly hostility of the whole tribe of ship-underlings—master-at-arms, ship's corporals, and boatswain's mates,—both to the poet and his casket. They hated his box, as if it had been Pandora's, crammed to the very lid with hurricanes and gales. They hunted out his hiding-places like pointers, and gave him no peace night or day.

Still, the long twenty-four-pounders on the main-deck offered some promise of a hiding-place to the box; and, accordingly, it was often tucked away behind the carriages, among the side tackles; its black color blending with the ebon hue of the guns.

But Quoin, one of the quarter-gunners, had eyes like a ferret. Quoin was a little old man-of-war's man, hardly five feet high, with a complexion like a gun-shot wound after it is healed. He was indefatigable in attending to his duties; which consisted in taking care of one division of the guns, embracing ten of the aforesaid twenty-four-pounders. Ranged up against the ship's side at regular intervals, they resembled not a little a stud of sable chargers in their stalls. Among this iron stud little Quoin was continually running in and out, currying them down, now and then, with an old rag, or keeping the flies off with a brush. To Quoin, the honor and dignity of the United States of America seemed indissolubly linked with the keeping his guns unspotted and glossy. He himself was black as a chimney-sweep with continually tending them, and rubbing them down with black paint. He would sometimes get outside of the port-holes and peer into their muzzles, as a monkey into a bottle. Or, like a dentist, he seemed intent upon examining their teeth. Quite as often, he would be brushing out their touch-holes with a little wisp of oakum, like a Chinese barber in Canton, cleaning a patient's ear.

Such was his solicitude, that it was a thousand pities he was not able to dwarf himself still more, so as to creep in at the touch-hole, and examining the whole interior of the tube, emerge at last from the muzzle. Quoin swore by his guns, and slept by their side. Woe betide the man whom he found leaning against them, or in any way soiling them. He seemed seized with the crazy fancy, that his darling twenty-four-pounders were fragile, and might break, like glass retorts.

Now, from this Quoin's vigilance, how could my poor friend the poet hope to escape with his box? Twenty times a week it was pounced upon, with a "here's that d——d pill-box again!" and a loud threat, to pitch it overboard the next time, without a moment's warning, or benefit of clergy. Like many poets, Lemsford was nervous, and upon these occasions he trembled like a leaf. Once, with an inconsolable countenance, he came to me, saying that his casket was nowhere to be found; he had sought for it in his hiding-place, and it was not there.

I asked him where he had hidden it?

"Among the guns," he replied.

"Then depend upon it, Lemsford, that Quoin has been the death of it."

Straight to Quoin went the poet. But Quoin knew nothing about it. For ten mortal days the poet was not to be comforted; dividing his leisure time between cursing Quoin and lamenting his loss. The world is undone, he must have thought; no such calamity has befallen it since the Deluge;— my verses are perished.

But though Quoin, as it afterward turned out, had indeed found the box, it so happened that he had not destroyed it; which no doubt led Lemsford to infer that a superintending Providence had interposed to preserve to posterity his invaluable casket. It was found at last, lying exposed near the galley.

Lemsford was not the only literary man on board the Neversink. There were three or four persons who kept journals of the cruise. One of these journalists embellished his work— which was written in a large blank account-book—with various colored illustrations of the harbors and bays at which the frigate had touched; and also, with small crayon sketches of comical incidents on board the frigate itself. He would frequently read passages of his book to an admiring circle of the more refined sailors, between the guns. They pronounced the whole performance a miracle of art. As the author declared to them that it was all to be printed and published so soon as the vessel reached home, they vied with each other in procuring interesting items, to be incorporated into additional chapters. But it having been rumored abroad that this journal was to be ominously entitled "*The Cruise of the Neversink, or a Paixhan Shot into Naval Abuses;*" and it having also reached the ears of the Ward-room that the work contained reflections somewhat derogatory to the dignity of the officers, the volume was seized by the master-at-arms, armed with a warrant from the Captain. A few days after, a large nail was driven straight through the two covers, and clinched on the other side, and, thus everlastingly sealed, the book was committed to the deep. The ground taken by the authorities on this occasion was, perhaps, that the book was obnoxious to a certain clause in the Articles of War, forbidding any person in the Navy to bring any other person in the Navy into contempt, which the suppressed volume undoubtedly did.

Chapter 12

THE GOOD OR BAD TEMPER OF MEN-OF-WAR'S MEN,
IN A GREAT DEGREE, ATTRIBUTABLE TO THEIR PAR-
TICULAR STATIONS AND DUTIES ABOARD SHIP

QUOIN, the quarter-gunner, was the representative of a class on board the Neversink, altogether too remarkable to be left astern, without further notice, in the rapid wake of these chapters.

As has been seen, Quoin was full of unaccountable whimsies; he was, withal, a very cross, bitter, ill-natured, inflammable little old man. So, too, were all the members of the gunner's gang; including the two gunner's mates, and all the quarter-gunners. Every one of them had the same dark brown complexion; all their faces looked like smoked hams. They were continually grumbling and growling about the batteries; running in and out among the guns; driving the sailors away from them; and cursing and swearing as if all their consciences had been powder-singed, and made callous, by their calling. Indeed they were a most unpleasant set of men; especially Priming, the nasal-voiced gunner's mate, with the hare-lip; and Cylinder, his stuttering coadjutor, with the clubbed foot. But you will always observe, that the gunner's gang of every man-of-war are invariably ill-tempered, ugly featured, and quarrelsome. Once when I visited an English line-of-battle ship, the gunner's gang were at work fore and aft, polishing up the batteries, which, according to the Admiral's fancy, had been painted white as snow. Fidgeting round the great thirty-two-pounders, and making stinging remarks at the sailors and each other, they reminded one of a swarm of black wasps, buzzing about rows of white headstones in a church-yard.

Now, there can be little doubt, that their being so much among the guns is the very thing that makes a gunner's gang so cross and quarrelsome. Indeed, this was once proved to the satisfaction of our whole company of main-top-men. A fine top-mate of ours, a most merry and companionable fellow, chanced to be promoted to a quarter-gunner's berth. A few days afterward, some of us main-top-men, his old comrades, went to pay him a visit, while he was going his regular rounds through the division of guns allotted to his care. But instead of greeting us with his usual heartiness, and cracking his pleasant jokes, to our amazement, he did little else but scowl; and at last, when we rallied him upon his ill-temper, he seized a long black rammer from overhead, and drove us on deck; threatening to report us, if we ever dared to be familiar with him again.

My top-mates thought that this remarkable metamorphose was the effect produced upon a weak, vain character, suddenly elevated from the level of a mere seaman to the dignified position of a *petty-officer*. But though, in similar cases, I had seen such effects produced upon some of the crew; yet, in the present instance, I knew better than that;—it was solely brought about by his consorting with those villainous, irritable, ill-tempered cannon; more especially from his being subject to the orders of those deformed blunderbusses, Priming and Cylinder.

The truth seems to be, indeed, that all people should be very careful in selecting their callings and vocations; very careful in seeing to it, that they surround themselves by good-humored, pleasant-looking objects; and agreeable, temper-soothing sounds. Many an angelic disposition has had its even edge turned, and hacked like a saw; and many a sweet draught of piety has soured on the heart, from people's choosing ill-natured employments, and omitting to gather round them good-natured landscapes. Gardeners are almost always pleasant, affable people to converse with; but beware of quarter-gunners, keepers of arsenals, and lonely light-house men. And though you will generally observe, that people living in arsenals and light-houses endeavor to cultivate a few flowers in pots, and perhaps a few cabbages in patches, by way of keeping up, if possible, some gayety of spirits; yet, it will not do; their going among great guns and muskets, everlastingly mildews the blossoms of the one; and how can even cabbages thrive in a soil, whereunto the moldering keels of shipwrecked vessels have imparted the loam?

It would be advisable for any man, who from an unlucky

choice of a profession, which it is too late to change for another, should find his temper souring, to endeavor to counteract that misfortune, by filling his private chamber with amiable, pleasurable sights and sounds. In summer time, an Æolian harp can be placed in your window at a very trifling expense; a conch-shell might stand on your mantel, to be taken up and held to the ear, that you may be soothed by its continual lulling sound, when you feel the blue fit stealing over you. For sights, a gay-painted punch-bowl, or Dutch tankard—never mind about filling it—might be recommended. It should be placed on a bracket in the pier. Nor is an old-fashioned silver ladle, nor a chased dinner-castor, nor a fine portly demijohn, nor any thing, indeed, that savors of eating and drinking, bad to drive off the spleen. But perhaps the best of all is a shelf of merrily-bound books, containing comedies, farces, songs, and humorous novels. You need never open them; only have the titles in plain sight. For this purpose, Peregrine Pickle is a good book; so is Gil Blas; so is Goldsmith.

But of all chamber furniture in the world, best calculated to cure a bad temper, and breed a pleasant one, is the sight of a lovely wife. If you have children, however, that are teething, the nursery should be a good way up stairs; at sea, it ought to be in the mizzen-top. Indeed, teething children play the very deuce with a husband's temper. I have known three promising young husbands completely spoil on their wives' hands, by reason of a teething child, whose worrisomeness happened to be aggravated at the time by the summer-complaint. With a breaking heart, and my handkerchief to my eyes, I followed those three hapless young husbands, one after the other, to their premature graves.

Gossiping scenes breed gossips. Who so chatty as hotel-clerks, market-women, auctioneers, bar-keepers, apothecaries, newspaper-reporters, monthly-nurses, and all those who live in bustling crowds, or are present at scenes of chatty interest.

Solitude breeds taciturnity; *that* every body knows; who so taciturn as authors, taken as a race?

A forced, interior quietude, in the midst of great outward commotion, breeds moody people. Who so moody as rail-road-brakemen, steam-boat engineers, helmsmen, and tenders of power-looms in cotton factories? For all these must hold their peace while employed, and let the machinery do the chatting; they can not even edge in a single syllable.

Now, this theory about the wondrous influence of habitual sights and sounds upon the human temper, was suggested by my experiences on board our frigate. And although I regard the example furnished by our quarter-gunners—especially him who had once been our top-mate—as by far the strongest argument in favor of the general theory; yet, the entire ship abounded with illustrations of its truth. Who were more liberal-hearted, lofty-minded, gayer, more jocund, elastic, adventurous, given to fun and frolic, than the top-men of the fore, main, and mizzen masts? The reason of their liberal-heartedness was, that they were daily called upon to expatiate themselves all over the rigging. The reason of their lofty-mindedness was, that they were high lifted above the petty tumults, carping cares, and paltrinesses of the decks below.

And I feel persuaded in my inmost soul, that it is to the fact of my having been a main-top-man; and especially my particular post being on the loftiest yard of the frigate, the main-royal-yard; that I am now enabled to give such a free, broad, off-hand, bird's-eye, and, more than all, impartial account of our man-of-war world; withholding nothing; inventing nothing; nor flattering, nor scandalizing any; but meting out to all—commodore and messenger-boy alike— their precise descriptions and deserts.

The reason of the mirthfulness of these top-men was, that they always looked out upon the blue, boundless, dimpled, laughing, sunny sea. Nor do I hold, that it militates against this theory, that of a stormy day, when the face of the ocean was black, and overcast, that some of them would grow moody, and chose to sit apart. On the contrary, it only proves the thing which I maintain. For even on shore, there are many people, naturally gay and light-hearted, who, whenever the autumnal wind begins to bluster round the corners, and roar along the chimney-stacks, straight become cross, petulant, and irritable. What is more mellow than fine old ale? Yet thunder will sour the best nut-brown ever brewed.

The *Holders* of our frigate, the Troglodytes, who lived down in the tarry cellars and caves below the berth-deck, were, nearly all of them, men of gloomy dispositions, taking sour views of things; one of them was a blue-light Calvinist. Whereas, the old sheet-anchor-men, who spent their time in the bracing sea-air and broad-cast sunshine of the forecastle, were free, generous-hearted, charitable, and full of good-will to all hands; though some of them, to tell the truth, proved sad exceptions; but exceptions only prove the rule.

The "steady-cooks" on the berth-deck, the "steady-sweepers," and "steady-spit-box-musterers," in all divisions of the frigate, fore and aft, were a narrow-minded set; with contracted souls; imputable, no doubt, to their groveling duties. More especially was this evinced in the case of those odious ditchers and night scavengers, the ignoble "Waisters."

The members of the band, some ten or twelve in number, who had nothing to do but keep their instruments polished, and play a lively air now and then, to stir the stagnant current in our poor old Commodore's torpid veins, were the most gleeful set of fellows you ever saw. They were Portuguese, who had been shipped at the Cape De Verd islands, on the passage out. They messed by themselves; forming a dinner-party, not to be exceeded in mirthfulness, by a club of young bridegrooms, three months after marriage, completely satisfied with their bargains, after testing them.

But what made them, now, so full of fun? What indeed but their merry, martial, mellow calling. Who could be a churl, and play a flageolet? who mean and spiritless, braying forth the souls of thousand heroes from his brazen trump? But still more efficacious, perhaps, in ministering to the light spirits of the band, was the consoling thought, that should the ship ever go into action, they would be exempted from the perils of battle. In ships of war, the members of the "music," as the band is called, are generally non-combatants; and mostly ship, with the express understanding, that as soon as the vessel comes within long gun-shot of an enemy, they shall have the privilege of burrowing down in the cable-tiers, or sea coal-hole. Which shows that they are inglorious, but uncommonly sensible fellows.

Look at the barons of the gun-room—Lieutenants, Purser, Marine officers, Sailing-master—all of them gentlemen with stiff upper lips, and aristocratic cut noses. Why was this? Will any one deny, that from their living so long in high military life, served by a crowd of menial stewards and cot-boys, and always accustomed to command right and left; will any one deny, I say, that by reason of this, their very noses had become thin, peaked, aquiline, and aristocratically cartilaginous? Even old Cuticle, the Surgeon, had a Roman nose.

But I never could account how it came to be, that our gray-headed First Lieutenant was a little lop-sided; that is, one of his shoulders disproportionately drooped. And when I observed, that nearly all the First Lieutenants I saw in other men-of-war, besides many Second and Third Lieutenants, were similarly lop-sided; I knew, that there must be some general law which induced the phenomenon; and I put myself to studying it out, as an interesting problem. At last, I came to the conclusion—to which I still adhere—that their so long wearing only one epaulet (for to only one does their rank entitle them) was the infallible clew to this mystery. And when any one reflects upon so well-known a fact, that many sea Lieutenants grow decrepit from age, without attaining a Captaincy and wearing *two* epaulets, which would strike the balance between their shoulders, the above reason assigned will not appear unwarrantable.

Chapter 13

A Man-of-war Hermit in a Mob

THE ALLUSION to the poet Lemsford in a previous chapter, leads me to speak of our mutual friends, Nord and Williams, who, with Lemsford himself, Jack Chase, and my comrades of the main-top, comprised almost the only persons with whom I unreservedly consorted while on board the frigate. For I had not been long on board ere I found that it would not do to be intimate with every body. An indiscriminate intimacy with all hands leads to sundry annoyances and scrapes, too often ending with a dozen at the gang-way. Though I was above a year in the frigate, there were scores of men who to the last remained perfect strangers to me, whose very names I did not know, and whom I would hardly be able to recognize now should I happen to meet them in the streets.

In the dog-watches at sea, during the early part of the evening, the main-deck is generally filled with crowds of pedestrians, promenading up and down past the guns, like people taking the air in Broadway. At such times, it is curious to see the men nodding to each other's recognitions (they might not have seen each other for a week); exchanging a pleasant word with a friend; making a hurried appointment to meet him somewhere aloft on the morrow, or passing group after group without deigning the slightest salutation. Indeed, I was not at all singular in having but comparatively few acquaintances on board, though certainly carrying my fastidiousness to an unusual extent.

My friend Nord was a somewhat remarkable character; and if mystery includes romance, he certainly was a very romantic one. Before seeking an introduction to him through Lemsford, I had often marked his tall, spare, upright figure stalking like Don Quixote among the pigmies of the After-guard, to which he belonged. At first I found him exceedingly reserved and taciturn; his saturnine brow wore a scowl; he was almost repelling in his demeanor. In a word, he seemed desirous of hinting, that his list of man-of-war friends was already made up, complete, and full; and there was no room for more. But observing that the only man he ever consorted with was Lemsford, I had too much magnanimity, by going off in a pique at his coldness, to let him lose forever the chance of making so capital an acquaintance as myself. Besides, I saw it in his eye, that the man had been a reader of good books; I would have staked my life on it, that he seized the right meaning of Montaigne. I saw that he was an earnest thinker; I more than suspected that he had been bolted in the mill of adversity. For all these things, my heart yearned toward him; I determined to know him.

At last I succeeded; it was during a profoundly quiet midnight watch, when I perceived him walking alone in the waist, while most of the men were dozing on the carronade-slides.

That night we scoured all the prairies of reading; dived into the bosoms of authors, and tore out their hearts; and that night White-Jacket learned more than he has ever done in any single night since.

The man was a marvel. He amazed me, as much as Coleridge did the troopers among whom he enlisted. What could have induced such a man to enter a man-of-war, all my sapience can not fathom. And how he managed to preserve his dignity, as he did, among such a rabble rout was equally a mystery. For he was no sailor; as ignorant of a ship, indeed, as a man from the sources of the Niger. Yet the officers respected him; and the men were afraid of him. This much was observable, however, that he faithfully discharged whatever special duties devolved upon him; and was so fortunate as never to render himself liable to a reprimand. Doubtless, he took the same view of the thing that another of the crew did; and had early resolved, so to conduct himself as never to run the risk of the scourge. And this it must have been—added to whatever incommunicable grief which might have been his—that made this Nord such a wandering recluse, even among our man-of-war mob. Nor could he have long swung his hammock on board, ere he must have found that, to insure his exemption from that thing which alone affrighted him, he must be content for the most part to turn a man-hater, and socially expatriate himself from many things, which might have rendered his situation more tolerable. Still more, several events that took place must have horrified him, at times, with the thought that, however he might isolate and entomb himself, yet for all this, the improbability of his being overtaken by what he most dreaded never advanced to the infallibility of the impossible.

In my intercourse with Nord, he never made allusions to his past career—a subject upon which most high-bred cast-aways in a man-of-war are very diffuse; relating their adventures at the gaming-table; the recklessness with which they have run through the amplest fortunes in a single season; their alms-givings, and gratuities to porters and poor relations; and above all, their youthful indiscretions, and broken-hearted ladies they have left behind. No such tales had Nord to tell. Concerning the past, he was barred and locked up like the specie vaults of the Bank of England. For any thing that dropped from him, none of us could be sure that he had ever existed till now. Altogether, he was a remarkable man.

My other friend, Williams, was a thorough-going Yankee from Maine, who had been both a peddler and a pedagogue in his day. He had all manner of stories to tell about nice little country frolics, and would run over an endless list of his sweet-hearts. He was honest, acute, witty, full of mirth and good humor—a laughing philosopher. He was invaluable as a pill against the spleen; and, with the view of extending the advantages of his society to the saturnine Nord, I introduced them to each other; but Nord cut him dead the very same evening, when we sallied out from between the guns for a walk on the main-deck.

Chapter 14

A Drought in a Man-of-war

W E WERE NOT many days out of port, when a rumor was set afloat that dreadfully alarmed many tars. It was this: that, owing to some unprecedented oversight in the Purser, or some equally unprecedented remissness in the Naval-store-keeper at Callao, the frigate's supply of that delectable beverage, called "grog," was well-nigh expended.

In the American Navy, the law allows one gill of spirits per day to every seaman. In two portions, it is served out just previous to breakfast and dinner. At the roll of the drum, the sailors assemble round a large tub, or cask, filled with the liquid; and, as their names are called off by a midshipman, they step up and regale themselves from a little tin measure called a "tot." No high-liver helping himself to Tokay off a well-polished side-board, smacks his lips with more mighty satisfaction than the sailor does over this *tot*. To many of them, indeed, the thought of their daily *tots* forms a perpetual perspective of ravishing landscapes, indefinitely receding in the distance. It is their great "prospect in life." Take away their grog, and life possesses no further charms for them. It is hardly to be doubted, that the controlling inducement which keeps many men in the Navy, is the unbounded confidence they have in the ability of the United States government to supply them, regularly and unfailingly, with their daily allowance of this beverage. I have known several forlorn individuals, shipping as landsmen, who have confessed to me, that having contracted a love for ardent spirits, which they could not renounce, and having by their foolish courses been brought into the most abject poverty—insomuch that they could no longer gratify their thirst ashore—they incontinently entered the Navy; regarding it as the asylum for all drunkards, who might there prolong their lives by regular hours and exercise, and twice every day quench their thirst by moderate and undeviating doses.

When I once remonstrated with an old toper of a top-man

about this daily dram-drinking; when I told him it was ruining him, and advised him to *stop his grog* and receive the money for it, in addition to his wages, as provided by law, he turned about on me, with an irresistibly waggish look, and said, "Give up my grog? And why? Because it is ruining me? No, no; I am a good Christian, White-Jacket, and love my enemy too much to drop his acquaintance."

It may be readily imagined, therefore, what consternation and dismay pervaded the gun-deck at the first announcement of the tidings that the grog was expended.

"The grog gone!" roared an old Sheet-anchor-man.

"Oh! Lord! what a pain in my stomach!" cried a Main-top-man.

"It's worse than the Cholera!" cried a man of the After-guard.

"I'd sooner the water-casks would give out!" said a Captain of the Hold.

"Are we ganders and geese, that we can live without grog?" asked a Corporal of Marines.

"Ay, we must now drink with the ducks!" cried a Quarter-master.

"Not a tot left?" groaned a Waister.

"Not a toothful!" sighed a Holder, from the bottom of his boots.

Yes, the fatal intelligence proved true. The drum was no longer heard rolling the men to the tub, and deep gloom and dejection fell like a cloud. The ship was like a great city, when some terrible calamity has overtaken it. The men stood apart, in groups, discussing their woes, and mutually condoling. No longer, of still moon-light nights, was the song heard from the giddy tops; and few and far between were the stories that were told.

It was during this interval, so dismal to many, that, to the amazement of all hands, ten men were reported by the master-at-arms to be intoxicated. They were brought up to the mast, and at their appearance the doubts of the most skeptical were dissipated; but whence they had obtained their liquor no one could tell. It was observed, however, at the time, that the tarry knaves all smelled of lavender, like so many dandies.

After their examination they were ordered into the "brig,"

a jail-house between two guns on the main-deck, where prisoners are kept. Here they laid for some time, stretched out stark and stiff, with their arms folded over their breasts, like so many effigies of the Black Prince on his monument in Canterbury Cathedral.

Their first slumbers over, the marine sentry who stood guard over them had as much as he could do to keep off the crowd, who were all eagerness to find out how, in such a time of want, the prisoners had managed to drink themselves into oblivion. In due time they were liberated, and the secret simultaneously leaked out.

It seemed that an enterprising man of their number, who had suffered severely from the common deprivation, had all at once been struck by a brilliant idea. It had come to his knowledge that the purser's steward was supplied with a large quantity of *Eau-de-Cologne*, clandestinely brought out in the ship, for the purpose of selling it, on his own account, to the people of the coast; but the supply proving larger than the demand, and having no customers on board the frigate but Lieutenant Selvagee, he was now carrying home more than a third of his original stock. To make a short story of it, this functionary, being called upon in secret, was readily prevailed upon to part with a dozen bottles, with whose contents the intoxicated party had regaled themselves.

The news spread far and wide among the men, being only kept secret from the officers and underlings, and that night the long, crane-necked Cologne bottles jingled in out-of-the-way corners and by-places, and, being emptied, were sent flying out of the ports. With brown sugar, taken from the mess-chests, and hot water begged from the galley-cooks, the men made all manner of punches, toddies, and cocktails, letting fall therein a small drop of tar, like a bit of brown toast, by way of imparting a flavor. Of course, the thing was managed with the utmost secrecy; and as a whole dark night elapsed after their orgies, the revelers were, in a good measure, secure from detection; and those who indulged too freely had twelve long hours to get sober before daylight obtruded.

Next day, fore and aft, the whole frigate smelled like a lady's toilet; the very tar-buckets were fragrant; and from the mouth of many a grim, grizzled old quarter-gunner came the most fragrant of breaths. The amazed Lieutenants went about snuffing up the gale; and, for once, Selvagee had no further need to flourish his perfumed handkerchief. It was as if we were sailing by some odoriferous shore, in the vernal season of violets. Sabæan odors!

> "For many a league,
> Cheered with the grateful smell, old Ocean smiled."

But, alas! all this perfume could not be wasted for nothing; and the master-at-arms and ship's corporals, putting this and that together, very soon burrowed into the secret. The purser's steward was called to account, and no more lavender punches and Cologne toddies were drank on board the Neversink.

Chapter 15

A SALT-JUNK CLUB IN A MAN-OF-WAR, WITH A
NOTICE TO QUIT

IT WAS ABOUT the period of the Cologne-water excitement that my self-conceit was not a little wounded, and my sense of delicacy altogether shocked, by a polite hint received from the cook of the mess to which I happened to belong. To understand the matter, it is needful to enter into preliminaries.

The common seamen in a large frigate are divided into some thirty or forty messes, put down on the purser's books as *Mess No. 1*, *Mess No. 2*, *Mess No. 3*, &c. The members of each mess club their rations of provisions, and breakfast, dine, and sup together in allotted intervals between the guns on the main-deck. In undeviating rotation, the members of each mess (excepting the petty-officers) take their turn in performing the functions of cook and steward. And for the time being, all the affairs of the club are subject to their inspection and control.

It is the cook's business, also, to have an eye to the general interests of his mess; to see that, when the aggregated allowances of beef, bread, &c., are served out by one of the master's mates, the mess over which he presides receives its full share, without stint or subtraction. Upon the berth-deck he has a chest, in which to keep his pots, pans, spoons, and small stores of sugar, molasses, tea, and flour.

But though entitled a cook, strictly speaking, the head of the mess is no cook at all; for the cooking for the crew is all done by a high and mighty functionary, officially called the "*ship's cook*," assisted by several deputies. In our frigate, this personage was a dignified colored gentleman, whom the men dubbed "*Old Coffee*;" and his assistants, negroes also, went by the poetical appellations of "*Sunshine*," "*Rose-water*," and "*May-day*."

Now the *ship's cooking* required very little science, though old Coffee often assured us that he had graduated at the New

York Astor House, under the immediate eye of the celebrated
Coleman and Stetson. All he had to do was, in the first place,
to keep bright and clean the three huge coppers, or caldrons,
in which many hundred pounds of beef were daily boiled. To
this end, Rose-water, Sunshine, and May-day every morning
sprang into their respective apartments, stripped to the waist,
and well provided with bits of soap-stone and sand. By exercising these in a very vigorous manner, they threw themselves
into a violent perspiration, and put a fine polish upon the
interior of the coppers.

Sunshine was the bard of the trio; and while all three
would be busily employed clattering their soap-stones against
the metal, he would exhilarate them with some remarkable St.
Domingo melodies; one of which was the following:

"Oh! I los' my shoes in an old canoe,
     Johnio! come Winum so!
 Oh! I los' my boot in a pilot-boat,
     Johnio! come Winum so!
 Den rub-a-dub de copper, oh!
 Oh! copper rub-a-dub-a-oh!"

When I listened to these jolly Africans, thus making gleeful
their toil by their cheering songs, I could not help murmuring
against that immemorial rule of men-of-war, which forbids
the sailors to sing out, as in merchant-vessels, when pulling
ropes, or occupied at any other ship's duty. Your only music,
at such times, is the shrill pipe of the boatswain's mate, which
is almost worse than no music at all. And if the boatswain's
mate is not by, you must pull the ropes, like convicts, in profound silence; or else endeavor to impart unity to the exertions of all hands, by singing out mechanically, *one*, *two*,
three, and then pulling all together.

Now, when Sunshine, Rose-water, and May-day have so
polished the ship's coppers, that a white kid glove might be
drawn along the inside and show no stain, they leap out of
their holes, and the water is poured in for the coffee. And the
coffee being boiled, and decanted off in buckets-full, the
cooks of the messes march up with their salt beef for dinner,
strung upon strings and tallied with labels; all of which are

plunged together into the self-same coppers, and there boiled. When, upon the beef being fished out with a huge pitch-fork, the water for the evening's tea is poured in; which, consequently, possesses a flavor not unlike that of shank-soup.

From this it will be seen, that, so far as cooking is concerned, a "*cook of the mess*" has very little to do; merely carrying his provisions to and from the grand democratic cookery. Still, in some things, his office involves many annoyances. Twice a week butter and cheese are served out—so much to each man—and the mess-cook has the sole charge of these delicacies. The great difficulty consists in so catering for the mess, touching these luxuries, as to satisfy all. Some guzzlers are for devouring the butter at a meal, and finishing off with the cheese the same day; others contend for saving it up against *Banyan Day*, when there is nothing but beef and bread; and others, again, are for taking a very small bit of butter and cheese, by way of dessert, to each and every meal through the week. All this gives rise to endless disputes, debates, and altercations.

Sometimes, with his mess-cloth—a square of painted canvas—set out on deck between the guns, garnished with pots, and pans, and *kids*, you see the mess-cook seated on a match-tub at its head, his trowser legs rolled up and arms bared, presiding over the convivial party.

"Now, men, you can't have any butter to-day. I'm saving it up for to-morrow. You don't know the value of butter, men. You, Jim, take your hoof off the cloth! Devil take me, if some of you chaps haven't no more manners than so many swines! Quick, men, quick; bear a hand, and '*scoff*' (eat) away.—I've got my to-morrow's *duff* to make yet, and some of you fellows keep *scoffing* as if I had nothing to do but sit still here on this here tub here, and look on. There, there, men, you've all had enough; so sail away out of this, and let me clear up the wreck."

In this strain would one of the periodical cooks of mess No. 15 talk to us. He was a tall, resolute fellow, who had once been a breakman on a rail-road, and he kept us all pretty straight; from his fiat there was no appeal.

But it was not thus when the turn came to others among us. Then it was, *look out for squalls*. The business of dining became a bore, and digestion was seriously impaired by the unamiable discourse we had over our *salt horse*.

I sometimes thought that the junks of lean pork—which were boiled in their own bristles, and looked gaunt and grim, like pickled chins of half-famished, unwashed Cossacks—had something to do with creating the bristling bitterness at times prevailing in our mess. The men tore off the tough hide from their pork, as if they were Indians scalping Christians.

Some cursed the cook for a rogue, who kept from us our butter and cheese, in order to make away with it himself in an underhand manner; selling it as a premium to other messes, and thus accumulating a princely fortune at our expense. Others anathematized him for his slovenliness, casting hypercritical glances into their pots and pans, and scraping them with their knives. Then he would be railed at for his miserable "duffs," and other short-coming preparations.

Marking all this from the beginning, I, White-Jacket, was sorely troubled with the idea, that, in the course of time, my own turn would come round to undergo the same objurgations. How to escape, I knew not. However, when the dreaded period arrived, I received the keys of office (the keys of the mess-chest) with a resigned temper, and offered up a devout ejaculation for fortitude under the trial. I resolved, please Heaven, to approve myself an unexceptionable caterer, and the most impartial of stewards.

The first day there was "*duff*" to make—a business which devolved upon the mess-cooks, though the boiling of it pertained to Old Coffee and his deputies. I made up my mind to lay myself out on that *duff*; to centre all my energies upon it; to put the very soul of art into it, and achieve an unrivaled *duff*—a *duff* that should put out of conceit all other *duffs*, and forever make my administration memorable.

From the proper functionary the flour was obtained, and the raisins; the beef-fat, or "*slush*," from Old Coffee; and the requisite supply of water from the scuttle-butt. I then went among the various cooks, to compare their receipts for making "duffs;" and having well weighed them all, and gathered from each a choice item to make an original receipt of my own, with due deliberation and solemnity I proceeded to business. Placing the component parts in a tin pan, I kneaded them together for an hour, entirely reckless as to pulmonary considerations, touching the ruinous expenditure of breath; and having decanted the semi-liquid dough into a canvas-bag, secured the muzzle, tied on the talley, and delivered it to Rose-water, who dropped the precious bag into the coppers, along with a score or two of others.

Eight bells had struck. The boatswain and his mates had piped the hands to dinner; my mess-cloth was set out, and my messmates were assembled, knife in hand, all ready to precipitate themselves upon the devoted *duff*. Waiting at the grand cookery till my turn came, I received the bag of pudding, and gallanting it into the mess, proceeded to loosen the string.

It was an anxious, I may say, a fearful moment. My hands trembled; every eye was upon me; my reputation and credit were at stake. Slowly I undressed the *duff*, dandling it upon my knee, much as a nurse does a baby about bed-time. The excitement increased, as I curled down the bag from the pudding; it became intense, when at last I plumped it into the pan, held up to receive it by an eager hand. Bim! it fell like a man shot down in a riot. Distraction! It was harder than a sinner's heart; yea, tough as the cock that crowed on the morn that Peter told a lie.

"Gentlemen of the mess, for heaven's sake! permit me one word. I have done my duty by that duff—I have—"

But they beat down my excuses with a storm of criminations. One present proposed that the fatal pudding should be tied round my neck, like a mill-stone, and myself pushed overboard. No use, no use; I had failed; ever after, that duff lay heavy at my stomach and my heart.

After this, I grew desperate; despised popularity; returned scorn for scorn; till at length my week expired, and in the duff-bag I transferred the keys of office to the next man on the roll.

Somehow, there had never been a very cordial feeling between this mess and me; all along they had nourished a prejudice against my white jacket. They must have harbored the silly fancy that in it I gave myself airs, and wore it in order to look consequential; perhaps, as a cloak to cover pilferings of tit-bits from the mess. But to out with the plain truth, they themselves were not a very irreproachable set. Considering the sequel I am coming to, this avowal may be deemed sheer malice; but for all that, I can not avoid speaking my mind.

After my week of office, the mess gradually changed their behavior to me; they cut me to the heart; they became cold and reserved; seldom or never addressed me at meal-times, without invidious allusions to my *duff*, and also to my jacket, and its dripping in wet weather upon the mess-cloth. However, I had no idea that any thing serious, on their part, was brewing; but alas! so it turned out.

We were assembled at supper one evening, when I noticed certain winks and silent hints tipped to the cook, who presided. He was a little, oily fellow, who had once kept an oyster-cellar ashore; he bore me a grudge. Looking down on the mess-cloth, he observed that some fellows never knew when their room was better than their company. This being a maxim of indiscriminate application, of course I silently assented to it, as any other reasonable man would have done. But this remark was followed up by another, to the effect that, not only did some fellows never know when their room was better than their company, but they persisted in staying when their company wasn't wanted; and by so doing disturbed the serenity of society at large. But this, also, was a general observation that could not be gainsayed. A long and ominous pause ensued; during which I perceived every eye upon me, and my white jacket; while the cook went on to enlarge upon the disagreeableness of a perpetually damp garment in the mess, especially when that garment was white. This was coming nearer home.

Yes, they were going to black-ball me; but I resolved to sit it out a little longer; never dreaming that my moralist would proceed to extremities, while all hands were present. But bethinking him that by going this roundabout way he would never get at his object, he went off on another tack; apprising me, in substance, that he was instructed by the whole mess, then and there assembled, to give me warning to seek out another club, as they did not longer fancy the society either of myself or my jacket.

I was shocked. Such a want of tact and delicacy! Common propriety suggested that a point-blank intimation of that nature should be conveyed in a private interview; or, still better, by note. I immediately rose, tucked my jacket about me, bowed, and departed.

And now, to do myself justice, I must add that, the next day, I was received with open arms by a glorious set of fellows—mess No. 1!—numbering, among the rest, my noble Captain Jack Chase.

This mess was principally composed of the headmost men of the gun-deck; and, out of a pardonable self-conceit, they called themselves the "*Forty-two-pounder Club*;" meaning that they were, one and all, fellows of large intellectual and corporeal calibre. Their mess-cloth was well located. On their starboard hand was *Mess No.* 2, embracing sundry rare jokers and high livers, who waxed gay and epicurean over their salt fare, and were known as the "Society for the *Destruction of Beef and Pork*." On the larboard hand was *Mess No.* 31, made up entirely of fore-top-men, a dashing, blaze-away set of men-of-war's-men, who called themselves the "*Cape Horn Snorters and Neversink Invincibles*." Opposite, was one of the marine messes, mustering the aristocracy of the marine corps—the two corporals, the drummer and fifer, and some six or eight rather gentlemanly privates, native-born Americans, who had served in the Seminole campaigns of Florida; and they now enlivened their salt fare with stories of wild ambushes in the everglades; and one of them related a surprising tale of his hand-to-hand encounter with Osceola, the Indian chief, whom he fought one morning from daybreak till breakfast time. This slashing private also boasted that he could take a chip from between your teeth at twenty paces; he offered to bet any amount on it; and as he could get no one to hold the chip, his boast remained forever good.

Besides many other attractions which the *Forty-two-pounder Club* furnished, it had this one special advantage, that, owing to there being so many *petty officers* in it, all the members of the mess were exempt from doing duty as cooks and stewards. A fellow called a *steady-cook*, attended to that business during the entire cruise. He was a long, lank, pallid varlet, going by the name of Shanks. In very warm weather this Shanks would sit at the foot of the mess-cloth, fanning himself with the front flap of his frock or shirt, which he inelegantly wore over his trowsers. Jack Chase, the President of the Club, frequently remonstrated against this breach of good manners; but the *steady-cook* had somehow contracted the habit, and it proved incurable. For a time, Jack Chase, out of a polite nervousness touching myself, as a newly-elected member of the club, would frequently endeavor to excuse to me the vulgarity of Shanks. One day he wound up his remarks by the philosophic reflection—"But White-Jacket, my dear fellow, what can you expect of him? Our real misfortune is, that our noble club should be obliged to dine with its cook."

There were several of these *steady-cooks* on board; men of no mark or consideration whatever in the ship; lost to all noble promptings; sighing for no worlds to conquer, and perfectly contented with mixing their *duffs*, and spreading their mess-cloths, and mustering their pots and pans together three times every day for a three years' cruise. They were very seldom to be seen on the spar-deck, but kept below out of sight.

Chapter 16

GENERAL TRAINING IN A MAN-OF-WAR

To a quiet, contemplative character, averse to uproar, undue exercise of his bodily members, and all kind of useless confusion, nothing can be more distressing than a proceeding in all men-of-war called "*general quarters*." And well may it be so called, since it amounts to a general drawing and quartering of all the parties concerned.

As the specific object for which a man-of-war is built and put into commission is to fight and fire off cannon, it is, of course, deemed indispensable that the crew should be duly instructed in the art and mystery involved. Hence these "general quarters," which is a mustering of all hands to their stations at the guns on the several decks, and a sort of sham-fight with an imaginary foe.

The summons is given by the ship's drummer, who strikes a peculiar beat—short, broken, rolling, shuffling—like the sound made by the march into battle of iron-heeled grenadiers. It is a regular tune, with a fine song composed to it; the words of the chorus, being most artistically arranged, may give some idea of the air:

> "Hearts of oak are our ships, jolly tars are our men,
>   We always are ready, steady, boys, steady,
>   To fight and to conquer, again and again."

In warm weather this pastime at the guns is exceedingly unpleasant, to say the least, and throws a quiet man into a violent passion and perspiration. For one, I ever abominated it.

I have a heart like Julius Cæsar, and upon occasion would fight like Caius Marcius Coriolanus. If my beloved and forever glorious country should be ever in jeopardy from invaders, let Congress put me on a war-horse, in the van-guard, and *then* see how I will acquit myself. But to toil and sweat in a fictitious encounter; to squander the precious breath of my precious body in a ridiculous fight of shams and pretensions; to hurry about the decks, pretending to carry the killed and wounded below; to be told that I must consider the ship blowing up, in order to exercise myself in presence of mind, and prepare for a real explosion; all this I despise, as beneath a true tar and man of valor.

These were my sentiments at the time, and these remain my sentiments still; but as, while on board the frigate, my liberty of thought did not extend to liberty of expression, I was obliged to keep these sentiments to myself; though, indeed, I had some thoughts of addressing a letter, marked *Private and Confidential*, to his Honor the Commodore, on the subject.

My station at the batteries was at one of the thirty-two-pound carronades, on the starboard side of the quarter-deck.*

I did not fancy this station at all; for it is well known on shipboard that, in time of action, the quarter-deck is one of the most dangerous posts of a man-of-war. The reason is, that the officers of the highest rank are there stationed; and the enemy have an ungentlemanly way of target-shooting at their buttons. If we should chance to engage a ship, then, who could tell but some bungling small-arm marksman in the enemy's tops might put a bullet through *me* instead of the Commodore? If they hit *him*, no doubt he would not feel it

---

*For the benefit of a Quaker reader here and there, a word or two in explanation of a carronade may not be amiss. The carronade is a gun comparatively short and light for its calibre. A carronade throwing a thirty-two-pound shot weighs considerably less than a long-gun only throwing a twenty-four-pound shot. It further differs from a long-gun, in working with a joint and bolt underneath, instead of the short arms or *trunnions* at the sides. Its *carriage*, likewise, is quite different from that of a long-gun, having a sort of sliding apparatus, something like an extension dining-table; the goose on it, however, is a tough one, and villainously stuffed with most indigestible dumplings. Point-blank, the range of a carronade does not exceed one hundred and fifty yards, much less than the range of a long-gun. When of large calibre, however, it throws within that limit, Paixhan shot, all manner of shells and combustibles, with great effect, being a very destructive engine at close quarters. This piece is now very generally found mounted in the batteries of the English and American navies. The quarter-deck armaments of most modern frigates wholly consist of carronades. The name is derived from the village of Carron, in Scotland, at whose celebrated founderies this iron Attila was first cast.

much, for he was used to that sort of thing, and, indeed, had a bullet in him already. Whereas, *I* was altogether unaccustomed to having blue pills playing round my head in such an indiscriminate way. Besides, ours was a flag-ship; and every one knows what a peculiarly dangerous predicament the quarter-deck of Nelson's flag-ship was in at the battle of Trafalgar; how the lofty tops of the enemy were full of soldiers, peppering away at the English Admiral and his officers. Many a poor sailor, at the guns of that quarter-deck, must have received a bullet intended for some wearer of an epaulet.

By candidly confessing my feelings on this subject, I do by no means invalidate my claims to being held a man of prodigious valor. I merely state my invincible repugnance to being shot for somebody else. If I am shot, be it with the express understanding in the shooter that I am the identical person intended so to be served. That Thracian who, with his compliments, sent an arrow into the King of Macedon, superscribed "*For Philip's right eye,*" set a fine example to all warriors. The hurried, hasty, indiscriminate, reckless, abandoned manner in which both sailors and soldiers nowadays fight is really painful to any serious-minded, methodical old gentleman, especially if he chance to have systematized his mind as an accountant. There is little or no skill and bravery about it. Two parties, armed with lead and old iron, envelop themselves in a cloud of smoke, and pitch their lead and old iron about in all directions. If you happen to be in the way, you are hit; possibly, killed; if not, you escape. In sea-actions, if by good or bad luck, as the case may be, a round shot, fired at random through the smoke, happens to send overboard your fore-mast, another to unship your rudder, there you lie crippled, pretty much at the mercy of your foe; who, accordingly, pronounces himself victor, though that honor properly belongs to the Law of Gravitation operating on the enemy's balls in the smoke. Instead of tossing this old lead and iron into the air, therefore, it would be much better amicably to toss up a copper and let heads win.

The carronade at which I was stationed was known as "Gun No. 5," on the First Lieutenant's quarter-bill. Among our gun's crew, however, it was known as *Black Bet*. This name was bestowed by the captain of the gun—a fine negro

—in honor of his sweet-heart, a colored lady of Philadelphia. Of Black Bet I was rammer-and-sponger; and ram and sponge I did, like a good fellow. I have no doubt that, had I and my gun been at the battle of the Nile, we would mutually have immortalized ourselves; the ramming-pole would have been hung up in Westminster Abbey; and I, ennobled by the king, besides receiving the illustrious honor of an autograph letter from his majesty through the perfumed right hand of his private secretary.

But it was terrible work to help run in and out of the porthole that amazing mass of metal, especially as the thing must be done in a trice. Then, at the summons of a horrid, rasping rattle, swayed by the Captain in person, we were made to rush from our guns, seize pikes and pistols, and repel an imaginary army of boarders, who, by a fiction of the officers, were supposed to be assailing all sides of the ship at once. After cutting and slashing at them a while, we jumped back to our guns, and again went to jerking our elbows.

Meantime, a loud cry is heard of "Fire! fire! fire!" in the fore-top; and a regular engine, worked by a set of Bowery-boy tars, is forthwith set to playing streams of water aloft. And now it is "Fire! fire! fire!" on the main-deck; and the entire ship is in as great a commotion as if a whole city ward were in a blaze.

Are our officers of the Navy utterly unacquainted with the laws of good health? Do they not know that this violent exercise, taking place just after a hearty dinner, as it generally does, is eminently calculated to breed the dyspepsia? There was no satisfaction in dining; the flavor of every mouthful was destroyed by the thought that the next moment the cannonading drum might be beating to quarters.

Such a sea-martinet was our Captain, that sometimes we were roused from our hammocks at night; when a scene would ensue that it is not in the power of pen and ink to describe. Five hundred men spring to their feet, dress themselves, take up their bedding, and run to the nettings and stow it; then hie to their stations—each man jostling his neighbor—some alow, some aloft; some this way, some that; and in less than five minutes the frigate is ready for action, and still as the grave; almost every man precisely where he would be were an enemy actually about to be engaged. The Gunner, like a Cornwall miner in a cave, is burrowing down in the magazine under the Ward-room, which is lighted by battle-lanterns, placed behind glazed glass bull's-eyes inserted in the bulkhead. The *powder-monkeys*, or boys, who fetch and carry cartridges, are scampering to and fro among the guns; and the *first and second loaders* stand ready to receive their supplies.

These *Powder-monkeys*, as they are called, enact a curious part in time of action. The entrance to the magazine on the berth-deck, where they procure their food for the guns, is guarded by a wooden screen; and a gunner's mate, standing behind it, thrusts out the cartridges through a small arm-hole in this screen. The enemy's shot (perhaps red hot) are flying in all directions; and to protect their cartridges, the powder-monkeys hurriedly wrap them up in their jackets; and with all haste scramble up the ladders to their respective guns, like eating-house waiters hurrying along with hot cakes for breakfast.

At *general quarters* the shot-boxes are uncovered; showing the grape-shot—aptly so called, for they precisely resemble bunches of the fruit; though, to receive a bunch of iron grapes in the abdomen would be but a sorry dessert; and also showing the canister-shot—old iron of various sorts, packed in a tin case, like a tea-caddy.

Imagine some midnight craft sailing down on her enemy thus; twenty-four pounders leveled, matches lighted, and each captain of his gun at his post!

But if verily going into action, then would the Neversink have made still further preparations; for however alike in some things, there is always a vast difference—if you sound them—between a reality and a sham. Not to speak of the pale sternness of the men at their guns at such a juncture, and the choked thoughts at their hearts, the ship itself would here and there present a far different appearance. Something like that of an extensive mansion preparing for a grand entertainment, when folding-doors are withdrawn, chambers converted into drawing-rooms, and every inch of available space thrown into one continuous whole. For previous to an action, every bulk-head in a man-of-war is knocked down; great guns are run

out of the Commodore's parlor windows; nothing separates
the ward-room officers' quarters from those of the men, but
an ensign used for a curtain. The sailors' mess-chests are tumbled down into the hold; and the hospital cots—of which all
men-of-war carry a large supply—are dragged forth from the
sail-room, and piled near at hand to receive the wounded;
amputation-tables are ranged in the *cock-pit* or in the *tiers*,
whereon to carve the bodies of the maimed. The yards are
slung in chains; fire-screens distributed here and there; hill-
ocks of cannon-balls piled between the guns; shot-plugs suspended within easy reach from the beams; and solid masses
of wads, big as Dutch cheeses, braced to the cheeks of the
gun-carriages.

No small difference, also, would be visible in the ward-robe
of both officers and men. The officers generally fight as dandies dance, namely, in silk stockings; inasmuch as, in case of
being wounded in the leg, the silk-hose can be more easily
drawn off by the Surgeon; cotton sticks, and works into the
wound. An economical captain, while taking care to case his
legs in silk, might yet see fit to save his best suit, and fight in
his old clothes. For, besides that an old garment might much
better be cut to pieces than a new one, it must be a mighty
disagreeable thing to die in a stiff, tight-breasted coat, not yet
worked easy under the armpits. At such times, a man should
feel free, unencumbered, and perfectly at his ease in point of
straps and suspenders. No ill-will concerning his tailor,
should intrude upon his thoughts of eternity. Seneca understood this, when he chose to die naked in a bath. And men-
of-war's-men understand it, also; for most of them, in battle,
strip to the waist-bands; wearing nothing but a pair of duck
trowsers, and a handkerchief round their head.

A captain combining a heedful patriotism with economy,
would probably "bend" his old topsails before going into battle, instead of exposing his best canvas to be riddled to pieces;
for it is generally the case that the enemy's shot flies high.
Unless allowance is made for it in pointing the tube, at long-
gun distance, the slightest roll of the ship, at the time of
firing, would send a shot, meant for the hull, high over the
top-gallant yards.

But besides these differences between a sham-fight at *gen-*

eral quarters and a real cannonading, the aspect of the ship, at the beating of the retreat, would, in the latter case, be very dissimilar to the neatness and uniformity in the former.

Then our bulwarks might look like the walls of the houses in West Broadway in New York, after being broken into and burned out by the Negro Mob. Our stout masts and yards might be lying about decks, like tree boughs after a tornado in a piece of woodland; our dangling ropes, cut and sundered in all directions, would be bleeding tar at every yarn; and strewn with jagged splinters from our wounded planks, the gun-deck might resemble a carpenter's shop. *Then*, when all was over, and all hands would be piped to take down the hammocks from the exposed nettings (where they play the part of the cotton bales at New Orleans), we might find bits of broken shot, iron bolts, and bullets in our blankets. And, while smeared with blood like butchers, the surgeon and his mates would be amputating arms and legs on the berth-deck, an underling of the carpenter's gang would be new-legging and arming the broken chairs and tables in the Commodore's cabin; while the rest of his *squad* would be *splicing* and *fishing* the shattered masts and yards. The scupper-holes having discharged the last rivulet of blood, the decks would be washed down; and the galley-cooks would be going fore and aft, sprinkling them with hot vinegar, to take out the shambles' smell from the planks; which, unless some such means are employed, often create a highly offensive effluvia for weeks after a fight.

Then, upon mustering the men, and calling the quarter-bills by the light of a battle-lantern, many a wounded seaman, with his arm in a sling, would answer for some poor shipmate who could never more make answer for himself:

"Tom Brown?"

"Killed, sir."

"Jack Jewel?"

"Killed, sir."

"Joe Hardy?"

"Killed, sir."

And opposite all these poor fellows' names, down would go on the quarter-bills the bloody marks of red ink—a murderer's fluid, fitly used on these occasions.

Chapter 17

Away! Second, Third, and Fourth Cutters, away!

IT WAS THE MORNING succeeding one of these *general quarters* that we picked up a life-buoy, descried floating by.

It was a circular mass of cork, about eight inches thick and four feet in diameter, covered with tarred canvas. All round its circumference there trailed a number of knotted ropes'-ends, terminating in fanciful Turks' heads. These were the life-lines, for the drowning to clutch. Inserted into the middle of the cork was an upright, carved pole, somewhat shorter than a pike-staff. The whole buoy was embossed with barnacles, and its sides festooned with sea-weed. Dolphins were sporting and flashing around it, and one white bird was hovering over the top of the pole. Long ago, this thing must have been thrown overboard to save some poor wretch, who must have been drowned; while even the life-buoy itself had drifted away out of sight.

The forecastle-men fished it up from the bows, and the seamen thronged round it.

"Bad luck! bad luck!" cried the Captain of the Head; "we'll number one less before long."

The ship's cooper strolled by: he, to whose department it belongs to see that the ship's life-buoys are kept in good order.

In men-of-war, night and day, week in and week out, two life-buoys are kept depending from the stern; and two men, with hatchets in their hands, pace up and down, ready at the first cry to cut the cord and drop the buoys overboard. Every two hours they are regularly relieved, like sentinels on guard. No similar precautions are adopted in the merchant or whaling service.

Thus deeply solicitous to preserve human life are the regulations of men-of-war; and seldom has there been a better illustration of this solicitude than at the battle of Trafalgar, when, after "several thousand" French seamen had been destroyed, according to Lord Collingwood, and, by the official returns, sixteen hundred and ninety Englishmen were killed or wounded, the Captains of the surviving ships ordered the life-buoy sentries from their death-dealing guns to their vigilant posts, as officers of the Humane Society.

"There, Bungs!" cried Scrimmage, a sheet-anchor-man,* "there's a good pattern for you; make us a brace of life-buoys like that; something that will save a man, and not fill and sink under him, as those leaky quarter-casks of yours will the first time there's occasion to drop 'em. I came near pitching off the bowsprit the other day; and, when I scrambled inboard again, I went aft to get a squint at 'em. Why, Bungs, they are all open between the staves. Shame on you! Suppose you yourself should fall overboard, and find yourself going down with buoys under you of your own making—what then?"

"I never go aloft, and don't intend to fall overboard," replied Bungs.

"Don't believe it!" cried the sheet-anchor-man; "you lopers that live about the decks here are nearer the bottom of the sea than the light hand that looses the main-royal. Mind your eye, Bungs—mind your eye!"

"I will," retorted Bungs; "and you mind yours!"

Next day, just at dawn, I was startled from my hammock by the cry of *"All hands about ship and shorten sail!"* Springing up the ladders, I found that an unknown man had fallen overboard from the chains; and darting a glance toward the poop, perceived, from their gestures, that the life-sentries there had cut away the buoys.

It was blowing a fresh breeze; the frigate was going fast through the water. But the one thousand arms of five hundred men soon tossed her about on the other tack, and checked her further headway.

"Do you see him?" shouted the officer of the watch through his trumpet, hailing the main-mast-head. "Man or *buoy*, do you see either?"

"See nothing, sir," was the reply.

"Clear away the cutters!" was the next order. "Bugler! call

*In addition to the *Bower-anchors* carried on her bows, a frigate carries large anchors in her fore-chains, called *Sheet-anchors*. Hence, the old seamen stationed in that part of a man-of-war are called *Sheet-anchor-men*.

away the second, third, and fourth cutters' crews. Hands by the tackles!"

In less than three minutes the three boats were down. More hands were wanted in one of them, and, among others, I jumped in to make up the deficiency.

"Now, men, give way! and each man look out along his oar, and look sharp!" cried the officer of our boat. For a time, in perfect silence, we slid up and down the great seething swells of the sea, but saw nothing.

"There, it's no use," cried the officer; "he's gone, whoever he is. Pull away, men—pull away! they'll be recalling us soon."

"Let him drown!" cried the strokesman; "he's spoiled my watch below for me."

"Who the devil is he?" cried another.

"He's one who'll never have a coffin!" replied a third.

"No, no! they'll never sing out, *'All hands bury the dead!'* for him, my hearties!" cried a fourth.

"Silence," said the officer, "and look along your oars." But the sixteen oarsmen still continued their talk; and, after pulling about for two or three hours, we spied the recall-signal at the frigate's fore-t'-gallant-mast-head, and returned on board, having seen no sign even of the life-buoys.

The boats were hoisted up, the yards braced forward, and away we bowled—one man less.

"Muster all hands!" was now the order; when, upon calling the roll, the cooper was the only man missing.

"I told you so, men," cried the Captain of the Head; "I said we would lose a man before long."

"Bungs, is it?" cried Scrimmage, the sheet-anchor-man; "I told him his buoys wouldn't save a drowning man; and now he has proved it!"

Chapter 18

A Man-of-war Full as a Nut

I T WAS NECESSARY to supply the lost cooper's place; accordingly, word was passed for all who belonged to that calling to muster at the main-mast, in order that one of them might be selected. Thirteen men obeyed the summons—a circumstance illustrative of the fact that many good handicraftsmen are lost to their trades and the world by serving in men-of-war. Indeed, from a frigate's crew might be culled out men of all callings and vocations, from a backslidden parson to a broken-down comedian. The Navy is the asylum for the perverse, the home of the unfortunate. Here the sons of adversity meet the children of calamity, and here the children of calamity meet the offspring of sin. Bankrupt brokers, boot-blacks, blacklegs, and blacksmiths here assemble together; and castaway tinkers, watch-makers, quill-drivers, cobblers, doctors, farmers, and lawyers compare past experiences and talk of old times. Wrecked on a desert shore, a man-of-war's crew could quickly found an Alexandria by themselves, and fill it with all the things which go to make up a capital.

Frequently, at one and the same time, you see every trade in operation on the gun-deck—coopering, carpentering, tailoring, tinkering, blacksmithing, rope-making, preaching, gambling, and fortune-telling.

In truth, a man-of-war is a city afloat, with long avenues set out with guns instead of trees, and numerous shady lanes, courts, and by-ways. The quarter-deck is a grand square, park, or parade ground, with a great Pittsfield elm, in the shape of the main-mast, at one end, and fronted at the other by the palace of the Commodore's cabin.

Or, rather, a man-of-war is a lofty, walled, and garrisoned town, like Quebec, where the thoroughfares are mostly ramparts, and peaceable citizens meet armed sentries at every corner.

Or it is like the lodging-houses in Paris, turned upside down; the first floor, or deck, being rented by a lord; the second, by a select club of gentlemen; the third, by crowds of artisans; and the fourth, by a whole rabble of common people.

For even thus is it in a frigate, where the commander has a whole cabin to himself on the spar-deck, the lieutenants their ward-room underneath, and the mass of sailors swing their hammocks under all.

And with its long rows of port-hole casements, each revealing the muzzle of a cannon, a man-of-war resembles a three-story house in a suspicious part of the town, with a basement of indefinite depth, and ugly-looking fellows gazing out at the windows.

Chapter 19

The Jacket Aloft

AGAIN must I call attention to my white jacket, which about this time came near being the death of me.

I am of a meditative humor, and at sea used often to mount aloft at night, and, seating myself on one of the upper yards, tuck my jacket about me and give loose to reflection. In some ships in which I have done this, the sailors used to fancy that I must be studying astronomy—which, indeed, to some extent, was the case—and that my object in mounting aloft was to get a nearer view of the stars, supposing me, of course, to be short-sighted. A very silly conceit of theirs, some may say, but not so silly after all; for surely the advantage of getting nearer an object by two hundred feet is not to be underrated. Then, to study the stars upon the wide, boundless sea, is divine as it was to the Chaldean Magi, who observed their revolutions from the plains.

And it is a very fine feeling, and one that fuses us into the universe of things, and makes us a part of the All, to think that, wherever we ocean-wanderers rove, we have still the same glorious old stars to keep us company; that they still shine onward and on, forever beautiful and bright, and luring us, by every ray, to die and be glorified with them.

Ay, ay! we sailors sail not in vain. We expatriate ourselves to nationalize with the universe; and in all our voyages round the world, we are still accompanied by those old circumnavigators, the stars, who are shipmates and fellow-sailors of ours—sailing in heaven's blue, as we on the azure main. Let genteel generations scoff at our hardened hands, and finger-nails tipped with tar—did they ever clasp truer palms than ours? Let them feel of our sturdy hearts, beating like sledge-hammers in those hot smithies, our bosoms; with their amber-headed canes, let them feel of our generous pulses, and swear that they go off like thirty-two-pounders.

Oh, give me again the rover's life—the joy, the thrill, the whirl! Let me feel thee again, old sea! let me leap into thy saddle once more. I am sick of these terra firma toils and cares; sick of the dust and reek of towns. Let me hear the clatter of hailstones on icebergs, and not the dull tramp of these plodders, plodding their dull way from their cradles to their graves. Let me snuff thee up, sea-breeze! and whinny in thy spray. Forbid it, sea-gods! intercede for me with Neptune, O sweet Amphitrite, that no dull clod may fall on my coffin! Be mine the tomb that swallowed up Pharaoh and all his hosts; let me lie down with Drake, where he sleeps in the sea.

But when White-Jacket speaks of the rover's life, he means not life in a man-of-war, which, with its martial formalities and thousand vices, stabs to the heart the soul of all free-and-easy honorable rovers.

I have said that I was wont to mount up aloft and muse; and thus was it with me the night following the loss of the cooper. Ere my watch in the top had expired, high up on the main-royal-yard I reclined, the white jacket folded around me like Sir John Moore in his frosted cloak.

Eight bells had struck, and my watchmates had hied to their hammocks, and the other watch had gone to their stations, and the *top* below me was full of strangers, and still one hundred feet above even *them* I lay entranced; now dozing, now dreaming; now thinking of things past, and anon of the life to come. Well-timed was the latter thought, for the life to come was much nearer to overtaking me than I then could imagine. Perhaps I was half conscious at last of a tremulous voice hailing the main-royal-yard from the *top*. But if so, the consciousness glided away from me, and left me in Lethe. But when, like lightning, the yard dropped under me, and instinctively I clung with both hands to the "*tie*," then I came to myself with a rush, and felt something like a choking hand on my throat. For an instant I thought the Gulf Stream in my head was whirling me away to eternity; but the next moment I found myself standing; the yard had descended to the *cap*; and shaking myself in my jacket, I felt that I was unharmed and alive.

Who had done this? who had made this attempt on my life? thought I, as I ran down the rigging.

"Here it comes!—Lord! Lord! here it comes! See, see! it is white as a hammock."

"Who's coming?" I shouted, springing down into the top; "who's white as a hammock?"

"Bless my soul, Bill, it's only White-Jacket—that infernal White-Jacket again!"

It seems they had spied a moving white spot there aloft, and, sailor-like, had taken me for the ghost of the cooper; and after hailing me, and bidding me descend, to test my corporeality, and getting no answer, they had lowered the halyards in affright.

In a rage I tore off the jacket, and threw it on the deck.

"Jacket," cried I, "you must change your complexion! you must hie to the dyers and be dyed, that I may live. I have but one poor life, White Jacket, and that life I can not spare. I can not consent to die for *you*, but be dyed you must for me. You can dye many times without injury; but I can not die without irreparable loss, and running the eternal risk."

So in the morning, jacket in hand, I repaired to the First Lieutenant, and related the narrow escape I had had during the night. I enlarged upon the general perils I ran in being taken for a ghost, and earnestly besought him to relax his commands for once, and give me an order on Brush, the captain of the paint-room, for some black paint, that my jacket might be painted of that color.

"Just look at it, sir," I added, holding it up; "did you ever see any thing whiter? Consider how it shines of a night, like a bit of the Milky Way. A little paint, sir, you can not refuse."

"The ship has no paint to spare," he said; "you must get along without it."

"Sir, every rain gives me a soaking;—Cape Horn is at hand—six brushes-full would make it water-proof; and no longer would I be in peril of my life!"

"Can't help it, sir; depart!"

I fear it will not be well with me in the end; for if my own sins are to be forgiven only as I forgive that hard-hearted and unimpressible First Lieutenant, then pardon there is none for me.

What! when but one dab of paint would make a man of a ghost, and a Mackintosh of a herring-net—to refuse it!

I am full. I can say no more.

Chapter 20

How they Sleep in a Man-of-war

No more of my luckless jacket for a while; let me speak of my hammock, and the tribulations I endured therefrom.

Give me plenty of room to swing it in; let me swing it between two date-trees on an Arabian plain; or extend it diagonally from Moorish pillar to pillar, in the open marble Court of the Lions in Granada's Alhambra: let me swing it on a high bluff of the Mississippi—one swing in the pure ether for every swing over the green grass; or let me oscillate in it beneath the cool dome of St. Peter's; or drop me in it, as in a balloon, from the zenith, with the whole firmament to rock and expatiate in; and I would not exchange my coarse canvas hammock for the grand state-bed, like a stately coach-and-four, in which they tuck in a king when he passes a night at Blenheim Castle.

When you have the requisite room, you always have "spreaders" in your hammock; that is, two horizontal sticks, one at each end, which serve to keep the sides apart, and create a wide vacancy between, wherein you can turn over and over—lay on this side or that; on your back, if you please; stretch out your legs; in short, take your ease in your hammock; for of all inns, your bed is the best.

But when, with five hundred other hammocks, yours is crowded and jammed in on all sides, on a frigate berth-deck, the third from above; when "*spreaders*" are prohibited by an express edict from the Captain's cabin; and every man about you is jealously watchful of the rights and privileges of his own proper hammock, as settled by law and usage; *then* your hammock is your Bastile and canvas jug; into which, or out of which, it is very hard to get; and where sleep is but a mockery and a name.

Eighteen inches a man is all they allow you; eighteen inches in width; in *that* you must swing. Dreadful! they give you more swing than that at the gallows.

During warm nights in the Tropics, your hammock is as a stew-pan; where you stew and stew, till you can almost hear yourself hiss. Vain are all stratagems to widen your accommodations. Let them catch you insinuating your boots or other articles in the head of your hammock, by way of a "spreader." Near and far, the whole rank and file of the row to which you belong feel the encroachment in an instant, and are clamorous till the guilty one is found out, and his pallet brought back to its bearings.

In platoons and squadrons, they all lie on a level; their hammock *clews* crossing and recrossing in all directions, so as to present one vast field-bed, midway between the ceiling and the floor; which are about five feet asunder.

One extremely warm night, during a calm, when it was so hot that only a skeleton could keep cool (from the free current of air through its bones), after being drenched in my own perspiration, I managed to wedge myself out of my hammock; and with what little strength I had left, lowered myself gently to the deck. Let me see now, thought I, whether my ingenuity can not devise some method whereby I can have room to breathe and sleep at the same time. I have it. I will lower my hammock underneath all these others; and then—upon that separate and independent level, at least—I shall have the whole berth-deck to myself. Accordingly, I lowered away my pallet to the desired point —about three inches from the floor—and crawled into it again.

But, alas! this arrangement made such a sweeping semicircle of my hammock, that, while my head and feet were at par, the small of my back was settling down indefinitely; I felt as if some gigantic archer had hold of me for a bow.

But there was another plan left. I triced up my hammock with all my strength, so as to bring it wholly *above* the tiers of pallets around me. This done, by a last effort, I hoisted myself into it; but alas! it was much worse than before. My luckless hammock was stiff and straight as a board; and there I was—laid out in it, with my nose against the ceiling, like a dead man's against the lid of his coffin.

So at last I was fain to return to my old level, and moralize upon the folly, in all arbitrary governments, of striving to get either *below* or *above* those whom legislation has placed upon an equality with yourself.

Speaking of hammocks, recalls a circumstance that happened one night in the Neversink. It was three or four times repeated, with various but not fatal results.

The watch below was fast asleep on the berth-deck, where perfect silence was reigning, when a sudden shock and a groan roused up all hands; and the hem of a pair of white trowsers vanished up one of the ladders at the fore-hatchway.

We ran toward the groan, and found a man lying on the deck; one end of his hammock having given way, pitching his head close to three twenty-four-pound cannon shot, which must have been purposely placed in that position. When it was discovered that this man had long been suspected of being an *informer* among the crew, little surprise and less pleasure were evinced at his narrow escape.

Chapter 21

I CAN NOT quit this matter of the hammocks without making mention of a grievance among the sailors that ought
to be redressed.

In a man-of-war at sea, the sailors have *watch and watch*;
that is, through every twenty-four hours, they are on and off
duty every four hours. Now, the hammocks are piped down
from the nettings (the open space for stowing them, running
round the top of the bulwarks) a little after sunset, and piped
up again when the forenoon watch is called, at eight o'clock
in the morning; so that during the daytime they are inaccessible as pallets. This would be all well enough, did the sailors
have a complete night's rest; but every other night at sea, one
watch have only four hours in their hammocks. Indeed, deducting the time allowed for the other watch to turn out; for
yourself to arrange your hammock, get into it, and fairly get
asleep; it may be said that, every other night, you have but
three hours' sleep in your hammock. Having then been on
deck for twice four hours, at eight o'clock in the morning
your *watch-below* comes round, and you are not liable to duty
until noon. Under like circumstances, a merchant seaman
goes to his *bunk*, and has the benefit of a good long sleep.
But in a man-of-war you can do no such thing; your hammock is very neatly stowed in the nettings, and there it must
remain till nightfall.

But perhaps there is a corner for you somewhere along the
batteries on the gun-deck, where you may enjoy a snug nap.
But as no one is allowed to recline on the larboard side of the
gun-deck (which is reserved as a corridor for the officers
when they go forward to their smoking-room at the *bridle-
port*), the starboard side only is left to the seamen. But most
of this side, also, is occupied by the carpenters, sail-makers,
barbers, and coopers. In short, so few are the corners where
you can snatch a nap during daytime in a frigate, that not one

in ten of the watch, who have been on deck eight hours, can get a wink of sleep till the following night. Repeatedly, after by good fortune securing a corner, I have been roused from it by some functionary commissioned to keep it clear.

Off Cape Horn, what before had been very uncomfortable became a serious hardship. Drenched through and through by the spray of the sea at night, I have sometimes slept standing on the spar-deck—and shuddered as I slept—for the want of sufficient sleep in my hammock.

During three days of the stormiest weather, we were given the privilege of the *berth-deck* (at other times strictly interdicted), where we were permitted to spread our jackets, and take a nap in the morning after the eight hours' night exposure. But this privilege was but a beggarly one, indeed. Not to speak of our jackets—used for blankets—being soaking wet, the spray, coming down the hatchways, kept the planks of the berth-deck itself constantly wet; whereas, had we been permitted our hammocks, we might have swung dry over all this deluge. But we endeavored to make ourselves as warm and comfortable as possible, chiefly by close stowing, so as to generate a little steam, in the absence of any fire-side warmth. You have seen, perhaps, the way in which they box up subjects intended to illustrate the winter lectures of a professor of surgery. Just so we laid; heel and point, face to back, dovetailed into each other at every ham and knee. The wet of our jackets, thus densely packed, would soon begin to distill. But it was like pouring hot water on you to keep you from freezing. It was like being "packed" between the soaked sheets in a Water-cure Establishment.

Such a posture could not be preserved for any considerable period without shifting side for side. Three or four times during the four hours I would be startled from a wet doze by the hoarse cry of a fellow who did the duty of a corporal at the after-end of my file, *"Sleepers ahoy! stand by to slew round!"* and, with a double shuffle, we all rolled in concert, and found ourselves facing the taffrail instead of the bowsprit. But, however you turned, your nose was sure to stick to one or other of the steaming backs on your two flanks. There was some little relief in the change of odor consequent upon this.

But what is the reason that, after battling out eight stormy hours on deck at night, men-of-war's-men are not allowed the poor boon of a dry four hours' nap during the day following? What is the reason? The Commodore, Captain, and First Lieutenant, Chaplain, Purser, and scores of others, have *all night in*, just as if they were staying at a hotel on shore. And the junior Lieutenants not only have their cots to go to at any time; but as only one of them is required to head the watch, and there are so many of them among whom to divide that duty, they are only on deck four hours to twelve hours below. In some cases the proportion is still greater. Whereas, with *the people* it is four hours in and four hours off continually.

What is the reason, then, that the common seamen should fare so hard in this matter? It would seem but a simple thing to let them get down their hammocks during the day for a nap. But no; such a proceeding would mar the uniformity of daily events in a man-of-war. It seems indispensable to the picturesque effect of the spar-deck, that the hammocks should invariably remain stowed in the nettings between sunrise and sundown. But the chief reason is this—a reason which has sanctioned many an abuse in this world—*precedents are against it*; such a thing as sailors sleeping in their hammocks in the daytime, after being eight hours exposed to a night-storm, was hardly ever heard of in the navy. Though, to the immortal honor of some captains be it said, the fact is upon navy record that, off Cape Horn, they *have* vouchsafed the morning hammocks to their crew. Heaven bless such tender-hearted officers; and may they and their descendants—ashore or afloat—have sweet and pleasant slumbers while they live, and an undreaming siesta when they die.

It is concerning such things as the subject of this chapter that special enactments of Congress are demanded. Health and comfort—so far as duly attainable under the circumstances—should be legally guaranteed to the man-of-war's-man; and not left to the discretion or caprice of their commanders.

Chapter 22

BESIDES the other tribulations connected with your hammock, you must keep it snow-white and clean; who has not observed the long rows of spotless hammocks exposed in a frigate's nettings, where, through the day, their outsides, at least, are kept airing?

Hence it comes that there are regular mornings appointed for the scrubbing of hammocks; and such mornings are called *scrub-hammock-mornings*; and desperate is the scrubbing that ensues.

Before daylight the operation begins. All hands are called, and at it they go. Every deck is spread with hammocks, fore and aft; and lucky are you if you can get sufficient superficies to spread your own hammock in. Down on their knees are five hundred men, scrubbing away with brushes and brooms; jostling, and crowding, and quarreling about using each other's suds; when all their Purser's soap goes to create one indiscriminate yeast.

Sometimes you discover that, in the dark, you have been all the while scrubbing your next neighbor's hammock instead of your own. But it is too late to begin over again; for now the word is passed for every man to advance with his hammock, that it may be tied to a net-like frame-work of clothes-lines, and hoisted aloft to dry.

That done, without delay you get together your frocks and trowsers, and on the already flooded deck embark in the laundry business. You have no special bucket or basin to yourself—the ship being one vast wash-tub, where all hands wash and rinse out, and rinse out and wash, till at last the word is passed again, to make fast your clothes, that they, also, may be elevated to dry.

Then on all three decks the operation of holy-stoning begins, so called from the queer name bestowed upon the principal instruments employed. These are ponderous flat stones with long ropes at each end, by which the stones are slidden about, to and fro, over the wet and sanded decks; a most wearisome, dog-like, galley-slave employment. For the by-ways and corners about the masts and guns, smaller stones are used, called *prayer-books*; inasmuch as the devout operator has to down with them on his knees.

Finally, a grand flooding takes place, and the decks are remorselessly thrashed with dry swabs. After which an extraordinary implement—a sort of leathern hoe called a "*squilgee*"—is used to scrape and squeeze the last dribblings of water from the planks. Concerning this "squilgee," I think something of drawing up a memoir, and reading it before the Academy of Arts and Sciences. It is a most curious affair.

By the time all these operations are concluded it is *eight bells*, and all hands are piped to breakfast upon the damp and every-way disagreeable decks.

Now, against this invariable daily flooding of the three decks of a frigate, as a man-of-war's-man, White-Jacket most earnestly protests. In sunless weather it keeps the sailor's quarters perpetually damp; so much so, that you can scarce sit down without running the risk of getting the lumbago. One rheumatic old sheet-anchor-man among us was driven to the extremity of sewing a piece of tarred canvas on the seat of his trowsers.

Let those neat and tidy officers who so love to see a ship kept spick and span clean; who institute vigorous search after the man who chances to drop the crumb of a biscuit on deck, when the ship is rolling in a sea-way; let all such swing their hammocks with the sailors, and they would soon get sick of this daily damping of the decks.

Is a ship a wooden platter, that it is to be scrubbed out every morning before breakfast, even if the thermometer be at zero, and every sailor goes barefooted through the flood with the chilblains? And all the while the ship carries a doctor, well aware of Boerhaave's great maxim "*keep the feet dry.*" He has plenty of pills to give you when you are down with a fever, the consequences of these things; but enters no protest at the outset—as it is his duty to do—against the cause that induces the fever.

During the pleasant night watches, the promenading officers, mounted on their high-heeled boots, pass dry-shod, like the Israelites, over the decks; but by daybreak the roaring tide sets back, and the poor sailors are almost overwhelmed in it, like the Egyptians in the Red Sea.

Oh! the chills, colds, and agues that are caught. No snug stove, grate, or fire-place to go to; no, your only way to keep warm is to keep in a blazing passion, and anathematize the custom that every morning makes a wash-house of a man-of-war.

Look at it. Say you go on board a line-of-battle-ship: you see every thing scrupulously neat; you see all the decks clear and unobstructed as the sidewalks of Wall Street of a Sunday morning; you see no trace of a sailor's dormitory; you marvel by what magic all this is brought about. And well you may. For consider, that in this unobstructed fabric nearly one thousand mortal men have to sleep, eat, wash, dress, cook, and perform all the ordinary functions of humanity. The same number of men ashore would expand themselves into a township. Is it credible, then, that this extraordinary neatness, and especially this *unobstructedness* of a man-of-war, can be brought about, except by the most rigorous edicts, and a very serious sacrifice, with respect to the sailors, of the domestic comforts of life? To be sure, sailors themselves do not often complain of these things; they are used to them; but man can become used even to the hardest usage. And it is because he *is* used to it, that sometimes he does not complain of it.

Of all men-of-war, the American ships are the most excessively neat, and have the greatest reputation for it. And of all men-of-war the general discipline of the American ships is the most arbitrary.

In the English navy, the men liberally mess on tables, which, between meals, are triced up out of the way. The American sailors mess on the deck, and peck up their broken biscuit, or *midshipmen's nuts*, like fowls in a barn-yard.

But if this unobstructedness in an American fighting-ship be, at all hazards, so desirable, why not imitate the Turks? In the Turkish navy they have no mess-chests; the sailors roll their mess things up in a rug, and thrust them under a gun. Nor do they have any hammocks; they sleep any where about the decks in their *gregoes*. Indeed, come to look at it, what more does a man-of-war's-man absolutely require to live in

than his own skin? That's room enough; and room enough
to turn in, if he but knew how to shift his spine, end for end,
like a ramrod, without disturbing his next neighbor.

Among all men-of-war's-men, it is a maxim that over-neat
vessels are Tartars to the crew; and perhaps it may be safely
laid down that, when you see such a ship, some sort of tyranny is not very far off.

In the Neversink, as in other national ships, the business of
holy-stoning the decks was often prolonged, by way of punishment to the men, particularly of a raw, cold morning. This is
one of the punishments which a lieutenant of the watch may
easily inflict upon the crew, without infringing the statute
which places the power of punishment solely in the hands of
the Captain.

The abhorrence which men-of-war's-men have for this protracted *holy-stoning* in cold, comfortless weather—with their
bare feet exposed to the splashing inundations—is shown in
a strange story, rife among them, curiously tinctured with
their proverbial superstitions.

The First Lieutenant of an English sloop of war, a severe
disciplinarian, was uncommonly particular concerning the
whiteness of the quarter-deck. One bitter winter morning at
sea, when the crew had washed that part of the vessel, as
usual, and put away their holy-stones, this officer came on
deck, and after inspecting it, ordered the *holy-stones* and
prayer-books up again. Once more slipping off the shoes from
their frosted feet, and rolling up their trowsers, the crew
kneeled down to their task; and in that suppliant posture,
silently invoked a curse upon their tyrant; praying, as he went
below, that he might never more come out of the ward-room
alive. The prayer seemed answered; for being shortly after visited with a paralytic stroke at his breakfast-table, the First
Lieutenant next morning was carried out of the ward-room
feet foremost, dead. As they dropped him over the side—so
goes the story—the marine sentry at the gangway turned his
back upon the corpse.

To the credit of the humane and sensible portion of the
roll of American navy-captains, be it added, that *they* are not
so particular in keeping the decks spotless at all times, and in
all weathers; nor do they torment the men with scraping

bright-wood and polishing ring-bolts; but give all such gin-gerbread-work a hearty coat of black paint, which looks more warlike, is a better preservative, and exempts the sailors from a perpetual annoyance.

Chapter 23

Theatricals in a Man-of-War

THE NEVERSINK had summered out her last Christmas on the Equator; she was now destined to winter out the Fourth of July not very far from the frigid latitudes of Cape Horn.

It is sometimes the custom in the American Navy to celebrate this national holiday by doubling the allowance of spirits to the men; that is, if the ship happen to be lying in harbor. The effects of this patriotic plan may be easily imagined: the whole ship is converted into a dram-shop; and the intoxicated sailors reel about, on all three decks, singing, howling, and fighting. This is the time that, owing to the relaxed discipline of the ship, old and almost forgotten quarrels are revived, under the stimulus of drink; and, fencing themselves up between the guns—so as to be sure of a clear space with at least three walls—the combatants, two and two, fight out their hate, cribbed and cabined like soldiers dueling in a sentry-box. In a word, scenes ensue which would not for a single instant be tolerated by the officers upon any other occasion. This is the time that the most venerable of quarter-gunners and quarter-masters, together with the smallest apprentice boys, and men never known to have been previously intoxicated during the cruise—this is the time that they all roll together in the same muddy trough of drunkenness.

In emulation of the potentates of the Middle Ages, some Captains augment the din by authorizing a grand jail-delivery of all the prisoners who, on that auspicious Fourth of the month, may happen to be confined in the ship's prison—"*the brig.*"

But from scenes like these the Neversink was happily delivered. Besides that she was now approaching a most perilous part of the ocean—which would have made it madness to intoxicate the sailors—her complete destitution of *grog*, even for ordinary consumption, was an obstacle altogether insuperable, even had the Captain felt disposed to indulge his man-of-war's-men by the most copious libations.

For several days previous to the advent of the holiday, frequent conferences were held on the gun-deck touching the melancholy prospects before the ship.

"Too bad—too bad!" cried a top-man. "Think of it, shipmates—a Fourth of July without grog!"

"I'll hoist the Commodore's pennant at half-mast that day," sighed the signal-quarter-master.

"And I'll turn my best uniform jacket wrong side out, to keep company with the pennant, old Ensign," sympathetically responded an after-guard's-man.

"Ay, do!" cried a forecastle-man. "I could almost pipe my eye to think on't."

"No grog on de day dat tried men's souls!" blubbered Sunshine, the galley-cook.

"Who would be a *Jankee* now?" roared a Hollander of the fore-top, more Dutch than sour-crout.

"Is this the *riglar* fruits of liberty?" touchingly inquired an Irish waister of an old Spanish sheet-anchor-man.

You will generally observe that, of all Americans, your foreign-born citizens are the most patriotic—especially toward the Fourth of July.

But how could Captain Claret, the father of his crew, behold the grief of his ocean children with indifference? He could not. Three days before the anniversary—it still continuing very pleasant weather for these latitudes—it was publicly announced that free permission was given to the sailors to get up any sort of theatricals they desired, wherewith to honor the Fourth.

Now, some weeks prior to the Neversink's sailing from home—nearly three years before the time here spoken of—some of the seamen had clubbed together, and made up a considerable purse, for the purpose of purchasing a theatrical outfit; having in view to diversify the monotony of lying in foreign harbors for weeks together, by an occasional display on the boards—though if ever there was a continual theatre in the world, playing by night and by day, and without intervals between the acts, a man-of-war is that theatre, and her planks are the *boards* indeed.

The sailors who originated this scheme had served in other American frigates, where the privilege of having theatricals was allowed to the crew. What was their chagrin, then, when, upon making an application to the Captain, in a Peruvian harbor, for permission to present the much-admired drama of "*The Ruffian Boy*," under the Captain's personal patronage, that dignitary assured them that there were already enough *ruffian boys* on board, without conjuring up any more from the green-room.

The theatrical outfit, therefore, was stowed down in the bottom of the sailors' bags, who little anticipated *then* that it would ever be dragged out while Captain Claret had the sway.

But immediately upon the announcement that the embargo was removed, vigorous preparations were at once commenced to celebrate the Fourth with unwonted spirit. The half-deck was set apart for the theatre, and the signal-quarter-master was commanded to loan his flags to decorate it in the most patriotic style.

As the stage-struck portion of the crew had frequently during the cruise rehearsed portions of various plays, to while away the tedium of the night-watches, they needed no long time now to perfect themselves in their parts.

Accordingly, on the very next morning after the indulgence had been granted by the Captain, the following written placard, presenting a broadside of staring capitals, was found tacked against the main-mast on the gun-deck. It was as if a Drury-Lane bill had been posted upon the London Monument:

CAPE HORN THEATRE.

Grand Celebration of the Fourth of July.

DAY PERFORMANCE.

UNCOMMON ATTRACTION.

THE OLD WAGON PAID OFF!

JACK CHASE........PERCY ROYAL-MAST.

STARS OF THE FIRST MAGNITUDE.

For this time only,

THE TRUE YANKEE SAILOR.

The managers of the Cape Horn Theatre beg leave to inform the inhabitants of the Pacific and Southern Oceans that, on the afternoon of the Fourth of July, 184–, they will have the honor to present the admired drama of

THE OLD WAGON PAID OFF!

Commodore Bougee .... *Tom Brown, of the Fore-top.*
Captain Spy-glass .... *Ned Brace, of the After-Guard.*
Commodore's Cockswain .... *Joe Bunk, of the Launch.*
Old Luff .... *Quarter-master Coffin.*
Mayor .... *Seafull, of the Forecastle.*
PERCY ROYAL-MAST .... JACK CHASE.
Mrs. Lovelorn .... *Long-locks, of the After-Guard.*
Toddy Moll .... *Frank Jones.*
Gin and Sugar Sall................ *Dick Dash.*
Sailors, Marines, Bar-keepers, Crimps, Aldermen, Police-officers, Soldiers, Landsmen generally.

Long live the Commodore! ‖ Admission Free.

To conclude with the much-admired song by Dibdin, altered to suit all American Tars, entitled

THE TRUE YANKEE SAILOR.

True Yankee Sailor (in costume), Patrick Flinegan,
Captain of the Head.

Performance to commence with "Hail Columbia," by the Brass Band. Ensign rises at three bells, P.M. No sailor permitted to enter in his shirt-sleeves. Good order is expected to be maintained. The Master-at-arms and Ship's Corporals to be in attendance to keep the peace.

At the earnest entreaties of the seamen, Lemsford, the gun-deck poet, had been prevailed upon to draw up this bill. And upon this one occasion his literary abilities were far from being underrated, even by the least intellectual person on board. Nor must it be omitted that, before the bill was placarded, Captain Claret, enacting the part of censor and grand chamberlain, ran over a manuscript copy of "*The Old Wagon Paid Off,*" to see whether it contained any thing calculated to breed disaffection against lawful authority among the crew. He objected to some parts, but in the end let them all pass.

The morning of The Fourth—most anxiously awaited—dawned clear and fair. The breeze was steady; the air bracing cold; and one and all the sailors anticipated a gleeful afternoon. And thus was falsified the prophecies of certain old growlers averse to theatricals, who had predicted a gale of wind that would quash all the arrangements of the green-room.

As the men whose regular turns, at the time of the performance, would come round to be stationed in the tops, and at the various halyards and running ropes about the spar-deck, could not be permitted to partake in the celebration, there accordingly ensued, during the morning, many amusing scenes of tars who were anxious to procure substitutes at their posts. Through the day, many anxious glances were cast to windward; but the weather still promised fair.

At last *the people* were piped to dinner; two bells struck; and soon after, all who could be spared from their stations hurried to the half-deck. The capstan bars were placed on shot-boxes, as at prayers on Sundays, furnishing seats for the audience, while a low stage, rigged by the carpenter's gang, was built at one end of the open space. The curtain was composed of a large ensign, and the bulwarks round about were draperied with the flags of all nations. The ten or twelve members of the brass band were ranged in a row at the foot of the stage, their polished instruments in their hands, while the consequential Captain of the Band himself was elevated upon a gun-carriage.

At three bells precisely a group of ward-room officers emerged from the after-hatchway, and seated themselves upon camp-stools, in a central position, with the stars and stripes for a canopy. *That* was the royal box. The sailors looked round for the Commodore; but neither Commodore nor Captain honored *the people* with their presence.

At the call of a bugle the band struck up *Hail Columbia*, the whole audience keeping time, as at Drury Lane, when *God Save the King* is played after a great national victory.

At the discharge of a marine's musket the curtain rose, and four sailors, in the picturesque garb of Maltese mariners, staggered on the stage in a feigned state of intoxication. The truthfulness of the representation was much heightened by the roll of the ship.

"The Commodore," "Old Luff," "The Mayor," and "Gin and Sugar Sall," were played to admiration, and received great applause. But at the first appearance of that universal favorite, Jack Chase, in the chivalric character of "*Percy Royal-Mast*," the whole audience simultaneously rose to their feet, and greeted him with three hearty cheers, that almost took the main-top-sail aback.

Matchless Jack, *in full fig*, bowed again and again, with true quarter-deck grace and self-possession; and when five or six untwisted strands of rope and bunches of oakum were thrown to him, as substitutes for bouquets, he took them one by one, and gallantly hung them from the buttons of his jacket.

"Hurrah! hurrah! hurrah!—go on! go on!—stop hollering—hurrah!—go on!—stop hollering—hurrah!" was now heard on all sides, till at last, seeing no end to the enthusiasm of his ardent admirers, Matchless Jack stepped forward, and, with his lips moving in pantomime, plunged into the thick of the part. Silence soon followed, but was fifty times broken by uncontrollable bursts of applause. At length, when that heart-thrilling scene came on, where Percy Royal-Mast rescues fifteen oppressed sailors from the watch-house, in the teeth of a posse of constables, the audience leaped to their feet, overturned the capstan bars, and to a man hurled their hats on the stage in a delirium of delight. Ah Jack, that was a ten-stroke indeed!

The commotion was now terrific; all discipline seemed gone forever; the Lieutenants ran in among the men, the Captain darted from his cabin, and the Commodore nervously questioned the armed sentry at his door as to what the deuce *the people* were about. In the midst of all this, the trumpet of the officer-of-the-deck, commanding the top-gallant sails to be taken in, was almost completely drowned. A black squall was coming down on the weather-bow, and the boatswain's mates bellowed themselves hoarse at the main-hatchway. There is no knowing what would have ensued, had not the bass drum suddenly been heard, calling all hands to quarters, a summons not to be withstood. The sailors pricked their ears at it, as horses at the sound of a cracking whip, and confusedly stumbled up the ladders to their stations. The next moment all was silent but the wind, howling like a thousand devils in the cordage.

"Stand by to reef all three top-sails!—settle away the halyards!—haul out—so: make fast!—aloft, top-men! and reef away!"

Thus, in storm and tempest terminated that day's theatricals. But the sailors never recovered from the disappointment of not having the *"True Yankee Sailor"* sung by the Irish Captain of the Head.

And here White-Jacket must moralize a bit. The unwonted spectacle of the row of gun-room officers mingling with "the people" in applauding a mere seaman like Jack Chase, filled me at the time with the most pleasurable emotions. It is a sweet thing, thought I, to see these officers confess a human brotherhood with us, after all; a sweet thing to mark their cordial appreciation of the manly merits of my matchless Jack. Ah! they are noble fellows all round, and I do not know but I have wronged them sometimes in my thoughts.

Nor was it without similar pleasurable feelings that I witnessed the temporary rupture of the ship's stern discipline, consequent upon the tumult of the theatricals. I thought to myself, this now is as it should be. It is good to shake off, now and then, this iron yoke round our necks. And after having once permitted us sailors to be a little noisy, in a harmless way—somewhat merrily turbulent—the officers can not, with any good grace, be so excessively stern and unyielding as before. I began to think a man-of-war a man-of-peace-and-good-will, after all. But, alas! disappointment came.

Next morning the same old scene was enacted at the gangway. And beholding the row of uncompromising-looking officers there assembled with the Captain, to witness punishment—the same officers who had been so cheerfully disposed over night—an old sailor touched my shoulder, and said, "See, White-Jacket, all round they have *shipped their quarter-deck faces again*. But this is the way."

I afterward learned that this was an old man-of-war's-man's phrase, expressive of the facility with which a sea-officer falls back upon all the severity of his dignity, after a temporary suspension of it.

Chapter 24

INTRODUCTORY TO CAPE HORN

AND NOW, through drizzling fogs and vapors, and under damp, double-reefed top-sails, our wet-decked frigate drew nearer and nearer to the squally Cape.

Who has not heard of it? Cape Horn, Cape Horn—a *horn* indeed, that has tossed many a good ship. Was the descent of Orpheus, Ulysses, or Dante into Hell, one whit more hardy and sublime than the first navigator's weathering of that terrible Cape?

Turned on her heel by a fierce West Wind, many an outward-bound ship has been driven across the Southern Ocean to the Cape of Good Hope—*that* way to seek a passage to the Pacific. And that stormy Cape, I doubt not, has sent many a fine craft to the bottom, and told no tales. At those ends of the earth are no chronicles. What signify the broken spars and shrouds that, day after day, are driven before the prows of more fortunate vessels? or the tall masts, imbedded in icebergs, that are found floating by? They but hint the old story—of ships that have sailed from their ports, and never more have been heard of.

Impracticable Cape! You may approach it from this direction or that—in any way you please—from the East, or from the West; with the wind astern, or abeam, or on the quarter; and still Cape Horn is Cape Horn. Cape Horn it is that takes the conceit out of fresh-water sailors, and steeps in a still salter brine the saltest. Woe betide the tyro; the foolhardy, Heaven preserve!

Your Mediterranean captain, who with a cargo of oranges has hitherto made merry runs across the Atlantic, without so much as furling a t'-gallant-sail, oftentimes, off Cape Horn, receives a lesson which he carries to the grave; though the grave—as is too often the case—follows so hard on the lesson that no benefit comes from the experience.

Other strangers who draw nigh to this Patagonia termination of our Continent, with their souls full of its shipwrecks

and disasters—top-sails cautiously reefed, and every thing
guardedly snug—these strangers at first unexpectedly encountering a tolerably smooth sea, rashly conclude that the Cape,
after all, is but a bugbear; they have been imposed upon by
fables, and founderings and sinkings hereabouts are all cock-
and-bull stories.

"Out reefs, my hearties; fore and aft set t'-gallant-sails!
stand by to give her the fore-top-mast stun'-sail!"

But, Captain Rash, those sails of yours were much safer in
the sail-maker's loft. For now, while the heedless craft is
bounding over the billows, a black cloud rises out of the sea;
the sun drops down from the sky; a horrible mist far and
wide spreads over the water.

"Hands by the halyards! Let go! Clew up!"

Too late.

For ere the ropes' ends can be cast off from the pins, the tornado is blowing down to the bottom of their throats. The masts
are willows, the sails ribbons, the cordage wool; the whole ship
is brewed into the yeast of the gale.

And now, if, when the first green sea breaks over him, Captain Rash is not swept overboard, he has his hands full, be
sure. In all probability his three masts have gone by the
board, and, raveled into list, his sails are floating in the air.
Or, perhaps, the ship *broaches to*, or is *brought by the lee*. In
either case, Heaven help the sailors, their wives, and their little ones; and Heaven help the underwriters.

Familiarity with danger makes a brave man braver, but less
daring. Thus with seamen: he who goes the oftenest round
Cape Horn goes the most circumspectly. A veteran mariner is
never deceived by the treacherous breezes which sometimes
waft him pleasantly toward the latitude of the Cape. No
sooner does he come within a certain distance of it—previously fixed in his own mind—than all hands are turned to
setting the ship in storm-trim; and, never mind how light the
breeze, down come his t'-gallant-yards. He "bends" his
strongest storm-sails, and lashes every thing on deck securely.
The ship is then ready for the worst; and if, in reeling round
the headland, she receives a broadside, it generally goes well
with her. If ill, all hands go to the bottom with quiet consciences.

Among sea-captains, there are some who seem to regard the genius of the Cape as a willful, capricious jade, that must be courted and coaxed into complaisance. First, they come along under easy sail; do not steer boldly for the headland, but tack this way and that—sidling up to it. Now they woo the Jezebel with a t'-gallant-studding-sail; anon, they deprecate her wrath with double-reefed-top-sails. When, at length, her unappeasable fury is fairly aroused, and all round the dismantled ship the storm howls and howls for days together, they still persevere in their efforts. First, they try unconditional submission; furling every rag and *heaving to*; laying like a log, for the tempest to toss wheresoever it pleases.

This failing, they set a *spencer* or *try-sail*, and shift on the other tack. Equally vain! The gale sings as hoarsely as before. At last, the wind comes round fair; they drop the fore-sail; square the yards, and scud before it: their implacable foe chasing them with tornadoes, as if to show her insensibility to the last.

Other ships, without encountering these terrible gales, spend week after week endeavoring to turn this boisterous world-corner against a continual head-wind. Tacking hither and thither, in the language of sailors, they *polish* the Cape by beating about its edges so long.

Le Mair and Schouten, two Dutchmen, were the first navigators who weathered Cape Horn. Previous to this, passages had been made to the Pacific by the Straits of Magellan; nor, indeed, at that period, was it known to a certainty that there was any other route, or that the land now called Terra Del Fuego was an island. A few leagues southward from Terra Del Fuego is a cluster of small islands, the Diegoes; between which and the former island are the Straits of Le Mair, so called in honor of their discoverer, who first sailed through them into the Pacific. Le Mair and Schouten, in their small, clumsy vessels, encountered a series of tremendous gales, the prelude to the long train of similar hardships which most of their followers have experienced. It is a significant fact, that Schouten's vessel, the *Horne*, which gave its name to the Cape, was almost lost in weathering it.

The next navigator round the Cape was Sir Francis Drake, who, on Raleigh's Expedition, beholding for the first time, from the Isthmus of Darien, the "goodlie South Sea," like a true-born Englishman, vowed, please God, to sail an English ship thereon; which the gallant sailor did, to the sore discomfiture of the Spaniards on the coasts of Chili and Peru.

But perhaps the greatest hardships on record, in making this celebrated passage, were those experienced by Lord Anson's squadron in 1736. Three remarkable and most interesting narratives record their disasters and sufferings. The first, jointly written by the carpenter and gunner of the Wager; the second, by young Byron, a midshipman in the same ship; the third, by the chaplain of the Centurion. White-Jacket has them all; and they are fine reading of a boisterous March night, with the casement rattling in your ear, and the chimney-stacks blowing down upon the pavement, bubbling with rain-drops.

But if you want the best idea of Cape Horn, get my friend Dana's unmatchable "Two Years Before the Mast." But you can read, and so you must have read it. His chapters describing Cape Horn must have been written with an icicle.

At the present day the horrors of the Cape have somewhat abated. This is owing to a growing familiarity with it; but, more than all, to the improved condition of ships in all respects, and the means now generally in use of preserving the health of the crews in times of severe and prolonged exposure.

Chapter 25

COLDER AND COLDER; we are drawing nigh to the Cape. Now gregoes, pea jackets, monkey jackets, reefing jackets, storm jackets, oil jackets, paint jackets, round jackets, short jackets, long jackets, and all manner of jackets, are the order of the day, not excepting the immortal white jacket, which begins to be sturdily buttoned up to the throat, and pulled down vigorously at the skirts, to bring them well over the loins.

But, alas! those skirts were lamentably scanty; and though, with its quiltings, the jacket was stuffed out about the breasts like a Christmas turkey, and of a dry cold day kept the wearer warm enough in that vicinity, yet about the loins it was shorter than a ballet-dancer's skirts; so that while my chest was in the temperate zone, close adjoining the torrid, my hapless thighs were in Nova Zembla, hardly an icicle's toss from the Pole.

Then, again, the repeated soakings and dryings it had undergone, had by this time made it shrink woefully all over, especially in the arms, so that the wristbands had gradually crawled up near to the elbows; and it required an energetic thrust to push the arm through, in drawing the jacket on.

I endeavored to amend these misfortunes by sewing a sort of canvass ruffle round the skirts, by way of a continuation or supplement to the original work, and by doing the same with the wristbands.

This is the time for oil-skin suits, dread-naughts, tarred trowsers and overalls, sea-boots, comforters, mittens, woolen socks, Guernsey frocks, Havre shirts, buffalo-robe shirts, and moose-skin drawers. Every man's jacket is his wigwam, and every man's hat his caboose.

Perfect license is now permitted to the men respecting their clothing. Whatever they can rake and scrape together they put on—swaddling themselves in old sails, and drawing old socks over their heads for night-caps. This is the time for smiting your chest with your hand, and talking loud to keep up the circulation.

Colder, and colder, and colder, till at last we spoke a fleet of icebergs bound North. After that, it was one incessant "*cold snap*," that almost snapped off our fingers and toes. Cold! It was cold as *Blue Flujin*, where sailors say fire freezes.

And now coming up with the latitude of the Cape, we stood southward to give it a wide berth, and while so doing were becalmed; ay, becalmed off Cape Horn, which is worse, far worse, than being becalmed on the Line.

Here we lay forty-eight hours, during which the cold was intense. I wondered at the liquid sea, which refused to freeze in such a temperature. The clear, cold sky overhead looked like a steel-blue cymbal, that might ring, could you smite it. Our breath came and went like puffs of smoke from pipe-bowls. At first there was a long, gauky swell, that obliged us to furl most of the sails, and even send down t'-gallant-yards, for fear of pitching them overboard.

Out of sight of land, at this extremity of both the inhabitable and uninhabitable world, our peopled frigate, echoing with the voices of men, the bleating of lambs, the cackling of fowls, the gruntings of pigs, seemed like Noah's old ark itself, becalmed at the climax of the Deluge.

There was nothing to be done but patiently to await the pleasure of the elements, and "whistle for a wind," the usual practice of seamen in a calm. No fire was allowed, except for the indispensable purpose of cooking, and heating bottles of water to toast Selvagee's feet. He who possessed the largest stock of vitality, stood the best chance to escape freezing. It was horrifying. In such weather any man could have undergone amputation with great ease, and helped take up the arteries himself.

Indeed, this state of affairs had not lasted quite twenty-four hours, when the extreme frigidity of the air, united to our increased tendency to inactivity, would very soon have rendered some of us subjects for the surgeon and his mates, had not a humane proceeding of the Captain suddenly impelled us to vigorous exercise.

And here be it said, that the appearance of the Boatswain, with his silver whistle to his mouth, at the main hatchway of the gun-deck, is always regarded by the crew with the utmost curiosity, for this betokens that some general order is about to be promulgated through the ship. What now? is the question that runs on from man to man. A short preliminary whistle is then given by "Old Yarn," as they call him, which whistle serves to collect round him, from their various stations, his four mates. Then Yarn, or Pipes, as leader of the orchestra, begins a peculiar call, in which his assistants join. This over, the order, whatever it may be, is loudly sung out and prolonged, till the remotest corner echoes again. The Boatswain and his mates are the town-criers of a man-of-war.

The calm had commenced in the afternoon; and the following morning the ship's company were electrified by a general order, thus set forth and declared: *"D'ye hear there, fore and aft! all hands skylark!"*

This mandate, nowadays never used except upon very rare occasions, produced the same effect upon the men that Exhilarating Gas would have done, or an extra allowance of "grog." For a time, the wonted discipline of the ship was broken through, and perfect license allowed. It was a Babel here, a Bedlam there, and a Pandemonium every where. The Theatricals were nothing compared with it. Then the fainthearted and timorous crawled to their hiding-places, and the lusty and bold shouted forth their glee. Gangs of men, in all sorts of outlandish habiliments, wild as those worn at some crazy carnival, rushed to and fro, seizing upon whomsoever they pleased—warrant-officers and dangerous pugilists excepted— pulling and hauling the luckless tars about, till fairly baited into a genial warmth. Some were made fast to, and hoisted aloft with a will; others, mounted upon oars, were ridden fore and aft on a rail, to the boisterous mirth of the spectators, any one of whom might be the next victim. Swings were rigged from the tops, or the masts; and the most reluctant wights being purposely selected, spite of all struggles, were swung from East to West, in vast arcs of circles, till almost breathless. Hornpipes, fandangoes, Donnybrook-jigs, reels, and quadrilles, were danced under the very nose of the most mighty captain, and upon the very quarter-deck and poop. Sparring and wrestling, too, were all the vogue; *Kentucky bites* were given, and the *Indian hug* exchanged. The din frightened the sea-fowl, that flew by with accelerated wing.

It is worth mentioning that several casualties occurred, of which, however, I will relate but one. While the "skylarking" was at its height, one of the fore-top-men—an ugly-tempered devil of a Portuguese, looking on—swore that he would be the death of any man who laid violent hands upon his inviolable person. This threat being overheard, a band of desperadoes, coming up from behind, tripped him up in an instant, and in the twinkling of an eye the Portuguese was straddling an oar, borne aloft by an uproarious multitude, who rushed him along the deck at a rail-road gallop. The living mass of arms all round and beneath him was so dense, that every time he inclined to one side he was instantly pushed upright, but only to fall over again, to receive another push from the contrary direction. Presently, disengaging his hands from those who held them, the enraged seaman drew from his bosom an iron belaying-pin, and recklessly laid about him to right and left. Most of his persecutors fled; but some eight or ten still stood their ground, and, while bearing him aloft, endeavored to wrest the weapon from his hands. In this attempt, one man was struck on the head, and dropped insensible. He was taken up for dead, and carried below to Cuticle, the surgeon, while the Portuguese was put under guard. But the wound did not prove very serious; and in a few days the man was walking about the deck, with his head well bandaged.

This occurrence put an end to the "skylarking," further head-breaking being strictly prohibited. In due time the Portuguese paid the penalty of his rashness at the gangway; while once again the officers *shipped their quarter-deck faces*.

Chapter 26

THE PITCH OF THE CAPE

Ere the calm had yet left us, a sail had been discerned from the fore-top-mast-head, at a great distance, probably three leagues or more. At first it was a mere speck, altogether out of sight from the deck. By the force of attraction, or something else equally inscrutable, two ships in a calm, and equally affected by the currents, will always approximate, more or less. Though there was not a breath of wind, it was not a great while before the strange sail was descried from our bulwarks; gradually, it drew still nearer.

What was she, and whence? There is no object which so excites interest and conjecture, and, at the same time, baffles both, as a sail, seen as a mere speck on these remote seas off Cape Horn.

A breeze! a breeze! for lo! the stranger is now perceptibly nearing the frigate; the officer's spy-glass pronounces her a full-rigged ship, with all sail set, and coming right down to us, though in our own vicinity the calm still reigns.

She is bringing the wind with her. Hurrah! Ay, there it is! Behold how mincingly it creeps over the sea, just ruffling and crisping it.

Our top-men were at once sent aloft to loose the sails, and presently they faintly began to distend. As yet we hardly had steerage-way. Toward sunset the stranger bore down before the wind, a complete pyramid of canvass. Never before, I venture to say, was Cape Horn so audaciously insulted. Stun'-sails alow and aloft; royals, moon-sails, and every thing else. She glided under our stern, within hailing distance, and the signal-quarter-master ran up our ensign to the gaff.

"Ship ahoy!" cried the Lieutenant of the Watch, through his trumpet.

"Halloa!" bawled an old fellow in a green jacket, clapping one hand to his mouth, while he held on with the other to the mizzen-shrouds.

"What ship's that?"

"The Sultan, Indiaman, from New York, and bound to Callao and Canton, sixty days out, all well. What frigate's that?"

"The United States ship Neversink, homeward bound."

"Hurrah! hurrah! hurrah!" yelled our enthusiastic countryman, transported with patriotism.

By this time the Sultan had swept past, but the Lieutenant of the Watch could not withhold a parting admonition.

"D'ye hear? You'd better take in some of your flying-kites there. Look out for Cape Horn!"

But the friendly advice was lost in the now increasing wind. With a suddenness by no means unusual in these latitudes, the light breeze soon became a succession of sharp squalls, and our sail-proud braggadocio of an Indiaman was observed to let every thing go by the run, his t'-gallant stun'-sails and flying-jib taking quick leave of the spars; the flying-jib was swept into the air, rolled together for a few minutes, and tossed about in the squalls like a foot-ball. But the wind played no such pranks with the more prudently managed canvass of the Neversink, though before many hours it was stirring times with us.

About midnight, when the starboard watch, to which I belonged, was below, the boatswain's whistle was heard, followed by the shrill cry for "*All hands take in sail!* jump, men, and save ship!"

Springing from our hammocks, we found the frigate leaning over to it so steeply, that it was with difficulty we could climb the ladders leading to the upper deck.

Here the scene was awful. The vessel seemed to be sailing on her side. The main-deck guns had several days previous been run in and housed, and the port-holes closed, but the lee carronades on the quarter-deck and forecastle were plunging through the sea, which undulated over them in milk-white billows of foam. With every lurch to leeward the yard-arm-ends seemed to dip in the sea, while forward the spray dashed over the bows in cataracts, and drenched the men who were on the fore-yard. By this time the deck was alive with the whole strength of the ship's company, five hundred men, officers and all, mostly clinging to the weather bulwarks. The occasional phosphorescence of the yeasting sea cast a glare upon their uplifted faces, as a night fire in a populous city lights up the panic-stricken crowd.

In a sudden gale, or when a large quantity of sail is suddenly to be furled, it is the custom for the First Lieutenant to take the trumpet from whoever happens then to be officer of the deck. But Mad Jack had the trumpet that watch; nor did the First Lieutenant now seek to wrest it from his hands. Every eye was upon him, as if we had chosen him from among us all, to decide this battle with the elements, by single combat with the spirit of the Cape; for Mad Jack was the saving genius of the ship, and so proved himself that night. I owe this right hand, that is this moment flying over my sheet, and all my present being to Mad Jack. The ship's bows were now butting, battering, ramming, and thundering over and upon the head seas, and with a horrible wallowing sound our whole hull was rolling in the trough of the foam. The gale came athwart the deck, and every sail seemed bursting with its wild breath.

All the quarter-masters, and several of the forecastle-men, were swarming round the double-wheel on the quarter-deck. Some jumping up and down, with their hands upon the spokes; for the whole helm and galvanized keel were fiercely feverish, with the life imparted to them by the tempest.

"Hard *up* the helm!" shouted Captain Claret, bursting from his cabin like a ghost in his night-dress.

"Damn you!" raged Mad Jack to the quarter-masters; "hard *down*—hard *down*, I say, and be damned to you!"

Contrary orders! but Mad Jack's were obeyed. His object was to throw the ship into the wind, so as the better to admit of close-reefing the top-sails. But though the halyards were let go, it was impossible to clew down the yards, owing to the enormous horizontal strain on the canvass. It now blew a hurricane. The spray flew over the ship in floods. The gigantic masts seemed about to snap under the world-wide strain of the three entire top-sails.

"Clew down! clew down!" shouted Mad Jack, husky with excitement, and in a frenzy, beating his trumpet against one of the shrouds. But, owing to the slant of the ship, the thing could not be done. It was obvious that before many minutes something must go—either sails, rigging, or sticks; perhaps the hull itself, and all hands.

Presently a voice from the top exclaimed that there was a rent in the main-top-sail. And instantly we heard a report like two or three muskets discharged together; the vast sail was rent up and down like the Vail of the Temple. This saved the main-mast; for the yard was now clewed down with comparative ease, and the top-men laid out to stow the shattered canvass. Soon, the two remaining top-sails were also clewed down and close reefed.

Above all the roar of the tempest and the shouts of the crew, was heard the dismal tolling of the ship's bell—almost as large as that of a village church—which the violent rolling of the ship was occasioning. Imagination can not conceive the horror of such a sound in a night-tempest at sea.

"Stop that ghost!" roared Mad Jack; "away, one of you, and wrench off the clapper!"

But no sooner was this ghost gagged, than a still more appalling sound was heard, the rolling to and fro of the heavy shot, which, on the gun-deck, had broken loose from the gun-racks, and converted that part of the ship into an immense bowling-alley. Some hands were sent down to secure them; but it was as much as their lives were worth. Several were maimed; and the midshipmen who were ordered to see the duty performed reported it impossible, until the storm abated.

The most terrific job of all was to furl the main-sail, which, at the commencement of the squalls, had been clewed up, coaxed and quieted as much as possible with the bunt-lines and slab-lines. Mad Jack waited some time for a lull, ere he gave an order so perilous to be executed. For to furl this enormous sail, in such a gale, required at least fifty men on the yard; whose weight, superadded to that of the ponderous stick itself, still further jeopardized their lives. But there was no prospect of a cessation of the gale, and the order was at last given.

At this time a hurricane of slanting sleet and hail was descending upon us; the rigging was coated with a thin glare of ice, formed within the hour.

"Aloft, main-yard-men! and all you main-top-men! and furl the main-sail!" cried Mad Jack.

I dashed down my hat, slipped out of my quilted jacket in an instant, kicked the shoes from my feet, and, with a crowd of others, sprang for the rigging. Above the bulwarks (which in a frigate are so high as to afford much protection to those on deck) the gale was horrible. The sheer force of the wind flattened us to the rigging as we ascended, and every hand seemed congealing to the icy shrouds by which we held.

"Up—up, my brave hearties!" shouted Mad Jack; and up we got, some way or other, all of us, and groped our way out on the yard-arms.

"Hold on, every mother's son!" cried an old quarter-gunner at my side. He was bawling at the top of his compass; but in the gale, he seemed to be whispering; and I only heard him from his being right to windward of me.

But his hint was unnecessary; I dug my nails into the *jack-stays*, and swore that nothing but death should part me and them until I was able to turn round and look to windward. As yet, this was impossible; I could scarcely hear the man to leeward at my elbow; the wind seemed to snatch the words from his mouth and fly away with them to the South Pole.

All this while the sail itself was flying about, sometimes catching over our head, and threatening to tear us from the yard in spite of all our hugging. For about three quarters of an hour we thus hung suspended right over the rampant billows, which curled their very crests under the feet of some four or five of us clinging to the lee-yard-arm, as if to float us from our place.

Presently, the word passed along the yard from windward, that we were ordered to come down and leave the sail to blow, since it could not be furled. A midshipman, it seemed, had been sent up by the officer of the deck to give the order, as no trumpet could be heard where we were.

Those on the weather yard-arm managed to crawl upon the spar and scramble down the rigging; but with us, upon the extreme leeward side, this feat was out of the question; it was, literally, like climbing a precipice to get to windward in order to reach the shrouds; besides, the entire yard was now encased in ice, and our hands and feet were so numb that we dared not trust our lives to them. Nevertheless, by assisting each other, we contrived to throw ourselves prostrate along the yard, and embrace it with our arms and legs. In this position, the stun'-sail-booms greatly assisted in securing our hold. Strange as it may appear, I do not suppose that, at this moment, the slightest sensation of fear was felt by one man on that yard. We clung to it with might and main; but this was instinct. The truth is, that, in circumstances like these, the sense of fear is annihilated in the unutterable sights that fill all the eye, and the sounds that fill all the ear. You become identified with the tempest; your insignificance is lost in the riot of the stormy universe around.

Below us, our noble frigate seemed thrice its real length— a vast black wedge, opposing its widest end to the combined fury of the sea and wind.

At length the first fury of the gale began to abate, and we at once fell to pounding our hands, as a preliminary operation to going to work; for a gang of men had now ascended to help secure what was left of the sail; we somehow packed it away, at last, and came down.

About noon the next day, the gale so moderated that we shook two reefs out of the top-sails, set new courses, and stood due east, with the wind astern.

Thus, all the fine weather we encountered after first weighing anchor on the pleasant Spanish coast, was but the prelude to this one terrific night; more especially, that treacherous calm immediately preceding it. But how could we reach our long-promised homes without encountering Cape Horn? by what possibility avoid it? And though some ships have weathered it without these perils, yet by far the greater part must encounter them. Lucky it is that it comes about midway in the homeward-bound passage, so that the sailors have time to prepare for it, and time to recover from it after it is astern.

But, sailor or landsman, there is some sort of a Cape Horn for all. Boys! beware of it; prepare for it in time. Gray-beards! thank God it is passed. And ye lucky livers, to whom, by some rare fatality, your Cape Horns are placid as Lake Lemans, flatter not yourselves that good luck is judgment and discretion; for all the yolk in your eggs, you might have foundered and gone down, had the Spirit of the Cape said the word.

Chapter 27

SOME THOUGHTS GROWING OUT OF MAD JACK'S
COUNTERMANDING HIS SUPERIOR'S ORDER

IN TIME OF PERIL, like the needle to the load-stone, obedience, irrespective of rank, generally flies to him who is best
fitted to command. The truth of this seemed evinced in the
case of Mad Jack, during the gale, and especially at that perilous moment when he countermanded the Captain's order at
the helm. But every seaman knew, at the time, that the Captain's order was an unwise one in the extreme; perhaps worse
than unwise.

These two orders, given by the Captain and his Lieutenant,
exactly contrasted their characters. By putting the helm *hard
up*, the Captain was for *scudding*; that is, for flying away from
the gale. Whereas, Mad Jack was for running the ship into its
teeth. It is needless to say that, in almost all cases of similar
hard squalls and gales, the latter step, though attended with
more appalling appearances, is, in reality, the safer of the two,
and the most generally adopted.

Scudding makes you a slave to the blast, which drives you
headlong before it; but *running up into the wind's eye* enables
you, in a degree, to hold it at bay. Scudding exposes to the
gale your stern, the weakest part of your hull; the contrary
course presents to it your bows, your strongest part. As with
ships, so with men; he who turns his back to his foe gives
him an advantage. Whereas, our ribbed chests, like the ribbed
bows of a frigate, are as bulkheads to dam off an onset.

That night, off the pitch of the Cape, Captain Claret was
hurried forth from his disguises, and, at a manhood-testing
conjuncture, appeared in his true colors. A thing which every
man in the ship had long suspected that night was proved
true. Hitherto, in going about the ship, and casting his
glances among the men, the peculiarly lustreless repose of the
Captain's eye—his slow, even, unnecessarily methodical step,
and the forced firmness of his whole demeanor—though, to
a casual observer, seemingly expressive of the consciousness

of command and a desire to strike subjection among the crew—all this, to some minds, had only been deemed indications of the fact that Captain Claret, while carefully shunning positive excesses, continually kept himself in an uncertain equilibrio between soberness and its reverse; which equilibrio might be destroyed by the first sharp vicissitude of events.

And though this is only a surmise, nevertheless, as having some knowledge of brandy and mankind, White-Jacket will venture to state that, had Captain Claret been an out-and-out temperance man, he would never have given that most imprudent order to *hard up* the helm. He would either have held his peace, and stayed in his cabin, like his gracious majesty the Commodore, or else have anticipated Mad Jack's order, and thundered forth "Hard down the helm!"

To show how little real sway at times have the severest restrictive laws, and how spontaneous is the instinct of discretion in some minds, it must here be added, that though Mad Jack, under a hot impulse, had countermanded an order of his superior officer before his very face, yet that severe Article of War, to which he thus rendered himself obnoxious, was never enforced against him. Nor, so far as any of the crew ever knew, did the Captain even venture to reprimand him for his temerity.

It has been said that Mad Jack himself was a lover of strong drink. So he was. But here we only see the virtue of being placed in a station constantly demanding a cool head and steady nerves, and the misfortune of filling a post that does *not* at all times demand these qualities. So exact and methodical in most things was the discipline of the frigate, that, to a certain extent, Captain Claret was exempted from personal interposition in many of its current events, and thereby, perhaps, was he lulled into security, under the enticing lee of his decanter.

But as for Mad Jack, he must stand his regular watches, and pace the quarter-deck at night, and keep a sharp eye to windward. Hence, at sea, Mad Jack tried to make a point of keeping sober, though in very fine weather he was sometimes betrayed into a glass too many; and got himself into difficulties, as has been mentioned elsewhere. But with Cape Horn before him, he took the temperance pledge outright, till that perilous promontory should be far astern.

The leading incident of the gale irresistibly invites the question, Are there incompetent officers in the American navy?— that is, incompetent to the due performance of whatever duties may devolve upon them. But in that gallant marine, which, during the Late War, gained so much of what is called *glory*, can there possibly be to-day incompetent officers?

As in the camp ashore, so on the quarter-deck at sea—the trumpets of one victory drown the muffled drums of a thousand defeats. And, in degree, this holds true of those events of war which are neuter in their character, neither making renown nor disgrace. Besides, as a long array of ciphers, led by but one solitary numeral, swell, by mere force of aggregation, into an immense arithmetical sum, even so, in some brilliant actions, do a crowd of officers, each inefficient in himself, aggregate renown when banded together, and led by a numeral Nelson or a Wellington. And the renown of such heroes, by outliving themselves, descends as a heritage to their subordinate survivors. One large brain and one large heart have virtue sufficient to magnetize a whole fleet or an army. And if all the men who, since the beginning of the world, have mainly contributed to the warlike successes or reverses of nations, were now mustered together, we should be amazed to behold but a handful of heroes. For there is no heroism in merely running in and out a gun at a port-hole, enveloped in smoke or vapor, or in firing off muskets in platoons at the word of command. This kind of merely manual valor is often born of trepidation at the heart. There may be men, individually craven, who, united, may display even temerity. Yet it would be false to deny that, in some instances, the lowest privates have acquitted themselves with even more gallantry than their commodores. True heroism is not in the hand, but in the heart and the head.

But are there incompetent officers in the gallant American navy? For an American, the question is of no grateful cast. White-Jacket must again evade it, by referring to an historical fact in the history of a kindred marine, which, from its long standing and magnitude, furnishes many more examples of all kinds than our own. And this is the only reason why it is ever referred to in this narrative. I thank God I am free from all national invidiousness.

It is indirectly on record in the books of the English Admiralty, that in the year 1808—after the death of Lord Nelson—when Lord Collingwood commanded on the Mediterranean station, and his broken health induced him to solicit a furlough, that out of a list of upward of one hundred admirals, not a single officer was found who was deemed qualified to relieve the applicant with credit to the country. This fact Collingwood sealed with his life; for, hopeless of being recalled, he shortly after died, worn out, at his post. Now, if this was the case in so renowned a marine as England's, what must be inferred with respect to our own? But herein no special disgrace is involved. For the truth is, that to be an accomplished and skillful naval generalissimo needs natural capabilities of an uncommon order. Still more, it may safely be asserted, that, worthily to command even a frigate, requires a degree of natural heroism, talent, judgment, and integrity, that is denied to mediocrity. Yet these qualifications are not only required, but demanded; and no one has a right to be a naval captain unless he possesses them.

Regarding Lieutenants, there are not a few Selvagees and Paper Jacks in the American navy. Many Commodores know that they have seldom taken a line-of-battle ship to sea, without feeling more or less nervousness when some of the Lieutenants have the deck at night.

According to the last Navy Register (1849), there are now 68 Captains in the American navy, collectively drawing about $300,000 annually from the public treasury; also, 97 Commanders, drawing about $200,000; and 327 Lieutenants, drawing about half a million; and 451 Midshipmen (including Passed-midshipmen), also drawing nearly half a million. Considering the known facts, that some of these officers are seldom or never sent to sea, owing to the Navy Department being well aware of their inefficiency; that others are detailed for pen-and-ink work at observatories, and solvers of logarithms in the Coast Survey; while the really meritorious officers, who are accomplished practical seamen, are known to be sent from ship to ship, with but a small interval of a furlough; considering all this, it is not too much to say, that no small portion of the million and a half of money above mentioned is annually paid to national pensioners in disguise, who live on the navy without serving it.

Nothing like this can be even insinuated against the "*forward officers*"—Boatswains, Gunners, &c.; nor against the *petty officers*—Captains of the Tops, &c.; nor against the able seamen in the navy. For if any of *these* are found wanting, they are forthwith disrated or discharged.

True, all experience teaches that, whenever there is a great national establishment, employing large numbers of officials, the public must be reconciled to support many incompetent men; for such is the favoritism and nepotism always prevailing in the purlieus of these establishments, that some incompetent persons are always admitted, to the exclusion of many of the worthy.

Nevertheless, in a country like ours, boasting of the political equality of all social conditions, it is a great reproach that such a thing as a common seaman rising to the rank of a commissioned officer in our navy, is nowadays almost unheard-of. Yet, in former times, when officers have so risen to rank, they have generally proved of signal usefulness in the service, and sometimes have reflected solid honor upon the country. Instances in point might be mentioned.

Is it not well to have our institutions of a piece? Any American landsman may hope to become President of the Union—commodore of our squadron of states. And every American sailor should be placed in such a position, that he might freely aspire to command a squadron of frigates.

But if there is good reason to believe, that there are some incompetent officers in our navy; we have still better, and more abundant reason to know, that there are others, whom both nature and art have united in eminently qualifying for it; and whom the service does not so much honor, as they may be said to honor it.

And the only purpose of this chapter is, to point out as the peculiar desert of individuals, that generalized reputation, which most men, perhaps, are apt to ascribe in the gross, to one and all the members of a popular military establishment.

Chapter 28

Edging Away

RIGHT BEFORE THE WIND! Ay, blow, blow, ye breezes; so long as *ye* stay fair, and *we* are homeward bound, what care the jolly crew?

It is worth mentioning here that, in nineteen cases out of twenty, a passage from the Pacific round the Cape is almost sure to be much shorter, and attended with less hardship, than a passage undertaken from the Atlantic. The reason is, that the gales are mostly from the westward, also the currents.

But, after all, going before the wind in a frigate, in such a tempest, has its annoyances and drawbacks, as well as many other blessings. The disproportionate weight of metal upon the spar and gun decks induces a violent rolling, unknown to merchant ships. We rolled and rolled on our way, like the world in its orbit, shipping green seas on both sides, until the old frigate dipped and went into it like a diving-bell.

The hatchways of some armed vessels are but poorly secured in bad weather. This was peculiarly the case with those of the Neversink. They were merely spread over with an old tarpaulin, cracked and rent in every direction.

In fair weather, the ship's company messed on the gundeck; but as this was now flooded almost continually, we were obliged to take our meals upon the berth-deck, the next one below. One day, the messes of the starboard-watch were seated here at dinner; forming little groups, twelve or fifteen men in each, reclining about the beef-kids and their pots and pans; when all of a sudden the ship was seized with such a paroxysm of rolling that, in a single instant, every thing on the berth-deck—pots, kids, sailors, pieces of beef, bread-bags, clothes-bags, and barges—were tossed indiscriminately from side to side. It was impossible to stay one's self; there was nothing but the bare deck to cling to, which was slippery with the contents of the kids, and heaving under us as if there were a volcano in the frigate's hold. While we were yet sliding in uproarious crowds—all seated—the windows of the deck opened, and floods of brine descended, simultaneously with a violent lee-roll. The shower was hailed by the reckless tars with a hurricane of yells; although, for an instant, I really imagined we were about being swamped in the sea, such volumes of water came cascading down.

A day or two after, we had made sufficient Easting to stand to the northward, which we did, with the wind astern; thus fairly turning the corner without abating our rate of progress. Though we had seen no land since leaving Callao, Cape Horn was said to be somewhere to the West of us; and though there was no positive evidence of the fact, the weather encountered might be accounted pretty good presumptive proof.

The land near Cape Horn, however, is well worth seeing, especially Staten Land. Upon one occasion, the ship in which I then happened to be sailing drew near this place from the northward, with a fair, free wind, blowing steadily, through a bright translucent day, whose air was almost musical with the clear, glittering cold. On our starboard beam, like a pile of glaciers in Switzerland, lay this Staten Land, gleaming in snow-white barrenness and solitude. Unnumbered white albatross were skimming the sea near by, and clouds of smaller white wings fell through the air like snow-flakes. High, towering in their own turbaned snows, the far-inland pinnacles loomed up, like the boarder of some other world. Flashing walls and crystal battlements, like the diamond watch-towers along heaven's furthest frontier.

After leaving the latitude of the Cape, we had several storms of snow; one night a considerable quantity laid upon the decks, and some of the sailors enjoyed the juvenile diversion of snow-balling. Woe unto the "middy" who that night went forward of the booms. Such a target for snow-balls! The throwers could never be known. By some curious sleight in hurling the missiles, they seemed to be thrown on board by some hoydenish sea-nymphs outside the frigate.

At daybreak Midshipman Pert went below to the surgeon with an alarming wound, gallantly received in discharging his perilous duty on the forecastle. The officer of the deck had sent him on an errand, to tell the boatswain that he was wanted in the captain's cabin. While in the very act of performing the exploit of delivering the message, Mr. Pert was struck on the nose with a snow-ball of wondrous compactness. Upon being informed of the disaster, the rogues expressed the liveliest sympathy. Pert was no favorite.

After one of these storms, it was a curious sight to see the men relieving the uppermost deck of its load of snow. It became the duty of the captain of each gun to keep his own station clean; accordingly, with an old broom, or "squilgee," he proceeded to business, often quarreling with his next-door neighbors about their scraping their snow on his premises. It was like Broadway in winter, the morning after a storm, when rival shop-boys are at work cleaning the sidewalk.

Now and then, by way of variety, we had a fall of hail-stones, so big that sometimes we found ourselves dodging them.

The Commodore had a Polynesian servant on board, whose services he had engaged at the Society Islands. Unlike his countrymen, Wooloo was of a sedate, earnest, and philosophic temperament. Having never been outside of the tropics before, he found many phenomena off Cape Horn, which absorbed his attention, and set him, like other philosophers, to feign theories corresponding to the marvels he beheld. At the first snow, when he saw the deck covered all over with a white powder, as it were, he expanded his eyes into stew-pans; but upon examining the strange substance, he decided that this must be a species of superfine flour, such as was compounded into his master's "*duffs*," and other dainties. In vain did an experienced natural philosopher belonging to the fore-top maintain before his face, that in this hypothesis Wooloo was mistaken; Wooloo's opinion remained unchanged for some time.

As for the hailstones, they transported him; he went about with a bucket, making collections, and receiving contributions, for the purpose of carrying them home to his sweet-hearts for glass beads; but having put his bucket away, and returning to it again, and finding nothing but a little water, he accused the by-standers of stealing his precious stones.

This suggests another story concerning him. The first time he was given a piece of "duff" to eat, he was observed to pick out very carefully every raisin, and throw it away, with a gesture indicative of the highest disgust. It turned out that he had taken the raisins for bugs.

In our man-of-war, this semi-savage, wandering about the gun-deck in his barbaric robe, seemed a being from some other sphere. His tastes were our abominations: ours his. Our creed he rejected: his we. We thought him a loon: he fancied us fools. Had the case been reversed; had we been Polynesians and he an American, our mutual opinion of each other would still have remained the same. A fact proving that neither was wrong, but both right.

Chapter 29

THE NIGHT-WATCHES

THOUGH LEAVING the Cape behind us, the severe cold still continued, and one of its worst consequences was the almost incurable drowsiness induced thereby during the long night-watches. All along the decks, huddled between the guns, stretched out on the carronade slides, and in every accessible nook and corner, you would see the sailors wrapped in their monkey jackets, in a state of half-conscious torpidity, lying still and freezing alive, without the power to rise and shake themselves.

"Up—up, you lazy dogs!" our good-natured Third Lieutenant, a Virginian, would cry, rapping them with his speaking trumpet. "Get up, and stir about."

But in vain. They would rise for an instant, and as soon as his back was turned, down they would drop, as if shot through the heart.

Often I have lain thus, when the fact, that if I laid much longer I would actually freeze to death, would come over me with such overpowering force as to break the icy spell, and starting to my feet, I would endeavor to go through the combined manual and pedal exercise to restore the circulation. The first fling of my benumbed arm generally struck me in the face, instead of smiting my chest, its true destination. But in these cases one's muscles have their own way.

In exercising my other extremities, I was obliged to hold on to something, and leap with both feet; for my limbs seemed as destitute of joints as a pair of canvass pants spread to dry, and frozen stiff.

When an order was given to haul the braces—which required the strength of the entire watch, some two hundred men—a spectator would have supposed that all hands had received a stroke of the palsy. Roused from their state of enchantment, they came halting and limping across the decks, falling against each other, and, for a few moments, almost unable to handle the ropes. The slightest exertion seemed intolerable; and frequently a body of eighty or a hundred men, summoned to brace the main-yard, would hang over the rope for several minutes, waiting for some active fellow to pick it up and put it into their hands. Even then, it was some time before they were able to do any thing. They made all the motions usual in hauling a rope, but it was a long time before the yard budged an inch. It was to no purpose that the officers swore at them, or sent the midshipmen among them to find out who those "*horse-marines*" and "*sogers*" were. The sailors were so enveloped in monkey jackets, that in the dark night there was no telling one from the other.

"Here, *you*, sir!" cries little Mr. Pert, eagerly catching hold of the skirts of an old sea-dog, and trying to turn him round, so as to peer under his tarpaulin. "Who are *you*, sir? What's your name?"

"Find out, Milk-and-Water," was the impertinent rejoinder.

"Blast you! you old rascal; I'll have you licked for that! Tell me his name, some of you!" turning round to the bystanders.

"Gammon!" cries a voice at a distance.

"Hang me, but I know *you*, sir! and here's at you!" and, so saying, Mr. Pert drops the impenetrable unknown, and makes into the crowd after the bodiless voice. But the attempt to find an owner for that voice is quite as idle as the effort to discover the contents of the monkey jacket.

And here sorrowful mention must be made of something which, during this state of affairs, most sorely afflicted me. Most monkey jackets are of a dark hue; mine, as I have fifty times repeated, and say again, was white. And thus, in those long, dark nights, when it was my quarter-watch on deck, and not in the top, and others went skulking and "sogering" about the decks, secure from detection—their identity undiscoverable—my own hapless jacket forever proclaimed the name of its wearer. It gave me many a hard job, which otherwise I should have escaped. When an officer wanted a man for any particular duty—running aloft, say, to communicate some slight order to the captains of the tops—how easy, in that mob of incognitoes, to individualize "*that white jacket*," and dispatch him on the errand. Then, it would never do for me to hang back when the ropes were being pulled.

Indeed, upon all these occasions, such alacrity and cheerfulness was I obliged to display, that I was frequently held up as an illustrious example of activity, which the rest were called upon to emulate. "Pull—pull! you lazy lubbers! Look at White-Jacket, there; pull like him!"

Oh! how I execrated my luckless garment; how often I scoured the deck with it to give it a tawny hue; how often I supplicated the inexorable Brush, captain of the paint-room, for just one brushful of his invaluable pigment. Frequently, I meditated giving it a toss overboard; but I had not the resolution. Jacketless at sea! Jacketless so near Cape Horn! The thought was unendurable. And, at least, my garment was a jacket in name, if not in utility.

At length I essayed a "swap." "Here, Bob," said I, assuming all possible suavity, and accosting a mess-mate with a sort of diplomatic assumption of superiority, "suppose I was ready to part with this 'grego' of mine, and take yours in exchange—what would you give me to boot?"

"Give you to *boot*?" he exclaimed, with horror; "I wouldn't take your infernal jacket for a gift!"

How I hailed every snow-squall; for then—blessings on them!—many of the men became *white jackets* along with myself; and, powdered with the flakes, we all looked like millers.

We had six lieutenants, all of whom, with the exception of the First Lieutenant, by turns headed the watches. Three of these officers, including Mad Jack, were strict disciplinarians, and never permitted us to lay down on deck during the night. And, to tell the truth, though it caused much growling, it was far better for our health to be thus kept on our feet. So promenading was all the vogue. For some of us, however, it was like pacing in a dungeon; for, as we had to keep at our stations—some at the halyards, some at the braces, and elsewhere—and were not allowed to stroll about indefinitely, and fairly take the measure of the ship's entire keel, we were fain to confine ourselves to the space of a very few feet. But the worst of this was soon over. The suddenness of the change in the temperature consequent on leaving Cape Horn, and steering to the northward with a ten-knot breeze, is a noteworthy thing. To-day, you are assailed by a blast that seems to have edged itself on icebergs; but in a little more than a week, your jacket may be superfluous.

One word more about Cape Horn, and we have done with it.

Years hence, when a ship-canal shall have penetrated the Isthmus of Darien, and the traveler be taking his seat in the cars at Cape Cod for Astoria, it will be held a thing almost incredible that, for so long a period, vessels bound to the Nor'-west Coast from New York should, by going round Cape Horn, have lengthened their voyages some thousands of miles. "In those unenlightened days" (I quote, in advance, the language of some future philosopher), "entire years were frequently consumed in making the voyage to and from the Spice Islands, the present fashionable watering-place of the beau-monde of Oregon." Such must be our national progress.

Why, sir, that boy of yours will, one of these days, be sending your grandson to the salubrious city of Jeddo to spend his summer vacations.

Chapter 30

WHILE NOW running rapidly away from the bitter coast of Patagonia, battling with the night-watches—still cold—as best we may; come under the lee of my white jacket, reader, while I tell of the less painful sights to be seen in a frigate.

A hint has already been conveyed concerning the subterranean depths of the Neversink's hold. But there is no time here to speak of the *spirit-room*, a cellar down in the after-hold, where the sailor "grog" is kept; nor of the *cable-tiers*, where the great hawsers and chains are piled, as you see them at a large ship-chandler's on shore; nor of the grocer's vaults, where tierces of sugar, molasses, vinegar, rice, and flour are snugly stowed; nor of the *sail-room*, full as a sail-maker's loft ashore—piled up with great top-sails and top-gallant-sails, all ready-folded in their places, like so many white vests in a gentleman's wardrobe; nor of the copper and copper-fastened *magazine*, closely packed with kegs of powder, great-gun and small-arm cartridges; nor of the immense *shot-lockers,* or subterranean arsenals, full as a bushel of apples with twenty-four-pound balls; nor of the *bread-room,* a large apartment, tinned all round within to keep out the mice, where the hard biscuit destined for the consumption of five hundred men on a long voyage is stowed away by the cubic yard; nor of the vast iron *tanks* for fresh water in the hold, like the reservoir lakes at Fairmount, in Philadelphia; nor of the *paint-room,* where the kegs of white-lead, and casks of linseed oil, and all sorts of pots and brushes, are kept; nor of the *armoror's smithy*, where the ship's forges and anvils may be heard ringing at times; I say I have no time to speak of these things, and many more places of note.

But there is one very extensive warehouse among the rest that needs special mention—*the ship's Yeoman's store-room.* In the Neversink it was down in the ship's basement, beneath the berth-deck, and you went to it by way of the *Fore-passage*, a very dim, devious corridor, indeed. Entering—say at noon-day—you find yourself in a gloomy apartment, lit by a solitary lamp. On one side are shelves, filled with balls of *marline*, *ratlin-stuff*, *seizing-stuff*, *spun-yarn*, and numerous twines of assorted sizes. In another direction you see large cases containing heaps of articles, reminding one of a shoe-maker's furnishing-store—wooden *serving-mallets*, *fids*, *toggles*, and *heavers*; iron *prickers* and *marling-spikes*; in a third quarter you see a sort of hardware shop—shelves piled with all manner of hooks, bolts, nails, screws, and *thimbles*; and, in still another direction, you see a block-maker's store, heaped up with lignum-vitæ sheeves and wheels.

Through low arches in the bulk-head beyond, you peep in upon distant vaults and catacombs, obscurely lighted in the far end, and showing immense coils of new ropes, and other bulky articles, stowed in tiers, all savoring of tar.

But by far the most curious department of these mysterious store-rooms is the armory, where the pikes, cutlasses, pistols, and belts, forming the arms of the boarders in time of action, are hung against the walls, and suspended in thick rows from the beams overhead. Here, too, are to be seen scores of Colt's patent revolvers, which, though furnished with but one tube, multiply the fatal bullets, as the naval cat-o'-nine-tails, with a cannibal cruelty, in one blow nine times multiplies a culprit's lashes; so that, when a sailor is ordered one dozen lashes, the sentence should read one hundred and eight. All these arms are kept in the brightest order, wearing a fine polish, and may truly be said to *reflect* credit on the Yeoman and his mates.

Among the lower grade of officers in a man-of-war, that of Yeoman is not the least important. His responsibilities are denoted by his pay. While the *petty officers*, quarter-gunners, captains of the tops, and others, receive but fifteen and eighteen dollars a month—but little more than a mere able sea-man—the Yeoman in an American line-of-battle ship receives forty dollars, and in a frigate thirty-five dollars per month.

He is accountable for all the articles under his charge, and on no account must deliver a yard of twine or a tenpenny nail to the boatswain or carpenter, unless shown a written requisition and order from the Senior Lieutenant. The Yeoman is to be found burrowing in his under-ground store-rooms all the day long, in readiness to serve licensed customers. But in the counter, behind which he usually stands, there is no place for a till to drop the shillings in, which takes away not a little from the most agreeable part of a storekeeper's duties. Nor, among the musty, old account-books in his desk, where he registers all expenditures of his stuffs, is there any cash or check book.

The Yeoman of the Neversink was a somewhat odd specimen of a Troglodite. He was a little old man, round-shoul-dered, bald-headed, with great goggle-eyes, looking through portentous round spectacles, which he called his *barnacles*. He was imbued with a wonderful zeal for the naval service, and seemed to think that, in keeping his pistols and cutlasses free from rust, he preserved the national honor untarnished.

After *general quarters*, it was amusing to watch his anxious air as the various *petty officers* restored to him the arms used at the martial exercises of the crew. As successive bundles would be deposited on his counter, he would count over the pistols and cutlasses, like an old housekeeper telling over her silver forks and spoons in a pantry before retiring for the night. And often, with a sort of dark lantern in his hand, he might be seen poking into his furthest vaults and cellars, and counting over his great coils of ropes, as if they were all jolly puncheons of old Port and Madeira.

By reason of his incessant watchfulness and unaccountable bachelor oddities, it was very difficult for him to retain in his employment the various sailors who, from time to time, were billeted with him to do the duty of subalterns. In particular, he was always desirous of having at least one steady, faultless young man, of a literary taste, to keep an eye on his account-books, and swab out the armory every morning. It was an odious business this, to be immured all day in such a bottom-less hole, among tarry old ropes and villainous guns and pis-tols. It was with peculiar dread that I one day noticed the goggle-eyes of *Old Revolver*, as they called him, fastened upon me with a fatal glance of good-will and approbation. He had somehow heard of my being a very learned person, who could both read and write with extraordinary facility; and, moreover, that I was a rather reserved youth, who kept his modest, unassuming merits in the background. But though, from the keen sense of my situation as a man-of-war's-man, all this about my keeping myself in the *back* ground was true enough, yet I had no idea of hiding my diffident merits *under* ground. I became alarmed at the old Yeoman's goggling glances, lest he should drag me down into tarry perdition in his hideous store-rooms. But this fate was providentially averted, owing to mysterious causes which I never could fathom.

Chapter 31

The Gunner under Hatches

Among such a crowd of marked characters as were to be met with on board our frigate, many of whom moved in mysterious circles beneath the lowermost deck, and at long intervals flitted into sight like apparitions, and disappeared again for whole weeks together, there were some who inordinately excited my curiosity, and whose names, callings, and precise abodes I industriously sought out, in order to learn something satisfactory concerning them.

While engaged in these inquiries, often fruitless, or but partially gratified, I could not but regret that there was no public printed Directory for the Neversink, such as they have in large towns, containing an alphabetic list of all the crew, and where they might be found. Also, in losing myself in some remote, dark corner of the bowels of the frigate, in the vicinity of the various store-rooms, shops, and warehouses, I much lamented that no enterprising tar had yet thought of compiling a *Hand-book of the Neversink*, so that the tourist might have a reliable guide.

Indeed, there were several parts of the ship under hatches shrouded in mystery, and completely inaccessible to the sailor. Wondrous old doors, barred and bolted in dingy bulk-heads, must have opened into regions full of interest to a successful explorer.

They looked like the gloomy entrances to family vaults of buried dead; and when I chanced to see some unknown functionary insert his key, and enter these inexplicable apartments with a battle-lantern, as if on solemn official business, I almost quaked to dive in with him, and satisfy myself whether these vaults indeed contained the moldering relics of by-gone old Commodores and Post-captains. But the habitations of the living commodore and captain—their spacious and curtained cabins—were themselves almost as sealed volumes, and I passed them in hopeless wonderment, like a peasant before a prince's palace. Night and day armed sentries guarded their sacred portals, cutlass in hand; and had I dared to cross their path, I would infallibly have been cut down, as if in battle. Thus, though for a period of more than a year I was an inmate of this floating box of live-oak, yet there were numberless things in it that, to the last, remained wrapped in obscurity, or concerning which I could only lose myself in vague speculations. I was as a Roman Jew of the Middle Ages, confined to the Jews' quarter of the town, and forbidden to stray beyond my limits. Or I was as a modern traveler in the same famous city, forced to quit it at last without gaining ingress to the most mysterious haunts—the innermost shrine of the Pope, and the dungeons and cells of the Inquisition.

But among all the persons and things on board that puzzled me, and filled me most with strange emotions of doubt, misgivings, and mystery, was the Gunner—a short, square, grim man, his hair and beard grizzled and singed, as if with gunpowder. His skin was of a flecky brown, like the stained barrel of a fowling-piece, and his hollow eyes burned in his head like blue-lights. He it was who had access to many of those mysterious vaults I have spoken of. Often he might be seen groping his way into them, followed by his subalterns, the old quarter-gunners, as if intent upon laying a train of powder to blow up the ship. I remembered Guy Fawkes and the Parliament-house, and made earnest inquiry whether this gunner was a Roman Catholic. I felt relieved when informed that he was not.

A little circumstance which one of his *mates* once told me heightened the gloomy interest with which I regarded his chief. He told me that, at periodical intervals, his master the Gunner, accompanied by his phalanx, entered into the great Magazine under the Gun-room, of which he had sole custody and kept the key, nearly as big as the key of the Bastile, and provided with lanterns, something like Sir Humphrey Davy's Safety-lamp for coal mines, proceeded to turn, end for end, all the kegs of powder and packages of cartridges stored in this innermost explosive vault, lined throughout with sheets of copper. In the vestibule of the Magazine, against the paneling, were several pegs for slippers, and, before penetrating further than that vestibule, every man of the gunner's-gang silently removed his shoes, for fear that the nails in their heels might possibly create a spark, by striking against the coppered floor within. Then, with slippered feet and with hushed whispers, they stole into the heart of the place.

This turning of the powder was to preserve its inflammability. And surely it was a business full of direful interest, to be buried so deep below the sun, handling whole barrels of powder, any one of which, touched by the smallest spark, was powerful enough to blow up a whole street of warehouses.

The gunner went by the name of *Old Combustibles*, though I thought this an undignified name for so momentous a personage, who had all our lives in his hand.

While we lay in Callao, we received from shore several barrels of powder. So soon as the *launch* came alongside with them, orders were given to extinguish all lights and all fires in the ship; and the master-at-arms and his corporals inspected every deck to see that this order was obeyed; a very prudent precaution, no doubt, but not observed at all in the Turkish navy. The Turkish sailors will sit on their gun-carriages, tranquilly smoking, while kegs of powder are being rolled under their ignited pipe-bowls. This shows the great comfort there is in the doctrine of these Fatalists, and how such a doctrine, in some things at least, relieves men from nervous anxieties. But we are all Fatalists at bottom. Nor need we so much marvel at the heroism of that army officer, who challenged his personal foe to bestride a barrel of powder with him—the match to be placed between them—and be blown up in good company, for it is pretty certain that the whole earth itself is a vast hogshead, full of inflammable materials, and which we are always bestriding; at the same time, that all good Christians believe that at any minute the last day may come, and the terrible combustion of the entire planet ensue.

As if impressed with a befitting sense of the awfulness of his calling, our gunner always wore a fixed expression of solemnity, which was heightened by his grizzled hair and beard. But what imparted such a sinister look to him, and what wrought so upon my imagination concerning this man, was a frightful scar crossing his left cheek and forehead. He had been almost mortally wounded, they said, with a sabre-cut, during a frigate engagement in the last war with Britain.

He was the most methodical, exact, and punctual of all the forward officers. Among his other duties, it pertained to him, while in harbor, to see that at a certain hour in the evening one of the great guns was discharged from the forecastle, a ceremony only observed in a flag-ship. And always at the precise moment you might behold him blowing his match, then applying it; and with that booming thunder in his ear, and the smell of the powder in his hair, he retired to his hammock for the night. What dreams he must have had!

The same precision was observed when ordered to fire a gun to *bring to* some ship at sea; for, true to their name, and preserving its applicability, even in times of peace, all men-of-war are great bullies on the high seas. They domineer over the poor merchantmen, and with a hissing hot ball sent bowling across the ocean, compel them to stop their headway at pleasure.

It was enough to make you a man of method for life, to see the gunner superintending his subalterns, when preparing the main-deck batteries for a great national salute. While lying in harbor, intelligence reached us of the lamentable casualty that befell certain high officers of state, including the acting Secretary of the Navy himself, some other member of the President's cabinet, a Commodore, and others, all engaged in experimenting upon a new-fangled engine of war. At the same time with the receipt of this sad news, orders arrived to fire minute-guns for the deceased head of the naval department. Upon this occasion the gunner was more than usually ceremonious, in seeing that the long twenty-fours were thoroughly loaded and rammed down, and then accurately marked with chalk, so as to be discharged in undeviating rotation, first from the larboard side, and then from the starboard.

But as my ears hummed, and all my bones danced in me with the reverberating din, and my eyes and nostrils were almost suffocated with the smoke, and when I saw this grim old gunner firing away so solemnly, I thought it a strange mode of honoring a man's memory who had himself been slaughtered by a cannon. Only the smoke, that, after rolling in at the port-holes, rapidly drifted away to leeward, and was lost to view, seemed truly emblematical touching the personage thus honored, since that great non-combatant, the Bible, assures us that our life is but a vapor, that quickly passeth away.

Chapter 32

A Dish of Dunderfunk

IN MEN-OF-WAR, the space on the uppermost deck, round about the main-mast, is the Police-office, Court-house, and yard of execution, where all charges are lodged, causes tried, and punishment administered. In frigate phrase, to be *brought up to the mast*, is equivalent to being presented before the grand-jury, to see whether a true bill will be found against you.

From the merciless, inquisitorial *baiting*, which sailors, charged with offences, too often experience *at the mast*, that vicinity is usually known among them as the *bull-ring*.

The main-mast, moreover, is the only place where the sailor can hold formal communication with the captain and officers. If any one has been robbed; if any one has been evilly entreated; if any one's character has been defamed; if any one has a request to present; if any one has aught important for the executive of the ship to know—straight to the main-mast he repairs; and stands there—generally with his hat off—waiting the pleasure of the officer of the deck, to advance and communicate with him. Often, the most ludicrous scenes occur, and the most comical complaints are made.

One clear, cold morning, while we were yet running away from the Cape, a raw-boned, crack-pated Down Easter, belonging to the Waist, made his appearance at the mast, dolefully exhibiting a blackened tin pan, bearing a few crusty traces of some sort of a sea-pie, which had been cooked in it.

"Well, sir, what now?" said the Lieutenant of the Deck, advancing.

"They stole it, sir; all my nice *dunderfunk*, sir; they did, sir," whined the Down Easter, ruefully holding up his pan.

"Stole your *dundlefunk*! what's that?"

"*Dunderfunk*, sir, *dunderfunk*; a cruel nice dish as ever man put into him."

"Speak out, sir; what's the matter?"

"My *dunderfunk*, sir—as elegant a dish of *dunderfunk* as you ever see, sir— they stole it, sir!"

"Go forward, you rascal!" cried the Lieutenant, in a towering rage, "or else stop your whining. Tell me, what's the matter?"

"Why, sir, them 'ere two fellows, Dobs and Hodnose, stole my *dunderfunk*."

"Once more, sir, I ask what that *dundledunk* is? Speak!"

"As cruel a nice——"

"Be off, sir! sheer!" and muttering something about *non compos mentis*, the Lieutenant stalked away; while the Down Easter beat a melancholy retreat, holding up his pan like a tambourine, and making dolorous music on it as he went.

"Where are you going with that tear in your eye, like a traveling rat?" cried a top-man.

"Oh! he's going home to Down East," said another; "so far eastward, you know, *shippy*, that they have to pry up the sun with a handspike."

To make this anecdote plainer, be it said that, at sea, the monotonous round of salt beef and pork at the messes of the sailors—where but very few of the varieties of the season are to be found—induces them to adopt many contrivances in order to diversify their meals. Hence the various sea-rolls, made dishes, and Mediterranean pies, well known by man-of-war's-men— *Scouse, Lob-scouse, Soft-Tack, Soft-Tommy, Skillagalee, Burgoo, Dough-boys, Lob-Dominion, Dog's-Body,* and lastly, and least known, *Dunderfunk*; all of which come under the general denomination of *Manavalins*.

Dunderfunk is made of hard biscuit, hashed and pounded, mixed with beef fat, molasses, and water, and baked brown in a pan. And to those who are beyond all reach of shore delicacies, this *dunderfunk*, in the feeling language of the Down Easter, is certainly "*a cruel nice dish*."

Now the only way that a sailor, after preparing his *dunderfunk*, could get it cooked on board the Neversink, was by slily going to *Old Coffee*, the ship's cook, and bribing him to put it into his oven. And as some such dishes or other are well known to be all the time in the oven, a set of unprincipled gourmands are constantly on the look-out for the chance of stealing them. Generally, two or three league together, and while one engages *Old Coffee* in some interesting conversation touching his wife and family at home, another snatches the first thing he can lay hands on in the oven, and rapidly passes it to the third man, who at his earliest leisure disappears with it.

In this manner had the Down Easter lost his previous pie, and afterward found the empty pan knocking about the forecastle.

Chapter 33

A Flogging

IF YOU BEGIN the day with a laugh, you may, nevertheless, end it with a sob and a sigh.

Among the many who were exceedingly diverted with the scene between the Down Easter and the Lieutenant, none laughed more heartily than John, Peter, Mark, and Antone—four sailors of the starboard-watch. The same evening these four found themselves prisoners in the "brig," with a sentry standing over them. They were charged with violating a well-known law of the ship—having been engaged in one of those tangled, general fights sometimes occurring among sailors. They had nothing to anticipate but a flogging, at the captain's pleasure.

Toward evening of the next day, they were startled by the dread summons of the boatswain and his mates at the principal hatchway—a summons that ever sends a shudder through every manly heart in a frigate:

"All hands witness punishment, ahoy!"

The hoarseness of the cry, its unrelenting prolongation, its being caught up at different points, and sent through the lowermost depths of the ship; all this produces a most dismal effect upon every heart not calloused by long habituation to it.

However much you may desire to absent yourself from the scene that ensues, yet behold it you must; or, at least, stand near it you must; for the regulations enjoin the attendance of the entire ship's company, from the corpulent Captain himself to the smallest boy who strikes the bell.

"All hands witness punishment, ahoy!"

To the sensitive seaman that summons sounds like a doom. He knows that the same law which impels it—the same law by which the culprits of the day must suffer; that by that very law he also is liable at any time to be judged and condemned. And the inevitableness of his own presence at the scene; the strong arm that drags him in view of the scourge, and holds

488

him there till all is over; forcing upon his loathing eye and soul the sufferings and groans of men who have familiarly consorted with him, eaten with him, battled out watches with him—men of his own type and badge—all this conveys a terrible hint of the omnipotent authority under which he lives. Indeed, to such a man the naval summons to witness punishment carries a thrill, somewhat akin to what we may impute to the quick and the dead, when they shall hear the Last Trump, that is to bid them all arise in their ranks, and behold the final penalties inflicted upon the sinners of our race.

But it must not be imagined that to all men-of-war's-men this summons conveys such poignant emotions; but it is hard to decide whether one should be glad or sad that this is not the case; whether it is grateful to know that so much pain is avoided, or whether it is far sadder to think that, either from constitutional hard-heartedness or the multiplied searings of habit, hundreds of men-of-war's-men have been made proof against the sense of degradation, pity, and shame.

As if in sympathy with the scene to be enacted, the sun, which the day previous had merrily flashed upon the tin pan of the disconsolate Down Easter, was now setting over the dreary waters, veiling itself in vapors. The wind blew hoarsely in the cordage; the seas broke heavily against the bows; and the frigate, staggering under whole top-sails, strained as in agony on her way.

"All hands witness punishment, ahoy!"

At the summons the crew crowded round the main-mast; multitudes eager to obtain a good place on the booms, to overlook the scene; many laughing and chatting, others canvassing the case of the culprits; some maintaining sad, anxious countenances, or carrying a suppressed indignation in their eyes; a few purposely keeping behind to avoid looking on; in short, among five hundred men, there was every possible shade of character.

All the officers—midshipmen included—stood together in a group on the starboard side of the main-mast; the First Lieutenant in advance, and the surgeon, whose special duty it is to be present at such times, standing close by his side.

Presently the Captain came forward from his cabin, and

stood in the centre of this solemn group, with a small paper
in his hand. That paper was the daily report of offences, regularly laid upon his table every morning or evening, like the
day's journal placed by a bachelor's napkin at breakfast.

"Master-at-arms, bring up the prisoners," he said.

A few moments elapsed, during which the Captain, now
clothed in his most dreadful attributes, fixed his eyes severely
upon the crew, when suddenly a lane formed through the
crowd of seamen, and the prisoners advanced—the master-at-
arms, rattan in hand, on one side, and an armed marine on
the other—and took up their stations at the mast.

"You John, you Peter, you Mark, you Antone," said the
Captain, "were yesterday found fighting on the gun-deck.
Have you any thing to say?"

Mark and Antone, two steady, middle-aged men, whom I
had often admired for their sobriety, replied that they did not
strike the first blow; that they had submitted to much before
they had yielded to their passions; but as they acknowledged
that they had at last defended themselves, their excuse was
overruled.

John—a brutal bully, who, it seems, was the real author of
the disturbance—was about entering into a long extenuation,
when he was cut short by being made to confess, irrespective
of circumstances, that he had been in the fray.

Peter, a handsome lad about nineteen years old, belonging
to the mizzen-top, looked pale and tremulous. He was a great
favorite in his part of the ship, and especially in his own mess,
principally composed of lads of his own age. That morning
two of his young mess-mates had gone to his bag, taken out
his best clothes, and, obtaining the permission of the marine
sentry at the "brig," had handed them to him, to be put on
against being summoned to the mast. This was done to pro-
pitiate the Captain, as most captains love to see a tidy sailor.
But it would not do. To all his supplications the Captain
turned a deaf ear. Peter declared that he had been struck twice
before he had returned a blow. "No matter," said the Captain, "you struck at last, instead of reporting the case to an
officer. I allow no man to fight on board here but myself. *I*
do the fighting."

"Now, men," he added, "you all admit the charge; you

Chapter 34

SOME OF THE EVIL EFFECTS OF FLOGGING

THERE ARE incidental considerations touching this matter of flogging, which exaggerate the evil into a great enormity. Many illustrations might be given, but let us be content with a few.

One of the arguments advanced by officers of the Navy in favor of corporal punishment is this: it can be inflicted in a moment; it consumes no valuable time; and when the prisoner's shirt is put on, *that* is the last of it. Whereas, if another punishment were substituted, it would probably occasion a great waste of time and trouble, besides thereby begetting in the sailor an undue idea of his importance.

Absurd, or worse than absurd, as it may appear, all this is true; and if you start from the same premises with these officers, you must admit that they advance an irresistible argument. But in accordance with this principle, captains in the Navy, to a certain extent, inflict the scourge—which is ever at hand—for nearly all degrees of transgression. In offences not cognizable by a court martial, little, if any, discrimination is shown. It is of a piece with the penal laws that prevailed in England some sixty years ago, when one hundred and sixty different offences were declared by the statute-book to be capital, and the servant-maid who but pilfered a watch was hung beside the murderer of a family.

It is one of the most common punishments for very trivial offences in the Navy, to "stop" a seaman's *grog* for a day or a week. And as most seamen so cling to their *grog*, the loss of it is generally deemed by them a very serious penalty. You will sometimes hear them say, "I would rather have my wind *stopped* than my *grog*!"

But there are some sober seamen that would much rather draw the money for it, instead of the grog itself, as provided by law; but they are too often deterred from this by the thought of receiving a scourging for some inconsiderable offence, as a substitute for the stopping of their spirits. This is

a most serious obstacle to the cause of temperance in the
Navy. But, in many cases, even the reluctant drawing of his
grog can not exempt a prudent seaman from ignominy; for
besides the formal administering of the *"cat"* at the gangway
for petty offences, he is liable to the "colt," or rope's-end, a
bit of *ratlin-stuff*, indiscriminately applied—without stripping the victim—at any time, and in any part of the ship, at
the merest wink from the Captain. By an express order of that
officer, most boatswain's mates carry the "colt" coiled in their
hats, in readiness to be administered at a minute's warning upon
any offender. This was the custom in the Neversink. And until
so recent a period as the administration of President Polk, when
the historian Bancroft, Secretary of the Navy, officially interposed, it was an almost universal thing for the officers of the
watch, at their own discretion, to inflict chastisement upon a
sailor, and this, too, in the face of the ordinance restricting the
power of flogging solely to Captains and Courts Martial. Nor
was it a thing unknown for a Lieutenant, in a sudden outburst of
passion, perhaps inflamed by brandy, or smarting under the
sense of being disliked or hated by the seamen, to order a whole
watch of two hundred and fifty men, at dead of night, to undergo the indignity of the "colt."

It is believed that, even at the present day, there are instances of Commanders still violating the law, by delegating
the power of the colt to subordinates. At all events, it is certain that, almost to a man, the Lieutenants in the Navy bitterly rail against the officiousness of Bancroft, in so materially
abridging their usurped functions by snatching the colt from
their hands. At the time, they predicted that this rash and
most ill-judged interference of the Secretary would end in the
breaking up of all discipline in the Navy. But it has not so
proved. These officers *now* predict that, if the "cat" be abolished, the same unfulfilled prediction would be verified.

Concerning the license with which many captains violate
the express laws laid down by Congress for the government
of the Navy, a glaring instance may be quoted. For upward
of forty years there has been on the American Statute-book a
law prohibiting a Captain from inflicting, on his own authority, more than twelve lashes at one time, and for one offence.
If more are to be given, the sentence must be passed by a

Court Martial. Yet, for nearly half a century, this law has been frequently, and with almost perfect impunity, set at naught: though of late, through the exertions of Bancroft and others, it has been much better observed than formerly; indeed, at the present day, it is generally respected. Still, while the Neversink was lying in a South American port, on the cruise now written of, the seamen belonging to another American frigate informed us that their captain sometimes inflicted, upon his own authority, eighteen and twenty lashes. It is worth while to state that this frigate was vastly admired by the shore ladies for her wonderfully neat appearance. One of her forecastlemen told me that he had used up three jack-knives (charged to him on the books of the purser) in scraping the belaying-pins and the combings of the hatchways.

It is singular that while the Lieutenants of the Watch in American men-of-war so long usurped the power of inflicting corporal punishment with the *colt*, few or no similar abuses were known in the English Navy. And though the captain of an English armed ship is authorized to inflict, at his own discretion, *more* than a dozen lashes (I think three dozen), yet it is to be doubted whether, upon the whole, there is as much flogging at present in the English Navy as in the American. The chivalric Virginian, John Randolph of Roanoke, declared, in his place in Congress, that on board of the American man-of-war that carried him out Embassador to Russia he had witnessed more flogging than had taken place on his own plantation of five hundred African slaves in ten years. Certain it is, from what I have personally seen, that the English officers, as a general thing, seem to be less disliked by their crews than the American officers by theirs. The reason probably is, that many of them, from their station in life, have been more accustomed to social command; hence, quarter-deck authority sits more naturally on them. A coarse, vulgar man, who happens to rise to high naval rank by the exhibition of talents not incompatible with vulgarity, invariably proves a tyrant to his crew. It is a thing that American man-of-war's-men have often observed, that the Lieutenants from the Southern States, the descendants of the old Virginians, are much less severe, and much more gentle and gentlemanly in command, than the Northern officers, as a class.

According to the present laws and usages of the Navy, a seaman, for the most trivial alleged offences, of which he may be entirely innocent, must, without a trial, undergo a penalty the traces whereof he carries to the grave; for to a man-of-war's-man's experienced eye the marks of a naval scourging with the "*cat*" are through life discernible. And with these marks on his back, this image of his Creator must rise at the Last Day. Yet so untouchable is true dignity, that there are cases wherein to be flogged at the gangway is no dishonor; though, to abase and hurl down the last pride of some sailor who has piqued him, be sometimes the secret motive, with some malicious officer, in procuring him to be condemned to the lash. But this feeling of the innate dignity remaining untouched, though outwardly the body be scarred for the whole term of the natural life, is one of the hushed things, buried among the holiest privacies of the soul; a thing between a man's God and himself; and forever undiscernible by our fellow-men, who account *that* a degradation which seems so to the corporal eye. But what torments must that seaman undergo who, while his back bleeds at the gangway, bleeds agonized drops of shame from his soul! Are we not justified in immeasurably denouncing this thing? Join hands with me, then; and, in the name of that Being in whose image the flogged sailor is made, let us demand of Legislators, by what right they dare profane what God himself accounts sacred.

Is it lawful for you to scourge a man that is a Roman? asks the intrepid Apostle, well knowing, as a Roman citizen, that it was not. And now, eighteen hundred years after, is it lawful for you, my countrymen, to scourge a man that is an American? to scourge him round the world in your frigates?

It is to no purpose that you apologetically appeal to the general depravity of the man-of-war's-man. Depravity in the oppressed is no apology for the oppressor; but rather an additional stigma to him, as being, in a large degree, the effect, and not the cause and justification of oppression.

Chapter 35

FLOGGING NOT LAWFUL

I T IS NEXT TO IDLE, at the present day, merely to denounce an iniquity. Be ours, then, a different task.

If there are any three things opposed to the genius of the American Constitution, they are these: irresponsibility in a judge, unlimited discretionary authority in an executive, and the union of an irresponsible judge and an unlimited executive in one person.

Yet by virtue of an enactment of Congress, all the Commodores in the American Navy are obnoxious to these three charges, so far as concerns the punishment of the sailor for alleged misdemeanors not particularly set forth in the Articles of War.

Here is the enactment in question.

XXXII. *Of the Articles of War.*—"All crimes committed by persons belonging to the Navy, which are not specified in the foregoing articles, shall be punished according to the laws and customs in such cases at sea."

This is the article that, above all others, puts the scourge into the hands of the Captain, calls him to no account for its exercise, and furnishes him with an ample warrant for inflictions of cruelty upon the common sailor, hardly credible to landsmen.

By this article the Captain is made a legislator, as well as a judge and an executive. So far as it goes, it absolutely leaves to his discretion to decide what things shall be considered crimes, and what shall be the penalty; whether an accused person has been guilty of actions by him declared to be crimes; and how, when, and where the penalty shall be inflicted.

In the American Navy there is an everlasting suspension of the Habeas Corpus. Upon the bare allegation of misconduct, there is no law to restrain the Captain from imprisoning a seaman, and keeping him confined at his pleasure. While I was in the Neversink, the Captain of an American sloop of

war, from undoubted motives of personal pique, kept a seaman confined in the brig for upward of a month.

Certainly the necessities of navies warrant a code for its
government more stringent than the law that governs the
land; but that code should conform to the spirit of the political institutions of the country that ordains it. It should not
convert into slaves some of the citizens of a nation of freemen. Such objections can not be urged against the laws of the
Russian Navy (not essentially different from our own), because the laws of that Navy, creating the absolute one-man
power in the Captain, and vesting in him the authority to
scourge, conform in spirit to the territorial laws of Russia,
which is ruled by an autocrat, and whose courts inflict the
knout upon the subjects of the land. But with us it is different. Our institutions claim to be based upon broad principles
of political liberty and equality. Whereas, it would hardly affect one iota the condition on shipboard of an American man-
of-war's-man, were he transferred to the Russian Navy and
made a subject of the Czar.

As a sailor, he shares none of our civil immunities; the law
of our soil in no respect accompanies the national floating
timbers grown thereon, and to which he clings as his home.
For him our Revolution was in vain; to him our Declaration
of Independence is a lie.

It is not sufficiently borne in mind, perhaps, that though
the naval code comes under the head of the martial law, yet,
in time of peace, and in the thousand questions arising between man and man on board ship, this code, to a certain
extent, may not improperly be deemed municipal. With its
crew of 800 or 1000 men, a three-decker is a city on the sea.
But in most of these matters between man and man, the Captain, instead of being a magistrate, dispensing what the law
promulgates, is an absolute ruler, making and unmaking law
as he pleases.

It will be seen that the XXth of the Articles of War provides, that if any person in the Navy negligently perform the
duties assigned him, he shall suffer such punishment as a
court martial shall adjudge; but if the offender be a private
(common sailor), he may, at the discretion of the Captain, be
put in irons or flogged. It is needless to say, that in cases

where an officer commits a trivial violation of this law, a court martial is seldom or never called to sit upon his trial; but in the sailor's case, he is at once condemned to the lash. Thus, one set of sea-citizens is exempted from a law that is hung in terror over others. What would landsmen think, were the State of New York to pass a law against some offence, affixing a fine as a penalty, and then add to that law a section restricting its penal operation to mechanics and day laborers, exempting all gentlemen with an income of one thousand dollars? Yet thus, in the spirit of its practical operation, even thus, stands a good part of the naval laws wherein naval flogging is involved.

But a law should be "universal," and include in its possible penal operations the very judge himself who gives decisions upon it; nay, the very judge who expounds it. Had Sir William Blackstone violated the laws of England, he would have been brought before the bar over which he had presided, and would there have been tried, with the counsel for the crown reading to him, perhaps, from a copy of his own *Commentaries*. And should he have been found guilty, he would have suffered like the meanest subject, "according to law."

How is it in an American frigate? Let one example suffice. By the Articles of War, and especially by Article I., an American Captain may, and frequently does, inflict a severe and degrading punishment upon a sailor, while he himself is forever removed from the possibility of undergoing the like disgrace; and, in all probability, from undergoing any punishment whatever, even if guilty of the same thing—contention with his equals, for instance—for which he punishes another. Yet both sailor and captain are American citizens.

Now, in the language of Blackstone, again, there is a law, "coeval with mankind, dictated by God himself, superior in obligation to any other, and no human laws are of any validity if contrary to this." That law is the Law of Nature; among the three great principles of which Justinian includes "that to every man should be rendered his due." But we have seen that the laws involving flogging in the Navy do *not* render to every man his due, since in some cases they indirectly exclude the officers from any punishment whatever, and in all cases protect them from the scourge, which is inflicted upon the sailor. Therefore, according to Blackstone and Justinian, those laws have no binding force; and every American man-of-war's-man would be morally justified in resisting the scourge to the uttermost; and, in so resisting, would be religiously justified in what would be judicially styled "the act of mutiny" itself.

If, then, these scourging laws be for any reason necessary, make them binding upon all who of right come under their sway; and let us see an honest Commodore, duly authorized by Congress, condemning to the lash a transgressing Captain by the side of a transgressing sailor. And if the Commodore himself prove a transgressor, let us see one of his brother Commodores take up the lash against *him*, even as the boat-swain's mates, the navy executioners, are often called upon to scourge each other.

Or will you say that a navy officer is a man, but that an American-born citizen, whose grandsire may have ennobled him by pouring out his blood at Bunker Hill—will you say that, by entering the service of his country as a common seaman, and standing ready to fight her foes, he thereby loses his manhood at the very time he most asserts it? Will you say that, by so doing, he degrades himself to the liability of the scourge, but if he tarries ashore in time of danger, he is safe from that indignity? All our linked states, all four continents of mankind, unite in denouncing such a thought.

We plant the question, then, on the topmost argument of all. Irrespective of incidental considerations, we assert that flogging in the navy is opposed to the essential dignity of man, which no legislator has a right to violate; that it is oppressive, and glaringly unequal in its operations; that it is utterly repugnant to the spirit of our democratic institutions; indeed, that it involves a lingering trait of the worst times of a barbarous feudal aristocracy; in a word, we denounce it as religiously, morally, and immutably *wrong*.

No matter, then, what may be the consequences of its abolition; no matter if we have to dismantle our fleets, and our unprotected commerce should fall a prey to the spoiler, the awful admonitions of justice and humanity demand that abolition without procrastination; in a voice that is not to be mistaken, demand that abolition to-day. It is not a dollar-and-cent question of expediency; it is a matter of *right and wrong*. And if any man can lay his hand on his heart, and solemnly say that this scourging is right, let that man but once feel the lash on his own back, and in his agony you will hear the apostate call the seventh heavens to witness that it is *wrong*. And, in the name of immortal manhood, would to God that every man who upholds this thing were scourged at the gang-way till he recanted.

Chapter 36

Flogging not Necessary

B UT WHITE-JACKET is ready to come down from the lofty mast-head of an eternal principle, and fight you—Commodores and Captains of the navy—on your own quarter-deck, with your own weapons, at your own paces.

Exempt yourselves from the lash, you take Bible oaths to it that it is indispensable for others; you swear that, without the lash, no armed ship can be kept in suitable discipline. Be it proved to you, officers, and stamped upon your foreheads, that herein you are utterly wrong.

"Send them to Collingwood," said Lord Nelson, "and *he* will bring them to order." This was the language of that renowned Admiral, when his officers reported to him certain seamen of the fleet as wholly ungovernable. "Send them to Collingwood." And who was Collingwood, that, after these navy rebels had been imprisoned and scourged without being brought to order, Collingwood could convert them to docility?

Who Admiral Collingwood was, as an historical hero, history herself will tell you; nor, in whatever triumphal hall they may be hanging, will the captured flags of Trafalgar fail to rustle at the mention of that name. But what Collingwood was as a disciplinarian on board the ships he commanded perhaps needs to be said. He was an officer, then, who held in abhorrence all corporal punishment; who, though seeing more active service than any sea-officer of his time, yet, for years together, governed his men without inflicting the lash.

But these seamen of his must have been most exemplary saints to have proved docile under so lenient a sway. Were they saints? Answer, ye jails and alms-houses throughout the length and breadth of Great Britain, which, in Collingwood's time, were swept clean of the last lingering villain and pauper to man his majesty's fleets.

Still more, *that* was a period when the uttermost resources of England were taxed to the quick; when the masts of her multiplied fleets almost transplanted her forests, all standing to the sea; when British press-gangs not only boarded foreign ships on the high seas, and boarded foreign pier-heads, but boarded their own merchantmen at the mouth of the Thames, and boarded the very fire-sides along its banks; when Englishmen were knocked down and dragged into the navy, like cattle into the slaughter-house, with every mortal provocation to a mad desperation against the service that thus ran their unwilling heads into the muzzles of the enemy's cannon. *This* was the time, and *these* the men that Collingwood governed without the lash.

I know it has been said that Lord Collingwood began by inflicting severe punishments, and afterward ruling his sailors by the mere memory of a by-gone terror, which he could at pleasure revive; and that his sailors knew this, and hence their good behavior under a lenient sway. But, granting the quoted assertion to be true, how comes it that many American Captains, who, after inflicting as severe punishment as ever Collingwood could have authorized—how comes it that *they*, also, have not been able to maintain good order without subsequent floggings, after once showing to the crew with what terrible attributes they were invested? But it is notorious, and a thing that I myself, in several instances, *know* to have been the case, that in the American navy, where corporal punishment has been most severe, it has also been most frequent.

But it is incredible that, with such crews as Lord Collingwood's—composed, in part, of the most desperate characters, the rakings of the jails—it is incredible that such a set of men could have been governed by the mere *memory* of the lash. Some other influence must have been brought to bear; mainly, no doubt, the influence wrought by a powerful brain, and a determined, intrepid spirit over a miscellaneous rabble.

It is well known that Lord Nelson himself, in point of policy, was averse to flogging; and that, too, when he had witnessed the mutinous effects of government abuses in the navy—unknown in our times—and which, to the terror of all England, developed themselves at the great mutiny of the Nore: an outbreak that for several weeks jeopardized the very existence of the British navy.

But we may press this thing nearly two centuries further

back, for it is a matter of historical doubt whether, in Robert Blake's time, Cromwell's great admiral, such a thing as flogging was known at the gangways of his victorious fleets. And as in this matter we can not go further back than to Blake, so we can not advance further than to our own time, which shows Commodore Stockton, during the recent war with Mexico, governing the American squadron in the Pacific without employing the scourge.

But if of three famous English Admirals one has abhorred flogging, another almost governed his ships without it, and to the third it may be supposed to have been unknown, while an American Commander has, within the present year almost, been enabled to sustain the good discipline of an entire squadron in time of war without having an instrument of scourging on board, what inevitable inferences must be drawn, and how disastrous to the mental character of all advocates of navy flogging, who may happen to be navy officers themselves.

It can not have escaped the discernment of any observer of mankind, that, in the presence of its conventional inferiors, conscious imbecility in power often seeks to carry off that imbecility by assumptions of lordly severity. The amount of flogging on board an American man-of-war is, in many cases, in exact proportion to the professional and intellectual incapacity of her officers to command. Thus, in these cases, the law that authorizes flogging does but put a scourge into the hand of a fool. In most calamitous instances this has been shown.

It is a matter of record, that some English ships of war have fallen a prey to the enemy through the insubordination of the crew, induced by the witless cruelty of their officers; officers so armed by the law that they could inflict that cruelty without restraint. Nor have there been wanting instances where the seamen have ran away with their ships, as in the case of the Hermione and Danae, and forever rid themselves of the outrageous inflictions of their officers by sacrificing their lives to their fury.

Events like these aroused the attention of the British public at the time. But it was a tender theme, the public agitation of which the government was anxious to suppress. Nevertheless,

whenever the thing was privately discussed, these terrific mutinies, together with the then prevailing insubordination of
the men in the navy, were almost universally attributed to the
exasperating system of flogging. And the necessity for flogging was generally believed to be directly referable to the impressment of such crowds of dissatisfied men. And in high
quarters it was held that if, by any mode, the English fleet
could be manned without resource to coercive measures, then
the necessity of flogging would cease.

"If we abolish either impressment or flogging, the abolition
of the other will follow as a matter of course." This was the
language of the Edinburgh Review at a still later period, 1824.

If, then, the necessity of flogging in the British armed marine was solely attributed to the impressment of the seamen,
what faintest shadow of reason is there for the continuance of
this barbarity in the American service, which is wholly freed
from the reproach of impressment?

It is true that, during a long period of non-impressment,
and even down to the present day, flogging has been, and still
is, the law of the English navy. But in things of this kind
England should be nothing to us, except an example to be
shunned. Nor should wise legislators wholly govern themselves by precedents, and conclude that, since scourging has
so long prevailed, some virtue must reside in it. Not so. The
world has arrived at a period which renders it the part of
Wisdom to pay homage to the prospective precedents of the
Future in preference to those of the Past. The Past is dead,
and has no resurrection; but the Future is endowed with such
a life, that it lives to us even in anticipation. The Past is, in
many things, the foe of mankind; the Future is, in all things,
our friend. In the Past is no hope; the Future is both hope
and fruition. The Past is the text-book of tyrants; the Future
the Bible of the Free. Those who are solely governed by the
Past stand like Lot's wife, crystallized in the act of looking
backward, and forever incapable of looking before.

Let us leave the Past, then, to dictate laws to immovable
China; let us abandon it to the Chinese Legitimists of Europe. But for us, we will have another captain to rule over
us—that captain who ever marches at the head of his troop
and beckons them forward, not lingering in the rear, and

impeding their march with lumbering baggage-wagons of old precedents. *This* is the Past.

But in many things we Americans are driven to a rejection of the maxims of the Past, seeing that, ere long, the van of the nations must, of right, belong to ourselves. There are occasions when it is for America to make precedents, and not to obey them. We should, if possible, prove a teacher to posterity, instead of being the pupil of by-gone generations. More shall come after us than have gone before; the world is not yet middle-aged.

Escaped from the house of bondage, Israel of old did not follow after the ways of the Egyptians. To her was given an express dispensation; to her were given new things under the sun. And we Americans are the peculiar, chosen people—the Israel of our time; we bear the ark of the liberties of the world. Seventy years ago we escaped from thrall; and, besides our first birth-right—embracing one continent of earth— God has given to us, for a future inheritance, the broad domains of the political pagans, that shall yet come and lie down under the shade of our ark, without bloody hands being lifted. God has predestinated, mankind expects, great things from our race; and great things we feel in our souls. The rest of the nations must soon be in our rear. We are the pioneers of the world; the advance-guard, sent on through the wilderness of untried things, to break a new path in the New World that is ours. In our youth is our strength; in our inexperience, our wisdom. At a period when other nations have but lisped, our deep voice is heard afar. Long enough have we been skeptics with regard to ourselves, and doubted whether, indeed, the political Messiah had come. But he has come in *us*, if we would but give utterance to his promptings. And let us always remember that with ourselves, almost for the first time in the history of earth, national selfishness is unbounded philanthropy; for we can not do a good to America but we give alms to the world.

Chapter 37

WE HAD JUST slid into pleasant weather, drawing near to the Tropics, when all hands were thrown into a wonderful excitement by an event that eloquently appealed to many palates.

A man at the fore-top-sail-yard sung out that there were eight or ten dark objects floating on the sea, some three points off our lee-bow.

"Keep her off three points!" cried Captain Claret, to the quarter-master at the *cun*.

And thus, with all our batteries, store-rooms, and five hundred men, with their baggage, and beds, and provisions, at one move of a round bit of mahogany, our great-embattled ark edged away for the strangers, as easily as a boy turns to the right or left in pursuit of insects in the field.

Directly the man on the top-sail-yard reported the dark objects to be hogsheads. Instantly all the top-men were straining their eyes, in delirious expectation of having their long *grog-fast* broken at last, and that, too, by what seemed an almost miraculous intervention. It was a curious circumstance that, without knowing the contents of the hogsheads, they yet seemed certain that the staves encompassed the thing they longed for.

Sail was now shortened, our headway was stopped, and a cutter was lowered, with orders to tow the fleet of strangers alongside. The men sprang to their oars with a will, and soon five goodly puncheons lay wallowing in the sea, just under the main-chains. We got overboard the slings, and hoisted them out of the water.

It was a sight that Bacchus and his bacchanals would have gloated over. Each puncheon was of a deep-green color, so covered with minute barnacles and shell-fish, and streaming with sea-weed, that it needed long searching to find out their bung-holes; they looked like venerable old *loggerhead-turtles*.

How long they had been tossing about, and making voyages for the benefit of the flavor of their contents, no one could tell. In trying to raft them ashore, or on board of some merchant-ship, they must have drifted off to sea. This we inferred from the ropes that lengthwise united them, and which, from one point of view, made them resemble a section of a sea-serpent. They were *struck* into the gun-deck, where the eager crowd being kept off by sentries, the cooper was called with his tools.

"Bung up, and bilge free!" he cried, in an ecstasy, flourishing his driver and hammer.

Upon clearing away the barnacles and moss, a flat sort of shell-fish was found, closely adhering, like a California-shell, right over one of the bungs. Doubtless this shell-fish had there taken up his quarters, and thrown his own body into the breach, in order the better to preserve the precious contents of the cask. The by-standers were breathless, when at last this puncheon was canted over and a tin-pot held to the orifice. What was to come forth? salt-water or wine? But a rich purple tide soon settled the question, and the lieutenant assigned to taste it, with a loud and satisfactory smack of his lips, pronounced it Port!

"Oporto!" cried Mad Jack, "and no mistake!"

But, to the surprise, grief, and consternation of the sailors, an order now came from the quarter-deck to "strike the strangers down into the main-hold!" This proceeding occasioned all sorts of censorious observations upon the Captain, who, of course, had authorized it.

It must be related here that, on the passage out from home, the Neversink had touched at Madeira; and there, as is often the case with men-of-war, the Commodore and Captain had laid in a goodly stock of wines for their own private tables, and the benefit of their foreign visitors. And although the Commodore was a small, spare man, who evidently emptied but few glasses, yet Captain Claret was a portly gentleman, with a crimson face, whose father had fought at the battle of the Brandywine, and whose brother had commanded the well-known frigate named in honor of that engagement. And his whole appearance evinced that Captain Claret himself had fought many Brandywine battles ashore in honor of his sire's memory, and commanded in many bloodless Brandywine actions at sea.

It was therefore with some savor of provocation that the sailors held forth on the ungenerous conduct of Captain Claret, in stepping in between them and Providence, as it were, which by this lucky windfall, they held, seemed bent upon relieving their necessities; while Captain Claret himself, with an inexhaustible cellar, emptied his Madeira decanters at his leisure.

But next day all hands were electrified by the old familiar sound—so long hushed—of the drum rolling to grog.

After that the port was served out twice a day, till all was expended.

Chapter 38

The Chaplain and Chapel in a Man-of-war

THE NEXT DAY was Sunday; a fact set down in the almanac, spite of merchant seamen's maxim, that *there are no Sundays off soundings*.

No Sundays off soundings, indeed! No Sundays on shipboard! You may as well say there should be no Sundays in churches; for is not a ship modeled after a church? has it not three spires—three steeples? yea, and on the gun-deck, a bell and a belfry? And does not that bell merrily peal every Sunday morning, to summon the crew to devotions?

At any rate, there were Sundays on board this particular frigate of ours, and a clergyman also. He was a slender, middle-aged man, of an amiable deportment and irreproachable conversation; but I must say, that his sermons were but ill calculated to benefit the crew. He had drank at the mystic fountain of Plato; his head had been turned by the Germans; and this I will say, that White-Jacket himself saw him with Coleridge's Biographia Literaria in his hand.

Fancy, now, this transcendental divine standing behind a gun-carriage on the main-deck, and addressing five hundred salt-sea sinners upon the psychological phenomena of the soul, and the ontological necessity of every sailor's saving it at all hazards. He enlarged upon the follies of the ancient philosophers; learnedly alluded to the Phædon of Plato; exposed the follies of Simplicius's Commentary on Aristotle's "De Cœlo," by arraying against that clever Pagan author the admired tract of Tertullian—*De Præscriptionibus Hæreticorum*—and concluded by a Sanscrit invocation. He was particularly hard upon the Gnostics and Marcionites of the second century of the Christian era; but he never, in the remotest manner, attacked the every-day vices of the nineteenth century, as eminently illustrated in our man-of-war world. Concerning drunkenness, fighting, flogging, and oppression—things expressly or impliedly prohibited by Christianity—he never said aught. But the most mighty Commodore and Captain sat before him; and in general, if, in a monarchy, the state form the audience of the church, little evangelical piety will be preached. Hence, the harmless, non-committal abstrusities of our Chaplain were not to be wondered at. He was no Massillon, to thunder forth his ecclesiastical rhetoric, even when a Louis le Grand was enthroned among his congregation. Nor did the chaplains who preached on the quarter-deck of Lord Nelson ever allude to the guilty Felix, nor to Delilah, nor practically reason of righteousness, temperance, and judgment to come, when that renowned Admiral sat, sword-belted, before them.

During these Sunday discourses, the officers always sat in a circle round the chaplain, and, with a business-like air, steadily preserved the utmost propriety. In particular, our old Commodore himself made a point of looking intensely edified; and not a sailor on board but believed that the Commodore, being the greatest man present, must alone comprehend the mystic sentences that fell from our parson's lips.

Of all the noble lords in the ward-room, this lord-spiritual, with the exception of the Purser, was in the highest favor with the Commodore, who frequently conversed with him in a close and confidential manner. Nor, upon reflection, was this to be marveled at, seeing how efficacious, in all despotic governments, it is for the throne and altar to go hand-in-hand.

The accommodations of our chapel were very poor. We had nothing to sit on but the great gun-rammers and capstan-bars, placed horizontally upon shot-boxes. These seats were exceedingly uncomfortable, wearing out our trowsers and our tempers, and, no doubt, impeded the conversion of many valuable souls.

To say the truth, man-of-war's-men, in general, make but poor auditors upon these occasions, and adopt every possible means to elude them. Often the boatswain's-mates were obliged to drive the men to service, violently swearing upon these occasions, as upon every other.

"Go to prayers, d—n you! To prayers, you rascals—to prayers!" In this clerical invitation Captain Claret would frequently unite.

At this Jack Chase would sometimes make merry. "Come, boys, don't hang back," he would say; "come, let us go hear the parson talk about his Lord High Admiral Plato, and Commodore Socrates."

But, in one instance, grave exception was taken to this summons. A remarkably serious, but bigoted seaman, a sheet-anchor-man—whose private devotions may hereafter be alluded to—once touched his hat to the Captain, and respectfully said, "Sir, I am a Baptist; the chaplain is an Episcopalian; his form of worship is not mine; I do not believe with him, and it is against my conscience to be under his ministry. May I be allowed, sir, *not* to attend service on the half-deck?"

"You will be allowed, sir!" said the Captain, haughtily, "to obey the laws of the ship. If you absent yourself from prayers on Sunday mornings, you know the penalty."

According to the Articles of War, the Captain was perfectly right; but if any law requiring an American to attend divine service against his will be a law respecting the establishment of religion, then the Articles of War are, in this one particular, opposed to the American Constitution, which expressly says, "Congress shall make no law respecting the establishment of religion, or the free exercise thereof." But this is only one of several things in which the Articles of War are repugnant to that instrument. They will be glanced at in another part of the narrative.

The motive which prompts the introduction of chaplains into the Navy can not but be warmly responded to by every Christian. But it does not follow, that because chaplains are to be found in men-of-war, that, under the present system, they achieve much good, or that, under any other, they ever will.

How can it be expected that the religion of peace should flourish in an oaken castle of war? How can it be expected that the clergyman, whose pulpit is a forty-two-pounder, should convert sinners to a faith that enjoins them to turn the right cheek when the left is smitten? How is it to be expected that when, according to the XLII. of the Articles of War, as they now stand unrepealed on the Statute Book, "a bounty shall be paid" (to the officers and crew) "by the United States government of $20 for each person on board any ship of an enemy which shall be sunk or destroyed by any United States ship;" and when, by a subsequent section (vii.), it is provided, among other apportionings, that the chaplain shall receive "two twentieths" of this price paid for sinking and destroying ships full of human beings? How is it to be expected that a clergyman, thus provided for, should prove efficacious in enlarging upon the criminality of Judas, who, for thirty pieces of silver, betrayed his Master?

Although, by the regulations of the Navy, each seaman's mess on board the Neversink was furnished with a Bible, these Bibles were seldom or never to be seen, except on Sunday mornings, when usage demands that they shall be exhibited by the cooks of the messes, when the master-at-arms goes his rounds on the berth-deck. At such times, they usually surmounted a highly polished tin-pot placed on the lid of the chest.

Yet, for all this, the Christianity of man-of-war's-men, and their disposition to contribute to pious enterprises, are often relied upon. Several times subscription papers were circulated among the crew of the Neversink, while in harbor, under the direct patronage of the Chaplain. One was for the purpose of building a seaman's chapel in China; another to pay the salary of a tract-distributor in Greece; a third to raise a fund for the benefit of an African Colonization Society.

Where the Captain himself is a moral man, he makes a far better chaplain for his crew than any clergyman can be. This is sometimes illustrated in the case of sloops of war and armed brigs, which are not allowed a regular chaplain. I have known one crew, who were warmly attached to a naval commander worthy of their love, who have mustered even with alacrity to the call to prayer; and when their Captain would read the Church of England service to them, would present a congregation not to be surpassed for earnestness and devotion by any Scottish Kirk. It seemed like family devotions, where the head of the house is foremost in confessing himself before his Maker. But our own hearts are our best prayer-rooms, and the chaplains who can most help us are ourselves.

Chapter 39

The Frigate in Harbor • The Boats • Grand
State Reception of the Commodore

IN GOOD TIME we were up with the parallel of Rio de Ja-
neiro, and, standing in for the land, the mist soon cleared;
and high aloft the famed Sugar Loaf pinnacle was seen, our
bowsprit pointing for it straight as a die.

As we glided on toward our anchorage, the bands of the
various men-of-war in harbor saluted us with national airs,
and gallantly lowered their ensigns. Nothing can exceed the
courteous etiquette of these ships, of all nations, in greeting
their brethren. Of all men, your accomplished duellist is generally the most polite.

We lay in Rio some weeks, lazily taking in stores and otherwise preparing for the passage home. But though Rio is
one of the most magnificent bays in the world; though the
city itself contains many striking objects; and though much
might be said of the Sugar Loaf and Signal Hill heights; and
the little islet of Lucia; and the fortified Ilha das Cobras, or
Isle of the Snakes (though the only anacondas and adders
now found in the arsenals there are great guns and pistols);
and Lord Hood's Nose—a lofty eminence said by seamen to
resemble his lordship's conch-shell; and the Prays do Fla-
mingo—a noble tract of beach, so called from its having been
the resort, in olden times, of those gorgeous birds; and the
charming Bay of Botafogo, which, spite of its name, is fragrant as the neighboring Larangieros, or Valley of the Oranges; and the green Gloria Hill, surmounted by the belfries
of the queenly Church of Nossa Senora de Gloria; and the
iron-gray Benedictine convent near by; and the fine drive and
promenade, Passeo Publico; and the massive arch-over-arch
aqueduct, Arcos de Carico; and the Emperor's Palace; and
the Empress's Gardens; and the fine Church de Candelaria;
and the gilded throne on wheels, drawn by eight silken, sil-
ver-belled mules, in which, of pleasant evenings, his Imperial
Majesty is driven out of town to his Moorish villa of St.

514

Christova—ay, though much might be said of all this, yet must I forbear, if I may, and adhere to my one proper object, *the world in a man-of-war*.

Behold, now, the Neversink under a new aspect. With all her batteries, she is tranquilly lying in harbor, surrounded by English, French, Dutch, Portuguese, and Brazilian seventy-fours, moored in the deep-green water, close under the lee of that oblong, castellated mass of rock, Ilha das Cobras, which, with its port-holes and lofty flag-staffs, looks like another man-of-war, fast anchored in the bay. But what is an insular fortress, indeed, but an embattled land-slide into the sea from the world's Gibraltars and Quebecs? And what a main-land fortress but a few decks of a line-of-battle ship transplanted ashore? They are all one—all, as King David, men-of-war from their youth.

Ay, behold now the Neversink at her anchors, in many respects presenting a different appearance from what she presented at sea. Nor is the routine of life on board the same.

At sea there is more to employ the sailors, and less temptation to violations of the law. Whereas, in port, unless some particular service engages them, they lead the laziest of lives, beset by all the allurements of the shore, though perhaps that shore they may never touch.

Unless you happen to belong to one of the numerous boats, which, in a man-of-war in harbor, are continually plying to and from the land, you are mostly thrown upon your own resources to while away the time. Whole days frequently pass without your being individually called upon to lift a finger; for though, in the merchant-service, they make a point of keeping the men always busy about something or other, yet, to employ five hundred sailors when there is nothing definite to be done wholly surpasses the ingenuity of any First Lieutenant in the Navy.

As mention has just been made of the numerous boats employed in harbor, something more may as well be put down concerning them. Our frigate carried a very large boat—as big as a small sloop—called a *launch*, which was generally used for getting off wood, water, and other bulky articles. Besides this, she carried four boats of an arithmetical progression in point of size—the largest being known as the first cutter, the next largest the second cutter, then the third and fourth cutters. She also carried a Commodore's Barge, a Captain's Gig, and a "dingy," a small yawl, with a crew of apprentice boys. All these boats, except the "dingy," had their regular crews, who were subordinate to their cockswains, or steersmen—*petty officers*, receiving pay in addition to their seaman's wages.

The *launch* was manned by the old Tritons of the forecastle, who were no ways particular about their dress, while the other boats—commissioned for genteeler duties—were rowed by young fellows, mostly, who had a dandy eye to their personal appearance. Above all, the officers see to it that the Commodore's Barge and the Captain's Gig are manned by gentlemanly youths, who may do credit to their country, and form agreeable objects for the eyes of the Commodore or Captain to repose upon as he tranquilly sits in the stern, when pulled ashore by his barge-men or gig-men, as the case may be. Some sailors are very fond of belonging to the boats, and deem it a great honor to be a *Commodore's bargeman*; but others, perceiving no particular distinction in that office, do not court it so much.

On the second day after arriving at Rio, one of the gig-men fell sick, and, to my no small concern, I found myself temporarily appointed to his place.

"Come, White-Jacket, rig yourself in white—that's the gig's uniform to-day; you are a gig-man, my boy—give ye joy!" This was the first announcement of the fact that I heard; but soon after it was officially ratified.

I was about to seek the First Lieutenant, and plead the scantiness of my wardrobe, which wholly disqualified me to fill so distinguished a station, when I heard the bugler call away the "gig;" and, without more ado, I slipped into a clean frock, which a messmate doffed for my benefit, and soon after found myself pulling off his High Mightiness, the Captain, to an English seventy-four.

As we were bounding along, the cockswain suddenly cried "Oars!" At the word every oar was suspended in the air, while our Commodore's barge floated by, bearing that dignitary himself. At the sight, Captain Claret removed his chapeau, and saluted profoundly, our boat laying motionless on the water. But the barge never stopped; and the Commodore made but a slight return to the obsequious salute he had received.

We then resumed rowing, and presently I heard "Oars!" again; but from another boat, the second cutter, which turned out to be carrying a Lieutenant ashore. It was now Captain Claret's turn to be honored. The cutter lay still, and the Lieutenant off hat; while the Captain only nodded, and we kept on our way.

This naval etiquette is very much like the etiquette at the Grand Porte of Constantinople, where, after washing the Sublime Sultan's feet, the Grand Vizier avenges himself on an Emir, who does the same office for him.

When we arrived aboard the English seventy-four, the Captain was received with the usual honors, and the gig's crew were conducted below, and hospitably regaled with some spirits, served out by order of the officer of the deck.

Soon after, the English crew went to quarters; and as they stood up at their guns, all along the main-deck, a row of beef-fed Britons, stalwart-looking fellows, I was struck with the contrast they afforded to similar sights on board of the Neversink.

For on board of us our "*quarters*" showed an array of rather slender, lean-cheeked chaps. But then I made no doubt, that, in a sea-tussle, these lantern-jawed varlets would have approved themselves as slender Damascus blades, nimble and flexible; whereas these Britons would have been, perhaps, as sturdy broadswords. Yet every one remembers that story of Saladin and Richard trying their respective blades; how gallant Richard clove an anvil in twain, or something quite as ponderous, and Saladin elegantly severed a cushion; so that the two monarchs were even—each excelling in his way—though, unfortunately for my simile, in a patriotic point of view, Richard whipped Saladin's armies in the end.

There happened to be a lord on board of this ship—the younger son of an earl, they told me. He was a fine-looking fellow. I chanced to stand by when he put a question to an Irish captain of a gun; upon the seaman's inadvertently saying *sir* to him, his lordship looked daggers at the slight; and the sailor, touching his hat a thousand times, said, "Pardon, your honor; I meant to say *my lord*, sir!"

I was much pleased with an old white-headed musician, who stood at the main hatchway, with his enormous bass drum full before him, and thumping it sturdily to the tune of "God Save the King!" though small mercy did he have on his drum-heads. Two little boys were clashing cymbals, and another was blowing a fife, with his cheeks puffed out like the plumpest of his country's plum-puddings.

When we returned from this trip, there again took place that ceremonious reception of our captain on board the vessel he commanded, which always had struck me as exceedingly diverting.

In the first place, while in port, one of the quarter-masters is always stationed on the poop with a spy-glass, to look out for all boats approaching, and report the same to the officer of the deck; also, who it is that may be coming in them; so that preparations may be made accordingly. As soon, then, as the gig touched the side, a mightily shrill piping was heard, as if some boys were celebrating the Fourth of July with penny whistles. This proceeded from a boatswain's mate, who, standing at the gangway, was thus honoring the Captain's return after his long and perilous absence.

The Captain then slowly mounted the ladder, and gravely marching through a lane of "*side-boys*," so called—all in their best bibs and tuckers, and who stood making sly faces behind his back—was received by all the Lieutenants in a body, their hats in their hands, and making a prodigious scraping and bowing, as if they had just graduated at a French dancing-school. Meanwhile, preserving an erect, inflexible, and ram-rod carriage, and slightly touching his chapeau, the Captain made his ceremonious way to the cabin, disappearing behind the scenes, like the pasteboard ghost in Hamlet.

But these ceremonies are nothing to those in homage of the Commodore's arrival, even should he depart and arrive twenty times a day. Upon such occasions, the whole marine guard, except the sentries on duty, are marshaled on the quarter-deck, presenting arms as the Commodore passes them; while their commanding officer gives the military salute with his sword, as if making masonic signs. Meanwhile, the boatswain himself—not a *boatswain's mate*—is keeping up a persevering whistling with his silver pipe; for the Commodore is never greeted with the rude whistle of a boatswain's subaltern; *that* would be positively insulting. All the Lieutenants and Midshipmen, besides the Captain himself, are drawn up in a phalanx, and off hat together; and the *side-boys*, whose number is now increased to ten or twelve, make an imposing display at the gangway; while the whole brass band, elevated upon the poop, strike up "See! the Conquering Hero comes!" At least, this was the tune that our Captain always hinted, by a gesture, to the captain of the band, whenever the Commodore arrived from shore. It conveyed a complimentary appreciation, on the Captain's part, of the Commodore's heroism during the Late War.

To return to the gig. As I did not relish the idea of being a sort of body-servant to Captain Claret—since his gigmen were often called upon to scrub his cabin floor, and perform other duties for him—I made it my particular business to get rid of my appointment in his boat as soon as possible, and the next day after receiving it, succeeded in procuring a substitute, who was glad of the chance to fill the position I so much undervalued.

And thus, with our counterlikes and dislikes, most of us man-of-war's-men harmoniously dove-tail into each other, and, by our very points of opposition, unite in a clever whole, like the parts of a Chinese puzzle. But as, in a Chinese puzzle, many pieces are hard to place, so there are some unfortunate fellows who can never slip into their proper angles, and thus the whole puzzle becomes a puzzle indeed, which is the precise condition of the greatest puzzle in the world—this man-of-war world itself.

Chapter 40

SOME OF THE CEREMONIES IN A MAN-OF-WAR
UNNECESSARY AND INJURIOUS

THE CEREMONIALS of a man-of-war, some of which have been described in the preceding chapter, may merit a reflection or two.

The general usages of the American Navy are founded upon the usages that prevailed in the Navy of monarchical England more than a century ago; nor have they been materially altered since. And while both England and America have become greatly liberalized in the interval; while shore pomp in high places has come to be regarded by the more intelligent masses of men as belonging to the absurd, ridiculous, and mock-heroic; while that most truly august of all the majesties of earth, the President of the United States, may be seen entering his residence with his umbrella under his arm, and no brass band or military guard at his heels, and unostentatiously taking his seat by the side of the meanest citizen in a public conveyance; while this is the case, there still lingers in American men-of-war all the stilted etiquette and childish parade of the old-fashioned Spanish court of Madrid. Indeed, so far as the things that meet the eye are concerned, an American Commodore is by far a greater man than the President of twenty millions of freemen.

But we plain people ashore might very willingly be content to leave these commodores in the unmolested possession of their gilded penny whistles, rattles, and gewgaws, since they seem to take so much pleasure in them, were it not that all this is attended by consequences to their subordinates in the last degree to be deplored.

While hardly any one will question that a naval officer should be surrounded by circumstances calculated to impart a requisite dignity to his position, it is not the less certain that, by the excessive pomp he at present maintains, there is naturally and unavoidably generated a feeling of servility and debasement in the hearts of most of the seamen who continually behold a fellow-mortal flourishing over their heads like the archangel Michael with a thousand wings. And as, in degree, this same pomp is observed toward their inferiors by all the grades of commissioned officers, even down to a midshipman, the evil is proportionately multiplied.

It would not at all diminish a proper respect for the officers, and subordination to their authority among the seamen, were all this idle parade—only ministering to the arrogance of the officers, without at all benefiting the state—completely done away. But to do so, we voters and lawgivers ourselves must be no respecters of persons.

That saying about *leveling upward, and not downward*, may seem very fine to those who can not see its self-involved absurdity. But the truth is, that, to gain the true level, in some things, we *must* cut downward; for how can you make every sailor a commodore? or how raise the valleys, without filling them up with the superfluous tops of the hills?

Some discreet, but democratic, legislation in this matter is much to be desired. And by bringing down naval officers, in these things at least, without affecting their legitimate dignity and authority, we shall correspondingly elevate the common sailor, without relaxing the subordination, in which he should by all means be retained.

Chapter 41

A Man-of-war Library

NOWHERE does time pass more heavily than with most man-of-war's-men on board their craft in harbor.

One of my principal antidotes against *ennui* in Rio, was reading. There was a public library on board, paid for by government, and intrusted to the custody of one of the marine corporals, a little, dried-up man, of a somewhat literary turn. He had once been a clerk in a Post-office ashore; and, having been long accustomed to hand over letters when called for, he was now just the man to hand over books. He kept them in a large cask on the berth-deck, and, when seeking a particular volume, had to capsize it like a barrel of potatoes. This made him very cross and irritable, as most all Librarians are. Who had the selection of these books, I do not know, but some of them must have been selected by our Chaplain, who so pranced on Coleridge's "*High German horse*."

Mason Good's Book of Nature—a very good book, to be sure, but not precisely adapted to tarry tastes—was one of these volumes; and Machiavel's Art of War—which was very dry fighting; and a folio of Tillotson's Sermons—the best of reading for divines, indeed, but with little relish for a main-top-man; and Locke's Essays—incomparable essays, every body knows, but miserable reading at sea; and Plutarch's Lives—superexcellent biographies, which pit Greek against Roman in beautiful style, but then, in a sailor's estimation, not to be mentioned with the *Lives of the Admirals*; and Blair's Lectures, University Edition—a fine treatise on rhetoric, but having nothing to say about nautical phrases, such as "*splicing the main-brace*," "*passing a gammoning*," "*pudding-ing the dolphin*," and "*making a Carrick-bend*;" besides numerous invaluable but unreadable tomes, that might have been purchased cheap at the auction of some college-professor's library.

But I found ample entertainment in a few choice old authors, whom I stumbled upon in various parts of the ship, among the inferior officers. One was "*Morgan's History of Algiers*," a famous old quarto, abounding in picturesque narratives of corsairs, captives, dungeons, and sea-fights; and making mention of a cruel old Dey, who, toward the latter part of his life, was so filled with remorse for his cruelties and crimes that he could not stay in bed after four o'clock in the morning, but had to rise in great trepidation and walk off his bad feelings till breakfast time. And another venerable octavo, containing a certificate from Sir Christopher Wren to its authenticity, entitled "*Knox's Captivity in Ceylon*, 1681"—abounding in stories about the Devil, who was superstitiously supposed to tyrannize over that unfortunate land: to mollify him, the priests offered up buttermilk, red cocks, and sausages; and the Devil ran roaring about in the woods, frightening travelers out of their wits; insomuch that the Islanders bitterly lamented to Knox that their country was full of devils, and, consequently, there was no hope for their eventual well-being. Knox swears that he himself heard the Devil roar, though he did not see his horns; it was a terrible noise, he says, like the baying of a hungry mastiff.

Then there was Walpole's Letters—very witty, pert, and polite—and some odd volumes of plays, each of which was a precious casket of jewels of good things, shaming the trash nowadays passed off for dramas, containing "The Jew of Malta," "Old Fortunatus," "The City Madam," "Volpone," "The Alchymist," and other glorious old dramas of the age of Marlow and Jonson, and that literary Damon and Pythias, the magnificent, mellow old Beaumont and Fletcher, who have sent the long shadow of their reputation, side by side with Shakspeare's, far down the endless vale of posterity. And may that shadow never be less! but as for St. Shakspeare, may his never be more, lest the commentators arise, and settling upon his sacred text, like unto locusts, devour it clean up, leaving never a dot over an I.

I diversified this reading of mine, by borrowing Moore's "*Loves of the Angels*" from Rose-water, who recommended it as "*de charmingest of wolumes*;" and a Negro Song-book, containing *Sittin' on a Rail*, *Gumbo Squash*, and *Jim along Josey*, from Broadbit, a sheet-anchor-man. The sad taste of this old tar, in admiring such vulgar stuff, was much denounced by

Rose-water, whose own predilections were of a more elegant nature, as evinced by his exalted opinion of the literary merits of the "*Loves of the Angels.*"

I was by no means the only reader of books on board the Neversink. Several other sailors were diligent readers, though their studies did not lie in the way of belles-lettres. Their favorite authors were such as you may find at the book-stalls around Fulton Market; they were slightly physiological in their nature. My book experiences on board of the frigate proved an example of a fact which every book-lover must have experienced before me, namely, that though public libraries have an imposing air, and doubtless contain invaluable volumes, yet, somehow, the books that prove most agreeable, grateful, and companionable, are those we pick up by chance here and there; those which seem put into our hands by Providence; those which pretend to little, but abound in much.

Chapter 42

Killing Time in a Man-of-war in Harbor

READING was by no means the only method adopted by my shipmates in whiling away the long, tedious hours in harbor. In truth, many of them could not have read, had they wanted to ever so much; in early youth their primers had been sadly neglected. Still, they had other pursuits; some were expert at the needle, and employed their time in making elaborate shirts, stitching picturesque eagles, and anchors, and all the stars of the federated states in the collars thereof; so that when they at last completed and put on these shirts, they may be said to have hoisted the American colors.

Others excelled in *tattooing*, or *pricking*, as it is called in a man-of-war. Of these prickers, two had long been celebrated, in their way, as consummate masters of the art. Each had a small box full of tools and coloring matter; and they charged so high for their services, that at the end of the cruise they were supposed to have cleared upward of four hundred dollars. They would *prick* you to order a palm-tree, an anchor, a crucifix, a lady, a lion, an eagle, or any thing else you might want.

The Roman Catholic sailors on board had at least the crucifix pricked on their arms, and for this reason: If they chanced to die in a Catholic land, they would be sure of a decent burial in consecrated ground, as the priest would be sure to observe the symbol of Mother Church on their persons. They would not fare as Protestant sailors dying in Callao, who are shoved under the sands of St. Lorenzo, a solitary, volcanic island in the harbor, overrun with reptiles, their heretical bodies not being permitted to repose in the more genial loam of Lima.

And many sailors not Catholics were anxious to have the crucifix painted on them, owing to a curious superstition of theirs. They affirm—some of them—that if you have that mark tattooed upon all four limbs, you might fall overboard among seven hundred and seventy-five thousand white sharks, all dinnerless, and not one of them would so much as dare to smell at your little finger.

We had one fore-top-man on board, who, during the entire cruise, was having an endless cable *pricked* round and round his waist, so that, when his frock was off, he looked like a capstan with a hawser coiled round about it. This fore-top-man paid eighteen pence per link for the cable, besides being on the smart the whole cruise, suffering the effects of his repeated puncturings; so he paid very dear for his cable.

One other mode of passing time while in port was cleaning and polishing your *bright-work*; for it must be known that, in men-of-war, every sailor has some brass or steel of one kind or other to keep in high order—like house-maids, whose business it is to keep well-polished the knobs on the front-door railing and the parlor-grates.

Excepting the ring-bolts, eye-bolts, and belaying-pins scattered about the decks, this bright-work, as it is called, is principally about the guns, embracing the "*monkey-tails*" of the carronades, the screws, *prickers*, little irons, and other things.

The portion that fell to my own share I kept in superior order, quite equal in polish to Rogers's best cutlery. I received the most extravagant encomiums from the officers; one of whom offered to match me against any brasier or brass-polisher in her British majesty's Navy. Indeed, I devoted myself to the work body and soul, and thought no pains too painful, and no labor too laborious, to achieve the highest attainable polish possible for us poor lost sons of Adam to reach.

Upon one occasion, even, when woolen rags were scarce, and no burned-brick was to be had from the ship's-yeoman, I sacrificed the corners of my woolen shirt, and used some dentifrice I had, as substitutes for the rags and burned-brick. The dentifrice operated delightfully, and made the threading of my carronade screw shine and grin again, like a set of false teeth in an eager heiress-hunter's mouth.

Still another mode of passing time, was arraying yourself in your best "*togs*" and promenading up and down the gun-deck, admiring the shore scenery from the port-holes, which, in an amphitheatrical bay like Rio—belted about by the most varied and charming scenery of hill, dale, moss, meadow, court, castle, tower, grove, vine, vineyard, aqueduct, palace, square, island, fort—is very much like lounging round a circular cosmorama, and ever and anon lazily peeping through the glasses here and there. Oh! there is something worth living for, even in our man-of-war world; and one glimpse of a bower of grapes, though a cable's length off, is almost satisfaction for dining off a shank-bone salted down.

This promenading was chiefly patronized by the marines, and particularly by Colbrook, a remarkably handsome and very gentlemanly corporal among them. He was a complete lady's man; with fine black eyes, bright red cheeks, glossy jet whiskers, and a refined organization of the whole man. He used to array himself in his regimentals, and saunter about like an officer of the Cold-Stream Guards, strolling down to his club in St. James's. Every time he passed me, he would heave a sentimental sigh, and hum to himself "*The girl I left behind me.*" This fine corporal afterward became a representative in the Legislature of the State of New Jersey; for I saw his name returned about a year after my return home.

But, after all, there was not much room, while in port, for promenading, at least on the gun-deck, for the whole larboard side is kept clear for the benefit of the officers, who appreciate the advantages of having a clear stroll fore and aft; and they well know that the sailors had much better be crowded together on the other side than that the set of their own coat-tails should be impaired by brushing against their tarry trowsers.

One other way of killing time while in port is playing checkers; that is, when it is permitted; for it is not every navy captain who will allow such a scandalous proceeding. But, as for Captain Claret, though he *did* like his glass of Madeira uncommonly well, and was an undoubted descendant from the hero of the Battle of the Brandywine, and though he sometimes showed a suspiciously flushed face when superintending in person the flogging of a sailor for getting intoxicated against his particular orders, yet I will say for Captain Claret that, upon the whole, he was rather indulgent to his crew, so long as they were perfectly docile. He allowed them to play checkers as much as they pleased. More than once I have known him, when going forward to the fore-castle, pick his way carefully among scores of canvass checker-cloths spread upon the deck, so as not to tread upon the men—the checker-men and man-of-war's-men included; but, in a certain sense, they were both one; for, as the sailors used their checker-men, so, at quarters, their officers used these man-of-war's-men.

But Captain Claret's leniency in permitting checkers on board his ship might have arisen from the following little circumstance, confidentially communicated to me. Soon after the ship had sailed from home, checkers were prohibited; whereupon the sailors were exasperated against the Captain, and one night, when he was walking round the forecastle, bim! came an iron belaying-pin past his ears; and while he was dodging that, bim! came another, from the other side; so that, it being a very dark night, and nobody to be seen, and it being impossible to find out the trespassers, he thought it best to get back into his cabin as soon as possible. Some time after—just as if the belaying-pins had nothing to do with it—it was indirectly rumored that the checker-boards might be brought out again, which—as a philosophical shipmate observed—showed that Captain Claret was a man of a ready understanding, and could understand a hint as well as any other man, even when conveyed by several pounds of iron.

Some of the sailors were very precise about their checker-cloths, and even went so far that they would not let you play with them unless you first washed your hands, especially if so be you had just come from tarring down the rigging.

Another way of beguiling the tedious hours, is to get a cosy seat somewhere, and fall into as snug a little revery as you can. Or if a seat is not to be had—which is frequently the case—then get a tolerably comfortable *stand-up* against the bulwarks, and begin to think about home and bread and butter—always inseparably connected to a wanderer—which will very soon bring delicious tears into your eyes; for every one knows what a luxury is grief, when you can get a private closet to enjoy it in, and no Paul Prys intrude. Several of my shore friends, indeed, when suddenly overwhelmed by some disaster, always make a point of flying to the first oyster-cellar, and shutting themselves up in a box, with nothing but a

plate of stewed oysters, some crackers, the castor, and a decanter of old Port.

Still another way of killing time in harbor, is to lean over
the bulwarks, and speculate upon where, under the sun, you
are going to be that day next year, which is a subject full of
interest to every living soul; so much so, that there is a particular day of a particular month of the year, which, from my
earliest recollections, I have always kept the run of, so that I
can even now tell just where I was on that identical day of
every year past since I was twelve years old. And, when I am
all alone, to run over this almanac in my mind is almost as
entertaining as to read your own diary, and far more interesting than to peruse a table of logarithms on a rainy afternoon.
I always keep the anniversary of that day with lamb and peas,
and a pint of Sherry, for it comes in Spring. But when it came
round in the Neversink, I could get neither lamb, peas, nor
Sherry.

But perhaps the best way to drive the hours before you
four-in-hand, is to select a soft plank on the gun-deck, and
go to sleep. A fine specific, which seldom fails, unless, to be
sure, you have been sleeping all the twenty-four hours beforehand.

Whenever employed in killing time in harbor, I have
lifted myself up on my elbow and looked around me, and
seen so many of my shipmates all employed at the same
common business; all under lock and key; all hopeless prisoners like myself; all under martial law; all dieting on salt beef
and biscuit; all in one uniform; all yawning, gaping, and
stretching in concert, it was then that I used to feel a certain
love and affection for them, grounded, doubtless, on a fellow-
feeling.

And though, in a previous part of this narrative, I have
mentioned that I used to hold myself somewhat aloof from
the mass of seamen on board the Neversink; and though this
was true, and my real acquaintances were comparatively few,
and my intimates still fewer, yet, to tell the truth, it is quite
impossible to live so long with five hundred of your fellow-
beings, even if not of the best families in the land, and with
morals that would not be spoiled by further cultivation; it is
quite impossible, I say, to live with five hundred of your

fellow-beings, be they who they may, without feeling a common sympathy with them at the time, and ever after cherishing some sort of interest in their welfare.

The truth of this was curiously corroborated by a rather equivocal acquaintance of mine, who, among the men, went by the name of "*Shakings*." He belonged to the fore-hold, whence, of a dark night, he would sometimes emerge to chat with the sailors on deck. I never liked the man's looks; I protest it was a mere accident that gave me the honor of his acquaintance, and generally I did my best to avoid him, when he would come skulking, like a jail-bird, out of his den into the liberal, open air of the sky. Nevertheless, the anecdote this *holder* told me is well worth preserving, more especially the extraordinary frankness evinced in his narrating such a thing to a comparative stranger.

The substance of his story was as follows: Shakings, it seems, had once been a convict in the New York State's Prison at Sing Sing, where he had been for years confined for a crime, which he gave me his solemn word of honor he was wholly innocent of. He told me that, after his term had expired, and he went out into the world again, he never could stumble upon any of his old Sing Sing associates without dropping into a public house and talking over old times. And when fortune would go hard with him, and he felt out of sorts, and incensed at matters and things in general, he told me that, at such time, he almost wished he was back again in Sing Sing, where he was relieved from all anxieties about what he should eat and drink, and was supported, like the President of the United States and Prince Albert, at the public charge. He used to have such a snug little cell, he said, all to himself, and never felt afraid of house-breakers, for the walls were uncommonly thick, and his door was securely bolted for him, and a watchman was all the time walking up and down in the passage, while he himself was fast asleep and dreaming. To this, in substance, the *holder* added, that he narrated this anecdote because he thought it applicable to a man-of-war, which he scandalously asserted to be a sort of State Prison afloat.

Concerning the curious disposition to fraternize and be sociable, which this Shakings mentioned as characteristic of the convicts liberated from his old homestead at Sing Sing, it may well be asked, whether it may not prove to be some feeling, somehow akin to the reminiscent impulses which influenced them, that shall hereafter fraternally reunite all us mortals, when we shall have exchanged this State's Prison man-of-war world of ours for another and a better.

From the foregoing account of the great difficulty we had in killing time while in port, it must not be inferred that on board of the Neversink in Rio there was literally no work to be done. At long intervals the *launch* would come alongside with water-casks, to be emptied into iron tanks in the hold. In this way nearly fifty thousand gallons, as chronicled in the books of the master's mate, were decanted into the ship's bowels—a ninety days' allowance. With this huge Lake Ontario in us, the mighty Neversink might be said to resemble the united continent of the Eastern Hemisphere—floating in a vast ocean herself, and having a Mediterranean floating in her.

Chapter 43

SMUGGLING IN A MAN-OF-WAR

IT IS IN A GOOD DEGREE owing to the idleness just described, that, while lying in harbor, the man-of-war's-man is exposed to the most temptations, and gets into his saddest scrapes. For though his vessel be anchored a mile from the shore, and her sides are patrolled by sentries night and day, yet these things can not entirely prevent the seductions of the land from reaching him. The prime agent in working his calamities in port is his old arch-enemy, the ever-devilish god of grog.

Immured as the man-of-war's-man is, serving out his weary three years in a sort of sea-Newgate, from which he can not escape, either by the roof or burrowing under ground, he too often flies to the bottle to seek relief from the intolerable ennui of nothing to do, and nowhere to go. His ordinary government allowance of spirits, one gill per diem, is not enough to give a sufficient fillip to his listless senses; he pronounces his grog basely *watered*; he scouts at it, as *thinner than muslin*; he craves a more vigorous *nip at the cable*, a more sturdy *swig at the halyards*; and if opium were to be had, many would steep themselves a thousand fathoms down in the densest fumes of that oblivious drug. Tell him that the delirium tremens and the mania-a-potu lie in ambush for drunkards, he will say to you, "Let them bear down upon me, then, before the wind; any thing that smacks of life is better than to feel Davy Jones's chest-lid on your nose." He is reckless as an avalanche; and though his fall destroy himself and others, yet a ruinous commotion is better than being frozen fast in unendurable solitudes. No wonder, then, that he goes all lengths to procure the thing he craves; no wonder that he pays the most exorbitant prices, breaks through all law, and braves the ignominious lash itself, rather than be deprived of his stimulus.

Now, concerning no one thing in a man-of-war, are the regulations more severe than respecting the smuggling of grog, and being found intoxicated. For either offence there is but one penalty, invariably enforced; and that is, the degradation of the gangway.

All conceivable precautions are taken by most frigate-executives to guard against the secret admission of spirits into the vessel. In the first place, no shore-boat whatever is allowed to approach a man-of-war in a foreign harbor without permission from the officer of the deck. Even the *bum-boats*, the small craft licensed by the officers to bring off fruit for the sailors, to be bought out of their own money—these are invariably inspected before permitted to hold intercourse with the ship's company. And not only this, but every one of the numerous ship's boats—kept almost continually plying to and from the shore—are similarly inspected, sometimes each boat twenty times in the day.

This inspection is thus performed: The boat being descried by the quarter-master from the poop, she is reported to the deck-officer, who thereupon summons the master-at-arms, the ship's Chief of Police. This functionary now stations himself at the gangway, and as the boat's crew, one by one, come up the side, he personally overhauls them, making them take off their hats, and then, placing both hands upon their heads, draws his palms slowly down to their feet, carefully feeling all unusual protuberances. If nothing suspicious is felt, the man is let pass; and so on, till the whole boat's crew, averaging about sixteen men, are examined. The Chief of Police then descends into the boat, and walks from stem to stern, eyeing it all over, and poking his long rattan into every nook and cranny. This operation concluded, and nothing found, he mounts the ladder, touches his hat to the deck-officer, and reports the boat *clean*; whereupon she is hauled out to the booms.

Thus it will be seen that not a man of the ship's company ever enters the vessel from shore without it being rendered next to impossible, apparently, that he should have succeeded in smuggling any thing. Those individuals who are permitted to board the ship without undergoing this ordeal, are only persons whom it would be preposterous to search—such as the Commodore himself, the Captain, Lieutenants, &c., and gentlemen and ladies coming as visitors.

For any thing to be clandestinely thrust through the lower port-holes at night, is rendered very difficult, from the watchfulness of the quarter-master in hailing all boats that approach, long before they draw alongside, and the vigilance of the sentries, posted on platforms overhanging the water, whose orders are to fire into a strange boat which, after being warned to withdraw, should still persist in drawing nigh. Moreover, thirty-two-pound shot are slung to ropes, and suspended over the bows, to drop a hole into and sink any small craft, which, spite of all precautions, by strategy should succeed in getting under the bows with liquor by night. Indeed, the whole power of martial law is enlisted in this matter; and every one of the numerous officers of the ship, besides his general zeal in enforcing the regulations, adds to that a personal feeling, since the sobriety of the men abridges his own cares and anxieties.

How then, it will be asked, in the face of an argus-eyed police, and in defiance even of bayonets and bullets, do man-of-war's-men contrive to smuggle their spirits? Not to enlarge upon minor stratagems—every few days detected, and rendered naught (such as rolling up, in a neckerchief, a long, slender "skin" of grog, like a sausage, and in that manner ascending to the deck out of a boat just from shore; or openly bringing on board cocoa-nuts and melons, procured from a knavish bum-boat, filled with spirits, instead of milk or water)—we will only mention here two or three other modes, coming under my own observation.

While in Rio, a fore-top-man, belonging to the second cutter, paid down the money, and made an arrangement with a person encountered at the Palace-landing ashore, to the following effect. Of a certain moonless night, he was to bring off three gallons of spirits, *in skins*, and moor them to the frigate's anchor-buoy—some distance from the vessel—attaching something heavy, to sink them out of sight. In the middle watch of the night, the fore-top-man slips out of his hammock, and by creeping along in the shadows, eludes the vigilance of the master-at-arms and his mates, gains a port-hole, and softly lowers himself into the water, almost without creating a ripple—the sentries marching to and fro on their overhanging platform above him. He is an expert swimmer, and paddles along under the surface, every now and then rising a little, and lying motionless on his back to breathe—little but his nose exposed. The buoy gained, he cuts the skins adrift, ties them round his body, and in the same adroit manner makes good his return.

This feat is very seldom attempted, for it needs the utmost caution, address, and dexterity; and no one but a super-expert burglar, and faultless Leander of a swimmer, could achieve it.

From the greater privileges which they enjoy, the "*forward officers*," that is, the Gunner, Boatswain, &c., have much greater opportunities for successful smuggling than the common seamen. Coming alongside one night in a cutter, Yarn, our boatswain, in some inexplicable way, contrived to slip several skins of brandy through the air-port of his own state-room. The feat, however, must have been perceived by one of the boat's crew, who immediately, on gaining the deck, sprung down the ladders, stole into the boatswain's room, and made away with the prize, not three minutes before the rightful owner entered to claim it. Though, from certain circumstances, the thief was known to the aggrieved party, yet the latter could say nothing, since he himself had infringed the law. But the next day, in the capacity of captain of the ship's executioners, Yarn had the satisfaction (it was so to him), of standing over the robber at the gangway; for, being found intoxicated with the very liquor the boatswain himself had smuggled, the man had been condemned to a flogging.

This recalls another instance, still more illustrative of the knotted, trebly intertwisted villainy, accumulating at a sort of compound interest in a man-of-war. The cockswain of the Commodore's barge takes his crew apart, one by one, and cautiously sounds them as to their fidelity—not to the United States of America, but to himself. Three individuals, whom he deems doubtful—that is, faithful to the United States of America—he procures to be discharged from the barge, and men of his own selection are substituted; for he is always an influential character, this cockswain of the Commodore's barge. Previous to this, however, he has seen to it well, that no Temperance men—that is, sailors who do not draw their government ration of grog, but take the money for it—he has seen to it, that none of these *balkers* are numbered among

his crew. Having now proved his men, he divulges his plan
to the assembled body; a solemn oath of secrecy is obtained,
and he waits the first fit opportunity to carry into execution
his nefarious designs.

At last it comes. One afternoon the barge carries the Commodore across the Bay to a fine water-side settlement of noblemen's seats, called Praya Grande. The Commodore is
visiting a Portuguese marquis, and the pair linger long over
their dinner in an arbor in the garden. Meanwhile, the cockswain has liberty to roam about where he pleases. He searches
out a place where some choice *red-eye* (brandy) is to be had,
purchases six large bottles, and conceals them among the
trees. Under the pretence of filling the boat-keg with water,
which is always kept in the barge to refresh the crew, he now
carries it off into the grove, knocks out the head, puts the
bottles inside, reheads the keg, fills it with water, carries it
down to the boat, and audaciously restores it to its conspicuous position in the middle, with its bung-hole up. When the
Commodore comes down to the beach, and they pull off for
the ship, the Cockswain, in a loud voice, commands the nearest man to take that bung out of the keg—that precious water will spoil. Arrived alongside the frigate, the boat's crew
are overhauled, as usual, at the gangway; and nothing being
found on them, are passed. The master-at-arms now descending into the barge, and finding nothing suspicious, reports it
clean, having put his finger into the open bung of the keg
and tasted that the water was pure. The barge is ordered out
to the booms, and deep night is waited for, ere the Cockswain essays to snatch the bottles from the keg.

But, unfortunately for the success of this masterly smuggler, one of his crew is a weak-pated fellow, who, having
drank somewhat freely ashore, goes about the gun-deck
throwing out profound, tipsy hints concerning some unutterable proceeding on the ship's anvil. A knowing old sheet-
anchor-man, an unprincipled fellow, putting this, that, and
the other together, ferrets out the mystery; and straightway
resolves to reap the goodly harvest which the Cockswain has
sowed. He seeks him out, takes him to one side, and ad-
dresses him thus:

"Cockswain, you have been smuggling off some *red-eye*,

which at this moment is in your barge at the booms. Now, Cockswain, I have stationed two of my mess-mates at the port-holes, on that side of the ship; and if they report to me that you, or any of your bargemen, offer to enter that barge before morning, I will immediately report you as a smuggler to the officer of the deck."

The Cockswain is astounded; for, to be reported to the deck-officer as a smuggler, would inevitably procure him a sound flogging, and be the disgraceful *breaking* of him as a petty officer, receiving four dollars a month beyond his pay as an able seaman. He attempts to bribe the other to secrecy, by promising half the profits of the enterprise; but the sheet-anchor-man's integrity is like a rock; he is no mercenary, to be bought up for a song. The Cockswain, therefore, is forced to swear that neither himself, nor any of his crew, shall enter the barge before morning. This done, the sheet-anchor-man goes to his confidants, and arranges his plans. In a word, he succeeds in introducing the six brandy bottles into the ship; five of which he sells at eight dollars a bottle; and then, with the sixth, between two guns, he secretly regales himself and confederates; while the helpless Cockswain, stifling his rage, bitterly eyes them from afar.

Thus, though they say that there is honor among thieves, there is little among man-of-war smugglers.

Chapter 44

A KNAVE IN OFFICE IN A MAN-OF-WAR

THE LAST smuggling story now about to be related also occurred while we lay in Rio. It is the more particularly presented, since it furnishes the most curious evidence of the almost incredible corruption pervading nearly all ranks in some men-of-war.

For some days, the number of intoxicated sailors collared and brought up to the mast by the master-at-arms, to be reported to the deck-officers—previous to a flogging at the gangway—had, in the last degree, excited the surprise and vexation of the Captain and senior officers. So strict were the Captain's regulations concerning the suppression of grog-smuggling, and so particular had he been in charging the matter upon all the Lieutenants, and every under-strapper official in the frigate, that he was wholly at a loss how so large a quantity of spirits could have been spirited into the ship, in the face of all these checks, guards, and precautions.

Still additional steps were adopted to detect the smugglers; and Bland, the master-at-arms, together with his corporals, were publicly harangued at the mast by the Captain in person, and charged to exert their best powers in suppressing the traffic. Crowds were present at the time, and saw the master-at-arms touch his cap in obsequious homage, as he solemnly assured the Captain that he would still continue to do his best; as, indeed, he said, he had always done. He concluded with a pious ejaculation, expressive of his personal abhorrence of smuggling and drunkenness, and his fixed resolution, so help him Heaven, to spend his last wink in setting up by night, to spy out all deeds of darkness.

"I do not doubt you, master-at-arms," returned the Captain; "now go to your duty." This master-at-arms was a favorite of the Captain's.

The next morning, before breakfast, when the market-boat came off (that is, one of the ship's boats regularly deputed to bring off the daily fresh provisions for the officers)—when

538

this boat came off, the master-at-arms, as usual, after carefully examining both her and her crew, reported them to the deck-officer to be free from suspicion. The provisions were then hoisted out, and among them came a good-sized wooden box, addressed to "Mr. ——, Purser of the United States ship Neversink." Of course, any private matter of this sort, destined for a gentleman of the ward-room, was sacred from examination, and the master-at-arms commanded one of his corporals to carry it down into the Purser's state-room. But recent occurrences had sharpened the vigilance of the deck-officer to an unwonted degree, and seeing the box going down the hatchway, he demanded what that was, and whom it was for.

"All right, sir," said the master-at-arms, touching his cap; "stores for the Purser, sir."

"Let it remain on deck," said the Lieutenant. "Mr. Montgomery!" calling a midshipman, "ask the Purser whether there is any box coming off for him this morning."

"Ay, ay, sir," said the middy, touching his cap.

Presently he returned, saying that the Purser was ashore.

"Very good, then; Mr. Montgomery, have that box put into the 'brig,' with strict orders to the sentry not to suffer any one to touch it."

"Had I not better take it down into my mess, sir, till the Purser comes off?" said the master-at-arms, deferentially.

"I have given my orders, sir!" said the Lieutenant, turning away.

When the Purser came on board, it turned out that he knew nothing at all about the box. He had never so much as heard of it in his life. So it was again brought up before the deck-officer, who immediately summoned the master-at-arms.

"Break open that box!"

"Certainly, sir!" said the master-at-arms; and, wrenching off the cover, twenty-five brown jugs, like a litter of twenty-five brown pigs, were found snugly nestled in a bed of straw.

"The smugglers are at work, sir," said the master-at-arms, looking up.

"Uncork and taste it," said the officer.

The master-at-arms did so; and, smacking his lips after a puzzled fashion, was a little doubtful whether it was American whisky or Holland gin; but he said he was not used to liquor.

"Brandy; I know it by the smell," said the officer; "return the box to the brig."

"Ay, ay, sir," said the master-at-arms, redoubling his activity.

The affair was at once reported to the Captain, who, incensed at the audacity of the thing, adopted every plan to detect the guilty parties. Inquiries were made ashore; but by whom the box had been brought down to the market-boat there was no finding out. Here the matter rested for a time.

Some days after, one of the boys of the mizzen-top was flogged for drunkenness, and, while suspended in agony at the gratings, was made to reveal from whom he had procured his spirits. The man was called, and turned out to be an old superannuated marine, one Scriggs, who did the cooking for the marine-sergeants and master-at-arms' mess. This marine was one of the most villainous-looking fellows in the ship, with a squinting, pick-lock, gray eye, and hang-dog gallows gait. How such a most unmartial vagabond had insinuated himself into the honorable marine corps was a perfect mystery. He had always been noted for his personal uncleanliness, and among all hands, fore and aft, had the reputation of being a notorious old miser, who denied himself the few comforts, and many of the common necessaries of a man-of-war life.

Seeing no escape, Scriggs fell on his knees before the Captain, and confessed the charge of the boy. Observing the fellow to be in an agony of fear at the sight of the boatswain's mates and their lashes, and all the striking parade of public punishment, the Captain must have thought this a good opportunity for completely pumping him of all his secrets. This terrified marine was at length forced to reveal his having been for some time an accomplice in a complicated system of underhand villainy, the head of which was no less a personage than the indefatigable chief of police, the master-at-arms himself. It appeared that this official had his confidential agents ashore, who supplied him with spirits, and in various boxes, packages, and bundles—addressed to the Purser and others—brought them down to the frigate's boats at the landing. Ordinarily, the appearance of these things for the Purser and other ward-room gentlemen occasioned no surprise; for almost every day some bundle or other is coming off for them, especially for the Purser; and, as the master-at-arms was always present on these occasions, it was an easy matter for him to hurry the smuggled liquor out of sight, and, under pretence of carrying the box or bundle down to the Purser's room, hide it away upon his own premises.

The miserly marine, Scriggs, with the pick-lock eye, was the man who clandestinely sold the spirits to the sailors, thus completely keeping the master-at-arms in the background. The liquor sold at the most exorbitant prices; at one time reaching twelve dollars the bottle in cash, and thirty dollars a bottle in orders upon the Purser, to be honored upon the frigate's arrival home. It may seem incredible that such prices should have been given by the sailors; but when some man-of-war's-men crave liquor, and it is hard to procure, they would almost barter ten years of their lifetime for but one solitary "*tot*," if they could.

The sailors who became intoxicated with the liquor thus smuggled on board by the master-at-arms, were, in almost numberless instances, officially seized by that functionary and scourged at the gangway. In a previous place it has been shown how conspicuous a part the master-at-arms enacts at this scene.

The ample profits of this iniquitous business were divided between all the parties concerned in it; Scriggs, the marine, coming in for one third. His cook's mess-chest being brought on deck, four canvass bags of silver were found in it, amounting to a sum something short of as many hundred dollars.

The guilty parties were scourged, double-ironed, and for several weeks were confined in the "brig," under a sentry; all but the master-at-arms, who was merely cashiered and imprisoned for a time, with bracelets at his wrists. Upon being liberated, he was turned adrift among the ship's company; and, by way of disgracing him still more, was thrust into the *waist*, the most inglorious division of the ship.

Upon going to dinner one day, I found him soberly seated at my own mess; and at first I could not but feel some very serious scruples about dining with him. Nevertheless, he was

a man to study and digest; so, upon a little reflection, I was
not displeased at his presence. It amazed me, however, that
he had wormed himself into the mess, since so many of the
other messes had declined the honor; until at last, I ascertained that he had induced a mess-mate of ours, a distant relation of his, to prevail upon the cook to admit him.

Now it would not have answered for hardly any other mess
in the ship to have received this man among them, for it
would have torn a huge rent in their reputation; but our
mess, A. No. 1—the Forty-two-pounder Club—was composed of so fine a set of fellows; so many captains of tops,
and quarter-masters—men of undeniable mark on board
ship—of long-established standing and consideration on the
gun-deck; that, with impunity, we could do so many equivocal things, utterly inadmissible for messes of inferior preten-
sion. Besides, though we all abhorred the monster of Sin
itself, yet, from our social superiority, highly rarified education in our lofty top, and large and liberal sweep of the aggregate of things, we were in a good degree free from those
useless, personal prejudices, and galling hatreds against conspicuous *sinners*—not *Sin*—which so widely prevail among
men of warped understandings and unchristian and uncharitable hearts. No; the superstitions and dogmas concerning Sin
had not laid their withering maxims upon our hearts. We perceived how that evil was but good disguised, and a knave a
saint in his way; how that in other planets, perhaps, what we
deem wrong, may there be deemed right; even as some substances, without undergoing any mutations in themselves, utterly change their color, according to the light thrown upon
them. We perceived that the anticipated millennium must
have begun upon the morning the first worlds were created;
and that, taken all in all, our man-of-war world itself was as
eligible a round-sterned craft as any to be found in the Milky
Way. And we fancied that though some of us, of the gun-
deck, were at times condemned to sufferings and slights, and
all manner of tribulation and anguish, yet, no doubt, it was
only our misapprehension of these things that made us take
them for woeful pains instead of the most agreeable pleasures.
I have dreamed of a sphere, says Pinzella, where to break a

man on the wheel is held the most exquisite of delights you can confer upon him; where for one gentleman in any way to vanquish another, is accounted an everlasting dishonor; where to tumble one into a pit after death, and then throw cold clods upon his upturned face, is a species of contumely, only inflicted upon the most notorious criminals.

But whatever we mess-mates thought, in whatever circumstances we found ourselves, we never forgot that our frigate, bad as it was, was homeward-bound. Such, at least, were our reveries at times, though sorely jarred, now and then, by events that took our philosophy aback. For after all, philosophy—that is, the best wisdom that has ever in any way been revealed to our man-of-war world—is but a slough and a mire, with a few tufts of good footing here and there.

But there was one man in the mess who would have naught to do with our philosophy—a churlish, ill-tempered, unphilosophical, superstitious old bear of a quarter-gunner; a believer in Tophet, for which he was accordingly preparing himself. Priming was his name; but methinks I have spoken of him before.

Besides, this Bland, the master-at-arms, was no vulgar, dirty knave. In him—to modify Burke's phrase—vice *seemed*, but only seemed, to lose half its seeming evil by losing all its apparent grossness. He was a neat and gentlemanly villain, and broke his biscuit with a dainty hand. There was a fine polish about his whole person, and a pliant, insinuating style in his conversation, that was, socially, quite irresistible. Save my noble captain, Jack Chase, he proved himself the most entertaining, I had almost said the most companionable man in the mess. Nothing but his mouth, that was somewhat small, Moorish-arched, and wickedly delicate, and his snaky, black eye, that at times shone like a dark-lantern in a jeweler-shop at midnight, betokened the accomplished scoundrel within. But in his conversation there was no trace of evil; nothing equivocal; he studiously shunned an indelicacy, never swore, and chiefly abounded in passing puns and witticisms, varied with humorous contrasts between ship and shore life, and many agreeable and racy anecdotes, very tastefully narrated. In short—in a merely psychological point of view, at least—he was a charming blackleg. Ashore, such a man might have been an irreproachable mercantile swindler, circulating in polite society.

But he was still more than this. Indeed, I claim for this master-at-arms a lofty and honorable niche in the Newgate Calender of history. His intrepidity, coolness, and wonderful self-possession in calmly resigning himself to a fate that thrust him from an office in which he had tyrannized over five hundred mortals, many of whom hated and loathed him, passed all belief; his intrepidity, I say, in now fearlessly glid-ing among them, like a disarmed sword-fish among ferocious white-sharks; this, surely, bespoke no ordinary man. While in office, even, his life had often been secretly attempted by the seamen whom he had brought to the gangway. Of dark nights they had dropped shot down the hatchways, destined "to damage his pepper-box," as they phrased it; they had made ropes with a hangman's noose at the end, and tried to *lasso* him in dark corners. And now he was adrift among them, under notorious circumstances of superlative villainy, at last dragged to light; and yet he blandly smiled, politely offered his cigar-holder to a perfect stranger, and laughed and chatted to right and left, as if springy, buoyant, and elastic, with an angelic conscience, and sure of kind friends wherever he went, both in this life and the life to come.

While he was lying ironed in the "brig," gangs of the men were sometimes overheard whispering about the terrible re-ception they would give him when he should be set at large. Nevertheless, when liberated, they seemed confounded by his erect and cordial assurance, his gentlemanly sociability and fearless companionableness. From being an implacable police-man, vigilant, cruel, and remorseless in his office, however polished in his phrases, he was now become a disinterested, sauntering man of leisure, winking at all improprieties, and ready to laugh and make merry with any one. Still, at first, the men gave him a wide berth, and returned scowls for his smiles; but who can forever resist the very Devil himself, when he comes in the guise of a gentleman, free, fine, and frank? Though Goëthe's pious Margaret hates the Devil in his horns and harpooneer's tail, yet she smiles and nods to the engaging fiend in the persuasive, winning, oily, wholly harmless Mephistophiles. But, however it was, I, for one, regarded this master-at-arms with mixed feelings of detestation, pity, admiration, and something opposed to enmity. I could not but abominate him when I thought of his conduct; but I pitied the continual gnawing which, under all his deftly-donned disguises, I saw lying at the bottom of his soul. I admired his heroism in sustaining himself so well under such reverses. And when I thought how arbitrary the *Articles of War* are in defining a man-of-war villain; how much unde-tected guilt might be sheltered by the aristocratic awning of our quarter-deck; how many florid pursers, ornaments of the ward-room, had been legally protected in defrauding *the peo-ple*, I could not but say to myself, Well, after all, though this man is a most wicked one indeed, yet is he even more luckless than depraved.

Besides, a studied observation of Bland convinced me that he was an organic and irreclaimable scoundrel, who did wicked deeds as the cattle browse the herbage, because wicked deeds seemed the legitimate operation of his whole infernal organization. Phrenologically, he was without a soul. Is it to be wondered at, that the devils are irreligious? What, then, thought I, who is to blame in this matter? For one, I will not take the Day of Judgment upon me by authoritatively pronouncing upon the essential criminality of any man-of-war's-man; and Christianity has taught me that, at the last day, man-of-war's-men will not be judged by the *Articles of War*, nor by the *United States Statutes at Large*, but by im-mutable laws, ineffably beyond the comprehension of the honorable Board of Commodores and Navy Commissioners.

But though I will stand by even a man-of-war thief, and defend him from being seized up at the gangway, if I can—remembering that my Savior once hung between two thieves, promising one life-eternal—yet I would not, after the plain conviction of a villain, again let him entirely loose to prey upon honest seamen, fore and aft all three decks. But this did Captain Claret; and though the thing may not perhaps be credited, nevertheless, here it shall be recorded.

After the master-at-arms had been adrift among the ship's company for several weeks, and we were within a few days' sail of home, he was summoned to the mast, and publicly reinstated in his office as the ship's chief of police. Perhaps Captain Claret had read the Memoirs of Vidocq, and believed in the old saying, *set a rogue to catch a rogue*. Or, perhaps, he was a man of very tender feelings, highly susceptible to the soft emotions of gratitude, and could not bear to leave in disgrace a person who, out of the generosity of his heart, had, about a year previous, presented him with a rare snuff-box, fabricated from a sperm-whale's tooth, with a curious silver hinge, and cunningly wrought in the shape of a whale; also a splendid gold-mounted cane, of a costly Brazilian wood, with a gold plate, bearing the Captain's name and rank in the service, the place and time of his birth, and with a vacancy underneath—no doubt providently left for his heirs to record his decease.

Certain it was that, some months previous to the master-at-arms' disgrace, he had presented these articles to the Captain, with his best love and compliments; and the Captain had received them, and seldom went ashore without the cane, and never took snuff but out of that box. With some Captains, a sense of propriety might have induced them to return these presents, when the generous donor had proved himself unworthy of having them retained; but it was not Captain Claret who would inflict such a cutting wound upon any officer's sensibilities, though long-established naval customs had habituated him to scourging *the people* upon an emergency.

Now had Captain Claret deemed himself constitutionally bound to decline all presents from his subordinates, the sense of gratitude would not have operated to the prejudice of justice. And, as some of the subordinates of a man-of-war captain are apt to invoke his good wishes and mollify his conscience by making him friendly gifts, it would perhaps have been an excellent thing for him to adopt the plan pursued by the President of the United States, when he received a present of lions and Arabian chargers from the Sultan of Muscat. Being forbidden by his sovereign lords and masters, the imperial people, to accept of any gifts from foreign powers, the President sent them to an auctioneer, and the proceeds were deposited in the Treasury. In the same manner, when Captain Claret received his snuff-box and cane, he might have accepted them very kindly, and then sold them off to the highest bidder, perhaps to the donor himself, who in that case would never have tempted him again.

Upon his return home, Bland was paid off for his full term, not deducting the period of his suspension. He again entered the service in his old capacity.

As no further allusion will be made to this affair, it may as well be stated now that, for the very brief period elapsing between his restoration and being paid off in port by the Purser, the master-at-arms conducted himself with infinite discretion, artfully steering between any relaxation of discipline—which would have awakened the displeasure of the officers—and any unwise severity—which would have revived, in ten-fold force, all the old grudges of the seamen under his command.

Never did he show so much talent and tact as when vibrating in this his most delicate predicament; and plenty of cause was there for the exercise of his cunningest abilities; for, upon the discharge of our man-of-war's-men at home, should he *then* be held by them as an enemy, as free and independent citizens they would waylay him in the public streets, and take purple vengeance for all his iniquities, past, present, and possible in the future. More than once a master-at-arms ashore has been seized by night by an exasperated crew, and served as Origen served himself, or as his enemies served Abelard.

But though, under extreme provocation, *the people* of a man-of-war have been guilty of the maddest vengeance, yet, at other times, they are very placable and milky-hearted, even to those who may have outrageously abused them; many things in point might be related, but I forbear.

This account of the master-at-arms can not better be concluded than by denominating him, in the vivid language of the Captain of the Fore-top, as "*the two ends and middle of the thrice-laid strand of a bloody rascal*," which was intended for a terse, well-knit, and all-comprehensive assertion, without omission or reservation. It was also asserted that, had Tophet itself been raked with a fine-tooth comb, such another ineffable villain could not by any possibility have been caught.

Chapter 45

PUBLISHING POETRY IN A MAN-OF-WAR

A DAY OR TWO after our arrival in Rio, a rather amusing incident occurred to a particular acquaintance of mine, young Lemsford, the gun-deck bard.

The great guns of an armed ship have blocks of wood, called *tompions*, painted black, inserted in their muzzles, to keep out the spray of the sea. These tompions slip in and out very handily, like covers to butter firkins.

By advice of a friend, Lemsford, alarmed for the fate of his box of poetry, had latterly made use of a particular gun on the main-deck, in the tube of which he thrust his manuscripts, by simply crawling partly out of the port-hole, removing the tompion, inserting his papers, tightly rolled, and making all snug again. Little Quoin, the quarter-gunner, was on the "sick-list" then.

Breakfast over, Lemsford and I were reclining in the main-top—where, by permission of my noble master, Jack Chase, I had invited him—when, of a sudden, we heard a cannonading. It was our own ship.

"Ah!" said a top-man, "returning the shore salute they gave us yesterday."

"O Lord!" cried Lemsford, "my *Songs of the Sirens*!" and he ran down the rigging to the batteries; but just as he touched the gun-deck, gun No. 20—his literary strong box—went off with a terrific report.

"Well, my after-guard Virgil," said Jack Chase to him, as he slowly returned up the rigging, "did you get it? You need not answer; I see you were too late. But never mind, my boy; no printer could do the business for you better. That's the way to publish, White-Jacket," turning to me—"fire it right into 'em; every canto a twenty-four-pound shot; *hull* the blockheads, whether they will or no. And mind you, Lemsford, when your shot does the most execution, you hear the least from the foe. A killed man can not even lisp."

"Glorious Jack!" cried Lemsford, running up and snatching

him by the hand, "say that again, Jack! look me in the eyes. By all the Homers, Jack, you have made my soul mount like a balloon! Jack, I'm a poor devil of a poet. Not two months before I shipped aboard here, I published a volume of poems, very aggressive on the world, Jack. Heaven knows what it cost me. I published it, Jack, and the cursed publisher sued me for damages; my friends looked sheepish; one or two who liked it were non-committal; and as for the addle-pated mob and rabble, they thought they had found out a fool. Blast them, Jack, what they call the public is a monster, like the idol we saw in Owhyhee, with the head of a jackass, the body of a baboon, and the tail of a scorpion!"

"I don't like that," said Jack; "when I'm ashore, I myself am part of the public."

"Your pardon, Jack; you are not. You are then a part of the people, just as you are aboard the frigate here. The public is one thing, Jack, and the people another."

"You are right," said Jack; "right as this leg. Virgil, you are a trump; you are a jewel, my boy. The public and the people! Ay, ay, my lads, let us hate the one and cleave to the other."

Chapter 46

A DAY OR TWO after the publication of Lemsford's "Songs of the Sirens," a sad accident befell a mess-mate of mine, one of the captains of the mizzen-top. He was a fine little Scot, who, from the premature loss of the hair on the top of his head, always went by the name of *Baldy*. This baldness was no doubt, in great part, attributable to the same cause that early thins the locks of most man-of-war's-men—namely, the hard, unyielding, and ponderous man-of-war and navy-regulation tarpaulin hat, which, when new, is stiff enough to sit upon, and indeed, in lieu of his thumb, sometimes serves the common sailor for a bench.

Now, there is nothing upon which the Commodore of a squadron more prides himself than upon the celerity with which his men can handle the sails, and go through with all the evolutions pertaining thereto. This is especially manifested in harbor, when other vessels of his squadron are near, and perhaps the armed ships of rival nations.

Upon these occasions, surrounded by his post-captain satraps—each of whom in his own floating island is king—the Commodore domineers over all—emperor of the whole oaken archipelago; yea, magisterial and magnificent as the Sultan of the Isles of Sooloo.

But, even as so potent an emperor and Cæsar to boot as the great Don of Germany, Charles the Fifth, was used to divert himself in his dotage by watching the gyrations of the springs and cogs of a long row of clocks, even so does an elderly Commodore while away his leisure in harbor, by what is called "*exercising guns*," and also "*exercising yards and sails*;" causing the various spars of all the ships under his command to be "braced," "topped," and "cock billed" in concert, while the Commodore himself sits, something like King Canute, on an arm-chest on the poop of his flag-ship.

But far more regal than any descendant of Charlemagne,

more haughty than any Mogul of the East, and almost mysterious and voiceless in his authority as the Great Spirit of the Five Nations, the Commodore deigns not to verbalize his commands; they are imparted by signal.

And as for old Charles the Fifth, again, the gay-pranked, colored suits of cards were invented, to while away his dotage, even so, doubtless, must these pretty little signals of blue and red spotted *bunting* have been devised to cheer the old age of all Commodores.

By the Commodore's side stands the signal-midshipman, with a sea-green bag swung on his shoulder (as a sportsman bears his game-bag), the signal-book in one hand, and the signal-spy-glass in the other. As this signal-book contains the Masonic signs and tokens of the navy, and would therefore be invaluable to an enemy, its binding is always bordered with lead, so as to insure its sinking in case the ship should be captured. Not the only book this, that might appropriately be bound in lead, though there be many where the author, and not the bookbinder, furnishes the metal.

As White-Jacket understands it, these signals consist of variously-colored flags, each standing for a certain number. Say there are ten flags, representing the cardinal numbers—the red flag, No. 1; the blue flag, No. 2; the green flag, No. 3, and so forth; then, by mounting the blue flag over the red, that would stand for No. 21: if the green flag were set underneath, it would then stand for 213. How easy, then, by endless transpositions, to multiply the various numbers that may be exhibited at the mizzen-peak, even by only three or four of these flags.

To each number a particular meaning is applied. No. 100, for instance, may mean, "*Beat to quarters.*" No. 150, "*All hands to grog.*" No. 2000, "*Strike top-gallant-yards.*" No. 2110, "*See any thing to windward?*" No. 2800, "*No.*"

And as every man-of-war is furnished with a signal-book, where all these things are set down in order, therefore, though two American frigates—almost perfect strangers to each other—came from the opposite Poles, yet at a distance of more than a mile they could carry on a very liberal conversation in the air.

When several men-of-war of one nation lie at anchor in one

port, forming a wide circle round their lord and master, the flagship, it is a very interesting sight to see them all obeying the Commodore's orders, who meanwhile never opens his lips.

Thus was it with us in Rio, and hereby hangs the story of my poor mess-mate Baldy.

One morning, in obedience to a signal from our flag-ship, the various vessels belonging to the American squadron then in harbor simultaneously loosened their sails to dry. In the evening, the signal was set to furl them. Upon such occasions, great rivalry exists between the First Lieutenants of the different ships; they vie with each other who shall first have his sails stowed on the yards. And this rivalry is shared between all the officers of each vessel, who are respectively placed over the different top-men; so that the main-mast is all eagerness to vanquish the fore-mast, and the mizzen-mast to vanquish them both. Stimulated by the shouts of their officers, the sailors throughout the squadron exert themselves to the utmost.

"Aloft, top-men! lay out! furl!" cried the First Lieutenant of the Neversink.

At the word the men sprang into the rigging, and on all three masts were soon climbing about the yards, in reckless haste, to execute their orders.

Now, in furling top-sails or courses, the point of honor, and the hardest work, is in the *bunt*, or middle of the yard; this post belongs to the first captain of the top.

"What are you 'bout there, mizzen-top-men?" roared the First Lieutenant, through his trumpet. "D—n you, you are clumsy as Russian bears! don't you see the main-top-men are nearly off the yard? Bear a hand, bear a hand, or I'll stop your grog all round! You, Baldy! are you going to sleep there in the bunt?"

While this was being said, poor Baldy—his hat off, his face streaming with perspiration—was franticly exerting himself, piling up the ponderous folds of canvass in the middle of the yard; ever and anon glancing at victorious Jack Chase, hard at work at the main-topsail-yard before him.

At last, the sail being well piled up, Baldy jumped with both feet into the *bunt*, holding on with one hand to the chain "*tie*," and in that manner was violently treading down the canvass, to pack it close.

"D—n you, Baldy, why don't you move, you crawling caterpillar?" roared the First Lieutenant.

Baldy brought his whole weight to bear on the rebellious sail, and in his frenzied heedlessness let go his hold on the *tie*.

"You, Baldy! are you afraid of falling?" cried the First Lieutenant.

At that moment, with all his force, Baldy jumped down upon the sail; the *bunt-gasket* parted; and a dark form dropped through the air. Lighting upon the *top-rim*, it rolled off; and the next instant, with a horrid crash of all his bones, Baldy came, like a thunder-bolt, upon the deck.

Aboard of most large men-of-war there is a stout oaken platform, about four feet square, on each side of the quarter-deck. You ascend to it by three or four steps; on top, it is railed in at the sides, with horizontal brass bars. It is called *the Horse Block*; and there the officer of the deck usually stands, in giving his orders at sea.

It was one of these horse blocks, now unoccupied, that broke poor Baldy's fall. He fell lengthwise across the brass bars, bending them into elbows, and crushing the whole oaken platform, steps and all, right down to the deck in a thousand splinters.

He was picked up for dead, and carried below to the surgeon. His bones seemed like those of a man broken on the wheel, and no one thought he would survive the night. But with the surgeon's skillful treatment he at last promised recovery. Surgeon Cuticle devoted all his science to this case.

A curious frame-work of wood was made for the maimed man; and placed in this, with all his limbs stretched out, Baldy lay flat on the floor of the Sick-bay, for many weeks. Upon our arrival home, he was able to hobble ashore on crutches; but from a hale, hearty little man, with bronzed cheeks, he was become a mere dislocated skeleton, white as foam; but ere this, perhaps, his broken bones are healed and whole in the last repose of the man-of-war's-man.

Not many days after Baldy's accident in furling sails—in this same frenzied manner, under the stimulus of a shouting officer—a seaman fell from the main-royal-yard of an English line-of-battle ship near us, and buried his ankle-bones in the deck, leaving two indentations there, as if scooped out by a carpenter's gouge.

The royal-yard forms a cross with the mast, and falling from that lofty cross in a line-of-battle ship is almost like falling from the cross of St. Paul's; almost like falling as Lucifer from the well-spring of morning down to the Phlegethon of night.

In some cases, a man, hurled thus from a yard, has fallen upon his own shipmates in the tops, and dragged them down with him to the same destruction with himself.

Hardly ever will you hear of a man-of-war returning home after a cruise, without the loss of some of her crew from aloft, whereas similar accidents in the merchant service—considering the much greater number of men employed in it—are comparatively few.

Why mince the matter? The death of most of these man-of-war's-men lies at the door of the souls of those officers, who, while safely standing on deck themselves, scruple not to sacrifice an immortal man or two, in order to show off the excelling discipline of the ship. And thus do *the people* of the gun-deck suffer, that the Commodore on the poop may be glorified.

Chapter 47

AN AUCTION IN A MAN-OF-WAR

SOME ALLUSION has been made to the weariness experienced by the man-of-war's-man while lying at anchor; but there are scenes now and then that serve to relieve it. Chief among these are the Purser's auctions, taking place while in harbor. Some weeks, or perhaps months, after a sailor dies in an armed vessel, his bag of clothes is in this manner sold, and the proceeds transferred to the account of his heirs or executors.

One of these auctions came off in Rio, shortly after the sad accident of Baldy.

It was a dreamy, quiet afternoon, and the crew were listlessly lying around, when suddenly the Boatswain's whistle was heard, followed by the announcement, "D'ye hear there, fore and aft! Purser's auction on the spar-deck!"

At the sound, the sailors sprang to their feet and mustered round the main-mast. Presently up came the Purser's steward, marshaling before him three or four of his subordinates, carrying several clothes' bags, which were deposited at the base of the mast.

Our Purser's steward was a rather gentlemanly man in his way. Like many young Americans of his class, he had at various times assumed the most opposite functions for a livelihood, turning from one to the other with all the facility of a light-hearted, clever adventurer. He had been a clerk in a steamer on the Mississippi River; an auctioneer in Ohio; a stock actor at the Olympic Theatre in New York; and now he was Purser's steward in the Navy. In the course of this diversified career his natural wit and waggery had been highly spiced, and every way improved; and he had acquired the last and most difficult art of the joker, the art of lengthening his own face while widening those of his hearers, preserving the utmost solemnity while setting them all in a roar. He was quite a favorite with the sailors, which, in a good degree, was owing to his humor; but

likewise to his off-hand, irresistible, romantic, theatrical
manner of addressing them.

With a dignified air, he now mounted the pedestal of the
main-top-sail sheet-bitts, imposing silence by a theatrical wave
of his hand; meantime, his subordinates were rummaging the
bags, and assorting their contents before him.

"Now, my noble hearties," he began, "we will open this
auction by offering to your impartial competition a very superior pair of old boots;" and so saying, he dangled aloft one
clumsy cowhide cylinder, almost as large as a fire bucket, as a
specimen of the complete pair.

"What shall I have now, my noble tars, for this superior
pair of sea-boots?"

"Where's t'other boot?" cried a suspicious-eyed waister. "I
remember them 'ere boots. They were old Bob's the quarter-
gunner's; there was two on 'em, too. I want to see t'other
boot."

"My sweet and pleasant fellow," said the auctioneer, with
his blandest accents, "the other boot is not just at hand, but
I give you my word of honor that it in all respects corresponds to the one you here see—it does, I assure you. Yes: I
solemnly guarantee, my noble sea-fencibles," he added, turning round upon all, "that the other boot is the exact counterpart of this. Now, then, say the word, my fine fellows. What
shall I have? Ten dollars, did you say?" politely bowing toward some indefinite person in the background.

"No; ten cents," responded a voice.

"Ten cents! ten cents! gallant sailors, for this noble pair of
boots," exclaimed the auctioneer, with affected horror; "I
must close the auction, my tars of Columbia; this will never
do. But let's have another bid; now, come," he added, coax-
ingly and soothingly. "What is it? One dollar? One dollar,
then—one dollar; going at one dollar; going, going—going.
Just see how it vibrates"—swinging the boot to and fro—
"this superior pair of sea-boots vibrating at one dollar;
wouldn't pay for the nails in their heels; going, going—
gone!" And down went the boots.

"Ah, what a sacrifice! what a sacrifice!" he sighed, tearfully
eyeing the solitary fire-bucket, and then glancing round the
company for sympathy.

"A sacrifice, indeed!" exclaimed Jack Chase, who stood by; "Purser's Steward, you are Mark Antony over the body of Julius Cæsar."

"So I am, so I am," said the auctioneer, without moving a muscle. "And look!" he exclaimed, suddenly seizing the boot, and exhibiting it on high, "look, my noble tars, if you have tears, prepare to shed them now. You all do know this boot. I remember the first time ever old Bob put it on. 'Twas on a winter evening, off Cape Horn, between the starboard carronades—that day his precious grog was stopped. Look! in this place a mouse has nibbled through; see what a rent some envious rat has made; through this another filed, and, as he plucked his cursed rasp away, mark how the bootleg gaped. This was the unkindest cut of all. But whose are the boots?" suddenly assuming a business-like air; "yours? yours? yours?"

But not a friend of the lamented Bob stood by.

"Tars of Columbia," said the auctioneer, imperatively, "these boots must be sold; and if I can't sell them one way, I must sell them another. How much *a pound*, now, for this superior pair of old boots? going by *the pound* now, remember, my gallant sailors! what shall I have? one cent, do I hear? going now at one cent a pound—going—going—going—*gone!*"

"Whose are they? Yours, Captain of the Waist? Well, my sweet and pleasant friend, I will have them weighed out to you when the auction is over."

In like manner all the contents of the bags were disposed of, embracing old frocks, trowsers, and jackets, the various sums for which they went being charged to the bidders on the books of the Purser.

Having been present at this auction, though not a purchaser, and seeing with what facility the most dismantled old garments went off, through the magical cleverness of the accomplished auctioneer, the thought occurred to me, that if ever I calmly and positively decided to dispose of my famous white jacket, this would be the very way to do it. I turned the matter over in my mind a long time.

The weather in Rio was genial and warm, and that I would ever again need such a thing as a heavy quilted jacket—and such a jacket as the white one, too—seemed almost impos-

sible. Yet I remembered the American coast, and that it would
probably be Autumn when we should arrive there. Yes, I
thought of all that, to be sure; nevertheless, the ungovernable
whim seized me to sacrifice my jacket and recklessly abide the
consequences. Besides, was it not a horrible jacket? To how
many annoyances had it subjected me? How many scrapes
had it dragged me into? Nay, had it not once jeopardized my
very existence? And I had a dreadful presentiment that, if I
persisted in retaining it, it would do so again. Enough! I will
sell it, I muttered; and, so muttering, I thrust my hands further down in my waistband, and walked the main-top in the
stern concentration of an inflexible purpose. Next day, hearing that another auction was shortly to take place, I repaired
to the office of the Purser's steward, with whom I was upon
rather friendly terms. After vaguely and delicately hinting at
the object of my visit, I came roundly to the point, and asked
him whether he could slip my jacket into one of the bags of
clothes next to be sold, and so dispose of it by public auction.
He kindly acquiesced, and the thing was done.

In due time all hands were again summoned round the
main-mast; the Purser's steward mounted his post, and the
ceremony began. Meantime, I lingered out of sight, but still
within hearing, on the gun-deck below, gazing up, unperceived, at the scene.

As it is now so long ago, I will here frankly make confession that I had privately retained the services of a friend—
Williams, the Yankee pedagogue and peddler—whose business it would be to linger near the scene of the auction, and,
if the bids on the jacket loitered, to start it roundly himself;
and if the bidding then became brisk, he was continually to
strike in with the most pertinacious and infatuated bids, and
so exasperate competition into the maddest and most extravagant overtures.

A variety of other articles having been put up, the white
jacket was slowly produced, and, held high aloft between the
auctioneer's thumb and fore-finger, was submitted to the inspection of the discriminating public.

Here it behooves me once again to describe my jacket; for,
as a portrait taken at one period of life will not answer for a
later stage; much more this jacket of mine, undergoing so

many changes, needs to be painted again and again, in order truly to present its actual appearance at any given period.

A premature old age had now settled upon it; all over it bore melancholy scars of the masoned-up pockets that had once trenched it in various directions. Some parts of it were slightly mildewed from dampness; on one side several of the buttons were gone, and others were broken or cracked; while, alas! my many mad endeavors to rub it black on the decks had now imparted to the whole garment an exceedingly untidy appearance. Such as it was, with all its faults, the auctioneer displayed it.

"You venerable sheet-anchor-men! and you, gallant fore-top-men! and you, my fine waisters! what do you say now for this superior old jacket? Buttons and sleeves, lining and skirts, it must this day be sold without reservation. How much for it, my gallant tars of Columbia? say the word, and how much?"

"My eyes!" exclaimed a fore-top-man, "don't that 'ere bunch of old swabs belong to Jack Chase's pet? Arn't that *the white jacket*?"

"*The white jacket!*" cried fifty voices in response; "*the white jacket!*" The cry ran fore and aft the ship like a slogan, completely overwhelming the solitary voice of my private friend Williams, while all hands gazed at it with straining eyes, wondering how it came among the bags of deceased mariners.

"Ay, noble tars," said the auctioneer, "you may well stare at it; you will not find another jacket like this on either side of Cape Horn, I assure you. Why, just look at it! How much, now? Give me a bid—but don't be rash; be prudent, be prudent, men; remember your Purser's accounts, and don't be betrayed into extravagant bids."

"Purser's Steward!" cried Grummet, one of the quarter-gunners, slowly shifting his quid from one cheek to the other, like a ballast-stone, "I won't bid on that 'ere bunch of old swabs, unless you put up ten pounds of soap with it."

"Don't mind that old fellow," said the auctioneer. "How much for the jacket, my noble tars?"

"Jacket!" cried a dandy *bone-polisher* of the gun-room. "The sail-maker was the tailor, then. How many fathoms of canvass in it, Purser's Steward?"

"How much for this *jacket*?" reiterated the auctioneer, emphatically.

"*Jacket* do you call it!" cried a captain of the hold. "Why not call it a white-washed man-of-war schooner? Look at the port-holes, to let in the air of cold nights."

"A reg'lar herring-net," chimed in Grummet.

"Gives me the *fever-nagur* to look at it," echoed a mizzen-top-man.

"Silence!" cried the auctioneer. "Start it now—start it, boys; any thing you please, my fine fellows! it *must* be sold. Come, what ought I to have on it, now?"

"Why, Purser's Steward," cried a waister, "you ought to have new sleeves, a new lining, and a new body on it, afore you try to shove it off on a green-horn."

"What are you busin' that 'ere garment for?" cried an old sheet-anchor-man. "Don't you see it's a 'uniform mustering jacket'—three buttons on one side, and none on t'other?"

"Silence!" again cried the auctioneer. "How much, my sea-fencibles, for this superior old jacket?"

"Well," said Grummet, "I'll take it for cleaning-rags at one cent."

"Oh, come, give us a bid! say something, Columbians."

"Well, then," said Grummet, all at once bursting into genuine indignation, "if you want us to say something, then heave that bunch of old swabs overboard, *say I*, and show us something worth looking at."

"No one will give me a bid, then? Very good; here, shove it aside. Let's have something else there."

While this scene was going forward, and my white jacket was thus being abused, how my heart swelled within me! Thrice was I on the point of rushing out of my hiding-place, and bearing it off from derision; but I lingered, still flattering myself that all would be well, and the jacket find a purchaser at last. But no, alas! there was no getting rid of it, except by rolling a forty-two-pound shot in it, and committing it to the deep. But though, in my desperation, I had once contemplated something of that sort, yet I had now become unaccountably averse to it, from certain involuntary superstitious considerations. If I sink my jacket, thought I, it will be sure to spread itself into a bed at the bottom of the sea, upon which I shall sooner or later recline, a dead man. So, unable to conjure it into the possession of another, and withheld from burying it out of sight forever, my jacket stuck to me like the fatal shirt on Nessus.

Chapter 48

PURSER, PURSER'S STEWARD, AND POSTMASTER
IN A MAN-OF-WAR

As THE PURSER'S STEWARD so conspicuously figured at the
unsuccessful auction of my jacket, it reminds me of how
important a personage that official is on board of all men-of-
war. He is the right-hand man and confidential deputy and
clerk of the Purser, who intrusts to him all his accounts with
the crew, while, in most cases, he himself, snug and comfortable in his state-room, glances over a file of newspapers instead of overhauling his ledgers.

Of all the non-combatants of a man-of-war, the Purser, perhaps, stands foremost in importance. Though he is but a
member of the gun-room mess, yet usage seems to assign him
a conventional station somewhat above that of his equals in
navy rank—the Chaplain, Surgeon, and Professor. Moreover,
he is frequently to be seen in close conversation with the
Commodore, who, in the Neversink, was more than once
known to be slightly jocular with our Purser. Upon several
occasions, also, he was called into the Commodore's cabin,
and remained closeted there for several minutes together. Nor
do I remember that there ever happened a cabinet meeting of
the ward-room barons, the Lieutenants, in the Commodore's
cabin, but the Purser made one of the party. Doubtless the
important fact of the Purser having under his charge all the
financial affairs of a man-of-war, imparts to him the great importance he enjoys. Indeed, we find in every government—
monarchies and republics alike—that the personage at the
head of the finances invariably occupies a commanding position. Thus, in point of station, the Secretary of the Treasury
of the United States is deemed superior to the other heads of
departments. Also, in England, the real office held by the
great Premier himself is—as every one knows—that of First
Lord of the Treasury.

Now, under this high functionary of state, the official
known as the Purser's Steward was head clerk of the frigate's

fiscal affairs. Upon the berth-deck he had a regular counting-room, full of ledgers, journals, and day-books. His desk was as much littered with papers as any Pearl Street merchant's, and much time was devoted to his accounts. For hours together you would see him, through the window of his subterranean office, writing by the light of his perpetual lamp.

Ex-officio, the Purser's Steward of most ships is a sort of Postmaster, and his office the Post-office. When the letter-bags for the squadron—almost as large as those of the United States mail—arrived on board the Neversink, it was the Purser's Steward that sat at his little window on the berth-deck and handed you your letter or paper—if any there were to your address. Some disappointed applicants among the sailors would offer to buy the epistles of their more fortunate shipmates, while yet the seal was unbroken—maintaining that the sole and confidential reading of a fond, long, domestic letter from any man's home, was far better than no letter at all.

In the vicinity of the office of the Purser's Steward are the principal store-rooms of the Purser, where large quantities of goods of every description are to be found. On board of those ships where goods are permitted to be served out to the crew for the purpose of selling them ashore, to raise money, more business is transacted at the office of a Purser's Steward in one *Liberty-day* morning than all the dry goods shops in a considerable village would transact in a week.

Once a month, with undeviating regularity, this official has his hands more than usually full. For, once a month, certain printed bills, called Mess-bills, are circulated among the crew, and whatever you may want from the Purser—be it tobacco, soap, duck, dungeree, needles, thread, knives, belts, calico, ribbon, pipes, paper, pens, hats, ink, shoes, socks, or whatever it may be—down it goes on the mess-bill, which, being the next day returned to the office of the Steward, the "slops," as they are called, are served out to the men and charged to their accounts.

Lucky is it for man-of-war's-men that the outrageous impositions to which, but a very few years ago, they were subjected from the abuses in this department of the service, and the unscrupulous cupidity of many of the Pursers—lucky is it for them that *now* these things are in a great degree done away. The Pursers, instead of being at liberty to make almost what they pleased from the sale of their wares, are now paid by regular stipends laid down by law.

Under the exploded system, the profits of some of these officers were almost incredible. In one cruise up the Mediterranean, the Purser of an American line-of-battle ship was, on good authority, said to have cleared the sum of $50,000. Upon that he quitted the service, and retired into the country. Shortly after, his three daughters—not very lovely—married extremely well.

The ideas that sailors entertain of Pursers is expressed in a rather inelegant but expressive saying of theirs: "The Purser is a conjuror; he can make a dead man chew tobacco"—insinuating that the accounts of a dead man are sometimes subjected to post-mortem charges. Among sailors, also, Pursers commonly go by the name of *nip-cheeses*.

No wonder that on board of the old frigate Java, upon her return from a cruise extending over a period of more than four years, one thousand dollars paid off eighty of her crew, though the aggregate wages of the eighty for the voyage must have amounted to about sixty thousand dollars. Even under the present system, the Purser of a line-of-battle ship, for instance, is far better paid than any other officer, short of Captain or Commodore. While the Lieutenant commonly receives but eighteen hundred dollars, the Surgeon of the fleet but fifteen hundred, the Chaplain twelve hundred, the Purser of a line-of-battle ship receives thirty-five hundred dollars. In considering his salary, however, his responsibilities are not to be overlooked; they are by no means insignificant.

There are Pursers in the Navy whom the sailors exempt from the insinuations above mentioned, nor, as a class, are they so obnoxious to them now as formerly; for one, the florid old Purser of the Neversink—never coming into disciplinary contact with the seamen, and being withal a jovial and apparently good-hearted gentleman—was something of a favorite with many of the crew.

Chapter 49

Rumors of a War, and how they were received by the Population of the Neversink

WHILE LYING in the harbor of Callao, in Peru, certain rumors had come to us touching a war with England, growing out of the long-vexed Northeastern Boundary Question. In Rio these rumors were increased; and the probability of hostilities induced our Commodore to authorize proceedings that closely brought home to every man on board the Neversink his liability at any time to be killed at his gun.

Among other things, a number of men were detailed to pass up the rusty cannon-balls from the shot-lockers in the hold, and scrape them clean for service. The Commodore was a very neat gentleman, and would not fire a dirty shot into his foe.

It was an interesting occasion for a tranquil observer; nor was it altogether neglected. Not to recite the precise remarks made by the seamen while pitching the shot up the hatchway from hand to hand, like schoolboys playing ball ashore, it will be enough to say that, from the general drift of their discourse—jocular as it was—it was manifest that, almost to a man, they abhorred the idea of going into action.

And why should they desire a war? Would their wages be raised? Not a cent. The prize-money, though, ought to have been an inducement. But of all the "rewards of virtue," prize-money is the most uncertain; and this the man-of-war's-man knows. What, then, has he to expect from war? What but harder work, and harder usage than in peace; a wooden leg or arm; mortal wounds, and death? Enough, however, that by far the majority of the common sailors of the Neversink were plainly concerned at the prospect of war, and were plainly averse to it.

But with the officers of the quarter-deck it was just the reverse. None of them, to be sure, in my hearing at least, verbally expressed their gratification; but it was unavoidably betrayed by the increased cheerfulness of their demeanor toward each other, their frequent fraternal conferences, and their unwonted animation for several days in issuing their orders. The voice of Mad Jack—always a belfry to hear—now resounded like that famous bell of England, Great Tom of Oxford. As for Selvagee, he wore his sword with a jaunty air, and his servant daily polished the blade.

But why this contrast between the forecastle and the quarter-deck, between the man-of-war's-man and his officer? Because, though war would equally jeopardize the lives of both, yet, while it held out to the sailor no promise of promotion, and what is called *glory*, these things fired the breast of his officers.

It is no pleasing task, nor a thankful one, to dive into the souls of some men; but there are occasions when, to bring up the mud from the bottom, reveals to us on what soundings we are, on what coast we adjoin.

How were these officers to gain glory? How but by a distinguished slaughtering of their fellow-men. How were they to be promoted? How but over the buried heads of killed comrades and mess-mates.

This hostile contrast between the feelings with which the common seamen and the officers of the Neversink looked forward to this more than possible war, is one of many instances that might be quoted to show the antagonism of their interests, the incurable antagonism in which they dwell. But can men, whose interests are diverse, ever hope to live together in a harmony uncoerced? Can the brotherhood of the race of mankind ever hope to prevail in a man-of-war, where one man's bane is almost another's blessing? By abolishing the scourge, shall we do away tyranny; *that* tyranny which must ever prevail, where of two essentially antagonist classes in perpetual contact, one is immeasurably the stronger? Surely it seems all but impossible. And as the very object of a man-of-war, as its name implies, is to fight the very battles so naturally averse to the seamen; so long as a man-of-war exists, it must ever remain a picture of much that is tyrannical and repelling in human nature.

Being an establishment much more extensive than the American Navy, the English armed marine furnishes a yet more striking example of this thing, especially as the existence of war produces so vast an augmentation of her naval force compared with what it is in time of peace. It is well known what joy the news of Bonaparte's sudden return from Elba created among crowds of British naval officers, who had previously been expecting to be sent ashore on half-pay. Thus, when all the world wailed, these officers found occasion for thanksgiving. I urge it not against them as *men*—their feelings belonged to their profession. Had they not been naval officers, they had not been rejoicers in the midst of despair.

When shall the time come, how much longer will God postpone it, when the clouds, which at times gather over the horizons of nations, shall not be hailed by any class of humanity, and invoked to burst as a bomb? Standing navies, as well as standing armies, serve to keep alive the spirit of war even in the meek heart of peace. In its very embers and smoulderings, they nourish that fatal fire, and half-pay officers, as the priests of Mars, yet guard the temple, though no god be there.

Chapter 50

THE BAY OF ALL BEAUTIES

I HAVE SAID that I must pass over Rio without a description; but just now such a flood of scented reminiscences steals over me, that I must needs yield and recant, as I inhale that musky air.

More than one hundred and fifty miles' circuit of living green hills imbosoms a translucent expanse, so gemmed in by sierras of grass, that among the Indian tribes the place was known as "The Hidden Water." On all sides, in the distance, rise high conical peaks, which at sunrise and sunset burn like vast tapers; and down from the interior, through vineyards and forests, flow radiating streams, all emptying into the harbor.

Talk not of Bahia de Todos os Santos—the Bay of All Saints; for though that be a glorious haven, yet Rio is the Bay of all Rivers—the Bay of all Delights—the Bay of all Beauties. From circumjacent hill-sides, untiring summer hangs perpetually in terraces of vivid verdure; and, embossed with old mosses, convent and castle nestle in valley and glen.

All round, deep inlets run into the green mountain land, and, overhung with wild Highlands, more resemble Loch Katrines than Lake Lemans. And though Loch Katrine has been sung by the bonneted Scott, and Lake Leman by the coroneted Byron; yet here, in Rio, both the loch and the lake are but two wild flowers in a prospect that is almost unlimited. For, behold! far away and away, stretches the broad blue of the water, to yonder soft-swelling hills of light green, backed by the purple pinnacles and pipes of the grand Organ Mountains; fitly so called, for in thunder-time they roll cannonades down the bay, drowning the blended bass of all the cathedrals in Rio. Shout amain, exalt your voices, stamp your feet, jubilate, Organ Mountains! and roll your Te Deums round the world!

What though, for more than five thousand five hundred years, this grand harbor of Rio lay hid in the hills, unknown by the Catholic Portuguese? Centuries ere Haydn performed before emperors and kings, these Organ Mountains played his Oratorio of the Creation, before the Creator himself. But nervous Haydn could not have endured that cannonading choir, since this composer of thunder-bolts himself died at last through the crashing commotion of Napoleon's bombardment of Vienna.

But all mountains are Organ Mountains: the Alps and the Himmelahs; the Appalachian Chain, the Ural, the Andes, the Green Hills and the White. All of them play anthems forever: The Messiah, and Samson, and Israel in Egypt, and Saul, and Judas Maccabeus, and Solomon.

Archipelago Rio! ere Noah on old Ararat anchored his ark, there lay anchored in you all these green, rocky isles I now see. But God did not build on you, isles! those long lines of batteries; nor did our blessed Savior stand godfather at the christening of yon frowning fortress of Santa Cruz, though named in honor of himself, the divine Prince of Peace!

Amphitheatrical Rio! in your broad expanse might be held the Resurrection and Judgment-day of the whole world's men-of-war, represented by the flag-ships of fleets—the flag-ships of the Phœnician armed galleys of Tyre and Sidon; of King Solomon's annual squadrons that sailed to Ophir; whence in after times, perhaps, sailed the Acapulco fleets of the Spaniards, with golden ingots for ballasting; the flag-ships of all the Greek and Persian craft that exchanged the war-hug at Salamis; of all the Roman and Egyptian galleys that, eagle-like, with blood-dripping prows, beaked each other at Actium; of all the Danish keels of the Vikings; of all the musquito craft of Abba Thule, king of the Pelews, when he went to vanquish Artingall; of all the Venetian, Genoese, and Papal fleets that came to the shock at Lepanto; of both horns of the crescent of the Spanish Armada; of the Portuguese squadron that, under the gallant Gama, chastised the Moors, and discovered the Moluccas; of all the Dutch navies led by Van Tromp, and sunk by Admiral Hawke; of the forty-seven French and Spanish sail-of-the-line that, for three months, essayed to batter down Gibraltar; of all Nelson's seventy-fours that thunder-bolted off St. Vincent's, at the Nile, Copenhagen, and Trafalgar; of all the frigate-merchantmen of the

East India Company; of Perry's war-brigs, sloops, and schooners that scattered the British armament on Lake Erie; of all the Barbary corsairs captured by Bainbridge; of the war-canoes of the Polynesian kings, Tammahammaha and Pomare —ay! one and all, with Commodore Noah for their Lord High Admiral—in this abounding Bay of Rio these flag-ships might all come to anchor, and swing round in concert to the first of the flood.

Rio is a small Mediterranean; and what was fabled of the entrance to that sea, in Rio is partly made true; for here, at the mouth, stands one of Hercules' Pillars, the Sugar-Loaf Mountain, one thousand feet high, inclining over a little, like the Leaning Tower of Pisa. At its base crouch, like mastiffs, the batteries of Jose and Theodosia; while opposite, you are menaced by a rock-founded fort.

The channel between—the sole inlet to the bay—seems but a biscuit's toss over; you see naught of the land-locked sea within till fairly in the strait. But, then, what a sight is beheld! Diversified as the harbor of Constantinople, but a thousand-fold grander. When the Neversink swept in, word was passed, "Aloft, top-men! and furl the t'-gallant-sails and royals!"

At the sound I sprang into the rigging, and was soon at my perch. How I hung over that main-royal-yard in a rapture! High in air, poised over that magnificent bay, a new world to my ravished eyes, I felt like the foremost of a flight of angels, new-lighted upon earth, from some star in the Milky Way.

Chapter 51

One of "the People" has an Audience with the Commodore and the Captain on the Quarter-deck

WE HAD NOT lain in Rio long, when in the innermost recesses of the mighty soul of my noble Captain of the Top—incomparable Jack Chase—the deliberate opinion was formed, and rock-founded, that our ship's company must have at least one day's "*liberty*" to go ashore ere we weighed anchor for home.

Here it must be mentioned that, concerning any thing of this kind, no sailor in a man-of-war ever presumes to be an agitator, unless he is of a rank superior to a mere able-seaman; and no one short of a petty officer—that is, a captain of the top, a quarter-gunner, or boatswain's mate—ever dreams of being a spokesman to the supreme authority of the vessel in soliciting any kind of favor for himself and shipmates.

After canvassing the matter thoroughly with several old quarter-masters and other dignified sea-fencibles, Jack, hat in hand, made his appearance, one fine evening, at the mast, and, waiting till Captain Claret drew nigh, bowed, and addressed him in his own off-hand, polished, and poetical style. In his intercourse with the quarter-deck, he always presumed upon his being such a universal favorite.

"Sir, this Rio is a charming harbor, and we poor mariners—your trusty sea-warriors, valiant Captain! who, with *you* at their head, would board the Rock of Gibraltar itself, and carry it by storm—we poor fellows, valiant Captain! have gazed round upon this ravishing landscape till we can gaze no more. Will Captain Claret vouchsafe one day's liberty, and so assure himself of eternal felicity, since, in our flowing cups, he will be ever after freshly remembered?"

As Jack thus rounded off with a snatch from Shakspeare, he saluted the Captain with a gallant flourish of his tarpaulin, and then, bringing the rim to his mouth, with his head bowed, and his body thrown into a fine negligent attitude, stood a picture of eloquent but passive appeal. He seemed to say, Magnanimous Captain Claret, we fine fellows, and hearts of oak, throw ourselves upon your unparalleled goodness.

"And what do you want to go ashore for?" asked the Captain, evasively, and trying to conceal his admiration of Jack by affecting some haughtiness.

"Ah! sir," sighed Jack, "why do the thirsty camels of the desert desire to lap the waters of the fountain and roll in the green grass of the oasis? Are we not but just from the ocean Sahara? and is not this Rio a verdant spot, noble Captain? Surely you will not keep us always tethered at anchor, when a little more cable would admit of our cropping the herbage! And it is a weary thing, Captain Claret, to be imprisoned month after month on the gun-deck, without so much as smelling a citron. Ah! Captain Claret, what sings sweet Waller:

> 'But who can always on the billows lie?
> The watery wilderness yields no supply.'

Compared with such a prisoner, noble Captain,

> 'Happy, thrice happy, who, in battle slain,
> Press'd in Atrides' cause the Trojan plain!'

Pope's version, sir, not the original Greek."

And so saying, Jack once more brought his hat-rim to his mouth, and slightly bending forward, stood mute.

At this juncture the Most Serene Commodore himself happened to emerge from the after-gangway, his gilded buttons, epaulets, and the gold lace on his chapeau glittering in the flooding sunset. Attracted by the scene between Captain Claret and so well-known and admired a commoner as Jack Chase, he approached, and assuming for the moment an air of pleasant condescension—never shown to his noble barons the officers of the ward-room—he said, with a smile, "Well, Jack, you and your shipmates are after some favor, I suppose—a day's liberty, is it not?"

Whether it was the horizontal setting sun, streaming along the deck, that blinded Jack, or whether it was in sun-worshipping homage of the mighty Commodore, there is no telling;

but just at this juncture noble Jack was standing reverentially holding his hat to his brow, like a man with weak eyes.

"Valiant Commodore," said he, at last, "this audience is indeed an honor undeserved. I almost sink beneath it. Yes, valiant Commodore, your sagacious mind has truly divined our object. Liberty, sir; liberty is, indeed, our humble prayer. I trust your honorable wound, received in glorious battle, valiant Commodore, pains you less to-day than common."

"Ah! cunning Jack!" cried the Commodore, by no means blind to the bold sortie of his flattery, but not at all displeased with it. In more respects than one, our Commodore's wound was his weak side.

"I think we must give them liberty," he added, turning to Captain Claret; who thereupon, waving Jack further off, fell into confidential discourse with his superior.

"Well, Jack, we will see about it," at last cried the Commodore, advancing. "I think we must let you go."

"To your duty, captain of the main-top!" said the Captain, rather stiffly. He wished to neutralize somewhat the effect of the Commodore's condescension. Besides, he had much rather the Commodore had been in his cabin. His presence, for the time, affected his own supremacy in his ship. But Jack was noways cast down by the Captain's coldness; he felt safe enough; so he proceeded to offer his acknowledgments.

" 'Kind gentlemen,' " he sighed, " 'your pains are registered where every day I turn the leaf to read'—Macbeth, valiant Commodore and Captain!—what the Thane says to the noble lords, Rosse and Angus."

And long and lingeringly bowing to the two noble officers, Jack backed away from their presence, still shading his eyes with the broad rim of his hat.

"Jack Chase forever!" cried his shipmates, as he carried the grateful news of liberty to them on the forecastle. "Who can talk to Commodores like our matchless Jack!"

Chapter 52

IT WAS THE NEXT MORNING after matchless Jack's interview with the Commodore and Captain, that a little incident occurred, soon forgotten by the crew at large, but long remembered by the few seamen who were in the habit of closely scrutinizing every-day proceedings. Upon the face of it, it was but a common event—at least in a man-of-war—the flogging of a man at the gangway. But the under-current of circumstances in the case were of a nature that magnified this particular flogging into a matter of no small importance. The story itself can not here be related; it would not well bear recital: enough that the person flogged was a middle-aged man of the Waist—a forlorn, broken-down, miserable object, truly; one of those wretched landsmen sometimes driven into the Navy by their unfitness for all things else, even as others are driven into the work-house. He was flogged at the complaint of a midshipman; and hereby hangs the drift of the thing. For though this waister was so ignoble a mortal, yet his being scourged on this one occasion indirectly proceeded from the mere wanton spite and unscrupulousness of the midshipman in question—a youth, who was apt to indulge at times in undignified familiarities with some of the men, who, sooner or later, almost always suffered from his capricious preferences.

But the leading principle that was involved in this affair is far too mischievous to be lightly dismissed.

In most cases, it would seem to be a cardinal principle with a Navy Captain that his subordinates are disintegrated parts of himself, detached from the main body on special service, and that the order of the minutest midshipman must be as deferentially obeyed by the seamen as if proceeding from the Commodore on the poop. This principle was once emphasized in a remarkable manner by the valiant and handsome Sir Peter Parker, upon whose death, on a national arson expedition on the shores of Chesapeake Bay, in 1812 or 1813, Lord

Byron wrote his well-known stanzas. "By the god of war!" said Sir Peter to his sailors, "I'll make you touch your hat to a midshipman's coat, if it's only hung on a broomstick to dry!"

That the king, in the eye of the law, can do no wrong, is the well-known fiction of despotic states; but it has remained for the navies of Constitutional Monarchies and Republics to magnify this fiction, by indirectly extending it to all the quarter-deck subordinates of an armed ship's chief magistrate. And though judicially unrecognized, and unacknowledged by the officers themselves, yet this is the principle that pervades the fleet; this is the principle that is every hour acted upon, and to sustain which, thousands of seamen have been flogged at the gangway.

However childish, ignorant, stupid, or idiotic a midshipman, if he but orders a sailor to perform even the most absurd action, that man is not only bound to render instant and unanswering obedience, but he would refuse at his peril. And if, having obeyed, he should then complain to the Captain, and the Captain, in his own mind, should be thoroughly convinced of the impropriety, perhaps of the illegality of the order, yet, in nine cases out of ten, he would not publicly reprimand the midshipman, nor by the slightest token admit before the complainant that, in this particular thing, the midshipman had done otherwise than perfectly right.

Upon a midshipman's complaining of a seaman to Lord Collingwood, when Captain of a line-of-battle ship, he ordered the man for punishment; and, in the interval, calling the midshipman aside, said to him, "In all probability, now, the fault is yours—you know; therefore, when the man is brought to the mast, you had better ask for his pardon."

Accordingly, upon the lad's public intercession, Collingwood, turning to the culprit, said, "This young gentleman has pleaded so humanely for you, that, in the hope you feel a due gratitude to him for his benevolence, I will, for this time, overlook your offence." This story is related by the editor of the Admiral's "Correspondence," to show the Admiral's kindheartedness.

Now Collingwood was, in reality, one of the most just, humane, and benevolent admirals that ever hoisted a flag. For a sea-officer, Collingwood was a man in a million. But if a man like him, swayed by old usages, could thus violate the commonest principle of justice—with however good motives at bottom—what must be expected from other Captains not so eminently gifted with noble traits as Collingwood?

And if the corps of American midshipmen is mostly replenished from the nursery, the counter, and the lap of unrestrained indulgence at home; and if most of them at least, by their impotency as officers, in all important functions at sea, by their boyish and overweening conceit of their gold lace, by their overbearing manner toward the seamen, and by their peculiar aptitude to construe the merest trivialities of manner into set affronts against their dignity; if by all this they sometimes contract the ill-will of the seamen; and if, in a thousand ways, the seamen can not but betray it—how easy for any of these midshipmen, who may happen to be unrestrained by moral principle, to resort to spiteful practices in procuring vengeance upon the offenders, in many instances to the extremity of the lash; since, as we have seen, the tacit principle in the Navy seems to be that, in his ordinary intercourse with the sailors, a midshipman can do nothing obnoxious to the public censure of his superiors.

"You fellow, I'll get you *licked* before long," is often heard from a midshipman to a sailor who, in some way not open to the judicial action of the Captain, has chanced to offend him.

At times you will see one of these lads, not five feet high, gazing up with inflamed eye at some venerable six-footer of a forecastle-man, cursing and insulting him by every epithet deemed most scandalous and unendurable among men. Yet that man's indignant tongue is treble-knotted by the law, that suspends death itself over his head should his passion discharge the slightest blow at the boy-worm that spits at his feet.

But since what human nature is, and what it must forever continue to be, is well enough understood for most practical purposes, it needs no special example to prove that, where the merest boys, indiscriminately snatched from the human family, are given such authority over mature men, the results must be proportionable in monstrousness to the custom that authorizes this worse than cruel absurdity.

Nor is it unworthy of remark that, while the noblest-minded and most heroic sea-officers—men of the topmost stature, including Lord Nelson himself—have regarded flogging in the Navy with the deepest concern, and not without weighty scruples touching its general necessity, still, one who has seen much of midshipmen can truly say that he has seen but few midshipmen who were not enthusiastic advocates and admirers of scourging. It would almost seem that they themselves, having so recently escaped the posterior discipline of the nursery and the infant school, are impatient to recover from those smarting reminiscences by mincing the backs of full-grown American freemen.

It should not be omitted here, that the midshipmen in the English Navy are not permitted to be quite so imperious as in the American ships. They are divided into three (I think) probationary classes of "volunteers," instead of being at once advanced to a warrant. Nor will you fail to remark, when you see an English cutter officered by one of these volunteers, that the boy does not so strut and slap his dirk-hilt with a Bobadil air, and anticipatingly feel of the place where his warlike whiskers are going to be, and sputter out oaths so at the men, as is too often the case with the little boys wearing best-bower anchors on their lapels in the American Navy.

Yet it must be confessed that at times you see midshipmen who are noble little fellows, and not at all disliked by the crew. Besides three gallant youths, one black-eyed little lad in particular, in the Neversink, was such a one. From his diminutiveness, he went by the name of *Boat Plug* among the seamen. Without being exactly familiar with them, he had yet become a general favorite, by reason of his kindness of manner, and never cursing them. It was amusing to hear some of the older Tritons invoke blessings upon the youngster, when his kind tones fell on their weather-beaten ears. "Ah, good luck to you, sir!" touching their hats to the little man; "you have a soul to be saved, sir!" There was a wonderful deal of meaning involved in the latter sentence. *You have a soul to be saved*, is the phrase which a man-of-war's-man peculiarly applies to a humane and kind-hearted officer. It also implies that the majority of quarter-deck officers are regarded by them in such a light that they deny to them the possession of souls.

Ah! but these plebeians sometimes have a sublime vengeance upon patricians. Imagine an outcast old sailor seriously cherishing the purely speculative conceit that some bully in epaulets, who orders him to and fro like a slave, is of an organization immeasurably inferior to himself; must at last perish with the brutes, while he goes to his immortality in heaven.

But from what has been said in this chapter, it must not be inferred that a midshipman leads a lord's life in a man-of-war. Far from it. He lords it over those below him, while lorded over himself by his superiors. It is as if with one hand a school-boy snapped his fingers at a dog, and at the same time received upon the other the discipline of the usher's ferule. And though, by the American Articles of War, a Navy Captain can not, of his own authority, legally punish a midshipman, otherwise than by suspension from duty (the same as with respect to the Ward-room officers), yet this is one of those sea-statutes which the Captain, to a certain extent, observes or disregards at his pleasure. Many instances might be related of the petty mortifications and official insults inflicted by some Captains upon their midshipmen; far more severe, in one sense, than the old-fashioned punishment of sending them to the mast-head, though not so arbitrary as sending them before the mast, to do duty with the common sailors— a custom, in former times, pursued by Captains in the English Navy.

Captain Claret himself had no special fondness for midshipmen. A tall, overgrown young midshipman, about sixteen years old, having fallen under his displeasure, he interrupted the humble apologies he was making, by saying, "Not a word, sir! I'll not hear a word! Mount the netting, sir, and stand there till you are ordered to come down!"

The midshipman obeyed; and, in full sight of the entire ship's company, Captain Claret promenaded to and fro below his lofty perch, reading him a most aggravating lecture upon his alleged misconduct. To a lad of sensibility, such treatment must have been almost as stinging as the lash itself would have been.

In another case a midshipman attempted to carry the day by speaking up to his superior; but in a most unexpected manner he paid the penalty of his indiscretion.

Seeing a reefer's hammock in the quarter-netting, and observing it to be rather equivocally discolored, the Captain demanded to know what particular midshipman was the proprietor of that hammock. When the lad appeared, he said to him, "What do you call that, sir?" pointing at the discoloration.

"Captain Claret," said the unabashed reefer, looking him full in the eye, "you know what that is, sir, as well as I do."

"So I do, sir. Quarter-master! pitch that hammock overboard."

The midshipman started, and, hurrying up to it, turned round, and said, "Captain Claret, I have a purse lashed up here; it's the only safe way I can keep it."

"Did you hear me, quarter-master?" said the Captain; and overboard went the hammock and purse.

The same afternoon, this midshipman reported his *cot-boy* as having neglected to scrub this identical hammock, though repeatedly ordered to do so by his master. Though called a cot-*boy*, the person thus designated happened to be, in fact, a full-grown man. The case being fully laid before the Captain at the mast, and the midshipman's charge having been heard, this cot-boy, spite of his protestations, and altogether through the midshipman's instrumentality, was condemned to a flogging.

Thus it will be seen, that though the Captain permits himself to domineer over a midshipman, and, in cases of personal contact with him, does not scruple to pronounce him an egregious wrong-doer, and treats him accordingly; yet, in *other* cases, involving the immediate relationship between the midshipman and the sailor, he still sustains the principle that a midshipman can neither say nor do any wrong.

It is to be remembered that, wherever these chapters treat of midshipmen, the officers known as passed-midshipmen are not at all referred to. In the American Navy, these officers form a class of young men, who, having seen sufficient service at sea as midshipmen to pass an examination before a Board of Commodores, are promoted to the rank of passed-midshipmen, introductory to that of lieutenant. They are supposed to be qualified to do duty as lieutenants, and in some cases temporarily serve as such. The difference between a passed-midshipman and a midshipman may be also inferred from their respective rates of pay. The former, upon sea-service, receives $750 a year; the latter, $400. There were no passed-midshipmen in the Neversink.

Chapter 53

SEA-FARING PERSONS PECULIARLY SUBJECT TO BEING
UNDER THE WEATHER • THE EFFECTS OF THIS
UPON A MAN-OF-WAR CAPTAIN

IT HAS BEEN SAID that some midshipmen, in certain cases, are guilty of spiteful practices against the man-of-war's-man. But as these midshipmen are presumed to have received the liberal and lofty breeding of gentlemen, it would seem all but incredible that any of their corps could descend to the paltriness of cherishing personal malice against so convention-ally degraded a being as a sailor. So, indeed, it would seem. But when all the circumstances are considered, it will not ap-pear extraordinary that some of them should thus cast dis-credit upon the warrants they wear. Title, and rank, and wealth, and education can not unmake human nature; the same in cabin-boy and commodore, its only differences lie in the different modes of development.

At sea, a frigate houses and homes five hundred mortals in a space so contracted that they can hardly so much as move but they touch. Cut off from all those outward passing things which ashore employ the eyes, tongues, and thoughts of landsmen, the inmates of a frigate are thrown upon them-selves and each other, and all their ponderings are introspec-tive. A morbidness of mind is often the consequence, especially upon long voyages, accompanied by foul weather, calms, or head-winds. Nor does this exempt from its evil in-fluence any rank on board. Indeed, high station only minis-ters to it the more, since the higher the rank in a man-of-war, the less companionship.

It is an odious, unthankful, repugnant thing to dwell upon a subject like this; nevertheless, be it said, that, through these jaundiced influences, even the captain of a frigate is, in some cases, indirectly induced to the infliction of corporal punish-ment upon a seaman. Never sail under a navy captain whom you suspect of being dyspeptic, or constitutionally prone to hypochondria.

The manifestation of these things is sometimes remarkable. In the earlier part of the cruise, while making a long, tedious run from Mazatlan to Callao on the Main, baffled by light head winds and frequent intermitting calms, when all hands were heartily wearied by the torrid, monotonous sea, a good-natured fore-top-man, by the name of Candy—quite a character in his way—standing in the waist among a crowd of seamen, touched me, and said, "D'ye see the old man there, White-Jacket, walking the poop? Well, don't he look as if he wanted to flog some one? Look at him once."

But to me, at least, no such indications were visible in the deportment of the Captain, though his thrashing the arm-chest with the slack of the spanker-out-haul looked a little suspicious. But any one might have been doing that to pass away a calm.

"Depend on it," said the top-man, "he must somehow have thought I was making sport of *him* a while ago, when I was only taking off old Priming, the gunner's mate. Just look at him once, White-Jacket, while I make believe coil this here rope; if there arn't a dozen in that 'ere Captain's top-lights, my name is *horse-marine*. If I could only touch my tile to him now, and take my Bible oath on it, that I was only taking off Priming, and not *him*, he wouldn't have such hard thoughts of me. But that can't be done; he'd think I meant to insult him. Well, it can't be helped; I suppose I must look out for a baker's dozen afore long."

I had an incredulous laugh at this. But two days afterward, when we were hoisting the main-top-mast stun'-sail, and the Lieutenant of the Watch was reprimanding the crowd of seamen at the halyards for their laziness—for the sail was but just crawling up to its place, owing to the languor of the men, induced by the heat—the Captain, who had been impatiently walking the deck, suddenly stopped short, and darting his eyes among the seamen, suddenly fixed them, crying out, "You, Candy, and be damned to you, you don't pull an ounce, you blackguard! Stand up to that gun, sir; I'll teach you to be grinning over a rope that way, without lending your pound of beef to it. Boatswain's mate, where's your *colt*? Give that man a dozen."

Removing his hat, the boatswain's mate looked into the

crown aghast; the coiled rope, usually worn there, was not to be found; but the next instant it slid from the top of his head to the deck. Picking it up, and straightening it out, he advanced toward the sailor.

"Sir," said Candy, touching and retouching his cap to the Captain, "I was pulling, sir, as much as the rest, sir; I was, indeed, sir."

"Stand up to that gun," cried the Captain. "Boatswain's mate, do your duty."

Three stripes were given, when the Captain raised his finger. "You———,* do you dare stand up to be flogged with your hat on! Take it off, sir, instantly."

Candy dropped it on deck.

"Now go on, boatswain's mate." And the sailor received his dozen.

With his hand to his back he came up to me, where I stood among the by-standers, saying, "O Lord, O Lord! that boatswain's mate, too, had a spite agin me; he always thought it was *me* that set afloat that yarn about his wife in Norfolk. O Lord! just run your hand under my shirt, will you, White-Jacket? There! didn't he have a spite agin me, to raise such bars as them? And my shirt all cut to pieces, too—arn't it, White-Jacket? Damn me, but these coltings puts the tin in the Purser's pocket. O Lord! my back feels as if there was a red-hot gridiron lashed to it. But I told you so—a widow's curse on him, say I—he thought I meant *him*, and not Priming."

*The phrase here used I have never seen either written or printed, and should not like to be the first person to introduce it to the public.

Chapter 54

Whenever, in intervals of mild benevolence, or yielding to mere politic dictates, Kings and Commodores relax the yoke of servitude, they should see to it well that the concession seem not too sudden or unqualified; for, in the commoner's estimation, that might argue feebleness or fear.

Hence it was, perhaps, that, though noble Jack had carried the day captive in his audience at the mast, yet more than thirty-six hours elapsed ere any thing official was heard of the "liberty" his shipmates so earnestly coveted. Some of the people began to growl and grumble.

"It's turned out all gammon, Jack," said one.

"Blast the Commodore!" cried another, "he bamboozled you, Jack."

"Lay on your oars a while," answered Jack, "and we shall see; we've struck for liberty, and liberty we'll have! I'm your tribune, boys; I'm your Rienzi. The Commodore must keep his word."

Next day, about breakfast-time, a mighty whistling and piping was heard at the main-hatchway, and presently the boatswain's voice was heard: "D'ye hear there, fore and aft! all you starboard-quarter watch! get ready to go ashore on liberty!"

In a paroxysm of delight, a young mizzen-top-man, standing by at the time, whipped the tarpaulin from his head, and smashed it like a pancake on the deck. "Liberty!" he shouted, leaping down into the berth-deck after his bag.

At the appointed hour, the quarter-watch mustered round the capstan, at which stood our old First Lord of the Treasury and Pay-Master-General, the Purser, with several goodly buck-skin bags of dollars, piled up on the capstan. He helped us all round to half a handful or so, and then the boats were manned, and, like so many Esterhazys, we were pulled ashore

by our shipmates. All their lives lords may live in listless state;
but give the commoners a holiday, and they out-lord the
Commodore himself.

The ship's company were divided into four sections or
quarter-watches, only one of which were on shore at a time,
the rest remaining to garrison the frigate—the term of liberty
for each being twenty-four hours.

With Jack Chase and a few other discreet and gentlemanly
top-men, I went ashore on the first day, with the first quarter-
watch. Our own little party had a charming time; we saw
many fine sights; fell in—as all sailors must—with dashing
adventures. But, though not a few good chapters might be
written on this head, I must again forebear; for in this book
I have nothing to do with the shore further than to glance at
it, now and then, from the water; my man-of-war world alone
must supply me with the staple of my matter; I have taken an
oath to keep afloat to the last letter of my narrative.

Had they all been as punctual as Jack Chase's party, the
whole quarter-watch of liberty-men had been safe on board
the frigate at the expiration of the twenty-four hours. But this
was not the case; and during the entire day succeeding, the
midshipmen and others were engaged in ferreting them out
of their hiding-places on shore, and bringing them off in scattered detachments to the ship.

They came in all imaginable stages of intoxication; some
with blackened eyes and broken heads; some still more severely injured, having been stabbed in frays with the Portuguese soldiers. Others, unharmed, were immediately dropped
on the gun-deck, between the guns, where they lay snoring
for the rest of the day. As a considerable degree of license is
invariably permitted to man-of-war's-men just "off liberty,"
and as man-of-war's-men well know this to be the case, they
occasionally avail themselves of the privilege to talk very
frankly to the officers when they first cross the gangway,
taking care, meanwhile, to reel about very industriously, so
that there shall be no doubt about their being seriously intoxicated, and altogether *non compos* for the time. And though
but few of them have cause to feign intoxication, yet some
individuals may be suspected of enacting a studied part upon
these occasions. Indeed—judging by certain symptoms—

even when really inebriated, some of the sailors must have previously determined upon their conduct; just as some persons who, before taking the exhilarating gas, secretly make up their minds to perform certain mad feats while under its influence, which feats consequently come to pass precisely as if the actors were not accountable for them.

For several days, while the other quarter-watches were given liberty, the Neversink presented a sad scene. She was more like a mad-house than a frigate; the gun-deck resounded with frantic fights, shouts, and songs. All visitors from shore were kept at a cable's length.

These scenes, however, are nothing to those which have repeatedly been enacted in American men-of-war upon other stations. But the custom of introducing women on board, in harbor, is now pretty much discontinued, both in the English and American Navy, unless a ship, commanded by some dissolute Captain, happens to lie in some far away, outlandish port, in the Pacific or Indian Ocean.

The British line-of-battle ship, Royal George, which in 1782 sunk at her anchors at Spithead, carried down three hundred English women among the one thousand souls that were drowned on that memorable morning.

When, at last, after all the mad tumult and contention of "Liberty," the reaction came, our frigate presented a very different scene. The men looked jaded and wan, lethargic and lazy; and many an old mariner, with hand upon abdomen, called upon the Flag-staff to witness that there were more *hot coppers* in the Neversink than those in the ship's galley.

Such are the lamentable effects of suddenly and completely releasing "*the people*" of a man-of-war from arbitrary discipline. It shows that, to such, "liberty," at first, must be administered in small and moderate quantities, increasing with the patient's capacity to make a good use of it.

Of course, while we lay in Rio, our officers frequently went ashore for pleasure, and, as a general thing, conducted themselves with propriety. But it is a sad thing to say, that, as for Lieutenant Mad Jack, he enjoyed himself so delightfully for three consecutive days in the town, that, upon returning to the ship, he sent his card to the Surgeon, with his compliments, begging him to drop into his state-room the first time he happened to pass that way in the ward-room.

But one of our Surgeon's mates, a young medico of fine family but slender fortune, must have created by far the strongest impression among the hidalgoes of Rio. He had read Don Quixote, and, instead of curing him of his Quixotism, as it ought to have done, it only made him still more Quixotic. Indeed, there are some natures concerning whose moral maladies the grand maxim of Mr. Similia Similibus Curantur Hahneman does not hold true, since, with them, *like cures* not *like*, but only aggravates *like*. Though, on the other hand, so incurable are the moral maladies of such persons, that the antagonist maxim, *contraria contrariis curantur*, often proves equally false.

Of a warm tropical day, this Surgeon's mate must needs go ashore in his blue cloth boat-cloak, wearing it, with a gallant Spanish toss, over his cavalier shoulder. By noon, he perspired very freely; but then his cloak attracted all eyes, and that was huge satisfaction. Nevertheless, his being knock-kneed, and spavined of one leg, sorely impaired the effect of this hidalgo cloak, which, by-the-way, was somewhat rusty in front, where his chin rubbed against it, and a good deal bedraggled all over, from his having used it as a counterpane off Cape Horn.

As for the midshipmen, there is no knowing what their mammas would have said to their conduct in Rio. Three of them drank a good deal too much; and when they came on board, the Captain ordered them to be sewed up in their hammocks, to cut short their obstreperous capers till sober.

This shows how unwise it is to allow children yet in their teens to wander so far from home. It more especially illustrates the folly of giving them long holidays in a foreign land, full of seductive dissipation. Port for men, claret for boys, cried Dr. Johnson. Even so, men only should drink the strong drink of travel; boys should still be kept on milk and water at home. Middies! you may despise your mother's leading-strings, but they are the *man-ropes*, my lads, by which many youngsters have steadied the giddiness of youth, and saved themselves from lamentable falls. And middies! know this, that as infants, being too early put on their feet, grow up bandy-legged, and curtailed of their fair proportions, even so, my dear middies, does it morally prove with some of you, who prematurely are sent off to sea.

These admonitions are solely addressed to the more diminutive class of midshipmen—those under five feet high, and under seven stone in weight.

Truly, the records of the steerages of men-of-war are full of most melancholy examples of early dissipation, disease, disgrace, and death. Answer, ye shades of fine boys, who in the soils of all climes, the round world over, far away sleep from your homes.

Mothers of men! If your hearts have been cast down when your boys have fallen in the way of temptations ashore, how much more bursting your grief, did you know that those boys were, far from your arms, cabined and cribbed in by all manner of iniquities. But this some of you can not believe. It is, perhaps, well that it is so.

But, hold them fast—all those who have not yet weighed their anchors for the Navy—round and round, hitch over hitch, bind your leading-strings on them, and, clinching a ring-bolt into your chimney-jam, moor your boys fast to that best of harbors, the hearth-stone.

But if youth be giddy, old age is staid; even as young saplings, in the litheness of their limbs, toss to their roots in the fresh morning air; but, stiff and unyielding with age, mossy trunks never bend. With pride and pleasure be it said, that, as for our old Commodore, though he might treat himself to as many "*liberty days*" as he pleased, yet throughout our stay in Rio he conducted himself with the utmost discretion.

But he was an old, old man; physically, a very small man; his spine was as an unloaded musket-barrel—not only attenuated, but destitute of a solitary cartridge, and his ribs were as the ribs of a weasel.

Besides, he was Commodore of the fleet, supreme lord of the Commons in Blue. It beseemed him, therefore, to erect himself into an ensample of virtue, and show the gun-deck what virtue was. But alas! when Virtue sits high aloft on a frigate's poop, when Virtue is crowned in the cabin a Commodore, when Virtue rules by compulsion, and domineers over Vice as a slave, then Virtue, though her mandates be outwardly observed, bears little interior sway. To be efficacious, Virtue must come down from aloft, even as our blessed Redeemer came down to redeem our whole man-of-war world; to that end, mixing with its sailors and sinners as equals.

Chapter 55

MIDSHIPMEN ENTERING THE NAVY EARLY

THE ALLUSION in the preceding chapter to the early age at which some of the midshipmen enter the Navy, suggests some thoughts relative to more important considerations.

A very general modern impression seems to be, that, in order to learn the profession of a sea-officer, a boy can hardly be sent to sea too early. To a certain extent, this may be a mistake. Other professions, involving a knowledge of technicalities and things restricted to one particular field of action, are frequently mastered by men who begin after the age of twenty-one, or even at a later period of life. It was only about the middle of the seventeenth century that the British military and naval services were kept distinct. Previous to that epoch the king's officers commanded indifferently either by sea or by land.

Robert Blake, perhaps one of the most accomplished, and certainly one of the most successful Admirals that ever hoisted a flag, was more than half a century old (fifty-one years) before he entered the naval service, or had aught to do, professionally, with a ship. He was of a studious turn, and, after leaving Oxford, resided quietly on his estate, a country gentleman, till his forty-second year, soon after which he became connected with the Parliamentary army.

The historian Clarendon says of him, "He was the first man that made it manifest that the science (seamanship) might be attained in less time than was imagined." And doubtless it was to his shore sympathies that the well-known humanity and kindness which Blake evinced in his intercourse with the sailors is in a large degree to be imputed.

Midshipmen sent into the Navy at a very early age are exposed to the passive reception of all the prejudices of the quarter-deck in favor of ancient usages, however useless or pernicious; those prejudices grow up with them, and solidify with their very bones. As they rise in rank, they naturally carry them up, whence the inveterate repugnance of many Commodores and Captains to the slightest innovations in the service, however salutary they may appear to landsmen.

It is hardly to be doubted that, in matters connected with the general welfare of the Navy, government has paid rather too much deference to the opinions of the officers of the Navy, considering them as men almost born to the service, and therefore far better qualified to judge concerning any and all questions touching it than people on shore. But in a nation under a liberal Constitution, it must ever be unwise to make too distinct and peculiar the profession of either branch of its military men. True, in a country like ours, nothing is at present to be apprehended of their gaining political rule; but not a little is to be apprehended concerning their perpetuating or creating abuses among their subordinates, unless civilians have full cognizance of their administrative affairs, and account themselves competent to the complete overlooking and ordering them.

We do wrong when we in any way contribute to the prevailing mystification that has been thrown about the internal affairs of the national sea-service. Hitherto those affairs have been regarded even by some high state functionaries as things beyond their insight—altogether too technical and mysterious to be fully comprehended by landsmen. And this it is that has perpetuated in the Navy many evils that otherwise would have been abolished in the general amelioration of other things. The army is sometimes remodeled, but the Navy goes down from generation to generation almost untouched and unquestioned, as if its code were infallible, and itself a piece of perfection that no statesman could improve. When a Secretary of the Navy ventures to innovate upon its established customs, you hear some of the Navy officers say, "What does this landsman know about our affairs? Did he ever head a watch? He does not know starboard from larboard, girt-line from back-stay."

While we deferentially and cheerfully leave to navy officers the sole conduct of making and shortening sail, tacking ship, and performing other nautical maneuvres, as may seem to them best; let us beware of abandoning to their discretion those general municipal regulations touching the well-being of the great body of men before the mast; let us beware of being too much influenced by their opinions in matters where it is but natural to suppose that their long-established prejudices are enlisted.

Chapter 56

A Shore Emperor on board a Man-of-war

WHILE WE LAY in Rio, we sometimes had company from shore; but an unforeseen honor awaited us. One day, the young Emperor, Don Pedro II., and suite—making a circuit of the harbor, and visiting all the men-of-war in rotation—at last condescendingly visited the Neversink.

He came in a splendid barge, rowed by thirty African slaves, who, after the Brazilian manner, in concert rose upright to their oars at every stroke; then sank backward again to their seats with a simultaneous groan.

He reclined under a canopy of yellow silk, looped with tassels of green, the national colors. At the stern waved the Brazilian flag, bearing a large diamond figure in the centre, emblematical, perhaps, of the mines of precious stones in the interior; or, it may be, a magnified portrait of the famous "Portuguese diamond" itself, which was found in Brazil, in the district of Tejuco, on the banks of the Rio Belmonte.

We gave them a grand salute, which almost made the ship's live-oak *knees* knock together with the tremendous concussions. We manned the yards, and went through a long ceremonial of paying the Emperor homage. Republicans are often more courteous to royalty than royalists themselves. But doubtless this springs from a noble magnanimity.

At the gangway, the Emperor was received by our Commodore in person, arrayed in his most resplendent coat and finest French epaulets. His servant had devoted himself to polishing every button that morning with rotten-stone and rags—your sea air is a sworn foe to metallic glosses; whence it comes that the swords of sea-officers have, of late, so rusted in their scabbards that they are with difficulty drawn.

It was a fine sight to see this Emperor and Commodore complimenting each other. Both wore *chapeaux-de-bras*, and both continually waved them. By instinct, the Emperor knew that the venerable personage before him was as much a monarch afloat as he himself was ashore. Did not our Commodore

593

carry the sword of state by his side? For though not borne before him, it must have been a sword of state, since it looked far too lustrous ever to have been his fighting sword. *That* was naught but a limber steel blade, with a plain, serviceable handle, like the handle of a slaughter-house knife.

Who ever saw a star when the noon sun was in sight? But you seldom see a king without satellites. In the suite of the youthful Emperor came a princely train; so brilliant with gems, that they seemed just emerged from the mines of the Rio Belmonte.

You have seen cones of crystallized salt? Just so flashed these Portuguese Barons, Marquises, Viscounts, and Counts. Were it not for their titles, and being seen in the train of their lord, you would have sworn they were eldest sons of jewelers all, who had run away with their fathers' cases on their backs.

Contrasted with these lamp-lustres of Barons of Brazil, how waned the gold lace of our barons of the frigate, the officers of the gun-room! and compared with the long, jewel-hilted rapiers of the Marquises, the little dirks of our cadets of noble houses—the middies—looked like gilded tenpenny nails in their girdles.

But there they stood! Commodore and Emperor, Lieutenants and Marquises, middies and pages! The brazen band on the poop struck up; the marine guard presented arms; and high aloft, looking down on this scene, all *the people* vigorously hurraed. A top-man next me on the main-royal-yard removed his hat, and diligently manipulated his head in honor of the event; but he was so far out of sight in the clouds, that this ceremony went for nothing.

A great pity it was, that in addition to all these honors, that admirer of Portuguese literature, Viscount Strangford, of Great Britain—who, I believe, once went out Embassador Extraordinary to the Brazils—it was a pity that he was not present on this occasion, to yield his tribute of "A Stanza to Braganza!" For our royal visitor was an undoubted Braganza, allied to nearly all the great families of Europe. His grandfather, John VI., had been King of Portugal; his own sister, Maria, was now its queen. He was, indeed, a distinguished young gentleman, entitled to high consideration, and that consideration was most cheerfully accorded him.

He wore a green dress-coat, with one regal morning-star at the breast, and white pantaloons. In his chapeau was a single, bright, golden-hued feather of the Imperial Toucan fowl, a magnificent, omnivorous, broad-billed bandit bird of prey, a native of Brazil. Its perch is on the loftiest trees, whence it looks down upon all humbler fowls, and, hawk-like, flies at their throats. The Toucan once formed part of the savage regalia of the Indian caciques of the country, and, upon the establishment of the empire, was symbolically retained by the Portuguese sovereigns.

His Imperial Majesty was yet in his youth; rather corpulent, if any thing, with a care-free, pleasant face, and a polite, indifferent, and easy address. His manners, indeed, were entirely unexceptionable.

Now here, thought I, is a very fine lad, with very fine prospects before him. He is supreme Emperor of all these Brazils; he has no stormy night-watches to stand; he can lay abed of mornings just as long as he pleases. Any gentleman in Rio would be proud of his personal acquaintance, and the prettiest girl in all South America would deem herself honored with the least glance from the acutest angle of his eye.

Yes: this young Emperor will have a fine time of this life, even so long as he condescends to exist. Every one jumps to obey him; and see, as I live, there is an old nobleman in his suit—the Marquis d'Acarty they call him, old enough to be his grandfather—who, in the hot sun, is standing bareheaded before him, while the Emperor carries his hat on his head.

"I suppose that old gentleman, now," said a young New England tar beside me, "would consider it a great honor to put on his Royal Majesty's boots; and yet, White-Jacket, if yonder Emperor and I were to strip and jump overboard for a bath, it would be hard telling which was of the blood royal when we should once be in the water. Look you, Don Pedro II.," he added, "how do you come to be Emperor? Tell me that. You can not pull as many pounds as I on the main-topsail-halyards; you are not as tall as I; your nose is a pug, and mine is a cut-water; and how do you come to be a '*brigand*,' with that thin pair of spars? A *brigand*, indeed!"

"*Braganza*, you mean," said I, willing to correct the

rhetoric of so fierce a republican, and, by so doing, chastise his censoriousness.

"Braganza! *bragger* it is," he replied; "and a bragger, indeed. See that feather in his cap! See how he struts in that coat! He may well wear a green one, top-mates—he's a green-looking swab at the best."

"Hush, Jonathan," said I; "there's the *First Luff* looking up. Be still! the Emperor will hear you;" and I put my hand on his mouth.

"Take your hand away, White-Jacket," he cried; "there's no law up aloft here. I say, you Emperor—you green-horn in the green coat, there—look you, you can't raise a pair of whiskers yet; and see what a pair of homeward-bounders I have on my jowls! *Don Pedro*, eh? What's that, after all, but plain Peter—reckoned a shabby name in my country. Damn me, White-Jacket, I wouldn't call my dog Peter!"

"Clap a stopper on your jaw-tackle, will you?" cried Ringbolt, the sailor on the other side of him. "You'll be getting us all into darbies for this."

"I won't trice up my red rag for nobody," retorted Jonathan. "So you had better take a round turn with yours, Ringbolt, and let me alone, or I'll fetch you such a swat over your figure-head, you'll think a Long Wharf truck-horse kicked you with all four shoes on one hoof! You Emperor—you counter-jumping son of a gun—cock your weather eye up aloft here, and see your betters! I say, top-mates, he ain't any Emperor at all—*I'm* the rightful Emperor. Yes, by the Commodore's boots! they stole me out of my cradle here in the palace at Rio, and put that green-horn in my place. Ay, you timber-head, you, I'm Don Pedro II., and by good rights you ought to be a main-top-man here, with your fist in a tar-bucket! Look you, I say, that crown of yours ought to be on my head; or, if you don't believe *that*, just heave it into the ring once, and see who's the best man."

"What's this hurra's nest here aloft?" cried Jack Chase, coming up the t'-gallant rigging from the top-sail yard. "Can't you behave yourself, royal-yard-men, when an Emperor's on board?"

"It's this here Jonathan," answered Ringbolt; "he's been

blackguarding the young nob in the green coat, there. He says Don Pedro stole his hat."

"How?"

"Crown, he means, noble Jack," said a top-man.

"Jonathan don't call himself an Emperor, does he?" asked Jack.

"Yes," cried Jonathan; "that green-horn, standing there by the Commodore, is sailing under false colors; he's an impostor, I say; he wears my crown."

"Ha! ha!" laughed Jack, now seeing into the joke, and willing to humor it; "though I'm born a Briton, boys, yet, by the mast! these Don Pedros are all Perkin Warbecks. But I say, Jonathan, my lad, don't pipe your eye now about the loss of your crown; for, look you, we all wear crowns, from our cradles to our graves, and though in *double-darbies* in the *brig*, the Commodore himself can't unking us."

"A riddle, noble Jack."

"Not a bit; every man who has a sole to his foot has a crown to his head. Here's mine;" and so saying, Jack, removing his tarpaulin, exhibited a bald spot, just about the bigness of a crown-piece, on the summit of his curly and classical head.

Chapter 57

I BEG their royal highnesses' pardons all round, but I had almost forgotten to chronicle the fact, that with the Emperor came several other royal Princes—kings for aught we knew—since it was just after the celebration of the nuptials of a younger sister of the Brazilian monarch to some European royalty. Indeed, the Emperor and his suite formed a sort of bridal party, only the bride herself was absent.

The first reception over, the smoke of the cannonading salute having cleared away, and the martial outburst of the brass band having also rolled off to leeward, the people were called down from the yards, and the drum beat to quarters.

To quarters we went; and there we stood up by our iron bull-dogs, while our royal and noble visitors promenaded along the batteries, breaking out into frequent exclamations at our warlike array, the extreme neatness of our garments, and, above all, the extraordinary polish of the *bright-work* about the great guns, and the marvelous whiteness of the decks.

"Que gosto!" cried a Marquis, with several dry goods samples of ribbon, tallied with bright buttons, hanging from his breast.

"Que gloria!" cried a crooked, coffee-colored Viscount, spreading both palms.

"Que alegria!" cried a little Count, mincingly circumnavigating a shot-box.

"Que contentamento he o meu!" cried the Emperor himself, complacently folding his royal arms, and serenely gazing along our ranks.

Pleasure, *Glory*, and *Joy*—this was the burden of the three noble courtiers. *And very pleasing indeed*—was the simple rendering of Don Pedro's imperial remark.

"Ay, ay," growled a grim rammer-and-sponger behind me; "it's all devilish fine for you nobs to look at; but what would you say if you had to holy-stone the deck yourselves, and wear out your elbows in polishing this cursed old iron, besides getting a dozen at the gangway, if you dropped a grease-spot on deck in your mess? Ay, ay, devilish fine for you, but devilish dull for us!"

In due time the drums beat the retreat, and the ship's company scattered over the decks.

Some of the officers now assumed the part of cicerones, to show the distinguished strangers the bowels of the frigate, concerning which several of them showed a good deal of intelligent curiosity. A guard of honor, detached from the marine corps, accompanied them, and they made the circuit of the berth-deck, where, at a judicious distance, the Emperor peeped down into the cable-tier, a very subterranean vault.

The Captain of the Main-Hold, who there presided, made a polite bow in the twilight, and respectfully expressed a desire for His Royal Majesty to step down and honor him with a call; but, with his handkerchief to his Imperial nose, his Majesty declined. The party then commenced the ascent to the spar-deck; which, from so great a depth in a frigate, is something like getting up to the top of Bunker Hill Monument from the basement.

While a crowd of the people was gathered about the forward part of the booms, a sudden cry was heard from below; a lieutenant came running forward to learn the cause, when an old sheet-anchor-man, standing by, after touching his hat, hitched up his waistbands, and replied, "I don't know, sir, but I'm thinking as how one o' them 'ere kings has been tumblin' down the hatchway."

And something like this it turned out. In ascending one of the narrow ladders leading from the berth-deck to the gun-deck, the Most Noble Marquis of Silva, in the act of elevating the Imperial coat-tails, so as to protect them from rubbing against the newly-painted combings of the hatchway, this Noble Marquis's sword, being an uncommonly long one, had caught between his legs, and tripped him head over heels down into the fore-passage.

"Onde ides?" (where are you going?) said his royal master, tranquilly peeping down toward the falling Marquis; "and what did you let go of my coat-tails for?" he suddenly added, in a passion, glancing round at the same time, to see if they had suffered from the unfaithfulness of his train-bearer.

"Oh, Lord!" sighed the Captain of the Fore-top, "who would be a Marquis of Silva?"

Upon being assisted to the spar-deck, the unfortunate Marquis was found to have escaped without serious harm; but, from the marked coolness of his royal master, when the Marquis drew near to apologize for his awkwardness, it was plain that he was condemned to languish for a time under the royal displeasure.

Shortly after, the Imperial party withdrew, under another grand national salute.

Chapter 58

A Quarter-deck Officer before the Mast

As we were somewhat short-handed while we lay in Rio, we received a small draft of men from a United States sloop of war, whose three years' term of service would expire about the time of our arrival in America.

Under guard of an armed Lieutenant and four midshipmen, they came on board in the afternoon. They were immediately mustered in the starboard gangway, that Mr. Bridewell, our First Lieutenant, might take down their names, and assign them their stations.

They stood in a mute and solemn row; the officer advanced, with his memorandum-book and pencil.

My casual friend, Shakings, the holder, happened to be by at the time. Touching my arm, he said, "White-Jacket, this here reminds me of Sing-Sing, when a draft of fellows, in darbies, came on from the State Prison at Auburn for a change of scene like, you know!"

After taking down four or five names, Mr. Bridewell accosted the next man, a rather good-looking person, but, from his haggard cheek and sunken eye, he seemed to have been in the sad habit, all his life, of sitting up rather late at night; and though all sailors do certainly keep late hours enough—standing watches at midnight—yet there is no small difference between keeping late hours at sea and keeping late hours ashore.

"What's your name?" asked the officer, of this rather rakish-looking recruit.

"Mandeville, sir," said the man, courteously touching his cap. "You must remember me, sir," he added, in a low, confidential tone, strangely dashed with servility; "we sailed together once in the old Macedonian, sir. I wore an epaulet then; we had the same state-room, you know, sir. I'm your old chum, Mandeville, sir," and he again touched his cap.

"I remember an *officer* by that name," said the First Lieutenant, emphatically, "and I know *you*, fellow. But I know you henceforth for a common sailor. I can show no favoritism here. If you ever violate the ship's rules, you shall be flogged like any other seaman. I place you in the fore-top; go forward to your duty."

It seemed this Mandeville had entered the Navy when very young, and had risen to be a lieutenant, as he said. But brandy had been his bane. One night, when he had the deck of a line-of-battle ship, in the Mediterranean, he was seized with a fit of mania-a-potu, or something like that; and, being out of his senses for the time, went below and turned into his berth, leaving the deck without a commanding officer. For this unpardonable offence he was broken.

Having no fortune, and no other profession than the sea, upon his disgrace he entered the merchant-service as a chief mate; but his love of strong drink still pursuing him, he was again cashiered at sea, and degraded before the mast by the Captain. After this, in a state of intoxication, he re-entered the Navy at Pensacola as a common sailor. But all these lessons, so biting-bitter to learn, could not cure him of his sin. He had hardly been a week on board the Neversink, when he was found intoxicated with smuggled spirits. They lashed him to the gratings, and ignominiously scourged him under the eye of his old friend and comrade, the First Lieutenant.

This took place while we lay in port, which reminds me of the circumstance, that when punishment is about to be inflicted in harbor, all strangers are ordered ashore; and the sentries at the side have it in strict charge to waive off all boats drawing near.

Chapter 59

A Man-of-war Button divides two Brothers

THE CONDUCT of Mandeville, in claiming the acquaintance of the First Lieutenant under such disreputable circumstances, was strongly contrasted by the behavior of another person on board, placed for a time in a somewhat similar situation.

Among the genteel youths of the after-guard was a lad of about sixteen, a very handsome young fellow, with starry eyes, curly hair of a golden color, and a bright, sunshiny complexion: he must have been the son of some goldsmith. He was one of the few sailors—not in the main-top—whom I used to single out for occasional conversation. After several friendly interviews he became quite frank, and communicated certain portions of his history. There is some charm in the sea, which induces most persons to be very communicative concerning themselves.

We had lain in Rio but a day, when I observed that this lad—whom I shall here call Frank—wore an unwonted expression of sadness, mixed with apprehension. I questioned him as to the cause, but he chose to conceal it. Not three days after, he abruptly accosted me on the gun-deck, where I happened to be taking a promenade.

"I can't keep it to myself any more," he said; "I must have a confidant, or I shall go mad!"

"What is the matter?" said I, in alarm.

"Matter enough—look at this!" and he handed me a torn half sheet of an old New York Herald, putting his finger upon a particular word in a particular paragraph. It was the announcement of the sailing from the Brooklyn Navy-yard of a United States Store Ship, with provisions for the squadron in Rio. It was upon a particular name, in the list of officers and midshipmen, that Frank's finger was placed.

"That is my own brother," said he; "he must have got a reefer's warrant since I left home. Now, White-Jacket, what's to be done? I have calculated that the Store Ship may be expected here every day; my brother will then see me—he an officer and I a miserable sailor that any moment may be flogged at the gangway, before his very eyes. Heavens! White-Jacket, what shall I do? Would you run? Do you think there is any chance to desert? I won't see him, by Heaven, with this sailor's frock on, and he with the anchor button!"

"Why, Frank," said I, "I do not really see sufficient cause for this fit you are in. Your brother is an officer—very good; and you are nothing but a sailor—but that is no disgrace. If he comes on board here, go up to him, and take him by the hand; believe me, he will be glad enough to see you!"

Frank started from his desponding attitude, and fixing his eyes full upon mine, with clasped hands exclaimed, "White-Jacket, I have been from home nearly three years; in that time I have never heard one word from my family, and, though God knows how I love them, yet I swear to you, that though my brother can tell me whether my sisters are still alive, yet, rather than accost him in this *lined-frock*, I would go ten centuries without hearing one syllable from home!"

Amazed at his earnestness, and hardly able to account for it altogether, I stood silent a moment; then said, "Why, Frank, this midshipman is your own brother, you say; now, do you really think that your own flesh and blood is going to give himself airs over you, simply because he sports large brass buttons on his coat? Never believe it. If he does, he can be no brother, and ought to be hanged—that's all!"

"Don't say that again," said Frank, resentfully; "my brother is a noble-hearted fellow; I love him as I do myself. You don't understand me, White-Jacket; don't you see, that when my brother arrives, he must consort more or less with our chuckle-headed reefers on board here? There's that namby-pamby Miss Nancy of a white-face, Stribbles, who, the other day, when Mad Jack's back was turned, ordered me to hand him the spy-glass, as if he were a Commodore. Do you suppose, now, I want my brother to see me a lackey aboard here? By Heaven, it is enough to drive one distracted! What's to be done?" he cried, fiercely.

Much more passed between us, but all my philosophy was in vain, and at last Frank departed, his head hanging down in despondency.

For several days after, whenever the quarter-master reported a sail entering the harbor, Frank was foremost in the rigging to observe it. At length, one afternoon, a vessel drawing near was reported to be the long-expected store ship. I looked round for Frank on the spar-deck, but he was nowhere to be seen. He must have been below, gazing out of a port-hole. The vessel was hailed from our poop, and came to anchor within a biscuit's toss of our batteries.

That evening I heard that Frank had ineffectually endeavored to get removed from his place as an oarsman in the First-Cutter—a boat which, from its size, is generally employed with the *launch* in carrying ship-stores. When I thought that, the very next day, perhaps, this boat would be plying between the store ship and our frigate, I was at no loss to account for Frank's attempts to get rid of his oar, and felt heartily grieved at their failure.

Next morning the bugler called away the First-Cutter's crew, and Frank entered the boat with his hat slouched over his eyes. Upon his return, I was all eagerness to learn what had happened, and, as the communication of his feelings was a grateful relief, he poured his whole story into my ear.

It seemed that, with his comrades, he mounted the store ship's side, and hurried forward to the forecastle. Then, turning anxiously toward the quarter-deck, he spied two midshipmen leaning against the bulwarks, conversing. One was the officer of his boat—was the other his brother? No; he was too tall—too large. Thank Heaven! it was *not* him. And perhaps his brother had not sailed from home, after all; there might have been some mistake. But suddenly the strange midshipman laughed aloud, and that laugh Frank had heard a thousand times before. It was a free, hearty laugh—a brother's laugh; but it carried a pang to the heart of poor Frank.

He was now ordered down to the main-deck to assist in removing the stores. The boat being loaded, he was ordered into her, when, looking toward the gangway, he perceived the two midshipmen lounging upon each side of it, so that no one could pass them without brushing their persons. But again pulling his hat over his eyes, Frank, darting between them, gained his oar. "How my heart thumped," he said, "when I actually *felt* him so near me; but I wouldn't look at him—no! I'd have died first!"

To Frank's great relief, the store ship at last moved further up the bay, and it fortunately happened that he saw no more of his brother while in Rio; and while there, he never in any way made himself known to him.

Chapter 60

A Man-of-war's-man Shot at

THERE WAS a seaman belonging to the fore-top—a mess-mate, though not a top-mate of mine, and no favorite of the Captain's—who, for certain venial transgressions, had been prohibited from going ashore on liberty when the ship's company went. Enraged at the deprivation—for he had not touched earth in upward of a year—he, some nights after, lowered himself overboard, with the view of gaining a canoe, attached by a rope to a Dutch galiot some cables'-length distant. In this canoe he proposed paddling himself ashore. Not being a very expert swimmer, the commotion he made in the water attracted the ear of the sentry on that side of the ship, who, turning about in his walk, perceived the faint white spot where the fugitive was swimming in the frigate's shadow. He hailed it; but no reply.

"Give the word, or I fire!"

Not a word was heard.

The next instant there was a red flash, and, before it had completely ceased illuminating the night, the white spot was changed into crimson. Some of the officers, returning from a party at the Beach of the Flamingoes, happened to be drawing near the ship in one of her cutters. They saw the flash, and the bounding body it revealed. In a moment the top-man was dragged into the boat, a handkerchief was used for a tourniquet, and the wounded fugitive was soon on board the frigate, when, the surgeon being called, the necessary attentions were rendered.

Now, it appeared, that at the moment the sentry fired, the top-man—in order to elude discovery, by manifesting the completest quietude—was floating on the water, straight and horizontal, as if reposing on a bed. As he was not far from the ship at the time, and the sentry was considerably elevated above him—pacing his platform, on a level with the upper part of the hammock-nettings—the ball struck with great force, with a downward obliquity, entering the right thigh just above the knee, and, penetrating some inches, glanced upward along the bone, burying itself somewhere, so that it could not be felt by outward manipulation. There was no dusky discoloration to mark its internal track, as in the case when a partly-spent ball—obliquely hitting—after entering the skin, courses on, just beneath the surface, without penetrating further. Nor was there any mark on the opposite part of the thigh to denote its place, as when a ball forces itself straight through a limb, and lodges, perhaps, close to the skin on the other side. Nothing was visible but a small, ragged puncture, bluish about the edges, as if the rough point of a tenpenny nail had been forced into the flesh, and withdrawn. It seemed almost impossible, that through so small an aperture, a musket-bullet could have penetrated.

The extreme misery and general prostration of the man, caused by the great effusion of blood—though, strange to say, at first he said he felt no pain from the wound itself—induced the Surgeon, very reluctantly, to forego an immediate search for the ball, to extract it, as that would have involved the dilating of the wound by the knife; an operation which, at that juncture, would have been almost certainly attended with fatal results. A day or two, therefore, was permitted to pass, while simple dressings were applied.

The Surgeons of the other American ships of war in harbor occasionally visited the Neversink, to examine the patient, and incidentally to listen to the expositions of our own Surgeon, their senior in rank. But Cadwallader Cuticle, who, as yet, has been but incidentally alluded to, now deserves a chapter by himself.

Chapter 61

THE SURGEON OF THE FLEET

CADWALLADER CUTICLE, M.D., and Honorary Member of the most distinguished Colleges of Surgeons both in Europe and America, was our Surgeon of the Fleet. Nor was he at all blind to the dignity of his position; to which, indeed, he was rendered peculiarly competent, if the reputation he enjoyed was deserved. He had the name of being the foremost Surgeon in the Navy, a gentleman of remarkable science, and a veteran practitioner.

He was a small, withered man, nearly, perhaps quite, sixty years of age. His chest was shallow, his shoulders bent, his pantaloons hung round skeleton legs, and his face was singularly attenuated. In truth, the corporeal vitality of this man seemed, in a good degree, to have died out of him. He walked abroad, a curious patch-work of life and death, with a wig, one glass eye, and a set of false teeth, while his voice was husky and thick; but his mind seemed undebilitated as in youth; it shone out of his remaining eye with basilisk brilliancy.

Like most old physicians and surgeons who have seen much service, and have been promoted to high professional place for their scientific attainments, this Cuticle was an enthusiast in his calling. In private, he had once been heard to say, confidentially, that he would rather cut off a man's arm than dismember the wing of the most delicate pheasant. In particular, the department of Morbid Anatomy was his peculiar love; and in his state-room below he had a most unsightly collection of Parisian casts, in plaster and wax, representing all imaginable malformations of the human members, both organic and induced by disease. Chief among these was a cast, often to be met with in the Anatomical Museums of Europe, and no doubt an unexaggerated copy of a genuine original; it was the head of an elderly woman, with an aspect singularly gentle and meek, but at the same time wonderfully expressive of a gnawing sorrow, never to be relieved. You would almost have thought it the face of some abbess, for some unspeakable crime voluntarily sequestered from human society, and leading a life of agonized penitence without hope; so marvelously sad and tearfully pitiable was this head. But when you first beheld it, no such emotions ever crossed your mind. All your eyes and all your horrified soul were fast fascinated and frozen by the sight of a hideous, crumpled horn, like that of a ram, downward growing out from the forehead, and partly shadowing the face; but as you gazed, the freezing fascination of its horribleness gradually waned, and then your whole heart burst with sorrow, as you contemplated those aged features, ashy pale and wan. The horn seemed the mark of a curse for some mysterious sin, conceived and committed before the spirit had entered the flesh. Yet that sin seemed something imposed, and not voluntarily sought; some sin growing out of the heartless necessities of the predestination of things; some sin under which the sinner sank in sinless woe.

But no pang of pain, not the slightest touch of concern, ever crossed the bosom of Cuticle when he looked on this cast. It was immovably fixed to a bracket, against the partition of his state-room, so that it was the first object that greeted his eyes when he opened them from his nightly sleep. Nor was it to hide the face, that upon retiring, he always hung his Navy cap upon the upward curling extremity of the horn, for that obscured it but little.

The Surgeon's cot-boy, the lad who made up his swinging bed and took care of his room, often told us of the horror he sometimes felt when he would find himself alone in his master's retreat. At times he was seized with the idea that Cuticle was a preternatural being; and once entering his room in the middle watch of the night, he started at finding it enveloped in a thick, bluish vapor, and stifling with the odors of brimstone. Upon hearing a low groan from the smoke, with a wild cry he darted from the place, and, rousing the occupants of the neighboring state-rooms, it was found that the vapor proceeded from smoldering bunches of Lucifer matches, which had become ignited through the carelessness of the Surgeon. Cuticle, almost dead, was dragged from the suffocating atmosphere, and it was several days ere he completely recovered from its effects. This accident took place immediately over the powder magazine; but as Cuticle, during his sickness, paid dearly enough for transgressing the laws prohibiting combustibles in the gun-room, the Captain contented himself with privately remonstrating with him.

Well knowing the enthusiasm of the Surgeon for all specimens of morbid anatomy, some of the ward-room officers used to play upon his credulity, though, in every case, Cuticle was not long in discovering their deceptions. Once, when they had some sago pudding for dinner, and Cuticle chanced to be ashore, they made up a neat parcel of this bluish-white, firm, jelly-like preparation, and placing it in a tin box, carefully sealed with wax, they deposited it on the gun-room table, with a note, purporting to come from an eminent physician in Rio, connected with the Grand National Museum on the Praca d'Acclamacao, begging leave to present the scientific Senhor Cuticle—with the donor's compliments— an uncommonly fine specimen of a cancer.

Descending to the ward-room, Cuticle spied the note, and no sooner read it, than, clutching the case, he opened it, and exclaimed, "Beautiful! splendid! I have never seen a finer specimen of this most interesting disease."

"What have you there, Surgeon Cuticle?" said a Lieutenant, advancing.

"Why, sir, look at it; did you ever see any thing more exquisite?"

"Very exquisite indeed; let me have a bit of it, will you, Cuticle?"

"Let you have a bit of it!" shrieked the Surgeon, starting back. "Let you have one of my limbs! I wouldn't mar so large a specimen for a hundred dollars; but what can you want of it? You are not making collections!"

"I'm fond of the article," said the Lieutenant; "it's a fine cold relish to bacon or ham. You know, I was in New Zealand last cruise, Cuticle, and got into sad dissipation there among the cannibals; come, let's have a bit, if it's only a mouthful."

"Why, you infernal Feejee!" shouted Cuticle, eyeing the other with a confounded expression; "you don't really mean to eat a piece of this cancer?"

"Hand it to me, and see whether I will not," was the reply.

"In God's name, take it!" cried the Surgeon, putting the case into his hands, and then standing with his own uplifted.

"Steward!" cried the Lieutenant, "the castor—quick! I always use plenty of pepper with this dish, Surgeon; it's oystery. Ah! this is really delicious," he added, smacking his lips over a mouthful. "Try it now, Surgeon, and you'll never keep such a fine dish as this, lying uneaten on your hands, as a mere scientific curiosity."

Cuticle's whole countenance changed; and, slowly walking up to the table, he put his nose close to the tin case, then touched its contents with his finger and tasted it. Enough. Buttoning up his coat, in all the tremblings of an old man's rage he burst from the ward-room, and, calling for a boat, was not seen again for twenty-four hours.

But though, like all other mortals, Cuticle was subject at times to these fits of passion—at least under outrageous provocation—nothing could exceed his coolness when actually employed in his eminent vocation. Surrounded by moans and shrieks, by features distorted with anguish inflicted by himself, he yet maintained a countenance almost supernaturally calm; and unless the intense interest of the operation flushed his wan face with a momentary tinge of professional enthusiasm, he toiled away, untouched by the keenest misery coming under a fleet-surgeon's eye. Indeed, long habituation to the dissecting-room and the amputation-table had made him seemingly impervious to the ordinary emotions of humanity. Yet you could not say that Cuticle was essentially a cruel-hearted man. His apparent heartlessness must have been of a purely scientific origin. It is not to be imagined even that Cuticle would have harmed a fly, unless he could procure a microscope powerful enough to assist him in experimenting on the minute vitals of the creature.

But notwithstanding his marvelous indifference to the sufferings of his patients, and spite even of his enthusiasm in his vocation—not cooled by frosting old age itself—Cuticle, on some occasions, would affect a certain disrelish of his profession, and declaim against the necessity that forced a man of his humanity to perform a surgical operation. Especially was it apt to be thus with him, when the case was one of more than ordinary interest. In discussing it, previous to setting about it, he would vail his eagerness under an aspect of great circumspection, curiously marred, however, by continual sallies of unsuppressible impatience. But the knife once in his hand, the compassionless surgeon himself, undisguised, stood before you. Such was Cadwallader Cuticle, our Surgeon of the Fleet.

Chapter 62

A CONSULTATION OF MAN-OF-WAR SURGEONS

IT SEEMS customary for the Surgeon of the Fleet, when any important operation in his department is on the anvil, and there is nothing to absorb professional attention from it, to invite his brother surgeons, if at hand at the time, to a ceremonious consultation upon it. And this, in courtesy, his brother surgeons expect.

In pursuance of this custom, then, the surgeons of the neighboring American ships of war were requested to visit the Neversink in a body, to advise concerning the case of the top-man, whose situation had now become critical. They assembled on the half-deck, and were soon joined by their respected senior, Cuticle. In a body they bowed as he approached, and accosted him with deferential regard.

"Gentlemen," said Cuticle, unostentatiously seating himself on a camp-stool, handed him by his cot-boy, "we have here an extremely interesting case. You have all seen the patient, I believe. At first I had hopes that I should have been able to cut down to the ball, and remove it; but the state of the patient forbade. Since then, the inflammation and sloughing of the part has been attended with a copious suppuration, great loss of substance, extreme debility and emaciation. From this, I am convinced that the ball has shattered and deadened the bone, and now lies impacted in the medullary canal. In fact, there can be no doubt that the wound is incurable, and that amputation is the only resource. But, gentlemen, I find myself placed in a very delicate predicament. I assure you I feel no professional anxiety to perform the operation. I desire your advice, and if you will now again visit the patient with me, we can then return here, and decide what is best to be done. Once more, let me say, that I feel no personal anxiety whatever to use the knife."

The assembled surgeons listened to this address with the most serious attention, and, in accordance with their superior's desire, now descended to the sick-bay, where the patient was languishing. The examination concluded, they returned to the half-deck, and the consultation was renewed.

"Gentlemen," began Cuticle, again seating himself, "you have now just inspected the limb; you have seen that there is no resource but amputation; and now, gentlemen, what do you say? Surgeon Bandage, of the Mohawk, will you express your opinion?"

"The wound is a very serious one," said Bandage—a corpulent man, with a high German forehead—shaking his head solemnly.

"Can any thing save him but amputation?" demanded Cuticle.

"His constitutional debility is extreme," observed Bandage, "but I have seen more dangerous cases."

"Surgeon Wedge, of the Malay," said Cuticle, in a pet, "be pleased to give *your* opinion; and let it be definitive, I entreat:" this was said with a severe glance toward Bandage.

"If I thought," began Wedge, a very spare, tall man, elevating himself still higher on his toes, "that the ball had shattered and divided the whole *femur*, including the *Greater* and *Lesser Trochanter*, the *Linear aspera*, the *Digital fossa*, and the *Intertrochanteric*, I should certainly be in favor of amputation; but that, sir, permit me to observe, is not my opinion."

"Surgeon Sawyer, of the Buccaneer," said Cuticle, drawing in his thin lower lip with vexation, and turning to a round-faced, florid, frank, sensible-looking man, whose uniform coat very handsomely fitted him, and was adorned with an unusual quantity of gold lace; "Surgeon Sawyer, of the Buccaneer, let us now hear *your* opinion, if you please. Is not amputation the only resource, sir?"

"Excuse me," said Sawyer, "I am decidedly opposed to it; for if hitherto the patient has not been strong enough to undergo the extraction of the ball, I do not see how he can be expected to endure a far more severe operation. As there is no immediate danger of mortification, and you say the ball can not be reached without making large incisions, I should support him, I think, for the present, with tonics, and gentle antiphlogistics, locally applied. On no account would I proceed to amputation until further symptoms are exhibited."

"Surgeon Patella, of the Algerine," said Cuticle, in an ill-

suppressed passion, abruptly turning round on the person addressed, "will *you* have the kindness to say whether *you* do
not think that amputation is the only resource?"

Now Patella was the youngest of the company, a modest
man, filled with a profound reverence for the science of Cuticle, and desirous of gaining his good opinion, yet not wishing to commit himself altogether by a decided reply, though,
like Surgeon Sawyer, in his own mind he might have been
clearly against the operation.

"What you have remarked, Mr. Surgeon of the Fleet," said
Patella, respectfully hemming, "concerning the dangerous
condition of the limb, seems obvious enough; amputation
would certainly be a cure to the wound; but then, as, notwithstanding his present debility, the patient seems to have a
strong constitution, he might rally as it is, and by your scientific treatment, Mr. Surgeon of the Fleet"—bowing—"be
entirely made whole, without risking an amputation. Still, it
is a very critical case, and amputation may be indispensable;
and if it *is* to be performed, there ought to be no delay whatever. That is my view of the case, Mr. Surgeon of the Fleet."

"Surgeon Patella, then, gentlemen," said Cuticle, turning
round triumphantly, "is clearly of opinion that amputation
should be immediately performed. For my own part—individually, I mean, and without respect to the patient—I am
sorry to have it so decided. But this settles the question, gentlemen—in my own mind, however, it was settled before. At
ten o'clock to-morrow morning the operation will be performed. I shall be happy to see you all on the occasion, and
also your juniors" (alluding to the absent *Assistant Surgeons*).
"Good-morning, gentlemen; at ten o'clock, remember."

And Cuticle retreated to the Ward-room.

Chapter 63

THE OPERATION

NEXT MORNING, at the appointed hour, the surgeons arrived in a body. They were accompanied by their juniors, young men ranging in age from nineteen years to thirty. Like the senior surgeons, these young gentlemen were arrayed in their blue navy uniforms, displaying a profusion of bright buttons, and several broad bars of gold lace about the wristbands. As in honor of the occasion, they had put on their best coats; they looked exceedingly brilliant.

The whole party immediately descended to the half-deck, where preparations had been made for the operation. A large garrison-ensign was stretched across the ship by the mainmast, so as completely to screen the space behind. This space included the whole extent aft to the bulk-head of the Commodore's cabin, at the door of which the marine-orderly paced, in plain sight, cutlass in hand.

Upon two gun-carriages, dragged amidships, the Death-board (used for burials at sea) was horizontally placed, covered with an old royal-stun'-sail. Upon this occasion, to do duty as an amputation-table, it was widened by an additional plank. Two match-tubs, near by, placed one upon another, at either end supported another plank, distinct from the table, whereon was exhibited an array of saws and knives of various and peculiar shapes and sizes; also, a sort of steel, something like the dinner-table implement, together with long needles, crooked at the end for taking up the arteries, and large darning-needles, thread and bee's-wax, for sewing up a wound.

At the end nearest the larger table was a tin basin of water, surrounded by small sponges, placed at mathematical intervals. From the long horizontal pole of a great-gun rammer—fixed in its usual place overhead—hung a number of towels, with "U. S." marked in the corners.

All these arrangements had been made by the "Surgeon's steward," a person whose important functions in a man-of-war will, in a future chapter, be entered upon at large. Upon the present occasion, he was bustling about, adjusting and readjusting the knives, needles, and carver, like an over-conscientious butler fidgeting over a dinner-table just before the convivialists enter.

But by far the most striking object to be seen behind the ensign was a human skeleton, whose every joint articulated with wires. By a rivet at the apex of the skull, it hung dangling from a hammock-hook fixed in a beam above. Why this object was here, will presently be seen; but why it was placed immediately at the foot of the amputation-table, only Surgeon Cuticle can tell.

While the final preparations were being made, Cuticle stood conversing with the assembled Surgeons and Assistant Surgeons, his invited guests.

"Gentlemen," said he, taking up one of the glittering knives and artistically drawing the steel across it; "Gentlemen, though these scenes are very unpleasant, and in some moods, I may say, repulsive to me—yet how much better for our patient to have the contusions and lacerations of his present wound—with all its dangerous symptoms—converted into a clean incision, free from these objections, and occasioning so much less subsequent anxiety to himself and the Surgeon. Yes," he added, tenderly feeling the edge of his knife, "amputation is our only resource. Is it not so, Surgeon Patella?" turning toward that gentleman, as if relying upon some sort of an assent, however clogged with conditions.

"Certainly," said Patella, "amputation is your only resource, Mr. Surgeon of the Fleet; that is, I mean, if you are fully persuaded of its necessity."

The other surgeons said nothing, maintaining a somewhat reserved air, as if conscious that they had no positive authority in the case, whatever might be their own private opinions; but they seemed willing to behold, and, if called upon, to assist at the operation, since it could not now be averted.

The young men, their Assistants, looked very eager, and cast frequent glances of awe upon so distinguished a practitioner as the venerable Cuticle.

"They say he can drop a leg in one minute and ten seconds from the moment the knife touches it," whispered one of them to another.

"We shall see," was the reply, and the speaker clapped his hand to his fob, to see if his watch would be forthcoming when wanted.

"Are you all ready here?" demanded Cuticle, now advancing to his steward; "have not those fellows got through yet?" pointing to three men of the carpenter's gang, who were placing bits of wood under the gun-carriages supporting the central table.

"They are just through, sir," respectfully answered the Steward, touching his hand to his forehead, as if there were a cap-front there.

"Bring up the patient, then," said Cuticle.

"Young gentlemen," he added, turning to the row of Assistant Surgeons, "seeing you here reminds me of the classes of students once under my instruction at the Philadelphia College of Physicians and Surgeons. Ah, those were happy days!" he sighed, applying the extreme corner of his handkerchief to his glass eye. "Excuse an old man's emotions, young gentlemen; but when I think of the numerous rare cases that then came under my treatment, I can not but give way to my feelings. The town, the city, the metropolis, young gentlemen, is the place for you students; at least in these dull times of peace, when the army and navy furnish no inducements for a youth ambitious of rising in our honorable profession. Take an old man's advice, and if the war now threatening between the States and Mexico should break out, exchange your Navy commissions for commissions in the army. From having no military marine herself, Mexico has always been backward in furnishing subjects for the amputation-tables of foreign navies. The cause of science has languished in her hands. The army, young gentlemen, is your best school; depend upon it. You will hardly believe it, Surgeon Bandage," turning to that gentleman, "but this is my first important case of surgery in a nearly three years' cruise. I have been almost wholly confined in this ship to doctor's practice— prescribing for fevers and fluxes. True, the other day a man fell from the mizzen-top-sail yard; but that was merely an aggravated case of dislocations and bones splintered and broken. No one, sir, could have made an amputation of it, without severely contusing his conscience. And mine—I may say it, gentlemen, without ostentation—is peculiarly susceptible."

And so saying, the knife and carver touchingly dropped to his sides, and he stood for a moment fixed in a tender reverie. But a commotion being heard beyond the curtain, he started, and, briskly crossing and recrossing the knife and carver, exclaimed, "Ah, here comes our patient; surgeons, this side of the table, if you please; young gentlemen, a little further off, I beg. Steward, take off my coat—so; my neckerchief now; I must be perfectly unencumbered, Surgeon Patella, or I can do nothing whatever."

These articles being removed, he snatched off his wig, placing it on the gun-deck capstan; then took out his set of false teeth, and placed it by the side of the wig; and, lastly, putting his forefinger to the inner angle of his blind eye, spirited out the glass optic with professional dexterity, and deposited that, also, next to the wig and false teeth.

Thus divested of nearly all inorganic appurtenances, what was left of the Surgeon slightly shook itself, to see whether any thing more could be spared to advantage.

"Carpenter's mates," he now cried, "will you never get through with that job?"

"Almost through, sir—just through," they replied, staring round in search of the strange, unearthly voice that addressed them; for the absence of his teeth had not at all improved the conversational tones of the Surgeon of the Fleet.

With natural curiosity, these men had purposely been lingering, to see all they could; but now, having no further excuse, they snatched up their hammers and chisels, and—like the stage-builders decamping from a public meeting at the eleventh hour, after just completing the rostrum in time for the first speaker—the Carpenter's gang withdrew.

The broad ensign now lifted, revealing a glimpse of the crowd of man-of-war's-men outside, and the patient, borne in the arms of two of his mess-mates, entered the place. He was much emaciated, weak as an infant, and every limb visibly trembled, or rather jarred, like the head of a man with the palsy. As if an organic and involuntary apprehension of death had seized the wounded leg, its nervous motions were so violent that one of the mess-mates was obliged to keep his hand upon it.

The top-man was immediately stretched upon the table, the attendants steadying his limbs, when, slowly opening his eyes, he glanced about at the glittering knives and saws, the towels and sponges, the armed sentry at the Commodore's cabin-door, the row of eager-eyed students, the meagre death's-head of a Cuticle, now with his shirt sleeves rolled up upon his withered arms and knife in hand, and, finally, his eye settled in horror upon the skeleton, slowly vibrating and jingling before him, with the slow, slight roll of the frigate in the water.

"I would advise perfect repose of your every limb, my man," said Cuticle, addressing him; "the precision of an operation is often impaired by the inconsiderate restlessness of the patient. But if you consider, my good fellow," he added, in a patronizing and almost sympathetic tone, and slightly pressing his hand on the limb, "if you consider how much better it is to live with three limbs than to die with four, and especially if you but knew to what torments both sailors and soldiers were subjected before the time of Celsus, owing to the lamentable ignorance of surgery then prevailing, you would certainly thank God from the bottom of your heart that *your* operation has been postponed to the period of this enlightened age, blessed with a Bell, a Brodie, and a Larrey. My man, before Celsus's time, such was the general ignorance of our noble science, that, in order to prevent the excessive effusion of blood, it was deemed indispensable to operate with a red-hot knife"—making a professional movement toward the thigh—"and pour scalding oil upon the parts"—elevating his elbow, as if with a tea-pot in his hand—"still further to sear them, after amputation had been performed."

"He is fainting!" said one of his mess-mates; "quick! some water!" The steward immediately hurried to the top-man with the basin.

Cuticle took the top-man by the wrist, and feeling it a while, observed, "Don't be alarmed, men," addressing the two mess-mates; "he'll recover presently; this fainting very generally takes place." And he stood for a moment, tranquilly eying the patient.

Now the Surgeon of the Fleet and the top-man presented

a spectacle which, to a reflecting mind, was better than a church-yard sermon on the mortality of man.

Here was a sailor, who, four days previous, had stood erect—a pillar of life—with an arm like a royal-mast and a thigh like a windlass. But the slightest conceivable finger-touch of a bit of crooked trigger had eventuated in stretching him out, more helpless than an hour-old babe, with a blasted thigh, utterly drained of its brawn. And who was it that now stood over him like a superior being, and, as if clothed himself with the attributes of immortality, indifferently discoursed of carving up his broken flesh, and thus piecing out his abbreviated days? Who was it, that in capacity of Surgeon, seemed enacting the part of a Regenerator of life? The withered, shrunken, one-eyed, toothless, hairless Cuticle; with a trunk half dead—a *memento mori* to behold!

And while, in those soul-sinking and panic-striking premonitions of speedy death which almost invariably accompany a severe gun-shot wound, even with the most intrepid spirits; while thus drooping and dying, this once robust topman's eye was now waning in his head like a Lapland moon being eclipsed in clouds—Cuticle, who for years had still lived in his withered tabernacle of a body—Cuticle, no doubt sharing in the common self-delusion of old age—Cuticle must have felt his hold of life as secure as the grim hug of a grizzly bear. Verily, Life is more awful than Death; and let no man, though his live heart beat in him like a cannon—let him not hug his life to himself; for, in the predestinated necessities of things, that bounding life of his is not a whit more secure than the life of a man on his death-bed. To-day we inhale the air with expanding lungs, and life runs through us like a thousand Niles; but to-morrow we may collapse in death, and all our veins be dry as the Brook Kedron in a drought.

"And now, young gentlemen," said Cuticle, turning to the Assistant Surgeons, "while the patient is coming to, permit me to describe to you the highly-interesting operation I am about to perform."

"Mr. Surgeon of the Fleet," said Surgeon Bandage, "if you are about to lecture, permit me to present you with your teeth; they will make your discourse more readily understood." And so saying, Bandage, with a bow, placed the two semicircles of ivory into Cuticle's hands.

"Thank you, Surgeon Bandage," said Cuticle, and slipped the ivory into its place.

"In the first place, now, young gentlemen, let me direct your attention to the excellent preparation before you. I have had it unpacked from its case, and set up here from my state-room, where it occupies the spare berth; and all this for your express benefit, young gentlemen. This skeleton I procured in person from the Hunterian department of the Royal College of Surgeons in London. It is a master-piece of art. But we have no time to examine it now. Delicacy forbids that I should amplify at a juncture like this"—casting an almost be-nignant glance toward the patient, now beginning to open his eyes; "but let me point out to you upon this thigh-bone"—disengaging it from the skeleton, with a gentle twist—"the precise place where I propose to perform the op-eration. *Here*, young gentlemen, *here* is the place. You per-ceive it is very near the point of articulation with the trunk."

"Yes," interposed Surgeon Wedge, rising on his toes, "yes, young gentlemen, the point of articulation with the *acetabu-lum* of the *os innominatum*."

"Where's your 'Bell on Bones,' Dick?" whispered one of the assistants to the student next him. "Wedge has been spending the whole morning over it, getting out the hard names."

"Surgeon Wedge," said Cuticle, looking round severely, "we will dispense with your commentaries, if you please, at present. Now, young gentlemen, you can not but perceive, that the point of operation being so near the trunk and the vitals, it becomes an unusually beautiful one, demanding a steady hand and a true eye; and, after all, the patient may die under my hands."

"Quick, Steward! water, water; he's fainting again!" cried the two mess-mates.

"Don't be alarmed for your comrade, men," said Cuticle, turning round. "I tell you it is not an uncommon thing for the patient to betray some emotion upon these occasions—most usually manifested by swooning; it is quite natural it should be so. But we must not delay the operation. Steward, that knife—no, the next one—there, that's it. He is coming to, I think"—feeling the top-man's wrist. "Are you all ready, sir?"

This last observation was addressed to one of the Never-sink's assistant surgeons, a tall, lank, cadaverous young man, arrayed in a sort of shroud of white canvass, pinned about his throat, and completely enveloping his person. He was seated on a match-tub—the skeleton swinging near his head—at the foot of the table, in readiness to grasp the limb, as when a plank is being severed by a carpenter and his apprentice.

"The sponges, Steward," said Cuticle, for the last time taking out his teeth, and drawing up his shirt sleeve still further. Then, taking the patient by the wrist, "Stand by, now, you mess-mates; keep hold of his arms; pin him down. Steward, put your hand on the artery; I shall commence as soon as his pulse begins to— *now, now!*" Letting fall the wrist, feeling the thigh carefully, and bowing over it an instant, he drew the fatal knife unerringly across the flesh. As it first touched the part, the row of surgeons simultaneously dropped their eyes to the watches in their hands, while the patient lay, with eyes horribly distended, in a kind of waking trance. Not a breath was heard; but as the quivering flesh parted in a long, lingering gash, a spring of blood welled up between the living walls of the wound, and two thick streams, in opposite directions, coursed down the thigh. The sponges were instantly dipped in the purple pool; every face present was pinched to a point with suspense; the limb writhed; the man shrieked; his mess-mates pinioned him; while round and round the leg went the unpitying cut.

"The saw!" said Cuticle.

Instantly it was in his hand.

Full of the operation, he was about to apply it, when, look-ing up, and turning to the assistant surgeons, he said, "Would any of you young gentlemen like to apply the saw? A splendid subject!"

Several volunteered; when, selecting one, Cuticle surren-dered the instrument to him, saying, "Don't be hurried, now; be steady."

While the rest of the assistants looked upon their comrade with glances of envy, he went rather timidly to work; and Cuticle, who was earnestly regarding him, suddenly snatched the saw from his hand. "Away, butcher! you disgrace the profession. Look at *me*!"

For a few moments the thrilling, rasping sound was heard; and then the top-man seemed parted in twain at the hip, as the leg slowly slid into the arms of the pale, gaunt man in the shroud, who at once made away with it, and tucked it out of sight under one of the guns.

"Surgeon Sawyer," now said Cuticle, courteously turning to the surgeon of the Buccaneer, "would you like to take up the arteries? They are quite at your service, sir."

"Do, Sawyer; be prevailed upon," said Surgeon Bandage.

Sawyer complied; and while, with some modesty, he was conducting the operation, Cuticle, turning to the row of assistants, said, "Young gentlemen, we will now proceed with our illustration. Hand me that bone, Steward." And taking the thigh-bone in his still bloody hands, and holding it conspicuously before his auditors, the Surgeon of the Fleet began:

"Young gentlemen, you will perceive that precisely at this spot— *here*—to which I previously directed your attention— at the corresponding spot precisely—the operation has been performed. About here, young gentlemen, *here*"—lifting his hand some inches from the bone—"about *here* the great artery was. But you noticed that I did not use the tourniquet; I never do. The forefinger of my steward is far better than a tourniquet, being so much more manageable, and leaving the smaller veins uncompressed. But I have been told, young gentlemen, that a certain Seignior Seignioroni, a surgeon of Seville, has recently invented an admirable substitute for the clumsy, old-fashioned tourniquet. As I understand it, it is something like a pair of *calipers*, working with a small Archimedes screw—a very clever invention, according to all accounts. For the padded points at the end of the arches"— arching his forefinger and thumb—"can be so worked as to approximate in such a way, as to—but you don't attend to me, young gentlemen," he added, all at once starting.

Being more interested in the active proceedings of Surgeon Sawyer, who was now threading a needle to sew up the overlapping of the stump, the young gentlemen had not scrupled to turn away their attention altogether from the lecturer.

A few moments more, and the top-man, in a swoon, was removed below into the sick-bay. As the curtain settled again after the patient had disappeared, Cuticle, still holding the thigh-bone of the skeleton in his ensanguined hands, proceeded with his remarks upon it; and having concluded them, added, "Now, young gentlemen, not the least interesting consequence of this operation will be the finding of the ball, which, in case of non-amputation, might have long eluded the most careful search. That ball, young gentlemen, must have taken a most circuitous route. Nor, in cases where the direction is oblique, is this at all unusual. Indeed, the learned Hennen gives us a most remarkable—I had almost said an incredible—case of a soldier's neck, where the bullet, entering at the part called Adam's Apple—"

"Yes," said Surgeon Wedge, elevating himself, "the *pomum Adami*."

"Entering the point called *Adam's Apple*," continued Cuticle, severely emphasizing the last two words, "ran completely round the neck, and, emerging at the same hole it had entered, shot the next man in the ranks. It was afterward extracted, says Hennen, from the second man, and pieces of the other's skin were found adhering to it. But examples of foreign substances being received into the body with a ball, young gentlemen, are frequently observed. Being attached to a United States ship at the time, I happened to be near the spot of the battle of Ayacucho, in Peru. The day after the action, I saw in the barracks of the wounded a trooper, who, having been severely injured in the brain, went crazy, and, with his own holster-pistol, committed suicide in the hospital. The ball drove inward a portion of his woolen night-cap—"

"In the form of a *cul-de-sac*, doubtless," said the undaunted Wedge.

"For once, Surgeon Wedge, you use the only term that can be employed; and let me avail myself of this opportunity to say to you, young gentlemen, that a man of true science"—expanding his shallow chest a little—"uses but few hard words, and those only when none other will answer his purpose; whereas the smatterer in science"—slightly glancing toward Wedge—"thinks, that by mouthing hard words, he proves that he understands hard things. Let this sink deep in your minds, young gentlemen; and, Surgeon Wedge"—with a stiff bow—"permit me to submit the reflection to yourself. Well, young gentlemen, the bullet was afterward extracted by pulling upon the external parts of the *cul-de-sac*—a simple, but exceedingly beautiful operation. There is a fine example, somewhat similar, related in Guthrie; but, of course, you must have met with it, in so well-known a work as his Treatise upon Gun-shot Wounds. When, upward of twenty years ago, I was with Lord Cochrane, then Admiral of the fleets of this very country"—pointing shoreward, out of a porthole—"a sailor of the vessel to which I was attached, during the blockade of Bahia, had his leg—" But by this time the fidgets had completely taken possession of his auditors, especially of the senior surgeons; and turning upon them abruptly, he added, "But I will not detain you longer, gentlemen"—turning round upon all the surgeons—"your dinners must be waiting you on board your respective ships. But, Surgeon Sawyer, perhaps you may desire to wash your hands before you go. There is the basin, sir; you will find a clean towel on the rammer. For myself, I seldom use them"—taking out his handkerchief. "I must leave you now, gentlemen"—bowing. "To-morrow, at ten, the limb will be upon the table, and I shall be happy to see you all upon the occasion. Who's there?" turning to the curtain, which then rustled.

"Please, sir," said the Steward, entering, "the patient is dead."

"The body also, gentlemen, at ten precisely," said Cuticle, once more turning round upon his guests. "I predicted that the operation might prove fatal; he was very much run down. Good-morning;" and Cuticle departed.

"He does not, surely, mean to touch the body?" exclaimed Surgeon Sawyer, with much excitement.

"Oh, no!" said Patella, "that's only his way; he means, doubtless, that it may be inspected previous to being taken ashore for burial."

The assemblage of gold-laced surgeons now ascended to the quarter-deck; the second cutter was called away by the bugler, and, one by one, they were dropped aboard of their respective ships.

The following evening the mess-mates of the top-man rowed his remains ashore, and buried them in the ever-vernal Protestant cemetery, hard by the Beach of the Flamingoes, in plain sight from the bay.

Chapter 64

MAN-OF-WAR TROPHIES

WHEN the second cutter pulled about among the ships, dropping the surgeons aboard the American men-of-war here and there—as a pilot-boat distributes her pilots at the mouth of the harbor—she passed several foreign frigates, two of which, an Englishman and a Frenchman, had excited not a little remark on board the Neversink. These vessels often loosed their sails and exercised yards simultaneously with ourselves, as if desirous of comparing the respective efficiency of the crews.

When we were nearly ready for sea, the English frigate, weighing her anchor, made all sail with the sea-breeze, and began showing off her paces by gliding about among all the men-of-war in harbor, and particularly by running down under the Neversink's stern. Every time she drew near, we complimented her by lowering our ensign a little, and invariably she courteously returned the salute. She was inviting us to a sailing-match; and it was rumored that, when we should leave the bay, our Captain would have no objections to gratify her; for, be it known, the Neversink was accounted the fleetest keeled craft sailing under the American long-pennant. Perhaps this was the reason why the stranger challenged us.

It may have been that a portion of our crew were the more anxious to race with this frigate, from a little circumstance which a few of them deemed rather galling. Not many cables'-length distant from our Commodore's cabin lay the frigate President, with the red cross of St. George flying from her peak. As its name imported, this fine craft was an American born; but having been captured during the last war with Britain, she now sailed the salt seas as a trophy.

Think of it, my gallant countrymen, one and all, down the sea-coast and along the endless banks of the Ohio and Columbia—think of the twinges we sea-patriots must have felt to behold the live-oak of the Floridas and the pines of green Maine built into the oaken walls of Old England! But, to some of the sailors, there was a counterbalancing thought, as grateful as the other was galling, and that was, that somewhere, sailing under the stars and stripes, was the frigate Macedonian, a British-born craft which had once sported the battle-banner of Britain.

It has ever been the custom to spend almost any amount of money in repairing a captured vessel, in order that she may long survive to commemorate the heroism of the conqueror. Thus, in the English Navy, there are many Monsieurs of seventy-fours won from the Gaul. But we Americans can show but few similar trophies, though, no doubt, we would much like to be able so to do.

But I never have beheld any of these floating trophies without being reminded of a scene once witnessed in a pioneer village on the western bank of the Mississippi. Not far from this village, where the stumps of aboriginal trees yet stand in the market-place, some years ago lived a portion of the remnant tribes of the Sioux Indians, who frequently visited the white settlements to purchase trinkets and cloths.

One florid crimson evening in July, when the red-hot sun was going down in a blaze, and I was leaning against a corner in my huntsman's frock, lo! there came stalking out of the crimson West a gigantic red-man, erect as a pine, with his glittering tomahawk, big as a broad-ax, folded in martial repose across his chest. Moodily wrapped in his blanket, and striding like a king on the stage, he promenaded up and down the rustic streets, exhibiting on the back of his blanket a crowd of human hands, rudely delineated in red; one of them seemed recently drawn.

"Who is this warrior?" asked I; "and why marches he here? and for what are these bloody hands?"

"That warrior is the *Red-Hot Coal*," said a pioneer in moccasins, by my side. "He marches here to show off his last trophy; every one of those hands attests a foe scalped by his tomahawk; and he has just emerged from Ben Brown's, the painter, who has sketched the last red hand that you see; for last night this *Red-Hot Coal* outburned the *Yellow Torch*, the chief of a band of the Foxes."

Poor savage! thought I; and is this the cause of your lofty gait? Do you straighten yourself to think that you have committed a murder, when a chance-falling stone has often done the same? Is it a proud thing to topple down six feet perpendicular of immortal manhood, though that lofty living tower needed perhaps thirty good growing summers to bring it to maturity? Poor savage! And you account it so glorious, do you, to mutilate and destroy what God himself was more than a quarter of a century in building?

And yet, fellow-Christians, what is the American frigate Macedonian, or the English frigate President, but as two bloody red hands painted on this poor savage's blanket?

Are there no Moravians in the Moon, that not a missionary has yet visited this poor pagan planet of ours, to civilize civilization and christianize Christendom?

Chapter 65

A Man-of-war Race

WE LAY in Rio so long—for what reason the Commodore only knows—that a saying went abroad among the impatient sailors that our frigate would at last ground on the beef-bones daily thrown overboard by the cooks.

But at last the good tidings came. "All hands up anchor, ahoy!" And bright and early in the morning up came our old iron, as the sun rose in the East.

The land-breeze at Rio—by which alone vessels may emerge from the bay—is ever languid and faint. It comes from gardens of citrons and cloves, spiced with all the spices of the Tropic of Capricorn. And, like that old exquisite, Mohammed, who so much loved to snuff perfumes and essences, and used to lounge out of the conservatories of Khadija, his wife, to give battle to the robust sons of Koriesh; even so this Rio land-breeze comes jaded with sweet-smelling savors, to wrestle with the wild Tartar breezes of the sea.

Slowly we dropped and dropped down the bay, glided like a stately swan through the outlet, and were gradually rolled by the smooth, sliding billows broad out upon the deep. Straight in our wake came the tall main-mast of the English fighting-frigate, terminating, like a steepled cathedral, in the bannered cross of the religion of peace; and straight after *her* came the rainbow banner of France, sporting God's token that no more would he make war on the earth.

Both Englishman and Frenchman were resolved on a race; and we Yankees swore by our top-sails and royals to sink their blazing banners that night among the Southern constellations we should daily be extinguishing behind us in our run to the North.

"Ay," said Mad Jack, "St. George's banner shall be as the *Southern Cross*, out of sight, leagues down the horizon, while our gallant stars, my brave boys, shall burn all alone in the North, like the Great Bear at the Pole! Come on, Rainbow and Cross!"

But the wind was long languid and faint, not yet recovered from its night's dissipation ashore, and noon advanced, with the Sugar-Loaf pinnacle in sight.

Now it is not with ships as with horses; for though, if a horse walk well and fast, it generally furnishes good token that he is not bad at a gallop, yet the ship that in a light breeze is outstripped, may sweep the stakes, so soon as a t'-gallant breeze enables her to strike into a canter. Thus fared it with us. First, the Englishman glided ahead, and bluffly passed on; then the Frenchman politely bade us adieu, while the old Neversink lingered behind, railing at the effeminate breeze. At one time, all three frigates were irregularly abreast, forming a diagonal line; and so near were all three, that the stately officers on the poops stiffly saluted by touching their caps, though refraining from any further civilities. At this juncture, it was a noble sight to behold those fine frigates, with dripping breast-hooks, all rearing and nodding in concert, and to look through their tall spars and wilderness of rigging, that seemed like inextricably-entangled, gigantic cobwebs against the sky.

Toward sundown the ocean pawed its white hoofs to the spur of its helter-skelter rider, a strong blast from the Eastward, and, giving three cheers from decks, yards, and tops, we crowded all sail on St. George and St. Denis.

But it is harder to overtake than outstrip; night fell upon us, still in the rear—still where the little boat was, which, at the eleventh hour, according to a Rabbinical tradition, pushed after the ark of old Noah.

It was a misty, cloudy night; and though at first our look-outs kept the chase in dim sight, yet at last so thick became the atmosphere, that no sign of a strange spar was to be seen. But the worst of it was, that, when last discerned, the Frenchman was broad on our weather-bow, and the Englishman gallantly leading his van.

The breeze blew fresher and fresher; but, with even our main-royal set, we dashed along through a cream-colored ocean of illuminated foam. White-Jacket was then in the top; and it was glorious to look down and see our black hull butting the white sea with its broad bows like a ram.

"We must beat them with such a breeze, dear Jack," said I to our noble Captain of the Top.

"But the same breeze blows for John Bull, remember," replied Jack, who, being a Briton, perhaps favored the Englishman more than the Neversink.

"But how we boom through the billows!" cried Jack, gazing over the top-rail; then, flinging forth his arm, recited,

> " 'Aslope, and gliding on the leeward side,
> The bounding vessel cuts the roaring tide.'

Camoens! White-Jacket, Camoens! Did you ever read him? The Lusiad, I mean? It's the man-of-war epic of the world, my lad. Give me Gama for a Commodore, say I—Noble Gama! And Mickle, White-Jacket, did you ever read of him? William Julius Mickle? Camoen's Translator? A disappointed man though, White-Jacket. Besides his version of the Lusiad, he wrote many forgotten things. Did you ever see his ballad of Cumnor Hall?—No?—Why, it gave Sir Walter Scott the hint of Kenilworth. My father knew Mickle when he went to sea on board the old Romney man-of-war. How many great men have been sailors, White-Jacket! They say Homer himself was once a tar, even as his hero, Ulysses, was both a sailor and a shipwright. I'll swear Shakspeare was once a captain of the forecastle. Do you mind the first scene in *The Tempest*, White-Jacket? And the world-finder, Christopher Columbus, was a sailor! and so was Camoens, who went to sea with Gama, else we had never had the Lusiad, White-Jacket. Yes, I've sailed over the very track that Camoens sailed—round the East Cape into the Indian Ocean. I've been in Don Jose's garden, too, in Macao, and bathed my feet in the blessed dew of the walks where Camoens wandered before me. Yes, White-Jacket, and I have seen and sat in the cave at the end of the flowery, winding way, where Camoens, according to tradition, composed certain parts of his Lusiad. Ay, Camoens was a sailor once! Then, there's Falconer, whose 'Shipwreck' will never founder, though he himself, poor fellow, was lost at sea in the Aurora frigate. Old Noah was the first sailor. And St. Paul, too, knew how to box the compass, my lad! mind you that chapter in Acts? I couldn't spin the yarn better myself. Were you ever in Malta? They called it Melita in the

Apostle's day. I have been in Paul's cave there, White-Jacket. They say a piece of it is good for a charm against shipwreck; but I never tried it. There's Shelley, he was quite a sailor. Shelley—poor lad! a Percy, too—but they ought to have let him sleep in his sailor's grave—he was drowned in the Mediterranean, you know, near Leghorn—and not burn his body, as they did, as if he had been a bloody Turk. But many people thought him so, White-Jacket, because he didn't go to mass, and because he wrote Queen Mab. Trelawny was by at the burning; and he was an ocean-rover, too! Ay, and Byron helped put a piece of a keel on the fire; for it was made of bits of a wreck, they say; one wreck burning another! And was not Byron a sailor? an amateur forecastle-man, White-Jacket! so he was; else how bid the ocean heave and fall in that grand, majestic way? I say, White-Jacket, d'ye mind me? there never was a very great man yet who spent all his life inland. A snuff of the sea, my boy, is inspiration; and having been once out of sight of land, has been the making of many a true poet and the blasting of many pretenders; for, d'ye see, there's no gammon about the ocean; it knocks the false keel right off a pretender's bows; it tells him just what he is, and makes him feel it, too. A sailor's life, I say, is the thing to bring us mortals out. What does the blessed Bible say? Don't it say that we main-top-men alone see the marvelous sights and wonders? Don't deny the blessed Bible, now! don't do it! How it rocks up here, my boy!" holding on to a shroud; "but it only proves what I've been saying—the sea is the place to cradle genius! Heave and fall, old sea!"

"And *you*, also, noble Jack," said I, "what are you but a sailor?"

"You're merry, my boy," said Jack, looking up with a glance like that of a sentimental archangel doomed to drag out his eternity in disgrace. "But mind you, White-Jacket, there are many great men in the world besides Commodores and Captains. I've that here, White-Jacket"—touching his forehead—"which, under happier skies—perhaps in yon solitary star there, peeping down from those clouds—might have made a Homer of me. But Fate is Fate, White-Jacket; and we Homers who happen to be captains of tops must write our odes in our hearts, and publish them in our heads.

But look! the Captain's on the poop."

It was now midnight; but all the officers were on deck.

"Jib-boom, there!" cried the Lieutenant of the Watch, going forward and hailing the headmost look-out. "D'ye see any thing of those fellows now?"

"See nothing, sir."

"See nothing, sir," said the Lieutenant, approaching the Captain, and touching his cap.

"Call all hands!" roared the Captain. "This keel sha'n't be beat while I stride it."

All hands were called, and the hammocks stowed in the nettings for the rest of the night, so that no one could lie between blankets.

Now, in order to explain the means adopted by the Captain to insure us the race, it needs to be said of the Neversink, that, for some years after being launched, she was accounted one of the slowest vessels in the American Navy. But it chanced upon a time, that, being on a cruise in the Mediterranean, she happened to sail out of Port Mahon in what was then supposed to be very bad trim for the sea. Her bows were rooting in the water, and her stern kicking up its heels in the air. But, wonderful to tell, it was soon discovered that in this comical posture she sailed like a shooting-star; she outstripped every vessel on the station. Thenceforward all her Captains, on all cruises, *trimmed her by the head*; and the Neversink gained the name of a clipper.

To return. All hands being called, they were now made use of by Captain Claret as make-weights, to trim the ship, scientifically, to her most approved bearings. Some were sent forward on the spar-deck, with twenty-four-pound shot in their hands, and were judiciously scattered about here and there, with strict orders not to budge an inch from their stations, for fear of marring the Captain's plans. Others were distributed along the gun and berth decks, with similar orders; and, to crown all, several carronade guns were unshipped from their carriages, and swung in their breechings from the beams of the main-deck, so as to impart a sort of vibratory briskness and oscillating buoyancy to the frigate.

And thus we five hundred make-weights stood out that whole night, some of us exposed to a drenching rain, in order that the Neversink might not be beaten. But the comfort and consolation of all make-weights is as dust in the balance in the estimation of the rulers of our man-of-war world.

The long, anxious night at last came to an end, and, with the first peep of day, the look-out on the jib-boom was hailed; but nothing was in sight. At last it was broad day; yet still not a bow was to be seen in our rear, nor a stern in our van.

"Where are they?" cried the Captain.

"Out of sight, astern, to be sure, sir," said the officer of the deck.

"Out of sight, *ahead*, to be sure, sir," muttered Jack Chase, in the top.

Precisely thus stood the question: whether we beat them, or whether they beat us, no mortal can tell to this hour, since we never saw them again; but for one, White-Jacket will lay his two hands on the bow-chasers of the Neversink, and take his ship's oath that we Yankees carried the day.

Chapter 66

FUN IN A MAN-OF-WAR

AFTER THE RACE (our man-of-war Derby) we had many days fine weather, during which we continued running before the Trades toward the north. Exhilarated by the thought of being homeward-bound, many of the seamen became joyous, and the discipline of the ship, if any thing, became a little relaxed. Many pastimes served to while away the *Dog-Watches* in particular. These *Dog-Watches* (embracing two hours in the early part of the evening) form the only authorized play-time for the crews of most ships at sea.

Among other diversions at present licensed by authority in the Neversink, were those of single-stick, sparring, hammer-and-anvil, and head-bumping. All these were under the direct patronage of the Captain, otherwise—seeing the consequences they sometimes led to—they would undoubtedly have been strictly prohibited. It is a curious coincidence, that when a navy captain does not happen to be an admirer of the *Fistiana*, his crew seldom amuse themselves in that way.

Single-stick, as every one knows, is a delightful pastime, which consists in two men standing a few feet apart, and rapping each other over the head with long poles. There is a good deal of fun in it, so long as you are not hit; but a hit—in the judgment of discreet persons—spoils the sport completely. When this pastime is practiced by connoisseurs ashore, they wear heavy, wired helmets, to break the force of the blows. But the only helmets of our tars were those with which nature had furnished them. They played with great gun-rammers.

Sparring consists in playing single-stick with bone poles instead of wooden ones. Two men stand apart, and pommel each other with their fists (a hard bunch of knuckles permanently attached to the arms, and made globular, or extended into a palm, at the pleasure of the proprietor), till one of them, finding himself sufficiently thrashed, cries *enough*.

Hammer-and-anvil is thus practiced by amateurs: Patient

638

No. 1 gets on all-fours, and stays so; while patient No. 2 is taken up by his arms and legs, and his base is swung against the base of patient No. 1, till patient No. 1, with the force of the final blow, is sent flying along the deck.

Head-bumping, as patronized by Captain Claret, consists in two negroes (whites will not answer) butting at each other like rams. This pastime was an especial favorite with the Captain. In the Dog-Watches, Rose-Water and May-Day were repeatedly summoned into the lee waist to tilt at each other, for the benefit of the Captain's health.

May-Day was a full-blooded "*bull-negro*," so the sailors called him, with a skull like an iron tea-kettle, wherefore May-Day much fancied the sport. But Rose-Water, he was a slender and rather handsome mulatto, and abhorred the pastime. Nevertheless, the Captain must be obeyed; so at the word poor Rose-Water was fain to put himself in a posture of defence, else May-Day would incontinently have bumped him out of a port-hole into the sea. I used to pity poor Rose-Water from the bottom of my heart. But my pity was almost aroused into indignation at a sad sequel to one of these gladiatorial scenes.

It seems that, lifted up by the unaffected, though verbally unexpressed applause of the Captain, May-Day had begun to despise Rose-Water as a poltroon—a fellow all brains and no skull; whereas he himself was a great warrior, all skull and no brains.

Accordingly, after they had been bumping one evening to the Captain's content, May-Day confidentially told Rose-Water that he considered him a "*nigger*," which, among some blacks, is held a great term of reproach. Fired at the insult, Rose-Water gave May-Day to understand that he utterly erred; for his mother, a black slave, had been one of the mistresses of a Virginia planter belonging to one of the oldest families in that state. Another insulting remark followed this innocent disclosure; retort followed retort; in a word, at last they came together in mortal combat.

The master-at-arms caught them in the act, and brought them up to the mast. The Captain advanced.

"Please, sir," said poor Rose-Water, "it all come of dat 'ar bumping; May-Day, here, aggrawated me 'bout it."

"Master-at-arms," said the Captain, "did you see them fighting?"

"Ay, sir," said the master-at-arms, touching his cap.

"Rig the gratings," said the Captain. "I'll teach you two men that, though I now and then permit you to *play*, I will have no *fighting*. Do your duty, boatswain's mate!" And the negroes were flogged.

Justice commands that the fact of the Captain's not showing any leniency to May-Day—a decided favorite of his, at least while in the ring—should not be passed over. He flogged both culprits in the most impartial manner.

As in the matter of the scene at the gangway, shortly after the Cape Horn theatricals, when my attention had been directed to the fact that the officers had *shipped their quarter-deck faces*—upon that occasion, I say, it was seen with what facility a sea-officer assumes his wonted severity of demeanor after a casual relaxation of it. This was especially the case with Captain Claret upon the present occasion. For any landsman to have beheld him in the lee waist, of a pleasant Dog-Watch, with a genial, good-humored countenance, observing the gladiators in the ring, and now and then indulging in a playful remark—that landsman would have deemed Captain Claret the indulgent father of his crew, perhaps permitting the excess of his kind-heartedness to encroach upon the appropriate dignity of his station. He would have deemed Captain Claret a fine illustration of those two well-known poetical comparisons between a sea-captain and a father, and between a sea-captain and the master of apprentices, instituted by those eminent maritime jurists, the noble Lords Tenterden and Stowell.

But surely, if there is any thing hateful, it is this *shipping of the quarter-deck face* after wearing a merry and good-natured one. How can they have the heart? Methinks, if but once I smiled upon a man—never mind how much beneath me—I could not bring myself to condemn him to the shocking misery of the lash. Oh officers! all round the world, if this quarter-deck face you wear at all, then never unship it for another, to be merely sported for a moment. Of all insults, the temporary condescension of a master to a slave is the most outrageous and galling. That potentate who most condescends, mark him well; for that potentate, if occasion come, will prove your uttermost tyrant.

Chapter 67

White-Jacket arraigned at the Mast

W HEN with five hundred others I made one of the compelled spectators at the scourging of poor Rose-Water, I little thought what Fate had ordained for myself the next day.

Poor mulatto! thought I, one of an oppressed race, they degrade you like a hound. Thank God! I am a white. Yet I had seen whites also scourged; for, black or white, all my shipmates were liable to that. Still, there is something in us, somehow, that, in the most degraded condition, we snatch at a chance to deceive ourselves into a fancied superiority to others, whom we suppose lower in the scale than ourselves.

Poor Rose-Water! thought I; poor mulatto! Heaven send you a release from your humiliation!

To make plain the thing about to be related, it needs to repeat what has somewhere been previously mentioned, that in *tacking ship* every seaman in a man-of-war has a particular station assigned him. What that station is, should be made known to him by the First Lieutenant; and when the word is passed to *tack* or *wear*, it is every seaman's duty to be found at his post. But among the various *numbers* and *stations* given to me by the senior Lieutenant, when I first came on board the frigate, he had altogether omitted informing me of my particular place at those times, and, up to the precise period now written of, I had hardly known that I should have had any special place then at all. For the rest of the men, they seemed to me to catch hold of the first rope that offered, as in a merchantman upon similar occasions. Indeed, I subsequently discovered, that such was the state of discipline—in this one particular, at least—that very few of the seamen could tell where their proper stations were, at *tacking* or *wearing*.

"All hands tack ship, ahoy!" such was the announcement made by the boatswain's mates at the hatchways the morning after the hard fate of Rose-Water. It was just eight bells—

noon, and springing from my white jacket, which I had spread between the guns for a bed on the main-deck, I ran up the ladders, and, as usual, seized hold of the main-brace, which fifty hands were streaming along forward. When *main-top-sail haul!* was given through the trumpet, I pulled at this brace with such heartiness and good-will, that I almost flattered myself that my instrumentality in getting the frigate round on the other tack, deserved a public vote of thanks, and a silver tankard from Congress.

But something happened to be in the way aloft when the yards swung round; a little confusion ensued; and, with anger on his brow, Captain Claret came forward to see what occasioned it. No one to let go the weather-lift of the main-yard! The rope was cast off, however, by a hand, and the yards, unobstructed, came round.

When the last rope was coiled away, the Captain desired to know of the First Lieutenant who it might be that was stationed at the weather (then the starboard) main-lift. With a vexed expression of countenance the First Lieutenant sent a midshipman for the Station Bill, when, upon glancing it over, my own name was found put down at the post in question.

At the time I was on the gun-deck below, and did not know of these proceedings; but a moment after, I heard the boatswain's mates bawling my name at all the hatchways, and along all three decks. It was the first time I had ever heard it so sent through the furthest recesses of the ship, and well knowing what this generally betokened to other seamen, my heart jumped to my throat, and I hurriedly asked Flute, the boatswain's mate at the fore-hatchway, what was wanted of me.

"Captain wants ye at the mast," he replied. "Going to flog ye, I guess."

"What for?"

"My eyes! you've been chalking your face, hain't ye?"

"What am I wanted for?" I repeated.

But at that instant my name was again thundered forth by the other boatswain's mate, and Flute hurried me away, hinting that I would soon find out what the Captain desired of me.

I swallowed down my heart in me as I touched the spar-deck, for a single instant balanced myself on my best centre, and then, wholly ignorant of what was going to be alleged against me, advanced to the dread tribunal of the frigate.

As I passed through the gangway, I saw the quarter-master rigging the gratings; the boatswain with his green bag of scourges; the master-at-arms ready to help off some one's shirt.

Again I made a desperate swallow of my whole soul in me, and found myself standing before Captain Claret. His flushed face obviously showed him in ill humor. Among the group of officers by his side was the First Lieutenant, who, as I came aft, eyed me in such a manner, that I plainly perceived him to be extremely vexed at me for having been the innocent means of reflecting upon the manner in which he kept up the discipline of the ship.

"Why were you not at your station, sir?" asked the Captain.

"What station do you mean, sir?" said I.

It is generally the custom with man-of-war's-men to stand obsequiously touching their hat at every sentence they address to the Captain. But as this was not obligatory upon me by the Articles of War, I did not do so upon the present occasion, and previously, I had never had the dangerous honor of a personal interview with Captain Claret.

He quickly noticed my omission of the homage usually rendered him, and instinct told me, that to a certain extent, it set his heart against me.

"What station, sir, do you mean?" said I.

"You pretend ignorance," he replied; "it will not help you, sir."

Glancing at the Captain, the First Lieutenant now produced the Station Bill, and read my name in connection with that of the starboard main-lift.

"Captain Claret," said I, "it is the first time I ever heard of my being assigned to that post."

"How is this, Mr. Bridewell?" he said, turning to the First Lieutenant, with a fault-finding expression.

"It is impossible, sir," said that officer, striving to hide his vexation, "but this man must have known his station."

"I have never known it before this moment, Captain Claret," said I.

"Do you contradict my officer?" he returned. "I shall flog you."

I had now been on board the frigate upward of a year, and remained unscourged; the ship was homeward-bound, and in a few weeks, at most, I would be a freeman. And now, after making a hermit of myself in some things, in order to avoid the possibility of the scourge, here it was hanging over me for a thing utterly unforeseen, for a crime of which I was as utterly innocent. But all that was as naught. I saw that my case was hopeless; my solemn disclaimer was thrown in my teeth, and the boatswain's mate stood curling his fingers through the *cat*.

There are times when wild thoughts enter a man's heart, when he seems almost irresponsible for his act and his deed. The Captain stood on the weather-side of the deck. Sideways, on an unobstructed line with him, was the opening of the lee-gangway, where the side-ladders are suspended in port. Nothing but a slight bit of sinnate-stuff served to rail in this opening, which was cut right down to the level of the Captain's feet, showing the far sea beyond. I stood a little to windward of him, and, though he was a large, powerful man, it was certain that a sudden rush against him, along the slanting deck, would infallibly pitch him headforemost into the ocean, though he who so rushed must needs go over with him. My blood seemed clotting in my veins; I felt icy cold at the tips of my fingers, and a dimness was before my eyes. But through that dimness the boatswain's mate, scourge in hand, loomed like a giant, and Captain Claret, and the blue sea seen through the opening at the gangway, showed with an awful vividness. I can not analyze my heart, though it then stood still within me. But the thing that swayed me to my purpose was not altogether the thought that Captain Claret was about to degrade me, and that I had taken an oath with my soul that he should not. No, I felt my man's manhood so bottomless within me, that no word, no blow, no scourge of Captain Claret could cut me deep enough for that. I but swung to an instinct in me—the instinct diffused through all animated nature, the same that prompts even a worm to turn under the heel. Locking souls with him, I meant to drag Captain Claret from this earthly tribunal of his to that of Jehovah, and let

Him decide between us. No other way could I escape the scourge.

Nature has not implanted any power in man that was not meant to be exercised at times, though too often our powers have been abused. The privilege, inborn and inalienable, that every man has, of dying himself, and inflicting death upon another, was not given to us without a purpose. These are the last resources of an insulted and unendurable existence.

"To the gratings, sir!" said Captain Claret; "do you hear?"

My eye was measuring the distance between him and the sea.

"Captain Claret," said a voice advancing from the crowd. I turned to see who this might be, that audaciously interposed at a juncture like this. It was the same remarkably handsome and gentlemanly corporal of marines, Colbrook, who has been previously alluded to, in the chapter describing killing time in a man-of-war.

"I know that man," said Colbrook, touching his cap, and speaking in a mild, firm, but extremely deferential manner; "and I know that he would not be found absent from his station, if he knew where it was."

This speech was almost unprecedented. Seldom or never before had a marine dared to speak to the Captain of a frigate in behalf of a seaman at the mast. But there was something so unostentatiously commanding in the calm manner of the man, that the Captain, though astounded, did not in any way reprimand him. The very unusualness of his interference seemed Colbrook's protection.

Taking heart, perhaps, from Colbrook's example, Jack Chase interposed, and in a manly but carefully respectful manner, in substance repeated the corporal's remark, adding that he had never found me wanting in the top.

Captain Claret looked from Chase to Colbrook, and from Colbrook to Chase—one the foremost man among the seamen, the other the foremost man among the soldiers—then all round upon the packed and silent crew, and, as if a slave to Fate, though supreme Captain of a frigate, he turned to the First Lieutenant, made some indifferent remark, and saying to me *you may go*, sauntered aft into his cabin; while I, who, in the desperation of my soul, had but just escaped being a murderer and a suicide, almost burst into tears of thanksgiving where I stood.

Chapter 68

A Man-of-war Fountain,
and other Things

LET US FORGET the scourge and the gangway a while, and
jot down in our memories a few little things pertaining
to our man-of-war world. I let nothing slip, however small;
and feel myself actuated by the same motive which has
prompted many worthy old chroniclers, to set down the merest trifles concerning things that are destined to pass away
entirely from the earth, and which, if not preserved in the
nick of time, must infallibly perish from the memories of
man. Who knows that this humble narrative may not hereafter prove the history of an obsolete barbarism? Who knows
that, when men-of-war shall be no more, "White-Jacket" may
not be quoted to show to the people in the Millennium what
a man-of-war was? God hasten the time! Lo! ye years, escort
it hither, and bless our eyes ere we die.

There is no part of a frigate where you will see more going
and coming of strangers, and overhear more greetings and
gossipings of acquaintances, than in the immediate vicinity of
the scuttle-butt, just forward of the main-hatchway, on the
gun-deck.

The scuttle-butt is a goodly, round, painted cask, standing
on end, and with its upper head removed, showing a narrow,
circular shelf within, where rest a number of tin cups for the
accommodation of drinkers. Central, within the scuttle-butt
itself, stands an iron pump, which, connecting with the immense water-tanks in the hold, furnishes an unfailing supply
of the much-admired Pale Ale, first brewed in the brooks of
the Garden of Eden, and stamped with the *brand* of our old
father Adam, who never knew what wine was. We are indebted to the old vintner Noah for that. The scuttle-butt is
the only fountain in the ship; and here alone can you drink,
unless at your meals. Night and day an armed sentry paces
before it, bayonet in hand, to see that no water is taken away,
except according to law. I wonder that they station no sen-

tries at the port-holes, to see that no air is breathed, except according to Navy regulations.

As five hundred men come to drink at this scuttle-butt; as it is often surrounded by officer's servants drawing water for their masters to wash; by the cooks of the range, who hither come to fill their coffee-pots; and by the cooks of the ship's messes to procure water for their *duffs*; the scuttle-butt may be denominated the town-pump of the ship. And would that my fine countryman, Hawthorne of Salem, had but served on board a man-of-war in his time, that he might give us the reading of a "*rill*" from the scuttle-butt.

*   *   *

As in all extensive establishments—abbeys, arsenals, colleges, treasuries, metropolitan post-offices, and monasteries—there are many snug little niches, wherein are ensconced certain superannuated old pensioner officials; and, more especially, as in most ecclesiastical establishments, a few choice prebendary stalls are to be found, furnished with well-filled mangers and racks; so, in a man-of-war, there are a variety of similar snuggeries for the benefit of decrepit or rheumatic old tars. Chief among these is the office of *mast-man*.

There is a stout rail on deck, at the base of each mast, where a number of *braces*, *lifts*, and *buntlines* are belayed to the pins. It is the sole duty of the mast-man to see that these ropes are always kept clear, to preserve his premises in a state of the greatest attainable neatness, and every Sunday morning to dispose his ropes in neat *Flemish coils*.

The *main-mast-man* of the Neversink was a very aged seaman, who well deserved his comfortable berth. He had seen more than half a century of the most active service, and, through all, had proved himself a good and faithful man. He furnished one of the very rare examples of a sailor in a green old age; for, with most sailors, old age comes in youth, and Hardship and Vice carry them on an early bier to the grave.

As in the evening of life, and at the close of the day, old Abraham sat at the door of his tent, biding his time to die, so sits our old mast-man on the *coat of the mast*, glancing round him with patriarchal benignity. And that mild expression of his sets off very strangely a face that has been burned almost black by the torrid suns that shone fifty years ago—a face that is seamed with three sabre cuts. You would almost think this old mast-man had been blown out of Vesuvius, to look alone at his scarred, blackened forehead, chin, and cheeks. But gaze down into his eye, and though all the snows of Time have drifted higher and higher upon his brow, yet deep down in that eye you behold an infantile, sinless look, the same that answered the glance of this old man's mother when first she cried for the babe to be laid by her side. That look is the fadeless, ever infantile immortality within.

*   *   *

The Lord Nelsons of the sea, though but Barons in the state, yet oftentimes prove more potent than their royal masters; and at such scenes as Trafalgar—dethroning this Emperor and reinstating that—enact on the ocean the proud part of mighty Richard Nevil, the king-making Earl of the land. And as Richard Nevil entrenched himself in his moated old man-of-war castle of Warwick, which, underground, was traversed with vaults, hewn out of the solid rock, and intricate as the wards of the old keys of Calais surrendered to Edward III.; even so do these King-Commodores house themselves in their water-rimmed, cannon-sentried frigates, oaken dug, deck under deck, as cell under cell. And as the old Middle-Age warders of Warwick, every night at curfew, patrolled the battlements, and dove down into the vaults to see that all lights were extinguished, even so do the master-at-arms and ship's corporals of a frigate perambulate all the decks of a man-of-war, blowing out all tapers but those burning in the legalized battle-lanterns. Yea, in these things, so potent is the authority of these sea-wardens, that, though almost the lowest subalterns in the ship, yet should they find the Senior Lieutenant himself sitting up late in his state-room, reading Bowditch's Navigator, or D'Anton "*On Gunpowder and Fire-arms*," they would infallibly blow the light out under his very nose; nor durst that Grand-Vizier resent the indignity.

But, unwittingly, I have ennobled, by grand historical comparisons, this prying, pettifogging, Irish-informer of a master-at-arms.

You have seen some slim, slip-shod housekeeper, at midnight, ferreting over a rambling old house in the country, starting at fancied witches and ghosts, yet intent on seeing every door bolted, every smouldering ember in the fire-places smothered, every loitering domestic abed, and every light made dark. This is the master-at-arms taking his night-rounds in a frigate.

*   *   *

It may be thought that but little is seen of the Commodore in these chapters, and that, since he so seldom appears on the stage, he can not be so august a personage, after all. But the mightiest potentates keep the most behind the vail. You might tarry in Constantinople a month, and never catch a glimpse of the Sultan. The Grand Lama of Thibet, according to some accounts, is never beheld by the people. But if any one doubts the majesty of a Commodore, let him know that, according to XLII. of the Articles of War, he is invested with a prerogative which, according to monarchical jurists, is inseparable from the throne—the plenary pardoning power. He may pardon all offences committed in the squadron under his command.

But this prerogative is only his while at sea, or on a foreign station. A circumstance peculiarly significant of the great difference between the stately absolutism of a Commodore enthroned on his poop in a foreign harbor, and an unlaced Commodore negligently reclining in an easy-chair in the bosom of his family at home.

*   *   *

In the histories of some old states we read of *tasters* being appointed to the court, by way of precaution against poisonings. This taster's business consisted in tasting all dishes previous to his royal master's dining. In modern navies this custom is reversed. Every day, at precisely seven bells of the forenoon watch, (half-past eleven o'clock,) the ship's cook of the Neversink would slowly emerge from the main-hatchway, bearing a capacious tin pan, containing a sample of the salt-beef or pork—as the case might be—that day cooked for the people's messes. Inserted uprightly in the steaming meat would be seen a knife and fork. Advancing to the main-mast, the cook deposits the pan on the belaying rail, and solemnly touching his hat, awaits the pleasure of the officer of the deck. It is a ceremony that attracts all eyes; for of all persons in the world, the sailors in a man-of-war are the most keenly anxious for the dinner-time to come; and Old Coffee's inevitable appearance with his pan, at precisely seven bells, was always hailed by them with delight. To myself, he was better than a clock. Nor was Old Coffee at all blind to the dignity and importance of the ceremony, in which he enacted so conspicuous a part. He preserved the utmost rectitude of carriage; and when it was "Duff Day," he would advance with his tin truncheon borne high aloft, exhibiting a pale, round duff surmounting the blood-red mass of beef;—he looked something like the figure in the old painting of the executioner presenting the head of St. John the Baptist in a charger.

In due time, the officer of the deck draws near, spreads his feet apart at the belaying rails, and squares himself to the inspection. Drawing out the knife and fork from the beef, he cuts himself a choice piece; masticates it rapidly, while looking the cook full in the eye; and if the flavor seems agreeable to him, he sticks the knife and fork into the beef again, and exclaims, "Very good: serve it up." Thus, in a man-of-war, the lords may be said to be tasters to the commons.

The ostensible reason of this ceremony is this, that the officer of the deck may be sure that the ship's cook has faithfully cooked his meat. But as all the meat is not inspected, and the cook may select what piece he pleases for inspection, the test is by no means a thorough one. A picked and pounded bit of the breast is not a fair specimen of a radically tough goose.

Chapter 69

PRAYERS AT THE GUNS

T HE TRAINING-DAYS, or general quarters, now and then taking place in our frigate, have already been described, also the Sunday devotions on the half-deck; but nothing has yet been said concerning the daily morning and evening quarters, when the men silently stand at their guns, and the chaplain simply offers up a prayer.

Let us now enlarge upon this matter. We have plenty of time; the occasion invites; for behold! the homeward-bound Neversink bowls along over a jubilant sea.

Shortly after breakfast the drum beats to quarters; and among five hundred men, scattered over all three decks, and engaged in all manner of ways, that sudden rolling march is magical as the monitory sound to which every good Mussulman at sunset drops to the ground whatsoever his hands might have found to do, and, throughout all Turkey, the people in concert kneel toward their holy Mecca.

The sailors run to and fro—some up the deck-ladders, some down—to gain their respective stations in the shortest possible time. In three minutes all is composed. One by one, the various officers stationed over the separate divisions of the ship then approach the First Lieutenant on the quarter-deck, and report their respective men at their quarters. It is curious to watch their countenances at this time. A profound silence prevails; and, emerging through the hatchway, from one of the lower decks, a slender young officer appears, hugging his sword to his thigh, and advances through the long lanes of sailors at their guns, his serious eye all the time fixed upon the First Lieutenant's—his polar star. Sometimes he essays a stately and graduated step, an erect and martial bearing, and seems full of the vast national importance of what he is about to communicate.

But when at last he gains his destination, you are amazed to perceive that all he has to say is imparted by a Free-mason touch of his cap, and a bow. He then turns and makes off to his division, perhaps passing several brother Lieutenants, all bound on the same errand he himself has just achieved. For about five minutes these officers are coming and going, bringing in thrilling intelligence from all quarters of the frigate; most stoically received, however, by the First Lieutenant. With his legs apart, so as to give a broad foundation for the superstructure of his dignity, this gentleman stands stiff as a pike-staff on the quarter-deck. One hand holds his sabre—an appurtenance altogether unnecessary at the time; and which he accordingly tucks, point backward, under his arm, like an umbrella on a sunshiny day. The other hand is continually bobbing up and down to the leather front of his cap, in response to the reports and salutes of his subordinates, to whom he never deigns to vouchsafe a syllable; merely going through the motions of accepting their news, without bestowing thanks for their pains.

This continual touching of caps between officers on board a man-of-war is the reason why you invariably notice that the glazed fronts of their caps look jaded, lack-lustre, and worn; sometimes slightly oleaginous—though, in other respects, the cap may appear glossy and fresh. But as for the First Lieutenant, he ought to have extra pay allowed to him, on account of his extraordinary outlays in cap fronts; for he it is to whom all day long, reports of various kinds are incessantly being made by the junior Lieutenants; and no report is made by them, however trivial, but caps are touched on the occasion. It is obvious that these individual salutes must be greatly multiplied and aggregated upon the senior Lieutenant, who must return them all. Indeed, when a subordinate officer is first promoted to that rank, he generally complains of the same exhaustion about the shoulder and elbow that La Fayette mourned over, when, in visiting America, he did little else but shake the sturdy hands of patriotic farmers from sunrise to sunset.

The various officers of divisions having presented their respects, and made good their return to their stations, the First Lieutenant turns round, and, marching aft, endeavors to catch the eye of the Captain, in order to touch his own cap to that personage, and thereby, without adding a word of explanation, communicate the fact of all hands being at their guns.

He is a sort of retort, or receiver general, to concentrate the whole sum of the information imparted to him, and discharge it upon his superior at one touch of his cap front.

But sometimes the Captain feels out of sorts, or in ill-humor, or is pleased to be somewhat capricious, or has a fancy to show a touch of his omnipotent supremacy; or, per-adventure, it has so happened that the First Lieutenant has, in some way, piqued or offended him, and he is not unwilling to show a slight specimen of his dominion over him, even before the eyes of all hands; at all events, only by some one of these suppositions can the singular circumstance be accounted for, that frequently Captain Claret would pertinaciously promenade up and down the poop, purposely averting his eye from the First Lieutenant, who would stand below in the most awkward suspense, waiting the first wink from his superior's eye.

"Now I have him!" he must have said to himself, as the Captain would turn toward him in his walk; "now's my time!" and up would go his hand to his cap; but, alas! the Captain was off again; and the men at the guns would cast sly winks at each other as the embarrassed Lieutenant would bite his lips with suppressed vexation.

Upon some occasions this scene would be repeated several times, till at last Captain Claret, thinking, that in the eyes of all hands, his dignity must by this time be pretty well bolstered, would stalk toward his subordinate, looking him full in the eyes; whereupon up goes his hand to the cap front, and the Captain, nodding his acceptance of the report, descends from his perch to the quarter-deck.

By this time the stately Commodore slowly emerges from his cabin, and soon stands leaning alone against the brass rails of the after-hatchway. In passing him, the Captain makes a profound salutation, which his superior returns, in token that the Captain is at perfect liberty to proceed with the ceremonies of the hour.

Marching on, Captain Claret at last halts near the main-mast, at the head of a group of the ward-room officers, and by the side of the Chaplain. At a sign from his finger, the brass band strikes up the Portuguese hymn. This over, from Commodore to hammock-boy, all hands uncover, and the

Chaplain reads a prayer. Upon its conclusion, the drum beats the retreat, and the ship's company disappear from the guns. At sea or in harbor, this ceremony is repeated every morning and evening.

By those stationed on the quarter-deck the Chaplain is distinctly heard; but the quarter-deck gun division embraces but a tenth part of the ship's company, many of whom are below, on the main-deck, where not one syllable of the prayer can be heard. This seemed a great misfortune; for I well knew myself how blessed and soothing it was to mingle twice every day in these peaceful devotions, and, with the Commodore, and Captain, and smallest boy, unite in acknowledging Almighty God. There was also a touch of the temporary equality of the Church about it, exceedingly grateful to a man-of-war's-man like me.

My carronade-gun happened to be directly opposite the brass railing against which the Commodore invariably leaned at prayers. Brought so close together, twice every day, for more than a year, we could not but become intimately acquainted with each other's faces. To this fortunate circumstance it is to be ascribed, that some time after reaching home, we were able to recognize each other when we chanced to meet in Washington, at a ball given by the Russian Minister, the Baron de Bodisco. And though, while on board the frigate, the Commodore never in any manner personally addressed me—nor did I him—yet, at the Minister's social entertainment, we *there* became exceedingly chatty; nor did I fail to observe, among that crowd of foreign dignitaries and magnates from all parts of America, that my worthy friend did not appear so exalted as when leaning, in solitary state, against the brass railing of the Neversink's quarter-deck. Like many other gentlemen, he appeared to the best advantage, and was treated with the most deference in the bosom of his home, the frigate.

Our morning and evening quarters were agreeably diversified for some weeks by a little circumstance, which to some of us at least, always seemed very pleasing.

At Callao, half of the Commodore's cabin had been hospitably yielded to the family of a certain aristocratic-looking magnate, who was going embassador from Peru to the Court of the Brazils, at Rio. This dignified diplomatist sported a long, twirling mustache, that almost enveloped his mouth. The sailors said, he looked like a rat with his teeth through a bunch of oakum, or a St. Jago monkey peeping through a prickly-pear bush.

He was accompanied by a very beautiful wife, and a still more beautiful little daughter, about six years old. Between this dark-eyed little gipsy and our chaplain there soon sprung up a cordial love and good feeling, so much so, that they were seldom apart. And whenever the drum beat to quarters, and the sailors were hurrying to their stations, this little signorita would outrun them all to gain her own quarters at the capstan, where she would stand by the chaplain's side, grasping his hand, and looking up archly in his face.

It was a sweet relief from the domineering sternness of our martial discipline—a sternness not relaxed even at our devotions before the altar of the common God of commodore and cabin-boy—to see that lovely little girl standing among the thirty-two-pounders, and now and then casting a wondering, commiserating glance at the array of grim seamen around her.

Chapter 70

MONTHLY MUSTER ROUND THE CAPSTAN

B ESIDES general quarters, and the regular morning and evening quarters for prayers on board the Neversink, on the first Sunday of every month we had a grand "*muster round the capstan*," when we passed in solemn review before the Captain and officers, who closely scanned our frocks and trowsers, to see whether they were according to the Navy cut. In some ships, every man is required to bring his bag and hammock along for inspection.

This ceremony acquires its chief solemnity, and, to a novice, is rendered even terrible, by the reading of the Articles of War by the Captain's clerk before the assembled ship's company, who, in testimony of their enforced reverence for the code, stand bareheaded till the last sentence is pronounced.

To a mere amateur reader the quiet perusal of these Articles of War would be attended with some nervous emotions. Imagine, then, what *my* feelings must have been, when, with my hat deferentially in my hand, I stood before my lord and master, Captain Claret, and heard these Articles read as the law and gospel, the infallible, unappealable dispensation and code, whereby I lived, and moved, and had my being on board of the United States ship Neversink.

Of some twenty offences—made penal—that a seaman may commit, and which are specified in this code, thirteen are punishable by death.

"*Shall suffer death!*" This was the burden of nearly every Article read by the Captain's clerk; for he seemed to have been instructed to omit the longer Articles, and only present those which were brief and to the point.

"*Shall suffer death!*" The repeated announcement falls on your ear like the intermitting discharge of artillery. After it has been repeated again and again, you listen to the reader as he deliberately begins a new paragraph; you hear him reciting the involved, but comprehensive and clear arrangement of the sentence, detailing all possible particulars of the offence described, and you breathlessly await, whether *that* clause also is going to be concluded by the discharge of the terrible minute-gun. When, lo! it again booms on your ear—*shall suffer death!* No reservations, no contingencies; not the remotest promise of pardon or reprieve; not a glimpse of commutation of the sentence; all hope and consolation is shut out—*shall suffer death!* that is the simple fact for you to digest; and it is a tougher morsel, believe White-Jacket when he says it, than a forty-two-pound cannon-ball.

But there is a glimmering of an alternative to the sailor who infringes these Articles. Some of them thus terminate: *"Shall suffer death, or such punishment as a court-martial shall adjudge."* But hints this at a penalty still more serious? Perhaps it means *"death, or worse punishment."*

Your honors of the Spanish Inquisition, Loyola and Torquemada! produce, reverend gentlemen, your most secret code, and match these Articles of War, if you can. Jack Ketch, *you* also are experienced in these things! Thou most benevolent of mortals, who standest by us, and hangest round our necks, when all the rest of this world are against us—tell us, hangman, what punishment is this, horribly hinted at as being worse than death? Is it, upon an empty stomach, to read the Articles of War every morning, for the term of one's natural life? Or is it to be imprisoned in a cell, with its walls papered from floor to ceiling with printed copies, in italics, of these Articles of War?

But it needs not to dilate upon the pure, bubbling milk of human kindness, and Christian charity, and forgiveness of injuries which pervade this charming document, so thoroughly imbued, as a Christian code, with the benignant spirit of the Sermon on the Mount. But as it is very nearly alike in the foremost states of Christendom, and as it is nationally set forth by those states, it indirectly becomes an index to the true condition of the present civilization of the world.

As, month after month, I would stand bareheaded among my shipmates, and hear this document read, I have thought to myself, Well, well, White-Jacket, you are in a sad box, indeed. But prick your ears, there goes another minute-gun. It admonishes you to take all bad usage in good part, and never to join in any public meeting that may be held on the gun-deck for a redress of grievances. Listen:

Art. XIII. *"If any person in the navy shall make, or attempt to make, any mutinous assembly, he shall, on conviction thereof by a court martial, suffer death."*

Bless me, White-Jacket, are you a great gun yourself, that you so recoil, to the extremity of your breechings, at that discharge?

But give ear again. Here goes another minute-gun. It indirectly admonishes you to receive the grossest insult, and stand still under it:

Art. XIV. *"No private in the navy shall disobey the lawful orders of his superior officer, or strike him, or draw, or offer to draw, or raise any weapon against him, while in the execution of the duties of his office, on pain of death."*

Do not hang back there by the bulwarks, White-Jacket; come up to the mark once more; for here goes still another minute-gun, which admonishes you never to be caught napping:

Part of Art. XX. *"If any person in the navy shall sleep upon his watch, he shall suffer death."*

Murderous! But then, in time of peace, they do not enforce these blood-thirsty laws? Do they not, indeed? What happened to those three men on board an American armed vessel a few years ago, quite within your memory, White-Jacket; yea, while you yourself were yet serving on board this very frigate, the Neversink? What happened to those three Americans, White-Jacket—those three men, even as you, who once were alive, but now are dead? *"Shall suffer death!"* those were the three words that hung those three men.

Have a care, then, have a care, lest you come to a sad end, even the end of a rope; lest, with a black-and-blue throat, you turn a dumb diver after pearl-shells; put to bed forever, and tucked in, in your own hammock, at the bottom of the sea. And there you will lie, White-Jacket, while hostile navies are playing cannon-ball billiards over your grave.

By the main-mast! then, in a time of profound peace, I am subject to the cut-throat martial law! And when my own brother, who happens to be dwelling ashore, and does not serve his country as I am now doing—when *he* is at liberty to call personally upon the President of the United States, and express his disapprobation of the whole national administration, here am *I*, liable at any time to be run up at the yard-arm, with a necklace, made by no jeweler, round my neck!

A hard case, truly, White-Jacket; but it can not be helped. Yes; you live under this same martial law. Does not every thing around you din the fact in your ears? Twice every day do you not jump to your quarters at the sound of a drum? Every morning, in port, are you not roused from your hammock by the *reveille*, and sent to it again at nightfall by the *tattoo*? Every Sunday are you not commanded in the mere matter of the very dress you shall wear through that blessed day? Can your shipmates so much as drink their "tot of grog?" nay, can they even drink but a cup of water at the scuttle-butt, without an armed sentry standing over them? Does not every officer wear a sword instead of a cane? You live and move among twenty-four-pounders, White-Jacket; the very cannon-balls are deemed an ornament around you, serving to embellish the hatchways; and should you come to die at sea, White-Jacket, still two cannon-balls would bear you company when you would be committed to the deep. Yea, by all methods, and devices, and inventions, you are momentarily admonished of the fact that you live under the Articles of War. And by virtue of them it is, White-Jacket, that, without a hearing and without a trial, you may, at a wink from the Captain, be condemned to the scourge.

Speak you true? Then let me fly!

Nay, White-Jacket, the landless horizon hoops you in.

Some tempest, then, surge all the sea against us! hidden reefs and rocks, arise and dash the ship to chips! I was not born a serf, and will not live a slave! Quick! cork-screw whirlpools, suck us down! world's end whelm us!

Nay, White-Jacket, though this frigate laid her broken bones upon the Antarctic shores of Palmer's Land; though not two planks adhered; though all her guns were spiked by sword-fish blades, and at her yawning hatchways mouth-yawning sharks swam in and out; yet, should you escape the wreck and scramble to the beach, this Martial Law would meet you still, and snatch you by the throat. Hark!

Art. XLII. Part of Sec. 3.—*"In all cases where the crews of the ships or vessels of the United States shall be separated from their vessels by the latter being wrecked, lost, or destroyed, all the command, power, and authority given to the officers of such ships or vessels shall remain, and be in full force, as effectually as if such ship or vessel were not so wrecked, lost, or destroyed."*

Hear you that, White-Jacket! I tell you there is no escape. Afloat or wrecked the Martial Law relaxes not its gripe. And though, by that self-same warrant, for some offence therein set down, you were indeed to "suffer death," even then the Martial Law might hunt you straight through the other world, and out again at its other end, following you through all eternity, like an endless thread on the inevitable track of its own point, passing unnumbered needles through.

Chapter 71

THE GENEALOGY OF THE ARTICLES
OF WAR

As THE ARTICLES OF WAR form the ark and constitution of the penal laws of the American Navy, in all sobriety and earnestness it may be well to glance at their origin. Whence came they? And how is it that one arm of the national defences of a Republic comes to be ruled by a Turkish code, whose every section almost, like each of the tubes of a revolving pistol, fires nothing short of death into the heart of an offender? How comes it that, by virtue of a law solemnly ratified by a Congress of freemen, the representatives of freemen, thousands of Americans are subjected to the most despotic usages, and, from the dock-yards of a republic, absolute monarchies are launched, with the "glorious stars and stripes" for an ensign? By what unparalleled anomaly, by what monstrous grafting of tyranny upon freedom did these Articles of War ever come to be so much as heard of in the American Navy?

Whence came they? They can not be the indigenous growth of those political institutions, which are based upon that arch-democrat Thomas Jefferson's Declaration of Independence? No; they are an importation from abroad, even from Britain, whose laws we Americans hurled off as tyrannical, and yet retained the most tyrannical of all.

But we stop not here; for these Articles of War had their congenial origin in a period of the history of Britain when the Puritan Republic had yielded to a monarchy restored; when a hangman George Jeffreys sentenced a world's champion like Algernon Sidney to the block; when one of a race—by some deemed accursed of God—even a Stuart, was on the throne; and a Stuart, also, was at the head of the Navy, as Lord High Admiral. One, the son of a King beheaded for encroaching on the rights of his people, and the other, his own brother, a king, James II., who was hurled from the throne for his tyranny. This is the origin of the

62

Articles of War; and it carries with it an unmistakable clew to their despotism.*

Nor is it a dumb thing that the men who, in democratic Cromwell's time, first proved to the nations the toughness of the British oak and the hardihood of the British sailor—that in Cromwell's time, whose fleets struck terror into the cruisers of France, Spain, Portugal, and Holland, and the corsairs of Algiers and the Levant; in Cromwell's time, when Robert Blake swept the Narrow Seas of all the keels of a Dutch Admiral who insultingly carried a broom at his fore-mast; it is not a dumb thing that, at a period deemed so glorious to the British Navy, these Articles of War were unknown.

Nevertheless, it is granted that some laws or other must have governed Blake's sailors at that period; but they must have been far less severe than those laid down in the written code which superseded them, since, according to the father-in-law of James II., the Historian of the Rebellion, the English Navy, prior to the enforcement of the new code, was

*The first Naval Articles of War in the English language were passed in the thirteenth year of the reign of Charles the Second, under the title of *"An act for establishing Articles and Orders for the regulating and better Government of his Majesty's Navies, Ships-of-War, and Forces by Sea."* This act was repealed, and, so far as concerned the officers, a modification of it substituted, in the twenty-second year of the reign of George the Second, shortly after the Peace of Aix la Chapelle, just one century ago. This last act, it is believed, comprises, in substance, the Articles of War at this day in force in the British Navy. It is not a little curious, nor without meaning, that neither of these acts explicitly empowers an officer to inflict the lash. It would almost seem as if, in this case, the British lawgivers were willing to leave such a stigma out of an organic statute, and bestow the power of the lash in some less solemn, and perhaps less public manner. Indeed, the only broad enactments directly sanctioning naval scourging at sea are to be found in the United States Statute Book and in the "Sea Laws" of the absolute monarch, Louis le Grand, of France.[1]

Taking for their basis the above-mentioned British Naval Code, and ingrafting upon it the positive scourging laws, which Britain was loth to recognize as organic statutes, our American lawgivers, in the year 1800, framed the Articles of War now governing the American Navy. They may be found in the second volume of the "United States Statutes at Large," under chapter xxxiii.—"An act for the *better* government of the Navy of the United States."

[1]For reference to the latter (L'Ord. de la Marine), *vide* Curtis's "Treatise on the Rights and Duties of Merchant-Seamen, according to the General Maritime Law," Part ii., c. i.

full of officers and sailors who, of all men, were the most republican. Moreover, the same author informs us that the first work undertaken by his respected son-in-law, then Duke of York, upon entering on the duties of Lord High Admiral, was to have a grand re-christening of the men-of-war, which still carried on their sterns names too democratic to suit his high-tory ears.

But if these Articles of War were unknown in Blake's time, and also during the most brilliant period of Admiral Benbow's career, what inference must follow? That such tyrannical ordinances are not indispensable—even during war—to the highest possible efficiency of a military marine.

Chapter 72

"HEREIN ARE THE GOOD ORDINANCES OF THE SEA,
WHICH WISE MEN, WHO VOYAGED ROUND THE
WORLD, GAVE TO OUR ANCESTORS, AND WHICH
CONSTITUTE THE BOOKS OF THE SCIENCE OF
GOOD CUSTOMS."

—*The Consulate of the Sea*

THE PRESENT usages of the American Navy are such that, though there is no government enactment to that effect, yet, in many respects, its Commanders seem virtually invested with the power to observe or violate, as seems to them fit, several of the Articles of War.

According to Article XV., *"No person in the Navy shall quarrel with any other person in the Navy, nor use provoking or reproachful words, gestures, or menaces, on pain of such punishment as a court-martial shall adjudge."*

"Provoking or reproachful words!" Officers of the Navy, answer me! Have you not, many of you, a thousand times violated this law, and addressed to men, whose tongues were tied by this very Article, language which no landsman would ever hearken to without flying at the throat of his insulter? I know that worse words than *you* ever used are to be heard addressed by a merchant-captain to his crew; but the merchant-captain does not live under this XV.th Article of War.

Not to make an example of him, nor to gratify any personal feeling, but to furnish one certain illustration of what is here asserted, I honestly declare that Captain Claret, of the Neversink, repeatedly violated this law in his own proper person.

According to Article III., no officer, or other person in the Navy, shall be guilty of "oppression, fraud, profane swearing, drunkenness, or any other scandalous conduct."

Again let me ask you, officers of the Navy, whether many of you have not repeatedly, and in more than one particular, violated this law? And here, again, as a certain illustration, I must once more cite Captain Claret as an offender, especially in the matter of profane swearing. I must also cite four of the

665

lieutenants, some eight of the midshipmen, and nearly all the seamen.

Additional Articles might be quoted that are habitually violated by the officers, while nearly all those *exclusively* referring to the sailors are unscrupulously enforced. Yet those Articles, by which the sailor is scourged at the gangway, are not one whit more laws than those *other* Articles, binding upon the officers, that have become obsolete from immemorial disuse; while still other Articles, to which the sailors alone are obnoxious, are observed or violated at the caprice of the Captain. Now, if it be not so much the severity as the certainty of punishment that deters from transgression, how fatal to all proper reverence for the enactments of Congress must be this disregard of its statutes.

Still more. This violation of the law, on the part of the officers, in many cases involves oppression to the sailor. But throughout the whole naval code, which so hems in the mariner by law upon law, and which invests the Captain with so much judicial and administrative authority over him—in most cases entirely discretionary—not one solitary clause is to be found which in any way provides means for a seaman deeming himself aggrieved to obtain redress. Indeed, both the written and unwritten laws of the American Navy are as destitute of individual guarantees to the mass of seamen as the Statute Book of the despotic Empire of Russia.

Who put this great gulf between the American Captain and the American sailor? Or is the Captain a creature of like passions with ourselves? Or is he an infallible archangel, incapable of the shadow of error? Or has a sailor no mark of humanity, no attribute of manhood, that, bound hand and foot, he is cast into an American frigate shorn of all rights and defences, while the notorious lawlessness of the Commander has passed into a proverb, familiar to man-of-war's-men, *the law was not made for the Captain!* Indeed, he may almost be said to put off the citizen when he touches his quarter-deck; and, almost exempt from the law of the land himself, he comes down upon others with a judicial severity unknown on the national soil. With the Articles of War in one hand, and the cat-o'-nine-tails in the other, he stands an undignified parody upon Mohammed enforcing Moslemism with the sword and the Koran.

The concluding sections of the Articles of War treat of the naval courts-martial before which officers are tried for serious offences as well as the seamen. The oath administered to members of these courts—which sometimes sit upon matters of life and death—explicitly enjoins that the members shall not *"at any time divulge the vote or opinion of any particular member of the court, unless required so to do before a court of justice in due course of law."*

Here, then, is a Council of Ten and a Star Chamber indeed! Remember, also, that though the sailor is sometimes tried for his life before a tribunal like this, in no case do his fellow-sailors, his peers, form part of the court. Yet that a man should be tried by his peers is the fundamental principle of all civilized jurisprudence. And not only tried by his peers, but his peers must be unanimous to render a verdict; whereas, in a court-martial, the concurrence of a majority of conventional and social superiors is all that is requisite.

In the English Navy, it is said, they had a law which authorized the sailor to appeal, if he chose, from the decision of the Captain—even in a comparatively trivial case—to the higher tribunal of a court-martial. It was an English seaman who related this to me. When I said that such a law must be a fatal clog to the exercise of the penal power in the Captain, he, in substance, told me the following story.

A top-man guilty of drunkenness being sent to the gratings, and the scourge about to be inflicted, he turned round and demanded a court-martial. The Captain smiled, and ordered him to be taken down and put into the "brig." There he was kept in irons some weeks, when, despairing of being liberated, he offered to compromise at two dozen lashes. "Sick of your bargain, then, are you?" said the Captain. "No, no! a court-martial you demanded, and a court-martial you shall have!" Being at last tried before the bar of quarter-deck officers, he was condemned to two hundred lashes. What for? for his having been drunk? No! for his having had the insolence to appeal from an authority, in maintaining which the men who tried and condemned him had so strong a sympathetic interest.

Whether this story be wholly true or not, or whether the particular law involved prevails, or ever did prevail, in the English Navy, the thing, nevertheless, illustrates the ideas that man-of-war's-men themselves have touching the tribunals in question.

What can be expected from a court whose deeds are done in the darkness of the recluse courts of the Spanish Inquisition? when that darkness is solemnized by an oath on the Bible? when an oligarchy of epaulets sits upon the bench, and a plebeian top-man, without a jury, stands judicially naked at the bar?

In view of these things, and especially in view of the fact that, in several cases, the degree of punishment inflicted upon a man-of-war's-man is absolutely left to the discretion of the court, what shame should American legislators take to themselves, that with perfect truth we may apply to the entire body of American man-of-war's-men that infallible principle of Sir Edward Coke: *"It is one of the genuine marks of servitude to have the law either concealed or precarious."* But still better may we subscribe to the saying of Sir Matthew Hale in his History of the Common Law, that *"the Martial Law, being based upon no settled principles, is, in truth and reality, no law, but something indulged rather than allowed as a law."*

I know it may be said that the whole nature of this naval code is purposely adapted to the war exigencies of the Navy. But waiving the grave question that might be raised concerning the moral, not judicial, lawfulness of this arbitrary code, even in time of war; be it asked, why is it in force during a time of peace? The United States has now existed as a nation upward of seventy years, and in all that time the alleged necessity for the operation of the naval code—in cases deemed capital—has only existed during a period of two or three years at most.

Some may urge that the severest operations of the code are tacitly made null in time of peace. But though with respect to several of the Articles this holds true, yet at any time any and all of them may be legally enforced. Nor have there been wanting recent instances, illustrating the spirit of this code, even in cases where the letter of the code was not altogether observed. The well-known case of a United States brig fur-

THE GOOD ORDINANCES OF THE SEA 669

nishes a memorable example, which at any moment may be repeated. Three men, in a time of peace, were then hung at the yard-arm, merely because, in the Captain's judgment, it became necessary to hang them. To this day the question of their complete guilt is socially discussed.

How shall we characterize such a deed? Says Blackstone, "If any one that hath commission of martial authority doth, in time of peace, hang, or otherwise execute any man by color of martial law, this is murder; for it is against Magna Charta."*

Magna Charta! We moderns, who may be landsmen, may justly boast of civil immunities not possessed by our fore-fathers; but our remoter forefathers who happened to be mariners may straighten themselves even in their ashes to think that their lawgivers were wiser and more humane in their generation than our lawgivers in ours. Compare the sea-laws of our Navy with the Roman and Rhodian ocean ordinances; compare them with the "Consulate of the Sea;" compare them with the Laws of the Hanse Towns; compare them with the ancient Wisbury laws. In the last we find that they were ocean democrats in those days. "If he strikes, he ought to receive blow for blow." Thus speak out the Wisbury laws concerning a Gothland sea-captain.

In final reference to all that has been said in previous chapters touching the severity and unusualness of the laws of the American Navy, and the large authority vested in its commanding officers, be it here observed, that White-Jacket is not unaware of the fact, that the responsibility of an officer commanding at sea—whether in the merchant service or the national marine—is unparalleled by that of any other relation in which man may stand to man. Nor is he unmindful that both wisdom and humanity dictate that, from the peculiarity of his position, a sea-officer in command should be clothed with a degree of authority and discretion inadmissible in any master ashore. But, at the same time, these principles—recognized by all writers on maritime law—have undoubtedly furnished warrant for clothing modern sea-commanders and naval courts-martial with powers which exceed the due limits

*Commentaries, b. i., c. xiii.

of reason and necessity. Nor is this the only instance where right and salutary principles, in themselves almost self-evident and infallible, have been advanced in justification of things, which in themselves are just as self-evidently wrong and pernicious.

Be it here, once and for all, understood, that no sentimental and theoretic love for the common sailor; no romantic belief in that peculiar noble-heartedness and exaggerated generosity of disposition fictitiously imputed to him in novels; and no prevailing desire to gain the reputation of being his friend, have actuated me in any thing I have said, in any part of this work, touching the gross oppression under which I know that the sailor suffers. Indifferent as to who may be the parties concerned, I but desire to see wrong things righted, and equal justice administered to all.

Nor, as has been elsewhere hinted, is the general ignorance or depravity of any race of men to be alleged as an apology for tyranny over them. On the contrary, it can not admit of a reasonable doubt, in any unbiased mind conversant with the interior life of a man-of-war, that most of the sailor iniquities practiced therein are indirectly to be ascribed to the morally debasing effects of the unjust, despotic, and degrading laws under which the man-of-war's-man lives.

Chapter 73

M ention has already been made that the game of draughts, or checkers, was permitted to be played on board the Neversink. At the present time, while there was little or no ship-work to be done, and all hands, in high spirits, were sailing homeward over the warm, smooth sea of the tropics; so numerous became the players, scattered about the decks, that our First Lieutenant used ironically to say that it was a pity they were not tesselated with squares of white and black marble, for the express benefit and convenience of the players. Had this gentleman had his way, our checker-boards would very soon have been pitched out of the ports. But the Captain—unusually lenient in some things—permitted them, and so Mr. Bridewell was fain to hold his peace.

But, although this one game was allowable in the frigate, all kinds of gambling were strictly interdicted, under the penalty of the gangway; nor were cards or dice tolerated in any way whatever. This regulation was indispensable, for, of all human beings, man-of-war's-men are perhaps the most inclined to gambling. The reason must be obvious to any one who reflects upon their condition on shipboard. And gambling—the most mischievous of vices any where—in a man-of-war operates still more perniciously than on shore. But quite as often as the law against smuggling spirits is transgressed by the unscrupulous sailors, the statutes against cards and dice are evaded.

Sable night, which, since the beginning of the world, has winked and looked on at so many deeds of iniquity—night is the time usually selected for their operations by man-of-war gamblers. The place pitched upon is generally the berth-deck, where the hammocks are swung, and which is lighted so stintedly as not to disturb the sleeping seamen with any obtruding glare. In so spacious an area the two lanterns swinging from the stanchions diffuse a subdued illumination, like a nighttaper in the apartment of some invalid. Owing to their position, also, these lanterns are far from shedding an impartial light, however dim, but fling long angular rays here and there, like burglar's dark-lanterns in the fifty-acre vaults of the West India Docks on the Thames.

It may well be imagined, therefore, how well adapted is this mysterious and subterranean Hall of Eblis to the clandestine proceedings of gamblers, especially as the hammocks not only hang thickly, but many of them swing very low, within two feet of the floor, thus forming innumerable little canvass glens, grottoes, nooks, corners, and crannies, where a good deal of wickedness may be practiced by the wary with considerable impunity.

Now the master-at-arms, assisted by his mates, the ship's corporals, reigns supreme in these bowels of the ship. Throughout the night these policemen relieve each other at standing guard over the premises; and, except when the watches are called, they sit in the midst of a profound silence, only invaded by trumpeter's snores, or the ramblings of some old sheet-anchor-man in his sleep.

The two ship's corporals went among the sailors by the names of Leggs and Pounce; Pounce had been a policeman, it was said, in Liverpool; Leggs, a turnkey attached to "The Tombs" in New York. Hence their education eminently fitted them for their stations; and Bland, the master-at-arms, ravished with their dexterity in prying out offenders, used to call them his two right hands.

When man-of-war's-men desire to gamble, they appoint the hour, and select some certain corner, in some certain shadow, behind some certain hammock. They then contribute a small sum toward a joint fund, to be invested in a bribe for some argus-eyed shipmate, who shall play the part of a spy upon the master-at-arms and corporals while the gaming is in progress. In nine cases out of ten these arrangements are so cunning and comprehensive, that the gamblers, eluding all vigilance, conclude their game unmolested. But now and then, seduced into unwariness, or perhaps, from parsimony, being unwilling to employ the services of a spy, they are suddenly lighted upon by the constables, remorselessly collared, and dragged into the *brig*, there to await a dozen lashes in the morning.

Several times at midnight I have been startled out of a sound sleep by a sudden, violent rush under my hammock, caused by the abrupt breaking up of some nest of gamblers, who have scattered in all directions, brushing under the tiers of swinging pallets, and setting them all in a rocking commotion.

It is, however, while laying in port that gambling most thrives in a man-of-war. Then the men frequently practice their dark deeds in the light of the day, and the additional guards which, at such times, they deem indispensable, are not unworthy of note. More especially, their extra precautions in engaging the services of several spies, necessitate a considerable expenditure, so that, in port, the diversion of gambling rises to the dignity of a nabob luxury.

During the day the master-at-arms and his corporals are continually prowling about on all three decks, eager to spy out iniquities. At one time, for example, you see Leggs switching his magisterial rattan, and lurking round the foremast on the spar-deck; the next moment, perhaps, he is three decks down, out of sight, prowling among the cable-tiers. Just so with his master, and Pounce his coadjutor; they are here, there, and every where, seemingly gifted with ubiquity.

In order successfully to carry on their proceedings by day, the gamblers must see to it that each of these constables is relentlessly dogged wherever he goes; so that, in case of his approach toward the spot where themselves are engaged, they may be warned of the fact in time to make good their escape. Accordingly, light and active scouts are selected to follow the constable about. From their youthful alertness and activity, the boys of the mizzen-top are generally chosen for this purpose.

But this is not all. On board of most men-of-war there is a set of sly, knavish foxes among the crew, destitute of every principle of honor, and on a par with Irish informers. In man-of-war parlance, they come under the denomination of *fancy-men* and *white-mice*. They are called *fancy-men*, because, from their zeal in craftily reporting offenders, they are presumed to be regarded with high favor by some of the officers. Though it is seldom that these informers can be certainly individualized, so secret and subtle are they in laying their information, yet certain of the crew, and especially certain of the marines, are invariably suspected to be *fancy-men* and *white-mice*, and are accordingly more or less hated by their comrades.

Now, in addition to having an eye on the master-at-arms and his aids, the day-gamblers must see to it, that every person suspected of being a *white-mouse* or *fancy-man*, is likewise dogged wherever he goes. Additional scouts are retained constantly to snuff at their trail. But the mysteries of man-of-war vice are wonderful; and it is now to be recorded, that, from long habit and observation, and familiarity with the *guardo moves* and *maneuvres* of a frigate, the master-at-arms and his aids can almost invariably tell when any gambling is going on by day; though, in the crowded vessel, abounding in decks, tops, dark places, and outlandish corners of all sorts, they may not be able to pounce upon the identical spot where the gamblers are hidden.

During the period that Bland was suspended from his office as master-at-arms, a person who, among the sailors, went by the name of Sneak, having been long suspected to have been a *white-mouse*, was put in Bland's place. He proved a hang-dog, sidelong catch-thief, but gifted with a marvelous perseverance in ferreting out culprits; following in their track like an inevitable Cuba blood-hound, with his noiseless nose. When disconcerted, however, you sometimes heard his bay.

"The muffled dice are somewhere around," Sneak would say to his aids; "there are them three chaps, there, been dogging me about for the last half hour. I say, Pounce, has any one been scouting around *you* this morning?"

"Four on 'em," says Pounce. "I know'd it; I know'd the muffled dice was rattlin'!"

"Leggs!" says the master-at-arms to his other aid, "Leggs, how is it with *you*—any spies?"

"Ten on 'em," says Leggs. "There's one on 'em now—that fellow stitching a hat."

"Halloo, you sir!" cries the master-at-arms, "top your boom and sail large, now. If I see you about me again, I'll have you up to the mast."

"What am I a doin' now?" says the hat-stitcher, with a face as long as a rope-walk. "Can't a feller be workin' here, without being 'spected of Tom Coxe's traverse, up one ladder and down t'other?"

"Oh, I know the moves, sir; I have been on board a *guardo*. Top your boom, I say, and be off, or I'll have you hauled up and riveted in a clinch—both fore-tacks over the main-yard, and no bloody knife to cut the seizing. Sheer! or I'll pitch into you like a shin of beef into a beggar's wallet."

It is often observable, that, in vessels of all kinds, the men who talk the most sailor lingo are the least sailor-like in reality. You may sometimes hear even marines jerk out more salt phrases than the Captain of the Forecastle himself. On the other hand, when not actively engaged in his vocation, you would take the best specimen of a seaman for a landsman. When you see a fellow yawing about the docks like a homeward-bound Indiaman, a long Commodore's pennant of black ribbon flying from his mast-head, and fetching up at a grog-shop with a slew of his hull, as if an Admiral were coming alongside a three-decker in his barge; you may put that man down for what man-of-war's-men call a *damn-my-eyes-tar*, that is, a humbug. And many damn-my-eyes humbugs there are in this man-of-war world of ours.

Chapter 74

THE MAIN-TOP AT NIGHT

THE WHOLE of our run from Rio to the Line was one delightful yachting, so far as fine weather and the ship's sailing were concerned. It was especially pleasant when our quarter-watch lounged in the main-top, diverting ourselves in many agreeable ways. Removed from the immediate presence of the officers, we there harmlessly enjoyed ourselves, more than in any other part of the ship. By day, many of us were very industrious, making hats or mending our clothes. But by night we became more romantically inclined.

Often Jack Chase, an enthusiastic admirer of sea-scenery, would direct our attention to the moonlight on the waves, by fine snatches from his catalogue of poets. I shall never forget the lyric air with which, one morning, at dawn of day, when all the East was flushed with red and gold, he stood leaning against the top-mast shrouds, and, stretching his bold hand over the sea, exclaimed, "Here comes Aurora: top-mates, see!" And, in a liquid, long-lingering tone, he recited the lines,

> "With gentle hand, as seeming oft to pause,
> The purple curtains of the morn she draws."

"Commodore Camoens, White-Jacket.—But bear a hand there; we must rig out that stun'-sail boom—the wind is shifting."

From our lofty perch, of a moonlight night, the frigate itself was a glorious sight. She was going large before the wind, her stun'-sails set on both sides, so that the canvass on the main-mast and fore-mast presented the appearance of two majestic, tapering pyramids, more than a hundred feet broad at the base, and terminating in the clouds with the light cope-stone of the royals. That immense area of snow-white canvass sliding along the sea was indeed a magnificent spectacle. The three shrouded masts looked like the apparitions of three gigantic Turkish Emirs striding over the ocean.

Nor, at times, was the sound of music wanting, to augment the poetry of the scene. The whole band would be assembled on the poop, regaling the officers, and incidentally ourselves, with their fine old airs. To these, some of us would occasionally dance in the *top*, which was almost as large as an ordinary-sized parlor. When the instrumental melody of the band was not to be had, our nightingales mustered their voices, and gave us a song.

Upon these occasions Jack Chase was often called out, and regaled us, in his own free and noble style, with the "*Spanish Ladies*"—a favorite thing with British man-of-war's-men—and many other salt-sea ballads and ditties, including,

> "Sir Patrick Spens was the best sail*or*
> That ever sailed the sea."

Also,

> "And three times around spun our gallant ship;
> Three times around spun she;
> Three times around spun our gallant ship,
> And she went to the bottom of the sea—
> The sea, the sea, the sea,
> And she went to the bottom of the sea!"

These songs would be varied by sundry *yarns* and *twisters* of the top-men. And it was at these times that I always endeavored to draw out the oldest Tritons into narratives of the war-service they had seen. There were but few of them, it is true, who had been in action; but that only made their narratives the more valuable.

There was an old negro, who went by the name of Tawney, a sheet-anchor-man, whom we often invited into our top of tranquil nights, to hear him discourse. He was a staid and sober seaman, very intelligent, with a fine, frank bearing, one of the best men in the ship, and held in high estimation by every one.

It seems that, during the last war between England and America, he had, with several others, been "impressed" upon the high seas, out of a New England merchantman. The ship that impressed him was an English frigate, the Macedonian, afterward taken by the Neversink, the ship in which we were sailing.

It was the holy Sabbath, according to Tawney, and, as the Briton bore down on the American—her men at their quarters—Tawney and his countrymen, who happened to be stationed at the quarter-deck battery, respectfully accosted the captain—an old man by the name of Cardan—as he passed them, in his rapid promenade, his spy-glass under his arm. Again they assured him that they were not Englishmen, and that it was a most bitter thing to lift their hands against the flag of that country which harbored the mothers that bore them. They conjured him to release them from their guns, and allow them to remain neutral during the conflict. But when a ship of any nation is running into action, it is no time for argument, small time for justice, and not much time for humanity. Snatching a pistol from the belt of a boarder standing by, the Captain leveled it at the heads of the three sailors, and commanded them instantly to their quarters, under penalty of being shot on the spot. So, side by side with his country's foes, Tawney and his companions toiled at the guns, and fought out the fight to the last; with the exception of one of them, who was killed at his post by one of his own country's balls.

At length, having lost her fore and main-top-masts, and her mizzen-mast having been shot away to the deck, and her fore-yard lying in two pieces on her shattered forecastle, and in a hundred places having been *hulled* with round shot, the English frigate was reduced to the last extremity. Captain Cardan ordered his signal quarter-master to strike the flag.

Tawney was one of those who, at last, helped pull him on board the Neversink. As he touched the deck, Cardan saluted Decatur, the hostile commander, and offered his sword; but it was courteously declined. Perhaps the victor remembered the dinner parties that he and the Englishman had enjoyed together in Norfolk, just previous to the breaking out of hostilities—and while both were in command of the very frigates now crippled on the sea. The Macedonian, it seems, had gone into Norfolk with dispatches. *Then* they had laughed and joked over their wine, and a wager of a beaver hat was said to have been made between them upon the event of the hostile meeting of their ships.

Gazing upon the heavy batteries before him, Cardan said to Decatur, "This is a seventy-four, not a frigate; no wonder the day is yours!"

This remark was founded upon the Neversink's superiority in guns. The Neversink's main-deck-batteries then consisted, as now, of twenty-four-pounders; the Macedonian's of only eighteens. In all, the Neversink numbered fifty-four guns and four hundred and fifty men; the Macedonian, forty-nine guns and three hundred men; a very great disparity, which, united to the other circumstances of this action, deprives the victory of all claims to glory beyond those that might be set up by a river-horse getting the better of a seal.

But if Tawney spoke truth—and he was a truth-telling man—this fact seemed counterbalanced by a circumstance he related. When the guns of the Englishman were examined, after the engagement, in more than one instance the wad was found rammed against the cartridge, without intercepting the ball. And though, in a frantic sea-fight, such a thing might be imputed to hurry and remissness, yet Tawney, a stickler for his tribe, always ascribed it to quite a different and less honorable cause. But, even granting the cause he assigned to have been the true one, it does not involve any thing inimical to the general valor displayed by the British crew. Yet, from all that may be learned from candid persons who have been in sea-fights, there can be but little doubt that on board of all ships, of whatever nation, in time of action, no very small number of the men are exceedingly nervous, to say the least, at the guns; ramming and sponging at a venture. And what special patriotic interest could an impressed man, for instance, take in a fight, into which he had been dragged from the arms of his wife? Or is it to be wondered at that impressed English seamen have not scrupled, in time of war, to cripple the arm that has enslaved them?

During the same general war which prevailed at and previous to the period of the frigate-action here spoken of, a British flag-officer, in writing to the Admiralty, said, "Every thing appears to be quiet in the fleet; but, in preparing for battle last week, several of the guns in the after part of the ship were found to be spiked;" that is to say, rendered useless. Who had spiked them? The dissatisfied seamen. Is it altogether improbable, then, that the guns to which Tawney referred were manned by men who purposely refrained from making them tell on the foe; that, in this one action, the victory America gained was partly won for her by the sulky insubordination of the enemy himself?

During this same period of general war, it was frequently the case that the guns of English armed ships were found in the mornings with their breechings cut over night. This maiming of the guns, and for the time incapacitating them, was only to be imputed to that secret spirit of hatred to the service which induced the spiking above referred to. But even in cases where no deep-seated dissatisfaction was presumed to prevail among the crew, and where a seaman, in time of action, impelled by pure fear, "shirked from his gun;" it seems but flying in the face of Him who made such a seaman what he constitutionally was, to sew *coward* upon his back, and degrade and agonize the already trembling wretch in numberless other ways. Nor seems it a practice warranted by the Sermon on the Mount, for the officer of a battery, in time of battle, to stand over the men with his drawn sword (as was done in the Macedonian), and run through on the spot the first seaman who showed a semblance of fear. Tawney told me that he distinctly heard this order given by the English Captain to his officers of divisions. Were the secret history of all sea-fights written, the laurels of sea-heroes would turn to ashes on their brows.

And how nationally disgraceful, in every conceivable point of view, is the IV. of our American Articles of War: "If any person in the Navy shall pusillanimously cry for quarter, he shall suffer death." Thus, with death before his face from the foe, and death behind his back from his countrymen, the best valor of a man-of-war's-man can never assume the merit of a noble spontaneousness. In this, as in every other case, the Articles of War hold out no reward for good conduct, but only compel the sailor to fight, like a hired murderer, for his pay, by digging his grave before his eyes if he hesitates.

But this Article IV. is open to still graver objections. Courage is the most common and vulgar of the virtues; the only one shared with us by the beasts of the field; the one most apt, by excess, to run into viciousness. And since Nature generally takes away with one hand to counterbalance her gifts with the other, excessive animal courage, in many cases, only finds room in a character vacated of loftier things. But in a naval officer, animal courage is exalted to the loftiest merit, and often procures him a distinguished command.

Hence, if some brainless bravo be Captain of a frigate in action, he may fight her against invincible odds, and seek to crown himself with the glory of the shambles, by permitting his hopeless crew to be butchered before his eyes, while at the same time that crew must consent to be slaughtered by the foe, under penalty of being murdered by the law. Look at the engagement between the American frigate Essex with the two English cruisers, the Phœbe and Cherub, off the Bay of Valparaiso, during the late war. It is admitted on all hands that the American Captain continued to fight his crippled ship against a greatly superior force; and when, at last, it became physically impossible that he could ever be otherwise than vanquished in the end; and when, from peculiarly unfortunate circumstances, his men merely stood up to their nearly useless batteries to be dismembered and blown to pieces by the incessant fire of the enemy's long guns. Nor, by thus continuing to fight, did this American frigate, one iota, promote the true interests of her country. I seek not to underrate any reputation which the American Captain may have gained by this battle. He was a brave man; *that* no sailor will deny. But the whole world is made up of brave men. Yet I would not be at all understood as impugning his special good name. Nevertheless, it is not to be doubted, that if there were any common-sense sailors at the guns of the Essex, however valiant they may have been, those common-sense sailors must have greatly preferred to strike their flag, when they saw the day was fairly lost, than postpone that inevitable act till there were few American arms left to assist in hauling it down. Yet had these men, under these circumstances, "pusillanimously cried for quarter," by the IV. Article of War they might have been legally hung.

According to the negro, Tawney, when the Captain of the Macedonian—seeing that the Neversink had his vessel completely in her power—gave the word to strike the flag, one of his officers, a man hated by the seamen for his tyranny, howled out the most terrific remonstrances, swearing that, for his part, he would not give up, but was for sinking the Macedonian alongside the enemy. Had he been Captain, doubtless he would have done so; thereby gaining the name of a hero in this world;—but what would they have called him in the next?

But as the whole matter of war is a thing that smites common sense and Christianity in the face; so every thing connected with it is utterly foolish, unchristian, barbarous, brutal, and savoring of the Feejee Islands, cannibalism, saltpetre, and the devil.

It is generally the case in a man-of-war when she strikes her flag that all discipline is at an end, and the men for a time are ungovernable. This was so on board of the English frigate. The spirit-room was broken open, and buckets of grog were passed along the decks, where many of the wounded were lying between the guns. These mariners seized the buckets, and, spite of all remonstrances, gulped down the burning spirits, till, as Tawney said, the blood suddenly spirted out of their wounds, and they fell dead to the deck.

The negro had many more stories to tell of this fight; and frequently he would escort me along our main-deck batteries—still mounting the same guns used in the battle—pointing out their ineffaceable indentations and scars. Coated over with the accumulated paint of more than thirty years, they were almost invisible to a casual eye; but Tawney knew them all by heart; for he had returned home in the Neversink, and had beheld these scars shortly after the engagement.

One afternoon, I was walking with him along the gun-deck, when he paused abreast of the main-mast. "This part of the ship," said he, "we called the *slaughter-house* on board the Macedonian. Here the men fell, five and six at a time. An enemy always directs its shot here, in order to hurl over the mast, if possible. The beams and carlines overhead in the Macedonian *slaughter-house* were spattered with blood and brains. About the hatchways it looked like a butcher's stall; bits of human flesh sticking in the ring-bolts. A pig that ran about the decks escaped unharmed, but his hide was so clotted with blood, from rooting among the pools of gore, that when the ship struck the sailors hove the animal overboard, swearing that it would be rank cannibalism to eat him."

Another quadruped, a goat, lost its fore legs in this fight.

The sailors who were killed—according to the usual custom—were ordered to be thrown overboard as soon as they fell; no doubt, as the negro said, that the sight of so many corpses lying around might not appall the survivors at the guns. Among other instances, he related the following. A shot entering one of the port-holes, dashed dead two thirds of a gun's crew. The captain of the next gun, dropping his lockstring, which he had just pulled, turned over the heap of bodies to see who they were; when, perceiving an old mess-mate, who had sailed with him in many cruises, he burst into tears, and, taking the corpse up in his arms, and going with it to the side, held it over the water a moment, and eying it, cried, "Oh God! Tom!"—"D—n your prayers over that thing! overboard with it, and down to your gun!" roared a wounded Lieutenant. The order was obeyed, and the heart-stricken sailor returned to his post.

Tawney's recitals were enough to snap this man-of-war world's sword in its scabbard. And thinking of all the cruel carnal glory wrought out by naval heroes in scenes like these, I asked myself whether, indeed, that was a glorious coffin in which Lord Nelson was entombed—a coffin presented to him, during life, by Captain Hallowell; it had been dug out of the main-mast of the French line-of-battle ship L'Orient, which, burning up with British fire, destroyed hundreds of Frenchmen at the battle of the Nile.

Peace to Lord Nelson where he sleeps in his moldering mast! but rather would I be urned in the trunk of some green tree, and even in death have the vital sap circulating round me, giving of my dead body to the living foliage that shaded my peaceful tomb.

Chapter 75

"Sink, Burn, and Destroy"
—*Printed Admiralty orders in time of war*

A MONG innumerable "*yarns and twisters*" reeled off in our main-top during our pleasant run to the North, none could match those of Jack Chase, our captain.

Never was there better company than ever-glorious Jack. The things which most men only read of, or dream about, he had seen and experienced. He had been a dashing smuggler in his day, and could tell of a long nine-pounder rammed home with wads of French silks; of cartridges stuffed with the finest gunpowder tea; of cannister-shot full of West India sweet-meats; of sailor frocks and trowsers, quilted inside with costly laces; and table legs, hollow as musket barrels, compactly stowed with rare drugs and spices. He could tell of a wicked widow, too—a beautiful receiver of smuggled goods upon the English coast—who smiled so sweetly upon the smugglers when they sold her silks and laces, cheap as tape and ginghams. She called them gallant fellows, hearts of game; and bade them bring her more.

He could tell of desperate fights with his British majesty's cutters, in midnight coves upon a stormy coast; of the capture of a reckless band, and their being drafted on board a man-of-war; of their swearing that their chief was slain; of a writ of habeas corpus sent on board for one of them for a debt—a reserved and handsome man—and his going ashore, strongly suspected of being the slaughtered captain, and this a successful scheme for his escape.

But more than all, Jack could tell of the battle of Navarino, for he had been a captain of one of the main-deck guns on board Admiral Codrington's flag-ship, the Asia. Were mine the style of stout old Chapman's Homer, even then I would scarce venture to give noble Jack's own version of this fight, wherein, on the 20th of October, A.D. 1827, thirty-two sail of Englishmen, Frenchmen, and Russians, attacked and vanquished in the Levant an Ottoman fleet of three ships-of-the-line, twenty-five frigates, and a swarm of fire ships and hornet craft.

"We bayed to be at them," said Jack; "and when we *did* open fire, we were like dolphin among the flying-fish. 'Every man take his bird' was the cry, when we trained our guns. And those guns all smoked like rows of Dutch pipe-bowls, my hearties! My gun's crew carried small flags in their bosoms, to nail to the mast in case the ship's colors were shot away. Stripped to the waistbands, we fought like skinned tigers, and bowled down the Turkish frigates like nine-pins. Among their shrouds—swarming thick with small-arm men, like flights of pigeons lighted on pine-trees—our marines sent their leaden pease and gooseberries, like a shower of hailstones in Labrador. It was a stormy time, my hearties! The blasted Turks pitched into the old Asia's hull a whole quarry of marble shot, each ball one hundred and fifty pounds. They knocked three port-holes into one. But we gave them better than they sent. 'Up and at them, my bull-dog!' said I, patting my gun on the breech; 'tear open hatchways in their Moslem sides!' White-Jacket, my lad, you ought to have been there. The bay was covered with masts and yards, as I have seen a raft of snags in the Arkansas River. Showers of burned rice and olives from the exploding foe fell upon us like manna in the wilderness. *'Allah! Allah! Mohammed! Mohammed!'* split the air; some cried it out from the Turkish port-holes; others shrieked it forth from the drowning waters, their top-knots floating on their shaven skulls, like black-snakes on half-tide rocks. By those top-knots they believed that their Prophet would drag them up to Paradise, but they sank fifty fathoms, my hearties, to the bottom of the bay. 'Ain't the bloody 'Hometons going to strike yet?' cried my first loader, a Guernsey man, thrusting his neck out of the port-hole, and looking at the Turkish line-of-battle ship near by. That instant his head blew by me like a bursting Paixhan shot, and the flag of Ned Knowles himself was hauled down forever. We dragged his hull to one side, and avenged him with the cooper's anvil, which, endways, we rammed home; a mess-mate shoved in the dead man's bloody Scotch cap for the wad, and sent it flying into the line-of-battle ship. By the god of war! boys, we hardly left enough of that craft to boil a pot of water with. It was a hard day's work—a sad day's work, my hearties. That night, when all was over, I slept sound enough, with a box of cannister shot for my pillow! But you ought to have seen the boat-load of Turkish flags one of our captains carried home; he swore to dress his father's orchard in colors with them, just as our spars are dressed for a gala day."

"Though you tormented the Turks at Navarino, noble Jack, yet you came off yourself with only the loss of a splinter, it seems," said a top-man, glancing at our captain's maimed hand.

"Yes; but I and one of the Lieutenants had a narrower escape than that. A shot struck the side of my port-hole, and sent the splinters right and left. One took off my hat rim clean to my brow; another *razeed* the Lieutenant's left boot, by slicing off the heel; a third shot killed my powder-monkey without touching him."

"How, Jack?"

"It *whizzed* the poor babe dead. He was seated on a *cheese of wads* at the time, and after the dust of the powdered bulwarks had blown away, I noticed he yet sat still, his eyes wide open. *'My little hero!'* cried I, and I clapped him on the back; but he fell on his face at my feet. I touched his heart, and found he was dead. There was not a little finger mark on him."

Silence now fell upon the listeners for a time, broken at last by the Second Captain of the Top.

"Noble Jack, I know you never brag, but tell us what you did yourself that day?"

"Why, my hearties, I did not do quite as much as my gun. But I flatter myself it was that gun that brought down the Turkish Admiral's main-mast; and the stump left wasn't long enough to make a wooden leg for Lord Nelson."

"How? but I thought, by the way you pull a lock-string on board here, and look along the sight, that you can steer a shot about right—hey, Jack?"

"It was the Admiral of the Fleet—God Almighty—who directed the shot that dismasted the Turkish Admiral," said Jack; "I only pointed the gun."

"But how did you feel, Jack, when the musket-ball carried away one of your hooks there?"

"Feel! only a finger the lighter. I have seven more left, besides thumbs; and they did good service, too, in the torn rigging the day after the fight; for you must know, my hearties, that the hardest work comes after the guns are run in. Three days I helped work, with one hand, in the rigging, in the same trowsers that I wore in the action; the blood had dried and stiffened; they looked like glazed red morocco."

Now, this Jack Chase had a heart in him like a mastodon's. I have seen him weep when a man has been flogged at the gangway; yet, in relating the story of the Battle of Navarino, he plainly showed that he held the God of the blessed Bible to have been the British Commodore in the Levant, on the bloody 20th of October, A.D. 1827. And thus it would seem that war almost makes blasphemers of the best of men, and brings them all down to the Feejee standard of humanity. Some man-of-war's-men have confessed to me, that as a battle has raged more and more, their hearts have hardened in infernal harmony; and, like their own guns, they have fought without a thought.

Soldier or sailor, the fighting man is but a fiend; and the staff and body-guard of the Devil musters many a baton. But war at times is inevitable. Must the national honor be trampled under foot by an insolent foe?

Say on, say on; but know you this, and lay it to heart, war-voting Bench of Bishops, that He on whom we believe *himself* has enjoined us to turn the left cheek if the right be smitten. Never mind what follows. That passage you can not expunge from the Bible; that passage is as binding upon us as any other; that passage embodies the soul and substance of the Christian faith; without it, Christianity were like any other faith. And that passage will yet, by the blessing of God, turn the world. But in some things we must turn Quakers first.

But though unlike most scenes of carnage, which have proved useless murders of men, Admiral Codrington's victory undoubtedly achieved the emancipation of Greece, and terminated the Turkish atrocities in that tomahawked state, yet who shall lift his hand and swear that a Divine Providence led the van of the combined fleets of England, France, and Russia at the battle of Navarino? For if this be so, then it led the van against the Church's own elect—the persecuted Waldenses in Switzerland—and kindled the Smithfield fires in bloody Mary's time.

But all events are mixed in a fusion indistinguishable. What we call Fate is even, heartless, and impartial; not a fiend to kindle bigot flames, nor a philanthropist to espouse the cause of Greece. We may fret, fume, and fight; but the thing called Fate everlastingly sustains an armed neutrality.

Yet though all this be so, nevertheless, in our own hearts, we mold the whole world's hereafters; and in our own hearts we fashion our own gods. Each mortal casts his vote for whom he will to rule the worlds; I have a voice that helps to shape eternity; and my volitions stir the orbits of the furthest suns. In two senses, we are precisely what we worship. Ourselves are Fate.

Chapter 76

THE CHAINS

WHEN WEARIED with the tumult and occasional contention of the gun-deck of our frigate, I have often retreated to a port-hole, and calmed myself down by gazing
broad off upon a placid sea. After the battle-din of the last
two chapters, let us now do the like, and, in the sequestered
fore-chains of the Neversink, tranquillize ourselves, if we may.

Notwithstanding the domestic communism to which the
seamen in a man-of-war are condemned, and the publicity in
which actions the most diffident and retiring in their nature
must be performed, there is yet an odd corner or two where
you may sometimes steal away, and, for a few moments, almost be private.

Chief among these places is the *chains*, to which I would
sometimes hie during our pleasant homeward-bound glide
over those pensive tropical latitudes. After hearing my fill of
the wild yarns of our top, here would I recline—if not disturbed—serenely concocting information into wisdom.

The chains designates the small platform outside of the
hull, at the base of the large shrouds leading down from the
three mast-heads to the bulwarks. At present they seem to be
getting out of vogue among merchant-vessels, along with the
fine, old-fashioned quarter-galleries, little turret-like appurtenances, which, in the days of the old Admirals, set off the
angles of an armed ship's stern. Here a naval officer might
lounge away an hour after action, smoking a cigar, to drive
out of his whiskers the villainous smoke of the gunpowder.
The picturesque, delightful stern-gallery, also, a broad balcony overhanging the sea, and entered from the Captain's
cabin, much as you might enter a bower from a lady's chamber; this charming balcony, where, sailing over summer seas
in the days of the old Peruvian viceroys, the Spanish cavalier
Mendanna, of Lima, made love to the Lady Isabella, as they
voyaged in quest of the Solomon Islands, the fabulous Ophir,
the Grand Cyclades; and the Lady Isabella, at sunset, blushed

like the Orient, and gazed down to the gold-fish and silver-hued flying-fish, that wove the woof and warp of their wakes in bright, scaly tartans and plaids underneath where the Lady reclined; this charming balcony—exquisite retreat—has been cut away by Vandalic innovations. Ay, that claw-footed old gallery is no longer in fashion; in Commodore's eyes, is no longer genteel.

Out on all furniture fashions but those that are past! Give me my grandfather's old arm-chair, planted upon four carved frogs, as the Hindoos fabled the world to be supported upon four tortoises; give me his cane, with the gold-loaded top—a cane that, like the musket of General Washington's father and the broad-sword of William Wallace, would break down the back of the switch-carrying dandies of these spindle-shank days; give me his broad-breasted vest, coming bravely down over the hips, and furnished with two strong-boxes of pockets to keep guineas in; toss this toppling cylinder of a beaver overboard, and give me my grandfather's gallant, gable-ended, cocked hat.

But though the quarter-galleries and the stern-gallery of a man-of-war are departed, yet the *chains* still linger; nor can there be imagined a more agreeable retreat. The huge blocks and lanyards forming the pedestals of the shrouds divide the chains into numerous little chapels, alcoves, niches, and altars, where you lazily lounge—outside of the ship, though on board. But there are plenty to divide a good thing with you in this man-of-war world. Often, when snugly seated in one of these little alcoves, gazing off to the horizon, and thinking of Cathay, I have been startled from my repose by some old quarter-gunner, who, having newly painted a parcel of match-tubs, wanted to set them to dry.

At other times, one of the tattooing artists would crawl over the bulwarks, followed by his sitter; and then a bare arm or leg would be extended, and the disagreeable business of "*pricking*" commence, right under my eyes; or an irruption of tars, with ditty-bags or sea-reticules, and piles of old trowsers to mend, would break in upon my seclusion, and, forming a sewing-circle, drive me off with their chatter.

But once—it was a Sunday afternoon—I was pleasantly reclining in a particularly shady and secluded little niche between two lanyards, when I heard a low, supplicating voice. Peeping through the narrow space between the ropes, I perceived an aged seaman on his knees, his face turned seaward, with closed eyes, buried in prayer. Softly rising, I stole through a port-hole, and left the venerable worshiper alone.

He was a sheet-anchor-man, an earnest Baptist, and was well known, in his own part of the ship, to be constant in his solitary devotions in the *chains*. He reminded me of St. Anthony going out into the wilderness to pray.

This man was captain of the starboard bow-chaser, one of the two long twenty-four-pounders on the forecastle. In time of action, the command of that iron Thalaba the Destroyer would devolve upon *him*. It would be his business to "train" it properly; to see it well loaded; the grape and cannister rammed home; also, to "prick the cartridge," "take the sight," and give the word for the match-man to apply his wand; bidding a sudden hell to flash forth from the muzzle, in wide combustion and death.

Now, this captain of the bow-chaser was an upright old man, a sincere, humble believer, and he but earned his bread in being captain of that gun; but how, with those hands of his begrimed with powder, could he break that *other* and most peaceful and penitent bread of the Supper? though in that hallowed sacrament, it seemed, he had often partaken ashore. The omission of this rite in a man-of-war—though there is a chaplain to preside over it, and at least a few communicants to partake—must be ascribed to a sense of religious propriety, in the last degree to be commended.

Ah! the best righteousness of our man-of-war world seems but an unrealized ideal, after all; and those maxims which, in the hope of bringing about a Millennium, we busily teach to the heathen, we Christians ourselves disregard. In view of the whole present social frame-work of our world, so ill adapted to the practical adoption of the meekness of Christianity, there seems almost some ground for the thought, that although our blessed Savior was full of the wisdom of heaven, yet his gospel seems lacking in the practical wisdom of earth—in a due appreciation of the necessities of nations at times demanding bloody massacres and wars; in a proper estimation of the value of rank, title, and money. But all this only the more crowns the divine consistency of Jesus; since Burnet and the best theologians demonstrate, that his nature was not merely human—was not that of a mere man of the world.

Chapter 77

THE HOSPITAL IN A MAN-OF-WAR

AFTER RUNNING with a fine steady breeze up to the Line, it fell calm, and there we lay, three days enchanted on the sea. We were a most puissant man-of-war, no doubt, with our five hundred men, Commodore and Captain, backed by our long batteries of thirty-two and twenty-four pounders; yet, for all that, there we lay rocking, helpless as an infant in the cradle. Had it only been a gale instead of a calm, gladly would we have charged upon it with our gallant bowsprit, as with a stout lance in rest; but, as with mankind, this serene, passive foe—unresisting and irresistible—lived it out, unconquered to the last.

All these three days the heat was excessive; the sun drew the tar from the seams of the ship; the awnings were spread fore and aft; the decks were kept constantly sprinkled with water. It was during this period that a sad event occurred, though not an unusual one on shipboard. But in order to prepare for its narration, some account of a part of the ship called the "*sick-bay*" must needs be presented.

The *sick-bay* is that part of a man-of-war where the invalid seamen are placed; in many respects it answers to a public hospital ashore. As with most frigates, the sick-bay of the Neversink was on the berth-deck—the third deck from above. It was in the extreme forward part of that deck, embracing the triangular area in the bows of the ship. It was, therefore, a subterranean vault, into which scarce a ray of heaven's glad light ever penetrated, even at noon.

In a sea-going frigate that has all her armament and stores on board, the floor of the berth-deck is partly below the surface of the water. But in a smooth harbor, some circulation of air is maintained by opening large auger-holes in the upper portion of the sides, called "air-ports," not much above the water level. Before going to sea, however, these air-ports must be closed, caulked, and the seams hermetically sealed with pitch. These places for ventilation being shut, the sick-bay is entirely barred against the free, natural admission of fresh air. In the Neversink, a few lungsful were forced down by artificial means. But as the ordinary *wind-sail* was the only method adopted, the quantity of fresh air sent down was regulated by the force of the wind. In a calm there was none to be had, while in a severe gale the wind-sail had to be hauled up, on account of the violent draught blowing full upon the cots of the sick. An open-work partition divided our sick-bay from the rest of the deck, where the hammocks of the watch were slung; it, therefore, was exposed to all the uproar that ensued upon the watches being relieved.

An official, called the surgeon's steward, assisted by subordinates, presided over the place. He was the same individual alluded to as officiating at the amputation of the top-man. He was always to be found at his post, by night and by day.

This surgeon's steward deserves a description. He was a small, pale, hollow-eyed young man, with that peculiar Lazarus-like expression so often noticed in hospital attendants. Seldom or never did you see him on deck, and when he *did* emerge into the light of the sun, it was with an abashed look, and an uneasy, winking eye. The sun was not made for *him*. His nervous organization was confounded by the sight of the robust old sea-dogs on the forecastle and the general tumult of the spar-deck, and he mostly buried himself below in an atmosphere which long habit had made congenial.

This young man never indulged in frivolous conversation; he only talked of the surgeon's prescriptions; his every word was a bolus. He never was known to smile; nor did he even look sober in the ordinary way; but his countenance ever wore an aspect of cadaverous resignation to his fate. Strange! that so many of those who would fain minister to our own health should look so much like invalids themselves.

Connected with the sick-bay, over which the surgeon's steward presided—but removed from it in place, being next door to the counting-room of the purser's steward—was a regular apothecary's shop, of which he kept the key. It was fitted up precisely like an apothecary's on shore, displaying tiers of shelves on all four sides filled with green bottles and gallipots; beneath were multitudinous drawers, bearing incomprehensible gilded inscriptions in abbreviated Latin.

He generally opened his shop for an hour or two every morning and evening. There was a Venetian blind in the upper part of the door, which he threw up when inside, so as to admit a little air. And there you would see him, with a green shade over his eyes, seated on a stool, and pounding his pestle in a great iron mortar that looked like a howitzer, mixing some jallapy compound. A smoky lamp shed a flickering, yellow-fever tinge upon his pallid face and the closely-packed regiments of gallipots.

Several times when I felt in need of a little medicine, but was not ill enough to report myself to the surgeon at his levees, I would call of a morning upon his steward at the Sign of the Mortar, and beg him to give me what I wanted; when, without speaking a word, this cadaverous young man would mix me my potion in a tin cup, and hand it out through the little opening in his door, like the boxed-up treasurer giving you your change at the ticket-office of a theatre.

But there was a little shelf against the wall of the door, and upon this I would set the tin cup for a while, and survey it; for I never was a Julius Cæsar at taking medicine; and to take it in this way, without a single attempt at disguising it; with no counteracting little morsel to hurry down after it; in short, to go to the very apothecary's in person, and there, at the counter, swallow down your dose, as if it were a nice mint-julep taken at the bar of a hotel—*this* was a bitter bolus indeed. But, then, this pallid young apothecary charged nothing for it, and *that* was no small satisfaction; for is it not remarkable, to say the least, that a shore apothecary should actually charge you money—round dollars and cents—for giving you a horrible nausea?

My tin cup would wait a long time on that little shelf; yet "Pills," as the sailors called him, never heeded my lingering, but in sober, silent sadness continued pounding his mortar or folding up his powders; until at last some other customer would appear, and then, in a sudden frenzy of resolution, I would gulp down my sherry-cobbler, and carry its unspeakable flavor with me far up into the frigate's main-top. I do not know whether it was the wide roll of the ship, as felt in that giddy perch, that occasioned it, but I always got sea-sick after taking medicine and going aloft with it. Seldom or never did it do me any lasting good.

Now the Surgeon's Steward was only a subordinate of Surgeon Cuticle himself, who lived in the ward-room among the Lieutenants, Sailing-master, Chaplain, and Purser.

The Surgeon is, by law, charged with the business of overlooking the general sanitary affairs of the ship. If any thing is going on in any of its departments which he judges to be detrimental to the healthfulness of the crew, he has a right to protest against it formally to the Captain. When a man is being scourged at the gangway, the Surgeon stands by; and if he thinks that the punishment is becoming more than the culprit's constitution can well bear, he has a right to interfere and demand its cessation for the time.

But though the Navy regulations nominally vest him with this high discretionary authority over the very Commodore himself, how seldom does he exercise it in cases where humanity demands it! Three years is a long time to spend in one ship, and to be at swords' points with its Captain and Lieutenants during such a period, must be very unsocial and every way irksome. No otherwise than thus, at least, can the remissness of some surgeons in remonstrating against cruelty be accounted for.

Not to speak again of the continual dampness of the decks consequent upon flooding them with salt water, when we were driving near to Cape Horn, it needs only to be mentioned that, on board of the Neversink, men known to be in consumptions gasped under the scourge of the boatswain's mate, when the Surgeon and his two attendants stood by and never interposed. But where the unscrupulousness of martial discipline is maintained, it is in vain to attempt softening its rigor by the ordaining of humanitarian laws. Sooner might you tame the grizzly bear of Missouri than humanize a thing so essentially cruel and heartless.

But the Surgeon has yet other duties to perform. Not a seaman enters the Navy without undergoing a corporal examination, to test his soundness in wind and limb.

One of the first places into which I was introduced when I first entered on board the Neversink was the sick-bay, where I found one of the Assistant Surgeons seated at a green-baize table. It was his turn for visiting the apartment. Having been commanded by the deck officer to report my business to the functionary before me, I accordingly hemmed, to attract his attention, and then catching his eye, politely intimated that I called upon him for the purpose of being accurately laid out and surveyed.

"Strip!" was the answer, and, rolling up his gold-laced cuff, he proceeded to manipulate me. He punched me in the ribs, smote me across the chest, commanded me to stand on one leg and hold out the other horizontally. He asked me whether any of my family were consumptive; whether I ever felt a tendency to a rush of blood to the head; whether I was gouty; how often I had been bled during my life; how long I had been ashore; how long I had been afloat; with several other questions which have altogether slipped my memory. He concluded his interrogatories with this extraordinary and unwarranted one—"Are you pious?"

It was a leading question which somewhat staggered me, but I said not a word; when, feeling of my calves, he looked up and incomprehensibly said, "I am afraid you are not."

At length he declared me a sound animal, and wrote a certificate to that effect, with which I returned to the deck.

This Assistant Surgeon turned out to be a very singular character, and when I became more acquainted with him, I ceased to marvel at the curious question with which he had concluded his examination of my person.

He was a thin, knock-kneed man, with a sour, saturnine expression, rendered the more peculiar from his shaving his beard so remorselessly, that his chin and cheeks always looked blue, as if pinched with cold. His long familiarity with nautical invalids seemed to have filled him full of theological hypoes concerning the state of their souls. He was at once the physician and priest of the sick, washing down his boluses with ghostly consolation, and among the sailors went by the name of The Pelican, a fowl whose hanging pouch imparts to it a most chop-fallen, lugubrious expression.

The privilege of going off duty and lying by when you are sick, is one of the few points in which a man-of-war is far better for the sailor than a merchantman. But, as with every other matter in the Navy, the whole thing is subject to the general discipline of the vessel, and is conducted with a severe, unyielding method and regularity, making no allowances for exceptions to rules.

During the half hour preceding morning quarters, the Surgeon of a frigate is to be found in the sick-bay, where, after going his rounds among the invalids, he holds a levee for the benefit of all new candidates for the sick-list. If, after looking at your tongue, and feeling of your pulse, he pronounces you a proper candidate, his secretary puts you down on his books, and you are thenceforth relieved from all duty, and have abundant leisure in which to recover your health. Let the boatswain blow; let the deck officer bellow; let the captain of your gun hunt you up; yet, if it can be answered by your mess-mates that you are "*down on the list*," you ride it all out with impunity. The Commodore himself has then no authority over you. But you must not be too much elated, for your immunities are only secure while you are immured in the dark hospital below. Should you venture to get a mouthful of fresh air on the spar-deck, and be there discovered by an officer, you will in vain plead your illness; for it is quite impossible, it seems, that any true man-of-war invalid can be hearty enough to crawl up the ladders. Besides, the raw sea air, as they will tell you, is not good for the sick.

But, notwithstanding all this, notwithstanding the darkness and closeness of the Sick-bay, in which an alleged invalid must be content to shut himself up till the Surgeon pronounces him cured, many instances occur, especially in protracted bad weather, where pretended invalids will submit to this dismal hospital durance, in order to escape hard work and wet jackets.

There is a story told somewhere of the Devil taking down the confessions of a woman on a strip of parchment, and being obliged to stretch it longer and longer with his teeth, in order to find room for all the lady had to say. Much thus was it with our Surgeon's Steward, who had to lengthen out his manuscript Sick-list, in order to accommodate all the names which were presented to him while we were off the pitch of Cape Horn. What sailors call the "*Cape Horn Fever*," alarmingly prevailed; though it disappeared altogether when we got into fine weather, which, as with many other invalids, was solely to be imputed to the wonder-working effects of an entire change of climate.

It seems very strange, but it is really true, that off Cape Horn some "*sogers*" of sailors will stand cupping, and bleeding, and blistering, before they will budge. On the other hand, there are cases where a man actually sick and in need of medicine will refuse to go on the Sick-list, because in that case his allowance of *grog* must be stopped.

On board of every American man-of-war, bound for sea, there is a goodly supply of wines and various delicacies put on board—according to law—for the benefit of the sick, whether officers or sailors. And one of the chicken-coops is always reserved for the Government chickens, destined for a similar purpose. But, on board of the Neversink, the only delicacies given to invalid sailors was a little sago or arrow-root, and they did not get *that* unless severely ill; but, so far as I could learn, no wine, in any quantity, was ever prescribed for them, though the Government bottles often went into the Ward-room, for the benefit of indisposed officers.

And though the Government chicken-coop was replenished at every port, yet not four pair of drum-sticks were ever boiled into broth for sick sailors. Where the chickens went, some one must have known; but, as I can not vouch for it myself, I will not here back the hardy assertion of the men, which was that the pious Pelican—true to his name—was extremely fond of poultry. I am the still less disposed to believe this scandal, from the continued leanness of the Pelican, which could hardly have been the case did he nourish himself by so nutritious a dish as the drum-sticks of fowls, a diet prescribed to pugilists in training. But who can avoid being suspicious of a very suspicious person? Pelican! I rather suspect you still.

Chapter 78

Dismal Times in the Mess

IT WAS on the first day of the long, hot calm which we had on the Equator, that a mess-mate of mine, by the name of Shenly, who had been for some weeks complaining, at length went on the Sick-list.

An old gunner's mate of the mess—Priming, the man with the hare-lip, who, true to his tribe, was charged to the muzzle with bile, and, moreover, rammed home on top of it a wad of sailor superstition—this gunner's mate indulged in some gloomy and savage remarks—strangely tinged with genuine feeling and grief—at the announcement of the sickness of Shenly, coming as it did not long after the almost fatal accident befalling poor Baldy, captain of the mizzen-top, another mess-mate of ours, and the dreadful fate of the amputated fore-top-man whom we buried in Rio, also our mess-mate.

We were cross-legged seated at dinner, between the guns, when the sad news concerning Shenly was first communicated.

"I know'd it, I know'd it," said Priming, through his nose. "Blast ye, I told ye so; poor fellow! But dam'me, I know'd it. This comes of having *thirteen* in the mess. I hope he arn't dangerous, men? Poor Shenly! But, blast it, it warn't till White-Jacket there comed into the mess that these here things began. I don't believe there'll be more nor three of us left by the time we strike soundings, men. But how is he now? Have you been down to see him, any on ye? Damn you, you Jonah! I don't see how you can sleep in your hammock, knowing as you do that by making an odd number in the mess you have been the death of one poor fellow, and ruined Baldy for life, and here's poor Shenly keeled up. Blast you, and your jacket, say I."

"My dear mess-mate," I cried, "don't blast me any more, for Heaven's sake. Blast my jacket you may, and I'll join you in *that*; but don't blast *me*; for if you do, I shouldn't wonder if I myself was the next man to keel up."

"Gunner's mate!" said Jack Chase, helping himself to a slice of beef, and sandwiching it between two large biscuits— "Gunner's mate! White-Jacket there is my particular friend, and I would take it as a particular favor if you would *knock off* blasting him. It's in bad taste, rude, and unworthy a gentleman."

"Take your back away from that 'ere gun-carriage, will ye now, Jack Chase?" cried Priming, in reply, just then Jack happening to lean up against it. "Must I be all the time cleaning after you fellows? Blast ye! I spent an hour on that 'ere gun-carriage this very mornin'. But it all comes of White-Jacket there. If it warn't for having one too many, there wouldn't be any crowding and jamming in the mess. I'm blessed if we ar'n't about chock a' block here! Move further up there, I'm sitting on my leg!"

"For God's sake, gunner's mate," cried I, "if it will content you, I and my jacket will leave the mess."

"I wish you would, and be —— to you!" he replied.

"And if he does, you will mess alone, gunner's mate," said Jack Chase.

"That you will," cried all.

"And I wish to the Lord you'd let me!" growled Priming, irritably rubbing his head with the handle of his sheath-knife.

"You are an old bear, gunner's mate," said Jack Chase.

"I am an old Turk," he replied, drawing the flat blade of his knife between his teeth, thereby producing a whetting, grating sound.

"Let him alone, let him alone, men," said Jack Chase. "Only keep off the tail of a rattlesnake, and he'll not rattle."

"Look out he don't bite, though," said Priming, snapping his teeth; and with that he rolled off, growling as he went.

Though I did my best to carry off my vexation with an air of indifference, need I say how I cursed my jacket, that it thus seemed the means of fastening on me the murder of one of my shipmates, and the probable murder of two more. For, had it not been for my jacket, doubtless, I had yet been a member of my old mess, and so have escaped making the luckless odd number among my present companions.

All I could say in private to Priming had no effect; though I often took him aside, to convince him of the philosophical impossibility of my having been accessary to the misfortunes of Baldy, the buried sailor in Rio, and Shenly. But Priming knew better; nothing could move him; and he ever afterward eyed me as virtuous citizens do some notorious underhand villain going unhung of justice.

Jacket! jacket! thou hast much to answer for, jacket!

Chapter 79

HOW MAN-OF-WAR'S-MEN DIE AT SEA

S HENLY, my sick mess-mate, was a middle-aged, handsome, intelligent seaman, whom some hard calamity, or
perhaps some unfortunate excess, must have driven into the
Navy. He told me he had a wife and two children in Portsmouth, in the state of New Hampshire. Upon being examined by Cuticle, the surgeon, he was, on purely scientific
grounds, reprimanded by that functionary for not having previously appeared before him. He was immediately consigned
to one of the invalid cots as a serious case. His complaint was
of long standing; a pulmonary one, now attended with general prostration.

The same evening he grew so much worse, that, according
to man-of-war usage, we, his mess-mates, were officially notified that we must take turns at sitting up with him through
the night. We at once made our arrangements, allotting two
hours for a watch. Not till the third night did my own turn
come round. During the day preceding, it was stated at the
mess that our poor mess-mate was run down completely; the
surgeon had given him up.

At four bells (two o'clock in the morning), I went down to relieve one of my mess-mates at the sick man's cot. The profound
quietude of the calm pervaded the entire frigate through all her
decks. The watch on duty were dozing on the carronade-slides,
far above the sick-bay; and the watch below were fast asleep in
their hammocks, on the same deck with the invalid.

Groping my way under these two hundred sleepers, I entered
the hospital. A dim lamp was burning on the table, which was
screwed down to the floor. This light shed dreary shadows over
the white-washed walls of the place, making it look like a whited
sepulchre under ground. The wind-sail had collapsed, and lay
motionless on the deck. The low groans of the sick were the only
sounds to be heard; and as I advanced, some of them rolled
upon me their sleepless, silent, tormented eyes.

"Fan him, and keep his forehead wet with this sponge,"

whispered my mess-mate, whom I came to relieve, as I drew near to Shenly's cot, "and wash the foam from his mouth; nothing more can be done for him. If he dies before your watch is out, call the Surgeon's steward; he sleeps in that hammock," pointing it out. "Good-by, good-by, mess-mate," he then whispered, stooping over the sick man; and so saying, he left the place.

Shenly was lying on his back. His eyes were closed, forming two dark-blue pits in his face; his breath was coming and going with a slow, long-drawn, mechanical precision. It was the mere foundering hull of a man that was before me; and though it presented the well-known features of my mess-mate, yet I knew that the living soul of Shenly never more would look out of those eyes.

So warm had it been during the day, that the Surgeon himself, when visiting the sick-bay, had entered it in his shirt sleeves; and so warm was now the night, that even in the lofty top I had worn but a loose linen frock and trowsers. But in this subterranean sick-bay, buried in the very bowels of the ship, and at sea cut off from all ventilation, the heat of the night calm was intense. The sweat dripped from me as if I had just emerged from a bath; and stripping myself naked to the waist, I sat by the side of the cot, and with a bit of crumpled paper—put into my hand by the sailor I had relieved—kept fanning the motionless white face before me.

I could not help thinking, as I gazed, whether this man's fate had not been accelerated by his confinement in this heated furnace below; and whether many a sick man round me might not soon improve, if but permitted to swing his hammock in the airy vacancies of the half-deck above, open to the port-holes, but reserved for the promenade of the officers.

At last the heavy breathing grew more and more irregular, and gradually dying away, left forever the unstirring form of Shenly.

Calling the Surgeon's steward, he at once told me to rouse the master-at-arms, and four or five of my mess-mates. The master-at-arms approached, and immediately demanded the dead man's bag, which was accordingly dragged into the bay. Having been laid on the floor, and washed with a bucket of water which I drew from the ocean, the body was then dressed in a white frock, trowsers, and neckerchief, taken out of the bag. While this was going on, the master-at-arms— standing over the operation with his rattan, and directing myself and mess-mates—indulged in much discursive levity, intended to manifest his fearlessness of death.

Pierre, who had been a "*chummy*" of Shenly's, spent much time in tying the neckkerchief in an elaborate bow, and affectionately adjusting the white frock and trowsers; but the master-at-arms put an end to this by ordering us to carry the body up to the gun-deck. It was placed on the death-board (used for that purpose), and we proceeded with it toward the main hatchway, awkwardly crawling under the tiers of hammocks, where the entire watch-below was sleeping. As, unavoidably, we rocked their pallets, the man-of-war's-men would cry out against us; through the mutterings of curses, the corpse reached the hatchway. Here the board slipped, and some time was spent in readjusting the body. At length we deposited it on the gun-deck, between two guns, and a union-jack being thrown over it for a pall, I was left again to watch by its side.

I had not been seated on my shot-box three minutes, when the messenger-boy passed me on his way forward; presently the slow, regular stroke of the ship's great bell was heard, proclaiming through the calm the expiration of the watch; it was four o'clock in the morning.

Poor Shenly! thought I, that sounds like your knell! and here you lie becalmed, in the last calm of all!

Hardly had the brazen din died away, when the Boatswain and his mates mustered round the hatchway, within a yard or two of the corpse, and the usual thundering call was given for the watch below to turn out.

"All the starboard-watch, ahoy! On deck there, below! Wide awake there, sleepers!"

But the dreamless sleeper by my side, who had so often sprung from his hammock at that summons, moved not a limb; the blue sheet over him lay unwrinkled.

A mess-mate of the other watch now came to relieve me; but I told him I chose to remain where I was till daylight came.

Chapter 80

THE LAST STITCH

JUST BEFORE DAYBREAK, two of the sail-maker's gang drew near, each with a lantern, carrying some canvass, two large shot, needles, and twine. I knew their errand; for in men-of-war the sail-maker is the undertaker.

They laid the body on deck, and, after fitting the canvass to it, seated themselves, cross-legged like tailors, one on each side, and, with their lanterns before them, went to stitching away, as if mending an old sail. Both were old men, with grizzled hair and beard, and shrunken faces. They belonged to that small class of aged seamen who, for their previous long and faithful services, are retained in the Navy more as pensioners upon its merited bounty than any thing else. They are set to light and easy duties.

"Ar'n't this the fore-top-man, Shenly?" asked the foremost, looking full at the frozen face before him.

"Ay, ay, old Ringrope," said the other, drawing his hand far back with a long thread, "I thinks it's him; and he's further aloft now, I hope, than ever he was at the fore-truck. But I only hopes; I'm afeard this ar'n't the last on him!"

"His hull here will soon be going out of sight below hatches, though, old Thrummings," replied Ringrope, placing two heavy cannon-balls in the foot of the canvass shroud.

"I don't know that, old man; I never yet sewed up a shipmate but he spooked me arterward. I tell ye, Ringrope, these 'ere corpses is cunning. You think they sinks deep, but they comes up agin as soon as you sails over 'em. They lose the number of their mess, and their mess-mates sticks their spoons in the rack; but no good—no good, old Ringrope; they ar'n't dead yet. I tell ye, now, ten best-bower-anchors wouldn't sink this 'ere top-man. He'll be soon coming in the wake of the thirty-nine spooks what spooks me every night in my hammock—jist afore the mid-watch is called. Small thanks I gets for my pains; and every one on 'em looks so 'proachful-like, with a sail-maker's needle through his nose.

I've been thinkin', old Ringrope, it's all wrong that 'ere last stitch we takes. Depend on't, they don't like it—none on 'em."

I was standing leaning over a gun, gazing at the two old men. The last remark reminded me of a superstitious custom generally practiced by most sea-undertakers upon these occasions. I resolved that, if I could help it, it should not take place upon the remains of Shenly.

"Thrummings," said I, advancing to the last speaker, "you are right. That last thing you do to the canvass is the very reason, be sure of it, that brings the ghosts after you, as you say. So don't do it to this poor fellow, I entreat. Try once, now, how it goes not to do it."

"What do you say to the youngster, old man?" said Thrummings, holding up his lantern into his comrade's wrinkled face, as if deciphering some ancient parchment.

"I'm agin all innowations," said Ringrope; "it's a good old fashion, that last stitch; it keeps 'em snug, d'ye see, youngster. I'm blest if they could sleep sound, if it wa'n't for that. No, no, Thrummings! no innowations; I won't hear on't. I goes for the last stitch!"

"S'pose you was going to be sewed up yourself, old Ringrope, would you like the last stitch then? You are an old gun, Ringrope; you can't stand looking out at your port-hole much longer," said Thrummings, as his own palsied hands were quivering over the canvass.

"Better say that to yourself, old man," replied Ringrope, stooping close to the light to thread his coarse needle, which trembled in his withered hands like the needle in a compass of a Greenland ship near the Pole. "You ain't long for the sarvice. I wish I could give you some o' the blood in my veins, old man!"

"Ye ain't got ne'er a tea-spoonful to spare," said Thrummings. "It will go hard, and I wouldn't want to do it; but I'm afear'd I'll have the sewing on ye up afore long!"

"Sew *me* up? Me dead and you alive, old man?" shrieked Ringrope. "Well, I've he'rd the parson of the old Independence say as how old age was deceitful; but I never seed it so true afore this blessed night. I'm sorry for ye, old man—to see you so innocent-like, and Death all the while turning in and out with you in your hammock, for all the world like a hammock-mate."

"You lie! old man," cried Thrummings, shaking with rage. "It's *you* that have Death for a hammock-mate; it's *you* that will make a hole in the shot-locker soon."

"Take that back!" cried Ringrope, huskily, leaning far over the corpse, and, needle in hand, menacing his companion with his aguish fist. "Take that back, or I'll throttle your lean bag of wind for ye!"

"Blast ye! old chaps, ain't ye any more manners than to be fighting over a dead man?" cried one of the sail-maker's mates, coming down from the spar-deck. "Bear a hand!— bear a hand! and get through with that job!"

"Only one more stitch to take," muttered Ringrope, creeping near the face.

"Drop your '*palm*,' then, and let Thrummings take it; follow me—the foot of the main-sail wants mending—must do it afore a breeze springs up. D'ye hear, old chap! I say, drop your *palm*, and follow me."

At the reiterated command of his superior, Ringrope rose, and, turning to his comrade, said, "I take it all back, Thrummings, and I'm sorry for it, too. But mind ye, take that 'ere last stitch, now; if ye don't, there's no tellin' the consekenses."

As the mate and his man departed, I stole up to Thrummings, "Don't do it—don't do it, now, Thrummings—depend on it, it's wrong!"

"Well, youngster, I'll try this here one without it for jist this here once; and if, arter that, he don't spook me, I'll be dead agin the last stitch as long as my name is Thrummings."

So, without mutilation, the remains were replaced between the guns, the union jack again thrown over them, and I reseated myself on the shot-box.

Chapter 81

How they Bury a Man-of-war's-man at Sea

QUARTERS over in the morning, the boatswain and his four mates stood round the main hatchway, and after giving the usual whistle, made the customary announcement—*"All hands bury the dead, ahoy!"*

In a man-of-war, every thing, even to a man's funeral and burial, proceeds with the unrelenting promptitude of the martial code. And whether it is *all hands bury the dead!* or *all hands splice the main-brace*, the order is given in the same hoarse tones.

Both officers and men assembled in the lee waist, and through that bareheaded crowd the mess-mates of Shenly brought his body to the same gangway where it had thrice winced under the scourge. But there is something in death that ennobles even a pauper's corpse; and the Captain himself stood bareheaded before the remains of a man whom, with his hat on, he had sentenced to the ignominious gratings when alive.

"I am the resurrection and the life!" solemnly began the Chaplain, in full canonicals, the prayer-book in his hand.

"Damn you! off those booms!" roared a boatswain's mate to a crowd of top-men, who had elevated themselves to gain a better view of the scene.

"We commit this body to the deep!" At the word, Shenly's mess-mates tilted the board, and the dead sailor sank in the sea.

"Look aloft," whispered Jack Chase. "See that bird! it is the spirit of Shenly."

Gazing upward, all beheld a snow-white, solitary fowl, which—whence coming no one could tell—had been hovering over the main-mast during the service, and was now sailing far up into the depths of the sky.

Chapter 82

WHAT REMAINS OF A MAN-OF-WAR'S-MAN AFTER
HIS BURIAL AT SEA

UPON EXAMINING Shenly's bag, a will was found, scratched in pencil, upon a blank leaf in the middle of his Bible; or, to use the phrase of one of the seamen, in the midships, atween the Bible and Testament, where the Pothecary (Apocrypha) uses to be.

The will was comprised in one solitary sentence, exclusive of the dates and signatures: *"In case I die on the voyage, the Purser will please pay over my wages to my wife, who lives in Portsmouth, New Hampshire."*

Besides the testator's, there were two signatures of witnesses.

This last will and testament being shown to the Purser, who, it seems, had been a notary, or surrogate, or some sort of cosy chamber practitioner in his time, he declared that it must be "proved." So the witnesses were called, and after recognizing their hands to the paper; for the purpose of additionally testing their honesty, they were interrogated concerning the day on which they had signed—whether it was *Banyan Day*, or *Duff Day*, or *Swamp-seed Day*; for among the sailors on board a man-of-war, the land terms, *Monday*, *Tuesday*, *Wednesday*, are almost unknown. In place of these they substitute nautical names, some of which are significant of the daily bill of fare at dinner for the week.

The two witnesses were somewhat puzzled by the attorney-like questions of the Purser, till a third party came along, one of the ship's barbers, and declared, of his own knowledge, that Shenly executed the instrument on a *Shaving Day*; for the deceased seaman had informed him of the circumstance, when he came to have his beard reaped on the morning of the event.

In the Purser's opinion, this settled the question; and it is to be hoped that the widow duly received her husband's death-earned wages.

Shenly was dead and gone; and what was Shenly's epitaph?
                    —"D. D."—
opposite his name in the Purser's books, in "*Black's best
Writing Fluid*"—funereal name and funereal hue—meaning
"Discharged, Dead."

Chapter 83

A Man-of-war College

In our man-of-war world, Life comes in at one gangway and Death goes overboard at the other. Under the man-of-war scourge, curses mix with tears; and the sigh and the sob furnish the bass to the shrill octave of those who laugh to drown buried griefs of their own. Checkers were played in the waist at the time of Shenly's burial; and as the body plunged, a player swept the board. The bubbles had hardly burst, when all hands were *piped down* by the Boatswain, and the old jests were heard again, as if Shenly himself were there to hear.

This man-of-war life has not left me unhardened. I can not stop to weep over Shenly now; that would be false to the life I depict; wearing no mourning weeds, I resume the task of portraying our man-of-war world.

Among the various other vocations, all driven abreast on board of the Neversink, was that of the schoolmaster. There were two academies in the frigate. One comprised the apprentice boys, who, upon certain days of the week, were indoctrinated in the mysteries of the primer by an invalid corporal of marines, a slender, wizzen-cheeked man, who had received a liberal infant-school education.

The other school was a far more pretentious affair—a sort of army and navy seminary combined, where mystical mathematical problems were solved by the midshipmen, and great ships-of-the-line were navigated over imaginary shoals by unimaginable observations of the moon and the stars, and learned lectures were delivered upon great guns, small arms, and the curvilinear lines described by bombs in the air.

"*The Professor*" was the title bestowed upon the erudite gentleman who conducted this seminary, and by that title alone was he known throughout the ship. He was domiciled in the Ward-room, and circulated there on a social par with the Purser, Surgeon, and other *non-combatants* and Quakers. By being advanced to the dignity of a peerage in the Ward-room,

Science and Learning were ennobled in the person of this Professor, even as divinity was honored in the Chaplain enjoying the rank of a spiritual peer.

Every other afternoon, while at sea, the Professor assembled his pupils on the half-deck, near the long twenty-four pounders. A bass drum-head was his desk, his pupils forming a semicircle around him, seated on shot-boxes and match-tubs.

They were in the jelly of youth, and this learned Professor poured into their susceptible hearts all the gentle, gunpowder maxims of war. Presidents of Peace Societies and Superintendents of Sabbath Schools, must it not have been a most interesting sight?

But the Professor himself was a noteworthy person. A tall, thin, spectacled man, about forty years old, with a student's stoop in his shoulders, and wearing uncommonly scanty pantaloons, exhibiting an undue proportion of his boots. In early life he had been a cadet in the military academy of West Point; but, becoming very weak-sighted, and thereby in a good manner disqualified for active service in the field, he had declined entering the army, and accepted the office of Professor in the Navy.

His studies at West Point had thoroughly grounded him in a knowledge of gunnery; and, as he was not a little of a pedant, it was sometimes amusing, when the sailors were at quarters, to hear him criticise their evolutions at the batteries. He would quote Dr. Hutton's Tracts on the subject, also, in the original, "*The French Bombardier*," and wind up by Italian passages from the "*Prattica Manuale dell' Artiglieria.*"

Though not required by the Navy regulations to instruct his scholars in aught but the application of mathematics to navigation, yet besides this, and besides instructing them in the theory of gunnery, he also sought to root them in the theory of frigate and fleet tactics. To be sure, he himself did not know how to splice a rope or furl a sail; and, owing to his partiality for strong coffee, he was apt to be nervous when we fired salutes; yet all this did not prevent him from delivering lectures on cannonading and "breaking the enemy's line."

He had arrived at his knowledge of tactics by silent, solitary study, and earnest meditation in the sequestered retreat of his state-room. His case was somewhat parallel to the Scotchman's—John Clerk, Esq., of Eldin—who, though he had never been to sea, composed a quarto treatise on fleet-fighting, which to this day remains a text-book; and he also originated a nautical maneuvre, which has given to England many a victory over her foes.

Now there was a large black-board, something like a great-gun target—only it was square—which during the professor's lectures was placed upright on the gun-deck, supported behind by three boarding-pikes. And here he would chalk out diagrams of great fleet engagements; making marks, like the soles of shoes, for the ships, and drawing a dog-vane in one corner to denote the assumed direction of the wind. This done, with a cutlass he would point out every spot of interest.

"Now, young gentlemen, the board before you exhibits the disposition of the British West Indian squadron under Rodney, when, early on the morning of the 9th of April, in the year of our blessed Lord 1782, he discovered part of the French fleet, commanded by the Count de Grasse, lying under the north end of the Island of Dominica. It was at this juncture that the Admiral gave the signal for the British line to prepare for battle, and stand on. D'ye understand, young gentlemen? Well, the British van having nearly fetched up with the centre of the enemy—who, be it remembered, were then on the starboard tack—and Rodney's centre and rear being yet becalmed under the lee of the land—the question I ask you is, What should Rodney now do?"

"Blaze away, by all means!" responded a rather confident reefer,—Mr. Pert,—who had zealously been observing the diagram.

"But, sir, his centre and rear are still becalmed, and his van has not yet closed with the enemy."

"Wait till he *does* come in range, and *then* blaze away," said the reefer.

"Permit me to remark, Mr. Pert, that '*blaze away*' is not a strictly technical term; and also permit me to hint, Mr. Pert, that you should consider the subject rather more deeply before you hurry forward your opinion."

This rebuke not only abashed Mr. Pert, but for a time intimidated the rest; and the professor was obliged to proceed, and extricate the British fleet by himself. He concluded by awarding Admiral Rodney the victory, which must have been exceedingly gratifying to the family pride of the surviving relatives and connections of that distinguished hero.

"Shall I clean the board, sir?" now asked Mr. Pert, brightening up.

"No, sir; not till you have saved that crippled French ship in the corner. That ship, young gentlemen, is the Glorieuse; you perceive she is cut off from her consorts, and the whole British fleet is giving chase to her. Her bowsprit is gone; her rudder is torn away; she has one hundred round shot in her hull, and two thirds of her men are dead or dying. What's to be done? the wind being at northeast by north?"

"Well, sir," said Mr. Dash, a chivalric young gentleman from Virginia, "I wouldn't strike yet; I'd nail my colors to the main-royal-mast! I would, by Jove!"

"That would not save your ship, sir; besides, your mainmast has gone by the board."

"I think, sir," said Mr. Slim, a diffident youth, "I think, sir, I would haul back the fore-top-sail."

"And why so? of what service would *that* be, I should like to know, Mr. Slim?"

"I can't tell exactly; but I think it would help her a little," was the timid reply.

"Not a whit, sir—not one particle; besides, you can't haul back your fore-top-sail—your fore-mast is lying across your forecastle."

"Haul back the main-top-sail, then," suggested another.

"Can't be done; your main-mast, also, has gone by the board!"

"Mizzen-top-sail?" meekly suggested little Boat-Plug.

"Your mizzen-top-mast, let me inform you, sir, was shot down in the first of the fight!"

"Well, sir," cried Mr. Dash, "I'd tack ship, any way; bid 'em good-by with a broadside; nail my flag to the keel, if there was no other place; and blow my brains out on the poop!"

"Idle, idle, sir! worse than idle! you are carried away, Mr. Dash, by your ardent Southern temperament! Let me inform you, young gentleman, that this ship," touching it with his cutlass, "can *not* be saved."

Then, throwing down his cutlass, "Mr. Pert, have the goodness to hand me one of those cannon-balls from the rack."

Balancing the iron sphere in one hand, the learned professor began fingering it with the other, like Columbus illustrating the rotundity of the globe before the Royal Commission of Castilian Ecclesiastics.

"Young gentlemen, I resume my remarks on the passage of a shot *in vacuo*, which remarks were interrupted yesterday by general quarters. After quoting that admirable passage in 'Spearman's British Gunner,' I then laid it down, you remember, that the path of a shot *in vacuo* describes a parabolic curve. I now add that, agreeably to the method pursued by the illustrious Newton in treating the subject of curvilinear motion, I consider the *trajectory* or curve described by a moving body in space as consisting of a series of right lines, described in successive intervals of time, and constituting the diagonals of parallelograms formed in a vertical plane between the vertical deflections caused by gravity and the production of the line of motion which has been described in each preceding interval of time. This must be obvious; for, if you say that the passage *in vacuo* of this cannon-ball, now held in my hand, would describe otherwise than a series of right lines, &c., then you are brought to the *Reductio ad Absurdum*, that the diagonals of parallelograms are—"

"All hands reef top-sails!" was now thundered forth by the boatswain's mates. The shot fell from the professor's palm; his spectacles dropped on his nose, and the school tumultuously broke up, the pupils scrambling up the ladders with the sailors, who had been overhearing the lecture.

Chapter 84

MAN-OF-WAR BARBERS

THE ALLUSION to one of the ship's barbers in a previous chapter, together with the recollection of how conspicuous a part they enacted in a tragical drama soon to be related, leads me now to introduce them to the reader.

Among the numerous artists and professors of polite trades in the Navy, none are held in higher estimation or drive a more profitable business than these barbers. And it may well be imagined that the five hundred heads of hair and five hundred beards of a frigate should furnish no small employment for those to whose faithful care they may be intrusted. As every thing connected with the domestic affairs of a man-of-war comes under the supervision of the martial executive, so certain barbers are formally licensed by the First Lieutenant. The better to attend to the profitable duties of their calling, they are exempted from all ship's duty except that of standing night-watches at sea, mustering at quarters, and coming on deck when all hands are called. They are rated as *able seamen* or *ordinary seamen*, and receive their wages as such; but in addition to this, they are liberally recompensed for their professional services. Herein their rate of pay is fixed for every sailor manipulated—so much per quarter, which is charged to the sailor, and credited to his barber on the books of the Purser.

It has been seen that while a man-of-war barber is shaving his customers at so much per chin, his wages as a seaman are still running on, which makes him a sort of *sleeping partner* of a sailor; nor are the sailor wages he receives altogether to be reckoned as earnings. Considering the circumstances, however, not much objection can be made to the barbers on this score. But there were instances of men in the Neversink receiving government money in part pay for work done for private individuals. Among these were several accomplished tailors, who nearly the whole cruise sat cross-legged on the half-deck, making coats, pantaloons, and vests for the quarter-deck officers. Some of these men, though knowing little or nothing about sailor duties, and seldom or never performing them, stood upon the ship's books as ordinary seamen, entitled to ten dollars a month. Why was this? Previous to shipping they had divulged the fact of their being tailors. True, the officers who employed them upon their wardrobes paid them for their work, but some of them in such a way as to elicit much grumbling from the tailors. At any rate, these makers and menders of clothes did not receive from some of these officers an amount equal to what they could have fairly earned ashore by doing the same work. It was a considerable saving to the officers to have their clothes made on board.

The men belonging to the carpenter's gang furnished another case in point. There were some six or eight allotted to this department. All the cruise they were hard at work. At what? Mostly making chests of drawers, canes, little ships and schooners, swifts, and other elaborated trifles, chiefly for the Captain. What did the Captain pay them for their trouble? Nothing. But the United States government paid them; two of them (the mates) at nineteen dollars a month, and the rest receiving the pay of able seamen, twelve dollars.

To return.

The regular days upon which the barbers shall exercise their vocation are set down on the ship's calendar, and known as *shaving days*. On board of the Neversink these days are Wednesdays and Saturdays; when, immediately after breakfast, the barbers' shops were opened to customers. They were in different parts of the gun-deck, between the long twenty-four pounders. Their furniture, however, was not very elaborate, hardly equal to the sumptuous appointments of metropolitan barbers. Indeed, it merely consisted of a match-tub, elevated upon a shot-box, as a barber's chair for the patient. No Psyche glasses; no hand-mirror; no ewer and basin; no comfortable padded footstool; nothing, in short, that makes a shore "*shave*" such a luxury.

Nor are the implements of these man-of-war barbers out of keeping with the rude appearance of their shops. Their razors are of the simplest patterns, and, from their jaggedness, would seem better fitted for the preparing and harrowing of the soil than for the ultimate reaping of the crop. But this is no matter for wonder, since so many chins are to be shaven, and a razor-case holds but two razors. For only two razors does a man-of-war barber have, and, like the marine sentries at the gangways in port, these razors go off and on duty in rotation. One brush, too, brushes every chin, and one lather lathers them all. No private brushes and boxes; no reservations whatever.

As it would be altogether too much trouble for a man-of-war's-man to keep his own shaving-tools and shave himself at sea, and since, therefore, nearly the whole ship's company patronize the ship's barbers, and as the seamen must be shaven by evening quarters of the days appointed for the business, it may be readily imagined what a scene of bustle and confusion there is when the razors are being applied. First come, first served, is the motto; and often you have to wait for hours together, sticking to your position (like one of an Indian file of merchants' clerks getting letters out of the post-office), ere you have a chance to occupy the pedestal of the match-tub. Often the crowd of quarrelsome candidates wrangle and fight for precedency, while at all times the interval is employed by the garrulous in every variety of ship-gossip.

As the shaving days are unalterable, they often fall upon days of high seas and tempestuous winds, when the vessel pitches and rolls in a frightful manner. In consequence, many valuable lives are jeopardized from the razor being plied under such untoward circumstances. But these sea-barbers pride themselves upon their sea-legs, and often you will see them standing over their patients, with their feet wide apart, and scientifically swaying their bodies to the motion of the ship, as they flourish their edge-tools about the lips, nostrils, and jugular.

As I looked upon the practitioner and patient at such times, I could not help thinking that, if the sailor had any insurance on his life, it would certainly be deemed forfeited should the president of the Company chance to lounge by and behold him in that imminent peril. For myself, I accounted it an excellent preparation for going into a sea-fight, where fortitude in standing up to your gun and running the risk of all splinters, comprise part of the practical qualities that make up an efficient man-of-war's-man.

It remains to be related, that these barbers of ours had their labors considerably abridged by a fashion prevailing among many of the crew, of wearing very large whiskers; so that, in most cases, the only parts needing a shave were the upper lip and suburbs of the chin. This had been more or less the custom during the whole three years' cruise; but for some time previous to our weathering Cape Horn, very many of the seamen had redoubled their assiduity in cultivating their beards, preparatory to their return to America. There they anticipated creating no small impression by their immense and magnificent *homeward-bounders*—so they called the long fly-brushes at their chins. In particular, the more aged sailors, embracing the Old Guard of sea grenadiers on the forecastle, and the begrimed gunner's mates and quarter-gunners, sported most venerable beards of an exceeding length and hoariness, like long, trailing moss hanging from the bough of some aged oak. Above all, the Captain of the Forecastle, old Ushant—a fine specimen of a sea sexagenarian—wore a wide, spreading beard, grizzled and gray, that flowed over his breast, and often became tangled and knotted with tar. This Ushant, in all weathers, was ever alert at his duty; intrepidly mounting the fore-yard in a gale, his long beard streaming like Neptune's. Off Cape Horn it looked like a miller's, being all over powdered with frost: sometimes it glittered with minute icicles in the pale, cold, moonlit Patagonian nights. But though he was so active in time of tempest, yet when his duty did not call for exertion, he was a remarkably staid, reserved, silent, and majestic old man, holding himself aloof from noisy revelry, and never participating in the boisterous sports of the crew. He resolutely set his beard against their boyish frolickings, and often held forth like an oracle concerning the vanity thereof. Indeed, at times he was wont to talk philosophy to his ancient companions—the old sheet-anchor-men around him—as well as to the hare-brained tenants of the fore-top, and the giddy lads in the mizzen.

Nor was his philosophy to be despised; it abounded in wisdom. For this Ushant was an old man, of strong natural sense, who had seen nearly the whole terraqueous globe, and could reason of civilized and savage, of Gentile and Jew, of Christian and Moslem. The long night-watches of the sailor are eminently adapted to draw out the reflective faculties of any serious-minded man, however humble or uneducated. Judge, then, what half a century of battling out watches on the ocean must have done for this fine old tar. He was a sort of sea-Socrates, in his old age "pouring out his last philosophy and life," as sweet Spenser has it; and I never could look at him, and survey his right reverend beard, without bestowing upon him that title which, in one of his satires, Persius gives to the immortal quaffer of the hemlock—*Magister Barbatus*—the bearded master.

Not a few of the ship's company had also bestowed great pains upon their hair, which some of them—especially the genteel young sailor bucks of the after-guard—wore over their shoulders like the ringleted Cavaliers. Many sailors, with naturally tendril locks, prided themselves upon what they call *love curls*, worn at the side of the head, just before the ear—a custom peculiar to tars, and which seems to have filled the vacated place of the old-fashioned Lord Rodney cue, which they used to wear some fifty years ago.

But there were others of the crew laboring under the misfortune of long, lank, Winnebago locks, or carroty bunches of hair, or rebellious bristles of a sandy hue. Ambitious of redundant mops, these still suffered their carrots to grow, spite of all ridicule. They looked like Huns and Scandinavians; and one of them, a young Down Easter, the unenvied proprietor of a thick crop of inflexible yellow bamboos, went by the name of *Peter the Wild Boy*; for, like Peter the Wild Boy in France, it was supposed that he must have been caught like a catamount in the pine woods of Maine. But there were many fine, flowing heads of hair to counterbalance such sorry exhibitions as Peter's.

What with long whiskers and venerable beards, then, of every variety of cut—Charles the Fifth's and Aurelian's—and endless *goatees* and *imperials*; and what with abounding locks, our crew seemed a company of Merovingians or Long-haired kings, mixed with savage Lombards or Longobardi, so called from their lengthy beards.

Chapter 85

THE GREAT MASSACRE OF THE BEARDS

THE PRECEDING chapter fitly paves the way for the present, wherein it sadly befalls White-Jacket to chronicle a calamitous event, which filled the Neversink with long lamentations, that echoed through all her decks and tops. After dwelling upon our redundant locks and thrice-noble beards, fain would I cease, and let the sequel remain undisclosed, but truth and fidelity forbid.

As I now deviously hover and lingeringly skirmish about the frontiers of this melancholy recital, a feeling of sadness comes over me that I can not withstand. Such a heartless massacre of hair! Such a Bartholomew's Day and Sicilian Vespers of assassinated beards! Ah! who would believe it! With intuitive sympathy I feel of my own brown beard while I write, and thank my kind stars that each precious hair is forever beyond the reach of the ruthless barbers of a man-of-war!

It needs that this sad and most serious matter should be faithfully detailed. Throughout the cruise, many of the officers had expressed their abhorrence of the impunity with which the most extensive plantations of hair were cultivated under their very noses; and they frowned upon every beard with even greater dislike. They said it was unseamanlike; not *ship-shape*; in short, it was disgraceful to the Navy. But as Captain Claret said nothing, and as the officers, of themselves, had no authority to preach a crusade against whiskerandoes, the Old Guard on the forecastle still complacently stroked their beards, and the sweet youths of the After-guard still lovingly threaded their fingers through their curls.

Perhaps the Captain's generosity in thus far permitting our beards sprung from the fact that he himself wore a small speck of a beard upon his own imperial cheek; which, if rumor said true, was to hide something, as Plutarch relates of the Emperor Adrian. But, to do him justice—as I always have done—the Captain's beard did not exceed the limits prescribed by the Navy Department.

According to a then recent ordinance at Washington, the beards of both officers and seamen were to be accurately laid out and surveyed, and on no account must come lower than the mouth, so as to correspond with the Army standard—a regulation directly opposed to the theocratical law laid down in the nineteenth chapter and twenty-seventh verse of Leviticus, where it is expressly ordained, *"Thou shalt not mar the corners of thy beard."* But legislators do not always square their statutes by those of the Bible.

At last, when we had crossed the Northern Tropic, and were standing up to our guns at evening quarters, and when the setting sun, streaming in at the port-holes, lit up every hair, till, to an observer on the quarter-deck, the two long, even lines of beards seemed one dense grove; in that evil hour it must have been, that a cruel thought entered into the heart of our Captain.

A pretty set of savages, thought he, am I taking home to America; people will think them all catamounts and Turks. Besides, now that I think of it, it's against the law. It will never do. They must be shaven and shorn—that's flat.

There is no knowing, indeed, whether these were the very words in which the Captain meditated that night; for it is yet a mooted point among metaphysicians, whether we think in words or whether we think in thoughts. But something like the above must have been the Captain's cogitations. At any rate, that very evening the ship's company were astounded by an extraordinary announcement made at the main-hatchway of the gun-deck, by the Boatswain's mate there stationed. He was afterward discovered to have been tipsy at the time.

"D'ye hear there, fore and aft? All you that have hair on your heads, shave them off; and all you that have beards, trim 'em small!"

Shave off our Christian heads! And then, placing them between our knees, trim small our worshiped beards! The Captain was mad.

But directly the Boatswain came rushing to the hatchway, and, after soundly rating his tipsy mate, thundered forth a true version of the order that had issued from the quarter-deck. As amended, it ran thus:

"D'ye hear there, fore and aft? All you that have long hair,

cut it short; and all you that have large whiskers, trim them
down, according to the Navy regulations."

This was an amendment, to be sure; but what barbarity,
after all! What! not thirty days' run from home, and lose our
magnificent homeward-bounders! The homeward-bounders
we had been cultivating so long! Lose them at one fell
swoop? Were the vile barbers of the gun-deck to reap our
long, nodding harvests, and expose our innocent chins to the
chill air of the Yankee coast? And our viny locks! were they
also to be shorn? Was a grand sheep-shearing, such as they
annually have at Nantucket, to take place; and our ignoble
barbers to carry off the fleece?

Captain Claret! in cutting our beards and our hair, you cut
us the unkindest cut of all! Were we going into action, Captain Claret—going to fight the foe with our hearts of flame
and our arms of steel, then would we gladly offer up our
beards to the terrific God of War, and *that* we would account
but a wise precaution against having them tweaked by the
foe. *Then*, Captain Claret, you would but be imitating the
example of Alexander, who had his Macedonians all shaven,
that in the hour of battle their beards might not be handles
to the Persians. But *now*, Captain Claret! when after our long,
long cruise, we are returning to our homes, tenderly stroking
the fine tassels on our chins, and thinking of father or mother,
or sister or brother, or daughter or son; to cut off our beards
now—the very beards that were frosted white off the pitch of
Patagonia—*this* is too bitterly bad, Captain Claret! and, by
Heaven, we will not submit. Train your guns inboard, let the
marines fix their bayonets, let the officers draw their swords;
we *will not* let our beards be reaped—the last insult inflicted
upon a vanquished foe in the East!

Where are you, sheet-anchor-men! Captains of the tops!
gunner's mates! mariners, all! Muster round the capstan your
venerable beards, and while you braid them together in token
of brotherhood, cross hands and swear that we will enact over
again the mutiny of the Nore, and sooner perish than yield
up a hair!

The excitement was intense throughout that whole evening. Groups of tens and twenties were scattered about all the
decks, discussing the mandate, and inveighing against its bar-

barous author. The long area of the gun-deck was something like a populous street of brokers, when some terrible commercial tidings have newly arrived. One and all, they resolved not to succumb, and every man swore to stand by his beard and his neighbor.

Twenty-four hours after—at the next evening quarters—the Captain's eye was observed to wander along the men at their guns—not a beard was shaven!

When the drum beat the retreat, the Boatswain—now attended by all four of his mates, to give additional solemnity to the announcement—repeated the previous day's order, and concluded by saying, that twenty-four hours would be given for all to acquiesce.

But the second day passed, and at quarters, untouched, every beard bristled on its chin. Forthwith Captain Claret summoned the midshipmen, who, receiving his orders, hurried to the various divisions of the guns, and communicated them to the Lieutenants respectively stationed over divisions.

The officer commanding mine turned upon us, and said, "Men, if to-morrow night I find any of you with long hair, or whiskers of a standard violating the Navy regulations, the names of such offenders shall be put down on the report."

The affair had now assumed a most serious aspect. The Captain was in earnest. The excitement increased ten-fold; and a great many of the older seamen, exasperated to the uttermost, talked about *knocking off duty* till the obnoxious mandate was revoked. I thought it impossible that they would seriously think of such a folly; but there is no knowing what man-of-war's-men will sometimes do, under provocation—witness Parker and the Nore.

That same night, when the first watch was set, the men in a body drove the two boatswain's mates from their stations at the fore and main hatchways, and unshipped the ladders; thus cutting off all communication between the gun and spar decks, forward of the main-mast.

Mad Jack had the trumpet; and no sooner was this incipient mutiny reported to him, than he jumped right down among the mob, and fearlessly mingling with them, exclaimed, "What do you mean, men? don't be fools! This is no way to get what you want. Turn to, my lads, turn to! Boatswain's mate, ship that ladder! So! up you tumble, now, my hearties! away you go!"

His gallant, off-handed, confident manner, recognizing no attempt at mutiny, operated upon the sailors like magic. They *tumbled up*, as commanded; and for the rest of that night contented themselves with privately fulminating their displeasure against the Captain, and publicly emblazoning every anchor-button on the coat of admired Mad Jack.

Captain Claret happened to be taking a nap in his cabin at the moment of the disturbance; and it was quelled so soon, that he knew nothing of it till it was officially reported to him. It was afterward rumored through the ship that he reprimanded Mad Jack for acting as he did. He maintained that he should at once have summoned the marines, and charged upon the "mutineers." But if the sayings imputed to the Captain were true, he nevertheless refrained from subsequently noticing the disturbance, or attempting to seek out and punish the ringleaders. This was but wise; for there are times when even the most potent governor must wink at transgression, in order to preserve the laws inviolate for the future. And great care is to be taken, by timely management, to avert an incontestable act of mutiny, and so prevent men from being roused, by their own consciousness of transgression, into all the fury of an unbounded insurrection. *Then*, for the time, both soldiers and sailors are irresistible; as even the valor of Cæsar was made to know, and the prudence of Germanicus, when their legions rebelled. And not all the concessions of Earl Spencer, as First Lord of the Admiralty, nor the threats and entreaties of Lord Bridport, the Admiral of the Fleet—no, nor his gracious majesty's plenary pardon in prospective, could prevail upon the Spithead mutineers (when at last fairly lashed up to the mark) to succumb, until deserted by their own mess-mates, and a handful was left in the breach.

Therefore, Mad Jack! you did right, and no one else could have acquitted himself better. By your crafty simplicity, good-natured daring, and off-handed air (as if nothing was happening) you perhaps quelled a very serious affair in the bud, and prevented the disgrace to the American Navy of a tragical mutiny, growing out of whiskers, soap-suds, and razors. Think of it, if future historians should devote a long chapter to the great *Rebellion of the Beards* on board the United States ship Neversink. Why, through all time thereafter, barbers would cut down their spiralized poles, and substitute miniature main-masts for the emblems of their calling.

And here is ample scope for some pregnant instruction, how that events of vast magnitude in our man-of-war world may originate in the pettiest of trifles. But that is an old theme; we waive it, and proceed.

On the morning following, though it was not a regular shaving day, the gun-deck barbers were observed to have their shops open, their match-tub accommodations in readiness, and their razors displayed. With their brushes, raising a mighty lather in their tin pots, they stood eying the passing throng of seamen, silently inviting them to walk in and be served. In addition to their usual implements, they now flourished at intervals a huge pair of sheep-shears, by way of more forcibly reminding the men of the edict which that day must be obeyed, or woe betide them.

For some hours the seamen paced to and fro in no very good humor, vowing not to sacrifice a hair. Beforehand, they denounced that man who should abase himself by compliance. But habituation to discipline is magical; and ere long an old forecastle-man was discovered elevated upon a match-tub, while, with a malicious grin, his barber—a fellow who, from his merciless rasping, was called Blue-Skin—seized him by his long beard, and at one fell stroke cut it off and tossed it out of the port-hole behind him. This forecastle-man was ever afterward known by a significant title—in the main equivalent to that name of reproach fastened upon that Athenian who, in Alexander's time, previous to which all the Greeks sported beards, first submitted to the deprivation of his own. But, spite of all the contempt hurled on our forecastle-man, so prudent an example was soon followed; presently all the barbers were busy.

Sad sight! at which any one but a barber or a Tartar would have wept! Beards three years old; *goatees* that would have graced a Chamois of the Alps; *imperials* that Count D'Orsay would have envied; and *love-curls* and man-of-war ringlets that would have measured, inch for inch, with the longest tresses of The Fair One with the Golden Locks—all went by the board! Captain Claret! how can you rest in your hammock! By this brown beard which now waves from my chin—the illustrious successor to that first, young, vigorous beard I yielded to your tyranny—by this manly beard, I swear, it was barbarous!

My noble captain, Jack Chase, was indignant. Not even all the special favors he had received from Captain Claret, and the plenary pardon extended to him for his desertion into the Peruvian service, could restrain the expression of his feelings. But in his cooler moments, Jack was a wise man; he at last deemed it but wisdom to succumb.

When he went to the barber he almost drew tears from his eyes. Seating himself mournfully on the match-tub, he looked sideways, and said to the barber, who was *slithering* his sheep-shears in readiness to begin: "My friend, I trust your scissors are consecrated. Let them not touch this beard if they have yet to be dipped in holy water; beards are sacred things, barber. Have you no feeling for beards, my friend? think of it;" and mournfully he laid his deep-dyed, russet cheek upon his hand. "Two summers have gone by since my chin has been reaped. I was in Coquimbo then, on the Spanish Main; and when the husbandman was sowing his Autumnal grain on the Vega, I started this blessed beard; and when the vine-dressers were trimming their vines in the vineyards, I first trimmed it to the sound of a flute. Ah! barber, have you no heart? This beard has been caressed by the snow-white hand of the lovely Tomasita of Tombez—the Castilian belle of all Lower Peru. Think of *that*, barber! I have worn it as an officer on the quarter-deck of a Peruvian man-of-war. I have sported it at brilliant fandangoes in Lima. I have been alow and aloft with it at sea. Yea, barber! it has streamed like an Admiral's pennant at the mast-head of this same gallant frigate, the Neversink! Oh! barber, barber! it stabs me to the heart!—Talk not of hauling down your ensigns and standards when vanquished—what is *that*, barber! to striking the flag that Nature herself has nailed to the mast!"

Here noble Jack's feelings overcame him; he drooped from the animated attitude into which his enthusiasm had momentarily transported him; his proud head sunk upon his chest, and his long, sad beard almost grazed the deck.

"Ay! trail your beards in grief and dishonor, oh crew of the Neversink!" sighed Jack. "Barber, come closer—now, tell me, my friend, have you obtained absolution for this deed you are about to commit? You have not? Then, barber, *I* will absolve you; your hands shall be washed of this sin; it is not you, but another; and though you are about to shear off my manhood, yet, barber, I freely forgive you; kneel, kneel, barber! that I may bless you, in token that I cherish no malice!"

So when this barber, who was the only tender-hearted one of his tribe, had kneeled, been absolved, and then blessed, Jack gave up his beard into his hands, and the barber, clipping it off with a sigh, held it high aloft, and, parodying the style of the boatswain's mates, cried aloud, "D'ye hear, fore and aft? This is the beard of our matchless Jack Chase, the noble captain of this frigate's main-top!"

Chapter 86

The Rebels brought to the Mast

Though many heads of hair were shorn, and many fine beards reaped that day, yet several still held out, and vowed to defend their sacred hair to the last gasp of their breath. These were chiefly old sailors—some of them petty officers—who, presuming upon their age or rank, doubtless thought that, after so many had complied with the Captain's commands, *they*, being but a handful, would be exempted from compliance, and remain a monument of our master's clemency.

That same evening, when the drum beat to quarters, the sailors went sullenly to their guns, and the old tars who still sported their beards stood up, grim, defying, and motionless, as the rows of sculptured Assyrian kings, who, with their magnificent beards, have recently been exhumed by Layard.

When the proper time arrived, their names were taken down by the officers of divisions, and they were afterward summoned in a body to the mast, where the Captain stood ready to receive them. The whole ship's company crowded to the spot, and, amid the breathless multitude, the venerable rebels advanced and unhatted.

It was an imposing display. They were old and venerable mariners; their cheeks had been burned brown in all latitudes, wherever the sun sends a tropical ray. Reverend old tars, one and all; some of them might have been grandsires, with grandchildren in every port round the world. They ought to have commanded the veneration of the most frivolous or magisterial beholder. Even Captain Claret they ought to have humiliated into deference. But a Scythian is touched with no reverential promptings; and, as the Roman student well knows, the august Senators themselves, seated in the Senate-house, on the majestic hill of the Capitol, had their holy beards tweaked by the insolent chief of the Goths.

Such an array of beards! spade-shaped, hammer-shaped, dagger-shaped, triangular, square, peaked, round, hemi-

730

spherical, and forked. But chief among them all, was old Ushant's, the ancient Captain of the Forecastle. Of a Gothic venerableness, it fell upon his breast like a continual iron-gray storm.

Ah! old Ushant, Nestor of the crew! it promoted my longevity to behold you.

He was a man-of-war's-man of the old Benbow school. He wore a short cue, which the wags of the mizzen-top called his "*plug of pig-tail*." About his waist was a broad boarder's belt, which he wore, he said, to brace his main-mast, meaning his backbone; for at times he complained of rheumatic twinges in the spine, consequent upon sleeping on deck, now and then, during the night-watches of upward of half a century. His sheath-knife was an antique—a sort of old-fashioned pruning-hook; its handle—a sperm whale's tooth—was carved all over with ships, cannon, and anchors. It was attached to his neck by a *lanyard*, elaborately worked into "rose-knots" and "Turks' heads" by his own venerable fingers.

Of all the crew, this Ushant was most beloved by my glorious Captain, Jack Chase, who one day pointed him out to me as the old man was slowly coming down the rigging from the fore-top.

"There, White-Jacket! isn't that old Chaucer's shipman?

" 'A dagger hanging by a las hadde he,
     About his nekke, under his arm adown;
     The hote sommer hadde made his beard all brown.
  Hardy he is, and wise; I undertake
  With many a tempest has his beard be shake.'

From the Canterbury Tales, White-Jacket! and must not old Ushant have been living in Chaucer's time, that Chaucer could draw his portrait so well?"

Chapter 87

OLD USHANT AT THE GANGWAY

THE REBEL BEARDS, headed by old Ushant's, streaming like a Commodore's *bougee*, now stood in silence at the mast.

"You knew the order!" said the Captain, eying them severely; "what does that hair on your chins?"

"Sir," said the Captain of the Forecastle, "did old Ushant ever refuse doing his duty? did he ever yet miss his muster? But, sir, old Ushant's beard is his own!"

"What's that, sir? Master-at-arms, put that man into the brig."

"Sir," said the old man, respectfully, "the three years for which I shipped are expired; and though I am perhaps bound to work the ship home, yet, as matters are, I think my beard might be allowed me. It is but a few days, Captain Claret."

"Put him into the brig!" cried the Captain; "and now, you old rascals!" he added, turning round upon the rest, "I give you fifteen minutes to have those beards taken off; if they then remain on your chins, I'll flog you—every mother's son of you—though you were all my own godfathers!"

The band of beards went forward, summoned their barbers, and their glorious pennants were no more. In obedience to orders, they then paraded themselves at the mast, and, addressing the Captain, said, "Sir, our *muzzle-lashings* are cast off!"

Nor is it unworthy of being chronicled, that not a single sailor who complied with the general order but refused to sport the vile *regulation-whiskers* prescribed by the Navy Department. No! like heroes they cried, "Shave me clean! I will not wear a hair, since I can not wear all!"

On the morrow, after breakfast, Ushant was taken out of irons, and, with the master-at-arms on one side and an armed sentry on the other, was escorted along the gun-deck and up the ladder to the main-mast. There the Captain stood, firm as before. They must have guarded the old man thus to prevent his escape to the shore, something less than a thousand miles distant at the time.

"Well, sir, will you have that beard taken off? you have slept over it a whole night now; what do you say? I don't want to flog an old man like you, Ushant!"

"My beard is my own, sir!" said the old man, lowly.

"Will you take it off?"

"It is mine, sir!" said the old man, tremulously.

"Rig the gratings!" roared the Captain. "Master-at-arms, strip him! quarter-masters, seize him up! boatswain's mates, do your duty!"

While these executioners were employed, the Captain's excitement had a little time to abate; and when, at last, old Ushant was tied up by the arms and legs, and his venerable back was exposed—that back which had bowed at the guns of the frigate Constitution when she captured the Guer-riere—the Captain seemed to relent.

"You are a very old man," he said, "and I am sorry to flog you; but my orders must be obeyed. I will give you one more chance; will you have that beard taken off?"

"Captain Claret," said the old man, turning round painfully in his bonds, "you may flog me, if you will; but, sir, in this one thing I can *not* obey you."

"Lay on! I'll see his backbone!" roared the Captain in a sudden fury.

"By Heaven!" thrillingly whispered Jack Chase, who stood by, "it's only a halter; I'll strike him!"

"Better not," said a top-mate; "it's death, or worse punishment, remember."

"There goes the lash!" cried Jack. "Look at the old man! By G—d, I can't stand it! Let me go, men!" and with moist eyes Jack forced his way to one side.

"You, boatswain's mate," cried the Captain, "you are favoring that man! Lay on soundly, sir, or I'll have your own *cat* laid soundly on you."

One, two, three, four, five, six, seven, eight, nine, ten, eleven, twelve lashes were laid on the back of that heroic old man. He only bowed over his head, and stood as the Dying Gladiator lies.

"Cut him down," said the Captain.

"And now go and cut your own throat," hoarsely whispered an old sheet-anchor-man, a mess-mate of Ushant's.

When the master-at-arms advanced with the prisoner's shirt, Ushant waived him off with the dignified air of a Brahim, saying, "Do you think, master-at-arms, that I am hurt? I will put on my own garment. I am never the worse for it, man; and 'tis no dishonor when he who would dishonor you, only dishonors himself."

"What says he?" cried the Captain; "what says that tarry old philosopher with the smoking back? Tell it to me, sir, if you dare! Sentry, take that man back to the brig. Stop! John Ushant, you have been Captain of the Forecastle; I break you. And now you go into the brig, there to remain till you consent to have that beard taken off."

"My beard is my own," said the old man, quietly. "Sentry, I am ready."

And back he went into durance between the guns; but after lying some four or five days in irons, an order came to remove them; but he was still kept confined.

Books were allowed him, and he spent much time in reading. But he also spent many hours in braiding his beard, and interweaving with it strips of red bunting, as if he desired to dress out and adorn the thing which had triumphed over all opposition.

He remained a prisoner till we arrived in America; but the very moment he heard the chain rattle out of the hawse-hole, and the ship swing to her anchor, he started to his feet, dashed the sentry aside, and gaining the deck, exclaimed, "At home, with my beard!"

His term of service having some months previous expired, and the ship being now in harbor, he was beyond the reach of naval law, and the officers durst not molest him. But without unduly availing himself of these circumstances, the old man merely got his bag and hammock together, hired a boat, and throwing himself into the stern, was rowed ashore, amid the unsuppressible cheers of all hands. It was a glorious conquest over the Conqueror himself, as well worthy to be celebrated as the Battle of the Nile.

Though, as I afterward learned, Ushant was earnestly entreated to put the case into some lawyer's hands, he firmly declined, saying, "I have won the battle, my friends, and I do not care for the prize-money." But even had he complied with these entreaties, from precedents in similar cases, it is almost certain that not a sou's worth of satisfaction would have been received.

I know not in what frigate you sail now, old Ushant; but Heaven protect your storied old beard, in whatever Typhoon it may blow. And if ever it must be shorn, old man, may it fare like the royal beard of Henry I., of England, and be clipped by the right reverend hand of some Archbishop of Sees.

As for Captain Claret, let it not be supposed that it is here sought to impale him before the world as a cruel, black-hearted man. Such he was not. Nor was he, upon the whole, regarded by his crew with any thing like the feelings which man-of-war's-men sometimes cherish toward signally tyrannical commanders. In truth, the majority of the Neversink's crew—in previous cruises habituated to flagrant misusage—deemed Captain Claret a lenient officer. In many things he certainly refrained from oppressing them. It has been related what privileges he accorded to the seamen respecting the free playing of checkers—a thing almost unheard of in most American men-of-war. In the matter of overseeing the men's clothing, also, he was remarkably indulgent, compared with the conduct of other Navy Captains, who, by sumptuary regulations, oblige their sailors to run up large bills with the Purser for clothes. In a word, of whatever acts Captain Claret might have been guilty in the Neversink, perhaps none of them proceeded from any personal, organic hard-heartedness. What he was, the usages of the Navy had made him. Had he been a mere landsman—a merchant, say—he would no doubt have been considered a kind-hearted man.

There may be some who shall read of this Bartholomew Massacre of beards who will yet marvel, perhaps, that the loss of a few hairs, more or less, should provoke such hostility from the sailors, lash them into so frothing a rage; indeed, come near breeding a mutiny.

But these circumstances are not without precedent. Not to speak of the riots, attended with the loss of life, which once occurred in Madrid, in resistance to an arbitrary edict of the king's, seeking to suppress the cloaks of the Cavaliers; and, not to make mention of other instances that might be quoted, it needs only to point out the rage of the Saxons in the time of William the Conqueror, when that despot commanded the hair on their upper lips to be shaven off—the hereditary mustaches which whole generations had sported. The multitude of the dispirited vanquished were obliged to acquiesce; but many Saxon Franklins and gentlemen of spirit, choosing rather to lose their castles than their mustaches, voluntarily deserted their fire-sides, and went into exile. All this is indignantly related by the stout Saxon friar, Matthew Paris, in his *Historia Major*, beginning with the Norman Conquest.

And that our man-of-war's-men were right in desiring to perpetuate their beards, as martial appurtenances, must seem very plain, when it is considered that, as the beard is the token of manhood, so, in some shape or other, has it ever been held the true badge of a warrior. Bonaparte's grenadiers were stout whiskerandoes; and perhaps, in a charge, those fierce whiskers of theirs did as much to appall the foe as the sheen of their bayonets. Most all fighting creatures sport either whiskers or beards; it seems a law of Dame Nature. Witness the boar, the tiger, the cougar, man, the leopard, the ram, the cat—all warriors, and all whiskerandoes. Whereas, the peace-loving tribes have mostly enameled chins.

Chapter 88

Flogging through the Fleet

THE FLOGGING of an old man like Ushant, most landsmen will probably regard with abhorrence. But though, from peculiar circumstances, his case occasioned a good deal of indignation among the people of the Neversink, yet, upon its own proper grounds, they did not denounce it. Man-of-war's-men are so habituated to what landsmen would deem excessive cruelties, that they are almost reconciled to inferior severities.

And here, though the subject of punishment in the Navy has been canvassed in previous chapters, and though the thing is every way a most unpleasant and grievous one to enlarge upon, and though I painfully nerve myself to it while I write, a feeling of duty compels me to enter upon a branch of the subject till now undiscussed. I would not be like the man, who, seeing an outcast perishing by the road-side, turned about to his friend, saying, "Let us cross the way; my soul so sickens at this sight, that I can not endure it."

There are certain enormities in this man-of-war world that often secure impunity by their very excessiveness. Some ignorant people will refrain from permanently removing the cause of a deadly malaria, for fear of the temporary spread of its offensiveness. Let us not be of such. The more repugnant and repelling, the greater the evil. Leaving our women and children behind, let us freely enter this Golgotha.

Years ago there was a punishment inflicted in the English, and I believe in the American Navy, called *keel-hauling*—a phrase still employed by man-of-war's-men when they would express some signal vengeance upon a personal foe. The practice still remains in the French national marine, though it is by no means resorted to so frequently as in times past. It consists of attaching tackles to the two extremities of the main-yard, and passing the rope under the ship's bottom. To one end of this rope the culprit is secured; his own shipmates are then made to run him up and down, first on this side,

then on that—now scraping the ship's hull under water—
anon, hoisted, stunned and breathless, into the air.

But though this barbarity is now abolished from the English and American navies, there still remains another practice
which, if any thing, is even worse than *keel-hauling*. This remnant of the Middle Ages is known in the Navy as "*flogging
through the fleet*." It is never inflicted except by authority of a
court-martial upon some trespasser deemed guilty of a flagrant offence. Never, that I know of, has it been inflicted by
an American man-of-war on the home station. The reason,
probably, is, that the officers well know that such a spectacle
would raise a mob in any American sea-port.

By XLI. of the Articles of War, a court-martial shall not,
"for any one offence not capital," inflict a punishment beyond
one hundred lashes. In cases "not capital" this law may be,
and has been, quoted in judicial justification of the infliction
of more than one hundred lashes. Indeed, it would cover a
thousand. Thus: One act of a sailor may be construed into
the commission of ten different transgressions, for each of
which he may be legally condemned to a hundred lashes, to
be inflicted without intermission. It will be perceived, that in
any case deemed "capital," a sailor, under the above Article,
may legally be flogged to the death.

But neither by the Articles of War, nor by any other enactment of Congress, is there any direct warrant for the extraordinary cruelty of the mode in which punishment is inflicted,
in cases of flogging through the fleet. But as in numerous
other instances, the incidental aggravations of this penalty are
indirectly covered by other clauses in the Articles of War; one
of which authorizes the authorities of a ship—in certain indefinite cases—to correct the guilty "*according to the usages of
the sea-service*."

One of these "usages" is the following:

All hands being called "to witness punishment" in the ship
to which the culprit belongs, the sentence of the court-martial
condemning him is read, when, with the usual solemnities, a
portion of the punishment is inflicted. In order that it shall
not lose in severity by the slightest exhaustion in the arm of
the executioner, a fresh boatswain's mate is called out at every
dozen.

As the leading idea is to strike terror into the beholders, the greatest number of lashes is inflicted on board the culprit's own ship, in order to render him the more shocking spectacle to the crews of the other vessels.

The first infliction being concluded, the culprit's shirt is thrown over him; he is put into a boat—the Rogue's March being played meanwhile—and rowed to the next ship of the squadron. All hands of that ship are then called to man the rigging, and another portion of the punishment is inflicted by the boatswain's mates of that ship. The bloody shirt is again thrown over the seaman; and thus he is carried through the fleet or squadron till the whole sentence is inflicted.

In other cases, the launch—the largest of the boats—is rigged with a platform (like a headsman's scaffold), upon which halberds, something like those used in the English army, are erected. They consist of two stout poles, planted upright. Upon the platform stand a Lieutenant, a Surgeon, a Master-at-arms, and the executioners with their "cats." They are rowed through the fleet, stopping at each ship, till the whole sentence is inflicted, as before.

In some cases, the attending surgeon has professionally interfered before the last lash has been given, alleging that immediate death must ensue if the remainder should be administered without a respite. But instead of humanely remitting the remaining lashes, in a case like this, the man is generally consigned to his cot for ten or twelve days; and when the surgeon officially reports him capable of undergoing the rest of the sentence, it is forthwith inflicted. Shylock must have his pound of flesh.

To say, that after being flogged through the fleet, the prisoner's back is sometimes puffed up like a pillow; or to say that in other cases it looks as if burned black before a roasting fire; or to say that you may track him through the squadron by the blood on the bulwarks of every ship, would only be saying what many seamen have seen.

Several weeks, sometimes whole months, elapse before the sailor is sufficiently recovered to resume his duties. During the greater part of that interval he lies in the sick-bay, groaning out his days and nights; and unless he has the hide and constitution of a rhinoceros, he never is the man he was before, but, broken and shattered to the marrow of his bones, sinks into death before his time. Instances have occurred where he has expired the day after the punishment. No wonder that the Englishman, Dr. Granville—himself once a surgeon in the Navy—declares, in his work on Russia, that the barbarian "knout" itself is not a greater torture to undergo than the Navy cat-o'-nine-tails.

Some years ago a fire broke out near the powder magazine in an American national ship, one of a squadron at anchor in the Bay of Naples. The utmost alarm prevailed. A cry went fore and aft that the ship was about to blow up. One of the seamen sprang overboard in affright. At length the fire was got under, and the man was picked up. He was tried before a court-martial, found guilty of cowardice, and condemned to be flogged through the fleet. In due time the squadron made sail for Algiers, and in that harbor, once haunted by pirates, the punishment was inflicted—the Bay of Naples, though washing the shores of an absolute king, not being deemed a fit place for such an exhibition of American naval law.

While the Neversink was in the Pacific, an American sailor, who had deposited a vote for General Harrison for President of the United States, was flogged through the fleet.

Chapter 89

THE SOCIAL STATE IN A MAN-OF-WAR

BUT THE FLOGGINGS at the gangway and the floggings through the fleet, the stealings, highway robberies, swearings, gamblings, blasphemings, thimble-riggings, smugglings, and tipplings of a man-of-war, which throughout this narrative have been here and there sketched from the life, by no means comprise the whole catalogue of evil. One single feature is full of significance.

All large ships of war carry soldiers, called marines. In the Neversink there were something less than fifty, two thirds of whom were Irishmen. They were officered by a Lieutenant, an Orderly Sergeant, two Sergeants, and two Corporals, with a drummer and fifer. The custom, generally, is to have a marine to each gun; which rule usually furnishes the scale for distributing the soldiers in vessels of different force.

Our marines had no other than martial duty to perform; excepting that, at sea, they stood watches like the sailors, and now and then lazily assisted in pulling the ropes. But they never put foot in rigging or hand in tar-bucket.

On the quarter-bills, these men were stationed at none of the great guns; on the station-bills, they had no posts at the ropes. What, then, were they for? To serve their country in time of battle? Let us see. When a ship is running into action, her marines generally lie flat on their faces behind the bulwarks (the sailors are sometimes ordered to do the same), and when the vessel is fairly engaged, they are usually drawn up in the ship's waist—like a company reviewing in the Park. At close quarters, their muskets may pick off a seaman or two in the rigging, but at long-gun distance they must passively stand in their ranks and be decimated at the enemy's leisure. Only in one case in ten—that is, when their vessel is attempted to be boarded by a large party, are these marines of any essential service as fighting-men; with their bayonets they are then called upon to "repel!"

If comparatively so useless as soldiers, why have marines at all in the Navy? Know, then, that what standing armies are to nations, what turnkeys are to jails, these marines are to the seamen in all large men-of-war. Their muskets are their keys. With those muskets they stand guard over the fresh water; over the grog, when doled; over the provisions, when being served out by the Master's mate; over the "brig" or jail; at the Commodore's and Captain's cabin doors; and, in port, at both gangways and forecastle.

Surely, the crowd of sailors, who besides having so many sea-officers over them, are thus additionally guarded by soldiers, even when they quench their thirst—surely these man-of-war's-men must be desperadoes indeed; or else the naval service must be so tyrannical that the worst is feared from their possible insubordination. Either reason holds good, or both, according to the character of the officers and crew.

It must be evident that the man-of-war's-man casts but an evil eye on a marine. To call a man a "horse-marine," is, among seamen, one of the greatest terms of contempt.

But the mutual contempt, and even hatred, subsisting between these two bodies of men—both clinging to one keel, both lodged in one household—is held by most Navy officers as the height of the perfection of Navy discipline. It is regarded as the button that caps the uttermost point on their main-mast.

Thus they reason: Secure of this antagonism between the marine and the sailor, we can always rely upon it, that if the sailor mutinies, it needs no great incitement for the marine to thrust his bayonet through his heart; if the marine revolts, the pike of the sailor is impatient to charge. Checks and balances, blood against blood, *that* is the cry and the argument.

What applies to the relation in which the marine and sailor stand toward each other—the mutual repulsion implied by a system of checks—will, in degree, apply to nearly the entire interior of a man-of-war's discipline. The whole body of this discipline is emphatically a system of cruel cogs and wheels, systematically grinding up in one common hopper all that might minister to the moral well-being of the crew.

It is the same with both officers and men. If a Captain have a grudge against a Lieutenant, or a Lieutenant against a midshipman, how easy to torture him by official treatment, which shall not lay open the superior officer to legal rebuke. And if a midshipman bears a grudge against a sailor, how easy for him, by cunning practices, born of a boyish spite, to have him degraded at the gangway. Through all the endless ramifications of rank and station, in most men-of-war there runs a sinister vein of bitterness, not exceeded by the fire-side hatreds in a family of step-sons ashore. It were sickening to detail all the paltry irritabilities, jealousies, and cabals, the spiteful detractions and animosities, that lurk far down, and cling to the very kelson of the ship. It is unmanning to think of. The immutable ceremonies and iron etiquette of a man-of-war; the spiked barriers separating the various grades of rank; the delegated absolutism of authority on all hands; the impossibility, on the part of the common seaman, of appeal from incidental abuses, and many more things that might be enumerated, all tend to beget in most armed ships a general social condition which is the precise reverse of what any Christian could desire. And though there are vessels, that in some measure furnish exceptions to this; and though, in other ships, the thing may be glazed over by a guarded, punctilious exterior, almost completely hiding the truth from casual visitors, while the worst facts touching the common sailor are systematically kept in the background, yet it is certain that what has here been said of the domestic interior of a man-of-war will, in a greater or less degree, apply to most vessels in the Navy. It is not that the officers are so malevolent, nor, altogether, that the man-of-war's-man is so vicious. Some of these evils are unavoidably generated through the operation of the Naval code; others are absolutely organic to a Navy establishment, and, like other organic evils, are incurable, except when they dissolve with the body they live in.

These things are undoubtedly heightened by the close cribbing and confinement of so many mortals in one oaken box on the sea. Like pears closely packed, the crowded crew mutually decay through close contact, and every plague-spot is contagious. Still more, from this same close confinement—so far as it affects the common sailors—arise other evils, so direful that they will hardly bear even so much as an allusion. What too many seamen are when ashore is very well known; but what some of them become when completely cut off from shore indulgences can hardly be imagined by landsmen. The sins for which the cities of the plain were overthrown still linger in some of these wooden-walled Gomorrahs of the deep. More than once complaints were made at the mast in the Neversink, from which the deck officer would turn away with loathing, refuse to hear them, and command the complainant out of his sight. There are evils in men-of-war, which, like the suppressed domestic drama of Horace Walpole, will neither bear representing, nor reading, and will hardly bear thinking of. The landsman who has neither read Walpole's *Mysterious Mother*, nor Sophocles's *Œdipus Tyrannus*, nor the Roman story of *Count Cenci*, dramatized by Shelley, let that landsman guardedly remain in his ignorance of even worse horrors than these, and forever abstain from seeking to draw aside this veil.

Chapter 90

THE MANNING OF NAVIES

"THE GALLOWS and the sea refuse nothing," is a very old sea saying; and, among all the wondrous prints of Hogarth, there is none remaining more true at the present day than that dramatic boat-scene, where after consorting with harlots and gambling on tomb-stones, the Idle Apprentice, with the villainous low forehead, is at last represented as being pushed off to sea, with a ship and a gallows in the distance. But Hogarth should have converted the ship's masts themselves into Tyburn-trees, and thus, with the ocean for a background, closed the career of his hero. It would then have had all the dramatic force of the opera of Don Juan, who, after running his impious courses, is swept from our sight in a tornado of devils.

For the sea is the true Tophet and bottomless pit of many workers of iniquity; and, as the German mystics feign Gehennas within Gehennas, even so are men-of-war familiarly known among sailors as "Floating Hells." And as the sea, according to old Fuller, is the stable of brute monsters, gliding hither and thither in unspeakable swarms, even so is it the home of many moral monsters, who fitly divide its empire with the snake, the shark, and the worm.

Nor are sailors, and man-of-war's-men especially, at all blind to a true sense of these things. "*Purser rigged and parish damned,*" is the sailor saying in the American Navy, when the tyro first mounts the linen frock and blue jacket, aptly manufactured for him in a State Prison ashore.

No wonder, that lured by some *crimp* into a service so galling, and, perhaps, persecuted by a vindictive lieutenant, some repentant sailors have actually jumped into the sea to escape from their fate, or set themselves adrift on the wide ocean on the gratings, without compass or rudder.

In one case, a young man, after being nearly cut into dog's meat at the gangway, loaded his pockets with shot and walked overboard.

Some years ago, I was in a whaling ship lying in a harbor of the Pacific, with three French men-of-war alongside. One dark, moody night, a suppressed cry was heard from the face of the waters, and, thinking it was some one drowning, a boat was lowered, when two French sailors were picked up, half dead from exhaustion, and nearly throttled by a bundle of their clothes tied fast to their shoulders. In this manner they had attempted their escape from their vessel. When the French officers came in pursuit, these sailors, rallying from their exhaustion, fought like tigers to resist being captured. Though this story concerns a French armed ship, it is not the less applicable, in degree, to those of other nations.

Mix with the men in an American armed ship; mark how many foreigners there are, though it is against the law to enlist them. Nearly one third of the petty officers of the Neversink were born east of the Atlantic. Why is this? Because the same principle that operates in hindering Americans from hiring themselves out as menial domestics also restrains them, in a great measure, from voluntarily assuming a far worse servitude in the Navy. "*Sailors wanted for the Navy*" is a common announcement along the wharves of our sea-ports. They are always "*wanted.*" It may have been, in part, owing to this scarcity of man-of-war's-men, that not many years ago, black slaves were frequently to be found regularly enlisted with the crew of an American frigate, their masters receiving their pay. This was in the teeth of a law of Congress expressly prohibiting slaves in the Navy. This law, indirectly, means black slaves, nothing being said concerning white ones. But in view of what John Randolph of Roanoke said about the frigate that carried him to Russia, and in view of what most armed vessels actually are at present, the American Navy is not altogether an inappropriate place for hereditary bondmen. Still, the circumstance of their being found in it is of such a nature, that to some it may hardly appear credible. The incredulity of such persons, nevertheless, must yield to the fact, that on board of the United States ship Neversink, during the present cruise, there was a Virginian slave regularly shipped as a seaman, his owner receiving his wages. Guinea—such was his name among the crew—belonged to the Purser, who was a southern gentleman; he was employed as his body servant.

Never did I feel my condition as a man-of-war's-man so keenly as when seeing this Guinea freely circulating about the decks in citizen's clothes, and, through the influence of his master, almost entirely exempted from the disciplinary degradation of the Caucasian crew. Faring sumptuously in the ward-room; sleek and round, his ebon face fairly polished with content; ever gay and hilarious; ever ready to laugh and joke, that African slave was actually envied by many of the seamen. There were times when I almost envied him myself. Lemsford once envied him outright. "Ah, Guinea!" he sighed, "you have peaceful times; you never opened the book I read in."

One morning, when all hands were called to witness punishment, the Purser's slave, as usual, was observed to be hurrying down the ladders toward the ward-room, his face wearing that peculiar, pinched blueness, which, in the negro, answers to the paleness caused by nervous agitation in the white. "Where are you going, Guinea?" cried the deck-officer, a humorous gentleman, who sometimes diverted himself with the Purser's slave, and well knew what answer he would now receive from him. "Where are you going, Guinea?" said this officer; "turn about; don't you hear the call, sir?" " 'Scuse me, massa!" said the slave, with a low salutation; "I can't 'tand it; I can't, indeed, massa!" and, so saying, he disappeared beyond the hatchway. He was the only person on board, except the hospital-steward and the invalids of the sick-bay, who was exempted from being present at the administering of the scourge. Accustomed to light and easy duties from his birth, and so fortunate as to meet with none but gentle masters, Guinea, though a bondman, liable to be saddled with a mortgage, like a horse—Guinea, in India-rubber manacles, enjoyed the liberties of the world.

Though his body-and-soul proprietor, the Purser, never in any way individualized me while I served on board the frigate, and never did me a good office of any kind (it was hardly in his power), yet, from his pleasant, kind, indulgent manner toward his slave, I always imputed to him a generous heart, and cherished an involuntary friendliness toward him. Upon our arrival home, his treatment of Guinea, under circumstances peculiarly calculated to stir up the resentment of a slave-owner, still more augmented my estimation of the Purser's good heart.

Mention has been made of the number of foreigners in the American Navy; but it is not in the American Navy alone that foreigners bear so large a proportion to the rest of the crew, though in no navy, perhaps, have they ever borne so large a proportion as in our own. According to an English estimate, the foreigners serving in the King's ships at one time amounted to one eighth of the entire body of seamen. How it is in the French Navy, I can not with certainty say; but I have repeatedly sailed with English seamen who have served in it.

One of the effects of the free introduction of foreigners into any Navy can not be sufficiently deplored. During the period I lived in the Neversink, I was repeatedly struck by the lack of patriotism in many of my shipmates. True, they were mostly foreigners who unblushingly avowed, that were it not for the difference of pay, they would as lief man the guns of an English ship as those of an American or Frenchman. Nevertheless, it was evident, that as for any high-toned patriotic feeling, there was comparatively very little—hardly any of it—evinced by our sailors as a body. Upon reflection, this was not to be wondered at. From their roving career, and the sundering of all domestic ties, many sailors, all the world over, are like the "Free Companions," who some centuries ago wandered over Europe, ready to fight the battles of any prince who could purchase their swords. The only patriotism is born and nurtured in a stationary home, and upon an immovable hearth-stone; but the man-of-war's-man, though in his voyagings he weds the two Poles and brings both Indies together, yet, let him wander where he will, he carries his one only home along with him: that home is his hammock. *"Born under a gun, and educated on the bowsprit,"* according to a phrase of his own, the man-of-war's-man rolls round the world like a billow, ready to mix with any sea, or be sucked down to death in the Maelstrom of any war.

Yet more. The dread of the general discipline of a man-of-war; the special obnoxiousness of the gangway; the protracted confinement on board ship, with so few "liberty days;" and the pittance of pay (much less than what can always be had in the Merchant Service), these things contrive to deter from the navies of all countries by far the majority of their best seamen. This will be obvious, when the following statistical facts, taken from Macpherson's Annals of Commerce, are considered. At one period, upon the Peace Establishment, the number of men employed in the English Navy was 25,000; at the same time, the English Merchant Service was employing 118,952. But while the necessities of a merchantman render it indispensable that the greater part of her crew be able seamen, the circumstances of a man-of-war admit of her mustering a crowd of landsmen, soldiers, and boys in her service. By a statement of Captain Marryat's, in his pamphlet (A.D. 1822) "On the Abolition of Impressment," it appears that, at the close of the Bonaparte wars, a full third of all the crews of his Majesty's fleets consisted of landsmen and boys.

Far from entering with enthusiasm into the King's ships when their country was menaced, the great body of English seamen, appalled at the discipline of the Navy, adopted unheard-of devices to escape its press-gangs. Some even hid themselves in caves, and lonely places inland, fearing to run the risk of seeking a berth in an outward-bound merchantman, that might have carried them beyond sea. In the true narrative of "John Nichol, Mariner," published in 1822 by Blackwood in Edinburgh, and Cadell in London, and which every where bears the spontaneous impress of truth, the old sailor, in the most artless, touching, and almost uncomplaining manner, tells of his "skulking like a thief" for whole years in the country round about Edinburgh, to avoid the press-gangs, prowling through the land like bandits and Burkers. At this time (Bonaparte's wars), according to "Steel's List," there were forty-five regular press-gang stations in Great Britain.*

---

*Besides this domestic kidnapping, British frigates, in friendly or neutral harbors, in some instances pressed into their service foreign sailors of all nations from the public wharves. In certain cases, where Americans were concerned, when "*protections*" were found upon their persons, these were destroyed; and to prevent the American consul from claiming his sailor countrymen, the press-gang generally went on shore the night previous to the sailing of the frigate, so that the kidnapped seamen were far out to sea before

In a later instance, a large body of British seamen solemnly assembled upon the eve of an anticipated war, and together determined, that in case of its breaking out, they would at once flee to America, to avoid being pressed into the service of their country—a service which degraded her own guardians at the gangway.

At another time, long previous to this, according to an English Navy officer, Lieutenant Tomlinson, three thousand seamen, impelled by the same motive, fled ashore in a panic from the colliers between Yarmouth Roads and the Nore. Elsewhere, he says, in speaking of some of the men on board the King's ships, that "they were most miserable objects." This remark is perfectly corroborated by other testimony referring to another period. In alluding to the lamented scarcity of good English seamen during the wars of 1808, &c., the author of a pamphlet on "Naval Subjects" says, that all the best seamen, the steadiest and best-behaved men, generally succeeded in avoiding the impress. This writer was, or had been, himself a Captain in the British fleet.

Now it may be easily imagined who are the men, and of what moral character they are, who, even at the present day, are willing to enlist as full-grown adults in a service so galling to all shore-manhood as the Navy. Hence it comes that the skulkers and scoundrels of all sorts in a man-of-war are chiefly composed not of regular seamen, but of these "dock-lopers" of landsmen, men who enter the Navy to draw their grog and murder their time in the notorious idleness of a frigate. But if so idle, why not reduce the number of a man-of-war's crew, and reasonably keep employed the rest? It can not be done.

---

they could be missed by their friends. It is not intended to revive old feuds. In one sense, let by-gones be by-gones. But these things should be known; for in case the English government again goes to war with its fleets, and should again resort to indiscriminate impressment to man them, it is well that both Englishmen and Americans, that all the world be prepared to put down an iniquity outrageous and insulting to God and man. It is hardly to be anticipated, however, that in case of war the English government would again attempt to revive measures, which some of its own statesmen must have deplored from the beginning; and which, at the present day, must surely seem iniquitous to the great body of Englishmen. Indeed, it is perhaps to be doubted, whether Englishmen could again be brought to submit even to domestic impressment.

In the first place, the magnitude of most of these ships requires a large number of hands to brace the heavy yards, hoist the enormous top-sails, and weigh the ponderous anchor. And though the occasion for the employment of so many men comes but seldom, it is true, yet when that occasion *does* come—and come it may at any moment—this multitude of men are indispensable.

But besides this, and to crown all, the batteries must be manned. There must be enough men to work all the guns at one time. And thus, in order to have a sufficiency of mortals at hand to "sink, burn, and destroy;" a man-of-war—besides, through her vices, hopelessly depraving the volunteer landsmen and ordinary seamen of good habits, who occasionally enlist—must feed at the public cost a multitude of persons, who, if they did not find a home in the Navy, would probably fall on the parish, or linger out their days in a prison.

Among others, these are the men into whose mouths Dibdin puts his patriotic verses, full of sea-chivalry and romance. With an exception in the last line, they might be sung with equal propriety by both English and American man-of-war's-men.

"As for me, in all weathers, all times, tides, and ends,
    Naught's a trouble from duty that springs;
For my heart is my Poll's, and my rhino's my friend's,
    And as for my life, it's the king's.

To rancour unknown, to no passion a slave,
    Nor unmanly, nor mean, nor a railer," &c.

I do not unite with a high critical authority in considering Dibdin's ditties as "slang songs," for most of them breathe the very poetry of the ocean. But it is remarkable that those songs—which would lead one to think that man-of-war's-men are the most care-free, contented, virtuous, and patriotic of mankind—were composed at a time when the English Navy was principally manned by felons and paupers, as mentioned in a former chapter. Still more, these songs are pervaded by a true Mohammedan sensualism; a reckless acquiescence in fate, and an implicit, unquestioning, dog-like devotion to whoever may be lord and master. Dibdin was a man of genius; but no wonder Dibdin was a government pensioner at £200 per annum.

But notwithstanding the iniquities of a man-of-war, men are to be found in them, at times, so used to a hard life; so drilled and disciplined to servitude, that, with an incomprehensible philosophy, they seem cheerfully to resign themselves to their fate. They have plenty to eat; spirits to drink; clothing to keep them warm; a hammock to sleep in; tobacco to chew; a doctor to medicine them; a parson to pray for them; and, to a penniless castaway, must not all this seem as a luxurious Bill of Fare?

There was on board of the Neversink a fore-top-man by the name of Landless, who, though his back was cross-barred, and plaided with the ineffaceable scars of all the floggings accumulated by a reckless tar during a ten years' service in the Navy, yet he perpetually wore a hilarious face, and at joke and repartee was a very Joe Miller.

That man, though a sea-vagabond, was not created in vain. He enjoyed life with the zest of everlasting adolescence; and, though cribbed in an oaken prison, with the turnkey sentries all round him, yet he paced the gun-deck as if it were broad as a prairie, and diversified in landscape as the hills and valleys of the Tyrol. Nothing ever disconcerted him; nothing could transmute his laugh into any thing like a sigh. Those glandular secretions, which in other captives sometimes go to the formation of tears, in *him* were expectorated from the mouth, tinged with the golden juice of a weed, wherewith he solaced and comforted his ignominious days.

"Rum and tobacco!" said Landless, "what more does a sailor want?"

His favorite song was "*Dibdin's True English Sailor*," beginning,

> "Jack dances and sings, and is always content,
>   In his vows to his lass he'll ne'er fail her;
>   His anchor's atrip when his money's all spent,
>   And this is the life of a sailor."

But poor Landless danced quite as often at the gangway, under the lash, as in the sailor dance-houses ashore.

Another of his songs, also set to the significant tune of *The King, God bless him!* mustered the following lines among many similar ones:

"Oh, when safely landed in Boston or 'York,
 Oh how I will tipple and jig it;
And toss off my glass while my rhino holds out,
 In drinking success to our frigate!"

During the many idle hours when our frigate was lying in harbor, this man was either merrily playing at checkers, or mending his clothes, or snoring like a trumpeter under the lee of the booms. When fast asleep, a national salute from our batteries could hardly move him. Whether ordered to the main-truck in a gale; or rolled by the drum to the grog-tub; or commanded to walk up to the gratings and be lashed, Landless always obeyed with the same invincible indifference.

His advice to a young lad, who shipped with us at Valparaiso, embodies the pith and marrow of that philosophy which enables some man-of-war's-men to wax jolly in the service.

"Shippy!" said Landless, taking the pale lad by his neckerchief, as if he had him by the halter; "Shippy, I've seen sarvice with Uncle Sam—I've sailed in many *Andrew Millers*. Now take my advice, and steer clear of all trouble. D'ye see, touch your tile whenever a swob (officer) speaks to you. And never mind how much they rope's-end you, keep your red-rag belayed; for you must know as how they don't fancy sea-lawyers; and when the sarving out of slops comes round, stand up to it stiffly; it's only an oh Lord! or two, and a few oh my Gods!—that's all. And what then? Why, you sleeps it off in a few nights, and turns out at last all ready for your grog."

This Landless was a favorite with the officers, among whom he went by the name of "*Happy Jack*." And it is just such Happy Jacks as Landless that most sea-officers profess to admire; a fellow without shame, without a soul, so dead to the least dignity of manhood that he could hardly be called a man. Whereas, a seaman who exhibits traits of moral sensitiveness, whose demeanor shows some dignity within; this is the man they, in many cases, instinctively dislike. The reason is, they feel such a man to be a continual reproach to them, as being mentally superior to their power. He has no business in a man-of-war; they do not want such men. To them there is an insolence in his manly freedom, contempt in his very carriage. He is unendurable, as an erect, lofty-minded African would be to some slave-driving planter.

Let it not be supposed, however, that the remarks in this and the preceding chapter apply to *all* men-of-war. There are some vessels blessed with patriarchal, intellectual Captains, gentlemanly and brotherly officers, and docile and Christianized crews. The peculiar usages of such vessels insensibly soften the tyrannical rigor of the Articles of War; in them, scourging is unknown. To sail in such ships is hardly to realize that you live under the martial law, or that the evils above mentioned can any where exist.

And Jack Chase, old Ushant, and several more fine tars that might be added, sufficiently attest, that in the Neversink at least, there was more than one noble man-of-war's-man who almost redeemed all the rest.

Wherever, throughout this narrative, the American Navy, in any of its bearings, has formed the theme of a general discussion, hardly one syllable of admiration for what is accounted illustrious in its achievements has been permitted to escape me. The reason is this: I consider, that so far as what is called military renown is concerned, the American Navy needs no eulogist but History. It were superfluous for White-Jacket to tell the world what it knows already. The office imposed upon me is of another cast; and, though I foresee and feel that it may subject me to the pillory in the hard thoughts of some men, yet, supported by what God has given me, I tranquilly abide the event, whatever it may prove.

Chapter 91

THERE IS a fable about a painter moved by Jove to the
painting of the head of Medusa. Though the picture was
true to the life, yet the poor artist sickened at the sight of
what his forced pencil had drawn. Thus, borne through my
task toward the end, my own soul now sinks at what I myself
have portrayed. But let us forget past chapters, if we may,
while we paint less repugnant things.

Metropolitan gentlemen have their club; provincial gossipers their news-room; village quidnuncs their barber's shop;
the Chinese their opium-houses; American Indians their
council-fire; and even cannibals their *Noojona*, or Talk-Stone,
where they assemble at times to discuss the affairs of the day.
Nor is there any government, however despotic, that ventures
to deny to the least of its subjects the privilege of a sociable
chat. Not the Thirty Tyrants even—the clubbed post-captains
of old Athens—could stop the wagging tongues at the street-
corners. For chat man must; and by our immortal Bill of
Rights, that guarantees to us liberty of speech, chat we Yankees will, whether on board a frigate, or on board our own
terra-firma plantations.

In men-of-war, the Galley, or Cookery, on the gun-deck is
the grand centre of gossip and news among the sailors. Here
crowds assemble to chat away the half hour elapsing after
every meal. The reason why this place and these hours are
selected rather than others is this: in the neighborhood of the
galley alone, and only after meals, is the man-of-war's-man
permitted to regale himself with a smoke.

A sumptuary edict, truly, that deprived White-Jacket, for
one, of a luxury to which he had long been attached. For how
can the mystical motives, the capricious impulses of a luxurious smoker go and come at the beck of a Commodore's command? No! when I smoke, be it because of my sovereign
good pleasure I choose so to do, though at so unseasonable

an hour that I send round the town for a brasier of coals. What! smoke by a sun-dial? Smoke on compulsion? Make a trade, a business, a vile recurring calling of smoking? And, perhaps, when those sedative fumes have steeped you in the grandest of reveries, and, circle over circle, solemnly rises some immeasurable dome in your soul—far away, swelling and heaving into the vapor you raise—as if from one of Mozart's grandest marches a temple were rising, like Venus from the sea—at such a time, to have your whole Parthenon tumbled about your ears by the knell of the ship's bell announcing the expiration of the half hour for smoking! Whip me, ye Furies! toast me in saltpetre! smite me, some thunder-bolt! charge upon me, endless squadrons of Mamalukes! devour me, Feejees! but preserve me from a tyranny like this.

No! though I smoked like an Indian summer ere I entered the Neversink, so abhorrent was this sumptuary law that I altogether abandoned the luxury rather than enslave it to a time and a place. Herein did I not right, Ancient and Honorable Old Guard of Smokers all round the world?

But there were others of the crew not so fastidious as myself. After every meal, they hied to the galley and solaced their souls with a whiff.

Now a bunch of cigars, all banded together, is a type and a symbol of the brotherly love between smokers. Likewise, for the time, in a community of pipes is a community of hearts. Nor was it an ill thing for the Indian Sachems to circulate their calumet tobacco-bowl—even as our own forefathers circulated their punch-bowl—in token of peace, charity, and good-will, friendly feelings, and sympathizing souls. And this it was that made the gossipers of the galley so loving a club, so long as the vapory bond united them.

It was a pleasant sight to behold them. Grouped in the recesses between the guns, they chatted and laughed like rows of convivialists in the boxes of some vast dining-saloon. Take a Flemish kitchen full of good fellows from Teniers; add a fire-side group from Wilkie; throw in a naval sketch from Cruikshank; and then stick a short pipe into every mother's son's mouth, and you have the smoking scene at the galley of the Neversink.

Not a few were politicians; and, as there were some

thoughts of a war with England at the time, their discussions waxed warm.

"I tell you what it is, *shippies*!" cried the old captain of gun No. 1 on the forecastle, "if that 'ere President of ourn don't luff up into the wind, by the Battle of the Nile! he'll be getting us into a grand fleet engagement afore the Yankee nation has rammed home her cartridges—let alone blowing the match!"

"Who talks of luffing?" roared a roystering fore-top-man. "Keep our Yankee nation large before the wind, say I, till you come plump on the enemy's bows, and then board him in the smoke," and with that, there came forth a mighty blast from his pipe.

"Who says the old man at the helm of the Yankee nation can't steer his *trick* as well as George Washington himself?" cried a sheet-anchor-man.

"But they say he's a cold water customer, Bill," cried another; "and sometimes o' nights I somehow has a presentation that he's goin' to stop our grog."

"D'ye hear there, fore and aft!" roared the boatswain's mates at the gangway, "all hands tumble up, and 'bout ship!"

"That's the talk!" cried the captain of gun No. 1, as, in obedience to the summons, all hands dropped their pipes and crowded toward the ladders, "and that's what the President must do—go in stays, my lads, and put the Yankee nation on the other tack."

But these political discussions by no means supplied the staple of conversation for the gossiping smokers of the galley. The interior affairs of the frigate itself formed their principal theme. Rumors about the private life of the Commodore in his cabin; about the Captain, in his; about the various officers in the Ward-room; about the *reefers* in the steerage, and their madcap frolickings, and about a thousand other matters touching the crew themselves; all these—forming the eternally shifting, domestic by-play of a man-of-war—proved inexhaustible topics for our quidnuncs.

The animation of these scenes was very much heightened as we drew nearer and nearer our port; it rose to a climax when the frigate was reported to be only twenty-four hours' sail from the land. What they should do when they landed;

how they should invest their wages; what they should eat; what they should drink; and what lass they should marry— these were the topics which absorbed them.

"Sink the sea!" cried a forecastle man. "Once more ashore, and you'll never again catch old Boombolt afloat. I mean to settle down in a sail-loft."

"Cable-tier pinches blister all tarpaulin hats!" cried a young after-guard's-man; "I mean to go back to the counter."

"Shipmates! take me by the arms, and swab up the lee-scuppers with me, but I mean to steer a clam-cart before I go again to a ship's wheel. Let the Navy go by the board—to sea again, I won't!"

"Start my soul-bolts, maties, if any more Blue Peters and sailing signals fly at my fore!" cried the Captain of the Head. "My wages will buy a wheelbarrow, if nothing more."

"I have taken my last dose of salts," said the Captain of the Waist, "and after this mean to stick to fresh water. Ay, maties, ten of us Waisters mean to club together and buy a *serving-mallet boat*, d'ye see; and if ever we drown, it will be in the 'raging canal!' Blast the sea, shipmates! say I."

"Profane not the holy element!" said Lemsford, the poet of the gun-deck, leaning over a cannon. "Know ye not, man-of-war's-men! that by the Parthian magi the ocean was held sacred? Did not Tiridates, the Eastern monarch, take an immense land circuit to avoid desecrating the Mediterranean, in order to reach his imperial master, Nero, and do homage for his crown?"

"What lingo is that?" cried the Captain of the Waist.

"Who's Commodore Tiddery-eye?" cried the forecastle-man.

"Hear me out," resumed Lemsford. "Like Tiridates, I venerate the sea, and venerate it so highly, shipmates, that ever-more I shall abstain from crossing it. In *that* sense, Captain of the Waist, I echo your cry."

It was, indeed, a remarkable fact, that nine men out of every ten of the Neversink's crew had formed some plan or other to keep themselves ashore for life, or, at least, on fresh water, after the expiration of the present cruise. With all the experiences of that cruise accumulated in one intense recollec-tion of a moment; with the smell of tar in their nostrils; out of sight of land; with a stout ship under foot, and snuffing the ocean air; with all the things of the sea surrounding them; in their cool, sober moments of reflection; in the silence and solitude of the deep, during the long night-watches, when all their holy home associations were thronging round their hearts; in the spontaneous piety and devotion of the last hours of so long a voyage; in the fullness and the frankness of their souls; when there was naught to jar the well-poised equilibrium of their judgment—under all these circumstances, at least nine tenths of a crew of five hundred man-of-war's-men resolved forever to turn their backs on the sea. But do men ever hate the thing they love? Do men forswear the hearth and the homestead? What, then, must the Navy be?

But, alas for the man-of-war's-man, who, though he may take a Hannibal oath against the service; yet, cruise after cruise, and after forswearing it again and again, he is driven back to the spirit-tub and the gun-deck by his old hereditary foe, the ever-devilish god of grog.

On this point, let some of the crew of the Neversink be called to the stand.

You, Captain of the Waist! and you, seamen of the foretop! and you, After-guard's-men and others! how came you here at the guns of the North Carolina, after registering your solemn vows at the galley of the Neversink?

They all hang their heads. I know the cause; poor fellows! perjure yourselves not again; swear not at all hereafter.

Ay, these very tars—the foremost in denouncing the Navy; who had bound themselves by the most tremendous oaths— these very men, not three days after getting ashore, were rolling round the streets in penniless drunkenness; and next day many of them were to be found on board of the *guardo* or receiving-ship. Thus, in part, is the Navy manned.

But what was still more surprising, and tended to impart a new and strange insight into the character of sailors, and overthrow some long-established ideas concerning them as a class, was this: numbers of men who, during the cruise, had passed for exceedingly prudent, nay, parsimonious persons, who would even refuse you a patch, or a needleful of thread, and, from their stinginess, procured the name of *Ravelings*— no sooner were these men fairly adrift in harbor, and under the influence of frequent quaffings, than their three-years'-earned wages flew right and left; they summoned whole boarding-houses of sailors to the bar, and treated them over and over again. Fine fellows! generous-hearted tars! Seeing this sight, I thought to myself, Well, these generous-hearted tars on shore were the greatest curmudgeons afloat! it's the bottle that's generous, not they! Yet the popular conceit concerning a sailor is derived from his behavior ashore; whereas, ashore he is no longer a sailor, but a landsman for the time. A man-of-war's-man is only a man-of-war's-man at sea; and the sea is the place to learn what he is. But we have seen that a man-of-war is but this old-fashioned world of ours afloat, full of all manner of characters—full of strange contradictions; and though boasting some fine fellows here and there, yet, upon the whole, charged to the combings of her hatchways with the spirit of Belial and all unrighteousness.

Chapter 92

THE LAST OF THE JACKET

ALREADY has White-Jacket chronicled the mishaps and inconveniences, troubles and tribulations of all sorts brought upon him by that unfortunate but indispensable garment of his. But now it befalls him to record how this jacket, for the second and last time, came near proving his shroud.

Of a pleasant midnight, our good frigate, now somewhere off the Capes of Virginia, was running on bravely, when the breeze, gradually dying, left us slowly gliding toward our still invisible port.

Headed by Jack Chase, the quarter-watch were reclining in the top, talking about the shore delights into which they intended to plunge, while our captain often broke in with allusions to similar conversations when he was on board the English line-of-battle ship, the Asia, drawing nigh to Portsmouth, in England, after the battle of Navarino.

Suddenly an order was given to set the main-top-gallant-stun'-sail, and the halyards not being rove, Jack Chase assigned to me that duty. Now this reeving of the halyards of a main-top-gallant-stun'-sail is a business that eminently demands sharpsightedness, skill, and celerity.

Consider that the end of a line, some two hundred feet long, is to be carried aloft, in your teeth, if you please, and dragged far out on the giddiest of yards, and after being wormed and twisted about through all sorts of intricacies—turning abrupt corners at the abruptest of angles—is to be dropped, clear of all obstructions, in a straight plumb-line right down to the deck. In the course of this business, there is a multitude of sheeve-holes and blocks, through which you must pass it; often the rope is a very tight fit, so as to make it like threading a fine cambric needle with rather coarse thread. Indeed, it is a thing only deftly to be done, even by day. Judge, then, what it must be to be threading cambric needles by night, and at sea, upward of a hundred feet aloft in the air.

With the end of the line in one hand, I was mounting the top-mast shrouds, when our Captain of the Top told me that I had better off jacket; but though it was not a very cold night, I had been reclining so long in the top, that I had become somewhat chilly, so I thought best not to comply with the hint.

Having reeved the line through all the inferior blocks, I went out with it to the end of the weather-top-gallant-yard-arm, and was in the act of leaning over and passing it through the suspended jewel-block there, when the ship gave a plunge in the sudden swells of the calm sea, and pitching me still further over the yard, threw the heavy skirts of my jacket right over my head, completely muffling me. Somehow I thought it was the sail that had flapped, and, under that impression, threw up my hands to drag it from my head, re-lying upon the sail itself to support me meanwhile. Just then the ship gave another sudden jerk, and, head foremost, I pitched from the yard. I knew where I was, from the rush of the air by my ears, but all else was a nightmare. A bloody film was before my eyes, through which, ghost-like, passed and repassed my father, mother, and sisters. An unutterable nau-sea oppressed me; I was conscious of gasping; there seemed no breath in my body. It was over one hundred feet that I fell—down, down, with lungs collapsed as in death. Ten thousand pounds of shot seemed tied to my head, as the ir-resistible law of gravitation dragged me, head foremost and straight as a die, toward the infallible centre of this terr-aqueous globe. All I had seen, and read, and heard, and all I had thought and felt in my life, seemed intensified in one fixed idea in my soul. But dense as this idea was, it was made up of atoms. Having fallen from the projecting yard-arm end, I was conscious of a collected satisfaction in feeling, that I should not be dashed on the deck, but would sink into the speechless profound of the sea.

With the bloody, blind film before my eyes, there was a still stranger hum in my head, as if a hornet were there; and I thought to myself, Great God! this is Death! Yet these thoughts were unmixed with alarm. Like frost-work that flashes and shifts its scared hues in the sun, all my braided, blended emotions were in themselves icy cold and calm.

So protracted did my fall seem, that I can even now recall the feeling of wondering how much longer it would be, ere all was over and I struck. Time seemed to stand still, and all the worlds seemed poised on their poles, as I fell, soul-becalmed, through the eddying whirl and swirl of the Maelstrom air.

At first, as I have said, I must have been precipitated head foremost; but I was conscious, at length, of a swift, flinging motion of my limbs, which involuntarily threw themselves out, so that at last I must have fallen in a heap. This is more likely, from the circumstance, that when I struck the sea, I felt as if some one had smote me slantingly across the shoulder and along part of my right side.

As I gushed into the sea, a thunder-boom sounded in my ear; my soul seemed flying from my mouth. The feeling of death flooded over me with the billows. The blow from the sea must have turned me, so that I sank almost feet foremost through a soft, seething, foamy lull. Some current seemed hurrying me away; in a trance I yielded, and sank deeper down with a glide. Purple and pathless was the deep calm now around me, flecked by summer lightnings in an azure afar. The horrible nausea was gone; the bloody, blind film turned a pale green; I wondered whether I was yet dead, or still dying. But of a sudden some fashionless form brushed my side—some inert, coiled fish of the sea; the thrill of being alive again tingled in my nerves, and the strong shunning of death shocked me through.

For one instant an agonizing revulsion came over me as I found myself utterly sinking. Next moment the force of my fall was expended; and there I hung, vibrating in the mid-deep. What wild sounds then rang in my ear! One was a soft moaning, as of low waves on the beach; the other wild and heartlessly jubilant, as of the sea in the height of a tempest. Oh soul! thou then heardest life and death: as he who stands upon the Corinthian shore hears both the Ionian and the Ægean waves. The life-and-death poise soon passed; and then I found myself slowly ascending, and caught a dim glimmering of light.

Quicker and quicker I mounted; till at last I bounded up like a buoy, and my whole head was bathed in the blessed air.

I had fallen in a line with the main-mast; I now found myself nearly abreast of the mizzen-mast, the frigate slowly gliding by like a black world in the water. Her vast hull loomed out of the night, showing hundreds of seamen in the hammock-nettings, some tossing over ropes, others madly flinging overboard the hammocks; but I was too far out from them immediately to reach what they threw. I essayed to swim toward the ship; but instantly I was conscious of a feeling like being pinioned in a feather-bed, and, moving my hands, felt my jacket puffed out above my tight girdle with water. I strove to tear it off; but it was looped together here and there, and the strings were not then to be sundered by hand. I whipped out my knife, that was tucked at my belt, and ripped my jacket straight up and down, as if I were ripping open myself. With a violent struggle I then burst out of it, and was free. Heavily soaked, it slowly sank before my eyes.

Sink! sink! oh shroud! thought I; sink forever! accursed jacket that thou art!

"See that white shark!" cried a horrified voice from the taffrail; "he'll have that man down his hatchway! Quick! the *grains!* the *grains!*"

The next instant that barbed bunch of harpoons pierced through and through the unfortunate jacket, and swiftly sped down with it out of sight.

Being now astern of the frigate, I struck out boldly toward the elevated pole of one of the life-buoys which had been cut away. Soon after, one of the cutters picked me up. As they dragged me out of the water into the air, the sudden transition of elements made my every limb feel like lead, and I helplessly sunk into the bottom of the boat.

Ten minutes after, I was safe on board, and, springing aloft, was ordered to reeve anew the stun'-sail-halyards, which, slipping through the blocks when I had let go the end, had unrove and fallen to the deck.

The sail was soon set; and, as if purposely to salute it, a gentle breeze soon came, and the Neversink once more glided over the water, a soft ripple at her bows, and leaving a tranquil wake behind.

Chapter 93

CABLE AND ANCHOR ALL CLEAR

A ND NOW that the white jacket has sunk to the bottom of the sea, and the blessed Capes of Virginia are believed to be broad on our bow—though still out of sight—our five hundred souls are fondly dreaming of home, and the iron throats of the guns round the galley re-echo with their songs and hurras—what more remains?

Shall I tell what conflicting and almost crazy surmisings prevailed concerning the precise harbor for which we were bound? For, according to rumor, our Commodore had received sealed orders touching that matter, which were not to be broken open till we gained a precise latitude of the coast. Shall I tell how, at last, all this uncertainty departed, and many a foolish prophecy was proved false, when our noble frigate—her longest pennant at her main—wound her stately way into the innermost harbor of Norfolk, like a plumed Spanish Grandee threading the corridors of the Escurial toward the throne-room within? Shall I tell how we kneeled upon the holy soil? How I begged a blessing of old Ushant, and one precious hair of his beard for a keepsake? How Lemsford, the gun-deck bard, offered up a devout ode as a prayer of thanksgiving? How saturnine Nord, the magnifico in disguise, refusing all companionship, stalked off into the woods, like the ghost of an old Calif of Bagdad? How I swayed and swung the hearty hand of Jack Chase, and nipped it to mine with a Carrick bend; yea, and kissed that noble hand of my liege lord and captain of my top, my sea-tutor and sire?

Shall I tell how the grand Commodore and Captain drove off from the pier-head? How the Lieutenants, in undress, sat down to their last dinner in the ward-room, and the Champagne, packed in ice, spirted and sparkled like the Hot Springs out of a snow-drift in Iceland? How the Chaplain went off in his cassock, without bidding the people adieu? How shrunken Cuticle, the Surgeon, stalked over the side, the wired skeleton carried in his wake by his cot-boy? How the Lieutenant of Marines sheathed his sword on the poop, and, calling for wax and a taper, sealed the end of the scabbard with his family crest and motto—*Denique Cœlum?* How the Purser in due time mustered his money-bags, and paid us all off on the quarter-deck—good and bad, sick and well, all receiving their wages; though, truth to tell, some reckless, improvident seamen, who had lived too fast during the cruise, had little or nothing now standing on the credit side of their Purser's accounts?

Shall I tell of the Retreat of the Five Hundred inland; not, alas! in battle-array, as at quarters, but scattered broadcast over the land?

Shall I tell how the Neversink was at last stripped of spars, shrouds, and sails—had her guns hoisted out—her powder-magazine, shot-lockers, and armories discharged—till not one vestige of a fighting thing was left in her, from furthest stem to uttermost stern?

No! let all this go by; for our anchor still hangs from our bows, though its eager flukes dip their points in the impatient waves. Let us leave the ship on the sea—still with the land out of sight—still with brooding darkness on the face of the deep. I love an indefinite, infinite background—a vast, heaving, rolling, mysterious rear!

It is night. The meagre moon is in her last quarter—that betokens the end of a cruise that is passing. But the stars look forth in their everlasting brightness—and *that* is the everlasting, glorious Future, forever beyond us.

We main-top-men are all aloft in the top; and round our mast we circle, a brother-band, hand in hand, all spliced together. We have reefed the last top-sail; trained the last gun; blown the last match; bowed to the last blast; been tranced in the last calm. We have mustered our last round the capstan; been rolled to grog the last time; for the last time swung in our hammocks; for the last time turned out at the sea-gull call of the watch. We have seen our last man scourged at the gangway; our last man gasp out the ghost in the stifling Sick-bay; our last man tossed to the sharks. Our last death-denouncing Article of War has been read; and far inland, in that blessed clime whitherward our frigate now glides, the last wrong in our frigate will be remembered no more; when down from our main-mast comes our Commodore's pennant, when down sinks its shooting stars from the sky.

"By the mark, nine!" sings the hoary old leadsman, in the chains. And thus, the mid-world Equator passed, our frigate strikes soundings at last.

Hand in hand we top-mates stand, rocked in our Pisgah top. And over the starry waves, and broad out into the blandly blue and boundless night, spiced with strange sweets from the long-sought land—the whole long cruise predestinated ours, though often in tempest-time we almost refused to believe in that far-distant shore—straight out into that fragrant night, ever-noble Jack Chase, matchless and unmatchable Jack Chase stretches forth his bannered hand, and, pointing shoreward, cries: "For the last time, hear Camoens, boys!

'How calm the waves, how mild the balmy gale!
The Halcyons call, ye Lusians spread the sail!
Appeased, old Ocean now shall rage no more;
Haste, point our bowsprit for yon shadowy shore.
Soon shall the transports of your natal soil
O'erwhelm in bounding joy the thoughts of every toil.' "

The End

As a MAN-OF-WAR that sails through the sea, so this earth that sails through the air. We mortals are all on board a fast-sailing, never-sinking world-frigate, of which God was the shipwright; and she is but one craft in a Milky-Way fleet, of which God is the Lord High Admiral. The port we sail from is forever astern. And though far out of sight of land, for ages and ages we continue to sail with sealed orders, and our last destination remains a secret to ourselves and our officers; yet our final haven was predestinated ere we slipped from the stocks at Creation.

Thus sailing with sealed orders, we ourselves are the repositories of the secret packet, whose mysterious contents we long to learn. There are no mysteries out of ourselves. But let us not give ear to the superstitious, gun-deck gossip about whither we may be gliding, for, as yet, not a soul on board of us knows—not even the Commodore himself; assuredly not the Chaplain; even our Professor's scientific surmisings are vain. On that point, the smallest cabin-boy is as wise as the Captain. And believe not the hypochondriac dwellers below hatches, who will tell you, with a sneer, that our world-frigate is bound to no final harbor whatever; that our voyage will prove an endless circumnavigation of space. Not so. For how can this world-frigate prove our eventual abiding place, when, upon our first embarkation, as infants in arms, her violent rolling—in after life unperceived—makes every soul of us sea-sick? Does not this show, too, that the very air we here inhale is uncongenial, and only becomes endurable at last through gradual habituation, and that some blessed, placid haven, however remote at present, must be in store for us all?

Glance fore and aft our flush decks. What a swarming crew! All told, they muster hard upon eight hundred millions of souls. Over these we have authoritative Lieutenants, a sword-belted Officer of Marines, a Chaplain, a Professor, a Purser, a Doctor, a Cook, a Master-at-arms.

Oppressed by illiberal laws, and partly oppressed by themselves, many of our people are wicked, unhappy, inefficient. We have skulkers and idlers all round, and brow-beaten waisters, who, for a pittance, do our craft's shabby work. Nevertheless, among our people we have gallant fore, main, and mizen top-men aloft, who, well treated or ill, still trim our craft to the blast.

We have a *brig* for trespassers; a bar by our main-mast, at which they are arraigned; a cat-o'-nine-tails and a gangway, to degrade them in their own eyes and in ours. These are not always employed to convert Sin to Virtue, but to divide them, and protect Virtue and legalized Sin from unlegalized Vice.

We have a Sick-bay for the smitten and helpless, whither we hurry them out of sight, and, however they may groan beneath hatches, we hear little of their tribulations on deck; we still sport our gay streamer aloft. Outwardly regarded, our craft is a lie; for all that is outwardly seen of it is the clean-swept deck, and oft-painted planks comprised above the water-line; whereas, the vast mass of our fabric, with all its store-rooms of secrets, forever slides along far under the surface.

When a shipmate dies, straightway we sew him up, and overboard he goes; our world-frigate rushes by, and never more do we behold him again; though, sooner or later, the everlasting under-tow sweeps him toward our own destination.

We have both a quarter-deck to our craft and a gun-deck; subterranean shot-lockers and gunpowder magazines; and the Articles of War form our domineering code.

Oh, shipmates and world-mates, all round! we the people suffer many abuses. Our gun-deck is full of complaints. In vain from Lieutenants do we appeal to the Captain; in vain—while on board our world-frigate—to the indefinite Navy Commissioners, so far out of sight aloft. Yet the worst of our evils we blindly inflict upon ourselves; our officers can not remove them, even if they would. From the last ills no being can save another; therein each man must be his own saviour. For the rest, whatever befall us, let us never train our murderous guns inboard; let us not mutiny with bloody pikes in our hands. Our Lord High Admiral will yet interpose; and though long ages should elapse, and leave our wrongs unredressed, yet, shipmates and world-mates! let us never forget, that,

> Whoever afflict us, whatever surround,
> Life is a voyage that's homeward-bound!

THE END

MOBY-DICK

or
The Whale

Contents

Etymology

(SUPPLIED BY A LATE CONSUMPTIVE USHER TO A
GRAMMAR SCHOOL.)

The pale Usher—threadbare in coat, heart, body, and brain; I see him now. He was ever dusting his old lexicons and grammars, with a queer handkerchief, mockingly embellished with all the gay flags of all the known nations of the world. He loved to dust his old grammars; it somehow mildly reminded him of his mortality.

Etymology

"While you take in hand to school others, and to teach them by what name a whale-fish is to be called in our tongue, leaving out, through ignorance, the letter H, which almost alone maketh up the signification of the word, you deliver that which is not true."

Hackluyt.

"WHALE. * * * Sw. and Dan. *hval*. This animal is named from roundness or rolling; for in Dan. *hvalt* is arched or vaulted."

Webster's Dictionary.

"WHALE. * * * It is more immediately from the Dut. and Ger. *Wallen*; A.S. *Walw-ian*, to roll, to wallow."

Richardson's Dictionary.

חן,	*Hebrew.*
κῆτος,	*Greek.*
CETUS,	*Latin.*
WHÆL,	*Anglo-Saxon.*
HVAL,	*Danish.*
WAL,	*Dutch.*
HWAL,	*Swedish.*
HVALUR,	*Icelandic.*
WHALE,	*English.*
BALEINE,	*French.*
BALLENA,	*Spanish.*
PEKEE-NUEE-NUEE,	*Fegee.*
PEHEE-NUEE-NUEE,	*Erromangoan.*

Extracts

(SUPPLIED BY A SUB-SUB-LIBRARIAN.)

It will be seen that this mere painstaking burrower and grub-worm of a poor devil of a Sub-Sub appears to have gone through the long Vaticans and street-stalls of the earth, picking up whatever random allusions to whales he could anyways find in any book whatsoever, sacred or profane. Therefore you must not, in every case at least, take the higgledy-piggledy whale statements, however authentic, in these extracts, for veritable gospel cetology. Far from it. As touching the ancient authors generally, as well as the poets here appearing, these extracts are solely valuable or entertaining, as affording a glancing bird's eye view of what has been promiscuously said, thought, fancied, and sung of Leviathan, by many nations and generations, including our own.

So fare thee well, poor devil of a Sub-Sub, whose commentator I am. Thou belongest to that hopeless, sallow tribe which no wine of this world will ever warm; and for whom even Pale Sherry would be too rosy-strong; but with whom one sometimes loves to sit, and feel poor-devilish, too; and grow convivial upon tears; and say to them bluntly, with full eyes and empty glasses, and in not altogether unpleasant sadness—Give it up, Sub-Subs! For by how much the more pains ye take to please the world, by so much the more shall ye for ever go thankless! Would that I could clear out Hampton Court and the Tuileries for ye! But gulp down your tears and hie aloft to the royal-mast with your hearts; for your friends who have gone before are clearing out the seven-storied heavens, and making refugees of long-pampered Gabriel, Michael, and Raphael, against your coming. Here ye strike but splintered hearts together—there, ye shall strike unsplinterable glasses!

Extracts

"And God created great whales."
Genesis.

"Leviathan maketh a path to shine after him;
One would think the deep to be hoary."
Job.

"Now the Lord had prepared a great fish to swallow up Jonah."
Jonah.

"There go the ships; there is that Leviathan whom thou hast made
to play therein."
Psalms.

"In that day, the Lord with his sore, and great, and strong sword,
shall punish Leviathan the piercing serpent, even Leviathan that
crooked serpent; and he shall slay the dragon that is in the sea."
Isaiah.

"And what thing soever besides cometh within the chaos of this
monster's mouth, be it beast, boat, or stone, down it goes all incontinently that foul great swallow of his, and perisheth in the bottomless gulf of his paunch."
Holland's Plutarch's Morals.

"The Indian Sea breedeth the most and the biggest fishes that are:
among which the Whales and Whirlpooles called Balænæ, take up as
much in length as four acres or arpens of land."
Holland's Pliny.

"Scarcely had we proceeded two days on the sea, when about sunrise a great many Whales and other monsters of the sea, appeared.
Among the former, one was of a most monstrous size. *   * This
came towards us, open-mouthed, raising the waves on all sides, and
beating the sea before him into a foam."
Tooke's Lucian.
"The True History."

"He visited this country also with a view of catching horse-whales,
which had bones of very great value for their teeth, of which he
brought some to the king.   *   *   *   The best whales were

catched in his own country, of which some were forty-eight, some fifty yards long. He said that he was one of six who had killed sixty in two days."   *Other or Octher's verbal narrative taken down from his mouth by King Alfred. A.D. 890.*

"And whereas all the other things, whether beast or vessel, that enter into the dreadful gulf of this monster's (whale's) mouth, are immediately lost and swallowed up, the sea-gudgeon retires into it in great security, and there sleeps."

MONTAIGNE.—*Apology for Raimond Sebond.*

"Let us fly, let us fly! Old Nick take me if it is not Leviathan described by the noble prophet Moses in the life of patient Job."

Rabelais.

"This whale's liver was two cart-loads."   *Stowe's Annals.*

"The great Leviathan that maketh the seas to seethe like boiling pan."   *Lord Bacon's Version of the Psalms.*

"Touching that monstrous bulk of the whale or ork we have received nothing certain. They grow exceeding fat, insomuch that an incredible quantity of oil will be extracted out of one whale."

Ibid. "History of Life and Death."

"The sovereignest thing on earth is parmacetti for an inward bruise."   *King Henry.*

"Very like a whale."   *Hamlet.*

"Which to recure, no skill of leach's art
Mote him availle, but to returne againe
To his wound's worker, that with lovely dart,
Dinting his breast, had bred his restless paine,
Like as the wounded whale to shore flies from the maine."

The Fairie Queen.

"Immense as whales, the motion of whose vast bodies can in a peaceful calm trouble the ocean till it boil."

Sir William Davenant. Preface to Gondibert.

"What spermacetti is, men might justly doubt, since the learned Hofmannus in his work of thirty years, saith plainly, *Nescio quid sit*."

Sir T. Browne. Of Sperma Ceti and the
Sperma Ceti Whale. Vide his V.E.

"Like Spencer's Talus with his iron flail
He threatens ruin with his ponderous tail.
*   *   *   *   *

Their fixed jav'lins in his side he wears,
And on his back a grove of pikes appears."

Waller's Battle of the Summer Islands.

"By art is created that great Leviathan, called a Commonwealth or State—(in Latin, Civitas) which is but an artificial man."

Opening sentence of Hobbes's Leviathan.

"Silly Mansoul swallowed it without chewing, as if it had been a sprat in the mouth of a whale."   *Holy War.*

"That sea beast
Leviathan, which God of all his works
Created hugest that swim the ocean stream."

Paradise Lost.

————"There Leviathan,
Hugest of living creatures, on the deep
Stretched like a promontory sleeps or swims,
And seems a moving land; and at his gills
Draws in, and at his trunk spouts out a sea."

Ibid.

"The mighty whales which swim in a sea of water, and have a sea of oil swimming in them."   *Fuller's Profane and Holy State.*

"So close behind some promontory lie
   The huge Leviathans to attend their prey,
And give no chace, but swallow in the fry,
   Which through their gaping jaws mistake the way."

Dryden's Annus Mirabilis.

"While the whale is floating at the stern of the ship, they cut off his head, and tow it with a boat as near the shore as it will come; but it will be aground in twelve or thirteen foot water."

Thomas Edge's Ten Voyages to Spitzbergen, in Purchass.

"In their way they saw many whales sporting in the ocean, and in wantonness fuzzing up the water through their pipes and vents, which nature has placed on their shoulders."

Sir T. Herbert's Voyages into Asia and Africa.
Harris Coll.

"Here they saw such huge shoals of whales, that they were forced to proceed with a great deal of caution for fear they should run their ship upon them." *Schouten's Sixth Circumnavigation.*

"We set sail from the Elbe, wind N. E. in the ship called The Jonas-in-the-Whale.   *   *   *

Some say the whale can't open his mouth, but that is a fable.
*   *   *

They frequently climb up the masts to see whether they can see a whale, for the first discoverer has a ducat for his pains.   *   *   *

I was told of a whale taken near Hitland, that had above a barrel of herrings in his belly.   *   *   *

One of our harpooneers told me that he caught once a whale in Spitzbergen that was white all over."

A Voyage to Greenland, A.D. 1671.
Harris Coll.

"Several whales have come in upon this coast (Fife). Anno 1652, one eighty foot in length of the whale-bone kind came in, which, (as I was informed) beside a vast quantity of oil, did afford 500 weight of baleen. The jaws of it stand for a gate in the garden of Pitfirren."

Sibbald's Fife and Kinross.

"Myself have agreed to try whether I can master and kill this Sperma-ceti whale, for I could never hear of any of that sort that was killed by any man, such is his fierceness and swiftness."

Richard Stafford's Letter from the Bermudas.
Phil. Trans. A.D. 1668.

"Whales in the sea
God's voice obey."

N. E. Primer.

"We saw also abundance of large whales, there being more in these southern seas, as I may say, by a hundred to one; than we have to the northward of us."

Captain Cowley's Voyage round the Globe. A.D. 1729.

*   *   *   *   *   "and the breath of the whale is frequently attended with such an insupportable smell, as to bring on a disorder of the brain." *Ulloa's South America.*

> "To fifty chosen sylphs of special note,
> We trust the important charge, the petticoat.
> Oft have we known that seven-fold fence to fail,
> Tho' stiff with hoops and armed with ribs of whale."
> *Rape of the Lock.*

"If we compare land animals in respect to magnitude, with those that take up their abode in the deep, we shall find they will appear contemptible in the comparison. The whale is doubtless the largest animal in creation." *Goldsmith, Nat. His.*

"If you should write a fable for little fishes, you would make them speak like great whales." *Goldsmith to Johnson.*

"In the afternoon we saw what was supposed to be a rock, but it was found to be a dead whale, which some Asiatics had killed, and were then towing ashore. They seemed to endeavor to conceal themselves behind the whale, in order to avoid being seen by us." *Cook's Voyages.*

"The larger whales, they seldom venture to attack. They stand in so great dread of some of them, that when out at sea they are afraid to mention even their names, and carry dung, brim-stone, juniper-wood, and some other articles of the same nature in their boats, in order to terrify and prevent their too near approach." *Uno Von Troil's Letters on Banks's and Solander's Voyage to Iceland in* 1772.

"The Spermacetti Whale found by the Nantuckois, is an active, fierce animal, and requires vast address and boldness in the fishermen." *Thomas Jefferson's Whale Memorial to the French minister in* 1788.

"And pray, sir, what in the world is equal to it?" *Edmund Burke's reference in Parliament to the Nantucket Whale-Fishery.*

"Spain——a great whale stranded on the shores of Europe."
                                        Edmund Burke. (somewhere.)

"A tenth branch of the king's ordinary revenue, said to be grounded on the consideration of his guarding and protecting the seas from pirates and robbers, is the right to *royal* fish, which are whale and sturgeon. And these, when either thrown ashore or caught near the coasts, are the property of the king."
                                        Blackstone.

"Soon to the sport of death the crews repair:
Rodmond unerring o'er his head suspends
The barbed steel, and every turn attends."
                                        Falconer's Shipwreck.

"Bright shone the roofs, the domes, the spires,
    And rockets flew self driven,
To hang their momentary fires
    Amid the vault of heaven.

"So fire with water to compare,
    The ocean serves on high,
Up-spouted by a whale in air,
    To express unwieldy joy."
                                        Cowper, on the Queen's Visit to London.

"Ten or fifteen gallons of blood are thrown out of the heart at a stroke, with immense velocity."
                                        John Hunter's account of the dissection
                                        of a whale. (A small sized one.)

"The aorta of a whale is larger in the bore than the main pipe of the water-works at London Bridge, and the water roaring in its passage through that pipe is inferior in impetus and velocity to the blood gushing from the whale's heart."   *Paley's Theology.*

"The whale is a mammiferous animal without hind feet."
                                        Baron Cuvier.

"In 40 degrees south, we saw Spermacetti Whales, but did not take any till the first of May, the sea being then covered with them."
                                        Colnett's Voyage for the Purpose of
                                        Extending the Spermacetti Whale Fishery.

"In the free element beneath me swam,
 Floundered and dived, in play, in chace, in battle,
 Fishes of every color, form, and kind;
 Which language cannot paint, and mariner
 Had never seen; from dread Leviathan
 To insect millions peopling every wave:
 Gather'd in shoals immense, like floating islands,
 Led by mysterious instinct through that waste
 And trackless region, though on every side
 Assaulted by voracious enemies,
 Whales, sharks, and monsters, arm'd in front or jaw,
 With swords, saws, spiral horns, or hooked fangs."

Montgomery's Pelican Island.

"Io! Pæan! Io! sing,
 To the finny people's king.
 Not a mightier whale than this
 In the vast Atlantic is;
 Not a fatter fish than he,
 Flounders round the Polar Sea."

Charles Lamb's Triumph of the Whale.

"In the year 1690 some persons were on a high hill observing the whales spouting and sporting with each other, when one observed; there—pointing to the sea—is a green pasture where our children's grand-children will go for bread."

Obed Macy's History of Nantucket.

"I built a cottage for Susan and myself and made a gateway in the form of a Gothic Arch, by setting up a whale's jaw bones."

Hawthorne's Twice Told Tales.

"She came to bespeak a monument for her first love, who had been killed by a whale in the Pacific ocean, no less than forty years ago."

Ibid.

"No, Sir, 'tis a Right Whale," answered Tom; "I saw his spout; he threw up a pair of as pretty rainbows as a Christian would wish to look at. He's a raal oil-butt, that fellow!"   *Cooper's Pilot.*

"The papers were brought in, and we saw in the Berlin Gazette that whales had been introduced on the stage there."

Eckermann's Conversations with Goethe.

"My God! Mr. Chase, what is the matter?" I answered, "we have been stove by a whale."

> *"Narrative of the Shipwreck of the Whale Ship Essex of Nantucket, which was attacked and finally destroyed by a large Sperm Whale in the Pacific Ocean." By Owen Chase of Nantucket, first mate of said vessel. New York. 1821.*

> "A mariner sat on the shrouds one night,
>   The wind was piping free;
>   Now bright, now dimmed, was the moonlight pale,
>   And the phosphor gleamed in the wake of the whale,
>   As it floundered in the sea."

Elizabeth Oakes Smith.

"The quantity of line withdrawn from the different boats engaged in the capture of this one whale, amounted altogether to 10,440 yards or nearly six English miles."   *   *   *

"Sometimes the whale shakes its tremendous tail in the air, which, cracking like a whip, resounds to the distance of three of four miles."

Scoresby.

"Mad with the agonies he endures from these fresh attacks, the infuriated Sperm Whale rolls over and over; he rears his enormous head, and with wide expanded jaw snaps at everything around him; he rushes at the boats with his head; they are propelled before him with vast swiftness, and sometimes utterly destroyed.

*   *   *   It is a matter of great astonishment that the consideration of the habits of so interesting, and, in a commercial point of view, of so important an animal (as the Sperm Whale) should have been so entirely neglected, or should have excited so little curiosity among the numerous, and many of them competent observers, that of late years must have possessed the most abundant and the most convenient opportunities of witnessing their habitudes."

Thomas Beale's History of the Sperm Whale, 1839.

"The Cachalot" (Sperm Whale) "is not only better armed than the True Whale" (Greenland or Right Whale) "in possessing a formidable weapon at either extremity of its body, but also more frequently displays a disposition to employ those weapons offensively, and in a manner at once so artful, bold, and mischievous, as to lead to its being regarded as the most dangerous to attack of all the known species of the whale tribe."

Frederick Debell Bennett's Whaling
Voyage Round the Globe. 1840.

October 13. "There she blows," was sung out from the mast-head.
"Where away?" demanded the captain.

"Three points off the lee bow, sir."

"Raise up your wheel. Steady!"

"Steady, sir."

"Mast-head ahoy! Do you see that whale now?"

"Ay ay, sir! A shoal of Sperm Whales! There she blows! There she breaches!"

"Sing out! sing out every time!"

"Ay ay, sir! There she blows! there—there—*thar* she blows— bowes—bo-o-o-s!"

"How far off?"

"Two miles and a half."

"Thunder and lightning! so near! Call all hands!"

> *J. Ross Browne's Etchings*
> *of a Whaling Cruise.* 1846.

"The Whale-ship Globe, on board of which vessel occurred the horrid transactions we are about to relate, belonged to the island of Nantucket."   *"Narrative of the Globe Mutiny," by*
> *Lay and Hussey, survivors. A.D.* 1828.

"Being once pursued by a whale which he had wounded, he parried the assault for some time with a lance; but the furious monster at length rushed on the boat; himself and comrades only being preserved by leaping into the water when they saw the onset was inevitable."   *Missionary Journal of Tyerman and Bennet.*

"Nantucket itself," said Mr. Webster, "is a very striking and peculiar portion of the National interest. There is a population of eight or nine thousand persons, living here in the sea, adding largely every year to the National wealth by the boldest and most persevering industry."

> *Report of Daniel Webster's Speech in the U. S. Senate, on the*
> *application for the Erection of a Breakwater at Nantucket.* 1828.

"The whale fell directly over him, and probably killed him in a moment."

> *"The Whale and his Captors, or The Whaleman's Adventures and*
> *the Whale's Biography, as gathered on the Homeward Cruise*
> *of the Commodore Preble." By Rev. Henry T. Cheever.*

"If you make the least damn bit of noise," replied Samuel, "I will send you to hell."

Life of Samuel Comstock (the mutineer), by his brother, William Comstock. Another Version of the whale-ship Globe narrative.

"The voyages of the Dutch and English to the Northern Ocean, in order, if possible, to discover a passage through it to India, though they failed of their main object, laid open the haunts of the whale."   *Mc Culloch's Commercial Dictionary.*

"These things are reciprocal; the ball rebounds, only to bound forward again; for now in laying open the haunts of the whale, the whalemen seem to have indirectly hit upon new clews to that same mystic North-West Passage."   *From "Something" unpublished.*

"It is impossible to meet a whale-ship on the ocean without being struck by her mere appearance. The vessel under short sail, with look-outs at the mast-heads, eagerly scanning the wide expanse around them, has a totally different air from those engaged in a regular voyage."   *Currents and Whaling. U.S. Ex. Ex.*

"Pedestrians in the vicinity of London and elsewhere may recollect having seen large curved bones set upright in the earth, either to form arches over gateways, or entrances to alcoves, and they may perhaps have been told that these were the ribs of whales."

*Tales of a Whale Voyager
to the Arctic Ocean.*

"It was not till the boats returned from the pursuit of these whales, that the whites saw their ship in bloody possession of the savages enrolled among the crew."

*Newspaper Account of the Taking and
Retaking of the Whale-ship Hobomock.*

"It is generally well known that out of the crews of Whaling vessels (American) few ever return in the ships on board of which they departed."   *Cruise in a Whale Boat.*

"Suddenly a mighty mass emerged from the water, and shot up perpendicularly into the air. It was the whale."

Miriam Coffin or the Whale Fishermen.

"The Whale is harpooned to be sure; but bethink you, how you would manage a powerful unbroken colt, with the mere appliance of a rope tied to the root of his tail."

A Chapter on Whaling in Ribs and Trucks.

"On one occasion I saw two of these monsters (whales) probably male and female, slowly swimming, one after the other, within less than a stone's throw of the shore" (Terra Del Fuego), "over which the beech tree extended its branches."

Darwin's Voyage of a Naturalist.

" 'Stern all!' exclaimed the mate, as upon turning his head, he saw the distended jaws of a large Sperm Whale close to the head of the boat, threatening it with instant destruction;—'Stern all, for your lives!' "   *Wharton the Whale Killer.*

"So be cheery, my lads, let your hearts never fail,
   While the bold harpooneer is striking the whale!"
Nantucket Song.

"Oh, the rare old Whale, mid storm and gale
   In his ocean home will be
 A giant in might, where might is right,
   And King of the boundless sea."
Whale Song.

Chapter 1

LOOMINGS

CALL ME ISHMAEL. Some years ago—never mind how long precisely—having little or no money in my purse, and nothing particular to interest me on shore, I thought I would sail about a little and see the watery part of the world. It is a way I have of driving off the spleen, and regulating the circulation. Whenever I find myself growing grim about the mouth; whenever it is a damp, drizzly November in my soul; whenever I find myself involuntarily pausing before coffin warehouses, and bringing up the rear of every funeral I meet; and especially whenever my hypos get such an upper hand of me, that it requires a strong moral principle to prevent me from deliberately stepping into the street, and methodically knocking people's hats off—then, I account it high time to get to sea as soon as I can. This is my substitute for pistol and ball. With a philosophical flourish Cato throws himself upon his sword; I quietly take to the ship. There is nothing surprising in this. If they but knew it, almost all men in their degree, some time or other, cherish very nearly the same feelings towards the ocean with me.

There now is your insular city of the Manhattoes, belted round by wharves as Indian isles by coral reefs—commerce surrounds it with her surf. Right and left, the streets take you waterward. Its extreme down-town is the Battery, where that noble mole is washed by waves, and cooled by breezes, which a few hours previous were out of sight of land. Look at the crowds of water-gazers there.

Circumambulate the city of a dreamy Sabbath afternoon. Go from Corlears Hook to Coenties Slip, and from thence, by Whitehall, northward. What do you see?—Posted like silent sentinels all around the town, stand thousands upon thousands of mortal men fixed in ocean reveries. Some leaning against the spiles; some seated upon the pier-heads; some looking over the bulwarks of ships from China; some high aloft in the rigging, as if striving to get a still better seaward peep. But these are all landsmen; of week days pent up in lath and plaster—tied to counters, nailed to benches, clinched to desks. How then is this? Are the green fields gone? What do they here?

But look! here come more crowds, pacing straight for the water, and seemingly bound for a dive. Strange! Nothing will content them but the extremest limit of the land; loitering under the shady lee of yonder warehouses will not suffice. No. They must get just as nigh the water as they possibly can without falling in. And there they stand—miles of them— leagues. Inlanders all, they come from lanes and alleys, streets and avenues—north, east, south, and west. Yet here they all unite. Tell me, does the magnetic virtue of the needles of the compasses of all those ships attract them thither?

Once more. Say, you are in the country; in some high land of lakes. Take almost any path you please, and ten to one it carries you down in a dale, and leaves you there by a pool in the stream. There is magic in it. Let the most absent-minded of men be plunged in his deepest reveries—stand that man on his legs, set his feet a-going, and he will infallibly lead you to water, if water there be in all that region. Should you ever be athirst in the great American desert, try this experiment, if your caravan happen to be supplied with a metaphysical pro- fessor. Yes, as every one knows, meditation and water are wedded for ever.

But here is an artist. He desires to paint you the dreamiest, shadiest, quietest, most enchanting bit of romantic landscape in all the valley of the Saco. What is the chief element he employs? There stand his trees, each with a hollow trunk, as if a hermit and a crucifix were within; and here sleeps his meadow, and there sleep his cattle; and up from yonder cot- tage goes a sleepy smoke. Deep into distant woodlands winds a mazy way, reaching to overlapping spurs of mountains bathed in their hill-side blue. But though the picture lies thus tranced, and though this pine-tree shakes down its sighs like leaves upon this shepherd's head, yet all were vain, unless the shepherd's eye were fixed upon the magic stream before him. Go visit the Prairies in June, when for scores on scores of miles you wade knee-deep among Tiger-lilies—what is the one charm wanting?—Water—there is not a drop of water there! Were Niagara but a cataract of sand, would you travel your thousand miles to see it? Why did the poor poet of Tennessee, upon suddenly receiving two handfuls of silver, deliberate whether to buy him a coat, which he sadly needed, or invest his money in a pedestrian trip to Rockaway Beach? Why is almost every robust healthy boy with a robust healthy soul in him, at some time or other crazy to go to sea? Why upon your first voyage as a passenger, did you yourself feel such a mystical vibration, when first told that you and your ship were now out of sight of land? Why did the old Persians hold the sea holy? Why did the Greeks give it a separate deity, and make him the own brother of Jove? Surely all this is not without meaning. And still deeper the meaning of that story of Narcissus, who because he could not grasp the tormenting, mild image he saw in the fountain, plunged into it and was drowned. But that same image, we ourselves see in all rivers and oceans. It is the image of the ungraspable phantom of life; and this is the key to it all.

Now, when I say that I am in the habit of going to sea whenever I begin to grow hazy about the eyes, and begin to be over conscious of my lungs, I do not mean to have it inferred that I ever go to sea as a passenger. For to go as a passenger you must needs have a purse, and a purse is but a rag unless you have something in it. Besides, passengers get sea-sick—grow quarrelsome—don't sleep of nights—do not enjoy themselves much, as a general thing;—no, I never go as a passenger; nor, though I am something of a salt, do I ever go to sea as a Commodore, or a Captain, or a Cook. I abandon the glory and distinction of such offices to those who like them. For my part, I abominate all honorable respectable toils, trials, and tribulations of every kind whatsoever. It is quite as much as I can do to take care of myself, without taking care of ships, barques, brigs, schooners, and what not. And as for going as cook,—though I confess there is considerable glory in that, a cook being a sort of officer on ship-board—yet, somehow, I never fancied broiling fowls;— though once broiled, judiciously buttered, and judgmatically salted and peppered, there is no one who will speak more respectfully, not to say reverentially, of a broiled fowl than I will. It is out of the idolatrous dotings of the old Egyptians upon broiled ibis and roasted river horse, that you see the mummies of those creatures in their huge bake-houses the pyramids.

No, when I go to sea, I go as a simple sailor, right before the mast, plumb down into the forecastle, aloft there to the royal mast-head. True, they rather order me about some, and make me jump from spar to spar, like a grasshopper in a May meadow. And at first, this sort of thing is unpleasant enough. It touches one's sense of honor, particularly if you come of an old established family in the land, the Van Rensselaers, or Randolphs, or Hardicanutes. And more than all, if just previous to putting your hand into the tar-pot, you have been lording it as a country schoolmaster, making the tallest boys stand in awe of you. The transition is a keen one, I assure you, from a schoolmaster to a sailor, and requires a strong decoction of Seneca and the Stoics to enable you to grin and bear it. But even this wears off in time.

What of it, if some old hunks of a sea-captain orders me to get a broom and sweep down the decks? What does that indignity amount to, weighed, I mean, in the scales of the New Testament? Do you think the archangel Gabriel thinks anything the less of me, because I promptly and respectfully obey that old hunks in that particular instance? Who aint a slave? Tell me that. Well, then, however the old sea-captains may order me about—however they may thump and punch me about, I have the satisfaction of knowing that it is all right; that everybody else is one way or other served in much the same way—either in a physical or metaphysical point of view, that is; and so the universal thump is passed round, and all hands should rub each other's shoulder-blades, and be content.

Again, I always go to sea as a sailor, because they make a point of paying me for my trouble, whereas they never pay passengers a single penny that I ever heard of. On the contrary, passengers themselves must pay. And there is all the difference in the world between paying and being paid. The act of paying is perhaps the most uncomfortable infliction that the two orchard thieves entailed upon us. But *being paid*,—what will compare with it? The urbane activity with which a man receives money is really marvellous, considering that we so earnestly believe money to be the root of all earthly ills, and that on no account can a monied man enter heaven. Ah! how cheerfully we consign ourselves to perdition!

Finally, I always go to sea as a sailor, because of the wholesome exercise and pure air of the forecastle deck. For as in this world, head winds are far more prevalent than winds from astern (that is, if you never violate the Pythagorean maxim), so for the most part the Commodore on the quarter-deck gets his atmosphere at second hand from the sailors on the forecastle. He thinks he breathes it first; but not so. In much the same way do the commonalty lead their leaders in many other things, at the same time that the leaders little suspect it. But wherefore it was that after having repeatedly smelt the sea as a merchant sailor, I should now take it into my head to go on a whaling voyage; this the invisible police officer of the Fates, who has the constant surveillance of me, and secretly dogs me, and influences me in some unaccountable way—he can better answer than any one else. And, doubtless, my going on this whaling voyage, formed part of the grand programme of Providence that was drawn up a long time ago. It came in as a sort of brief interlude and solo between more extensive performances. I take it that this part of the bill must have run something like this:

"*Grand Contested Election for the Presidency of the United States.*
"WHALING VOYAGE BY ONE ISHMAEL.
"BLOODY BATTLE IN AFFGHANISTAN."

Though I cannot tell why it was exactly that those stage managers, the Fates, put me down for this shabby part of a whaling voyage, when others were set down for magnificent parts in high tragedies, and short and easy parts in genteel comedies, and jolly parts in farces—though I cannot tell why this was exactly; yet, now that I recall all the circumstances, I think I can see a little into the springs and motives which being cunningly presented to me under various disguises, induced me to set about performing the part I did, besides cajoling me into the delusion that it was a choice resulting from my own unbiased freewill and discriminating judgment.

Chief among these motives was the overwhelming idea of

the great whale himself. Such a portentous and mysterious monster roused all my curiosity. Then the wild and distant seas where he rolled his island bulk; the undeliverable, name-less perils of the whale; these, with all the attending marvels of a thousand Patagonian sights and sounds, helped to sway me to my wish. With other men, perhaps, such things would not have been inducements; but as for me, I am tormented with an everlasting itch for things remote. I love to sail for-bidden seas, and land on barbarous coasts. Not ignoring what is good, I am quick to perceive a horror, and could still be social with it—would they let me—since it is but well to be on friendly terms with all the inmates of the place one lodges in.

By reason of these things, then, the whaling voyage was welcome; the great flood-gates of the wonder-world swung open, and in the wild conceits that swayed me to my purpose, two and two there floated into my inmost soul, endless processions of the whale, and, midmost of them all, one grand hooded phantom, like a snow hill in the air.

Chapter 2

THE CARPET-BAG

I STUFFED a shirt or two into my old carpet-bag, tucked it under my arm, and started for Cape Horn and the Pacific. Quitting the good city of old Manhatto, I duly arrived in New Bedford. It was on a Saturday night in December. Much was I disappointed upon learning that the little packet for Nantucket had already sailed, and that no way of reaching that place would offer, till the following Monday.

As most young candidates for the pains and penalties of whaling stop at this same New Bedford, thence to embark on their voyage, it may as well be related that I, for one, had no idea of so doing. For my mind was made up to sail in no other than a Nantucket craft, because there was a fine, boisterous something about everything connected with that famous old island, which amazingly pleased me. Besides though New Bedford has of late been gradually monopolizing the business of whaling, and though in this matter poor old Nantucket is now much behind her, yet Nantucket was her great original—the Tyre of this Carthage;—the place where the first dead American whale was stranded. Where else but from Nantucket did those aboriginal whalemen, the Red-Men, first sally out in canoes to give chase to the Leviathan? And where but from Nantucket, too, did that first adventurous little sloop put forth, partly laden with imported cobble-stones—so goes the story—to throw at the whales, in order to discover when they were nigh enough to risk a harpoon from the bowsprit?

Now having a night, a day, and still another night following before me in New Bedford, ere I could embark for my destined port, it became a matter of concernment where I was to eat and sleep meanwhile. It was a very dubious-looking, nay, a very dark and dismal night, bitingly cold and cheerless. I knew no one in the place. With anxious grapnels I had sounded my pocket, and only brought up a few pieces of silver,—So, wherever you go, Ishmael, said I to myself, as I stood in the middle of a dreary street shouldering my bag, and comparing the gloom towards the north with the darkness towards the south—wherever in your wisdom you may conclude to lodge for the night, my dear Ishmael, be sure to inquire the price, and don't be too particular.

With halting steps I paced the streets, and passed the sign of "The Crossed Harpoons"—but it looked too expensive and jolly there. Further on, from the bright red windows of the "Sword-Fish Inn," there came such fervent rays, that it seemed to have melted the packed snow and ice from before the house, for everywhere else the congealed frost lay ten inches thick in a hard, asphaltic pavement,—rather weary for me, when I struck my foot against the flinty projections, because from hard, remorseless service the soles of my boots were in a most miserable plight. Too expensive and jolly, again thought I, pausing one moment to watch the broad glare in the street, and hear the sounds of the tinkling glasses within. But go on, Ishmael, said I at last; don't you hear? get away from before the door; your patched boots are stopping the way. So on I went. I now by instinct followed the streets that took me waterward, for there, doubtless, were the cheapest, if not the cheeriest inns.

Such dreary streets! blocks of blackness, not houses, on either hand, and here and there a candle, like a candle moving about in a tomb. At this hour of the night, of the last day of the week, that quarter of the town proved all but deserted. But presently I came to a smoky light proceeding from a low, wide building, the door of which stood invitingly open. It had a careless look, as if it were meant for the uses of the public; so, entering, the first thing I did was to stumble over an ash-box in the porch. Ha! thought I, ha, as the flying particles almost choked me, are these ashes from that destroyed city, Gomorrah? But "The Crossed Harpoons," and "The Sword-Fish?"—this, then, must needs be the sign of "The Trap." However, I picked myself up and hearing a loud voice within, pushed on and opened a second, interior door.

It seemed the great Black Parliament sitting in Tophet. A hundred black faces turned round in their rows to peer; and beyond, a black Angel of Doom was beating a book in a pulpit. It was a negro church; and the preacher's text was about the blackness of darkness, and the weeping and wailing and teeth-gnashing there. Ha, Ishmael, muttered I, backing out, Wretched entertainment at the sign of "The Trap!"

Moving on, I at last came to a dim sort of out-hanging light not far from the docks, and heard a forlorn creaking in the air; and looking up, saw a swinging sign over the door with a white painting upon it, faintly representing a tall straight jet of misty spray, and these words underneath— "The Spouter-Inn:—Peter Coffin."

Coffin?—Spouter?—Rather ominous in that particular connexion, thought I. But it is a common name in Nantucket, they say, and I suppose this Peter here is an emigrant from there. As the light looked so dim, and the place, for the time, looked quiet enough, and the dilapidated little wooden house itself looked as if it might have been carted here from the ruins of some burnt district, and as the swinging sign had a poverty-stricken sort of creak to it, I thought that here was the very spot for cheap lodgings, and the best of pea coffee.

It was a queer sort of place—a gable-ended old house, one side palsied as it were, and leaning over sadly. It stood on a sharp bleak corner, where that tempestuous wind Euroclydon kept up a worse howling than ever it did about poor Paul's tossed craft. Euroclydon, nevertheless, is a mighty pleasant zephyr to any one in-doors, with his feet on the hob quietly toasting for bed. "In judging of that tempestuous wind called Euroclydon," says an old writer—of whose works I possess the only copy extant—"it maketh a marvellous difference, whether thou lookest out at it from a glass window where the frost is all on the outside, or whether thou observest it from that sashless window, where the frost is on both sides, and of which the wight Death is the only glazier." True enough, thought I, as this passage occurred to my mind—old black-letter, thou reasonest well. Yes, these eyes are windows, and this body of mine is the house. What a pity they didn't stop up the chinks and the crannies though, and thrust in a little lint here and there. But it's too late to make any improve-ments now. The universe is finished; the copestone is on, and the chips were carted off a million years ago. Poor Lazarus there, chattering his teeth against the curbstone for his pillow, and shaking off his tatters with his shiverings, he might plug up both ears with rags, and put a corn-cob into his mouth, and yet that would not keep out the tempestuous Euroclydon. Euroclydon! says old Dives, in his red silken wrapper (he had a redder one afterwards)—pooh, pooh! What a fine frosty night; how Orion glitters; what northern lights! Let them talk of their oriental summer climes of everlasting conservatories; give me the privilege of making my own summer with my own coals.

But what thinks Lazarus? Can he warm his blue hands by holding them up to the grand northern lights? Would not Lazarus rather be in Sumatra than here? Would he not far rather lay him down lengthwise along the line of the equator; yea, ye gods! go down to the fiery pit itself, in order to keep out this frost?

Now, that Lazarus should lie stranded there on the curbstone before the door of Dives, this is more wonderful than that an iceberg should be moored to one of the Moluccas. Yet Dives himself, he too lives like a Czar in an ice palace made of frozen sighs, and being a president of a temperance society, he only drinks the tepid tears of orphans.

But no more of this blubbering now, we are going a-whaling, and there is plenty of that yet to come. Let us scrape the ice from our frosted feet, and see what sort of a place this "Spouter" may be.

Chapter 3

ENTERING that gable-ended Spouter-Inn, you found yourself in a wide, low, straggling entry with old-fashioned wainscots, reminding one of the bulwarks of some condemned old craft. On one side hung a very large oil-painting so thoroughly besmoked, and every way defaced, that in the unequal cross-lights by which you viewed it, it was only by diligent study and a series of systematic visits to it, and careful inquiry of the neighbors, that you could any way arrive at an understanding of its purpose. Such unaccountable masses of shades and shadows, that at first you almost thought some ambitious young artist, in the time of the New England hags, had endeavored to delineate chaos bewitched. But by dint of much and earnest contemplation, and oft repeated ponderings, and especially by throwing open the little window towards the back of the entry, you at last came to the conclusion that such an idea, however wild, might not be altogether unwarranted.

But what most puzzled and confounded you was a long, limber, portentous, black mass of something hovering in the centre of the picture over three blue, dim, perpendicular lines floating in a nameless yeast. A boggy, soggy, squitchy picture truly, enough to drive a nervous man distracted. Yet was there a sort of indefinite, half-attained, unimaginable sublimity about it that fairly froze you to it, till you involuntarily took an oath with yourself to find out what that marvellous painting meant. Ever and anon a bright, but, alas, deceptive idea would dart you through.—It's the Black Sea in a midnight gale.—It's the unnatural combat of the four primal elements.—It's a blasted heath.—It's a Hyperborean winter scene.—It's the breaking-up of the ice-bound stream of Time. But at last all these fancies yielded to that one portentous something in the picture's midst. *That* once found out, and all the rest were plain. But stop; does it not bear a faint resemblance to a gigantic fish? even the great leviathan himself?

In fact, the artist's design seemed this: a final theory of my own, partly based upon the aggregated opinions of many aged persons with whom I conversed upon the subject. The picture represents a Cape-Horner in a great hurricane; the half-foundered ship weltering there with its three dismantled masts alone visible; and an exasperated whale, purposing to spring clean over the craft, is in the enormous act of impaling himself upon the three mast-heads.

The opposite wall of this entry was hung all over with a heathenish array of monstrous clubs and spears. Some were thickly set with glittering teeth resembling ivory saws; others were tufted with knots of human hair; and one was sickle-shaped, with a vast handle sweeping round like the segment made in the new-mown grass by a long-armed mower. You shuddered as you gazed, and wondered what monstrous cannibal and savage could ever have gone a death-harvesting with such a hacking, horrifying implement. Mixed with these were rusty old whaling lances and harpoons all broken and deformed. Some were storied weapons. With this once long lance, now wildly elbowed, fifty years ago did Nathan Swain kill fifteen whales between a sunrise and a sunset. And that harpoon—so like a corkscrew now—was flung in Javan seas, and run away with by a whale, years afterwards slain off the Cape of Blanco. The original iron entered nigh the tail, and, like a restless needle sojourning in the body of a man, travelled full forty feet, and at last was found imbedded in the hump.

Crossing this dusky entry, and on through yon low-arched way—cut through what in old times must have been a great central chimney with fire-places all round—you enter the public room. A still duskier place is this, with such low ponderous beams above, and such old wrinkled planks beneath, that you would almost fancy you trod some old craft's cockpits, especially of such a howling night, when this corner-anchored old ark rocked so furiously. On one side stood a long, low, shelf-like table covered with cracked glass cases, filled with dusty rarities gathered from this wide world's remotest nooks. Projecting from the further angle of the room stands a dark-looking den—the bar—a rude attempt at a right whale's head. Be that how it may, there stands the vast arched bone of the whale's jaw, so wide, a coach might almost drive beneath it. Within are shabby shelves, ranged round with old decanters, bottles, flasks; and in those jaws of swift destruction, like another cursed Jonah (by which name indeed they called him), bustles a little withered old man, who, for their money, dearly sells the sailors deliriums and death.

Abominable are the tumblers into which he pours his poison. Though true cylinders without—within, the villanous green goggling glasses deceitfully tapered downwards to a cheating bottom. Parallel meridians rudely pecked into the glass, surround these footpads' goblets. Fill to *this* mark, and your charge is but a penny; to *this* a penny more; and so on to the full glass—the Cape Horn measure, which you may gulph down for a shilling.

Upon entering the place I found a number of young seamen gathered about a table, examining by a dim light divers specimens of *skrimshander*. I sought the landlord, and telling him I desired to be accommodated with a room, received for answer that his house was full—not a bed unoccupied. "But avast," he added, tapping his forehead, "you haint no objections to sharing a harpooneer's blanket, have ye? I s'pose you are goin' a whalin', so you'd better get used to that sort of thing."

I told him that I never liked to sleep two in a bed; that if I should ever do so, it would depend upon who the harpooneer might be, and that if he (the landlord) really had no other place for me, and the harpooneer was not decidedly objectionable, why rather than wander further about a strange town on so bitter a night, I would put up with the half of any decent man's blanket.

"I thought so. All right; take a seat. Supper?—you want supper? Supper 'll be ready directly."

I sat down on an old wooden settle, carved all over like a bench on the Battery. At one end a ruminating tar was still further adorning it with his jack-knife, stooping over and diligently working away at the space between his legs. He was trying his hand at a ship under full sail, but he didn't make much headway, I thought.

At last some four or five of us were summoned to our meal in an adjoining room. It was cold as Iceland—no fire at all—

the landlord said he couldn't afford it. Nothing but two dismal tallow candles, each in a winding sheet. We were fain to button up our monkey jackets, and hold to our lips cups of scalding tea with our half frozen fingers. But the fare was of the most substantial kind—not only meat and potatoes, but dumplings; good heavens! dumplings for supper! One young fellow in a green box coat, addressed himself to these dumplings in a most direful manner.

"My boy," said the landlord, "you'll have the nightmare to a dead sartainty."

"Landlord," I whispered, "that aint the harpooneer, is it?"

"Oh, no," said he, looking a sort of diabolically funny, "the harpooner is a dark complexioned chap. He never eats dumplings, he don't—he eats nothing but steaks, and likes 'em rare."

"The devil he does," says I. "Where is that harpooneer? Is he here?"

"He'll be here afore long," was the answer.

I could not help it, but I began to feel suspicious of this "dark complexioned" harpooneer. At any rate, I made up my mind that if it so turned out that we should sleep together, he must undress and get into bed before I did.

Supper over, the company went back to the bar-room, when, knowing not what else to do with myself, I resolved to spend the rest of the evening as a looker on.

Presently a rioting noise was heard without. Starting up, the landlord cried, "That's the Grampus's crew. I seed her reported in the offing this morning; a four years' voyage, and a full ship. Hurrah, boys; now we'll have the latest news from the Feegees."

A tramping of sea boots was heard in the entry; the door was flung open, and in rolled a wild set of mariners enough. Enveloped in their shaggy watch coats, and with their heads muffled in woollen comforters, all bedarned and ragged, and their beards stiff with icicles, they seemed an eruption of bears from Labrador. They had just landed from their boat, and this was the first house they entered. No wonder, then, that they made a straight wake for the whale's mouth—the bar—when the wrinkled little old Jonah, there officiating, soon poured them out brimmers all round. One complained of a bad cold in his head, upon which Jonah mixed him a pitch-like potion of gin and molasses, which he swore was a sovereign cure for all colds and catarrhs whatsoever, never mind of how long standing, or whether caught off the coast of Labrador, or on the weather side of an ice-island.

The liquor soon mounted into their heads, as it generally does even with the arrantest topers newly landed from sea, and they began capering about most obstreperously.

I observed, however, that one of them held somewhat aloof, and though he seemed desirous not to spoil the hilarity of his shipmates by his own sober face, yet upon the whole he refrained from making as much noise as the rest. This man interested me at once; and since the sea-gods had ordained that he should soon become my shipmate (though but a sleeping-partner one, so far as this narrative is concerned), I will here venture upon a little description of him. He stood full six feet in height, with noble shoulders, and a chest like a coffer-dam. I have seldom seen such brawn in a man. His face was deeply brown and burnt, making his white teeth dazzling by the contrast; while in the deep shadows of his eyes floated some reminiscences that did not seem to give him much joy. His voice at once announced that he was a Southerner, and from his fine stature, I thought he must be one of those tall mountaineers from the Alleganian Ridge in Virginia. When the revelry of his companions had mounted to its height, this man slipped away unobserved, and I saw no more of him till he became my comrade on the sea. In a few minutes, however, he was missed by his shipmates, and being, it seems, for some reason a huge favorite with them, they raised a cry of "Bulkington! Bulkington! where's Bulkington?" and darted out of the house in pursuit of him.

It was now about nine o'clock, and the room seeming almost supernaturally quiet after these orgies, I began to congratulate myself upon a little plan that had occurred to me just previous to the entrance of the seamen.

No man prefers to sleep two in a bed. In fact, you would a good deal rather not sleep with your own brother. I don't know how it is, but people like to be private when they are sleeping. And when it comes to sleeping with an unknown stranger, in a strange inn, in a strange town, and that stranger a harpooneer, then your objections indefinitely multiply. Nor was there any earthly reason why I as a sailor should sleep two in a bed, more than anybody else; for sailors no more sleep two in a bed at sea, than bachelor Kings do ashore. To be sure they all sleep together in one apartment, but you have your own hammock, and cover yourself with your own blanket, and sleep in your own skin.

The more I pondered over this harpooneer, the more I abominated the thought of sleeping with him. It was fair to presume that being a harpooneer, his linen or woollen, as the case might be, would not be of the tidiest, certainly none of the finest. I began to twitch all over. Besides, it was getting late, and any decent harpooneer ought to be home and going bedwards. Suppose now, he should tumble in upon me at midnight—how could I tell from what vile hole he had been coming?

"Landlord! I've changed my mind about that harpooneer. —I shan't sleep with him. I'll try the bench here."

"Just as you please; I'm sorry I cant spare ye a table-cloth for a mattress, and it's a plaguy rough board here"—feeling of the knots and notches. "But wait a bit, Skrimshander; I've got a carpenter's plane there in the bar—wait, I say, and I'll make ye snug enough." So saying he procured the plane; and with his old silk handkerchief first dusting the bench, vigorously set to planing away at my bed, the while grinning like an ape. The shavings flew right and left; till at last the plane-iron came bump against an indestructible knot. The landlord was near spraining his wrist, and I told him for heaven's sake to quit—the bed was soft enough to suit me, and I did not know how all the planing in the world could make eider down of a pine plank. So gathering up the shavings with another grin, and throwing them into the great stove in the middle of the room, he went about his business, and left me in a brown study.

I now took the measure of the bench, and found that it was a foot too short; but that could be mended with a chair. But it was a foot too narrow, and the other bench in the room was about four inches higher than the planed one—so there was no yoking them. I then placed the first bench lengthwise along the only clear space against the wall, leaving a little interval between, for my back to settle down in. But I soon found that there came such a draught of cold air over me from under the sill of the window, that this plan would never do at all, especially as another current from the rickety door met the one from the window, and both together formed a series of small whirlwinds in the immediate vicinity of the spot where I had thought to spend the night.

The devil fetch that harpooneer, thought I, but stop, couldn't I steal a march on him—bolt his door inside, and jump into his bed, not to be wakened by the most violent knockings? It seemed no bad idea; but upon second thoughts I dismissed it. For who could tell but what the next morning, so soon as I popped out of the room, the harpooneer might be standing in the entry, all ready to knock me down!

Still, looking round me again, and seeing no possible chance of spending a sufferable night unless in some other person's bed, I began to think that after all I might be cherishing unwarrantable prejudices against this unknown harpooneer. Thinks I, I'll wait awhile; he must be dropping in before long. I'll have a good look at him then, and perhaps we may become jolly good bedfellows after all—there's no telling.

But though the other boarders kept coming in by ones, twos, and threes, and going to bed, yet no sign of my harpooneer.

"Landlord!" said I, "what sort of a chap is he—does he always keep such late hours?" It was now hard upon twelve o'clock.

The landlord chuckled again with his lean chuckle, and seemed to be mightily tickled at something beyond my comprehension. "No," he answered, "generally he's an airley bird—airley to bed and airley to rise—yes, he's the bird what catches the worm.—But to-night he went out a peddling, you see, and I don't see what on airth keeps him so late, unless, may be, he can't sell his head."

"Can't sell his head?—What sort of a bamboozling story is this you are telling me?" getting into a towering rage. "Do you pretend to say, landlord, that this harpooneer is actually engaged this blessed Saturday night, or rather Sunday morning, in peddling his head around this town?"

"That's precisely it," said the landlord, "and I told him he couldn't sell it here, the market's overstocked."

"With what?" shouted I.

"With heads to be sure; ain't there too many heads in the world?"

"I tell you what it is, landlord," said I, quite calmly, "you'd better stop spinning that yarn to me—I'm not green."

"May be not," taking out a stick and whittling a toothpick, "but I rayther guess you'll be done *brown* if that ere harpooneer hears you a slanderin' his head."

"I'll break it for him," said I, now flying into a passion again at this unaccountable farrago of the landlord's.

"It's broke a'ready," said he.

"Broke," said I—"*broke*, do you mean?"

"Sartain, and that's the very reason he can't sell it, I guess."

"Landlord," said I, going up to him as cool as Mt. Hecla in a snow storm,—"landlord, stop whittling. You and I must understand one another, and that too without delay. I come to your house and want a bed; you tell me you can only give me half a one; that the other half belongs to a certain harpooneer. And about this harpooneer, whom I have not yet seen, you persist in telling me the most mystifying and exasperating stories, tending to beget in me an uncomfortable feeling towards the man whom you design for my bedfellow—a sort of connexion, landlord, which is an intimate and confidential one in the highest degree. I now demand of you to speak out and tell me who and what this harpooneer is, and whether I shall be in all respects safe to spend the night with him. And in the first place, you will be so good as to unsay that story about selling his head, which if true I take to be good evidence that this harpooneer is stark mad, and I've no idea of sleeping with a madman; and you, sir, *you* I mean, landlord, *you*, sir, by trying to induce me to do so knowingly, would thereby render yourself liable to a criminal prosecution."

"Wall," said the landlord, fetching a long breath, "that's a purty long sarmon for a chap that rips a little now and then. But be easy, be easy, this here harpooneer I have been tellin' you of has just arrived from the south seas, where he bought up a lot of 'balmed New Zealand heads (great curios, you know), and he's sold all on 'em but one, and that one he's trying to sell to-night, cause to-morrow's Sunday, and it would not do to be sellin' human heads about the streets when folks is goin' to churches. He wanted to, last Sunday, but I stopped him just as he was goin' out of the door with four heads strung on a string, for all the airth like a string of inions."

This account cleared up the otherwise unaccountable mystery, and showed that the landlord, after all, had had no idea of fooling me—but at the same time what could I think of a harpooneer who stayed out of a Saturday night clean into the holy Sabbath, engaged in such a cannibal business as selling the heads of dead idolators?

"Depend upon it, landlord, that harpooneer is a dangerous man."

"He pays reg'lar," was the rejoinder. "But come, it's getting dreadful late, you had better be turning flukes—it's a nice bed: Sal and me slept in that ere bed the night we were spliced. There's plenty room for two to kick about in that bed; it's an almighty big bed that. Why, afore we give it up, Sal used to put our Sam and little Johnny in the foot of it. But I got a dreaming and sprawling about one night, and somehow, Sam got pitched on the floor, and came near breaking his arm. Arter that, Sal said it wouldn't do. Come along here, I'll give ye a glim in a jiffy;" and so saying he lighted a candle and held it towards me, offering to lead the way. But I stood irresolute; when looking at a clock in the corner, he exclaimed "I vum it's Sunday—you won't see that harpooneer to-night; he's come to anchor somewhere—come along then; *do* come; *won't* ye come?"

I considered the matter a moment, and then up stairs we went, and I was ushered into a small room, cold as a clam, and furnished, sure enough, with a prodigious bed, almost big enough indeed for any four harpooneers to sleep abreast.

"There," said the landlord, placing the candle on a crazy old sea chest that did double duty as a wash-stand and centre table; "there, make yourself comfortable now, and good night to ye." I turned round from eyeing the bed, but he had disappeared.

Folding back the counterpane, I stooped over the bed. Though none of the most elegant, it yet stood the scrutiny tolerably well. I then glanced round the room; and besides the bedstead and centre table, could see no other furniture belonging to the place, but a rude shelf, the four walls, and a papered fireboard representing a man striking a whale. Of things not properly belonging to the room, there was a hammock lashed up, and thrown upon the floor in one corner; also a large seaman's bag, containing the harpooneer's wardrobe no doubt, in lieu of a land trunk. Likewise, there was a parcel of outlandish bone fish hooks on the shelf over the fireplace, and a tall harpoon standing at the head of the bed.

But what is this on the chest? I took it up, and held it close to the light, and felt it, and smelt it, and tried every way possible to arrive at some satisfactory conclusion concerning it. I can compare it to nothing but a large door mat, ornamented at the edges with little tinkling tags something like the stained porcupine quills round an Indian moccasin. There was a hole or slit in the middle of this mat, the same as in South American ponchos. But could it be possible that any sober harpooneer would get into a door mat, and parade the streets of any Christian town in that sort of guise? I put it on, to try it, and it weighed me down like a hamper, being uncommonly shaggy and thick, and I thought a little damp, as though this mysterious harpooneer had been wearing it of a rainy day. I went up in it to a bit of glass stuck against the wall, and I never saw such a sight in my life. I tore myself out of it in such a hurry that I gave myself a kink in the neck.

I sat down on the side of the bed, and commenced thinking about this head-peddling harpooneer, and his door mat. After thinking some time on the bed-side, I got up and took off my monkey jacket, and then stood in the middle of the room thinking. I then took off my coat, and thought a little more in my shirt sleeves. But beginning to feel very cold now, half undressed as I was, and remembering what the landlord said about the harpooneer's not coming home at all that night, it being so very late, I made no more ado, but jumped out of my pantaloons and boots, and then blowing out the light tumbled into bed, and commended myself to the care of heaven.

Whether that mattress was stuffed with corn-cobs or broken crockery, there is no telling, but I rolled about a good deal, and could not sleep for a long time. At last I slid off into a light doze, and had pretty nearly made a good offing towards the land of Nod, when I heard a heavy footfall in the passage, and saw a glimmer of light come into the room from under the door.

Lord save me, thinks I, that must be the harpooneer, the infernal head-peddler. But I lay perfectly still, and resolved not to say a word till spoken to. Holding a light in one hand, and that identical New Zealand head in the other, the stranger entered the room, and without looking towards the bed, placed his candle a good way off from me on the floor in one corner, and then began working away at the knotted cords of the large bag I before spoke of as being in the room. I was all eagerness to see his face, but he kept it averted for some time while employed in unlacing the bag's mouth. This accomplished, however, he turned round—when, good heavens! what a sight! Such a face! It was of a dark, purplish, yellow color, here and there stuck over with large, blackish looking squares. Yes, it's just as I thought, he's a terrible bed-fellow; he's been in a fight, got dreadfully cut, and here he is, just from the surgeon. But at that moment he chanced to turn his face so towards the light, that I plainly saw they could not be sticking-plasters at all, those black squares on his cheeks. They were stains of some sort or other. At first I knew not what to make of this; but soon an inkling of the truth occurred to me. I remembered a story of a white man—a whaleman too—who, falling among the cannibals, had been tattooed by them. I concluded that this harpooneer, in the course of his distant voyages, must have met with a similar adventure. And what is it, thought I, after all! It's only his outside; a man can be honest in any sort of skin. But then, what to make of his unearthly complexion, that part of it, I mean, lying round about, and completely independent of the squares of tattooing. To be sure, it might be nothing but a good coat of tropical tanning; but I never heard of a hot sun's tanning a white man into a purplish yellow one. However, I had never been in the South Seas; and perhaps the sun there produced these extraordinary effects upon the skin. Now, while all these ideas were passing through me like lightning, this harpooneer never noticed me at all. But, after some difficulty having opened his bag, he commenced fumbling in it, and presently pulled out a sort of tomahawk, and a seal-skin wallet with the hair on. Placing these on the old chest in the middle of the room, he then took the New Zealand head—a ghastly thing enough—and crammed it down into the bag. He now took off his hat—a new beaver hat—when I came nigh singing out with fresh surprise. There was no hair on his head—none to speak of at least—nothing but a small scalp-knot twisted up on his forehead. His bald purplish head now looked for all the world like a mildewed skull. Had not the stranger stood between me and the door, I would have bolted out of it quicker than ever I bolted a dinner.

Even as it was, I thought something of slipping out of the window, but it was the second floor back. I am no coward, but what to make of this head-peddling purple rascal altogether passed my comprehension. Ignorance is the parent of fear, and being completely nonplussed and confounded about the stranger, I confess I was now as much afraid of him as if it was the devil himself who had thus broken into my room at the dead of night. In fact, I was so afraid of him that I was not game enough just then to address him, and demand a satisfactory answer concerning what seemed inexplicable in him.

Meanwhile, he continued the business of undressing, and at last showed his chest and arms. As I live, these covered parts of him were checkered with the same squares as his face; his back, too, was all over the same dark squares; he seemed to have been in a Thirty Years' War, and just escaped from it with a sticking-plaster shirt. Still more, his very legs were marked, as if a parcel of dark green frogs were running up the trunks of young palms. It was now quite plain that he must be some abominable savage or other shipped aboard of a whaleman in the South Seas, and so landed in this Christian country. I quaked to think of it. A peddler of heads too—perhaps the heads of his own brothers. He might take a fancy to mine—heavens! look at that tomahawk!

But there was no time for shuddering, for now the savage went about something that completely fascinated my attention, and convinced me that he must indeed be a heathen. Going to his heavy grego, or wrapall, or dreadnaught, which he had previously hung on a chair, he fumbled in the pockets, and produced at length a curious little deformed image with a hunch on its back, and exactly the color of a three days' old Congo baby. Remembering the embalmed head, at first I almost thought that this black manikin was a real baby preserved in some similar manner. But seeing that it was not at all limber, and that it glistened a good deal like polished ebony, I concluded that it must be nothing but a wooden idol, which indeed it proved to be. For now the savage goes up to the empty fire-place, and removing the papered fire-board, sets up this little hunchbacked image, like a tenpin, between the andirons. The chimney jambs and all the bricks inside were very sooty, so that I thought this fire-place made a very appropriate little shrine or chapel for his Congo idol.

I now screwed my eyes hard towards the half hidden image, feeling but ill at ease meantime—to see what was next to follow. First he takes about a double handful of shavings out of his grego pocket, and places them carefully before the idol; then laying a bit of ship biscuit on top and applying the flame from the lamp, he kindled the shavings into a sacrificial blaze. Presently, after many hasty snatches into the fire, and still hastier withdrawals of his fingers (whereby he seemed to be scorching them badly), he at last succeeded in drawing out the biscuit; then blowing off the heat and ashes a little, he made a polite offer of it to the little negro. But the little devil did not seem to fancy such dry sort of fare at all; he never moved his lips. All these strange antics were accompanied by still stranger guttural noises from the devotee, who seemed to be praying in a sing-song or else singing some pagan psalmody or other, during which his face twitched about in the most unnatural manner. At last extinguishing the fire, he took the idol up very unceremoniously, and bagged it again in his grego pocket as carelessly as if he were a sportsman bagging a dead woodcock.

All these queer proceedings increased my uncomfortableness, and seeing him now exhibiting strong symptoms of concluding his business operations, and jumping into bed with me, I thought it was high time, now or never, before the light was put out, to break the spell in which I had so long been bound.

But the interval I spent in deliberating what to say, was a fatal one. Taking up his tomahawk from the table, he examined the head of it for an instant, and then holding it to the light, with his mouth at the handle, he puffed out great clouds of tobacco smoke. The next moment the light was extinguished, and this wild cannibal, tomahawk between his teeth, sprang into bed with me. I sang out, I could not help it now; and giving a sudden grunt of astonishment he began feeling me.

Stammering out something, I knew not what, I rolled away from him against the wall, and then conjured him, whoever or whatever he might be, to keep quiet, and let me get up and light the lamp again. But his guttural responses satisfied me at once that he but ill comprehended my meaning.

"Who-e debel you?"—he at last said—"you no speak-e, dam-me, I kill-e." And so saying the lighted tomahawk began flourishing about me in the dark.

"Landlord, for God's sake, Peter Coffin!" shouted I. "Landlord! Watch! Coffin! Angels! save me!"

"Speak-e! tell-ee me who-ee be, or dam-me, I kill-e!" again growled the cannibal, while his horrid flourishings of the tomahawk scattered the hot tobacco ashes about me till I thought my linen would get on fire. But thank heaven, at that moment the landlord came into the room light in hand, and leaping from the bed I ran up to him.

"Don't be afraid now," said he, grinning again. "Queequeg here wouldn't harm a hair of your head."

"Stop your grinning," shouted I, "and why didn't you tell me that that infernal harpooneer was a cannibal?"

"I thought ye know'd it;—didn't I tell ye, he was a peddlin' heads around town?—but turn flukes again and go to sleep. Queequeg, look here—you sabbee me, I sabbee you—this man sleepe you—you sabbee?"—

"Me sabbee plenty"—grunted Queequeg, puffing away at his pipe and sitting up in bed.

"You gettee in," he added, motioning to me with his tomahawk, and throwing the clothes to one side. He really did this in not only a civil but a really kind and charitable way. I stood looking at him a moment. For all his tattooings he was on the whole a clean, comely looking cannibal. What's all this fuss I have been making about, thought I to myself—the man's a human being just as I am: he has just as much reason to fear me, as I have to be afraid of him. Better sleep with a sober cannibal than a drunken Christian.

"Landlord," said I, "tell him to stash his tomahawk there, or pipe, or whatever you call it; tell him to stop smoking, in short, and I will turn in with him. But I don't fancy having a man smoking in bed with me. It's dangerous. Besides, I aint insured."

This being told to Queequeg, he at once complied, and again politely motioned me to get into bed—rolling over to one side as much as to say—I wont touch a leg of ye.

"Good night, landlord," said I, "you may go."

I turned in, and never slept better in my life.

Chapter 4

THE COUNTERPANE

UPON WAKING next morning about daylight, I found Queequeg's arm thrown over me in the most loving and affectionate manner. You had almost thought I had been his wife. The counterpane was of patchwork, full of odd little parti-colored squares and triangles; and this arm of his tattooed all over with an interminable Cretan labyrinth of a figure, no two parts of which were of one precise shade—owing I suppose to his keeping his arm at sea unmethodically in sun and shade, his shirt sleeves irregularly rolled up at various times—this same arm of his, I say, looked for all the world like a strip of that same patchwork quilt. Indeed, partly lying on it as the arm did when I first awoke, I could hardly tell it from the quilt, they so blended their hues together; and it was only by the sense of weight and pressure that I could tell that Queequeg was hugging me.

My sensations were strange. Let me try to explain them. When I was a child, I well remember a somewhat similar circumstance that befell me; whether it was a reality or a dream, I never could entirely settle. The circumstance was this. I had been cutting up some caper or other—I think it was trying to crawl up the chimney, as I had seen a little sweep do a few days previous; and my stepmother who, somehow or other, was all the time whipping me, or sending me to bed supperless,—my mother dragged me by the legs out of the chimney and packed me off to bed, though it was only two o'clock in the afternoon of the 21st June, the longest day in the year in our hemisphere. I felt dreadfully. But there was no help for it, so up stairs I went to my little room in the third floor, undressed myself as slowly as possible so as to kill time, and with a bitter sigh got between the sheets.

I lay there dismally calculating that sixteen entire hours must elapse before I could hope for a resurrection. Sixteen hours in bed! the small of my back ached to think of it. And it was so light too; the sun shining in at the window, and a great rattling of coaches in the streets, and the sound of gay voices all over the house. I felt worse and worse—at last I got up, dressed, and softly going down in my stockinged feet, sought out my stepmother, and suddenly threw myself at her feet, beseeching her as a particular favor to give me a good slippering for my misbehavior; anything indeed but condemning me to lie abed such an unendurable length of time. But she was the best and most conscientious of stepmothers, and back I had to go to my room. For several hours I lay there broad awake, feeling a great deal worse than I have ever done since, even from the greatest subsequent misfortunes. At last I must have fallen into a troubled nightmare of a doze; and slowly waking from it—half steeped in dreams—I opened my eyes, and the before sun-lit room was now wrapped in outer darkness. Instantly I felt a shock running through all my frame; nothing was to be seen, and nothing was to be heard; but a supernatural hand seemed placed in mine. My arm hung over the counterpane, and the nameless, unimaginable, silent form or phantom, to which the hand belonged, seemed closely seated by my bedside. For what seemed ages piled on ages, I lay there, frozen with the most awful fears, not daring to drag away my hand; yet ever thinking that if I could but stir it one single inch, the horrid spell would be broken. I knew not how this consciousness at last glided away from me; but waking in the morning, I shuddceringly remembered it all, and for days and weeks and months afterwards I lost myself in confounding attempts to explain the mystery. Nay, to this very hour, I often puzzle myself with it.

Now, take away the awful fear, and my sensations at feeling the supernatural hand in mine were very similar, in their strangeness, to those which I experienced on waking up and seeing Queequeg's pagan arm thrown round me. But at length all the past night's events soberly recurred, one by one, in fixed reality, and then I lay only alive to the comical predicament. For though I tried to move his arm—unlock his bridegroom clasp—yet, sleeping as he was, he still hugged me tightly, as though naught but death should part us twain. I now strove to rouse him—"Queequeg!"—but his only answer was a snore. I then rolled over, my neck feeling as if it were in a horse-collar; and suddenly felt a slight scratch. Throwing aside the counterpane, there lay the tomahawk sleeping by the savage's side, as if it were a hatchet-faced baby. A pretty pickle, truly, thought I; abed here in a strange house in the broad day, with a cannibal and a tomahawk! "Queequeg!—in the name of goodness, Queequeg, wake!" At length, by dint of much wriggling, and loud and incessant expostulations upon the unbecomingness of his hugging a fellow male in that matrimonial sort of style, I succeeded in extracting a grunt; and presently, he drew back his arm, shook himself all over like a Newfoundland dog just from the water, and sat up in bed, stiff as a pike-staff, looking at me, and rubbing his eyes as if he did not altogether remember how I came to be there, though a dim consciousness of knowing something about me seemed slowly dawning over him. Meanwhile, I lay quietly eyeing him, having no serious misgivings now, and bent upon narrowly observing so curious a creature. When, at last, his mind seemed made up touching the character of his bedfellow, and he became, as it were, reconciled to the fact; he jumped out upon the floor, and by certain signs and sounds gave me to understand that, if it pleased me, he would dress first and then leave me to dress afterwards, having the whole apartment to myself. Thinks I, Queequeg, under the circumstances, this is a very civilized overture; but, the truth is, these savages have an innate sense of delicacy, say what you will; it is marvellous how essentially polite they are. I pay this particular compliment to Queequeg, because he treated me with so much civility and consideration, while I was guilty of great rudeness; staring at him from the bed, and watching all his toilette motions; for the time my curiosity getting the better of my breeding. Nevertheless, a man like Queequeg you don't see every day, he and his ways were well worth unusual regarding.

He commenced dressing at top by donning his beaver hat, a very tall one, by the by, and then—still minus his trowsers—he hunted up his boots. What under the heavens he did it for, I cannot tell, but his next movement was to crush himself—boots in hand, and hat on—under the bed; when, from sundry violent gaspings and strainings, I inferred he was hard at work booting himself; though by no law of propriety that I ever heard of, is any man required to be private when putting on his boots. But Queequeg, do you see, was a creature in the transition state—neither caterpillar nor butterfly. He was just enough civilized to show off his outlandishness in the strangest possible manner. His education was not yet completed. He was an undergraduate. If he had not been a small degree civilized, he very probably would not have troubled himself with boots at all; but then, if he had not been still a savage, he never would have dreamt of getting under the bed to put them on. At last, he emerged with his hat very much dented and crushed down over his eyes, and began creaking and limping about the room, as if, not being much accustomed to boots, his pair of damp, wrinkled cowhide ones—probably not made to order either—rather pinched and tormented him at the first go off of a bitter cold morning.

Seeing, now, that there were no curtains to the window, and that the street being very narrow, the house opposite commanded a plain view into the room, and observing more and more the indecorous figure that Queequeg made, staving about with little else but his hat and boots on; I begged him as well as I could, to accelerate his toilet somewhat, and particularly to get into his pantaloons as soon as possible. He complied, and then proceeded to wash himself. At that time in the morning any Christian would have washed his face; but Queequeg, to my amazement, contented himself with restricting his ablutions to his chest, arms, and hands. He then donned his waistcoat, and taking up a piece of hard soap on the wash-stand centre-table, dipped it into water and commenced lathering his face. I was watching to see where he kept his razor, when lo and behold, he takes the harpoon from the bed corner, slips out the long wooden stock, unsheathes the head, whets it a little on his boot, and striding up to the bit of mirror against the wall, begins a vigorous scraping, or rather harpooning of his cheeks. Thinks I, Queequeg, this is using Rogers's best cutlery with a vengeance. Afterwards I wondered the less at this operation when I came to know of what fine steel the head of a harpoon is made, and how exceedingly sharp the long straight edges are always kept.

The rest of his toilet was soon achieved, and he proudly marched out of the room, wrapped up in his great pilot monkey jacket, and sporting his harpoon like a marshal's baton.

Chapter 5

BREAKFAST

I QUICKLY followed suit, and descending into the bar-room accosted the grinning landlord very pleasantly. I cherished no malice towards him, though he had been skylarking with me not a little in the matter of my bedfellow.

However, a good laugh is a mighty good thing, and rather too scarce a good thing; the more's the pity. So, if any one man, in his own proper person, afford stuff for a good joke to anybody, let him not be backward, but let him cheerfully allow himself to spend and be spent in that way. And the man that has anything bountifully laughable about him, be sure there is more in that man than you perhaps think for.

The bar-room was now full of the boarders who had been dropping in the night previous, and whom I had not as yet had a good look at. They were nearly all whalemen; chief mates, and second mates, and third mates, and sea carpenters, and sea coopers, and sea blacksmiths, and harpooneers, and ship keepers; a brown and brawny company, with bosky beards; an unshorn, shaggy set, all wearing monkey jackets for morning gowns.

You could pretty plainly tell how long each one had been ashore. This young fellow's healthy cheek is like a sun-toasted pear in hue, and would seem to smell almost as musky; he cannot have been three days landed from his Indian voyage. That man next him looks a few shades lighter; you might say a touch of satin wood is in him. In the complexion of a third still lingers a tropic tawn, but slightly bleached withal; *he* doubtless has tarried whole weeks ashore. But who could show a cheek like Queequeg? which, barred with various tints, seemed like the Andes' western slope, to show forth in one array, contrasting climates, zone by zone.

"Grub, ho!" now cried the landlord, flinging open a door, and in we went to breakfast.

They say that men who have seen the world, thereby become quite at ease in manner, quite self-possessed in company. Not always, though: Ledyard, the great New England traveller, and Mungo Park, the Scotch one; of all men, they possessed the least assurance in the parlor. But perhaps the mere crossing of Siberia in a sledge drawn by dogs as Ledyard did, or the taking a long solitary walk on an empty stomach, in the negro heart of Africa, which was the sum of poor Mungo's performances—this kind of travel, I say, may not be the very best mode of attaining a high social polish. Still, for the most part, that sort of thing is to be had anywhere.

These reflections just here are occasioned by the circumstance that after we were all seated at the table, and I was preparing to hear some good stories about whaling; to my no small surprise, nearly every man maintained a profound silence. And not only that, but they looked embarrassed. Yes, here were a set of sea-dogs, many of whom without the slightest bashfulness had boarded great whales on the high seas —entire strangers to them—and duelled them dead without winking; and yet, here they sat at a social breakfast table —all of the same calling, all of kindred tastes—looking round as sheepishly at each other as though they had never been out of sight of some sheepfold among the Green Mountains. A curious sight; these bashful bears, these timid warrior whalemen!

But as for Queequeg—why, Queequeg sat there among them—at the head of the table, too, it so chanced; as cool as an icicle. To be sure I cannot say much for his breeding. His greatest admirer could not have cordially justified his bringing his harpoon into breakfast with him, and using it there without ceremony; reaching over the table with it, to the imminent jeopardy of many heads, and grappling the beefsteaks towards him. But *that* was certainly very coolly done by him, and every one knows that in most people's estimation, to do anything coolly is to do it genteelly.

We will not speak of all Queequeg's peculiarities here; how he eschewed coffee and hot rolls, and applied his undivided attention to beefsteaks, done rare. Enough, that when breakfast was over he withdrew like the rest into the public room, lighted his tomahawk-pipe, and was sitting there quietly digesting and smoking with his inseparable hat on, when I sallied out for a stroll.

Chapter 6

The Street

IF I had been astonished at first catching a glimpse of so outlandish an individual as Queequeg circulating among the polite society of a civilized town, that astonishment soon departed upon taking my first daylight stroll through the streets of New Bedford.

In thoroughfares nigh the docks, any considerable seaport will frequently offer to view the queerest looking nondescripts from foreign parts. Even in Broadway and Chestnut streets, Mediterranean mariners will sometimes jostle the affrighted ladies. Regent street is not unknown to Lascars and Malays; and at Bombay, in the Apollo Green, live Yankees have often scared the natives. But New Bedford beats all Water street and Wapping. In these last-mentioned haunts you see only sailors; but in New Bedford, actual cannibals stand chatting at street corners; savages outright; many of whom yet carry on their bones unholy flesh. It makes a stranger stare.

But, besides the Feegeeans, Tongatabooans, Erromanggoans, Pannangians, and Brighggians, and, besides the wild specimens of the whaling-craft which unheeded reel about the streets, you will see other sights still more curious, certainly more comical. There weekly arrive in this town scores of green Vermonters and New Hampshire men, all athirst for gain and glory in the fishery. They are mostly young, of stalwart frames; fellows who have felled forests, and now seek to drop the axe and snatch the whale-lance. Many are as green as the Green Mountains whence they came. In some things you would think them but a few hours old. Look there! that chap strutting round the corner. He wears a beaver hat and swallow-tailed coat, girdled with a sailor-belt and sheath-knife. Here comes another with a sou'-wester and a bombazine cloak.

No town-bred dandy will compare with a country-bred one—I mean a downright bumpkin dandy—a fellow that, in the dog-days, will mow his two acres in buckskin gloves for fear of tanning his hands. Now when a country dandy like this takes it into his head to make a distinguished reputation, and joins the great whale-fishery, you should see the comical things he does upon reaching the seaport. In bespeaking his sea-outfit, he orders bell-buttons to his waistcoats; straps to his canvas trowsers. Ah, poor Hay-Seed! how bitterly will burst those straps in the first howling gale, when thou art driven, straps, buttons, and all, down the throat of the tempest.

But think not that this famous town has only harpooneers, cannibals, and bumpkins to show her visitors. Not at all. Still New Bedford is a queer place. Had it not been for us whale-men, that tract of land would this day perhaps have been in as howling condition as the coast of Labrador. As it is, parts of her back country are enough to frighten one, they look so bony. The town itself is perhaps the dearest place to live in, in all New England. It is a land of oil, true enough: but not like Canaan; a land, also, of corn and wine. The streets do not run with milk; nor in the spring-time do they pave them with fresh eggs. Yet, in spite of this, nowhere in all America will you find more patrician-like houses; parks and gardens more opulent, than in New Bedford. Whence came they? how planted upon this once scraggy scoria of a country?

Go and gaze upon the iron emblematical harpoons round yonder lofty mansion, and your question will be answered. Yes; all these brave houses and flowery gardens came from the Atlantic, Pacific, and Indian oceans. One and all, they were harpooned and dragged up hither from the bottom of the sea. Can Herr Alexander perform a feat like that?

In New Bedford, fathers, they say, give whales for dowers to their daughters, and portion off their nieces with a few porpoises a-piece. You must go to New Bedford to see a brilliant wedding; for, they say, they have reservoirs of oil in every house, and every night recklessly burn their lengths in spermaceti candles.

In summer time, the town is sweet to see; full of fine maples—long avenues of green and gold. And in August, high in air, the beautiful and bountiful horse-chestnuts, candelabra-wise, proffer the passer-by their tapering upright cones of congregated blossoms. So omnipotent is art; which in many a district of New Bedford has superinduced bright terraces of flowers upon the barren refuse rocks thrown aside at creation's final day.

And the women of New Bedford, they bloom like their own red roses. But roses only bloom in summer; whereas the fine carnation of their cheeks is perennial as sunlight in the seventh heavens. Elsewhere match that bloom of theirs, ye cannot, save in Salem, where they tell me the young girls breathe such musk, their sailor sweethearts smell them miles off shore, as though they were drawing nigh the odorous Moluccas instead of the Puritanic sands.

Chapter 7

THE CHAPEL

IN THIS SAME New Bedford there stands a Whaleman's Chapel, and few are the moody fishermen, shortly bound for the Indian Ocean or Pacific, who fail to make a Sunday visit to the spot. I am sure that I did not.

Returning from my first morning stroll, I again sallied out upon this special errand. The sky had changed from clear, sunny cold, to driving sleet and mist. Wrapping myself in my shaggy jacket of the cloth called bearskin, I fought my way against the stubborn storm. Entering, I found a small scattered congregation of sailors, and sailors' wives and widows. A muffled silence reigned, only broken at times by the shrieks of the storm. Each silent worshipper seemed purposely sitting apart from the other, as if each silent grief were insular and incommunicable. The chaplain had not yet arrived; and there these silent islands of men and women sat steadfastly eyeing several marble tablets, with black borders, masoned into the wall on either side the pulpit. Three of them ran something like the following, but I do not pretend to quote:—

SACRED
To the Memory
OF
JOHN TALBOT,

Who, at the age of eighteen, was lost overboard,
Near the Isle of Desolation, off Patagonia,

November 1st, 1836.

THIS TABLET
Is erected to his Memory
BY HIS SISTER.

SACRED
To the Memory
OF
ROBERT LONG, WILLIS ELLERY,
NATHAN COLEMAN, WALTER CANNY, SETH MACY,
AND SAMUEL GLEIG,
Forming one of the boats' crews
OF
THE SHIP ELIZA,
Who were towed out of sight by a Whale,
On the Off-shore Ground in the
PACIFIC,
December 31st, 1839.
THIS MARBLE
Is here placed by their surviving
Shipmates.

———————

SACRED
To the Memory
OF
The late
CAPTAIN EZEKIEL HARDY,
Who in the bows of his boat was killed by a
Sperm Whale on the coast of Japan,
August 3d, 1833.
THIS TABLET
Is erected to his Memory
BY
HIS WIDOW.

Shaking off the sleet from my ice-glazed hat and jacket, I seated myself near the door, and turning sideways was surprised to see Queequeg near me. Affected by the solemnity of the scene, there was a wondering gaze of incredulous curiosity in his countenance. This savage was the only person present who seemed to notice my entrance; because he was the only one who could not read, and, therefore, was not reading

those frigid inscriptions on the wall. Whether any of the relatives of the seamen whose names appeared there were now
among the congregation, I knew not; but so many are the
unrecorded accidents in the fishery, and so plainly did several
women present wear the countenance if not the trappings of
some unceasing grief, that I feel sure that here before me were
assembled those, in whose unhealing hearts the sight of those
bleak tablets sympathetically caused the old wounds to bleed
afresh.

Oh! ye whose dead lie buried beneath the green grass; who
standing among flowers can say—here, *here* lies my beloved;
ye know not the desolation that broods in bosoms like these.
What bitter blanks in those black-bordered marbles which
cover no ashes! What despair in those immovable inscriptions! What deadly voids and unbidden infidelities in the lines
that seem to gnaw upon all Faith, and refuse resurrections to
the beings who have placelessly perished without a grave. As
well might those tablets stand in the cave of Elephanta as
here.

In what census of living creatures, the dead of mankind are
included; why it is that a universal proverb says of them, that
they tell no tales, though containing more secrets than the
Goodwin Sands; how it is that to his name who yesterday
departed for the other world, we prefix so significant and infidel a word, and yet do not thus entitle him, if he but embarks for the remotest Indies of this living earth; why the Life
Insurance Companies pay death-forfeitures upon immortals;
in what eternal, unstirring paralysis, and deadly, hopeless
trance, yet lies antique Adam who died sixty round centuries
ago; how it is that we still refuse to be comforted for those
who we nevertheless maintain are dwelling in unspeakable
bliss; why all the living so strive to hush all the dead; wherefore but the rumor of a knocking in a tomb will terrify a
whole city. All these things are not without their meanings.

But Faith, like a jackal, feeds among the tombs, and even
from these dead doubts she gathers her most vital hope.

It needs scarcely to be told, with what feelings, on the eve
of a Nantucket voyage, I regarded those marble tablets, and
by the murky light of that darkened, doleful day read the fate
of the whalemen who had gone before me. Yes, Ishmael, the

same fate may be thine. But somehow I grew merry again. Delightful inducements to embark, fine chance for promotion, it seems—aye, a stove boat will make me an immortal by brevet. Yes, there is death in this business of whaling—a speechlessly quick chaotic bundling of a man into Eternity. But what then? Methinks we have hugely mistaken this matter of Life and Death. Methinks that what they call my shadow here on earth is my true substance. Methinks that in looking at things spiritual, we are too much like oysters observing the sun through the water, and thinking that thick water the thinnest of air. Methinks my body is but the lees of my better being. In fact take my body who will, take it I say, it is not me. And therefore three cheers for Nantucket; and come a stove boat and stove body when they will, for stave my soul, Jove himself cannot.

Chapter 8

The Pulpit

I HAD NOT been seated very long ere a man of a certain venerable robustness entered; immediately as the storm-pelted door flew back upon admitting him, a quick regardful eyeing of him by all the congregation, sufficiently attested that this fine old man was the chaplain. Yes, it was the famous Father Mapple, so called by the whalemen, among whom he was a very great favorite. He had been a sailor and a harpoon-eer in his youth, but for many years past had dedicated his life to the ministry. At the time I now write of, Father Mapple was in the hardy winter of a healthy old age; that sort of old age which seems merging into a second flowering youth, for among all the fissures of his wrinkles, there shone certain mild gleams of a newly developing bloom—the spring ver-dure peeping forth even beneath February's snow. No one having previously heard his history, could for the first time behold Father Mapple without the utmost interest, because there were certain engrafted clerical peculiarities about him, imputable to that adventurous maritime life he had led. When he entered I observed that he carried no umbrella, and cer-tainly had not come in his carriage, for his tarpaulin hat ran down with melting sleet, and his great pilot cloth jacket seemed almost to drag him to the floor with the weight of the water it had absorbed. However, hat and coat and over-shoes were one by one removed, and hung up in a little space in an adjacent corner; when, arrayed in a decent suit, he qui-etly approached the pulpit.

Like most old fashioned pulpits, it was a very lofty one, and since a regular stairs to such a height would, by its long angle with the floor, seriously contract the already small area of the chapel, the architect, it seemed, had acted upon the hint of Father Mapple, and finished the pulpit without a stairs, substituting a perpendicular side ladder, like those used in mounting a ship from a boat at sea. The wife of a whaling captain had provided the chapel with a handsome pair of red worsted man-ropes for this ladder, which, being itself nicely headed, and stained with a mahogany color, the whole contrivance, considering what manner of chapel it was, seemed by no means in bad taste. Halting for an instant at the foot of the ladder, and with both hands grasping the ornamental knobs of the man-ropes, Father Mapple cast a look upwards, and then with a truly sailor-like but still reverential dexterity, hand over hand, mounted the steps as if ascending the maintop of his vessel.

The perpendicular parts of this side ladder, as is usually the case with swinging ones, were of cloth-covered rope, only the rounds were of wood, so that at every step there was a joint. At my first glimpse of the pulpit, it had not escaped me that however convenient for a ship, these joints in the present instance seemed unnecessary. For I was not prepared to see Father Mapple after gaining the height, slowly turn round, and stooping over the pulpit, deliberately drag up the ladder step by step, till the whole was deposited within, leaving him impregnable in his little Quebec.

I pondered some time without fully comprehending the reason for this. Father Mapple enjoyed such a wide reputation for sincerity and sanctity, that I could not suspect him of courting notoriety by any mere tricks of the stage. No, thought I, there must be some sober reason for this thing; furthermore, it must symbolize something unseen. Can it be, then, that by that act of physical isolation, he signifies his spiritual withdrawal for the time, from all outward worldly ties and connexions? Yes, for replenished with the meat and wine of the word, to the faithful man of God, this pulpit, I see, is a self-containing stronghold—a lofty Ehrenbreitstein, with a perennial well of water within the walls.

But the side ladder was not the only strange feature of the place, borrowed from the chaplain's former sea-farings. Between the marble cenotaphs on either hand of the pulpit, the wall which formed its back was adorned with a large painting representing a gallant ship beating against a terrible storm off a lee coast of black rocks and snowy breakers. But high above the flying scud and dark-rolling clouds, there floated a little isle of sunlight, from which beamed forth an angel's face; and this bright face shed a distinct spot of radiance upon the ship's tossed deck, something like that silver plate now inserted into the Victory's plank where Nelson fell. "Ah, noble ship," the angel seemed to say, "beat on, beat on, thou noble ship, and bear a hardy helm; for lo! the sun is breaking through; the clouds are rolling off—serenest azure is at hand."

Nor was the pulpit itself without a trace of the same seataste that had achieved the ladder and the picture. Its panelled front was in the likeness of a ship's bluff bows, and the Holy Bible rested on a projecting piece of scroll work, fashioned after a ship's fiddle-headed beak.

What could be more full of meaning?—for the pulpit is ever this earth's foremost part; all the rest comes in its rear; the pulpit leads the world. From thence it is the storm of God's quick wrath is first descried, and the bow must bear the earliest brunt. From thence it is the God of breezes fair or foul is first invoked for favorable winds. Yes, the world's a ship on its passage out, and not a voyage complete; and the pulpit is its prow.

Chapter 9

THE SERMON

FATHER MAPPLE rose, and in a mild voice of unassuming authority ordered the scattered people to condense. "Starboard gangway, there! side away to larboard—larboard gangway to starboard! Midships! midships!"

There was a low rumbling of heavy sea-boots among the benches, and a still slighter shuffling of women's shoes, and all was quiet again, and every eye on the preacher.

He paused a little; then kneeling in the pulpit's bows, folded his large brown hands across his chest, uplifted his closed eyes, and offered a prayer so deeply devout that he seemed kneeling and praying at the bottom of the sea.

This ended, in prolonged solemn tones, like the continual tolling of a bell in a ship that is foundering at sea in a fog—in such tones he commenced reading the following hymn; but changing his manner towards the concluding stanzas, burst forth with a pealing exultation and joy—

> "The ribs and terrors in the whale,
>   Arched over me a dismal gloom,
> While all God's sun-lit waves rolled by,
>   And left me deepening down to doom.

> "I saw the opening maw of hell,
>   With endless pains and sorrows there;
> Which none but they that feel can tell—
>   Oh, I was plunging to despair.

> "In black distress, I called my God,
>   When I could scarce believe him mine,
> He bowed his ear to my complaints—
>   No more the whale did me confine.

> "With speed he flew to my relief,
>   As on a radiant dolphin borne;

Awful, yet bright, as lightning shone
   The face of my Deliverer God.

"My song for ever shall record
   That terrible, that joyful hour;
I give the glory to my God,
   His all the mercy and the power."

Nearly all joined in singing this hymn, which swelled high above the howling of the storm. A brief pause ensued; the preacher slowly turned over the leaves of the Bible, and at last, folding his hand down upon the proper page, said: "Beloved shipmates, clinch the last verse of the first chapter of Jonah—'And God had prepared a great fish to swallow up Jonah.'

"Shipmates, this book, containing only four chapters—four yarns—is one of the smallest strands in the mighty cable of the Scriptures. Yet what depths of the soul does Jonah's deep sea-line sound! what a pregnant lesson to us is this prophet! What a noble thing is that canticle in the fish's belly! How billow-like and boisterously grand! We feel the floods surging over us; we sound with him to the kelpy bottom of the waters; sea-weed and all the slime of the sea is about us! But *what* is this lesson that the book of Jonah teaches? Shipmates, it is a two-stranded lesson; a lesson to us all as sinful men, and a lesson to me as a pilot of the living God. As sinful men, it is a lesson to us all, because it is a story of the sin, hard-heartedness, suddenly awakened fears, the swift punishment, repentance, prayers, and finally the deliverance and joy of Jonah. As with all sinners among men, the sin of this son of Amittai was in his wilful disobedience of the command of God—never mind now what that command was, or how conveyed—which he found a hard command. But all the things that God would have us do are hard for us to do—remember that—and hence, he oftener commands us than endeavors to persuade. And if we obey God, we must disobey ourselves; and it is in this disobeying ourselves, wherein the hardness of obeying God consists.

"With this sin of disobedience in him, Jonah still further flouts at God, by seeking to flee from Him. He thinks that a ship made by men, will carry him into countries where God does not reign, but only the Captains of this earth. He skulks about the wharves of Joppa, and seeks a ship that's bound for Tarshish. There lurks, perhaps, a hitherto unheeded meaning here. By all accounts Tarshish could have been no other city than the modern Cadiz. That's the opinion of learned men. And where is Cadiz, shipmates? Cadiz is in Spain; as far by water, from Joppa, as Jonah could possibly have sailed in those ancient days, when the Atlantic was an almost unknown sea. Because Joppa, the modern Jaffa, shipmates, is on the most easterly coast of the Mediterranean, the Syrian; and Tarshish or Cadiz more than two thousand miles to the westward from that, just outside the Straits of Gibraltar. See ye not then, shipmates, that Jonah sought to flee world-wide from God? Miserable man! Oh! most contemptible and worthy of all scorn; with slouched hat and guilty eye, skulking from his God; prowling among the shipping like a vile burglar hastening to cross the seas. So disordered, self-condemning is his look, that had there been policemen in those days, Jonah, on the mere suspicion of something wrong, had been arrested ere he touched a deck. How plainly he's a fugitive! no baggage, not a hat-box, valise, or carpet-bag,—no friends accompany him to the wharf with their adieux. At last, after much dodging search, he finds the Tarshish ship receiving the last items of her cargo; and as he steps on board to see its Captain in the cabin, all the sailors for the moment desist from hoisting in the goods, to mark the stranger's evil eye. Jonah sees this; but in vain he tries to look all ease and confidence; in vain essays his wretched smile. Strong intuitions of the man assure the mariners he can be no innocent. In their gamesome but still serious way, one whispers to the other—'Jack, he's robbed a widow;' or, 'Joe, do you mark him; he's a bigamist;' or, 'Harry lad, I guess he's the adulterer that broke jail in old Gomorrah, or belike, one of the missing murderers from Sodom.' Another runs to read the bill that's stuck against the spile upon the wharf to which the ship is moored, offering five hundred gold coins for the apprehension of a parricide, and containing a description of his person. He reads, and looks from Jonah to the bill; while all his sympathetic shipmates now crowd round Jonah, prepared to lay their hands upon him. Frighted Jonah trembles, and summoning all his boldness to his face, only looks so much the more a coward. He will not confess himself suspected; but that itself is strong suspicion. So he makes the best of it; and when the sailors find him not to be the man that is advertised, they let him pass, and he descends into the cabin.

" 'Who's there?' cries the Captain at his busy desk, hurriedly making out his papers for the Customs—'Who's there?' Oh! how that harmless question mangles Jonah! For the instant he almost turns to flee again. But he rallies. 'I seek a passage in this ship to Tarshish; how soon sail ye, sir?' Thus far the busy Captain had not looked up to Jonah, though the man now stands before him; but no sooner does he hear that hollow voice, than he darts a scrutinizing glance. 'We sail with the next coming tide,' at last he slowly answered, still intently eyeing him. 'No sooner, sir?'—'Soon enough for any honest man that goes a passenger.' Ha! Jonah, that's another stab. But he swiftly calls away the Captain from that scent. 'I'll sail with ye,'—he says,—'the passage money, how much is that?—I'll pay now.' For it is particularly written, shipmates, as if it were a thing not to be overlooked in this history, 'that he paid the fare thereof' ere the craft did sail. And taken with the context, this is full of meaning.

"Now Jonah's Captain, shipmates, was one whose discernment detects crime in any, but whose cupidity exposes it only in the penniless. In this world, shipmates, sin that pays its way can travel freely, and without a passport; whereas Virtue, if a pauper, is stopped at all frontiers. So Jonah's Captain prepares to test the length of Jonah's purse, ere he judge him openly. He charges him thrice the usual sum; and it's assented to. Then the Captain knows that Jonah is a fugitive; but at the same time resolves to help a flight that paves its rear with gold. Yet when Jonah fairly takes out his purse, prudent suspicions still molest the Captain. He rings every coin to find a counterfeit. Not a forger, any way, he mutters; and Jonah is put down for his passage. 'Point out my stateroom, Sir,' says Jonah now, 'I'm travel-weary; I need sleep.' 'Thou look'st like it,' says the Captain, 'there's thy room.' Jonah enters, and would lock the door, but the lock contains no key. Hearing him foolishly fumbling there, the Captain laughs lowly to himself, and mutters something about the doors of convicts' cells being never allowed to be locked within. All dressed and dusty as he is, Jonah throws himself into his berth, and finds the little state-room ceiling almost resting on his forehead. The air is close, and Jonah gasps. Then, in that contracted hole, sunk, too, beneath the ship's water-line, Jonah feels the heralding presentiment of that stifling hour, when the whale shall hold him in the smallest of his bowel's wards.

"Screwed at its axis against the side, a swinging lamp slightly oscillates in Jonah's room; and the ship, heeling over towards the wharf with the weight of the last bales received, the lamp, flame and all, though in slight motion, still maintains a permanent obliquity with reference to the room; though, in truth, infallibly straight itself, it but made obvious the false, lying levels among which it hung. The lamp alarms and frightens Jonah; as lying in his berth his tormented eyes roll round the place, and this thus far successful fugitive finds no refuge for his restless glance. But that contradiction in the lamp more and more appals him. The floor, the ceiling, and the side, are all awry. 'Oh! so my conscience hangs in me!' he groans, 'straight upward, so it burns; but the chambers of my soul are all in crookedness!'

"Like one who after a night of drunken revelry hies to his bed, still reeling, but with conscience yet pricking him, as the plungings of the Roman race-horse but so much the more strike his steel tags into him; as one who in that miserable plight still turns and turns in giddy anguish, praying God for annihilation until the fit be passed; and at last amid the whirl of woe he feels, a deep stupor steals over him, as over the man who bleeds to death, for conscience is the wound, and there's naught to staunch it; so, after sore wrestlings in his berth, Jonah's prodigy of ponderous misery drags him drowning down to sleep.

"And now the time of tide has come; the ship casts off her cables; and from the deserted wharf the uncheered ship for Tarshish, all careening, glides to sea. That ship, my friends, was the first of recorded smugglers! the contraband was Jonah. But the sea rebels; he will not bear the wicked burden. A dreadful storm comes on, the ship is like to break. But now when the boatswain calls all hands to lighten her; when boxes, bales, and jars are clattering overboard; when the wind is shrieking, and the men are yelling, and every plank thunders with trampling feet right over Jonah's head; in all this raging tumult, Jonah sleeps his hideous sleep. He sees no black sky and raging sea, feels not the reeling timbers, and little hears he or heeds he the far rush of the mighty whale, which even now with open mouth is cleaving the seas after him. Aye, shipmates, Jonah was gone down into the sides of the ship—a berth in the cabin as I have taken it, and was fast asleep. But the frightened master comes to him, and shrieks in his dead ear, 'What meanest thou, O sleeper! arise!' Startled from his lethargy by that direful cry, Jonah staggers to his feet, and stumbling to the deck, grasps a shroud, to look out upon the sea. But at that moment he is sprung upon by a panther billow leaping over the bulwarks. Wave after wave thus leaps into the ship, and finding no speedy vent runs roaring fore and aft, till the mariners come nigh to drowning while yet afloat. And ever, as the white moon shows her affrighted face from the steep gullies in the blackness overhead, aghast Jonah sees the rearing bowsprit pointing high upward, but soon beat downward again towards the tormented deep.

"Terrors upon terrors run shouting through his soul. In all his cringing attitudes, the God-fugitive is now too plainly known. The sailors mark him; more and more certain grow their suspicions of him, and at last, fully to test the truth, by referring the whole matter to high Heaven, they fall to casting lots, to see for whose cause this great tempest was upon them. The lot is Jonah's; that discovered, then how furiously they mob him with their questions. 'What is thine occupation? Whence comest thou? Thy country? What people?' But mark now, my shipmates, the behavior of poor Jonah. The eager mariners but ask him who he is, and where from; whereas, they not only receive an answer to those questions, but likewise another answer to a question not put by them, but the unsolicited answer is forced from Jonah by the hard hand of God that is upon him.

" 'I am a Hebrew,' he cries—and then—'I fear the Lord the God of Heaven who hath made the sea and the dry land!' Fear him, O Jonah? Aye, well mightest thou fear the Lord

God *then*! Straightway, he now goes on to make a full confession; whereupon the mariners become more and more appalled, but still are pitiful. For when Jonah, not yet supplicating God for mercy, since he but too well knew the darkness of his deserts,—when wretched Jonah cries out to them to take him and cast him forth into the sea, for he knew that for *his* sake this great tempest was upon them; they mercifully turn from him, and seek by other means to save the ship. But all in vain; the indignant gale howls louder; then, with one hand raised invokingly to God, with the other they not unreluctantly lay hold of Jonah.

"And now behold Jonah taken up as an anchor and dropped into the sea; when instantly an oily calmness floats out from the east, and the sea is still, as Jonah carries down the gale with him, leaving smooth water behind. He goes down in the whirling heart of such a masterless commotion that he scarce heeds the moment when he drops seething into the yawning jaws awaiting him; and the whale shoots-to all his ivory teeth, like so many white bolts, upon his prison. Then Jonah prayed unto the Lord out of the fish's belly. But observe his prayer, and learn a weighty lesson. For sinful as he is, Jonah does not weep and wail for direct deliverance. He feels that his dreadful punishment is just. He leaves all his deliverance to God, contenting himself with this, that spite of all his pains and pangs, he will still look towards His holy temple. And here, shipmates, is true and faithful repentance; not clamorous for pardon, but grateful for punishment. And how pleasing to God was this conduct in Jonah, is shown in the eventual deliverance of him from the sea and the whale. Shipmates, I do not place Jonah before you to be copied for his sin but I do place him before you as a model for repentance. Sin not; but if you do, take heed to repent of it like Jonah."

While he was speaking these words, the howling of the shrieking, slanting storm without seemed to add new power to the preacher, who, when describing Jonah's sea-storm, seemed tossed by a storm himself. His deep chest heaved as with a ground-swell; his tossed arms seemed the warring elements at work; and the thunders that rolled away from off his swarthy brow, and the light leaping from his eye, made all his simple hearers look on him with a quick fear that was strange to them.

There now came a lull in his look, as he silently turned over the leaves of the Book once more; and, at last, standing motionless, with closed eyes, for the moment, seemed communing with God and himself.

But again he leaned over towards the people, and bowing his head lowly, with an aspect of the deepest yet manliest humility, he spake these words:

"Shipmates, God has laid but one hand upon you; both his hands press upon me. I have read ye by what murky light may be mine the lesson that Jonah teaches to all sinners; and therefore to ye, and still more to me, for I am a greater sinner than ye. And now how gladly would I come down from this mast-head and sit on the hatches there where you sit, and listen as you listen, while some one of you reads *me* that other and more awful lesson which Jonah teaches to *me*, as a pilot of the living God. How being an anointed pilot-prophet, or speaker of true things, and bidden by the Lord to sound those unwelcome truths in the ears of a wicked Nineveh, Jonah, appalled at the hostility he should raise, fled from his mission, and sought to escape his duty and his God by taking ship at Joppa. But God is everywhere; Tarshish he never reached. As we have seen, God came upon him in the whale, and swallowed him down to living gulfs of doom, and with swift slantings tore him along 'into the midst of the seas,' where the eddying depths sucked him ten thousand fathoms down, and 'the weeds were wrapped about his head,' and all the watery world of woe bowled over him. Yet even then beyond the reach of any plummet—'out of the belly of hell'—when the whale grounded upon the ocean's utmost bones, even then, God heard the engulphed, repenting prophet when he cried. Then God spake unto the fish; and from the shuddering cold and blackness of the sea, the whale came breeching up towards the warm and pleasant sun, and all the delights of air and earth; and 'vomited out Jonah upon the dry land;' when the word of the Lord came a second time; and Jonah, bruised and beaten—his ears, like two sea-shells, still multitudinously murmuring of the ocean—Jonah did the Almighty's bidding. And what was that, shipmates? To preach the Truth to the face of Falsehood! That was it!

"This, shipmates, this is that other lesson; and woe to that pilot of the living God who slights it. Woe to him whom this world charms from Gospel duty! Woe to him who seeks to pour oil upon the waters when God has brewed them into a gale! Woe to him who seeks to please rather than to appal! Woe to him whose good name is more to him than goodness! Woe to him who, in this world, courts not dishonor! Woe to him who would not be true, even though to be false were salvation! Yea, woe to him who, as the great Pilot Paul has it, while preaching to others is himself a castaway!"

He drooped and fell away from himself for a moment; then lifting his face to them again, showed a deep joy in his eyes, as he cried out with a heavenly enthusiasm,—"But oh! shipmates! on the starboard hand of every woe, there is a sure delight; and higher the top of that delight, than the bottom of the woe is deep. Is not the main-truck higher than the kelson is low? Delight is to him—a far, far upward, and inward delight—who against the proud gods and commodores of this earth, ever stands forth his own inexorable self. Delight is to him whose strong arms yet support him, when the ship of this base treacherous world has gone down beneath him. Delight is to him, who gives no quarter in the truth, and kills, burns, and destroys all sin though he pluck it out from under the robes of Senators and Judges. Delight,—top-gallant delight is to him, who acknowledges no law or lord, but the Lord his God, and is only a patriot to heaven. Delight is to him, whom all the waves of the billows of the seas of the boisterous mob can never shake from this sure Keel of the Ages. And eternal delight and deliciousness will be his, who coming to lay him down, can say with his final breath—O Father!—chiefly known to me by Thy rod—mortal or immortal, here I die. I have striven to be Thine, more than to be this world's, or mine own. Yet this is nothing; I leave eternity to Thee; for what is man that he should live out the lifetime of his God?"

He said no more, but slowly waving a benediction, covered his face with his hands, and so remained, kneeling, till all the people had departed, and he was left alone in the place.

Chapter 10

A Bosom Friend

Returning to the Spouter-Inn from the Chapel, I found Queequeg there quite alone; he having left the Chapel before the benediction some time. He was sitting on a bench before the fire, with his feet on the stove hearth, and in one hand was holding close up to his face that little negro idol of his; peering hard into its face, and with a jack-knife gently whittling away at its nose, meanwhile humming to himself in his heathenish way.

But being now interrupted, he put up the image; and pretty soon, going to the table, took up a large book there, and placing it on his lap began counting the pages with deliberate regularity; at every fiftieth page—as I fancied—stopping a moment, looking vacantly around him, and giving utterance to a long-drawn gurgling whistle of astonishment. He would then begin again at the next fifty; seeming to commence at number one each time, as though he could not count more than fifty, and it was only by such a large number of fifties being found together, that his astonishment at the multitude of pages was excited.

With much interest I sat watching him. Savage though he was, and hideously marred about the face—at least to my taste—his countenance yet had a something in it which was by no means disagreeable. You cannot hide the soul. Through all his unearthly tattooings, I thought I saw the traces of a simple honest heart; and in his large, deep eyes, fiery black and bold, there seemed tokens of a spirit that would dare a thousand devils. And besides all this, there was a certain lofty bearing about the Pagan, which even his uncouthness could not altogether maim. He looked like a man who had never cringed and never had had a creditor. Whether it was, too, that his head being shaved, his forehead was drawn out in freer and brighter relief, and looked more expansive than it otherwise would, this I will not venture to decide; but certain it was his head was phrenologically an excellent one. It may seem ridiculous, but it reminded me of General Washington's head, as seen in the popular busts of him. It had the same long regularly graded retreating slope from above the brows, which were likewise very projecting, like two long promontories thickly wooded on top. Queequeg was George Washington cannibalistically developed.

Whilst I was thus closely scanning him, half-pretending meanwhile to be looking out at the storm from the casement, he never heeded my presence, never troubled himself with so much as a single glance; but appeared wholly occupied with counting the pages of the marvellous book. Considering how sociably we had been sleeping together the night previous, and especially considering the affectionate arm I had found thrown over me upon waking in the morning, I thought this indifference of his very strange. But savages are strange beings; at times you do not know exactly how to take them. At first they are overawing; their calm self-collectedness of simplicity seems a Socratic wisdom. I had noticed also that Queequeg never consorted at all, or but very little, with the other seamen in the inn. He made no advances whatever; appeared to have no desire to enlarge the circle of his acquaintances. All this struck me as mighty singular; yet, upon second thoughts, there was something almost sublime in it. Here was a man some twenty thousand miles from home, by the way of Cape Horn, that is—which was the only way he could get there—thrown among people as strange to him as though he were in the planet Jupiter; and yet he seemed entirely at his ease; preserving the utmost serenity; content with his own companionship; always equal to himself. Surely this was a touch of fine philosophy; though no doubt he had never heard there was such a thing as that. But, perhaps, to be true philosophers, we mortals should not be conscious of so living or so striving. So soon as I hear that such or such a man gives himself out for a philosopher, I conclude that, like the dyspeptic old woman, he must have "broken his digester."

As I sat there in that now lonely room; the fire burning low, in that mild stage when, after its first intensity has warmed the air, it then only glows to be looked at; the evening shades and phantoms gathering round the casements, and peering in upon us silent, solitary twain; the storm

booming without in solemn swells; I began to be sensible of
strange feelings. I felt a melting in me. No more my splintered heart and maddened hand were turned against the wolfish world. This soothing savage had redeemed it. There he
sat, his very indifference speaking a nature in which there
lurked no civilized hypocrisies and bland deceits. Wild he
was; a very sight of sights to see; yet I began to feel myself
mysteriously drawn towards him. And those same things that
would have repelled most others, they were the very magnets
that thus drew me. I'll try a pagan friend, thought I, since
Christian kindness has proved but hollow courtesy. I drew
my bench near him, and made some friendly signs and hints,
doing my best to talk with him meanwhile. At first he little
noticed these advances; but presently, upon my referring to
his last night's hospitalities, he made out to ask me whether
we were again to be bedfellows. I told him yes; whereat I
thought he looked pleased, perhaps a little complimented.

We then turned over the book together, and I endeavored
to explain to him the purpose of the printing, and the meaning of the few pictures that were in it. Thus I soon engaged
his interest; and from that we went to jabbering the best we
could about the various outer sights to be seen in this famous
town. Soon I proposed a social smoke; and, producing his
pouch and tomahawk, he quietly offered me a puff. And then
we sat exchanging puffs from that wild pipe of his, and keeping it regularly passing between us.

If there yet lurked any ice of indifference towards me in the
Pagan's breast, this pleasant, genial smoke we had, soon
thawed it out, and left us cronies. He seemed to take to me
quite as naturally and unbiddenly as I to him; and when our
smoke was over, he pressed his forehead against mine, clasped
me round the waist, and said that henceforth we were married; meaning, in his country's phrase, that we were bosom
friends; he would gladly die for me, if need should be. In a
countryman, this sudden flame of friendship would have
seemed far too premature, a thing to be much distrusted; but
in this simple savage those old rules would not apply.

After supper, and another social chat and smoke, we went
to our room together. He made me a present of his embalmed head; took out his enormous tobacco wallet, and

groping under the tobacco, drew out some thirty dollars in silver; then spreading them on the table, and mechanically dividing them into two equal portions, pushed one of them towards me, and said it was mine. I was going to remonstrate; but he silenced me by pouring them into my trowsers' pockets. I let them stay. He then went about his evening prayers, took out his idol, and removed the paper fireboard. By certain signs and symptoms, I thought he seemed anxious for me to join him; but well knowing what was to follow, I deliberated a moment whether, in case he invited me, I would comply or otherwise.

I was a good Christian; born and bred in the bosom of the infallible Presbyterian Church. How then could I unite with this wild idolator in worshipping his piece of wood? But what is worship? thought I. Do you suppose now, Ishmael, that the magnanimous God of heaven and earth—pagans and all included—can possibly be jealous of an insignificant bit of black wood? Impossible! But what is worship?—to do the will of God—*that* is worship. And what is the will of God?—to do to my fellow man what I would have my fellow man to do to me—*that* is the will of God. Now, Queequeg is my fellow man. And what do I wish that this Queequeg would do to me? Why, unite with me in my particular Presbyterian form of worship. Consequently, I must then unite with him in his; ergo, I must turn idolator. So I kindled the shavings; helped prop up the innocent little idol; offered him burnt biscuit with Queequeg; salamed before him twice or thrice; kissed his nose; and that done, we undressed and went to bed, at peace with our own consciences and all the world. But we did not go to sleep without some little chat.

How it is I know not; but there is no place like a bed for confidential disclosures between friends. Man and wife, they say, there open the very bottom of their souls to each other; and some old couples often lie and chat over old times till nearly morning. Thus, then, in our hearts' honeymoon, lay I and Queequeg—a cosy, loving pair.

Chapter 11

W E HAD lain thus in bed, chatting and napping at short intervals, and Queequeg now and then affectionately throwing his brown tattooed legs over mine, and then drawing them back; so entirely sociable and free and easy were we; when, at last, by reason of our confabulations, what little nappishness remained in us altogether departed, and we felt like getting up again, though day-break was yet some way down the future.

Yes, we became very wakeful; so much so that our recumbent position began to grow wearisome, and by little and little we found ourselves sitting up; the clothes well tucked around us, leaning against the head-board with our four knees drawn up close together, and our two noses bending over them, as if our knee-pans were warming-pans. We felt very nice and snug, the more so since it was so chilly out of doors; indeed out of bed-clothes too, seeing that there was no fire in the room. The more so, I say, because truly to enjoy bodily warmth, some small part of you must be cold, for there is no quality in this world that is not what it is merely by contrast. Nothing exists in itself. If you flatter yourself that you are all over comfortable, and have been so a long time, then you cannot be said to be comfortable any more. But if, like Queequeg and me in the bed, the tip of your nose or the crown of your head be slightly chilled, why then, indeed, in the general consciousness you feel most delightfully and unmistakably warm. For this reason a sleeping apartment should never be furnished with a fire, which is one of the luxurious discomforts of the rich. For the height of this sort of deliciousness is to have nothing but the blanket between you and your snugness and the cold of the outer air. Then there you lie like the one warm spark in the heart of an arctic crystal.

We had been sitting in this crouching manner for some time, when all at once I thought I would open my eyes; for when between sheets, whether by day or by night, and whether asleep or awake, I have a way of always keeping my eyes shut, in order the more to concentrate the snugness of being in bed. Because no man can ever feel his own identity aright except his eyes be closed; as if darkness were indeed the proper element of our essences, though light be more congenial to our clayey part. Upon opening my eyes then, and coming out of my own pleasant and self-created darkness into the imposed and coarse outer gloom of the unilluminated twelve-o'clock-at-night, I experienced a disagreeable revulsion. Nor did I at all object to the hint from Queequeg that perhaps it were best to strike a light, seeing that we were so wide awake; and besides he felt a strong desire to have a few quiet puffs from his Tomahawk. Be it said, that though I had felt such a strong repugnance to his smoking in the bed the night before, yet see how elastic our stiff prejudices grow when love once comes to bend them. For now I liked nothing better than to have Queequeg smoking by me, even in bed, because he seemed to be full of such serene household joy then. I no more felt unduly concerned for the landlord's policy of insurance. I was only alive to the condensed confidential comfortableness of sharing a pipe and a blanket with a real friend. With our shaggy jackets drawn about our shoulders, we now passed the Tomahawk from one to the other, till slowly there grew over us a blue hanging tester of smoke, illuminated by the flame of the new-lit lamp.

Whether it was that this undulating tester rolled the savage away to far distant scenes, I know not, but he now spoke of his native island; and, eager to hear his history, I begged him to go on and tell it. He gladly complied. Though at the time I but ill comprehended not a few of his words, yet subsequent disclosures, when I had become more familiar with his broken phraseology, now enable me to present the whole story such as it may prove in the mere skeleton I give.

Chapter 12

BIOGRAPHICAL

Q UEEQUEG was a native of Kokovoko, an island far away
to the West and South. It is not down in any map;
true places never are.

When a new-hatched savage running wild about his native
woodlands in a grass clout, followed by the nibbling goats, as
if he were a green sapling; even then, in Queequeg's ambitious soul, lurked a strong desire to see something more of
Christendom than a specimen whaler or two. His father was
a High Chief, a King; his uncle a High Priest; and on the
maternal side he boasted aunts who were the wives of unconquerable warriors. There was excellent blood in his veins—
royal stuff; though sadly vitiated, I fear, by the cannibal propensity he nourished in his untutored youth.

A Sag Harbor ship visited his father's bay, and Queequeg
sought a passage to Christian lands. But the ship, having her
full complement of seamen, spurned his suit; and not all the
King his father's influence could prevail. But Queequeg
vowed a vow. Alone in his canoe, he paddled off to a distant
strait, which he knew the ship must pass through when she
quitted the island. On one side was a coral reef; on the other
a low tongue of land, covered with mangrove thickets that
grew out into the water. Hiding his canoe, still afloat, among
these thickets, with its prow seaward, he sat down in the
stern, paddle low in hand; and when the ship was gliding by,
like a flash he darted out; gained her side; with one backward
dash of his foot capsized and sank his canoe; climbed up the
chains; and throwing himself at full length upon the deck,
grappled a ring-bolt there, and swore not to let it go, though
hacked in pieces.

In vain the captain threatened to throw him overboard;
suspended a cutlass over his naked wrists; Queequeg was the
son of a King, and Queequeg budged not. Struck by his desperate dauntlessness, and his wild desire to visit Christendom,
the captain at last relented, and told him he might make him-

self at home. But this fine young savage—this sea Prince of Wales, never saw the captain's cabin. They put him down among the sailors, and made a whaleman of him. But like Czar Peter content to toil in the shipyards of foreign cities, Queequeg disdained no seeming ignominy, if thereby he might haply gain the power of enlightening his untutored countrymen. For at bottom—so he told me—he was actuated by a profound desire to learn among the Christians, the arts whereby to make his people still happier than they were; and more than that, still better than they were. But, alas! the practices of whalemen soon convinced him that even Christians could be both miserable and wicked; infinitely more so, than all his father's heathens. Arrived at last in old Sag Harbor; and seeing what the sailors did there; and then going on to Nantucket, and seeing how they spent their wages in *that* place also, poor Queequeg gave it up for lost. Thought he, it's a wicked world in all meridians; I'll die a pagan.

And thus an old idolator at heart, he yet lived among these Christians, wore their clothes, and tried to talk their gibberish. Hence the queer ways about him, though now some time from home.

By hints, I asked him whether he did not propose going back, and having a coronation; since he might now consider his father dead and gone, he being very old and feeble at the last accounts. He answered no, not yet; and added that he was fearful Christianity, or rather Christians, had unfitted him for ascending the pure and undefiled throne of thirty pagan Kings before him. But by and by, he said, he would return,—as soon as he felt himself baptized again. For the nonce, however, he proposed to sail about, and sow his wild oats in all four oceans. They had made a harpooneer of him, and that barbed iron was in lieu of a sceptre now.

I asked him what might be his immediate purpose, touching his future movements. He answered, to go to sea again, in his old vocation. Upon this, I told him that whaling was my own design, and informed him of my intention to sail out of Nantucket, as being the most promising port for an adventurous whaleman to embark from. He at once resolved to accompany me to that island, ship aboard the same vessel, get into the same watch, the same boat, the same mess with me, in short to share my every hap; with both my hands in his, boldly dip into the Potluck of both worlds. To all this I joyously assented; for besides the affection I now felt for Queequeg, he was an experienced harpooneer, and as such, could not fail to be of great usefulness to one, who, like me, was wholly ignorant of the mysteries of whaling, though well acquainted with the sea, as known to merchant seamen.

His story being ended with his pipe's last dying puff, Queequeg embraced me, pressed his forehead against mine, and blowing out the light, we rolled over from each other, this way and that, and very soon were sleeping.

Chapter 13

WHEELBARROW

NEXT MORNING, Monday, after disposing of the embalmed head to a barber, for a block, I settled my own and comrade's bill; using, however, my comrade's money. The grinning landlord, as well as the boarders, seemed amazingly tickled at the sudden friendship which had sprung up between me and Queequeg—especially as Peter Coffin's cock and bull stories about him had previously so much alarmed me concerning the very person whom I now companied with.

We borrowed a wheelbarrow, and embarking our things, including my own poor carpet-bag, and Queequeg's canvas sack and hammock, away we went down to "the Moss," the little Nantucket packet schooner moored at the wharf. As we were going along the people stared; not at Queequeg so much—for they were used to seeing cannibals like him in their streets,—but at seeing him and me upon such confidential terms. But we heeded them not, going along wheeling the barrow by turns, and Queequeg now and then stopping to adjust the sheath on his harpoon barbs. I asked him why he carried such a troublesome thing with him ashore, and whether all whaling ships did not find their own harpoons. To this, in substance, he replied, that though what I hinted was true enough, yet he had a particular affection for his own harpoon, because it was of assured stuff, well tried in many a mortal combat, and deeply intimate with the hearts of whales. In short, like many inland reapers and mowers, who go into the farmers' meadows armed with their own scythes—though in no wise obliged to furnish them—even so, Queequeg, for his own private reasons, preferred his own harpoon.

Shifting the barrow from my hand to his, he told me a funny story about the first wheelbarrow he had ever seen. It was in Sag Harbor. The owners of his ship, it seems, had lent him one, in which to carry his heavy chest to his boarding house. Not to seem ignorant about the thing—though in truth he was entirely so, concerning the precise way in which to manage the barrow—Queequeg puts his chest upon it; lashes it fast; and then shoulders the barrow and marches up the wharf. "Why," said I, "Queequeg, you might have known better than that, one would think. Didn't the people laugh?"

Upon this, he told me another story. The people of his island of Kokovoko, it seems, at their wedding feasts express the fragrant water of young cocoanuts into a large stained calabash like a punchbowl; and this punchbowl always forms the great central ornament on the braided mat where the feast is held. Now a certain grand merchant ship once touched at Kokovoko, and its commander—from all accounts, a very stately punctilious gentleman, at least for a sea captain—this commander was invited to the wedding feast of Queequeg's sister, a pretty young princess just turned of ten. Well; when all the wedding guests were assembled at the bride's bamboo cottage, this Captain marches in, and being assigned the post of honor, placed himself over against the punchbowl, and between the High Priest and his majesty the King, Queequeg's father. Grace being said,—for those people have their grace as well as we—though Queequeg told me that unlike us, who at such times look downwards to our platters, they, on the contrary, copying the ducks, glance upwards to the great Giver of all feasts—Grace, I say, being said, the High Priest opens the banquet by the immemorial ceremony of the island; that is, dipping his consecrated and consecrating fingers into the bowl before the blessed beverage circulates. Seeing himself placed next the Priest, and noting the ceremony, and thinking himself—being Captain of a ship—as having plain precedence over a mere island King, especially in the King's own house—the Captain coolly proceeds to wash his hands in the punch bowl;—taking it I suppose for a huge finger-glass. "Now," said Queequeg, "what you tink now?—Didn't our people laugh?"

At last, passage paid, and luggage safe, we stood on board the schooner. Hoisting sail, it glided down the Acushnet river. On one side, New Bedford rose in terraces of streets, their ice-covered trees all glittering in the clear, cold air. Huge hills and mountains of casks on casks were piled upon her wharves, and side by side the world-wandering whale ships lay silent and safely moored at last; while from others came a sound of carpenters and coopers, with blended noises of fires and forges to melt the pitch, all betokening that new cruises were on the start; that one most perilous and long voyage ended, only begins a second; and a second ended, only begins a third, and so on, for ever and for aye. Such is the endlessness, yea, the intolerableness of all earthy effort.

Gaining the more open water, the bracing breeze waxed fresh; the little Moss tossed the quick foam from her bows, as a young colt his snortings. How I snuffed that Tartar air!—how I spurned that turnpike earth!—that common highway all over dented with the marks of slavish heels and hoofs; and turned me to admire the magnanimity of the sea which will permit no records.

At the same foam-fountain, Queequeg seemed to drink and reel with me. His dusky nostrils swelled apart; he showed his filed and pointed teeth. On, on we flew; and our offing gained, the Moss did homage to the blast; ducked and dived her bows as a slave before the Sultan. Sideways leaning, we sideways darted; every ropeyarn tingling like a wire; the two tall masts buckling like Indian canes in land tornadoes. So full of this reeling scene were we, as we stood by the plunging bowsprit, that for some time we did not notice the jeering glances of the passengers, a lubber-like assembly, who marvelled that two fellow beings should be so companionable; as though a white man were anything more dignified than a whitewashed negro. But there were some boobies and bumpkins there, who, by their intense greenness, must have come from the heart and centre of all verdure. Queequeg caught one of these young saplings mimicking him behind his back. I thought the bumpkin's hour of doom was come. Dropping his harpoon, the brawny savage caught him in his arms, and by an almost miraculous dexterity and strength, sent him high up bodily into the air; then slightly tapping his stern in midsomerset, the fellow landed with bursting lungs upon his feet, while Queequeg, turning his back upon him, lighted his tomahawk pipe and passed it to me for a puff.

"Capting! Capting!" yelled the bumpkin, running towards that officer; "Capting, Capting, here's the devil."

"Hallo, *you* sir," cried the Captain, a gaunt rib of the sea, stalking up to Queequeg, "what in thunder do you mean by that? Don't you know you might have killed that chap?"

"What him say?" said Queequeg, as he mildly turned to me.

"He say," said I, "that you came near kill-e that man there," pointing to the still shivering greenhorn.

"Kill-e," cried Queequeg, twisting his tattooed face into an unearthly expression of disdain, "ah! him bery small-e fish-e; Queequeg no kill-e so small-e fish-e; Queequeg kill-e big whale!"

"Look you," roared the Captain, "I'll kill-e *you*, you cannibal, if you try any more of your tricks aboard here; so mind your eye."

But it so happened just then, that it was high time for the Captain to mind his own eye. The prodigious strain upon the main-sail had parted the weather-sheet, and the tremendous boom was now flying from side to side, completely sweeping the entire after part of the deck. The poor fellow whom Queequeg had handled so roughly, was swept overboard; all hands were in a panic; and to attempt snatching at the boom to stay it, seemed madness. It flew from right to left, and back again, almost in one ticking of a watch, and every instant seemed on the point of snapping into splinters. Nothing was done, and nothing seemed capable of being done; those on deck rushed towards the bows, and stood eyeing the boom as if it were the lower jaw of an exasperated whale. In the midst of this consternation, Queequeg dropped deftly to his knees, and crawling under the path of the boom, whipped hold of a rope, secured one end to the bulwarks, and then flinging the other like a lasso, caught it round the boom as it swept over his head, and at the next jerk, the spar was that way trapped, and all was safe. The schooner was run into the wind, and while the hands were clearing away the stern boat, Queequeg, stripped to the waist, darted from the side with a long living arc of a leap. For three minutes or more he was seen swimming like a dog, throwing his long arms straight out before him, and by turns revealing his brawny shoulders through the freezing foam. I looked at the grand and glorious fellow, but saw no one to be saved. The greenhorn had gone down. Shooting himself perpendicularly from the water, Queequeg now took an instant's glance around him, and seeming to see just how matters were, dived down and disappeared. A few minutes more, and he rose again, one arm still striking out, and with the other dragging a lifeless form. The boat soon picked them up. The poor bumpkin was restored. All hands voted Queequeg a noble trump; the captain begged his pardon. From that hour I clove to Queequeg like a barnacle; yea, till poor Queequeg took his last long dive.

Was there ever such unconsciousness? He did not seem to think that he at all deserved a medal from the Humane and Magnanimous Societies. He only asked for water—fresh water—something to wipe the brine off; that done, he put on dry clothes, lighted his pipe, and leaning against the bulwarks, and mildly eyeing those around him, seemed to be saying to himself—"It's a mutual, joint-stock world, in all meridians. We cannibals must help these Christians."

Chapter 14

NANTUCKET

NOTHING more happened on the passage worthy the mentioning; so, after a fine run, we safely arrived in Nantucket.

Nantucket! Take out your map and look at it. See what a real corner of the world it occupies; how it stands there, away off shore, more lonely than the Eddystone lighthouse. Look at it—a mere hillock, and elbow of sand; all beach, without a background. There is more sand there than you would use in twenty years as a substitute for blotting paper. Some gamesome wights will tell you that they have to plant weeds there, they don't grow naturally; that they import Canada thistles; that they have to send beyond seas for a spile to stop a leak in an oil cask; that pieces of wood in Nantucket are carried about like bits of the true cross in Rome; that people there plant toadstools before their houses, to get under the shade in summer time; that one blade of grass makes an oasis, three blades in a day's walk a prairie; that they wear quicksand shoes, something like Laplander snow-shoes; that they are so shut up, belted about, every way inclosed, surrounded, and made an utter island of by the ocean, that to their very chairs and tables small clams will sometimes be found adhering, as to the backs of sea turtles. But these extravaganzas only show that Nantucket is no Illinois.

Look now at the wondrous traditional story of how this island was settled by the red-men. Thus goes the legend. In olden times an eagle swooped down upon the New England coast, and carried off an infant Indian in his talons. With loud lament the parents saw their child borne out of sight over the wide waters. They resolved to follow in the same direction. Setting out in their canoes, after a perilous passage they discovered the island, and there they found an empty ivory casket,—the poor little Indian's skeleton.

What wonder, then, that these Nantucketers, born on a beach, should take to the sea for a livelihood! They first caught crabs and quohogs in the sand; grown bolder, they waded out with nets for mackerel; more experienced, they pushed off in boats and captured cod; and at last, launching a navy of great ships on the sea, explored this watery world; put an incessant belt of circumnavigations round it; peeped in at Bhering's Straits; and in all seasons and all oceans declared everlasting war with the mightiest animated mass that has survived the flood; most monstrous and most mountainous! That Himmalehan, salt-sea Mastodon, clothed with such portentousness of unconscious power, that his very panics are more to be dreaded than his most fearless and malicious assaults!

And thus have these naked Nantucketers, these sea hermits, issuing from their ant-hill in the sea, overrun and conquered the watery world like so many Alexanders; parcelling out among them the Atlantic, Pacific, and Indian oceans, as the three pirate powers did Poland. Let America add Mexico to Texas, and pile Cuba upon Canada; let the English overswarm all India, and hang out their blazing banner from the sun; two thirds of this terraqueous globe are the Nantucketer's. For the sea is his; he owns it, as Emperors own empires; other seamen having but a right of way through it. Merchant ships are but extension bridges; armed ones but floating forts; even pirates and privateers, though following the sea as highwaymen the road, they but plunder other ships, other fragments of the land like themselves, without seeking to draw their living from the bottomless deep itself. The Nantucketer, he alone resides and rests on the sea; he alone, in Bible language, goes down to it in ships; to and fro ploughing it as his own special plantation. *There* is his home; *there* lies his business, which a Noah's flood would not interrupt, though it overwhelmed all the millions in China. He lives on the sea, as prairie cocks in the prairie; he hides among the waves, he climbs them as chamois hunters climb the Alps. For years he knows not the land; so that when he comes to it at last, it smells like another world, more strangely than the moon would to an Earthsman. With the landless gull, that at sunset folds her wings and is rocked to sleep between billows; so at nightfall, the Nantucketer, out of sight of land, furls his sails, and lays him to his rest, while under his very pillow rush herds of walruses and whales.

Chapter 15

CHOWDER

IT WAS quite late in the evening when the little Moss came snugly to anchor, and Queequeg and I went ashore; so we could attend to no business that day, at least none but a supper and a bed. The landlord of the Spouter-Inn had recommended us to his cousin Hosea Hussey of the Try Pots, whom he asserted to be the proprietor of one of the best kept hotels in all Nantucket, and moreover he had assured us that cousin Hosea, as he called him, was famous for his chowders. In short, he plainly hinted that we could not possibly do better than try pot-luck at the Try Pots. But the directions he had given us about keeping a yellow warehouse on our starboard hand till we opened a white church to the larboard, and then keeping that on the larboard hand till we made a corner three points to the starboard, and that done, then ask the first man we met where the place was: these crooked directions of his very much puzzled us at first, especially as, at the outset, Queequeg insisted that the yellow warehouse—our first point of departure—must be left on the larboard hand, whereas I had understood Peter Coffin to say it was on the starboard. However, by dint of beating about a little in the dark, and now and then knocking up a peaceable inhabitant to inquire the way, we at last came to something which there was no mistaking.

Two enormous wooden pots painted black, and suspended by asses' ears, swung from the cross-trees of an old top-mast, planted in front of an old doorway. The horns of the cross-trees were sawed off on the other side, so that this old top-mast looked not a little like a gallows. Perhaps I was over sensitive to such impressions at the time, but I could not help staring at this gallows with a vague misgiving. A sort of crick was in my neck as I gazed up to the two remaining horns; yes, *two* of them, one for Queequeg, and one for me. It's ominous, thinks I. A Coffin my Innkeeper upon landing in my first whaling port; tombstones staring at me in the whalemen's chapel; and here a gallows! and a pair of prodigious black pots too! Are these last throwing out oblique hints touching Tophet?

I was called from these reflections by the sight of a freckled woman with yellow hair and a yellow gown, standing in the porch of the inn, under a dull red lamp swinging there, that looked much like an injured eye, and carrying on a brisk scolding with a man in a purple woollen shirt.

"Get along with ye," said she to the man, "or I'll be combing ye!"

"Come on, Queequeg," said I, "all right. There's Mrs. Hussey."

And so it turned out; Mr. Hosea Hussey being from home, but leaving Mrs. Hussey entirely competent to attend to all his affairs. Upon making known our desires for a supper and a bed, Mrs. Hussey, postponing further scolding for the present, ushered us into a little room, and seating us at a table spread with the relics of a recently concluded repast, turned round to us and said—"Clam or Cod?"

"What's that about Cods, ma'am?" said I, with much politeness.

"Clam or Cod?" she repeated.

"A clam for supper? a cold clam; is *that* what you mean, Mrs. Hussey?" says I; "but that's a rather cold and clammy reception in the winter time, ain't it, Mrs. Hussey?"

But being in a great hurry to resume scolding the man in the purple shirt, who was waiting for it in the entry, and seeming to hear nothing but the word "clam," Mrs. Hussey hurried towards an open door leading to the kitchen, and bawling out "clam for two," disappeared.

"Queequeg," said I, "do you think that we can make out a supper for us both on one clam?"

However, a warm savory steam from the kitchen served to belie the apparently cheerless prospect before us. But when that smoking chowder came in, the mystery was delightfully explained. Oh, sweet friends! hearken to me. It was made of small juicy clams, scarcely bigger than hazel nuts, mixed with pounded ship biscuit, and salted pork cut up into little flakes; the whole enriched with butter, and plentifully seasoned with pepper and salt. Our appetites being sharpened by the frosty voyage, and in particular, Queequeg seeing his favorite fishy food before him, and the chowder being surpassingly excellent, we despatched it with great expedition: when leaning back a moment and bethinking me of Mrs. Hussey's clam and cod announcement, I thought I would try a little experiment. Stepping to the kitchen door, I uttered the word "cod" with great emphasis, and resumed my seat. In a few moments the savory steam came forth again, but with a different flavor, and in good time a fine cod-chowder was placed before us.

We resumed business; and while plying our spoons in the bowl, thinks I to myself, I wonder now if this here has any effect on the head? What's that stultifying saying about chowder-headed people? "But look, Queequeg, ain't that a live eel in your bowl? Where's your harpoon?"

Fishiest of all fishy places was the Try Pots, which well deserved its name; for the pots there were always boiling chowders. Chowder for breakfast, and chowder for dinner, and chowder for supper, till you began to look for fish-bones coming through your clothes. The area before the house was paved with clam-shells. Mrs. Hussey wore a polished necklace of codfish vertebra; and Hosea Hussey had his account books bound in superior old shark-skin. There was a fishy flavor to the milk, too, which I could not at all account for, till one morning happening to take a stroll along the beach among some fishermen's boats, I saw Hosea's brindled cow feeding on fish remnants, and marching along the sand with each foot in a cod's decapitated head, looking very slip-shod, I assure ye.

Supper concluded, we received a lamp, and directions from Mrs. Hussey concerning the nearest way to bed; but, as Queequeg was about to precede me up the stairs, the lady reached forth her arm, and demanded his harpoon; she allowed no harpoon in her chambers. "Why not?" said I; "every true whaleman sleeps with his harpoon—but why not?" "Because it's dangerous," says she. "Ever since young Stiggs coming from that unfort'nt v'y'ge of his, when he was gone four years and a half, with ony three barrels of *ile*, was found dead in my first floor back, with his harpoon in his side; ever since then I allow no boarders to take such dangerous weepons in their rooms a-night. So, Mr. Queequeg" (for she had learned his name), "I will just take this here iron, and keep it for you till morning. But the chowder; clam or cod to-morrow for breakfast, men?"

"Both," says I; "and let's have a couple of smoked herring by way of variety."

Chapter 16

The Ship

IN BED we concocted our plans for the morrow. But to my surprise and no small concern, Queequeg now gave me to understand, that he had been diligently consulting Yojo—the name of his black little god—and Yojo had told him two or three times over, and strongly insisted upon it everyway, that instead of our going together among the whaling-fleet in harbor, and in concert selecting our craft; instead of this, I say, Yojo earnestly enjoined that the selection of the ship should rest wholly with me, inasmuch as Yojo purposed befriending us; and, in order to do so, had already pitched upon a vessel, which, if left to myself, I, Ishmael, should infallibly light upon, for all the world as though it had turned out by chance; and in that vessel I must immediately ship myself, for the present irrespective of Queequeg.

I have forgotten to mention that, in many things, Queequeg placed great confidence in the excellence of Yojo's judgment and surprising forecast of things; and cherished Yojo with considerable esteem, as a rather good sort of god, who perhaps meant well enough upon the whole, but in all cases did not succeed in his benevolent designs.

Now, this plan of Queequeg's, or rather Yojo's, touching the selection of our craft; I did not like that plan at all. I had not a little relied upon Queequeg's sagacity to point out the whaler best fitted to carry us and our fortunes securely. But as all my remonstrances produced no effect upon Queequeg, I was obliged to acquiesce; and accordingly prepared to set about this business with a determined rushing sort of energy and vigor, that should quickly settle that trifling little affair. Next morning early, leaving Queequeg shut up with Yojo in our little bedroom—for it seemed that it was some sort of Lent or Ramadan, or day of fasting, humiliation, and prayer with Queequeg and Yojo that day; *how* it was I never could find out, for, though I applied myself to it several times, I never could master his liturgies and XXXIX Articles—leaving

Queequeg, then, fasting on his tomahawk pipe, and Yojo warming himself at his sacrificial fire of shavings, I sallied out among the shipping. After much prolonged sauntering and many random inquiries, I learnt that there were three ships up for three-years' voyages—The Devil-dam, the Tit-bit, and the Pequod. *Devil-Dam*, I do not know the origin of; *Tit-bit* is obvious; *Pequod*, you will no doubt remember, was the name of a celebrated tribe of Massachusetts Indians, now extinct as the ancient Medes. I peered and pryed about the Devil-Dam; from her, hopped over to the Tit-bit; and, finally, going on board the Pequod, looked around her for a moment, and then decided that this was the very ship for us.

You may have seen many a quaint craft in your day, for aught I know;—square-toed luggers; mountainous Japanese junks; butter-box galliots, and what not; but take my word for it, you never saw such a rare old craft as this same rare old Pequod. She was a ship of the old school, rather small if anything; with an old fashioned claw-footed look about her. Long seasoned and weather-stained in the typhoons and calms of all four oceans, her old hull's complexion was darkened like a French grenadier's, who has alike fought in Egypt and Siberia. Her venerable bows looked bearded. Her masts—cut somewhere on the coast of Japan, where her original ones were lost overboard in a gale—her masts stood stiffly up like the spines of the three old kings of Cologne. Her ancient decks were worn and wrinkled, like the pilgrim-worshipped flag-stone in Canterbury Cathedral where Becket bled. But to all these her old antiquities, were added new and marvellous features, pertaining to the wild business that for more than half a century she had followed. Old Captain Peleg, many years her chief-mate, before he commanded another vessel of his own, and now a retired seaman, and one of the principal owners of the Pequod,—this old Peleg, during the term of his chief-mateship, had built upon her original grotesqueness, and inlaid it, all over, with a quaintness both of material and device, unmatched by anything except it be Thorkill-Hake's carved buckler or bedstead. She was apparelled like any barbaric Ethiopian emperor, his neck heavy with pendants of polished ivory. She was a thing of trophies. A cannibal of a craft, tricking herself forth in the chased bones of her enemies. All round, her unpanelled, open bulwarks were garnished like one continuous jaw, with the long sharp teeth of the sperm whale, inserted there for pins, to fasten her old hempen thews and tendons to. Those thews ran not through base blocks of land wood, but deftly travelled over sheaves of sea-ivory. Scorning a turnstile wheel at her reverend helm, she sported there a tiller; and that tiller was in one mass, curiously carved from the long narrow lower jaw of her hereditary foe. The helmsman who steered by that tiller in a tempest, felt like the Tartar, when he holds back his fiery steed by clutching its jaw. A noble craft, but somehow a most melancholy! All noble things are touched with that.

Now when I looked about the quarter-deck, for some one having authority, in order to propose myself as a candidate for the voyage, at first I saw nobody; but I could not well overlook a strange sort of tent, or rather wigwam, pitched a little behind the main-mast. It seemed only a temporary erection used in port. It was of a conical shape, some ten feet high; consisting of the long, huge slabs of limber black bone taken from the middle and highest part of the jaws of the right-whale. Planted with their broad ends on the deck, a circle of these slabs laced together, mutually sloped towards each other, and at the apex united in a tufted point, where the loose hairy fibres waved to and fro like the top-knot on some old Pottowottamie Sachem's head. A triangular opening faced towards the bows of the ship, so that the insider commanded a complete view forward.

And half concealed in this queer tenement, I at length found one who by his aspect seemed to have authority; and who, it being noon, and the ship's work suspended, was now enjoying respite from the burden of command. He was seated on an old-fashioned oaken chair, wriggling all over with curious carving; and the bottom of which was formed of a stout interlacing of the same elastic stuff of which the wigwam was constructed.

There was nothing so very particular, perhaps, about the appearance of the elderly man I saw; he was brown and brawny, like most old seamen, and heavily rolled up in blue pilot-cloth, cut in the Quaker style; only there was a fine and almost microscopic net-work of the minutest wrinkles interlacing round his eyes, which must have arisen from his continual sailings in many hard gales, and always looking to windward;—for this causes the muscles about the eyes to become pursed together. Such eye-wrinkles are very effectual in a scowl.

"Is this the Captain of the Pequod?" said I, advancing to the door of the tent.

"Supposing it be the Captain of the Pequod, what dost thou want of him?" he demanded.

"I was thinking of shipping."

"Thou wast, wast thou? I see thou art no Nantucketer— ever been in a stove boat?"

"No, Sir, I never have."

"Dost know nothing at all about whaling, I dare say—eh?"

"Nothing, Sir; but I have no doubt I shall soon learn. I've been several voyages in the merchant service, and I think that——"

"Marchant service be damned. Talk not that lingo to me. Dost see that leg?—I'll take that leg away from thy stern, if ever thou talkest of the marchant service to me again. Marchant service indeed! I suppose now ye feel considerable proud of having served in those marchant ships. But flukes! man, what makes thee want to go a whaling, eh?—it looks a little suspicious, don't it, eh?—Hast not been a pirate, hast thou?—Didst not rob thy last Captain, didst thou?—Dost not think of murdering the officers when thou gettest to sea?"

I protested my innocence of these things. I saw that under the mask of these half humorous inuendoes, this old seaman, as an insulated Quakerish Nantucketer, was full of his insular prejudices, and rather distrustful of all aliens, unless they hailed from Cape Cod or the Vineyard.

"But what takes thee a-whaling? I want to know that before I think of shipping ye."

"Well, sir, I want to see what whaling is. I want to see the world."

"Want to see what whaling is, eh? Have ye clapped eye on Captain Ahab?"

"Who is Captain Ahab, sir?"

"Aye, aye, I thought so. Captain Ahab is the Captain of this ship."

"I am mistaken then. I thought I was speaking to the Captain himself."

"Thou art speaking to Captain Peleg—that's who ye are speaking to, young man. It belongs to me and Captain Bildad to see the Pequod fitted out for the voyage, and supplied with all her needs, including crew. We are part owners and agents. But as I was going to say, if thou wantest to know what whaling is, as thou tellest ye do, I can put ye in a way of finding it out before ye bind yourself to it, past backing out. Clap eye on Captain Ahab, young man, and thou wilt find that he has only one leg."

"What do you mean, sir? Was the other one lost by a whale?"

"Lost by a whale! Young man, come nearer to me: it was devoured, chewed up, crunched by the monstrousest parmacetty that ever chipped a boat!—ah, ah!"

I was a little alarmed by his energy, perhaps also a little touched at the hearty grief in his concluding exclamation, but said as calmly as I could, "What you say is no doubt true enough, sir; but how could I know there was any peculiar ferocity in that particular whale, though indeed I might have inferred as much from the simple fact of the accident."

"Look ye now, young man, thy lungs are a sort of soft, d'ye see; thou dost not talk shark a bit. *Sure*, ye've been to sea before now; sure of that?"

"Sir," said I, "I thought I told you that I had been four voyages in the merchant——"

"Hard down out of that! Mind what I said about the marchant service—don't aggravate me—I won't have it. But let us understand each other. I have given thee a hint about what whaling is; do ye yet feel inclined for it?"

"I do, sir."

"Very good. Now, art thou the man to pitch a harpoon down a live whale's throat, and then jump after it? Answer, quick!"

"I am, sir, if it should be positively indispensable to do so; not to be got rid of, that is; which I don't take to be the fact."

"Good again. Now then, thou not only wantest to go a-whaling, to find out by experience what whaling is, but ye also want to go in order to see the world? Was not that what ye said? I thought so. Well then, just step forward there, and take a peep over the weather-bow, and then back to me and tell me what ye see there."

For a moment I stood a little puzzled by this curious request, not knowing exactly how to take it, whether humorously or in earnest. But concentrating all his crow's feet into one scowl, Captain Peleg started me on the errand.

Going forward and glancing over the weather bow, I perceived that the ship swinging to her anchor with the flood-tide, was now obliquely pointing towards the open ocean. The prospect was unlimited, but exceedingly monotonous and forbidding; not the slightest variety that I could see.

"Well, what's the report?" said Peleg when I came back; "what did ye see?"

"Not much," I replied—"nothing but water; considerable horizon though, and there's a squall coming up, I think."

"Well, what dost thou think then of seeing the world? Do ye wish to go round Cape Horn to see any more of it, eh? Can't ye see the world where you stand?"

I was a little staggered, but go a-whaling I must, and I would; and the Pequod was as good a ship as any—I thought the best—and all this I now repeated to Peleg. Seeing me so determined, he expressed his willingness to ship me.

"And thou mayest as well sign the papers right off," he added—"come along with ye." And so saying, he led the way below deck into the cabin.

Seated on the transom was what seemed to me a most uncommon and surprising figure. It turned out to be Captain Bildad, who along with Captain Peleg was one of the largest owners of the vessel; the other shares, as is sometimes the case in these ports, being held by a crowd of old annuitants; widows, fatherless children, and chancery wards; each owning about the value of a timber head, or a foot of plank, or a nail or two in the ship. People in Nantucket invest their money in whaling vessels, the same way that you do yours in approved state stocks bringing in good interest.

Now, Bildad, like Peleg, and indeed many other Nantucketers, was a Quaker, the island having been originally settled by that sect; and to this day its inhabitants in general retain

in an uncommon measure the peculiarities of the Quaker,
only variously and anomalously modified by things altogether
alien and heterogeneous. For some of these same Quakers are
the most sanguinary of all sailors and whale-hunters. They are
fighting Quakers; they are Quakers with a vengeance.

So that there are instances among them of men, who,
named with Scripture names—a singularly common fashion
on the island—and in childhood naturally imbibing the
stately dramatic thee and thou of the Quaker idiom; still,
from the audacious, daring, and boundless adventure of their
subsequent lives, strangely blend with these unoutgrown peculiarities, a thousand bold dashes of character, not unworthy
a Scandinavian sea-king, or a poetical Pagan Roman. And
when these things unite in a man of greatly superior natural
force, with a globular brain and a ponderous heart; who has
also by the stillness and seclusion of many long night-watches
in the remotest waters, and beneath constellations never seen
here at the north, been led to think untraditionally and inde-
pendently; receiving all nature's sweet or savage impressions
fresh from her own virgin, voluntary, and confiding breast,
and thereby chiefly, but with some help from accidental advantages, to learn a bold and nervous lofty language—that
man makes one in a whole nation's census—a mighty pageant
creature, formed for noble tragedies. Nor will it at all detract
from him, dramatically regarded, if either by birth or other
circumstances, he have what seems a half wilful over-ruling
morbidness at the bottom of his nature. For all men tragically
great are made so through a certain morbidness. Be sure of
this, O young ambition, all mortal greatness is but disease.
But, as yet we have not to do with such an one, but with
quite another; and still a man, who, if indeed peculiar, it only
results again from another phase of the Quaker, modified by
individual circumstances.

Like Captain Peleg, Captain Bildad was a well-to-do, retired whaleman. But unlike Captain Peleg—who cared not a
rush for what are called serious things, and indeed deemed
those self-same serious things the veriest of all trifles—Captain Bildad had not only been originally educated according
to the strictest sect of Nantucket Quakerism, but all his subsequent ocean life, and the sight of many unclad, lovely island

creatures, round the Horn—all that had not moved this native born Quaker one single jot, had not so much as altered one angle of his vest. Still, for all this immutableness, was there some lack of common consistency about worthy Captain Bildad. Though refusing, from conscientious scruples, to bear arms against land invaders, yet himself had illimitably invaded the Atlantic and Pacific; and though a sworn foe to human bloodshed, yet had he in his straight-bodied coat, spilled tuns upon tuns of leviathan gore. How now in the contemplative evening of his days, the pious Bildad reconciled these things in the reminiscence, I do not know; but it did not seem to concern him much, and very probably he had long since come to the sage and sensible conclusion that a man's religion is one thing, and this practical world quite another. This world pays dividends. Rising from a little cabin-boy in short clothes of the drabbest drab, to a harpooneer in a broad shad-bellied waistcoat; from that becoming boat-header, chief-mate, and captain, and finally a ship-owner; Bildad, as I hinted before, had concluded his adventurous career by wholly retiring from active life at the goodly age of sixty, and dedicating his remaining days to the quiet receiving of his well-earned income.

Now Bildad, I am sorry to say, had the reputation of being an incorrigible old hunks, and in his sea-going days, a bitter, hard task-master. They told me in Nantucket, though it certainly seems a curious story, that when he sailed the old Categut whaleman, his crew, upon arriving home, were mostly all carried ashore to the hospital, sore exhausted and worn out. For a pious man, especially for a Quaker, he was certainly rather hard-hearted, to say the least. He never used to swear, though, at his men, they said; but somehow he got an inordinate quantity of cruel, unmitigated hard work out of them. When Bildad was a chief-mate, to have his drab-colored eye intently looking at you, made you feel completely nervous, till you could clutch something—a hammer or a marling-spike, and go to work like mad, at something or other, never mind what. Indolence and idleness perished from before him. His own person was the exact embodiment of his utilitarian character. On his long, gaunt body, he carried no spare flesh, no superfluous beard, his chin having a soft, economical nap to it, like the worn nap of his broad-brimmed hat.

Such, then, was the person that I saw seated on the transom when I followed Captain Peleg down into the cabin. The space between the decks was small; and there, bolt-upright, sat old Bildad, who always sat so, and never leaned, and this to save his coat tails. His broad-brim was placed beside him; his legs were stiffly crossed; his drab vesture was buttoned up to his chin; and spectacles on nose, he seemed absorbed in reading from a ponderous volume.

"Bildad," cried Captain Peleg, "at it again, Bildad, eh? Ye have been studying those Scriptures, now, for the last thirty years, to my certain knowledge. How far ye got, Bildad?"

As if long habituated to such profane talk from his old shipmate, Bildad, without noticing his present irreverence, quietly looked up, and seeing me, glanced again inquiringly towards Peleg.

"He says he's our man, Bildad," said Peleg, "he wants to ship."

"Dost thee?" said Bildad, in a hollow tone, and turning round to me.

"I *dost*," said I unconsciously, he was so intense a Quaker.

"What do ye think of him, Bildad?" said Peleg.

"He'll do," said Bildad, eyeing me, and then went on spelling away at his book in a mumbling tone quite audible.

I thought him the queerest old Quaker I ever saw, especially as Peleg, his friend and old shipmate, seemed such a blusterer. But I said nothing, only looking round me sharply. Peleg now threw open a chest, and drawing forth the ship's articles, placed pen and ink before him, and seated himself at a little table. I began to think it was high time to settle with myself at what terms I would be willing to engage for the voyage. I was already aware that in the whaling business they paid no wages; but all hands, including the captain, received certain shares of the profits called *lays*, and that these lays were proportioned to the degree of importance pertaining to the respective duties of the ship's company. I was also aware that being a green hand at whaling, my own lay would not be very large; but considering that I was used to the sea, could steer a ship, splice a rope, and all that, I made no doubt that from all I had heard I should be offered at least the 275th lay—that is, the 275th part of the clear nett proceeds of the voyage, whatever that might eventually amount to. And though the 275th lay was what they call a rather *long lay*, yet it was better than nothing; and if we had a lucky voyage, might pretty nearly pay for the clothing I would wear out on it, not to speak of my three years' beef and board, for which I would not have to pay one stiver.

It might be thought that this was a poor way to accumulate a princely fortune—and so it was, a very poor way indeed. But I am one of those that never take on about princely fortunes, and am quite content if the world is ready to board and lodge me, while I am putting up at this grim sign of the Thunder Cloud. Upon the whole, I thought that the 275th lay would be about the fair thing, but would not have been surprised had I been offered the 200th, considering I was of a broad-shouldered make.

But one thing, nevertheless, that made me a little distrustful about receiving a generous share of the profits was this: Ashore, I had heard something of both Captain Peleg and his unaccountable old crony Bildad; how that they being the principal proprietors of the Pequod, therefore the other and more inconsiderable and scattered owners, left nearly the whole management of the ship's affairs to these two. And I did not know but what the stingy old Bildad might have a mighty deal to say about shipping hands, especially as I now found him on board the Pequod, quite at home there in the cabin, and reading his Bible as if at his own fireside. Now while Peleg was vainly trying to mend a pen with his jackknife, old Bildad, to my no small surprise, considering that he was such an interested party in these proceedings; Bildad never heeded us, but went on mumbling to himself out of his book, " '*Lay* not up for yourselves treasures upon earth, where moth—' "

"Well, Captain Bildad," interrupted Peleg, "what d'ye say, what lay shall we give this young man?"

"Thou knowest best," was the sepulchral reply, "the seven hundred and seventy-seventh wouldn't be too much, would it?—'where moth and rust do corrupt, but *lay*—' "

Lay, indeed, thought I, and such a lay! the seven hundred

and seventy-seventh! Well, old Bildad, you are determined that I, for one, shall not *lay* up many *lays* here below, where moth and rust do corrupt. It was an exceedingly *long lay* that, indeed; and though from the magnitude of the figure it might at first deceive a landsman, yet the slightest consideration will show that though seven hundred and seventy-seven is a pretty large number, yet, when you come to make a *teenth* of it, you will then see, I say, that the seven hundred and seventy-seventh part of a farthing is a good deal less than seven hundred and seventy-seven gold doubloons; and so I thought at the time.

"Why, blast your eyes, Bildad," cried Peleg, "thou dost not want to swindle this young man! he must have more than that."

"Seven hundred and seventy-seventh," again said Bildad, without lifting his eyes; and then went on mumbling—" 'for where your treasure is, there will your heart be also.' "

"I am going to put him down for the three hundredth," said Peleg, "do ye hear that, Bildad! The three hundredth lay, I say."

Bildad laid down his book, and turning solemnly towards him said, "Captain Peleg, thou hast a generous heart; but thou must consider the duty thou owest to the other owners of this ship—widows and orphans, many of them—and that if we too abundantly reward the labors of this young man, we may be taking the bread from those widows and those orphans. The seven hundred and seventy-seventh lay, Captain Peleg."

"Thou Bildad!" roared Peleg, starting up and clattering about the cabin. "Blast ye, Captain Bildad, if I had followed thy advice in these matters, I would afore now had a conscience to lug about that would be heavy enough to founder the largest ship that ever sailed round Cape Horn."

"Captain Peleg," said Bildad steadily, "thy conscience may be drawing ten inches of water, or ten fathoms, I can't tell; but as thou art still an impenitent man, Captain Peleg, I greatly fear lest thy conscience be but a leaky one; and will in the end sink thee foundering down to the fiery pit, Captain Peleg."

"Fiery pit! fiery pit! ye insult me, man; past all natural bearing, ye insult me. It's an all-fired outrage to tell any human creature that he's bound to hell. Flukes and flames! Bildad, say that again to me, and start my soul-bolts, but I'll—I'll—yes, I'll swallow a live goat with all his hair and horns on. Out of the cabin, ye canting, drab-colored son of a wooden gun—a straight wake with ye!"

As he thundered out this he made a rush at Bildad, but with a marvellous oblique, sliding celerity, Bildad for that time eluded him.

Alarmed at this terrible outburst between the two principal and responsible owners of the ship, and feeling half a mind to give up all idea of sailing in a vessel so questionably owned and temporarily commanded, I stepped aside from the door to give egress to Bildad, who, I made no doubt, was all eagerness to vanish from before the awakened wrath of Peleg. But to my astonishment, he sat down again on the transom very quietly, and seemed to have not the slightest intention of withdrawing. He seemed quite used to impenitent Peleg and his ways. As for Peleg, after letting off his rage as he had, there seemed no more left in him, and he, too, sat down like a lamb, though he twitched a little as if still nervously agitated. "Whew!" he whistled at last—"the squall's gone off to leeward, I think. Bildad, thou used to be good at sharpening a lance, mend that pen, will ye. My jack-knife here needs the grindstone. Thank ye; thank ye, Bildad. Now then, my young man, Ishmael's thy name, didn't ye say? Well then, down ye go here, Ishmael, for the three hundredth lay."

"Captain Peleg," said I, "I have a friend with me who wants to ship too—shall I bring him down to-morrow?"

"To be sure," said Peleg. "Fetch him along, and we'll look at him."

"What lay does *he* want?" groaned Bildad, glancing up from the book in which he had again been burying himself.

"Oh! never thee mind about that, Bildad," said Peleg. "Has he ever whaled it any?" turning to me.

"Killed more whales than I can count, Captain Peleg."

"Well, bring him along then."

And, after signing the papers, off I went; nothing doubting but that I had done a good morning's work, and that the Pequod was the identical ship that Yojo had provided to carry Queequeg and me round the Cape.

But I had not proceeded far, when I began to bethink me that the captain with whom I was to sail yet remained unseen by me; though, indeed, in many cases, a whale-ship will be completely fitted out, and receive all her crew on board, ere the captain makes himself visible by arriving to take command; for sometimes these voyages are so prolonged, and the shore intervals at home so exceedingly brief, that if the captain have a family, or any absorbing concernment of that sort, he does not trouble himself much about his ship in port, but leaves her to the owners till all is ready for sea. However, it is always as well to have a look at him before irrevocably committing yourself into his hands. Turning back I accosted Captain Peleg, inquiring where Captain Ahab was to be found.

"And what dost thou want of Captain Ahab? It's all right enough; thou art shipped."

"Yes, but I should like to see him."

"But I don't think thou wilt be able to at present. I don't know exactly what's the matter with him; but he keeps close inside the house; a sort of sick, and yet he don't look so. In fact, he ain't sick; but no, he isn't well either. Any how, young man, he won't always see me, so I don't suppose he will thee. He's a queer man, Captain Ahab—so some think— but a good one. Oh, thou'lt like him well enough; no fear, no fear. He's a grand, ungodly, god-like man, Captain Ahab; doesn't speak much; but, when he does speak, then you may well listen. Mark ye, be forewarned; Ahab's above the common; Ahab's been in colleges, as well as 'mong the cannibals; been used to deeper wonders than the waves; fixed his fiery lance in mightier, stranger foes than whales. His lance! aye, the keenest and the surest that, out of all our isle! Oh! he ain't Captain Bildad; no, and he ain't Captain Peleg; *he's Ahab*, boy; and Ahab of old, thou knowest, was a crowned king!"

"And a very vile one. When that wicked king was slain, the dogs, did they not lick his blood?"

"Come hither to me—hither, hither," said Peleg, with a significance in his eye that almost startled me. "Look ye, lad; never say that on board the Pequod. Never say it anywhere. Captain Ahab did not name himself. 'Twas a foolish, ignorant whim of his crazy, widowed mother, who died when he was

only a twelvemonth old. And yet the old squaw Tistig, at
Gay-head, said that the name would somehow prove prophetic. And, perhaps, other fools like her may tell thee the
same. I wish to warn thee. It's a lie. I know Captain Ahab
well; I've sailed with him as mate years ago; I know what he
is—a good man—not a pious, good man, like Bildad, but a
swearing good man—something like me—only there's a
good deal more of him. Aye, aye, I know that he was never
very jolly; and I know that on the passage home, he was a
little out of his mind for a spell; but it was the sharp shooting
pains in his bleeding stump that brought that about, as any
one might see. I know, too, that ever since he lost his leg last
voyage by that accursed whale, he's been a kind of moody—
desperate moody, and savage sometimes; but that will all pass
off. And once for all, let me tell thee and assure thee, young
man, it's better to sail with a moody good captain than a
laughing bad one. So good-bye to thee—and wrong not
Captain Ahab, because he happens to have a wicked name.
Besides, my boy, he has a wife—not three voyages wedded—
a sweet, resigned girl. Think of that; by that sweet girl that
old man has a child: hold ye then there can be any utter,
hopeless harm in Ahab? No, no, my lad; stricken, blasted, if
he be, Ahab has his humanities!"

As I walked away, I was full of thoughtfulness; what had
been incidentally revealed to me of Captain Ahab, filled me
with a certain wild vagueness of painfulness concerning him.
And somehow, at the time, I felt a sympathy and a sorrow
for him, but for I don't know what, unless it was the cruel
loss of his leg. And yet I also felt a strange awe of him; but
that sort of awe, which I cannot at all describe, was not exactly awe; I do not know what it was. But I felt it; and it did
not disincline me towards him; though I felt impatience at
what seemed like mystery in him, so imperfectly as he was
known to me then. However, my thoughts were at length
carried in other directions, so that for the present dark Ahab
slipped my mind.

Chapter 17

The Ramadan

As Queequeg's Ramadan, or Fasting and Humiliation, was to continue all day, I did not choose to disturb him till towards night-fall; for I cherish the greatest respect towards everybody's religious obligations, never mind how comical, and could not find it in my heart to undervalue even a congregation of ants worshipping a toad-stool; or those other creatures in certain parts of our earth, who with a degree of footmanism quite unprecedented in other planets, bow down before the torso of a deceased landed proprietor merely on account of the inordinate possessions yet owned and rented in his name.

I say, we good Presbyterian Christians should be charitable in these things, and not fancy ourselves so vastly superior to other mortals, pagans and what not, because of their half-crazy conceits on these subjects. There was Queequeg, now, certainly entertaining the most absurd notions about Yojo and his Ramadan;—but what of that? Queequeg thought he knew what he was about, I suppose; he seemed to be content; and there let him rest. All our arguing with him would not avail; let him be, I say: and Heaven have mercy on us all—Presbyterians and Pagans alike—for we are all somehow dreadfully cracked about the head, and sadly need mending.

Towards evening, when I felt assured that all his performances and rituals must be over, I went up to his room and knocked at the door; but no answer. I tried to open it, but it was fastened inside. "Queequeg," said I softly through the key-hole:—all silent. "I say, Queequeg! why don't you speak? It's I—Ishmael." But all remained still as before. I began to grow alarmed. I had allowed him such abundant time; I thought he might have had an apoplectic fit. I looked through the key-hole; but the door opening into an odd corner of the room, the key-hole prospect was but a crooked and sinister one. I could only see part of the foot-board of the bed and a line of the wall, but nothing more. I was surprised to behold resting against the wall the wooden shaft of Queequeg's harpoon, which the landlady the evening previous had taken from him, before our mounting to the chamber. That's strange, thought I; but at any rate, since the harpoon stands yonder, and he seldom or never goes abroad without it, therefore he must be inside here, and no possible mistake.

"Queequeg!—Queequeg!"—all still. Something must have happened. Apoplexy! I tried to burst open the door; but it stubbornly resisted. Running down stairs, I quickly stated my suspicions to the first person I met—the chamber-maid. "La! La!" she cried, "I thought something must be the matter. I went to make the bed after breakfast, and the door was locked; and not a mouse to be heard; and it's been just so silent ever since. But I thought, may be, you had both gone off and locked your baggage in for safe keeping. La! La, ma'am!—Mistress! murder! Mrs. Hussey! apoplexy!"—and with these cries, she ran towards the kitchen, I following.

Mrs. Hussey soon appeared, with a mustard-pot in one hand and a vinegar-cruet in the other, having just broken away from the occupation of attending to the castors, and scolding her little black boy meantime.

"Wood-house!" cried I, "which way to it? Run for God's sake, and fetch something to pry open the door—the axe!—the axe!—he's had a stroke; depend upon it!"—and so saying I was unmethodically rushing up stairs again empty-handed, when Mrs. Hussey interposed the mustard-pot and vinegar-cruet, and the entire castor of her countenance.

"What's the matter with you, young man?"

"Get the axe! For God's sake, run for the doctor, some one, while I pry it open!"

"Look here," said the landlady, quickly putting down the vinegar-cruet, so as to have one hand free; "look here; are you talking about prying open any of my doors?"—and with that she seized my arm. "What's the matter with you? What's the matter with you, shipmate?"

In as calm, but rapid a manner as possible, I gave her to understand the whole case. Unconsciously clapping the mustard-pot to one side of her nose, she ruminated for an instant; then exclaimed—"No! I haven't seen it since I put it there." Running to a little closet under the landing of the stairs, she glanced in, and returning, told me that Queequeg's harpoon was missing. "He's killed himself," she cried. "It's unfort'nate Stiggs done over again—there goes another counterpane— God pity his poor mother!—it will be the ruin of my house. Has the poor lad a sister? Where's that girl?—there, Betty, go to Snarles the Painter, and tell him to paint me a sign, with—'no suicides permitted here, and no smoking in the parlor;'—might as well kill both birds at once. Kill? The Lord be merciful to his ghost! What's that noise there? You, young man, avast there!"

And running up after me, she caught me as I was again trying to force open the door.

"I won't allow it; I won't have my premises spoiled. Go for the locksmith, there's one about a mile from here. But avast!" putting her hand in her side-pocket, "here's a key that'll fit, I guess; let's see." And with that, she turned it in the lock; but, alas! Queequeg's supplemental bolt remained unwithdrawn within.

"Have to burst it open," said I, and was running down the entry a little, for a good start, when the landlady caught at me, again vowing I should not break down her premises; but I tore from her, and with a sudden bodily rush dashed myself full against the mark.

With a prodigious noise the door flew open, and the knob slamming against the wall, sent the plaster to the ceiling; and there, good heavens! there sat Queequeg, altogether cool and self-collected; right in the middle of the room; squatting on his hams, and holding Yojo on top of his head. He looked neither one way nor the other way, but sat like a carved image with scarce a sign of active life.

"Queequeg," said I, going up to him, "Queequeg, what's the matter with you?"

"He hain't been a sittin' so all day, has he?" said the land-lady.

But all we said, not a word could we drag out of him; I almost felt like pushing him over, so as to change his position, for it was almost intolerable, it seemed so painfully and unnaturally constrained; especially, as in all probability he had been sitting so for upwards of eight or ten hours, going too without his regular meals.

"Mrs. Hussey," said I, "he's *alive* at all events; so leave us, if you please, and I will see to this strange affair myself."

Closing the door upon the landlady, I endeavored to prevail upon Queequeg to take a chair; but in vain. There he sat; and all I could do—for all my polite arts and blandishments—he would not move a peg, nor say a single word, nor even look at me, nor notice my presence in any the slightest way.

I wonder, thought I, if this can possibly be a part of his Ramadan; do they fast on their hams that way in his native island. It must be so; yes, it's part of his creed, I suppose; well, then, let him rest; he'll get up sooner or later, no doubt. It can't last for ever, thank God, and his Ramadan only comes once a year; and I don't believe it's very punctual then.

I went down to supper. After sitting a long time listening to the long stories of some sailors who had just come from a plum-pudding voyage, as they called it (that is, a short whaling-voyage in a schooner or brig, confined to the north of the line, in the Atlantic Ocean only); after listening to these plum-puddingers till nearly eleven o'clock, I went up stairs to go to bed, feeling quite sure by this time Queequeg must certainly have brought his Ramadan to a termination. But no; there he was just where I had left him; he had not stirred an inch. I began to grow vexed with him; it seemed so downright senseless and insane to be sitting there all day and half the night on his hams in a cold room, holding a piece of wood on his head.

"For heaven's sake, Queequeg, get up and shake yourself; get up and have some supper. You'll starve; you'll kill yourself, Queequeg." But not a word did he reply.

Despairing of him, therefore, I determined to go to bed and to sleep; and no doubt, before a great while, he would follow me. But previous to turning in, I took my heavy bearskin jacket, and threw it over him, as it promised to be a very cold night; and he had nothing but his ordinary round jacket on. For some time, do all I would, I could not get into the faintest doze. I had blown out the candle; and the mere thought of Queequeg—not four feet off—sitting there in that uneasy position, stark alone in the cold and dark; this made me really wretched. Think of it; sleeping all night in the

same room with a wide awake pagan on his hams in this
dreary, unaccountable Ramadan!

But somehow I dropped off at last, and knew nothing
more till break of day; when, looking over the bedside, there
squatted Queequeg, as if he had been screwed down to the
floor. But as soon as the first glimpse of sun entered the window, up he got, with stiff and grating joints, but with a
cheerful look; limped towards me where I lay; pressed his
forehead again against mine; and said his Ramadan was over.

Now, as I before hinted, I have no objection to any person's religion, be it what it may, so long as that person does
not kill or insult any other person, because that other person
don't believe it also. But when a man's religion becomes really
frantic; when it is a positive torment to him; and, in fine,
makes this earth of ours an uncomfortable inn to lodge in;
then I think it high time to take that individual aside and
argue the point with him.

And just so I now did with Queequeg. "Queequeg," said
I, "get into bed now, and lie and listen to me." I then went
on, beginning with the rise and progress of the primitive religions, and coming down to the various religions of the present time, during which time I labored to show Queequeg that
all these Lents, Ramadans, and prolonged ham-squattings in
cold, cheerless rooms were stark nonsense; bad for the health;
useless for the soul; opposed, in short, to the obvious laws of
Hygiene and common sense. I told him, too, that he being in
other things such an extremely sensible and sagacious savage,
it pained me, very badly pained me, to see him now so de-
plorably foolish about this ridiculous Ramadan of his. Besides, argued I, fasting makes the body cave in; hence the
spirit caves in; and all thoughts born of a fast must necessarily
be half-starved. This is the reason why most dyspeptic reli-
gionists cherish such melancholy notions about their hereafters. In one word, Queequeg, said I, rather digressively; hell
is an idea first born on an undigested apple-dumpling; and
since then perpetuated through the hereditary dyspepsias nurtured by Ramadans.

I then asked Queequeg whether he himself was ever troubled with dyspepsia; expressing the idea very plainly, so that
he could take it in. He said no; only upon one memorable

occasion. It was after a great feast given by his father the king, on the gaining of a great battle wherein fifty of the enemy had been killed by about two o'clock in the afternoon, and all cooked and eaten that very evening.

"No more, Queequeg," said I, shuddering; "that will do;" for I knew the inferences without his further hinting them. I had seen a sailor who had visited that very island, and he told me that it was the custom, when a great battle had been gained there, to barbecue all the slain in the yard or garden of the victor; and then, one by one, they were placed in great wooden trenchers, and garnished round like a pilau, with breadfruit and cocoanuts; and with some parsley in their mouths, were sent round with the victor's compliments to all his friends, just as though these presents were so many Christmas turkeys.

After all, I do not think that my remarks about religion made much impression upon Queequeg. Because, in the first place, he somehow seemed dull of hearing on that important subject, unless considered from his own point of view; and, in the second place, he did not more than one third understand me, couch my ideas simply as I would; and, finally, he no doubt thought he knew a good deal more about the true religion than I did. He looked at me with a sort of condescending concern and compassion, as though he thought it a great pity that such a sensible young man should be so hopelessly lost to evangelical pagan piety.

At last we rose and dressed; and Queequeg, taking a prodigiously hearty breakfast of chowders of all sorts, so that the landlady should not make much profit by reason of his Ramadan, we sallied out to board the Pequod, sauntering along, and picking our teeth with halibut bones.

Chapter 18

His Mark

As we were walking down the end of the wharf towards the ship, Queequeg carrying his harpoon, Captain Peleg in his gruff voice loudly hailed us from his wigwam, saying he had not suspected my friend was a cannibal, and furthermore announcing that he let no cannibals on board that craft, unless they previously produced their papers.

"What do you mean by that, Captain Peleg?" said I, now jumping on the bulwarks, and leaving my comrade standing on the wharf.

"I mean," he replied, "he must show his papers."

"Yea," said Captain Bildad in his hollow voice, sticking his head from behind Peleg's, out of the wigwam. "He must show that he's converted. Son of darkness," he added, turning to Queequeg, "art thou at present in communion with any christian church?"

"Why," said I, "he's a member of the First Congregational Church." Here be it said, that many tattooed savages sailing in Nantucket ships at last come to be converted into the churches.

"First Congregational Church," cried Bildad, "what! that worships in Deacon Deuteronomy Coleman's meeting-house?" and so saying, taking out his spectacles, he rubbed them with his great yellow bandana handkerchief, and putting them on very carefully, came out of the wigwam, and leaning stiffly over the bulwarks, took a good long look at Queequeg.

"How long hath he been a member?" he then said, turning to me; "not very long, I rather guess, young man."

"No," said Peleg, "and he hasn't been baptized right either, or it would have washed some of that devil's blue off his face."

"Do tell, now," cried Bildad, "is this Philistine a regular member of Deacon Deuteronomy's meeting? I never saw him going there, and I pass it every Lord's day."

"I don't know anything about Deacon Deuteronomy or his

meeting," said I, "all I know is, that Queequeg here is a born member of the First Congregational Church. He is a deacon himself, Queequeg is."

"Young man," said Bildad sternly, "thou art skylarking with me—explain thyself, thou young Hittite. What church dost thee mean? answer me."

Finding myself thus hard pushed, I replied, "I mean, sir, the same ancient Catholic Church to which you and I, and Captain Peleg there, and Queequeg here, and all of us, and every mother's son and soul of us belong; the great and everlasting First Congregation of this whole worshipping world; we all belong to that; only some of us cherish some queer crotchets noways touching the grand belief; in *that* we all join hands."

"Splice, thou mean'st *splice* hands," cried Peleg, drawing nearer. "Young man, you'd better ship for a missionary, instead of a fore-mast hand; I never heard a better sermon. Deacon Deuteronomy—why Father Mapple himself couldn't beat it, and he's reckoned something. Come aboard, come aboard; never mind about the papers. I say, tell Quohog there—what's that you call him? tell Quohog to step along. By the great anchor, what a harpoon he's got there! looks like good stuff that; and he handles it about right. I say, Quohog, or whatever your name is, did you ever stand in the head of a whale-boat? did you ever strike a fish?"

Without saying a word, Queequeg, in his wild sort of way, jumped upon the bulwarks, from thence into the bows of one of the whale-boats hanging to the side; and then bracing his left knee, and poising his harpoon, cried out in some such way as this:—

"Cap'ain, you see him small drop tar on water dere? You see him? well, spose him one whale eye, well, den!" and taking sharp aim at it, he darted the iron right over old Bildad's broad brim, clean across the ship's decks, and struck the glistening tar spot out of sight.

"Now," said Queequeg, quietly hauling in the line, "spos-ee him whale-e eye; why, dad whale dead."

"Quick, Bildad," said Peleg, to his partner, who, aghast at the close vicinity of the flying harpoon, had retreated towards the cabin gangway. "Quick, I say, you Bildad, and get the ship's papers. We must have Hedgehog there, I mean Quohog, in one of our boats. Look ye, Quohog, we'll give ye the ninetieth lay, and that's more than ever was given a harpooneer yet out of Nantucket."

So down we went into the cabin, and to my great joy Queequeg was soon enrolled among the same ship's company to which I myself belonged.

When all preliminaries were over and Peleg had got everything ready for signing, he turned to me and said, "I guess, Quohog there don't know how to write, does he? I say, Quohog, blast ye! dost thou sign thy name or make thy mark?"

But at this question, Queequeg, who had twice or thrice before taken part in similar ceremonies, looked no ways abashed; but taking the offered pen, copied upon the paper, in the proper place, an exact counterpart of a queer round figure which was tattooed upon his arm; so that through Captain Peleg's obstinate mistake touching his appellative, it stood something like this: —

Quohog.

his ✚ mark.

Meanwhile Captain Bildad sat earnestly and steadfastly eyeing Queequeg, and at last rising solemnly and fumbling in the huge pockets of his broad-skirted drab coat, took out a bundle of tracts, and selecting one entitled "The Latter Day Coming; or No Time to Lose," placed it in Queequeg's hands, and then grasping them and the book with both his, looked earnestly into his eyes, and said, "Son of darkness, I must do my duty by thee; I am part owner of this ship, and feel concerned for the souls of all its crew; if thou still clingest to thy Pagan ways, which I sadly fear, I beseech thee, remain not for aye a Belial bondsman. Spurn the idol Bel, and the hideous dragon; turn from the wrath to come; mind thine eye, I say; oh! goodness gracious! steer clear of the fiery pit!"

Something of the salt sea yet lingered in old Bildad's language, heterogeneously mixed with Scriptural and domestic phrases.

"Avast there, avast there, Bildad, avast now spoiling our harpooneer," cried Peleg. "Pious harpooneers never make good voyagers—it takes the shark out of 'em; no harpooneer is worth a straw who aint pretty sharkish. There was young Nat Swaine, once the bravest boat-header out of all Nantucket and the Vineyard; he joined the meeting, and never came to good. He got so frightened about his plaguy soul, that he shrinked and sheered away from whales, for fear of after-claps, in case he got stove and went to Davy Jones."

"Peleg! Peleg!" said Bildad, lifting his eyes and hands, "thou thyself, as I myself, hast seen many a perilous time; thou knowest, Peleg, what it is to have the fear of death; how, then, can'st thou prate in this ungodly guise. Thou beliest thine own heart, Peleg. Tell me, when this same Pequod here had her three masts overboard in that typhoon on Japan, that same voyage when thou went mate with Captain Ahab, did'st thou not think of Death and the Judgment then?"

"Hear him, hear him now," cried Peleg, marching across the cabin, and thrusting his hands far down into his pockets,—"hear him, all of ye. Think of that! When every moment we thought the ship would sink! Death and the Judgment then? What? With all three masts making such an everlasting thundering against the side; and every sea breaking over us, fore and aft. Think of Death and the Judgment then? No! no time to think about Death then. Life was what Captain Ahab and I was thinking of; and how to save all hands—how to rig jury-masts—how to get into the nearest port; that was what I was thinking of."

Bildad said no more, but buttoning up his coat, stalked on deck, where we followed him. There he stood, very quietly overlooking some sail-makers who were mending a top-sail in the waist. Now and then he stooped to pick up a patch, or save an end of the tarred twine, which otherwise might have been wasted.

Chapter 19

The Prophet

"S HIPMATES, have ye shipped in that ship?"

Queequeg and I had just left the Pequod, and were sauntering away from the water, for the moment each occupied with his own thoughts, when the above words were put to us by a stranger, who, pausing before us, levelled his massive fore-finger at the vessel in question. He was but shabbily apparelled in faded jacket and patched trowsers; a rag of a black handkerchief investing his neck. A confluent small-pox had in all directions flowed over his face, and left it like the complicated ribbed bed of a torrent, when the rushing waters have been dried up.

"Have ye shipped in her?" he repeated.

"You mean the ship Pequod, I suppose," said I, trying to gain a little more time for an uninterrupted look at him.

"Aye, the Pequod—that ship there," he said, drawing back his whole arm, and then rapidly shoving it straight out from him, with the fixed bayonet of his pointed finger darted full at the object.

"Yes," said I, "we have just signed the articles."

"Anything down there about your souls?"

"About what?"

"Oh, perhaps you hav'n't got any," he said quickly. "No matter though, I know many chaps that hav'n't got any,— good luck to 'em; and they are all the better off for it. A soul's a sort of a fifth wheel to a wagon."

"What are you jabbering about, shipmate?" said I.

"*He's* got enough, though, to make up for all deficiencies of that sort in other chaps," abruptly said the stranger, placing a nervous emphasis upon the word *he*.

"Queequeg," said I, "let's go; this fellow has broken loose from somewhere; he's talking about something and somebody we don't know."

"Stop!" cried the stranger. "Ye said true—ye hav'n't seen Old Thunder yet, have ye?"

"Who's Old Thunder?" said I, again riveted with the insane earnestness of his manner.

"Captain Ahab."

"What! the captain of our ship, the Pequod?"

"Aye, among some of us old sailor chaps, he goes by that name. Ye hav'n't seen him yet, have ye?"

"No, we hav'n't. He's sick they say, but is getting better, and will be all right again before long."

"All right again before long!" laughed the stranger, with a solemnly derisive sort of laugh. "Look ye; when captain Ahab is all right, then this left arm of mine will be all right; not before."

"What do you know about him?"

"What did they *tell* you about him? Say that!"

"They didn't tell much of anything about him; only I've heard that he's a good whale-hunter, and a good captain to his crew."

"That's true, that's true—yes, both true enough. But you must jump when he gives an order. Step and growl; growl and go—that's the word with Captain Ahab. But nothing about that thing that happened to him off Cape Horn, long ago, when he lay like dead for three days and nights; nothing about that deadly skrimmage with the Spaniard afore the altar in Santa?—heard nothing about that, eh? Nothing about the silver calabash he spat into? And nothing about his losing his leg last voyage, according to the prophecy? Didn't ye hear a word about them matters and something more, eh? No, I don't think ye did; how could ye? Who knows it? Not all Nantucket, I guess. But hows'ever, mayhap, ye've heard tell about the leg, and how he lost it; aye, ye have heard of that, I dare say. Oh yes, *that* every one knows a'most—I mean they know he's only one leg; and that a parmacetti took the other off."

"My friend," said I, "what all this gibberish of yours is about, I don't know, and I don't much care; for it seems to me that you must be a little damaged in the head. But if you are speaking of Captain Ahab, of that ship there, the Pequod, then let me tell you, that I know all about the loss of his leg."

"*All* about it, eh—sure you do?—all?"

"Pretty sure."

With finger pointed and eye levelled at the Pequod, the beggar-like stranger stood a moment, as if in a troubled reverie; then starting a little, turned and said:—"Ye've shipped, have ye? Names down on the papers? Well, well, what's signed, is signed; and what's to be, will be; and then again, perhaps it wont be, after all. Any how, it's all fixed and arranged a'ready; and some sailors or other must go with him, I suppose; as well these as any other men, God pity 'em! Morning to ye, shipmates, morning; the ineffable heavens bless ye; I'm sorry I stopped ye."

"Look here, friend," said I, "if you have anything important to tell us, out with it; but if you are only trying to bamboozle us, you are mistaken in your game; that's all I have to say."

"And it's said very well, and I like to hear a chap talk up that way; you are just the man for him—the likes of ye. Morning to ye, shipmates, morning! Oh! when ye get there, tell 'em I've concluded not to make one of 'em."

"Ah, my dear fellow, you can't fool us that way—you can't fool us. It is the easiest thing in the world for a man to look as if he had a great secret in him."

"Morning to ye, shipmates, morning."

"Morning it is," said I. "Come along, Queequeg, let's leave this crazy man. But stop, tell me your name, will you?"

"Elijah."

Elijah! thought I, and we walked away, both commenting, after each other's fashion, upon this ragged old sailor; and agreed that he was nothing but a humbug, trying to be a bugbear. But we had not gone perhaps above a hundred yards, when chancing to turn a corner, and looking back as I did so, who should be seen but Elijah following us, though at a distance. Somehow, the sight of him struck me so, that I said nothing to Queequeg of his being behind, but passed on with my comrade, anxious to see whether the stranger would turn the same corner that we did. He did; and then it seemed to me that he was dogging us, but with what intent I could not for the life of me imagine. This circumstance, coupled with his ambiguous, half-hinting, half-revealing, shrouded sort of talk, now begat in me all kinds of vague wonderments and half-apprehensions, and all connected with the Pequod;

and Captain Ahab; and the leg he had lost; and the Cape Horn fit; and the silver calabash; and what Captain Peleg had said of him, when I left the ship the day previous; and the prediction of the squaw Tistig; and the voyage we had bound ourselves to sail; and a hundred other shadowy things.

I was resolved to satisfy myself whether this ragged Elijah was really dogging us or not, and with that intent crossed the way with Queequeg, and on that side of it retraced our steps. But Elijah passed on, without seeming to notice us. This relieved me; and once more, and finally as it seemed to me, I pronounced him in my heart, a humbug.

Chapter 20

ALL ASTIR

A DAY OR TWO passed, and there was great activity aboard the Pequod. Not only were the old sails being mended, but new sails were coming on board, and bolts of canvas, and coils of rigging; in short, everything betokened that the ship's preparations were hurrying to a close. Captain Peleg seldom or never went ashore, but sat in his wigwam keeping a sharp look-out upon the hands: Bildad did all the purchasing and providing at the stores; and the men employed in the hold and on the rigging were working till long after night-fall.

On the day following Queequeg's signing the articles, word was given at all the inns where the ship's company were stopping, that their chests must be on board before night, for there was no telling how soon the vessel might be sailing. So Queequeg and I got down our traps, resolving, however, to sleep ashore till the last. But it seems they always give very long notice in these cases, and the ship did not sail for several days. But no wonder; there was a good deal to be done, and there is no telling how many things to be thought of, before the Pequod was fully equipped.

Every one knows what a multitude of things—beds, saucepans, knives and forks, shovels and tongs, napkins, nut-crackers, and what not, are indispensable to the business of housekeeping. Just so with whaling, which necessitates a three-years' housekeeping upon the wide ocean, far from all grocers, coster-mongers, doctors, bakers, and bankers. And though this also holds true of merchant vessels, yet not by any means to the same extent as with whalemen. For besides the great length of the whaling voyage, the numerous articles peculiar to the prosecution of the fishery, and the impossibility of replacing them at the remote harbors usually frequented, it must be remembered, that of all ships, whaling vessels are the most exposed to accidents of all kinds, and especially to the destruction and loss of the very things upon which the success of the voyage most depends. Hence, the spare boats, spare spars, and spare lines and harpoons, and spare everythings, almost, but a spare Captain and duplicate ship.

At the period of our arrival at the Island, the heaviest stowage of the Pequod had been almost completed; comprising her beef, bread, water, fuel, and iron hoops and staves. But, as before hinted, for some time there was a continual fetching and carrying on board of divers odds and ends of things, both large and small.

Chief among those who did this fetching and carrying was Captain Bildad's sister, a lean old lady of a most determined and indefatigable spirit, but withal very kindhearted, who seemed resolved that, if *she* could help it, nothing should be found wanting in the Pequod, after once fairly getting to sea. At one time she would come on board with a jar of pickles for the steward's pantry; another time with a bunch of quills for the chief mate's desk, where he kept his log; a third time with a roll of flannel for the small of some one's rheumatic back. Never did any woman better deserve her name, which was Charity—Aunt Charity, as everybody called her. And like a sister of charity did this charitable Aunt Charity bustle about hither and thither, ready to turn her hand and heart to anything that promised to yield safety, comfort, and consolation to all on board a ship in which her beloved brother Bildad was concerned, and in which she herself owned a score or two of well-saved dollars.

But it was startling to see this excellent hearted Quakeress coming on board, as she did the last day, with a long oil-ladle in one hand, and a still longer whaling lance in the other. Nor was Bildad himself nor Captain Peleg at all backward. As for Bildad, he carried about with him a long list of the articles needed, and at every fresh arrival, down went his mark opposite that article upon the paper. Every once and a while Peleg came running out of his whalebone den, roaring at the men down the hatchways, roaring up to the riggers at the mast-head, and then concluded by roaring back into his wigwam.

During these days of preparation, Queequeg and I often visited the craft, and as often I asked about Captain Ahab, and how he was, and when he was going to come on board his ship. To these questions they would answer, that he was getting better and better, and was expected aboard every day; meantime, the two Captains, Peleg and Bildad, could attend to everything necessary to fit the vessel for the voyage. If I had been downright honest with myself, I would have seen very plainly in my heart that I did but half fancy being committed this way to so long a voyage, without once laying my eyes on the man who was to be the absolute dictator of it, so soon as the ship sailed out upon the open sea. But when a man suspects any wrong, it sometimes happens that if he be already involved in the matter, he insensibly strives to cover up his suspicions even from himself. And much this way it was with me. I said nothing, and tried to think nothing.

At last it was given out that some time next day the ship would certainly sail. So next morning, Queequeg and I took a very early start.

Chapter 21

GOING ABOARD

IT WAS NEARLY six o'clock, but only grey imperfect misty dawn, when we drew nigh the wharf.

"There are some sailors running ahead there, if I see right," said I to Queequeg, "it can't be shadows; she's off by sunrise, I guess; come on!"

"Avast!" cried a voice, whose owner at the same time coming close behind us, laid a hand upon both our shoulders, and then insinuating himself between us, stood stooping forward a little, in the uncertain twilight, strangely peering from Queequeg to me. It was Elijah.

"Going aboard?"

"Hands off, will you," said I.

"Lookee here," said Queequeg, shaking himself, "go 'way!"

"Aint going aboard, then?"

"Yes, we are," said I, "but what business is that of yours? Do you know, Mr. Elijah, that I consider you a little impertinent?"

"No, no, no; I wasn't aware of that," said Elijah, slowly and wonderingly looking from me to Queequeg, with the most unaccountable glances.

"Elijah," said I, "you will oblige my friend and me by withdrawing. We are going to the Indian and Pacific Oceans, and would prefer not to be detained."

"Ye be, be ye? Coming back afore breakfast?"

"He's cracked, Queequeg," said I, "come on."

"Holloa!" cried stationary Elijah, hailing us when we had removed a few paces.

"Never mind him," said I, "Queequeg, come on."

But he stole up to us again, and suddenly clapping his hand on my shoulder, said—"Did ye see anything looking like men going towards that ship a while ago?"

Struck by this plain matter-of-fact question, I answered, saying "Yes, I thought I did see four or five men; but it was too dim to be sure."

"Very dim, very dim," said Elijah. "Morning to ye."

Once more we quitted him; but once more he came softly after us; and touching my shoulder again, said, "See if you can find 'em now, will ye?"

"Find who?"

"Morning to ye! morning to ye!" he rejoined, again moving off. "Oh! I was going to warn ye against—but never mind, never mind—it's all one, all in the family too;—sharp frost this morning, ain't it? Good bye to ye. Shan't see ye again very soon, I guess; unless it's before the Grand Jury." And with these cracked words he finally departed, leaving me, for the moment, in no small wonderment at his frantic impudence.

At last, stepping on board the Pequod, we found everything in profound quiet, not a soul moving. The cabin entrance was locked within; the hatches were all on, and lumbered with coils of rigging. Going forward to the forecastle, we found the slide of the scuttle open. Seeing a light, we went down, and found only an old rigger there, wrapped in a tattered pea-jacket. He was thrown at whole length upon two chests, his face downwards and inclosed in his folded arms. The profoundest slumber slept upon him.

"Those sailors we saw, Queequeg, where can they have gone to?" said I, looking dubiously at the sleeper. But it seemed that, when on the wharf, Queequeg had not at all noticed what I now alluded to; hence I would have thought myself to have been optically deceived in that matter, were it not for Elijah's otherwise inexplicable question. But I beat the thing down; and again marking the sleeper, jocularly hinted to Queequeg that perhaps we had best sit up with the body; telling him to establish himself accordingly. He put his hand upon the sleeper's rear, as though feeling if it was soft enough; and then, without more ado, sat quietly down there.

"Gracious! Queequeg, don't sit there," said I.

"Oh! perry dood seat," said Queequeg, "my country way; won't hurt him face."

"Face!" said I, "call that his face? very benevolent countenance then; but how hard he breathes, he's heaving himself; get off, Queequeg, you are heavy, it's grinding the face of the poor. Get off, Queequeg! Look, he'll twitch you off soon. I wonder he don't wake."

Queequeg removed himself to just beyond the head of the sleeper, and lighted his tomahawk pipe. I sat at the feet. We kept the pipe passing over the sleeper, from one to the other. Meanwhile, upon questioning him, in his broken fashion Queequeg gave me to understand that, in his land, owing to the absence of settees and sofas of all sorts, the king, chiefs, and great people generally, were in the custom of fattening some of the lower orders for ottomans; and to furnish a house comfortably in that respect, you had only to buy up eight or ten lazy fellows, and lay them round in the piers and alcoves. Besides, it was very convenient on an excursion; much better than those garden-chairs which are convertible into walking-sticks; upon occasion, a chief calling his atten-dant, and desiring him to make a settee of himself under a spreading tree, perhaps in some damp marshy place.

While narrating these things, every time Queequeg received the tomahawk from me, he flourished the hatchet-side of it over the sleeper's head.

"What's that for, Queequeg?"

"Perry easy, kill-e; oh! perry easy!"

He was going on with some wild reminiscences about his tomahawk-pipe, which, it seemed, had in its two uses both brained his foes and soothed his soul, when we were directly attracted to the sleeping rigger. The strong vapor now com-pletely filling the contracted hole, it began to tell upon him. He breathed with a sort of muffledness; then seemed troubled in the nose; then revolved over once or twice; then sat up and rubbed his eyes.

"Holloa!" he breathed at last, "who be ye smokers?"

"Shipped men," answered I, "when does she sail?"

"Aye, aye, ye are going in her, be ye? She sails to-day. The Captain came aboard last night."

"What Captain?—Ahab?"

"Who but him indeed?"

I was going to ask him some further questions concerning Ahab, when we heard a noise on deck.

"Holloa! Starbuck's astir," said the rigger. "He's a lively chief mate, that; good man, and a pious; but all alive now, I must turn to." And so saying he went on deck, and we followed.

It was now clear sunrise. Soon the crew came on board in twos and threes; the riggers bestirred themselves; the mates were actively engaged; and several of the shore people were busy in bringing various last things on board. Meanwhile Captain Ahab remained invisibly enshrined within his cabin.

Chapter 22

MERRY CHRISTMAS

A T LENGTH, towards noon, upon the final dismissal of the ship's riggers, and after the Pequod had been hauled out from the wharf, and after the ever-thoughtful Charity had come off in a whaleboat, with her last gifts—a night-cap for Stubb, the second mate, her brother-in-law, and a spare Bible for the steward—after all this, the two captains, Peleg and Bildad, issued from the cabin, and turning to the chief mate, Peleg said:

"Now, Mr. Starbuck, are you sure everything is right? Captain Ahab is all ready—just spoke to him—nothing more to be got from shore, eh? Well, call all hands, then. Muster 'em aft here—blast 'em!"

"No need of profane words, however great the hurry, Peleg," said Bildad, "but away with thee, friend Starbuck, and do our bidding."

How now! Here upon the very point of starting for the voyage, Captain Peleg and Captain Bildad were going it with a high hand on the quarter-deck, just as if they were to be joint-commanders at sea, as well as to all appearances in port. And, as for Captain Ahab, no sign of him was yet to be seen; only, they said he was in the cabin. But then, the idea was, that his presence was by no means necessary in getting the ship under weigh, and steering her well out to sea. Indeed, as that was not at all his proper business, but the pilot's; and as he was not yet completely recovered—so they said—therefore, Captain Ahab stayed below. And all this seemed natural enough; especially as in the merchant service many captains never show themselves on deck for a considerable time after heaving up the anchor, but remain over the cabin table, having a farewell merry-making with their shore friends, before they quit the ship for good with the pilot.

But there was not much chance to think over the matter, for Captain Peleg was now all alive. He seemed to do most of the talking and commanding, and not Bildad.

"Aft here, ye sons of bachelors," he cried, as the sailors lingered at the main-mast. "Mr. Starbuck, drive 'em aft."

"Strike the tent there!"—was the next order. As I hinted before, this whalebone marquee was never pitched except in port; and on board the Pequod, for thirty years, the order to strike the tent was well known to be the next thing to heaving up the anchor.

"Man the capstan! Blood and thunder!—jump!"—was the next command, and the crew sprang for the handspikes.

Now, in getting under weigh, the station generally occupied by the pilot is the forward part of the ship. And here Bildad, who, with Peleg, be it known, in addition to his other offices, was one of the licensed pilots of the port—he being suspected to have got himself made a pilot in order to save the Nantucket pilot-fee to all the ships he was concerned in, for he never piloted any other craft—Bildad, I say, might now be seen actively engaged in looking over the bows for the approaching anchor, and at intervals singing what seemed a dismal stave of psalmody, to cheer the hands at the windlass, who roared forth some sort of a chorus about the girls in Booble Alley, with hearty good will. Nevertheless, not three days previous, Bildad had told them that no profane songs would be allowed on board the Pequod, particularly in getting under weigh; and Charity, his sister, had placed a small choice copy of Watts in each seaman's berth.

Meantime, overseeing the other part of the ship, Captain Peleg ripped and swore astern in the most frightful manner. I almost thought he would sink the ship before the anchor could be got up; involuntarily I paused on my handspike, and told Queequeg to do the same, thinking of the perils we both ran, in starting on the voyage with such a devil for a pilot. I was comforting myself, however, with the thought that in pious Bildad might be found some salvation, spite of his seven hundred and seventy-seventh lay; when I felt a sudden sharp poke in my rear, and turning round, was horrified at the apparition of Captain Peleg in the act of withdrawing his leg from my immediate vicinity. That was my first kick.

"Is that the way they heave in the marchant service?" he roared. "Spring, thou sheep-head; spring, and break thy backbone! Why don't ye spring, I say, all of ye—spring! Quohog!

spring, thou chap with the red whiskers; spring there, Scotch-cap; spring, thou green pants. Spring, I say, all of ye, and spring your eyes out!" And so saying, he moved along the windlass, here and there using his leg very freely, while imperturbable Bildad kept leading off with his psalmody. Thinks I, Captain Peleg must have been drinking something to-day.

At last the anchor was up, the sails were set, and off we glided. It was a short, cold Christmas; and as the short northern day merged into night, we found ourselves almost broad upon the wintry ocean, whose freezing spray cased us in ice, as in polished armor. The long rows of teeth on the bulwarks glistened in the moonlight; and like the white ivory tusks of some huge elephant, vast curving icicles depended from the bows.

Lank Bildad, as pilot, headed the first watch, and ever and anon, as the old craft deep dived into the green seas, and sent the shivering frost all over her, and the winds howled, and the cordage rang, his steady notes were heard,—

> "Sweet fields beyond the swelling flood,
> Stand dressed in living green.
> So to the Jews old Canaan stood,
> While Jordan rolled between."

Never did those sweet words sound more sweetly to me than then. They were full of hope and fruition. Spite of this frigid winter night in the boisterous Atlantic, spite of my wet feet and wetter jacket, there was yet, it then seemed to me, many a pleasant haven in store; and meads and glades so eternally vernal, that the grass shot up by the spring, untrodden, unwilted, remains at midsummer.

At last we gained such an offing, that the two pilots were needed no longer. The stout sail-boat that had accompanied us began ranging alongside.

It was curious and not unpleasing, how Peleg and Bildad were affected at this juncture, especially Captain Bildad. For loath to depart, yet; very loath to leave, for good, a ship bound on so long and perilous a voyage—beyond both stormy Capes; a ship in which some thousands of his hard earned dollars were invested; a ship, in which an old shipmate

sailed as captain; a man almost as old as he, once more starting to encounter all the terrors of the pitiless jaw; loath to say
good-bye to a thing so every way brimful of every interest to
him,—poor old Bildad lingered long; paced the deck with
anxious strides; ran down into the cabin to speak another
farewell word there; again came on deck, and looked to windward; looked towards the wide and endless waters, only
bounded by the far-off unseen Eastern Continents; looked towards the land; looked aloft; looked right and left; looked
everywhere and nowhere; and at last, mechanically coiling a
rope upon its pin, convulsively grasped stout Peleg by the
hand, and holding up a lantern, for a moment stood gazing
heroically in his face, as much as to say, "Nevertheless, friend
Peleg, I can stand it; yes, I can."

As for Peleg himself, he took it more like a philosopher;
but for all his philosophy, there was a tear twinkling in his
eye, when the lantern came too near. And he, too, did not a
little run from cabin to deck—now a word below, and now
a word with Starbuck, the chief mate.

But, at last, he turned to his comrade, with a final sort of
look about him,—"Captain Bildad—come, old shipmate, we
must go. Back the main-yard there! Boat ahoy! Stand by to
come close alongside, now! Careful, careful!—come, Bildad,
boy—say your last. Luck to ye, Starbuck—luck to ye, Mr.
Stubb—luck to ye, Mr. Flask—good-bye, and good luck to
ye all—and this day three years I'll have a hot supper smoking for ye in old Nantucket. Hurrah and away!"

"God bless ye, and have ye in His holy keeping, men,"
murmured old Bildad, almost incoherently. "I hope ye'll have
fine weather now, so that Captain Ahab may soon be moving
among ye—a pleasant sun is all he needs, and ye'll have
plenty of them in the tropic voyage ye go. Be careful in the
hunt, ye mates. Don't stave the boats needlessly, ye harpooneers; good white cedar plank is raised full three per cent.
within the year. Don't forget your prayers, either. Mr. Starbuck, mind that cooper don't waste the spare staves. Oh! the
sail-needles are in the green locker! Don't whale it too much
a' Lord's days, men; but don't miss a fair chance either, that's
rejecting Heaven's good gifts. Have an eye to the molasses
tierce, Mr. Stubb; it was a little leaky, I thought. If ye touch

at the islands, Mr. Flask, beware of fornication. Good-bye, good-bye! Don't keep that cheese too long down in the hold, Mr. Starbuck; it'll spoil. Be careful with the butter—twenty cents the pound it was, and mind ye, if—"

"Come, come, Captain Bildad; stop palavering,—away!" and with that, Peleg hurried him over the side, and both dropt into the boat.

Ship and boat diverged; the cold, damp night breeze blew between; a screaming gull flew overhead; the two hulls wildly rolled; we gave three heavy-hearted cheers, and blindly plunged like fate into the lone Atlantic.

Chapter 23

THE LEE SHORE

S OME CHAPTERS BACK, one Bulkington was spoken of, a tall, new-landed mariner, encountered in New Bedford at the inn.

When on that shivering winter's night, the Pequod thrust her vindictive bows into the cold malicious waves, who should I see standing at her helm but Bulkington! I looked with sympathetic awe and fearfulness upon the man, who in midwinter just landed from a four years' dangerous voyage, could so unrestingly push off again for still another tempestuous term. The land seemed scorching to his feet. Wonderfullest things are ever the unmentionable; deep memories yield no epitaphs; this six-inch chapter is the stoneless grave of Bulkington. Let me only say that it fared with him as with the storm-tossed ship, that miserably drives along the leeward land. The port would fain give succor; the port is pitiful; in the port is safety, comfort, hearthstone, supper, warm blankets, friends, all that's kind to our mortalities. But in that gale, the port, the land, is that ship's direst jeopardy; she must fly all hospitality; one touch of land, though it but graze the keel, would make her shudder through and through. With all her might she crowds all sail off shore; in so doing, fights 'gainst the very winds that fain would blow her homeward; seeks all the lashed sea's landlessness again; for refuge's sake forlornly rushing into peril; her only friend her bitterest foe!

Know ye, now, Bulkington? Glimpses do ye seem to see of that mortally intolerable truth; that all deep, earnest thinking is but the intrepid effort of the soul to keep the open independence of her sea; while the wildest winds of heaven and earth conspire to cast her on the treacherous, slavish shore?

But as in landlessness alone resides the highest truth, shoreless, indefinite as God—so, better is it to perish in that howling infinite, than be ingloriously dashed upon the lee, even if that were safety! For worm-like, then, oh! who would craven crawl to land! Terrors of the terrible! is all this agony so vain?

Take heart, take heart, O Bulkington! Bear thee grimly, de-migod! Up from the spray of thy ocean-perishing— straight up, leaps thy apotheosis!

Chapter 24

The Advocate

As queequeg and I are now fairly embarked in this business of whaling; and as this business of whaling has somehow come to be regarded among landsmen as a rather unpoetical and disreputable pursuit; therefore, I am all anxiety to convince ye, ye landsmen, of the injustice hereby done to us hunters of whales.

In the first place, it may be deemed almost superfluous to establish the fact, that among people at large, the business of whaling is not accounted on a level with what are called the liberal professions. If a stranger were introduced into any miscellaneous metropolitan society, it would but slightly advance the general opinion of his merits, were he presented to the company as a harpooneer, say; and if in emulation of the naval officers he should append the initials S. W. F. (Sperm Whale Fishery) to his visiting card, such a procedure would be deemed pre-eminently presuming and ridculous.

Doubtless one leading reason why the world declines honoring us whalemen, is this: they think that, at best, our vocation amounts to a butchering sort of business; and that when actively engaged therein, we are surrounded by all manner of defilements. Butchers we are, that is true. But butchers, also, and butchers of the bloodiest badge have been all Martial Commanders whom the world invariably delights to honor. And as for the matter of the alleged uncleanliness of our business, ye shall soon be initiated into certain facts hitherto pretty generally unknown, and which, upon the whole, will triumphantly plant the sperm whale-ship at least among the cleanliest things of this tidy earth. But even granting the charge in question to be true; what disordered slippery decks of a whale-ship are comparable to the unspeakable carrion of those battle-fields from which so many soldiers return to drink in all ladies' plaudits? And if the idea of peril so much enhances the popular conceit of the soldier's profession; let me assure ye that many a veteran who has freely marched up to a battery, would quickly recoil at the apparition of the sperm whale's vast tail, fanning into eddies the air over his head. For what are the comprehensible terrors of man compared with the interlinked terrors and wonders of God!

But, though the world scouts at us whale hunters, yet does it unwittingly pay us the profoundest homage; yea, an all-abounding adoration! for almost all the tapers, lamps, and candles that burn round the globe, burn, as before so many shrines, to our glory!

But look at this matter in other lights; weigh it in all sorts of scales; see what we whalemen are, and have been.

Why did the Dutch in De Witt's time have admirals of their whaling fleets? Why did Louis XVI. of France, at his own personal expense, fit out whaling ships from Dunkirk, and politely invite to that town some score or two of families from our own island of Nantucket? Why did Britain between the years 1750 and 1788 pay to her whalemen in bounties upwards of £1,000,000? And lastly, how comes it that we whalemen of America now outnumber all the rest of the banded whalemen in the world; sail a navy of upwards of seven hundred vessels; manned by eighteen thousand men; yearly consuming 4,000,000 of dollars; the ships worth, at the time of sailing, $20,000,000; and every year importing into our harbors a well reaped harvest of $7,000,000. How comes all this, if there be not something puissant in whaling?

But this is not the half; look again.

I freely assert, that the cosmopolite philosopher cannot, for his life, point out one single peaceful influence, which within the last sixty years has operated more potentially upon the whole broad world, taken in one aggregate, than the high and mighty business of whaling. One way and another, it has begotten events so remarkable in themselves, and so continuously momentous in their sequential issues, that whaling may well be regarded as that Egyptian mother, who bore offspring themselves pregnant from her womb. It would be a hopeless, endless task to catalogue all these things. Let a handful suffice. For many years past the whale-ship has been the pioneer in ferreting out the remotest and least known parts of the earth. She has explored seas and archipelagoes which had no chart, where no Cook or Vancouver had ever sailed. If American and European men-of-war now peacefully ride in once savage harbors, let them fire salutes to the honor and the glory of the whale-ship, which originally showed them the way, and first interpreted between them and the savages. They may celebrate as they will the heroes of Exploring Expeditions, your Cooks, your Krusensterns; but I say that scores of anonymous Captains have sailed out of Nantucket, that were as great, and greater than your Cook and your Krusenstern. For in their succorless empty-handedness, they, in the heathenish sharked waters, and by the beaches of unrecorded, javelin islands, battled with virgin wonders and terrors that Cook with all his marines and muskets would not willingly have dared. All that is made such a flourish of in the old South Sea Voyages, those things were but the life-time commonplaces of our heroic Nantucketers. Often, adventures which Vancouver dedicates three chapters to, these men accounted unworthy of being set down in the ship's common log. Ah, the world! Oh, the world!

Until the whale fishery rounded Cape Horn, no commerce but colonial, scarcely any intercourse but colonial, was carried on between Europe and the long line of the opulent Spanish provinces on the Pacific coast. It was the whaleman who first broke through the jealous policy of the Spanish crown, touching those colonies; and, if space permitted, it might be distinctly shown how from those whalemen at last eventuated the liberation of Peru, Chili, and Bolivia from the yoke of Old Spain, and the establishment of the eternal democracy in those parts.

That great America on the other side of the sphere, Australia, was given to the enlightened world by the whaleman. After its first blunder-born discovery by a Dutchman, all other ships long shunned those shores as pestiferously barbarous; but the whale-ship touched there. The whale-ship is the true mother of that now mighty colony. Moreover, in the infancy of the first Australian settlement, the emigrants were several times saved from starvation by the benevolent biscuit of the whale-ship luckily dropping an anchor in their waters. The uncounted isles of all Polynesia confess the same truth, and do commercial homage to the whale-ship, that cleared the way for the missionary and the merchant, and in many cases carried the primitive missionaries to their first destinations. If that double-bolted land, Japan, is ever to become hospitable, it is the whale-ship alone to whom the credit will be due; for already she is on the threshold.

But if, in the face of all this, you still declare that whaling has no æsthetically noble associations connected with it, then am I ready to shiver fifty lances with you there, and unhorse you with a split helmet every time.

The whale has no famous author, and whaling no famous chronicler, you will say.

The whale no famous author, and whaling no famous chronicler? Who wrote the first account of our Leviathan? Who but mighty Job! And who composed the first narrative of a whaling-voyage? Who, but no less a prince than Alfred the Great, who, with his own royal pen, took down the words from Other, the Norwegian whale-hunter of those times! And who pronounced our glowing eulogy in Parliament? Who, but Edmund Burke!

True enough, but then whalemen themselves are poor devils; they have no good blood in their veins.

No good blood in their veins? They have something better than royal blood there. The grandmother of Benjamin Franklin was Mary Morrel; afterwards, by marriage, Mary Folger, one of the old settlers of Nantucket, and the ancestress to a long line of Folgers and harpooneers—all kith and kin to noble Benjamin—this day darting the barbed iron from one side of the world to the other.

Good again; but then all confess that somehow whaling is not respectable.

Whaling not respectable? Whaling is imperial! By old English statutory law, the whale is declared "a royal fish."*

Oh, that's only nominal! The whale himself has never figured in any grand imposing way.

The whale never figured in any grand imposing way? In one of the mighty triumphs given to a Roman general upon his entering the world's capital, the bones of a whale, brought all the way from the Syrian coast, were the most conspicuous object in the cymballed procession.*

---

*See subsequent chapters for something more on this head.

Grant it, since you cite it; but, say what you will, there is no real dignity in whaling.

No dignity in whaling? The dignity of our calling the very heavens attest. Cetus is a constellation in the South! No more! Drive down your hat in presence of the Czar, and take it off to Queequeg! No more! I know a man that, in his lifetime, has taken three hundred and fifty whales. I account that man more honorable than that great captain of antiquity who boasted of taking as many walled towns.

And, as for me, if, by any possibility, there be any as yet undiscovered prime thing in me; if I shall ever deserve any real repute in that small but high hushed world which I might not be unreasonably ambitious of; if hereafter I shall do anything that, upon the whole, a man might rather have done than to have left undone; if, at my death, my executors, or more properly my creditors, find any precious MSS. in my desk, then here I prospectively ascribe all the honor and the glory to whaling; for a whale-ship was my Yale College and my Harvard.

Chapter 25

POSTSCRIPT

IN BEHALF of the dignity of whaling, I would fain advance naught but substantiated facts. But after embattling his facts, an advocate who should wholly suppress a not unreasonable surmise, which might tell eloquently upon his cause—such an advocate, would he not be blameworthy?

It is well known that at the coronation of kings and queens, even modern ones, a certain curious process of seasoning them for their functions is gone through. There is a saltcellar of state, so called, and there may be a caster of state. How they use the salt, precisely—who knows? Certain I am, however, that a king's head is solemnly oiled at his coronation, even as a head of salad. Can it be, though, that they anoint it with a view of making its interior run well, as they anoint machinery? Much might be ruminated here, concerning the essential dignity of this regal process, because in common life we esteem but meanly and contemptibly a fellow who anoints his hair, and palpably smells of that anointing. In truth, a mature man who uses hair-oil, unless medicinally, that man has probably got a quoggy spot in him somewhere. As a general rule, he can't amount to much in his totality.

But the only thing to be considered here, is this—what kind of oil is used at coronations? Certainly it cannot be olive oil, nor macassar oil, nor castor oil, nor bear's oil, nor train oil, nor cod-liver oil. What then can it possibly be, but sperm oil in its unmanufactured, unpolluted state, the sweetest of all oils?

Think of that, ye loyal Britons! we whalemen supply your kings and queens with coronation stuff!

Chapter 26

Knights and Squires

THE CHIEF MATE of the Pequod was Starbuck, a native of Nantucket, and a Quaker by descent. He was a long, earnest man, and though born on an icy coast, seemed well adapted to endure hot latitudes, his flesh being hard as twice-baked biscuit. Transported to the Indies, his live blood would not spoil like bottled ale. He must have been born in some time of general drought and famine, or upon one of those fast days for which his state is famous. Only some thirty arid summers had he seen; those summers had dried up all his physical superfluousness. But this, his thinness, so to speak, seemed no more the token of wasting anxieties and cares, than it seemed the indication of any bodily blight. It was merely the condensation of the man. He was by no means ill-looking; quite the contrary. His pure tight skin was an excellent fit; and closely wrapped up in it, and embalmed with inner health and strength, like a revivified Egyptian, this Starbuck seemed prepared to endure for long ages to come, and to endure always, as now; for be it Polar snow or torrid sun, like a patent chronometer, his interior vitality was warranted to do well in all climates. Looking into his eyes, you seemed to see there the yet lingering images of those thousand-fold perils he had calmly confronted through life. A staid, steadfast man, whose life for the most part was a telling pantomime of action, and not a tame chapter of words. Yet, for all his hardy sobriety and fortitude, there were certain qualities in him which at times affected, and in some cases seemed well nigh to overbalance all the rest. Uncommonly conscientious for a seaman, and endued with a deep natural reverence, the wild watery loneliness of his life did therefore strongly incline him to superstition; but to that sort of superstition, which in some organizations seems rather to spring, somehow, from intelligence than from ignorance. Outward portents and inward presentiments were his. And if at times these things bent the welded iron of his soul, much more did his far-away domestic memories of his young Cape wife and child, tend to bend him still more from the original ruggedness of his nature, and open him still further to those latent influences which, in some honest-hearted men, restrain the gush of dare-devil daring, so often evinced by others in the more perilous vicissitudes of the fishery. "I will have no man in my boat," said Starbuck, "who is not afraid of a whale." By this, he seemed to mean, not only that the most reliable and useful courage was that which arises from the fair estimation of the encountered peril, but that an utterly fearless man is a far more dangerous comrade than a coward.

"Aye, aye," said Stubb, the second mate, "Starbuck, there, is as careful a man as you'll find anywhere in this fishery." But we shall ere long see what that word "careful" precisely means when used by a man like Stubb, or almost any other whale hunter.

Starbuck was no crusader after perils; in him courage was not a sentiment; but a thing simply useful to him, and always at hand upon all mortally practical occasions. Besides, he thought, perhaps, that in this business of whaling, courage was one of the great staple outfits of the ship, like her beef and her bread, and not to be foolishly wasted. Wherefore he had no fancy for lowering for whales after sun-down; nor for persisting in fighting a fish that too much persisted in fighting him. For, thought Starbuck, I am here in this critical ocean to kill whales for my living, and not to be killed by them for theirs; and that hundreds of men had been so killed Starbuck well knew. What doom was his own father's? Where, in the bottomless deeps, could he find the torn limbs of his brother?

With memories like these in him, and, moreover, given to a certain superstitiousness, as has been said; the courage of this Starbuck which could, nevertheless, still flourish, must indeed have been extreme. But it was not in reasonable nature that a man so organized, and with such terrible experiences and remembrances as he had; it was not in nature that these things should fail in latently engendering an element in him, which, under suitable circumstances, would break out from its confinement, and burn all his courage up. And brave as he might be, it was that sort of bravery, chiefly visible in some intrepid men, which, while generally abiding firm in the conflict with seas, or winds, or whales, or any of the ordinary irrational horrors of the world, yet cannot withstand those more terrific, because more spiritual terrors, which sometimes menace you from the concentrating brow of an enraged and mighty man.

But were the coming narrative to reveal, in any instance, the complete abasement of poor Starbuck's fortitude, scarce might I have the heart to write it; for it is a thing most sorrowful, nay shocking, to expose the fall of valor in the soul. Men may seem detestable as joint stock-companies and nations; knaves, fools, and murderers there may be; men may have mean and meagre faces; but man, in the ideal, is so noble and so sparkling, such a grand and glowing creature, that over any ignominious blemish in him all his fellows should run to throw their costliest robes. That immaculate manliness we feel within ourselves, so far within us, that it remains intact though all the outer character seem gone; bleeds with keenest anguish at the undraped spectacle of a valor-ruined man. Nor can piety itself, at such a shameful sight, completely stifle her upbraidings against the permitting stars. But this august dignity I treat of, is not the dignity of kings and robes, but that abounding dignity which has no robed investiture. Thou shalt see it shining in the arm that wields a pick or drives a spike; that democratic dignity which, on all hands, radiates without end from God; Himself! The great God absolute! The centre and circumference of all democracy! His omnipresence, our divine equality!

If, then, to meanest mariners, and renegades and castaways, I shall hereafter ascribe high qualities, though dark; weave round them tragic graces; if even the most mournful, perchance the most abased, among them all, shall at times lift himself to the exalted mounts; if I shall touch that workman's arm with some ethereal light; if I shall spread a rainbow over his disastrous set of sun; then against all mortal critics bear me out in it, thou just Spirit of Equality, which hast spread one royal mantle of humanity over all my kind! Bear me out in it, thou great democratic God! who didst not refuse to the swart convict, Bunyan, the pale, poetic pearl; Thou who didst clothe with doubly hammered leaves of finest gold, the stumped and paupered arm of old Cervantes; Thou who didst pick up Andrew Jackson from the pebbles; who didst hurl him upon a war-horse; who didst thunder him higher than a throne! Thou who, in all Thy mighty, earthly marchings, ever cullest Thy selectest champions from the kingly commons; bear me out in it, O God!

Chapter 27

KNIGHTS AND SQUIRES

STUBB was the second mate. He was a native of Cape Cod; and hence, according to local usage, was called a Cape-Cod-man. A happy-go-lucky; neither craven nor valiant; taking perils as they came with an indifferent air; and while engaged in the most imminent crisis of the chase, toiling away, calm and collected as a journeyman joiner engaged for the year. Good-humored, easy, and careless, he presided over his whale-boat as if the most deadly encounter were but a dinner, and his crew all invited guests. He was as particular about the comfortable arrangement of his part of the boat, as an old stage-driver is about the snugness of his box. When close to the whale, in the very death-lock of the fight, he handled his unpitying lance coolly and off-handedly, as a whistling tinker his hammer. He would hum over his old rigadig tunes while flank and flank with the most exasperated monster. Long usage had, for this Stubb, converted the jaws of death into an easy chair. What he thought of death itself, there is no telling. Whether he ever thought of it at all, might be a question; but, if he ever did chance to cast his mind that way after a comfortable dinner, no doubt, like a good sailor, he took it to be a sort of call of the watch to tumble aloft, and bestir themselves there, about something which he would find out when he obeyed the order, and not sooner.

What, perhaps, with other things, made Stubb such an easy-going, unfearing man, so cheerily trudging off with the burden of life in a world full of grave peddlers, all bowed to the ground with their packs; what helped to bring about that almost impious good-humor of his; that thing must have been his pipe. For, like his nose, his short, black little pipe was one of the regular features of his face. You would almost as soon have expected him to turn out of his bunk without his nose as without his pipe. He kept a whole row of pipes there ready loaded, stuck in a rack, within easy reach of his hand; and, whenever he turned in, he smoked them all out in succession, lighting one from the other to the end of the chapter; then loading them again to be in readiness anew. For, when Stubb dressed, instead of first putting his legs into his trowsers, he put his pipe into his mouth.

I say this continual smoking must have been one cause, at least, of his peculiar disposition; for every one knows that this earthly air, whether ashore or afloat, is terribly infected with the nameless miseries of the numberless mortals who have died exhaling it; and as in time of the cholera, some people go about with a camphorated handkerchief to their mouths; so, likewise, against all mortal tribulations, Stubb's tobacco smoke might have operated as a sort of disinfecting agent.

The third mate was Flask, a native of Tisbury, in Martha's Vineyard. A short, stout, ruddy young fellow, very pugnacious concerning whales, who somehow seemed to think that the great Leviathans had personally and hereditarily affronted him; and therefore it was a sort of point of honor with him, to destroy them whenever encountered. So utterly lost was he to all sense of reverence for the many marvels of their majestic bulk and mystic ways; and so dead to anything like an apprehension of any possible danger from encountering them; that in his poor opinion, the wondrous whale was but a species of magnified mouse, or at least water-rat, requiring only a little circumvention and some small application of time and trouble in order to kill and boil. This ignorant, unconscious fearlessness of his made him a little waggish in the matter of whales; he followed these fish for the fun of it; and a three years' voyage round Cape Horn was only a jolly joke that lasted that length of time. As a carpenter's nails are divided into wrought nails and cut nails; so mankind may be similarly divided. Little Flask was one of the wrought ones; made to clinch tight and last long. They called him King-Post on board of the Pequod; because, in form, he could be well likened to the short, square timber known by that name in Arctic whalers; and which by the means of many radiating side timbers inserted into it, serves to brace the ship against the icy concussions of those battering seas.

Now these three mates—Starbuck, Stubb, and Flask, were momentous men. They it was who by universal prescription commanded three of the Pequod's boats as headsmen. In that grand order of battle in which Captain Ahab would presently marshal his forces to descend on the whales, these three headsmen were as captains of companies. Or, being armed with their long keen whaling spears, they were as a picked trio of lancers; even as the harpooneers were flingers of javelins.

And since in this famous fishery, each mate or headsman, like a Gothic Knight of old, is always accompanied by his boat-steerer or harpooneer, who in certain conjunctures provides him with a fresh lance, when the former one has been badly twisted, or elbowed in the assault; and moreover, as there generally subsists between the two, a close intimacy and friendliness; it is therefore but meet, that in this place we set down who the Pequod's harpooneers were, and to what headsman each of them belonged.

First of all was Queequeg, whom Starbuck, the chief mate, had selected for his squire. But Queequeg is already known.

Next was Tashtego, an unmixed Indian from Gay Head, the most westerly promontory of Martha's Vineyard, where there still exists the last remnant of a village of red men, which has long supplied the neighboring island of Nantucket with many of her most daring harpooneers. In the fishery, they usually go by the generic name of Gay-Headers. Tashtego's long, lean, sable hair, his high cheek bones, and black rounding eyes—for an Indian, Oriental in their largeness, but Antarctic in their glittering expression—all this sufficiently proclaimed him an inheritor of the unvitiated blood of those proud warrior hunters, who, in quest of the great New England moose, had scoured, bow in hand, the aboriginal forests of the main. But no longer snuffing in the trail of the wild beasts of the woodland, Tashtego now hunted in the wake of the great whales of the sea; the unerring harpoon of the son fitly replacing the infallible arrow of the sires. To look at the tawny brawn of his lithe snaky limbs, you would almost have credited the superstitions of some of the earlier Puritans, and half believed this wild Indian to be a son of the Prince of the Powers of the Air. Tashtego was Stubb the second mate's squire.

Third among the harpooneers was Daggoo, a gigantic, coal-black negro-savage, with a lion-like tread—an Ahasuerus to behold. Suspended from his ears were two golden hoops, so large that the sailors called them ring-bolts, and would talk of securing the top-sail halyards to them. In his youth Daggoo had voluntarily shipped on board of a whaler, lying in a lonely bay on his native coast. And never having been anywhere in the world but in Africa, Nantucket, and the pagan harbors most frequented by whalemen; and having now led for many years the bold life of the fishery in the ships of owners uncommonly heedful of what manner of men they shipped; Daggoo retained all his barbaric virtues, and erect as a giraffe, moved about the decks in all the pomp of six feet five in his socks. There was a corporeal humility in looking up at him; and a white man standing before him seemed a white flag come to beg truce of a fortress. Curious to tell, this imperial negro, Ahasuerus Daggoo, was the Squire of little Flask, who looked like a chess-man beside him. As for the residue of the Pequod's company, be it said, that at the present day not one in two of the many thousand men before the mast employed in the American whale fishery, are Americans born, though pretty nearly all the officers are. Herein it is the same with the American whale fishery as with the American army and military and merchant navies, and the engineering forces employed in the construction of the American Canals and Railroads. The same, I say, because in all these cases the native American liberally provides the brains, the rest of the world as generously supplying the muscles. No small number of these whaling seamen belong to the Azores, where the outward bound Nantucket whalers frequently touch to augment their crews from the hardy peasants of those rocky shores. In like manner, the Greenland whalers sailing out of Hull or London, put in at the Shetland Islands, to receive the full complement of their crew. Upon the passage homewards, they drop them there again. How it is, there is no telling, but Islanders seem to make the best whalemen. They were nearly all Islanders in the Pequod, *Isolatoes* too, I call such, not acknowledging the common continent of men, but each *Isolato* living on a separate continent of his own. Yet now, federated along one keel, what a set these Isolatoes were! An Anacharsis Clootz deputation from all the isles of the sea, and all the ends of the earth, accompanying Old Ahab in the Pequod to lay the world's grievances before that bar from which not very many of them ever come back. Black Little Pip—he never did! Poor Alabama boy! On the grim Pequod's forecastle, ye shall ere long see him, beating his tambourine; prelusive of the eternal time, when sent for, to the great quarter-deck on high, he was bid strike in with angels, and beat his tambourine in glory; called a coward here, hailed a hero there!

Chapter 28

AHAB

FOR SEVERAL DAYS after leaving Nantucket, nothing above hatches was seen of Captain Ahab. The mates regularly relieved each other at the watches, and for aught that could be seen to the contrary, they seemed to be the only commanders of the ship; only they sometimes issued from the cabin with orders so sudden and peremptory, that after all it was plain they but commanded vicariously. Yes, their supreme lord and dictator was there, though hitherto unseen by any eyes not permitted to penetrate into the now sacred retreat of the cabin.

Every time I ascended to the deck from my watches below, I instantly gazed aft to mark if any strange face were visible; for my first vague disquietude touching the unknown captain, now in the seclusion of the sea, became almost a perturbation. This was strangely heightened at times by the ragged Elijah's diabolical incoherences uninvitedly recurring to me, with a subtle energy I could not have before conceived of. But poorly could I withstand them, much as in other moods I was almost ready to smile at the solemn whimsicalities of that outlandish prophet of the wharves. But whatever it was of apprehensiveness or uneasiness—to call it so—which I felt, yet whenever I came to look about me in the ship, it seemed against all warranty to cherish such emotions. For though the harpooneers, with the great body of the crew, were a far more barbaric, heathenish, and motley set than any of the tame merchant-ship companies which my previous experiences had made me acquainted with, still I ascribed this—and rightly ascribed it—to the fierce uniqueness of the very nature of that wild Scandinavian vocation in which I had so abandonedly embarked. But it was especially the aspect of the three chief officers of the ship, the mates, which was most forcibly calculated to allay these colorless misgivings, and induce confidence and cheerfulness in every presentment of the voyage. Three better, more likely sea-officers and men, each

923

in his own different way, could not readily be found, and they were every one of them Americans; a Nantucketer, a Vineyarder, a Cape man. Now, it being Christmas when the ship shot from out her harbor, for a space we had biting Polar weather, though all the time running away from it to the southward; and by every degree and minute of latitude which we sailed, gradually leaving that merciless winter, and all its intolerable weather behind us. It was one of those less lowering, but still grey and gloomy enough mornings of the transition, when with a fair wind the ship was rushing through the water with a vindictive sort of leaping and melancholy rapidity, that as I mounted to the deck at the call of the forenoon watch, so soon as I levelled my glance towards the taffrail, foreboding shivers ran over me. Reality outran apprehension; Captain Ahab stood upon his quarter-deck.

There seemed no sign of common bodily illness about him, nor of the recovery from any. He looked like a man cut away from the stake, when the fire has overrunningly wasted all the limbs without consuming them, or taking away one particle from their compacted aged robustness. His whole high, broad form, seemed made of solid bronze, and shaped in an unalterable mould, like Cellini's cast Perseus. Threading its way out from among his grey hairs, and continuing right down one side of his tawny scorched face and neck, till it disappeared in his clothing, you saw a slender rod-like mark, lividly whitish. It resembled that perpendicular seam sometimes made in the straight, lofty trunk of a great tree, when the upper lightning tearingly darts down it, and without wrenching a single twig, peels and grooves out the bark from top to bottom, ere running off into the soil, leaving the tree still greenly alive, but branded. Whether that mark was born with him, or whether it was the scar left by some desperate wound, no one could certainly say. By some tacit consent, throughout the voyage little or no allusion was made to it, especially by the mates. But once Tashtego's senior, an old Gay-Head Indian among the crew, superstitiously asserted that not till he was full forty years old did Ahab become that way branded, and then it came upon him, not in the fury of any mortal fray, but in an elemental strife at sea. Yet, this wild hint seemed inferentially negatived, by what a grey Manxman insinuated, an old sepulchral man, who, having never before sailed out of Nantucket, had never ere this laid eye upon wild Ahab. Nevertheless, the old sea-traditions, the immemorial credulities, popularly invested this old Manxman with preternatural powers of discernment. So that no white sailor seriously contradicted him when he said that if ever Captain Ahab should be tranquilly laid out—which might hardly come to pass, so he muttered—then, whoever should do that last office for the dead, would find a birth-mark on him from crown to sole.

So powerfully did the whole grim aspect of Ahab affect me, and the livid brand which streaked it, that for the first few moments I hardly noted that not a little of this overbearing grimness was owing to the barbaric white leg upon which he partly stood. It had previously come to me that this ivory leg had at sea been fashioned from the polished bone of the sperm whale's jaw. "Aye, he was dismasted off Japan," said the old Gay-Head Indian once; "but like his dismasted craft, he shipped another mast without coming home for it. He has a quiver of 'em."

I was struck with the singular posture he maintained. Upon each side of the Pequod's quarter deck, and pretty close to the mizen shrouds, there was an auger hole, bored about half an inch or so, into the plank. His bone leg steadied in that hole; one arm elevated, and holding by a shroud; Captain Ahab stood erect, looking straight out beyond the ship's ever-pitching prow. There was an infinity of firmest fortitude, a determinate, unsurrenderable wilfulness, in the fixed and fearless, forward dedication of that glance. Not a word he spoke; nor did his officers say aught to him; though by all their minutest gestures and expressions, they plainly showed the uneasy, if not painful, consciousness of being under a troubled master-eye. And not only that, but moody stricken Ahab stood before them with a crucifixion in his face; in all the nameless regal overbearing dignity of some mighty woe.

Ere long, from his first visit in the air, he withdrew into his cabin. But after that morning, he was every day visible to the crew; either standing in his pivot-hole, or seated upon an ivory stool he had; or heavily walking the deck. As the sky grew less gloomy; indeed, began to grow a little genial, he became still less and less a recluse; as if, when the ship had sailed from home, nothing but the dead wintry bleakness of the sea had then kept him so secluded. And, by and by, it came to pass, that he was almost continually in the air; but, as yet, for all that he said, or perceptibly did, on the at last sunny deck, he seemed as unnecessary there as another mast. But the Pequod was only making a passage now; not regularly cruising; nearly all whaling preparatives needing supervision the mates were fully competent to, so that there was little or nothing, out of himself, to employ or excite Ahab, now; and thus chase away, for that one interval, the clouds that layer upon layer were piled upon his brow, as ever all clouds choose the loftiest peaks to pile themselves upon.

Nevertheless, ere long, the warm, warbling persuasiveness of the pleasant, holiday weather we came to, seemed gradually to charm him from his mood. For, as when the red-cheeked, dancing girls, April and May, trip home to the wintry, misanthropic woods; even the barest, ruggedest, most thundercloven old oak will at least send forth some few green sprouts, to welcome such glad-hearted visitants; so Ahab did, in the end, a little respond to the playful allurings of that girlish air. More than once did he put forth the faint blossom of a look, which, in any other man, would have soon flowered out in a smile.

Chapter 29

ENTER AHAB; TO HIM, STUBB

SOME DAYS ELAPSED, and ice and icebergs all astern, the Pequod now went rolling through the bright Quito spring, which, at sea, almost perpetually reigns on the threshold of the eternal August of the Tropic. The warmly cool, clear, ringing, perfumed, overflowing, redundant days, were as crystal goblets of Persian sherbet, heaped up—flaked up, with rose-water snow. The starred and stately nights seemed haughty dames in jewelled velvets, nursing at home in lonely pride, the memory of their absent conquering Earls, the golden helmeted suns! For sleeping man, 'twas hard to choose between such winsome days and such seducing nights. But all the witcheries of that unwaning weather did not merely lend new spells and potencies to the outward world. Inward they turned upon the soul, especially when the still mild hours of eve came on; then, memory shot her crystals as the clear ice most forms of noiseless twilights. And all these subtle agencies, more and more they wrought on Ahab's texture.

Old age is always wakeful; as if, the longer linked with life, the less man has to do with aught that looks like death. Among sea-commanders, the old greybeards will oftenest leave their berths to visit the night-cloaked deck. It was so with Ahab; only that now, of late, he seemed so much to live in the open air, that truly speaking, his visits were more to the cabin, than from the cabin to the planks. "It feels like going down into one's tomb,"—he would mutter to himself,—"for an old captain like me to be descending this narrow scuttle, to go to my grave-dug berth."

So, almost every twenty-four hours, when the watches of the night were set, and the band on deck sentinelled the slumbers of the band below; and when if a rope was to be hauled upon the forecastle, the sailors flung it not rudely down, as by day, but with some cautiousness dropt it to its place, for fear of disturbing their slumbering shipmates; when this sort

of steady quietude would begin to prevail, habitually, the silent steersman would watch the cabin-scuttle; and ere long
the old man would emerge, griping at the iron banister, to
help his crippled way. Some considerating touch of humanity
was in him; for at times like these, he usually abstained from
patrolling the quarter-deck; because to his wearied mates,
seeking repose within six inches of his ivory heel, such would
have been the reverberating crack and din of that bony step,
that their dreams would have been of the crunching teeth of
sharks. But once, the mood was on him too deep for common
regardings; and as with heavy, lumber-like pace he was measuring the ship from taffrail to mainmast, Stubb, the odd second mate, came up from below, and with a certain unassured,
deprecating humorousness, hinted that if Captain Ahab was
pleased to walk the planks, then, no one could say nay; but
there might be some way of muffling the noise; hinting something indistinctly and hesitatingly about a globe of tow, and
the insertion into it, of the ivory heel. Ah! Stubb, thou did'st
not know Ahab then.

"Am I a cannon-ball, Stubb," said Ahab, "that thou
wouldst wad me that fashion? But go thy ways; I had forgot.
Below to thy nightly grave; where such as ye sleep between
shrouds, to use ye to the filling one at last.—Down, dog, and
kennel!"

Starting at the unforeseen concluding exclamation of the so
suddenly scornful old man, Stubb was speechless a moment;
then said excitedly, "I am not used to be spoken to that way,
sir; I do but less than half like it, sir."

"Avast!" gritted Ahab between his set teeth, and violently
moving away, as if to avoid some passionate temptation.

"No, sir; not yet," said Stubb, emboldened, "I will not
tamely be called a dog, sir."

"Then be called ten times a donkey, and a mule, and an ass,
and begone, or I'll clear the world of thee!"

As he said this, Ahab advanced upon him with such overbearing terrors in his aspect, that Stubb involuntarily retreated.

"I was never served so before without giving a hard blow
for it," muttered Stubb, as he found himself descending the
cabin-scuttle. "It's very queer. Stop, Stubb; somehow, now,
I don't well know whether to go back and strike him, or—

what's that?—down here on my knees and pray for him?
Yes, that was the thought coming up in me; but it would be
the first time I ever *did* pray. It's queer; very queer; and he's
queer too; aye, take him fore and aft, he's about the queerest
old man Stubb ever sailed with. How he flashed at me!—his
eyes like powder-pans! is he mad? Anyway there's something
on his mind, as sure as there must be something on a deck
when it cracks. He ain't in his bed now, either, more than
three hours out of the twenty-four; and he don't sleep then.
Didn't that Dough-Boy, the steward, tell me that of a morning he always finds the old man's hammock clothes all rumpled and tumbled, and the sheets down at the foot, and the
coverlid almost tied into knots, and the pillow a sort of frightful hot, as though a baked brick had been on it? A hot old
man! I guess he's got what some folks ashore call a conscience; it's a kind of Tic-Dolly-row they say—worse nor a
toothache. Well, well; I don't know what it is, but the Lord
keep me from catching it. He's full of riddles; I wonder what
he goes into the after hold for, every night, as Dough-Boy
tells me he suspects; what's that for, I should like to know?
Who's made appointments with him in the hold? Ain't that
queer, now? But there's no telling, it's the old game—Here
goes for a snooze. Damn me, it's worth a fellow's while to
be born into the world, if only to fall right asleep. And now
that I think of it, that's about the first thing babies do, and
that's a sort of queer, too. Damn me, but all things are queer,
come to think of 'em. But that's against my principles. Think
not, is my eleventh commandment; and sleep when you can,
is my twelfth—So here goes again. But how's that? didn't he
call me a dog? blazes! he called me ten times a donkey, and
piled a lot of jackasses on top of *that*! He might as well have
kicked me, and done with it. Maybe he *did* kick me, and I
didn't observe it, I was so taken all aback with his brow,
somehow. It flashed like a bleached bone. What the devil's
the matter with me? I don't stand right on my legs. Coming
afoul of that old man has a sort of turned me wrong side out.
By the Lord, I must have been dreaming, though—How?
how? how?—but the only way's to stash it; so here goes to
hammock again; and in the morning, I'll see how this plaguey
juggling thinks over by daylight."

Chapter 30

THE PIPE

W HEN STUBB had departed, Ahab stood for a while lean- ing over the bulwarks; and then, as had been usual with him of late, calling a sailor of the watch, he sent him below for his ivory stool, and also his pipe. Lighting the pipe at the binnacle lamp and planting the stool on the weather side of the deck, he sat and smoked.

In old Norse times, the thrones of the sea-loving Danish kings were fabricated, saith tradition, of the tusks of the nar- whale. How could one look at Ahab then, seated on that tri- pod of bones, without bethinking him of the royalty it symbolized? For a Khan of the plank, and a king of the sea, and a great lord of Leviathans was Ahab.

Some moments passed, during which the thick vapor came from his mouth in quick and constant puffs, which blew back again into his face. "How now," he soliloquized at last, with- drawing the tube, "this smoking no longer soothes. Oh, my pipe! hard must it go with me if thy charm be gone! Here have I been unconsciously toiling, not pleasuring,—aye, and ignorantly smoking to windward all the while; to windward, and with such nervous whiffs, as if, like the dying whale, my final jets were the strongest and fullest of trouble. What busi- ness have I with this pipe? This thing that is meant for se- reneness, to send up mild white vapors among mild white hairs, not among torn iron-grey locks like mine. I'll smoke no more—"

He tossed the still lighted pipe into the sea. The fire hissed in the waves; the same instant the ship shot by the bubble the sinking pipe made. With slouched hat, Ahab lurchingly paced the planks.

Chapter 31

Queen Mab

NEXT MORNING Stubb accosted Flask.

"Such a queer dream, King-Post, I never had. You know the old man's ivory leg, well I dreamed he kicked me with it; and when I tried to kick back, upon my soul, my little man, I kicked my leg right off! And then, presto! Ahab seemed a pyramid, and I, like a blazing fool, kept kicking at it. But what was still more curious, Flask—you know how curious all dreams are—through all this rage that I was in, I somehow seemed to be thinking to myself, that after all, it was not much of an insult, that kick from Ahab. 'Why,' thinks I, 'what's the row? It's not a real leg, only a false leg.' And there's a mighty difference between a living thump and a dead thump. That's what makes a blow from the hand, Flask, fifty times more savage to bear than a blow from a cane. The living member—that makes the living insult, my little man. And thinks I to myself all the while, mind, while I was stubbing my silly toes against that cursed pyramid—so confoundedly contradictory was it all, all the while, I say, I was thinking to myself, 'what's his leg now, but a cane—a whalebone cane. Yes,' thinks I, 'it was only a playful cudgelling—in fact, only a whaleboning that he gave me—not a base kick. Besides,' thinks I, 'look at it once; why, the end of it—the foot part— what a small sort of end it is; whereas, if a broad footed farmer kicked me, *there's* a devilish broad insult. But this insult is whittled down to a point only.' But now comes the greatest joke of the dream, Flask. While I was battering away at the pyramid, a sort of badger-haired old merman, with a hump on his back, takes me by the shoulders, and slews me round. 'What are you 'bout?' says he. 'Slid! man, but I was frightened. Such a phiz! But, somehow, next moment I was over the fright. 'What am I about?' says I at last. 'And what business is that of yours, I should like to know, Mr. Humpback? Do *you* want a kick?' By the lord, Flask, I had no sooner said that, than he turned round his stern to me, bent over, and dragging up a lot of sea-weed he

had for a clout—what do you think, I saw?—why thunder
alive, man, his stern was stuck full of marlinspikes, with the
points out. Says I, on second thoughts, 'I guess I won't kick you,
old fellow.' 'Wise Stubb,' said he, 'wise Stubb;' and kept muttering it all the time, a sort of eating of his own gums like a chimney
hag. Seeing he wasn't going to stop saying over his 'wise Stubb,
wise Stubb,' I thought I might as well fall to kicking the pyramid
again. But I had only just lifted my foot for it, when he roared
out, 'Stop that kicking!' 'Halloa,' says I, 'what's the matter now,
old fellow?' 'Look ye here,' says he; 'let's argue the insult. Captain Ahab kicked ye, didn't he?' 'Yes, he did,' says I—'right *here*
it was.' 'Very good,' says he—'he used his ivory leg, didn't he?'
'Yes, he did,' says I. 'Well then,' says he, 'wise Stubb, what have
you to complain of? Didn't he kick with right good will? it
wasn't a common pitch pine leg he kicked with, was it? No, you
were kicked by a great man, and with a beautiful ivory leg,
Stubb. It's an honor; I consider it an honor. Listen, wise Stubb.
In old England the greatest lords think it great glory to be
slapped by a queen, and made garter-knights of; but, be *your*
boast, Stubb, that ye were kicked by old Ahab, and made a wise
man of. Remember what I say; *be* kicked by him; account his
kicks honors; and on no account kick back; for you can't help
yourself, wise Stubb. Don't you see that pyramid?' With that, he
all of a sudden seemed somehow, in some queer fashion, to
swim off into the air. I snored; rolled over; and there I was in
my hammock! Now, what do you think of that dream, Flask?"

"I don't know; it seems a sort of foolish to me, tho'."

"May be; may be. But it's made a wise man of me, Flask.
D'ye see Ahab standing there, sideways looking over the
stern? Well, the best thing you can do, Flask, is to let that old
man alone; never speak quick to him, whatever he says. Halloa! what's that he shouts? Hark!"

"Mast-head, there! Look sharp, all of ye! There are whales
hereabouts! If ye see a white one, split your lungs for him!"

"What d'ye think of that now, Flask? ain't there a small
drop of something queer about that, eh? A white whale—did
ye mark that, man? Look ye—there's something special in the
wind. Stand by for it, Flask. Ahab has that that's bloody on
his mind. But, mum; he comes this way."

Chapter 32

CETOLOGY

ALREADY we are boldly launched upon the deep; but soon we shall be lost in its unshored, harborless immensities. Ere that come to pass; ere the Pequod's weedy hull rolls side by side with the barnacled hulls of the leviathan; at the outset it is but well to attend to a matter almost indispensable to a thorough appreciative understanding of the more special leviathanic revelations and allusions of all sorts which are to follow.

It is some systematized exhibition of the whale in his broad genera, that I would now fain put before you. Yet is it no easy task. The classification of the constituents of a chaos, nothing less is here essayed. Listen to what the best and latest authorities have laid down.

"No branch of Zoology is so much involved as that which is entitled Cetology," says Captain Scoresby, A. D. 1820.

"It is not my intention, were it in my power, to enter into the inquiry as to the true method of dividing the cetacea into groups and families. * * * Utter confusion exists among the historians of this animal" (sperm whale), says Surgeon Beale, A. D. 1839.

"Unfitness to pursue our research in the unfathomable waters." "Impenetrable veil covering our knowledge of the cetacea." "A field strewn with thorns." "All these incomplete indications but serve to torture us naturalists."

Thus speak of the whale, the great Cuvier, and John Hunter, and Lesson, those lights of zoology and anatomy. Nevertheless, though of real knowledge there be little, yet of books there are a plenty; and so in some small degree, with cetology, or the science of whales. Many are the men, small and great, old and new, landsmen and seamen, who have at large or in little, written of the whale. Run over a few: — The Authors of the Bible; Aristotle; Pliny; Aldrovandi; Sir Thomas Browne; Gesner; Ray; Linnæus; Rondeletius; Willoughby; Green; Artedi; Sibbald; Brisson; Marten; Lacépède;

Bonnatierre; Desmarest; Baron Cuvier; Frederick Cuvier; John Hunter; Owen; Scoresby; Beale; Bennett; J. Ross Browne; the Author of Miriam Coffin; Olmsted; and the Rev. Henry T. Cheever. But to what ultimate generalizing purpose all these have written, the above cited extracts will show.

Of the names in this list of whale authors, only those following Owen ever saw living whales; and but one of them was a real professional harpooneer and whaleman. I mean Captain Scoresby. On the separate subject of the Greenland or right-whale, he is the best existing authority. But Scoresby knew nothing and says nothing of the great sperm whale, compared with which the Greenland whale is almost unworthy mentioning. And here be it said, that the Greenland whale is an usurper upon the throne of the seas. He is not even by any means the largest of the whales. Yet, owing to the long priority of his claims, and the profound ignorance which, till some seventy years back, invested the then fabulous or utterly unknown sperm-whale; and which ignorance to this present day still reigns in all but some few scientific retreats and whale-ports; this usurpation has been every way complete. Reference to nearly all the leviathanic allusions in the great poets of past days, will satisfy you that the Greenland whale, without one rival, was to them the monarch of the seas. But the time has at last come for a new proclamation. This is Charing Cross; hear ye! good people all,—the Greenland whale is deposed,—the great sperm whale now reigneth!

There are only two books in being which at all pretend to put the living sperm whale before you, and at the same time, in the remotest degree succeed in the attempt. Those books are Beale's and Bennett's; both in their time surgeons to English South-Sea whale-ships, and both exact and reliable men. The original matter touching the sperm whale to be found in their volumes is necessarily small; but so far as it goes, it is of excellent quality, though mostly confined to scientific description. As yet, however, the sperm whale, scientific or poetic, lives not complete in any literature. Far above all other hunted whales, his is an unwritten life.

Now the various species of whales need some sort of popular comprehensive classification, if only an easy outline one for the present, hereafter to be filled in all its departments by subsequent laborers. As no better man advances to take this matter in hand, I hereupon offer my own poor endeavors. I promise nothing complete; because any human thing supposed to be complete, must for that very reason infallibly be faulty. I shall not pretend to a minute anatomical description of the various species, or—in this place at least—to much of any description. My object here is simply to project the draught of a systematization of cetology. I am the architect, not the builder.

But it is a ponderous task; no ordinary letter-sorter in the Post-office is equal to it. To grope down into the bottom of the sea after them; to have one's hands among the unspeakable foundations, ribs, and very pelvis of the world; this is a fearful thing. What am I that I should essay to hook the nose of this leviathan! The awful tauntings in Job might well appal me. "Will he (the leviathan) make a covenant with thee? Behold the hope of him is vain!" But I have swam through libraries and sailed through oceans; I have had to do with whales with these visible hands; I am in earnest; and I will try. There are some preliminaries to settle.

First: The uncertain, unsettled condition of this science of Cetology is in the very vestibule attested by the fact, that in some quarters it still remains a moot point whether a whale be a fish. In his System of Nature, A.D. 1766, Linnæus declares, "I hereby separate the whales from the fish." But of my own knowledge, I know that down to the year 1850, sharks and shad, alewives and herring, against Linnæus's express edict, were still found dividing the possession of the same seas with the Leviathan.

The grounds upon which Linnæus would fain have banished the whales from the waters, he states as follows: "On account of their warm bilocular heart, their lungs, their movable eyelids, their hollow ears, penem intrantem feminam mammis lactantem," and finally, "ex lege naturæ jure meritoque." I submitted all this to my friends Simeon Macey and Charley Coffin, of Nantucket, both messmates of mine in a certain voyage, and they united in the opinion that the reasons set forth were altogether insufficient. Charley profanely hinted they were humbug.

Be it known that, waiving all argument, I take the good old fashioned ground that the whale is a fish, and call upon holy Jonah to back me. This fundamental thing settled, the next point is, in what internal respect does the whale differ from other fish. Above, Linnæus has given you those items. But in brief, they are these: lungs and warm blood; whereas, all other fish are lungless and cold blooded.

Next: how shall we define the whale, by his obvious externals, so as conspicuously to label him for all time to come? To be short, then, a whale is *a spouting fish with a horizontal tail*. There you have him. However contracted, that definition is the result of expanded meditation. A walrus spouts much like a whale, but the walrus is not a fish, because he is amphibious. But the last term of the definition is still more cogent, as coupled with the first. Almost any one must have noticed that all the fish familiar to landsmen have not a flat, but a vertical, or up-and-down tail. Whereas, among spouting fish the tail, though it may be similarly shaped, invariably assumes a horizontal position.

By the above definition of what a whale is, I do by no means exclude from the leviathanic brotherhood any sea creature hitherto identified with the whale by the best informed Nantucketers; nor, on the other hand, link with it any fish hitherto authoritatively regarded as alien.* Hence, all the smaller, spouting, and horizontal tailed fish must be included in this ground-plan of Cetology. Now, then, come the grand divisions of the entire whale host.

First: According to magnitude I divide the whales into three primary BOOKS (subdivisible into CHAPTERS), and these shall comprehend them all, both small and large.

---

*I am aware that down to the present time, the fish styled Lamantins and Dugongs (Pig-fish and Sow-fish of the Coffins of Nantucket) are included by many naturalists among the whales. But as these pig-fish are a nosy, contemptible set, mostly lurking in the mouths of rivers, and feeding on wet hay, and especially as they do not spout, I deny their credentials as whales; and have presented them with their passports to quit the Kingdom of Cetology.

I. The FOLIO WHALE; II. the OCTAVO WHALE; III. the DUODECIMO WHALE.

As the type of the FOLIO I present the *Sperm Whale*; of the OCTAVO, the *Grampus*; of the DUODECIMO, the *Porpoise*.

FOLIOS. Among these I here include the following chapters:—I. The *Sperm Whale*; II. the *Right Whale*; III. the *Fin Back Whale*; IV. the *Hump-backed Whale*; V. the *Razor Back Whale*; VI. the *Sulphur Bottom Whale*.

BOOK I. (*Folio*), CHAPTER I. (*Sperm Whale*).—This whale, among the English of old vaguely known as the Trumpa whale, and the Physeter whale, and the Anvil Headed whale, is the present Cachalot of the French, and the Pottfisch of the Germans, and the Macrocephalus of the Long Words. He is, without doubt, the largest inhabitant of the globe; the most formidable of all whales to encounter; the most majestic in aspect; and lastly, by far the most valuable in commerce; he being the only creature from which that valuable substance, spermaceti, is obtained. All his peculiarities will, in many other places, be enlarged upon. It is chiefly with his name that I now have to do. Philologically considered, it is absurd. Some centuries ago, when the Sperm whale was almost wholly unknown in his own proper individuality, and when his oil was only accidentally obtained from the stranded fish; in those days spermaceti, it would seem, was popularly supposed to be derived from a creature identical with the one then known in England as the Greenland or Right Whale. It was the idea also, that this same spermaceti was that quickening humor of the Greenland Whale which the first syllable of the word literally expresses. In those times, also, spermaceti was exceedingly scarce, not being used for light, but only as an ointment and medicament. It was only to be had from the druggists as you nowadays buy an ounce of rhubarb. When, as I opine, in the course of time, the true nature of spermaceti became known, its original name was still retained by the dealers; no doubt to enhance its value by a notion so strangely significant of its scarcity. And so the appellation must at last have come to be bestowed upon the whale from which this spermaceti was really derived.

BOOK I. (*Folio*), CHAPTER II. (*Right Whale*).—In one respect this is the most venerable of the leviathans, being the one first regularly hunted by man. It yields the article commonly known as whalebone or baleen; and the oil specially known as "whale oil," an inferior article in commerce. Among the fishermen, he is indiscriminately designated by all the following titles: The Whale; the Greenland Whale; the Black Whale; the Great Whale; the True Whale; the Right Whale. There is a deal of obscurity concerning the identity of the species thus multitudinously baptized. What then is the whale, which I include in the second species of my Folios? It is the Great Mysticetus of the English naturalists; the Greenland Whale of the English whalemen; the Baleine Ordinaire of the French whalemen; the Gronlands Walfisk of the Swedes. It is the whale which for more than two centuries past has been hunted by the Dutch and English in the Arctic seas; it is the whale which the American fishermen have long pursued in the Indian ocean, on the Brazil Banks, on the Nor' West Coast, and various other parts of the world, designated by them Right Whale Cruising Grounds.

Some pretend to see a difference between the Greenland whale of the English and the right whale of the Americans. But they precisely agree in all their grand features; nor has there yet been presented a single determinate fact upon which to ground a radical distinction. It is by endless subdivisions based upon the most inconclusive differences, that some departments of natural history become so repellingly intricate. The right whale will be elsewhere treated of at some length, with reference to elucidating the sperm whale.

BOOK I. (*Folio*), CHAPTER III. (*Fin-Back*).—Under this head I reckon a monster which, by the various names of Fin-Back, Tall-Spout, and Long-John, has been seen almost in every sea and is commonly the whale whose distant jet is so often descried by passengers crossing the Atlantic, in the New York packet-tracks. In the length he attains, and in his baleen, the Fin-back resembles the right whale, but is of a less portly girth, and a lighter color, approaching to olive. His great lips present a cable-like aspect, formed by the intertwisting, slanting folds of large wrinkles. His grand distinguishing feature, the fin, from which he derives his name, is often a conspicuous object. This fin is some three or four feet long, growing vertically from the hinder part of the back, of an angular shape, and with a very sharp pointed end. Even if not the slightest other part of the creature be visible, this isolated fin will, at times, be seen plainly projecting from the surface. When the sea is moderately calm, and slightly marked with spherical ripples, and this gnomon-like fin stands up and casts shadows upon the wrinkled surface, it may well be supposed that the watery circle surrounding it somewhat resembles a dial, with its style and wavy hour-lines graved on it. On that Ahaz-dial the shadow often goes back. The Fin-Back is not gregarious. He seems a whale-hater, as some men are man-haters. Very shy; always going solitary; unexpectedly rising to the surface in the remotest and most sullen waters; his straight and single lofty jet rising like a tall misanthropic spear upon a barren plain; gifted with such wondrous power and velocity in swimming, as to defy all present pursuit from man; this leviathan seems the banished and unconquerable Cain of his race, bearing for his mark that style upon his back. From having the baleen in his mouth, the Fin-Back is sometimes included with the right whale, among a theoretic species denominated *Whalebone whales*, that is, whales with baleen. Of these so called Whalebone whales, there would seem to be several varieties, most of which, however, are little known. Broad-nosed whales and beaked whales; pike-headed whales; bunched whales; under-jawed whales and rostrated whales, are the fishermen's names for a few sorts.

In connexion with this appellative of "Whalebone whales," it is of great importance to mention, that however such a nomenclature may be convenient in facilitating allusions to some kind of whales, yet it is in vain to attempt a clear classification of the Leviathan, founded upon either his baleen, or hump, or fin, or teeth; notwithstanding that those marked parts or features very obviously seem better adapted to afford the basis for a regular system of Cetology than any other detached bodily distinctions, which the whale, in his kinds, presents. How then? The baleen, hump, back-fin, and teeth; these are things whose peculiarities are indiscriminately dispersed among all sorts of whales, without any regard to what may be the nature of their structure in other and more essential particulars. Thus, the sperm whale and the humpbacked whale, each has a hump; but there the similitude ceases.

Then, this same humpbacked whale and the Greenland whale, each of these has baleen; but there again the similitude ceases. And it is just the same with the other parts above mentioned. In various sorts of whales, they form such irregular combinations; or, in the case of any one of them detached, such an irregular isolation; as utterly to defy all general methodization formed upon such a basis. On this rock every one of the whale-naturalists has split.

But it may possibly be conceived that, in the internal parts of the whale, in his anatomy—there, at least, we shall be able to hit the right classification. Nay; what thing, for example, is there in the Greenland whale's anatomy more striking than his baleen? Yet we have seen that by his baleen it is impossible correctly to classify the Greenland whale. And if you descend into the bowels of the various leviathans, why there you will not find distinctions a fiftieth part as available to the systematizer as those external ones already enumerated. What then remains? nothing but to take hold of the whales bodily, in their entire liberal volume, and boldly sort them that way. And this is the Bibliographical system here adopted; and it is the only one that can possibly succeed, for it alone is practicable. To proceed.

BOOK I. (*Folio*), CHAPTER IV. (*Hump Back*).—This whale is often seen on the northern American coast. He has been frequently captured there, and towed into harbor. He has a great pack on him like a peddler; or you might call him the Elephant and Castle whale. At any rate, the popular name for him does not sufficiently distinguish him, since the sperm whale also has a hump, though a smaller one. His oil is not very valuable. He has baleen. He is the most gamesome and light-hearted of all the whales, making more gay foam and white water generally than any other of them.

BOOK I. (*Folio*), CHAPTER V. (*Razor Back*).—Of this whale little is known but his name. I have seen him at a distance off Cape Horn. Of a retiring nature, he eludes both hunters and philosophers. Though no coward, he has never yet shown any part of him but his back, which rises in a long sharp ridge. Let him go. I know little more of him, nor does anybody else.

BOOK I. (*Folio*), CHAPTER VI. (*Sulphur Bottom*).—Another retiring gentleman, with a brimstone belly, doubtless got by scraping along the Tartarian tiles in some of his profounder divings. He is seldom seen; at least I have never seen him except in the remoter southern seas, and then always at too great a distance to study his countenance. He is never chased; he would run away with rope-walks of line. Prodigies are told of him. Adieu, Sulphur Bottom! I can say nothing more that is true of ye, nor can the oldest Nantucketer.

Thus ends BOOK I. (*Folio*), and now begins BOOK II. (*Octavo*).

OCTAVOES.* These embrace the whales of middling magnitude, among which at present may be numbered:—I., the *Grampus*; II., the *Black Fish*; III., the *Narwhale*; IV., the *Killer*; V., the *Thrasher*.

BOOK II. (*Octavo*), CHAPTER I. (*Grampus*).—Though this fish, whose loud sonorous breathing, or rather blowing, has furnished a proverb to landsmen, is so well known a denizen of the deep, yet is he not popularly classed among whales. But possessing all the grand distinctive features of the leviathan, most naturalists have recognized him for one. He is of moderate octavo size, varying from fifteen to twenty-five feet in length, and of corresponding dimensions round the waist. He swims in herds; he is never regularly hunted, though his oil is considerable in quantity, and pretty good for light. By some fishermen his approach is regarded as premonitory of the advance of the great sperm whale.

BOOK II. (*Octavo*), CHAPTER II. (*Black Fish*).—I give the popular fishermen's names for all these fish, for generally they are the best. Where any name happens to be vague or inexpressive, I shall say so, and suggest another. I do so now, touching the Black Fish, so called, because blackness is the rule among almost all whales. So, call him the Hyena Whale, if you please. His voracity is well known, and from the circumstance that the inner angles of his lips are curved upwards, he carries an everlasting Mephistophelean grin on his

---

*Why this book of whales is not denominated the Quarto is very plain. Because, while the whales of this order, though smaller than those of the former order, nevertheless retain a proportionate likeness to them in figure, yet the bookbinder's Quarto volume in its diminished form does not preserve the shape of the Folio volume, but the Octavo volume does.

face. This whale averages some sixteen or eighteen feet in length. He is found in almost all latitudes. He has a peculiar way of showing his dorsal hooked fin in swimming, which looks something like a Roman nose. When not more profitably employed, the sperm whale hunters sometimes capture the Hyena whale, to keep up the supply of cheap oil for domestic employment—as some frugal housekeepers, in the absence of company, and quite alone by themselves, burn unsavory tallow instead of odorous wax. Though their blubber is very thin, some of these whales will yield you upwards of thirty gallons of oil.

BOOK II. (*Octavo*), CHAPTER III. (*Narwhale*), that is, *Nostril whale.*—Another instance of a curiously named whale, so named I suppose from his peculiar horn being originally mistaken for a peaked nose. The creature is some sixteen feet in length, while its horn averages five feet, though some exceed ten, and even attain to fifteen feet. Strictly speaking, this horn is but a lengthened tusk, growing out from the jaw in a line a little depressed from the horizontal. But it is only found on the sinister side, which has an ill effect, giving its owner something analogous to the aspect of a clumsy left-handed man. What precise purpose this ivory horn or lance answers, it would be hard to say. It does not seem to be used like the blade of the sword-fish and bill-fish; though some sailors tell me that the Narwhale employs it for a rake in turning over the bottom of the sea for food. Charley Coffin said it was used for an ice-piercer; for the Narwhale, rising to the surface of the Polar Sea, and finding it sheeted with ice, thrusts his horn up, and so breaks through. But you cannot prove either of these surmises to be correct. My own opinion is, that however this one-sided horn may really be used by the Narwhale—however that may be—it would certainly be very convenient to him for a folder in reading pamphlets. The Narwhale I have heard called the Tusked whale, the Horned whale, and the Unicorn whale. He is certainly a curious example of the Unicornism to be found in almost every kingdom of animated nature. From certain cloistered old authors I have gathered that this same sea-unicorn's horn was in ancient days regarded as the great antidote against poison, and as such, preparations of it brought immense prices. It was also distilled to a volatile salts for fainting ladies, the same way that the horns of the male deer are manufactured into hartshorn. Originally it was in itself accounted an object of great curiosity. Black Letter tells me that Sir Martin Frobisher on his return from that voyage, when Queen Bess did gallantly wave her jewelled hand to him from a window of Greenwich Palace, as his bold ship sailed down the Thames; "when Sir Martin returned from that voyage," saith Black Letter, "on bended knees he presented to her highness a prodigious long horn of the Narwhale, which for a long period after hung in the castle at Windsor." An Irish author avers that the Earl of Leicester, on bended knees, did likewise present to her highness another horn, pertaining to a land beast of the unicorn nature.

The Narwhale has a very picturesque, leopard-like look, being of a milk-white ground color, dotted with round and oblong spots of black. His oil is very superior, clear and fine; but there is little of it, and he is seldom hunted. He is mostly found in the circumpolar seas.

BOOK II. (*Octavo*), CHAPTER IV. (*Killer*).—Of this whale little is precisely known to the Nantucketer, and nothing at all to the professed naturalist. From what I have seen of him at a distance, I should say that he was about the bigness of a grampus. He is very savage—a sort of Feegee fish. He sometimes takes the great Folio whales by the lip, and hangs there like a leech, till the mighty brute is worried to death. The Killer is never hunted. I never heard what sort of oil he has. Exception might be taken to the name bestowed upon this whale, on the ground of its indistinctness. For we are all killers, on land and on sea; Bonapartes and Sharks included.

BOOK II. (*Octavo*), CHAPTER V. (*Thrasher*).—This gentleman is famous for his tail, which he uses for a ferule in thrashing his foes. He mounts the Folio whale's back, and as he swims, he works his passage by flogging him; as some schoolmasters get along in the world by a similar process. Still less is known of the Thrasher than of the Killer. Both are outlaws, even in the lawless seas.

Thus ends BOOK II. (*Octavo*), and begins BOOK III. (*Duodecimo*).

DUODECIMOES.—These include the smaller whales. I. The Huzza Porpoise. II. The Algerine Porpoise. III. The Mealy-mouthed Porpoise.

To those who have not chanced specially to study the subject, it may possibly seem strange, that fishes not commonly exceeding four or five feet should be marshalled among WHALES—a word, which, in the popular sense, always conveys an idea of hugeness. But the creatures set down above as Duodecimoes are infallibly whales, by the terms of my definition of what a whale is—i.e. a spouting fish, with a horizontal tail.

BOOK III. (*Duodecimo*), CHAPTER I. (*Huzza Porpoise*).— This is the common porpoise found almost all over the globe. The name is of my own bestowal; for there are more than one sort of porpoises, and something must be done to distinguish them. I call him thus, because he always swims in hilarious shoals, which upon the broad sea keep tossing themselves to heaven like caps in a Fourth-of-July crowd. Their appearance is generally hailed with delight by the mariner. Full of fine spirits, they invariably come from the breezy billows to windward. They are the lads that always live before the wind. They are accounted a lucky omen. If you yourself can withstand three cheers at beholding these vivacious fish, then heaven help ye; the spirit of godly gamesomeness is not in ye. A well-fed, plump Huzza Porpoise will yield you one good gallon of good oil. But the fine and delicate fluid extracted from his jaws is exceedingly valuable. It is in request among jewellers and watchmakers. Sailors put it on their hones. Porpoise meat is good eating, you know. It may never have occurred to you that a porpoise spouts. Indeed, his spout is so small that it is not very readily discernible. But the next time you have a chance, watch him; and you will then see the great Sperm whale himself in miniature.

BOOK III. (*Duodecimo*), CHAPTER II. (*Algerine Porpoise*).—A pirate. Very savage. He is only found, I think, in the Pacific. He is somewhat larger than the Huzza Porpoise, but much of the same general make. Provoke him, and he will buckle to a shark. I have lowered for him many times, but never yet saw him captured.

BOOK III. (*Duodecimo*), CHAPTER III. (*Mealy-mouthed Porpoise*).—The largest kind of Porpoise; and only found in the Pacific, so far as it is known. The only English name, by which he has hitherto been designated, is that of the fishers—Right-Whale Porpoise, from the circumstance that he is chiefly found in the vicinity of that Folio. In shape, he differs in some degree from the Huzza Porpoise, being of a less rotund and jolly girth; indeed, he is of quite a neat and gentlemanlike figure. He has no fins on his back (most other porpoises have), he has a lovely tail, and sentimental Indian eyes of a hazel hue. But his mealy-mouth spoils all. Though his entire back down to his side fins is of a deep sable, yet a boundary line, distinct as the mark in a ship's hull, called the "bright waist," that line streaks him from stem to stern, with two separate colors, black above and white below. The white comprises part of his head, and the whole of his mouth, which makes him look as if he had just escaped from a felonious visit to a meal-bag. A most mean and mealy aspect! His oil is much like that of the common porpoise.

*   *   *

Beyond the DUODECIMO, this system does not proceed, inasmuch as the Porpoise is the smallest of the whales. Above, you have all the Leviathans of note. But there are a rabble of uncertain, fugitive, half-fabulous whales, which, as an American whaleman, I know by reputation, but not personally. I shall enumerate them by their forecastle appellations; for possibly such a list may be valuable to future investigators, who may complete what I have here but begun. If any of the following whales, shall hereafter be caught and marked, then he can readily be incorporated into this System, according to his Folio, Octavo, or Duodecimo magnitude:—The Bottle-Nose Whale; the Junk Whale; the Pudding-Headed Whale; the Cape Whale; the Leading Whale; the Cannon Whale; the Scragg Whale; the Coppered Whale; the Elephant Whale; the Iceberg Whale; the Quog Whale; the Blue Whale; &c. From Icelandic, Dutch, and old English authorities, there might be quoted other lists of uncertain whales, blessed with all manner of uncouth names. But I omit them as altogether obsolete; and can hardly help suspecting them for mere sounds, full of Leviathanism, but signifying nothing.

Finally: It was stated at the outset, that this system would not be here, and at once, perfected. You cannot but plainly see that I have kept my word. But I now leave my cetological System standing thus unfinished, even as the great Cathedral of Cologne was left, with the crane still standing upon the top of the uncompleted tower. For small erections may be finished by their first architects; grand ones, true ones, ever leave the copestone to posterity. God keep me from ever completing anything. This whole book is but a draught—nay, but the draught of a draught. Oh, Time, Strength, Cash, and Patience!

Chapter 33

THE SPECKSYNDER

CONCERNING the officers of the whale-craft, this seems as good a place as any to set down a little domestic peculiarity on ship-board, arising from the existence of the harpooneer class of officers, a class unknown of course in any other marine than the whale-fleet.

The large importance attached to the harpooneer's vocation is evinced by the fact, that originally in the old Dutch Fishery, two centuries and more ago, the command of a whale ship was not wholly lodged in the person now called the captain, but was divided between him and an officer called the Specksynder. Literally this word means Fat-Cutter; usage, however, in time made it equivalent to Chief Harpooneer. In those days, the captain's authority was restricted to the navigation and general management of the vessel: while over the whale-hunting department and all its concerns, the Specksynder or Chief Harpooneer reigned supreme. In the British Greenland Fishery, under the corrupted title of Specksioneer, this old Dutch official is still retained, but his former dignity is sadly abridged. At present he ranks simply as senior Harpooneer; and as such, is but one of the captain's more inferior subalterns. Nevertheless, as upon the good conduct of the harpooneers the success of a whaling voyage largely depends, and since in the American Fishery he is not only an important officer in the boat, but under certain circumstances (night watches on a whaling ground) the command of the ship's deck is also his; therefore the grand political maxim of the sea demands, that he should nominally live apart from the men before the mast, and be in some way distinguished as their professional superior; though always, by them, familiarly regarded as their social equal.

Now, the grand distinction drawn between officer and man at sea, is this—the first lives aft, the last forward. Hence, in whale-ships and merchantmen alike, the mates have their quarters with the captain; and so, too, in most of the American whalers the harpooneers are lodged in the after part of the ship. That is to say, they take their meals in the captain's cabin, and sleep in a place indirectly communicating with it.

Though the long period of a Southern whaling voyage (by far the longest of all voyages now or ever made by man), the peculiar perils of it, and the community of interest prevailing among a company, all of whom, high or low, depend for their profits, not upon fixed wages, but upon their common luck, together with their common vigilance, intrepidity, and hard work; though all these things do in some cases tend to beget a less rigorous discipline than in merchantmen generally; yet, never mind how much like an old Mesopotamian family these whalemen may, in some primitive instances, live together; for all that, the punctilious externals, at least, of the quarter-deck are seldom materially relaxed, and in no instance done away. Indeed, many are the Nantucket ships in which you will see the skipper parading his quarter-deck with an elated grandeur not surpassed in any military navy; nay, extorting almost as much outward homage as if he wore the imperial purple, and not the shabbiest of pilot-cloth.

And though of all men the moody captain of the Pequod was the least given to that sort of shallowest assumption; and though the only homage he ever exacted, was implicit, instantaneous obedience; though he required no man to remove the shoes from his feet ere stepping upon the quarter-deck; and though there were times when, owing to peculiar circumstances connected with events hereafter to be detailed, he addressed them in unusual terms, whether of condescension or *in terrorem*, or otherwise; yet even Captain Ahab was by no means unobservant of the paramount forms and usages of the sea.

Nor, perhaps, will it fail to be eventually perceived, that behind those forms and usages, as it were, he sometimes masked himself; incidentally making use of them for other and more private ends than they were legitimately intended to subserve. That certain sultanism of his brain, which had otherwise in a good degree remained unmanifested; through those forms that same sultanism became incarnate in an irresistible dictatorship. For be a man's intellectual superiority what it will, it can never assume the practical, available supremacy over other men, without the aid of some sort of external arts and entrenchments, always, in themselves, more or less paltry and base. This is it, that for ever keeps God's true princes of the Empire from the world's hustings; and leaves the highest honors that this air can give, to those men who become famous more through their infinite inferiority to the choice hidden handful of the Divine Inert, than through their undoubted superiority over the dead level of the mass. Such large virtue lurks in these small things when extreme political superstitions invest them, that in some royal instances even to idiot imbecility they have imparted potency. But when, as in the case of Nicholas the Czar, the ringed crown of geographical empire encircles an imperial brain; then, the plebeian herds crouch abased before the tremendous centralization. Nor, will the tragic dramatist who would depict mortal indomitableness in its fullest sweep and direst swing, ever forget a hint, incidentally so important in his art, as the one now alluded to.

But Ahab, my Captain, still moves before me in all his Nantucket grimness and shagginess; and in this episode touching Emperors and Kings, I must not conceal that I have only to do with a poor old whale-hunter like him; and, therefore, all outward majestical trappings and housings are denied me. Oh, Ahab! what shall be grand in thee, it must needs be plucked at from the skies, and dived for in the deep, and featured in the unbodied air!

Chapter 34

The Cabin-Table

It is noon; and Dough-Boy, the steward, thrusting his pale loaf-of-bread face from the cabin-scuttle, announces dinner to his lord and master; who, sitting in the lee quarter-boat, has just been taking an observation of the sun; and is now mutely reckoning the latitude on the smooth, medallion-shaped tablet, reserved for that daily purpose on the upper part of his ivory leg. From his complete inattention to the tidings, you would think that moody Ahab had not heard his menial. But presently, catching hold of the mizen shrouds, he swings himself to the deck, and in an even, unexhilarated voice, saying, "Dinner, Mr. Starbuck," disappears into the cabin.

When the last echo of his sultan's step has died away, and Starbuck, the first Emir, has every reason to suppose that he is seated, then Starbuck rouses from his quietude, takes a few turns along the planks, and, after a grave peep into the binnacle, says, with some touch of pleasantness, "Dinner, Mr. Stubb," and descends the scuttle. The second Emir lounges about the rigging awhile, and then slightly shaking the main brace, to see whether it be all right with that important rope, he likewise takes up the old burden, and with a rapid "Dinner, Mr. Flask," follows after his predecessors.

But the third Emir, now seeing himself all alone on the quarter-deck, seems to feel relieved from some curious restraint; for, tipping all sorts of knowing winks in all sorts of directions, and kicking off his shoes, he strikes into a sharp but noiseless squall of a hornpipe right over the Grand Turk's head; and then, by a dexterous sleight, pitching his cap up into the mizen-top for a shelf, he goes down rollicking, so far at least as he remains visible from the deck, reversing all other processions, by bringing up the rear with music. But ere stepping into the cabin doorway below, he pauses, ships a new face altogether, and, then, independent, hilarious little Flask enters King Ahab's presence, in the character of Abjectus, or the Slave.

It is not the least among the strange things bred by the intense artificialness of sea-usages, that while in the open air of the deck some officers will, upon provocation, bear themselves boldly and defyingly enough towards their commander; yet, ten to one, let those very officers the next moment go down to their customary dinner in that same commander's cabin, and straightway their inoffensive, not to say deprecatory and humble air towards him, as he sits at the head of the table; this is marvellous, sometimes most comical. Wherefore this difference? A problem? Perhaps not. To have been Belshazzar, King of Babylon; and to have been Belshazzar, not haughtily but courteously, therein certainly must have been some touch of mundane grandeur. But he who in the rightly regal and intelligent spirit presides over his own private dinner-table of invited guests, that man's unchallenged power and dominion of individual influence for the time; that man's royalty of state transcends Belshazzar's, for Belshazzar was not the greatest. Who has but once dined his friends, has tasted what it is to be Cæsar. It is a witchery of social czarship which there is no withstanding. Now, if to this consideration you superadd the official supremacy of a ship-master, then, by inference, you will derive the cause of that peculiarity of sea-life just mentioned.

Over his ivory-inlaid table, Ahab presided like a mute, maned sea-lion on the white coral beach, surrounded by his war-like but still deferential cubs. In his own proper turn, each officer waited to be served. They were as little children before Ahab; and yet, in Ahab, there seemed not to lurk the smallest social arrogance. With one mind, their intent eyes all fastened upon the old man's knife, as he carved the chief dish before him. I do not suppose that for the world they would have profaned that moment with the slightest observation, even upon so neutral a topic as the weather. No! And when reaching out his knife and fork, between which the slice of beef was locked, Ahab thereby motioned Starbuck's plate towards him, the mate received his meat as though receiving alms; and cut it tenderly; and a little started if, perchance, the knife grazed against the plate; and chewed it noiselessly; and swallowed it, not without circumspection. For, like the Coronation banquet at Frankfort, where the German Emperor profoundly dines with the seven Imperial Electors, so these cabin meals were somehow solemn meals, eaten in awful silence; and yet at table old Ahab forbade not conversation; only he himself was dumb. What a relief it was to choking Stubb, when a rat made a sudden racket in the hold below. And poor little Flask, he was the youngest son, and little boy of this weary family party. His were the shinbones of the saline beef; his would have been the drumsticks. For Flask to have presumed to help himself, this must have seemed to him tantamount to larceny in the first degree. Had he helped himself at that table, doubtless, never more would he have been able to hold his head up in this honest world; nevertheless, strange to say, Ahab never forbade him. And had Flask helped himself, the chances were Ahab had never so much as noticed it. Least of all, did Flask presume to help himself to butter. Whether he thought the owners of the ship denied it to him, on account of its clotting his clear, sunny complexion; or whether he deemed that, on so long a voyage in such marketless waters, butter was at a premium, and therefore was not for him, a subaltern; however it was, Flask, alas! was a butterless man!

Another thing. Flask was the last person down at the dinner, and Flask is the first man up. Consider! For hereby Flask's dinner was badly jammed in point of time. Starbuck and Stubb both had the start of him; and yet they also have the privilege of lounging in the rear. If Stubb even, who is but a peg higher than Flask, happens to have but a small appetite, and soon shows symptoms of concluding his repast, then Flask must bestir himself, he will not get more than three mouthfuls that day; for it is against holy usage for Stubb to precede Flask to the deck. Therefore it was that Flask once admitted in private, that ever since he had arisen to the dignity of an officer, from that moment he had never known what it was to be otherwise than hungry, more or less. For what he ate did not so much relieve his hunger, as keep it immortal in him. Peace and satisfaction, thought Flask, have for ever departed from my stomach. I am an officer; but, how I wish I could fist a bit of old-fashioned beef in the forecastle, as I used to when I was before the mast. There's the fruits of promotion now; there's the vanity of glory: there's the insanity of life! Besides, if it were so that any mere sailor of the Pequod had a grudge against Flask in Flask's official capacity, all that sailor had to do, in order to obtain ample vengeance, was to go aft at dinner-time, and get a peep at Flask through the cabin sky-light, sitting silly and dumfoundered before awful Ahab.

Now, Ahab and his three mates formed what may be called the first table in the Pequod's cabin. After their departure, taking place in inverted order to their arrival, the canvas cloth was cleared, or rather was restored to some hurried order by the pallid steward. And then the three harpooneers were bidden to the feast, they being its residuary legatees. They made a sort of temporary servants' hall of the high and mighty cabin.

In strange contrast to the hardly tolerable constraint and nameless invisible domineerings of the captain's table, was the entire care-free license and ease, the almost frantic democracy of those inferior fellows the harpooneers. While their masters, the mates, seemed afraid of the sound of the hinges of their own jaws, the harpooneers chewed their food with such a relish that there was a report to it. They dined like lords; they filled their bellies like Indian ships all day loading with spices. Such portentous appetites had Queequeg and Tashtego, that to fill out the vacancies made by the previous repast, often the pale Dough-Boy was fain to bring on a great baron of salt-junk, seemingly quarried out of the solid ox. And if he were not lively about it, if he did not go with a nimble hop-skip-and-jump, then Tashtego had an ungentlemanly way of accelerating him by darting a fork at his back, harpoon-wise. And once Daggoo, seized with a sudden humor, assisted Dough-Boy's memory by snatching him up bodily, and thrusting his head into a great empty wooden trencher, while Tashtego, knife in hand, began laying out the circle preliminary to scalping him. He was naturally a very nervous, shuddering sort of 'little fellow, this bread-faced steward; the progeny of a bankrupt baker and a hospital nurse. And what with the standing spectacle of the black terrific Ahab, and the periodical tumultuous visitations of these three savages, Dough-Boy's whole life was one continual lip-quiver. Commonly, after seeing the harpooneers furnished with all things they demanded, he would escape from their clutches into his little pantry adjoining, and fearfully peep out at them through the blinds of its door, till all was over.

It was a sight to see Queequeg seated over against Tashtego, opposing his filed teeth to the Indian's: crosswise to them, Daggoo seated on the floor, for a bench would have brought his hearse-plumed head to the low carlines; at every motion of his colossal limbs, making the low cabin framework to shake, as when an African elephant goes passenger in a ship. But for all this, the great negro was wonderfully abstemious, not to say dainty. It seemed hardly possible that by such comparatively small mouthfuls he could keep up the vitality diffused through so broad, baronial, and superb a person. But, doubtless, this noble savage fed strong and drank deep of the abounding element of air; and through his dilated nostrils snuffed in the sublime life of the worlds. Not by beef or by bread, are giants made or nourished. But Queequeg, he had a mortal, barbaric smack of the lip in eating—an ugly sound enough—so much so, that the trembling Dough-Boy almost looked to see whether any marks of teeth lurked in his own lean arms. And when he would hear Tashtego singing out for him to produce himself, that his bones might be picked, the simple-witted Steward all but shattered the crockery hanging round him in the pantry, by his sudden fits of the palsy. Nor did the whetstones which the harpooneers carried in their pockets, for their lances and other weapons; and with which whetstones, at dinner, they would ostentatiously sharpen their knives; that grating sound did not at all tend to tranquillize poor Dough-Boy. How could he forget that in his Island days, Queequeg, for one, must certainly have been guilty of some murderous, convivial indiscretions. Alas! Dough-Boy! hard fares the white waiter who waits upon cannibals. Not a napkin should he carry on his arm, but a buckler. In good time, though, to his great delight, the three salt-sea warriors would rise and depart; to his credulous, fable-mongering ears, all their martial bones jingling in them at every step, like Moorish scimetars in scabbards.

But, though these barbarians dined in the cabin, and nominally lived there; still, being anything but sedentary in their habits, they were scarcely ever in it except at meal-times, and just before sleeping-time, when they passed through it to their own peculiar quarters.

In this one matter, Ahab seemed no exception to most American whale captains, who, as a set, rather incline to the opinion that by rights the ship's cabin belongs to them; and that it is by courtesy alone that anybody else is, at any time, permitted there. So that, in real truth, the mates and harpooneers of the Pequod might more properly be said to have lived out of the cabin than in it. For when they did enter it, it was something as a street-door enters a house; turning inwards for a moment, only to be turned out the next; and, as a permanent thing, residing in the open air. Nor did they lose much hereby; in the cabin was no companionship; socially, Ahab was inaccessible. Though nominally included in the census of Christendom, he was still an alien to it. He lived in the world, as the last of the Grisly Bears lived in settled Missouri. And as when Spring and Summer had departed, that wild Logan of the woods, burying himself in the hollow of a tree, lived out the winter there, sucking his own paws; so, in his inclement, howling old age, Ahab's soul, shut up in the caved trunk of his body, there fed upon the sullen paws of its gloom!

Chapter 35

THE MAST-HEAD

IT WAS DURING the more pleasant weather, that in due rotation with the other seamen my first mast-head came round.

In most American whalemen the mast-heads are manned almost simultaneously with the vessel's leaving her port; even though she may have fifteen thousand miles, and more, to sail ere reaching her proper cruising ground. And if, after a three, four, or five years' voyage she is drawing nigh home with anything empty in her—say, an empty vial even—then, her mast-heads are kept manned to the last; and not till her sky-sail-poles sail in among the spires of the port, does she altogether relinquish the hope of capturing one whale more.

Now, as the business of standing mast-heads, ashore or afloat, is a very ancient and interesting one, let us in some measure expatiate here. I take it, that the earliest standers of mast-heads were the old Egyptians; because, in all my researches, I find none prior to them. For though their progenitors, the builders of Babel, must doubtless, by their tower, have intended to rear the loftiest mast-head in all Asia, or Africa either; yet (ere the final truck was put to it) as that great stone mast of theirs may be said to have gone by the board, in the dread gale of God's wrath; therefore, we cannot give these Babel builders priority over the Egyptians. And that the Egyptians were a nation of mast-head standers, is an assertion based upon the general belief among archæologists, that the first pyramids were founded for astronomical purposes: a theory singularly supported by the peculiar stair-like formation of all four sides of those edifices; whereby, with prodigious long upliftings of their legs, those old astronomers were wont to mount to the apex, and sing out for new stars; even as the look-outs of a modern ship sing out for a sail, or a whale just bearing in sight. In Saint Stylites, the famous Christian hermit of old times, who built him a lofty stone pillar in the desert and spent the whole latter portion of his

life on its summit, hoisting his food from the ground with a
tackle; in him we have a remarkable instance of a dauntless
stander-of-mast-heads; who was not to be driven from his
place by fogs or frosts, rain, hail, or sleet; but valiantly facing
everything out to the last, literally died at his post. Of modern
standers-of-mast-heads we have but a lifeless set; mere stone,
iron, and bronze men; who, though well capable of facing
out a stiff gale, are still entirely incompetent to the business
of singing out upon discovering any strange sight. There is
Napoleon; who, upon the top of the column of Vendome,
stands with arms folded, some one hundred and fifty feet in
the air; careless, now, who rules the decks below; whether
Louis Philippe, Louis Blanc, or Louis the Devil. Great Washington, too, stands high aloft on his towering main-mast in
Baltimore, and like one of Hercules' pillars, his column marks
that point of human grandeur beyond which few mortals will
go. Admiral Nelson, also, on a capstan of gun-metal, stands
his mast-head in Trafalgar Square; and even when most obscured by that London smoke, token is yet given that a hidden hero is there; for where there is smoke, must be fire. But
neither great Washington, nor Napoleon, nor Nelson, will
answer a single hail from below, however madly invoked to
befriend by their counsels the distracted decks upon which
they gaze; however, it may be surmised, that their spirits penetrate through the thick haze of the future, and descry what
shoals and what rocks must be shunned.

It may seem unwarrantable to couple in any respect the
mast-head standers of the land with those of the sea; but that
in truth it is not so, is plainly evinced by an item for which
Obed Macy, the sole historian of Nantucket, stands accountable. The worthy Obed tells us, that in the early times of the
whale fishery, ere ships were regularly launched in pursuit of
the game, the people of that island erected lofty spars along
the sea-coast, to which the look-outs ascended by means of
nailed cleats, something as fowls go upstairs in a hen-house.
A few years ago this same plan was adopted by the Bay
whalemen of New Zealand, who, upon descrying the game,
gave notice to the ready-manned boats nigh the beach. But
this custom has now become obsolete; turn we then to the
one proper mast-head, that of a whale-ship at sea. The three

mast-heads are kept manned from sun-rise to sun-set; the sea-men taking their regular turns (as at the helm), and relieving each other every two hours. In the serene weather of the trop-ics it is exceedingly pleasant—the mast-head; nay, to a dreamy meditative man it is delightful. There you stand, a hundred feet above the silent decks, striding along the deep, as if the masts were gigantic stilts, while beneath you and between your legs, as it were, swim the hugest monsters of the sea, even as ships once sailed between the boots of the famous Colossus at old Rhodes. There you stand, lost in the infinite series of the sea, with nothing ruffled but the waves. The tranced ship indolently rolls; the drowsy trade winds blow; everything resolves you into languor. For the most part, in this tropic whaling life, a sublime uneventfulness in-vests you; you hear no news; read no gazettes; extras with startling accounts of commonplaces never delude you into un-necessary excitements; you hear of no domestic afflictions; bankrupt securities; fall of stocks; are never troubled with the thought of what you shall have for dinner—for all your meals for three years and more are snugly stowed in casks, and your bill of fare is immutable.

In one of those southern whalemen, on a long three or four years' voyage, as often happens, the sum of the various hours you spend at the mast-head would amount to several entire months. And it is much to be deplored that the place to which you devote so considerable a portion of the whole term of your natural life, should be so sadly destitute of anything approaching to a cosy inhabitiveness, or adapted to breed a comfortable localness of feeling, such as pertains to a bed, a hammock, a hearse, a sentry box, a pulpit, a coach, or any other of those small and snug contrivances in which men tem-porarily isolate themselves. Your most usual point of perch is the head of the t' gallant-mast, where you stand upon two thin parallel sticks (almost peculiar to whalemen) called the t' gallant cross-trees. Here, tossed about by the sea, the begin-ner feels about as cosy as he would standing on a bull's horns. To be sure, in coolish weather you may carry your house aloft with you, in the shape of a watch-coat; but properly speaking the thickest watch-coat is no more of a house than the unclad body; for as the soul is glued inside of its fleshly tabernacle, and cannot freely move about in it, nor even move out of it, without running great risk of perishing (like an ignorant pilgrim crossing the snowy Alps in winter); so a watch-coat is not so much of a house as it is a mere envelope, or additional skin encasing you. You cannot put a shelf or chest of drawers in your body, and no more can you make a convenient closet of your watch-coat.

Concerning all this, it is much to be deplored that the mast-heads of a southern whale ship are unprovided with those enviable little tents or pulpits, called *crow's-nests*, in which the look-outs of a Greenland whaler are protected from the inclement weather of the frozen seas. In the fire-side narrative of Captain Sleet, entitled "A Voyage among the Icebergs, in quest of the Greenland Whale, and incidentally for the re-discovery of the Lost Icelandic Colonies of Old Greenland;" in this admirable volume, all standers of mast-heads are furnished with a charmingly circumstantial account of the then recently invented *crow's-nest* of the Glacier, which was the name of Captain Sleet's good craft. He called it the *Sleet's crow's-nest*, in honor of himself; he being the original inventor and patentee, and free from all ridiculous false delicacy, and holding that if we call our own children after our own names (we fathers being the original inventors and patentees), so likewise should we denominate after ourselves any other apparatus we may beget. In shape, the Sleet's crow's-nest is something like a large tierce or pipe; it is open above, however, where it is furnished with a movable side-screen to keep to windward of your head in a hard gale. Being fixed on the summit of the mast, you ascend into it through a little trap-hatch in the bottom. On the after side, or side next the stern of the ship, is a comfortable seat, with a locker underneath for umbrellas, comforters, and coats. In front is a leather rack, in which to keep your speaking trumpet, pipe, telescope, and other nautical conveniences. When Captain Sleet in person stood his mast-head in this crow's nest of his, he tells us that he always had a rifle with him (also fixed in the rack), together with a powder flask and shot, for the purpose of popping off the stray narwhales, or vagrant sea unicorns infesting those waters; for you cannot successfully shoot at them from the deck owing to the resistance of the water, but to shoot

down upon them is a very different thing. Now, it was plainly
a labor of love for Captain Sleet to describe, as he does, all
the little detailed conveniences of his crow's-nest; but though
he so enlarges upon many of these, and though he treats us
to a very scientific account of his experiments in this crow's-
nest, with a small compass he kept there for the purpose of
counter-acting the errors resulting from what is called the "local attraction" of all binnacle magnets; an error ascribable to
the horizontal vicinity of the iron in the ship's planks, and in
the Glacier's case, perhaps, to there having been so many broken-down blacksmiths among her crew; I say, that though the
Captain is very discreet and scientific here, yet, for all his
learned "binnacle deviations," "azimuth compass observations," and "approximate errors," he knows very well, Captain
Sleet, that he was not so much immersed in those profound
magnetic meditations, as to fail being attracted occasionally
towards that well replenished little case-bottle, so nicely
tucked in on one side of his crow's nest, within easy reach of
his hand. Though, upon the whole, I greatly admire and even
love the brave, the honest, and learned Captain; yet I take it
very ill of him that he should so utterly ignore that case-
bottle, seeing what a faithful friend and comforter it must
have been, while with mittened fingers and hooded head he
was studying the mathematics aloft there in that bird's nest
within three or four perches of the pole.

But if we Southern whale-fishers are not so snugly housed
aloft as Captain Sleet and his Greenland-men were; yet that
disadvantage is greatly counterbalanced by the widely contrasting serenity of those seductive seas in which we Southern
fishers mostly float. For one, I used to lounge up the rigging
very leisurely, resting in the top to have a chat with Queequeg, or any one else off duty whom I might find there; then
ascending a little way further, and throwing a lazy leg over
the top-sail yard, take a preliminary view of the watery pastures, and so at last mount to my ultimate destination.

Let me make a clean breast of it here, and frankly admit
that I kept but sorry guard. With the problem of the universe
revolving in me, how could I—being left completely to myself at such a thought-engendering altitude,—how could I
but lightly hold my obligations to observe all whale-ships'

standing orders, "Keep your weather eye open, and sing out every time."

And let me in this place movingly admonish you, ye ship-owners of Nantucket! Beware of enlisting in your vigilant fisheries any lad with lean brow and hollow eye; given to unseasonable meditativeness; and who offers to ship with the Phædon instead of Bowditch in his head. Beware of such an one, I say: your whales must be seen before they can be killed; and this sunken-eyed young Platonist will tow you ten wakes round the world, and never make you one pint of sperm the richer. Nor are these monitions at all unneeded. For nowadays, the whale-fishery furnishes an asylum for many romantic, melancholy, and absent-minded young men, disgusted with the carking cares of earth, and seeking sentiment in tar and blubber. Childe Harold not unfrequently perches himself upon the mast-head of some luckless disappointed whale-ship, and in moody phrase ejaculates:—

"Roll on, thou deep and dark blue ocean, roll!
Ten thousand blubber-hunters sweep over thee in vain."

Very often do the captains of such ships take those absent-minded young philosophers to task, upbraiding them with not feeling sufficient "interest" in the voyage; half-hinting that they are so hopelessly lost to all honorable ambition, as that in their secret souls they would rather not see whales than otherwise. But all in vain; those young Platonists have a notion that their vision is imperfect; they are short-sighted; what use, then, to strain the visual nerve? They have left their opera-glasses at home.

"Why, thou monkey," said a harpooneer to one of these lads, "we've been cruising now hard upon three years, and thou hast not raised a whale yet. Whales are as scarce as hen's teeth whenever thou art up here." Perhaps they were; or perhaps there might have been shoals of them in the far horizon; but lulled into such an opium-like listlessness of vacant, unconscious reverie is this absent-minded youth by the blending cadence of waves with thoughts, that at last he loses his identity; takes the mystic ocean at his feet for the visible image of that deep, blue, bottomless soul, pervading mankind and nature; and every strange, half-seen, gliding, beautiful thing that eludes him; every dimly-discovered, uprising fin of some un-discernible form, seems to him the embodiment of those elusive thoughts that only people the soul by continually flitting through it. In this enchanted mood, thy spirit ebbs away to whence it came; becomes diffused through time and space; like Wickliff's sprinkled Pantheistic ashes, forming at last a part of every shore the round globe over.

There is no life in thee, now, except that rocking life imparted by a gently rolling ship; by her, borrowed from the sea; by the sea, from the inscrutable tides of God. But while this sleep, this dream is on ye, move your foot or hand an inch, slip your hold at all; and your identity comes back in horror. Over Descartian vortices you hover. And perhaps, at mid-day, in the fairest weather, with one half-throttled shriek you drop through that transparent air into the summer sea, no more to rise for ever. Heed it well, ye Pantheists!

Chapter 36

THE QUARTER-DECK

(Enter Ahab: Then, all.)

I^T WAS NOT a great while after the affair of the pipe, that one morning shortly after breakfast, Ahab, as was his wont, ascended the cabin-gangway to the deck. There most sea-captains usually walk at that hour, as country gentlemen, after the same meal, take a few turns in the garden.

Soon his steady, ivory stride was heard, as to and fro he paced his old rounds, upon planks so familiar to his tread, that they were all over dented, like geological stones, with the peculiar mark of his walk. Did you fixedly gaze, too, upon that ribbed and dented brow; there also, you would see still stranger foot-prints—the foot-prints of his one unsleeping, ever-pacing thought.

But on the occasion in question, those dents looked deeper, even as his nervous step that morning left a deeper mark. And, so full of his thought was Ahab, that at every uniform turn that he made, now at the main-mast and now at the binnacle, you could almost see that thought turn in him as he turned, and pace in him as he paced; so completely possessing him, indeed, that it all but seemed the inward mould of every outer movement.

"D'ye mark him, Flask?" whispered Stubb; "the chick that's in him pecks the shell. T'will soon be out."

The hours wore on;—Ahab now shut up within his cabin; anon, pacing the deck, with the same intense bigotry of purpose in his aspect.

It drew near the close of day. Suddenly he came to a halt by the bulwarks, and inserting his bone leg into the auger-hole there, and with one hand grasping a shroud, he ordered Starbuck to send everybody aft.

"Sir!" said the mate, astonished at an order seldom or never given on ship-board except in some extraordinary case.

"Send everybody aft," repeated Ahab. "Mast-heads, there! come down!"

When the entire ship's company were assembled, and with curious and not wholly unapprehensive faces, were eyeing him, for he looked not unlike the weather horizon when a storm is coming up, Ahab, after rapidly glancing over the bulwarks, and then darting his eyes among the crew, started from his stand-point; and as though not a soul were nigh him resumed his heavy turns upon the deck. With bent head and half-slouched hat he continued to pace, unmindful of the wondering whispering among the men; till Stubb cautiously whispered to Flask, that Ahab must have summoned them there for the purpose of witnessing a pedestrian feat. But this did not last long. Vehemently pausing, he cried: —

"What do ye do when ye see a whale, men?"

"Sing out for him!" was the impulsive rejoinder from a score of clubbed voices.

"Good!" cried Ahab, with a wild approval in his tones; observing the hearty animation into which his unexpected question had so magnetically thrown them.

"And what do ye next, men?"

"Lower away, and after him!"

"And what tune is it ye pull to, men?"

"A dead whale or a stove boat!"

More and more strangely and fiercely glad and approving, grew the countenance of the old man at every shout; while the mariners began to gaze curiously at each other, as if marvelling how it was that they themselves became so excited at such seemingly purposeless questions.

But, they were all eagerness again, as Ahab, now half-revolving in his pivot-hole, with one hand reaching high up a shroud, and tightly, almost convulsively grasping it, addressed them thus: —

"All ye mast-headers have before now heard me give orders about a white whale. Look ye! d'ye see this Spanish ounce of gold?"—holding up a broad bright coin to the sun—"it is a sixteen dollar piece, men,—a doubloon. D'ye see it? Mr. Starbuck, hand me yon top-maul."

While the mate was getting the hammer, Ahab, without speaking, was slowly rubbing the gold piece against the skirts of his jacket, as if to heighten its lustre, and without using any words was meanwhile lowly humming to himself, producing a sound so strangely muffled and inarticulate that it seemed the mechanical humming of the wheels of his vitality in him.

Receiving the top-maul from Starbuck, he advanced towards the main-mast with the hammer uplifted in one hand, exhibiting the gold with the other, and with a high raised voice exclaiming: "Whosoever of ye raises me a white-headed whale with a wrinkled brow and a crooked jaw; whosoever of ye raises me that white-headed whale, with three holes punctured in his starboard fluke—look ye, whosoever of ye raises me that same white whale, he shall have this gold ounce, my boys!"

"Huzza! huzza!" cried the seamen, as with swinging tarpaulins they hailed the act of nailing the gold to the mast.

"It's a white whale, I say," resumed Ahab, as he threw down the top-maul; "a white whale. Skin your eyes for him, men; look sharp for white water; if ye see but a bubble, sing out."

All this while Tashtego, Daggoo, and Queequeg had looked on with even more intense interest and surprise than the rest, and at the mention of the wrinkled brow and crooked jaw they had started as if each was separately touched by some specific recollection.

"Captain Ahab," said Tashtego, "that white whale must be the same that some call Moby Dick."

"Moby Dick?" shouted Ahab. "Do ye know the white whale then, Tash?"

"Does he fan-tail a little curious, sir, before he goes down?" said the Gay-Header deliberately.

"And has he a curious spout, too," said Daggoo, "very bushy, even for a parmacetty, and mighty quick, Captain Ahab?"

"And he have one, two, tree—oh! good many iron in him hide, too, Captain," cried Queequeg disjointedly, "all twisketee be-twisk, like him—him—" faltering hard for a word, and screwing his hand round and round as though uncorking a bottle—"like him—him—"

"Corkscrew!" cried Ahab, "aye, Queequeg, the harpoons lie all twisted and wrenched in him; aye, Daggoo, his spout is a big one, like a whole shock of wheat, and white as a pile of

our Nantucket wool after the great annual sheep-shearing;
aye, Tashtego, and he fan-tails like a split jib in a squall.
Death and devils! men, it is Moby Dick ye have seen—Moby
Dick—Moby Dick!"

"Captain Ahab," said Starbuck, who, with Stubb and Flask,
had thus far been eyeing his superior with increasing surprise,
but at last seemed struck with a thought which somewhat
explained all the wonder. "Captain Ahab, I have heard of
Moby Dick—but it was not Moby Dick that took off thy
leg?"

"Who told thee that?" cried Ahab; then pausing, "Aye,
Starbuck; aye, my hearties all round; it was Moby Dick that
dismasted me; Moby Dick that brought me to this dead
stump I stand on now. Aye, aye," he shouted with a terrific,
loud, animal sob, like that of a heart-stricken moose; "Aye,
aye! it was that accursed white whale that razeed me; made a
poor pegging lubber of me for ever and a day!" Then tossing
both arms, with measureless imprecations he shouted out:
"Aye, aye! and I'll chase him round Good Hope, and round
the Horn, and round the Norway Maelstrom, and round perdition's flames before I give him up. And this is what ye have
shipped for, men! to chase that white whale on both sides of
land, and over all sides of earth, till he spouts black blood and
rolls fin out. What say ye, men, will ye splice hands on it,
now? I think ye do look brave."

"Aye, aye!" shouted the harpooneers and seamen, running
closer to the excited old man: "A sharp eye for the White
Whale; a sharp lance for Moby Dick!"

"God bless ye," he seemed to half sob and half shout. "God
bless ye, men. Steward! go draw the great measure of grog.
But what's this long face about, Mr. Starbuck; wilt thou not
chase the white whale? art not game for Moby Dick?"

"I am game for his crooked jaw, and for the jaws of Death
too, Captain Ahab, if it fairly comes in the way of the business we follow; but I came here to hunt whales, not my commander's vengeance. How many barrels will thy vengeance
yield thee even if thou gettest it, Captain Ahab? it will not
fetch thee much in our Nantucket market."

"Nantucket market! Hoot! But come closer, Starbuck; thou
requirest a little lower layer. If money's to be the measurer,

man, and the accountants have computed their great count-ing-house the globe, by girdling it with guineas, one to every three parts of an inch; then, let me tell thee, that my ven-geance will fetch a great premium *here*!"

"He smites his chest," whispered Stubb, "what's that for? methinks it rings most vast, but hollow."

"Vengeance on a dumb brute!" cried Starbuck, "that simply smote thee from blindest instinct! Madness! To be enraged with a dumb thing, Captain Ahab, seems blasphemous."

"Hark ye yet again,—the little lower layer. All visible ob-jects, man, are but as pasteboard masks. But in each event— in the living act, the undoubted deed—there, some unknown but still reasoning thing puts forth the mouldings of its fea-tures from behind the unreasoning mask. If man will strike, strike through the mask! How can the prisoner reach outside except by thrusting through the wall? To me, the white whale is that wall, shoved near to me. Sometimes I think there's naught beyond. But 'tis enough. He tasks me; he heaps me; I see in him outrageous strength, with an inscrutable malice sinewing it. That inscrutable thing is chiefly what I hate; and be the white whale agent, or be the white whale principal, I will wreak that hate upon him. Talk not to me of blasphemy, man; I'd strike the sun if it insulted me. For could the sun do that, then could I do the other; since there is ever a sort of fair play herein, jealousy presiding over all creations. But not my master, man, is even that fair play. Who's over me? Truth hath no confines. Take off thine eye! more intolerable than fiends' glarings is a doltish stare! So, so; thou reddenest and palest; my heat has melted thee to anger-glow. But look ye, Starbuck, what is said in heat, that thing unsays itself. There are men from whom warm words are small indignity. I meant not to incense thee. Let it go. Look! see yonder Turkish cheeks of spotted tawn—living, breathing pictures painted by the sun. The Pagan leopards—the unrecking and unworshipping things, that live; and seek, and give no rea-sons for the torrid life they feel! The crew, man, the crew! Are they not one and all with Ahab, in this matter of the whale? See Stubb! he laughs! See yonder Chilian! he snorts to think of it. Stand up amid the general hurricane, thy one tost sapling cannot, Starbuck! And what is it? Reckon it. 'Tis but to help strike a fin; no wondrous feat for Starbuck. What is it more? From this one poor hunt, then, the best lance out of all Nantucket, surely he will not hang back, when every foremast-hand has clutched a whetstone? Ah! constrainings seize thee; I see! the billow lifts thee! Speak, but speak!— Aye, aye! thy silence, then, *that* voices thee. (*Aside*) Something shot from my dilated nostrils, he has inhaled it in his lungs. Starbuck now is mine; cannot oppose me now, without rebellion."

"God keep me!—keep us all!" murmured Starbuck, lowly.

But in his joy at the enchanted, tacit acquiescence of the mate, Ahab did not hear his foreboding invocation; nor yet the low laugh from the hold; nor yet the presaging vibrations of the winds in the cordage; nor yet the hollow flap of the sails against the masts, as for a moment their hearts sank in. For again Starbuck's downcast eyes lighted up with the stubbornness of life; the subterranean laugh died away; the winds blew on; the sails filled out; the ship heaved and rolled as before. Ah, ye admonitions and warnings! why stay ye not when ye come? But rather are ye predictions than warnings, ye shadows! Yet not so much predictions from without, as verifications of the foregoing things within. For with little external to constrain us, the innermost necessities in our being, these still drive us on.

"The measure! the measure!" cried Ahab.

Receiving the brimming pewter, and turning to the harpooneers, he ordered them to produce their weapons. Then ranging them before him near the capstan, with their harpoons in their hands, while his three mates stood at his side with their lances, and the rest of the ship's company formed a circle round the group; he stood for an instant searchingly eyeing every man of his crew. But those wild eyes met his, as the bloodshot eyes of the prairie wolves meet the eye of their leader, ere he rushes on at their head in the trail of the bison; but, alas! only to fall into the hidden snare of the Indian.

"Drink and pass!" he cried, handing the heavy charged flagon to the nearest seaman. "The crew alone now drink. Round with it, round! Short draughts—long swallows, men; 'tis hot as Satan's hoof. So, so; it goes round excellently. It spiralizes in ye; forks out at the serpent-snapping eye. Well done; almost drained. That way it went, this way it comes. Hand it me—here's a hollow! Men, ye seem the years; so brimming life is gulped and gone. Steward, refill!

"Attend now, my braves. I have mustered ye all round this capstan; and ye mates, flank me with your lances; and ye harpooneers, stand there with your irons; and ye, stout mariners, ring me in, that I may in some sort revive a noble custom of my fisherman fathers before me. O men, you will yet see that—— Ha! boy, come back? bad pennies come not sooner. Hand it me. Why, now, this pewter had run brimming again, wert not thou St. Vitus' imp—away, thou ague!

"Advance, ye mates! Cross your lances full before me. Well done! Let me touch the axis." So saying, with extended arm, he grasped the three level, radiating lances at their crossed centre; while so doing, suddenly and nervously twitched them; meanwhile, glancing intently from Starbuck to Stubb; from Stubb to Flask. It seemed as though, by some nameless, interior volition, he would fain have shocked into them the same fiery emotion accumulated within the Leyden jar of his own magnetic life. The three mates quailed before his strong, sustained, and mystic aspect. Stubb and Flask looked sideways from him; the honest eye of Starbuck fell downright.

"In vain!" cried Ahab; "but, maybe, 'tis well. For did ye three but once take the full-forced shock, then mine own electric thing, *that* had perhaps expired from out me. Perchance, too, it would have dropped ye dead. Perchance ye need it not. Down lances! And now, ye mates, I do appoint ye three cupbearers to my three pagan kinsmen there—yon three most honorable gentlemen and noblemen, my valiant harpooneers. Disdain the task? What, when the great Pope washes the feet of beggars, using his tiara for ewer? Oh, my sweet cardinals! your own condescension, *that* shall bend ye to it. I do not order ye; ye will it. Cut your seizings and draw the poles, ye harpooneers!"

Silently obeying the order, the three harpooneers now stood with the detached iron part of their harpoons, some three feet long, held, barbs up, before him.

"Stab me not with that keen steel! Cant them; cant them over! know ye not the goblet end? Turn up the socket! So, so; now, ye cup-bearers, advance. The irons! take them; hold them while I fill!" Forthwith, slowly going from one officer to the other, he brimmed the harpoon sockets with the fiery waters from the pewter.

"Now, three to three, ye stand. Commend the murderous chalices! Bestow them, ye who are now made parties to this indissoluble league. Ha! Starbuck! but the deed is done! Yon ratifying sun now waits to sit upon it. Drink, ye harpooneers! drink and swear, ye men that man the deathful whaleboat's bow—Death to Moby Dick! God hunt us all, if we do not hunt Moby Dick to his death!" The long, barbed steel goblets were lifted; and to cries and maledictions against the white whale, the spirits were simultaneously quaffed down with a hiss. Starbuck paled, and turned, and shivered. Once more, and finally, the replenished pewter went the rounds among the frantic crew; when, waving his free hand to them, they all dispersed; and Ahab retired within his cabin.

Chapter 37

SUNSET

(The cabin; by the stern windows; Ahab sitting alone, and gazing out.)

I LEAVE a white and turbid wake; pale waters, paler cheeks, where'er I sail. The envious billows sidelong swell to whelm my track; let them; but first I pass.

Yonder, by the ever-brimming goblet's rim, the warm waves blush like wine. The gold brow plumbs the blue. The diver sun—slow dived from noon,—goes down; my soul mounts up! she wearies with her endless hill. Is, then, the crown too heavy that I wear? this Iron Crown of Lombardy. Yet is it bright with many a gem; I, the wearer, see not its far flashings; but darkly feel that I wear that, that dazzlingly confounds. 'Tis iron—that I know—not gold. 'Tis split, too—that I feel; the jagged edge galls me so, my brain seems to beat against the solid metal; aye, steel skull, mine; the sort that needs no helmet in the most brain-battering fight!

Dry heat upon my brow? Oh! time was, when as the sunrise nobly spurred me, so the sunset soothed. No more. This lovely light, it lights not me; all loveliness is anguish to me, since I can ne'er enjoy. Gifted with the high perception, I lack the low, enjoying power; damned, most subtly and most malignantly! damned in the midst of Paradise! Good night—good night! *(waving his hand, he moves from the window.)*

'Twas not so hard a task. I thought to find one stubborn, at the least; but my one cogged circle fits into all their various wheels, and they revolve. Or, if you will, like so many anthills of powder, they all stand before me; and I their match. Oh, hard! that to fire others, the match itself must needs be wasting! What I've dared, I've willed; and what I've willed, I'll do! They think me mad—Starbuck does; but I'm demoniac, I am madness maddened! That wild madness that's only calm to comprehend itself! The prophecy was that I should be dismembered; and—Aye! I lost this leg. I now prophesy that I will dismember my dismemberer. Now, then, be the prophet and the fulfiller one. That's more than ye, ye great gods, ever were. I laugh and hoot at ye, ye cricket-players, ye pugilists, ye deaf Burkes and blinded Bendigoes! I will not say as schoolboys do to bullies,—Take some one of your own size; don't pommel *me*! No, ye've knocked me down, and I am up again; but *ye* have run and hidden. Come forth from behind your cotton bags! I have no long gun to reach ye. Come, Ahab's compliments to ye; come and see if ye can swerve me. Swerve me? ye cannot swerve me, else ye swerve yourselves! man has ye there. Swerve me? The path to my fixed purpose is laid with iron rails, whereon my soul is grooved to run. Over unsounded gorges, through the rifled hearts of mountains, under torrents' beds, unerringly I rush! Naught's an obstacle, naught's an angle to the iron way!

Chapter 38

DUSK

(By the Mainmast; Starbuck leaning against it.)

MY SOUL is more than matched; she's overmanned; and by a madman! Insufferable sting, that sanity should ground arms on such a field! But he drilled deep down, and blasted all my reason out of me! I think I see his impious end; but feel that I must help him to it. Will I, nill I, the ineffable thing has tied me to him; tows me with a cable I have no knife to cut. Horrible old man! Who's over him, he cries;— aye, he would be a democrat to all above; look, how he lords it over all below! Oh! I plainly see my miserable office,—to obey, rebelling; and worse yet, to hate with touch of pity! For in his eyes I read some lurid woe would shrivel me up, had I it. Yet is there hope. Time and tide flow wide. The hated whale has the round watery world to swim in, as the small gold-fish has its glassy globe. His heaven-insulting purpose, God may wedge aside. I would up heart, were it not like lead. But my whole clock's run down; my heart the all-controlling weight, I have no key to lift again.

(A burst of revelry from the forecastle.)

Oh, God! to sail with such a heathen crew that have small touch of human mothers in them! Whelped somewhere by the sharkish sea. The white whale is their demogorgon. Hark! the infernal orgies! that revelry is forward! mark the unfaltering silence aft! Methinks it pictures life. Foremost through the sparkling sea shoots on the gay, embattled, bantering bow, but only to drag dark Ahab after it, where he broods within his sternward cabin, builded over the dead water of the wake, and further on, hunted by its wolfish gurglings. The long howl thrills me through! Peace! ye revellers, and set the watch! Oh, life! 'tis in an hour like this, with soul beat down and held to knowledge,—as wild, untutored things are forced to feed—Oh, life! 'tis now that I do feel the latent horror in thee! but 'tis not me! that horror's out of me! and with the soft feeling of the human in me, yet will I try to fight ye, ye grim, phantom futures! Stand by me, hold me, bind me, O ye blessed influences!

Chapter 39

First Night-Watch

FORE-TOP.
(Stubb solus, and mending a brace.)

HA! HA! HA! HA! HEM! clear my throat!—I've been thinking over it ever since, and that ha, ha's the final consequence. Why so? Because a laugh's the wisest, easiest answer to all that's queer; and come what will, one comfort's always left—that unfailing comfort is, it's all predestinated. I heard not all his talk with Starbuck; but to my poor eye Starbuck then looked something as I the other evening felt. Be sure the old Mogul has fixed him, too. I twigged it, knew it; had had the gift, might readily have prophesied it—for when I clapped my eye upon his skull I saw it. Well, Stubb, *wise* Stubb—that's my title—well, Stubb, what of it, Stubb? Here's a carcase. I know not all that may be coming, but be it what it will, I'll go to it laughing. Such a waggish leering as lurks in all your horribles! I feel funny. Fa, la! lirra, skirra! What's my juicy little pear at home doing now? Crying its eyes out?—Giving a party to the last arrived harpooneers, I dare say, gay as a frigate's pennant, and so am I—fa, la! lirra, skirra! Oh—

> We'll drink to-night with hearts as light,
>   To loves as gay and fleeting
> As bubbles that swim, on the beaker's brim,
>   And break on the lips while meeting.

A brave stave that—who calls? Mr. Starbuck? Aye, aye, sir—(*Aside*) he's my superior, he has his too, if I'm not mistaken.—Aye, aye, sir, just through with this job—coming.

975

Chapter 40

Midnight, Forecastle

HARPOONEERS AND SAILORS.
*(Foresail rises and discovers the watch standing, lounging,
leaning, and lying in various attitudes, all singing in chorus.)*

> Farewell and adieu to you, Spanish ladies!
> Farewell and adieu to you, ladies of Spain!
> Our captain's commanded—

1ST NANTUCKET SAILOR.

Oh, boys, don't be sentimental; it's bad for the digestion!
Take a tonic, follow me!

> *(Sings, and all follow.)*
> Our captain stood upon the deck,
>   A spy-glass in his hand,
> A viewing of those gallant whales
>   That blew at every strand.
> Oh, your tubs in your boats, my boys,
>   And by your braces stand,
> And we'll have one of those fine whales,
>   Hand, boys, over hand!
> So, be cheery, my lads! may your hearts never fail!
> While the bold harpooneer is striking the whale!

MATE'S VOICE FROM THE QUARTER-DECK.

Eight bells there, forward!

2D NANTUCKET SAILOR.

Avast the chorus! Eight bells there! d'ye hear, bell-boy?
Strike the bell eight, thou Pip! thou blackling! and let me call
the watch. I've the sort of mouth for that—the hogshead
mouth. So, so, *(thrusts his head down the scuttle,)* Star—bo-
l-e-e-n-s, a-h-o-y! Eight bells there below! Tumble up!

DUTCH SAILOR.

Grand snoozing to-night, maty; fat night for that. I mark
this in our old Mogul's wine; it's quite as deadening to some

as filliping to others. We sing; they sleep—aye, lie down there, like ground-tier butts. At 'em again! There, take this copper-pump, and hail 'em through it. Tell 'em to avast dreaming of their lasses. Tell 'em it's the resurrection; they must kiss their last, and come to judgment. That's the way—*that's* it; thy throat ain't spoiled with eating Amsterdam butter.

FRENCH SAILOR.

Hist, boys! let's have a jig or two before we ride to anchor in Blanket Bay. What say ye? There comes the other watch. Stand by all legs! Pip! little Pip! hurrah with your tambourine!

PIP.
(Sulky and sleepy.)

Don't know where it is.

FRENCH SAILOR.

Beat thy belly, then, and wag thy ears. Jig it, men, I say; merry's the word; hurrah! Damn me, won't you dance? Form, now, Indian-file, and gallop into the double-shuffle? Throw yourselves! Legs! legs!

ICELAND SAILOR.

I don't like your floor, maty; it's too springy to my taste. I'm used to ice-floors. I'm sorry to throw cold water on the subject; but excuse me.

MALTESE SAILOR.

Me too; where's your girls? Who but a fool would take his left hand by his right, and say to himself, how d'ye do? Partners! I must have partners!

SICILIAN SAILOR.

Aye; girls and a green!—then I'll hop with ye; yea, turn grasshopper!

LONG-ISLAND SAILOR.

Well, well, ye sulkies, there's plenty more of us. Hoe corn when you may, say I. All legs go to harvest soon. Ah! here comes the music; now for it!

AZORE SAILOR.
(Ascending, and pitching the tambourine up the scuttle.)

Here you are, Pip; and there's the windlass-bitts; up you mount! Now, boys!

(The half of them dance to the tambourine; some go below; some sleep or lie among the coils of rigging. Oaths a-plenty.)

AZORE SAILOR.
(Dancing.)

Go it, Pip! Bang it, bell-boy! Rig it, dig it, stig it, quig it, bell-boy! Make fire-flies; break the jinglers!

PIP.

Jinglers, you say?—there goes another, dropped off; I pound it so.

CHINA SAILOR.

Rattle thy teeth, then, and pound away; make a pagoda of thyself.

FRENCH SAILOR.

Merry-mad! Hold up thy hoop, Pip, till I jump through it! Split jibs! tear yourselves!

TASHTEGO.
(Quietly smoking.)

That's a white man; he calls that fun: humph! I save my sweat.

OLD MANX SAILOR.

I wonder whether those jolly lads bethink them of what they are dancing over. I'll dance over your grave, I will— that's the bitterest threat of your night-women, that beat head-winds round corners. O Christ! to think of the green navies and the green-skulled crews! Well, well; belike the whole world's one ball, as your scholars have it; and so 'tis right to make one ball-room of it. Dance on, lads, you're young; I was once.

3D NANTUCKET SAILOR.

Spell oh!—whew! this is worse than pulling after whales in a calm—give us a whiff, Tash.

(They cease dancing, and gather in clusters. Meantime the sky darkens—the wind rises.)

LASCAR SAILOR.

By Brahma! boys, it'll be douse sail soon. The sky-born, high-tide Ganges turned to wind! Thou showest thy black brow, Seeva!

MALTESE SAILOR.
(Reclining and shaking his cap.)

It's the waves'—the snow-caps' turn to jig it now. They'll shake their tassels soon. Now would all the waves were women, then I'd go drown, and chassee with them evermore! There's naught so sweet on earth—heaven may not match it!—as those swift glances of warm, wild bosoms in the dance, when the over-arboring arms hide such ripe, bursting grapes.

SICILIAN SAILOR.
(Reclining.)

Tell me not of it! Hark ye, lad—fleet interlacings of the limbs—lithe swayings—coyings—flutterings! lip! heart! hip! all graze: unceasing touch and go! not taste, observe ye, else come satiety. Eh, Pagan? *(Nudging.)*

TAHITIAN SAILOR.
(Reclining on a mat.)

Hail, holy nakedness of our dancing girls!—the Heeva-Heeva! Ah! low valed, high palmed Tahiti! I still rest me on thy mat, but the soft soil has slid! I saw thee woven in the wood, my mat! green the first day I brought ye thence; now worn and wilted quite. Ah me!—not thou nor I can bear the change! How then, if so be transplanted to yon sky? Hear I the roaring streams from Pirohitee's peak of spears, when they leap down the crags and drown the villages?—The blast! the blast! Up, spine, and meet it! *(Leaps to his feet.)*

PORTUGUESE SAILOR.

How the sea rolls swashing 'gainst the side! Stand by for reefing, hearties! the winds are just crossing swords, pell-mell they'll go lunging presently.

DANISH SAILOR.

Crack, crack, old ship! so long as thou crackest, thou holdest! Well done! The mate there holds ye to it stiffly. He's no more afraid than the isle fort at Cattegat, put there to fight the Baltic with storm-lashed guns, on which the sea-salt cakes!

4TH NANTUCKET SAILOR.

He has his orders, mind ye that. I heard old Ahab tell him
he must always kill a squall, something as they burst a water-
spout with a pistol—fire your ship right into it!

ENGLISH SAILOR.

Blood! but that old man's a grand old cove! We are the
lads to hunt him up his whale!

ALL.

Aye! aye!

OLD MANX SAILOR.

How the three pines shake! Pines are the hardest sort of
tree to live when shifted to any other soil, and here there's
none but the crew's cursed clay. Steady, helmsman! steady.
This is the sort of weather when brave hearts snap ashore,
and keeled hulls split at sea. Our captain has his birth-mark;
look yonder, boys, there's another in the sky—lurid-like, ye
see, all else pitch black.

DAGGOO.

What of that? Who's afraid of black's afraid of me! I'm
quarried out of it!

SPANISH SAILOR.

(*Aside.*) He wants to bully, ah!—the old grudge makes me
touchy. (*Advancing.*) Aye, harpooneer, thy race is the undeniable dark side of mankind—devilish dark at that. No offence.

DAGGOO.
(*Grimly.*)

None.

ST. JAGO'S SAILOR.

That Spaniard's mad or drunk. But that can't be, or else in
his one case our old Mogul's fire-waters are somewhat long
in working.

5TH NANTUCKET SAILOR.
What's that I saw—lightning? Yes.

SPANISH SAILOR.
No; Daggoo showing his teeth.

DAGGOO.
(Springing.)
Swallow thine, mannikin! White skin, white liver!

SPANISH SAILOR.
(Meeting him.)
Knife thee heartily! big frame, small spirit!

ALL.
A row! a row! a row!

TASHTEGO.
(With a whiff.)
A row a'low, and a row aloft—Gods and men—both brawlers! Humph!

BELFAST SAILOR.
A row! arrah a row! The Virgin be blessed, a row! Plunge in with ye!

ENGLISH SAILOR.
Fair play! Snatch the Spaniard's knife! A ring, a ring!

OLD MANX SAILOR.
Ready formed. There! the ringed horizon. In that ring Cain struck Abel. Sweet work, right work! No? Why then, God, mad'st thou the ring?

MATE'S VOICE FROM THE QUARTER DECK.
Hands by the halyards! in top-gallant sails! Stand by to reef topsails!

ALL.
The squall! the squall! jump, my jollies! *(They scatter.)*

PIP.
(Shrinking under the windlass.)
Jollies? Lord help such jollies! Crish, crash! there goes the jib-stay! Blang-whang! God! Duck lower, Pip, here comes the royal yard! It's worse than being in the whirled woods, the last day of the year! Who'd go climbing after chestnuts now? But there they go, all cursing, and here I don't. Fine prospects to 'em; they're on the road to heaven. Hold on hard! Jimmini, what a squall! But those chaps there are worse yet—

they are your white squalls, they. White squalls? white whale, shirr! shirr! Here have I heard all their chat just now, and the white whale—shirr! shirr!—but spoken of once! and only this evening—it makes me jingle all over like my tambourine—that anaconda of an old man swore 'em in to hunt him! Oh, thou big white God aloft there somewhere in yon darkness, have mercy on this small black boy down here; preserve him from all men that have no bowels to feel fear!

*   *   *

Chapter 41

MOBY DICK

I ISHMAEL, was one of that crew; my shouts had gone up
,with the rest; my oath had been welded with theirs; and
stronger I shouted, and more did I hammer and clinch my
oath, because of the dread in my soul. A wild, mystical, sym-
pathetical feeling was in me; Ahab's quenchless feud seemed
mine. With greedy ears I learned the history of that murderous monster against whom I and all the others had taken our
oaths of violence and revenge.

For some time past, though at intervals only, the unaccompanied, secluded White Whale had haunted those uncivilized
seas mostly frequented by the Sperm Whale fishermen. But
not all of them knew of his existence; only a few of them,
comparatively, had knowingly seen him; while the number
who as yet had actually and knowingly given battle to him,
was small indeed. For, owing to the large number of whale-
cruisers; the disorderly way they were sprinkled over the
entire watery circumference, many of them adventurously
pushing their quest along solitary latitudes, so as seldom or
never for a whole twelvemonth or more on a stretch, to encounter a single news-telling sail of any sort; the inordinate
length of each separate voyage; the irregularity of the times
of sailing from home; all these, with other circumstances, direct and indirect, long obstructed the spread through the
whole world-wide whaling-fleet of the special individualizing
tidings concerning Moby Dick. It was hardly to be doubted,
that several vessels reported to have encountered, at such or
such a time, or on such or such a meridian, a Sperm Whale
of uncommon magnitude and malignity, which whale, after
doing great mischief to his assailants, had completely escaped
them; to some minds it was not an unfair presumption, I say,
that the whale in question must have been no other than
Moby Dick. Yet as of late the Sperm Whale fishery had been
marked by various and not unfrequent instances of great ferocity, cunning, and malice in the monster attacked; therefore

it was, that those who by accident ignorantly gave battle to
Moby Dick; such hunters, perhaps, for the most part, were
content to ascribe the peculiar terror he bred, more, as it
were, to the perils of the Sperm Whale fishery at large, than
to the individual cause. In that way, mostly, the disastrous
encounter between Ahab and the whale had hitherto been
popularly regarded.

And as for those who, previously hearing of the White
Whale, by chance caught sight of him; in the beginning of
the thing they had every one of them, almost, as boldly and
fearlessly lowered for him, as for any other whale of that species. But at length, such calamities did ensue in these assaults—not restricted to sprained wrists and ancles, broken
limbs, or devouring amputations—but fatal to the last degree
of fatality; those repeated disastrous repulses, all accumulating
and piling their terrors upon Moby Dick; those things had
gone far to shake the fortitude of many brave hunters, to
whom the story of the White Whale had eventually come.

Nor did wild rumors of all sorts fail to exaggerate, and still
the more horrify the true histories of these deadly encounters.
For not only do fabulous rumors naturally grow out of the
very body of all surprising terrible events,—as the smitten
tree gives birth to its fungi; but, in maritime life, far more
than in that of terra firma, wild rumors abound, wherever
there is any adequate reality for them to cling to. And as the
sea surpasses the land in this matter, so the whale fishery surpasses every other sort of maritime life, in the wonderfulness
and fearfulness of the rumors which sometimes circulate
there. For not only are whalemen as a body unexempt from
that ignorance and superstitiousness hereditary to all sailors;
but of all sailors, they are by all odds the most directly
brought into contact with whatever is appallingly astonishing
in the sea; face to face they not only eye its greatest marvels,
but, hand to jaw, give battle to them. Alone, in such remotest
waters, that though you sailed a thousand miles, and passed a
thousand shores, you would not come to any chiselled hearth-
stone, or aught hospitable beneath that part of the sun; in
such latitudes and longitudes, pursuing too such a calling as
he does, the whaleman is wrapped by influences all tending
to make his fancy pregnant with many a mighty birth.

No wonder, then, that ever gathering volume from the mere transit over the widest watery spaces, the outblown rumors of the White Whale did in the end incorporate with themselves all manner of morbid hints, and half-formed fœtal suggestions of supernatural agencies, which eventually invested Moby Dick with new terrors unborrowed from anything that visibly appears. So that in many cases such a panic did he finally strike, that few who by those rumors, at least, had heard of the White Whale, few of those hunters were willing to encounter the perils of his jaw.

But there were still other and more vital practical influences at work. Not even at the present day has the original prestige of the Sperm Whale, as fearfully distinguished from all other species of the leviathan, died out of the minds of the whalemen as a body. There are those this day among them, who, though intelligent and courageous enough in offering battle to the Greenland or Right whale, would perhaps—either from professional inexperience, or incompetency, or timidity, decline a contest with the Sperm Whale; at any rate, there are plenty of whalemen, especially among those whaling nations not sailing under the American flag, who have never hostilely encountered the Sperm Whale, but whose sole knowledge of the leviathan is restricted to the ignoble monster primitively pursued in the North; seated on their hatches, these men will hearken with a childish fire-side interest and awe, to the wild, strange tales of Southern whaling. Nor is the pre-eminent tremendousness of the great Sperm Whale anywhere more feelingly comprehended, than on board of those prows which stem him.

And as if the now tested reality of his might had in former legendary times thrown its shadow before it; we find some book naturalists—Olafsen and Povelsen—declaring the Sperm Whale not only to be a consternation to every other creature in the sea, but also to be so incredibly ferocious as continually to be athirst for human blood. Nor even down to so late a time as Cuvier's, were these or almost similar impressions effaced. For in his Natural History, the Baron himself affirms that at sight of the Sperm Whale, all fish (sharks included) are "struck with the most lively terror," and "often in the precipitancy of their flight dash themselves against the rocks with such violence as to cause instantaneous death." And however the general experiences in the fishery may amend such reports as these; yet in their full terribleness, even to the bloodthirsty item of Povelsen, the superstitious belief in them is, in some vicissitudes of their vocation, revived in the minds of the hunters.

So that overawed by the rumors and portents concerning him, not a few of the fishermen recalled, in reference to Moby Dick, the earlier days of the Sperm Whale fishery, when it was oftentimes hard to induce long practised Right whalemen to embark in the perils of this new and daring warfare; such men protesting that although other leviathans might be hopefully pursued, yet to chase and point lance at such an apparition as the Sperm Whale was not for mortal man. That to attempt it, would be inevitably to be torn into a quick eternity. On this head, there are some remarkable documents that may be consulted.

Nevertheless, some there were, who even in the face of these things were ready to give chase to Moby Dick; and a still greater number who, chancing only to hear of him distantly and vaguely, without the specific details of any certain calamity, and without superstitious accompaniments, were sufficiently hardy not to flee from the battle if offered.

One of the wild suggestings referred to, as at last coming to be linked with the White Whale in the minds of the superstitiously inclined, was the unearthly conceit that Moby Dick was ubiquitous; that he had actually been encountered in opposite latitudes at one and the same instant of time.

Nor, credulous as such minds must have been, was this conceit altogether without some faint show of superstitious probability. For as the secrets of the currents in the seas have never yet been divulged, even to the most erudite research; so the hidden ways of the Sperm Whale when beneath the surface remain, in great part, unaccountable to his pursuers; and from time to time have originated the most curious and contradictory speculations regarding them, especially concerning the mystic modes whereby, after sounding to a great depth, he transports himself with such vast swiftness to the most widely distant points.

It is a thing well known to both American and English

whale-ships, and as well a thing placed upon authoritative record years ago by Scoresby, that some whales have been captured far north in the Pacific, in whose bodies have been found the barbs of harpoons darted in the Greenland seas. Nor is it to be gainsaid, that in some of these instances it has been declared that the interval of time between the two assaults could not have exceeded very many days. Hence, by inference, it has been believed by some whalemen, that the Nor' West Passage, so long a problem to man, was never a problem to the whale. So that here, in the real living experience of living men, the prodigies related in old times of the inland Strella mountain in Portugal (near whose top there was said to be a lake in which the wrecks of ships floated up to the surface); and that still more wonderful story of the Arethusa fountain near Syracuse (whose waters were believed to have come from the Holy Land by an underground passage); these fabulous narrations are almost fully equalled by the realities of the whaleman.

Forced into familiarity, then, with such prodigies as these; and knowing that after repeated, intrepid assaults, the White Whale had escaped alive; it cannot be much matter of surprise that some whalemen should go still further in their superstitions; declaring Moby Dick not only ubiquitous, but immortal (for immortality is but ubiquity in time); that though groves of spears should be planted in his flanks, he would still swim away unharmed; or if indeed he should ever be made to spout thick blood, such a sight would be but a ghastly deception; for again in unensanguined billows hundreds of leagues away, his unsullied jet would once more be seen.

But even stripped of these supernatural surmisings, there was enough in the earthly make and incontestable character of the monster to strike the imagination with unwonted power. For, it was not so much his uncommon bulk that so much distinguished him from other sperm whales, but, as was elsewhere thrown out—a peculiar snow-white wrinkled forehead, and a high, pyramidical white hump. These were his prominent features; the tokens whereby, even in the limitless, uncharted seas, he revealed his identity, at a long distance, to those who knew him.

The rest of his body was so streaked, and spotted, and mar-bled with the same shrouded hue, that, in the end, he had gained his distinctive appellation of the White Whale; a name, indeed, literally justified by his vivid aspect, when seen gliding at high noon through a dark blue sea, leaving a milky-way wake of creamy foam, all spangled with golden gleamings.

Nor was it his unwonted magnitude, nor his remarkable hue, nor yet his deformed lower jaw, that so much invested the whale with natural terror, as that unexampled, intelligent malignity which, according to specific accounts, he had over and over again evinced in his assaults. More than all, his treacherous retreats struck more of dismay than perhaps aught else. For, when swimming before his exulting pursuers, with every apparent symptom of alarm, he had several times been known to turn round suddenly, and, bearing down upon them, either stave their boats to splinters, or drive them back in consternation to their ship.

Already several fatalities had attended his chase. But though similar disasters, however little bruited ashore, were by no means unusual in the fishery; yet, in most instances, such seemed the White Whale's infernal aforethought of ferocity, that every dismembering or death that he caused, was not wholly regarded as having been inflicted by an unintelligent agent.

Judge, then, to what pitches of inflamed, distracted fury the minds of his more desperate hunters were impelled, when amid the chips of chewed boats, and the sinking limbs of torn comrades, they swam out of the white curds of the whale's direful wrath into the serene, exasperating sunlight, that smiled on, as if at a birth or a bridal.

His three boats stove around him, and oars and men both whirling in the eddies; one captain, seizing the line-knife from his broken prow, had dashed at the whale, as an Arkansas duellist at his foe, blindly seeking with a six inch blade to reach the fathom-deep life of the whale. That captain was Ahab. And then it was, that suddenly sweeping his sickle-shaped lower jaw beneath him, Moby Dick had reaped away Ahab's leg, as a mower a blade of grass in the field. No turbaned Turk, no hired Venetian or Malay, could have smote him with more seeming malice. Small reason was there to doubt, then, that ever since that almost fatal encounter, Ahab had cherished a wild vindictiveness against the whale, all the more fell for that in his frantic morbidness he at last came to identify with him, not only all his bodily woes, but all his intellectual and spiritual exasperations. The White Whale swam before him as the monomaniac incarnation of all those malicious agencies which some deep men feel eating in them, till they are left living on with half a heart and half a lung. That intangible malignity which has been from the beginning; to whose dominion even the modern Christians ascribe one-half of the worlds; which the ancient Ophites of the east reverenced in their statue devil;—Ahab did not fall down and worship it like them; but deliriously transferring its idea to the abhorred white whale, he pitted himself, all mutilated, against it. All that most maddens and torments; all that stirs up the lees of things; all truth with malice in it; all that cracks the sinews and cakes the brain; all the subtle demonisms of life and thought; all evil, to crazy Ahab, were visibly personified, and made practically assailable in Moby Dick. He piled upon the whale's white hump the sum of all the general rage and hate felt by his whole race from Adam down; and then, as if his chest had been a mortar, he burst his hot heart's shell upon it.

It is not probable that this monomania in him took its instant rise at the precise time of his bodily dismemberment. Then, in darting at the monster, knife in hand, he had but given loose to a sudden, passionate, corporal animosity; and when he received the stroke that tore him, he probably but felt the agonizing bodily laceration, but nothing more. Yet, when by this collision forced to turn towards home, and for long months of days and weeks, Ahab and anguish lay stretched together in one hammock, rounding in mid winter that dreary, howling Patagonian Cape; then it was, that his torn body and gashed soul bled into one another; and so interfusing, made him mad. That it was only then, on the homeward voyage, after the encounter, that the final monomania seized him, seems all but certain from the fact that, at intervals during the passage, he was a raving lunatic; and, though unlimbed of a leg, yet such vital strength yet lurked in his Egyptian chest, and was moreover intensified by his delirium, that his mates were forced to lace him fast, even there, as he sailed, raving in his hammock. In a strait-jacket, he swung to the mad rockings of the gales. And, when running into more sufferable latitudes, the ship, with mild stun'sails spread, floated across the tranquil tropics, and, to all appearances, the old man's delirium seemed left behind him with the Cape Horn swells, and he came forth from his dark den into the blessed light and air; even then, when he bore that firm, collected front, however pale, and issued his calm orders once again; and his mates thanked God the direful madness was now gone; even then, Ahab, in his hidden self, raved on. Human madness is oftentimes a cunning and most feline thing. When you think it fled, it may have but become transfigured into some still subtler form. Ahab's full lunacy subsided not, but deepeningly contracted; like the unabated Hudson, when that noble Northman flows narrowly, but unfathomably through the Highland gorge. But, as in his narrow-flowing monomania, not one jot of Ahab's broad madness had been left behind; so in that broad madness, not one jot of his great natural intellect had perished. That before living agent, now became the living instrument. If such a furious trope may stand, his special lunacy stormed his general sanity, and carried it, and turned all its concentred cannon upon its own mad mark; so that far from having lost his strength, Ahab, to that one end, did now possess a thousand fold more potency than ever he had sanely brought to bear upon any one reasonable object.

This is much; yet Ahab's larger, darker, deeper part remains unhinted. But vain to popularize profundities, and all truth is profound. Winding far down from within the very heart of this spiked Hotel de Cluny where we here stand—however grand and wonderful, now quit it;—and take your way, ye nobler, sadder souls, to those vast Roman halls of Thermes; where far beneath the fantastic towers of man's upper earth, his root of grandeur, his whole awful essence sits in bearded state; an antique buried beneath antiquities, and throned on torsoes! So with a broken throne, the great gods mock that captive king; so like a Caryatid, he patient sits, upholding on his frozen brow the piled entablatures of ages. Wind ye down there, ye prouder, sadder souls! question that proud, sad king! A family likeness! aye, he did beget ye, ye young exiled royalties; and from your grim sire only will the old State-secret come.

Now, in his heart, Ahab had some glimpse of this, namely: all my means are sane, my motive and my object mad. Yet without power to kill, or change, or shun the fact; he likewise knew that to mankind he did long dissemble; in some sort, did still. But that thing of his dissembling was only subject to his perceptibility, not to his will determinate. Nevertheless, so well did he succeed in that dissembling, that when with ivory leg he stepped ashore at last, no Nantucketer thought him otherwise than but naturally grieved, and that to the quick, with the terrible casualty which had overtaken him.

The report of his undeniable delirium at sea was likewise popularly ascribed to a kindred cause. And so too, all the added moodiness which always afterwards, to the very day of sailing in the Pequod on the present voyage, sat brooding on his brow. Nor is it so very unlikely, that far from distrusting his fitness for another whaling voyage, on account of such dark symptoms, the calculating people of that prudent isle were inclined to harbor the conceit, that for those very reasons he was all the better qualified and set on edge, for a pursuit so full of rage and wildness as the bloody hunt of whales. Gnawed within and scorched without, with the infixed, unrelenting fangs of some incurable idea; such an one, could he be found, would seem the very man to dart his iron and lift his lance against the most appalling of all brutes. Or, if for any reason thought to be corporeally incapacitated for that, yet such an one would seem superlatively competent to cheer and howl on his underlings to the attack. But be all this as it may, certain it is, that with the mad secret of his unabated rage bolted up and keyed in him, Ahab had purposely sailed upon the present voyage with the one only and all-engrossing object of hunting the White Whale. Had any one of his old acquaintances on shore but half dreamed of what was lurking in him then, how soon would their aghast and righteous souls have wrenched the ship from such a fiendish man! They were bent on profitable cruises, the profit to be counted down in dollars from the mint. He was intent on an audacious, immitigable, and supernatural revenge.

Here, then, was this grey-headed, ungodly old man, chas-

ing with curses a Job's whale round the world, at the head of
a crew, too, chiefly made up of mongrel renegades, and cast-
aways, and cannibals—morally enfeebled also, by the incom-
petence of mere unaided virtue or right-mindedness in
Starbuck, the invulnerable jollity of indifference and recklessness in Stubb, and the pervading mediocrity in Flask. Such a
crew, so officered, seemed specially picked and packed by
some infernal fatality to help him to his monomaniac revenge.
How it was that they so aboundingly responded to the old
man's ire—by what evil magic their souls were possessed,
that at times his hate seemed almost theirs; the White Whale
as much their insufferable foe as his; how all this came to
be—what the White Whale was to them, or how to their
unconscious understandings, also, in some dim, unsuspected
way, he might have seemed the gliding great demon of the
seas of life,—all this to explain, would be to dive deeper than
Ishmael can go. The subterranean miner that works in us all,
how can one tell whither leads his shaft by the ever shifting,
muffled sound of his pick? Who does not feel the irresistible
arm drag? What skiff in tow of a seventy-four can stand still?
For one, I gave myself up to the abandonment of the time
and the place; but while yet all a-rush to encounter the whale,
could see naught in that brute but the deadliest ill.

Chapter 42

THE WHITENESS OF THE WHALE

W HAT the white whale was to Ahab, has been hinted; what, at times, he was to me, as yet remains unsaid.

Aside from those more obvious considerations touching Moby Dick, which could not but occasionally awaken in any man's soul some alarm, there was another thought, or rather vague, nameless horror concerning him, which at times by its intensity completely overpowered all the rest; and yet so mystical and well nigh ineffable was it, that I almost despair of putting it in a comprehensible form. It was the whiteness of the whale that above all things appalled me. But how can I hope to explain myself here; and yet, in some dim, random way, explain myself I must, else all these chapters might be naught.

Though in many natural objects, whiteness refiningly enhances beauty, as if imparting some special virtue of its own, as in marbles, japonicas, and pearls; and though various nations have in some way recognised a certain royal pre-eminence in this hue; even the barbaric, grand old kings of Pegu placing the title "Lord of the White Elephants" above all their other magniloquent ascriptions of dominion; and the modern kings of Siam unfurling the same snow-white quadruped in the royal standard; and the Hanoverian flag bearing the one figure of a snow-white charger; and the great Austrian Empire, Cæsarian heir to overlording Rome, having for the imperial color the same imperial hue; and though this pre-eminence in it applies to the human race itself, giving the white man ideal mastership over every dusky tribe; and though, besides all this, whiteness has been even made significant of gladness, for among the Romans a white stone marked a joyful day; and though in other mortal sympathies and symbolizings, this same hue is made the emblem of many touching, noble things—the innocence of brides, the benignity of age; though among the Red Men of America the giving of the white belt of wampum was the deepest pledge of

honor; though in many climes, whiteness typifies the majesty
of Justice in the ermine of the Judge, and contributes to the
daily state of kings and queens drawn by milk-white steeds;
though even in the higher mysteries of the most august religions it has been made the symbol of the divine spotlessness
and power; by the Persian fire worshippers, the white forked
flame being held the holiest on the altar; and in the Greek
mythologies, Great Jove himself being made incarnate in a
snow-white bull; and though to the noble Iroquois, the midwinter sacrifice of the sacred White Dog was by far the holiest
festival of their theology, that spotless, faithful creature being
held the purest envoy they could send to the Great Spirit with
the annual tidings of their own fidelity; and though directly
from the Latin word for white, all Christian priests derive the
name of one part of their sacred vesture, the alb or tunic,
worn beneath the cassock; and though among the holy
pomps of the Romish faith, white is specially employed in the
celebration of the Passion of our Lord; though in the Vision
of St. John, white robes are given to the redeemed, and the
four-and-twenty elders stand clothed in white before the great
white throne, and the Holy One that sitteth there white like
wool; yet for all these accumulated associations, with whatever is sweet, and honorable, and sublime, there yet lurks an
elusive something in the innermost idea of this hue, which
strikes more of panic to the soul than that redness which affrights in blood.

This elusive quality it is, which causes the thought of
whiteness, when divorced from more kindly associations, and
coupled with any object terrible in itself, to heighten that terror to the furthest bounds. Witness the white bear of the
poles, and the white shark of the tropics; what but their
smooth, flaky whiteness makes them the transcendent horrors
they are? That ghastly whiteness it is which imparts such an
abhorrent mildness, even more loathsome than terrific, to the
dumb gloating of their aspect. So that not the fierce-fanged
tiger in his heraldic coat can so stagger courage as the white-
shrouded bear or shark.*

*With reference to the Polar bear, it may possibly be urged by him who
would fain go still deeper into this matter, that it is not the whiteness, separately regarded, which heightens the intolerable hideousness of that brute;

Bethink thee of the albatross: whence come those clouds of spiritual wonderment and pale dread, in which that white phantom sails in all imaginations? Not Coleridge first threw that spell; but God's great, unflattering laureate, Nature.*

Most famous in our Western annals and Indian traditions is that of the White Steed of the Prairies; a magnificent milk-white charger, large-eyed, small-headed, bluff-chested, and

---

for, analysed, that heightened hideousness, it might be said, only arises from the circumstance, that the irresponsible ferociousness of the creature stands invested in the fleece of celestial innocence and love; and hence, by bringing together two such opposite emotions in our minds, the Polar bear frightens us with so unnatural a contrast. But even assuming all this to be true; yet, were it not for the whiteness, you would not have that intensified terror.

As for the white shark, the white gliding ghostliness of repose in that creature, when beheld in his ordinary moods, strangely tallies with the same quality in the Polar quadruped. This peculiarity is most vividly hit by the French in the name they bestow upon that fish. The Romish mass for the dead begins with "Requiem eternam" (eternal rest), whence *Requiem* denominating the mass itself, and any other funereal music. Now, in allusion to the white, silent stillness of death in this shark, and the mild deadliness of his habits, the French call him *Requin*.

*I remember the first albatross I ever saw. It was during a prolonged gale, in waters hard upon the Antarctic seas. From my forenoon watch below, I ascended to the overclouded deck; and there, dashed upon the main hatches, I saw a regal, feathery thing of unspotted whiteness, and with a hooked, Roman bill sublime. At intervals, it arched forth its vast archangel wings, as if to embrace some holy ark. Wondrous flutterings and throbbings shook it. Though bodily unharmed, it uttered cries, as some king's ghost in supernatural distress. Through its inexpressible, strange eyes, methought I peeped to secrets which took hold of God. As Abraham before the angels, I bowed myself; the white thing was so white, its wings so wide, and in those for ever exiled waters, I had lost the miserable warping memories of traditions and of towns. Long I gazed at that prodigy of plumage. I cannot tell, can only hint, the things that darted through me then. But at last I awoke; and turning, asked a sailor what bird was this. A goney, he replied. Goney! I never had heard that name before; is it conceivable that this glorious thing is utterly unknown to men ashore! never! But some time after, I learned that goney was some seaman's name for albatross. So that by no possibility could Coleridge's wild Rhyme have had aught to do with those mystical impressions which were mine, when I saw that bird upon our deck. For neither had I then read the Rhyme, nor knew the bird to be an albatross. Yet, in saying this, I do but indirectly burnish a little brighter the noble merit of the poem and the poet.

I assert, then, that in the wondrous bodily whiteness of the bird chiefly lurks the secret of the spell; a truth the more evinced in this, that by a sole-with the dignity of a thousand monarchs in his lofty, over-scorning carriage. He was the elected Xerxes of vast herds of wild horses, whose pastures in those days were only fenced by the Rocky Mountains and the Alleghanies. At their flaming head he westward trooped it like that chosen star which every evening leads on the hosts of light. The flashing cascade of his mane, the curving comet of his tail, invested him with housings more resplendent than gold and silver-beaters could have furnished him. A most imperial and archangelical apparition of that unfallen, western world, which to the eyes of the old trappers and hunters revived the glories of those primeval times when Adam walked majestic as a god, bluff-bowed and fearless as this mighty steed. Whether marching amid his aides and marshals in the van of countless cohorts that endlessly streamed it over the plains, like an Ohio; or whether with his circumambient subjects browsing all around at the horizon, the White Steed gallopingly reviewed them with warm nostrils reddening through his cool milkiness; in whatever aspect he presented himself, always to the bravest Indians he was the object of trembling reverence and awe. Nor can it be questioned from what stands on legendary record of this noble horse, that it was his spiritual whiteness chiefly, which so clothed him with divineness; and that this divineness had that in it which, though commanding worship, at the same time enforced a certain nameless terror.

But there are other instances where this whiteness loses all that accessory and strange glory which invests it in the White Steed and Albatross.

What is it that in the Albino man so peculiarly repels and often shocks the eye, as that sometimes he is loathed by his own kith and kin? It is that whiteness which invests him, a thing expressed by the name he bears. The Albino is as well

---

cism of terms there are birds called grey albatrosses; and these I have frequently seen, but never with such emotions as when I beheld the Antarctic fowl.

But how had the mystic thing been caught? Whisper it not, and I will tell; with a treacherous hook and line, as the fowl floated on the sea. At last the Captain made a postman of it; tying a lettered, leathern tally round its neck, with the ship's time and place; and then letting it escape. But I doubt not, that leathern tally, meant for man, was taken off in Heaven, when the white fowl flew to join the wing-folding, the invoking, and adoring cherubim!

made as other men—has no substantive deformity—and yet this mere aspect of all-pervading whiteness makes him more strangely hideous than the ugliest abortion. Why should this be so?

Nor, in quite other aspects, does Nature in her least palpable but not the less malicious agencies, fail to enlist among her forces this crowning attribute of the terrible. From its snowy aspect, the gauntleted ghost of the Southern Seas has been denominated the White Squall. Nor, in some historic instances, has the art of human malice omitted so potent an auxiliary. How wildly it heightens the effect of that passage in Froissart, when, masked in the snowy symbol of their faction, the desperate White Hoods of Ghent murder their bailiff in the market-place!

Nor, in some things, does the common, hereditary experience of all mankind fail to bear witness to the supernaturalism of this hue. It cannot well be doubted, that the one visible quality in the aspect of the dead which most appals the gazer, is the marble pallor lingering there; as if indeed that pallor were as much the badge of consternation in the other world, as of mortal trepidation here. And from that pallor of the dead, we borrow the expressive hue of the shroud in which we wrap them. Nor even in our superstitions do we fail to throw the same snowy mantle round our phantoms; all ghosts rising in a milk-white fog—Yea, while these terrors seize us, let us add, that even the king of terrors, when personified by the evangelist, rides on his pallid horse.

Therefore, in his other moods, symbolize whatever grand or gracious thing he will by whiteness, no man can deny that in its profoundest idealized significance it calls up a peculiar apparition to the soul.

But though without dissent this point be fixed, how is mortal man to account for it? To analyse it, would seem impossible. Can we, then, by the citation of some of those instances wherein this thing of whiteness—though for the time either wholly or in great part stripped of all direct associations calculated to impart to it aught fearful, but, nevertheless, is found to exert over us the same sorcery, however modified;—can we thus hope to light upon some chance clue to conduct us to the hidden cause we seek?

Let us try. But in a matter like this, subtlety appeals to subtlety, and without imagination no man can follow another into these halls. And though, doubtless, some at least of the imaginative impressions about to be presented may have been shared by most men, yet few perhaps were entirely conscious of them at the time, and therefore may not be able to recall them now.

Why to the man of untutored ideality, who happens to be but loosely acquainted with the peculiar character of the day, does the bare mention of Whitsuntide marshal in the fancy such long, dreary, speechless processions of slow-pacing pilgrims, down-cast and hooded with new-fallen snow? Or, to the unread, unsophisticated Protestant of the Middle American States, why does the passing mention of a White Friar or a White Nun, evoke such an eyeless statue in the soul?

Or what is there apart from the traditions of dungeoned warriors and kings (which will not wholly account for it) that makes the White Tower of London tell so much more strongly on the imagination of an untravelled American, than those other storied structures, its neighbors—the Byward Tower, or even the Bloody? And those sublimer towers, the White Mountains of New Hampshire, whence, in peculiar moods, comes that gigantic ghostliness over the soul at the bare mention of that name, while the thought of Virginia's Blue Ridge is full of a soft, dewy, distant dreaminess? Or why, irrespective of all latitudes and longitudes, does the name of the White Sea exert such a spectralness over the fancy, while that of the Yellow Sea lulls us with mortal thoughts of long lacquered mild afternoons on the waves, followed by the gaudiest and yet sleepiest of sunsets? Or, to choose a wholly unsubstantial instance, purely addressed to the fancy, why, in reading the old fairy tales of Central Europe, does "the tall pale man" of the Hartz forests, whose changeless pallor unrustlingly glides through the green of the groves—why is this phantom more terrible than all the whooping imps of the Blocksburg?

Nor is it, altogether, the remembrance of her cathedral-toppling earthquakes; nor the stampedoes of her frantic seas; nor the tearlessness of arid skies that never rain; nor the sight of her wide field of leaning spires, wrenched cope-stones, and crosses all adroop (like canted yards of anchored fleets); and her suburban avenues of house-walls lying over upon each other, as a tossed pack of cards;—it is not these things alone which make tearless Lima, the strangest, saddest city thou can'st see. For Lima has taken the white veil; and there is a higher horror in this whiteness of her woe. Old as Pizarro, this whiteness keeps her ruins for ever new; admits not the cheerful greenness of complete decay; spreads over her broken ramparts the rigid pallor of an apoplexy that fixes its own distortions.

I know that, to the common apprehension, this phenomenon of whiteness is not confessed to be the prime agent in exaggerating the terror of objects otherwise terrible; nor to the unimaginative mind is there aught of terror in those appearances whose awfulness to another mind almost solely consists in this one phenomenon, especially when exhibited under any form at all approaching to muteness or universality. What I mean by these two statements may perhaps be respectively elucidated by the following examples.

First: The mariner, when drawing nigh the coasts of foreign lands, if by night he hear the roar of breakers, starts to vigilance, and feels just enough of trepidation to sharpen all his faculties; but under precisely similar circumstances, let him be called from his hammock to view his ship sailing through a midnight sea of milky whiteness—as if from encircling headlands shoals of combed white bears were swimming round him, then he feels a silent, superstitious dread; the shrouded phantom of the whitened waters is horrible to him as a real ghost; in vain the lead assures him he is still off soundings; heart and helm they both go down; he never rests till blue water is under him again. Yet where is the mariner who will tell thee, "Sir, it was not so much the fear of striking hidden rocks, as the fear of that hideous whiteness that so stirred me?"

Second: To the native Indian of Peru, the continual sight of the snow-howdahed Andes conveys naught of dread, except, perhaps, in the mere fancying of the eternal frosted desolateness reigning at such vast altitudes, and the natural conceit of what a fearfulness it would be to lose oneself in such inhuman solitudes. Much the same is it with the backwoodsman of the West, who with comparative indifference views an unbounded prairie sheeted with driven snow, no shadow of tree or twig to break the fixed trance of whiteness. Not so the sailor, beholding the scenery of the Antarctic seas; where at times, by some infernal trick of legerdemain in the powers of frost and air, he, shivering and half shipwrecked, instead of rainbows speaking hope and solace to his misery, views what seems a boundless church-yard grinning upon him with its lean ice monuments and splintered crosses.

But thou sayest, methinks this white-lead chapter about whiteness is but a white flag hung out from a craven soul; thou surrenderest to a hypo, Ishmael.

Tell me, why this strong young colt, foaled in some peaceful valley of Vermont, far removed from all beasts of prey—why is it that upon the sunniest day, if you but shake a fresh buffalo robe behind him, so that he cannot even see it, but only smells its wild animal muskiness—why will he start, snort, and with bursting eyes paw the ground in phrensies of affright? There is no remembrance in him of any gorings of wild creatures in his green northern home, so that the strange muskiness he smells cannot recall to him anything associated with the experience of former perils; for what knows he, this New England colt, of the black bisons of distant Oregon?

No: but here thou beholdest even in a dumb brute, the instinct of the knowledge of the demonism in the world. Though thousands of miles from Oregon, still when he smells that savage musk, the rending, goring bison herds are as present as to the deserted wild foal of the prairies, which this instant they may be trampling into dust.

Thus, then, the muffled rollings of a milky sea; the bleak rustlings of the festooned frosts of mountains; the desolate shiftings of the windrowed snows of prairies; all these, to Ishmael, are as the shaking of that buffalo robe to the frightened colt!

Though neither knows where lie the nameless things of which the mystic sign gives forth such hints; yet with me, as with the colt, somewhere those things must exist. Though in many of its aspects this visible world seems formed in love, the invisible spheres were formed in fright.

But not yet have we solved the incantation of this whiteness, and learned why it appeals with such power to the soul;

and more strange and far more portentous—why, as we have seen, it is at once the most meaning symbol of spiritual things, nay, the very veil of the Christian's Deity; and yet should be as it is, the intensifying agent in things the most appalling to mankind.

Is it that by its indefiniteness it shadows forth the heartless voids and immensities of the universe, and thus stabs us from behind with the thought of annihilation, when beholding the white depths of the milky way? Or is it, that as in essence whiteness is not so much a color as the visible absence of color, and at the same time the concrete of all colors; is it for these reasons that there is such a dumb blankness, full of meaning, in a wide landscape of snows—a colorless, all-color of atheism from which we shrink? And when we consider that other theory of the natural philosophers, that all other earthly hues—every stately or lovely emblazoning—the sweet tinges of sunset skies and woods; yea, and the gilded velvets of but-terflies, and the butterfly cheeks of young girls; all these are but subtile deceits, not actually inherent in substances, but only laid on from without; so that all deified Nature abso-lutely paints like the harlot, whose allurements cover nothing but the charnel-house within; and when we proceed further, and consider that the mystical cosmetic which produces every one of her hues, the great principle of light, for ever remains white or colorless in itself, and if operating without medium upon matter, would touch all objects, even tulips and roses, with its own blank tinge—pondering all this, the palsied uni-verse lies before us a leper; and like wilful travellers in Lap-land, who refuse to wear colored and coloring glasses upon their eyes, so the wretched infidel gazes himself blind at the monumental white shroud that wraps all the prospect around him. And of all these things the Albino whale was the sym-bol. Wonder ye then at the fiery hunt?

Chapter 43

HARK!

"Hist! Did you hear that noise, Cabaco?"

It was the middle-watch: a fair moonlight; the seamen were standing in a cordon, extending from one of the fresh-water butts in the waist, to the scuttle-butt near the taffrail. In this manner, they passed the buckets to fill the scuttle-butt. Standing, for the most part, on the hallowed precincts of the quarter-deck, they were careful not to speak or rustle their feet. From hand to hand, the buckets went in the deepest silence, only broken by the occasional flap of a sail, and the steady hum of the unceasingly advancing keel.

It was in the midst of this repose, that Archy, one of the cordon, whose post was near the after-hatches, whispered to his neighbor, a Cholo, the words above.

"Hist! did you hear that noise, Cabaco?"

"Take the bucket, will ye, Archy? what noise d'ye mean?"

"There it is again—under the hatches—don't you hear it—a cough—it sounded like a cough."

"Cough be damned! Pass along that return bucket."

"There again—there it is!—it sounds like two or three sleepers turning over, now!"

"Caramba! have done, shipmate, will ye? It's the three soaked biscuits ye eat for supper turning over inside of ye—nothing else. Look to the bucket!"

"Say what ye will, shipmate; I've sharp ears."

"Aye, you are the chap, ain't ye, that heard the hum of the old Quakeress's knitting-needles fifty miles at sea from Nantucket; you're the chap."

"Grin away; we'll see what turns up. Hark ye, Cabaco, there is somebody down in the after-hold that has not yet been seen on deck; and I suspect our old Mogul knows something of it too. I heard Stubb tell Flask, one morning watch, that there was something of that sort in the wind."

"Tish! the bucket!"

Chapter 44

The Chart

HAD YOU FOLLOWED Captain Ahab down into his cabin after the squall that took place on the night succeeding that wild ratification of his purpose with his crew, you would have seen him go to a locker in the transom, and bringing out a large wrinkled roll of yellowish sea charts, spread them before him on his screwed-down table. Then seating himself before it, you would have seen him intently study the various lines and shadings which there met his eye; and with slow but steady pencil trace additional courses over spaces that before were blank. At intervals, he would refer to piles of old log-books beside him, wherein were set down the seasons and places in which, on various former voyages of various ships, sperm whales had been captured or seen.

While thus employed, the heavy pewter lamp suspended in chains over his head, continually rocked with the motion of the ship, and for ever threw shifting gleams and shadows of lines upon his wrinkled brow, till it almost seemed that while he himself was marking out lines and courses on the wrinkled charts, some invisible pencil was also tracing lines and courses upon the deeply marked chart of his forehead.

But it was not this night in particular that, in the solitude of his cabin, Ahab thus pondered over his charts. Almost every night they were brought out; almost every night some pencil marks were effaced, and others were substituted. For with the charts of all four oceans before him, Ahab was threading a maze of currents and eddies, with a view to the more certain accomplishment of that monomaniac thought of his soul.

Now, to any one not fully acquainted with the ways of the leviathans, it might seem an absurdly hopeless task thus to seek out one solitary creature in the unhooped oceans of this planet. But not so did it seem to Ahab, who knew the sets of all tides and currents; and thereby calculating the driftings of the sperm whale's food; and, also, calling to mind the regular,

ascertained seasons for hunting him in particular latitudes;
could arrive at reasonable surmises, almost approaching to
certainties, concerning the timeliest day to be upon this or
that ground in search of his prey.

So assured, indeed, is the fact concerning the periodicalness
of the sperm whale's resorting to given waters, that many
hunters believe that, could he be closely observed and studied
throughout the world; were the logs for one voyage of the
entire whale fleet carefully collated, then the migrations of the
sperm whale would be found to correspond in invariability to
those of the herring-shoals or the flights of swallows. On this
hint, attempts have been made to construct elaborate migra-
tory charts of the sperm whale.*

Besides, when making a passage from one feeding-ground
to another, the sperm whales, guided by some infallible instinct—say, rather, secret intelligence from the Deity—
mostly swim in *veins*, as they are called; continuing their way
along a given ocean-line with such undeviating exactitude,
that no ship ever sailed her course, by any chart, with one
tithe of such marvellous precision. Though, in these cases, the
direction taken by any one whale be straight as a surveyor's
parallel, and though the line of advance be strictly confined to
its own unavoidable, straight wake, yet the arbitrary *vein* in
which at these times he is said to swim, generally embraces
some few miles in width (more or less, as the vein is presumed to expand or contract); but never exceeds the visual
sweep from the whale-ship's mast-heads, when circumspectly
gliding along this magic zone. The sum is, that at particular
seasons within that breadth and along that path, migrating
whales may with great confidence be looked for.

And hence not only at substantiated times, upon well

*Since the above was written, the statement is happily borne out by an
official circular, issued by Lieutenant Maury, of the National Observatory,
Washington, April 16th, 1851. By that circular, it appears that precisely such a
chart is in course of completion; and portions of it are presented in the circular. "This chart divides the ocean into districts of five degrees of latitude
by five degrees of longitude; perpendicularly through each of which districts
are twelve columns for the twelve months; and horizontally through each of
which districts are three lines; one to show the number of days that have
been spent in each month in every district, and the two others to show the
number of days on which whales, sperm or right, have been seen."

known separate feeding-grounds, could Ahab hope to encounter his prey; but in crossing the widest expanses of water
between those grounds he could, by his art, so place and time
himself on his way, as even then not to be wholly without
prospect of a meeting.

There was a circumstance which at first sight seemed to
entangle his delirious but still methodical scheme. But not so
in the reality, perhaps. Though the gregarious sperm whales
have their regular seasons for particular grounds, yet in general you cannot conclude that the herds which haunted such
and such a latitude or longitude this year, say, will turn out
to be identically the same with those that were found there
the preceding season; though there are peculiar and unquestionable instances where the contrary of this has proved true.
In general, the same remark, only within a less wide limit,
applies to the solitaries and hermits among the matured, aged
sperm whales. So that though Moby Dick had in a former
year been seen, for example, on what is called the Seychelle
ground in the Indian ocean, or Volcano Bay on the Japanese
Coast; yet it did not follow, that were the Pequod to visit
either of those spots at any subsequent corresponding season,
she would infallibly encounter him there. So, too, with some
other feeding grounds, where he had at times revealed himself. But all these seemed only his casual stopping-places and
ocean-inns, so to speak, not his places of prolonged abode.
And where Ahab's chances of accomplishing his object have
hitherto been spoken of, allusion has only been made to
whatever way-side, antecedent, extra prospects were his, ere a
particular set time and place were attained, when all possibilities would become probabilities, and, as Ahab fondly
thought, every possibility the next thing to a certainty. That
particular set time and place were conjoined in the one technical phrase—the Season-on-the-Line. For there and then,
for several consecutive years, Moby Dick had been periodically descried, lingering in those waters for awhile, as the sun,
in its annual round, loiters for a predicted interval in any one
sign of the Zodiac. There it was, too, that most of the deadly
encounters with the white whale had taken place; there the
waves were storied with his deeds; there also was that tragic
spot where the monomaniac old man had found the awful

motive to his vengeance. But in the cautious comprehensiveness and unloitering vigilance with which Ahab threw his brooding soul into this unfaltering hunt, he would not permit himself to rest all his hopes upon the one crowning fact above mentioned, however flattering it might be to those hopes; nor in the sleeplessness of his vow could he so tranquillize his unquiet heart as to postpone all intervening quest.

Now, the Pequod had sailed from Nantucket at the very beginning of the Season-on-the-Line. No possible endeavor then could enable her commander to make the great passage southwards, double Cape Horn, and then running down sixty degrees of latitude arrive in the equatorial Pacific in time to cruise there. Therefore, he must wait for the next ensuing season. Yet the premature hour of the Pequod's sailing had, perhaps, been covertly selected by Ahab, with a view to this very complexion of things. Because, an interval of three hundred and sixty-five days and nights was before him; an interval which, instead of impatiently enduring ashore, he would spend in a miscellaneous hunt; if by chance the White Whale, spending his vacation in seas far remote from his periodical feeding-grounds, should turn up his wrinkled brow off the Persian Gulf, or in the Bengal Bay, or China Seas, or in any other waters haunted by his race. So that Monsoons, Pampas, Nor-Westers, Harmattans, Trades; any wind but the Levanter and Simoom, might blow Moby Dick into the devious zig-zag world-circle of the Pequod's circumnavigating wake.

But granting all this; yet, regarded discreetly and coolly, seems it not but a mad idea, this; that in the broad boundless ocean, one solitary whale, even if encountered, should be thought capable of individual recognition from his hunter, even as a white-bearded Mufti in the thronged thoroughfares of Constantinople? No. For the peculiar snow-white brow of Moby Dick, and his snow-white hump, could not but be unmistakable. And have I not tallied the whale, Ahab would mutter to himself, as after poring over his charts till long after midnight he would throw himself back in reveries—tallied him, and shall he escape? His broad fins are bored, and scalloped out like a lost sheep's ear! And here, his mad mind would run on in a breathless race; till a weariness and faintness of pondering came over him; and in the open air of the deck he would seek to recover his strength. Ah, God! what trances of torments does that man endure who is consumed with one unachieved revengeful desire. He sleeps with clenched hands; and wakes with his own bloody nails in his palms.

Often, when forced from his hammock by exhausting and intolerably vivid dreams of the night, which, resuming his own intense thoughts through the day, carried them on amid a clashing of phrensies, and whirled them round and round in his blazing brain, till the very throbbing of his life-spot became insufferable anguish; and when, as was sometimes the case, these spiritual throes in him heaved his being up from its base, and a chasm seemed opening in him, from which forked flames and lightnings shot up, and accursed fiends beckoned him to leap down among them; when this hell in himself yawned beneath him, a wild cry would be heard through the ship; and with glaring eyes Ahab would burst from his state room, as though escaping from a bed that was on fire. Yet these, perhaps, instead of being the unsuppressable symptoms of some latent weakness, or fright at his own resolve, were but the plainest tokens of its intensity. For, at such times, crazy Ahab, the scheming, unappeasedly steadfast hunter of the white whale; this Ahab that had gone to his hammock, was not the agent that so caused him to burst from it in horror again. The latter was the eternal, living principle or soul in him; and in sleep, being for the time dissociated from the characterizing mind, which at other times employed it for its outer vehicle or agent, it spontaneously sought escape from the scorching contiguity of the frantic thing, of which, for the time, it was no longer an integral. But as the mind does not exist unless leagued with the soul, therefore it must have been that, in Ahab's case, yielding up all his thoughts and fancies to his one supreme purpose; that purpose, by its own sheer inveteracy of will, forced itself against gods and devils into a kind of self-assumed, independent being of its own. Nay, could grimly live and burn, while the common vitality to which it was conjoined, fled horror-stricken from the unbidden and unfathered birth. Therefore, the tormented spirit that glared out of bodily eyes, when what seemed Ahab rushed from his room, was for the time but a vacated thing, a formless somnambulistic being, a ray of living light, to be sure, but without an object to color, and therefore a blankness in itself. God help thee, old man, thy thoughts have created a creature in thee; and he whose intense thinking thus makes him a Prometheus; a vulture feeds upon that heart for ever; that vulture the very creature he creates.

Chapter 45

THE AFFIDAVIT

S O FAR AS what there may be of a narrative in this book; and, indeed, as indirectly touching one or two very interesting and curious particulars in the habits of sperm whales, the foregoing chapter, in its earlier part, is as important a one as will be found in this volume; but the leading matter of it requires to be still further and more familiarly enlarged upon, in order to be adequately understood, and moreover to take away any incredulity which a profound ignorance of the entire subject may induce in some minds, as to the natural verity of the main points of this affair.

I care not to perform this part of my task methodically; but shall be content to produce the desired impression by separate citations of items, practically or reliably known to me as a whaleman; and from these citations, I take it—the conclusion aimed at will naturally follow of itself.

First: I have personally known three instances where a whale, after receiving a harpoon, has effected a complete escape; and, after an interval (in one instance of three years), has been again struck by the same hand, and slain; when the two irons, both marked by the same private cypher, have been taken from the body. In the instance where three years intervened between the flinging of the two harpoons; and I think it may have been something more than that; the man who darted them happening, in the interval, to go in a trading ship on a voyage to Africa, went ashore there, joined a discovery party, and penetrated far into the interior, where he travelled for a period of nearly two years, often endangered by serpents, savages, tigers, poisonous miasmas, with all the other common perils incident to wandering in the heart of unknown regions. Meanwhile, the whale he had struck must also have been on its travels; no doubt it had thrice circumnavigated the globe, brushing with its flanks all the coasts of Africa; but to no purpose. This man and this whale again came together, and the one vanquished the other. I say I, myself, have known three instances similar to this; that is in two of them I saw the whales struck; and, upon the second attack, saw the two irons with the respective marks cut in them, afterwards taken from the dead fish. In the three-year instance, it so fell out that I was in the boat both times, first and last, and the last time distinctly recognized a peculiar sort of huge mole under the whale's eye, which I had observed there three years previous. I say three years, but I am pretty sure it was more than that. Here are three instances, then, which I personally know the truth of; but I have heard of many other instances from persons whose veracity in the matter there is no good ground to impeach.

Secondly: It is well known in the Sperm Whale Fishery, however ignorant the world ashore may be of it, that there have been several memorable historical instances where a particular whale in the ocean has been at distant times and places popularly cognisable. Why such a whale became thus marked was not altogether and originally owing to his bodily peculiarities as distinguished from other whales; for however peculiar in that respect any chance whale may be, they soon put an end to his peculiarities by killing him, and boiling him down into a peculiarly valuable oil. No: the reason was this: that from the fatal experiences of the fishery there hung a terrible prestige of perilousness about such a whale as there did about Rinaldo Rinaldini, insomuch that most fishermen were content to recognise him by merely touching their tarpaulins when he would be discovered lounging by them on the sea, without seeking to cultivate a more intimate acquaintance. Like some poor devils ashore that happen to know an irascible great man, they make distant unobtrusive salutations to him in the street, lest if they pursued the acquaintance further, they might receive a summary thump for their presumption.

But not only did each of these famous whales enjoy great individual celebrity—nay, you may call it an ocean-wide renown; not only was he famous in life and now is immortal in forecastle stories after death, but he was admitted into all the rights, privileges, and distinctions of a name; had as much a name indeed as Cambyses or Cæsar. Was it not so, O Timor Jack! thou famed leviathan, scarred like an iceberg, who so

long did'st lurk in the Oriental straits of that name, whose
spout was oft seen from the palmy beach of Ombay? Was it
not so, O New Zealand Tom! thou terror of all cruisers that
crossed their wakes in the vicinity of the Tattoo Land? Was it
not so, O Morquan! King of Japan, whose lofty jet they say
at times assumed the semblance of a snow-white cross against
the sky? Was it not so, O Don Miguel! thou Chilian whale,
marked like an old tortoise with mystic hieroglyphics upon
the back! In plain prose, here are four whales as well known
to the students of Cetacean History as Marius or Sylla to the
classic scholar.

But this is not all. New Zealand Tom and Don Miguel,
after at various times creating great havoc among the boats of
different vessels, were finally gone in quest of, systematically
hunted out, chased and killed by valiant whaling captains,
who heaved up their anchors with that express object as much
in view, as in setting out through the Narragansett Woods,
Captain Church of old had it in his mind to capture that notorious murderous savage Annawon, the headmost warrior of
the Indian King Philip.

I do not know where I can find a better place than just
here, to make mention of one or two other things, which to
me seem important, as in printed form establishing in all respects the reasonableness of the whole story of the White
Whale, more especially the catastrophe. For this is one of
those disheartening instances where truth requires full as
much bolstering as error. So ignorant are most landsmen of
some of the plainest and most palpable wonders of the world,
that without some hints touching the plain facts, historical
and otherwise, of the fishery, they might scout at Moby Dick
as a monstrous fable, or still worse and more detestable, a
hideous and intolerable allegory.

First: Though most men have some vague flitting ideas of
the general perils of the grand fishery, yet they have nothing
like a fixed, vivid conception of those perils, and the fre-
quency with which they recur. One reason perhaps is, that
not one in fifty of the actual disasters and deaths by casualties
in the fishery, ever finds a public record at home, however
transient and immediately forgotten that record. Do you suppose that that poor fellow there, who this moment perhaps

caught by the whale-line off the coast of New Guinea, is being carried down to the bottom of the sea by the sounding leviathan—do you suppose that that poor fellow's name will appear in the newspaper obituary you will read to-morrow at your breakfast? No: because the mails are very irregular between here and New Guinea. In fact, did you ever hear what might be called regular news direct or indirect from New Guinea? Yet I tell you that upon one particular voyage which I made to the Pacific, among many others, we spoke thirty different ships, every one of which had had a death by a whale, some of them more than one, and three that had each lost a boat's crew. For God's sake, be economical with your lamps and candles! not a gallon you burn, but at least one drop of man's blood was spilled for it.

Secondly: People ashore have indeed some indefinite idea that a whale is an enormous creature of enormous power; but I have ever found that when narrating to them some specific example of this two-fold enormousness, they have significantly complimented me upon my facetiousness; when, I declare upon my soul, I had no more idea of being facetious than Moses, when he wrote the history of the plagues of Egypt.

But fortunately the special point I here seek can be established upon testimony entirely independent of my own. That point is this: The Sperm Whale is in some cases sufficiently powerful, knowing, and judiciously malicious, as with direct aforethought to stave in, utterly destroy, and sink a large ship; and what is more, the Sperm Whale *has* done it.

First: In the year 1820 the ship Essex, Captain Pollard, of Nantucket, was cruising in the Pacific Ocean. One day she saw spouts, lowered her boats, and gave chase to a shoal of sperm whales. Ere long, several of the whales were wounded; when, suddenly, a very large whale escaping from the boats, issued from the shoal, and bore directly down upon the ship. Dashing his forehead against her hull, he so stove her in, that in less than "ten minutes" she settled down and fell over. Not a surviving plank of her has been seen since. After the severest exposure, part of the crew reached the land in their boats. Being returned home at last, Captain Pollard once more sailed for the Pacific in command of another ship, but the gods shipwrecked him again upon unknown rocks and breakers; for the second time his ship was utterly lost, and forthwith forswearing the sea, he has never tempted it since. At this day Captain Pollard is a resident of Nantucket. I have seen Owen Chase, who was chief mate of the Essex at the time of the tragedy; I have read his plain and faithful narrative; I have conversed with his son; and all this within a few miles of the scene of the catastrophe.*

Secondly: The ship Union, also of Nantucket, was in the year 1807 totally lost off the Azores by a similar onset, but the authentic particulars of this catastrophe I have never chanced to encounter, though from the whale hunters I have now and then heard casual allusions to it.

Thirdly: Some eighteen or twenty years ago Commodore J—— then commanding an American sloop-of-war of the first class, happened to be dining with a party of whaling captains, on board a Nantucket ship in the harbor of Oahu, Sandwich Islands. Conversation turning upon whales, the

*The following are extracts from Chase's narrative: "Every fact seemed to warrant me in concluding that it was anything but chance which directed his operations; he made two several attacks upon the ship, at a short interval between them, both of which, according to their direction, were calculated to do us the most injury, by being made ahead, and thereby combining the speed of the two objects for the shock; to effect which, the exact manœuvres which he made were necessary. His aspect was most horrible, and such as indicated resentment and fury. He came directly from the shoal which we had just before entered, and in which we had struck three of his companions, as if fired with revenge for their sufferings." Again: "At all events, the whole circumstances taken together, all happening before my own eyes, and producing, at the time, impressions in my mind of decided, calculating mischief, on the part of the whale (many of which impressions I cannot now recall), induce me to be satisfied that I am correct in my opinion."

Here are his reflections some time after quitting the ship, during a black night in an open boat, when almost despairing of reaching any hospitable shore. "The dark ocean and swelling waters were nothing; the fears of being swallowed up by some dreadful tempest, or dashed upon hidden rocks, with all the other ordinary subjects of fearful contemplation, seemed scarcely entitled to a moment's thought; the dismal looking wreck, and *the horrid aspect and revenge of the whale*, wholly engrossed my reflections, until day again made its appearance."

In another place—p. 45,—he speaks of "*the mysterious and mortal attack of the animal*."

  * * * * * * * *
  * * * * * * * *

Commodore was pleased to be sceptical touching the amazing strength ascribed to them by the professional gentlemen present. He peremptorily denied for example, that any whale could so smite his stout sloop-of-war as to cause her to leak so much as a thimbleful. Very good; but there is more coming. Some weeks after, the commodore set sail in this impregnable craft for Valparaiso. But he was stopped on the way by a portly sperm whale, that begged a few moments' confidential business with him. That business consisted in fetching the Commodore's craft such a thwack, that with all his pumps going he made straight for the nearest port to heave down and repair. I am not superstitious, but I consider the Commodore's interview with that whale as providential. Was not Saul of Tarsus converted from unbelief by a similar fright? I tell you, the sperm whale will stand no nonsense.

I will now refer you to Langsdorff's Voyages for a little circumstance in point, peculiarly interesting to the writer hereof. Langsdorff, you must know by the way, was attached to the Russian Admiral Krusenstern's famous Discovery Expedition in the beginning of the present century. Captain Langsdorff thus begins his seventeenth chapter.

"By the thirteenth of May our ship was ready to sail, and the next day we were out in the open sea, on our way to Ochotsk. The weather was very clear and fine, but so intolerably cold that we were obliged to keep on our fur clothing. For some days we had very little wind; it was not till the nineteenth that a brisk gale from the northwest sprang up. An uncommon large whale, the body of which was larger than the ship itself, lay almost at the surface of the water, but was not perceived by any one on board till the moment when the ship, which was in full sail, was almost upon him, so that it was impossible to prevent its striking against him. We were thus placed in the most imminent danger, as this gigantic creature, setting up its back, raised the ship three feet at least out of the water. The masts reeled, and the sails fell altogether, while we who were below all sprang instantly upon the deck, concluding that we had struck upon some rock; instead of this we saw the monster sailing off with the utmost gravity and solemnity. Captain D'Wolf applied immediately to the pumps to examine whether or not the vessel had received any damage from the shock, but we found that very happily it had escaped entirely uninjured."

Now, the Captain D'Wolf here alluded to as commanding the ship in question, is a New Englander, who, after a long life of unusual adventures as a sea-captain, this day resides in the village of Dorchester near Boston. I have the honor of being a nephew of his. I have particularly questioned him concerning this passage in Langsdorff. He substantiates every word. The ship, however, was by no means a large one: a Russian craft built on the Siberian coast, and purchased by my uncle after bartering away the vessel in which he sailed from home.

In that up and down manly book of old-fashioned adventure, so full, too, of honest wonders—the voyage of Lionel Wafer, one of ancient Dampier's old chums—I found a little matter set down so like that just quoted from Langsdorff, that I cannot forbear inserting it here for a corroborative example, if such be needed.

Lionel, it seems, was on his way to "John Ferdinando," as he calls the modern Juan Fernandes. "In our way thither," he says, "about four o'clock in the morning, when we were about one hundred and fifty leagues from the Main of America, our ship felt a terrible shock, which put our men in such consternation that they could hardly tell where they were or what to think; but every one began to prepare for death. And, indeed, the shock was so sudden and violent, that we took it for granted the ship had struck against a rock; but when the amazement was a little over, we cast the lead, and sounded, but found no ground. * * * * * The suddenness of the shock made the guns leap in their carriages, and several of the men were shaken out of their hammocks. Captain Davis, who lay with his head over a gun, was thrown out of his cabin!" Lionel then goes on to impute the shock to an earthquake, and seems to substantiate the imputation by stating that a great earthquake, somewhere about that time, did actually do great mischief along the Spanish land. But I should not much wonder if, in the darkness of that early hour of the morning, the shock was after all caused by an unseen whale vertically bumping the hull from beneath.

I might proceed with several more examples, one way or another known to me, of the great power and malice at times of the sperm whale. In more than one instance, he has been known, not only to chase the assailing boats back to their ships, but to pursue the ship itself, and long withstand all the lances hurled at him from its decks. The English ship Pusie Hall can tell a story on that head; and, as for his strength, let me say, that there have been examples where the lines attached to a running sperm whale have, in a calm, been transferred to the ship, and secured there; the whale towing her great hull through the water, as a horse walks off with a cart. Again, it is very often observed that, if the sperm whale, once struck, is allowed time to rally, he then acts, not so often with blind rage, as with wilful, deliberate designs of destruction to his pursuers; nor is it without conveying some eloquent indication of his character, that upon being attacked he will frequently open his mouth, and retain it in that dread expansion for several consecutive minutes. But I must be content with only one more and a concluding illustration; a remarkable and most significant one, by which you will not fail to see, that not only is the most marvellous event in this book corroborated by plain facts of the present day, but that these marvels (like all marvels) are mere repetitions of the ages; so that for the millionth time we say amen with Solomon— Verily there is nothing new under the sun.

In the sixth Christian century lived Procopius, a Christian magistrate of Constantinople, in the days when Justinian was Emperor and Belisarius general. As many know, he wrote the history of his own times, a work every way of uncommon value. By the best authorities, he has always been considered a most trustworthy and unexaggerating historian, except in some one or two particulars, not at all affecting the matter presently to be mentioned.

Now, in this history of his, Procopius mentions that, during the term of his prefecture at Constantinople, a great sea-monster was captured in the neighboring Propontis, or Sea of Marmora, after having destroyed vessels at intervals in those waters for a period of more than fifty years. A fact thus set down in substantial history cannot easily be gainsaid. Nor is there any reason it should be. Of what precise species this sea-monster was, is not mentioned. But as he destroyed ships, as well as for other reasons, he must have been a whale; and I am strongly inclined to think a sperm whale. And I will tell you why. For a long time I fancied that the sperm whale had been always unknown in the Mediterranean and the deep waters connecting with it. Even now I am certain that those seas are not, and perhaps never can be, in the present constitution of things, a place for his habitual gregarious resort. But further investigations have recently proved to me, that in modern times there have been isolated instances of the presence of the sperm whale in the Mediterranean. I am told, on good authority, that on the Barbary coast, a Commander Davies of the British navy found the skeleton of a sperm whale. Now, as a vessel of war readily passes through the Dardanelles, hence a sperm whale could, by the same route, pass out of the Mediterranean into the Propontis.

In the Propontis, as far as I can learn, none of that peculiar substance called *brit* is to be found, the aliment of the right whale. But I have every reason to believe that the food of the sperm whale—squid or cuttle-fish—lurks at the bottom of that sea, because large creatures, but by no means the largest of that sort, have been found at its surface. If, then, you properly put these statements together, and reason upon them a bit, you will clearly perceive that, according to all human reasoning, Procopius's sea-monster, that for half a century stove the ships of a Roman Emperor, must in all probability have been a sperm whale.

Chapter 46

SURMISES

THOUGH, consumed with the hot fire of his purpose, Ahab in all his thoughts and actions ever had in view the ultimate capture of Moby Dick; though he seemed ready to sacrifice all mortal interests to that one passion; nevertheless it may have been that he was by nature and long habituation far too wedded to a fiery whaleman's ways, altogether to abandon the collateral prosecution of the voyage. Or at least if this were otherwise, there were not wanting other motives much more influential with him. It would be refining too much, perhaps, even considering his monomania, to hint that his vindictiveness towards the White Whale might have possibly extended itself in some degree to all sperm whales, and that the more monsters he slew by so much the more he multiplied the chances that each subsequently encountered whale would prove to be the hated one he hunted. But if such an hypothesis be indeed exceptionable, there were still additional considerations which, though not so strictly according with the wildness of his ruling passion, yet were by no means incapable of swaying him.

To accomplish his object Ahab must use tools; and of all tools used in the shadow of the moon, men are most apt to get out of order. He knew, for example, that however magnetic his ascendency in some respects was over Starbuck, yet that ascendency did not cover the complete spiritual man any more than mere corporeal superiority involves intellectual mastership; for to the purely spiritual, the intellectual but stands in a sort of corporeal relation. Starbuck's body and Starbuck's coerced will were Ahab's, so long as Ahab kept his magnet at Starbuck's brain; still he knew that for all this the chief mate, in his soul, abhorred his captain's quest, and could he, would joyfully disintegrate himself from it, or even frustrate it. It might be that a long interval would elapse ere the White Whale was seen. During that long interval Starbuck would ever be apt to fall into open relapses of rebellion against his captain's leadership, unless some ordinary, prudential, circumstantial influences were brought to bear upon him. Not only that, but the subtle insanity of Ahab respecting Moby Dick was noways more significantly manifested than in his superlative sense and shrewdness in foreseeing that, for the present, the hunt should in some way be stripped of that strange imaginative impiousness which naturally invested it; that the full terror of the voyage must be kept withdrawn into the obscure background (for few men's courage is proof against protracted meditation unrelieved by action); that when they stood their long night watches, his officers and men must have some nearer things to think of than Moby Dick. For however eagerly and impetuously the savage crew had hailed the announcement of his quest; yet all sailors of all sorts are more or less capricious and unreliable—they live in the varying outer weather, and they inhale its fickleness—and when retained for any object remote and blank in the pursuit, however promissory of life and passion in the end, it is above all things requisite that temporary interests and employments should intervene and hold them healthily suspended for the final dash.

Nor was Ahab unmindful of another thing. In times of strong emotion mankind disdain all base considerations; but such times are evanescent. The permanent constitutional condition of the manufactured man, thought Ahab, is sordidness. Granting that the White Whale fully incites the hearts of this my savage crew, and playing round their savageness even breeds a certain generous knight-errantism in them, still, while for the love of it they give chase to Moby Dick, they must also have food for their more common, daily appetites. For even the high lifted and chivalric Crusaders of old times were not content to traverse two thousand miles of land to fight for their holy sepulchre, without committing burglaries, picking pockets, and gaining other pious perquisites by the way. Had they been strictly held to their one final and romantic object—that final and romantic object, too many would have turned from in disgust. I will not strip these men, thought Ahab, of all hopes of cash—aye, cash. They may scorn cash now; but let some months go by, and no perspective promise of it to them, and then this same quiescent cash all at once mutinying in them, this same cash would soon cashier Ahab.

Nor was there wanting still another precautionary motive more related to Ahab personally. Having impulsively, it is probable, and perhaps somewhat prematurely revealed the prime but private purpose of the Pequod's voyage, Ahab was now entirely conscious that, in so doing, he had indirectly laid himself open to the unanswerable charge of usurpation; and with perfect impunity, both moral and legal, his crew if so disposed, and to that end competent, could refuse all further obedience to him, and even violently wrest from him the command. From even the barely hinted imputation of usurpation, and the possible consequences of such a suppressed impression gaining ground, Ahab must of course have been most anxious to protect himself. That protection could only consist in his own predominating brain and heart and hand, backed by a heedful, closely calculating attention to every minute atmospheric influence which it was possible for his crew to be subjected to.

For all these reasons then, and others perhaps too analytic to be verbally developed here, Ahab plainly saw that he must still in a good degree continue true to the natural, nominal purpose of the Pequod's voyage; observe all customary usages; and not only that, but force himself to evince all his well known passionate interest in the general pursuit of his profession.

Be all this as it may, his voice was now often heard hailing the three mast-heads and admonishing them to keep a bright look-out, and not omit reporting even a porpoise. This vigilance was not long without reward.

Chapter 47

The Mat-Maker

It was a cloudy, sultry afternoon; the seamen were lazily lounging about the decks, or vacantly gazing over into the lead-colored waters. Queequeg and I were mildly employed weaving what is called a sword-mat, for an additional lashing to our boat. So still and subdued and yet somehow preluding was all the scene, and such an incantation of revery lurked in the air, that each silent sailor seemed resolved into his own invisible self.

I was the attendant or page of Queequeg, while busy at the mat. As I kept passing and repassing the filling or woof of marline between the long yarns of the warp, using my own hand for the shuttle, and as Queequeg, standing sideways, ever and anon slid his heavy oaken sword between the threads, and idly looking off upon the water, carelessly and unthinkingly drove home every yarn: I say so strange a dreaminess did there then reign all over the ship and all over the sea, only broken by the intermitting dull sound of the sword, that it seemed as if this were the Loom of Time, and I myself were a shuttle mechanically weaving and weaving away at the Fates. There lay the fixed threads of the warp subject to but one single, ever returning, unchanging vibration, and that vibration merely enough to admit of the crosswise interblending of other threads with its own. This warp seemed necessity; and here, thought I, with my own hand I ply my own shuttle and weave my own destiny into these unalterable threads. Meantime, Queequeg's impulsive, indifferent sword, sometimes hitting the woof slantingly, or crookedly, or strongly, or weakly, as the case might be; and by this difference in the concluding blow producing a corresponding contrast in the final aspect of the completed fabric; this savage's sword, thought I, which thus finally shapes and fashions both warp and woof; this easy, indifferent sword must be chance—aye, chance, free will, and necessity—no wise incompatible—all interweavingly working together. The straight warp of necessity, not to be swerved from its ultimate course—its every alternating vibration, indeed, only tending to that; free will still free to ply her shuttle between given threads; and chance, though restrained in its play within the right lines of necessity, and sideways in its motions modified by free will, though thus prescribed to by both, chance by turns rules either, and has the last featuring blow at events.

* * *

Thus we were weaving and weaving away when I started at a sound so strange, long drawn, and musically wild and unearthly, that the ball of free will dropped from my hand, and I stood gazing up at the clouds whence that voice dropped like a wing. High aloft in the cross-trees was that mad Gay-Header, Tashtego. His body was reaching eagerly forward, his hand stretched out like a wand, and at brief sudden intervals he continued his cries. To be sure the same sound was that very moment perhaps being heard all over the seas, from hundreds of whalemen's look-outs perched as high in the air; but from few of those lungs could that accustomed old cry have derived such a marvellous cadence as from Tashtego the Indian's.

As he stood hovering over you half suspended in air, so wildly and eagerly peering towards the horizon, you would have thought him some prophet or seer beholding the shadows of Fate, and by those wild cries announcing their coming.

"There she blows! there! there! there! she blows! she blows!"

"Where-away?"

"On the lee-beam, about two miles off! a school of them!"

Instantly all was commotion.

The Sperm Whale blows as a clock ticks, with the same undeviating and reliable uniformity. And thereby whalemen distinguish this fish from other tribes of his genus.

"There go flukes!" was now the cry from Tashtego; and the whales disappeared.

"Quick, steward!" cried Ahab. "Time! time!"

Dough-Boy hurried below, glanced at the watch, and reported the exact minute to Ahab.

The ship was now kept away from the wind, and she went gently rolling before it. Tashtego reporting that the whales had gone down heading to leeward, we confidently looked to see them again directly in advance of our bows. For that singular craft at times evinced by the Sperm Whale when, sounding with his head in one direction, he nevertheless, while concealed beneath the surface, mills round, and swiftly swims off in the opposite quarter—this deceitfulness of his could not now be in action; for there was no reason to suppose that the fish seen by Tashtego had been in any way alarmed, or indeed knew at all of our vicinity. One of the men selected for shipkeepers—that is, those not appointed to the boats, by this time relieved the Indian at the main-mast head. The sailors at the fore and mizzen had come down; the line tubs were fixed in their places; the cranes were thrust out; the mainyard was backed, and the three boats swung over the sea like three samphire baskets over high cliffs. Outside of the bulwarks their eager crews with one hand clung to the rail, while one foot was expectantly poised on the gunwale. So look the long line of man-of-war's men about to throw themselves on board an enemy's ship.

But at this critical instant a sudden exclamation was heard that took every eye from the whale. With a start all glared at dark Ahab, who was surrounded by five dusky phantoms that seemed fresh formed out of air.

Chapter 48

THE FIRST LOWERING

THE PHANTOMS, for so they then seemed, were flitting on the other side of the deck, and, with a noiseless celerity, were casting loose the tackles and bands of the boat which swung there. This boat had always been deemed one of the spare boats, though technically called the captain's, on account of its hanging from the starboard quarter. The figure that now stood by its bows was tall and swart, with one white tooth evilly protruding from its steel-like lips. A rumpled Chinese jacket of black cotton funereally invested him, with wide black trowsers of the same dark stuff. But strangely crowning this ebonness was a glistening white plaited turban, the living hair braided and coiled round and round upon his head. Less swart in aspect, the companions of this figure were of that vivid, tiger-yellow complexion peculiar to some of the aboriginal natives of the Manillas;—a race notorious for a certain diabolism of subtilty, and by some honest white mariners supposed to be the paid spies and secret confidential agents on the water of the devil, their lord, whose counting-room they suppose to be elsewhere.

While yet the wondering ship's company were gazing upon these strangers, Ahab cried out to the white-turbaned old man at their head, "All ready there, Fedallah?"

"Ready," was the half-hissed reply.

"Lower away then; d'ye hear?" shouting across the deck. "Lower away there, I say."

Such was the thunder of his voice, that spite of their amazement the men sprang over the rail; the sheaves whirled round in the blocks; with a wallow, the three boats dropped into the sea; while, with a dexterous, off-handed daring, unknown in any other vocation, the sailors, goat-like, leaped down the rolling ship's side into the tossed boats below.

Hardly had they pulled out from under the ship's lee, when a fourth keel, coming from the windward side, pulled round under the stern, and showed the five strangers rowing Ahab, who, standing erect in the stern, loudly hailed Starbuck, Stubb, and Flask, to spread themselves widely, so as to cover a large expanse of water. But with all their eyes again riveted upon the swart Fedallah and his crew, the inmates of the other boats obeyed not the command.

"Captain Ahab?—" said Starbuck.

"Spread yourselves," cried Ahab; "give way, all four boats. Thou, Flask, pull out more to leeward!"

"Aye, aye, sir," cheerily cried little King-Post, sweeping round his great steering oar. "Lay back!" addressing his crew. "There!—there!—there again! There she blows right ahead, boys!—lay back!—Never heed yonder yellow boys, Archy."

"Oh, I don't mind 'em, sir," said Archy; "I knew it all before now. Didn't I hear 'em in the hold? And didn't I tell Cabaco here of it? What say ye, Cabaco? They are stowaways, Mr. Flask."

"Pull, pull, my fine hearts-alive; pull, my children; pull, my little ones," drawlingly and soothingly sighed Stubb to his crew, some of whom still showed signs of uneasiness. "Why don't you break your backbones, my boys? What is it you stare at? Those chaps in yonder boat? Tut! They are only five more hands come to help us—never mind from where—the more the merrier. Pull, then, do pull; never mind the brimstone—devils are good fellows enough. So, so; there you are now; that's the stroke for a thousand pounds; that's the stroke to sweep the stakes! Hurrah for the gold cup of sperm oil, my heroes! Three cheers, men—all hearts alive! Easy, easy; don't be in a hurry—don't be in a hurry. Why don't you snap your oars, you rascals? Bite something, you dogs! So, so, so, then;—softly, softly! That's it—that's it! long and strong. Give way there, give way! The devil fetch ye, ye ragamuffin rapscallions; ye are all asleep. Stop snoring, ye sleepers, and pull. Pull, will ye? pull, can't ye? pull, won't ye? Why in the name of gudgeons and ginger-cakes don't ye pull?— pull and break something! pull, and start your eyes out! Here!" whipping out the sharp knife from his girdle; "every mother's son of ye draw his knife, and pull with the blade between his teeth. That's it—that's it. Now ye do something; that looks like it, my steel-bits. Start her—start her, my silver-spoons! Start her, marling-spikes!"

Stubb's exordium to his crew is given here at large, because he had rather a peculiar way of talking to them in general, and especially in inculcating the religion of rowing. But you must not suppose from this specimen of his sermonizings that he ever flew into downright passions with his congregation. Not at all; and therein consisted his chief peculiarity. He would say the most terrific things to his crew, in a tone so strangely compounded of fun and fury, and the fury seemed so calculated merely as a spice to the fun, that no oarsman could hear such queer invocations without pulling for dear life, and yet pulling for the mere joke of the thing. Besides he all the time looked so easy and indolent himself, so loungingly managed his steering-oar, and so broadly gaped—open-mouthed at times—that the mere sight of such a yawning commander, by sheer force of contrast, acted like a charm upon the crew. Then again, Stubb was one of those odd sort of humorists, whose jollity is sometimes so curiously ambiguous, as to put all inferiors on their guard in the matter of obeying them.

In obedience to a sign from Ahab, Starbuck was now pulling obliquely across Stubb's bow; and when for a minute or so the two boats were pretty near to each other, Stubb hailed the mate.

"Mr. Starbuck! larboard boat there, ahoy! a word with ye, sir, if ye please!"

"Halloa!" returned Starbuck, turning round not a single inch as he spoke; still earnestly but whisperingly urging his crew; his face set like a flint from Stubb's.

"What think ye of those yellow boys, sir!"

"Smuggled on board, somehow, before the ship sailed. (Strong, strong, boys!)" in a whisper to his crew, then speaking out loud again: "A sad business, Mr. Stubb! (seethe her, seethe her, my lads!) but never mind, Mr. Stubb, all for the best. Let all your crew pull strong, come what will. (Spring, my men, spring!) There's hogsheads of sperm ahead, Mr. Stubb, and that's what ye came for. (Pull, my boys!) Sperm, sperm's the play! This at least is duty; duty and profit hand in hand!"

"Aye, aye, I thought as much," soliloquized Stubb, when the boats diverged, "as soon as I clapt eye on 'em, I thought so. Aye, and that's what he went into the after hold for, so often, as Dough-Boy long suspected. They were hidden down there. The White Whale's at the bottom of it. Well, well, so be it! Can't be helped! All right! Give way, men! It ain't the White Whale to-day! Give way!"

Now the advent of these outlandish strangers at such a critical instant as the lowering of the boats from the deck, this had not unreasonably awakened a sort of superstitious amazement in some of the ship's company; but Archy's fancied discovery having some time previous got abroad among them, though indeed not credited then, this had in some small measure prepared them for the event. It took off the extreme edge of their wonder; and so what with all this and Stubb's confident way of accounting for their appearance, they were for the time freed from superstitious surmisings; though the affair still left abundant room for all manner of wild conjectures as to dark Ahab's precise agency in the matter from the beginning. For me, I silently recalled the mysterious shadows I had seen creeping on board the Pequod during the dim Nantucket dawn, as well as the enigmatical hintings of the unaccountable Elijah.

Meantime, Ahab, out of hearing of his officers, having sided the furthest to windward, was still ranging ahead of the other boats; a circumstance bespeaking how potent a crew was pulling him. Those tiger yellow creatures of his seemed all steel and whalebone; like five trip-hammers they rose and fell with regular strokes of strength, which periodically started the boat along the water like a horizontal burst boiler out of a Mississippi steamer. As for Fedallah, who was seen pulling the harpooneer oar, he had thrown aside his black jacket, and displayed his naked chest with the whole part of his body above the gunwale, clearly cut against the alternating depressions of the watery horizon; while at the other end of the boat Ahab, with one arm, like a fencer's, thrown half backward into the air, as if to counterbalance any tendency to trip; Ahab was seen steadily managing his steering oar as in a thousand boat lowerings ere the White Whale had torn him. All at once the outstretched arm gave a peculiar motion and then remained fixed, while the boat's five oars were seen simultaneously peaked. Boat and crew sat motionless on the sea. Instantly the three spread boats in the rear paused on their way. The whales had irregularly settled bodily down into the blue, thus giving no distantly discernible token of the movement, though from his closer vicinity Ahab had observed it.

"Every man look out along his oar!" cried Starbuck. "Thou, Queequeg, stand up!"

Nimbly springing up on the triangular raised box in the bow, the savage stood erect there, and with intensely eager eyes gazed off towards the spot where the chase had last been descried. Likewise upon the extreme stern of the boat where it was also triangularly platformed level with the gunwale, Starbuck himself was seen coolly and adroitly balancing himself to the jerking tossings of his chip of a craft, and silently eyeing the vast blue eye of the sea.

Not very far distant Flask's boat was also lying breathlessly still; its commander recklessly standing upon the top of the loggerhead, a stout sort of post rooted in the keel, and rising some two feet above the level of the stern platform. It is used for catching turns with the whale line. Its top is not more spacious than the palm of a man's hand, and standing upon such a base as that, Flask seemed perched at the mast-head of some ship which had sunk to all but her trucks. But little King-Post was small and short, and at the same time little King-Post was full of a large and tall ambition, so that this loggerhead stand-point of his did by no means satisfy King-Post.

"I can't see three seas off; tip us up an oar there, and let me on to that."

Upon this, Daggoo, with either hand upon the gunwale to steady his way, swiftly slid aft, and then erecting himself volunteered his lofty shoulders for a pedestal.

"Good a mast-head as any, sir. Will you mount?"

"That I will, and thank ye very much, my fine fellow; only I wish you fifty feet taller."

Whereupon planting his feet firmly against two opposite planks of the boat, the gigantic negro, stooping a little, presented his flat palm to Flask's foot, and then putting Flask's hand on his hearse-plumed head and bidding him spring as he himself should toss, with one dexterous fling landed the little man high and dry on his shoulders. And here was Flask now standing, Daggoo with one lifted arm furnishing him with a breast-band to lean against and steady himself by.

At any time it is a strange sight to the tyro to see with what wondrous habitude of unconscious skill the whaleman will maintain an erect posture in his boat, even when pitched about by the most riotously perverse and cross-running seas. Still more strange to see him giddily perched upon the log-gerhead itself, under such circumstances. But the sight of little Flask mounted upon gigantic Daggoo was yet more curious; for sustaining himself with a cool, indifferent, easy, un-thought of, barbaric majesty, the noble negro to every roll of the sea harmoniously rolled his fine form. On his broad back, flaxen-haired Flask seemed a snow-flake. The bearer looked nobler than the rider. Though, truly, vivacious, tumultuous, ostentatious little Flask would now and then stamp with im-patience; but not one added heave did he thereby give to the negro's lordly chest. So have I seen Passion and Vanity stamping the living magnanimous earth, but the earth did not alter her tides and her seasons for that.

Meanwhile Stubb, the third mate, betrayed no such far-gazing solicitudes. The whales might have made one of their regular soundings, not a temporary dive from mere fright; and if that were the case, Stubb, as his wont in such cases, it seems, was resolved to solace the languishing interval with his pipe. He withdrew it from his hatband, where he always wore it aslant like a feather. He loaded it, and rammed home the loading with his thumb-end; but hardly had he ignited his match across the rough sand-paper of his hand, when Tash-tego, his harpooneer, whose eyes had been setting to wind-ward like two fixed stars, suddenly dropped like light from his erect attitude to his seat, crying out in a quick phrensy of hurry, "Down, down all, and give way!—there they are!"

To a landsman, no whale, nor any sign of a herring, would have been visible at that moment; nothing but a troubled bit of greenish white water, and thin scattered puffs of vapor hovering over it, and suffusingly blowing off to leeward, like the confused scud from white rolling billows. The air around suddenly vibrated and tingled, as it were, like the air over intensely heated plates of iron. Beneath this atmospheric waving and curling, and partially beneath a thin layer of water, also, the whales were swimming. Seen in advance of all the other indications, the puffs of vapor they spouted, seemed their forerunning couriers and detached flying outriders.

All four boats were now in keen pursuit of that one spot of troubled water and air. But it bade fair to outstrip them; it flew on and on, as a mass of interblending bubbles borne down a rapid stream from the hills.

"Pull, pull, my good boys," said Starbuck, in the lowest possible but intensest concentrated whisper to his men; while the sharp fixed glance from his eyes, darted straight ahead of the bow, almost seemed as two visible needles in two unerring binnacle compasses. He did not say much to his crew, though, nor did his crew say anything to him. Only the silence of the boat was at intervals startlingly pierced by one of his peculiar whispers, now harsh with command, now soft with entreaty.

How different the loud little King-Post. "Sing out and say something, my hearties. Roar and pull, my thunderbolts! Beach me, beach me on their black backs, boys; only do that for me, and I'll sign over to you my Martha's Vineyard plantation, boys; including wife and children, boys. Lay me on— lay me on! O Lord, Lord! but I shall go stark, staring mad: See! see that white water!" And so shouting, he pulled his hat from his head, and stamped up and down on it; then picking it up, flirted it far off upon the sea; and finally fell to rearing and plunging in the boat's stern like a crazed colt from the prairie.

"Look at that chap now," philosophically drawled Stubb, who, with his unlighted short pipe, mechanically retained between his teeth, at a short distance, followed after—"He's got fits, that Flask has. Fits? yes, give him fits—that's the very word—pitch fits into 'em. Merrily, merrily, hearts-alive. Pudding for supper, you know;—merry's the word. Pull, babes—pull, sucklings—pull, all. But what the devil are you hurrying about? Softly, softly, and steadily, my men. Only pull, and keep pulling; nothing more. Crack all your backbones, and bite your knives in two—that's all. Take it easy— why don't ye take it easy, I say, and burst all your livers and lungs!"

But what it was that inscrutable Ahab said to that tiger-yellow crew of his—these were words best omitted here; for you live under the blessed light of the evangelical land. Only the infidel sharks in the audacious seas may give ear to such words, when, with tornado brow, and eyes of red murder, and foam-glued lips, Ahab leaped after his prey.

Meanwhile, all the boats tore on. The repeated specific allusions of Flask to "that whale," as he called the fictitious monster which he declared to be incessantly tantalizing his boat's bow with its tail—these allusions of his were at times so vivid and life-like, that they would cause some one or two of his men to snatch a fearful look over the shoulder. But this was against all rule; for the oarsmen must put out their eyes, and ram a skewer through their necks; usage pronouncing that they must have no organs but ears, and no limbs but arms, in these critical moments.

It was a sight full of quick wonder and awe! The vast swells of the omnipotent sea; the surging, hollow roar they made, as they rolled along the eight gunwales, like gigantic bowls in a boundless bowling-green; the brief suspended agony of the boat, as it would tip for an instant on the knife-like edge of the sharper waves, that almost seemed threatening to cut it in two; the sudden profound dip into the watery glens and hollows; the keen spurrings and goadings to gain the top of the opposite hill; the headlong, sled-like slide down its other side;—all these, with the cries of the headsmen and harpooneers, and the shuddering gasps of the oarsmen, with the wondrous sight of the ivory Pequod bearing down upon her boats with outstretched sails, like a wild hen after her screaming brood;—all this was thrilling. Not the raw recruit, marching from the bosom of his wife into the fever heat of his first battle; not the dead man's ghost encountering the first unknown phantom in the other world;—neither of these can feel stranger and stronger emotions than that man does, who for the first time finds himself pulling into the charmed, churned circle of the hunted sperm whale.

The dancing white water made by the chase was now becoming more and more visible, owing to the increasing darkness of the dun cloud-shadows flung upon the sea. The jets of vapor no longer blended, but tilted everywhere to right and left; the whales seemed separating their wakes. The boats were pulled more apart; Starbuck giving chase to three whales running dead to leeward. Our sail was now set, and, with the still rising wind, we rushed along; the boat going with such madness through the water, that the lee oars could scarcely be worked rapidly enough to escape being torn from the row-locks.

Soon we were running through a suffusing wide veil of mist; neither ship nor boat to be seen.

"Give way, men," whispered Starbuck, drawing still further aft the sheet of his sail; "there is time to kill a fish yet before the squall comes. There's white water again!—close to! Spring!"

Soon after, two cries in quick succession on each side of us denoted that the other boats had got fast; but hardly were they overheard, when with a lightning-like hurtling whisper Starbuck said: "Stand up!" and Queequeg, harpoon in hand, sprang to his feet.

Though not one of the oarsmen was then facing the life and death peril so close to them ahead, yet with their eyes on the intense countenance of the mate in the stern of the boat, they knew that the imminent instant had come; they heard, too, an enormous wallowing sound as of fifty elephants stirring in their litter. Meanwhile the boat was still booming through the mist, the waves curling and hissing around us like the erected crests of enraged serpents.

"That's his hump. *There, there,* give it to him!" whispered Starbuck.

A short rushing sound leaped out of the boat; it was the darted iron of Queequeg. Then all in one welded commotion came an invisible push from astern, while forward the boat seemed striking on a ledge; the sail collapsed and exploded; a gush of scalding vapor shot up near by; something rolled and tumbled like an earthquake beneath us. The whole crew were half suffocated as they were tossed helter-skelter into the white curdling cream of the squall. Squall, whale, and harpoon had all blended together; and the whale, merely grazed by the iron, escaped.

Though completely swamped, the boat was nearly un-harmed. Swimming round it we picked up the floating oars, and lashing them across the gunwale, tumbled back to our places. There we sat up to our knees in the sea, the water covering every rib and plank, so that to our downward gazing eyes the suspended craft seemed a coral boat grown up to us from the bottom of the ocean.

The wind increased to a howl; the waves dashed their bucklers together; the whole squall roared, forked, and crackled around us like a white fire upon the prairie, in which, unconsumed, we were burning; immortal in these jaws of death! In vain we hailed the other boats; as well roar to the live coals down the chimney of a flaming furnace as hail those boats in that storm. Meanwhile the driving scud, rack, and mist, grew darker with the shadows of night; no sign of the ship could be seen. The rising sea forbade all attempts to bale out the boat. The oars were useless as propellers, performing now the office of life-preservers. So, cutting the lashing of the waterproof match keg, after many failures Starbuck contrived to ignite the lamp in the lantern; then stretching it on a waif pole, handed it to Queequeg as the standard-bearer of this forlorn hope. There, then, he sat, holding up that imbecile candle in the heart of that almighty forlornness. There, then, he sat, the sign and symbol of a man without faith, hopelessly holding up hope in the midst of despair.

Wet, drenched through, and shivering cold, despairing of ship or boat, we lifted up our eyes as the dawn came on. The mist still spread over the sea, the empty lantern lay crushed in the bottom of the boat. Suddenly Queequeg started to his feet, hollowing his hand to his ear. We all heard a faint creaking, as of ropes and yards hitherto muffled by the storm. The sound came nearer and nearer; the thick mists were dimly parted by a huge, vague form. Affrighted, we all sprang into the sea as the ship at last loomed into view, bearing right down upon us within a distance of not much more than its length.

Floating on the waves we saw the abandoned boat, as for one instant it tossed and gaped beneath the ship's bows like a chip at the base of a cataract; and then the vast hull rolled over it, and it was seen no more till it came up weltering astern. Again we swam for it, were dashed against it by the seas, and were at last taken up and safely landed on board.

Ere the squall came close to, the other boats had cut loose from their fish and returned to the ship in good time. The ship had given us up, but was still cruising, if haply it might light upon some token of our perishing,—an oar or a lance pole.

Chapter 49

THE HYENA

THERE ARE certain queer times and occasions in this strange mixed affair we call life when a man takes this whole universe for a vast practical joke, though the wit thereof he but dimly discerns, and more than suspects that the joke is at nobody's expense but his own. However, nothing dispirits, and nothing seems worth while disputing. He bolts down all events, all creeds, and beliefs, and persuasions, all hard things visible and invisible, never mind how knobby; as an ostrich of potent digestion gobbles down bullets and gun flints. And as for small difficulties and worryings, prospects of sudden disaster, peril of life and limb; all these, and death itself, seem to him only sly, good-natured hits, and jolly punches in the side bestowed by the unseen and unaccountable old joker. That odd sort of wayward mood I am speaking of, comes over a man only in some time of extreme tribulation; it comes in the very midst of his earnestness, so that what just before might have seemed to him a thing most momentous, now seems but a part of the general joke. There is nothing like the perils of whaling to breed this free and easy sort of genial, desperado philosophy; and with it I now regarded this whole voyage of the Pequod, and the great White Whale its object.

"Queequeg," said I, when they had dragged me, the last man, to the deck, and I was still shaking myself in my jacket to fling off the water; "Queequeg, my fine friend, does this sort of thing often happen?" Without much emotion, though soaked through just like me, he gave me to understand that such things did often happen.

"Mr. Stubb," said I, turning to that worthy, who, buttoned up in his oil-jacket, was now calmly smoking his pipe in the rain; "Mr. Stubb, I think I have heard you say that of all whalemen you ever met, our chief mate, Mr. Starbuck, is by far the most careful and prudent. I suppose then, that going plump on a flying whale with your sail set in a foggy squall is the height of a whaleman's discretion?"

"Certain. I've lowered for whales from a leaking ship in a gale off Cape Horn."

"Mr. Flask," said I, turning to little King-Post, who was standing close by; "you are experienced in these things, and I am not. Will you tell me whether it is an unalterable law in this fishery, Mr. Flask, for an oarsman to break his own back pulling himself back-foremost into death's jaws?"

"Can't you twist that smaller?" said Flask. "Yes, that's the law. I should like to see a boat's crew backing water up to a whale face foremost. Ha, ha! the whale would give them squint for squint, mind that!"

Here then, from three impartial witnesses, I had a deliberate statement of the entire case. Considering, therefore, that squalls and capsizings in the water and consequent bivouacks on the deep, were matters of common occurrence in this kind of life; considering that at the superlatively critical instant of going on to the whale I must resign my life into the hands of him who steered the boat—oftentimes a fellow who at that very moment is in his impetuousness upon the point of scuttling the craft with his own frantic stampings; considering that the particular disaster to our own particular boat was chiefly to be imputed to Starbuck's driving on to his whale almost in the teeth of a squall, and considering that Starbuck, notwithstanding, was famous for his great heedfulness in the fishery; considering that I belonged to this uncommonly prudent Starbuck's boat; and finally considering in what a devil's chase I was implicated, touching the White Whale: taking all things together, I say, I thought I might as well go below and make a rough draft of my will. "Queequeg," said I, "come along, you shall be my lawyer, executor, and legatee."

It may seem strange that of all men sailors should be tinkering at their last wills and testaments, but there are no people in the world more fond of that diversion. This was the fourth time in my nautical life that I had done the same thing. After the ceremony was concluded upon the present occasion, I felt all the easier; a stone was rolled away from my heart. Besides, all the days I should now live would be as good as the days that Lazarus lived after his resurrection; a supplementary clean gain of so many months or weeks as the case might be. I survived myself; my death and burial were locked up in my chest. I looked round me tranquilly and content-edly, like a quiet ghost with a clean conscience sitting inside the bars of a snug family vault.

Now then, thought I, unconsciously rolling up the sleeves of my frock, here goes for a cool, collected dive at death and destruction, and the devil fetch the hindmost.

Chapter 50

AHAB'S BOAT AND CREW • FEDALLAH

W HO WOULD have thought it, Flask!" cried Stubb; "if I had but one leg you would not catch me in a boat, unless maybe to stop the plug-hole with my timber toe. Oh! he's a wonderful old man!"

"I don't think it so strange, after all, on that account," said Flask. "If his leg were off at the hip, now, it would be a different thing. That would disable him; but he has one knee, and good part of the other left, you know."

"I don't know that, my little man; I never yet saw him kneel."

*   *   *

Among whale-wise people it has often been argued whether, considering the paramount importance of his life to the success of the voyage, it is right for a whaling captain to jeopardize that life in the active perils of the chase. So Tamerlane's soldiers often argued with tears in their eyes, whether that invaluable life of his ought to be carried into the thickest of the fight.

But with Ahab the question assumed a modified aspect. Considering that with two legs man is but a hobbling wight in all times of danger; considering that the pursuit of whales is always under great and extraordinary difficulties; that every individual moment, indeed, then comprises a peril; under these circumstances is it wise for any maimed man to enter a whale-boat in the hunt? As a general thing, the joint-owners of the Pequod must have plainly thought not.

Ahab well knew that although his friends at home would think little of his entering a boat in certain comparatively harmless vicissitudes of the chase, for the sake of being near the scene of action and giving his orders in person, yet for Captain Ahab to have a boat actually apportioned to him as a regular headsman in the hunt—above all for Captain Ahab to be supplied with five extra men, as that same boat's crew, he well knew that such generous conceits never entered the heads of the owners of the Pequod. Therefore he had not solicited a boat's crew from them, nor had he in any way hinted his desires on that head. Nevertheless he had taken private measures of his own touching all that matter. Until Archy's published discovery, the sailors had little foreseen it, though to be sure when, after being a little while out of port, all hands had concluded the customary business of fitting the whaleboats for service; when some time after this Ahab was now and then found bestirring himself in the matter of making thole-pins with his own hands for what was thought to be one of the spare boats, and even solicitously cutting the small wooden skewers, which when the line is running out are pinned over the groove in the bow: when all this was observed in him, and particularly his solicitude in having an extra coat of sheathing in the bottom of the boat, as if to make it better withstand the pointed pressure of his ivory limb; and also the anxiety he evinced in exactly shaping the thigh board, or clumsy cleat, as it is sometimes called, the horizontal piece in the boat's bow for bracing the knee against in darting or stabbing at the whale; when it was observed how often he stood up in that boat with his solitary knee fixed in the semi-circular depression in the cleat, and with the carpenter's chisel gouged out a little here and straightened it a little there; all these things, I say, had awakened much interest and curiosity at the time. But almost everybody supposed that this particular preparative heedfulness in Ahab must only be with a view to the ultimate chase of Moby Dick; for he had already revealed his intention to hunt that mortal monster in person. But such a supposition did by no means involve the remotest suspicion as to any boat's crew being assigned to that boat.

Now, with the subordinate phantoms, what wonder remained soon waned away; for in a whaler wonders soon wane. Besides, now and then such unaccountable odds and ends of strange nations come up from the unknown nooks and ash-holes of the earth to man these floating outlaws of whalers; and the ships themselves often pick up such queer castaway creatures found tossing about the open sea on planks, bits of wreck, oars, whale-boats, canoes, blown-off

Japanese junks, and what not; that Beelzebub himself might climb up the side and step down into the cabin to chat with the captain, and it would not create any unsubduable excitement in the forecastle.

But be all this as it may, certain it is that while the subordinate phantoms soon found their place among the crew, though still as it were somehow distinct from them, yet that hair-turbaned Fedallah remained a muffled mystery to the last. Whence he came in a mannerly world like this, by what sort of unaccountable tie he soon evinced himself to be linked with Ahab's peculiar fortunes; nay, so far as to have some sort of a half-hinted influence; Heaven knows, but it might have been even authority over him; all this none knew. But one cannot sustain an indifferent air concerning Fedallah. He was such a creature as civilized, domestic people in the temperate zone only see in their dreams, and that but dimly; but the like of whom now and then glide among the unchanging Asiatic communities, especially the Oriental isles to the east of the continent—those insulated, immemorial, unalterable countries, which even in these modern days still preserve much of the ghostly aboriginalness of earth's primal generations, when the memory of the first man was a distinct recollection, and all men his descendants, unknowing whence he came, eyed each other as real phantoms, and asked of the sun and the moon why they were created and to what end; when though, according to Genesis, the angels indeed consorted with the daughters of men, the devils also, add the uncanonical Rabbins, indulged in mundane amours.

Chapter 51

The Spirit-Spout

DAYS, WEEKS PASSED, and under easy sail, the ivory Pequod had slowly swept across four several cruising-
grounds; that off the Azores; off the Cape de Verdes; on the
Plate (so called), being off the mouth of the Rio de la Plata;
and the Carrol Ground, an unstaked, watery locality, southerly from St. Helena.

It was while gliding through these latter waters that one
serene and moonlight night, when all the waves rolled by like
scrolls of silver; and, by their soft, suffusing seethings, made
what seemed a silvery silence, not a solitude: on such a silent
night a silvery jet was seen far in advance of the white bubbles
at the bow. Lit up by the moon, it looked celestial; seemed
some plumed and glittering god uprising from the sea. Fedallah first descried this jet. For of these moonlight nights, it
was his wont to mount to the main-mast head, and stand a
look-out there, with the same precision as if it had been day.
And yet, though herds of whales were seen by night, not one
whaleman in a hundred would venture a lowering for them.
You may think with what emotions, then, the seamen beheld
this old Oriental perched aloft at such unusual hours; his turban and the moon, companions in one sky. But when, after
spending his uniform interval there for several successive
nights without uttering a single sound; when, after all this
silence, his unearthly voice was heard announcing that silvery,
moon-lit jet, every reclining mariner started to his feet as if
some winged spirit had lighted in the rigging, and hailed the
mortal crew. "There she blows!" Had the trump of judgment
blown, they could not have quivered more; yet still they felt
no terror; rather pleasure. For though it was a most unwonted hour, yet so impressive was the cry, and so deliriously
exciting, that almost every soul on board instinctively desired
a lowering.

Walking the deck with quick, side-lunging strides, Ahab
commanded the t'gallant sails and royals to be set, and every

stunsail spread. The best man in the ship must take the helm. Then, with every mast-head manned, the piled-up craft rolled down before the wind. The strange, upheaving, lifting tendency of the taffrail breeze filling the hollows of so many sails, made the buoyant, hovering deck to feel like air beneath the feet; while still she rushed along, as if two antagonistic influences were struggling in her—one to mount direct to heaven, the other to drive yawingly to some horizontal goal. And had you watched Ahab's face that night, you would have thought that in him also two different things were warring. While his one live leg made lively echoes along the deck, every stroke of his dead limb sounded like a coffin-tap. On life and death this old man walked. But though the ship so swiftly sped, and though from every eye, like arrows, the eager glances shot, yet the silvery jet was no more seen that night. Every sailor swore he saw it once, but not a second time.

This midnight-spout had almost grown a forgotten thing, when, some days after, lo! at the same silent hour, it was again announced: again it was descried by all; but upon making sail to overtake it, once more it disappeared as if it had never been. And so it served us night after night, till no one heeded it but to wonder at it. Mysteriously jetted into the clear moonlight, or starlight, as the case might be; disappearing again for one whole day, or two days, or three; and somehow seeming at every distinct repetition to be advancing still further and further in our van, this solitary jet seemed for ever alluring us on.

Nor with the immemorial superstition of their race, and in accordance with the preternaturalness, as it seemed, which in many things invested the Pequod, were there wanting some of the seamen who swore that whenever and wherever descried; at however remote times, or in however far apart latitudes and longitudes, that unnearable spout was cast by one self-same whale; and that whale, Moby Dick. For a time, there reigned, too, a sense of peculiar dread at this flitting apparition, as if it were treacherously beckoning us on and on, in order that the monster might turn round upon us, and rend us at last in the remotest and most savage seas.

These temporary apprehensions, so vague but so awful, derived a wondrous potency from the contrasting serenity of the weather, in which, beneath all its blue blandness, some thought there lurked a devilish charm, as for days and days we voyaged along, through seas so wearily, lonesomely mild, that all space, in repugnance to our vengeful errand, seemed vacating itself of life before our urn-like prow.

But, at last, when turning to the eastward, the Cape winds began howling around us, and we rose and fell upon the long, troubled seas that are there; when the ivory-tusked Pequod sharply bowed to the blast, and gored the dark waves in her madness, till, like showers of silver chips, the foam-flakes flew over her bulwarks; then all this desolate vacuity of life went away, but gave place to sights more dismal than before.

Close to our bows, strange forms in the water darted hither and thither before us; while thick in our rear flew the inscrutable sea-ravens. And every morning, perched on our stays, rows of these birds were seen; and spite of our hootings, for a long time obstinately clung to the hemp, as though they deemed our ship some drifting, uninhabited craft; a thing appointed to desolation, and therefore fit roosting-place for their homeless selves. And heaved and heaved, still unrestingly heaved the black sea, as if its vast tides were a conscience; and the great mundane soul were in anguish and remorse for the long sin and suffering it had bred.

Cape of Good Hope, do they call ye? Rather Cape Tormentoso, as called of yore; for long allured by the perfidious silences that before had attended us, we found ourselves launched into this tormented sea, where guilty beings transformed into those fowls and these fish, seemed condemned to swim on everlastingly without any haven in store, or beat that black air without any horizon. But calm, snow-white, and unvarying; still directing its fountain of feathers to the sky; still beckoning us on from before, the solitary jet would at times be descried.

During all this blackness of the elements, Ahab, though assuming for the time the almost continual command of the drenched and dangerous deck, manifested the gloomiest reserve; and more seldom than ever addressed his mates. In tempestuous times like these, after everything above and aloft has been secured, nothing more can be done but passively to await the issue of the gale. Then Captain and crew become practical fatalists. So, with his ivory leg inserted into its accustomed hole, and with one hand firmly grasping a shroud, Ahab for hours and hours would stand gazing dead to windward, while an occasional squall of sleet or snow would all but congeal his very eyelashes together. Meantime, the crew driven from the forward part of the ship by the perilous seas that burstingly broke over its bows, stood in a line along the bulwarks in the waist; and the better to guard against the leaping waves, each man had slipped himself into a sort of bowline secured to the rail, in which he swung as in a loosened belt. Few or no words were spoken; and the silent ship, as if manned by painted sailors in wax, day after day tore on through all the swift madness and gladness of the demoniac waves. By night the same muteness of humanity before the shrieks of the ocean prevailed; still in silence the men swung in the bowlines; still wordless Ahab stood up to the blast. Even when wearied nature seemed demanding repose he would not seek that repose in his hammock. Never could Starbuck forget the old man's aspect, when one night going down into the cabin to mark how the barometer stood, he saw him with closed eyes sitting straight in his floor-screwed chair; the rain and half-melted sleet of the storm from which he had some time before emerged, still slowly dripping from the unremoved hat and coat. On the table beside him lay unrolled one of those charts of tides and currents which have previously been spoken of. His lantern swung from his tightly clenched hand. Though the body was erect, the head was thrown back so that the closed eyes were pointed towards the needle of the tell-tale that swung from a beam in the ceiling.*

Terrible old man! thought Starbuck with a shudder, sleeping in this gale, still thou steadfastly eyest thy purpose.

---

*The cabin-compass is called the tell-tale, because without going to the compass at the helm, the Captain, while below, can inform himself of the course of the ship.

Chapter 52

THE ALBATROSS

S OUTH-EASTWARD from the Cape, off the distant Crozetts, a good cruising ground for Right Whalemen, a sail loomed ahead, the Goney (Albatross) by name. As she slowly drew nigh, from my lofty perch at the fore-mast-head, I had a good view of that sight so remarkable to a tyro in the far ocean fisheries—a whaler at sea, and long absent from home.

As if the waves had been fullers, this craft was bleached like the skeleton of a stranded walrus. All down her sides, this spectral appearance was traced with long channels of reddened rust, while all her spars and her rigging were like the thick branches of trees furred over with hoar-frost. Only her lower sails were set. A wild sight it was to see her long-bearded look-outs at those three mast-heads. They seemed clad in the skins of beasts, so torn and bepatched the raiment that had survived nearly four years of cruising. Standing in iron hoops nailed to the mast, they swayed and swung over a fathomless sea; and though, when the ship slowly glided close under our stern, we six men in the air came so nigh to each other that we might almost have leaped from the mast-heads of one ship to those of the other; yet, those forlorn-looking fishermen, mildly eyeing us as they passed, said not one word to our own look-outs, while the quarter-deck hail was being heard from below.

"Ship ahoy! Have ye seen the White Whale?"

But as the strange captain, leaning over the pallid bulwarks, was in the act of putting his trumpet to his mouth, it somehow fell from his hand into the sea; and the wind now rising amain, he in vain strove to make himself heard without it. Meantime his ship was still increasing the distance between. While in various silent ways the seamen of the Pequod were evincing their observance of this ominous incident at the first mere mention of the White Whale's name to another ship, Ahab for a moment paused; it almost seemed as though he would have lowered a boat to board the stranger, had not the threatening wind forbade. But taking advantage of his windward position, he again seized his trumpet, and knowing by her aspect that the stranger vessel was a Nantucketer and shortly bound home, he loudly hailed—"Ahoy there! This is the Pequod, bound round the world! Tell them to address all future letters to the Pacific ocean! and this time three years, if I am not at home, tell them to address them to ———"

At that moment the two wakes were fairly crossed, and instantly, then, in accordance with their singular ways, shoals of small harmless fish, that for some days before had been placidly swimming by our side, darted away with what seemed shuddering fins, and ranged themselves fore and aft with the stranger's flanks. Though in the course of his continual voyagings Ahab must often before have noticed a similar sight, yet, to any monomaniac man, the veriest trifles capriciously carry meanings.

"Swim away from me, do ye?" murmured Ahab, gazing over into the water. There seemed but little in the words, but the tone conveyed more of deep helpless sadness than the insane old man had ever before evinced. But turning to the steersman, who thus far had been holding the ship in the wind to diminish her headway, he cried out in his old lion voice,—"Up helm! Keep her off round the world!"

Round the world! There is much in that sound to inspire proud feelings; but whereto does all that circumnavigation conduct? Only through numberless perils to the very point whence we started, where those that we left behind secure, were all the time before us.

Were this world an endless plain, and by sailing eastward we could for ever reach new distances, and discover sights more sweet and strange than any Cyclades or Islands of King Solomon, then there were promise in the voyage. But in pursuit of those far mysteries we dream of, or in tormented chase of that demon phantom that, some time or other, swims before all human hearts; while chasing such over this round globe, they either lead us on in barren mazes or midway leave us whelmed.

Chapter 53

THE GAM

THE OSTENSIBLE REASON why Ahab did not go on board
of the whaler we had spoken was this: the wind and sea
betokened storms. But even had this not been the case, he
would not after all, perhaps, have boarded her—judging by
his subsequent conduct on similar occasions—if so it had
been that, by the process of hailing, he had obtained a negative answer to the question he put. For, as it eventually
turned out, he cared not to consort, even for five minutes,
with any stranger captain, except he could contribute some of
that information he so absorbingly sought. But all this might
remain inadequately estimated, were not something said here
of the peculiar usages of whaling-vessels when meeting each
other in foreign seas, and especially on a common cruising-
ground.

If two strangers crossing the Pine Barrens in New York
State, or the equally desolate Salisbury Plain in England; if
casually encountering each other in such inhospitable wilds,
these twain, for the life of them, cannot well avoid a mutual
salutation; and stopping for a moment to interchange the
news; and, perhaps, sitting down for a while and resting in
concert: then, how much more natural that upon the illimit-
able Pine Barrens and Salisbury Plains of the sea, two whaling
vessels descrying each other at the ends of the earth—off lone
Fanning's Island, or the far away King's Mills; how much
more natural, I say, that under such circumstances these ships
should not only interchange hails, but come into still closer,
more friendly and sociable contact. And especially would this
seem to be a matter of course, in the case of vessels owned in
one seaport, and whose captains, officers, and not a few of
the men are personally known to each other; and consequently, have all sorts of dear domestic things to talk about.

For the long absent ship, the outward-bounder, perhaps,
has letters on board; at any rate, she will be sure to let her
have some papers of a date a year or two later than the last

one on her blurred and thumb-worn files. And in return for that courtesy, the outward-bound ship would receive the latest whaling intelligence from the cruising-ground to which she may be destined, a thing of the utmost importance to her. And in degree, all this will hold true concerning whaling vessels crossing each other's track on the cruising-ground itself, even though they are equally long absent from home. For one of them may have received a transfer of letters from some third, and now far remote vessel; and some of those letters may be for the people of the ship she now meets. Besides, they would exchange the whaling news, and have an agreeable chat. For not only would they meet with all the sympathies of sailors, but likewise with all the peculiar congenialities arising from a common pursuit and mutually shared privations and perils.

Nor would difference of country make any very essential difference; that is, so long as both parties speak one language, as is the case with Americans and English. Though, to be sure, from the small number of English whalers, such meetings do not very often occur, and when they do occur there is too apt to be a sort of shyness between them; for your Englishman is rather reserved, and your Yankee, he does not fancy that sort of thing in anybody but himself. Besides, the English whalers sometimes affect a kind of metropolitan superiority over the American whalers; regarding the long, lean Nantucketer, with his nondescript provincialisms, as a sort of sea-peasant. But where this superiority in the English whalemen does really consist, it would be hard to say, seeing that the Yankees in one day, collectively, kill more whales than all the English, collectively, in ten years. But this is a harmless little foible in the English whale-hunters, which the Nantucketer does not take much to heart; probably, because he knows that he has a few foibles himself.

So, then, we see that of all ships separately sailing the sea, the whalers have most reason to be sociable—and they are so. Whereas, some merchant ships crossing each other's wake in the mid-Atlantic, will oftentimes pass on without so much as a single word of recognition, mutually cutting each other on the high seas, like a brace of dandies in Broadway; and all the time indulging, perhaps, in finical criticism upon each other's rig. As for Men-of-War, when they chance to meet at sea, they first go through such a string of silly bowings and scrapings, such a ducking of ensigns, that there does not seem to be much right-down hearty good-will and brotherly love about it at all. As touching Slave-ships meeting, why, they are in such a prodigious hurry, they run away from each other as soon as possible. And as for Pirates, when they chance to cross each other's cross-bones, the first hail is—"How many skulls?"—the same way that whalers hail—"How many barrels?" And that question once answered, pirates straightway steer apart, for they are infernal villains on both sides, and don't like to see overmuch of each other's villanous likenesses.

But look at the godly, honest, unostentatious, hospitable, sociable, free-and-easy whaler! What does the whaler do when she meets another whaler in any sort of decent weather? She has a "*Gam*," a thing so utterly unknown to all other ships that they never heard of the name even; and if by chance they should hear of it, they only grin at it, and repeat gamesome stuff about "spouters" and "blubber-boilers," and such like pretty exclamations. Why it is that all Merchant-seamen, and also all Pirates and Man-of-War's men, and Slave-ship sailors, cherish such a scornful feeling towards Whale-ships; this is a question it would be hard to answer. Because, in the case of pirates, say, I should like to know whether that profession of theirs has any peculiar glory about it. It sometimes ends in uncommon elevation, indeed; but only at the gallows. And besides, when a man is elevated in that odd fashion, he has no proper foundation for his superior altitude. Hence, I conclude, that in boasting himself to be high lifted above a whaleman, in that assertion the pirate has no solid basis to stand on.

But what is a *Gam*? You might wear out your index-finger running up and down the columns of dictionaries, and never find the word. Dr. Johnson never attained to that erudition; Noah Webster's ark does not hold it. Nevertheless, this same expressive word has now for many years been in constant use among some fifteen thousand true born Yankees. Certainly, it needs a definition, and should be incorporated into the Lexicon. With that view, let me learnedly define it.

GAM. NOUN—*A social meeting of two (or more) Whale-ships, generally on a cruising-ground; when, after exchanging hails, they exchange visits by boats' crews: the two captains remaining, for the time, on board of one ship, and the two chief mates on the other.*

There is another little item about Gamming which must not be forgotten here. All professions have their own little peculiarities of detail; so has the whale fishery. In a pirate, man-of-war, or slave ship, when the captain is rowed anywhere in his boat, he always sits in the stern sheets on a comfortable, sometimes cushioned seat there, and often steers himself with a pretty little milliner's tiller decorated with gay cords and ribbons. But the whale-boat has no seat astern, no sofa of that sort whatever, and no tiller at all. High times indeed, if whaling captains were wheeled about the water on castors like gouty old aldermen in patent chairs. And as for a tiller, the whale-boat never admits of any such effeminancy; and therefore as in gamming a complete boat's crew must leave the ship, and hence as the boat steerer or harpooneer is of the number, that subordinate is the steersman upon the occasion, and the captain, having no place to sit in, is pulled off to his visit all standing like a pine tree. And often you will notice that being conscious of the eyes of the whole visible world resting on him from the sides of the two ships, this standing captain is all alive to the importance of sustaining his dignity by maintaining his legs. Nor is this any very easy matter; for in his rear is the immense projecting steering oar hitting him now and then in the small of his back, the after-oar reciprocating by rapping his knees in front. He is thus completely wedged before and behind, and can only expand himself sideways by settling down on his stretched legs; but a sudden, violent pitch of the boat will often go far to topple him, because length of foundation is nothing without corresponding breadth. Merely make a spread angle of two poles, and you cannot stand them up. Then, again, it would never do in plain sight of the world's riveted eyes, it would never do, I say, for this straddling captain to be seen steadying himself the slightest particle by catching hold of anything with his hands; indeed, as token of his entire, buoyant self-command, he generally carries his hands in his trowsers' pockets;

but perhaps being generally very large, heavy hands, he carries them there for ballast. Nevertheless there have occurred instances, well authenticated ones too, where the captain has been known for an uncommonly critical moment or two, in a sudden squall say—to seize hold of the nearest oarsman's hair, and hold on there like grim death.

Chapter 54

THE TOWN-HO'S STORY
(As told at the Golden Inn.)

T HE Cape of Good Hope, and all the watery region round about there, is much like some noted four corners of a great highway, where you meet more travellers than in any other part.

It was not very long after speaking the Goney that another homeward-bound whaleman, the Town-Ho,* was encountered. She was manned almost wholly by Polynesians. In the short gam that ensued she gave us strong news of Moby Dick. To some the general interest in the White Whale was now wildly heightened by a circumstance of the Town-Ho's story, which seemed obscurely to involve with the whale a certain wondrous, inverted visitation of one of those so called judgments of God which at times are said to overtake some men. This latter circumstance, with its own particular accompaniments, forming what may be called the secret part of the tragedy about to be narrated, never reached the ears of Captain Ahab or his mates. For that secret part of the story was unknown to the captain of the Town-Ho himself. It was the private property of three confederate white seamen of that ship, one of whom, it seems, communicated it to Tashtego with Romish injunctions of secresy, but the following night Tashtego rambled in his sleep, and revealed so much of it in that way, that when he was wakened he could not well withhold the rest. Nevertheless, so potent an influence did this thing have on those seamen in the Pequod who came to the full knowledge of it, and by such a strange delicacy, to call it so, were they governed in this matter, that they kept the secret among themselves so that it never transpired abaft the Pequod's main-mast. Interweaving in its proper place this darker thread with the story as publicly narrated on the ship,

---

*The ancient whale-cry upon first sighting a whale from the mast-head, still used by whalemen in hunting the famous Gallipagos terrapin.

1052

the whole of this strange affair I now proceed to put on lasting record.

For my humor's sake, I shall preserve the style in which I once narrated it at Lima, to a lounging circle of my Spanish friends, one saint's eve, smoking upon the thick-gilt tiled piazza of the Golden Inn. Of those fine cavaliers, the young Dons, Pedro and Sebastian, were on the closer terms with me; and hence the interluding questions they occasionally put, and which are duly answered at the time.

"Some two years prior to my first learning the events which I am about rehearsing to you, gentlemen, the Town-Ho, Sperm Whaler of Nantucket, was cruising in your Pacific here, not very many days' sail westward from the eaves of this good Golden Inn. She was somewhere to the northward of the Line. One morning upon handling the pumps, according to daily usage, it was observed that she made more water in her hold than common. They supposed a sword-fish had stabbed her, gentlemen. But the captain, having some unusual reason for believing that rare good luck awaited him in those latitudes; and therefore being very averse to quit them, and the leak not being then considered at all dangerous, though, indeed, they could not find it after searching the hold as low down as was possible in rather heavy weather, the ship still continued her cruisings, the mariners working at the pumps at wide and easy intervals; but no good luck came; more days went by, and not only was the leak yet undiscovered, but it sensibly increased. So much so, that now taking some alarm, the captain, making all sail, stood away for the nearest harbor among the islands, there to have his hull hove out and repaired.

"Though no small passage was before her, yet, if the commonest chance favored, he did not at all fear that his ship would founder by the way, because his pumps were of the best, and being periodically relieved at them, those six-and-thirty men of his could easily keep the ship free; never mind if the leak should double on her. In truth, well nigh the whole of this passage being attended by very prosperous breezes, the Town-Ho had all but certainly arrived in perfect safety at her port without the occurrence of the least fatality, had it not been for the brutal overbearing of Radney, the mate, a Vineyarder, and the bitterly provoked vengeance of Steelkilt, a Lakeman and desperado from Buffalo."

"Lakeman!—Buffalo! Pray, what is a Lakeman, and where is Buffalo?" said Don Sebastian, rising in his swinging mat of grass.

"On the eastern shore of our Lake Erie, Don; but—I crave your courtesy—may be, you shall soon hear further of all that. Now, gentlemen, in square-sail brigs and three-masted ships, well nigh as large and stout as any that ever sailed out of your old Callao to far Manilla; this Lakeman, in the land-locked heart of our America, had yet been nurtured by all those agrarian freebooting impressions popularly connected with the open ocean. For in their interflowing aggregate, those grand fresh-water seas of ours,—Erie, and Ontario, and Huron, and Superior, and Michigan,—possess an ocean-like expansiveness, with many of the ocean's noblest traits; with many of its rimmed varieties of races and of climes. They contain round archipelagoes of romantic isles, even as the Polynesian waters do; in large part, are shored by two great contrasting nations, as the Atlantic is; they furnish long maritime approaches to our numerous territorial colonies from the East, dotted all round their banks; here and there are frowned upon by batteries, and by the goat-like craggy guns of lofty Mackinaw; they have heard the fleet thunderings of naval victories; at intervals, they yield their beaches to wild barbarians, whose red painted faces flash from out their peltry wigwams; for leagues and leagues are flanked by ancient and unentered forests, where the gaunt pines stand like serried lines of kings in Gothic genealogies; those same woods harboring wild Afric beasts of prey, and silken creatures whose exported furs give robes to Tartar Emperors; they mirror the paved capitals of Buffalo and Cleveland, as well as Winnebago villages; they float alike the full-rigged merchant ship, the armed cruiser of the State, the steamer, and the birch canoe; they are swept by Borean and dismasting blasts as direful as any that lash the salted wave; they know what shipwrecks are, for out of sight of land, however inland, they have drowned full many a midnight ship with all its shrieking crew. Thus, gentlemen, though an inlander, Steelkilt was wild-ocean born, and wild-ocean nurtured; as much of an audacious mariner as any. And for Radney, though in his infancy he may have laid him down on the lone Nantucket beach, to nurse at his maternal sea; though in after life he had long followed our austere Atlantic and your contemplative Pacific; yet was he quite as vengeful and full of social quarrel as the backwoods seaman, fresh from the latitudes of buck-horn handled Bowie-knives. Yet was this Nantucketer a man with some good-hearted traits; and this Lakeman, a mariner, who though a sort of devil indeed, might yet by inflexible firmness, only tempered by that common decency of human recognition which is the meanest slave's right; thus treated, this Steelkilt had long been retained harmless and docile. At all events, he had proved so thus far; but Radney was doomed and made mad, and Steelkilt—but, gentlemen, you shall hear.

"It was not more than a day or two at the furthest after pointing her prow for her island haven, that the Town-Ho's leak seemed again increasing, but only so as to require an hour or more at the pumps every day. You must know that in a settled and civilized ocean like our Atlantic, for example, some skippers think little of pumping their whole way across it; though of a still, sleepy night, should the officer of the deck happen to forget his duty in that respect, the probability would be that he and his shipmates would never again remember it, on account of all hands gently subsiding to the bottom. Nor in the solitary and savage seas far from you to the westward, gentlemen, is it altogether unusual for ships to keep clanging at their pump-handles in full chorus even for a voyage of considerable length; that is, if it lie along a tolerably accessible coast, or if any other reasonable retreat is afforded them. It is only when a leaky vessel is in some very out of the way part of those waters, some really landless latitude, that her captain begins to feel a little anxious.

"Much this way had it been with the Town-Ho; so when her leak was found gaining once more, there was in truth some small concern manifested by several of her company; especially by Radney the mate. He commanded the upper sails to be well hoisted, sheeted home anew, and every way expanded to the breeze. Now this Radney, I suppose, was as little of a coward, and as little inclined to any sort of nervous apprehensiveness touching his own person as any fearless, unthinking creature on land or on sea that you can conveniently imagine, gentlemen. Therefore when he betrayed this solicitude about the safety of the ship, some of the seamen declared that it was only on account of his being a part owner in her. So when they were working that evening at the pumps, there was on this head no small gamesomeness slily going on among them, as they stood with their feet continually overflowed by the rippling clear water; clear as any mountain spring, gentlemen—that bubbling from the pumps ran across the deck, and poured itself out in steady spouts at the lee scupper-holes.

"Now, as you well know, it is not seldom the case in this conventional world of ours—watery or otherwise; that when a person placed in command over his fellow-men finds one of them to be very significantly his superior in general pride of manhood, straightway against that man he conceives an unconquerable dislike and bitterness; and if he have a chance he will pull down and pulverize that subaltern's tower, and make a little heap of dust of it. Be this conceit of mine as it may, gentlemen, at all events Steelkilt was a tall and noble animal with a head like a Roman, and a flowing golden beard like the tasseled housings of your last viceroy's snorting charger; and a brain, and a heart, and a soul in him, gentlemen, which had made Steelkilt Charlemagne, had he been born son to Charlemagne's father. But Radney, the mate, was ugly as a mule; yet as hardy, as stubborn, as malicious. He did not love Steelkilt, and Steelkilt knew it.

"Espying the mate drawing near as he was toiling at the pump with the rest, the Lakeman affected not to notice him, but unawed, went on with his gay banterings.

" 'Aye, aye, my merry lads, it's a lively leak this; hold a cannikin, one of ye, and let's have a taste. By the Lord, it's worth bottling! I tell ye what, men, old Rad's investment must go for it! he had best cut away his part of the hull and tow it home. The fact is, boys, that sword-fish only began the job; he's come back again with a gang of ship-carpenters, saw-fish, and file-fish, and what not; and the whole posse of 'em are now hard at work cutting and slashing at the bottom; making improvements, I suppose. If old Rad were here now, I'd tell him to jump overboard and scatter 'em. They're playing the devil with his estate, I can tell him. But he's a simple old soul,—Rad, and a beauty too. Boys, they say the rest of his property is invested in looking-glasses. I wonder if he'd give a poor devil like me the model of his nose.'

" 'Damn your eyes! what's that pump stopping for?' roared Radney, pretending not to have heard the sailor's talk. 'Thunder away at it!'

" 'Aye, aye, sir,' said Steelkilt, merry as a cricket. 'Lively, boys, lively, now!' And with that the pump clanged like fifty fire-engines; the men tossed their hats off to it, and ere long that peculiar gasping of the lungs was heard which denotes the fullest tension of life's utmost energies.

"Quitting the pump at last, with the rest of his band, the Lakeman went forward all panting, and sat himself down on the windlass; his face fiery red, his eyes bloodshot, and wiping the profuse sweat from his brow. Now what cozening fiend it was, gentlemen, that possessed Radney to meddle with such a man in that corporeally exasperated state, I know not; but so it happened. Intolerably striding along the deck, the mate commanded him to get a broom and sweep down the planks, and also a shovel, and remove some offensive matters consequent upon allowing a pig to run at large.

"Now, gentlemen, sweeping a ship's deck at sea is a piece of household work which in all times but raging gales is regularly attended to every evening; it has been known to be done in the case of ships actually foundering at the time. Such, gentlemen, is the inflexibility of sea-usages and the instinctive love of neatness in seamen; some of whom would not willingly drown without first washing their faces. But in all vessels this broom business is the prescriptive province of the boys, if boys there be aboard. Besides, it was the stronger men in the Town-Ho that had been divided into gangs, taking turns at the pumps; and being the most athletic seaman of them all, Steelkilt had been regularly assigned captain of one of the gangs; consequently he should have been freed from any trivial business not connected with truly nautical duties, such being the case with his comrades. I mention all these particulars so that you may understand exactly how this affair stood between the two men.

"But there was more than this: the order about the shovel

was almost as plainly meant to sting and insult Steelkilt, as though Radney had spat in his face. Any man who has gone sailor in a whale-ship will understand this; and all this and doubtless much more, the Lakeman fully comprehended when the mate uttered his command. But as he sat still for a moment, and as he steadfastly looked into the mate's malignant eye and perceived the stacks of powder-casks heaped up in him and the slow-match silently burning along towards them; as he instinctively saw all this, that strange forbearance and unwillingness to stir up the deeper passionateness in any already ireful being—a repugnance most felt, when felt at all, by really valiant men even when aggrieved—this nameless phantom feeling, gentlemen, stole over Steelkilt.

"Therefore, in his ordinary tone, only a little broken by the bodily exhaustion he was temporarily in, he answered him saying that sweeping the deck was not his business, and he would not do it. And then, without at all alluding to the shovel, he pointed to three lads as the customary sweepers; who, not being billeted at the pumps, had done little or nothing all day. To this, Radney replied with an oath, in a most domineering and outrageous manner unconditionally reiterating his command; meanwhile advancing upon the still seated Lakeman, with an uplifted cooper's club hammer which he had snatched from a cask near by.

"Heated and irritated as he was by his spasmodic toil at the pumps, for all his first nameless feeling of forbearance the sweating Steelkilt could but ill brook this bearing in the mate; but somehow still smothering the conflagration within him, without speaking he remained doggedly rooted to his seat, till at last the incensed Radney shook the hammer within a few inches of his face, furiously commanding him to do his bidding.

"Steelkilt rose, and slowly retreating round the windlass, steadily followed by the mate with his menacing hammer, deliberately repeated his intention not to obey. Seeing, however, that his forbearance had not the slightest effect, by an awful and unspeakable intimation with his twisted hand he warned off the foolish and infatuated man; but it was to no purpose. And in this way the two went once slowly round the windlass; when, resolved at last no longer to retreat, bethinking him that he had now forborne as much as comported with his humor, the Lakeman paused on the hatches and thus spoke to the officer:

" 'Mr. Radney, I will not obey you. Take that hammer away, or look to yourself.' But the predestinated mate coming still closer to him, where the Lakeman stood fixed, now shook the heavy hammer within an inch of his teeth; meanwhile repeating a string of insufferable maledictions. Retreating not the thousandth part of an inch; stabbing him in the eye with the unflinching poniard of his glance, Steelkilt, clenching his right hand behind him and creepingly drawing it back, told his persecutor that if the hammer but grazed his cheek he (Steelkilt) would murder him. But, gentlemen, the fool had been branded for the slaughter by the gods. Immediately the hammer touched the cheek; the next instant the lower jaw of the mate was stove in his head; he fell on the hatch spouting blood like a whale.

"Ere the cry could go aft Steelkilt was shaking one of the backstays leading far aloft to where two of his comrades were standing their mast-heads. They were both Canallers."

"Canallers!" cried Don Pedro. "We have seen many whaleships in our harbors, but never heard of your Canallers. Pardon: who and what are they?"

"Canallers, Don, are the boatmen belonging to our grand Erie Canal. You must have heard of it."

"Nay, Senor; hereabouts in this dull, warm, most lazy, and hereditary land, we know but little of your vigorous North."

"Aye? Well then, Don, refill my cup. Your chicha's very fine; and ere proceeding further I will tell ye what our Canallers are; for such information may throw side-light upon my story.

"For three hundred and sixty miles, gentlemen, through the entire breadth of the state of New York; through numerous populous cities and most thriving villages; through long, dismal, uninhabited swamps, and affluent, cultivated fields, unrivalled for fertility; by billiard-room and bar-room; through the holy-of-holies of great forests; on Roman arches over Indian rivers; through sun and shade; by happy hearts or broken; through all the wide contrasting scenery of those noble Mohawk counties; and especially, by rows of snow-white chapels, whose spires stand almost like milestones, flows one continual stream of Venetianly corrupt and often lawless life. There's your true Ashantee, gentlemen; there howl your pagans; where you ever find them, next door to you; under the long-flung shadow, and the snug patronizing lee of churches. For by some curious fatality, as it is often noted of your metropolitan freebooters that they ever encamp around the halls of justice, so sinners, gentlemen, most abound in holiest vicinities."

"Is that a friar passing?" said Don Pedro, looking downwards into the crowded plaza, with humorous concern.

"Well for our northern friend, Dame Isabella's Inquisition wanes in Lima," laughed Don Sebastian. "Proceed, Senor."

"A moment! Pardon!" cried another of the company. "In the name of all us Limeese, I but desire to express to you, sir sailor, that we have by no means overlooked your delicacy in not substituting present Lima for distant Venice in your corrupt comparison. Oh! do not bow and look surprised; you know the proverb all along this coast—'Corrupt as Lima.' It but bears out your saying, too; churches more plentiful than billiard-tables, and for ever open—and 'Corrupt as Lima.' So, too, Venice; I have been there; the holy city of the blessed evangelist, St. Mark!—St. Dominic, purge it! Your cup! Thanks: here I refill; now, you pour out again."

"Freely depicted in his own vocation, gentlemen, the Canaller would make a fine dramatic hero, so abundantly and picturesquely wicked is he. Like Mark Antony, for days and days along his green-turfed, flowery Nile, he indolently floats, openly toying with his red-cheeked Cleopatra, ripening his apricot thigh upon the sunny deck. But ashore, all this effeminacy is dashed. The brigandish guise which the Canaller so proudly sports; his slouched and gaily-ribboned hat betoken his grand features. A terror to the smiling innocence of the villages through which he floats; his swart visage and bold swagger are not unshunned in cities. Once a vagabond on his own canal, I have received good turns from one of these Canallers; I thank him heartily; would fain be not ungrateful; but it is often one of the prime redeeming qualities of your man of violence, that at times he has as stiff an arm to back a poor stranger in a strait, as to plunder a wealthy one. In sum, gentlemen, what the wildness of this canal life is, is emphatically evinced by this; that our wild whale-fishery contains so many of its most finished graduates, and that scarce any race of mankind, except Sydney men, are so much distrusted by our whaling captains. Nor does it at all diminish the curiousness of this matter, that to many thousands of our rural boys and young men born along its line, the probationary life of the Grand Canal furnishes the sole transition between quietly reaping in a Christian corn-field, and recklessly ploughing the waters of the most barbaric seas."

"I see! I see!" impetuously exclaimed Don Pedro, spilling his chicha upon his silvery ruffles. "No need to travel! The world's one Lima. I had thought, now, that at your temperate North the generations were cold and holy as the hills.—But the story."

"I left off, gentlemen, where the Lakeman shook the backstay. Hardly had he done so, when he was surrounded by the three junior mates and the four harpooneers, who all crowded him to the deck. But sliding down the ropes like baleful comets, the two Canallers rushed into the uproar, and sought to drag their man out of it towards the forecastle. Others of the sailors joined with them in this attempt, and a twisted turmoil ensued; while standing out of harm's way, the valiant captain danced up and down with a whale-pike, calling upon his officers to manhandle that atrocious scoundrel, and smoke him along to the quarter-deck. At intervals, he ran close up to the revolving border of the confusion, and prying into the heart of it with his pike, sought to prick out the object of his resentment. But Steelkilt and his desperadoes were too much for them all; they succeeded in gaining the forecastle deck, where, hastily slewing about three or four large casks in a line with the windlass, these sea-Parisians entrenched themselves behind the barricade.

" 'Come out of that, ye pirates!' roared the captain, now menacing them with a pistol in each hand, just brought to him by the steward. 'Come out of that, ye cut-throats!'

"Steelkilt leaped on the barricade, and striding up and down there, defied the worst the pistols could do; but gave the captain to understand distinctly, that his (Steelkilt's) death would be the signal for a murderous mutiny on the part of all hands. Fearing in his heart lest this might prove but too true, the captain a little desisted, but still commanded the insurgents instantly to return to their duty.

" 'Will you promise not to touch us, if we do?' demanded their ringleader.

" 'Turn to! turn to!—I make no promise; to your duty! Do you want to sink the ship, by knocking off at a time like this? Turn to!' and he once more raised a pistol.

" 'Sink the ship?' cried Steelkilt. 'Aye, let her sink. Not a man of us turns to, unless you swear not to raise a rope-yarn against us. What say ye, men?' turning to his comrades. A fierce cheer was their response.

"The Lakeman now patrolled the barricade, all the while keeping his eye on the Captain, and jerking out such sentences as these:—'It's not our fault; we didn't want it; I told him to take his hammer away; it was boy's business; he might have known me before this; I told him not to prick the buffalo; I believe I have broken a finger here against his cursed jaw; ain't those mincing knives down in the forecastle there, men? look to those handspikes, my hearties. Captain, by God, look to yourself; say the word; don't be a fool; forget it all; we are ready to turn to; treat us decently, and we're your men; but we won't be flogged.'

" 'Turn to! I make no promises, turn to, I say!'

" 'Look ye, now,' cried the Lakeman, flinging out his arm towards him, 'there are a few of us here (and I am one of them) who have shipped for the cruise, d'ye see; now as you well know, sir, we can claim our discharge as soon as the anchor is down; so we don't want a row; it's not our interest; we want to be peaceable; we are ready to work, but we won't be flogged.'

" 'Turn to!' roared the Captain.

"Steelkilt glanced round him a moment, and then said:—'I tell you what it is now, Captain, rather than kill ye, and be hung for such a shabby rascal, we won't lift a hand against ye unless ye attack us; but till you say the word about not flogging us, we don't do a hand's turn.'

" 'Down into the forecastle then, down with ye, I'll keep ye there till ye're sick of it. Down ye go.'

" 'Shall we?' cried the ringleader to his men. Most of them

were against it; but at length, in obedience to Steelkilt, they preceded him down into their dark den, growlingly disappearing, like bears into a cave.

"As the Lakeman's bare head was just level with the planks, the Captain and his posse leaped the barricade, and rapidly drawing over the slide of the scuttle, planted their group of hands upon it, and loudly called for the steward to bring the heavy brass padlock belonging to the companion-way. Then opening the slide a little, the Captain whispered something down the crack, closed it, and turned the key upon them— ten in number—leaving on deck some twenty or more, who thus far had remained neutral.

"All night a wide-awake watch was kept by all the officers, forward and aft, especially about the forecastle scuttle and fore hatchway; at which last place it was feared the insurgents might emerge, after breaking through the bulkhead below. But the hours of darkness passed in peace; the men who still remained at their duty toiling hard at the pumps, whose clinking and clanking at intervals through the dreary night dismally resounded through the ship.

"At sunrise the Captain went forward, and knocking on the deck, summoned the prisoners to work; but with a yell they refused. Water was then lowered down to them, and a couple of handfuls of biscuit were tossed after it; when again turning the key upon them and pocketing it, the Captain returned to the quarter-deck. Twice every day for three days this was repeated; but on the fourth morning a confused wrangling, and then a scuffling was heard, as the customary summons was delivered; and suddenly four men burst up from the forecastle, saying they were ready to turn to. The fetid closeness of the air, and a famishing diet, united perhaps to some fears of ultimate retribution, had constrained them to surrender at discretion. Emboldened by this, the Captain reiterated his demand to the rest, but Steelkilt shouted up to him a terrific hint to stop his babbling and betake himself where he belonged. On the fifth morning three others of the mutineers bolted up into the air from the desperate arms below that sought to restrain them. Only three were left.

" 'Better turn to, now!' said the Captain with a heartless jeer.

" 'Shut us up again, will ye!' cried Steelkilt.

" 'Oh! certainly,' said the Captain, and the key clicked.

"It was at this point, gentlemen, that enraged by the defection of seven of his former associates, and stung by the mocking voice that had last hailed him, and maddened by his long entombment in a place as black as the bowels of despair; it was then that Steelkilt proposed to the two Canallers, thus far apparently of one mind with him, to burst out of their hole at the next summoning of the garrison; and armed with their keen mincing knives (long, crescentic, heavy implements with a handle at each end) run a muck from the bowsprit to the taffrail; and if by any devilishness of desperation possible, seize the ship. For himself, he would do this, he said, whether they joined him or not. That was the last night he should spend in that den. But the scheme met with no opposition on the part of the other two; they swore they were ready for that, or for any other mad thing, for anything in short but a surrender. And what was more, they each insisted upon being the first man on deck, when the time to make the rush should come. But to this their leader as fiercely objected, reserving that priority for himself; particularly as his two comrades would not yield, the one to the other, in the matter; and both of them could not be first, for the ladder would but admit one man at a time. And here, gentlemen, the foul play of these miscreants must come out.

"Upon hearing the frantic project of their leader, each in his own separate soul had suddenly lighted, it would seem, upon the same piece of treachery, namely: to be foremost in breaking out, in order to be the first of the three, though the last of the ten, to surrender; and thereby secure whatever small chance of pardon such conduct might merit. But when Steelkilt made known his determination still to lead them to the last, they in some way, by some subtle chemistry of villany, mixed their before secret treacheries together; and when their leader fell into a doze, verbally opened their souls to each other in three sentences; and bound the sleeper with cords, and gagged him with cords; and shrieked out for the Captain at midnight.

"Thinking murder at hand, and smelling in the dark for the blood, he and all his armed mates and harpooneers rushed for the forecastle. In a few minutes the scuttle was opened, and, bound hand and foot, the still struggling ringleader was shoved up into the air by his perfidious allies, who at once claimed the honor of securing a man who had been fully ripe for murder. But all three were collared, and dragged along the deck like dead cattle; and, side by side, were seized up into the mizen rigging, like three quarters of meat, and there they hung till morning. 'Damn ye,' cried the Captain, pacing to and fro before them, 'the vultures would not touch ye, ye villains!'

"At sunrise he summoned all hands; and separating those who had rebelled from those who had taken no part in the mutiny, he told the former that he had a good mind to flog them all round—thought, upon the whole, he would do so— he ought to—justice demanded it; but for the present, considering their timely surrender, he would let them go with a reprimand, which he accordingly administered in the vernacular.

" 'But as for you, ye carrion rogues,' turning to the three men in the rigging—'for you, I mean to mince ye up for the try-pots;' and, seizing a rope, he applied it with all his might to the backs of the two traitors, till they yelled no more, but lifelessly hung their heads sideways, as the two crucified thieves are drawn.

" 'My wrist is sprained with ye!' he cried, at last; 'but there is still rope enough left for you, my fine bantam, that wouldn't give up. Take that gag from his mouth, and let us hear what he can say for himself.'

"For a moment the exhausted mutineer made a tremulous motion of his cramped jaws, and then painfully twisting round his head, said in a sort of hiss, 'What I say is this— and mind it well—if you flog me, I murder you!'

" 'Say ye so? then see how ye frighten me'—and the Captain drew off with the rope to strike.

" 'Best not,' hissed the Lakeman.

" 'But I must,'—and the rope was once more drawn back for the stroke.

"Steelkilt here hissed out something, inaudible to all but the Captain; who, to the amazement of all hands, started back, paced the deck rapidly two or three times, and then suddenly throwing down his rope, said, 'I won't do it—let him go—cut him down: d'ye hear?'

"But as the junior mates were hurrying to execute the order, a pale man, with a bandaged head, arrested them—Radney the chief mate. Ever since the blow, he had lain in his berth; but that morning, hearing the tumult on the deck, he had crept out, and thus far had watched the whole scene. Such was the state of his mouth, that he could hardly speak; but mumbling something about *his* being willing and able to do what the captain dared not attempt, he snatched the rope and advanced to his pinioned foe.

" 'You are a coward!' hissed the Lakeman.

" 'So I am, but take that.' The mate was in the very act of striking, when another hiss stayed his uplifted arm. He paused: and then pausing no more, made good his word, spite of Steelkilt's threat, whatever that might have been. The three men were then cut down, all hands were turned to, and, sullenly worked by the moody seamen, the iron pumps clanged as before.

"Just after dark that day, when one watch had retired below, a clamor was heard in the forecastle; and the two trembling traitors running up, besieged the cabin door, saying they durst not consort with the crew. Entreaties, cuffs, and kicks could not drive them back, so at their own instance they were put down in the ship's run for salvation. Still, no sign of mutiny reappeared among the rest. On the contrary, it seemed, that mainly at Steelkilt's instigation, they had resolved to maintain the strictest peacefulness, obey all orders to the last, and, when the ship reached port, desert her in a body. But in order to insure the speediest end to the voyage, they all agreed to another thing—namely, not to sing out for whales, in case any should be discovered. For, spite of her leak, and spite of all her other perils, the Town-Ho still maintained her mast-heads, and her captain was just as willing to lower for a fish that moment, as on the day his craft first struck the cruising ground; and Radney the mate was quite as ready to change his berth for a boat, and with his bandaged mouth seek to gag in death the vital jaw of the whale.

"But though the Lakeman had induced the seamen to adopt this sort of passiveness in their conduct, he kept his own counsel (at least till all was over) concerning his own proper and private revenge upon the man who had stung him in the ventricles of his heart. He was in Radney the chief mate's watch; and as if the infatuated man sought to run more than half way to meet his doom, after the scene at the rigging, he insisted, against the express counsel of the captain, upon resuming the head of his watch at night. Upon this, and one or two other circumstances, Steelkilt systematically built the plan of his revenge.

"During the night, Radney had an unseamanlike way of sitting on the bulwarks of the quarter-deck, and leaning his arm upon the gunwale of the boat which was hoisted up there, a little above the ship's side. In this attitude, it was well known, he sometimes dozed. There was a considerable vacancy between the boat and the ship, and down beneath this was the sea. Steelkilt calculated his time, and found that his next trick at the helm would come round at two o'clock, in the morning of the third day from that in which he had been betrayed. At his leisure, he employed the interval in braiding something very carefully in his watches below.

" 'What are you making there?' said a shipmate.

" 'What do you think? what does it look like?'

" 'Like a lanyard for your bag; but it's an odd one, seems to me.'

" 'Yes, rather oddish,' said the Lakeman, holding it at arm's length before him; 'but I think it will answer. Shipmate, I haven't enough twine,—have you any?'

"But there was none in the forecastle.

" 'Then I must get some from old Rad;' and he rose to go aft.

" 'You don't mean to go a begging to *him*!' said a sailor.

" 'Why not? Do you think he won't do me a turn, when it's to help himself in the end, shipmate?' and going to the mate, he looked at him quietly, and asked him for some twine to mend his hammock. It was given him—neither twine nor lanyard were seen again; but the next night an iron ball, closely netted, partly rolled from the pocket of the Lakeman's monkey jacket, as he was tucking the coat into his hammock for a pillow. Twenty-four hours after, his trick at the silent helm—nigh to the man who was apt to doze over the grave always ready dug to the seaman's hand—that fatal hour was then to come; and in the fore-ordaining soul of Steelkilt, the mate was already stark and stretched as a corpse, with his forehead crushed in.

"But, gentlemen, a fool saved the would-be murderer from the bloody deed he had planned. Yet complete revenge he had, and without being the avenger. For by a mysterious fatality, Heaven itself seemed to step in to take out of his hands into its own the damning thing he would have done.

"It was just between daybreak and sunrise of the morning of the second day, when they were washing down the decks, that a stupid Teneriffe man, drawing water in the main-chains, all at once shouted out, 'There she rolls! there she rolls! Jesu, what a whale!' It was Moby Dick."

"'Moby Dick'!" cried Don Sebastian; "St. Dominic! Sir sailor, but do whales have christenings? Whom call you Moby Dick?"

"A very white, and famous, and most deadly immortal monster, Don;—but that would be too long a story."

"How? how?" cried all the young Spaniards, crowding.

"Nay, Dons, Dons—nay, nay! I cannot rehearse that now. Let me get more into the air, Sirs."

"The chicha! the chicha!" cried Don Pedro; "our vigorous friend looks faint;—fill up his empty glass!"

"No need, gentlemen; one moment, and I proceed.— Now, gentlemen, so suddenly perceiving the snowy whale within fifty yards of the ship—forgetful of the compact among the crew—in the excitement of the moment, the Teneriffe man had instinctively and involuntarily lifted his voice for the monster, though for some little time past it had been plainly beheld from the three sullen mast-heads. All was now a phrensy. 'The White Whale—the White Whale!' was the cry from captain, mates, and harpooneers, who, undeterred by fearful rumors, were all anxious to capture so famous and precious a fish; while the dogged crew eyed askance, and with curses, the appalling beauty of the vast milky mass, that lit up by a horizontal spangling sun, shifted and glistened like a living opal in the blue morning sea. Gentlemen, a strange fatality pervades the whole career of these events, as if verily mapped out before the world itself was charted. The mutineer was the bowsman of the mate, and when fast to a fish, it was his duty to sit next him, while Radney stood up with his lance in the prow, and haul in or slacken the line, at the word of command. Moreover, when the four boats were lowered, the mate's got the start; and none howled more fiercely with delight than did Steelkilt, as he strained at his oar. After a stiff pull, their harpooneer got fast, and, spear in hand, Radney sprang to the bow. He was always a furious man, it seems, in a boat. And now his bandaged cry was, to beach him on the whale's topmost back. Nothing loath, his bowsman hauled him up and up, through a blinding foam that blent two whitenesses together; till of a sudden the boat struck as against a sunken ledge, and keeling over, spilled out the standing mate. That instant, as he fell on the whale's slippery back, the boat righted, and was dashed aside by the swell, while Radney was tossed over into the sea, on the other flank of the whale. He struck out through the spray, and, for an instant, was dimly seen through that veil, wildly seeking to remove himself from the eye of Moby Dick. But the whale rushed round in a sudden maelstrom; seized the swimmer between his jaws; and rearing high up with him, plunged headlong again, and went down.

"Meantime, at the first tap of the boat's bottom, the Lakeman had slackened the line, so as to drop astern from the whirlpool; calmly looking on, he thought his own thoughts. But a sudden, terrific, downward jerking of the boat, quickly brought his knife to the line. He cut it; and the whale was free. But, at some distance, Moby Dick rose again, with some tatters of Radney's red woollen shirt, caught in the teeth that had destroyed him. All four boats gave chase again; but the whale eluded them, and finally wholly disappeared.

"In good time, the Town-Ho reached her port—a savage, solitary place—where no civilized creature resided. There, headed by the Lakeman, all but five or six of the foremastmen deliberately deserted among the palms; eventually, as it turned out, seizing a large double war-canoe of the savages, and setting sail for some other harbor.

"The ship's company being reduced to but a handful, the captain called upon the Islanders to assist him in the laborious business of heaving down the ship to stop the leak. But to

such unresting vigilance over their dangerous allies was this
small band of whites necessitated, both by night and by day, and
so extreme was the hard work they underwent, that upon the
vessel being ready again for sea, they were in such a weakened
condition that the captain durst not put off with them in so
heavy a vessel. After taking counsel with his officers, he anchored the ship as far off shore as possible; loaded and ran
out his two cannon from the bows; stacked his muskets on the
poop; and warning the Islanders not to approach the ship at
their peril, took one man with him, and setting the sail of his
best whaleboat, steered straight before the wind for Tahiti, five
hundred miles distant, to procure a reinforcement to his crew.

"On the fourth day of the sail, a large canoe was descried,
which seemed to have touched at a low isle of corals. He
steered away from it; but the savage craft bore down on him;
and soon the voice of Steelkilt hailed him to heave to, or he
would run him under water. The captain presented a pistol.
With one foot on each prow of the yoked war-canoes, the
Lakeman laughed him to scorn; assuring him that if the pistol
so much as clicked in the lock, he would bury him in bubbles
and foam.

" 'What do you want of me?' cried the captain.

" 'Where are you bound? and for what are you bound?'
demanded Steelkilt; 'no lies.'

" 'I am bound to Tahiti for more men.'

" 'Very good. Let me board you a moment—I come in
peace.' With that he leaped from the canoe, swam to the boat;
and climbing the gunwale, stood face to face with the captain.

" 'Cross your arms, sir; throw back your head. Now, repeat
after me. "As soon as Steelkilt leaves me, I swear to beach this
boat on yonder island, and remain there six days. If I do not,
may lightnings strike me!" '

" 'A pretty scholar,' laughed the Lakeman. 'Adios, Senor!'
and leaping into the sea, he swam back to his comrades.

"Watching the boat till it was fairly beached, and drawn up
to the roots of the cocoa-nut trees, Steelkilt made sail again,
and in due time arrived at Tahiti, his own place of destination. There, luck befriended him; two ships were about to sail
for France, and were providentially in want of precisely that
number of men which the sailor headed. They embarked; and

so for ever got the start of their former captain, had he been at all minded to work them legal retribution.

"Some ten days after the French ships sailed, the whale-boat arrived, and the captain was forced to enlist some of the more civilized Tahitians, who had been somewhat used to the sea. Chartering a small native schooner, he returned with them to his vessel; and finding all right there, again resumed his cruisings.

"Where Steelkilt now is, gentlemen, none know; but upon the island of Nantucket, the widow of Radney still turns to the sea which refuses to give up its dead; still in dreams sees the awful white whale that destroyed him." * * * *

"Are you through?" said Don Sebastian, quietly.

"I am, Don."

"Then I entreat you, tell me if to the best of your own convictions, this your story is in substance really true? It is so passing wonderful! Did you get it from an unquestionable source? Bear with me if I seem to press."

"Also bear with all of us, sir sailor; for we all join in Don Sebastian's suit," cried the company, with exceeding interest.

"Is there a copy of the Holy Evangelists in the Golden Inn, gentlemen?"

"Nay," said Don Sebastian; "but I know a worthy priest near by, who will quickly procure one for me. I go for it; but are you well advised? this may grow too serious."

"Will you be so good as to bring the priest also, Don?"

"Though there are no Auto-da-Fés in Lima now," said one of the company to another; "I fear our sailor friend runs risk of the archiepiscopacy. Let us withdraw more out of the moonlight. I see no need of this."

"Excuse me for running after you, Don Sebastian; but may I also beg that you will be particular in procuring the largest sized Evangelists you can."

* * *

"This is the priest, he brings you the Evangelists," said Don Sebastian, gravely, returning with a tall and solemn figure.

"Let me remove my hat. Now, venerable priest, further into the light, and hold the Holy Book before me that I may touch it.

"So help me Heaven, and on my honor, the story I have told ye, gentlemen, is in substance and its great items, true. I know it to be true; it happened on this ball; I trod the ship; I knew the crew; I have seen and talked with Steelkilt since the death of Radney."

Chapter 55

Of the Monstrous Pictures of Whales

I SHALL ere long paint to you as well as one can without canvas, something like the true form of the whale as he actually appears to the eye of the whaleman when in his own absolute body the whale is moored alongside the whale-ship so that he can be fairly stepped upon there. It may be worth while, therefore, previously to advert to those curious imaginary portraits of him which even down to the present day confidently challenge the faith of the landsman. It is time to set the world right in this matter, by proving such pictures of the whale all wrong.

It may be that the primal source of all those pictorial delusions will be found among the oldest Hindoo, Egyptian, and Grecian sculptures. For ever since those inventive but unscrupulous times when on the marble panellings of temples, the pedestals of statues, and on shields, medallions, cups, and coins, the dolphin was drawn in scales of chain-armor like Saladin's, and a helmeted head like St. George's; ever since then has something of the same sort of license prevailed, not only in most popular pictures of the whale, but in many scientific presentations of him.

Now, by all odds, the most ancient extant portrait anyways purporting to be the whale's, is to be found in the famous cavern-pagoda of Elephanta, in India. The Brahmins maintain that in the almost endless sculptures of that immemorial pagoda, all the trades and pursuits, every conceivable avocation of man, were prefigured ages before any of them actually came into being. No wonder then, that in some sort our noble profession of whaling should have been there shadowed forth. The Hindoo whale referred to, occurs in a separate department of the wall, depicting the incarnation of Vishnu in the form of leviathan, learnedly known as the Matse Avatar. But though this sculpture is half man and half whale, so as only to give the tail of the latter, yet that small section of him is all wrong. It looks more like the tapering tail of an anaconda, than the broad palms of the true whale's majestic flukes.

But go to the old Galleries, and look now at a great Christian painter's portrait of this fish; for he succeeds no better than the antediluvian Hindoo. It is Guido's picture of Perseus rescuing Andromeda from the sea-monster or whale. Where did Guido get the model of such a strange creature as that? Nor does Hogarth, in painting the same scene in his own "Perseus Descending," make out one whit better. The huge corpulence of that Hogarthian monster undulates on the surface, scarcely drawing one inch of water. It has a sort of howdah on its back, and its distended tusked mouth into which the billows are rolling, might be taken for the Traitors' Gate leading from the Thames by water into the Tower. Then, there are the Prodromus whales of old Scotch Sibbald, and Jonah's whale, as depicted in the prints of old Bibles and the cuts of old primers. What shall be said of these? As for the book-binder's whale winding like a vine-stalk round the stock of a descending anchor—as stamped and gilded on the backs and title-pages of many books both old and new—that is a very picturesque but purely fabulous creature, imitated, I take it, from the like figures on antique vases. Though universally denominated a dolphin, I nevertheless call this book-binder's fish an attempt at a whale; because it was so intended when the device was first introduced. It was introduced by an old Italian publisher somewhere about the 15th century, during the Revival of Learning; and in those days, and even down to a comparatively late period, dolphins were popularly supposed to be a species of the Leviathan.

In the vignettes and other embellishments of some ancient books you will at times meet with very curious touches at the whale, where all manner of spouts, jets d'eau, hot springs and cold, Saratoga and Baden-Baden, come bubbling up from his unexhausted brain. In the title-page of the original edition of the "Advancement of Learning" you will find some curious whales.

But quitting all these unprofessional attempts, let us glance at those pictures of leviathan purporting to be sober, scientific delineations, by those who know. In old Harris's collection of voyages there are some plates of whales extracted from a

Dutch book of voyages, A.D. 1671, entitled "A Whaling Voyage to Spitzbergen in the ship Jonas in the Whale, Peter Peterson of Friesland, master." In one of those plates the whales, like great rafts of logs, are represented lying among ice-isles, with white bears running over their living backs. In another plate, the prodigious blunder is made of representing the whale with perpendicular flukes.

Then again, there is an imposing quarto, written by one Captain Colnett, a Post Captain in the English navy, entitled "A Voyage round Cape Horn into the South Seas, for the purpose of extending the Spermaceti Whale Fisheries." In this book is an outline purporting to be a "Picture of a Physeter or Spermaceti whale, drawn by scale from one killed on the coast of Mexico, August, 1793, and hoisted on deck." I doubt not the captain had this veracious picture taken for the benefit of his marines. To mention but one thing about it, let me say that it has an eye which applied, according to the accompanying scale, to a full grown sperm whale, would make the eye of that whale a bow-window some five feet long. Ah, my gallant captain, why did ye not give us Jonah looking out of that eye!

Nor are the most conscientious compilations of Natural History for the benefit of the young and tender, free from the same heinousness of mistake. Look at that popular work "Goldsmith's Animated Nature." In the abridged London edition of 1807, there are plates of an alleged "whale" and a "narwhale." I do not wish to seem inelegant, but this unsightly whale looks much like an amputated sow; and, as for the narwhale, one glimpse at it is enough to amaze one, that in this nineteenth century such a hippogriff could be palmed for genuine upon any intelligent public of schoolboys.

Then, again, in 1825, Bernard Germain, Count de Lacépède, a great naturalist, published a scientific systemized whale book, wherein are several pictures of the different species of the Leviathan. All these are not only incorrect, but the picture of the Mysticetus or Greenland whale (that is to say, the Right whale), even Scoresby, a long experienced man as touching that species, declares not to have its counterpart in nature.

But the placing of the cap-sheaf to all this blundering busi-

ness was reserved for the scientific Frederick Cuvier, brother
to the famous Baron. In 1836, he published a Natural History
of Whales, in which he gives what he calls a picture of the
Sperm Whale. Before showing that picture to any Nantucketer, you had best provide for your summary retreat from
Nantucket. In a word, Frederick Cuvier's Sperm Whale is not
a Sperm Whale, but a squash. Of course, he never had the
benefit of a whaling voyage (such men seldom have), but
whence he derived that picture, who can tell? Perhaps he got
it as his scientific predecessor in the same field, Desmarest,
got one of his authentic abortions; that is, from a Chinese
drawing. And what sort of lively lads with the pencil those
Chinese are, many queer cups and saucers inform us.

As for the sign-painters' whales seen in the streets hanging
over the shops of oil-dealers, what shall be said of them? They
are generally Richard III. whales, with dromedary humps,
and very savage; breakfasting on three or four sailor tarts, that
is whaleboats full of mariners: their deformities floundering
in seas of blood and blue paint.

But these manifold mistakes in depicting the whale are not
so very surprising after all. Consider! Most of the scientific
drawings have been taken from the stranded fish; and these
are about as correct as a drawing of a wrecked ship, with
broken back, would correctly represent the noble animal itself
in all its undashed pride of hull and spars. Though elephants
have stood for their full-lengths, the living Leviathan has
never yet fairly floated himself for his portrait. The living
whale, in his full majesty and significance, is only to be seen
at sea in unfathomable waters; and afloat the vast bulk of him
is out of sight, like a launched line-of-battle ship; and out of
that element it is a thing eternally impossible for mortal man
to hoist him bodily into the air, so as to preserve all his
mighty swells and undulations. And, not to speak of the
highly presumable difference of contour between a young
sucking whale and a full-grown Platonian Leviathan; yet,
even in the case of one of those young sucking whales hoisted
to a ship's deck, such is then the outlandish, eel-like, lim-
bered, varying shape of him, that his precise expression the
devil himself could not catch.

But it may be fancied, that from the naked skeleton of the

stranded whale, accurate hints may be derived touching his true form. Not at all. For it is one of the more curious things about this Leviathan, that his skeleton gives very little idea of his general shape. Though Jeremy Bentham's skeleton, which hangs for candelabra in the library of one of his executors, correctly conveys the idea of a burly-browed utilitarian old gentleman, with all Jeremy's other leading personal characteristics; yet nothing of this kind could be inferred from any leviathan's articulated bones. In fact, as the great Hunter says, the mere skeleton of the whale bears the same relation to the fully invested and padded animal as the insect does to the chrysalis that so roundingly envelopes it. This peculiarity is strikingly evinced in the head, as in some part of this book will be incidentally shown. It is also very curiously displayed in the side fin, the bones of which almost exactly answer to the bones of the human hand, minus only the thumb. This fin has four regular bone-fingers, the index, middle, ring, and little finger. But all these are permanently lodged in their fleshy covering, as the human fingers in an artificial covering. "However recklessly the whale may sometimes serve us," said humorous Stubb one day, "he can never be truly said to handle us without mittens."

For all these reasons, then, any way you may look at it, you must needs conclude that the great Leviathan is that one creature in the world which must remain unpainted to the last. True, one portrait may hit the mark much nearer than another, but none can hit it with any very considerable degree of exactness. So there is no earthly way of finding out precisely what the whale really looks like. And the only mode in which you can derive even a tolerable idea of his living contour, is by going a whaling yourself; but by so doing, you run no small risk of being eternally stove and sunk by him. Wherefore, it seems to me you had best not be too fastidious in your curiosity touching this Leviathan.

Chapter 56

Of the Less Erroneous Pictures of Whales, and the True Pictures of Whaling Scenes

In connexion with the monstrous pictures of whales, I am strongly tempted here to enter upon those still more monstrous stories of them which are to be found in certain books, both ancient and modern, especially in Pliny, Purchas, Hackluyt, Harris, Cuvier, &c. But I pass that matter by.

I know of only four published outlines of the great Sperm Whale; Colnett's, Huggins's, Frederick Cuvier's, and Beale's. In the previous chapter Colnett and Cuvier have been referred to. Huggins's is far better than theirs; but, by great odds, Beale's is the best. All Beale's drawings of this whale are good, excepting the middle figure in the picture of three whales in various attitudes, capping his second chapter. His frontispiece, boats attacking Sperm Whales, though no doubt calculated to excite the civil scepticism of some parlor men, is admirably correct and life-like in its general effect. Some of the Sperm Whale drawings in J. Ross Browne are pretty correct in contour; but they are wretchedly engraved. That is not his fault though.

Of the Right Whale, the best outline pictures are in Scoresby; but they are drawn on too small a scale to convey a desirable impression. He has but one picture of whaling scenes, and this is a sad deficiency, because it is by such pictures only, when at all well done, that you can derive anything like a truthful idea of the living whale as seen by his living hunters.

But, taken for all in all, by far the finest, though in some details not the most correct, presentations of whales and whaling scenes to be anywhere found, are two large French engravings, well executed, and taken from paintings by one Garneray. Respectively, they represent attacks on the Sperm and Right Whale. In the first engraving a noble Sperm Whale is depicted in full majesty of might, just risen beneath the boat from the profundities of the ocean, and bearing high in the air upon his back the terrific wreck of the stoven planks.

The prow of the boat is partially unbroken, and is drawn just balancing upon the monster's spine; and standing in that prow, for that one single incomputable flash of time, you behold an oarsman, half shrouded by the incensed boiling spout of the whale, and in the act of leaping, as if from a precipice. The action of the whole thing is wonderfully good and true. The half-emptied line-tub floats on the whitened sea; the wooden poles of the spilled harpoons obliquely bob in it; the heads of the swimming crew are scattered about the whale in contrasting expressions of affright; while in the black stormy distance the ship is bearing down upon the scene. Serious fault might be found with the anatomical details of this whale, but let that pass; since, for the life of me, I could not draw so good a one.

In the second engraving, the boat is in the act of drawing alongside the barnacled flank of a large running Right Whale, that rolls his black weedy bulk in the sea like some mossy rock-slide from the Patagonian cliffs. His jets are erect, full, and black like soot; so that from so abounding a smoke in the chimney, you would think there must be a brave supper cooking in the great bowels below. Sea fowls are pecking at the small crabs, shell-fish, and other sea candies and maccaroni, which the Right Whale sometimes carries on his pestilent back. And all the while the thick-lipped leviathan is rushing through the deep, leaving tons of tumultuous white curds in his wake, and causing the slight boat to rock in the swells like a skiff caught nigh the paddle-wheels of an ocean steamer. Thus, the foreground is all raging commotion; but behind, in admirable artistic contrast, is the glassy level of a sea becalmed, the drooping unstarched sails of the powerless ship, and the inert mass of a dead whale, a conquered fortress, with the flag of capture lazily hanging from the whale-pole inserted into his spout-hole.

Who Garneray the painter is, or was, I know not. But my life for it he was either practically conversant with his subject, or else marvellously tutored by some experienced whaleman. The French are the lads for painting action. Go and gaze upon all the paintings of Europe, and where will you find such a gallery of living and breathing commotion on canvas, as in that triumphal hall at Versailles; where the beholder

fights his way, pell-mell, through the consecutive great battles
of France; where every sword seems a flash of the Northern
Lights, and the successive armed kings and Emperors dash
by, like a charge of crowned centaurs? Not wholly unworthy
of a place in that gallery, are these sea battle-pieces of Garneray.

The natural aptitude of the French for seizing the picturesqueness of things seems to be peculiarly evinced in what
paintings and engravings they have of their whaling scenes.
With not one tenth of England's experience in the fishery, and
not the thousandth part of that of the Americans, they have
nevertheless furnished both nations with the only finished
sketches at all capable of conveying the real spirit of the whale
hunt. For the most part, the English and American whale
draughtsmen seem entirely content with presenting the mechanical outline of things, such as the vacant profile of the
whale; which, so far as picturesqueness of effect is concerned,
is about tantamount to sketching the profile of a pyramid.
Even Scoresby, the justly renowned Right whaleman, after
giving us a stiff full length of the Greenland whale, and three
or four delicate miniatures of narwhales and porpoises, treats
us to a series of classical engravings of boat hooks, chopping
knives, and grapnels; and with the microscopic diligence of a
Leuwenhoeck submits to the inspection of a shivering world
ninety-six fac-similes of magnified Arctic snow crystals. I
mean no disparagement to the excellent voyager (I honor him
for a veteran), but in so important a matter it was certainly
an oversight not to have procured for every crystal a sworn
affidavit taken before a Greenland Justice of the Peace.

In addition to those fine engravings from Garneray, there
are two other French engravings worthy of note, by some one
who subscribes himself "H. Durand." One of them, though
not precisely adapted to our present purpose, nevertheless deserves mention on other accounts. It is a quiet noon-scene
among the isles of the Pacific; a French whaler anchored, in-
shore, in a calm, and lazily taking water on board; the loosened sails of the ship, and the long leaves of the palms in the
background, both drooping together in the breezeless air.
The effect is very fine, when considered with reference to its
presenting the hardy fishermen under one of their few aspects

of oriental repose. The other engraving is quite a different affair: the ship hove-to upon the open sea, and in the very heart of the Leviathanic life, with a Right Whale alongside; the vessel (in the act of cutting-in) hove over to the monster as if to a quay; and a boat, hurriedly pushing off from this scene of activity, is about giving chase to whales in the distance. The harpoons and lances lie levelled for use; three oarsmen are just setting the mast in its hole; while from a sudden roll of the sea, the little craft stands half-erect out of the water, like a rearing horse. From the ship, the smoke of the torments of the boiling whale is going up like the smoke over a village of smithies; and to windward, a black cloud, rising up with earnest of squalls and rains, seems to quicken the activity of the excited seamen.

Chapter 57

ON TOWER-HILL, as you go down to the London docks, you may have seen a crippled beggar (or *kedger*, as the sailors say) holding a painted board before him, representing the tragic scene in which he lost his leg. There are three whales and three boats; and one of the boats (presumed to contain the missing leg in all its original integrity) is being crunched by the jaws of the foremost whale. Any time these ten years, they tell me, has that man held up that picture, and exhibited that stump to an incredulous world. But the time of his justification has now come. His three whales are as good whales as were ever published in Wapping, at any rate; and his stump as unquestionable a stump as any you will find in the western clearings. But, though for ever mounted on that stump, never a stump-speech does the poor whaleman make; but, with downcast eyes, stands ruefully contemplating his own amputation.

Throughout the Pacific, and also in Nantucket, and New Bedford, and Sag Harbor, you will come across lively sketches of whales and whaling-scenes, graven by the fishermen themselves on Sperm Whale-teeth, or ladies' busks wrought out of the Right Whale-bone, and other like skrimshander articles, as the whalemen call the numerous little ingenious contrivances they elaborately carve out of the rough material, in their hours of ocean leisure. Some of them have little boxes of dentistical-looking implements, specially intended for the skrimshandering business. But, in general, they toil with their jack-knives alone; and, with that almost omnipotent tool of the sailor, they will turn you out anything you please, in the way of a mariner's fancy.

Long exile from Christendom and civilization inevitably restores a man to that condition in which God placed him, *i.e.* what is called savagery. Your true whale-hunter is as much a savage as an Iroquois. I myself am a savage, owning no allegiance but to the King of the Cannibals; and ready at any moment to rebel against him.

Now, one of the peculiar characteristics of the savage in his domestic hours, is his wonderful patience of industry. An ancient Hawaiian war-club or spear-paddle, in its full multiplicity and elaboration of carving, is as great a trophy of human perseverance as a Latin lexicon. For, with but a bit of broken sea-shell or a shark's tooth, that miraculous intricacy of wooden net-work has been achieved; and it has cost steady years of steady application.

As with the Hawaiian savage, so with the white sailor-savage. With the same marvellous patience, and with the same single shark's tooth, of his one poor jack-knife, he will carve you a bit of bone sculpture, not quite as workmanlike, but as close packed in its maziness of design, as the Greek savage, Achilles's shield; and full of barbaric spirit and suggestiveness, as the prints of that fine old Dutch savage, Albert Durer.

Wooden whales, or whales cut in profile out of the small dark slabs of the noble South Sea war-wood, are frequently met with in the forecastles of American whalers. Some of them are done with much accuracy.

At some old gable-roofed country houses you will see brass whales hung by the tail for knockers to the road-side door. When the porter is sleepy, the anvil-headed whale would be best. But these knocking whales are seldom remarkable as faithful essays. On the spires of some old-fashioned churches you will see sheet-iron whales placed there for weather-cocks; but they are so elevated, and besides that are to all intents and purposes so labelled with "*Hands off!*" you cannot examine them closely enough to decide upon their merit.

In bony, ribby regions of the earth, where at the base of high broken cliffs masses of rock lie strewn in fantastic groupings upon the plain, you will often discover images as of the petrified forms of the Leviathan partly merged in grass, which of a windy day breaks against them in a surf of green surges.

Then, again, in mountainous countries where the traveller is continually girdled by amphitheatrical heights; here and there from some lucky point of view you will catch passing glimpses of the profiles of whales defined along the undulating ridges. But you must be a thorough whaleman, to see these sights; and not only that, but if you wish to return to such a sight again, you must be sure and take the exact intersecting latitude and longitude of your first stand-point, else— so chance-like are such observations of the hills—your precise, previous stand-point would require a laborious re-discovery; like the Solomon islands, which still remain incognita, though once high-ruffed Mendanna trod them and old Figueroa chronicled them.

Nor when expandingly lifted by your subject, can you fail to trace out great whales in the starry heavens, and boats in pursuit of them; as when long filled with thoughts of war the Eastern nations saw armies locked in battle among the clouds. Thus at the North have I chased Leviathan round and round the Pole with the revolutions of the bright points that first defined him to me. And beneath the effulgent Antarctic skies I have boarded the Argo-Navis, and joined the chase against the starry Cetus far beyond the utmost stretch of Hydrus and the Flying Fish.

With a frigate's anchors for my bridle-bitts and fasces of harpoons for spurs, would I could mount that whale and leap the topmost skies, to see whether the fabled heavens with all their countless tents really lie encamped beyond my mortal sight!

Chapter 58

BRIT

Steering north-eastward from the Crozetts, we fell in with vast meadows of brit, the minute, yellow substance, upon which the Right Whale largely feeds. For leagues and leagues it undulated round us, so that we seemed to be sailing through boundless fields of ripe and golden wheat.

On the second day, numbers of Right Whales were seen, who, secure from the attack of a Sperm Whaler like the Pequod, with open jaws sluggishly swam through the brit, which, adhering to the fringing fibres of that wondrous Venetian blind in their mouths, was in that manner separated from the water that escaped at the lip.

As morning mowers, who side by side slowly and seethingly advance their scythes through the long wet grass of marshy meads; even so these monsters swam, making a strange, grassy, cutting sound; and leaving behind them endless swaths of blue upon the yellow sea.*

But it was only the sound they made as they parted the brit which at all reminded one of mowers. Seen from the mastheads, especially when they paused and were stationary for a while, their vast black forms looked more like lifeless masses of rock than anything else. And as in the great hunting countries of India, the stranger at a distance will sometimes pass on the plains recumbent elephants without knowing them to be such, taking them for bare, blackened elevations of the soil; even so, often, with him, who for the first time beholds this species of the leviathans of the sea. And even when recognised at last, their immense magnitude renders it very hard really to believe that such bulky masses of overgrowth can possibly be instinct, in all parts, with the same sort of life that lives in a dog or a horse.

*That part of the sea known among whalemen as the "Brazil Banks" does not bear that name as the Banks of Newfoundland do, because of there being shallows and soundings there, but because of this remarkable meadow-like appearance, caused by the vast drifts of brit continually floating in those latitudes, where the Right Whale is often chased.

Indeed, in other respects, you can hardly regard any creatures of the deep with the same feelings that you do those of the shore. For though some old naturalists have maintained that all creatures of the land are of their kind in the sea; and though taking a broad general view of the thing, this may very well be; yet coming to specialities, where, for example, does the ocean furnish any fish that in disposition answers to the sagacious kindness of the dog? The accursed shark alone can in any generic respect be said to bear comparative analogy to him.

But though, to landsmen in general, the native inhabitants of the seas have ever been regarded with emotions unspeakably unsocial and repelling; though we know the sea to be an everlasting terra incognita, so that Columbus sailed over numberless unknown worlds to discover his one superficial western one; though, by vast odds, the most terrific of all mortal disasters have immemorially and indiscriminately befallen tens and hundreds of thousands of those who have gone upon the waters; though but a moment's consideration will teach, that however baby man may brag of his science and skill, and however much, in a flattering future, that science and skill may augment; yet for ever and for ever, to the crack of doom, the sea will insult and murder him, and pulverize the stateliest, stiffest frigate he can make; nevertheless, by the continual repetition of these very impressions, man has lost that sense of the full awfulness of the sea which aboriginally belongs to it.

The first boat we read of, floated on an ocean, that with Portuguese vengeance had whelmed a whole world without leaving so much as a widow. That same ocean rolls now; that same ocean destroyed the wrecked ships of last year. Yea, foolish mortals, Noah's flood is not yet subsided; two thirds of the fair world it yet covers.

Wherein differ the sea and the land, that a miracle upon one is not a miracle upon the other? Preternatural terrors rested upon the Hebrews, when under the feet of Korah and his company the live ground opened and swallowed them up for ever; yet not a modern sun ever sets, but in precisely the same manner the live sea swallows up ships and crews.

But not only is the sea such a foe to man who is an alien

to it, but it is also a fiend to its own offspring; worse than the Persian host who murdered his own guests; sparing not the creatures which itself hath spawned. Like a savage tigress that tossing in the jungle overlays her own cubs, so the sea dashes even the mightiest whales against the rocks, and leaves them there side by side with the split wrecks of ships. No mercy, no power but its own controls it. Panting and snorting like a mad battle steed that has lost its rider, the masterless ocean overruns the globe.

Consider the subtleness of the sea; how its most dreaded creatures glide under water, unapparent for the most part, and treacherously hidden beneath the loveliest tints of azure. Consider also the devilish brilliance and beauty of many of its most remorseless tribes, as the dainty embellished shape of many species of sharks. Consider, once more, the universal cannibalism of the sea; all whose creatures prey upon each other, carrying on eternal war since the world began.

Consider all this; and then turn to this green, gentle, and most docile earth; consider them both, the sea and the land; and do you not find a strange analogy to something in yourself? For as this appalling ocean surrounds the verdant land, so in the soul of man there lies one insular Tahiti, full of peace and joy, but encompassed by all the horrors of the half known life. God keep thee! Push not off from that isle, thou canst never return!

Chapter 59

SQUID

S LOWLY wading through the meadows of brit, the Pequod still held on her way north-eastward towards the island of Java; a gentle air impelling her keel, so that in the surrounding serenity her three tall tapering masts mildly waved to that languid breeze, as three mild palms on a plain. And still, at wide intervals in the silvery night, the lonely, alluring jet would be seen.

But one transparent blue morning, when a stillness almost preternatural spread over the sea, however unattended with any stagnant calm; when the long burnished sun-glade on the waters seemed a golden finger laid across them, enjoining some secresy; when the slippered waves whispered together as they softly ran on; in this profound hush of the visible sphere a strange spectre was seen by Daggoo from the main-mast-head.

In the distance, a great white mass lazily rose, and rising higher and higher, and disentangling itself from the azure, at last gleamed before our prow like a snow-slide, new slid from the hills. Thus glistening for a moment, as slowly it subsided, and sank. Then once more arose, and silently gleamed. It seemed not a whale; and yet is this Moby Dick? thought Daggoo. Again the phantom went down, but on re-appearing once more, with a stiletto-like cry that startled every man from his nod, the negro yelled out—"There! there again! there she breaches! right ahead! The White Whale, the White Whale!"

Upon this, the seamen rushed to the yard-arms, as in swarming-time the bees rush to the boughs. Bare-headed in the sultry sun, Ahab stood on the bowsprit, and with one hand pushed far behind in readiness to wave his orders to the helmsman, cast his eager glance in the direction indicated aloft by the outstretched motionless arm of Daggoo.

Whether the flitting attendance of the one still and solitary jet had gradually worked upon Ahab, so that he was now prepared to connect the ideas of mildness and repose with the first sight of the particular whale he pursued; however this was, or whether his eagerness betrayed him; whichever way it might have been, no sooner did he distinctly perceive the white mass, than with a quick intensity he instantly gave orders for lowering.

The four boats were soon on the water; Ahab's in advance, and all swiftly pulling towards their prey. Soon it went down, and while, with oars suspended, we were awaiting its reappearance, lo! in the same spot where it sank, once more it slowly rose. Almost forgetting for the moment all thoughts of Moby Dick, we now gazed at the most wondrous phenomenon which the secret seas have hitherto revealed to mankind. A vast pulpy mass, furlongs in length and breadth, of a glancing cream-color, lay floating on the water, innumerable long arms radiating from its centre, and curling and twisting like a nest of anacondas, as if blindly to clutch at any hapless object within reach. No perceptible face or front did it have; no conceivable token of either sensation or instinct; but undulated there on the billows, an unearthly, formless, chance-like apparition of life.

As with a low sucking sound it slowly disappeared again, Starbuck still gazing at the agitated waters where it had sunk, with a wild voice exclaimed—"Almost rather had I seen Moby Dick and fought him, than to have seen thee, thou white ghost!"

"What was it, Sir?" said Flask.

"The great live squid, which, they say, few whale-ships ever beheld, and returned to their ports to tell of it."

But Ahab said nothing; turning his boat, he sailed back to the vessel; the rest as silently following.

Whatever superstitions the sperm whalemen in general have connected with the sight of this object, certain it is, that a glimpse of it being so very unusual, that circumstance has gone far to invest it with portentousness. So rarely is it beheld, that though one and all of them declare it to be the largest animated thing in the ocean, yet very few of them have any but the most vague ideas concerning its true nature and form; notwithstanding, they believe it to furnish to the sperm whale his only food. For though other species of whales find their food above water, and may be seen by man in the act of feeding, the spermaceti whale obtains his whole food in unknown zones below the surface; and only by inference is it that any one can tell of what, precisely, that food consists. At times, when closely pursued, he will disgorge what are supposed to be the detached arms of the squid; some of them thus exhibited exceeding twenty and thirty feet in length. They fancy that the monster to which these arms belonged ordinarily clings by them to the bed of the ocean; and that the sperm whale, unlike other species, is supplied with teeth in order to attack and tear it.

There seems some ground to imagine that the great Kraken of Bishop Pontoppidan may ultimately resolve itself into Squid. The manner in which the Bishop describes it, as alternately rising and sinking, with some other particulars he narrates, in all this the two correspond. But much abatement is necessary with respect to the incredible bulk he assigns it.

By some naturalists who have vaguely heard rumors of the mysterious creature, here spoken of, it is included among the class of cuttle-fish, to which, indeed, in certain external respects it would seem to belong, but only as the Anak of the tribe.

Chapter 60

THE LINE

WITH REFERENCE to the whaling scene shortly to be described, as well as for the better understanding of all similar scenes elsewhere presented, I have here to speak of the magical, sometimes horrible whale-line.

The line originally used in the fishery was of the best hemp, slightly vapored with tar, not impregnated with it, as in the case of ordinary ropes; for while tar, as ordinarily used, makes the hemp more pliable to the rope-maker, and also renders the rope itself more convenient to the sailor for common ship use; yet, not only would the ordinary quantity too much stiffen the whale-line for the close coiling to which it must be subjected; but as most seamen are beginning to learn, tar in general by no means adds to the rope's durability or strength, however much it may give it compactness and gloss.

Of late years the Manilla rope has in the American fishery almost entirely superseded hemp as a material for whale-lines; for, though not so durable as hemp, it is stronger, and far more soft and elastic; and I will add (since there is an æsthetics in all things), is much more handsome and becoming to the boat, than hemp. Hemp is a dusky, dark fellow, a sort of Indian; but Manilla is as a golden-haired Circassian to behold.

The whale line is only two thirds of an inch in thickness. At first sight, you would not think it so strong as it really is. By experiment its one and fifty yarns will each suspend a weight of one hundred and twelve pounds; so that the whole rope will bear a strain nearly equal to three tons. In length, the common sperm whale-line measures something over two hundred fathoms. Towards the stern of the boat it is spirally coiled away in the tub, not like the worm-pipe of a still though, but so as to form one round, cheese-shaped mass of densely bedded "sheaves," or layers of concentric spiralizations, without any hollow but the "heart," or minute vertical tube formed at the axis of the cheese. As the least tangle or kink in the coiling would, in running out, infallibly take somebody's arm, leg, or entire body off, the utmost precaution is used in stowing the line in its tub. Some harpooneers will consume almost an entire morning in this business, carrying the line high aloft and then reeving it downwards through a block towards the tub, so as in the act of coiling to free it from all possible wrinkles and twists.

In the English boats two tubs are used instead of one; the same line being continuously coiled in both tubs. There is some advantage in this; because these twin-tubs being so small they fit more readily into the boat, and do not strain it so much; whereas, the American tub, nearly three feet in diameter and of proportionate depth, makes a rather bulky freight for a craft whose planks are but one half-inch in thickness; for the bottom of the whale-boat is like critical ice, which will bear up a considerable distributed weight, but not very much of a concentrated one. When the painted canvas cover is clapped on the American line-tub, the boat looks as if it were pulling off with a prodigious great wedding-cake to present to the whales.

Both ends of the line are exposed; the lower end terminating in an eye-splice or loop coming up from the bottom against the side of the tub, and hanging over its edge completely disengaged from everything. This arrangement of the lower end is necessary on two accounts. First: In order to facilitate the fastening to it of an additional line from a neighboring boat, in case the stricken whale should sound so deep as to threaten to carry off the entire line originally attached to the harpoon. In these instances, the whale of course is shifted like a mug of ale, as it were, from the one boat to the other; though the first boat always hovers at hand to assist its consort. Second: This arrangement is indispensable for common safety's sake; for were the lower end of the line in any way attached to the boat, and were the whale then to run the line out to the end almost in a single, smoking minute as he sometimes does, he would not stop there, for the doomed boat would infallibly be dragged down after him into the profundity of the sea; and in that case no town-crier would ever find her again.

Before lowering the boat for the chase, the upper end of

the line is taken aft from the tub, and passing round the loggerhead there, is again carried forward the entire length of
the boat, resting crosswise upon the loom or handle of every
man's oar, so that it jogs against his wrist in rowing; and also
passing between the men, as they alternately sit at the opposite gunwales, to the leaded chocks or grooves in the extreme
pointed prow of the boat, where a wooden pin or skewer the
size of a common quill, prevents it from slipping out. From
the chocks it hangs in a slight festoon over the bows, and is
then passed inside the boat again; and some ten or twenty
fathoms (called box-line) being coiled upon the box in the
bows, it continues its way to the gunwale still a little further
aft, and is then attached to the short-warp—the rope which
is immediately connected with the harpoon; but previous to
that connexion, the short-warp goes through sundry mystifi-
cations too tedious to detail.

Thus the whale-line folds the whole boat in its complicated
coils, twisting and writhing around it in almost every direction. All the oarsmen are involved in its perilous contortions;
so that to the timid eye of the landsman, they seem as Indian
jugglers, with the deadliest snakes sportively festooning their
limbs. Nor can any son of mortal woman, for the first time,
seat himself amid those hempen intricacies, and while straining his utmost at the oar, bethink him that at any unknown
instant the harpoon may be darted, and all these horrible contortions be put in play like ringed lightnings; he cannot be
thus circumstanced without a shudder that makes the very
marrow in his bones to quiver in him like a shaken jelly. Yet
habit—strange thing! what cannot habit accomplish?—Gayer
sallies, more merry mirth, better jokes, and brighter repartees,
you never heard over your mahogany, than you will hear over
the half-inch white cedar of the whale-boat, when thus hung
in hangman's nooses; and, like the six burghers of Calais before King Edward, the six men composing the crew pull into
the jaws of death, with a halter around every neck, as you
may say.

Perhaps a very little thought will now enable you to account for those repeated whaling disasters—some few of
which are casually chronicled—of this man or that man being
taken out of the boat by the line, and lost. For, when the line

is darting out, to be seated then in the boat, is like being seated in the midst of the manifold whizzings of a steam-engine in full play, when every flying beam, and shaft, and wheel, is grazing you. It is worse; for you cannot sit motion-less in the heart of these perils, because the boat is rocking like a cradle, and you are pitched one way and the other, without the slightest warning; and only by a certain self-ad-justing buoyancy and simultaneousness of volition and action, can you escape being made a Mazeppa of, and run away with where the all-seeing sun himself could never pierce you out.

Again: as the profound calm which only apparently pre-cedes and prophesies of the storm, is perhaps more awful than the storm itself; for, indeed, the calm is but the wrapper and envelope of the storm; and contains it in itself, as the seem-ingly harmless rifle holds the fatal powder, and the ball, and the explosion; so the graceful repose of the line, as it silently serpentines about the oarsmen before being brought into ac-tual play—this is a thing which carries more of true terror than any other aspect of this dangerous affair. But why say more? All men live enveloped in whale-lines. All are born with halters round their necks; but it is only when caught in the swift, sudden turn of death, that mortals realize the silent, subtle, ever-present perils of life. And if you be a philosopher, though seated in the whale-boat, you would not at heart feel one whit more of terror, than though seated before your eve-ning fire with a poker, and not a harpoon, by your side.

Chapter 61

STUBB KILLS A WHALE

If to Starbuck the apparition of the Squid was a thing of portents, to Queequeg it was quite a different object.

"When you see him 'quid," said the savage, honing his harpoon in the bow of his hoisted boat, "then you quick see him 'parm whale."

The next day was exceedingly still and sultry, and with nothing special to engage them, the Pequod's crew could hardly resist the spell of sleep induced by such a vacant sea. For this part of the Indian Ocean through which we then were voyaging is not what whalemen call a lively ground; that is, it affords fewer glimpses of porpoises, dolphins, flying-fish, and other vivacious denizens of more stirring waters, than those off the Rio de la Plata, or the in-shore ground off Peru.

It was my turn to stand at the foremast-head; and with my shoulders leaning against the slackened royal shrouds, to and fro I idly swayed in what seemed an enchanted air. No resolution could withstand it; in that dreamy mood losing all consciousness, at last my soul went out of my body; though my body still continued to sway as a pendulum will, long after the power which first moved it is withdrawn.

Ere forgetfulness altogether came over me, I had noticed that the seamen at the main and mizen mast-heads were already drowsy. So that at last all three of us lifelessly swung from the spars, and for every swing that we made there was a nod from below from the slumbering helmsman. The waves, too, nodded their indolent crests; and across the wide trance of the sea, east nodded to west, and the sun over all.

Suddenly bubbles seemed bursting beneath my closed eyes; like vices my hands grasped the shrouds; some invisible, gracious agency preserved me; with a shock I came back to life. And lo! close under our lee, not forty fathoms off, a gigantic Sperm Whale lay rolling in the water like the capsized hull of a frigate, his broad, glossy back, of an Ethiopian hue, glistening in the sun's rays like a mirror. But lazily undulating in the trough of the sea, and ever and anon tranquilly spouting his vapory jet, the whale looked like a portly burgher smoking his pipe of a warm afternoon. But that pipe, poor whale, was thy last. As if struck by some enchanter's wand, the sleepy ship and every sleeper in it all at once started into wakefulness; and more than a score of voices from all parts of the vessel, simultaneously with the three notes from aloft, shouted forth the accustomed cry, as the great fish slowly and regularly spouted the sparkling brine into the air.

"Clear away the boats! Luff!" cried Ahab. And obeying his own order, he dashed the helm down before the helmsman could handle the spokes.

The sudden exclamations of the crew must have alarmed the whale; and ere the boats were down, majestically turning, he swam away to the leeward, but with such a steady tranquillity, and making so few ripples as he swam, that thinking after all he might not as yet be alarmed, Ahab gave orders that not an oar should be used, and no man must speak but in whispers. So seated like Ontario Indians on the gunwales of the boats, we swiftly but silently paddled along; the calm not admitting of the noiseless sails being set. Presently, as we thus glided in chase, the monster perpendicularly flitted his tail forty feet into the air, and then sank out of sight like a tower swallowed up.

"There go flukes!" was the cry, an announcement immediately followed by Stubb's producing his match and igniting his pipe, for now a respite was granted. After the full interval of his sounding had elapsed, the whale rose again, and being now in advance of the smoker's boat, and much nearer to it than to any of the others, Stubb counted upon the honor of the capture. It was obvious, now, that the whale had at length become aware of his pursuers. All silence of cautiousness was therefore no longer of use. Paddles were dropped, and oars came loudly into play. And still puffing at his pipe, Stubb cheered on his crew to the assault.

Yes, a mighty change had come over the fish. All alive to his jeopardy, he was going "head out;" that part obliquely projecting from the mad yeast which he brewed.*

*It will be seen in some other place of what a very light substance the entire interior of the sperm whale's enormous head consists. Though appar-

"Start her, start her, my men! Don't hurry yourselves; take plenty of time—but start her; start her like thunder-claps, that's all," cried Stubb, spluttering out the smoke as he spoke. "Start her, now; give 'em the long and strong stroke, Tashtego. Start her, Tash, my boy—start her, all; but keep cool, keep cool—cucumbers is the word—easy, easy—only start her like grim death and grinning devils, and raise the buried dead perpendicular out of their graves, boys—that's all. Start her!"

"Woo-hoo! Wa-hee!" screamed the Gay-Header in reply, raising some old war-whoop to the skies; as every oarsman in the strained boat involuntarily bounced forward with the one tremendous leading stroke which the eager Indian gave.

But his wild screams were answered by others quite as wild. "Kee-hee! Kee-hee!" yelled Daggoo, straining forwards and backwards on his seat, like a pacing tiger in his cage.

"Ka-la! Koo-loo!" howled Queequeg, as if smacking his lips over a mouthful of Grenadier's steak. And thus with oars and yells the keels cut the sea. Meanwhile, Stubb retaining his place in the van, still encouraged his men to the onset, all the while puffing the smoke from his mouth. Like desperadoes they tugged and they strained, till the welcome cry was heard—"Stand up, Tashtego!—give it to him!" The harpoon was hurled. "Stern all!" The oarsmen backed water; the same moment something went hot and hissing along every one of their wrists. It was the magical line. An instant before, Stubb had swiftly caught two additional turns with it round the loggerhead, whence, by reason of its increased rapid circlings, a hempen blue smoke now jetted up and mingled with the steady fumes from his pipe. As the line passed round and round the loggerhead; so also, just before reaching that point, it blisteringly passed through and through both of Stubb's hands, from which the hand-cloths, or squares of quilted

---

ently the most massive, it is by far the most buoyant part about him. So that with ease he elevates it in the air, and invariably does so when going at his utmost speed. Besides, such is the breadth of the upper part of the front of his head, and such the tapering cut-water formation of the lower part, that by obliquely elevating his head, he thereby may be said to transform himself from a bluff-bowed sluggish galliot into a sharp-pointed New York pilot-boat.

canvas sometimes worn at these times, had accidentally
dropped. It was like holding an enemy's sharp two-edged
sword by the blade, and that enemy all the time striving to
wrest it out of your clutch.

"Wet the line! wet the line!" cried Stubb to the tub oarsman (him seated by the tub) who, snatching off his hat,
dashed the sea-water into it.* More turns were taken, so that
the line began holding its place. The boat now flew through
the boiling water like a shark all fins. Stubb and Tashtego
here changed places—stem for stern—a staggering business
truly in that rocking commotion.

From the vibrating line extending the entire length of the
upper part of the boat, and from its now being more tight
than a harpstring, you would have thought the craft had two
keels—one cleaving the water, the other the air—as the boat
churned on through both opposing elements at once. A continual cascade played at the bows; a ceaseless whirling eddy
in her wake; and, at the slightest motion from within, even
but of a little finger, the vibrating, cracking craft canted over
her spasmodic gunwale into the sea. Thus they rushed; each
man with might and main clinging to his seat, to prevent
being tossed to the foam; and the tall form of Tashtego at
the steering oar crouching almost double, in order to bring
down his centre of gravity. Whole Atlantics and Pacifics
seemed passed as they shot on their way, till at length the
whale somewhat slackened his flight.

"Haul in—haul in!" cried Stubb to the bowsman; and, facing round towards the whale, all hands began pulling the
boat up to him, while yet the boat was being towed on. Soon
ranging up by his flank, Stubb, firmly planting his knee in the
clumsy cleat, darted dart after dart into the flying fish; at the
word of command, the boat alternately sterning out of the
way of the whale's horrible wallow, and then ranging up for
another fling.

The red tide now poured from all sides of the monster like
brooks down a hill. His tormented body rolled not in brine

---

*Partly to show the indispensableness of this act, it may here be stated,
that, in the old Dutch fishery, a mop was used to dash the running line with
water; in many other ships, a wooden piggin, or bailer, is set apart for that
purpose. Your hat, however, is the most convenient.

but in blood, which bubbled and seethed for furlongs behind in their wake. The slanting sun playing upon this crimson pond in the sea, sent back its reflection into every face, so that they all glowed to each other like red men. And all the while, jet after jet of white smoke was agonizingly shot from the spiracle of the whale, and vehement puff after puff from the mouth of the excited headsman; as at every dart, hauling in upon his crooked lance (by the line attached to it), Stubb straightened it again and again, by a few rapid blows against the gunwale, then again and again sent it into the whale.

"Pull up—pull up!" he now cried to the bowsman, as the waning whale relaxed in his wrath. "Pull up!—close to!" and the boat ranged along the fish's flank. When reaching far over the bow, Stubb slowly churned his long sharp lance into the fish, and kept it there, carefully churning and churning, as if cautiously seeking to feel after some gold watch that the whale might have swallowed, and which he was fearful of breaking ere he could hook it out. But that gold watch he sought was the innermost life of the fish. And now it is struck; for, starting from his trance into that unspeakable thing called his "flurry," the monster horribly wallowed in his blood, overwrapped himself in impenetrable, mad, boiling spray, so that the imperilled craft, instantly dropping astern, had much ado blindly to struggle out from that phrensied twilight into the clear air of the day.

And now abating in his flurry, the whale once more rolled out into view; surging from side to side; spasmodically dilating and contracting his spout-hole, with sharp, cracking, agonized respirations. At last, gush after gush of clotted red gore, as if it had been the purple lees of red wine, shot into the frighted air; and falling back again, ran dripping down his motionless flanks into the sea. His heart had burst!

"He's dead, Mr. Stubb," said Tashtego.

"Yes; both pipes smoked out!" and withdrawing his own from his mouth, Stubb scattered the dead ashes over the water; and, for a moment, stood thoughtfully eyeing the vast corpse he had made.

Chapter 62

THE DART

A WORD concerning an incident in the last chapter.
According to the invariable usage of the fishery,
the whale-boat pushes off from the ship, with the headsman
or whale-killer as temporary steersman, and the harpooneer or
whale-fastener pulling the foremost oar, the one known as the
harpooneer-oar. Now it needs a strong, nervous arm to strike
the first iron into the fish; for often, in what is called a long
dart, the heavy implement has to be flung to the distance of
twenty or thirty feet. But however prolonged and exhausting
the chase, the harpooneer is expected to pull his oar meanwhile to the uttermost; indeed, he is expected to set an example of superhuman activity to the rest, not only by
incredible rowing, but by repeated loud and intrepid exclamations; and what it is to keep shouting at the top of one's
compass, while all the other muscles are strained and half
started—what that is none know but those who have tried it.
For one, I cannot bawl very heartily and work very recklessly
at one and the same time. In this straining, bawling state,
then, with his back to the fish, all at once the exhausted harpooneer hears the exciting cry—"Stand up, and give it to
him!" He now has to drop and secure his oar, turn round on
his centre half way, seize his harpoon from the crotch, and
with what little strength may remain, he essays to pitch it
somehow into the whale. No wonder, taking the whole fleet
of whalemen in a body, that out of fifty fair chances for a
dart, not five are successful; no wonder that so many hapless
harpooneers are madly cursed and disrated; no wonder that
some of them actually burst their blood-vessels in the boat;
no wonder that some sperm whalemen are absent four years
with four barrels; no wonder that to many ship owners, whaling is but a losing concern; for it is the harpooneer that
makes the voyage, and if you take the breath out of his body
how can you expect to find it there when most wanted!

Again, if the dart be successful, then at the second critical instant, that is, when the whale starts to run, the boat-header and harpooneer likewise start to running fore and aft, to the imminent jeopardy of themselves and every one else. It is then they change places; and the headsman, the chief officer of the little craft, takes his proper station in the bows of the boat.

Now, I care not who maintains the contrary, but all this is both foolish and unnecessary. The headsman should stay in the bows from first to last; he should both dart the harpoon and the lance, and no rowing whatever should be expected of him, except under circumstances obvious to any fisherman. I know that this would sometimes involve a slight loss of speed in the chase; but long experience in various whalemen of more than one nation has convinced me that in the vast majority of failures in the fishery, it has not by any means been so much the speed of the whale as the before described exhaustion of the harpooneer that has caused them.

To insure the greatest efficiency in the dart, the harpooneers of this world must start to their feet from out of idleness, and not from out of toil.

Chapter 63

THE CROTCH

O UT OF THE TRUNK, the branches grow; out of them, the twigs. So, in productive subjects, grow the chapters.

The crotch alluded to on a previous page deserves independent mention. It is a notched stick of a peculiar form, some two feet in length, which is perpendicularly inserted into the starboard gunwale near the bow, for the purpose of furnishing a rest for the wooden extremity of the harpoon, whose other naked, barbed end slopingly projects from the prow. Thereby the weapon is instantly at hand to its hurler, who snatches it up as readily from its rest as a backwoodsman swings his rifle from the wall. It is customary to have two harpoons reposing in the crotch, respectively called the first and second irons.

But these two harpoons, each by its own cord, are both connected with the line; the object being this: to dart them both, if possible, one instantly after the other into the same whale; so that if, in the coming drag, one should draw out, the other may still retain a hold. It is a doubling of the chances. But it very often happens that owing to the instantaneous, violent, convulsive running of the whale upon receiving the first iron, it becomes impossible for the harpooneer, however lightning-like in his movements, to pitch the second iron into him. Nevertheless, as the second iron is already connected with the line, and the line is running, hence that weapon must, at all events, be anticipatingly tossed out of the boat, somehow and somewhere; else the most terrible jeopardy would involve all hands. Tumbled into the water, it accordingly is in such cases; the spare coils of box line (mentioned in a preceding chapter) making this feat, in most instances, prudently practicable. But this critical act is not always unattended with the saddest and most fatal casualties.

Furthermore: you must know that when the second iron is thrown overboard, it thenceforth becomes a dangling, sharp-edged terror, skittishly curvetting about both boat and whale, entangling the lines, or cutting them, and making a prodigious sensation in all directions. Nor, in general, is it possible to secure it again until the whale is fairly captured and a corpse.

Consider, now, how it must be in the case of four boats all engaging one unusually strong, active, and knowing whale; when owing to these qualities in him, as well as to the thousand concurring accidents of such an audacious enterprise, eight or ten loose second irons may be simultaneously dangling about him. For, of course, each boat is supplied with several harpoons to bend on to the line should the first one be ineffectually darted without recovery. All these particulars are faithfully narrated here, as they will not fail to elucidate several most important, however intricate passages, in scenes hereafter to be painted.

Chapter 64

STUBB'S SUPPER

S TUBB'S WHALE had been killed some distance from the ship. It was a calm; so, forming a tandem of three boats, we commenced the slow business of towing the trophy to the Pequod. And now, as we eighteen men with our thirty-six arms, and one hundred and eighty thumbs and fingers, slowly toiled hour after hour upon that inert, sluggish corpse in the sea; and it seemed hardly to budge at all, except at long intervals; good evidence was hereby furnished of the enormousness of the mass we moved. For, upon the great canal of Hang-Ho, or whatever they call it, in China, four or five laborers on the foot-path will draw a bulky freighted junk at the rate of a mile an hour; but this grand argosy we towed heavily forged along, as if laden with pig-lead in bulk.

Darkness came on; but three lights up and down in the Pequod's main-rigging dimly guided our way; till drawing nearer we saw Ahab dropping one of several more lanterns over the bulwarks. Vacantly eyeing the heaving whale for a moment, he issued the usual orders for securing it for the night, and then handing his lantern to a seaman, went his way into the cabin, and did not come forward again until morning.

Though, in overseeing the pursuit of this whale, Captain Ahab had evinced his customary activity, to call it so; yet now that the creature was dead, some vague dissatisfaction, or impatience, or despair, seemed working in him; as if the sight of that dead body reminded him that Moby Dick was yet to be slain; and though a thousand other whales were brought to his ship, all that would not one jot advance his grand, monomaniac object. Very soon you would have thought from the sound on the Pequod's decks, that all hands were preparing to cast anchor in the deep; for heavy chains are being dragged along the deck, and thrust rattling out of the port-holes. But by those clanking links, the vast corpse itself, not the ship, is to be moored. Tied by the head to the stern, and by the tail to the bows, the whale now lies with its black hull close to the vessel's, and seen through the darkness of the night, which obscured the spars and rigging aloft, the two—ship and whale, seemed yoked together like colossal bullocks, whereof one reclines while the other remains standing.*

If moody Ahab was now all quiescence, at least so far as could be known on deck, Stubb, his second mate, flushed with conquest, betrayed an unusual but still good-natured excitement. Such an unwonted bustle was he in that the staid Starbuck, his official superior, quietly resigned to him for the time the sole management of affairs. One small, helping cause of all this liveliness in Stubb, was soon made strangely manifest. Stubb was a high liver; he was somewhat intemperately fond of the whale as a flavorish thing to his palate.

"A steak, a steak, ere I sleep! You, Daggoo! overboard you go, and cut me one from his small!"

Here be it known, that though these wild fishermen do not, as a general thing, and according to the great military maxim, make the enemy defray the current expenses of the war (at least before realizing the proceeds of the voyage), yet now and then you find some of these Nantucketers who have a genuine relish for that particular part of the Sperm Whale designated by Stubb; comprising the tapering extremity of the body.

About midnight that steak was cut and cooked; and lighted by two lanterns of sperm oil, Stubb stoutly stood up to his spermaceti supper at the capstan-head, as if that capstan were a sideboard. Nor was Stubb the only banqueter on whale's flesh that night. Mingling their mumblings with his own mas-

*A little item may as well be related here. The strongest and most reliable hold which the ship has upon the whale when moored alongside, is by the flukes or tail; and as from its greater density that part is relatively heavier than any other (excepting the side-fins), its flexibility even in death, causes it to sink low beneath the surface; so that with the hand you cannot get at it from the boat, in order to put the chain round it. But this difficulty is ingeniously overcome: a small, strong line is prepared with a wooden float at its outer end, and a weight in its middle, while the other end is secured to the ship. By adroit management the wooden float is made to rise on the other side of the mass, so that now having girdled the whale, the chain is readily made to follow suit; and being slipped along the body, is at last locked fast round the smallest part of the tail, at the point of junction with its broad flukes or lobes.

tications, thousands on thousands of sharks, swarming round the dead leviathan, smackingly feasted on its fatness. The few sleepers below in their bunks were often startled by the sharp slapping of their tails against the hull, within a few inches of the sleepers' hearts. Peering over the side you could just see them (as before you heard them) wallowing in the sullen, black waters, and turning over on their backs as they scooped out huge globular pieces of the whale of the bigness of a human head. This particular feat of the shark seems all but miraculous. How, at such an apparently unassailable surface, they contrive to gouge out such symmetrical mouth-fuls, remains a part of the universal problem of all things. The mark they thus leave on the whale, may best be likened to the hollow made by a carpenter in countersinking for a screw.

Though amid all the smoking horror and diabolism of a sea-fight, sharks will be seen longingly gazing up to the ship's decks, like hungry dogs round a table where red meat is being carved, ready to bolt down every killed man that is tossed to them; and though, while the valiant butchers over the deck-table are thus cannibally carving each other's live meat with carving-knives all gilded and tasselled, the sharks, also, with their jewel-hilted mouths, are quarrelsomely carving away un-der the table at the dead meat; and though, were you to turn the whole affair upside down, it would still be pretty much the same thing, that is to say, a shocking sharkish business enough for all parties; and though sharks also are the invari-able outriders of all slave ships crossing the Atlantic, system-atically trotting alongside, to be handy in case a parcel is to be carried anywhere, or a dead slave to be decently buried; and though one or two other like instances might be set down, touching the set terms, places, and occasions, when sharks do most socially congregate, and most hilariously feast; yet is there no conceivable time or occasion when you will find them in such countless numbers, and in gayer or more jovial spirits, than around a dead sperm whale, moored by night to a whale-ship at sea. If you have never seen that sight, then suspend your decision about the propriety of devil-worship, and the expediency of conciliating the devil.

But, as yet, Stubb heeded not the mumblings of the ban-

quet that was going on so nigh him, no more than the sharks
heeded the smacking of his own epicurean lips.

"Cook, cook!—where's that old Fleece?" he cried at length,
widening his legs still further, as if to form a more secure base
for his supper; and, at the same time, darting his fork into
the dish, as if stabbing with his lance; "cook, you cook!—sail
this way, cook!"

The old black, not in any very high glee at having been
previously roused from his warm hammock at a most unseasonable hour, came shambling along from his galley, for, like
many old blacks, there was something the matter with his
knee-pans, which he did not keep well scoured like his other
pans; this old Fleece, as they called him, came shuffling and
limping along, assisting his step with his tongs, which, after
a clumsy fashion, were made of straightened iron hoops; this
old Ebony floundered along, and in obedience to the word of
command, came to a dead stop on the opposite side of
Stubb's sideboard; when, with both hands folded before him,
and resting on his two-legged cane, he bowed his arched back
still further over, at the same time sideways inclining his head,
so as to bring his best ear into play.

"Cook," said Stubb, rapidly lifting a rather reddish morsel
to his mouth, "don't you think this steak is rather overdone?
You've been beating this steak too much, cook; it's too tender. Don't I always say that to be good, a whale-steak must
be tough? There are those sharks now over the side, don't
you see they prefer it tough and rare? What a shindy they are
kicking up! Cook, go and talk to 'em; tell 'em they are welcome to help themselves civilly, and in moderation, but they
must keep quiet. Blast me, if I can hear my own voice. Away,
cook, and deliver my message. Here, take this lantern,"
snatching one from his sideboard; "now then, go and preach
to 'em!"

Sullenly taking the offered lantern, old Fleece limped across
the deck to the bulwarks; and then, with one hand dropping
his light low over the sea, so as to get a good view of his
congregation, with the other hand he solemnly flourished his
tongs, and leaning far over the side in a mumbling voice began addressing the sharks, while Stubb, softly crawling behind, overheard all that was said.

"Fellow-critters: I'se ordered here to say dat you must stop dat dam noise dare. You hear? Stop dat dam smackin' ob de lip! Massa Stubb say dat you can fill your dam bellies up to de hatchings, but by Gor! you must stop dat dam racket!"

"Cook," here interposed Stubb, accompanying the word with a sudden slap on the shoulder,—"Cook! why, damn your eyes, you mustn't swear that way when you're preaching. That's no way to convert sinners, Cook!"

"Who dat? Den preach to him yourself," sullenly turning to go.

"No, Cook; go on, go on."

"Well, den, Belubed fellow-critters:"—

"Right!" exclaimed Stubb, approvingly, "coax 'em to it; try that," and Fleece continued.

"Dough you is all sharks, and by natur wery woracious, yet I zay to you, fellow-critters, dat dat woraciousness—'top dat dam slappin' ob de tail! How you tink to hear, 'spose you keep up such a dam slappin' and bitin' dare?"

"Cook," cried Stubb, collaring him, "I wont have that swearing. Talk to 'em gentlemanly."

Once more the sermon proceeded.

"Your woraciousness, fellow-critters, I don't blame ye so much for; dat is natur, and can't be helped; but to gobern dat wicked natur, dat is de pint. You is sharks, sartin; but if you gobern de shark in you, why den you be angel; for all angel is not'ing more dan de shark well goberned. Now, look here, bred'ren, just try wonst to be cibil, a helping yourselbs from dat whale. Don't be tearin' de blubber out your neighbour's mout, I say. Is not one shark good right as toder to dat whale? And, by Gor, none on you has de right to dat whale; dat whale belong to some one else. I know some o' you has berry brig mout, brigger dan oders; but den de brig mouts sometimes has de small bellies; so dat de brigness ob de mout is not to swallar wid, but to bite off de blubber for de small fry ob sharks, dat can't get into de scrouge to help demselves."

"Well done, old Fleece!" cried Stubb, "that's Christianity; go on."

"No use goin' on; de dam willains will keep a scrougin' and slappin' each oder, Massa Stubb; dey don't hear one word;

no use a-preachin' to such dam g'uttons as you call 'em, till
dare bellies is full, and dare bellies is bottomless; and when
dey do get em full, dey wont hear you den; for den dey sink
in de sea, go fast to sleep on de coral, and can't hear not'ing
at all, no more, for eber and eber."

"Upon my soul, I am about of the same opinion; so give
the benediction, Fleece, and I'll away to my supper."

Upon this, Fleece, holding both hands over the fishy mob,
raised his shrill voice, and cried—

"Cussed fellow-critters! Kick up de damndest row as ever
you can; fill your dam' bellies 'till dey bust—and den die."

"Now, cook," said Stubb, resuming his supper at the capstan; "Stand just where you stood before, there, over against
me, and pay particular attention."

"All dention," said Fleece, again stooping over upon his
tongs in the desired position.

"Well," said Stubb, helping himself freely meanwhile; "I
shall now go back to the subject of this steak. In the first
place, how old are you, cook?"

"What dat do wid de 'teak," said the old black, testily.

"Silence! How old are you, cook?"

" 'Bout ninety, dey say," he gloomily muttered.

"And have you lived in this world hard upon one hundred
years, cook, and don't know yet how to cook a whale-steak?"
rapidly bolting another mouthful at the last word, so that that
morsel seemed a continuation of the question. "Where were
you born, cook?"

" 'Hind de hatchway, in ferry-boat, goin' ober de Roanoke."

"Born in a ferry-boat! That's queer, too. But I want to
know what country you were born in, cook?"

"Didn't I say de Roanoke country?" he cried, sharply.

"No, you didn't cook; but I'll tell you what I'm coming to,
cook. You must go home and be born over again; you don't
know how to cook a whale-steak yet."

"Bress my soul, if I cook noder one," he growled, angrily,
turning round to depart.

"Come back, cook;—here, hand me those tongs;—now
take that bit of steak there, and tell me if you think that steak
cooked as it should be? Take it, I say"—holding the tongs
towards him—"take it, and taste it."

Faintly smacking his withered lips over it for a moment, the old negro muttered, "Best cooked 'teak I eber taste; joosy, berry joosy."

"Cook," said Stubb, squaring himself once more; "do you belong to the church?"

"Passed one once in Cape-Down," said the old man sullenly.

"And you have once in your life passed a holy church in Cape-Town, where you doubtless overheard a holy parson addressing his hearers as his beloved fellow-creatures, have you, cook! And yet you come here, and tell me such a dreadful lie as you did just now, eh?" said Stubb. "Where do you expect to go to, cook?"

"Go to bed berry soon," he mumbled, half-turning as he spoke.

"Avast! heave to! I mean when you die, cook. It's an awful question. Now what's your answer?"

"When dis old brack man dies," said the negro slowly, changing his whole air and demeanor, "he hisself won't go nowhere; but some bressed angel will come and fetch him."

"Fetch him? How? In a coach and four, as they fetched Elijah? And fetch him where?"

"Up dere," said Fleece, holding his tongs straight over his head, and keeping it there very solemnly.

"So, then, you expect to go up into our main-top, do you, cook, when you are dead? But don't you know the higher you climb, the colder it gets? Main-top eh?"

"Didn't say dat t'all," said Fleece, again in the sulks.

"You said up there, didn't you? and now look yourself, and see where your tongs are pointing. But, perhaps you expect to get into heaven by crawling through the lubber's hole, cook; but, no, no, cook, you don't get there, except you go the regular way, round by the rigging. It's a ticklish business, but must be done, or else it's no go. But none of us are in heaven yet. Drop your tongs, cook, and hear my orders. Do ye hear? Hold your hat in one hand, and clap t'other a'top of your heart, when I'm giving my orders, cook. What! that your heart, there?—that's your gizzard! Aloft! aloft!—that's it—now you have it. Hold it there now, and pay attention."

"All 'dention," said the old black, with both hands placed

as desired, vainly wriggling his grizzled head, as if to get both ears in front at one and the same time.

"Well then, cook, you see this whale-steak of yours was so very bad, that I have put it out of sight as soon as possible; you see that, don't you? Well, for the future, when you cook another whale-steak for my private table here, the capstan, I'll tell you what to do so as not to spoil it by overdoing. Hold the steak in one hand, and show a live coal to it with the other; that done, dish it; d'ye hear? And now to-morrow, cook, when we are cutting in the fish, be sure you stand by to get the tips of his fins; have them put in pickle. As for the ends of the flukes, have them soused, cook. There, now ye may go."

But Fleece had hardly got three paces off, when he was recalled.

"Cook, give me cutlets for supper to-morrow night in the mid-watch. D'ye hear? away you sail, then.—Halloa! stop! make a bow before you go.—Avast heaving again! Whale-balls for breakfast—don't forget."

"Wish, by gor! whale eat him, 'stead of him eat whale. I'm bressed if he ain't more of shark dan Massa Shark hisself," muttered the old man, limping away; with which sage ejaculation he went to his hammock.

Chapter 65

THE WHALE AS A DISH

THAT MORTAL MAN should feed upon the creature that feeds his lamp, and, like Stubb, eat him by his own light, as you may say; this seems so outlandish a thing that one must needs go a little into the history and philosophy of it.

It is upon record, that three centuries ago the tongue of the Right Whale was esteemed a great delicacy in France, and commanded large prices there. Also, that in Henry VIIIth's time, a certain cook of the court obtained a handsome reward for inventing an admirable sauce to be eaten with barbacued porpoises, which, you remember, are a species of whale. Porpoises, indeed, are to this day considered fine eating. The meat is made into balls about the size of billiard balls, and being well seasoned and spiced might be taken for turtle-balls or veal balls. The old monks of Dunfermline were very fond of them. They had a great porpoise grant from the crown.

The fact is, that among his hunters at least, the whale would by all hands be considered a noble dish, were there not so much of him; but when you come to sit down before a meat-pie nearly one hundred feet long, it takes away your appetite. Only the most unprejudiced of men like Stubb, nowadays partake of cooked whales; but the Esquimaux are not so fastidious. We all know how they live upon whales, and have rare old vintages of prime old train oil. Zogranda, one of their most famous doctors, recommends strips of blubber for infants, as being exceedingly juicy and nourishing. And this reminds me that certain Englishmen, who long ago were accidentally left in Greenland by a whaling vessel—that these men actually lived for several months on the mouldy scraps of whales which had been left ashore after trying out the blubber. Among the Dutch whalemen these scraps are called "fritters;" which, indeed, they greatly resemble, being brown and crisp, and smelling something like old Amsterdam housewives' dough-nuts or oly-cooks, when fresh. They have such an eatable look that the most self-denying stranger can hardly keep his hands off.

But what further depreciates the whale as a civilized dish, is his exceeding richness. He is the great prize ox of the sea, too fat to be delicately good. Look at his hump, which would be as fine eating as the buffalo's (which is esteemed a rare dish), were it not such a solid pyramid of fat. But the spermaceti itself, how bland and creamy that is; like the transparent, half-jellied, white meat of a cocoanut in the third month of its growth, yet far too rich to supply a substitute for butter. Nevertheless, many whalemen have a method of absorbing it into some other substance, and then partaking of it. In the long try watches of the night it is a common thing for the seamen to dip their ship-biscuit into the huge oil-pots and let them fry there awhile. Many a good supper have I thus made.

In the case of a small Sperm Whale the brains are accounted a fine dish. The casket of the skull is broken into with an axe, and the two plump, whitish lobes being withdrawn (precisely resembling two large puddings), they are then mixed with flour, and cooked into a most delectable mess, in flavor somewhat resembling calves' head, which is quite a dish among some epicures; and every one knows that some young bucks among the epicures, by continually dining upon calves' brains, by and by get to have a little brains of their own, so as to be able to tell a calf's head from their own heads; which, indeed, requires uncommon discrimination. And that is the reason why a young buck with an intelligent looking calf's head before him, is somehow one of the saddest sights you can see. The head looks a sort of reproachfully at him, with an "Et tu Brute!" expression.

It is not, perhaps, entirely because the whale is so excessively unctuous that landsmen seem to regard the eating of him with abhorrence; that appears to result, in some way, from the consideration before mentioned: i.e. that a man should eat a newly murdered thing of the sea, and eat it too by its own light. But no doubt the first man that ever murdered an ox was regarded as a murderer; perhaps he was hung; and if he had been put on his trial by oxen, he certainly would have been; and he certainly deserved it if any murderer does. Go to the meat-market of a Saturday night and see the crowds of live bipeds staring up at the long rows of dead quadrupeds. Does not that sight take a tooth out of the cannibal's jaw? Cannibals? who is not a cannibal? I tell you it will be more tolerable for the Fejee that salted down a lean missionary in his cellar against a coming famine; it will be more tolerable for that provident Fejee, I say, in the day of judgment, than for thee, civilized and enlightened gourmand, who nailest geese to the ground and feastest on their bloated livers in thy paté-de-foie-gras.

But Stubb, he eats the whale by its own light, does he? and that is adding insult to injury, is it? Look at your knife-handle, there, my civilized and enlightened gourmand dining off that roast beef, what is that handle made of?—what but the bones of the brother of the very ox you are eating? And what do you pick your teeth with, after devouring that fat goose? With a feather of the same fowl. And with what quill did the Secretary of the Society for the Suppression of Cruelty to Ganders formerly indite his circulars? It is only within the last month or two that that society passed a resolution to patronize nothing but steel pens.

Chapter 66

THE SHARK MASSACRE

WHEN in the Southern Fishery, a captured Sperm Whale, after long and weary toil, is brought alongside late at night, it is not, as a general thing at least, customary to proceed at once to the business of cutting him in. For that business is an exceedingly laborious one; is not very soon completed; and requires all hands to set about it. Therefore, the common usage is to take in all sail; lash the helm a'lee; and then send every one below to his hammock till daylight, with the reservation that, until that time, anchor-watches shall be kept; that is, two and two, for an hour each couple, the crew in rotation shall mount the deck to see that all goes well.

But sometimes, especially upon the Line in the Pacific, this plan will not answer at all; because such incalculable hosts of sharks gather round the moored carcase, that were he left so for six hours, say, on a stretch, little more than the skeleton would be visible by morning. In most other parts of the ocean, however, where these fish do not so largely abound, their wondrous voracity can be at times considerably diminished, by vigorously stirring them up with sharp whaling-spades, a procedure notwithstanding, which, in some instances, only seems to tickle them into still greater activity. But it was not thus in the present case with the Pequod's sharks; though, to be sure, any man unaccustomed to such sights, to have looked over her side that night, would have almost thought the whole round sea was one huge cheese, and those sharks the maggots in it.

Nevertheless, upon Stubb setting the anchor-watch after his supper was concluded; and when, accordingly, Queequeg and a forecastle seaman came on deck, no small excitement was created among the sharks; for immediately suspending the cutting stages over the side, and lowering three lanterns, so that they cast long gleams of light over the turbid sea, these two mariners, darting their long whaling-spades, kept up an incessant murdering of the sharks,* by striking the keen steel deep into their skulls, seemingly their only vital part. But in the foamy confusion of their mixed and struggling hosts, the marksmen could not always hit their mark; and this brought about new revelations of the incredible ferocity of the foe. They viciously snapped, not only at each other's disembowelments, but like flexible bows, bent round, and bit their own; till those entrails seemed swallowed over and over again by the same mouth, to be oppositely voided by the gaping wound. Nor was this all. It was unsafe to meddle with the corpses and ghosts of these creatures. A sort of generic or Pantheistic vitality seemed to lurk in their very joints and bones, after what might be called the individual life had departed. Killed and hoisted on deck for the sake of his skin, one of these sharks almost took poor Queequeg's hand off, when he tried to shut down the dead lid of his murderous jaw.

"Queequeg no care what god made him shark," said the savage, agonizingly lifting his hand up and down; "wedder Fejee god or Nantucket god; but de god wat made shark must be one dam Ingin."

*The whaling-spade used for cutting-in is made of the very best steel; is about the bigness of a man's spread hand; and in general shape, corresponds to the garden implement after which it is named; only its sides are perfectly flat, and its upper end considerably narrower than the lower. This weapon is always kept as sharp as possible; and when being used is occasionally honed, just like a razor. In its socket, a stiff pole, from twenty to thirty feet long, is inserted for a handle.

Chapter 67

CUTTING IN

IT WAS a Saturday night, and such a Sabbath as followed! Ex officio professors of Sabbath breaking are all whalemen. The ivory Pequod was turned into what seemed a shamble; every sailor a butcher. You would have thought we were offering up ten thousand red oxen to the sea gods.

In the first place, the enormous cutting tackles, among other ponderous things comprising a cluster of blocks generally painted green, and which no single man can possibly lift—this vast bunch of grapes was swayed up to the maintop and firmly lashed to the lower mast-head, the strongest point anywhere above a ship's deck. The end of the hawser-like rope winding through these intricacies, was then conducted to the windlass, and the huge lower block of the tackles was swung over the whale; to this block the great blubber hook, weighing some one hundred pounds, was attached. And now suspended in stages over the side, Starbuck and Stubb, the mates, armed with their long spades, began cutting a hole in the body for the insertion of the hook just above the nearest of the two side-fins. This done, a broad, semicircular line is cut round the hole, the hook is inserted, and the main body of the crew striking up a wild chorus, now commence heaving in one dense crowd at the windlass. When instantly, the entire ship careens over on her side; every bolt in her starts like the nail-heads of an old house in frosty weather; she trembles, quivers, and nods her frighted mast-heads to the sky. More and more she leans over to the whale, while every gasping heave of the windlass is answered by a helping heave from the billows; till at last, a swift, startling snap is heard; with a great swash the ship rolls upwards and backwards from the whale, and the triumphant tackle rises into sight dragging after it the disengaged semicircular end of the first strip of blubber. Now as the blubber envelopes the whale precisely as the rind does an orange, so is it stripped off from the body precisely as an orange is sometimes

stripped by spiralizing it. For the strain constantly kept up by
the windlass continually keeps the whale rolling over and over
in the water, and as the blubber in one strip uniformly peels
off along the line called the "scarf," simultaneously cut by the
spades of Starbuck and Stubb, the mates; and just as fast as it
is thus peeled off, and indeed by that very act itself, it is all
the time being hoisted higher and higher aloft till its upper
end grazes the main-top; the men at the windlass then cease
heaving, and for a moment or two the prodigious blood-
dripping mass sways to and fro as if let down from the sky,
and every one present must take good heed to dodge it when
it swings, else it may box his ears and pitch him headlong
overboard.

One of the attending harpooneers now advances with a
long, keen weapon called a boarding-sword, and watching his
chance he dexterously slices out a considerable hole in the
lower part of the swaying mass. Into this hole, the end of the
second alternating great tackle is then hooked so as to retain
a hold upon the blubber, in order to prepare for what follows. Whereupon, this accomplished swordsman, warning all
hands to stand off, once more makes a scientific dash at the
mass, and with a few sidelong, desperate, lunging slicings,
severs it completely in twain; so that while the short lower
part is still fast, the long upper strip, called a blanket-piece,
swings clear, and is all ready for lowering. The heavers forward now resume their song, and while the one tackle is peel-
ing and hoisting a second strip from the whale, the other is
slowly slackened away, and down goes the first strip through
the main hatchway right beneath, into an unfurnished parlor
called the blubber-room. Into this twilight apartment sundry
nimble hands keep coiling away the long blanket-piece as if it
were a great live mass of plaited serpents. And thus the work
proceeds; the two tackles hoisting and lowering simultaneously; both whale and windlass heaving, the heavers singing, the blubber-room gentlemen coiling, the mates scarfing,
the ship straining, and all hands swearing occasionally, by
way of assuaging the general friction.

Chapter 68

THE BLANKET

I HAVE GIVEN no small attention to that not unvexed subject, the skin of the whale. I have had controversies about it with experienced whalemen afloat, and learned naturalists ashore. My original opinion remains unchanged; but it is only an opinion.

The question is, what and where is the skin of the whale? Already you know what his blubber is. That blubber is something of the consistence of firm, close-grained beef, but tougher, more elastic and compact, and ranges from eight or ten to twelve and fifteen inches in thickness.

Now, however preposterous it may at first seem to talk of any creature's skin as being of that sort of consistence and thickness, yet in point of fact these are no arguments against such a presumption; because you cannot raise any other dense enveloping layer from the whale's body but that same blubber; and the outermost enveloping layer of any animal, if reasonably dense, what can that be but the skin? True, from the unmarred dead body of the whale, you may scrape off with your hand an infinitely thin, transparent substance, somewhat resembling the thinnest shreds of isinglass, only it is almost as flexible and soft as satin; that is, previous to being dried, when it not only contracts and thickens, but becomes rather hard and brittle. I have several such dried bits, which I use for marks in my whale-books. It is transparent, as I said before; and being laid upon the printed page, I have sometimes pleased myself with fancying it exerted a magnifying influence. At any rate, it is pleasant to read about whales through their own spectacles, as you may say. But what I am driving at here is this. That same infinitely thin, isinglass substance, which, I admit, invests the entire body of the whale, is not so much to be regarded as the skin of the creature, as the skin of the skin, so to speak; for it were simply ridiculous to say, that the proper skin of the tremendous whale is thinner and more tender than the skin of a new-born child. But no more of this.

Assuming the blubber to be the skin of the whale; then, when this skin, as in the case of a very large Sperm Whale, will yield the bulk of one hundred barrels of oil; and, when it is considered that, in quantity, or rather weight, that oil, in its expressed state, is only three fourths, and not the entire substance of the coat; some idea may hence be had of the enormousness of that animated mass, a mere part of whose mere integument yields such a lake of liquid as that. Reckoning ten barrels to the ton, you have ten tons for the net weight of only three quarters of the stuff of the whale's skin.

In life, the visible surface of the Sperm Whale is not the least among the many marvels he presents. Almost invariably it is all over obliquely crossed and re-crossed with numberless straight marks in thick array, something like those in the finest Italian line engravings. But these marks do not seem to be impressed upon the isinglass substance above mentioned, but seem to be seen through it, as if they were engraved upon the body itself. Nor is this all. In some instances, to the quick, observant eye, those linear marks, as in a veritable engraving, but afford the ground for far other delineations. These are hieroglyphical; that is, if you call those mysterious cyphers on the walls of pyramids hieroglyphics, then that is the proper word to use in the present connexion. By my retentive memory of the hieroglyphics upon one Sperm Whale in particular, I was much struck with a plate representing the old Indian characters chiselled on the famous hieroglyphic palisades on the banks of the Upper Mississippi. Like those mystic rocks, too, the mystic-marked whale remains undecipherable. This allusion to the Indian rocks reminds me of another thing. Besides all the other phenomena which the exterior of the Sperm Whale presents, he not seldom displays the back, and more especially his flanks, effaced in great part of the regular linear appearance, by reason of numerous rude scratches, altogether of an irregular, random aspect. I should say that those New England rocks on the sea-coast, which Agassiz imagines to bear the marks of violent scraping contact with vast floating icebergs—I should say, that those rocks must not a little resemble the Sperm Whale in this particular. It also seems to me that such scratches in the whale are probably made by hostile contact with other whales; for I have most remarked them in the large, full-grown bulls of the species.

A word or two more concerning this matter of the skin or blubber of the whale. It has already been said, that it is stript from him in long pieces, called blanket-pieces. Like most sea-terms, this one is very happy and significant. For the whale is indeed wrapt up in his blubber as in a real blanket or counterpane; or, still better, an Indian poncho slipt over his head, and skirting his extremity. It is by reason of this cosy blanketing of his body, that the whale is enabled to keep himself comfortable in all weathers, in all seas, times, and tides. What would become of a Greenland whale, say, in those shuddering, icy seas of the North, if unsupplied with his cosy surtout? True, other fish are found exceedingly brisk in those Hyperborean waters; but these, be it observed, are your cold-blooded, lungless fish, whose very bellies are refrigerators; creatures, that warm themselves under the lee of an iceberg, as a traveller in winter would bask before an inn fire; whereas, like man, the whale has lungs and warm blood. Freeze his blood, and he dies. How wonderful is it then—except after explanation—that this great monster, to whom corporeal warmth is as indispensable as it is to man; how wonderful that he should be found at home, immersed to his lips for life in those Arctic waters! where, when seamen fall overboard, they are sometimes found, months afterwards, perpendicularly frozen into the hearts of fields of ice, as a fly is found glued in amber. But more surprising is it to know, as has been proved by experiment, that the blood of a Polar whale is warmer than that of a Borneo negro in summer.

It does seem to me, that herein we see the rare virtue of a strong individual vitality, and the rare virtue of thick walls, and the rare virtue of interior spaciousness. Oh, man! admire and model thyself after the whale! Do thou, too, remain warm among ice. Do thou, too, live in this world without being of it. Be cool at the equator; keep thy blood fluid at the Pole. Like the great dome of St. Peter's, and like the great whale, retain, O man! in all seasons a temperature of thine own.

But how easy and how hopeless to teach these fine things! Of erections, how few are domed like St. Peter's! of creatures, how few vast as the whale!

Chapter 69

THE FUNERAL

"HAUL IN THE CHAINS! Let the carcase go astern!"

The vast tackles have now done their duty. The peeled white body of the beheaded whale flashes like a marble sepulchre; though changed in hue, it has not perceptibly lost anything in bulk. It is still colossal. Slowly it floats more and more away, the water round it torn and splashed by the insatiate sharks, and the air above vexed with rapacious flights of screaming fowls, whose beaks are like so many insulting poniards in the whale. The vast white headless phantom floats further and further from the ship, and every rod that it so floats, what seem square roods of sharks and cubic roods of fowls, augment the murderous din. For hours and hours from the almost stationary ship that hideous sight is seen. Beneath the unclouded and mild azure sky, upon the fair face of the pleasant sea, wafted by the joyous breezes, that great mass of death floats on and on, till lost in infinite perspectives.

There's a most doleful and most mocking funeral! The sea-vultures all in pious mourning, the air-sharks all punctiliously in black or speckled. In life but few of them would have helped the whale, I ween, if peradventure he had needed it; but upon the banquet of his funeral they most piously do pounce. Oh, horrible vulturism of earth! from which not the mightiest whale is free.

Nor is this the end. Desecrated as the body is, a vengeful ghost survives and hovers over it to scare. Espied by some timid man-of-war or blundering discovery-vessel from afar, when the distance obscuring the swarming fowls, nevertheless still shows the white mass floating in the sun, and the white spray heaving high against it; straightway the whale's unharming corpse, with trembling fingers is set down in the log—*shoals, rocks, and breakers hereabouts: beware!* And for years afterwards, perhaps, ships shun the place; leaping over it as silly sheep leap over a vacuum, because their leader originally leaped there when a stick was held. There's your law of precedents; there's your utility of traditions; there's the story of your obstinate survival of old beliefs never bottomed on the earth, and now not even hovering in the air! There's orthodoxy!

Thus, while in life the great whale's body may have been a real terror to his foes, in his death his ghost becomes a powerless panic to a world.

Are you a believer in ghosts, my friend? There are other ghosts than the Cock-Lane one, and far deeper men than Doctor Johnson who believe in them.

Chapter 70

THE SPHYNX

IT SHOULD NOT have been omitted that previous to completely stripping the body of the leviathan, he was beheaded. Now, the beheading of the Sperm Whale is a scientific anatomical feat, upon which experienced whale surgeons very much pride themselves: and not without reason.

Consider that the whale has nothing that can properly be called a neck; on the contrary, where his head and body seem to join, there, in that very place, is the thickest part of him. Remember, also, that the surgeon must operate from above, some eight or ten feet intervening between him and his subject, and that subject almost hidden in a discolored, rolling, and oftentimes tumultuous and bursting sea. Bear in mind, too, that under these untoward circumstances he has to cut many feet deep in the flesh; and in that subterranean manner, without so much as getting one single peep into the ever-contracting gash thus made, he must skilfully steer clear of all adjacent, interdicted parts, and exactly divide the spine at a critical point hard by its insertion into the skull. Do you not marvel, then, at Stubb's boast, that he demanded but ten minutes to behead a sperm whale?

When first severed, the head is dropped astern and held there by a cable till the body is stripped. That done, if it belong to a small whale it is hoisted on deck to be deliberately disposed of. But, with a full grown leviathan this is impossible; for the sperm whale's head embraces nearly one third of his entire bulk, and completely to suspend such a burden as that, even by the immense tackles of a whaler, this were as vain a thing as to attempt weighing a Dutch barn in jewellers' scales.

The Pequod's whale being decapitated and the body stripped, the head was hoisted against the ship's side — about half way out of the sea, so that it might yet in great part be buoyed up by its native element. And there with the strained craft steeply leaning over to it, by reason of the enormous downward drag from the lower mast-head, and every yard-arm on that side projecting like a crane over the waves; there, that blood-dripping head hung to the Pequod's waist like the giant Holofernes's from the girdle of Judith.

When this last task was accomplished it was noon, and the seamen went below to their dinner. Silence reigned over the before tumultuous but now deserted deck. An intense copper calm, like a universal yellow lotus, was more and more un-folding its noiseless measureless leaves upon the sea.

A short space elapsed, and up into this noiselessness came Ahab alone from his cabin. Taking a few turns on the quarter-deck, he paused to gaze over the side, then slowly getting into the main-chains he took Stubb's long spade—still remaining there after the whale's decapitation—and striking it into the lower part of the half-suspended mass, placed its other end crutch-wise under one arm, and so stood leaning over with eyes attentively fixed on this head.

It was a black and hooded head; and hanging there in the midst of so intense a calm, it seemed the Sphynx's in the desert. "Speak, thou vast and venerable head," muttered Ahab, "which, though ungarnished with a beard, yet here and there lookest hoary with mosses; speak, mighty head, and tell us the secret thing that is in thee. Of all divers, thou hast dived the deepest. That head upon which the upper sun now gleams, has moved amid this world's foundations. Where un-recorded names and navies rust, and untold hopes and an-chors rot; where in her murderous hold this frigate earth is ballasted with bones of millions of the drowned; there, in that awful water-land, there was thy most familiar home. Thou hast been where bell or diver never went; hast slept by many a sailor's side, where sleepless mothers would give their lives to lay them down. Thou saw'st the locked lovers when leap-ing from their flaming ship; heart to heart they sank beneath the exulting wave; true to each other, when heaven seemed false to them. Thou saw'st the murdered mate when tossed by pirates from the midnight deck; for hours he fell into the deeper midnight of the insatiate maw; and his murderers still sailed on unharmed—while swift lightnings shivered the neighboring ship that would have borne a righteous husband to outstretched, longing arms. O head! thou hast seen enough to split the planets and make an infidel of Abraham, and not one syllable is thine!"

"Sail ho!" cried a triumphant voice from the main-mast-head.

"Aye? Well, now, that's cheering," cried Ahab, suddenly erecting himself, while whole thunder-clouds swept aside from his brow. "That lively cry upon this deadly calm might almost convert a better man.—Where away?"

"Three points on the starboard bow, sir, and bringing down her breeze to us!"

"Better and better, man. Would now St. Paul would come along that way, and to my breezelessness bring his breeze! O Nature, and O soul of man! how far beyond all utterance are your linked analogies! not the smallest atom stirs or lives in matter, but has its cunning duplicate in mind."

Chapter 71

THE JEROBOAM'S STORY

HAND IN HAND, ship and breeze blew on; but the breeze came faster than the ship, and soon the Pequod began to rock.

By and by, through the glass the stranger's boats and manned mast-heads proved her a whale-ship. But as she was so far to windward, and shooting by, apparently making a passage to some other ground, the Pequod could not hope to reach her. So the signal was set to see what response would be made.

Here be it said, that like the vessels of military marines, the ships of the American Whale Fleet have each a private signal; all which signals being collected in a book with the names of the respective vessels attached, every captain is provided with it. Thereby, the whale commanders are enabled to recognise each other upon the ocean, even at considerable distances, and with no small facility.

The Pequod's signal was at last responded to by the stranger's setting her own; which proved the ship to be the Jeroboam of Nantucket. Squaring her yards, she bore down, ranged abeam under the Pequod's lee, and lowered a boat; it soon drew nigh; but, as the side-ladder was being rigged by Starbuck's order to accommodate the visiting captain, the stranger in question waved his hand from his boat's stern in token of that proceeding being entirely unnecessary. It turned out that the Jeroboam had a malignant epidemic on board, and that Mayhew, her captain, was fearful of infecting the Pequod's company. For, though himself and boat's crew remained untainted, and though his ship was half a rifle-shot off, and an incorruptible sea and air rolling and flowing between; yet conscientiously adhering to the timid quarantine of the land, he peremptorily refused to come into direct contact with the Pequod.

But this did by no means prevent all communication. Preserving an interval of some few yards between itself and the ship, the Jeroboam's boat by the occasional use of its oars contrived to keep parallel to the Pequod, as she heavily forged through the sea (for by this time it blew very fresh), with her main-top-sail aback; though, indeed, at times by the sudden onset of a large rolling wave, the boat would be pushed some way ahead; but would be soon skilfully brought to her proper bearings again. Subject to this, and other the like interruptions now and then, a conversation was sustained between the two parties; but at intervals not without still another interruption of a very different sort.

Pulling an oar in the Jeroboam's boat, was a man of a singular appearance, even in that wild whaling life where individual notabilities make up all totalities. He was a small, short, youngish man, sprinkled all over his face with freckles, and wearing redundant yellow hair. A long-skirted, cabalistically-cut coat of a faded walnut tinge enveloped him; the overlapping sleeves of which were rolled up on his wrists. A deep, settled, fanatic delirium was in his eyes.

So soon as this figure had been first descried, Stubb had exclaimed—"That's he! that's he!—the long-togged scaramouch the Town-Ho's company told us of!" Stubb here alluded to a strange story told of the Jeroboam, and a certain man among her crew, some time previous when the Pequod spoke the Town-Ho. According to this account and what was subsequently learned, it seemed that the scaramouch in question had gained a wonderful ascendency over almost everybody in the Jeroboam. His story was this:

He had been originally nurtured among the crazy society of Niskyeuna Shakers, where he had been a great prophet; in their cracked, secret meetings having several times descended from heaven by the way of a trap-door, announcing the speedy opening of the seventh vial, which he carried in his vest-pocket; but, which, instead of containing gunpowder, was supposed to be charged with laudanum. A strange, apostolic whim having seized him, he had left Niskyeuna for Nantucket, where, with that cunning peculiar to craziness, he assumed a steady, common sense exterior, and offered himself as a green-hand candidate for the Jeroboam's whaling voyage. They engaged him; but straightway upon the ship's getting out of sight of land, his insanity broke out in a freshet. He announced himself as the archangel Gabriel, and commanded the captain to jump overboard. He published his manifesto, whereby he set himself forth as the deliverer of the isles of the sea and vicar-general of all Oceanica. The unflinching earnestness with which he declared these things:—the dark, daring play of his sleepless, excited imagination, and all the preternatural terrors of real delirium, united to invest this Gabriel in the minds of the majority of the ignorant crew, with an atmosphere of sacredness. Moreover, they were afraid of him. As such a man, however, was not of much practical use in the ship, especially as he refused to work except when he pleased, the incredulous captain would fain have been rid of him; but apprised that that individual's intention was to land him in the first convenient port, the archangel forthwith opened all his seals and vials—devoting the ship and all hands to unconditional perdition, in case this intention was carried out. So strongly did he work upon his disciples among the crew, that at last in a body they went to the captain and told him if Gabriel was sent from the ship, not a man of them would remain. He was therefore forced to relinquish his plan. Nor would they permit Gabriel to be any way maltreated, say or do what he would; so that it came to pass that Gabriel had the complete freedom of the ship. The consequence of all this was, that the archangel cared little or nothing for the captain and mates; and since the epidemic had broken out, he carried a higher hand than ever; declaring that the plague, as he called it, was at his sole command; nor should it be stayed but according to his good pleasure. The sailors, mostly poor devils, cringed, and some of them fawned before him; in obedience to his instructions, sometimes rendering him personal homage, as to a god. Such things may seem incredible; but, however wondrous, they are true. Nor is the history of fanatics half so striking in respect to the measureless self-deception of the fanatic himself, as his measureless power of deceiving and bedevilling so many others. But it is time to return to the Pequod.

"I fear not thy epidemic, man," said Ahab from the bulwarks, to Captain Mayhew, who stood in the boat's stern; "come on board."

But now Gabriel started to his feet.

"Think, think of the fevers, yellow and bilious! Beware of the horrible plague!"

"Gabriel, Gabriel!" cried Captain Mayhew; "thou must

either—" But that instant a headlong wave shot the boat far ahead, and its seethings drowned all speech.

"Hast thou seen the White Whale?" demanded Ahab, when the boat drifted back.

"Think, think of thy whale-boat, stoven and sunk! Beware of the horrible tail!"

"I tell thee again, Gabriel, that—" But again the boat tore ahead as if dragged by fiends. Nothing was said for some moments, while a succession of riotous waves rolled by, which by one of those occasional caprices of the seas were tumbling, not heaving it. Meantime, the hoisted sperm whale's head jogged about very violently, and Gabriel was seen eyeing it with rather more apprehensiveness than his archangel nature seemed to warrant.

When this interlude was over, Captain Mayhew began a dark story concerning Moby Dick; not, however, without frequent interruptions from Gabriel, whenever his name was mentioned, and the crazy sea that seemed leagued with him.

It seemed that the Jeroboam had not long left home, when upon speaking a whale-ship, her people were reliably apprised of the existence of Moby Dick, and the havoc he had made. Greedily sucking in this intelligence, Gabriel solemnly warned the captain against attacking the White Whale, in case the monster should be seen; in his gibbering insanity, pronouncing the White Whale to be no less a being than the Shaker God incarnated; the Shakers receiving the Bible. But when, some year or two afterwards, Moby Dick was fairly sighted from the mast-heads, Macey, the chief mate, burned with ardor to encounter him; and the captain himself being not unwilling to let him have the opportunity, despite all the archangel's denunciations and forewarnings, Macey succeeded in persuading five men to man his boat. With them he pushed off; and, after much weary pulling, and many perilous, unsuccessful onsets, he at last succeeded in getting one iron fast. Meantime, Gabriel, ascending to the main-royal mast-head, was tossing one arm in frantic gestures, and hurling forth prophecies of speedy doom to the sacrilegious assailants of his divinity. Now, while Macey, the mate, was standing up in his boat's bow, and with all the reckless energy of his tribe was venting his wild exclamations upon the whale, and essaying to get a fair chance for his poised lance, lo! a broad white shadow rose from the sea; by its quick, fanning motion, temporarily taking the breath out of the bodies of the oarsmen. Next instant, the luckless mate, so full of furious life, was smitten bodily into the air, and making a long arc in his descent, fell into the sea at the distance of about fifty yards. Not a chip of the boat was harmed, nor a hair of any oarsman's head; but the mate for ever sank.

It is well to parenthesize here, that of the fatal accidents in the Sperm-Whale Fishery, this kind is perhaps almost as frequent as any. Sometimes, nothing is injured but the man who is thus annihilated; oftener the boat's bow is knocked off, or the thigh-board, in which the headsman stands, is torn from its place and accompanies the body. But strangest of all is the circumstance, that in more instances than one, when the body has been recovered, not a single mark of violence is discernible; the man being stark dead.

The whole calamity, with the falling form of Macey, was plainly descried from the ship. Raising a piercing shriek—"The vial! the vial!" Gabriel called off the terror-stricken crew from the further hunting of the whale. This terrible event clothed the archangel with added influence; because his credulous disciples believed that he had specifically foreannounced it, instead of only making a general prophecy, which any one might have done, and so have chanced to hit one of many marks in the wide margin allowed. He became a nameless terror to the ship.

Mayhew having concluded his narration, Ahab put such questions to him, that the stranger captain could not forbear inquiring whether he intended to hunt the White Whale, if opportunity should offer. To which Ahab answered—"Aye." Straightway, then, Gabriel once more started to his feet, glaring upon the old man, and vehemently exclaimed, with downward pointed finger—"Think, think of the blasphemer—dead, and down there!—beware of the blasphemer's end!"

Ahab stolidly turned aside; then said to Mayhew, "Captain, I have just bethought me of my letter-bag; there is a letter for one of thy officers, if I mistake not. Starbuck, look over the bag."

Every whale-ship takes out a goodly number of letters for various ships, whose delivery to the persons to whom they may be addressed, depends upon the mere chance of encountering them in the four oceans. Thus, most letters never reach their mark; and many are only received after attaining an age of two or three years or more.

Soon Starbuck returned with a letter in his hand. It was sorely tumbled, damp, and covered with a dull, spotted, green mould, in consequence of being kept in a dark locker of the cabin. Of such a letter, Death himself might well have been the post-boy.

"Can'st not read it?" cried Ahab. "Give it me, man. Aye, aye, it's but a dim scrawl;—what's this?" As he was studying it out, Starbuck took a long cutting-spade pole, and with his knife slightly split the end, to insert the letter there, and in that way, hand it to the boat, without its coming any closer to the ship.

Meantime, Ahab holding the letter, muttered, "Mr. Har—yes, Mr. Harry—(a woman's pinny hand,—the man's wife, I'll wager)—Aye—Mr. Harry Macey, Ship Jeroboam;—why it's Macey, and he's dead!"

"Poor fellow! poor fellow! and from his wife," sighed Mayhew; "but let me have it."

"Nay, keep it thyself," cried Gabriel to Ahab; "thou art soon going that way."

"Curses throttle thee!" yelled Ahab. "Captain Mayhew, stand by now to receive it;" and taking the fatal missive from Starbuck's hands, he caught it in the slit of the pole, and reached it over towards the boat. But as he did so, the oarsmen expectantly desisted from rowing; the boat drifted a little towards the ship's stern; so that, as if by magic, the letter suddenly ranged along with Gabriel's eager hand. He clutched it in an instant, seized the boat-knife, and impaling the letter on it, sent it thus loaded back into the ship. It fell at Ahab's feet. Then Gabriel shrieked out to his comrades to give way with their oars, and in that manner the mutinous boat rapidly shot away from the Pequod.

As, after this interlude, the seamen resumed their work upon the jacket of the whale, many strange things were hinted in reference to this wild affair.

Chapter 72

THE MONKEY-ROPE

IN THE TUMULTUOUS business of cutting-in and attending to a whale, there is much running backwards and forwards among the crew. Now hands are wanted here, and then again hands are wanted there. There is no staying in any one place; for at one and the same time everything has to be done everywhere. It is much the same with him who endeavors the description of the scene. We must now retrace our way a little. It was mentioned that upon first breaking ground in the whale's back, the blubber-hook was inserted into the original hole there cut by the spades of the mates. But how did so clumsy and weighty a mass as that same hook get fixed in that hole? It was inserted there by my particular friend Queequeg, whose duty it was, as harpooneer, to descend upon the monster's back for the special purpose referred to. But in very many cases, circumstances require that the harpooneer shall remain on the whale till the whole flensing or stripping operation is concluded. The whale, be it observed, lies almost entirely submerged, excepting the immediate parts operated upon. So down there, some ten feet below the level of the deck, the poor harpooneer flounders about, half on the whale and half in the water, as the vast mass revolves like a tread-mill beneath him. On the occasion in question, Queequeg figured in the Highland costume—a shirt and socks—in which to my eyes, at least, he appeared to uncommon advantage; and no one had a better chance to observe him, as will presently be seen.

Being the savage's bowsman, that is, the person who pulled the bow-oar in his boat (the second one from forward), it was my cheerful duty to attend upon him while taking that hard-scrabble scramble upon the dead whale's back. You have seen Italian organ-boys holding a dancing-ape by a long cord. Just so, from the ship's steep side, did I hold Queequeg down there in the sea, by what is technically called in the fishery a monkey-rope, attached to a strong strip of canvas belted round his waist.

It was a humorously perilous business for both of us. For, before we proceed further, it must be said that the monkey-rope was fast at both ends; fast to Queequeg's broad canvas belt, and fast to my narrow leather one. So that for better or for worse, we two, for the time, were wedded; and should poor Queequeg sink to rise no more, then both usage and honor demanded, that instead of cutting the cord, it should drag me down in his wake. So, then, an elongated Siamese ligature united us. Queequeg was my own inseparable twin brother; nor could I any way get rid of the dangerous liabilities which the hempen bond entailed.

So strongly and metaphysically did I conceive of my situation then, that while earnestly watching his motions, I seemed distinctly to perceive that my own individuality was now merged in a joint stock company of two: that my free will had received a mortal wound; and that another's mistake or misfortune might plunge innocent me into unmerited disaster and death. Therefore, I saw that here was a sort of interregnum in Providence; for its even-handed equity never could have sanctioned so gross an injustice. And yet still further pondering—while I jerked him now and then from between the whale and the ship, which would threaten to jam him—still further pondering, I say, I saw that this situation of mine was the precise situation of every mortal that breathes; only, in most cases, he, one way or other, has this Siamese connexion with a plurality of other mortals. If your banker breaks, you snap; if your apothecary by mistake sends you poison in your pills, you die. True, you may say that, by exceeding caution, you may possibly escape these and the multitudinous other evil chances of life. But handle Queequeg's monkey-rope heedfully as I would, sometimes he jerked it so, that I came very near sliding overboard. Nor could I possibly forget that, do what I would, I only had the management of one end of it.*

I have hinted that I would often jerk poor Queequeg from

---

*The monkey-rope is found in all whalers; but it was only in the Pequod that the monkey and his holder were ever tied together. This improvement upon the original usage was introduced by no less a man than Stubb, in order to afford to the imperilled harpooneer the strongest possible guarantee for the faithfulness and vigilance of his monkey-rope holder.

between the whale and the ship—where he would occasionally fall, from the incessant rolling and swaying of both. But this was not the only jamming jeopardy he was exposed to. Unappalled by the massacre made upon them during the night, the sharks now freshly and more keenly allured by the before pent blood which began to flow from the carcase—the rabid creatures swarmed round it like bees in a beehive.

And right in among those sharks was Queequeg; who often pushed them aside with his floundering feet. A thing altogether incredible were it not that attracted by such prey as a dead whale, the otherwise miscellaneously carnivorous shark will seldom touch a man.

Nevertheless, it may well be believed that since they have such a ravenous finger in the pie, it is deemed but wise to look sharp to them. Accordingly, besides the monkey-rope, with which I now and then jerked the poor fellow from too close a vicinity to the maw of what seemed a peculiarly ferocious shark—he was provided with still another protection. Suspended over the side in one of the stages, Tashtego and Daggoo continually flourished over his head a couple of keen whale-spades, wherewith they slaughtered as many sharks as they could reach. This procedure of theirs, to be sure, was very disinterested and benevolent of them. They meant Queequeg's best happiness, I admit; but in their hasty zeal to befriend him, and from the circumstance that both he and the sharks were at times half hidden by the blood-mudded water, those indiscreet spades of theirs would come nearer amputating a leg than a tail. But poor Queequeg, I suppose, straining and gasping there with that great iron hook—poor Queequeg, I suppose, only prayed to his Yojo, and gave up his life into the hands of his gods.

Well, well, my dear comrade and twin-brother, thought I, as I drew in and then slacked off the rope to every swell of the sea—what matters it, after all? Are you not the precious image of each and all of us men in this whaling world? That unsounded ocean you gasp in, is Life; those sharks, your foes; those spades, your friends; and what between sharks and spades you are in a sad pickle and peril, poor lad.

But courage! there is good cheer in store for you, Queequeg. For now, as with blue lips and bloodshot eyes the ex-

hausted savage at last climbs up the chains and stands all
dripping and involuntarily trembling over the side; the steward advances, and with a benevolent, consolatory glance
hands him—what? Some hot Cogniac? No! hands him, ye
gods! hands him a cup of tepid ginger and water!

"Ginger? Do I smell ginger?" suspiciously asked Stubb,
coming near. "Yes, this must be ginger," peering into the as
yet untasted cup. Then standing as if incredulous for a while,
he calmly walked towards the astonished steward slowly
saying, "Ginger? ginger? and will you have the goodness
to tell me, Mr. Dough-Boy, where lies the virtue of ginger?
Ginger! is ginger the sort of fuel you use, Dough-Boy, to
kindle a fire in this shivering cannibal? Ginger!—what the
devil is ginger?—sea-coal?—fire-wood?—lucifer matches?—
tinder?—gunpowder?—what the devil is ginger, I say, that
you offer this cup to our poor Queequeg here?"

"There is some sneaking Temperance Society movement
about this business," he suddenly added, now approaching
Starbuck, who had just come from forward. "Will you look
at that kannakin, sir: smell of it, if you please." Then watching the mate's countenance, he added: "The steward, Mr.
Starbuck, had the face to offer that calomel and jalap to Queequeg, there, this instant off the whale. Is the steward an
apothecary, sir? and may I ask whether this is the sort of bellows by which he blows back the breath into a half-drowned
man?"

"I trust not," said Starbuck, "it is poor stuff enough."

"Aye, aye, steward," cried Stubb, "we'll teach you to drug
a harpooneer; none of your apothecary's medicine here; you
want to poison us, do ye? You have got out insurances on
our lives and want to murder us all, and pocket the proceeds,
do ye?"

"It was not me," cried Dough-Boy, "it was Aunt Charity
that brought the ginger on board; and bade me never give
the harpooneers any spirits, but only this ginger-jub—so she
called it."

"Ginger-jub! you gingerly rascal! take that! and run along
with ye to the lockers, and get something better. I hope I do
no wrong, Mr. Starbuck. It is the captain's orders—grog for
the harpooneer on a whale."

"Enough," replied Starbuck, "only don't hit him again, but—"

"Oh, I never hurt when I hit, except when I hit a whale or something of that sort; and this fellow's a weazel. What were you about saying, sir?"

"Only this: go down with him, and get what thou wantest thyself."

When Stubb reappeared, he came with a dark flask in one hand, and a sort of tea-caddy in the other. The first contained strong spirits, and was handed to Queequeg; the second was Aunt Charity's gift, and that was freely given to the waves.

Chapter 73

Stubb and Flask kill a Right Whale; and Then Have a Talk over Him

IT MUST be borne in mind that all this time we have a Sperm Whale's prodigious head hanging to the Pequod's side. But we must let it continue hanging there a while till we can get a chance to attend to it. For the present other matters press, and the best we can do now for the head, is to pray heaven the tackles may hold.

Now, during the past night and forenoon, the Pequod had gradually drifted into a sea, which, by its occasional patches of yellow brit, gave unusual tokens of the vicinity of Right Whales, a species of the Leviathan that but few supposed to be at this particular time lurking anywhere near. And though all hands commonly disdained the capture of those inferior creatures; and though the Pequod was not commissioned to cruise for them at all, and though she had passed numbers of them near the Crozetts without lowering a boat; yet now that a Sperm Whale had been brought alongside and beheaded, to the surprise of all, the announcement was made that a Right Whale should be captured that day, if opportunity offered.

Nor was this long wanting. Tall spouts were seen to lee-ward; and two boats, Stubb's and Flask's, were detached in pursuit. Pulling further and further away, they at last became almost invisible to the men at the mast-head. But suddenly in the distance, they saw a great heap of tumultuous white water, and soon after news came from aloft that one or both the boats must be fast. An interval passed and the boats were in plain sight, in the act of being dragged right towards the ship by the towing whale. So close did the monster come to the hull, that at first it seemed as if he meant it malice; but suddenly going down in a maelstrom, within three rods of the planks, he wholly disappeared from view, as if diving under the keel. "Cut, cut!" was the cry from the ship to the boats, which, for one instant, seemed on the point of being brought with a deadly dash against the vessel's side. But having plenty of line yet in the tubs, and the whale not sounding very rapidly, they paid out abundance of rope, and at the same time pulled with all their might so as to get ahead of the ship. For a few minutes the struggle was intensely critical; for while they still slacked out the tightened line in one direction, and still plied their oars in another, the contending strain threatened to take them under. But it was only a few feet advance they sought to gain. And they stuck to it till they did gain it; when instantly, a swift tremor was felt running like lightning along the keel, as the strained line, scraping beneath the ship, suddenly rose to view under her bows, snapping and quivering; and so flinging off its drippings, that the drops fell like bits of broken glass on the water, while the whale beyond also rose to sight, and once more the boats were free to fly. But the fagged whale abated his speed, and blindly altering his course, went round the stern of the ship towing the two boats after him, so that they performed a complete circuit.

Meantime, they hauled more and more upon their lines, till close flanking him on both sides, Stubb answered Flask with lance for lance; and thus round and round the Pequod the battle went, while the multitudes of sharks that had before swum round the Sperm Whale's body, rushed to the fresh blood that was spilled, thirstily drinking at every new gash, as the eager Israelites did at the new bursting fountains that poured from the smitten rock.

At last his spout grew thick, and with a frightful roll and vomit, he turned upon his back a corpse.

While the two headsmen were engaged in making fast cords to his flukes, and in other ways getting the mass in readiness for towing, some conversation ensued between them.

"I wonder what the old man wants with this lump of foul lard," said Stubb, not without some disgust at the thought of having to do with so ignoble a leviathan.

"Wants with it?" said Flask, coiling some spare line in the boat's bow, "did you never hear that the ship which but once has a Sperm Whale's head hoisted on her starboard side, and at the same time a Right Whale's on the larboard; did you never hear, Stubb, that that ship can never afterwards capsize?"

"Why not?"

"I don't know, but I heard that gamboge ghost of a Fedallah saying so, and he seems to know all about ships' charms. But I sometimes think he'll charm the ship to no good at last. I don't half like that chap, Stubb. Did you ever notice how that tusk of his is a sort of carved into a snake's head, Stubb?"

"Sink him! I never look at him at all; but if ever I get a chance of a dark night, and he standing hard by the bulwarks, and no one by; look down there, Flask"—pointing into the sea with a peculiar motion of both hands—"Aye, will I! Flask, I take that Fedallah to be the devil in disguise. Do you believe that cock and bull story about his having been stowed away on board ship? He's the devil, I say. The reason why you don't see his tail, is because he tucks it up out of sight; he carries it coiled away in his pocket, I guess. Blast him! now that I think of it, he's always wanting oakum to stuff into the toes of his boots."

"He sleeps in his boots, don't he? He hasn't got any hammock; but I've seen him lay of nights in a coil of rigging."

"No doubt, and it's because of his cursed tail; he coils it down, do ye see, in the eye of the rigging."

"What's the old man have so much to do with him for?"

"Striking up a swap or a bargain, I suppose."

"Bargain?—about what?"

"Why, do ye see, the old man is hard bent after that White Whale, and the devil there is trying to come round him, and get him to swap away his silver watch, or his soul, or something of that sort, and then he'll surrender Moby Dick."

"Pooh! Stubb, you are skylarking; how can Fedallah do that?"

"I don't know, Flask, but the devil is a curious chap, and a wicked one, I tell ye. Why, they say as how he went a sauntering into the old flag-ship once, switching his tail about devilish easy and gentlemanlike, and inquiring if the old governor was at home. Well, he was at home, and asked the devil what he wanted. The devil, switching his hoofs, up and says, 'I want John.' 'What for?' says the old governor. 'What business is that of yours,' says the devil, getting mad,—'I want to use him.' 'Take him,' says the governor—and by the Lord,

Flask, if the devil didn't give John the Asiatic cholera before he got through with him, I'll eat this whale in one mouthful. But look sharp—aint you all ready there? Well, then, pull ahead, and let's get the whale alongside."

"I think I remember some such story as you were telling," said Flask, when at last the two boats were slowly advancing with their burden towards the ship, "but I can't remember where."

"Three Spaniards? Adventures of those three bloody-minded soldadoes? Did ye read it there, Flask? I guess ye did?"

"No: never saw such a book; heard of it, though. But now, tell me, Stubb, do you suppose that that devil you was speaking of just now, was the same you say is now on board the Pequod?"

"Am I the same man that helped kill this whale? Doesn't the devil live for ever; who ever heard that the devil was dead? Did you ever see any parson a wearing mourning for the devil? And if the devil has a latch-key to get into the admiral's cabin, don't you suppose he can crawl into a porthole? Tell me that, Mr. Flask?"

"How old do you suppose Fedallah is, Stubb?"

"Do you see that mainmast there?" pointing to the ship; "well, that's the figure one; now take all the hoops in the Pequod's hold, and string 'em along in a row with that mast, for oughts, do you see; well, that wouldn't begin to be Fedallah's age. Nor all the coopers in creation couldn't show hoops enough to make oughts enough."

"But see here, Stubb, I thought you a little boasted just now, that you meant to give Fedallah a sea-toss, if you got a good chance. Now, if he's so old as all those hoops of yours come to, and if he is going to live for ever, what good will it do to pitch him overboard—tell me that?"

"Give him a good ducking, anyhow."

"But he'd crawl back."

"Duck him again; and keep ducking him."

"Suppose he should take it into his head to duck you, though—yes, and drown you—what then?"

"I should like to see him try it; I'd give him such a pair of black eyes that he wouldn't dare to show his face in the admiral's cabin again for a long while, let alone down in the orlop there, where he lives, and hereabouts on the upper decks where he sneaks so much. Damn the devil, Flask; do you suppose I'm afraid of the devil? Who's afraid of him, except the old governor who daresn't catch him and put him in double-darbies, as he deserves, but lets him go about kidnapping people; aye, and signed a bond with him, that all the people the devil kidnapped, he'd roast for him? There's a governor!"

"Do you suppose Fedallah wants to kidnap Captain Ahab?"

"Do I suppose it? You'll know it before long, Flask. But I am going now to keep a sharp look-out on him; and if I see anything very suspicious going on, I'll just take him by the nape of his neck, and say—Look here, Beelzebub, you don't do it; and if he makes any fuss, by the Lord I'll make a grab into his pocket for his tail, take it to the capstan, and give him such a wrenching and heaving, that his tail will come short off at the stump—do you see; and then, I rather guess when he finds himself docked in that queer fashion, he'll sneak off without the poor satisfaction of feeling his tail between his legs."

"And what will you do with the tail, Stubb?"

"Do with it? Sell it for an ox whip when we get home;—what else?"

"Now, do you mean what you say, and have been saying all along, Stubb?"

"Mean or not mean, here we are at the ship."

The boats were here hailed, to tow the whale on the larboard side, where fluke chains and other necessaries were already prepared for securing him.

"Didn't I tell you so?" said Flask; "yes, you'll soon see this right whale's head hoisted up opposite that parmacetti's."

In good time, Flask's saying proved true. As before, the Pequod steeply leaned over towards the sperm whale's head, now, by the counterpoise of both heads, she regained her even keel; though sorely strained, you may well believe. So, when on one side you hoist in Locke's head, you go over that way; but now, on the other side, hoist in Kant's and you come back again; but in very poor plight. Thus, some minds for ever keep trimming boat. Oh, ye foolish! throw all these thunder-heads overboard, and then you will float light and right.

In disposing of the body of a right whale, when brought alongside the ship, the same preliminary proceedings commonly take place as in the case of a sperm whale; only, in the latter instance, the head is cut off whole, but in the former the lips and tongue are separately removed and hoisted on deck, with all the well known black bone attached to what is called the crown-piece. But nothing like this, in the present case, had been done. The carcases of both whales had dropped astern; and the head-laden ship not a little resembled a mule carrying a pair of overburdening panniers.

Meantime, Fedallah was calmly eyeing the right whale's head, and ever and anon glancing from the deep wrinkles there to the lines in his own hand. And Ahab chanced so to stand, that the Parsee occupied his shadow; while, if the Parsee's shadow was there at all it seemed only to blend with, and lengthen Ahab's. As the crew toiled on, Laplandish speculations were bandied among them, concerning all these passing things.

Chapter 74

THE SPERM WHALE'S HEAD—CONTRASTED VIEW

HERE, NOW, are two great whales, laying their heads together; let us join them, and lay together our own.

Of the grand order of folio leviathans, the Sperm Whale and the Right Whale are by far the most noteworthy. They are the only whales regularly hunted by man. To the Nantucketer, they present the two extremes of all the known varieties of the whale. As the external difference between them is mainly observable in their heads; and as a head of each is this moment hanging from the Pequod's side; and as we may freely go from one to the other, by merely stepping across the deck:—where, I should like to know, will you obtain a better chance to study practical cetology than here?

In the first place, you are struck by the general contrast between these heads. Both are massive enough in all conscience; but there is a certain mathematical symmetry in the Sperm Whale's which the Right Whale's sadly lacks. There is more character in the Sperm Whale's head. As you behold it, you involuntarily yield the immense superiority to him, in point of pervading dignity. In the present instance, too, this dignity is heightened by the pepper and salt color of his head at the summit, giving token of advanced age and large experience. In short, he is what the fishermen technically call a "greyheaded whale."

Let us now note what is least dissimilar in these heads—namely, the two most important organs, the eye and the ear. Far back on the side of the head, and low down, near the angle of either whale's jaw, if you narrowly search, you will at last see a lashless eye, which you would fancy to be a young colt's eye; so out of all proportion is it to the magnitude of the head.

Now, from this peculiar sideway position of the whale's eyes, it is plain that he can never see an object which is exactly ahead, no more than he can one exactly astern. In a word, the position of the whale's eyes corresponds to that of a man's ears; and you may fancy, for yourself, how it would fare with you, did you sideways survey objects through your ears. You would find that you could only command some thirty degrees of vision in advance of the straight side-line of sight; and about thirty more behind it. If your bitterest foe were walking straight towards you, with dagger uplifted in broad day, you would not be able to see him, any more than if he were stealing upon you from behind. In a word, you would have two backs, so to speak; but, at the same time, also, two fronts (side fronts): for what is it that makes the front of a man— what, indeed, but his eyes?

Moreover, while in most other animals that I can now think of, the eyes are so planted as imperceptibly to blend their visual power, so as to produce one picture and not two to the brain; the peculiar position of the whale's eyes, effectually divided as they are by many cubic feet of solid head, which towers between them like a great mountain separating two lakes in valleys; this, of course, must wholly separate the impressions which each independent organ imparts. The whale, therefore, must see one distinct picture on this side, and another distinct picture on that side; while all between must be profound darkness and nothingness to him. Man may, in effect, be said to look out on the world from a sentry-box with two joined sashes for his window. But with the whale, these two sashes are separately inserted, making two distinct windows, but sadly impairing the view. This peculiarity of the whale's eyes is a thing always to be borne in mind in the fishery; and to be remembered by the reader in some subsequent scenes.

A curious and most puzzling question might be started concerning this visual matter as touching the Leviathan. But I must be content with a hint. So long as a man's eyes are open in the light, the act of seeing is involuntary; that is, he cannot then help mechanically seeing whatever objects are before him. Nevertheless, any one's experience will teach him, that though he can take in an undiscriminating sweep of things at one glance, it is quite impossible for him, attentively, and completely, to examine any two things—however large or however small—at one and the same instant of time; never mind if they lie side by side and touch each other. But if you now come to separate these two objects, and surround each by a circle of profound darkness; then, in order to see one of them, in such a manner as to bring your mind to bear on it, the other will be utterly excluded from your contemporary consciousness. How is it, then, with the whale? True, both his eyes, in themselves, must simultaneously act; but is his brain so much more comprehensive, combining, and subtle than man's, that he can at the same moment of time attentively examine two distinct prospects, one on one side of him, and the other in an exactly opposite direction? If he can, then is it as marvellous a thing in him, as if a man were able simultaneously to go through the demonstrations of two distinct problems in Euclid. Nor, strictly investigated, is there any incongruity in this comparison.

It may be but an idle whim, but it has always seemed to me, that the extraordinary vacillations of movement displayed by some whales when beset by three or four boats; the timidity and liability to queer frights, so common to such whales; I think that all this indirectly proceeds from the helpless perplexity of volition, in which their divided and diametrically opposite powers of vision must involve them.

But the ear of the whale is full as curious as the eye. If you are an entire stranger to their race, you might hunt over these two heads for hours, and never discover that organ. The ear has no external leaf whatever; and into the hole itself you can hardly insert a quill, so wondrously minute is it. It is lodged a little behind the eye. With respect to their ears, this important difference is to be observed between the sperm whale and the right. While the ear of the former has an external opening, that of the latter is entirely and evenly covered over with a membrane, so as to be quite imperceptible from without.

Is it not curious, that so vast a being as the whale should see the world through so small an eye, and hear the thunder through an ear which is smaller than a hare's? But if his eyes were broad as the lens of Herschel's great telescope; and his ears capacious as the porches of cathedrals; would that make him any longer of sight, or sharper of hearing? Not at all.— Why then do you try to "enlarge" your mind? Subtilize it.

Let us now with whatever levers and steam-engines we have at hand, cant over the sperm whale's head, so that it may lie bottom up; then, ascending by a ladder to the summit, have a peep down the mouth; and were it not that the body is now completely separated from it, with a lantern we might descend into the great Kentucky Mammoth Cave of his stomach. But let us hold on here by this tooth, and look about us where we are. What a really beautiful and chaste-looking mouth! from floor to ceiling, lined, or rather papered with a glistening white membrane, glossy as bridal satins.

But come out now, and look at this portentous lower jaw, which seems like the long narrow lid of an immense snuff-box, with the hinge at one end, instead of one side. If you pry it up, so as to get it overhead, and expose its rows of teeth, it seems a terrific portcullis; and such, alas! it proves to many a poor wight in the fishery, upon whom these spikes fall with impaling force. But far more terrible is it to behold, when fathoms down in the sea, you see some sulky whale, floating there suspended, with his prodigious jaw, some fifteen feet long, hanging straight down at right-angles with his body, for all the world like a ship's jib-boom. This whale is not dead; he is only dispirited; out of sorts, perhaps; hypochondriac; and so supine, that the hinges of his jaw have relaxed, leaving him there in that ungainly sort of plight, a reproach to all his tribe, who must, no doubt, imprecate lock-jaws upon him.

In most cases this lower jaw—being easily unhinged by a practised artist—is disengaged and hoisted on deck for the purpose of extracting the ivory teeth, and furnishing a supply of that hard white whalebone with which the fishermen fashion all sorts of curious articles, including canes, umbrella-stocks, and handles to riding-whips.

With a long, weary hoist the jaw is dragged on board, as if it were an anchor; and when the proper time comes—some few days after the other work—Queequeg, Daggoo, and Tashtego, being all accomplished dentists, are set to drawing teeth. With a keen cutting-spade, Queequeg lances the gums; then the jaw is lashed down to ringbolts, and a tackle being rigged from aloft, they drag out these teeth, as Michigan oxen drag stumps of old oaks out of wild wood-lands. There are generally forty-two teeth in all; in old whales, much worn down, but undecayed; nor filled after our artificial fashion. The jaw is afterwards sawn into slabs, and piled away like joists for building houses.

Chapter 75

THE RIGHT WHALE'S HEAD—CONTRASTED VIEW

CROSSING THE DECK, let us now have a good long look at the Right Whale's head.

As in general shape the noble Sperm Whale's head may be compared to a Roman war-chariot (especially in front, where it is so broadly rounded); so, at a broad view, the Right Whale's head bears a rather inelegant resemblance to a gigantic galliot-toed shoe. Two hundred years ago an old Dutch voyager likened its shape to that of a shoemaker's last. And in this same last or shoe, that old woman of the nursery tale, with the swarming brood, might very comfortably be lodged, she and all her progeny.

But as you come nearer to this great head it begins to assume different aspects, according to your point of view. If you stand on its summit and look at these two *f*-shaped spout-holes, you would take the whole head for an enormous bass-viol, and these spiracles, the apertures in its sounding-board. Then, again, if you fix your eye upon this strange, crested, comb-like incrustation on the top of the mass—this green, barnacled thing, which the Greenlanders call the "crown," and the Southern fishers the "bonnet" of the Right Whale; fixing your eyes solely on this, you would take the head for the trunk of some huge oak, with a bird's nest in its crotch. At any rate, when you watch those live crabs that nestle here on this bonnet, such an idea will be almost sure to occur to you; unless, indeed, your fancy has been fixed by the technical term "crown" also bestowed upon it; in which case you will take great interest in thinking how this mighty monster is actually a diademed king of the sea, whose green crown has been put together for him in this marvellous manner. But if this whale be a king, he is a very sulky looking fellow to grace a diadem. Look at that hanging lower lip! what a huge sulk and pout is there! a sulk and pout, by carpenter's measurement, about twenty feet long and five feet deep; a sulk and pout that will yield you some 500 gallons of oil and more.

A great pity, now, that this unfortunate whale should be hare-lipped. The fissure is about a foot across. Probably the mother during an important interval was sailing down the Peruvian coast, when earthquakes caused the beach to gape. Over this lip, as over a slippery threshold, we now slide into the mouth. Upon my word were I at Mackinaw, I should take this to be the inside of an Indian wigwam. Good Lord! is this the road that Jonah went? The roof is about twelve feet high, and runs to a pretty sharp angle, as if there were a regular ridge-pole there; while these ribbed, arched, hairy sides, present us with those wondrous, half vertical, scimetar-shaped slats of whalebone, say three hundred on a side, which depending from the upper part of the head or crown bone, form those Venetian blinds which have elsewhere been cursorily mentioned. The edges of these bones are fringed with hairy fibres, through which the Right Whale strains the water, and in whose intricacies he retains the small fish, when open-mouthed he goes through the seas of brit in feeding time. In the central blinds of bone, as they stand in their natural order, there are certain curious marks, curves, hollows, and ridges, whereby some whalemen calculate the creature's age, as the age of an oak by its circular rings. Though the certainty of this criterion is far from demonstrable, yet it has the savor of analogical probability. At any rate, if we yield to it, we must grant a far greater age to the Right Whale than at first glance will seem reasonable.

In old times, there seem to have prevailed the most curious fancies concerning these blinds. One voyager in Purchas calls them the wondrous "whiskers" inside of the whale's mouth;* another, "hogs' bristles;" a third old gentleman in Hackluyt uses the following elegant language: "There are about two hundred and fifty fins growing on each side of his upper *chop*, which arch over his tongue on each side of his mouth."

As every one knows, these same "hogs' bristles," "fins," "whiskers," "blinds," or whatever you please, furnish to the

---

*This reminds us that the Right Whale really has a sort of whisker, or rather a moustache, consisting of a few scattered white hairs on the upper part of the outer end of the lower jaw. Sometimes these tufts impart a rather brigandish expression to his otherwise solemn countenance.

ladies their busks and other stiffening contrivances. But in this particular, the demand has long been on the decline. It was in Queen Anne's time that the bone was in its glory, the farthingale being then all the fashion. And as those ancient dames moved about gaily, though in the jaws of the whale, as you may say; even so, in a shower, with the like thoughtlessness, do we nowadays fly under the same jaws for protection; the umbrella being a tent spread over the same bone.

But now forget all about blinds and whiskers for a moment, and, standing in the Right Whale's mouth, look around you afresh. Seeing all these colonnades of bone so methodically ranged about, would you not think you were inside of the great Haarlem organ, and gazing upon its thousand pipes? For a carpet to the organ we have a rug of the softest Turkey—the tongue, which is glued, as it were, to the floor of the mouth. It is very fat and tender, and apt to tear in pieces in hoisting it on deck. This particular tongue now before us; at a passing glance I should say it was a six-barreler; that is, it will yield you about that amount of oil.

Ere this, you must have plainly seen the truth of what I started with—that the Sperm Whale and the Right Whale have almost entirely different heads. To sum up, then: in the Right Whale's there is no great well of sperm; no ivory teeth at all; no long, slender mandible of a lower jaw, like the Sperm Whale's. Nor in the Sperm Whale are there any of those blinds of bone; no huge lower lip; and scarcely anything of a tongue. Again, the Right Whale has two external spout-holes, the Sperm Whale only one.

Look your last, now, on these venerable hooded heads, while they yet lie together; for one will soon sink, unrecorded, in the sea; the other will not be very long in following.

Can you catch the expression of the Sperm Whale's there? It is the same he died with, only some of the longer wrinkles in the forehead seem now faded away. I think his broad brow to be full of a prairie-like placidity, born of a speculative indifference as to death. But mark the other head's expression. See that amazing lower lip, pressed by accident against the vessel's side, so as firmly to embrace the jaw. Does not this whole head seem to speak of an enormous practical resolution in facing death? This Right Whale I take to have been a Stoic; the Sperm Whale, a Platonian, who might have taken up Spinoza in his latter years.

Chapter 76

THE BATTERING-RAM

E RE QUITTING, for the nonce, the Sperm Whale's head, I
would have you, as a sensible physiologist, simply—
particularly remark its front aspect, in all its compacted col-
lectedness. I would have you investigate it now with the sole
view of forming to yourself some unexaggerated, intelligent
estimate of whatever battering-ram power may be lodged
there. Here is a vital point; for you must either satisfactorily
settle this matter with yourself, or for ever remain an infidel
as to one of the most appalling, but not the less true events,
perhaps anywhere to be found in all recorded history.

You observe that in the ordinary swimming position of the
Sperm Whale, the front of his head presents an almost wholly
vertical plane to the water; you observe that the lower part of
that front slopes considerably backwards, so as to furnish
more of a retreat for the long socket which receives the
boom-like lower jaw; you observe that the mouth is entirely
under the head, much in the same way, indeed, as though
your own mouth were entirely under your chin. Moreover
you observe that the whale has no external nose; and that
what nose he has—his spout hole—is on the top of his head;
you observe that his eyes and ears are at the sides of his head,
nearly one third of his entire length from the front. Wherefore, you must now have perceived that the front of the
Sperm Whale's head is a dead, blind wall, without a single
organ or tender prominence of any sort whatsoever. Furthermore, you are now to consider that only in the extreme,
lower, backward sloping part of the front of the head, is there
the slightest vestige of bone; and not till you get near twenty
feet from the forehead do you come to the full cranial development. So that this whole enormous boneless mass is as one
wad. Finally, though, as will soon be revealed, its contents
partly comprise the most delicate oil; yet, you are now to be
apprised of the nature of the substance which so impregnably
invests all that apparent effeminacy. In some previous place I

have described to you how the blubber wraps the body of the whale, as the rind wraps an orange. Just so with the head; but with this difference: about the head this envelope, though not so thick, is of a boneless toughness, inestimable by any man who has not handled it. The severest pointed harpoon, the sharpest lance darted by the strongest human arm, impotently rebounds from it. It is as though the forehead of the Sperm Whale were paved with horses' hoofs. I do not think that any sensation lurks in it.

Bethink yourself also of another thing. When two large, loaded Indiamen chance to crowd and crush towards each other in the docks, what do the sailors do? They do not suspend between them, at the point of coming contact, any merely hard substance, like iron or wood. No, they hold there a large, round wad of tow and cork, enveloped in the thickest and toughest of ox-hide. That bravely and uninjured takes the jam which would have snapped all their oaken handspikes and iron crow-bars. By itself this sufficiently illustrates the obvious fact I drive at. But supplementary to this, it has hypothetically occurred to me, that as ordinary fish possess what is called a swimming bladder in them, capable, at will, of distension or contraction; and as the Sperm Whale, as far as I know, has no such provision in him; considering, too, the otherwise inexplicable manner in which he now depresses his head altogether beneath the surface, and anon swims with it high elevated out of the water; considering the unobstructed elasticity of its envelop; considering the unique interior of his head; it has hypothetically occurred to me, I say, that those mystical lung-celled honeycombs there may possibly have some hitherto unknown and unsuspected connexion with the outer air, so as to be susceptible to atmospheric distension and contraction. If this be so, fancy the irresistibleness of that might, to which the most impalpable and destructive of all elements contributes.

Now, mark. Unerringly impelling this dead, impregnable, uninjurable wall, and this most buoyant thing within; there swims behind it all a mass of tremendous life, only to be adequately estimated as piled wood is—by the cord; and all obedient to one volition, as the smallest insect. So that when I shall hereafter detail to you all the specialities and concen-

trations of potency everywhere lurking in this expansive monster; when I shall show you some of his more inconsiderable
braining feats; I trust you will have renounced all ignorant
incredulity, and be ready to abide by this; that though the
Sperm Whale stove a passage through the Isthmus of Darien,
and mixed the Atlantic with the Pacific, you would not elevate one hair of your eye-brow. For unless you own the
whale, you are but a provincial and sentimentalist in Truth.
But clear Truth is a thing for salamander giants only to encounter; how small the chances for the provincials then?
What befel the weakling youth lifting the dread goddess's veil
at Sais?

Chapter 77

The Great Heidelburgh Tun

Now comes the Baling of the Case. But to comprehend it aright, you must know something of the curious internal structure of the thing operated upon.

Regarding the Sperm Whale's head as a solid oblong, you may, on an inclined plane, sideways divide it into two quoins,* whereof the lower is the bony structure, forming the cranium and jaws, and the upper an unctuous mass wholly free from bones; its broad forward end forming the expanded vertical apparent forehead of the whale. At the middle of the forehead horizontally subdivide this upper quoin, and then you have two almost equal parts, which before were naturally divided by an internal wall of a thick tendinous substance.

The lower subdivided part, called the junk, is one immense honeycomb of oil, formed by the crossing and re-crossing, into ten thousand infiltrated cells, of tough elastic white fibres throughout its whole extent. The upper part, known as the Case, may be regarded as the great Heidelburgh Tun of the Sperm Whale. And as that famous great tierce is mystically carved in front, so the whale's vast plaited forehead forms innumerable strange devices for the emblematical adornment of his wondrous tun. Moreover, as that of Heidelburgh was always replenished with the most excellent of the wines of the Rhenish valleys, so the tun of the whale contains by far the most precious of all his oily vintages; namely, the highly-prized spermaceti, in its absolutely pure, limpid, and odoriferous state. Nor is this precious substance found unalloyed in any other part of the creature. Though in life it remains perfectly fluid, yet, upon exposure to the air, after death, it soon begins to concrete; sending forth beautiful crystalline shoots, as when the first thin delicate ice is just forming in water. A

---

*Quoin is not a Euclidean term. It belongs to the pure nautical mathematics. I know not that it has been defined before. A quoin is a solid which differs from a wedge in having its sharp end formed by the steep inclination of one side, instead of the mutual tapering of both sides.

large whale's case generally yields about five hundred gallons of sperm, though from unavoidable circumstances, considerable of it is spilled, leaks, and dribbles away, or is otherwise irrevocably lost in the ticklish business of securing what you can.

I know not with what fine and costly material the Heidelburgh Tun was coated within, but in superlative richness that coating could not possibly have compared with the silken pearl-colored membrane, like the lining of a fine pelisse, forming the inner surface of the Sperm Whale's case.

It will have been seen that the Heidelburgh Tun of the Sperm Whale embraces the entire length of the entire top of the head; and since—as has been elsewhere set forth—the head embraces one third of the whole length of the creature, then setting that length down at eighty feet for a good sized whale, you have more than twenty-six feet for the depth of the tun, when it is lengthwise hoisted up and down against a ship's side.

As in decapitating the whale, the operator's instrument is brought close to the spot where an entrance is subsequently forced into the spermaceti magazine; he has, therefore, to be uncommonly heedful, lest a careless, untimely stroke should invade the sanctuary and wastingly let out its invaluable contents. It is this decapitated end of the head, also, which is at last elevated out of the water, and retained in that position by the enormous cutting tackles, whose hempen combinations, on one side, make quite a wilderness of ropes in that quarter.

Thus much being said, attend now, I pray you, to that marvellous and—in this particular instance—almost fatal operation whereby the Sperm Whale's great Heidelburgh Tun is tapped.

Chapter 78

CISTERN AND BUCKETS

NIMBLE AS A CAT, Tashtego mounts aloft; and without altering his erect posture, runs straight out upon the overhanging main-yard-arm, to the part where it exactly projects over the hoisted Tun. He has carried with him a light tackle called a whip, consisting of only two parts, travelling through a single-sheaved block. Securing this block, so that it hangs down from the yard-arm, he swings one end of the rope, till it is caught and firmly held by a hand on deck. Then, hand-over-hand, down the other part, the Indian drops through the air, till dexterously he lands on the summit of the head. There—still high elevated above the rest of the company, to whom he vivaciously cries—he seems some Turkish Muezzin calling the good people to prayers from the top of a tower. A short-handled sharp spade being sent up to him, he diligently searches for the proper place to begin breaking into the Tun. In this business he proceeds very heedfully, like a treasure-hunter in some old house, sounding the walls to find where the gold is masoned in. By the time this cautious search is over, a stout iron-bound bucket, precisely like a well-bucket, has been attached to one end of the whip; while the other end, being stretched across the deck, is there held by two or three alert hands. These last now hoist the bucket within grasp of the Indian, to whom another person has reached up a very long pole. Inserting this pole into the bucket, Tashtego downward guides the bucket into the Tun, till it entirely disappears; then giving the word to the seamen at the whip, up comes the bucket again, all bubbling like a dairy-maid's pail of new milk. Carefully lowered from its height, the full-freighted vessel is caught by an appointed hand, and quickly emptied into a large tub. Then re-mounting aloft, it again goes through the same round until the deep cistern will yield no more. Towards the end, Tashtego has to ram his long pole harder and harder, and deeper and deeper into the Tun, until some twenty feet of the pole have gone down.

Now, the people of the Pequod had been baling some time in this way; several tubs had been filled with the fragrant sperm; when all at once a queer accident happened. Whether it was that Tashtego, that wild Indian, was so heedless and reckless as to let go for a moment his one-handed hold on the great cabled tackles suspending the head; or whether the place where he stood was so treacherous and oozy; or whether the Evil One himself would have it to fall out so, without stating his particular reasons; how it was exactly, there is no telling now; but, on a sudden, as the eightieth or ninetieth bucket came suckingly up—my God! poor Tashtego—like the twin reciprocating bucket in a veritable well, dropped head-foremost down into this great Tun of Heidelburgh, and with a horrible oily gurgling, went clean out of sight!

"Man overboard!" cried Daggoo, who amid the general consternation first came to his senses. "Swing the bucket this way!" and putting one foot into it, so as the better to secure his slippery hand-hold on the whip itself, the hoisters ran him high up to the top of the head, almost before Tashtego could have reached its interior bottom. Meantime, there was a terrible tumult. Looking over the side, they saw the before lifeless head throbbing and heaving just below the surface of the sea, as if that moment seized with some momentous idea; whereas it was only the poor Indian unconsciously revealing by those struggles the perilous depth to which he had sunk.

At this instant, while Daggoo, on the summit of the head, was clearing the whip—which had somehow got foul of the great cutting tackles—a sharp cracking noise was heard; and to the unspeakable horror of all, one of the two enormous hooks suspending the head tore out, and with a vast vibration the enormous mass sideways swung, till the drunk ship reeled and shook as if smitten by an iceberg. The one remaining hook, upon which the entire strain now depended, seemed every instant to be on the point of giving way; an event still more likely from the violent motions of the head.

"Come down, come down!" yelled the seamen to Daggoo, but with one hand holding on to the heavy tackles, so that if the head should drop, he would still remain suspended; the negro having cleared the foul line, rammed down the bucket into the now collapsed well, meaning that the buried harpooneer should grasp it, and so be hoisted out.

"In heaven's name, man," cried Stubb, "are you ramming home a cartridge there?—Avast! How will that help him; jamming that iron-bound bucket on top of his head? Avast, will ye!"

"Stand clear of the tackle!" cried a voice like the bursting of a rocket.

Almost in the same instant, with a thunder-boom, the enormous mass dropped into the sea, like Niagara's Table-Rock into the whirlpool; the suddenly relieved hull rolled away from it, to far down her glittering copper; and all caught their breath, as half swinging—now over the sailors' heads, and now over the water—Daggoo, through a thick mist of spray, was dimly beheld clinging to the pendulous tackles, while poor, buried-alive Tashtego was sinking utterly down to the bottom of the sea! But hardly had the blinding vapor cleared away, when a naked figure with a boarding-sword in its hand, was for one swift moment seen hovering over the bulwarks. The next, a loud splash announced that my brave Queequeg had dived to the rescue. One packed rush was made to the side, and every eye counted every ripple, as moment followed moment, and no sign of either the sinker or the diver could be seen. Some hands now jumped into a boat alongside, and pushed a little off from the ship.

"Ha! ha!" cried Daggoo, all at once, from his now quiet, swinging perch overhead; and looking further off from the side, we saw an arm thrust upright from the blue waves; a sight strange to see, as an arm thrust forth from the grass over a grave.

"Both! both!—it is both!"—cried Daggoo again with a joyful shout; and soon after, Queequeg was seen boldly striking out with one hand, and with the other clutching the long hair of the Indian. Drawn into the waiting boat, they were quickly brought to the deck; but Tashtego was long in coming to, and Queequeg did not look very brisk.

Now, how had this noble rescue been accomplished? Why,

diving after the slowly descending head, Queequeg with his keen sword had made side lunges near its bottom, so as to scuttle a large hole there; then dropping his sword, had thrust his long arm far inwards and upwards, and so hauled out our poor Tash by the head. He averred, that upon first thrusting in for him, a leg was presented; but well knowing that that was not as it ought to be, and might occasion great trouble;—he had thrust back the leg, and by a dexterous heave and toss, had wrought a somerset upon the Indian; so that with the next trial, he came forth in the good old way—head foremost. As for the great head itself, that was doing as well as could be expected.

And thus, through the courage and great skill in obstetrics of Queequeg, the deliverance, or rather, delivery of Tashtego, was successfully accomplished, in the teeth, too, of the most untoward and apparently hopeless impediments; which is a lesson by no means to be forgotten. Midwifery should be taught in the same course with fencing and boxing, riding and rowing.

I know that this queer adventure of the Gay-Header's will be sure to seem incredible to some landsmen, though they themselves may have either seen or heard of some one's falling into a cistern ashore; an accident which not seldom happens, and with much less reason too than the Indian's, considering the exceeding slipperiness of the curb of the Sperm Whale's well.

But, peradventure, it may be sagaciously urged, how is this? We thought the tissued, infiltrated head of the Sperm Whale, was the lightest and most corky part about him; and yet thou makest it sink in an element of a far greater specific gravity than itself. We have thee there. Not at all, but I have ye; for at the time poor Tash fell in, the case had been nearly emptied of its lighter contents, leaving little but the dense tendinous wall of the well—a double welded, hammered substance, as I have before said, much heavier than the sea water, and a lump of which sinks in it like lead almost. But the tendency to rapid sinking in this substance was in the present instance materially counteracted by the other parts of the head remaining undetached from it, so that it sank very slowly and deliberately indeed, affording Queequeg a fair chance for performing his agile obstetrics on the run, as you may say. Yes, it was a running delivery, so it was.

Now, had Tashtego perished in that head, it had been a very precious perishing; smothered in the very whitest and daintiest of fragrant spermaceti; coffined, hearsed, and tombed in the secret inner chamber and sanctum sanctorum of the whale. Only one sweeter end can readily be recalled— the delicious death of an Ohio honey-hunter, who seeking honey in the crotch of a hollow tree, found such exceeding store of it, that leaning too far over, it sucked him in, so that he died embalmed. How many, think ye, have likewise fallen into Plato's honey head, and sweetly perished there?

Chapter 79

THE PRAIRIE

To SCAN the lines of his face, or feel the bumps on the head of this Leviathan; this is a thing which no Physiognomist or Phrenologist has as yet undertaken. Such an enterprise would seem almost as hopeful as for Lavater to have scrutinized the wrinkles on the Rock of Gibraltar, or for Gall to have mounted a ladder and manipulated the Dome of the Pantheon. Still, in that famous work of his, Lavater not only treats of the various faces of men, but also attentively studies the faces of horses, birds, serpents, and fish; and dwells in detail upon the modifications of expression discernible therein. Nor have Gall and his disciple Spurzheim failed to throw out some hints touching the phrenological characteristics of other beings than man. Therefore, though I am but ill qualified for a pioneer, in the application of these two semi-sciences to the whale, I will do my endeavor. I try all things; I achieve what I can.

Physiognomically regarded, the Sperm Whale is an anomalous creature. He has no proper nose. And since the nose is the central and most conspicuous of the features; and since it perhaps most modifies and finally controls their combined expression; hence it would seem that its entire absence, as an external appendage, must very largely affect the countenance of the whale. For as in landscape gardening, a spire, cupola, monument, or tower of some sort, is deemed almost indispensable to the completion of the scene; so no face can be physiognomically in keeping without the elevated open-work belfry of the nose. Dash the nose from Phidias's marble Jove, and what a sorry remainder! Nevertheless, Leviathan is of so mighty a magnitude, all his proportions are so stately, that the same deficiency which in the sculptured Jove were hideous, in him is no blemish at all. Nay, it is an added grandeur. A nose to the whale would have been impertinent. As on your physiognomical voyage you sail round his vast head in your jolly-boat, your noble conceptions of him are never in-

sulted by the reflection that he has a nose to be pulled. A
pestilent conceit, which so often will insist upon obtruding
even when beholding the mightiest royal beadle on his
throne.

In some particulars, perhaps the most imposing physiognomical view to be had of the Sperm Whale, is that of the
full front of his head. This aspect is sublime.

In thought, a fine human brow is like the East when troubled with the morning. In the repose of the pasture, the
curled brow of the bull has a touch of the grand in it. Pushing
heavy cannon up mountain defiles, the elephant's brow is
majestic. Human or animal, the mystical brow is as that great
golden seal affixed by the German emperors to their decrees.
It signifies—"God: done this day by my hand." But in most
creatures, nay in man himself, very often the brow is but a
mere strip of alpine land lying along the snow line. Few are
the foreheads which like Shakspeare's or Melancthon's rise so
high, and descend so low, that the eyes themselves seem clear,
eternal, tideless mountain lakes; and all above them in the
forehead's wrinkles, you seem to track the antlered thoughts
descending there to drink, as the Highland hunters track the
snow prints of the deer. But in the great Sperm Whale, this
high and mighty god-like dignity inherent in the brow is so
immensely amplified, that gazing on it, in that full front view,
you feel the Deity and the dread powers more forcibly than
in beholding any other object in living nature. For you see
no one point precisely; not one distinct feature is revealed; no
nose, eyes, ears, or mouth; no face; he has none, proper;
nothing but that one broad firmament of a forehead, pleated
with riddles; dumbly lowering with the doom of boats, and
ships, and men. Nor, in profile, does this wondrous brow
diminish; though that way viewed, its grandeur does not
domineer upon you so. In profile, you plainly perceive that
horizontal, semi-crescentic depression in the forehead's middle, which, in man, is Lavater's mark of genius.

But how? Genius in the Sperm Whale? Has the Sperm
Whale ever written a book, spoken a speech? No, his great
genius is declared in his doing nothing particular to prove it.
It is moreover declared in his pyramidical silence. And this
reminds me that had the great Sperm Whale been known to

the young Orient World, he would have been deified by their child-magian thoughts. They deified the crocodile of the Nile, because the crocodile is tongueless; and the Sperm Whale has no tongue, or at least it is so exceedingly small, as to be incapable of protrusion. If hereafter any highly cultured, poetical nation shall lure back to their birth-right, the merry Mayday gods of old; and livingly enthrone them again in the now egotistical sky; in the now unhaunted hill; then be sure, exalted to Jove's high seat, the great Sperm Whale shall lord it.

Champollion deciphered the wrinkled granite hieroglyphics. But there is no Champollion to decipher the Egypt of every man's and every being's face. Physiognomy, like every other human science, is but a passing fable. If then, Sir William Jones, who read in thirty languages, could not read the simplest peasant's face in its profounder and more subtle meanings, how may unlettered Ishmael hope to read the awful Chaldee of the Sperm Whale's brow? I but put that brow before you. Read it if you can.

Chapter 80

THE NUT

IF THE SPERM WHALE be physiognomically a Sphinx, to the
phrenologist his brain seems that geometrical circle which
it is impossible to square.

In the full-grown creature the skull will measure at least
twenty feet in length. Unhinge the lower jaw, and the side
view of this skull is as the side view of a moderately inclined
plane resting throughout on a level base. But in life—as we
have elsewhere seen—this inclined plane is angularly filled
up, and almost squared by the enormous superincumbent
mass of the junk and sperm. At the high end the skull forms
a crater to bed that part of the mass; while under the long
floor of this crater—in another cavity seldom exceeding ten
inches in length and as many in depth—reposes the mere
handful of this monster's brain. The brain is at least twenty
feet from his apparent forehead in life; it is hidden away behind its vast outworks, like the innermost citadel within the
amplified fortifications of Quebec. So like a choice casket is it
secreted in him, that I have known some whalemen who peremptorily deny that the Sperm Whale has any other brain
than that palpable semblance of one formed by the cubic-
yards of his sperm magazine. Lying in strange folds, courses,
and convolutions, to their apprehensions, it seems more in
keeping with the idea of his general might to regard that mystic part of him as the seat of his intelligence.

It is plain, then, that phrenologically the head of this Leviathan, in the creature's living intact state, is an entire delusion. As for his true brain, you can then see no indications of
it, nor feel any. The whale, like all things that are mighty,
wears a false brow to the common world.

If you unload his skull of its spermy heaps and then take a
rear view of its rear end, which is the high end, you will be
struck by its resemblance to the human skull, beheld in the
same situation, and from the same point of view. Indeed,
place this reversed skull (scaled down to the human magni-

tude) among a plate of men's skulls, and you would involuntarily confound it with them; and remarking the depressions on one part of its summit, in phrenological phrase you would say—This man had no self-esteem, and no veneration. And by those negations, considered along with the affirmative fact of his prodigious bulk and power, you can best form to yourself the truest, though not the most exhilarating conception of what the most exalted potency is.

But if from the comparative dimensions of the whale's proper brain, you deem it incapable of being adequately charted, then I have another idea for you. If you attentively regard almost any quadruped's spine, you will be struck with the resemblance of its vertebræ to a strung necklace of dwarfed skulls, all bearing rudimental resemblance to the skull proper. It is a German conceit, that the vertebræ are absolutely undeveloped skulls. But the curious external resemblance, I take it the Germans were not the first men to perceive. A foreign friend once pointed it out to me, in the skeleton of a foe he had slain, and with the vertebræ of which he was inlaying, in a sort of basso-relievo, the beaked prow of his canoe. Now, I consider that the phrenologists have omitted an important thing in not pushing their investigations from the cerebellum through the spinal canal. For I believe that much of a man's character will be found betokened in his backbone. I would rather feel your spine than your skull, whoever you are. A thin joist of a spine never yet upheld a full and noble soul. I rejoice in my spine, as in the firm audacious staff of that flag which I fling half out to the world.

Apply this spinal branch of phrenology to the Sperm Whale. His cranial cavity is continuous with the first neck-vertebra; and in that vertebra the bottom of the spinal canal will measure ten inches across, being eight in height, and of a triangular figure with the base downwards. As it passes through the remaining vertebræ the canal tapers in size, but for a considerable distance remains of large capacity. Now, of course, this canal is filled with much the same strangely fibrous substance—the spinal cord—as the brain; and directly communicates with the brain. And what is still more, for many feet after emerging from the brain's cavity, the spinal cord remains of an undecreasing girth, almost equal to that of the brain. Under all these circumstances, would it be unreasonable to survey and map out the whale's spine phrenologically? For, viewed in this light, the wonderful comparative smallness of his brain proper is more than compensated by the wonderful comparative magnitude of his spinal cord.

But leaving this hint to operate as it may with the phrenologists, I would merely assume the spinal theory for a moment, in reference to the Sperm Whale's hump. This august hump, if I mistake not, rises over one of the larger vertebræ, and is, therefore, in some sort, the outer convex mould of it. From its relative situation then, I should call this high hump the organ of firmness or indomitableness in the Sperm Whale. And that the great monster is indomitable, you will yet have reason to know.

Chapter 81

THE PEQUOD MEETS THE VIRGIN

THE PREDESTINATED DAY arrived, and we duly met the ship Jungfrau, Derick De Deer, master, of Bremen.

At one time the greatest whaling people in the world, the Dutch and Germans are now among the least; but here and there at very wide intervals of latitude and longitude, you still occasionally meet with their flag in the Pacific.

For some reason, the Jungfrau seemed quite eager to pay her respects. While yet some distance from the Pequod, she rounded to, and dropping a boat, her captain was impelled towards us, impatiently standing in the bows instead of the stern.

"What has he in his hand there?" cried Starbuck, pointing to something wavingly held by the German. "Impossible!—a lamp-feeder!"

"Not that," said Stubb, "no, no, it's a coffee-pot, Mr. Starbuck; he's coming off to make us our coffee, is the Yarman; don't you see that big tin can there alongside of him?—that's his boiling water. Oh! he's all right, is the Yarman."

"Go along with you," cried Flask, "it's a lamp-feeder and an oil-can. He's out of oil, and has come a-begging."

However curious it may seem for an oil-ship to be borrowing oil on the whale-ground, and however much it may invertedly contradict the old proverb about carrying coals to Newcastle, yet sometimes such a thing really happens; and in the present case Captain Derick De Deer did indubitably conduct a lamp-feeder as Flask did declare.

As he mounted the deck, Ahab abruptly accosted him, without at all heeding what he had in his hand; but in his broken lingo, the German soon evinced his complete ignorance of the White Whale; immediately turning the conversation to his lamp-feeder and oil can, with some remarks touching his having to turn into his hammock at night in profound darkness—his last drop of Bremen oil being gone, and not a single flying-fish yet captured to supply the deficiency; concluding by hinting that his ship was indeed what in the Fishery is technically called a *clean* one (that is, an empty one), well deserving the name of Jungfrau or the Virgin.

His necessities supplied, Derick departed; but he had not gained his ship's side, when whales were almost simultaneously raised from the mast-heads of both vessels; and so eager for the chase was Derick, that without pausing to put his oil-can and lamp-feeder aboard, he slewed round his boat and made after the leviathan lamp-feeders.

Now, the game having risen to leeward, he and the other three German boats that soon followed him, had considerably the start of the Pequod's keels. There were eight whales, an average pod. Aware of their danger, they were going all abreast with great speed straight before the wind, rubbing their flanks as closely as so many spans of horses in harness. They left a great, wide wake, as though continually unrolling a great wide parchment upon the sea.

Full in this rapid wake, and many fathoms in the rear, swam a huge, humped old bull, which by his comparatively slow progress, as well as by the unusual yellowish incrustations overgrowing him, seemed afflicted with the jaundice, or some other infirmity. Whether this whale belonged to the pod in advance, seemed questionable; for it is not customary for such venerable leviathans to be at all social. Nevertheless, he stuck to their wake, though indeed their back water must have retarded him, because the white-bone or swell at his broad muzzle was a dashed one, like the swell formed when two hostile currents meet. His spout was short, slow, and laborious; coming forth with a choking sort of gush, and spending itself in torn shreds, followed by strange subterranean commotions in him, which seemed to have egress at his other buried extremity, causing the waters behind him to up-bubble.

"Who's got some paregoric?" said Stubb, "he has the stomach-ache, I'm afraid. Lord, think of having half an acre of stomach-ache! Adverse winds are holding mad Christmas in him, boys. It's the first foul wind I ever knew to blow from astern; but look, did ever whale yaw so before? it must be, he's lost his tiller."

As an overladen Indiaman bearing down the Hindostan coast with a deck load of frightened horses, careens, buries, rolls, and wallows on her way; so did this old whale heave his aged bulk, and now and then partly turning over on his cumbrous rib-ends, expose the cause of his devious wake in the unnatural stump of his starboard fin. Whether he had lost that fin in battle, or had been born without it, it were hard to say.

"Only wait a bit, old chap, and I'll give ye a sling for that wounded arm," cried cruel Flask, pointing to the whale-line near him.

"Mind he don't sling thee with it," cried Starbuck. "Give way, or the German will have him."

With one intent all the combined rival boats were pointed for this one fish, because not only was he the largest, and therefore the most valuable whale, but he was nearest to them, and the other whales were going with such great velocity, moreover, as almost to defy pursuit for the time. At this juncture, the Pequod's keels had shot by the three German boats last lowered; but from the great start he had had, Derick's boat still led the chase, though every moment neared by his foreign rivals. The only thing they feared, was, that from being already so nigh to his mark, he would be enabled to dart his iron before they could completely overtake and pass him. As for Derick, he seemed quite confident that this would be the case, and occasionally with a deriding gesture shook his lamp-feeder at the other boats.

"The ungracious and ungrateful dog!" cried Starbuck; "he mocks and dares me with the very poor-box I filled for him not five minutes ago!"—then in his old intense whisper—"give way, greyhounds! Dog to it!"

"I tell ye what it is, men"—cried Stubb to his crew—"It's against my religion to get mad; but I'd like to eat that villanous Yarman—Pull—wont ye? Are ye going to let that rascal beat ye? Do ye love brandy? A hogshead of brandy, then, to the best man. Come, why don't some of ye burst a blood-vessel? Who's that been dropping an anchor overboard—we don't budge an inch—we're becalmed. Halloo, here's grass growing in the boat's bottom—and by the Lord, the mast there's budding. This won't do, boys. Look at that Yarman! The short and long of it is, men, will ye spit fire or not?"

"Oh! see the suds he makes!" cried Flask, dancing up and down—"What a hump—Oh, *do* pile on the beef—lays like a log! Oh! my lads, *do* spring—slap-jacks and quohogs for supper, you know, my lads—baked clams and muffins—oh, *do*, *do*, spring—he's a hundred barreler—don't lose him now—don't, oh, *don't!*—see that Yarman—Oh! won't ye pull for your duff, my lads—such a sog! such a sogger! Don't ye love sperm? There goes three thousand dollars, men!—a bank!—a whole bank! The bank of England!—Oh, *do*, *do*, *do!*—What's that Yarman about now?"

At this moment Derick was in the act of pitching his lamp-feeder at the advancing boats, and also his oil-can; perhaps with the double view of retarding his rivals' way, and at the same time economically accelerating his own by the momentary impetus of the backward toss.

"The unmannerly Dutch dogger!" cried Stubb. "Pull now, men, like fifty thousand line-of-battle-ship loads of red-haired devils. What d'ye say, Tashtego; are you the man to snap your spine in two-and-twenty pieces for the honor of old Gayhead? What d'ye say?"

"I say, pull like god-dam,"—cried the Indian.

Fiercely but evenly, incited by the taunts of the German, the Pequod's three boats now began ranging almost abreast; and, so disposed, momentarily neared him. In that fine, loose, chivalrous attitude of the headsman when drawing near to his prey, the three mates stood up proudly, occasionally backing the after oarsman with an exhilarating cry of, "There she slides, now! Hurrah for the white-ash breeze! Down with the Yarman! Sail over him!"

But so decided an original start had Derick had, that spite of all their gallantry, he would have proved the victor in this race, had not a righteous judgment descended upon him in a crab which caught the blade of his midship oarsman. While this clumsy lubber was striving to free his white-ash, and while, in consequence, Derick's boat was nigh to capsizing, and he thundering away at his men in a mighty rage;—that was a good time for Starbuck, Stubb, and Flask. With a shout, they took a mortal start forwards, and slantingly ranged up on the German's quarter. An instant more, and all four boats were diagonally in the whale's immediate wake, while stretching from them, on both sides, was the foaming swell that he made.

It was a terrific, most pitiable, and maddening sight. The whale was now going head out, and sending his spout before him in a continual tormented jet; while his one poor fin beat his side in an agony of fright. Now to this hand, now to that, he yawed in his faltering flight, and still at every billow that he broke, he spasmodically sank in the sea, or sideways rolled towards the sky his one beating fin. So have I seen a bird with clipped wing, making affrighted broken circles in the air, vainly striving to escape the piratical hawks. But the bird has a voice, and with plaintive cries will make known her fear; but the fear of this vast dumb brute of the sea, was chained up and enchanted in him; he had no voice, save that choking respiration through his spiracle, and this made the sight of him unspeakably pitiable; while still, in his amazing bulk, portcullis jaw, and omnipotent tail, there was enough to appal the stoutest man who so pitied.

Seeing now that but a very few moments more would give the Pequod's boats the advantage, and rather than be thus foiled of his game, Derick chose to hazard what to him must have seemed a most unusually long dart, ere the last chance would for ever escape.

But no sooner did his harpooneer stand up for the stroke, than all three tigers—Queequeg, Tashtego, Daggoo—instinctively sprang to their feet, and standing in a diagonal row, simultaneously pointed their barbs; and, darted over the head of the German harpooneer, their three Nantucket irons entered the whale. Blinding vapors of foam and white-fire! The three boats, in the first fury of the whale's headlong rush, bumped the German's aside with such force, that both Derick and his baffled harpooneer were spilled out, and sailed over by the three flying keels.

"Don't be afraid, my butter-boxes," cried Stubb, casting a passing glance upon them as he shot by; "ye'll be picked up presently—all right—I saw some sharks astern—St. Bernard's dogs, you know—relieve distressed travellers. Hurrah! this is the way to sail now. Every keel a sun-beam! Hurrah!— Here we go like three tin kettles at the tail of a mad cougar! This puts me in mind of fastening to an elephant in a tilbury on a plain—makes the wheel-spokes fly, boys, when you fasten to him that way; and there's danger of being pitched out too, when you strike a hill. Hurrah! this is the way a fellow feels when he's going to Davy Jones—all a rush down an endless inclined plane! Hurrah! this whale carries the everlasting mail!"

But the monster's run was a brief one. Giving a sudden gasp, he tumultuously sounded. With a grating rush, the three lines flew round the loggerheads with such a force as to gouge deep grooves in them; while so fearful were the harpooneers that this rapid sounding would soon exhaust the lines, that using all their dexterous might, they caught repeated smoking turns with the rope to hold on; till at last—owing to the perpendicular strain from the lead-lined chocks of the boats, whence the three ropes went straight down into the blue—the gunwales of the bows were almost even with the water, while the three sterns tilted high in the air. And the whale soon ceasing to sound, for some time they remained in that attitude, fearful of expending more line, though the position was a little ticklish. But though boats have been taken down and lost in this way, yet it is this "holding on," as it is called; this hooking up by the sharp barbs of his live flesh from the back; this it is that often torments the Leviathan into soon rising again to meet the sharp lance of his foes. Yet not to speak of the peril of the thing, it is to be doubted whether this course is always the best; for it is but reasonable to presume, that the longer the stricken whale stays under water, the more he is exhausted. Because, owing to the enormous surface of him—in a full grown sperm whale something less than 2000 square feet—the pressure of the water is immense. We all know what an astonishing atmospheric weight we ourselves stand up under; even here, above-ground, in the air; how vast, then, the burden of a whale, bearing on his back a column of two hundred fathoms of ocean! It must at least equal the weight of fifty atmospheres. One whaleman has estimated it at the weight of twenty line-of-battle ships, with all their guns, and stores, and men on board.

As the three boats lay there on that gently rolling sea, gazing down into its eternal blue noon; and as not a single groan or cry of any sort, nay, not so much as a ripple or a bubble came up from its depths; what landsman would have thought, that beneath all that silence and placidity, the utmost monster of the seas was writhing and wrenching in agony! Not eight inches of perpendicular rope were visible at the bows. Seems it credible that by three such thin threads the great Leviathan was suspended like the big weight to an eight day clock. Suspended? and to what? To three bits of board. Is this the creature of whom it was once so triumphantly said—"Canst thou fill his skin with barbed irons? or his head with fish-spears? The sword of him that layeth at him cannot hold, the spear, the dart, nor the habergeon: he esteemeth iron as straw; the arrow cannot make him flee; darts are counted as stubble; he laugheth at the shaking of a spear!" This the creature? this he? Oh! that unfulfilments should follow the prophets. For with the strength of a thousand thighs in his tail, Leviathan had run his head under the mountains of the sea, to hide him from the Pequod's fish-spears!

In that sloping afternoon sunlight, the shadows that the three boats sent down beneath the surface, must have been long enough and broad enough to shade half Xerxes' army. Who can tell how appalling to the wounded whale must have been such huge phantoms flitting over his head!

"Stand by, men; he stirs," cried Starbuck, as the three lines suddenly vibrated in the water, distinctly conducting upwards to them, as by magnetic wires, the life and death throbs of the whale, so that every oarsman felt them in his seat. The next moment, relieved in great part from the downward strain at the bows, the boats gave a sudden bounce upwards, as a small ice-field will, when a dense herd of white bears are scared from it into the sea.

"Haul in! Haul in!" cried Starbuck again; "he's rising."

The lines, of which, hardly an instant before, not one hand's breadth could have been gained, were now in long quick coils flung back all dripping into the boats, and soon the whale broke water within two ship's lengths of the hunters.

His motions plainly denoted his extreme exhaustion. In most land animals there are certain valves or flood-gates in many of their veins, whereby when wounded, the blood is in some degree at least instantly shut off in certain directions. Not so with the whale; one of whose peculiarities it is, to have an entire non-valvular structure of the blood-vessels, so that when pierced even by so small a point as a harpoon, a deadly drain is at once begun upon his whole arterial system; and when this is heightened by the extraordinary pressure of water at a great distance below the surface, his life may be said to pour from him in incessant streams. Yet so vast is the quantity of blood in him, and so distant and numerous its interior fountains, that he will keep thus bleeding and bleeding for a considerable period; even as in a drought a river will flow, whose source is in the well-springs of far-off and undiscernible hills. Even now, when the boats pulled upon this whale, and perilously drew over his swaying flukes, and the lances were darted into him, they were followed by steady jets from the new made wound, which kept continually playing, while the natural spout-hole in his head was only at intervals, however rapid, sending its affrighted moisture into the air. From this last vent no blood yet came, because no vital part of him had thus far been struck. His life, as they significantly call it, was untouched.

As the boats now more closely surrounded him, the whole upper part of his form, with much of it that is ordinarily submerged, was plainly revealed. His eyes, or rather the places where his eyes had been, were beheld. As strange misgrown masses gather in the knot-holes of the noblest oaks when prostrate, so from the points which the whale's eyes had once occupied, now protruded blind bulbs, horribly pitiable to see. But pity there was none. For all his old age, and his one arm, and his blind eyes, he must die the death and be murdered, in order to light the gay bridals and other merry-makings of men, and also to illuminate the solemn churches that preach unconditional inoffensiveness by all to all. Still rolling in his blood, at last he partially disclosed a strangely discolored bunch or protuberance, the size of a bushel, low down on the flank.

"A nice spot," cried Flask; "just let me prick him there once."

"Avast!" cried Starbuck, "there's no need of that!"

But humane Starbuck was too late. At the instant of the

dart an ulcerous jet shot from this cruel wound, and goaded by it into more than sufferable anguish, the whale now spouting thick blood, with swift fury blindly darted at the craft, bespattering them and their glorying crews all over with showers of gore, capsizing Flask's boat and marring the bows. It was his death stroke. For, by this time, so spent was he by loss of blood, that he helplessly rolled away from the wreck he had made; lay panting on his side, impotently flapped with his stumped fin, then over and over slowly revolved like a waning world; turned up the white secrets of his belly; lay like a log, and died. It was most piteous, that last expiring spout. As when by unseen hands the water is gradually drawn off from some mighty fountain, and with half-stifled melancholy gurglings the spray-column lowers and lowers to the ground—so the last long dying spout of the whale.

Soon, while the crews were awaiting the arrival of the ship, the body showed symptoms of sinking with all its treasures unrifled. Immediately, by Starbuck's orders, lines were secured to it at different points, so that ere long every boat was a buoy; the sunken whale being suspended a few inches beneath them by the cords. By very heedful management, when the ship drew nigh, the whale was transferred to her side, and was strongly secured there by the stiffest fluke-chains, for it was plain that unless artificially upheld, the body would at once sink to the bottom.

It so chanced that almost upon first cutting into him with the spade, the entire length of a corroded harpoon was found imbedded in his flesh, on the lower part of the bunch before described. But as the stumps of harpoons are frequently found in the dead bodies of captured whales, with the flesh perfectly healed around them, and no prominence of any kind to denote their place; therefore, there must needs have been some other unknown reason in the present case fully to account for the ulceration alluded to. But still more curious was the fact of a lance-head of stone being found in him, not far from the buried iron, the flesh perfectly firm about it. Who had darted that stone lance? And when? It might have been darted by some Nor' West Indian long before America was discovered.

What other marvels might have been rummaged out of this

monstrous cabinet there is no telling. But a sudden stop was put to further discoveries, by the ship's being unprecedentedly dragged over sideways to the sea, owing to the body's immensely increasing tendency to sink. However, Starbuck, who had the ordering of affairs, hung on to it to the last; hung on to it so resolutely, indeed, that when at length the ship would have been capsized, if still persisting in locking arms with the body; then, when the command was given to break clear from it, such was the immovable strain upon the timber-heads to which the fluke-chains and cables were fastened, that it was impossible to cast them off. Meantime everything in the Pequod was aslant. To cross to the other side of the deck was like walking up the steep gabled roof of a house. The ship groaned and gasped. Many of the ivory inlayings of her bulwarks and cabins were started from their places, by the unnatural dislocation. In vain handspikes and crows were brought to bear upon the immovable fluke-chains, to pry them adrift from the timber-heads; and so low had the whale now settled that the submerged ends could not be at all approached, while every moment whole tons of ponderosity seemed added to the sinking bulk, and the ship seemed on the point of going over.

"Hold on, hold on, won't ye?" cried Stubb to the body, "don't be in such a devil of a hurry to sink! By thunder, men, we must do something or go for it. No use prying there; avast, I say with your handspikes, and run one of ye for a prayer book and a pen-knife, and cut the big chains."

"Knife? Aye, aye," cried Queequeg, and seizing the carpenter's heavy hatchet, he leaned out of a porthole, and steel to iron, began slashing at the largest fluke-chains. But a few strokes, full of sparks, were given, when the exceeding strain effected the rest. With a terrific snap, every fastening went adrift; the ship righted, the carcase sank.

Now, this occasional inevitable sinking of the recently killed Sperm Whale is a very curious thing; nor has any fisherman yet adequately accounted for it. Usually the dead Sperm Whale floats with great buoyancy, with its side or belly considerably elevated above the surface. If the only whales that thus sank were old, meagre, and broken-hearted creatures, their pads of lard diminished and all their bones heavy and rheumatic; then you might with some reason assert that this sinking is caused by an uncommon specific gravity in the fish so sinking, consequent upon this absence of buoyant matter in him. But it is not so. For young whales, in the highest health, and swelling with noble aspirations, prematurely cut off in the warm flush and May of life, with all their panting lard about them; even these brawny, buoyant heroes do sometimes sink.

Be it said, however, that the Sperm Whale is far less liable to this accident than any other species. Where one of that sort go down, twenty Right Whales do. This difference in the species is no doubt imputable in no small degree to the greater quantity of bone in the Right Whale; his Venetian blinds alone sometimes weighing more than a ton; from this incumbrance the Sperm Whale is wholly free. But there are instances where, after the lapse of many hours or several days, the sunken whale again rises, more buoyant than in life. But the reason of this is obvious. Gases are generated in him; he swells to a prodigious magnitude; becomes a sort of animal balloon. A line-of-battle ship could hardly keep him under then. In the Shore Whaling, on soundings, among the Bays of New Zealand, when a Right Whale gives token of sinking, they fasten buoys to him, with plenty of rope; so that when the body has gone down, they know where to look for it when it shall have ascended again.

It was not long after the sinking of the body that a cry was heard from the Pequod's mast-heads, announcing that the Jungfrau was again lowering her boats; though the only spout in sight was that of a Fin-Back, belonging to the species of uncapturable whales, because of its incredible power of swimming. Nevertheless, the Fin-Back's spout is so similar to the Sperm Whale's, that by unskilful fishermen it is often mistaken for it. And consequently Derick and all his host were now in valiant chase of this unnearable brute. The Virgin crowding all sail, made after her four young keels, and thus they all disappeared far to leeward, still in bold, hopeful chase.

Oh! many are the Fin-Backs, and many are the Dericks, my friend.

Chapter 82

THE HONOR AND GLORY OF WHALING

THERE ARE some enterprises in which a careful disorderliness is the true method.

The more I dive into this matter of whaling, and push my researches up to the very spring-head of it, so much the more am I impressed with its great honorableness and antiquity; and especially when I find so many great demi-gods and heroes, prophets of all sorts, who one way or other have shed distinction upon it, I am transported with the reflection that I myself belong, though but subordinately, to so emblazoned a fraternity.

The gallant Perseus, a son of Jupiter, was the first whaleman; and to the eternal honor of our calling be it said, that the first whale attacked by our brotherhood was not killed with any sordid intent. Those were the knightly days of our profession, when we only bore arms to succor the distressed, and not to fill men's lamp-feeders. Every one knows the fine story of Perseus and Andromeda; how the lovely Andromeda, the daughter of a king, was tied to a rock on the sea-coast, and as Leviathan was in the very act of carrying her off, Perseus, the prince of whalemen, intrepidly advancing, harpooned the monster, and delivered and married the maid. It was an admirable artistic exploit, rarely achieved by the best harpooneers of the present day; inasmuch as this Leviathan was slain at the very first dart. And let no man doubt this Arkite story; for in the ancient Joppa, now Jaffa, on the Syrian coast, in one of the Pagan temples, there stood for many ages the vast skeleton of a whale, which the city's legends and all the inhabitants asserted to be the identical bones of the monster that Perseus slew. When the Romans took Joppa, the same skeleton was carried to Italy in triumph. What seems most singular and suggestively important in this story, is this: it was from Joppa that Jonah set sail.

Akin to the adventure of Perseus and Andromeda—indeed, by some supposed to be indirectly derived from it—is that famous story of St. George and the Dragon; which dragon I maintain to have been a whale; for in many old chronicles whales and dragons are strangely jumbled together, and often stand for each other. "Thou art as a lion of the waters, and as a dragon of the sea," saith Ezekiel; hereby, plainly meaning a whale; in truth, some versions of the Bible use that word itself. Besides, it would much subtract from the glory of the exploit had St. George but encountered a crawling reptile of the land, instead of doing battle with the great monster of the deep. Any man may kill a snake, but only a Perseus, a St. George, a Coffin, have the heart in them to march boldly up to a whale.

Let not the modern paintings of this scene mislead us; for though the creature encountered by that valiant whaleman of old is vaguely represented of a griffin-like shape, and though the battle is depicted on land and the saint on horseback, yet considering the great ignorance of those times, when the true form of the whale was unknown to artists; and considering that as in Perseus' case, St. George's whale might have crawled up out of the sea on the beach; and considering that the animal ridden by St. George might have been only a large seal, or sea-horse; bearing all this in mind, it will not appear altogether incompatible with the sacred legend and the ancientest draughts of the scene, to hold this so-called dragon no other than the great Leviathan himself. In fact, placed before the strict and piercing truth, this whole story will fare like that fish, flesh, and fowl idol of the Philistines, Dagon by name; who being planted before the ark of Israel, his horse's head and both the palms of his hands fell off from him, and only the stump or fishy part of him remained. Thus, then, one of our own noble stamp, even a whaleman, is the tutelary guardian of England; and by good rights, we harpooneers of Nantucket should be enrolled in the most noble order of St. George. And therefore, let not the knights of that honorable company (none of whom, I venture to say, have ever had to do with a whale like their great patron), let them never eye a Nantucketer with disdain, since even in our woollen frocks and tarred trowsers we are much better entitled to St. George's decoration than they.

Whether to admit Hercules among us or not, concerning

this I long remained dubious: for though according to the
Greek mythologies, that antique Crockett and Kit Carson—
that brawny doer of rejoicing good deeds, was swallowed
down and thrown up by a whale; still, whether that strictly
makes a whaleman of him, that might be mooted. It nowhere
appears that he ever actually harpooned his fish, unless, indeed, from the inside. Nevertheless, he may be deemed a sort
of involuntary whaleman; at any rate the whale caught him,
if he did not the whale. I claim him for one of our clan.

But, by the best contradictory authorities, this Grecian
story of Hercules and the whale is considered to be derived
from the still more ancient Hebrew story of Jonah and the
whale; and vice versâ; certainly they are very similar. If I claim
the demi-god then, why not the prophet?

Nor do heroes, saints, demigods, and prophets alone comprise the whole roll of our order. Our grand master is still to
be named; for like royal kings of old times, we find the head-
waters of our fraternity in nothing short of the great gods
themselves. That wondrous oriental story is now to be rehearsed from the Shaster, which gives us the dread Vishnoo,
one of the three persons in the godhead of the Hindoos;
gives us this divine Vishnoo himself for our Lord;—Vishnoo, who, by the first of his ten earthly incarnations, has for
ever set apart and sanctified the whale. When Bramha, or the
God of Gods, saith the Shaster, resolved to recreate the world
after one of its periodical dissolutions, he gave birth to Vishnoo, to preside over the work; but the Vedas, or mystical
books, whose perusal would seem to have been indispensable
to Vishnoo before beginning the creation, and which therefore must have contained something in the shape of practical
hints to young architects, these Vedas were lying at the bottom of the waters; so Vishnoo became incarnate in a whale,
and sounding down in him to the uttermost depths, rescued
the sacred volumes. Was not this Vishnoo a whaleman, then?
even as a man who rides a horse is called a horseman?

Perseus, St. George, Hercules, Jonah, and Vishnoo! there's
a member-roll for you! What club but the whaleman's can
head off like that?

Chapter 83

REFERENCE was made to the historical story of Jonah and the whale in the preceding chapter. Now some Nantucketers rather distrust this historical story of Jonah and the whale. But then there were some sceptical Greeks and Romans, who, standing out from the orthodox pagans of their times, equally doubted the story of Hercules and the whale, and Arion and the dolphin; and yet their doubting those traditions did not make those traditions one whit the less facts, for all that.

One old Sag-Harbor whaleman's chief reason for questioning the Hebrew story was this:—He had one of those quaint old-fashioned Bibles, embellished with curious, unscientific plates; one of which represented Jonah's whale with two spouts in his head—a peculiarity only true with respect to a species of the Leviathan (the Right Whale, and the varieties of that order), concerning which the fishermen have this saying, "A penny roll would choke him;" his swallow is so very small. But, to this, Bishop Jebb's anticipative answer is ready. It is not necessary, hints the Bishop, that we consider Jonah as tombed in the whale's belly, but as temporarily lodged in some part of his mouth. And this seems reasonable enough in the good Bishop. For truly, the Right Whale's mouth would accommodate a couple of whist-tables, and comfortably seat all the players. Possibly, too, Jonah might have ensconced himself in a hollow tooth; but, on second thoughts, the Right Whale is toothless.

Another reason which Sag-Harbor (he went by that name) urged for his want of faith in this matter of the prophet, was something obscurely in reference to his incarcerated body and the whale's gastric juices. But this objection likewise falls to the ground, because a German exegetist supposes that Jonah must have taken refuge in the floating body of a *dead* whale—even as the French soldiers in the Russian campaign turned their dead horses into tents, and crawled into them.

Besides, it has been divined by other continental commentators, that when Jonah was thrown overboard from the Joppa
ship, he straightway effected his escape to another vessel near
by, some vessel with a whale for a figure-head; and, I would
add, possibly called "The Whale," as some craft are nowadays
christened the "Shark," the "Gull," the "Eagle." Nor have
there been wanting learned exegetists who have opined that
the whale mentioned in the book of Jonah merely meant a
life-preserver—an inflated bag of wind—which the endangered prophet swam to, and so was saved from a watery
doom. Poor Sag-Harbor, therefore, seems worsted all round.
But he had still another reason for his want of faith. It was
this, if I remember right: Jonah was swallowed by the whale
in the Mediterranean Sea, and after three days he was vomited
up somewhere within three days' journey of Nineveh, a city
on the Tigris, very much more than three days' journey across
from the nearest point of the Mediterranean coast. How is
that?

But was there no other way for the whale to land the
prophet within that short distance of Nineveh? Yes. He might
have carried him round by the way of the Cape of Good
Hope. But not to speak of the passage through the whole
length of the Mediterranean, and another passage up the Persian Gulf and Red Sea, such a supposition would involve the
complete circumnavigation of all Africa in three days, not to
speak of the Tigris waters, near the site of Nineveh, being too
shallow for any whale to swim in. Besides, this idea of Jonah's
weathering the Cape of Good Hope at so early a day would
wrest the honor of the discovery of that great headland from
Bartholomew Diaz, its reputed discoverer, and so make modern history a liar.

But all these foolish arguments of old Sag-Harbor only
evinced his foolish pride of reason—a thing still more reprehensible in him, seeing that he had but little learning except
what he had picked up from the sun and the sea. I say it only
shows his foolish, impious pride, and abominable, devilish rebellion against the reverend clergy. For by a Portuguese Catholic priest, this very idea of Jonah's going to Nineveh viâ the
Cape of Good Hope was advanced as a signal magnification
of the general miracle. And so it was. Besides, to this day, the

highly enlightened Turks devoutly believe in the historical story of Jonah. And some three centuries ago, an English traveller in old Harris's Voyages, speaks of a Turkish Mosque built in honor of Jonah, in which mosque was a miraculous lamp that burnt without any oil.

Chapter 84

PITCHPOLING

TO MAKE THEM run easily and swiftly, the axles of carriages are anointed; and for much the same purpose, some whalers perform an analogous operation upon their boat; they grease the bottom. Nor is it to be doubted that as such a procedure can do no harm, it may possibly be of no contemptible advantage; considering that oil and water are hostile; that oil is a sliding thing, and that the object in view is to make the boat slide bravely. Queequeg believed strongly in anointing his boat, and one morning not long after the German ship Jungfrau disappeared, took more than customary pains in that occupation; crawling under its bottom, where it hung over the side, and rubbing in the unctuousness as though diligently seeking to insure a crop of hair from the craft's bald keel. He seemed to be working in obedience to some particular presentiment. Nor did it remain unwarranted by the event.

Towards noon whales were raised; but so soon as the ship sailed down to them, they turned and fled with swift precipitancy; a disordered flight, as of Cleopatra's barges from Actium.

Nevertheless, the boats pursued, and Stubb's was foremost. By great exertion, Tashtego at last succeeded in planting one iron; but the stricken whale, without at all sounding, still continued his horizontal flight, with added fleetness. Such unintermitted strainings upon the planted iron must sooner or later inevitably extract it. It became imperative to lance the flying whale, or be content to lose him. But to haul the boat up to his flank was impossible, he swam so fast and furious. What then remained?

Of all the wondrous devices and dexterities, the sleights of hand and countless subtleties, to which the veteran whaleman is so often forced, none exceed that fine manœuvre with the lance called pitchpoling. Small sword, or broad sword, in all its exercises boasts nothing like it. It is only indispensable with an inveterate running whale; its grand fact and feature is the wonderful distance to which the long lance is accurately darted from a violently rocking, jerking boat, under extreme headway. Steel and wood included, the entire spear is some ten or twelve feet in length; the staff is much slighter than that of the harpoon, and also of a lighter material—pine. It is furnished with a small rope called a warp, of considerable length, by which it can be hauled back to the hand after darting.

But before going further, it is important to mention here, that though the harpoon may be pitchpoled in the same way with the lance, yet it is seldom done; and when done, is still less frequently successful, on account of the greater weight and inferior length of the harpoon as compared with the lance, which in effect become serious drawbacks. As a general thing, therefore, you must first get fast to a whale, before any pitchpoling comes into play.

Look now at Stubb; a man who from his humorous, deliberate coolness and equanimity in the direst emergencies, was specially qualified to excel in pitchpoling. Look at him; he stands upright in the tossed bow of the flying boat; wrapt in fleecy foam, the towing whale is forty feet ahead. Handling the long lance lightly, glancing twice or thrice along its length to see if it be exactly straight, Stubb whistlingly gathers up the coil of the warp in one hand, so as to secure its free end in his grasp, leaving the rest unobstructed. Then holding the lance full before his waistband's middle, he levels it at the whale; when, covering him with it, he steadily depresses the butt-end in his hand, thereby elevating the point till the weapon stands fairly balanced upon his palm, fifteen feet in the air. He minds you somewhat of a juggler, balancing a long staff on his chin. Next moment with a rapid, nameless impulse, in a superb lofty arch the bright steel spans the foaming distance, and quivers in the life spot of the whale. Instead of sparkling water, he now spouts red blood.

"That drove the spigot out of him!" cries Stubb. "'Tis July's immortal Fourth; all fountains must run wine to-day! Would now, it were old Orleans whiskey, or old Ohio, or unspeakable old Monongahela! Then, Tashtego, lad, I'd have ye hold a canakin to the jet, and we'd drink round it! Yea, verily, hearts alive, we'd brew choice punch in the spread of his spout-hole there, and from that live punch-bowl quaff the living stuff!"

Again and again to such gamesome talk, the dexterous dart is repeated, the spear returning to its master like a greyhound held in skilful leash. The agonized whale goes into his flurry; the tow-line is slackened, and the pitchpoler dropping astern, folds his hands, and mutely watches the monster die.

Chapter 85

The Fountain

THAT for six thousand years—and no one knows how many millions of ages before—the great whales should have been spouting all over the sea, and sprinkling and mistifying the gardens of the deep, as with so many sprinkling or mistifying pots; and that for some centuries back, thousands of hunters should have been close by the fountain of the whale, watching these sprinklings and spoutings—that all this should be, and yet, that down to this blessed minute (fifteen and a quarter minutes past one o'clock P.M. of this sixteenth day of December, A.D. 1850), it should still remain a problem, whether these spoutings are, after all, really water, or nothing but vapor—this is surely a noteworthy thing.

Let us, then, look at this matter, along with some interesting items contingent. Every one knows that by the peculiar cunning of their gills, the finny tribes in general breathe the air which at all times is combined with the element in which they swim; hence, a herring or a cod might live a century, and never once raise its head above the surface. But owing to his marked internal structure which gives him regular lungs, like a human being's, the whale can only live by inhaling the disengaged air in the open atmosphere. Wherefore the necessity for his periodical visits to the upper world. But he cannot in any degree breathe through his mouth, for, in his ordinary attitude, the Sperm Whale's mouth is buried at least eight feet beneath the surface; and what is still more, his windpipe has no connexion with his mouth. No, he breathes through his spiracle alone; and this is on the top of his head.

If I say, that in any creature breathing is only a function indispensable to vitality, inasmuch as it withdraws from the air a certain element, which being subsequently brought into contact with the blood imparts to the blood its vivifying principle, I do not think I shall err; though I may possibly use some superfluous scientific words. Assume it, and it follows that if all the blood in a man could be aerated with one breath, he might then seal up his nostrils and not fetch another for a considerable time. That is to say, he would then live without breathing. Anomalous as it may seem, this is precisely the case with the whale, who systematically lives, by intervals, his full hour and more (when at the bottom) without drawing a single breath, or so much as in any way inhaling a particle of air; for, remember, he has no gills. How is this? Between his ribs and on each side of his spine he is supplied with a remarkable involved Cretan labyrinth of vermicelli-like vessels, which vessels, when he quits the surface, are completely distended with oxygenated blood. So that for an hour or more, a thousand fathoms in the sea, he carries a surplus stock of vitality in him, just as the camel crossing the waterless desert carries a surplus supply of drink for future use in its four supplementary stomachs. The anatomical fact of this labyrinth is indisputable; and that the supposition founded upon it is reasonable and true, seems the more cogent to me, when I consider the otherwise inexplicable obstinacy of that leviathan in *having his spoutings out*, as the fishermen phrase it. This is what I mean. If unmolested, upon rising to the surface, the Sperm Whale will continue there for a period of time exactly uniform with all his other unmolested risings. Say he stays eleven minutes, and jets seventy times, that is, respires seventy breaths; then whenever he rises again, he will be sure to have his seventy breaths over again, to a minute. Now, if after he fetches a few breaths you alarm him, so that he sounds, he will be always dodging up again to make good his regular allowance of air. And not till those seventy breaths are told, will he finally go down to stay out his full term below. Remark, however, that in different individuals these rates are different; but in any one they are alike. Now, why should the whale thus insist upon having his spoutings out, unless it be to replenish his reservoir of air, ere descending for good? How obvious is it, too, that this necessity for the whale's rising exposes him to all the fatal hazards of the chase. For not by hook or by net could this vast leviathan be caught, when sailing a thousand fathoms beneath the sunlight. Not so much thy skill, then, O hunter, as the great necessities, that strike the victory to thee!

In man, breathing is incessantly going on—one breath

only serving for two or three pulsations; so that whatever other business he has to attend to, waking or sleeping, breathe he must, or die he will. But the Sperm Whale only breathes about one seventh or Sunday of his time.

It has been said that the whale only breathes through his spout-hole; if it could truthfully be added that his spouts are mixed with water, then I opine we should be furnished with the reason why his sense of smell seems obliterated in him; for the only thing about him that at all answers to his nose is that identical spout-hole; and being so clogged with two elements, it could not be expected to have the power of smelling. But owing to the mystery of the spout—whether it be water or whether it be vapor—no absolute certainty can as yet be arrived at on this head. Sure it is, nevertheless, that the Sperm Whale has no proper olfactories. But what does he want of them? No roses, no violets, no Cologne-water in the sea.

Furthermore, as his windpipe solely opens into the tube of his spouting canal, and as that long canal—like the grand Erie Canal—is furnished with a sort of locks (that open and shut) for the downward retention of air or the upward exclusion of water, therefore the whale has no voice; unless you insult him by saying, that when he so strangely rumbles, he talks through his nose. But then again, what has the whale to say? Seldom have I known any profound being that had anything to say to this world, unless forced to stammer out something by way of getting a living. Oh! happy that the world is such an excellent listener!

Now, the spouting canal of the Sperm Whale, chiefly intended as it is for the conveyance of air, and for several feet laid along, horizontally, just beneath the upper surface of his head, and a little to one side; this curious canal is very much like a gas-pipe laid down in a city on one side of a street. But the question returns whether this gas-pipe is also a water-pipe; in other words, whether the spout of the Sperm Whale is the mere vapor of the exhaled breath, or whether that exhaled breath is mixed with water taken in at the mouth, and discharged through the spiracle. It is certain that the mouth indirectly communicates with the spouting canal; but it cannot be proved that this is for the purpose of discharging water through the spiracle. Because the greatest necessity for so doing would seem to be, when in feeding he accidentally takes in water. But the Sperm Whale's food is far beneath the surface, and there he cannot spout even if he would. Besides, if you regard him very closely, and time him with your watch, you will find that when unmolested, there is an undeviating rhyme between the periods of his jets and the ordinary periods of respiration.

But why pester one with all this reasoning on the subject? Speak out! You have seen him spout; then declare what the spout is; can you not tell water from air? My dear sir, in this world it is not so easy to settle these plain things. I have ever found your plain things the knottiest of all. And as for this whale spout, you might almost stand in it, and yet be undecided as to what it is precisely.

The central body of it is hidden in the snowy sparkling mist enveloping it; and how can you certainly tell whether any water falls from it, when, always, when you are close enough to a whale to get a close view of his spout, he is in a prodigious commotion, the water cascading all around him. And if at such times you should think that you really perceived drops of moisture in the spout, how do you know that they are not merely condensed from its vapor; or how do you know that they are not those identical drops superficially lodged in the spout-hole fissure, which is countersunk into the summit of the whale's head? For even when tranquilly swimming through the mid-day sea in a calm, with his elevated hump sun-dried as a dromedary's in the desert; even then, the whale always carries a small basin of water on his head, as under a blazing sun you will sometimes see a cavity in a rock filled up with rain.

Nor is it at all prudent for the hunter to be over curious touching the precise nature of the whale spout. It will not do for him to be peering into it, and putting his face in it. You cannot go with your pitcher to this fountain and fill it, and bring it away. For even when coming into slight contact with the outer, vapory shreds of the jet, which will often happen, your skin will feverishly smart, from the acridness of the thing so touching it. And I know one, who coming into still closer contact with the spout, whether with some scientific object in view, or otherwise, I cannot say, the skin peeled off from his cheek and arm. Wherefore, among whalemen, the spout is deemed poisonous; they try to evade it. Another thing; I have heard it said, and I do not much doubt it, that if the jet is fairly spouted into your eyes, it will blind you. The wisest thing the investigator can do then, it seems to me, is to let this deadly spout alone.

Still, we can hypothesize, even if we cannot prove and establish. My hypothesis is this: that the spout is nothing but mist. And besides other reasons, to this conclusion I am impelled, by considerations touching the great inherent dignity and sublimity of the Sperm Whale; I account him no common, shallow being, inasmuch as it is an undisputed fact that he is never found on soundings, or near shores; all other whales sometimes are. He is both ponderous and profound. And I am convinced that from the heads of all ponderous profound beings, such as Plato, Pyrrho, the Devil, Jupiter, Dante, and so on, there always goes up a certain semi-visible steam, while in the act of thinking deep thoughts. While composing a little treatise on Eternity, I had the curiosity to place a mirror before me; and ere long saw reflected there, a curious involved worming and undulation in the atmosphere over my head. The invariable moisture of my hair, while plunged in deep thought, after six cups of hot tea in my thin shingled attic, of an August noon; this seems an additional argument for the above supposition.

And how nobly it raises our conceit of the mighty, misty monster, to behold him solemnly sailing through a calm tropical sea; his vast, mild head overhung by a canopy of vapor, engendered by his incommunicable contemplations, and that vapor—as you will sometimes see it—glorified by a rainbow, as if Heaven itself had put its seal upon his thoughts. For, d'ye see, rainbows do not visit the clear air; they only irradiate vapor. And so, through all the thick mists of the dim doubts in my mind, divine intuitions now and then shoot, enkindling my fog with a heavenly ray. And for this I thank God; for all have doubts; many deny; but doubts or denials, few along with them, have intuitions. Doubts of all things earthly, and intuitions of some things heavenly; this combination makes neither believer nor infidel, but makes a man who regards them both with equal eye.

Chapter 86

THE TAIL

OTHER POETS have warbled the praises of the soft eye of the antelope, and the lovely plumage of the bird that never alights; less celestial, I celebrate a tail.

Reckoning the largest sized Sperm Whale's tail to begin at that point of the trunk where it tapers to about the girth of a man, it comprises upon its upper surface alone, an area of at least fifty square feet. The compact round body of its root expands into two broad, firm, flat palms or flukes, gradually shoaling away to less than an inch in thickness. At the crotch or junction, these flukes slightly overlap, then sideways recede from each other like wings, leaving a wide vacancy between. In no living thing are the lines of beauty more exquisitely defined than in the crescentic borders of these flukes. At its utmost expansion in the full grown whale, the tail will considerably exceed twenty feet across.

The entire member seems a dense webbed bed of welded sinews; but cut into it, and you find that three distinct strata compose it:—upper, middle, and lower. The fibres in the upper and lower layers, are long and horizontal; those of the middle one, very short, and running crosswise between the outside layers. This triune structure, as much as anything else, imparts power to the tail. To the student of old Roman walls, the middle layer will furnish a curious parallel to the thin course of tiles always alternating with the stone in those wonderful relics of the antique, and which undoubtedly contribute so much to the great strength of the masonry.

But as if this vast local power in the tendinous tail were not enough, the whole bulk of the leviathan is knit over with a warp and woof of muscular fibres and filaments, which passing on either side the loins and running down into the flukes, insensibly blend with them, and largely contribute to their might; so that in the tail the confluent measureless force of the whole whale seems concentrated to a point. Could annihilation occur to matter, this were the thing to do it.

Nor does this—its amazing strength, at all tend to cripple the graceful flexion of its motions; where infantileness of ease undulates through a Titanism of power. On the contrary, those motions derive their most appalling beauty from it. Real strength never impairs beauty or harmony, but it often bestows it; and in everything imposingly beautiful, strength has much to do with the magic. Take away the tied tendons that all over seem bursting from the marble in the carved Hercules, and its charm would be gone. As devout Ecker-mann lifted the linen sheet from the naked corpse of Goethe, he was overwhelmed with the massive chest of the man, that seemed as a Roman triumphal arch. When Angelo paints even God the Father in human form, mark what robustness is there. And whatever they may reveal of the divine love in the Son, the soft, curled, hermaphroditical Italian pictures, in which his idea has been most successfully embodied; these pictures, so destitute as they are of all brawniness, hint noth-ing of any power, but the mere negative, feminine one of submission and endurance, which on all hands it is conceded, form the peculiar practical virtues of his teachings.

Such is the subtle elasticity of the organ I treat of, that whether wielded in sport, or in earnest, or in anger, whatever be the mood it be in, its flexions are invariably marked by exceeding grace. Therein no fairy's arm can transcend it.

Five great motions are peculiar to it. First, when used as a fin for progression; Second, when used as a mace in battle; Third, in sweeping; Fourth, in lobtailing; Fifth, in peaking flukes.

First: Being horizontal in its position, the Leviathan's tail acts in a different manner from the tails of all other sea crea-tures. It never wriggles. In man or fish, wriggling is a sign of inferiority. To the whale, his tail is the sole means of propul-sion. Scroll-wise coiled forwards beneath the body, and then rapidly sprung backwards, it is this which gives that singular darting, leaping motion to the monster when furiously swim-ming. His side-fins only serve to steer by.

Second: It is a little significant, that while one sperm whale only fights another sperm whale with his head and jaw, nev-ertheless, in his conflicts with man, he chiefly and contemp-tuously uses his tail. In striking at a boat, he swiftly curves away his flukes from it, and the blow is only inflicted by the recoil. If it be made in the unobstructed air, especially if it descend to its mark, the stroke is then simply irresistible. No ribs of man or boat can withstand it. Your only salvation lies in eluding it; but if it comes sideways through the opposing water, then partly owing to the light buoyancy of the whale-boat, and the elasticity of its materials, a cracked rib or a dashed plank or two, a sort of stitch in the side, is generally the most serious result. These submerged side blows are so often received in the fishery, that they are accounted mere child's play. Some one strips off a frock, and the hole is stopped.

Third: I cannot demonstrate it, but it seems to me, that in the whale the sense of touch is concentrated in the tail; for in this respect there is a delicacy in it only equalled by the daintiness of the elephant's trunk. This delicacy is chiefly evinced in the action of sweeping, when in maidenly gentleness the whale with a certain soft slowness moves his immense flukes from side to side upon the surface of the sea; and if he feel but a sailor's whisker, woe to that sailor, whiskers and all. What tenderness there is in that preliminary touch! Had this tail any prehensile power, I should straightway bethink me of Darmonodes' elephant that so frequented the flower-market, and with low salutations presented nosegays to damsels, and then caressed their zones. On more accounts than one, a pity it is that the whale does not possess this prehensile virtue in his tail; for I have heard of yet another elephant, that when wounded in the fight, curved round his trunk and extracted the dart.

Fourth: Stealing unawares upon the whale in the fancied security of the middle of solitary seas, you find him unbent from the vast corpulence of his dignity, and kitten-like, he plays on the ocean as if it were a hearth. But still you see his power in his play. The broad palms of his tail are flirted high into the air; then smiting the surface, the thunderous concussion resounds for miles. You would almost think a great gun had been discharged; and if you noticed the light wreath of vapor from the spiracle at his other extremity, you would think that that was the smoke from the touch-hole.

Fifth: As in the ordinary floating posture of the leviathan the flukes lie considerably below the level of his back, they are then completely out of sight beneath the surface; but when he is about to plunge into the deeps, his entire flukes with at least thirty feet of his body are tossed erect in the air, and so remain vibrating a moment, till they downwards shoot out of view. Excepting the sublime *breach*—somewhere else to be described—this peaking of the whale's flukes is perhaps the grandest sight to be seen in all animated nature. Out of the bottomless profundities the gigantic tail seems spasmodically snatching at the highest heaven. So in dreams, have I seen majestic Satan thrusting forth his tormented colossal claw from the flame Baltic of Hell. But in gazing at such scenes, it is all in all what mood you are in; if in the Dantean, the devils will occur to you; if in that of Isaiah, the archangels. Standing at the mast-head of my ship during a sunrise that crimsoned sky and sea, I once saw a large herd of whales in the east, all heading towards the sun, and for a moment vibrating in concert with peaked flukes. As it seemed to me at the time, such a grand embodiment of adoration of the gods was never beheld, even in Persia, the home of the fire worshippers. As Ptolemy Philopater testified of the African elephant, I then testified of the whale, pronouncing him the most devout of all beings. For according to King Juba, the military elephants of antiquity often hailed the morning with their trunks uplifted in the profoundest silence.

The chance comparison in this chapter, between the whale and the elephant, so far as some aspects of the tail of the one and the trunk of the other are concerned, should not tend to place those two opposite organs on an equality, much less the creatures to which they respectively belong. For as the mightiest elephant is but a terrier to Leviathan, so, compared with Leviathan's tail, his trunk is but the stalk of a lily. The most direful blow from the elephant's trunk were as the playful tap of a fan, compared with the measureless crush and crash of the sperm whale's ponderous flukes, which in repeated instances have one after the other hurled entire boats with all their oars and crews into the air, very much as an Indian juggler tosses his balls.*

*Though all comparison in the way of general bulk between the whale and the elephant is preposterous, inasmuch as in that particular the elephant stands in much the same respect to the whale that a dog does to the elephant;

The more I consider this mighty tail, the more do I deplore my inability to express it. At times there are gestures in it, which, though they would well grace the hand of man, remain wholly inexplicable. In an extensive herd, so remarkable, occasionally, are these mystic gestures, that I have heard hunters who have declared them akin to Free-Mason signs and symbols; that the whale, indeed, by these methods intelligently conversed with the world. Nor are there wanting other motions of the whale in his general body, full of strangeness, and unaccountable to his most experienced assailant. Dissect him how I may, then, I but go skin deep; I know him not, and never will. But if I know not even the tail of this whale, how understand his head? much more, how comprehend his face, when face he has none? Thou shalt see my back parts, my tail, he seems to say, but my face shall not be seen. But I cannot completely make out his back parts; and hint what he will about his face, I say again he has no face.

---

nevertheless, there are not wanting some points of curious similitude; among these is the spout. It is well known that the elephant will often draw up water or dust in his trunk, and then elevating it, jet it forth in a stream.

Chapter 87

THE GRAND ARMADA

THE LONG and narrow peninsula of Malacca, extending south-eastward from the territories of Birmah, forms the most southerly point of all Asia. In a continuous line from that peninsula stretch the long islands of Sumatra, Java, Bally, and Timor; which, with many others, form a vast mole, or rampart, lengthwise connecting Asia with Australia, and dividing the long unbroken Indian ocean from the thickly studded oriental archipelagoes. This rampart is pierced by several sally-ports for the convenience of ships and whales; conspicuous among which are the straits of Sunda and Malacca. By the straits of Sunda, chiefly, vessels bound to China from the west, emerge into the China seas.

Those narrow straits of Sunda divide Sumatra from Java; and standing midway in that vast rampart of islands, buttressed by that bold green promontory, known to seamen as Java Head; they not a little correspond to the central gateway opening into some vast walled empire: and considering the inexhaustible wealth of spices, and silks, and jewels, and gold, and ivory, with which the thousand islands of that oriental sea are enriched, it seems a significant provision of nature, that such treasures, by the very formation of the land, should at least bear the appearance, however ineffectual, of being guarded from the all-grasping western world. The shores of the Straits of Sunda are unsupplied with those domineering fortresses which guard the entrances to the Mediterranean, the Baltic, and the Propontis. Unlike the Danes, these Orientals do not demand the obsequious homage of lowered topsails from the endless procession of ships before the wind, which for centuries past, by night and by day, have passed between the islands of Sumatra and Java, freighted with the costliest cargoes of the east. But while they freely waive a ceremonial like this, they do by no means renounce their claim to more solid tribute.

Time out of mind the piratical proas of the Malays, lurking among the low shaded coves and islets of Sumatra, have sallied out upon the vessels sailing through the straits, fiercely demanding tribute at the point of their spears. Though by the repeated bloody chastisements they have received at the hands of European cruisers, the audacity of these corsairs has of late been somewhat repressed; yet, even at the present day, we occasionally hear of English and American vessels, which, in those waters, have been remorselessly boarded and pillaged.

With a fair, fresh wind, the Pequod was now drawing nigh to these straits; Ahab purposing to pass through them into the Javan sea, and thence, cruising northwards, over waters known to be frequented here and there by the Sperm Whale, sweep inshore by the Philippine Islands, and gain the far coast of Japan, in time for the great whaling season there. By these means, the circumnavigating Pequod would sweep almost all the known Sperm Whale cruising grounds of the world, previous to descending upon the Line in the Pacific; where Ahab, though everywhere else foiled in his pursuit, firmly counted upon giving battle to Moby Dick, in the sea he was most known to frequent; and at a season when he might most reasonably be presumed to be haunting it.

But how now? in this zoned quest, does Ahab touch no land? does his crew drink air? Surely, he will stop for water. Nay. For a long time, now, the circus-running sun has raced within his fiery ring, and needs no sustenance but what's in himself. So Ahab. Mark this, too, in the whaler. While other hulls are loaded down with alien stuff, to be transferred to foreign wharves; the world-wandering whaleship carries no cargo but herself and crew, their weapons and their wants. She has a whole lake's contents bottled in her ample hold. She is ballasted with utilities; not altogether with unusable pig-lead and kentledge. She carries years' water in her. Clear old prime Nantucket water; which, when three years afloat, the Nantucketer, in the Pacific, prefers to drink before the brackish fluid, but yesterday rafted off in casks, from the Peruvian or Indian streams. Hence it is, that, while other ships may have gone to China from New York, and back again, touching at a score of ports, the whale-ship, in all that interval, may not have sighted one grain of soil; her crew having seen no man but floating seamen like themselves. So that did you carry them the news that another flood had come; they would only answer—"Well, boys, here's the ark!"

Now, as many Sperm Whales had been captured off the western coast of Java, in the near vicinity of the Straits of Sunda; indeed, as most of the ground, roundabout, was generally recognised by the fishermen as an excellent spot for cruising; therefore, as the Pequod gained more and more upon Java Head, the look-outs were repeatedly hailed, and admonished to keep wide awake. But though the green palmy cliffs of the land soon loomed on the starboard bow, and with delighted nostrils the fresh cinnamon was snuffed in the air, yet not a single jet was descried. Almost renouncing all thought of falling in with any game hereabouts, the ship had well nigh entered the straits, when the customary cheering cry was heard from aloft, and ere long a spectacle of singular magnificence saluted us.

But here be it premised, that owing to the unwearied activity with which of late they have been hunted over all four oceans, the Sperm Whales, instead of almost invariably sailing in small detached companies, as in former times, are now frequently met with in extensive herds, sometimes embracing so great a multitude, that it would almost seem as if numerous nations of them had sworn solemn league and covenant for mutual assistance and protection. To this aggregation of the Sperm Whale into such immense caravans, may be imputed the circumstance that even in the best cruising grounds, you may now sometimes sail for weeks and months together, without being greeted by a single spout; and then be suddenly saluted by what sometimes seems thousands on thousands.

Broad on both bows, at the distance of some two or three miles, and forming a great semicircle, embracing one half of the level horizon, a continuous chain of whale-jets were up-playing and sparkling in the noon-day air. Unlike the straight perpendicular twin-jets of the Right Whale, which, dividing at top, fall over in two branches, like the cleft drooping boughs of a willow, the single forward-slanting spout of the

Sperm Whale presents a thick curled bush of white mist, continually rising and falling away to leeward.

Seen from the Pequod's deck, then, as she would rise on a high hill of the sea, this host of vapory spouts, individually curling up into the air, and beheld through a blending atmosphere of bluish haze, showed like the thousand cheerful chimneys of some dense metropolis, descried of a balmy autumnal morning, by some horseman on a height.

As marching armies approaching an unfriendly defile in the mountains, accelerate their march, all eagerness to place that perilous passage in their rear, and once more expand in comparative security upon the plain; even so did this vast fleet of whales now seem hurrying forward through the straits; gradually contracting the wings of their semicircle, and swimming on, in one solid, but still crescentic centre.

Crowding all sail the Pequod pressed after them; the harpooneers handling their weapons, and loudly cheering from the heads of their yet suspended boats. If the wind only held, little doubt had they, that chased through these Straits of Sunda, the vast host would only deploy into the Oriental seas to witness the capture of not a few of their number. And who could tell whether, in that congregated caravan, Moby Dick himself might not temporarily be swimming, like the worshipped white-elephant in the coronation procession of the Siamese! So with stun-sail piled on stun-sail, we sailed along, driving these leviathans before us; when, of a sudden, the voice of Tashtego was heard, loudly directing attention to something in our wake.

Corresponding to the crescent in our van, we beheld another in our rear. It seemed formed of detached white vapors, rising and falling something like the spouts of the whales; only they did not so completely come and go; for they constantly hovered, without finally disappearing. Levelling his glass at this sight, Ahab quickly revolved in his pivot-hole, crying, "Aloft there, and rig whips and buckets to wet the sails;—Malays, sir, and after us!"

As if too long lurking behind the headlands, till the Pequod should fairly have entered the straits, these rascally Asiatics were now in hot pursuit, to make up for their over-cautious delay. But when the swift Pequod, with a fresh leading wind,

was herself in hot chase; how very kind of these tawny phi-
lanthropists to assist in speeding her on to her own chosen
pursuit,—mere riding-whips and rowels to her, that they
were. As with glass under arm, Ahab to-and-fro paced the
deck; in his forward turn beholding the monsters he chased,
and in the after one the bloodthirsty pirates chasing *him*;
some such fancy as the above seemed his. And when he
glanced upon the green walls of the watery defile in which
the ship was then sailing, and bethought him that through
that gate lay the route to his vengeance, and beheld, how that
through that same gate he was now both chasing and being
chased to his deadly end; and not only that, but a herd of
remorseless wild pirates and inhuman atheistical devils were
infernally cheering him on with their curses;—when all these
conceits had passed through his brain, Ahab's brow was left
gaunt and ribbed, like the black sand beach after some stormy
tide has been gnawing it, without being able to drag the firm
thing from its place.

But thoughts like these troubled very few of the reckless
crew; and when, after steadily dropping and dropping the
pirates astern, the Pequod at last shot by the vivid green
Cockatoo Point on the Sumatra side, emerging at last upon
the broad waters beyond; then, the harpooneers seemed more
to grieve that the swift whales had been gaining upon the
ship, than to rejoice that the ship had so victoriously gained
upon the Malays. But still driving on in the wake of the
whales, at length they seemed abating their speed; gradually
the ship neared them; and the wind now dying away, word
was passed to spring to the boats. But no sooner did the
herd, by some presumed wonderful instinct of the Sperm
Whale, become notified of the three keels that were after
them,—though as yet a mile in their rear,—than they rallied
again, and forming in close ranks and battalions, so that their
spouts all looked like flashing lines of stacked bayonets,
moved on with redoubled velocity.

Stripped to our shirts and drawers, we sprang to the white-
ash, and after several hours' pulling were almost disposed to
renounce the chase, when a general pausing commotion
among the whales gave animating token that they were now
at last under the influence of that strange perplexity of inert

irresolution, which, when the fishermen perceive it in the whale, they say he is *gallied*.* The compact martial columns in which they had been hitherto rapidly and steadily swimming, were now broken up in one measureless rout; and like King Porus' elephants in the Indian battle with Alexander, they seemed going mad with consternation. In all directions expanding in vast irregular circles, and aimlessly swimming hither and thither, by their short thick spoutings, they plainly betrayed their distraction of panic. This was still more strangely evinced by those of their number, who, completely paralysed as it were, helplessly floated like water-logged dismantled ships on the sea. Had these leviathans been but a flock of simple sheep, pursued over the pasture by three fierce wolves, they could not possibly have evinced such excessive dismay. But this occasional timidity is characteristic of almost all herding creatures. Though banding together in tens of thousands, the lion-maned buffaloes of the West have fled before a solitary horseman. Witness, too, all human beings, how when herded together in the sheepfold of a theatre's pit, they will, at the slightest alarm of fire, rush helter-skelter for the outlets, crowding, trampling, jamming, and remorselessly dashing each other to death. Best, therefore, withhold any amazement at the strangely gallied whales before us, for there is no folly of the beasts of the earth which is not infinitely outdone by the madness of men.

Though many of the whales, as has been said, were in violent motion, yet it is to be observed that as a whole the herd

---

*To *gally*, or *gallow*, is to frighten excessively,—to confound with fright. It is an old Saxon word. It occurs once in Shakspere:—

> "The wrathful skies
> *Gallow* the very wanderers of the dark,
> And make them keep their caves."
>
> *Lear*, Act III. sc. ii.

To common land usages, the word is now completely obsolete. When the polite landsman first hears it from the gaunt Nantucketer, he is apt to set it down as one of the whaleman's self-derived savageries. Much the same is it with many other sinewy Saxonisms of this sort, which emigrated to the New-England rocks with the noble brawn of the old English emigrants in the time of the Commonwealth. Thus, some of the best and furthest-descended English words—the etymological Howards and Percys—are now democratised, nay, plebeianised—so to speak—in the New World.

neither advanced nor retreated, but collectively remained in one place. As is customary in those cases, the boats at once separated, each making for some one lone whale on the out-skirts of the shoal. In about three minutes' time, Queequeg's harpoon was flung; the stricken fish darted blinding spray in our faces, and then running away with us like light, steered straight for the heart of the herd. Though such a movement on the part of the whale struck under such circumstances, is in no wise unprecedented; and indeed is almost always more or less anticipated; yet does it present one of the more peril-ous vicissitudes of the fishery. For as the swift monster drags you deeper and deeper into the frantic shoal, you bid adieu to circumspect life and only exist in a delirious throb.

As, blind and deaf, the whale plunged forward, as if by sheer power of speed to rid himself of the iron leech that had fastened to him; as we thus tore a white gash in the sea, on all sides menaced as we flew, by the crazed creatures to and fro rushing about us; our beset boat was like a ship mobbed by ice-isles in a tempest, and striving to steer through their complicated channels and straits, knowing not at what mo-ment it may be locked in and crushed.

But not a bit daunted, Queequeg steered us manfully; now sheering off from this monster directly across our route in advance; now edging away from that, whose colossal flukes were suspended overhead, while all the time, Starbuck stood up in the bows, lance in hand, pricking out of our way what-ever whales he could reach by short darts, for there was no time to make long ones. Nor were the oarsmen quite idle, though their wonted duty was now altogether dispensed with. They chiefly attended to the shouting part of the busi-ness. "Out of the way, Commodore!" cried one, to a great dromedary that of a sudden rose bodily to the surface, and for an instant threatened to swamp us. "Hard down with your tail, there!" cried a second to another, which, close to our gunwale, seemed calmly cooling himself with his own fan-like extremity.

All whaleboats carry certain curious contrivances, originally invented by the Nantucket Indians, called druggs. Two thick squares of wood of equal size are stoutly clenched together, so that they cross each other's grain at right angles; a line of considerable length is then attached to the middle of this block, and the other end of the line being looped, it can in a moment be fastened to a harpoon. It is chiefly among gallied whales that this drugg is used. For then, more whales are close round you than you can possibly chase at one time. But sperm whales are not every day encountered; while you may, then, you must kill all you can. And if you cannot kill them all at once, you must wing them, so that they can be afterwards killed at your leisure. Hence it is, that at times like these the drugg comes into requisition. Our boat was furnished with three of them. The first and second were successfully darted, and we saw the whales staggeringly running off, fettered by the enormous sidelong resistance of the towing drugg. They were cramped like malefactors with the chain and ball. But upon flinging the third, in the act of tossing overboard the clumsy wooden block, it caught under one of the seats of the boat, and in an instant tore it out and carried it away, dropping the oarsman in the boat's bottom as the seat slid from under him. On both sides the sea came in at the wounded planks, but we stuffed two or three drawers and shirts in, and so stopped the leaks for the time.

It had been next to impossible to dart these drugged-harpoons, were it not that as we advanced into the herd, our whale's way greatly diminished; moreover, that as we went still further and further from the circumference of commotion, the direful disorders seemed waning. So that when at last the jerking harpoon drew out, and the towing whale sideways vanished; then, with the tapering force of his parting momentum, we glided between two whales into the innermost heart of the shoal, as if from some mountain torrent we had slid into a serene valley lake. Here the storms in the roaring glens between the outermost whales, were heard but not felt. In this central expanse the sea presented that smooth satin-like surface, called a sleek, produced by the subtle moisture thrown off by the whale in his more quiet moods. Yes, we were now in that enchanted calm which they say lurks at the heart of every commotion. And still in the distracted distance we beheld the tumults of the outer concentric circles, and saw successive pods of whales, eight or ten in each, swiftly going round and round, like multiplied spans of horses in a ring; and so closely shoulder to shoulder, that a Titanic circus-rider might easily have overarched the middle ones, and so have gone round on their backs. Owing to the density of the crowd of reposing whales, more immediately surrounding the embayed axis of the herd, no possible chance of escape was at present afforded us. We must watch for a breach in the living wall that hemmed us in; the wall that had only admitted us in order to shut us up. Keeping at the centre of the lake, we were occasionally visited by small tame cows and calves; the women and children of this routed host.

Now, inclusive of the occasional wide intervals between the revolving outer circles, and inclusive of the spaces between the various pods in any one of those circles, the entire area at this juncture, embraced by the whole multitude, must have contained at least two or three square miles. At any rate— though indeed such a test at such a time might be deceptive—spoutings might be discovered from our low boat that seemed playing up almost from the rim of the horizon. I mention this circumstance, because, as if the cows and calves had been purposely locked up in this innermost fold; and as if the wide extent of the herd had hitherto prevented them from learning the precise cause of its stopping; or, possibly, being so young, unsophisticated, and every way innocent and inexperienced; however it may have been, these smaller whales—now and then visiting our becalmed boat from the margin of the lake—evinced a wondrous fearlessness and confidence, or else a still, becharmed panic which it was impossible not to marvel at. Like household dogs they came snuffling round us, right up to our gunwales, and touching them; till it almost seemed that some spell had suddenly domesticated them. Queequeg patted their foreheads; Starbuck scratched their backs with his lance; but fearful of the consequences, for the time refrained from darting it.

But far beneath this wondrous world upon the surface, another and still stranger world met our eyes as we gazed over the side. For, suspended in those watery vaults, floated the forms of the nursing mothers of the whales, and those that by their enormous girth seemed shortly to become mothers. The lake, as I have hinted, was to a considerable depth exceedingly transparent; and as human infants while suckling

will calmly and fixedly gaze away from the breast, as if leading
two different lives at the time; and while yet drawing mortal
nourishment, be still spiritually feasting upon some unearthly
reminiscence;—even so did the young of these whales seem
looking up towards us, but not at us, as if we were but a bit
of Gulf-weed in their new-born sight. Floating on their sides,
the mothers also seemed quietly eyeing us. One of these little
infants, that from certain queer tokens seemed hardly a day
old, might have measured some fourteen feet in length, and
some six feet in girth. He was a little frisky; though as yet his
body seemed scarce yet recovered from that irksome position
it had so lately occupied in the maternal reticule; where, tail
to head, and all ready for the final spring, the unborn whale
lies bent like a Tartar's bow. The delicate side-fins, and the
palms of his flukes, still freshly retained the plaited crumpled
appearance of a baby's ears newly arrived from foreign parts.

"Line! line!" cried Queequeg, looking over the gunwale;
"him fast! him fast!—Who line him! Who struck?—Two
whale; one big, one little!"

"What ails ye, man?" cried Starbuck.

"Look-e here," said Queequeg pointing down.

As when the stricken whale, that from the tub has reeled
out hundreds of fathoms of rope; as, after deep sounding, he
floats up again, and shows the slackened curling line buoy-
antly rising and spiralling towards the air; so now, Starbuck
saw long coils of the umbilical cord of Madame Leviathan,
by which the young cub seemed still tethered to its dam. Not
seldom in the rapid vicissitudes of the chase, this natural line,
with the maternal end loose, becomes entangled with the
hempen one, so that the cub is thereby trapped. Some of the
subtlest secrets of the seas seemed divulged to us in this enchanted pond. We saw young Leviathan amours in the deep.*

And thus, though surrounded by circle upon circle of con-
sternations and affrights, did these inscrutable creatures at the
centre freely and fearlessly indulge in all peaceful concern-

*The sperm whale, as with all other species of the Leviathan, but unlike
most other fish, breeds indifferently at all seasons; after a gestation which
may probably be set down at nine months, producing but one at a time;
though in some few known instances giving birth to an Esau and Jacob:—a
contingency provided for in suckling by two teats, curiously situated, one on

ments; yea, serenely revelled in dalliance and delight. But
even so, amid the tornadoed Atlantic of my being, do I myself
still for ever centrally disport in mute calm; and while ponderous planets of unwaning woe revolve round me, deep
down and deep inland there I still bathe me in eternal mildness of joy.

Meanwhile, as we thus lay entranced, the occasional sudden
frantic spectacles in the distance evinced the activity of the
other boats, still engaged in drugging the whales on the frontier of the host; or possibly carrying on the war within the
first circle, where abundance of room and some convenient
retreats were afforded them. But the sight of the enraged
drugged whales now and then blindly darting to and fro
across the circles, was nothing to what at last met our eyes. It
is sometimes the custom when fast to a whale more than commonly powerful and alert, to seek to hamstring him, as it
were, by sundering or maiming his gigantic tail-tendon. It is
done by darting a short-handled cutting-spade, to which is
attached a rope for hauling it back again. A whale wounded
(as we afterwards learned) in this part, but not effectually, as
it seemed, had broken away from the boat, carrying along
with him half of the harpoon line; and in the extraordinary
agony of the wound, he was now dashing among the revolving circles like the lone mounted desperado Arnold, at the
battle of Saratoga, carrying dismay wherever he went.

But agonizing as was the wound of this whale, and an appalling spectacle enough, any way; yet the peculiar horror
with which he seemed to inspire the rest of the herd, was
owing to a cause which at first the intervening distance obscured from us. But at length we perceived that by one of the
unimaginable accidents of the fishery, this whale had become
entangled in the harpoon-line that he towed; he had also run
away with the cutting spade in him; and while the free end

---

each side of the anus; but the breasts themselves extend upwards from that.
When by chance these precious parts in a nursing whale are cut by the hunter's lance, the mother's pouring milk and blood rivallingly discolor the sea
for rods. The milk is very sweet and rich; it has been tasted by man; it might
do well with strawberries. When overflowing with mutual esteem, the whales
salute *more hominum*.

of the rope attached to that weapon, had permanently caught in the coils of the harpoon-line round his tail, the cutting-spade itself had worked loose from his flesh. So that tormented to madness, he was now churning through the water, violently flailing with his flexible tail, and tossing the keen spade about him, wounding and murdering his own comrades.

This terrific object seemed to recall the whole herd from their stationary fright. First, the whales forming the margin of our lake began to crowd a little, and tumble against each other, as if lifted by half spent billows from afar; then the lake itself began faintly to heave and swell; the submarine bridal-chambers and nurseries vanished; in more and more contracting orbits the whales in the more central circles began to swim in thickening clusters. Yes, the long calm was departing. A low advancing hum was soon heard; and then like to the tumultuous masses of block-ice when the great river Hudson breaks up in Spring, the entire host of whales came tumbling upon their inner centre, as if to pile themselves up in one common mountain. Instantly Starbuck and Queequeg changed places; Starbuck taking the stern.

"Oars! Oars!" he intensely whispered, seizing the helm—"gripe your oars, and clutch your souls, now! My God, men, stand by! Shove him off, you Queequeg—the whale there!—prick him!—hit him! Stand up—stand up, and stay so! Spring, men—pull, men; never mind their backs—scrape them!—scrape away!"

The boat was now all but jammed between two vast black bulks, leaving a narrow Dardanelles between their long lengths. But by desperate endeavor we at last shot into a temporary opening; then giving way rapidly, and at the same time earnestly watching for another outlet. After many similar hair-breadth escapes, we at last swiftly glided into what had just been one of the outer circles, but now crossed by random whales, all violently making for one centre. This lucky salvation was cheaply purchased by the loss of Queequeg's hat, who, while standing in the bows to prick the fugitive whales, had his hat taken clean from his head by the air-eddy made by the sudden tossing of a pair of broad flukes close by.

Riotous and disordered as the universal commotion now

was, it soon resolved itself into what seemed a systematic movement; for having clumped together at last in one dense body, they then renewed their onward flight with augmented fleetness. Further pursuit was useless; but the boats still lingered in their wake to pick up what drugged whales might be dropped astern, and likewise to secure one which Flask had killed and waifed. The waif is a pennoned pole, two or three of which are carried by every boat; and which, when additional game is at hand, are inserted upright into the floating body of a dead whale, both to mark its place on the sea, and also as token of prior possession, should the boats of any other ship draw near.

The result of this lowering was somewhat illustrative of that sagacious saying in the Fishery,—the more whales the less fish. Of all the drugged whales only one was captured. The rest contrived to escape for the time, but only to be taken, as will hereafter be seen, by some other craft than the Pequod.

Chapter 88

SCHOOLS AND SCHOOLMASTERS

THE PREVIOUS chapter gave account of an immense body or herd of Sperm Whales, and there was also then given the probable cause inducing those vast aggregations.

Now, though such great bodies are at times encountered, yet, as must have been seen, even at the present day, small detached bands are occasionally observed, embracing from twenty to fifty individuals each. Such bands are known as schools. They generally are of two sorts; those composed almost entirely of females, and those mustering none but young vigorous males, or bulls, as they are familiarly designated.

In cavalier attendance upon the school of females, you invariably see a male of full grown magnitude, but not old; who, upon any alarm, evinces his gallantry by falling in the rear and covering the flight of his ladies. In truth, this gentleman is a luxurious Ottoman, swimming about over the watery world, surroundingly accompanied by all the solaces and endearments of the harem. The contrast between this Ottoman and his concubines is striking; because, while he is always of the largest leviathanic proportions, the ladies, even at full growth, are not more than one third of the bulk of an average-sized male. They are comparatively delicate, indeed; I dare say, not to exceed half a dozen yards round the waist. Nevertheless, it cannot be denied, that upon the whole they are hereditarily entitled to *en bon point.*

It is very curious to watch this harem and its lord in their indolent ramblings. Like fashionables, they are for ever on the move in leisurely search of variety. You meet them on the Line in time for the full flower of the Equatorial feeding season, having just returned, perhaps, from spending the summer in the Northern seas, and so cheating summer of all unpleasant weariness and warmth. By the time they have lounged up and down the promenade of the Equator awhile, they start for the Oriental waters in anticipation of the cool season there, and so evade the other excessive temperature of the year.

When serenely advancing on one of these journeys, if any strange suspicious sights are seen, my lord whale keeps a wary eye on his interesting family. Should any unwarrantably pert young Leviathan coming that way, presume to draw confidentially close to one of the ladies, with what prodigious fury the Bashaw assails him, and chases him away! High times, indeed, if unprincipled young rakes like him are to be permitted to invade the sanctity of domestic bliss; though do what the Bashaw will, he cannot keep the most notorious Lothario out of his bed; for, alas! all fish bed in common. As ashore, the ladies often cause the most terrible duels among their rival admirers; just so with the whales, who sometimes come to deadly battle, and all for love. They fence with their long lower jaws, sometimes locking them together, and so striving for the supremacy like elks that warringly interweave their antlers. Not a few are captured having the deep scars of these encounters,—furrowed heads, broken teeth, scolloped fins; and in some instances, wrenched and dislocated mouths.

But supposing the invader of domestic bliss to betake himself away at the first rush of the harem's lord, then is it very diverting to watch that lord. Gently he insinuates his vast bulk among them again and revels there awhile, still in tantalizing vicinity to young Lothario, like pious Solomon devoutly worshipping among his thousand concubines. Granting other whales to be in sight, the fishermen will seldom give chase to one of these Grand Turks; for these Grand Turks are too lavish of their strength, and hence their unctuousness is small. As for the sons and the daughters they beget, why, those sons and daughters must take care of themselves; at least, with only the maternal help. For like certain other omnivorous roving lovers that might be named, my Lord Whale has no taste for the nursery, however much for the bower; and so, being a great traveller, he leaves his anonymous babies all over the world; every baby an exotic. In good time, nevertheless, as the ardor of youth declines; as years and dumps increase; as reflection lends her solemn pauses; in short, as a general lassitude overtakes the sated Turk; then a love of ease and virtue supplants the love for maidens; our Ottoman enters upon the impotent, repentant, admonitory stage of life, forswears, disbands the harem, and grown to an exemplary, sulky old soul, goes about all alone among the meridians and parallels saying his prayers, and warning each young Leviathan from his amorous errors.

Now, as the harem of whales is called by the fishermen a school, so is the lord and master of that school technically known as the schoolmaster. It is therefore not in strict character, however admirably satirical, that after going to school himself, he should then go abroad inculcating not what he learned there, but the folly of it. His title, schoolmaster, would very naturally seem derived from the name bestowed upon the harem itself, but some have surmised that the man who first thus entitled this sort of Ottoman whale, must have read the memoirs of Vidocq, and informed himself what sort of a country-schoolmaster that famous Frenchman was in his younger days, and what was the nature of those occult lessons he inculcated into some of his pupils.

The same secludedness and isolation to which the schoolmaster whale betakes himself in his advancing years, is true of all aged Sperm Whales. Almost universally, a lone whale—as a solitary Leviathan is called—proves an ancient one. Like venerable moss-bearded Daniel Boone, he will have no one near him but Nature herself; and her he takes to wife in the wilderness of waters, and the best of wives she is, though she keeps so many moody secrets.

The schools composing none but young and vigorous males, previously mentioned, offer a strong contrast to the harem schools. For while those female whales are characteristically timid, the young males, or forty-barrel-bulls, as they call them, are by far the most pugnacious of all Leviathans, and proverbially the most dangerous to encounter; excepting those wondrous greyheaded, grizzled whales, sometimes met, and these will fight you like grim fiends exasperated by a penal gout.

The Forty-barrel-bull schools are larger than the harem schools. Like a mob of young collegians, they are full of fight, fun, and wickedness, tumbling round the world at such a reckless, rollicking rate, that no prudent underwriter would insure them any more than he would a riotous lad at Yale or

Harvard. They soon relinquish this turbulence though, and when about three fourths grown, break up, and separately go about in quest of settlements, that is, harems.

Another point of difference between the male and female schools is still more characteristic of the sexes. Say you strike a Forty-barrel-bull—poor devil! all his comrades quit him. But strike a member of the harem school, and her companions swim around her with every token of concern, sometimes lingering so near her and so long, as themselves to fall a prey.

Chapter 89

THE ALLUSION to the waifs and waif-poles in the last chapter but one, necessitates some account of the laws and regulations of the whale fishery, of which the waif may be deemed the grand symbol and badge.

It frequently happens that when several ships are cruising in company, a whale may be struck by one vessel; then escape, and be finally killed and captured by another vessel; and herein are indirectly comprised many minor contingencies, all partaking of this one grand feature. For example,—after a weary and perilous chase and capture of a whale, the body may get loose from the ship by reason of a violent storm; and drifting far away to leeward, be retaken by a second whaler, who, in a calm, snugly tows it alongside, without risk of life or line. Thus the most vexatious and violent disputes would often arise between the fishermen, were there not some written or unwritten, universal, undisputed law applicable to all cases.

Perhaps the only formal whaling code authorized by legislative enactment, was that of Holland. It was decreed by the States-General in A.D. 1695. But though no other nation has ever had any written whaling law, yet the American fishermen have been their own legislators and lawyers in this matter. They have provided a system which for terse comprehensiveness surpasses Justinian's Pandects and the By-laws of the Chinese Society for the Suppression of Meddling with other People's Business. Yes; these laws might be engraven on a Queen Anne's farthing, or the barb of a harpoon, and worn round the neck, so small are they.

I. A Fast-Fish belongs to the party fast to it.

II. A Loose-Fish is fair game for anybody who can soonest catch it.

But what plays the mischief with this masterly code is the admirable brevity of it, which necessitates a vast volume of commentaries to expound it.

First: What is a Fast-Fish? Alive or dead a fish is technically fast, when it is connected with an occupied ship or boat, by any medium at all controllable by the occupant or occupants,—a mast, an oar, a nine-inch cable, a telegraph wire, or a strand of cobweb, it is all the same. Likewise a fish is technically fast when it bears a waif, or any other recognised symbol of possession; so long as the party waifing it plainly evince their ability at any time to take it alongside, as well as their intention so to do.

These are scientific commentaries; but the commentaries of the whalemen themselves sometimes consist in hard words and harder knocks—the Coke-upon-Littleton of the fist. True, among the more upright and honorable whalemen allowances are always made for peculiar cases, where it would be an outrageous moral injustice for one party to claim possession of a whale previously chased or killed by another party. But others are by no means so scrupulous.

Some fifty years ago there was a curious case of whale-trover litigated in England, wherein the plaintiffs set forth that after a hard chase of a whale in the Northern seas, they (the plaintiffs) had succeeded in harpooning the fish; but at last, through peril of their lives, were obliged to forsake not only their lines, but their boat itself. Ultimately the defendants (the crew of another ship) came up with the whale; struck, killed, seized, and finally appropriated it before the very eyes of the plaintiffs. And when those defendants were remonstrated with, their captain snapped his fingers in the plaintiffs' teeth, and assured them that by way of doxology to the deed he had done, he would now retain their line, harpoons, and boat, which had remained attached to the whale at the time of the seizure. Wherefore the plaintiffs now sued for the recovery of the value of their whale, line, harpoons, and boat.

Mr. Erskine was counsel for the defendants; Lord Ellenborough was the judge. In the course of the defence, the witty Erskine went on to illustrate his position, by alluding to a recent crim. con. case, wherein a gentleman, after in vain trying to bridle his wife's viciousness, had at last abandoned her upon the seas of life; but in the course of years, repenting of that step, he instituted an action to recover possession of

her. Erskine was on the other side; and he then supported it
by saying, that though the gentleman had originally harpooned the lady, and had once had her fast, and only by reason of the great stress of her plunging viciousness, had at last
abandoned her; yet abandon her he did, so that she became a
loose-fish; and therefore when a subsequent gentleman re-
harpooned her, the lady then became that subsequent gentleman's property, along with whatever harpoon might have
been found sticking in her.

Now in the present case Erskine contended that the examples of the whale and the lady were reciprocally illustrative of
each other.

These pleadings, and the counter pleadings, being duly
heard, the very learned judge in set terms decided, to wit,—
That as for the boat, he awarded it to the plaintiffs, because
they had merely abandoned it to save their lives; but that with
regard to the controverted whale, harpoons, and line, they
belonged to the defendants; the whale, because it was a
Loose-Fish at the time of the final capture; and the harpoons
and line because when the fish made off with them, it (the
fish) acquired a property in those articles; and hence anybody
who afterwards took the fish had a right to them. Now the
defendants afterwards took the fish; ergo, the aforesaid articles were theirs.

A common man looking at this decision of the very learned
Judge, might possibly object to it. But ploughed up to the
primary rock of the matter, the two great principles laid down
in the twin whaling laws previously quoted, and applied and
elucidated by Lord Ellenborough in the above cited case;
these two laws touching Fast-Fish and Loose-Fish, I say, will,
on reflection, be found the fundamentals of all human jurisprudence; for notwithstanding its complicated tracery of
sculpture, the Temple of the Law, like the Temple of the Philistines, has but two props to stand on.

Is it not a saying in every one's mouth, Possession is half
of the law: that is, regardless of how the thing came into
possession? But often possession is the whole of the law.
What are the sinews and souls of Russian serfs and Republican slaves but Fast-Fish, whereof possession is the whole of
the law? What to the rapacious landlord is the widow's last

mite but a Fast-Fish? What is yonder undetected villain's marble mansion with a door-plate for a waif; what is that but a Fast-Fish? What is the ruinous discount which Mordecai, the broker, gets from poor Woebegone, the bankrupt, on a loan to keep Woebegone's family from starvation; what is that ruinous discount but a Fast-Fish? What is the Archbishop of Savesoul's income of £100,000 seized from the scant bread and cheese of hundreds of thousands of broken-backed laborers (all sure of heaven without any of Savesoul's help) what is that globular 100,000 but a Fast-Fish? What are the Duke of Dunder's hereditary towns and hamlets but Fast-Fish? What to that redoubted harpooneer, John Bull, is poor Ireland, but a Fast-Fish? What to that apostolic lancer, Brother Jonathan, is Texas but a Fast-Fish? And concerning all these, is not Possession the whole of the law?

But if the doctrine of Fast-Fish be pretty generally applicable, the kindred doctrine of Loose-Fish is still more widely so. That is internationally and universally applicable.

What was America in 1492 but a Loose-Fish, in which Columbus struck the Spanish standard by way of waifing it for his royal master and mistress? What was Poland to the Czar? What Greece to the Turk? What India to England? What at last will Mexico be to the United States? All Loose-Fish.

What are the Rights of Man and the Liberties of the World but Loose-Fish? What all men's minds and opinions but Loose-Fish? What is the principle of religious belief in them but a Loose-Fish? What to the ostentatious smuggling verbalists are the thoughts of thinkers but Loose-Fish? What is the great globe itself but a Loose-Fish? And what are you, reader, but a Loose-Fish and a Fast-Fish, too?

Chapter 90

HEADS OR TAILS

"De balena vero sufficit, si rex habeat caput, et regina caudam."
Bracton, l. 3, c. 3.

LATIN from the books of the Laws of England, which taken along with the context, means, that of all whales captured by anybody on the coast of that land, the King, as Honorary Grand Harpooneer, must have the head, and the Queen be respectfully presented with the tail. A division which, in the whale, is much like halving an apple; there is no intermediate remainder. Now as this law, under a modified form, is to this day in force in England; and as it offers in various respects a strange anomaly touching the general law of Fast and Loose-Fish, it is here treated of in a separate chapter, on the same courteous principle that prompts the English railways to be at the expense of a separate car, specially reserved for the accommodation of royalty. In the first place, in curious proof of the fact that the above-mentioned law is still in force, I proceed to lay before you a circumstance that happened within the last two years.

It seems that some honest mariners of Dover, or Sandwich, or some one of the Cinque Ports, had after a hard chase succeeded in killing and beaching a fine whale which they had originally descried afar off from the shore. Now the Cinque Ports are partially or somehow under the jurisdiction of a sort of policeman or beadle, called a Lord Warden. Holding the office directly from the crown, I believe, all the royal emoluments incident to the Cinque Port territories become by assignment his. By some writers this office is called a sinecure. But not so. Because the Lord Warden is busily employed at times in fobbing his perquisites; which are his chiefly by virtue of that same fobbing of them.

Now when these poor sun-burnt mariners, bare-footed, and with their trowsers rolled high up on their eely legs, had wearily hauled their fat fish high and dry, promising themselves a good £150 from the precious oil and bone; and in fantasy sipping rare tea with their wives, and good ale with their cronies, upon the strength of their respective shares; up steps a very learned and most Christian and charitable gentleman, with a copy of Blackstone under his arm; and laying it upon the whale's head, he says—"Hands off! this fish, my masters, is a Fast-Fish. I seize it as the Lord Warden's." Upon this the poor mariners in their respectful consternation—so truly English—knowing not what to say, fall to vigorously scratching their heads all round; meanwhile ruefully glancing from the whale to the stranger. But that did in nowise mend the matter, or at all soften the hard heart of the learned gentleman with the copy of Blackstone. At length one of them, after long scratching about for his ideas, made bold to speak.

"Please, sir, who is the Lord Warden?"

"The Duke."

"But the duke had nothing to do with taking this fish?"

"It is his."

"We have been at great trouble, and peril, and some expense, and is all that to go to the Duke's benefit; we getting nothing at all for our pains but our blisters?"

"It is his."

"Is the Duke so very poor as to be forced to this desperate mode of getting a livelihood?"

"It is his."

"I thought to relieve my old bed-ridden mother by part of my share of this whale."

"It is his."

"Won't the Duke be content with a quarter or a half?"

"It is his."

In a word, the whale was seized and sold, and his Grace the Duke of Wellington received the money. Thinking that viewed in some particular lights, the case might by a bare possibility in some small degree be deemed, under the circumstances, a rather hard one, an honest clergyman of the town respectfully addressed a note to his Grace, begging him to take the case of those unfortunate mariners into full consideration. To which my Lord Duke in substance replied (both letters were published) that he had already done so, and received the money, and would be obliged to the reverend gentleman if for the future he (the reverend gentleman) would decline meddling with other people's business. Is this the still militant old man, standing at the corners of the three kingdoms, on all hands coercing alms of beggars?

It will readily be seen that in this case the alleged right of the Duke to the whale was a delegated one from the Sovereign. We must needs inquire then on what principle the Sovereign is originally invested with that right. The law itself has already been set forth. But Plowdon gives us the reason for it. Says Plowdon, the whale so caught belongs to the King and Queen, "because of its superior excellence." And by the soundest commentators this has ever been held a cogent argument in such matters.

But why should the King have the head, and the Queen the tail? A reason for that, ye lawyers!

In his treatise on "Queen-Gold," or Queen-pinmoney, an old King's Bench author, one William Prynne, thus discourseth: "Yᵉ tail is yᵉ Queen's, that yᵉ Queen's wardrobe may be supplied with yᵉ whalebone." Now this was written at a time when the black limber bone of the Greenland or Right whale was largely used in ladies' bodices. But this same bone is not in the tail; it is in the head, which is a sad mistake for a sagacious lawyer like Prynne. But is the Queen a mermaid, to be presented with a tail? An allegorical meaning may lurk here.

There are two royal fish so styled by the English law writers—the whale and the sturgeon; both royal property under certain limitations, and nominally supplying the tenth branch of the crown's ordinary revenue. I know not that any other author has hinted of the matter; but by inference it seems to me that the sturgeon must be divided in the same way as the whale, the King receiving the highly dense and elastic head peculiar to that fish, which, symbolically regarded, may possibly be humorously grounded upon some presumed congeniality. And thus there seems a reason in all things, even in law.

Chapter 91

The Pequod meets the Rose-bud

"In vain it was to rake for Ambergriese in the paunch of this Leviathan, insufferable fetor denying that inquiry."

Sir T. Browne, V.E.

I<small>T WAS</small> a week or two after the last whaling scene recounted, and when we were slowly sailing over a sleepy, vapory, mid-day sea, that the many noses on the Pequod's deck proved more vigilant discoverers than the three pairs of eyes aloft. A peculiar and not very pleasant smell was smelt in the sea.

"I will bet something now," said Stubb, "that somewhere hereabouts are some of those drugged whales we tickled the other day. I thought they would keel up before long."

Presently, the vapors in advance slid aside; and there in the distance lay a ship, whose furled sails betokened that some sort of whale must be alongside. As we glided nearer, the stranger showed French colors from his peak; and by the eddying cloud of vulture sea-fowl that circled, and hovered, and swooped around him, it was plain that the whale alongside must be what the fishermen call a blasted whale, that is, a whale that has died unmolested on the sea, and so floated an unappropriated corpse. It may well be conceived, what an unsavory odor such a mass must exhale; worse than an Assyrian city in the plague, when the living are incompetent to bury the departed. So intolerable indeed is it regarded by some, that no cupidity could persuade them to moor alongside of it. Yet are there those who will still do it; notwithstanding the fact that the oil obtained from such subjects is of a very inferior quality, and by no means of the nature of attar-of-rose.

Coming still nearer with the expiring breeze, we saw that the Frenchman had a second whale alongside; and this second whale seemed even more of a nosegay than the first. In truth, it turned out to be one of those problematical whales that seem to dry up and die with a sort of prodigious dyspepsia,

or indigestion; leaving their defunct bodies almost entirely
bankrupt of anything like oil. Nevertheless, in the proper
place we shall see that no knowing fisherman will ever turn
up his nose at such a whale as this, however much he may
shun blasted whales in general.

The Pequod had now swept so nigh to the stranger, that
Stubb vowed he recognised his cutting spade-pole entangled
in the lines that were knotted round the tail of one of these
whales.

"There's a pretty fellow, now," he banteringly laughed,
standing in the ship's bows, "there's a jackal for ye! I well
know that these Crappoes of Frenchmen are but poor devils
in the fishery; sometimes lowering their boats for breakers,
mistaking them for Sperm Whale spouts; yes, and sometimes
sailing from their port with their hold full of boxes of tallow
candles, and cases of snuffers, foreseeing that all the oil they
will get won't be enough to dip the Captain's wick into; aye,
we all know these things; but look ye, here's a Crappo that is
content with our leavings, the drugged whale there, I mean;
aye, and is content too with scraping the dry bones of that
other precious fish he has there. Poor devil! I say, pass round
a hat, some one, and let's make him a present of a little oil
for dear charity's sake. For what oil he'll get from that
drugged whale there, wouldn't be fit to burn in a jail; no, not
in a condemned cell. And as for the other whale, why, I'll
agree to get more oil by chopping up and trying out these
three masts of ours, than he'll get from that bundle of bones;
though, now that I think of it, it may contain something
worth a good deal more than oil; yes, ambergris. I wonder
now if our old man has thought of that. It's worth trying.
Yes, I'm in for it;" and so saying he started for the quarter-
deck.

By this time the faint air had become a complete calm; so
that whether or no, the Pequod was now fairly entrapped in
the smell, with no hope of escaping except by its breezing up
again. Issuing from the cabin, Stubb now called his boat's
crew, and pulled off for the stranger. Drawing across her
bow, he perceived that in accordance with the fanciful French
taste, the upper part of her stem-piece was carved in the likeness of a huge drooping stalk, was painted green, and for

thorns had copper spikes projecting from it here and there; the whole terminating in a symmetrical folded bulb of a bright red color. Upon her head boards, in large gilt letters, he read "Bouton de Rose,"—Rose-button, or Rose-bud; and this was the romantic name of this aromatic ship.

Though Stubb did not understand the *Bouton* part of the inscription, yet the word *rose*, and the bulbous figure-head put together, sufficiently explained the whole to him.

"A wooden rose-bud, eh?" he cried with his hand to his nose, "that will do very well; but how like all creation it smells!"

Now in order to hold direct communication with the people on deck, he had to pull round the bows to the starboard side, and thus come close to the blasted whale; and so talk over it.

Arrived then at this spot, with one hand still to his nose, he bawled—"Bouton-de-Rose, ahoy! are there any of you Bouton-de-Roses that speak English?"

"Yes," rejoined a Guernsey-man from the bulwarks, who turned out to be the chief-mate.

"Well, then, my Bouton-de-Rose-bud, have you seen the White Whale?"

"*What* whale?"

"The *White* Whale—a Sperm Whale—Moby Dick, have ye seen him?"

"Never heard of such a whale. Cachalot Blanche! White Whale—no."

"Very good, then; good bye now, and I'll call again in a minute."

Then rapidly pulling back towards the Pequod, and seeing Ahab leaning over the quarter-deck rail awaiting his report, he moulded his two hands into a trumpet and shouted—"No, Sir! No!" Upon which Ahab retired, and Stubb returned to the Frenchman.

He now perceived that the Guernsey-man, who had just got into the chains, and was using a cutting-spade, had slung his nose in a sort of bag.

"What's the matter with your nose, there?" said Stubb. "Broke it?"

"I wish it was broken, or that I didn't have any nose at all!"

answered the Guernsey-man, who did not seem to relish the job he was at very much. "But what are you holding *yours* for?"

"Oh, nothing! It's a wax nose; I have to hold it on. Fine day, aint it? Air rather gardenny, I should say; throw us a bunch of posies, will ye, Bouton-de-Rose?"

"What in the devil's name do you want here?" roared the Guernsey-man, flying into a sudden passion.

"Oh! keep cool—cool? yes, that's the word; why don't you pack those whales in ice while you're working at 'em? But joking aside, though; do you know, Rose-bud, that it's all nonsense trying to get any oil out of such whales? As for that dried up one, there, he hasn't a gill in his whole carcase."

"I know that well enough; but, d'ye see, the Captain here won't believe it; this is his first voyage; he was a Cologne manufacturer before. But come aboard, and mayhap he'll believe you, if he won't me; and so I'll get out of this dirty scrape."

"Anything to oblige ye, my sweet and pleasant fellow," rejoined Stubb, and with that he soon mounted to the deck. There a queer scene presented itself. The sailors, in tasselled caps of red worsted, were getting the heavy tackles in readiness for the whales. But they worked rather slow and talked very fast, and seemed in anything but a good humor. All their noses upwardly projected from their faces like so many jib-booms. Now and then pairs of them would drop their work, and run up to the mast-head to get some fresh air. Some thinking they would catch the plague, dipped oakum in coal-tar, and at intervals held it to their nostrils. Others having broken the stems of their pipes almost short off at the bowl, were vigorously puffing tobacco-smoke, so that it constantly filled their olfactories.

Stubb was struck by a shower of outcries and anathemas proceeding from the Captain's round-house abaft; and looking in that direction saw a fiery face thrust from behind the door, which was held ajar from within. This was the tormented surgeon, who, after in vain remonstrating against the proceedings of the day, had betaken himself to the Captain's round-house (*cabinet* he called it) to avoid the pest; but still, could not help yelling out his entreaties and indignations at times.

Marking all this, Stubb augured well for his scheme, and turning to the Guernsey-man had a little chat with him, during which the stranger mate expressed his detestation of his Captain as a conceited ignoramus, who had brought them all into so unsavory and unprofitable a pickle. Sounding him carefully, Stubb further perceived that the Guernsey-man had not the slightest suspicion concerning the ambergris. He therefore held his peace on that head, but otherwise was quite frank and confidential with him, so that the two quickly concocted a little plan for both circumventing and satirizing the Captain, without his at all dreaming of distrusting their sincerity. According to this little plan of theirs, the Guernsey-man, under cover of an interpreter's office, was to tell the Captain what he pleased, but as coming from Stubb; and as for Stubb, he was to utter any nonsense that should come uppermost in him during the interview.

By this time their destined victim appeared from his cabin. He was a small and dark, but rather delicate looking man for a sea-captain, with large whiskers and moustache, however; and wore a red cotton velvet vest with watch-seals at his side. To this gentleman, Stubb was now politely introduced by the Guernsey-man, who at once ostentatiously put on the aspect of interpreting between them.

"What shall I say to him first?" said he.

"Why," said Stubb, eyeing the velvet vest and the watch and seals, "you may as well begin by telling him that he looks a sort of babyish to me, though I don't pretend to be a judge."

"He says, Monsieur," said the Guernsey-man, in French, turning to his captain, "that only yesterday his ship spoke a vessel, whose captain and chief-mate, with six sailors, had all died of a fever caught from a blasted whale they had brought alongside."

Upon this the captain started, and eagerly desired to know more.

"What now?" said the Guernsey-man to Stubb.

"Why, since he takes it so easy, tell him that now I have eyed him carefully, I'm quite certain that he's no more fit to command a whale-ship than a St. Jago monkey. In fact, tell him from me he's a baboon."

"He vows and declares, Monsieur, that the other whale, the dried one, is far more deadly than the blasted one; in fine, Monsieur, he conjures us, as we value our lives, to cut loose from these fish."

Instantly the captain ran forward, and in a loud voice commanded his crew to desist from hoisting the cutting-tackles, and at once cast loose the cables and chains confining the whales to the ship.

"What now?" said the Guernsey-man, when the captain had returned to them.

"Why, let me see; yes, you may as well tell him now that— that—in fact, tell him I've diddled him, and (aside to himself) perhaps somebody else."

"He says, Monsieur, that he's very happy to have been of any service to us."

Hearing this, the captain vowed that they were the grateful parties (meaning himself and mate) and concluded by inviting Stubb down into his cabin to drink a bottle of Bordeaux.

"He wants you to take a glass of wine with him," said the interpreter.

"Thank him heartily; but tell him it's against my principles to drink with the man I've diddled. In fact, tell him I must go."

"He says, Monsieur, that his principles won't admit of his drinking; but that if Monsieur wants to live another day to drink, then Monsieur had best drop all four boats, and pull the ship away from these whales, for it's so calm they won't drift."

By this time Stubb was over the side, and getting into his boat, hailed the Guernsey-man to this effect,—that having a long tow-line in his boat, he would do what he could to help them, by pulling out the lighter whale of the two from the ship's side. While the Frenchman's boats, then, were engaged in towing the ship one way, Stubb benevolently towed away at his whale the other way, ostentatiously slacking out a most unusually long tow-line.

Presently a breeze sprang up; Stubb feigned to cast off from the whale; hoisting his boats, the Frenchman soon increased his distance, while the Pequod slid in between him and Stubb's whale. Whereupon Stubb quickly pulled to the floating body, and hailing the Pequod to give notice of his intentions, at once proceeded to reap the fruit of his unrighteous cunning. Seizing his sharp boat-spade, he commenced an excavation in the body, a little behind the side fin. You would almost have thought he was digging a cellar there in the sea; and when at length his spade struck against the gaunt ribs, it was like turning up old Roman tiles and pottery buried in fat English loam. His boat's crew were all in high excitement, eagerly helping their chief, and looking as anxious as gold-hunters.

And all the time numberless fowls were diving, and ducking, and screaming, and yelling, and fighting around them. Stubb was beginning to look disappointed, especially as the horrible nosegay increased, when suddenly from out the very heart of this plague, there stole a faint stream of perfume, which flowed through the tide of bad smells without being absorbed by it, as one river will flow into and then along with another, without at all blending with it for a time.

"I have it, I have it," cried Stubb, with delight, striking something in the subterranean regions, "a purse! a purse!"

Dropping his spade, he thrust both hands in, and drew out handfuls of something that looked like ripe Windsor soap, or rich mottled old cheese; very unctuous and savory withal. You might easily dent it with your thumb; it is of a hue between yellow and ash color. And this, good friends, is ambergris, worth a gold guinea an ounce to any druggist. Some six handfuls were obtained; but more was unavoidably lost in the sea, and still more, perhaps, might have been secured were it not for impatient Ahab's loud command to Stubb to desist, and come on board, else the ship would bid them good bye.

Chapter 92

AMBERGRIS

Now this ambergris is a very curious substance, and so important as an article of commerce, that in 1791 a certain Nantucket-born Captain Coffin was examined at the bar of the English House of Commons on that subject. For at that time, and indeed until a comparatively late day, the precise origin of ambergris remained, like amber itself, a problem to the learned. Though the word ambergris is but the French compound for grey amber, yet the two substances are quite distinct. For amber, though at times found on the sea-coast, is also dug up in some far inland soils, whereas ambergris is never found except upon the sea. Besides, amber is a hard, transparent, brittle, odorless substance, used for mouth-pieces to pipes, for beads and ornaments; but ambergris is soft, waxy, and so highly fragrant and spicy, that it is largely used in perfumery, in pastiles, precious candles, hair-powders, and pomatum. The Turks use it in cooking, and also carry it to Mecca, for the same purpose that frankincense is carried to St. Peter's in Rome. Some wine merchants drop a few grains into claret, to flavor it.

Who would think, then, that such fine ladies and gentlemen should regale themselves with an essence found in the inglorious bowels of a sick whale! Yet so it is. By some, ambergris is supposed to be the cause, and by others the effect, of the dyspepsia in the whale. How to cure such a dyspepsia it were hard to say, unless by administering three or four boat loads of Brandreth's pills, and then running out of harm's way, as laborers do in blasting rocks.

I have forgotten to say that there were found in this ambergris, certain hard, round, bony plates, which at first Stubb thought might be sailors' trousers buttons; but it afterwards turned out that they were nothing more than pieces of small squid bones embalmed in that manner.

Now that the incorruption of this most fragrant ambergris should be found in the heart of such decay; is this nothing?

Bethink thee of that saying of St. Paul in Corinthians, about corruption and incorruption; how that we are sown in dishonor, but raised in glory. And likewise call to mind that saying of Paracelsus about what it is that maketh the best musk. Also forget not the strange fact that of all things of ill-savor, Cologne-water, in its rudimental manufacturing stages, is the worst.

I should like to conclude the chapter with the above appeal, but cannot, owing to my anxiety to repel a charge often made against whalemen, and which, in the estimation of some already biased minds, might be considered as indirectly substantiated by what has been said of the Frenchman's two whales. Elsewhere in this volume the slanderous aspersion has been disproved, that the vocation of whaling is throughout a slatternly, untidy business. But there is another thing to rebut. They hint that all whales always smell bad. Now how did this odious stigma originate?

I opine, that it is plainly traceable to the first arrival of the Greenland whaling ships in London, more than two centuries ago. Because those whalemen did not then, and do not now, try out their oil at sea as the Southern ships have always done; but cutting up the fresh blubber in small bits, thrust it through the bung holes of large casks, and carry it home in that manner; the shortness of the season in those Icy Seas, and the sudden and violent storms to which they are exposed, forbidding any other course. The consequence is, that upon breaking into the hold, and unloading one of these whale cemeteries, in the Greenland dock, a savor is given forth somewhat similar to that arising from excavating an old city grave-yard, for the foundations of a Lying-in Hospital.

I partly surmise also, that this wicked charge against whalers may be likewise imputed to the existence on the coast of Greenland, in former times, of a Dutch village called Schmerenburgh or Smeerenberg, which latter name is the one used by the learned Fogo Von Slack, in his great work on Smells, a text-book on that subject. As its name imports (smeer, fat; berg, to put up), this village was founded in order to afford a place for the blubber of the Dutch whale fleet to be tried out, without being taken home to Holland for that purpose. It was a collection of furnaces, fat-kettles, and oil sheds; and when the works were in full operation certainly gave forth no very pleasant savor. But all this is quite different with a South Sea Sperm Whaler; which in a voyage of four years perhaps, after completely filling her hold with oil, does not, perhaps, consume fifty days in the business of boiling out; and in the state that it is casked, the oil is nearly scentless. The truth is, that living or dead, if but decently treated, whales as a species are by no means creatures of ill odor; nor can whalemen be recognised, as the people of the middle ages affected to detect a Jew in the company, by the nose. Nor indeed can the whale possibly be otherwise than fragrant, when, as a general thing, he enjoys such high health; taking abundance of exercise; always out of doors; though, it is true, seldom in the open air. I say, that the motion of a Sperm Whale's flukes above water dispenses a perfume, as when a musk-scented lady rustles her dress in a warm parlor. What then shall I liken the Sperm Whale to for fragrance, considering his magnitude? Must it not be to that famous elephant, with jewelled tusks, and redolent with myrrh, which was led out of an Indian town to do honor to Alexander the Great?

Chapter 93

THE CASTAWAY

IT WAS but some few days after encountering the Frenchman, that a most significant event befell the most insignificant of the Pequod's crew; an event most lamentable; and which ended in providing the sometimes madly merry and predestinated craft with a living and ever accompanying prophecy of whatever shattered sequel might prove her own.

Now, in the whale ship, it is not every one that goes in the boats. Some few hands are reserved called ship-keepers, whose province it is to work the vessel while the boats are pursuing the whale. As a general thing, these ship-keepers are as hardy fellows as the men comprising the boats' crews. But if there happen to be an unduly slender, clumsy, or timorous wight in the ship, that wight is certain to be made a ship-keeper. It was so in the Pequod with the little negro Pippin by nick-name, Pip by abbreviation. Poor Pip! ye have heard of him before; ye must remember his tambourine on that dramatic midnight, so gloomy-jolly.

In outer aspect, Pip and Dough-Boy made a match, like a black pony and a white one, of equal developments, though of dissimilar color, driven in one eccentric span. But while hapless Dough-Boy was by nature dull and torpid in his intellects, Pip, though over tender-hearted, was at bottom very bright, with that pleasant, genial, jolly brightness peculiar to his tribe; a tribe, which ever enjoy all holidays and festivities with finer, freer relish than any other race. For blacks, the year's calendar should show naught but three hundred and sixty-five Fourth of Julys and New Year's Days. Nor smile so, while I write that this little black was brilliant, for even blackness has its brilliancy; behold yon lustrous ebony, panelled in king's cabinets. But Pip loved life, and all life's peaceable securities; so that the panic-striking business in which he had somehow unaccountably become entrapped, had most sadly blurred his brightness; though, as ere long will be seen, what was thus temporarily subdued in him, in the end was destined to be luridly illumined by strange wild fires, that fictitiously showed him off to ten times the natural lustre with which in his native Tolland County in Connecticut, he had once enlivened many a fiddler's frolic on the green; and at melodious even-tide, with his gay ha-ha! had turned the round horizon into one star-belled tambourine. So, though in the clear air of day, suspended against a blue-veined neck, the pure-watered diamond drop will healthful glow; yet, when the cunning jeweller would show you the diamond in its most impressive lustre, he lays it against a gloomy ground, and then lights it up, not by the sun, but by some unnatural gases. Then come out those fiery effulgences, infernally superb; then the evil-blazing diamond, once the divinest symbol of the crystal skies, looks like some crown-jewel stolen from the King of Hell. But let us to the story.

It came to pass, that in the ambergris affair Stubb's after-oarsman chanced so to sprain his hand, as for a time to become quite maimed; and, temporarily, Pip was put into his place.

The first time Stubb lowered with him, Pip evinced much nervousness; but happily, for that time, escaped close contact with the whale; and therefore came off not altogether discreditably; though Stubb observing him, took care, afterwards, to exhort him to cherish his courageousness to the utmost, for he might often find it needful.

Now upon the second lowering, the boat paddled upon the whale; and as the fish received the darted iron, it gave its customary rap, which happened, in this instance, to be right under poor Pip's seat. The involuntary consternation of the moment caused him to leap, paddle in hand, out of the boat; and in such a way, that part of the slack whale line coming against his chest, he breasted it overboard with him, so as to become entangled in it, when at last plumping into the water. That instant the stricken whale started on a fierce run, the line swiftly straightened; and presto! poor Pip came all foaming up to the chocks of the boat, remorselessly dragged there by the line, which had taken several turns around his chest and neck.

Tashtego stood in the bows. He was full of the fire of the hunt. He hated Pip for a poltroon. Snatching the boat-knife from its sheath, he suspended its sharp edge over the line, and turning towards Stubb, exclaimed interrogatively, "Cut?" Meantime Pip's blue, choked face plainly looked, Do, for God's sake! All passed in a flash. In less than half a minute, this entire thing happened.

"Damn him, cut!" roared Stubb; and so the whale was lost and Pip was saved.

So soon as he recovered himself, the poor little negro was assailed by yells and execrations from the crew. Tranquilly permitting these irregular cursings to evaporate, Stubb then in a plain, business-like, but still half humorous manner, cursed Pip officially; and that done, unofficially gave him much wholesome advice. The substance was, Never jump from a boat, Pip, except—but all the rest was indefinite, as the soundest advice ever is. Now, in general, *Stick to the boat*, is your true motto in whaling; but cases will sometimes happen when *Leap from the boat*, is still better. Moreover, as if perceiving at last that if he should give undiluted conscientious advice to Pip, he would be leaving him too wide a margin to jump in for the future; Stubb suddenly dropped all advice, and concluded with a peremptory command, "Stick to the boat, Pip, or by the Lord, I wont pick you up if you jump; mind that. We can't afford to lose whales by the likes of you; a whale would sell for thirty times what you would, Pip, in Alabama. Bear that in mind, and don't jump any more." Hereby perhaps Stubb indirectly hinted, that though man loves his fellow, yet man is a money-making animal, which propensity too often interferes with his benevolence.

But we are all in the hands of the Gods; and Pip jumped again. It was under very similar circumstances to the first performance; but this time he did not breast out the line; and hence, when the whale started to run, Pip was left behind on the sea, like a hurried traveller's trunk. Alas! Stubb was but too true to his word. It was a beautiful, bounteous, blue day; the spangled sea calm and cool, and flatly stretching away, all round, to the horizon, like gold-beater's skin hammered out to the extremest. Bobbing up and down in that sea, Pip's ebon head showed like a head of cloves. No boat-knife was lifted when he fell so rapidly astern. Stubb's inexorable back was turned upon him; and the whale was winged. In three minutes, a whole mile of shoreless ocean was between Pip and Stubb. Out from the centre of the sea, poor Pip turned his crisp, curling, black head to the sun, another lonely castaway, though the loftiest and the brightest.

Now, in calm weather, to swim in the open ocean is as easy to the practised swimmer as to ride in a spring-carriage ashore. But the awful lonesomeness is intolerable. The intense concentration of self in the middle of such a heartless immensity, my God! who can tell it? Mark, how when sailors in a dead calm bathe in the open sea—mark how closely they hug their ship and only coast along her sides.

But had Stubb really abandoned the poor little negro to his fate? No; he did not mean to, at least. Because there were two boats in his wake, and he supposed, no doubt, that they would of course come up to Pip very quickly, and pick him up; though, indeed, such considerateness towards oarsmen jeopardized through their own timidity, is not always manifested by the hunters in all similar instances; and such instances not unfrequently occur; almost invariably in the fishery, a coward, so called, is marked with the same ruthless detestation peculiar to military navies and armies.

But it so happened, that those boats, without seeing Pip, suddenly spying whales close to them on one side, turned, and gave chase; and Stubb's boat was now so far away, and he and all his crew so intent upon his fish, that Pip's ringed horizon began to expand around him miserably. By the merest chance the ship itself at last rescued him; but from that hour the little negro went about the deck an idiot; such, at least, they said he was. The sea had jeeringly kept his finite body up, but drowned the infinite of his soul. Not drowned entirely, though. Rather carried down alive to wondrous depths, where strange shapes of the unwarped primal world glided to and fro before his passive eyes; and the miser-merman, Wisdom, revealed his hoarded heaps; and among the joyous, heartless, ever-juvenile eternities, Pip saw the multitudinous, God-omnipresent, coral insects, that out of the firmament of waters heaved the colossal orbs. He saw God's foot upon the treadle of the loom, and spoke it; and therefore his shipmates called him mad. So man's insanity is heaven's sense; and wandering from all mortal reason, man comes at last to that celestial thought, which, to reason, is absurd and frantic; and weal or woe, feels then uncompromised, indifferent as his God.

For the rest, blame not Stubb too hardly. The thing is common in that fishery; and in the sequel of the narrative, it will then be seen what like abandonment befell myself.

Chapter 94

A Squeeze of the Hand

THAT WHALE of Stubb's, so dearly purchased, was duly brought to the Pequod's side, where all those cutting and hoisting operations previously detailed, were regularly gone through, even to the baling of the Heidelburgh Tun, or Case.

While some were occupied with this latter duty, others were employed in dragging away the larger tubs, so soon as filled with the sperm; and when the proper time arrived, this same sperm was carefully manipulated ere going to the try-works, of which anon.

It had cooled and crystallized to such a degree, that when, with several others, I sat down before a large Constantine's bath of it, I found it strangely concreted into lumps, here and there rolling about in the liquid part. It was our business to squeeze these lumps back into fluid. A sweet and unctuous duty! No wonder that in old times this sperm was such a favorite cosmetic. Such a clearer! such a sweetener! such a softener! such a delicious mollifier! After having my hands in it for only a few minutes, my fingers felt like eels, and began, as it were, to serpentine and spiralize.

As I sat there at my ease, cross-legged on the deck; after the bitter exertion at the windlass; under a blue tranquil sky; the ship under indolent sail, and gliding so serenely along; as I bathed my hands among those soft, gentle globules of infil-trated tissues, woven almost within the hour; as they richly broke to my fingers, and discharged all their opulence, like fully ripe grapes their wine; as I snuffed up that uncontaminated aroma,—literally and truly, like the smell of spring violets; I declare to you, that for the time I lived as in a musky meadow; I forgot all about our horrible oath; in that inexpressible sperm, I washed my hands and my heart of it; I almost began to credit the old Paracelsan superstition that sperm is of rare virtue in allaying the heat of anger: while bathing in that bath, I felt divinely free from all ill-will, or petulance, or malice, of any sort whatsoever.

Squeeze! squeeze! squeeze! all the morning long; I squeezed that sperm till I myself almost melted into it; I squeezed that sperm till a strange sort of insanity came over me; and I found myself unwittingly squeezing my co-laborers' hands in it, mistaking their hands for the gentle globules. Such an abounding, affectionate, friendly, loving feeling did this avocation beget; that at last I was continually squeezing their hands, and looking up into their eyes sentimentally; as much as to say,—Oh! my dear fellow beings, why should we longer cherish any social acerbities, or know the slightest ill-humor or envy! Come; let us squeeze hands all round; nay, let us all squeeze ourselves into each other; let us squeeze ourselves universally into the very milk and sperm of kindness.

Would that I could keep squeezing that sperm for ever! For now, since by many prolonged, repeated experiences, I have perceived that in all cases man must eventually lower, or at least shift, his conceit of attainable felicity; not placing it anywhere in the intellect or the fancy; but in the wife, the heart, the bed, the table, the saddle, the fire-side, the country; now that I have perceived all this, I am ready to squeeze case eternally. In thoughts of the visions of the night, I saw long rows of angels in paradise, each with his hands in a jar of spermaceti.

*   *   *

Now, while discoursing of sperm, it behooves to speak of other things akin to it, in the business of preparing the sperm whale for the try-works.

First comes white-horse, so called, which is obtained from the tapering part of the fish, and also from the thicker portions of his flukes. It is tough with congealed tendons—a wad of muscle—but still contains some oil. After being severed from the whale, the white-horse is first cut into portable oblongs ere going to the mincer. They look much like blocks of Berkshire marble.

Plum-pudding is the term bestowed upon certain fragmentary parts of the whale's flesh, here and there adhering to the blanket of blubber, and often participating to a considerable degree in its unctuousness. It is a most refreshing, convivial, beautiful object to behold. As its name imports, it is of an exceedingly rich, mottled tint, with a bestreaked snowy and golden ground, dotted with spots of the deepest crimson and purple. It is plums of rubies, in pictures of citron. Spite of reason, it is hard to keep yourself from eating it. I confess, that once I stole behind the foremast to try it. It tasted something as I should conceive a royal cutlet from the thigh of Louis le Gros might have tasted, supposing him to have been killed the first day after the venison season, and that particular venison season contemporary with an unusually fine vintage of the vineyards of Champagne.

There is another substance, and a very singular one, which turns up in the course of this business, but which I feel it to be very puzzling adequately to describe. It is called slobgollion; an appellation original with the whalemen, and even so is the nature of the substance. It is an ineffably oozy, stringy affair, most frequently found in the tubs of sperm, after a prolonged squeezing, and subsequent decanting. I hold it to be the wondrously thin, ruptured membranes of the case, coalescing.

Gurry, so called, is a term properly belonging to right whalemen, but sometimes incidentally used by the sperm fishermen. It designates the dark, glutinous substance which is scraped off the back of the Greenland or right whale, and much of which covers the decks of those inferior souls who hunt that ignoble Leviathan.

Nippers. Strictly this word is not indigenous to the whale's vocabulary. But as applied by whalemen, it becomes so. A whaleman's nipper is a short firm strip of tendinous stuff cut from the tapering part of Leviathan's tail: it averages an inch in thickness, and for the rest, is about the size of the iron part of a hoe. Edgewise moved along the oily deck, it operates like a leathern squilgee; and by nameless blandishments, as of magic, allures along with it all impurities.

But to learn all about these recondite matters, your best way is at once to descend into the blubber-room, and have a long talk with its inmates. This place has previously been mentioned as the receptacle for the blanket-pieces, when stript and hoisted from the whale. When the proper time arrives for cutting up its contents, this apartment is a scene of terror to all tyros, especially by night. On one side, lit by a dull lantern, a space has been left clear for the workmen. They generally go in pairs,—a pike-and-gaff-man and a spade-man. The whaling-pike is similar to a frigate's boarding-weapon of the same name. The gaff is something like a boat-hook. With his gaff, the gaffman hooks on to a sheet of blubber, and strives to hold it from slipping, as the ship pitches and lurches about. Meanwhile, the spade-man stands on the sheet itself, perpendicularly chopping it into the portable horse-pieces. This spade is sharp as hone can make it; the spademan's feet are shoeless; the thing he stands on will sometimes irresistibly slide away from him, like a sledge. If he cuts off one of his own toes, or one of his assistant's, would you be very much astonished? Toes are scarce among veteran blubber-room men.

Chapter 95

THE CASSOCK

HAD YOU stepped on board the Pequod at a certain juncture of this post-mortemizing of the whale; and had you strolled forward nigh the windlass, pretty sure am I that you would have scanned with no small curiosity a very strange, enigmatical object, which you would have seen there, lying along lengthwise in the lee scuppers. Not the wondrous cistern in the whale's huge head; not the prodigy of his unhinged lower jaw; not the miracle of his symmetrical tail; none of these would so surprise you, as half a glimpse of that unaccountable cone,—longer than a Kentuckian is tall, nigh a foot in diameter at the base, and jet-black as Yojo, the ebony idol of Queequeg. And an idol, indeed, it is; or, rather, in old times, its likeness was. Such an idol as that found in the secret groves of Queen Maachah in Judea; and for worshipping which, king Asa, her son, did depose her, and destroyed the idol, and burnt it for an abomination at the brook Kedron, as darkly set forth in the 15th chapter of the first book of Kings.

Look at the sailor, called the mincer, who now comes along, and assisted by two allies, heavily backs the grandissimus, as the mariners call it, and with bowed shoulders, staggers off with it as if he were a grenadier carrying a dead comrade from the field. Extending it upon the forecastle deck, he now proceeds cylindrically to remove its dark pelt, as an African hunter the pelt of a boa. This done he turns the pelt inside out, like a pantaloon leg; gives it a good stretching, so as almost to double its diameter; and at last hangs it, well spread, in the rigging, to dry. Ere long, it is taken down; when removing some three feet of it, towards the pointed extremity, and then cutting two slits for arm-holes at the other end, he lengthwise slips himself bodily into it. The mincer now stands before you invested in the full canonicals of his calling. Immemorial to all his order, this investiture alone will adequately protect him, while employed in the peculiar functions of his office.

That office consists in mincing the horse-pieces of blubber for the pots; an operation which is conducted at a curious wooden horse, planted endwise against the bulwarks, and with a capacious tub beneath it, into which the minced pieces drop, fast as the sheets from a rapt orator's desk. Arrayed in decent black; occupying a conspicuous pulpit; intent on bible leaves; what a candidate for an archbishoprick, what a lad for a Pope were this mincer!*

*Bible leaves! Bible leaves! This is the invariable cry from the mates to the mincer. It enjoins him to be careful, and cut his work into as thin slices as possible, inasmuch as by so doing the business of boiling out the oil is much accelerated, and its quantity considerably increased, besides perhaps improving it in quality.

Chapter 96

THE TRY-WORKS

BESIDES her hoisted boats, an American whaler is out-wardly distinguished by her try-works. She presents the curious anomaly of the most solid masonry joining with oak and hemp in constituting the completed ship. It is as if from the open field a brick-kiln were transported to her planks.

The try-works are planted between the foremast and main-mast, the most roomy part of the deck. The timbers beneath are of a peculiar strength, fitted to sustain the weight of an almost solid mass of brick and mortar, some ten feet by eight square, and five in height. The foundation does not penetrate the deck, but the masonry is firmly secured to the surface by ponderous knees of iron bracing it on all sides, and screwing it down to the timbers. On the flanks it is cased with wood, and at top completely covered by a large, sloping, battened hatchway. Removing this hatch we expose the great try-pots, two in number, and each of several barrels' capacity. When not in use, they are kept remarkably clean. Sometimes they are polished with soapstone and sand, till they shine within like silver punch-bowls. During the night-watches some cynical old sailors will crawl into them and coil themselves away there for a nap. While employed in polishing them—one man in each pot, side by side—many confidential communications are carried on, over the iron lips. It is a place also for profound mathematical meditation. It was in the left hand try-pot of the Pequod, with the soapstone diligently circling round me, that I was first indirectly struck by the remarkable fact, that in geometry all bodies gliding along the cycloid, my soapstone for example, will descend from any point in precisely the same time.

Removing the fire-board from the front of the try-works, the bare masonry of that side is exposed, penetrated by the two iron mouths of the furnaces, directly underneath the pots. These mouths are fitted with heavy doors of iron. The intense heat of the fire is prevented from communicating itself to the deck, by means of a shallow reservoir extending under the entire inclosed surface of the works. By a tunnel inserted at the rear, this reservoir is kept replenished with water as fast as it evaporates. There are no external chimneys; they open direct from the rear wall. And here let us go back for a moment.

It was about nine o'clock at night that the Pequod's try-works were first started on this present voyage. It belonged to Stubb to oversee the business.

"All ready there? Off hatch, then, and start her. You cook, fire the works." This was an easy thing, for the carpenter had been thrusting his shavings into the furnace throughout the passage. Here be it said that in a whaling voyage the first fire in the try-works has to be fed for a time with wood. After that no wood is used, except as a means of quick ignition to the staple fuel. In a word, after being tried out, the crisp, shrivelled blubber, now called scraps or fritters, still contains considerable of its unctuous properties. These fritters feed the flames. Like a plethoric burning martyr, or a self-consuming misanthrope, once ignited, the whale supplies his own fuel and burns by his own body. Would that he consumed his own smoke! for his smoke is horrible to inhale, and inhale it you must, and not only that, but you must live in it for the time. It has an unspeakable, wild, Hindoo odor about it, such as may lurk in the vicinity of funereal pyres. It smells like the left wing of the day of judgment; it is an argument for the pit.

By midnight the works were in full operation. We were clear from the carcase; sail had been made; the wind was freshening; the wild ocean darkness was intense. But that darkness was licked up by the fierce flames, which at intervals forked forth from the sooty flues, and illuminated every lofty rope in the rigging, as with the famed Greek fire. The burning ship drove on, as if remorselessly commissioned to some vengeful deed. So the pitch and sulphur-freighted brigs of the bold Hydriote, Canaris, issuing from their midnight harbors, with broad sheets of flame for sails, bore down upon the Turkish frigates, and folded them in conflagrations.

The hatch, removed from the top of the works, now afforded a wide hearth in front of them. Standing on this were the Tartarean shapes of the pagan harpooneers, always the whale-ship's stokers. With huge pronged poles they pitched hissing masses of blubber into the scalding pots, or stirred up the fires beneath, till the snaky flames darted, curling, out of the doors to catch them by the feet. The smoke rolled away in sullen heaps. To every pitch of the ship there was a pitch of the boiling oil, which seemed all eagerness to leap into their faces. Opposite the mouth of the works, on the further side of the wide wooden hearth, was the windlass. This served for a sea-sofa. Here lounged the watch, when not otherwise employed, looking into the red heat of the fire, till their eyes felt scorched in their heads. Their tawny features, now all be-grimed with smoke and sweat, their matted beards, and the contrasting barbaric brilliancy of their teeth, all these were strangely revealed in the capricious emblazonings of the works. As they narrated to each other their unholy adventures, their tales of terror told in words of mirth; as their uncivilized laughter forked upwards out of them, like the flames from the furnace; as to and fro, in their front, the harpooneers wildly gesticulated with their huge pronged forks and dippers; as the wind howled on, and the sea leaped, and the ship groaned and dived, and yet steadfastly shot her red hell further and further into the blackness of the sea and the night, and scornfully champed the white bone in her mouth, and viciously spat round her on all sides; then the rushing Pequod, freighted with savages, and laden with fire, and burning a corpse, and plunging into that blackness of darkness, seemed the material counterpart of her monomaniac commander's soul.

So seemed it to me, as I stood at her helm, and for long hours silently guided the way of this fire-ship on the sea. Wrapped, for that interval, in darkness myself, I but the better saw the redness, the madness, the ghastliness of others. The continual sight of the fiend shapes before me, capering half in smoke and half in fire, these at last begat kindred visions in my soul, so soon as I began to yield to that unaccountable drowsiness which ever would come over me at a midnight helm.

But that night, in particular, a strange (and ever since inexplicable) thing occurred to me. Starting from a brief standing sleep, I was horribly conscious of something fatally wrong. The jaw-bone tiller smote my side, which leaned against it; in my ears was the low hum of sails, just beginning to shake in the wind; I thought my eyes were open; I was half conscious of putting my fingers to the lids and mechanically stretching them still further apart. But, spite of all this, I could see no compass before me to steer by; though it seemed but a minute since I had been watching the card, by the steady binnacle lamp illuminating it. Nothing seemed before me but a jet gloom, now and then made ghastly by flashes of redness. Uppermost was the impression, that whatever swift, rushing thing I stood on was not so much bound to any haven ahead as rushing from all havens astern. A stark, bewildered feeling, as of death, came over me. Convulsively my hands grasped the tiller, but with the crazy conceit that the tiller was, somehow, in some enchanted way, inverted. My God! what is the matter with me? thought I. Lo! in my brief sleep I had turned myself about, and was fronting the ship's stern, with my back to her prow and the compass. In an instant I faced back, just in time to prevent the vessel from flying up into the wind, and very probably capsizing her. How glad and how grateful the relief from this unnatural hallucination of the night, and the fatal contingency of being brought by the lee!

Look not too long in the face of the fire, O man! Never dream with thy hand on the helm! Turn not thy back to the compass; accept the first hint of the hitching tiller; believe not the artificial fire, when its redness makes all things look ghastly. To-morrow, in the natural sun, the skies will be bright; those who glared like devils in the forking flames, the morn will show in far other, at least gentler, relief; the glorious, golden, glad sun, the only true lamp—all others but liars!

Nevertheless the sun hides not Virginia's Dismal Swamp, nor Rome's accursed Campagna, nor wide Sahara, nor all the millions of miles of deserts and of griefs beneath the moon. The sun hides not the ocean, which is the dark side of this earth, and which is two thirds of this earth. So, therefore, that mortal man who hath more of joy than sorrow in him, that mortal man cannot be true—not true, or undeveloped. With books the same. The truest of all men was the Man of Sorrows, and the truest of all books is Solomon's, and Ecclesiastes is the fine hammered steel of woe. "All is vanity." ALL. This wilful world hath not got hold of unchristian Solomon's wisdom yet. But he who dodges hospitals and jails, and walks fast crossing grave-yards, and would rather talk of operas than hell; calls Cowper, Young, Pascal, Rousseau, poor devils all of sick men; and throughout a care-free lifetime swears by Rabelais as passing wise, and therefore jolly;—not that man is fitted to sit down on tomb-stones, and break the green damp mould with unfathomably wondrous Solomon.

But even Solomon, he says, "the man that wandereth out of the way of understanding shall remain" (*i.e.* even while living) "in the congregation of the dead." Give not thyself up, then, to fire, lest it invert thee, deaden thee; as for the time it did me. There is a wisdom that is woe; but there is a woe that is madness. And there is a Catskill eagle in some souls that can alike dive down into the blackest gorges, and soar out of them again and become invisible in the sunny spaces. And even if he for ever flies within the gorge, that gorge is in the mountains; so that even in his lowest swoop the mountain eagle is still higher than other birds upon the plain, even though they soar.

Chapter 97

THE LAMP

HAD YOU DESCENDED from the Pequod's try-works to the Pequod's forecastle, where the off duty watch were sleeping, for one single moment you would have almost thought you were standing in some illuminated shrine of canonized kings and counsellors. There they lay in their triangular oaken vaults, each mariner a chiselled muteness; a score of lamps flashing upon his hooded eyes.

In merchantmen, oil for the sailor is more scarce than the milk of queens. To dress in the dark, and eat in the dark, and stumble in the darkness to his pallet, this is his usual lot. But the whaleman, as he seeks the food of light, so he lives in light. He makes his berth an Aladdin's lamp, and lays him down in it; so that in the pitchiest night the ship's black hull still houses an illumination.

See with what entire freedom the whaleman takes his handful of lamps—often but old bottles and vials, though—to the copper cooler at the try-works, and replenishes them there, as mugs of ale at a vat. He burns, too, the purest of oil, in its unmanufactured, and, therefore, unvitiated state; a fluid unknown to solar, lunar, or astral contrivances ashore. It is sweet as early grass butter in April. He goes and hunts for his oil, so as to be sure of its freshness and genuineness, even as the traveller on the prairie hunts up his own supper of game.

Chapter 98

STOWING DOWN AND CLEARING UP

ALREADY has it been related how the great leviathan is afar off descried from the mast-head; how he is chased over the watery moors, and slaughtered in the valleys of the deep; how he is then towed alongside and beheaded; and how (on the principle which entitled the headsman of old to the garments in which the beheaded was killed) his great padded surtout becomes the property of his executioner; how, in due time, he is condemned to the pots, and, like Shadrach, Meshach, and Abednego, his spermaceti, oil, and bone pass unscathed through the fire;—but now it remains to conclude the last chapter of this part of the description by rehearsing— singing, if I may—the romantic proceeding of decanting off his oil into the casks and striking them down into the hold, where once again leviathan returns to his native profundities, sliding along beneath the surface as before; but, alas! never more to rise and blow.

While still warm, the oil, like hot punch, is received into the six-barrel casks; and while, perhaps, the ship is pitching and rolling this way and that in the midnight sea, the enormous casks are slewed round and headed over, end for end, and sometimes perilously scoot across the slippery deck, like so many land slides, till at last man-handled and stayed in their course; and all round the hoops, rap, rap, go as many hammers as can play upon them, for now, *ex officio*, every sailor is a cooper.

At length, when the last pint is casked, and all is cool, then the great hatchways are unsealed, the bowels of the ship are thrown open, and down go the casks to their final rest in the sea. This done, the hatches are replaced, and hermetically closed, like a closet walled up.

In the sperm fishery, this is perhaps one of the most remarkable incidents in all the business of whaling. One day the planks stream with freshets of blood and oil; on the sacred quarter-deck enormous masses of the whale's head are pro-

1250

fancly piled; great rusty casks lie about, as in a brewery yard;
the smoke from the try-works has besooted all the bulwarks;
the mariners go about suffused with unctuousness; the entire
ship seems great leviathan himself; while on all hands the din
is deafening.

But a day or two after, you look about you, and prick your
ears in this self-same ship; and were it not for the tell-tale
boats and try-works, you would all but swear you trod some
silent merchant vessel, with a most scrupulously neat commander. The unmanufactured sperm oil possesses a singularly
cleansing virtue. This is the reason why the decks never look
so white as just after what they call an affair of oil. Besides,
from the ashes of the burned scraps of the whale, a potent ley
is readily made; and whenever any adhesiveness from the back
of the whale remains clinging to the side, that ley quickly
exterminates it. Hands go diligently along the bulwarks, and
with buckets of water and rags restore them to their full tidi-
ness. The soot is brushed from the lower rigging. All the numerous implements which have been in use are likewise
faithfully cleansed and put away. The great hatch is scrubbed
and placed upon the try-works, completely hiding the pots;
every cask is out of sight; all tackles are coiled in unseen
nooks; and when by the combined and simultaneous industry
of almost the entire ship's company, the whole of this conscientious duty is at last concluded, then the crew themselves
proceed to their own ablutions; shift themselves from top to
toe; and finally issue to the immaculate deck, fresh and all
aglow, as bridegrooms new-leaped from out the daintiest
Holland.

Now, with elated step, they pace the planks in twos and
threes, and humorously discourse of parlors, sofas, carpets,
and fine cambrics; propose to mat the deck; think of having
hangings to the top; object not to taking tea by moonlight
on the piazza of the forecastle. To hint to such musked mariners of oil, and bone, and blubber, were little short of audacity. They know not the thing you distantly allude to. Away,
and bring us napkins!

But mark: aloft there, at the three mast heads, stand three
men intent on spying out more whales, which, if caught, infallibly will again soil the old oaken furniture, and drop at

least one small grease-spot somewhere. Yes; and many is the time, when, after the severest uninterrupted labors, which know no night; continuing straight through for ninety-six hours; when from the boat, where they have swelled their wrists with all day rowing on the Line,—they only step to the deck to carry vast chains, and heave the heavy windlass, and cut and slash, yea, and in their very sweatings to be smoked and burned anew by the combined fires of the equatorial sun and the equatorial try-works; when, on the heel of all this, they have finally bestirred themselves to cleanse the ship, and make a spotless dairy room of it; many is the time the poor fellows, just buttoning the necks of their clean frocks, are startled by the cry of "There she blows!" and away they fly to fight another whale, and go through the whole weary thing again. Oh! my friends, but this is man-killing! Yet this is life. For hardly have we mortals by long toilings extracted from this world's vast bulk its small but valuable sperm; and then, with weary patience, cleansed ourselves from its defilements, and learned to live here in clean tabernacles of the soul; hardly is this done, when—*There she blows!*—the ghost is spouted up, and away we sail to fight some other world, and go through young life's old routine again.

Oh! the metempsychosis! Oh! Pythagoras, that in bright Greece, two thousand years ago, did die, so good, so wise, so mild; I sailed with thee along the Peruvian coast last voyage—and, foolish as I am, taught thee, a green simple boy, how to splice a rope!

Chapter 99

THE DOUBLOON

E RE NOW it has been related how Ahab was wont to pace his quarter-deck, taking regular turns at either limit, the binnacle and mainmast; but in the multiplicity of other things requiring narration it has not been added how that sometimes in these walks, when most plunged in his mood, he was wont to pause in turn at each spot, and stand there strangely eyeing the particular object before him. When he halted before the binnacle, with his glance fastened on the pointed needle in the compass, that glance shot like a javelin with the pointed intensity of his purpose; and when resuming his walk he again paused before the mainmast, then, as the same riveted glance fastened upon the riveted gold coin there, he still wore the same aspect of nailed firmness, only dashed with a certain wild longing, if not hopefulness.

But one morning, turning to pass the doubloon, he seemed to be newly attracted by the strange figures and inscriptions stamped on it, as though now for the first time beginning to interpret for himself in some monomaniac way whatever significance might lurk in them. And some certain significance lurks in all things, else all things are little worth, and the round world itself but an empty cipher, except to sell by the cartload, as they do hills about Boston, to fill up some morass in the Milky Way.

Now this doubloon was of purest, virgin gold, raked somewhere out of the heart of gorgeous hills, whence, east and west, over golden sands, the head-waters of many a Pactolus flow. And though now nailed amidst all the rustiness of iron bolts and the verdigris of copper spikes, yet, untouchable and immaculate to any foulness, it still preserved its Quito glow. Nor, though placed amongst a ruthless crew and every hour passed by ruthless hands, and through the livelong nights shrouded with thick darkness which might cover any pilfering approach, nevertheless every sunrise found the doubloon where the sunset left it last. For it was set apart and sanctified to one awe-striking end; and however wanton in their sailor ways, one and all, the mariners revered it as the white whale's talisman. Sometimes they talked it over in the weary watch by night, wondering whose it was to be at last, and whether he would ever live to spend it.

Now those noble golden coins of South America are as medals of the sun and tropic token-pieces. Here palms, alpacas, and volcanoes; sun's disks and stars; ecliptics, horns-of-plenty, and rich banners waving, are in luxuriant profusion stamped; so that the precious gold seems almost to derive an added preciousness and enhancing glories, by passing through those fancy mints, so Spanishly poetic.

It so chanced that the doubloon of the Pequod was a most wealthy example of these things. On its round border it bore the letters, REPUBLICA DEL ECUADOR: QUITO. So this bright coin came from a country planted in the middle of the world, and beneath the great equator, and named after it; and it had been cast midway up the Andes, in the unwaning clime that knows no autumn. Zoned by those letters you saw the likeness of three Andes' summits; from one a flame; a tower on another; on the third a crowing cock; while arching over all was a segment of the partitioned zodiac, the signs all marked with their usual cabalistics, and the keystone sun entering the equinoctial point at Libra.

Before this equatorial coin, Ahab, not unobserved by others, was now pausing.

"There's something ever egotistical in mountain-tops and towers, and all other grand and lofty things; look here,— three peaks as proud as Lucifer. The firm tower, that is Ahab; the volcano, that is Ahab; the courageous, the undaunted, and victorious fowl, that, too, is Ahab; all are Ahab; and this round gold is but the image of the rounder globe, which, like a magician's glass, to each and every man in turn but mirrors back his own mysterious self. Great pains, small gains for those who ask the world to solve them; it cannot solve itself. Methinks now this coined sun wears a ruddy face; but see! aye, he enters the sign of storms, the equinox! and but six months before he wheeled out of a former equinox at Aries! From storm to storm! So be it, then. Born in throes, 'tis fit that man should live in pains and die in pangs! So be it, then! Here's stout stuff for woe to work on. So be it, then."

"No fairy fingers can have pressed the gold, but devil's claws must have left their mouldings there since yesterday," murmured Starbuck to himself, leaning against the bulwarks. "The old man seems to read Belshazzar's awful writing. I have never marked the coin inspectingly. He goes below; let me read. A dark valley between three mighty, heaven-abiding peaks, that almost seem the Trinity, in some faint earthly symbol. So in this vale of Death, God girds us round; and over all our gloom, the sun of Righteousness still shines a beacon and a hope. If we bend down our eyes, the dark vale shows her mouldy soil; but if we lift them, the bright sun meets our glance half way, to cheer. Yet, oh, the great sun is no fixture; and if, at midnight, we would fain snatch some sweet solace from him, we gaze for him in vain! This coin speaks wisely, mildly, truly, but still sadly to me. I will quit it, lest Truth shake me falsely."

"There now's the old Mogul," soliloquized Stubb by the try-works, "he's been twigging it; and there goes Starbuck from the same, and both with faces which I should say might be somewhere within nine fathoms long. And all from looking at a piece of gold, which did I have it now on Negro Hill or in Corlaer's Hook, I'd not look at it very long ere spending it. Humph! in my poor, insignificant opinion, I regard this as queer. I have seen doubloons before now in my voyagings; your doubloons of old Spain, your doubloons of Peru, your doubloons of Chili, your doubloons of Bolivia, your doubloons of Popayan; with plenty of gold moidores and pistoles, and joes, and half joes, and quarter joes. What then should there be in this doubloon of the Equator that is so killing wonderful? By Golconda! let me read it once. Halloa! here's signs and wonders truly! That, now, is what old Bowditch in his Epitome calls the zodiac, and what my almanack below calls ditto. I'll get the almanack; and as I have heard devils can be raised with Daboll's arithmetic, I'll try my hand at raising a meaning out of these queer curvicues here with the Massachusetts calendar. Here's the book. Let's see now. Signs and wonders; and the sun, he's always among

'em. Hem, hem, hem; here they are—here they go—all
alive:—Aries, or the Ram; Taurus, or the Bull;—and Jimini!
here's Gemini himself, or the Twins. Well; the sun he wheels
among 'em. Aye, here on the coin he's just crossing the
threshold between two of twelve sitting-rooms all in a ring.
Book! you lie there; the fact is, you books must know your
places. You'll do to give us the bare words and facts, but we
come in to supply the thoughts. That's my small experience,
so far as the Massachusetts calendar, and Bowditch's navigator, and Daboll's arithmetic go. Signs and wonders, eh? Pity
if there is nothing wonderful in signs, and significant in wonders! There's a clue somewhere; wait a bit; hist—hark! By
Jove, I have it! Look you, Doubloon, your zodiac here is the
life of man in one round chapter; and now I'll read it off,
straight out of the book. Come, Almanack! To begin: there's
Aries, or the Ram—lecherous dog, he begets us; then, Taurus, or the Bull—he bumps us the first thing; then Gemini,
or the Twins—that is, Virtue and Vice; we try to reach Virtue, when lo! comes Cancer the Crab, and drags us back; and
here, going from Virtue, Leo, a roaring Lion, lies in the
path—he gives a few fierce bites and surly dabs with his paw;
we escape, and hail Virgo, the Virgin! that's our first love;
we marry and think to be happy for aye, when pop comes
Libra, or the Scales—happiness weighed and found wanting;
and while we are very sad about that, Lord! how we suddenly
jump, as Scorpio, or the Scorpion, stings us in rear; we are
curing the wound, when whang come the arrows all round;
Sagittarius, or the Archer, is amusing himself. As we pluck
out the shafts, stand aside! here's the battering-ram, Capricor-
nus, or the Goat; full tilt, he comes rushing, and headlong we
are tossed; when Aquarius, or the Water-bearer, pours out his
whole deluge and drowns us; and, to wind up, with Pisces,
or the Fishes, we sleep. There's a sermon now, writ in high
heaven, and the sun goes through it every year, and yet comes
out of it all alive and hearty. Jollily he, aloft there, wheels
through toil and trouble; and so, alow here, does jolly Stubb.
Oh, jolly's the word for aye! Adieu, Doubloon! But stop;
here comes little King-Post; dodge round the try-works, now,
and let's hear what he'll have to say. There; he's before it;
he'll out with something presently. So, so; he's beginning."

"I see nothing here, but a round thing made of gold, and whoever raises a certain whale, this round thing belongs to him. So, what's all this staring been about? It is worth sixteen dollars, that's true; and at two cents the cigar, that's nine hundred and sixty cigars. I wont smoke dirty pipes like Stubb, but I like cigars, and here's nine hundred and sixty of them; so here goes Flask aloft to spy 'em out."

"Shall I call that wise or foolish, now; if it be really wise it has a foolish look to it; yet, if it be really foolish, then has it a sort of wiseish look to it. But, avast; here comes our old Manxman—the old hearse-driver, he must have been, that is, before he took to the sea. He luffs up before the doubloon; halloa, and goes round on the other side of the mast; why, there's a horse-shoe nailed on that side; and now he's back again; what does that mean? Hark! he's muttering—voice like an old worn-out coffee-mill. Prick ears, and listen!"

"If the White Whale be raised, it must be in a month and a day, when the sun stands in some one of these signs. I've studied signs, and know their marks; they were taught me two score years ago, by the old witch in Copenhagen. Now, in what sign will the sun then be? The horse-shoe sign; for there it is, right opposite the gold. And what's the horse-shoe sign? The lion is the horse-shoe sign—the roaring and devouring lion. Ship, old ship! my old head shakes to think of thee."

"There's another rendering now; but still one text. All sorts of men in one kind of world, you see. Dodge again! here comes Queequeg—all tattooing—looks like the signs of the Zodiac himself. What says the Cannibal? As I live he's comparing notes; looking at his thigh bone; thinks the sun is in the thigh, or in the calf, or in the bowels, I suppose, as the old women talk Surgeon's Astronomy in the back country. And by Jove, he's found something there in the vicinity of his thigh—I guess it's Sagittarius, or the Archer. No: he don't know what to make of the doubloon; he takes it for an old button off some king's trowsers. But, aside again! here comes that ghost-devil, Fedallah; tail coiled out of sight as usual, oakum in the toes of his pumps as usual. What does he say, with that look of his? Ah, only makes a sign to the sign and bows himself; there is a sun on the coin—fire worshipper, depend upon it. Ho! more and more. This way comes Pip—poor boy! would he had died, or I; he's half horrible to me. He too has been watching all of these interpreters—myself included—and look now, he comes to read, with that unearthly idiot face. Stand away again and hear him. Hark!"

"I look, you look, he looks; we look, ye look, they look."

"Upon my soul, he's been studying Murray's Grammar! Improving his mind, poor fellow! But what's that he says now—hist!"

"I look, you look, he looks; we look, ye look, they look."

"Why, he's getting it by heart—hist! again."

"I look, you look, he looks; we look, ye look, they look."

"Well, that's funny."

"And I, you, and he; and we, ye, and they, are all bats; and I'm a crow, especially when I stand a'top of this pine tree here. Caw! caw! caw! caw! caw! caw! Ain't I a crow? And where's the scare-crow? There he stands; two bones stuck into a pair of old trowsers, and two more poked into the sleeves of an old jacket."

"Wonder if he means me?—complimentary!—poor lad!—I could go hang myself. Any way, for the present, I'll quit Pip's vicinity. I can stand the rest, for they have plain wits; but he's too crazy-witty for my sanity. So, so, I leave him muttering."

"Here's the ship's navel, this doubloon here, and they are all on fire to unscrew it. But, unscrew your navel, and what's the consequence? Then again, if it stays here, that is ugly, too, for when aught's nailed to the mast it's a sign that things grow desperate. Ha, ha! old Ahab! the White Whale; he'll nail ye! This is a pine tree. My father, in old Tolland county, cut down a pine tree once, and found a silver ring grown over in it; some old darkey's wedding ring. How did it get there? And so they'll say in the resurrection, when they come to fish up this old mast, and find a doubloon lodged in it, with bedded oysters for the shaggy bark. Oh, the gold! the precious, precious gold!—the green miser 'll hoard ye soon! Hish! hish! God goes 'mong the worlds blackberrying. Cook! ho, cook! and cook us! Jenny! hey, hey, hey, hey, hey, Jenny, Jenny! and get your hoe-cake done!"

Chapter 100

"SHIP, AHOY! Hast seen the White Whale?"

So cried Ahab, once more hailing a ship showing English colors, bearing down under the stern. Trumpet to mouth, the old man was standing in his hoisted quarter-boat, his ivory leg plainly revealed to the stranger captain, who was carelessly reclining in his own boat's bow. He was a darkly-tanned, burly, good-natured, fine-looking man, of sixty or thereabouts, dressed in a spacious roundabout, that hung round him in festoons of blue pilot-cloth; and one empty arm of this jacket streamed behind him like the broidered arm of a huzzar's surcoat.

"Hast seen the White Whale?"

"See you this?" and withdrawing it from the folds that had hidden it, he held up a white arm of sperm whale bone, terminating in a wooden head like a mallet.

"Man my boat!" cried Ahab, impetuously, and tossing about the oars near him—"Stand by to lower!"

In less than a minute, without quitting his little craft, he and his crew were dropped to the water, and were soon alongside of the stranger. But here a curious difficulty presented itself. In the excitement of the moment, Ahab had forgotten that since the loss of his leg he had never once stepped on board of any vessel at sea but his own, and then it was always by an ingenious and very handy mechanical contrivance peculiar to the Pequod, and a thing not to be rigged and shipped in any other vessel at a moment's warning. Now, it is no very easy matter for anybody—except those who are almost hourly used to it, like whalemen—to clamber up a ship's side from a boat on the open sea; for the great swells now lift the boat high up towards the bulwarks, and then instantaneously drop it half way down to the kelson. So, deprived of one leg, and the strange ship of course being altogether unsupplied with the kindly invention, Ahab now found himself abjectly reduced to a clumsy landsman again; hopelessly eyeing the uncertain changeful height he could hardly hope to attain.

It has before been hinted, perhaps, that every little untoward circumstance that befel him, and which indirectly sprang from his luckless mishap, almost invariably irritated or exasperated Ahab. And in the present instance, all this was heightened by the sight of the two officers of the strange ship, leaning over the side, by the perpendicular ladder of nailed cleets there, and swinging towards him a pair of tastefully-ornamented man-ropes; for at first they did not seem to bethink them that a one-legged man must be too much of a cripple to use their sea bannisters. But this awkwardness only lasted a minute, because the strange captain, observing at a glance how affairs stood, cried out, "I see, I see!—avast heaving there! Jump, boys, and swing over the cutting-tackle."

As good luck would have it, they had had a whale alongside a day or two previous, and the great tackles were still aloft, and the massive curved blubber-hook, now clean and dry, was still attached to the end. This was quickly lowered to Ahab, who at once comprehending it all, slid his solitary thigh into the curve of the hook (it was like sitting in the fluke of an anchor, or the crotch of an apple tree), and then giving the word, held himself fast, and at the same time also helped to hoist his own weight, by pulling hand-over-hand upon one of the running parts of the tackle. Soon he was carefully swung inside the high bulwarks, and gently landed upon the capstan head. With his ivory arm frankly thrust forth in welcome, the other captain advanced, and Ahab, putting out his ivory leg, and crossing the ivory arm (like two sword-fish blades) cried out in his walrus way, "Aye, aye, hearty! let us shake bones together!—an arm and a leg!—an arm that never can shrink, d'ye see; and a leg that never can run. Where did'st thou see the White Whale?—how long ago?"

"The White Whale," said the Englishman, pointing his ivory arm towards the East, and taking a rueful sight along it, as if it had been a telescope; "There I saw him, on the Line, last season."

"And he took that arm off, did he?" asked Ahab, now

sliding down from the capstan, and resting on the English-man's shoulder, as he did so.

"Aye, he was the cause of it, at least; and that leg, too?"

"Spin me the yarn," said Ahab; "how was it?"

"It was the first time in my life that I ever cruised on the Line," began the Englishman. "I was ignorant of the White Whale at that time. Well, one day we lowered for a pod of four or five whales, and my boat fastened to one of them; a regular circus horse he was, too, that went milling and milling round so, that my boat's crew could only trim dish, by sitting all their sterns on the outer gunwale. Presently up breaches from the bottom of the sea a bouncing great whale, with a milky-white head and hump, all crows' feet and wrinkles."

"It was he, it was he!" cried Ahab, suddenly letting out his suspended breath.

"And harpoons sticking in near his starboard fin."

"Aye, aye—they were mine—*my* irons," cried Ahab, exult-ingly—"but on!"

"Give me a chance, then," said the Englishman, good-humoredly. "Well, this old great-grandfather, with the white head and hump, runs all afoam into the pod, and goes to snapping furiously at my fast-line."

"Aye, I see!—wanted to part it; free the fast-fish—an old trick—I know him."

"How it was exactly," continued the one-armed com-mander, "I do not know; but in biting the line, it got foul of his teeth, caught there somehow; but we didn't know it then; so that when we afterwards pulled on the line, bounce we came plump on to his hump! instead of the other whale's that went off to windward, all fluking. Seeing how matters stood, and what a noble great whale it was—the noblest and biggest I ever saw, sir, in my life—I resolved to capture him, spite of the boiling rage he seemed to be in. And thinking the hap-hazard line would get loose, or the tooth it was tangled to might draw (for I have a devil of a boat's crew for a pull on a whale-line); seeing all this, I say, I jumped into my first mate's boat—Mr. Mounttop's here (by the way, Captain—Mounttop; Mounttop—the captain);—as I was saying, I jumped into Mounttop's boat, which, d'ye see, was gunwale and gunwale with mine, then; and snatching the first harpoon, let this old great-grandfather have it. But, Lord, look you, sir—hearts and souls alive, man—the next instant, in a jiff, I was blind as a bat—both eyes out—all befogged and bedeadened with black foam—the whale's tail looming straight up out of it, perpendicular in the air, like a marble steeple. No use sterning all, then; but as I was groping at midday, with a blinding sun, all crown-jewels; as I was groping, I say, after the second iron, to toss it overboard—down comes the tail like a Lima tower, cutting my boat in two, leaving each half in splinters; and, flukes first, the white hump backed through the wreck, as though it was all chips. We all struck out. To escape his terrible flailings, I seized hold of my harpoon-pole sticking in him, and for a moment clung to that like a sucking fish. But a combing sea dashed me off, and at the same instant, the fish, taking one good dart forwards, went down like a flash; and the barb of that cursed second iron towing along near me caught me here" (clapping his hand just below his shoulder); "yes, caught me just here, I say, and bore me down to Hell's flames, I was thinking; when, when, all of a sudden, thank the good God, the barb ript its way along the flesh—clear along the whole length of my arm—came out nigh my wrist, and up I floated;—and that gentleman there will tell you the rest (by the way, captain—Dr. Bunger, ship's surgeon: Bunger, my lad,—the captain). Now, Bunger boy, spin your part of the yarn."

The professional gentleman thus familiarly pointed out, had been all the time standing near them, with nothing specific visible, to denote his gentlemanly rank on board. His face was an exceedingly round but sober one; he was dressed in a faded blue woollen frock or shirt, and patched trowsers; and had thus far been dividing his attention between a marlingspike he held in one hand, and a pill-box held in the other, occasionally casting a critical glance at the ivory limbs of the two crippled captains. But, at his superior's introduction of him to Ahab, he politely bowed, and straightway went on to do his captain's bidding.

"It was a shocking bad wound," began the whale-surgeon; "and, taking my advice, Captain Boomer here, stood our old Sammy—"

"Samuel Enderby is the name of my ship," interrupted the one-armed captain, addressing Ahab; "go on, boy."

"Stood our old Sammy off to the northward, to get out of the blazing hot weather there on the Line. But it was no use—I did all I could; sat up with him nights; was very severe with him in the matter of diet—"

"Oh, very severe!" chimed in the patient himself; then suddenly altering his voice, "Drinking hot rum toddies with me every night, till he couldn't see to put on the bandages; and sending me to bed, half seas over, about three o'clock in the morning. Oh, ye stars! he sat up with me indeed, and was very severe in my diet. Oh! a great watcher, and very dietetically severe, is Dr. Bunger. (Bunger, you dog, laugh out! why don't ye? You know you're a precious jolly rascal.) But, heave ahead, boy, I'd rather be killed by you than kept alive by any other man."

"My captain, you must have ere this perceived, respected sir"—said the imperturbable godly-looking Bunger, slightly bowing to Ahab—"is apt to be facetious at times; he spins us many clever things of that sort. But I may as well say—en passant, as the French remark—that I myself—that is to say, Jack Bunger, late of the reverend clergy—am a strict total abstinence man; I never drink—"

"Water!" cried the captain; "he never drinks it; it's a sort of fits to him; fresh water throws him into the hydrophobia; but go on—go on with the arm story."

"Yes, I may as well," said the surgeon, coolly. "I was about observing, sir, before Captain Boomer's facetious interruption, that spite of my best and severest endeavors, the wound kept getting worse and worse; the truth was, sir, it was as ugly gaping wound as surgeon ever saw; more than two feet and several inches long. I measured it with the lead line. In short, it grew black; I knew what was threatened, and off it came. But I had no hand in shipping that ivory arm there; that thing is against all rule"—pointing at it with the marlingspike—"that is the captain's work, not mine; he ordered the carpenter to make it; he had that club-hammer there put to the end, to knock some one's brains out with, I suppose, as he tried mine once. He flies into diabolical passions sometimes. Do ye see this dent, sir"—removing his hat, and brushing aside his hair, and exposing a bowl-like cavity in his skull, but which bore not the slightest scarry trace, or any token of ever having been a wound—"Well, the captain there will tell you how that came here; he knows."

"No, I don't," said the captain, "but his mother did; he was born with it. Oh, you solemn rogue, you—you Bunger! was there ever such another Bunger in the watery world? Bunger, when you die, you ought to die in pickle, you dog; you should be preserved to future ages, you rascal."

"What became of the White Whale?" now cried Ahab, who thus far had been impatiently listening to this bye-play between the two Englishmen.

"Oh!" cried the one-armed captain, "Oh, yes! Well; after he sounded, we didn't see him again for some time; in fact, as I before hinted, I didn't then know what whale it was that had served me such a trick, till some time afterwards, when coming back to the Line, we heard about Moby Dick—as some call him—and then I knew it was he."

"Did'st thou cross his wake again?"

"Twice."

"But could not fasten?"

"Didn't want to try to: ain't one limb enough? What should I do without this other arm? And I'm thinking Moby Dick doesn't bite so much as he swallows."

"Well, then," interrupted Bunger, "give him your left arm for bait to get the right. Do you know, gentlemen"—very gravely and mathematically bowing to each Captain in succession—"Do you know, gentlemen, that the digestive organs of the whale are so inscrutably constructed by Divine Providence, that it is quite impossible for him to completely digest even a man's arm? And he knows it too. So that what you take for the White Whale's malice is only his awkwardness. For he never means to swallow a single limb; he only thinks to terrify by feints. But sometimes he is like the old juggling fellow, formerly a patient of mine in Ceylon, that making believe swallow jack-knives, once upon a time let one drop into him in good earnest, and there it stayed for a twelvemonth or more; when I gave him an emetic, and he heaved it up in small tacks, d'ye see. No possible way for him to digest that jack-knife, and fully incorporate it into his general bodily system. Yes, Captain Boomer, if you are quick enough about it, and have a mind to pawn one arm for the sake of the privilege of giving decent burial to the other, why in that case the arm is yours; only let the whale have another chance at you shortly, that's all."

"No, thank ye, Bunger," said the English Captain, "he's welcome to the arm he has, since I can't help it, and didn't know him then; but not to another one. No more White Whales for me; I've lowered for him once, and that has satisfied me. There would be great glory in killing him, I know that; and there is a ship-load of precious sperm in him, but, hark ye, he's best let alone; don't you think so, Captain?"— glancing at the ivory leg.

"He is. But he will still be hunted, for all that. What is best let alone, that accursed thing is not always what least allures. He's all a magnet! How long since thou saw'st him last? Which way heading?"

"Bless my soul, and curse the foul fiend's," cried Bunger, stoopingly walking around Ahab, and like a dog, strangely snuffing; "this man's blood—bring the thermometer!—it's at the boiling point!—his pulse makes these planks beat!— sir!"—taking a lancet from his pocket, and drawing near to Ahab's arm.

"Avast!" roared Ahab, dashing him against the bulwarks— "Man the boat! Which way heading?"

"Good God!" cried the English Captain, to whom the question was put. "What's the matter? He was heading east, I think.—Is your Captain crazy?" whispering Fedallah.

But Fedallah, putting a finger on his lip, slid over the bulwarks to take the boat's steering oar, and Ahab, swinging the cutting-tackle towards him, commanded the ship's sailors to stand by to lower.

In a moment he was standing in the boat's stern, and the Manilla men were springing to their oars. In vain the English Captain hailed him. With back to the stranger ship, and face set like a flint to his own, Ahab stood upright till alongside of the Pequod.

Chapter 101

THE DECANTER

ERE THE English ship fades from sight, be it set down here, that she hailed from London, and was named after the late Samuel Enderby, merchant of that city, the original of the famous whaling house of Enderby & Sons; a house which in my poor whaleman's opinion, comes not far behind the united royal houses of the Tudors and Bourbons, in point of real historical interest. How long, prior to the year of our Lord 1775, this great whaling house was in existence, my numerous fish-documents do not make plain; but in that year (1775) it fitted out the first English ships that ever regularly hunted the Sperm Whale; though for some score of years previous (ever since 1726) our valiant Coffins and Maceys of Nantucket and the Vineyard had in large fleets pursued that Leviathan, but only in the North and South Atlantic: not elsewhere. Be it distinctly recorded here, that the Nantucketers were the first among mankind to harpoon with civilized steel the great Sperm Whale; and that for half a century they were the only people of the whole globe who so harpooned him.

In 1788, a fine ship, the Amelia, fitted out for the express purpose, and at the sole charge of the vigorous Enderbys, boldly rounded Cape Horn, and was the first among the nations to lower a whale-boat of any sort in the great South Sea. The voyage was a skilful and lucky one; and returning to her berth with her hold full of the precious sperm, the Amelia's example was soon followed by other ships, English and American, and thus the vast Sperm Whale grounds of the Pacific were thrown open. But not content with this good deed, the indefatigable house again bestirred itself: Samuel and all his Sons—how many, their mother only knows—and under their immediate auspices, and partly, I think, at their expense, the British government was induced to send the sloop-of-war Rattler on a whaling voyage of discovery into the South Sea. Commanded by a naval Post-Captain, the Rattler made a rattling voyage of it, and did some service; how much does not appear. But this is not all. In 1819, the same house fitted out a discovery whale ship of their own, to go on a testing cruise to the remote waters of Japan. That ship—well called the "Syren"—made a noble experimental cruise; and it was thus that the great Japanese Whaling Ground first became generally known. The Syren in this famous voyage was commanded by a Captain Coffin, a Nantucketer.

All honor to the Enderbies, therefore, whose house, I think, exists to the present day; though doubtless the original Samuel must long ago have slipped his cable for the great South Sea of the other world.

The ship named after him was worthy of the honor, being a very fast sailer and a noble craft every way. I boarded her once at midnight somewhere off the Patagonian coast, and drank good flip down in the forecastle. It was a fine gam we had, and they were all trumps—every soul on board. A short life to them, and a jolly death. And that fine gam I had— long, very long after old Ahab touched her planks with his ivory heel—it minds me of the noble, solid, Saxon hospitality of that ship; and may my parson forget me, and the devil remember me, if I ever lose sight of it. Flip? Did I say we had flip? Yes, and we flipped it at the rate of ten gallons the hour; and when the squall came (for it's squally off there by Patagonia), and all hands—visitors and all—were called to reef topsails, we were so top-heavy that we had to swing each other aloft in bowlines; and we ignorantly furled the skirts of our jackets into the sails, so that we hung there, reefed fast in the howling gale, a warning example to all drunken tars. However, the masts did not go overboard; and by and bye we scrambled down, so sober, that we had to pass the flip again, though the savage salt spray bursting down the forecastle scuttle, rather too much diluted and pickled it to my taste.

The beef was fine—tough, but with body in it. They said it was bull-beef; others, that it was dromedary beef; but I do not know, for certain, how that was. They had dumplings too; small, but substantial, symmetrically globular, and indestructible dumplings. I fancied that you could feel them, and roll them about in you after they were swallowed. If you stooped over too far forward, you risked their pitching out of you like billard-balls. The bread—but that couldn't be helped; besides, it was an anti-scorbutic; in short, the bread contained the only fresh fare they had. But the forecastle was not very light, and it was very easy to step over into a dark corner when you ate it. But all in all, taking her from truck to helm, considering the dimensions of the cook's boilers, including his own live parchment boilers; fore and aft, I say, the Samuel Enderby was a jolly ship; of good fare and plenty; fine flip and strong; crack fellows all, and capital from boot heels to hat-band.

But why was it, think ye, that the Samuel Enderby, and some other English whalers I know of—not all though— were such famous, hospitable ships; that passed round the beef, and the bread, and the can, and the joke; and were not soon weary of eating, and drinking, and laughing? I will tell you. The abounding good cheer of these English whalers is matter for historical research. Nor have I been at all sparing of historical whale research, when it has seemed needed.

The English were preceded in the whale fishery by the Hollanders, Zealanders, and Danes; from whom they derived many terms still extant in the fishery; and what is yet more, their fat old fashions, touching plenty to eat and drink. For, as a general thing, the English merchant-ship scrimps her crew; but not so the English whaler. Hence, in the English, this thing of whaling good cheer is not normal and natural, but incidental and particular; and, therefore, must have some special origin, which is here pointed out, and will be still further elucidated.

During my researches in the Leviathanic histories, I stumbled upon an ancient Dutch volume, which, by the musty whaling smell of it, I knew must be about whalers. The title was, "Dan Coopman," wherefore I concluded that this must be the invaluable memoirs of some Amsterdam cooper in the fishery, as every whale ship must carry its cooper. I was reinforced in this opinion by seeing that it was the production of one "Fitz Swackhammer." But my friend Dr. Snodhead, a very learned man, professor of Low Dutch and High German in the college of Santa Claus and St. Pott's, to whom I handed the work for translation, giving him a box of sperm candles for his trouble—this same Dr. Snodhead, so soon as he spied the book, assured me that "Dan Coopman" did not mean "The Cooper," but "The Merchant." In short, this ancient and learned Low Dutch book treated of the commerce of Holland; and, among other subjects, contained a very interesting account of its whale fishery. And in this chapter it was, headed "Smeer," or "Fat," that I found a long detailed list of the outfits for the larders and cellars of 180 sail of Dutch whalemen; from which list, as translated by Dr. Snodhead, I transcribe the following:

400,000	lbs. of beef.
60,000	lbs. Friesland pork.
150,000	lbs. of stock fish.
550,000	lbs. of biscuit.
72,000	lbs. of soft bread.
2,800	firkins of butter.
20,000	lbs. Texel & Leyden cheese.
144,000	lbs. cheese (probably an inferior article).
550	ankers of Geneva.
10,800	barrels of beer.

Most statistical tables are parchingly dry in the reading; not so in the present case, however, where the reader is flooded with whole pipes, barrels, quarts, and gills of good gin and good cheer.

At the time, I devoted three days to the studious digesting of all this beer, beef, and bread, during which many profound thoughts were incidentally suggested to me, capable of a transcendental and Platonic application; and, furthermore, I compiled supplementary tables of my own, touching the probable quantity of stock-fish, &c., consumed by every Low Dutch harpooneer in that ancient Greenland and Spitzbergen whale fishery. In the first place, the amount of butter, and Texel and Leyden cheese consumed, seems amazing. I impute it, though, to their naturally unctuous natures, being rendered still more unctuous by the nature of their vocation, and especially by their pursuing their game in those frigid Polar Seas, on the very coasts of that Esquimaux country where the convivial natives pledge each other in bumpers of train oil.

The quantity of beer, too, is very large, 10,800 barrels. Now, as those polar fisheries could only be prosecuted in the short summer of that climate, so that the whole cruise of one of these Dutch whalemen, including the short voyage to and from the Spitzbergen sea, did not much exceed three months, say, and reckoning 30 men to each of their fleet of 180 sail, we have 5,400 Low Dutch seamen in all; therefore, I say, we have precisely two barrels of beer per man, for a twelve weeks' allowance, exclusive of his fair proportion of that 550 ankers of gin. Now, whether these gin and beer harpooneers, so fuddled as one might fancy them to have been, were the right sort of men to stand up in a boat's head, and take good aim at flying whales; this would seem somewhat improbable. Yet they did aim at them, and hit them too. But this was very far North, be it remembered, where beer agrees well with the constitution; upon the Equator, in our southern fishery, beer would be apt to make the harpooneer sleepy at the mast-head and boozy in his boat; and grievous loss might ensue to Nantucket and New Bedford.

But no more; enough has been said to show that the old Dutch whalers of two or three centuries ago were high livers; and that the English whalers have not neglected so excellent an example. For, say they, when cruising in an empty ship, if you can get nothing better out of the world, get a good dinner out of it, at least. And this empties the decanter.

Chapter 102

A Bower in the Arsacides

HITHERTO, in descriptively treating of the Sperm Whale, I have chiefly dwelt upon the marvels of his outer aspect; or separately and in detail upon some few interior structural features. But to a large and thorough sweeping comprehension of him, it behoves me now to unbutton him still further, and untagging the points of his hose, unbuckling his garters, and casting loose the hooks and the eyes of the joints of his innermost bones, set him before you in his ultimatum; that is to say, in his unconditional skeleton.

But how now, Ishmael? How is it, that you, a mere oarsman in the fishery, pretend to know aught about the subterranean parts of the whale? Did erudite Stubb, mounted upon your capstan, deliver lectures on the anatomy of the Cetacea; and by help of the windlass, hold up a specimen rib for exhibition? Explain thyself, Ishmael. Can you land a full-grown whale on your deck for examination, as a cook dishes a roast-pig? Surely not. A veritable witness have you hitherto been, Ishmael; but have a care how you seize the privilege of Jonah alone; the privilege of discoursing upon the joists and beams; the rafters, ridge-pole, sleepers, and under-pinnings, making up the frame-work of leviathan; and belike of the tallow-vats, dairy-rooms, butteries, and cheeseries in his bowels.

I confess, that since Jonah, few whalemen have penetrated very far beneath the skin of the adult whale; nevertheless, I have been blessed with an opportunity to dissect him in miniature. In a ship I belonged to, a small cub Sperm Whale was once bodily hoisted to the deck for his poke or bag, to make sheaths for the barbs of the harpoons, and for the heads of the lances. Think you I let that chance go, without using my boat-hatchet and jack-knife, and breaking the seal and reading all the contents of that young cub?

And as for my exact knowledge of the bones of the leviathan in their gigantic, full grown development, for that rare knowledge I am indebted to my late royal friend Tranquo, king of Tranque, one of the Arsacides. For being at Tranque, years ago, when attached to the trading-ship Dey of Algiers, I was invited to spend part of the Arsacidean holidays with the lord of Tranque, at his retired palm villa at Pupella; a seaside glen not very far distant from what our sailors called Bamboo-Town, his capital.

Among many other fine qualities, my royal friend Tranquo, being gifted with a devout love for all matters of barbaric vertù, had brought together in Pupella whatever rare things the more ingenious of his people could invent; chiefly carved woods of wonderful devices, chiselled shells, inlaid spears, costly paddles, aromatic canoes; and all these distributed among whatever natural wonders, the wonder-freighted, tribute-rendering waves had cast upon his shores.

Chief among these latter was a great Sperm Whale, which, after an unusually long raging gale, had been found dead and stranded, with his head against a cocoa-nut tree, whose plumage-like, tufted droopings seemed his verdant jet. When the vast body had at last been stripped of its fathom-deep enfoldings, and the bones become dust dry in the sun, then the skeleton was carefully transported up the Pupella glen, where a grand temple of lordly palms now sheltered it.

The ribs were hung with trophies; the vertebræ were carved with Arsacidean annals, in strange hieroglyphics; in the skull, the priests kept up an unextinguished aromatic flame, so that the mystic head again sent forth its vapory spout; while, suspended from a bough, the terrific lower jaw vibrated over all the devotees, like the hair-hung sword that so affrighted Damocles.

It was a wondrous sight. The wood was green as mosses of the Icy Glen; the trees stood high and haughty, feeling their living sap; the industrious earth beneath was as a weaver's loom, with a gorgeous carpet on it, whereof the ground-vine tendrils formed the warp and woof, and the living flowers the figures. All the trees, with all their laden branches; all the shrubs, and ferns, and grasses; the message-carrying air; all these unceasingly were active. Through the lacings of the leaves, the great sun seemed a flying shuttle weaving the unwearied verdure. Oh, busy weaver! unseen weaver!—pause!—one word!—whither flows the fabric? what palace may it deck? wherefore all these ceaseless toilings? Speak, weaver!—stay thy hand!—but one single word with thee! Nay—the shuttle flies—the figures float from forth the loom; the freshet-rushing carpet for ever slides away. The weaver-god, he weaves; and by that weaving is he deafened, that he hears no mortal voice; and by that humming, we, too, who look on the loom are deafened; and only when we escape it shall we hear the thousand voices that speak through it. For even so it is in all material factories. The spoken words that are inaudible among the flying spindles; those same words are plainly heard without the walls, bursting from the opened casements. Thereby have villanies been detected. Ah, mortal! then, be heedful; for so, in all this din of the great world's loom, thy subtlest thinkings may be overheard afar.

Now, amid the green, life-restless loom of that Arsacidean wood, the great, white, worshipped skeleton lay lounging—a gigantic idler! Yet, as the ever-woven verdant warp and woof intermixed and hummed around him, the mighty idler seemed the cunning weaver; himself all woven over with the vines; every month assuming greener, fresher verdure; but himself a skeleton. Life folded Death; Death trellised Life; the grim god wived with youthful Life, and begat him curly-headed glories.

Now, when with royal Tranquo I visited this wondrous whale, and saw the skull an altar, and the artificial smoke ascending from where the real jet had issued, I marvelled that the king should regard a chapel as an object of vertù. He laughed. But more I marvelled that the priests should swear that smoky jet of his was genuine. To and fro I paced before this skeleton—brushed the vines aside—broke through the ribs—and with a ball of Arsacidean twine, wandered, eddied long amid its many winding, shaded colonnades and arbors. But soon my line was out; and following it back, I emerged from the opening where I entered. I saw no living thing within; naught was there but bones.

Cutting me a green measuring-rod, I once more dived within the skeleton. From their arrow-slit in the skull, the priests perceived me taking the altitude of the final rib. "How now!" they shouted; "Dar'st thou measure this our god! That's for us." "Aye, priests—well, how long do ye make him, then?" But hereupon a fierce contest rose among them, concerning feet and inches; they cracked each other's sconces with their yard-sticks—the great skull echoed—and seizing that lucky chance, I quickly concluded my own admeasurements.

These admeasurements I now propose to set before you. But first, be it recorded, that, in this matter, I am not free to utter any fancied measurement I please. Because there are skeleton authorities you can refer to, to test my accuracy. There is a Leviathanic Museum, they tell me, in Hull, England, one of the whaling ports of that country, where they have some fine specimens of fin-backs and other whales. Likewise, I have heard that in the museum of Manchester, in New Hampshire, they have what the proprietors call "the only perfect specimen of a Greenland or River Whale in the United States." Moreover, at a place in Yorkshire, England, Burton Constable by name, a certain Sir Clifford Constable has in his possession the skeleton of a Sperm Whale, but of moderate size, by no means of the full-grown magnitude of my friend King Tranquo's.

In both cases, the stranded whales to which these two skeletons belonged, were originally claimed by their proprietors upon similar grounds. King Tranquo seizing his because he wanted it; and Sir Clifford, because he was lord of the seignories of those parts. Sir Clifford's whale has been articulated throughout; so that, like a great chest of drawers, you can open and shut him, in all his bony cavities—spread out his ribs like a gigantic fan—and swing all day upon his lower jaw. Locks are to be put upon some of his trap-doors and shutters; and a footman will show round future visitors with a bunch of keys at his side. Sir Clifford thinks of charging twopence for a peep at the whispering gallery in the spinal column; threepence to hear the echo in the hollow of his cerebellum; and sixpence for the unrivalled view from his forehead.

The skeleton dimensions I shall now proceed to set down are copied verbatim from my right arm, where I had them tattooed; as in my wild wanderings at that period, there was no other secure way of preserving such valuable statistics. But as I was crowded for space, and wished the other parts of my

body to remain a blank page for a poem I was then composing—at least, what untattooed parts might remain—I did
not trouble myself with the odd inches; nor, indeed, should
inches at all enter into a congenial admeasurement of the
whale.

Chapter 103

Measurement of the Whale's Skeleton

In the first place, I wish to lay before you a particular, plain statement, touching the living bulk of this leviathan, whose skeleton we are briefly to exhibit. Such a statement may prove useful here.

According to a careful calculation I have made, and which I partly base upon Captain Scoresby's estimate, of seventy tons for the largest sized Greenland whale of sixty feet in length; according to my careful calculation, I say, a Sperm Whale of the largest magnitude, between eighty-five and ninety feet in length, and something less than forty feet in its fullest circumference, such a whale will weigh at least ninety tons; so that, reckoning thirteen men to a ton, he would considerably outweigh the combined population of a whole village of one thousand one hundred inhabitants.

Think you not then that brains, like yoked cattle, should be put to this leviathan, to make him at all budge to any landsman's imagination?

Having already in various ways put before you his skull, spout-hole, jaw, teeth, tail, forehead, fins, and divers other parts, I shall now simply point out what is most interesting in the general bulk of his unobstructed bones. But as the colossal skull embraces so very large a proportion of the entire extent of the skeleton; as it is by far the most complicated part; and as nothing is to be repeated concerning it in this chapter, you must not fail to carry it in your mind, or under your arm, as we proceed, otherwise you will not gain a complete notion of the general structure we are about to view.

In length, the Sperm Whale's skeleton at Tranque measured seventy-two feet; so that when fully invested and extended in life, he must have been ninety feet long; for in the whale, the skeleton loses about one fifth in length compared with the living body. Of this seventy-two feet, his skull and jaw comprised some twenty feet, leaving some fifty feet of plain backbone. Attached to this back-bone, for something less than a third of its length, was the mighty circular basket of ribs which once enclosed his vitals.

To me this vast ivory-ribbed chest, with the long, unrelieved spine, extending far away from it in a straight line, not a little resembled the embryo hull of a great ship new-laid upon the stocks, when only some twenty of her naked bowribs are inserted, and the keel is otherwise, for the time, but a long, disconnected timber.

The ribs were ten on a side. The first, to begin from the neck, was nearly six feet long; the second, third, and fourth were each successively longer, till you came to the climax of the fifth, or one of the middle ribs, which measured eight feet and some inches. From that part, the remaining ribs diminished, till the tenth and last only spanned five feet and some inches. In general thickness, they all bore a seemly correspondence to their length. The middle ribs were the most arched. In some of the Arsacides they are used for beams whereon to lay foot-path bridges over small streams.

In considering these ribs, I could not but be struck anew with the circumstance, so variously repeated in this book, that the skeleton of the whale is by no means the mould of his invested form. The largest of the Tranque ribs, one of the middle ones, occupied that part of the fish which, in life, is greatest in depth. Now, the greatest depth of the invested body of this particular whale must have been at least sixteen feet; whereas, the corresponding rib measured but little more than eight feet. So that this rib only conveyed half of the true notion of the living magnitude of that part. Besides, for some way, where I now saw but a naked spine, all that had been once wrapped round with tons of added bulk in flesh, muscle, blood, and bowels. Still more, for the ample fins, I here saw but a few disordered joints; and in place of the weighty and majestic, but boneless flukes, an utter blank!

How vain and foolish, then, thought I, for timid untravelled man to try to comprehend aright this wondrous whale, by merely poring over his dead attenuated skeleton, stretched in this peaceful wood. No. Only in the heart of quickest perils; only when within the eddyings of his angry flukes; only on the profound unbounded sea, can the fully invested whale be truly and livingly found out.

But the spine. For that, the best way we can consider it is, with a crane, to pile its bones high up on end. No speedy enterprise. But now it's done, it looks much like Pompey's Pillar.

There are forty and odd vertebræ in all, which in the skeleton are not locked together. They mostly lie like the great knobbed blocks on a Gothic spire, forming solid courses of heavy masonry. The largest, a middle one, is in width something less than three feet, and in depth more than four. The smallest, where the spine tapers away into the tail, is only two inches in width, and looks something like a white billiard-ball. I was told that there were still smaller ones, but they had been lost by some little cannibal urchins, the priest's children, who had stolen them to play marbles with. Thus we see how that the spine of even the hugest of living things tapers off at last into simple child's play.

Chapter 104

The Fossil Whale

FROM HIS MIGHTY BULK the whale affords a most congenial theme whereon to enlarge, amplify, and generally expatiate. Would you, you could not compress him. By good rights he should only be treated of in imperial folio. Not to tell over again his furlongs from spiracle to tail, and the yards he measures about the waist; only think of the gigantic involutions of his intestines, where they lie in him like great cables and hausers coiled away in the subterranean orlop-deck of a line-of-battle-ship.

Since I have undertaken to manhandle this Leviathan, it behoves me to approve myself omnisciently exhaustive in the enterprise; not overlooking the minutest seminal germs of his blood, and spinning him out to the uttermost coil of his bowels. Having already described him in most of his present habitatory and anatomical peculiarities, it now remains to magnify him in an archæological, fossiliferous, and antediluvian point of view. Applied to any other creature than the Leviathan—to an ant or a flea—such portly terms might justly be deemed unwarrantably grandiloquent. But when Leviathan is the text, the case is altered. Fain am I to stagger to this emprise under the weightiest words of the dictionary. And here be it said, that whenever it has been convenient to consult one in the course of these dissertations, I have invariably used a huge quarto edition of Johnson, expressly purchased for that purpose; because that famous lexicographer's uncommon personal bulk more fitted him to compile a lexicon to be used by a whale author like me.

One often hears of writers that rise and swell with their subject, though it may seem but an ordinary one. How, then, with me, writing of this Leviathan? Unconsciously my chirography expands into placard capitals. Give me a condor's quill! Give me Vesuvius' crater for an inkstand! Friends, hold my arms! For in the mere act of penning my thoughts of this Leviathan, they weary me, and make me faint with their out-reaching comprehensiveness of sweep, as if to include the whole circle of the sciences, and all the generations of whales, and men, and mastodons, past, present, and to come, with all the revolving panoramas of empire on earth, and throughout the whole universe, not excluding its suburbs. Such, and so magnifying, is the virtue of a large and liberal theme! We expand to its bulk. To produce a mighty book, you must choose a mighty theme. No great and enduring volume can ever be written on the flea, though many there be who have tried it.

Ere entering upon the subject of Fossil Whales, I present my credentials as a geologist, by stating that in my miscellaneous time I have been a stone-mason, and also a great digger of ditches, canals and wells, wine-vaults, cellars, and cisterns of all sorts. Likewise, by way of preliminary, I desire to remind the reader, that while in the earlier geological strata there are found the fossils of monsters now almost completely extinct; the subsequent relics discovered in what are called the Tertiary formations seem the connecting, or at any rate intercepted links, between the antechronical creatures, and those whose remote posterity are said to have entered the Ark; all the Fossil Whales hitherto discovered belong to the Tertiary period, which is the last preceding the superficial formations. And though none of them precisely answer to any known species of the present time, they are yet sufficiently akin to them in general respects, to justify their taking rank as Cetacean fossils.

Detached broken fossils of pre-adamite whales, fragments of their bones and skeletons, have within thirty years past, at various intervals, been found at the base of the Alps, in Lombardy, in France, in England, in Scotland, and in the States of Louisiana, Mississippi, and Alabama. Among the more curious of such remains is part of a skull, which in the year 1779 was disinterred in the Rue Dauphine in Paris, a short street opening almost directly upon the palace of the Tuileries; and bones disinterred in excavating the great docks of Antwerp, in Napoleon's time. Cuvier pronounced these fragments to have belonged to some utterly unknown Leviathanic species.

But by far the most wonderful of all cetacean relics was the almost complete vast skeleton of an extinct monster, found in the year 1842, on the plantation of Judge Creagh, in Alabama. The awe-stricken credulous slaves in the vicinity took it for the bones of one of the fallen angels. The Alabama doctors declared it a huge reptile, and bestowed upon it the name of Basilosaurus. But some specimen bones of it being taken across the sea to Owen, the English Anatomist, it turned out that this alleged reptile was a whale, though of a departed species. A significant illustration of the fact, again and again repeated in this book, that the skeleton of the whale furnishes but little clue to the shape of his fully invested body. So Owen rechristened the monster Zeuglodon; and in his paper read before the London Geological Society, pronounced it, in substance, one of the most extraordinary creatures which the mutations of the globe have blotted out of existence.

When I stand among these mighty Leviathan skeletons, skulls, tusks, jaws, ribs, and vertebræ, all characterized by partial resemblances to the existing breeds of sea-monsters; but at the same time bearing on the other hand similar affinities to the annihilated antechronical Leviathans, their incalculable seniors; I am, by a flood, borne back to that wondrous period, ere time itself can be said to have begun; for time began with man. Here Saturn's grey chaos rolls over me, and I obtain dim, shuddering glimpses into those Polar eternities; when wedged bastions of ice pressed hard upon what are now the Tropics; and in all the 25,000 miles of this world's circumference, not an inhabitable hand's breadth of land was visible. Then the whole world was the whale's; and, king of creation, he left his wake along the present lines of the Andes and the Himmalehs. Who can show a pedigree like Leviathan? Ahab's harpoon had shed older blood than the Pharaohs'. Methuselah seems a schoolboy. I look round to shake hands with Shem. I am horror-struck at this antemosaic, unsourced existence of the unspeakable terrors of the whale, which, having been before all time, must needs exist after all humane ages are over.

But not alone has this Leviathan left his pre-adamite traces in the stereotype plates of nature, and in limestone and marl bequeathed his ancient bust; but upon Egyptian tablets, whose antiquity seems to claim for them an almost fossiliferous character, we find the unmistakable print of his fin. In an apartment of the great temple of Denderah, some fifty years ago, there was discovered upon the granite ceiling a sculptured and painted planisphere, abounding in centaurs, griffins, and dolphins, similar to the grotesque figures on the celestial globe of the moderns. Gliding among them, old Leviathan swam as of yore; was there swimming in that planisphere, centuries before Solomon was cradled.

Nor must there be omitted another strange attestation of the antiquity of the whale, in his own osseous post-diluvian reality, as set down by the venerable John Leo, the old Barbary traveller.

"Not far from the Sea-side, they have a Temple, the Rafters and Beams of which are made of Whale-Bones; for Whales of a monstrous size are oftentimes cast up dead upon that shore. The Common People imagine, that by a secret Power bestowed by God upon the Temple, no Whale can pass by it without immediate death. But the truth of the Matter is, that on either side of the Temple, there are Rocks that shoot two Miles into the Sea, and wound the Whales when they light upon 'em. They keep a Whale's Rib of an incredible length for a Miracle, which lying upon the Ground with its convex part uppermost, makes an Arch, the Head of which cannot be reached by a Man upon a Camel's Back. This Rib (says John Leo) is said to have layn there a hundred Years before I saw it. Their Historians affirm, that a Prophet who prophesy'd of Mahomet, came from this Temple, and some do not stand to assert, that the Prophet Jonas was cast forth by the Whale at the Base of the Temple."

In this Afric Temple of the Whale I leave you, reader, and if you be a Nantucketer, and a whaleman, you will silently worship there.

Chapter 105

DOES THE WHALE'S MAGNITUDE DIMINISH?—
WILL HE PERISH?

INASMUCH, then, as this Leviathan comes floundering down
upon us from the head-waters of the Eternities, it may be
fitly inquired, whether, in the long course of his generations,
he has not degenerated from the original bulk of his sires.

But upon investigation we find, that not only are the
whales of the present day superior in magnitude to those
whose fossil remains are found in the Tertiary system (embracing a distinct geological period prior to man), but of the
whales found in that Tertiary system, those belonging to its
latter formations exceed in size those of its earlier ones.

Of all the pre-adamite whales yet exhumed, by far the largest is the Alabama one mentioned in the last chapter, and that
was less than seventy feet in length in the skeleton. Whereas,
we have already seen, that the tape-measure gives seventy-two
feet for the skeleton of a large sized modern whale. And I
have heard, on whalemen's authority, that Sperm Whales
have been captured near a hundred feet long at the time of
capture.

But may it not be, that while the whales of the present
hour are an advance in magnitude upon those of all previous
geological periods; may it not be, that since Adam's time they
have degenerated?

Assuredly, we must conclude so, if we are to credit the accounts of such gentlemen as Pliny, and the ancient naturalists
generally. For Pliny tells us of whales that embraced acres of
living bulk, and Aldrovandus of others which measured eight
hundred feet in length—Rope Walks and Thames Tunnels of
Whales! And even in the days of Banks and Solander, Cook's
naturalists, we find a Danish member of the Academy of Sciences setting down certain Iceland Whales (reydar-fiskur, or
Wrinkled Bellies) at one hundred and twenty yards; that is,
three hundred and sixty feet. And Lacépède, the French naturalist, in his elaborate history of whales, in the very begin-

ning of his work (page 3), sets down the Right Whale at one hundred metres, three hundred and twenty-eight feet. And this work was published so late as A.D. 1825.

But will any whaleman believe these stories? No. The whale of to-day is as big as his ancestors in Pliny's time. And if ever I go where Pliny is, I, a whaleman (more than he was), will make bold to tell him so. Because I cannot understand how it is, that while the Egyptian mummies that were buried thousands of years before even Pliny was born, do not measure so much in their coffins as a modern Kentuckian in his socks; and while the cattle and other animals sculptured on the oldest Egyptian and Nineveh tablets, by the relative proportions in which they are drawn, just as plainly prove that the high-bred, stall-fed, prize cattle of Smithfield, not only equal, but far exceed in magnitude the fattest of Pharaoh's fat kine; in the face of all this, I will not admit that of all animals the whale alone should have degenerated.

But still another inquiry remains; one often agitated by the more recondite Nantucketers. Whether owing to the almost omniscient look-outs at the mast-heads of the whale-ships, now penetrating even through Behring's straits, and into the remotest secret drawers and lockers of the world; and the thousand harpoons and lances darted along all continental coasts; the moot point is, whether Leviathan can long endure so wide a chase, and so remorseless a havoc; whether he must not at last be exterminated from the waters, and the last whale, like the last man, smoke his last pipe, and then himself evaporate in the final puff.

Comparing the humped herds of whales with the humped herds of buffalo, which, not forty years ago, overspread by tens of thousands the prairies of Illinois and Missouri, and shook their iron manes and scowled with their thunder-clotted brows upon the sites of populous river-capitals, where now the polite broker sells you land at a dollar an inch; in such a comparison an irresistible argument would seem furnished, to show that the hunted whale cannot now escape speedy extinction.

But you must look at this matter in every light. Though so short a period ago—not a good life-time—the census of the buffalo in Illinois exceeded the census of men now in London, and though at the present day not one horn or hoof of them remains in all that region; and though the cause of this wondrous extermination was the spear of man; yet the far different nature of the whale-hunt peremptorily forbids so inglorious an end to the Leviathan. Forty men in one ship hunting the Sperm Whale for forty-eight months think they have done extremely well, and thank God, if at last they carry home the oil of forty fish. Whereas, in the days of the old Canadian and Indian hunters and trappers of the West, when the far west (in whose sunset suns still rise) was a wilderness and a virgin, the same number of moccasined men, for the same number of months, mounted on horse instead of sailing in ships, would have slain not forty, but forty thousand and more buffaloes; a fact that, if need were, could be statistically stated.

Nor, considered aright, does it seem any argument in favor of the gradual extinction of the Sperm Whale, for example, that in former years (the latter part of the last century, say) these Leviathans, in small pods, were encountered much oftener than at present, and, in consequence, the voyages were not so prolonged, and were also much more remunerative. Because, as has been elsewhere noticed, those whales, influenced by some views to safety, now swim the seas in immense caravans, so that to a large degree the scattered solitaries, yokes, and pods, and schools of other days are now aggregated into vast but widely separated, unfrequent armies. That is all. And equally fallacious seems the conceit, that because the so-called whale-bone whales no longer haunt many grounds in former years abounding with them, hence that species also is declining. For they are only being driven from promontory to cape; and if one coast is no longer enlivened with their jets, then, be sure, some other and remoter strand has been very recently startled by the unfamiliar spectacle.

Furthermore: concerning these last mentioned Leviathans, they have two firm fortresses, which, in all human probability, will for ever remain impregnable. And as upon the invasion of their valleys, the frosty Swiss have retreated to their mountains; so, hunted from the savannas and glades of the middle seas, the whale-bone whales can at last resort to their Polar citadels, and diving under the ultimate glassy barriers and walls there, come up among icy fields and floes; and in a charmed circle of everlasting December, bid defiance to all pursuit from man.

But as perhaps fifty of these whale-bone whales are harpooned for one cachalot, some philosophers of the forecastle have concluded that this positive havoc has already very seriously diminished their battalions. But though for some time past a number of these whales, not less than 13,000, have been annually slain on the nor' west coast by the Americans alone; yet there are considerations which render even this circumstance of little or no account as an opposing argument in this matter.

Natural as it is to be somewhat incredulous concerning the populousness of the more enormous creatures of the globe, yet what shall we say to Horto, the historian of Goa, when he tells us that at one hunting the King of Siam took 4000 elephants; that in those regions elephants are numerous as droves of cattle in the temperate climes. And there seems no reason to doubt that if these elephants, which have now been hunted for thousands of years, by Semiramis, by Porus, by Hannibal, and by all the successive monarchs of the East—if they still survive there in great numbers, much more may the great whale outlast all hunting, since he has a pasture to expatiate in, which is precisely twice as large as all Asia, both Americas, Europe and Africa, New Holland, and all the Isles of the sea combined.

Moreover: we are to consider, that from the presumed great longevity of whales, their probably attaining the age of a century and more, therefore at any one period of time, several distinct adult generations must be contemporary. And what that is, we may soon gain some idea of, by imagining all the grave-yards, cemeteries, and family vaults of creation yielding up the live bodies of all the men, women, and children who were alive seventy-five years ago; and adding this countless host to the present human population of the globe.

Wherefore, for all these things, we account the whale immortal in his species, however perishable in his individuality. He swam the seas before the continents broke water; he once swam over the site of the Tuileries, and Windsor Castle, and the Kremlin. In Noah's flood he despised Noah's Ark; and if ever the world is to be again flooded, like the Netherlands, to kill off its rats, then the eternal whale will still survive, and rearing upon the topmost crest of the equatorial flood, spout his frothed defiance to the skies.

Chapter 106

AHAB'S LEG

THE PRECIPITATING MANNER in which Captain Ahab had quitted the Samuel Enderby of London, had not been unattended with some small violence to his own person. He had lighted with such energy upon a thwart of his boat that his ivory leg had received a half-splintering shock. And when after gaining his own deck, and his own pivot-hole there, he so vehemently wheeled round with an urgent command to the steersman (it was, as ever, something about his not steering inflexibly enough); then, the already shaken ivory received such an additional twist and wrench, that though it still remained entire, and to all appearances lusty, yet Ahab did not deem it entirely trustworthy.

And, indeed, it seemed small matter for wonder, that for all his pervading, mad recklessness, Ahab did at times give careful heed to the condition of that dead bone upon which he partly stood. For it had not been very long prior to the Pequod's sailing from Nantucket, that he had been found one night lying prone upon the ground, and insensible; by some unknown, and seemingly inexplicable, unimaginable casualty, his ivory limb having been so violently displaced, that it had stake-wise smitten, and all but pierced his groin; nor was it without extreme difficulty that the agonizing wound was entirely cured.

Nor, at the time, had it failed to enter his monomaniac mind, that all the anguish of that then present suffering was but the direct issue of a former woe; and he too plainly seemed to see, that as the most poisonous reptile of the marsh perpetuates his kind as inevitably as the sweetest songster of the grove; so, equally with every felicity, all miserable events do naturally beget their like. Yea, more than equally, thought Ahab; since both the ancestry and posterity of Grief go further than the ancestry and posterity of Joy. For, not to hint of this: that it is an inference from certain canonic teachings, that while some natural enjoyments here shall have no children born to them for the other world, but, on the contrary, shall be followed by the joy-childlessness of all hell's despair; whereas, some guilty mortal miseries shall still fertilely beget to themselves an eternally progressive progeny of griefs beyond the grave; not at all to hint of this, there still seems an inequality in the deeper analysis of the thing. For, thought Ahab, while even the highest earthly felicities ever have a certain unsignifying pettiness lurking in them, but, at bottom, all heart-woes, a mystic significance, and, in some men, an archangelic grandeur; so do their diligent tracings-out not belie the obvious deduction. To trail the genealogies of these high mortal miseries, carries us at last among the sourceless primogenitures of the gods; so that, in the face of all the glad, hay-making suns, and soft-cymballing, round harvest-moons, we must needs give in to this: that the gods themselves are not for ever glad. The ineffaceable, sad birth-mark in the brow of man, is but the stamp of sorrow in the signers.

Unwittingly here a secret has been divulged, which perhaps might more properly, in set way, have been disclosed before. With many other particulars concerning Ahab, always had it remained a mystery to some, why it was, that for a certain period, both before and after the sailing of the Pequod, he had hidden himself away with such Grand-Lama-like exclusiveness; and, for that one interval, sought speechless refuge, as it were, among the marble senate of the dead. Captain Peleg's bruited reason for this thing appeared by no means adequate; though, indeed, as touching all Ahab's deeper part, every revelation partook more of significant darkness than of explanatory light. But, in the end, it all came out; this one matter did, at least. That direful mishap was at the bottom of his temporary recluseness. And not only this, but to that ever-contracting, dropping circle ashore, who, for any reason, possessed the privilege of a less banned approach to him; to that timid circle the above hinted casualty—remaining, as it did moodily unaccounted for by Ahab—invested itself with terrors, not entirely underived from the land of spirits and of wails. So that, through their zeal for him, they had all conspired, so far as in them lay, to muffle up the knowledge of this thing from others; and hence it was, that not till a considerable interval had elapsed, did it transpire upon the Pequod's decks.

But be all this as it may; let the unseen, ambiguous synod in the air, or the vindictive princes and potentates of fire, have to do or not with earthly Ahab, yet, in this present matter of his leg, he took plain practical procedures;—he called the carpenter.

And when that functionary appeared before him, he bade him without delay set about making a new leg, and directed the mates to see him supplied with all the studs and joists of jaw-ivory (Sperm Whale) which had thus far been accumulated on the voyage, in order that a careful selection of the stoutest, clearest-grained stuff might be secured. This done, the carpenter received orders to have the leg completed that night; and to provide all the fittings for it, independent of those pertaining to the distrusted one in use. Moreover, the ship's forge was ordered to be hoisted out of its temporary idleness in the hold; and, to accelerate the affair, the blacksmith was commanded to proceed at once to the forging of whatever iron contrivances might be needed.

Chapter 107

THE CARPENTER

S EAT THYSELF sultanically among the moons of Saturn, and take high abstracted man alone; and he seems a wonder, a grandeur, and a woe. But from the same point, take mankind in mass, and for the most part, they seem a mob of unnecessary duplicates, both contemporary and hereditary. But most humble though he was, and far from furnishing an example of the high, humane abstraction; the Pequod's carpenter was no duplicate; hence, he now comes in person on this stage.

Like all sea-going ship carpenters, and more especially those belonging to whaling vessels, he was, to a certain offhanded, practical extent, alike experienced in numerous trades and callings collateral to his own; the carpenter's pursuit being the ancient and outbranching trunk of all those numerous handicrafts which more or less have to do with wood as an auxiliary material. But, besides the application to him of the generic remark above, this carpenter of the Pequod was singularly efficient in those thousand nameless mechanical emergencies continually recurring in a large ship, upon a three or four years' voyage, in uncivilized and far-distant seas. For not to speak of his readiness in ordinary duties:—repairing stove boats, sprung spars, reforming the shape of clumsy-bladed oars, inserting bull's eyes in the deck, or new tree-nails in the side planks, and other miscellaneous matters more directly pertaining to his special business; he was moreover unhesitatingly expert in all manner of conflicting aptitudes, both useful and capricious.

The one grand stage where he enacted all his various parts so manifold, was his vice-bench; a long rude ponderous table furnished with several vices, of different sizes, and both of iron and of wood. At all times except when whales were alongside, this bench was securely lashed athwartships against the rear of the Try-works.

A belaying pin is found too large to be easily inserted into its hold: the carpenter claps it into one of his ever-ready vices, and straightway files it smaller. A lost land-bird of strange plumage strays on board, and is made a captive: out of clean shaved rods of right-whale bone, and cross-beams of sperm whale ivory, the carpenter makes a pagoda-looking cage for it. An oarsman sprains his wrist: the carpenter concocts a soothing lotion. Stubb longs for vermillion stars to be painted upon the blade of his every oar: screwing each oar in his big vice of wood, the carpenter symmetrically supplies the con-stellation. A sailor takes a fancy to wear shark-bone ear-rings: the carpenter drills his ears. Another has the toothache: the carpenter out pincers, and clapping one hand upon his bench bids him be seated there; but the poor fellow unmanageably winces under the unconcluded operation; whirling round the handle of his wooden vice, the carpenter signs him to clap his jaw in that, if he would have him draw the tooth.

Thus, this carpenter was prepared at all points, and alike indifferent and without respect in all. Teeth he accounted bits of ivory; heads he deemed but top-blocks; men themselves he lightly held for capstans. But while now upon so wide a field thus variously accomplished, and with such liveliness of ex-pertness in him, too; all this would seem to argue some un-common vivacity of intelligence. But not precisely so. For nothing was this man more remarkable, than for a certain im-personal stolidity as it were; impersonal, I say; for it so shaded off into the surrounding infinite of things, that it seemed one with the general stolidity discernible in the whole visible world; which while pauselessly active in uncounted modes, still eternally holds its peace, and ignores you, though you dig foundations for cathedrals. Yet was this half-horrible stolidity in him, involving, too, as it appeared, an all-ramify-ing heartlessness;—yet was it oddly dashed at times, with an old, crutch-like, antediluvian, wheezing humorousness, not unstreaked now and then with a certain grizzled wittiness; such as might have served to pass the time during the mid-night watch on the bearded forecastle of Noah's ark. Was it that this old carpenter had been a life-long wanderer, whose much rolling, to and fro, not only had gathered no moss; but what is more, had rubbed off whatever small outward cling-ings might have originally pertained to him? He was a strip abstract; an unfractioned integral; uncompromised as a new-born babe; living without premeditated reference to this world or the next. You might almost say, that this strange uncompromisedness in him involved a sort of unintelligence; for in his numerous trades, he did not seem to work so much by reason or by instinct, or simply because he had been tutored to it, or by any intermixture of all these, even or uneven; but merely by a kind of deaf and dumb, spontaneous literal process. He was a pure manipulator; his brain, if he had ever had one, must have early oozed along into the muscles of his fingers. He was like one of those unreasoning but still highly useful, *multum in parvo*, Sheffield contrivances, assuming the exterior—though a little swelled—of a common pocket knife; but containing, not only blades of various sizes, but also screw-drivers, cork-screws, tweezers, awls, pens, rulers, nail-filers, countersinkers. So, if his superiors wanted to use the carpenter for a screw-driver, all they had to do was to open that part of him, and the screw was fast: or if for tweezers, take him up by the legs, and there they were.

Yet, as previously hinted, this omnitooled, open-and-shut carpenter, was, after all, no mere machine of an automaton. If he did not have a common soul in him, he had a subtle something that somehow anomalously did its duty. What that was, whether essence of quicksilver, or a few drops of hartshorn, there is no telling. But there it was; and there it had abided for now some sixty years or more. And this it was, this same unaccountable, cunning life-principle in him; this it was, that kept him a great part of the time soliloquizing; but only like an unreasoning wheel, which also hummingly soliloquizes; or rather, his body was a sentry-box and this soliloquizer on guard there, and talking all the time to keep himself awake.

Chapter 108

(Carpenter standing before his vice-bench, and by the light of two lanterns busily filing the ivory joist for the leg, which joist is firmly fixed in the vice. Slabs of ivory, leather straps, pads, screws, and various tools of all sorts lying about the bench. Forward, the red flame of the forge is seen, where the blacksmith is at work.)

DRAT THE FILE, and drat the bone! That is hard which should be soft, and that is soft which should be hard. So we go, who file old jaws and shinbones. Let's try another. Aye, now, this works better *(sneezes)*. Halloa, this bone dust is *(sneezes)*—why it's *(sneezes)*—yes it's *(sneezes)*—bless my soul, it won't let me speak! This is what an old fellow gets now for working in dead lumber. Saw a live tree, and you don't get this dust; amputate a live bone, and you don't get it *(sneezes)*. Come, come, you old Smut, there, bear a hand, and let's have that ferule and buckle-screw; I'll be ready for them presently. Lucky now *(sneezes)* there's no knee-joint to make; that might puzzle a little; but a mere shinbone—why it's easy as making hop-poles; only I should like to put a good finish on. Time, time; if I but only had the time, I could turn him out as neat a leg now as ever *(sneezes)* scraped to a lady in a parlor. Those buckskin legs and calves of legs I've seen in shop windows wouldn't compare at all. They soak water, they do; and of course get rheumatic, and have to be doctored *(sneezes)* with washes and lotions, just like live legs. There; before I saw it off, now, I must call his old Mogulship, and see whether the length will be all right; too short, if anything, I guess. Ha! that's the heel; we are in luck; here he comes, or it's somebody else, that's certain.

AHAB *(advancing)*.
(During the ensuing scene, the carpenter continues sneezing at times.)

Well, manmaker!

Just in time, sir. If the captain pleases, I will now mark the length. Let me measure, sir.

Measured for a leg! good. Well, it's not the first time. About it! There; keep thy finger on it. This is a cogent vice thou hast here, carpenter; let me feel its grip once. So, so; it does pinch some.

Oh, sir, it will break bones—beware, beware!

No fear; I like a good grip; I like to feel something in this slippery world that can hold, man. What's Prometheus about there?—the blacksmith, I mean—what's he about?

He must be forging the buckle-screw, sir, now.

Right. It's a partnership; he supplies the muscle part. He makes a fierce red flame there!

Aye, sir; he must have the white heat for this kind of fine work.

Um-m. So he must. I do deem it now a most meaning thing, that that old Greek, Prometheus, who made men, they say, should have been a blacksmith, and animated them with fire; for what's made in fire must properly belong to fire; and so hell's probable. How the soot flies! This must be the remainder the Greek made the Africans of. Carpenter, when he's through with that buckle, tell him to forge a pair of steel shoulder-blades; there's a pedlar aboard with a crushing pack.

Sir?

Hold; while Prometheus is about it, I'll order a complete man after a desirable pattern. Imprimis, fifty feet high in his socks; then, chest modelled after the Thames Tunnel; then, legs with roots to 'em, to stay in one place; then, arms three feet through the wrist; no heart at all, brass forehead, and about a quarter of an acre of fine brains; and let me see— shall I order eyes to see outwards? No, but put a sky-light on top of his head to illuminate inwards. There, take the order, and away.

Now, what's he speaking about, and who's he speaking to, I should like to know? Shall I keep standing here? *(aside.)*

'Tis but indifferent architecture to make a blind dome; here's one. No, no, no; I must have a lantern.

Ho, ho! That's it, hey? Here are two, sir; one will serve my turn.

What art thou thrusting that thief-catcher into my face for, man? Thrusted light is worse than presented pistols.

I thought, sir, that you spoke to carpenter.

Carpenter? why that's—but no;—a very tidy, and, I may say, an extremely gentlemanlike sort of business thou art in here, carpenter;—or would'st thou rather work in clay?

Sir?—Clay? clay, sir? That's mud; we leave clay to ditchers, sir.

The fellow's impious! What art thou sneezing about?

Bone is rather dusty, sir.

Take the hint, then; and when thou art dead, never bury thyself under living people's noses.

Sir?—oh! ah!—I guess so;—yes—oh, dear!

Look ye, carpenter, I dare say thou callest thyself a right good workmanlike workman, eh? Well, then, will it speak thoroughly well for thy work, if, when I come to mount this leg thou makest, I shall nevertheless feel another leg in the same identical place with it; that is, carpenter, my old lost leg; the flesh and blood one, I mean. Canst thou not drive that old Adam away?

Truly, sir, I begin to understand somewhat now. Yes, I have heard something curious on that score, sir; how that a dismasted man never entirely loses the feeling of his old spar, but it will be still pricking him at times. May I humbly ask if it be really so, sir?

It is, man. Look, put thy live leg here in the place where mine once was; so, now, here is only one distinct leg to the eye, yet two to the soul. Where thou feelest tingling life; there, exactly there, there to a hair, do I. Is't a riddle?

I should humbly call it a poser, sir.

Hist, then. How dost thou know that some entire, living, thinking thing may not be invisibly and uninterpenetratingly standing precisely where thou now standest; aye, and stand-ing there in thy spite? In thy most solitary hours, then, dost thou not fear eavesdroppers? Hold, don't speak! And if I still feel the smart of my crushed leg, though it be now so long dissolved; then, why mayst not thou, carpenter, feel the fiery pains of hell for ever, and without a body? Hah!

Good Lord! Truly, sir, if it comes to that, I must calculate over again; I think I didn't carry a small figure, sir.

Look ye, pudding-heads should never grant premises.— How long before the leg is done?

Perhaps an hour, sir.

Bungle away at it then, and bring it to me *(turns to go)*. Oh, Life! Here I am, proud as a Greek god, and yet standing debtor to this blockhead for a bone to stand on! Cursed be that mortal inter-indebtedness which will not do away with ledgers. I would be free as air; and I'm down in the whole world's books. I am so rich, I could have given bid for bid with the wealthiest Prætorians at the auction of the Roman empire (which was the world's); and yet I owe for the flesh in the tongue I brag with. By heavens! I'll get a crucible, and into it, and dissolve myself down to one small, compendious vertebra. So.

CARPENTER.

(Resuming his work.)

Well, well, well! Stubb knows him best of all, and Stubb always says he's queer; says nothing but that one sufficient little word queer; he's queer, says Stubb; he's queer—queer, queer; and keeps dinning it into Mr. Starbuck all the time— queer, sir—queer, queer, very queer. And here's his leg! Yes, now that I think of it, here's his bedfellow! has a stick of whale's jaw-bone for a wife! And this is his leg; he'll stand on this. What was that now about one leg standing in three places, and all three places standing in one hell—how was that? Oh! I don't wonder he looked so scornful at me! I'm a sort of strange-thoughted sometimes, they say; but that's only haphazard-like. Then, a short, little old body like me, should never undertake to wade out into deep waters with tall, heron-built captains; the water chucks you under the chin pretty quick, and there's a great cry for life-boats. And here's the heron's leg! long and slim, sure enough! Now, for most folks one pair of legs lasts a lifetime, and that must be because they use them mercifully, as a tender-hearted old lady uses her roly-poly old coach-horses. But Ahab; oh he's a hard driver. Look, driven one leg to death, and spavined the other for life, and now wears out bone legs by the cord. Halloa, there, you Smut! bear a hand there with those screws, and let's finish it before the resurrection fellow comes a-calling with his horn for all legs, true or false, as brewery-men go round collecting old beer barrels, to fill 'em up again. What a leg this is! It looks like a real live leg, filed down to nothing but the core; he'll be standing on this to-morrow; he'll be taking altitudes on it. Halloa! I almost forgot the little oval slate, smoothed ivory, where he figures up the latitude. So, so; chisel, file, and sand-paper, now!

Chapter 109

ACCORDING to usage they were pumping the ship next morning; and lo! no inconsiderable oil came up with the water; the casks below must have sprung a bad leak. Much concern was shown; and Starbuck went down into the cabin to report this unfavorable affair.*

Now, from the South and West the Pequod was drawing nigh to Formosa and the Bashee Isles, between which lies one of the tropical outlets from the China waters into the Pacific. And so Starbuck found Ahab with a general chart of the oriental archipelagoes spread before him; and another separate one representing the long eastern coasts of the Japanese islands—Niphon, Matsmai, and Sikoke. With his snow-white new ivory leg braced against the screwed leg of his table, and with a long pruning-hook of a jack-knife in his hand, the wondrous old man, with his back to the gangway door, was wrinkling his brow, and tracing his old courses again.

"Who's there?" hearing the footstep at the door, but not turning round to it. "On deck! Begone!"

"Captain Ahab mistakes; it is I. The oil in the hold is leaking, sir. We must up Burtons and break out."

"Up Burtons and break out? Now that we are nearing Japan; heave-to here for a week to tinker a parcel of old hoops?"

"Either do that, sir, or waste in one day more oil than we may make good in a year. What we come twenty thousand miles to get is worth saving, sir."

"So it is, so it is; if we get it."

"I was speaking of the oil in the hold, sir."

"And I was not speaking or thinking of that at all. Begone!

*In Sperm-whalemen with any considerable quantity of oil on board, it is a regular semi-weekly duty to conduct a hose into the hold, and drench the casks with sea-water; which afterwards, at varying intervals, is removed by the ship's pumps. Hereby the casks are sought to be kept damply tight; while by the changed character of the withdrawn water, the mariners readily detect any serious leakage in the precious cargo.

Let it leak! I'm all aleak myself. Aye! leaks in leaks! not only full of leaky casks, but those leaky casks are in a leaky ship; and that's a far worse plight than the Pequod's, man. Yet I don't stop to plug my leak; for who can find it in the deep-loaded hull; or how hope to plug it, even if found, in this life's howling gale? Starbuck! I'll not have the Burtons hoisted."

"What will the owners say, sir?"

"Let the owners stand on Nantucket beach and outyell the Typhoons. What cares Ahab? Owners, owners? Thou art always prating to me, Starbuck, about those miserly owners, as if the owners were my conscience. But look ye, the only real owner of anything is its commander; and hark ye, my conscience is in this ship's keel.—On deck!"

"Captain Ahab," said the reddening mate, moving further into the cabin, with a daring so strangely respectful and cautious that it almost seemed not only every way seeking to avoid the slightest outward manifestation of itself, but within also seemed more than half distrustful of itself; "A better man than I might well pass over in thee what he would quickly enough resent in a younger man; aye, and in a happier, Captain Ahab."

"Devils! Dost thou then so much as dare to critically think of me?—On deck!"

"Nay, sir, not yet; I do entreat. And I do dare, sir—to be forbearing! Shall we not understand each other better than hitherto, Captain Ahab?"

Ahab seized a loaded musket from the rack (forming part of most South-Sea-men's cabin furniture), and pointing it towards Starbuck, exclaimed: "There is one God that is Lord over the earth, and one Captain that is lord over the Pequod.—On deck!"

For an instant in the flashing eyes of the mate, and his fiery cheeks, you would have almost thought that he had really received the blaze of the levelled tube. But, mastering his emotion, he half calmly rose, and as he quitted the cabin, paused for an instant and said: "Thou hast outraged, not insulted me, sir; but for that I ask thee not to beware of Starbuck; thou wouldst but laugh; but let Ahab beware of Ahab; beware of thyself, old man."

"He waxes brave, but nevertheless obeys; most careful bravery that!" murmured Ahab, as Starbuck disappeared. "What's that he said—Ahab beware of Ahab—there's something there!" Then unconsciously using the musket for a staff, with an iron brow he paced to and fro in the little cabin; but presently the thick plaits of his forehead relaxed, and returning the gun to the rack, he went to the deck.

"Thou art but too good a fellow, Starbuck," he said lowly to the mate; then raising his voice to the crew: "Furl the t'gallant-sails, and close-reef the top-sails, fore and aft; back the main-yard; up Burtons, and break out in the main-hold."

It were perhaps vain to surmise exactly why it was, that as respecting Starbuck, Ahab thus acted. It may have been a flash of honesty in him; or mere prudential policy which, under the circumstance, imperiously forbade the slightest symptom of open disaffection, however transient, in the important chief officer of his ship. However it was, his orders were executed; and the Burtons were hoisted.

Chapter 110

QUEEQUEG IN HIS COFFIN

U PON SEARCHING, it was found that the casks last struck into the hold were perfectly sound, and that the leak must be further off. So, it being calm weather, they broke out deeper and deeper, disturbing the slumbers of the huge ground-tier butts; and from that black midnight sending those gigantic moles into the daylight above. So deep did they go; and so ancient, and corroded, and weedy the aspect of the lowermost puncheons, that you almost looked next for some mouldy corner-stone cask containing coins of Captain Noah, with copies of the posted placards, vainly warning the infatuated old world from the flood. Tierce after tierce, too, of water, and bread, and beef, and shooks of staves, and iron bundles of hoops, were hoisted out, till at last the piled decks were hard to get about; and the hollow hull echoed under foot, as if you were treading over empty catacombs, and reeled and rolled in the sea like an air-freighted demijohn. Top-heavy was the ship as a dinnerless student with all Aristotle in his head. Well was it that the Typhoons did not visit them then.

Now, at this time it was that my poor pagan companion, and fast bosom-friend, Queequeg, was seized with a fever, which brought him nigh to his endless end.

Be it said, that in this vocation of whaling, sinecures are unknown; dignity and danger go hand in hand; till you get to be Captain, the higher you rise the harder you toil. So with poor Queequeg, who, as harpooneer, must not only face all the rage of the living whale, but—as we have elsewhere seen—mount his dead back in a rolling sea; and finally descend into the gloom of the hold, and bitterly sweating all day in that subterraneous confinement, resolutely manhandle the clumsiest casks and see to their stowage. To be short, among whalemen, the harpooneers are the holders, so called.

Poor Queequeg! when the ship was about half disembowelled, you should have stooped over the hatchway, and peered

down upon him there; where, stripped to his woollen drawers, the tattooed savage was crawling about amid that dampness and slime, like a green spotted lizard at the bottom of a
well. And a well, or an ice-house, it somehow proved to him,
poor pagan; where, strange to say, for all the heat of his
sweatings, he caught a terrible chill which lapsed into a fever;
and at last, after some days' suffering, laid him in his hammock, close to the very sill of the door of death. How he
wasted and wasted away in those few long-lingering days, till
there seemed but little left of him but his frame and tattooing.
But as all else in him thinned, and his cheek-bones grew
sharper, his eyes, nevertheless, seemed growing fuller and
fuller; they became of a strange softness of lustre; and mildly
but deeply looked out at you there from his sickness, a wondrous testimony to that immortal health in him which could
not die, or be weakened. And like circles on the water, which,
as they grow fainter, expand; so his eyes seemed rounding
and rounding, like the rings of Eternity. An awe that cannot
be named would steal over you as you sat by the side of this
waning savage, and saw as strange things in his face, as any
beheld who were bystanders when Zoroaster died. For whatever is truly wondrous and fearful in man, never yet was put
into words or books. And the drawing near of Death, which
alike levels all, alike impresses all with a last revelation, which
only an author from the dead could adequately tell. So that—
let us say it again—no dying Chaldee or Greek had higher
and holier thoughts than those, whose mysterious shades you
saw creeping over the face of poor Queequeg, as he quietly
lay in his swaying hammock, and the rolling sea seemed
gently rocking him to his final rest, and the ocean's invisible
flood-tide lifted him higher and higher towards his destined
heaven.

Not a man of the crew but gave him up; and, as for Queequeg himself, what he thought of his case was forcibly shown
by a curious favor he asked. He called one to him in the grey
morning watch, when the day was just breaking, and taking
his hand, said that while in Nantucket he had chanced to see
certain little canoes of dark wood, like the rich war-wood of
his native isle; and upon inquiry, he had learned that all
whalemen who died in Nantucket, were laid in those same

dark canoes, and that the fancy of being so laid had much
pleased him; for it was not unlike the custom of his own race,
who, after embalming a dead warrior, stretched him out in
his canoe, and so left him to be floated away to the starry
archipelagoes; for not only do they believe that the stars are
isles, but that far beyond all visible horizons, their own mild,
uncontinented seas, interflow with the blue heavens; and so
form the white breakers of the milky way. He added, that he
shuddered at the thought of being buried in his hammock,
according to the usual sea-custom, tossed like something vile
to the death-devouring sharks. No: he desired a canoe like
those of Nantucket, all the more congenial to him, being a
whaleman, that like a whale-boat these coffin-canoes were
without a keel; though that involved but uncertain steering,
and much lee-way adown the dim ages.

Now, when this strange circumstance was made known aft,
the carpenter was at once commanded to do Queequeg's bidding, whatever it might include. There was some heathenish,
coffin-colored old lumber aboard, which, upon a long previous voyage, had been cut from the aboriginal groves of the
Lackaday islands, and from these dark planks the coffin was
recommended to be made. No sooner was the carpenter apprised of the order, than taking his rule, he forthwith with all
the indifferent promptitude of his character, proceeded into
the forecastle and took Queequeg's measure with great accuracy, regularly chalking Queequeg's person as he shifted the
rule.

"Ah! poor fellow! he'll have to die now," ejaculated the
Long Island sailor.

Going to his vice-bench, the carpenter for convenience'
sake and general reference, now transferringly measured on it
the exact length the coffin was to be, and then made the transfer permanent by cutting two notches at its extremities. This
done, he marshalled the planks and his tools, and to work.

When the last nail was driven, and the lid duly planed
and fitted, he lightly shouldered the coffin and went forward
with it, inquiring whether they were ready for it yet in that
direction.

Overhearing the indignant but half-humorous cries with
which the people on deck began to drive the coffin away,

Queequeg, to every one's consternation, commanded that the thing should be instantly brought to him, nor was there any denying him; seeing that, of all mortals, some dying men are the most tyrannical; and certainly, since they will shortly trouble us so little for evermore, the poor fellows ought to be indulged.

Leaning over in his hammock, Queequeg long regarded the coffin with an attentive eye. He then called for his harpoon, had the wooden stock drawn from it, and then had the iron part placed in the coffin along with one of the paddles of his boat. All by his own request, also, biscuits were then ranged round the sides within: a flask of fresh water was placed at the head, and a small bag of woody earth scraped up in the hold at the foot; and a piece of sail-cloth being rolled up for a pillow, Queequeg now entreated to be lifted into his final bed, that he might make trial of its comforts, if any it had. He lay without moving a few minutes, then told one to go to his bag and bring out his little god, Yojo. Then crossing his arms on his breast with Yojo between, he called for the coffin lid (hatch he called it) to be placed over him. The head part turned over with a leather hinge, and there lay Queequeg in his coffin with little but his composed countenance in view. "Rarmai" (it will do; it is easy), he murmured at last, and signed to be replaced in his hammock.

But ere this was done, Pip, who had been slily hovering near by all this while, drew nigh to him where he lay, and with soft sobbings, took him by the hand; in the other, holding his tambourine.

"Poor rover! will ye never have done with all this weary roving? where go ye now? But if the currents carry ye to those sweet Antilles where the beaches are only beat with water-lilies, will ye do one little errand for me? Seek out one Pip, who's now been missing long: I think he's in those far Antilles. If ye find him, then comfort him; for he must be very sad; for look! he's left his tambourine behind;—I found it. Rig-a-dig, dig, dig! Now, Queequeg, die; and I'll beat ye your dying march."

"I have heard," murmured Starbuck, gazing down the scuttle, "that in violent fevers, men, all ignorance, have talked in ancient tongues; and that when the mystery is probed, it turns out always that in their wholly forgotten childhood those ancient tongues had been really spoken in their hearing by some lofty scholars. So, to my fond faith, poor Pip, in this strange sweetness of his lunacy, brings heavenly vouchers of all our heavenly homes. Where learned he that, but there?— Hark! he speaks again: but more wildly now."

"Form two and two! Let's make a General of him! Ho, where's his harpoon? Lay it across here.—Rig-a-dig, dig, dig! huzza! Oh for a game cock now to sit upon his head and crow! Queequeg dies game!—mind ye that; Queequeg dies game!—take ye good heed of that; Queequeg dies game! I say; game, game, game! but base little Pip, he died a coward; died all a'shiver;—out upon Pip! Hark ye; if ye find Pip, tell all the Antilles he's a runaway; a coward, a coward, a coward! Tell them he jumped from a whale-boat! I'd never beat my tambourine over base Pip, and hail him General, if he were once more dying here. No, no! shame upon all cowards— shame upon them! Let 'em go drown like Pip, that jumped from a whale-boat. Shame! shame!"

During all this, Queequeg lay with closed eyes, as if in a dream. Pip was led away, and the sick man was replaced in his hammock.

But now that he had apparently made every preparation for death; now that his coffin was proved a good fit, Queequeg suddenly rallied; soon there seemed no need of the carpenter's box: and thereupon, when some expressed their delighted surprise, he, in substance, said, that the cause of his sudden convalescence was this;—at a critical moment, he had just recalled a little duty ashore, which he was leaving undone; and therefore had changed his mind about dying: he could not die yet, he averred. They asked him, then, whether to live or die was a matter of his own sovereign will and pleasure. He answered, certainly. In a word, it was Queequeg's conceit, that if a man made up his mind to live, mere sickness could not kill him: nothing but a whale, or a gale, or some violent, ungovernable, unintelligent destroyer of that sort.

Now, there is this noteworthy difference between savage and civilized; that while a sick, civilized man may be six months convalescing, generally speaking, a sick savage is almost half-well again in a day. So, in good time my Queequeg gained strength; and at length after sitting on the windlass for a few indolent days (but eating with a vigorous appetite) he suddenly leaped to his feet, threw out arms and legs, gave himself a good stretching, yawned a little bit, and then springing into the head of his hoisted boat, and poising a harpoon, pronounced himself fit for a fight.

With a wild whimsiness, he now used his coffin for a sea-chest; and emptying into it his canvas bag of clothes, set them in order there. Many spare hours he spent, in carving the lid with all manner of grotesque figures and drawings; and it seemed that hereby he was striving, in his rude way, to copy parts of the twisted tattooing on his body. And this tattooing, had been the work of a departed prophet and seer of his island, who, by those hieroglyphic marks, had written out on his body a complete theory of the heavens and the earth, and a mystical treatise on the art of attaining truth; so that Queequeg in his own proper person was a riddle to unfold; a wondrous work in one volume; but whose mysteries not even himself could read, though his own live heart beat against them; and these mysteries were therefore destined in the end to moulder away with the living parchment whereon they were inscribed, and so be unsolved to the last. And this thought it must have been which suggested to Ahab that wild exclamation of his, when one morning turning away from surveying poor Queequeg—"Oh, devilish tantalization of the gods!"

Chapter III

THE PACIFIC

WHEN GLIDING by the Bashee isles we emerged at last upon the great South Sea; were it not for other things, I could have greeted my dear Pacific with uncounted thanks, for now the long supplication of my youth was answered; that serene ocean rolled eastwards from me a thousand leagues of blue.

There is, one knows not what sweet mystery about this sea, whose gently awful stirrings seem to speak of some hidden soul beneath; like those fabled undulations of the Ephesian sod over the buried Evangelist St. John. And meet it is, that over these sea-pastures, wide-rolling watery prairies and Potters' Fields of all four continents, the waves should rise and fall, and ebb and flow unceasingly; for here, millions of mixed shades and shadows, drowned dreams, somnambulisms, reveries; all that we call lives and souls, lie dreaming, dreaming, still; tossing like slumberers in their beds; the ever-rolling waves but made so by their restlessness.

To any meditative Magian rover, this serene Pacific, once beheld, must ever after be the sea of his adoption. It rolls the midmost waters of the world, the Indian ocean and Atlantic being but its arms. The same waves wash the moles of the new-built Californian towns, but yesterday planted by the recentest race of men, and lave the faded but still gorgeous skirts of Asiatic lands, older than Abraham; while all between float milky-ways of coral isles, and low-lying, endless, unknown Archipelagoes, and impenetrable Japans. Thus this mysterious, divine Pacific zones the world's whole bulk about; makes all coasts one bay to it; seems the tide-beating heart of earth. Lifted by those eternal swells, you needs must own the seductive god, bowing your head to Pan.

But few thoughts of Pan stirred Ahab's brain, as standing like an iron statue at his accustomed place beside the mizen rigging, with one nostril he unthinkingly snuffed the sugary musk from the Bashee isles (in whose sweet woods mild lovers must be walking), and with the other consciously inhaled the salt breath of the new found sea; that sea in which the hated White Whale must even then be swimming. Launched at length upon these almost final waters, and gliding towards the Japanese cruising-ground, the old man's purpose intensified itself. His firm lips met like the lips of a vice; the Delta of his forehead's veins swelled like overladen brooks; in his very sleep, his ringing cry ran through the vaulted hull, "Stern all! the White Whale spouts thick blood!"

Chapter 112

THE BLACKSMITH

AVAILING HIMSELF of the mild, summer-cool weather that now reigned in these latitudes, and in preparation for the peculiarly active pursuits shortly to be anticipated, Perth, the begrimed, blistered old blacksmith, had not removed his portable forge to the hold again, after concluding his contributory work for Ahab's leg, but still retained it on deck, fast lashed to ringbolts by the foremast; being now almost incessantly invoked by the headsmen, and harpooneers, and bowsmen to do some little job for them; altering, or repairing, or new shaping their various weapons and boat furniture. Often he would be surrounded by an eager circle, all waiting to be served; holding boat-spades, pike-heads, harpoons, and lances, and jealously watching his every sooty movement, as he toiled. Nevertheless, this old man's was a patient hammer wielded by a patient arm. No murmur, no impatience, no petulance did come from him. Silent, slow, and solemn; bowing over still further his chronically broken back, he toiled away, as if toil were life itself, and the heavy beating of his hammer the heavy beating of his heart. And so it was.—Most miserable!

A peculiar walk in this old man, a certain slight but painful appearing yawing in his gait, had at an early period of the voyage excited the curiosity of the mariners. And to the importunity of their persisted questionings he had finally given in; and so it came to pass that every one now knew the shameful story of his wretched fate.

Belated, and not innocently, one bitter winter's midnight, on the road running between two country towns, the blacksmith half-stupidly felt the deadly numbness stealing over him, and sought refuge in a leaning, dilapidated barn. The issue was, the loss of the extremities of both feet. Out of this revelation, part by part, at last came out the four acts of the gladness, and the one long, and as yet uncatastrophied fifth act of the grief of his life's drama.

He was an old man, who, at the age of nearly sixty, had postponedly encountered that thing in sorrow's technicals called ruin. He had been an artisan of famed excellence, and with plenty to do; owned a house and garden; embraced a youthful, daughter-like, loving wife, and three blithe, ruddy children; every Sunday went to a cheerful-looking church, planted in a grove. But one night, under cover of darkness, and further concealed in a most cunning disguisement, a desperate burglar slid into his happy home, and robbed them all of everything. And darker yet to tell, the blacksmith himself did ignorantly conduct this burglar into his family's heart. It was the Bottle Conjuror! Upon the opening of that fatal cork, forth flew the fiend, and shrivelled up his home. Now, for prudent, most wise, and economic reasons, the blacksmith's shop was in the basement of his dwelling, but with a separate entrance to it; so that always had the young and loving healthy wife listened with no unhappy nervousness, but with vigorous pleasure, to the stout ringing of her young-armed old husband's hammer; whose reverberations, muffled by passing through the floors and walls, came up to her, not unsweetly, in her nursery; and so, to stout Labor's iron lullaby, the blacksmith's infants were rocked to slumber.

Oh, woe on woe! Oh, Death, why canst thou not sometimes be timely? Hadst thou taken this old blacksmith to thyself ere his full ruin came upon him, then had the young widow had a delicious grief, and her orphans a truly venerable, legendary sire to dream of in their after years; and all of them a care-killing competency. But Death plucked down some virtuous elder brother, on whose whistling daily toil solely hung the responsibilities of some other family, and left the worse than useless old man standing, till the hideous rot of life should make him easier to harvest.

Why tell the whole? The blows of the basement hammer every day grew more and more between; and each blow every day grew fainter than the last; the wife sat frozen at the window, with tearless eyes, glitteringly gazing into the weeping faces of her children; the bellows fell; the forge choked up with cinders; the house was sold; the mother dived down into the long church-yard grass; her children twice followed her thither; and the houseless, familyless old man staggered off a vagabond in crape; his every woe unreverenced; his grey head a scorn to flaxen curls!

Death seems the only desirable sequel for a career like this; but Death is only a launching into the region of the strange Untried; it is but the first salutation to the possibilities of the immense Remote, the Wild, the Watery, the Unshored; therefore, to the death-longing eyes of such men, who still have left in them some interior compunctions against suicide, does the all-contributed and all-receptive ocean alluringly spread forth his whole plain of unimaginable, taking terrors, and wonderful, new-life adventures; and from the hearts of infinite Pacifics, the thousand mermaids sing to them— "Come hither, broken-hearted; here is another life without the guilt of intermediate death; here are wonders supernatural, without dying for them. Come hither! bury thyself in a life which, to your now equally abhorred and abhorring, landed world, is more oblivious than death. Come hither! put up *thy* grave-stone, too, within the churchyard, and come hither, till we marry thee!"

Hearkening to these voices, East and West, by early sunrise, and by fall of eve, the blacksmith's soul responded, Aye, I come! And so Perth went a-whaling.

Chapter 113

THE FORGE

WITH MATTED BEARD, and swathed in a bristling
shark-skin apron, about mid-day, Perth was standing
between his forge and anvil, the latter placed upon an iron-
wood log, with one hand holding a pike-head in the coals,
and with the other at his forge's lungs, when Captain Ahab
came along, carrying in his hand a small rusty-looking leathern bag. While yet a little distance from the forge, moody
Ahab paused; till at last, Perth, withdrawing his iron from the
fire, began hammering it upon the anvil—the red mass sending off the sparks in thick hovering flights, some of which
flew close to Ahab.

"Are these thy Mother Carey's chickens, Perth? they are
always flying in thy wake; birds of good omen, too, but not
to all;—look here, they burn; but thou—thou liv'st among
them without a scorch."

"Because I am scorched all over, Captain Ahab," answered
Perth, resting for a moment on his hammer; "I am past
scorching; not easily can'st thou scorch a scar."

"Well, well; no more. Thy shrunk voice sounds too calmly,
sanely woful to me. In no Paradise myself, I am impatient of
all misery in others that is not mad. Thou should'st go mad,
blacksmith; say, why dost thou not go mad? How can'st thou
endure without being mad? Do the heavens yet hate thee,
that thou can'st not go mad?—What wert thou making
there?"

"Welding an old pike-head, sir; there were seams and dents
in it."

"And can'st thou make it all smooth again, blacksmith,
after such hard usage as it had?"

"I think so, sir."

"And I suppose thou can'st smoothe almost any seams and
dents; never mind how hard the metal, blacksmith?"

"Aye, sir, I think I can; all seams and dents but one."

"Look ye here, then," cried Ahab, passionately advancing,

and leaning with both hands on Perth's shoulders; "look ye here—*here*—can ye smoothe out a seam like this, blacksmith," sweeping one hand across his ribbed brow; "if thou could'st, blacksmith, glad enough would I lay my head upon thy anvil, and feel thy heaviest hammer between my eyes. Answer! Can'st thou smoothe this seam?"

"Oh! that is the one, sir! Said I not all seams and dents but one?"

"Aye, blacksmith, it is the one; aye, man, it is unsmoothable; for though thou only see'st it here in my flesh, it has worked down into the bone of my skull—*that* is all wrinkles! But, away with child's play; no more gaffs and pikes to-day. Look ye here!" jingling the leathern bag, as if it were full of gold coins. "I, too, want a harpoon made; one that a thousand yoke of fiends could not part, Perth; something that will stick in a whale like his own fin-bone. There's the stuff," flinging the pouch upon the anvil. "Look ye, blacksmith, these are the gathered nail-stubbs of the steel shoes of racing horses."

"Horse-shoe stubbs, sir? Why, Captain Ahab, thou hast here, then, the best and stubbornest stuff we blacksmiths ever work."

"I know it, old man; these stubbs will weld together like glue from the melted bones of murderers. Quick! forge me the harpoon. And forge me first, twelve rods for its shank; then wind, and twist, and hammer these twelve together like the yarns and strands of a tow-line. Quick! I'll blow the fire."

When at last the twelve rods were made, Ahab tried them, one by one, by spiralling them, with his own hand, round a long, heavy iron bolt. "A flaw!" rejecting the last one. "Work that over again, Perth."

This done, Perth was about to begin welding the twelve into one, when Ahab stayed his hand, and said he would weld his own iron. As, then, with regular, gasping hems, he hammered on the anvil, Perth passing to him the glowing rods, one after the other, and the hard pressed forge shooting up its intense straight flame, the Parsee passed silently, and bowing over his head towards the fire, seemed invoking some curse or some blessing on the toil. But, as Ahab looked up, he slid aside.

"What's that bunch of lucifers dodging about there for?"

muttered Stubb, looking on from the forecastle. "That Parsee smells fire like a fusee; and smells of it himself, like a hot musket's powder-pan."

At last the shank, in one complete rod, received its final heat; and as Perth, to temper it, plunged it all hissing into the cask of water near by, the scalding steam shot up into Ahab's bent face.

"Would'st thou brand me, Perth?" wincing for a moment with the pain; "have I been but forging my own branding-iron, then?"

"Pray God, not that; yet I fear something, Captain Ahab. Is not this harpoon for the White Whale?"

"For the white fiend! But now for the barbs; thou must make them thyself, man. Here are my razors—the best of steel; here, and make the barbs sharp as the needle-sleet of the Icy Sea."

For a moment, the old blacksmith eyed the razors as though he would fain not use them.

"Take them, man, I have no need for them; for I now neither shave, sup, nor pray till——but here—to work!"

Fashioned at last into an arrowy shape, and welded by Perth to the shank, the steel soon pointed the end of the iron; and as the blacksmith was about giving the barbs their final heat, prior to tempering them, he cried to Ahab to place the water-cask near.

"No, no—no water for that; I want it of the true death-temper. Ahoy, there! Tashtego, Queequeg, Daggoo! What say ye, pagans! Will ye give me as much blood as will cover this barb?" holding it high up. A cluster of dark nods replied, Yes. Three punctures were made in the heathen flesh, and the White Whale's barbs were then tempered.

"Ego non baptizo te in nomine patris, sed in nomine dia-boli!" deliriously howled Ahab, as the malignant iron scorch-ingly devoured the baptismal blood.

Now, mustering the spare poles from below, and selecting one of hickory, with the bark still investing it, Ahab fitted the end to the socket of the iron. A coil of new tow-line was then unwound, and some fathoms of it taken to the windlass, and stretched to a great tension. Pressing his foot upon it, till the rope hummed like a harp-string, then eagerly bending over it, and seeing no strandings, Ahab exclaimed, "Good! and now for the seizings."

At one extremity the rope was unstranded, and the separate spread yarns were all braided and woven round the socket of the harpoon; the pole was then driven hard up into the socket; from the lower end the rope was traced half way along the pole's length, and firmly secured so, with intertwistings of twine. This done, pole, iron, and rope—like the Three Fates—remained inseparable, and Ahab moodily stalked away with the weapon; the sound of his ivory leg, and the sound of the hickory pole, both hollowly ringing along every plank. But ere he entered his cabin, a light, unnatural, half-bantering, yet most piteous sound was heard. Oh, Pip! thy wretched laugh, thy idle but unresting eye; all thy strange mummeries not unmeaningly blended with the black tragedy of the melancholy ship, and mocked it!

Chapter 114

THE GILDER

PENETRATING further and further into the heart of the Japanese cruising ground, the Pequod was soon all astir in the fishery. Often, in mild, pleasant weather, for twelve, fifteen, eighteen, and twenty hours on the stretch, they were engaged in the boats, steadily pulling, or sailing, or paddling after the whales, or for an interlude of sixty or seventy minutes calmly awaiting their uprising; though with but small success for their pains.

At such times, under an abated sun; afloat all day upon smooth, slow heaving swells; seated in his boat, light as a birch canoe; and so sociably mixing with the soft waves themselves, that like hearth-stone cats they purr against the gunwale; these are the times of dreamy quietude, when beholding the tranquil beauty and brilliancy of the ocean's skin, one forgets the tiger heart that pants beneath it; and would not willingly remember, that this velvet paw but conceals a remorseless fang.

These are the times, when in his whale-boat the rover softly feels a certain filial, confident, land-like feeling towards the sea; that he regards it as so much flowery earth; and the distant ship revealing only the tops of her masts, seems struggling forward, not through high rolling waves, but through the tall grass of a rolling prairie: as when the western emigrants' horses only show their erected ears, while their hidden bodies widely wade through the amazing verdure.

The long-drawn virgin vales; the mild blue hill-sides; as over these there steals the hush, the hum; you almost swear that play-wearied children lie sleeping in these solitudes, in some glad May-time, when the flowers of the woods are plucked. And all this mixes with your most mystic mood; so that fact and fancy, half-way meeting, interpenetrate, and form one seamless whole.

Nor did such soothing scenes, however temporary, fail of at least as temporary an effect on Ahab. But if these secret golden keys did seem to open in him his own secret golden treasuries, yet did his breath upon them prove but tarnishing.

"Oh, grassy glades! oh, ever vernal endless landscapes in the soul; in ye,—though long parched by the dead drought of the earthy life,—in ye, men yet may roll, like young horses in new morning clover; and for some few fleeting moments, feel the cool dew of the life immortal on them. Would to God these blessed calms would last. But the mingled, mingling threads of life are woven by warp and woof: calms crossed by storms, a storm for every calm. There is no steady unretracing progress in this life; we do not advance through fixed gradations, and at the last one pause:—through infancy's unconscious spell, boyhood's thoughtless faith, adolescence' doubt (the common doom), then scepticism, then disbelief, resting at last in manhood's pondering repose of If. But once gone through, we trace the round again; and are infants, boys, and men, and Ifs eternally. Where lies the final harbor, whence we unmoor no more? In what rapt ether sails the world, of which the weariest will never weary? Where is the foundling's father hidden? Our souls are like those orphans whose unwedded mothers die in bearing them: the secret of our paternity lies in their grave, and we must there to learn it."

And that same day, too, gazing far down from his boat's side into that same golden sea, Starbuck lowly murmured:—

"Loveliness unfathomable, as ever lover saw in his young bride's eye!—Tell me not of thy teeth-tiered sharks, and thy kidnapping cannibal ways. Let faith oust fact; let fancy oust memory; I look deep down and do believe."

And Stubb, fish-like, with sparkling scales, leaped up in that same golden light:—

"I am Stubb, and Stubb has his history; but here Stubb takes oaths that he has always been jolly!"

Chapter 115

THE PEQUOD MEETS THE BACHELOR

AND JOLLY ENOUGH were the sights and the sounds that came bearing down before the wind, some few weeks after Ahab's harpoon had been welded.

It was a Nantucket ship, the Bachelor, which had just wedged in her last cask of oil, and bolted down her bursting hatches; and now, in glad holiday apparel, was joyously, though somewhat vain-gloriously, sailing round among the widely-separated ships on the ground, previous to pointing her prow for home.

The three men at her mast-heads wore long streamers of narrow red bunting at their hats; from the stern, a whale-boat was suspended, bottom up; and hanging captive from the bowsprit was seen the long lower jaw of the last whale they had slain. Signals, ensigns, and jacks of all colors were flying from her rigging, on every side. Sideways lashed in each of her three basketed tops were two barrels of sperm; above which, in her top-mast cross-trees, you saw slender breakers of the same precious fluid; and nailed to her main truck was a brazen lamp.

As was afterwards learned, the Bachelor had met with the most surprising success; all the more wonderful, for that while cruising in the same seas numerous other vessels had gone entire months without securing a single fish. Not only had barrels of beef and bread been given away to make room for the far more valuable sperm, but additional supplemental casks had been bartered for, from the ships she had met; and these were stowed along the deck, and in the captain's and officers' state-rooms. Even the cabin table itself had been knocked into kindling-wood; and the cabin mess dined off the broad head of an oil-butt, lashed down to the floor for a centrepiece. In the forecastle, the sailors had actually caulked and pitched their chests, and filled them; it was humorously added, that the cook had clapped a head on his largest boiler, and filled it; that the steward had plugged his spare coffee-pot and filled it; that the harpooneers had headed the sockets of their irons and filled them; that indeed everything was filled with sperm, except the captain's pantaloons pockets, and those he reserved to thrust his hands into, in self-complacent testimony of his entire satisfaction.

As this glad ship of good luck bore down upon the moody Pequod, the barbarian sound of enormous drums came from her forecastle; and drawing still nearer, a crowd of her men were seen standing round her huge try-pots, which, covered with the parchment-like *poke* or stomach skin of the black fish, gave forth a loud roar to every stroke of the clenched hands of the crew. On the quarter-deck, the mates and har-pooneers were dancing with the olive-hued girls who had eloped with them from the Polynesian Isles; while suspended in an ornamented boat, firmly secured aloft between the fore-mast and mainmast, three Long Island negroes, with glitter-ing fiddle-bows of whale ivory, were presiding over the hilarious jig. Meanwhile, others of the ship's company were tumultuously busy at the masonry of the try-works, from which the huge pots had been removed. You would have al-most thought they were pulling down the cursed Bastile, such wild cries they raised, as the now useless brick and mortar were being hurled into the sea.

Lord and master over all this scene, the captain stood erect on the ship's elevated quarter-deck, so that the whole rejoic-ing drama was full before him, and seemed merely contrived for his own individual diversion.

And Ahab, he too was standing on his quarter-deck, shaggy and black, with a stubborn gloom; and as the two ships crossed each other's wakes—one all jubilations for things passed, the other all forebodings as to things to come—their two captains in themselves impersonated the whole striking contrast of the scene.

"Come aboard, come aboard!" cried the gay Bachelor's commander, lifting a glass and a bottle in the air.

"Hast seen the White Whale?" gritted Ahab in reply.

"No; only heard of him; but don't believe in him at all," said the other good-humoredly. "Come aboard!"

"Thou art too damned jolly. Sail on. Hast lost any men?"

"Not enough to speak of—two islanders, that's all;—but

come aboard, old hearty, come along. I'll soon take that black from your brow. Come along, will ye (merry's the play); a full ship and homeward-bound."

"How wondrous familiar is a fool!" muttered Ahab; then aloud, "Thou art a full ship and homeward bound, thou sayst; well, then, call me an empty ship, and outward-bound. So go thy ways, and I will mine. Forward there! Set all sail, and keep her to the wind!"

And thus, while the one ship went cheerily before the breeze, the other stubbornly fought against it; and so the two vessels parted; the crew of the Pequod looking with grave, lingering glances towards the receding Bachelor; but the Bachelor's men never heeding their gaze for the lively revelry they were in. And as Ahab, leaning over the taffrail, eyed the homeward-bound craft, he took from his pocket a small vial of sand, and then looking from the ship to the vial, seemed thereby bringing two remote associations together, for that vial was filled with Nantucket soundings.

Chapter 116

THE DYING WHALE

NOT SELDOM in this life, when, on the right side, for-tune's favorites sail close by us, we, though all adroop before, catch somewhat of the rushing breeze, and joyfully feel our bagging sails fill out. So seemed it with the Pequod. For next day after encountering the gay Bachelor, whales were seen and four were slain; and one of them by Ahab.

It was far down the afternoon; and when all the spearings of the crimson fight were done: and floating in the lovely sunset sea and sky, sun and whale both stilly died together; then, such a sweetness and such plaintiveness, such inwreath-ing orisons curled up in that rosy air, that it almost seemed as if far over from the deep green convent valleys of the Ma-nilla isles, the Spanish land-breeze, wantonly turned sailor, had gone to sea, freighted with these vesper hymns.

Soothed again, but only soothed to deeper gloom, Ahab, who had sterned off from the whale, sat intently watching his final wanings from the now tranquil boat. For that strange spectacle observable in all sperm whales dying—the turning sunwards of the head, and so expiring—that strange specta-cle, beheld of such a placid evening, somehow to Ahab con-veyed a wondrousness unknown before.

"He turns and turns him to it,—how slowly, but how steadfastly, his homage-rendering and invoking brow, with his last dying motions. He too worships fire; most faithful, broad, baronial vassal of the sun!—Oh that these too-favor-ing eyes should see these too-favoring sights. Look! here, far water-locked; beyond all hum of human weal or woe; in these most candid and impartial seas; where to traditions no rocks furnish tablets; where for long Chinese ages, the billows have still rolled on speechless and unspoken to, as stars that shine upon the Niger's unknown source; here, too, life dies sun-wards full of faith; but see! no sooner dead, than death whirls round the corpse, and it heads some other way.—

"Oh, thou dark Hindoo half of nature, who of drowned

1322

bones hast builded thy separate throne somewhere in the heart of these unverdured seas; thou art an infidel, thou queen, and too truly speakest to me in the wide-slaughtering Typhoon, and the hushed burial of its after calm. Nor has this thy whale sunwards turned his dying head, and then gone round again, without a lesson to me.

"Oh, trebly hooped and welded hip of power! Oh, high aspiring, rainbowed jet!—that one striveth, this one jetteth all in vain! In vain, oh whale, dost thou seek intercedings with yon all-quickening sun, that only calls forth life, but gives it not again. Yet dost thou, darker half, rock me with a prouder, if a darker faith. All thy unnamable imminglings float beneath me here; I am buoyed by breaths of once living things, exhaled as air, but water now.

"Then hail, for ever hail, O sea, in whose eternal tossings the wild fowl finds his only rest. Born of earth, yet suckled by the sea; though hill and valley mothered me, ye billows are my foster-brothers!"

Chapter 117

THE WHALE WATCH

THE FOUR WHALES slain that evening had died wide apart; one, far to windward; one, less distant, to leeward; one ahead; one astern. These last three were brought alongside ere nightfall; but the windward one could not be reached till morning; and the boat that had killed it lay by its side all night; and that boat was Ahab's.

The waif-pole was thrust upright into the dead whale's spout-hole; and the lantern hanging from its top, cast a troubled flickering glare upon the black, glossy back, and far out upon the midnight waves, which gently chafed the whale's broad flank, like soft surf upon a beach.

Ahab and all his boat's crew seemed asleep but the Parsee; who crouching in the bow, sat watching the sharks, that spectrally played round the whale, and tapped the light cedar planks with their tails. A sound like the moaning in squadrons over Asphaltites of unforgiven ghosts of Gomorrah, ran shuddering through the air.

Started from his slumbers, Ahab, face to face, saw the Parsee; and hooped round by the gloom of the night they seemed the last men in a flooded world. "I have dreamed it again," said he.

"Of the hearses? Have I not said, old man, that neither hearse nor coffin can be thine?"

"And who are hearsed that die on the sea?"

"But I said, old man, that ere thou couldst die on this voyage, two hearses must verily be seen by thee on the sea; the first not made by mortal hands; and the visible wood of the last one must be grown in America."

"Aye, aye! a strange sight that, Parsee:—a hearse and its plumes floating over the ocean with the waves for the pallbearers. Ha! Such a sight we shall not soon see."

"Believe it or not, thou canst not die till it be seen, old man."

"And what was that saying about thyself?"

"Though it come to the last, I shall still go before thee thy pilot."

"And when thou art so gone before—if that ever befall—then ere I can follow, thou must still appear to me, to pilot me still?—Was it not so? Well, then, did I believe all ye say, oh my pilot! I have here two pledges that I shall yet slay Moby Dick and survive it."

"Take another pledge, old man," said the Parsee, as his eyes lighted up like fire-flies in the gloom—"Hemp only can kill thee."

"The gallows, ye mean.—I am immortal then, on land and on sea," cried Ahab, with a laugh of derision;—"Immortal on land and on sea!"

Both were silent again, as one man. The grey dawn came on, and the slumbering crew arose from the boat's bottom, and ere noon the dead whale was brought to the ship.

Chapter 118

THE QUADRANT

THE SEASON for the Line at length drew near; and every day when Ahab, coming from his cabin, cast his eyes aloft, the vigilant helmsman would ostentatiously handle his spokes, and the eager mariners quickly run to the braces, and would stand there with all their eyes centrally fixed on the nailed doubloon; impatient for the order to point the ship's prow for the equator. In good time the order came. It was hard upon high noon; and Ahab, seated in the bows of his high-hoisted boat, was about taking his wonted daily observation of the sun to determine his latitude.

Now, sometimes, in that Japanese sea, the days in summer are as freshets of effulgences. That unblinkingly vivid Japanese sun seems the blazing focus of the glassy ocean's immeasurable burning-glass. The sky looks lacquered; clouds there are none; the horizon floats; and this nakedness of unrelieved radiance is as the insufferable splendors of God's throne. Well that Ahab's quadrant was furnished with colored glasses, through which to take sight of that solar fire. So, swinging his seated form to the roll of the ship, and with his astrological-looking instrument placed to his eye, he remained in that posture for some moments to catch the precise instant when the sun should gain its precise meridian. Meantime while his whole attention was absorbed, the Parsee was kneeling beneath him on the ship's deck, and with face thrown up like Ahab's, was eyeing the same sun with him; only the lids of his eyes half hooded their orbs, and his wild face was subdued to an earthly passionlessness. At length the desired observation was taken; and with his pencil upon his ivory leg, Ahab soon calculated what his latitude must be at that precise instant. Then falling into a moment's revery, he again looked up towards the sun and murmured to himself: "Thou seamark! thou high and mighty Pilot! thou tellest me truly where I *am*—but canst thou cast the least hint where I *shall* be? Or canst thou tell where some other thing besides me is this moment living? Where is Moby Dick? This instant thou must be eyeing him. These eyes of mine look into the very eye that is even now beholding him; aye, and into the eye that is even now equally beholding the objects on the unknown, thither side of thee, thou sun!"

Then gazing at his quadrant, and handling, one after the other, its numerous cabalistical contrivances, he pondered again, and muttered: "Foolish toy! babies' plaything of haughty Admirals, and Commodores, and Captains; the world brags of thee, of thy cunning and might; but what after all canst thou do, but tell the poor, pitiful point, where thou thyself happenest to be on this wide planet, and the hand that holds thee: no! not one jot more! Thou canst not tell where one drop of water or one grain of sand will be to-morrow noon; and yet with thy impotence thou insultest the sun! Science! Curse thee, thou vain toy; and cursed be all the things that cast man's eyes aloft to that heaven, whose live vividness but scorches him, as these old eyes are even now scorched with thy light, O sun! Level by nature to this earth's horizon are the glances of man's eyes; not shot from the crown of his head, as if God had meant him to gaze on his firmament. Curse thee, thou quadrant!" dashing it to the deck, "no longer will I guide my earthly way by thee; the level ship's compass, and the level dead-reckoning, by log and by line; *these* shall conduct me, and show me my place on the sea. Aye," lighting from the boat to the deck, "thus I trample on thee, thou paltry thing that feebly pointest on high; thus I split and destroy thee!"

As the frantic old man thus spoke and thus trampled with his live and dead feet, a sneering triumph that seemed meant for Ahab, and a fatalistic despair that seemed meant for himself—these passed over the mute, motionless Parsee's face. Unobserved he rose and glided away; while, awestruck by the aspect of their commander, the seamen clustered together on the forecastle, till Ahab, troubledly pacing the deck, shouted out—"To the braces! Up helm!—square in!"

In an instant the yards swung round; and as the ship half-wheeled upon her heel, her three firm-seated graceful masts erectly poised upon her long, ribbed hull, seemed as the three Horatii pirouetting on one sufficient steed.

Standing between the knight-heads, Starbuck watched the Pequod's tumultuous way, and Ahab's also, as he went lurching along the deck.

"I have sat before the dense coal fire and watched it all aglow, full of its tormented flaming life; and I have seen it wane at last, down, down, to dumbest dust. Old man of oceans! of all this fiery life of thine, what will at length remain but one little heap of ashes!"

"Aye," cried Stubb, "but sea-coal ashes—mind ye that, Mr. Starbuck—sea-coal, not your common charcoal. Well, well; I heard Ahab mutter, 'Here some one thrusts these cards into these old hands of mine; swears that I must play them, and no others.' And damn me, Ahab, but thou actest right; live in the game, and die in it!"

Chapter 119

The Candles

WARMEST CLIMES but nurse the cruellest fangs: the tiger of Bengal crouches in spiced groves of ceaseless verdure. Skies the most effulgent but basket the deadliest thunders: gorgeous Cuba knows tornadoes that never swept tame northern lands. So, too, it is, that in these resplendent Japanese seas the mariner encounters the direst of all storms, the Typhoon. It will sometimes burst from out that cloudless sky, like an exploding bomb upon a dazed and sleepy town.

Towards evening of that day, the Pequod was torn of her canvas, and bare-poled was left to fight a Typhoon which had struck her directly ahead. When darkness came on, sky and sea roared and split with the thunder, and blazed with the lightning, that showed the disabled masts fluttering here and there with the rags which the first fury of the tempest had left for its after sport.

Holding by a shroud, Starbuck was standing on the quarter-deck; at every flash of the lightning glancing aloft, to see what additional disaster might have befallen the intricate hamper there; while Stubb and Flask were directing the men in the higher hoisting and firmer lashing of the boats. But all their pains seemed naught. Though lifted to the very top of the cranes, the windward quarter boat (Ahab's) did not escape. A great rolling sea, dashing high up against the reeling ship's high tetering side, stove in the boat's bottom at the stern, and left it again, all dripping through like a sieve.

"Bad work, bad work! Mr. Starbuck," said Stubb, regarding the wreck, "but the sea will have its way. Stubb, for one, can't fight it. You see, Mr. Starbuck, a wave has such a great long start before it leaps, all round the world it runs, and then comes the spring! But as for me, all the start I have to meet it, is just across the deck here. But never mind; it's all in fun: so the old song says;"— *(sings.)*

> Oh! jolly is the gale,
> And a joker is the whale,
> A' flourishin' his tail,—
Such a funny, sporty, gamy, jesty, joky, hoky-poky lad, is
the Ocean, oh!

> The scud all a flyin',
> That's his flip only foamin';
> When he stirs in the spicin',—
Such a funny, sporty, gamy, jesty, joky, hoky-poky lad, is
the Ocean, oh!

> Thunder splits the ships,
> But he only smacks his lips,
> A tastin' of this flip,—
Such a funny, sporty, gamy, jesty, joky, hoky-poky lad, is
the Ocean, oh!

"Avast Stubb," cried Starbuck, "let the Typhoon sing, and
strike his harp here in our rigging; but if thou art a brave
man thou wilt hold thy peace."

"But I am not a brave man; never said I was a brave man;
I am a coward; and I sing to keep up my spirits. And I tell
you what it is, Mr. Starbuck, there's no way to stop my singing in this world but to cut my throat. And when that's done,
ten to one I sing ye the doxology for a wind-up."

"Madman! look through my eyes if thou hast none of thine
own."

"What! how can you see better of a dark night than anybody else, never mind how foolish?"

"Here!" cried Starbuck, seizing Stubb by the shoulder, and
pointing his hand towards the weather bow, "markest thou
not that the gale comes from the eastward, the very course
Ahab is to run for Moby Dick? the very course he swung to
this day noon? now mark his boat there; where is that stove?
In the stern-sheets, man; where he is wont to stand—his
stand-point is stove, man! Now jump overboard, and sing
away, if thou must!"

"I don't half understand ye: what's in the wind?"

"Yes, yes, round the Cape of Good Hope is the shortest

way to Nantucket," soliloquized Starbuck suddenly, heedless of Stubb's question. "The gale that now hammers at us to stave us, we can turn it into a fair wind that will drive us towards home. Yonder, to windward, all is blackness of doom; but to leeward, homeward—I see it lightens up there; but not with the lightning."

At that moment in one of the intervals of profound darkness, following the flashes, a voice was heard at his side; and almost at the same instant a volley of thunder peals rolled overhead.

"Who's there?"

"Old Thunder!" said Ahab, groping his way along the bulwarks to his pivot-hole; but suddenly finding his path made plain to him by elbowed lances of fire.

Now, as the lightning rod to a spire on shore is intended to carry off the perilous fluid into the soil; so the kindred rod which at sea some ships carry to each mast, is intended to conduct it into the water. But as this conductor must descend to considerable depth, that its end may avoid all contact with the hull; and as moreover, if kept constantly towing there, it would be liable to many mishaps, besides interfering not a little with some of the rigging, and more or less impeding the vessel's way in the water; because of all this, the lower parts of a ship's lightning-rods are not always overboard; but are generally made in long slender links, so as to be the more readily hauled up into the chains outside, or thrown down into the sea, as occasion may require.

"The rods! the rods!" cried Starbuck to the crew, suddenly admonished to vigilance by the vivid lightning that had just been darting flambeaux, to light Ahab to his post. "Are they overboard? drop them over, fore and aft. Quick!"

"Avast!" cried Ahab; "let's have fair play here, though we be the weaker side. Yet I'll contribute to raise rods on the Himmalehs and Andes, that all the world may be secured; but out on privileges! Let them be, sir."

"Look aloft!" cried Starbuck. "The corpusants! the corpusants!"

All the yard-arms were tipped with a pallid fire; and touched at each tri-pointed lightning-rod-end with three tapering white flames, each of the three tall masts was silently

burning in that sulphurous air, like three gigantic wax tapers
before an altar.

"Blast the boat! let it go!" cried Stubb at this instant, as a
swashing sea heaved up under his own little craft, so that its
gunwale violently jammed his hand, as he was passing a lashing. "Blast it!"—but slipping backward on the deck, his
uplifted eyes caught the flames; and immediately shifting his
tone, he cried—"The corpusants have mercy on us all!"

To sailors, oaths are household words; they will swear in
the trance of the calm, and in the teeth of the tempest; they
will imprecate curses from the topsail-yard-arms, when most
they teter over to a seething sea; but in all my voyagings,
seldom have I heard a common oath when God's burning
finger has been laid on the ship; when His "Mene, Mene,
Tekel, Upharsin" has been woven into the shrouds and the
cordage.

While this pallidness was burning aloft, few words were
heard from the enchanted crew; who in one thick cluster
stood on the forecastle, all their eyes gleaming in that pale
phosphorescence, like a far away constellation of stars. Relieved against the ghostly light, the gigantic jet negro, Daggoo, loomed up to thrice his real stature, and seemed the
black cloud from which the thunder had come. The parted
mouth of Tashtego revealed his shark-white teeth, which
strangely gleamed as if they too had been tipped by corpusants; while lit up by the preternatural light, Queequeg's tattooing burned like Satanic blue flames on his body.

The tableau all waned at last with the pallidness aloft; and
once more the Pequod and every soul on her decks were
wrapped in a pall. A moment or two passed, when Starbuck,
going forward, pushed against some one. It was Stubb.
"What thinkest thou now, man; I heard thy cry; it was not
the same in the song."

"No, no, it wasn't; I said the corpusants have mercy on us
all; and I hope they will, still. But do they only have mercy
on long faces?—have they no bowels for a laugh? And look
ye, Mr. Starbuck—but it's too dark to look. Hear me, then:
I take that mast-head flame we saw for a sign of good luck;
for those masts are rooted in a hold that is going to be chock
a' block with sperm-oil, d'ye see; and so, all that sperm will

work up into the masts, like sap in a tree. Yes, our three masts will yet be as three spermaceti candles—that's the good promise we saw."

At that moment Starbuck caught sight of Stubb's face slowly beginning to glimmer into sight. Glancing upwards, he cried: "See! see!" and once more the high tapering flames were beheld with what seemed redoubled supernaturalness in their pallor.

"The corpusants have mercy on us all," cried Stubb, again.

At the base of the mainmast, full beneath the doubloon and the flame, the Parsee was kneeling in Ahab's front, but with his head bowed away from him; while near by, from the arched and overhanging rigging, where they had just been engaged securing a spar, a number of the seamen, arrested by the glare, now cohered together, and hung pendulous, like a knot of numbed wasps from a drooping, orchard twig. In various enchanted attitudes, like the standing, or stepping, or running skeletons in Herculaneum, others remained rooted to the deck; but all their eyes upcast.

"Aye, aye, men!" cried Ahab. "Look up at it; mark it well; the white flame but lights the way to the White Whale! Hand me those main-mast links there; I would fain feel this pulse, and let mine beat against it; blood against fire! So."

Then turning—the last link held fast in his left hand, he put his foot upon the Parsee; and with fixed upward eye, and high-flung right arm, he stood erect before the lofty tri-pointed trinity of flames.

"Oh! thou clear spirit of clear fire, whom on these seas I as Persian once did worship, till in the sacramental act so burned by thee, that to this hour I bear the scar; I now know thee, thou clear spirit, and I now know that thy right worship is defiance. To neither love nor reverence wilt thou be kind; and e'en for hate thou canst but kill; and all are killed. No fearless fool now fronts thee. I own thy speechless, placeless power; but to the last gasp of my earthquake life will dispute its un-conditional, unintegral mastery in me. In the midst of the personified impersonal, a personality stands here. Though but a point at best; whencesoe'er I came; wheresoe'er I go; yet while I earthly live, the queenly personality lives in me, and feels her royal rights. But war is pain, and hate is woe. Come in thy lowest form of love, and I will kneel and kiss thee; but at thy highest, come as mere supernal power; and though thou launchest navies of full-freighted worlds, there's that in here that still remains indifferent. Oh, thou clear spirit, of thy fire thou madest me, and like a true child of fire, I breathe it back to thee."

(Sudden, repeated flashes of lightning; the nine flames leap lengthwise to thrice their previous height; Ahab, with the rest, closes his eyes, his right hand pressed hard upon them.)

"I own thy speechless, placeless power; said I not so? Nor was it wrung from me; nor do I now drop these links. Thou canst blind; but I can then grope. Thou canst consume; but I can then be ashes. Take the homage of these poor eyes, and shutter-hands. I would not take it. The lightning flashes through my skull; mine eye-balls ache and ache; my whole beaten brain seems as beheaded, and rolling on some stunning ground. Oh, oh! Yet blindfold, yet will I talk to thee. Light though thou be, thou leapest out of darkness; but I am darkness leaping out of light, leaping out of thee! The javelins cease; open eyes; see, or not? There burn the flames! Oh, thou magnanimous! now I do glory in my genealogy. But thou art but my fiery father; my sweet mother, I know not. Oh, cruel! what hast thou done with her? There lies my puzzle; but thine is greater. Thou knowest not how came ye, hence callest thyself unbegotten; certainly knowest not thy beginning, hence callest thyself unbegun. I know that of me, which thou knowest not of thyself, oh, thou omnipotent. There is some unsuffusing thing beyond thee, thou clear spirit, to whom all thy eternity is but time, all thy creativeness mechanical. Through thee, thy flaming self, my scorched eyes do dimly see it. Oh, thou foundling fire, thou hermit immemorial, thou too hast thy incommunicable riddle, thy unparticipated grief. Here again with haughty agony, I read my sire. Leap! leap up, and lick the sky! I leap with thee; I burn with thee; would fain be welded with thee; defyingly I worship thee!"

"The boat! the boat!" cried Starbuck, "look at thy boat, old man!"

Ahab's harpoon, the one forged at Perth's fire, remained firmly lashed in its conspicuous crotch, so that it projected beyond his whale-boat's bow; but the sea that had stove its bottom had caused the loose leather sheath to drop off; and from the keen steel barb there now came a levelled flame of pale, forked fire. As the silent harpoon burned there like a serpent's tongue, Starbuck grasped Ahab by the arm—"God, God is against thee, old man; forbear! t' is an ill voyage! ill begun, ill continued; let me square the yards, while we may, old man, and make a fair wind of it homewards, to go on a better voyage than this."

Overhearing Starbuck, the panic-stricken crew instantly ran to the braces—though not a sail was left aloft. For the moment all the aghast mate's thoughts seemed theirs; they raised a half mutinous cry. But dashing the rattling lightning links to the deck, and snatching the burning harpoon, Ahab waved it like a torch among them; swearing to transfix with it the first sailor that but cast loose a rope's end. Petrified by his aspect, and still more shrinking from the fiery dart that he held, the men fell back in dismay, and Ahab again spoke:—

"All your oaths to hunt the White Whale are as binding as mine; and heart, soul, and body, lungs and life, old Ahab is bound. And that ye may know to what tune this heart beats: look ye here; thus I blow out the last fear!" And with one blast of his breath he extinguished the flame.

As in the hurricane that sweeps the plain, men fly the neighborhood of some lone, gigantic elm, whose very height and strength but render it so much the more unsafe, because so much the more a mark for thunderbolts; so at those last words of Ahab's many of the mariners did run from him in a terror of dismay.

Chapter 120

The Deck towards the End of the First Night Watch

(Ahab standing by the helm. Starbuck approaching him.)

WE must send down the main-top-sail yard, sir. The band is working loose, and the lee lift is half-stranded. Shall I strike it, sir?"

"Strike nothing; lash it. If I had sky-sail poles, I'd sway them up now."

"Sir?—in God's name!—sir?"

"Well."

"The anchors are working, sir. Shall I get them inboard?"

"Strike nothing, and stir nothing, but lash everything. The wind rises, but it has not got up to my table-lands yet. Quick, and see to it.—By masts and keels! he takes me for the hunchbacked skipper of some coasting smack. Send down my main-top-sail yard! Ho, gluepots! Loftiest trucks were made for wildest winds, and this brain-truck of mine now sails amid the cloud-scud. Shall I strike that? Oh, none but cowards send down their brain-trucks in tempest time. What a hoo-roosh aloft there! I would e'en take it for sublime, did I not know that the colic is a noisy malady. Oh, take medicine, take medicine!"

Chapter 121

(Stubb and Flask mounted on them, and passing additional lashings over the anchors there hanging.)

NO, STUBB; you may pound that knot there as much as you please, but you will never pound into me what you were just now saying. And how long ago is it since you said the very contrary? Didn't you once say that whatever ship Ahab sails in, that ship should pay something extra on its insurance policy, just as though it were loaded with powder barrels aft and boxes of lucifers forward? Stop, now; didn't you say so?"

"Well, suppose I did? What then? I've part changed my flesh since that time, why not my mind? Besides, supposing we *are* loaded with powder barrels aft and lucifers forward; how the devil could the lucifers get afire in this drenching spray here? Why, my little man, you have pretty red hair, but you couldn't get afire now. Shake yourself; you're Aquarius, or the water-bearer, Flask; might fill pitchers at your coat collar. Don't you see, then, that for these extra risks the Marine Insurance companies have extra guarantees? Here are hydrants, Flask. But hark, again, and I'll answer ye the other thing. First take your leg off from the crown of the anchor here, though, so I can pass the rope; now listen. What's the mighty difference between holding a mast's lightning-rod in the storm, and standing close by a mast that hasn't got any lightning-rod at all in a storm? Don't you see, you timber-head, that no harm can come to the holder of the rod, unless the mast is first struck? What are you talking about, then? Not one ship in a hundred carries rods, and Ahab,—aye, man, and all of us,—were in no more danger then, in my poor opinion, than all the crews in ten thousand ships now sailing the seas. Why, you King-Post, you, I suppose you would have every man in the world go about with a small lightning-rod running up the corner of his hat, like a militia officer's skewered feather, and trailing behind like his sash. Why don't ye be sensible, Flask? it's easy to be sensible; why don't ye, then? any man with half an eye can be sensible."

"I don't know that, Stubb. You sometimes find it rather hard."

"Yes, when a fellow's soaked through, it's hard to be sensible, that's a fact. And I am about drenched with this spray. Never mind; catch the turn there, and pass it. Seems to me we are lashing down these anchors now as if they were never going to be used again. Tying these two anchors here, Flask, seems like tying a man's hands behind him. And what big generous hands they are, to be sure. These are your iron fists, hey? What a hold they have, too! I wonder, Flask, whether the world is anchored anywhere; if she is, she swings with an uncommon long cable, though. There, hammer that knot down, and we've done. So; next to touching land, lighting on deck is the most satisfactory. I say, just wring out my jacket skirts, will ye? Thank ye. They laugh at long-togs so, Flask; but seems to me, a long tailed coat ought always to be worn in all storms afloat. The tails tapering down that way, serve to carry off the water, d'ye see. Same with cocked hats; the cocks form gable-end eave-troughs, Flask. No more monkey-jackets and tarpaulins for me; I must mount a swallow-tail, and drive down a beaver; so. Halloa! whew! there goes my tarpaulin overboard; Lord, Lord, that the winds that come from heaven should be so unmannerly! This is a nasty night, lad."

Chapter 122

Midnight Aloft—Thunder and Lightning

(The Main-top-sail yard. —Tashtego passing new lashings around it.)

UM, UM, UM. Stop that thunder! Plenty too much thunder up here. What's the use of thunder? Um, um, um. We don't want thunder; we want rum; give us a glass of rum. Um, um, um!"

Chapter 123

THE MUSKET

D URING the most violent shocks of the Typhoon, the man at the Pequod's jaw-bone tiller had several times been reelingly hurled to the deck by its spasmodic motions, even though preventer tackles had been attached to it—for they were slack—because some play to the tiller was indispensable.

In a severe gale like this, while the ship is but a tossed shuttle-cock to the blast, it is by no means uncommon to see the needles in the compasses, at intervals, go round and round. It was thus with the Pequod's; at almost every shock the helmsman had not failed to notice the whirling velocity with which they revolved upon the cards; it is a sight that hardly any one can behold without some sort of unwonted emotion.

Some hours after midnight, the Typhoon abated so much, that through the strenuous exertions of Starbuck and Stubb—one engaged forward and the other aft—the shivered remnants of the jib and fore and main-top-sails were cut adrift from the spars, and went eddying away to leeward, like the feathers of an albatross, which sometimes are cast to the winds when that storm-tossed bird is on the wing.

The three corresponding new sails were now bent and reefed, and a storm-trysail was set further aft; so that the ship soon went through the water with some precision again; and the course—for the present, East-south-east—which he was to steer, if practicable, was once more given to the helmsman. For during the violence of the gale, he had only steered according to its vicissitudes. But as he was now bringing the ship as near her course as possible, watching the compass meanwhile, lo! a good sign! the wind seemed coming round astern; aye, the foul breeze became fair!

Instantly the yards were squared, to the lively song of *"Ho! the fair wind! oh-he-yo, cheerly, men!"* the crew singing for joy, that so promising an event should so soon have falsified the evil portents preceding it.

In compliance with the standing order of his commander—to report immediately, and at any one of the twenty-four hours, any decided change in the affairs of the deck,—Starbuck had no sooner trimmed the yards to the breeze—however reluctantly and gloomily,—than he mechanically went below to apprise Captain Ahab of the circumstance.

Ere knocking at his state-room, he involuntarily paused before it a moment. The cabin lamp—taking long swings this way and that—was burning fitfully, and casting fitful shadows upon the old man's bolted door,—a thin one, with fixed blinds inserted, in place of upper panels. The isolated subterraneousness of the cabin made a certain humming silence to reign there, though it was hooped round by all the roar of the elements. The loaded muskets in the rack were shiningly revealed, as they stood upright against the forward bulkhead. Starbuck was an honest, upright man; but out of Starbuck's heart, at that instant when he saw the muskets, there strangely evolved an evil thought; but so blent with its neutral or good accompaniments that for the instant he hardly knew it for itself.

"He would have shot me once," he murmured, "yes, there's the very musket that he pointed at me;—that one with the studded stock; let me touch it—lift it. Strange, that I, who have handled so many deadly lances, strange, that I should shake so now. Loaded? I must see. Aye, aye; and powder in the pan;—that's not good. Best spill it?—wait. I'll cure myself of this. I'll hold the musket boldly while I think.—I come to report a fair wind to him. But how fair? Fair for death and doom,—*that's* fair for Moby Dick. It's a fair wind that's only fair for that accursed fish.—The very tube he pointed at me!—the very one; *this* one—I hold it here; he would have killed me with the very thing I handle now.—Aye and he would fain kill all his crew. Does he not say he will not strike his spars to any gale? Has he not dashed his heavenly quadrant? and in these same perilous seas, gropes he not his way by mere dead reckoning of the error-abounding log? and in this very Typhoon, did he not swear that he would have no lightning-rods? But shall this crazed old man be tamely suffered to drag a whole ship's company down to doom with him?—Yes, it would make him the wilful murderer of thirty

men and more, if this ship come to any deadly harm; and come to deadly harm, my soul swears this ship will, if Ahab have his way. If, then, he were this instant—put aside, that crime would not be his. Ha! is he muttering in his sleep? Yes, just there,—in there, he's sleeping. Sleeping? aye, but still alive, and soon awake again. I can't withstand thee, then, old man. Not reasoning; not remonstrance; not entreaty wilt thou hearken to; all this thou scornest. Flat obedience to thy own flat commands, this is all thou breathest. Aye, and say'st the men have vow'd thy vow; say'st all of us are Ahabs. Great God forbid!—But is there no other way? no lawful way?— Make him a prisoner to be taken home? What! hope to wrest this old man's living power from his own living hands? Only a fool would try it. Say he were pinioned even; knotted all over with ropes and hawsers; chained down to ring-bolts on this cabin floor; he would be more hideous than a caged tiger, then. I could not endure the sight; could not possibly fly his howlings; all comfort, sleep itself, inestimable reason would leave me on the long intolerable voyage. What, then, remains? The land is hundreds of leagues away, and locked Japan the nearest. I stand alone here upon an open sea, with two oceans and a whole continent between me and law.— Aye, aye, 'tis so.—Is heaven a murderer when its lightning strikes a would-be murderer in his bed, tindering sheets and skin together?—And would I be a murderer, then, if"
————and slowly, stealthily, and half sideways looking, he placed the loaded musket's end against the door.

"On this level, Ahab's hammock swings within; his head this way. A touch, and Starbuck may survive to hug his wife and child again.—Oh Mary! Mary!—boy! boy! boy!— But if I wake thee not to death, old man, who can tell to what unsounded deeps Starbuck's body this day week may sink, with all the crew! Great God, where art thou? Shall I? shall I?————The wind has gone down and shifted, sir; the fore and main topsails are reefed and set; she heads her course."

"Stern all! Oh Moby Dick, I clutch thy heart at last!"

Such were the sounds that now came hurtling from out the old man's tormented sleep, as if Starbuck's voice had caused the long dumb dream to speak.

The yet levelled musket shook like a drunkard's arm against the panel; Starbuck seemed wrestling with an angel; but turning from the door, he placed the death-tube in its rack, and left the place.

"He's too sound asleep, Mr. Stubb; go thou down, and wake him, and tell him. I must see to the deck here. Thou know'st what to say."

Chapter 124

THE NEEDLE

NEXT MORNING the not-yet-subsided sea rolled in long slow billows of mighty bulk, and striving in the Pequod's gurgling track, pushed her on like giants' palms outspread. The strong, unstaggering breeze abounded so, that sky and air seemed vast outbellying sails; the whole world boomed before the wind. Muffled in the full morning light, the invisible sun was only known by the spread intensity of his place; where his bayonet rays moved on in stacks. Emblazonings, as of crowned Babylonian kings and queens, reigned over everything. The sea was as a crucible of molten gold, that bubblingly leaps with light and heat.

Long maintaining an enchanted silence, Ahab stood apart; and every time the tetering ship loweringly pitched down her bowsprit, he turned to eye the bright sun's rays produced ahead; and when she profoundly settled by the stern, he turned behind, and saw the sun's rearward place, and how the same yellow rays were blending with his undeviating wake.

"Ha, ha, my ship! thou mightest well be taken now for the sea-chariot of the sun. Ho, ho! all ye nations before my prow, I bring the sun to ye! Yoke on the further billows; hallo! a tandem, I drive the sea!"

But suddenly reined back by some counter thought, he hurried towards the helm, huskily demanding how the ship was heading.

"East-sou-east, sir," said the frightened steersman.

"Thou liest!" smiting him with his clenched fist. "Heading East at this hour in the morning, and the sun astern?"

Upon this every soul was confounded; for the phenomenon just then observed by Ahab had unaccountably escaped every one else; but its very blinding palpableness must have been the cause.

Thrusting his head half way into the binnacle, Ahab caught one glimpse of the compasses; his uplifted arm slowly fell; for a moment he almost seemed to stagger. Standing behind him

Starbuck looked, and lo! the two compasses pointed East, and the Pequod was as infallibly going West.

But ere the first wild alarm could get out abroad among the crew, the old man with a rigid laugh exclaimed, "I have it! It has happened before. Mr. Starbuck, last night's thunder turned our compasses—that's all. Thou hast before now heard of such a thing, I take it."

"Aye; but never before has it happened to me, sir," said the pale mate, gloomily.

Here, it must needs be said, that accidents like this have in more than one case occurred to ships in violent storms. The magnetic energy, as developed in the mariner's needle, is, as all know, essentially one with the electricity beheld in heaven; hence it is not to be much marvelled at, that such things should be. In instances where the lightning has actually struck the vessel, so as to smite down some of the spars and rigging, the effect upon the needle has at times been still more fatal; all its loadstone virtue being annihilated, so that the before magnetic steel was of no more use than an old wife's knitting needle. But in either case, the needle never again, of itself, recovers the original virtue thus marred or lost; and if the binnacle compasses be affected, the same fate reaches all the others that may be in the ship; even were the lowermost one inserted into the kelson.

Deliberately standing before the binnacle, and eyeing the transpointed compasses, the old man, with the sharp of his extended hand, now took the precise bearing of the sun, and satisfied that the needles were exactly inverted, shouted out his orders for the ship's course to be changed accordingly. The yards were braced hard up; and once more the Pequod thrust her undaunted bows into the opposing wind, for the supposed fair one had only been juggling her.

Meanwhile, whatever were his own secret thoughts, Starbuck said nothing, but quietly he issued all requisite orders; while Stubb and Flask—who in some small degree seemed then to be sharing his feelings—likewise unmurmuringly acquiesced. As for the men, though some of them lowly rumbled, their fear of Ahab was greater than their fear of Fate. But as ever before, the pagan harpooneers remained almost wholly unimpressed; or if impressed, it was only with a cer-

tain magnetism shot into their congenial hearts from inflexible Ahab's.

For a space the old man walked the deck in rolling reveries.
But chancing to slip with his ivory heel, he saw the crushed
copper sight-tubes of the quadrant he had the day before
dashed to the deck.

"Thou poor, proud heaven-gazer and sun's pilot! yesterday
I wrecked thee, and to-day the compasses would feign have
wrecked me. So, so. But Ahab is lord over the level loadstone
yet. Mr. Starbuck—a lance without the pole; a top-maul, and
the smallest of the sail-maker's needles. Quick!"

Accessory, perhaps, to the impulse dictating the thing he
was now about to do, were certain prudential motives, whose
object might have been to revive the spirits of his crew by a
stroke of his subtile skill, in a matter so wondrous as that of
the inverted compasses. Besides, the old man well knew that
to steer by transpointed needles, though clumsily practicable,
was not a thing to be passed over by superstitious sailors,
without some shudderings and evil portents.

"Men," said he, steadily turning upon the crew, as the mate
handed him the things he had demanded, "my men, the thunder turned old Ahab's needles; but out of this bit of steel
Ahab can make one of his own, that will point as true as any."

Abashed glances of servile wonder were exchanged by the
sailors, as this was said; and with fascinated eyes they awaited
whatever magic might follow. But Starbuck looked away.

With a blow from the top-maul Ahab knocked off the steel
head of the lance, and then handing to the mate the long iron
rod remaining, bade him hold it upright, without its touching
the deck. Then, with the maul, after repeatedly smiting the
upper end of this iron rod, he placed the blunted needle endwise on the top of it, and less strongly hammered that, several
times, the mate still holding the rod as before. Then going
through some small strange motions with it—whether indispensable to the magnetizing of the steel, or merely intended
to augment the awe of the crew, is uncertain—he called for
linen thread; and moving to the binnacle, slipped out the two
reversed needles there, and horizontally suspended the sail-
needle by its middle, over one of the compass-cards. At first,
the steel went round and round, quivering and vibrating at

either end; but at last it settled to its place, when Ahab, who had been intently watching for this result, stepped frankly back from the binnacle, and pointing his stretched arm towards it, exclaimed,—"Look ye, for yourselves, if Ahab be not lord of the level loadstone! The sun is East, and that compass swears it!"

One after another they peered in, for nothing but their own eyes could persuade such ignorance as theirs, and one after another they slunk away.

In his fiery eyes of scorn and triumph, you then saw Ahab in all his fatal pride.

Chapter 125

THE LOG AND LINE

WHILE NOW the fated Pequod had been so long afloat this voyage, the log and line had but very seldom been in use. Owing to a confident reliance upon other means of determining the vessel's place, some merchantmen, and many whalemen, especially when cruising, wholly neglect to heave the log; though at the same time, and frequently more for form's sake than anything else, regularly putting down upon the customary slate the course steered by the ship, as well as the presumed average rate of progression every hour. It had been thus with the Pequod. The wooden reel and angular log attached hung, long untouched, just beneath the railing of the after bulwarks. Rains and spray had damped it; sun and wind had warped it; all the elements had combined to rot a thing that hung so idly. But heedless of all this, his mood seized Ahab, as he happened to glance upon the reel, not many hours after the magnet scene, and he remembered how his quadrant was no more, and recalled his frantic oath about the level log and line. The ship was sailing plungingly; astern the billows rolled in riots.

"Forward, there! Heave the log!"

Two seamen came. The golden-hued Tahitian and the grizzly Manxman. "Take the reel, one of ye, I'll heave."

They went towards the extreme stern, on the ship's lee side, where the deck, with the oblique energy of the wind, was now almost dipping into the creamy, sidelong-rushing sea.

The Manxman took the reel, and holding it high up, by the projecting handle-ends of the spindle, round which the spool of line revolved, so stood with the angular log hanging downwards, till Ahab advanced to him.

Ahab stood before him, and was lightly unwinding some thirty or forty turns to form a preliminary hand-coil to toss overboard, when the old Manxman, who was intently eyeing both him and the line, made bold to speak.

"Sir, I mistrust it; this line looks far gone, long heat and wet have spoiled it."

"'Twill hold, old gentleman. Long heat and wet, have they spoiled thee? Thou seem'st to hold. Or, truer perhaps, life holds thee; not thou it."

"I hold the spool, sir. But just as my captain says. With these grey hairs of mine 'tis not worth while disputing, 'specially with a superior, who'll ne'er confess."

"What's that? There now's a patched professor in Queen Nature's granite-founded College; but methinks he's too subservient. Where wert thou born?"

"In the little rocky Isle of Man, sir."

"Excellent! Thou'st hit the world by that."

"I know not, sir, but I was born there."

"In the Isle of Man, hey? Well, the other way, it's good. Here's a man from Man; a man born in once independent Man, and now unmanned of Man; which is sucked in—by what? Up with the reel! The dead, blind wall butts all inquiring heads at last. Up with it! So."

The log was heaved. The loose coils rapidly straightened out in a long dragging line astern, and then, instantly, the reel began to whirl. In turn, jerkingly raised and lowered by the rolling billows, the towing resistance of the log caused the old reelman to stagger strangely.

"Hold hard!"

Snap! the overstrained line sagged down in one long festoon; the tugging log was gone.

"I crush the quadrant, the thunder turns the needles, and now the mad sea parts the log-line. But Ahab can mend all. Haul in here, Tahitian; reel up, Manxman. And look ye, let the carpenter make another log, and mend thou the line. See to it."

"There he goes now; to him nothing's happened; but to me, the skewer seems loosening out of the middle of the world. Haul in, haul in, Tahitian! These lines run whole, and whirling out: come in broken, and dragging slow. Ha, Pip? come to help; eh, Pip?"

"Pip? whom call ye Pip? Pip jumped from the whale-boat. Pip's missing. Let's see now if ye haven't fished him up here, fisherman. It drags hard; I guess he's holding on. Jerk him,

Tahiti! Jerk him off; we haul in no cowards here. Ho! there's
his arm just breaking water. A hatchet! a hatchet! cut it off—
we haul in no cowards here. Captain Ahab! sir, sir! here's Pip,
trying to get on board again."

"Peace, thou crazy loon," cried the Manxman, seizing him
by the arm. "Away from the quarter-deck!"

"The greater idiot ever scolds the lesser," muttered Ahab,
advancing. "Hands off from that holiness! Where sayest thou
Pip was, boy?"

"Astern there, sir, astern! Lo, lo!"

"And who art thou, boy? I see not my reflection in the
vacant pupils of thy eyes. Oh God! that man should be a
thing for immortal souls to sieve through! Who art thou, boy?"

"Bell-boy, sir; ship's-crier; ding, dong, ding! Pip! Pip! Pip!
One hundred pounds of clay! reward for Pip; five feet high—
looks cowardly—quickest known by that! Ding, dong, ding!
Who's seen Pip the coward?"

"There can be no hearts above the snow-line. Oh, ye frozen
heavens! look down here. Ye did beget this luckless child, and
have abandoned him, ye creative libertines. Here, boy; Ahab's
cabin shall be Pip's home henceforth, while Ahab lives. Thou
touchest my inmost centre, boy; thou art tied to me by cords
woven of my heart-strings. Come, let's down."

"What's this? here's velvet shark-skin," intently gazing at
Ahab's hand, and feeling it. "Ah, now, had poor Pip but felt
so kind a thing as this, perhaps he had ne'er been lost! This
seems to me, sir, as a man-rope; something that weak souls
may hold by. Oh, sir, let old Perth now come and rivet these
two hands together; the black one with the white, for I will
not let this go."

"Oh, boy, nor will I thee, unless I should thereby drag thee
to worse horrors than are here. Come, then, to my cabin. Lo!
ye believers in gods all goodness, and in man all ill, lo you!
see the omniscient gods oblivious of suffering man; and
man, though idiotic, and knowing not what he does, yet full
of the sweet things of love and gratitude. Come! I feel prouder
leading thee by thy black hand, than though I grasped an
Emperor's!"

"There go two daft ones now," muttered the old Manxman. "One daft with strength, the other daft with weakness.

But here's the end of the rotten line—all dripping, too. Mend it, eh? I think we had best have a new line altogether. I'll see Mr. Stubb about it."

Chapter 126

THE LIFE-BUOY

S TEERING now south-eastward by Ahab's levelled steel,
and her progress solely determined by Ahab's level log
and line; the Pequod held on her path towards the Equator.
Making so long a passage through such unfrequented waters,
descrying no ships, and ere long, sideways impelled by unvarying trade winds, over waves monotonously mild; all these
seemed the strange calm things preluding some riotous and
desperate scene.

At last, when the ship drew near to the outskirts, as it were,
of the Equatorial fishing-ground, and in the deep darkness
that goes before the dawn, was sailing by a cluster of rocky
islets; the watch—then headed by Flask—was startled by a
cry so plaintively wild and unearthly—like half-articulated
wailings of the ghosts of all Herod's murdered Innocents—
that one and all, they started from their reveries, and for the
space of some moments stood, or sat, or leaned all trans-
fixedly listening, like the carved Roman slave, while that wild
cry remained within hearing. The Christian or civilized part
of the crew said it was mermaids, and shuddered; but the
pagan harpooneers remained unappalled. Yet the grey Manxman—the oldest mariner of all—declared that the wild thrilling sounds that were heard, were the voices of newly
drowned men in the sea.

Below in his hammock, Ahab did not hear of this till grey
dawn, when he came to the deck; it was then recounted to
him by Flask, not unaccompanied with hinted dark meanings.
He hollowly laughed, and thus explained the wonder.

Those rocky islands the ship had passed were the resort of
great numbers of seals, and some young seals that had lost
their dams, or some dams that had lost their cubs, must have
risen nigh the ship and kept company with her, crying and
sobbing with their human sort of wail. But this only the more
affected some of them, because most mariners cherish a very
superstitious feeling about seals, arising not only from their

peculiar tones when in distress, but also from the human look of their round heads and semi-intelligent faces, seen peeringly uprising from the water alongside. In the sea, under certain circumstances, seals have more than once been mistaken for men.

But the bodings of the crew were destined to receive a most plausible confirmation in the fate of one of their number that morning. At sun-rise this man went from his hammock to his mast-head at the fore; and whether it was that he was not yet half waked from his sleep (for sailors sometimes go aloft in a transition state), whether it was thus with the man, there is now no telling; but, be that as it may, he had not been long at his perch, when a cry was heard—a cry and a rushing—and looking up, they saw a falling phantom in the air; and looking down, a little tossed heap of white bubbles in the blue of the sea.

The life-buoy—a long slender cask—was dropped from the stern, where it always hung obedient to a cunning spring; but no hand rose to seize it, and the sun having long beat upon this cask it had shrunken, so that it slowly filled, and the parched wood also filled at its every pore; and the studded iron-bound cask followed the sailor to the bottom, as if to yield him his pillow, though in sooth but a hard one.

And thus the first man of the Pequod that mounted the mast to look out for the White Whale, on the White Whale's own peculiar ground; that man was swallowed up in the deep. But few, perhaps, thought of that at the time. Indeed, in some sort, they were not grieved at this event, at least as a portent; for they regarded it, not as a foreshadowing of evil in the future, but as the fulfilment of an evil already presaged. They declared that now they knew the reason of those wild shrieks they had heard the night before. But again the old Manxman said nay.

The lost life-buoy was now to be replaced; Starbuck was directed to see to it; but as no cask of sufficient lightness could be found, and as in the feverish eagerness of what seemed the approaching crisis of the voyage, all hands were impatient of any toil but what was directly connected with its final end, whatever that might prove to be; therefore, they were going to leave the ship's stern unprovided with a buoy, when by certain strange signs and inuendoes Queequeg hinted a hint concerning his coffin.

"A life-buoy of a coffin!" cried Starbuck, starting.

"Rather queer, that, I should say," said Stubb.

"It will make a good enough one," said Flask, "the carpenter here can arrange it easily."

"Bring it up; there's nothing else for it," said Starbuck, after a melancholy pause. "Rig it, carpenter; do not look at me so—the coffin, I mean. Dost thou hear me? Rig it."

"And shall I nail down the lid, sir?" moving his hand as with a hammer.

"Aye."

"And shall I caulk the seams, sir?" moving his hand as with a caulking-iron.

"Aye."

"And shall I then pay over the same with pitch, sir?" moving his hand as with a pitch-pot.

"Away! what possesses thee to this? Make a life-buoy of the coffin, and no more.—Mr. Stubb, Mr. Flask, come forward with me."

"He goes off in a huff. The whole he can endure; at the parts he baulks. Now I don't like this. I make a leg for Captain Ahab, and he wears it like a gentleman; but I make a bandbox for Queequeg, and he wont put his head into it. Are all my pains to go for nothing with that coffin? And now I'm ordered to make a life-buoy of it. It's like turning an old coat; going to bring the flesh on the other side now. I don't like this cobbling sort of business—I don't like it at all; it's undignified; it's not my place. Let tinkers' brats do tinkerings; we are their betters. I like to take in hand none but clean, virgin, fair-and-square mathematical jobs, something that regularly begins at the beginning, and is at the middle when midway, and comes to an end at the conclusion; not a cobbler's job, that's at an end in the middle, and at the beginning at the end. It's the old woman's tricks to be giving cobbling jobs. Lord! what an affection all old women have for tinkers. I know an old woman of sixty-five who ran away with a bald-headed young tinker once. And that's the reason I never would work for lonely widow old women ashore, when I kept my job-shop in the Vineyard; they might have taken it into their lonely old heads to run off with me. But heigh-ho! there are no caps at sea but snow-caps. Let me see. Nail down the lid; caulk the seams; pay over the same with pitch; batten them down tight, and hang it with the snap-spring over the ship's stern. Were ever such things done before with a coffin? Some superstitious old carpenters, now, would be tied up in the rigging, ere they would do the job. But I'm made of knotty Aroostook hemlock; I don't budge. Cruppered with a coffin! Sailing about with a grave-yard tray! But never mind. We workers in woods make bridal-bedsteads and card-tables, as well as coffins and hearses. We work by the month, or by the job, or by the profit; not for us to ask the why and wherefore of our work, unless it be too confounded cobbling, and then we stash it if we can. Hem! I'll do the job, now, tenderly. I'll have me—let's see—how many in the ship's company, all told? But I've forgotten. Any way, I'll have me thirty separate, Turk's-headed life-lines, each three feet long hanging all round to the coffin. Then, if the hull go down, there'll be thirty lively fellows all fighting for one coffin, a sight not seen very often beneath the sun! Come hammer, calking-iron, pitch-pot, and marling-spike! Let's to it."

Chapter 127

THE DECK

(The coffin laid upon two line-tubs, between the vice-bench and the open hatchway; the Carpenter calking its seams; the string of twisted oakum slowly unwinding from a large roll of it placed in the bosom of his frock. —Ahab comes slowly from the cabin-gangway, and hears Pip following him.)

BACK, lad; I will be with ye again presently. He goes! Not this hand complies with my humor more genially than that boy.—Middle aisle of a church! What's here?"

"Life-buoy, sir. Mr. Starbuck's orders. Oh, look, sir! Beware the hatchway!"

"Thank ye, man. Thy coffin lies handy to the vault."

"Sir? The hatchway? oh! So it does, sir, so it does."

"Art not thou the leg-maker? Look, did not this stump come from thy shop?"

"I believe it did, sir; does the ferrule stand, sir?"

"Well enough. But art thou not also the undertaker?"

"Aye, sir; I patched up this thing here as a coffin for Queequeg; but they've set me now to turning it into something else."

"Then tell me; art thou not an arrant, all-grasping, intermeddling, monopolizing, heathenish old scamp, to be one day making legs, and the next day coffins to clap them in, and yet again life-buoys out of those same coffins? Thou art as unprincipled as the gods, and as much of a jack-of-all-trades."

"But I do not mean anything, sir. I do as I do."

"The gods again. Hark ye, dost thou not ever sing working about a coffin? The Titans, they say, hummed snatches when chipping out the craters for volcanoes; and the grave-digger in the play sings, spade in hand. Dost thou never?"

"Sing, sir? Do I sing? Oh, I'm indifferent enough, sir, for that; but the reason why the grave-digger made music must have been because there was none in his spade, sir. But the calking mallet is full of it. Hark to it."

"Aye, and that's because the lid there's a sounding-board; and what in all things makes the sounding-board is this—there's naught beneath. And yet, a coffin with a body in it rings pretty much the same, Carpenter. Hast thou ever helped carry a bier, and heard the coffin knock against the church-yard gate, going in?"

"Faith, sir, I've———"

"Faith? What's that?"

"Why, faith, sir, it's only a sort of exclamation-like—that's all, sir."

"Um, um; go on."

"I was about to say, sir, that———"

"Art thou a silk-worm? Dost thou spin thy own shroud out of thyself? Look at thy bosom! Despatch! and get these traps out of sight."

"He goes aft. That was sudden, now; but squalls come sudden in hot latitudes. I've heard that the Isle of Albemarle, one of the Gallipagos, is cut by the Equator right in the middle. Seems to me some sort of Equator cuts yon old man, too, right in his middle. He's always under the Line—fiery hot, I tell ye! He's looking this way—come, oakum; quick. Here we go again. This wooden mallet is the cork, and I'm the professor of musical glasses—tap, tap!"

(Ahab to himself.)

"There's a sight! There's a sound! The greyheaded wood-pecker tapping the hollow tree! Blind and deaf might well be envied now. See! that thing rests on two line-tubs, full of tow-lines. A most malicious wag, that fellow. Rat-tat! So man's seconds tick! Oh! how immaterial are all materials! What things real are there, but imponderable thoughts? Here now's the very dreaded symbol of grim death, by a mere hap, made the expressive sign of the help and hope of most endangered life. A life-buoy of a coffin! Does it go further? Can it be that in some spiritual sense the coffin is, after all, but an immortality-preserver! I'll think of that. But no. So far gone am I in the dark side of earth, that its other side, the theoretic bright one, seems but uncertain twilight to me. Will ye never have done, Carpenter, with that accursed sound? I go below; let me not see that thing here when I return again. Now, then, Pip, we'll talk this over; I do suck most wondrous philosophies from thee! Some unknown conduits from the unknown worlds must empty into thee!"

Chapter 128

THE PEQUOD MEETS THE RACHEL

N EXT DAY, a large ship, the Rachel, was descried, bearing directly down upon the Pequod, all her spars thickly clustering with men. At the time the Pequod was making good speed through the water; but as the broad-winged windward stranger shot nigh to her, the boastful sails all fell together as blank bladders that are burst, and all life fled from the smitten hull.

"Bad news; she brings bad news," muttered the old Manxman. But ere her commander, who, with trumpet to mouth, stood up in his boat; ere he could hopefully hail, Ahab's voice was heard.

"Hast seen the White Whale?"

"Aye, yesterday. Have ye seen a whale-boat adrift?"

Throttling his joy, Ahab negatively answered this unexpected question; and would then have fain boarded the stranger, when the stranger captain himself, having stopped his vessel's way, was seen descending her side. A few keen pulls, and his boat-hook soon clinched the Pequod's main-chains, and he sprang to the deck. Immediately he was recognised by Ahab for a Nantucketer he knew. But no formal salutation was exchanged.

"Where was he?—not killed!—not killed!" cried Ahab, closely advancing. "How was it?"

It seemed that somewhat late on the afternoon of the day previous, while three of the stranger's boats were engaged with a shoal of whales, which had led them some four or five miles from the ship; and while they were yet in swift chase to windward, the white hump and head of Moby Dick had suddenly loomed up out of the blue water, not very far to leeward; whereupon, the fourth rigged boat—a reserved one—had been instantly lowered in chase. After a keen sail before the wind, this fourth boat—the swiftest keeled of all—seemed to have succeeded in fastening—at least, as well as the man at the mast-head could tell anything about it. In the

distance he saw the diminished dotted boat; and then a swift
gleam of bubbling white water; and after that nothing more;
whence it was concluded that the stricken whale must have
indefinitely run away with his pursuers, as often happens.
There was some apprehension, but no positive alarm, as yet.
The recall signals were placed in the rigging; darkness came
on; and forced to pick up her three far to windward boats—
ere going in quest of the fourth one in the precisely opposite
direction—the ship had not only been necessitated to leave
that boat to its fate till near midnight, but, for the time, to
increase her distance from it. But the rest of her crew being
at last safe aboard, she crowded all sail—stunsail on stun-
sail—after the missing boat; kindling a fire in her try-pots for
a beacon; and every other man aloft on the look-out. But
though when she had thus sailed a sufficient distance to gain
the presumed place of the absent ones when last seen; though
she then paused to lower her spare boats to pull all around
her; and not finding anything, had again dashed on; again
paused, and lowered her boats; and though she had thus continued doing till day light; yet not the least glimpse of the
missing keel had been seen.

The story told, the stranger Captain immediately went on
to reveal his object in boarding the Pequod. He desired that
ship to unite with his own in the search; by sailing over the
sea some four or five miles apart, on parallel lines, and so
sweeping a double horizon, as it were.

"I will wager something now," whispered Stubb to Flask,
"that some one in that missing boat wore off that Captain's
best coat; mayhap, his watch—he's so cursed anxious to get
it back. Who ever heard of two pious whale-ships cruising
after one missing whale-boat in the height of the whaling season? See, Flask, only see how pale he looks—pale in the very
buttons of his eyes—look—it wasn't the coat—it must have
been the—"

"My boy, my own boy is among them. For God's sake—I
beg, I conjure"—here exclaimed the stranger Captain to
Ahab, who thus far had but icily received his petition. "For
eight-and-forty hours let me charter your ship—I will gladly
pay for it, and roundly pay for it—if there be no other way—

for eight-and-forty hours only—only that—you must, oh, you must, and you *shall* do this thing."

"His son!" cried Stubb, "oh, it's his son he's lost! I take back the coat and watch—what says Ahab? We must save that boy."

"He's drowned with the rest on 'em, last night," said the old Manx sailor standing behind them; "I heard; all of ye heard their spirits."

Now, as it shortly turned out, what made this incident of the Rachel's the more melancholy, was the circumstance, that not only was one of the Captain's sons among the number of the missing boat's crew; but among the number of the other boats' crews, at the same time, but on the other hand, separated from the ship during the dark vicissitudes of the chase, there had been still another son; as that for a time, the wretched father was plunged to the bottom of the cruellest perplexity; which was only solved for him by his chief mate's instinctively adopting the ordinary procedure of a whale-ship in such emergencies, that is, when placed between jeopardized but divided boats, always to pick up the majority first. But the captain, for some unknown constitutional reason, had refrained from mentioning all this, and not till forced to it by Ahab's iciness did he allude to his one yet missing boy; a little lad, but twelve years old, whose father with the earnest but unmisgiving hardihood of a Nantucketer's paternal love, had thus early sought to initiate him in the perils and wonders of a vocation almost immemorially the destiny of all his race. Nor does it unfrequently occur, that Nantucket captains will send a son of such tender age away from them, for a protracted three or four years' voyage in some other ship than their own; so that their first knowledge of a whaleman's career shall be unenervated by any chance display of a father's natural but untimely partiality, or undue apprehensiveness and concern.

Meantime, now the stranger was still beseeching his poor boon of Ahab; and Ahab still stood like an anvil, receiving every shock, but without the least quivering of his own.

"I will not go," said the stranger, "till you say *aye* to me. Do to me as you would have me do to you in the like case.

For *you* too have a boy, Captain Ahab—though but a child, and nestling safely at home now—a child of your old age too—Yes, yes, you relent; I see it—run, run, men, now, and stand by to square in the yards."

"Avast," cried Ahab—"touch not a rope-yarn;" then in a voice that prolongingly moulded every word—"Captain Gardiner, I will not do it. Even now I lose time. Good bye, good bye. God bless ye, man, and may I forgive myself, but I must go. Mr. Starbuck, look at the binnacle watch, and in three minutes from this present instant warn off all strangers: then brace forward again, and let the ship sail as before."

Hurriedly turning, with averted face, he descended into his cabin, leaving the strange captain transfixed at this unconditional and utter rejection of his so earnest suit. But starting from his enchantment, Gardiner silently hurried to the side; more fell than stepped into his boat, and returned to his ship.

Soon the two ships diverged their wakes; and long as the strange vessel was in view, she was seen to yaw hither and thither at every dark spot, however small, on the sea. This way and that her yards were swung round; starboard and larboard, she continued to tack; now she beat against a head sea; and again it pushed her before it; while all the while, her masts and yards were thickly clustered with men, as three tall cherry trees, when the boys are cherrying among the boughs.

But by her still halting course and winding, woful way, you plainly saw that this ship that so wept with spray, still remained without comfort. She was Rachel, weeping for her children, because they were not.

Chapter 129

The Cabin

(Ahab moving to go on deck; Pip catches him by the hand to follow.)

LAD, LAD, I tell thee thou must not follow Ahab now. The hour is coming when Ahab would not scare thee from him, yet would not have thee by him. There is that in thee, poor lad, which I feel too curing to my malady. Like cures like; and for this hunt, my malady becomes my most desired health. Do thou abide below here, where they shall serve thee, as if thou wert the captain. Aye, lad, thou shalt sit here in my own screwed chair; another screw to it, thou must be."

"No, no, no! ye have not a whole body, sir; do ye but use poor me for your one lost leg; only tread upon me, sir; I ask no more, so I remain a part of ye."

"Oh! spite of million villains, this makes me a bigot in the fadeless fidelity of man!—and a black! and crazy!—but methinks like-cures-like applies to him too; he grows so sane again."

"They tell me, sir, that Stubb did once desert poor little Pip, whose drowned bones now show white, for all the blackness of his living skin. But I will never desert ye, sir, as Stubb did him. Sir, I must go with ye."

"If thou speakest thus to me much more, Ahab's purpose keels up in him. I tell thee no; it cannot be."

"Oh good master, master, master!"

"Weep so, and I will murder thee! have a care, for Ahab too is mad. Listen, and thou wilt often hear my ivory foot upon the deck, and still know that I am there. And now I quit thee. Thy hand!—Met! True art thou, lad, as the circumference to its centre. So: God for ever bless thee; and if it come to that,—God for ever save thee, let what will befall."

(Ahab goes; Pip steps one step forward.)

"Here he this instant stood; I stand in his air,—but I'm alone. Now were even poor Pip here I could endure it, but he's missing. Pip! Pip! Ding, dong, ding! Who's seen Pip?

He must be up here; let's try the door. What? neither lock, nor bolt, nor bar; and yet there's no opening it. It must be the spell; he told me to stay here: Aye, and told me this screwed chair was mine. Here, then, I'll seat me, against the transom, in the ship's full middle, all her keel and her three masts before me. Here, our old sailors say, in their black seventy-fours great admirals sometimes sit at table, and lord it over rows of captains and lieutenants. Ha! what's this? epaulets! epaulets! the epaulets all come crowding! Pass round the decanters; glad to see ye; fill up, monsieurs! What an odd feeling, now, when a black boy's host to white men with gold lace upon their coats!—Monsieurs, have ye seen one Pip?—a little negro lad, five feet high, hang-dog look, and cowardly! Jumped from a whale-boat once;—seen him? No! Well then, fill up again, captains, and let's drink shame upon all cowards! I name no names. Shame upon them! Put one foot upon the table. Shame upon all cowards.—Hist! above there, I hear ivory—Oh, master! master! I am indeed down-hearted when you walk over me. But here I'll stay, though this stern strikes rocks; and they bulge through; and oysters come to join me."

Chapter 130

The Hat

A<small>ND</small> N<small>OW</small> that at the proper time and place, after so long
and wide a preliminary cruise, Ahab,—all other whal-
ing waters swept—seemed to have chased his foe into an
ocean-fold, to slay him the more securely there; now, that he
found himself hard by the very latitude and longitude where
his tormenting wound had been inflicted; now that a vessel
had been spoken which on the very day preceding had actually encountered Moby Dick;—and now that all his successive meetings with various ships contrastingly concurred to
show the demoniac indifference with which the white whale
tore his hunters, whether sinning or sinned against; now it
was that there lurked a something in the old man's eyes,
which it was hardly sufferable for feeble souls to see. As the
unsetting polar star, which through the livelong, arctic, six
months' night sustains its piercing, steady, central gaze; so
Ahab's purpose now fixedly gleamed down upon the constant
midnight of the gloomy crew. It domineered above them so,
that all their bodings, doubts, misgivings, fears, were fain to
hide beneath their souls, and not sprout forth a single spear
or leaf.

In this foreshadowing interval too, all humor, forced or
natural, vanished. Stubb no more strove to raise a smile; Starbuck no more strove to check one. Alike, joy and sorrow,
hope and fear, seemed ground to finest dust, and powdered,
for the time, in the clamped mortar of Ahab's iron soul. Like
machines, they dumbly moved about the deck, ever conscious
that the old man's despot eye was on them.

But did you deeply scan him in his more secret confidential
hours; when he thought no glance but one was on him; then
you would have seen that even as Ahab's eyes so awed the
crew's, the inscrutable Parsee's glance awed his; or somehow,
at least, in some wild way, at times affected it. Such an added,
gliding strangeness began to invest the thin Fedallah now;
such ceaseless shudderings shook him; that the men looked

dubious at him; half uncertain, as it seemed, whether indeed
he were a mortal substance, or else a tremulous shadow cast
upon the deck by some unseen being's body. And that
shadow was always hovering there. For not by night, even,
had Fedallah ever certainly been known to slumber, or go
below. He would stand still for hours: but never sat or
leaned; his wan but wondrous eyes did plainly say—We two
watchmen never rest.

Nor, at any time, by night or day could the mariners now
step upon the deck, unless Ahab was before them; either
standing in his pivot-hole, or exactly pacing the planks between two undeviating limits,—the main-mast and the
mizen; or else they saw him standing in the cabin-scuttle,—
his living foot advanced upon the deck, as if to step; his hat
slouched heavily over his eyes; so that however motionless he
stood, however the days and nights were added on, that he
had not swung in his hammock; yet hidden beneath that
slouching hat, they could never tell unerringly whether, for
all this, his eyes were really closed at times: or whether he
was still intently scanning them; no matter, though he stood
so in the scuttle for a whole hour on the stretch, and the
unheeded night-damp gathered in beads of dew upon that
stone-carved coat and hat. The clothes that the night had wet,
the next day's sunshine dried upon him; and so, day after day,
and night after night; he went no more beneath the planks;
whatever he wanted from the cabin that thing he sent for.

He ate in the same open air; that is, his two only meals,—
breakfast and dinner: supper he never touched; nor reaped his
beard; which darkly grew all gnarled, as unearthed roots of
trees blown over, which still grow idly on at naked base,
though perished in the upper verdure. But though his whole
life was now become one watch on deck; and though the
Parsee's mystic watch was without intermission as his own;
yet these two never seemed to speak—one man to the
other—unless at long intervals some passing unmomentous
matter made it necessary. Though such a potent spell seemed
secretly to join the twain; openly, and to the awe-struck crew,
they seemed pole-like asunder. If by day they chanced to
speak one word; by night, dumb men were both, so far as
concerned the slightest verbal interchange. At times, for long-

est hours, without a single hail, they stood far parted in the starlight; Ahab in his scuttle, the Parsee by the mainmast; but still fixedly gazing upon each other; as if in the Parsee Ahab saw his forethrown shadow, in Ahab the Parsee his abandoned substance.

And yet, somehow, did Ahab—in his own proper self, as daily, hourly, and every instant, commandingly revealed to his subordinates,—Ahab seemed an independent lord; the Parsee but his slave. Still again both seemed yoked together, and an unseen tyrant driving them; the lean shade siding the solid rib. For be this Parsee what he may, all rib and keel was solid Ahab.

At the first faintest glimmering of the dawn, his iron voice was heard from aft—"Man the mast-heads!"—and all through the day, till after sunset and after twilight, the same voice every hour, at the striking of the helmsman's bell, was heard—"What d'ye see?—sharp! sharp!"

But when three or four days had slided by, after meeting the children-seeking Rachel; and no spout had yet been seen; the monomaniac old man seemed distrustful of his crew's fidelity; at least, of nearly all except the Pagan harpooneers; he seemed to doubt, even, whether Stubb and Flask might not willingly overlook the sight he sought. But if these suspicions were really his, he sagaciously refrained from verbally expressing them, however his actions might seem to hint them.

"I will have the first sight of the whale myself,"—he said. "Aye! Ahab must have the doubloon!" and with his own hands he rigged a nest of basketed bowlines; and sending a hand aloft, with a single sheaved block, to secure to the main-mast head, he received the two ends of the downward-reeved rope; and attaching one to his basket prepared a pin for the other end, in order to fasten it at the rail. This done, with that end yet in his hand and standing beside the pin, he looked round upon his crew, sweeping from one to the other; pausing his glance long upon Daggoo, Queequeg, Tashtego; but shunning Fedallah; and then settling his firm relying eye upon the chief mate, said,—"Take the rope, sir—I give it into thy hands, Starbuck." Then arranging his person in the basket, he gave the word for them to hoist him to his perch, Starbuck being the one who secured the rope at last; and afterwards stood near it. And thus, with one hand clinging round the royal mast, Ahab gazed abroad upon the sea for miles and miles,—ahead, astern, this side, and that,—within the wide expanded circle commanded at so great a height.

When in working with his hands at some lofty almost isolated place in the rigging, which chances to afford no foothold, the sailor at sea is hoisted up to that spot, and sustained there by the rope; under these circumstances, its fastened end on deck is always given in strict charge to some one man who has the special watch of it. Because in such a wilderness of running rigging, whose various different relations aloft cannot always be infallibly discerned by what is seen of them at the deck; and when the deck-ends of these ropes are being every few minutes cast down from the fastenings, it would be but a natural fatality, if, unprovided with a constant watchman, the hoisted sailor should by some carelessness of the crew be cast adrift and fall all swooping to the sea. So Ahab's proceedings in this matter were not unusual; the only strange thing about them seemed to be, that Starbuck, almost the one only man who had ever ventured to oppose him with anything in the slightest degree approaching to decision—one of those too, whose faithfulness on the look-out he had seemed to doubt somewhat;—it was strange, that this was the very man he should select for his watchman; freely giving his whole life into such an otherwise distrusted person's hands.

Now, the first time Ahab was perched aloft; ere he had been there ten minutes; one of those red-billed savage seahawks which so often fly incommodiously close round the manned mast-heads of whalemen in these latitudes; one of these birds came wheeling and screaming round his head in a maze of untrackably swift circlings. Then it darted a thousand feet straight up into the air; then spiralized downwards, and went eddying again round his head.

But with his gaze fixed upon the dim and distant horizon, Ahab seemed not to mark this wild bird; nor, indeed, would any one else have marked it much, it being no uncommon circumstance; only now almost the least heedful eye seemed to see some sort of cunning meaning in almost every sight.

"Your hat, your hat, sir!" suddenly cried the Sicilian seaman, who being posted at the mizen-mast-head, stood directly behind Ahab, though somewhat lower than his level, and with a deep gulf of air dividing them.

But already the sable wing was before the old man's eyes; the long hooked bill at his head: with a scream, the black hawk darted away with his prize.

An eagle flew thrice round Tarquin's head, removing his cap to replace it, and thereupon Tanaquil, his wife, declared that Tarquin would be king of Rome. But only by the replacing of the cap was that omen accounted good. Ahab's hat was never restored; the wild hawk flew on and on with it; far in advance of the prow: and at last disappeared; while from the point of that disappearance, a minute black spot was dimly discerned, falling from that vast height into the sea.

Chapter 131

The Pequod meets the Delight

THE INTENSE Pequod sailed on; the rolling waves and days went by; the life-buoy-coffin still lightly swung; and another ship, most miserably misnamed the Delight, was descried. As she drew nigh, all eyes were fixed upon her broad beams, called shears, which, in some whaling-ships, cross the quarter-deck at the height of eight or nine feet; serving to carry the spare, unrigged, or disabled boats.

Upon the stranger's shears were beheld the shattered, white ribs, and some few splintered planks, of what had once been a whale-boat; but you now saw through this wreck, as plainly as you see through the peeled, half-unhinged, and bleaching skeleton of a horse.

"Hast seen the White Whale?"

"Look!" replied the hollow-cheeked captain from his taffrail; and with his trumpet he pointed to the wreck.

"Hast killed him?"

"The harpoon is not yet forged that will ever do that," answered the other, sadly glancing upon a rounded hammock on the deck, whose gathered sides some noiseless sailors were busy in sewing together.

"Not forged!" and snatching Perth's levelled iron from the crotch, Ahab held it out, exclaiming—"Look ye, Nantucketer; here in this hand I hold his death! Tempered in blood, and tempered by lightning are these barbs; and I swear to temper them triply in that hot place behind the fin, where the White Whale most feels his accursed life!"

"Then God keep thee, old man—see'st thou that"—pointing to the hammock—"I bury but one of five stout men, who were alive only yesterday; but were dead ere night. Only *that* one I bury; the rest were buried before they died; you sail upon their tomb." Then turning to his crew—"Are ye ready there? place the plank then on the rail, and lift the body; so, then—Oh! God"—advancing towards the hammock with uplifted hands—"may the resurrection and the life——"

1370

"Brace forward! Up helm!" cried Ahab like lightning to his men.

But the suddenly started Pequod was not quick enough to escape the sound of the splash that the corpse soon made as it struck the sea; not so quick, indeed, but that some of the flying bubbles might have sprinkled her hull with their ghostly baptism.

As Ahab now glided from the dejected Delight, the strange life-buoy hanging at the Pequod's stern came into conspicuous relief.

"Ha! yonder! look yonder, men!" cried a foreboding voice in her wake. "In vain, oh, ye strangers, ye fly our sad burial; ye but turn us your taffrail to show us your coffin!"

Chapter 132

THE SYMPHONY

It was a clear steel-blue day. The firmaments of air and sea were hardly separable in that all-pervading azure; only, the pensive air was transparently pure and soft, with a woman's look, and the robust and man-like sea heaved with long, strong, lingering swells, as Samson's chest in his sleep.

Hither, and thither, on high, glided the snow-white wings of small, unspeckled birds; these were the gentle thoughts of the feminine air; but to and fro in the deeps, far down in the bottomless blue, rushed mighty leviathans, sword-fish, and sharks; and these were the strong, troubled, murderous thinkings of the masculine sea.

But though thus contrasting within, the contrast was only in shades and shadows without; those two seemed one; it was only the sex, as it were, that distinguished them.

Aloft, like a royal czar and king, the sun seemed giving this gentle air to this bold and rolling sea; even as bride to groom. And at the girdling line of the horizon, a soft and tremulous motion—most seen here at the equator—denoted the fond, throbbing trust, the loving alarms, with which the poor bride gave her bosom away.

Tied up and twisted; gnarled and knotted with wrinkles; haggardly firm and unyielding; his eyes glowing like coals, that still glow in the ashes of ruin; untottering Ahab stood forth in the clearness of the morn; lifting his splintered helmet of a brow to the fair girl's forehead of heaven.

Oh, immortal infancy, and innocency of the azure! Invisible winged creatures that frolic all round us! Sweet childhood of air and sky! how oblivious were ye of old Ahab's close-coiled woe! But so have I seen little Miriam and Martha, laughing-eyed elves, heedlessly gambol around their old sire; sporting with the circle of singed locks which grew on the marge of that burnt-out crater of his brain.

Slowly crossing the deck from the scuttle, Ahab leaned over the side, and watched how his shadow in the water sank and sank to his gaze, the more and the more that he strove to pierce the profundity. But the lovely aromas in that enchanted air did at last seem to dispel, for a moment, the cankerous thing in his soul. That glad, happy air, that winsome sky, did at last stroke and caress him; the step-mother world, so long cruel—forbidding—now threw affectionate arms round his stubborn neck, and did seem to joyously sob over him, as if over one, that however wilful and erring, she could yet find it in her heart to save and to bless. From beneath his slouched hat Ahab dropped a tear into the sea; nor did all the Pacific contain such wealth as that one wee drop.

Starbuck saw the old man; saw him, how he heavily leaned over the side; and he seemed to hear in his own true heart the measureless sobbing that stole out of the centre of the serenity around. Careful not to touch him, or be noticed by him, he yet drew near to him, and stood there.

Ahab turned.

"Starbuck!"

"Sir."

"Oh, Starbuck! it is a mild, mild wind, and a mild looking sky. On such a day—very much such a sweetness as this— I struck my first whale—a boy-harpooneer of eighteen! Forty—forty—forty years ago!—ago! Forty years of continual whaling! forty years of privation, and peril, and storm-time! forty years on the pitiless sea! for forty years has Ahab forsaken the peaceful land, for forty years to make war on the horrors of the deep! Aye and yes, Starbuck, out of those forty years I have not spent three ashore. When I think of this life I have led; the desolation of solitude it has been; the ma-soned, walled-town of a Captain's exclusiveness, which admits but small entrance to any sympathy from the green country without—oh, weariness! heaviness! Guinea-coast slavery of solitary command!—when I think of all this; only half-sus-pected, not so keenly known to me before—and how for forty years I have fed upon dry salted fare—fit emblem of the dry nourishment of my soul!—when the poorest landsman has had fresh fruit to his daily hand, and broken the world's fresh bread, to my mouldy crusts—away, whole oceans away, from that young girl-wife I wedded past fifty, and sailed for Cape Horn the next day, leaving but one dent in my marriage

pillow—wife? wife?—rather a widow with her husband
alive! Aye, I widowed that poor girl when I married her, Starbuck; and then, the madness, the frenzy, the boiling blood
and the smoking brow, with which, for a thousand lowerings
old Ahab has furiously, foamingly chased his prey—more a
demon than a man!—aye, aye! what a forty years' fool—
fool—old fool, has old Ahab been! Why this strife of the
chase? why weary, and palsy the arm at the oar, and the iron,
and the lance? how the richer or better is Ahab now? Behold.
Oh, Starbuck! is it not hard, that with this weary load I bear,
one poor leg should have been snatched from under me?
Here, brush this old hair aside; it blinds me, that I seem to
weep. Locks so grey did never grow but from out some
ashes! But do I look very old, so very, very old, Starbuck? I
feel deadly faint, bowed, and humped, as though I were
Adam, staggering beneath the piled centuries since Paradise.
God! God! God!—crack my heart!—stave my brain!—
mockery! mockery! bitter, biting mockery of grey hairs, have
I lived enough joy to wear ye; and seem and feel thus intolerably old? Close! stand close to me, Starbuck; let me look
into a human eye; it is better than to gaze into sea or sky;
better than to gaze upon God. By the green land; by the
bright hearth-stone! this is the magic glass, man; I see my
wife and my child in thine eye. No, no; stay on board, on
board!—lower not when I do; when branded Ahab gives
chase to Moby Dick. That hazard shall not be thine. No, no!
not with the far away home I see in that eye!"

"Oh, my Captain! my Captain! noble soul! grand old
heart, after all! why should any one give chase to that
hated fish! Away with me! let us fly these deadly waters! let
us home! Wife and child, too, are Starbuck's—wife and
child of his brotherly, sisterly, play-fellow youth; even as
thine, sir, are the wife and child of thy loving, longing, paternal old age! Away! let us away!—this instant let me alter
the course! How cheerily, how hilariously, O my Captain,
would we bowl on our way to see old Nantucket again! I
think, sir, they have some such mild blue days, even as this,
in Nantucket."

"They have, they have. I have seen them—some summer
days in the morning. About this time—yes, it is his noon

nap now—the boy vivaciously wakes; sits up in bed; and his mother tells him of me, of cannibal old me; how I am abroad upon the deep, but will yet come back to dance him again."

"'Tis my Mary, my Mary herself! She promised that my boy, every morning, should be carried to the hill to catch the first glimpse of his father's sail! Yes, yes! no more! it is done! we head for Nantucket! Come, my Captain, study out the course, and let us away! See, see! the boy's face from the window! the boy's hand on the hill!"

But Ahab's glance was averted; like a blighted fruit tree he shook, and cast his last, cindered apple to the soil.

"What is it, what nameless, inscrutable, unearthly thing is it; what cozening, hidden lord and master, and cruel, remorseless emperor commands me; that against all natural lovings and longings, I so keep pushing, and crowding, and jamming myself on all the time; recklessly making me ready to do what in my own proper, natural heart, I durst not so much as dare? Is Ahab, Ahab? Is it I, God, or who, that lifts this arm? But if the great sun move not of himself; but is as an errand-boy in heaven; nor one single star can revolve, but by some invisible power; how then can this one small heart beat; this one small brain think thoughts; unless God does that beating, does that thinking, does that living, and not I. By heaven, man, we are turned round and round in this world, like yonder windlass, and Fate is the handspike. And all the time, lo! that smiling sky, and this unsounded sea! Look! see yon Albicore! who put it into him to chase and fang that flying-fish? Where do murderers go, man! Who's to doom, when the judge himself is dragged to the bar? But it is a mild, mild wind, and a mild looking sky; and the air smells now, as if it blew from a far-away meadow; they have been making hay somewhere under the slopes of the Andes, Starbuck, and the mowers are sleeping among the new-mown hay. Sleeping? Aye, toil we how we may, we all sleep at last on the field. Sleep? Aye, and rust amid greenness; as last year's scythes flung down, and left in the half-cut swaths— Starbuck!"

But blanched to a corpse's hue with despair, the Mate had stolen away.

Ahab crossed the deck to gaze over on the other side; but started at two reflected, fixed eyes in the water there. Fedallah was motionlessly leaning over the same rail.

Chapter 133

THE CHASE—FIRST DAY

THAT NIGHT, in the mid-watch, when the old man—as his wont at intervals—stepped forth from the scuttle in which he leaned, and went to his pivot-hole, he suddenly thrust out his face fiercely, snuffing up the sea air as a sagacious ship's dog will, in drawing nigh to some barbarous isle. He declared that a whale must be near. Soon that peculiar odor, sometimes to a great distance given forth by the living sperm whale, was palpable to all the watch; nor was any mariner surprised when, after inspecting the compass, and then the dog-vane, and then ascertaining the precise bearing of the odor as nearly as possible, Ahab rapidly ordered the ship's course to be slightly altered, and the sail to be shortened.

The acute policy dictating these movements was sufficiently vindicated at daybreak, by the sight of a long sleek on the sea directly and lengthwise ahead, smooth as oil, and resembling in the pleated watery wrinkles bordering it, the polished metallic-like marks of some swift tide-rip, at the mouth of a deep, rapid stream.

"Man the mast-heads! Call all hands!"

Thundering with the butts of three clubbed handspikes on the forecastle deck, Daggoo roused the sleepers with such judgment claps that they seemed to exhale from the scuttle, so instantaneously did they appear with their clothes in their hands.

"What d'ye see?" cried Ahab, flattening his face to the sky.

"Nothing, nothing, sir!" was the sound hailing down in reply.

"T'gallant sails!—stunsails! alow and aloft, and on both sides!"

All sail being set, he now cast loose the life-line, reserved for swaying him to the main royal-mast head; and in a few moments they were hoisting him thither, when, while but two thirds of the way aloft, and while peering ahead through the horizontal vacancy between the main-top-sail and top-gallant-sail, he raised a gull-like cry in the air, "There she blows!—there she blows! A hump like a snow-hill! It is Moby Dick!"

Fired by the cry which seemed simultaneously taken up by the three look-outs, the men on deck rushed to the rigging to behold the famous whale they had so long been pursuing. Ahab had now gained his final perch, some feet above the other look-outs, Tashtego standing just beneath him on the cap of the top-gallant-mast, so that the Indian's head was almost on a level with Ahab's heel. From this height the whale was now seen some mile or so ahead, at every roll of the sea revealing his high sparkling hump, and regularly jetting his silent spout into the air. To the credulous mariners it seemed the same silent spout they had so long ago beheld in the moonlit Atlantic and Indian Oceans.

"And did none of ye see it before?" cried Ahab, hailing the perched men all around him.

"I saw him almost that same instant, sir, that Captain Ahab did, and I cried out," said Tashtego.

"Not the same instant; not the same—no, the doubloon is mine, Fate reserved the doubloon for me. *I* only; none of ye could have raised the White Whale first. There she blows! there she blows!—there she blows! There again!—there again!" he cried, in long-drawn, lingering, methodic tones, attuned to the gradual prolongings of the whale's visible jets. "He's going to sound! In stunsails! Down top-gallant-sails! Stand by three boats. Mr. Starbuck, remember, stay on board, and keep the ship. Helm there! Luff, luff a point! So; steady, man, steady! There go flukes! No, no; only black water! All ready the boats there? Stand by, stand by! Lower me, Mr. Starbuck; lower, lower,—quick, quicker!" and he slid through the air to the deck.

"He is heading straight to leeward, sir," cried Stubb, "right away from us; cannot have seen the ship yet."

"Be dumb, man! Stand by the braces! Hard down the helm!—brace up! Shiver her!—shiver her! So; well that! Boats, boats!"

Soon all the boats but Starbuck's were dropped; all the boat-sails set—all the paddles plying; with rippling swiftness, shooting to leeward; and Ahab heading the onset. A pale, death-glimmer lit up Fedallah's sunken eyes; a hideous motion gnawed his mouth.

Like noiseless nautilus shells, their light prows sped through the sea; but only slowly they neared the foe. As they neared him, the ocean grew still more smooth; seemed drawing a carpet over its waves; seemed a noon-meadow, so serenely it spread. At length the breathless hunter came so nigh his seemingly unsuspecting prey, that his entire dazzling hump was distinctly visible, sliding along the sea as if an isolated thing, and continually set in a revolving ring of finest, fleecy, greenish foam. He saw the vast, involved wrinkles of the slightly projecting head beyond. Before it, far out on the soft Turkish-rugged waters, went the glistening white shadow from his broad, milky forehead, a musical rippling playfully accompanying the shade; and behind, the blue waters interchangeably flowed over into the moving valley of his steady wake; and on either hand bright bubbles arose and danced by his side. But these were broken again by the light toes of hundreds of gay fowl softly feathering the sea, alternate with their fitful flight; and like to some flag-staff rising from the painted hull of an argosy, the tall but shattered pole of a recent lance projected from the white whale's back; and at intervals one of the cloud of soft-toed fowls hovering, and to and fro skimming like a canopy over the fish, silently perched and rocked on this pole, the long tail feathers streaming like pennons.

A gentle joyousness—a mighty mildness of repose in swiftness, invested the gliding whale. Not the white bull Jupiter swimming away with ravished Europa clinging to his graceful horns; his lovely, leering eyes sideways intent upon the maid; with smooth bewitching fleetness, rippling straight for the nuptial bower in Crete; not Jove, not that great majesty Supreme! did surpass the glorified White Whale as he so divinely swam.

On each soft side—coincident with the parted swell, that but once laving him, then flowed so wide away—on each bright side, the whale shed off enticings. No wonder there had been some among the hunters who namelessly transported and allured by all this serenity, had ventured to assail it; but had fatally found that quietude but the vesture of tornadoes. Yet calm, enticing calm, oh, whale! thou glidest on, to all who for the first time eye thee, no matter how many in that same way thou may'st have bejuggled and destroyed before.

And thus, through the serene tranquillities of the tropical sea, among waves whose hand-clappings were suspended by exceeding rapture, Moby Dick moved on, still withholding from sight the full terrors of his submerged trunk, entirely hiding the wrenched hideousness of his jaw. But soon the fore part of him slowly rose from the water; for an instant his whole marbleized body formed a high arch, like Virginia's Natural Bridge, and warningly waving his bannered flukes in the air, the grand god revealed himself, sounded, and went out of sight. Hoveringly halting, and dipping on the wing, the white sea-fowls longingly lingered over the agitated pool that he left.

With oars apeak, and paddles down, the sheets of their sails adrift, the three boats now stilly floated, awaiting Moby Dick's reappearance.

"An hour," said Ahab, standing rooted in his boat's stern; and he gazed beyond the whale's place, towards the dim blue spaces and wide wooing vacancies to leeward. It was only an instant; for again his eyes seemed whirling round in his head as he swept the watery circle. The breeze now freshened; the sea began to swell.

"The birds!—the birds!" cried Tashtego.

In long Indian file, as when herons take wing, the white birds were now all flying towards Ahab's boat; and when within a few yards began fluttering over the water there, wheeling round and round, with joyous, expectant cries. Their vision was keener than man's; Ahab could discover no sign in the sea. But suddenly as he peered down and down into its depths, he profoundly saw a white living spot no bigger than a white weasel, with wonderful celerity uprising, and magnifying as it rose, till it turned, and then there were plainly revealed two long crooked rows of white, glistening teeth, floating up from the undiscoverable bottom. It was Moby Dick's open mouth and scrolled jaw; his vast, shadowed bulk still half blending with the blue of the sea. The glittering mouth yawned beneath the boat like an open-

doored marble tomb; and giving one sidelong sweep with his
steering oar, Ahab whirled the craft aside from this tremendous apparition. Then, calling upon Fedallah to change places
with him, went forward to the bows, and seizing Perth's harpoon, commanded his crew to grasp their oars and stand by
to stern.

Now, by reason of this timely spinning round the boat
upon its axis, its bow, by anticipation, was made to face the
whale's head while yet under water. But as if perceiving this
stratagem, Moby Dick, with that malicious intelligence ascribed to him, sidelingly transplanted himself, as it were, in
an instant, shooting his pleated head lengthwise beneath the
boat.

Through and through; through every plank and each rib, it
thrilled for an instant, the whale obliquely lying on his back,
in the manner of a biting shark, slowly and feelingly taking
its bows full within his mouth, so that the long, narrow,
scrolled lower jaw curled high up into the open air, and one
of the teeth caught in a row-lock. The bluish pearl-white of
the inside of the jaw was within six inches of Ahab's head,
and reached higher than that. In this attitude the White
Whale now shook the slight cedar as a mildly cruel cat her
mouse. With unastonished eyes Fedallah gazed, and crossed
his arms; but the tiger-yellow crew were tumbling over each
other's heads to gain the uttermost stern.

And now, while both elastic gunwales were springing in
and out, as the whale dallied with the doomed craft in this
devilish way; and from his body being submerged beneath
the boat, he could not be darted at from the bows, for the
bows were almost inside of him, as it were; and while the
other boats involuntarily paused, as before a quick crisis impossible to withstand, then it was that monomaniac Ahab,
furious with this tantalizing vicinity of his foe, which placed
him all alive and helpless in the very jaws he hated; frenzied
with all this, he seized the long bone with his naked hands,
and wildly strove to wrench it from its gripe. As now he thus
vainly strove, the jaw slipped from him; the frail gunwales
bent in, collapsed, and snapped, as both jaws, like an enormous shears, sliding further aft, bit the craft completely in
twain, and locked themselves fast again in the sea, midway

between the two floating wrecks. These floated aside, the broken ends drooping, the crew at the stern-wreck clinging to the gunwales, and striving to hold fast to the oars to lash them across.

At that preluding moment, ere the boat was yet snapped, Ahab, the first to perceive the whale's intent, by the crafty upraising of his head, a movement that loosed his hold for the time; at that moment his hand had made one final effort to push the boat out of the bite. But only slipping further into the whale's mouth, and tilting over sideways as it slipped, the boat had shaken off his hold on the jaw; spilled him out of it, as he leaned to the push; and so he fell flat-faced upon the sea.

Ripplingly withdrawing from his prey, Moby Dick now lay at a little distance, vertically thrusting his oblong white head up and down in the billows; and at the same time slowly revolving his whole spindled body; so that when his vast wrinkled forehead rose—some twenty or more feet out of the water—the now rising swells, with all their confluent waves, dazzlingly broke against it; vindictively tossing their shivered spray still higher into the air.* So, in a gale, the but half baffled Channel billows only recoil from the base of the Eddy-stone, triumphantly to overleap its summit with their scud.

But soon resuming his horizontal attitude, Moby Dick swam swiftly round and round the wrecked crew; sideways churning the water in his vengeful wake, as if lashing himself up to still another and more deadly assault. The sight of the splintered boat seemed to madden him, as the blood of grapes and mulberries cast before Antiochus's elephants in the book of Maccabees. Meanwhile Ahab half smothered in the foam of the whale's insolent tail, and too much of a cripple to swim,—though he could still keep afloat, even in the heart of such a whirlpool as that; helpless Ahab's head was seen, like a tossed bubble which the least chance shock might burst. From the boat's fragmentary stern, Fedallah incuriously and

---

*This motion is peculiar to the sperm whale. It receives its designation (pitchpoling) from its being likened to that preliminary up-and-down poise of the whale-lance, in the exercise called pitchpoling, previously described. By this motion the whale must best and most comprehensively view whatever objects may be encircling him.

mildly eyed him; the clinging crew, at the other drifting end, could not succor him; more than enough was it for them to look to themselves. For so revolvingly appalling was the White Whale's aspect, and so planetarily swift the ever-contracting circles he made, that he seemed horizontally swooping upon them. And though the other boats, unharmed, still hovered hard by; still they dared not pull into the eddy to strike, lest that should be the signal for the instant destruction of the jeopardized castaways, Ahab and all; nor in that case could they themselves hope to escape. With straining eyes, then, they remained on the outer edge of the direful zone, whose centre had now become the old man's head.

Meantime, from the beginning all this had been descried from the ship's mast heads; and squaring her yards, she had borne down upon the scene; and was now so nigh, that Ahab in the water hailed her;—"Sail on the"—but that moment a breaking sea dashed on him from Moby Dick, and whelmed him for the time. But struggling out of it again, and chancing to rise on a towering crest, he shouted,—"Sail on the whale!—Drive him off!"

The Pequod's prow was pointed; and breaking up the charmed circle, she effectually parted the white whale from his victim. As he sullenly swam off, the boats flew to the rescue.

Dragged into Stubb's boat with blood-shot, blinded eyes, the white brine caking in his wrinkles; the long tension of Ahab's bodily strength did crack, and helplessly he yielded to his body's doom: for a time, lying all crushed in the bottom of Stubb's boat, like one trodden under foot of herds of elephants. Far inland, nameless wails came from him, as desolate sounds from out ravines.

But this intensity of his physical prostration did but so much the more abbreviate it. In an instant's compass, great hearts sometimes condense to one deep pang, the sum total of those shallow pains kindly diffused through feebler men's whole lives. And so, such hearts, though summary in each one suffering; still, if the gods decree it, in their life-time aggregate a whole age of woe, wholly made up of instantaneous intensities; for even in their pointless centres, those noble natures contain the entire circumferences of inferior souls.

"The harpoon," said Ahab, half way rising, and draggingly leaning on one bended arm—"is it safe?"

"Aye, sir, for it was not darted; this is it," said Stubb, showing it.

"Lay it before me;—any missing men?"

"One, two, three, four, five;—there were five oars, sir, and here are five men."

"That's good.—Help me, man; I wish to stand. So, so, I see him! there! there! going to leeward still; what a leaping spout!—Hands off from me! The eternal sap runs up in Ahab's bones again! Set the sail; out oars; the helm!"

It is often the case that when a boat is stove, its crew, being picked up by another boat, help to work that second boat; and the chase is thus continued with what is called double-banked oars. It was thus now. But the added power of the boat did not equal the added power of the whale, for he seemed to have treble-banked his every fin; swimming with a velocity which plainly showed, that if now, under these circumstances, pushed on, the chase would prove an indefinitely prolonged, if not a hopeless one; nor could any crew endure for so long a period, such an unintermitted, intense straining at the oar; a thing barely tolerable only in some one brief vicissitude. The ship itself, then, as it sometimes happens, offered the most promising intermediate means of overtaking the chase. Accordingly, the boats now made for her, and were soon swayed up to their cranes—the two parts of the wrecked boat having been previously secured by her—and then hoisting everything to her side, and stacking her canvas high up, and sideways outstretching it with stun-sails, like the double-jointed wings of an albatross; the Pequod bore down in the leeward wake of Moby Dick. At the well known, methodic intervals, the whale's glittering spout was regularly announced from the manned mast-heads; and when he would be reported as just gone down, Ahab would take the time, and then pacing the deck, binnacle-watch in hand, so soon as the last second of the allotted hour expired, his voice was heard.—"Whose is the doubloon now? D'ye see him?" and if the reply was, No, sir! straightway he commanded them to lift him to his perch. In this way the day wore on; Ahab, now aloft and motionless; anon, unrestingly pacing the planks.

As he was thus walking, uttering no sound, except to hail the men aloft, or to bid them hoist a sail still higher, or to spread one to a still greater breadth—thus to and fro pacing, beneath his slouched hat, at every turn he passed his own wrecked boat, which had been dropped upon the quarter-deck, and lay there reversed; broken bow to shattered stern. At last he paused before it; and as in an already over-clouded sky fresh troops of clouds will sometimes sail across, so over the old man's face there now stole some such added gloom as this.

Stubb saw him pause; and perhaps intending, not vainly, though, to evince his own unabated fortitude, and thus keep up a valiant place in his Captain's mind, he advanced, and eyeing the wreck exclaimed—"The thistle the ass refused; it pricked his mouth too keenly, sir; ha! ha!"

"What soulless thing is this that laughs before a wreck? Man, man! did I not know thee brave as fearless fire (and as mechanical) I could swear thou wert a poltroon. Groan nor laugh should be heard before a wreck."

"Aye sir," said Starbuck drawing near, " 'tis a solemn sight; an omen, and an ill one."

"Omen? omen?—the dictionary! If the gods think to speak outright to man, they will honorably speak outright; not shake their heads, and give an old wives' darkling hint.—Be-gone! Ye two are the opposite poles of one thing; Starbuck is Stubb reversed, and Stubb is Starbuck; and ye two are all mankind; and Ahab stands alone among the millions of the peopled earth, nor gods nor men his neighbors! Cold, cold—I shiver!—How now? Aloft there! D'ye see him? Sing out for every spout, though he spout ten times a second!"

The day was nearly done; only the hem of his golden robe was rustling. Soon, it was almost dark, but the look-out men still remained unset.

"Can't see the spout now, sir;—too dark"—cried a voice from the air.

"How heading when last seen?"

"As before, sir,—straight to leeward."

"Good! he will travel slower now 'tis night. Down royals and top-gallant stun-sails, Mr. Starbuck. We must not run over him before morning; he's making a passage now, and may heave-to a while. Helm there! keep her full before the wind!—Aloft! come down!—Mr. Stubb, send a fresh hand to the fore-mast head, and see it manned till morning."— Then advancing towards the doubloon in the main-mast— "Men, this gold is mine, for I earned it; but I shall let it abide here till the White Whale is dead; and then, whosoever of ye first raises him, upon the day he shall be killed, this gold is that man's; and if on that day I shall again raise him, then, ten times its sum shall be divided among all of ye! Away now!—the deck is thine, sir."

And so saying, he placed himself half way within the scuttle, and slouching his hat, stood there till dawn, except when at intervals rousing himself to see how the night wore on.

Chapter 134

THE CHASE—SECOND DAY

A T DAY-BREAK, the three mast-heads were punctually manned afresh.

"D'ye see him?" cried Ahab, after allowing a little space for the light to spread.

"See nothing, sir."

"Turn up all hands and make sail! he travels faster than I thought for;—the top-gallant sails!—aye, they should have been kept on her all night. But no matter—'tis but resting for the rush."

Here be it said, that this pertinacious pursuit of one particular whale, continued through day into night, and through night into day, is a thing by no means unprecedented in the South sea fishery. For such is the wonderful skill, prescience of experience, and invincible confidence acquired by some great natural geniuses among the Nantucket commanders; that from the simple observation of a whale when last descried, they will, under certain given circumstances, pretty accurately foretell both the direction in which he will continue to swim for a time, while out of sight, as well as his probable rate of progression during that period. And, in these cases, somewhat as a pilot, when about losing sight of a coast, whose general trending he well knows, and which he desires shortly to return to again, but at some further point; like as this pilot stands by his compass, and takes the precise bearing of the cape at present visible, in order the more certainly to hit aright the remote, unseen headland, eventually to be visited: so does the fisherman, at his compass, with the whale; for after being chased, and diligently marked, through several hours of daylight, then, when night obscures the fish, the creature's future wake through the darkness is almost as established to the sagacious mind of the hunter, as the pilot's coast is to him. So that to this hunter's wondrous skill, the proverbial evanescence of a thing writ in water, a wake, is to all desired purposes well nigh as reliable as the steadfast land.

And as the mighty iron Leviathan of the modern railway is so familiarly known in its every pace, that, with watches in their hands, men time his rate as doctors that of a baby's pulse; and lightly say of it, the up train or the down train will reach such or such a spot, at such or such an hour; even so, almost, there are occasions when these Nantucketers time that other Leviathan of the deep, according to the observed humor of his speed; and say to themselves, so many hours hence this whale will have gone two hundred miles, will have about reached this or that degree of latitude or longitude. But to render this acuteness at all successful in the end, the wind and the sea must be the whaleman's allies; for of what present avail to the becalmed or windbound mariner is the skill that assures him he is exactly ninety-three leagues and a quarter from his port? Inferable from these statements, are many collateral subtile matters touching the chase of whales.

The ship tore on; leaving such a furrow in the sea as when a cannon-ball, missent, becomes a plough-share and turns up the level field.

"By salt and hemp!" cried Stubb, "but this swift motion of the deck creeps up one's legs and tingles at the heart. This ship and I are two brave fellows!—Ha! ha! Some one take me up, and launch me, spine-wise, on the sea,—for by live-oaks! my spine's a keel. Ha, ha! we go the gait that leaves no dust behind!"

"There she blows—she blows!—she blows!—right ahead!" was now the mast-head cry.

"Aye, aye!" cried Stubb, "I knew it—ye can't escape—blow on and split your spout, O whale! the mad fiend himself is after ye! blow your trump—blister your lungs!—Ahab will dam off your blood, as a miller shuts his water-gate upon the stream!"

And Stubb did but speak out for well nigh all that crew. The frenzies of the chase had by this time worked them bubblingly up, like old wine worked anew. Whatever pale fears and forebodings some of them might have felt before; these were not only now kept out of sight through the growing awe of Ahab, but they were broken up, and on all sides routed, as timid prairie hares that scatter before the bounding bison. The hand of Fate had snatched all their souls; and by the stirring perils of the previous day; the rack of the past night's suspense; the fixed, unfearing, blind, reckless way in which their wild craft went plunging towards its flying mark; by all these things, their hearts were bowled along. The wind that made great bellies of their sails, and rushed the vessel on by arms invisible as irresistible; this seemed the symbol of that unseen agency which so enslaved them to the race.

They were one man, not thirty. For as the one ship that held them all; though it was put together of all contrasting things—oak, and maple, and pine wood; iron, and pitch, and hemp—yet all these ran into each other in the one concrete hull, which shot on its way, both balanced and directed by the long central keel; even so, all the individualities of the crew, this man's valor, that man's fear; guilt and guiltlessness, all varieties were welded into oneness, and were all directed to that fatal goal which Ahab their one lord and keel did point to.

The rigging lived. The mast-heads, like the tops of tall palms, were outspreadingly tufted with arms and legs. Clinging to a spar with one hand, some reached forth the other with impatient wavings; others, shading their eyes from the vivid sunlight, sat far out on the rocking yards; all the spars in full bearing of mortals, ready and ripe for their fate. Ah! how they still strove through that infinite blueness to seek out the thing that might destroy them!

"Why sing ye not out for him, if ye see him?" cried Ahab, when, after the lapse of some minutes since the first cry, no more had been heard. "Sway me up, men; ye have been deceived; not Moby Dick casts one odd jet that way, and then disappears."

It was even so; in their headlong eagerness, the men had mistaken some other thing for the whale-spout, as the event itself soon proved; for hardly had Ahab reached his perch; hardly was the rope belayed to its pin on deck, when he struck the key-note to an orchestra, that made the air vibrate as with the combined discharges of rifles. The triumphant halloo of thirty buckskin lungs was heard, as—much nearer to the ship than the place of the imaginary jet, less than a mile ahead—Moby Dick bodily burst into view! For not by any calm and indolent spoutings; not by the peaceable gush of that mystic fountain in his head, did the White Whale now reveal his vicinity; but by the far more wondrous phenomenon of breaching. Rising with his utmost velocity from the furthest depths, the Sperm Whale thus booms his entire bulk into the pure element of air, and piling up a mountain of dazzling foam, shows his place to the distance of seven miles and more. In those moments, the torn, enraged waves he shakes off, seem his mane; in some cases, this breaching is his act of defiance.

"There she breaches! there she breaches!" was the cry, as in his immeasurable bravadoes the White Whale tossed himself salmon-like to Heaven. So suddenly seen in the blue plain of the sea, and relieved against the still bluer margin of the sky, the spray that he raised, for the moment, intolerably glittered and glared like a glacier; and stood there gradually fading and fading away from its first sparkling intensity, to the dim mistiness of an advancing shower in a vale.

"Aye, breach your last to the sun, Moby Dick!" cried Ahab, "thy hour and thy harpoon are at hand!—Down! down all of ye, but one man at the fore. The boats!—stand by!"

Unmindful of the tedious rope-ladders of the shrouds, the men, like shooting stars, slid to the deck, by the isolated backstays and halyards; while Ahab, less dartingly, but still rapidly was dropped from his perch.

"Lower away," he cried, so soon as he had reached his boat—a spare one, rigged the afternoon previous. "Mr. Starbuck, the ship is thine—keep away from the boats, but keep near them. Lower, all!"

As if to strike a quick terror into them, by this time being the first assailant himself, Moby Dick had turned, and was now coming for the three crews. Ahab's boat was central; and cheering his men, he told them he would take the whale head-and-head,—that is, pull straight up to his forehead,—a not uncommon thing; for when within a certain limit, such a course excludes the coming onset from the whale's sidelong vision. But ere that close limit was gained, and while yet all three boats were plain as the ship's three masts to his eye; the White Whale churning himself into furious speed, almost in an instant as it were, rushing among the boats with open jaws, and a lashing tail, offered appalling battle on every side;

and heedless of the irons darted at him from every boat, seemed only intent on annihilating each separate plank of which those boats were made. But skilfully manœuvred, incessantly wheeling like trained chargers in the field; the boats for a while eluded him; though, at times, but by a plank's breadth; while all the time, Ahab's unearthly slogan tore every other cry but his to shreds.

But at last in his untraceable evolutions, the White Whale so crossed and recrossed, and in a thousand ways entangled the slack of the three lines now fast to him, that they foreshortened, and, of themselves, warped the devoted boats towards the planted irons in him; though now for a moment the whale drew aside a little, as if to rally for a more tremendous charge. Seizing that opportunity, Ahab first paid out more line: and then was rapidly hauling and jerking in upon it again—hoping that way to disencumber it of some snarls—when lo!—a sight more savage than the embattled teeth of sharks!

Caught and twisted—corkscrewed in the mazes of the line, loose harpoons and lances, with all their bristling barbs and points, came flashing and dripping up to the chocks in the bows of Ahab's boat. Only one thing could be done. Seizing the boat-knife, he critically reached within—through—and then, without—the rays of steel; dragged in the line beyond, passed it, inboard, to the bowsman, and then, twice sundering the rope near the chocks—dropped the intercepted fagot of steel into the sea; and was all fast again. That instant, the White Whale made a sudden rush among the remaining tangles of the other lines; by so doing, irresistibly dragged the more involved boats of Stubb and Flask towards his flukes; dashed them together like two rolling husks on a surf-beaten beach, and then, diving down into the sea, disappeared in a boiling maelstrom, in which, for a space, the odorous cedar chips of the wrecks danced round and round, like the grated nutmeg in a swiftly stirred bowl of punch.

While the two crews were yet circling in the waters, reaching out after the revolving line-tubs, oars, and other floating furniture, while aslope little Flask bobbed up and down like an empty vial, twitching his legs upwards to escape the dreaded jaws of sharks; and Stubb was lustily singing out for some one to ladle him up; and while the old man's line—now parting—admitted of his pulling into the creamy pool to rescue whom he could;—in that wild simultaneousness of a thousand concreted perils,—Ahab's yet unstricken boat seemed drawn up towards Heaven by invisible wires,—as, arrow-like, shooting perpendicularly from the sea, the White Whale dashed his broad forehead against its bottom, and sent it, turning over and over, into the air; till it fell again—gunwale downwards—and Ahab and his men struggled out from under it, like seals from a sea-side cave.

The first uprising momentum of the whale—modifying its direction as he struck the surface—involuntarily launched him along it, to a little distance from the centre of the destruction he had made; and with his back to it, he now lay for a moment slowly feeling with his flukes from side to side; and whenever a stray oar, bit of plank, the least chip or crumb of the boats touched his skin, his tail swiftly drew back, and came sideways smiting the sea. But soon, as if satisfied that his work for that time was done, he pushed his pleated forehead through the ocean, and trailing after him the intertangled lines, continued his leeward way at a traveller's methodic pace.

As before, the attentive ship having descried the whole fight, again came bearing down to the rescue, and dropping a boat, picked up the floating mariners, tubs, oars, and whatever else could be caught at, and safely landed them on her decks. Some sprained shoulders, wrists, and ankles; livid contusions; wrenched harpoons and lances; inextricable intricacies of rope; shattered oars and planks; all these were there; but no fatal or even serious ill seemed to have befallen any one. As with Fedallah the day before, so Ahab was now found grimly clinging to his boat's broken half, which afforded a comparatively easy float; nor did it so exhaust him as the previous day's mishap.

But when he was helped to the deck, all eyes were fastened upon him; as instead of standing by himself he still half-hung upon the shoulder of Starbuck, who had thus far been the foremost to assist him. His ivory leg had been snapped off, leaving but one short sharp splinter.

"Aye aye, Starbuck, 'tis sweet to lean sometimes, be the

leaner who he will; and would old Ahab had leaned oftener than he has."

"The ferrule has not stood, sir," said the carpenter, now coming up; "I put good work into that leg."

"But no bones broken, sir, I hope," said Stubb with true concern.

"Aye! and all splintered to pieces, Stubb!—d'ye see it.— But even with a broken bone, old Ahab is untouched; and I account no living bone of mine one jot more me, than this dead one that's lost. Nor white whale, nor man, nor fiend, can so much as graze old Ahab in his own proper and inaccessible being. Can any lead touch yonder floor, any mast scrape yonder roof?—Aloft there! which way?"

"Dead to leeward, sir."

"Up helm, then; pile on the sail again, ship keepers! down the rest of the spare boats and rig them—Mr. Starbuck away, and muster the boats' crews."

"Let me first help thee towards the bulwarks, sir."

"Oh, oh, oh! how this splinter gores me now! Accursed fate! that the unconquerable captain in the soul should have such a craven mate!"

"Sir?"

"My body, man, not thee. Give me something for a cane— there, that shivered lance will do. Muster the men. Surely I have not seen him yet. By heaven it cannot be!—missing?— quick! call them all."

The old man's hinted thought was true. Upon mustering the company, the Parsee was not there.

"The Parsee!" cried Stubb—"he must have been caught in——"

"The black vomit wrench thee!—run all of ye above, alow, cabin, forecastle—find him—not gone—not gone!"

But quickly they returned to him with the tidings that the Parsee was nowhere to be found.

"Aye, sir," said Stubb—"caught among the tangles of your line—I thought I saw him dragging under."

"*My* line! *my* line? Gone?—gone? What means that little word?—What death-knell rings in it, that old Ahab shakes as if he were the belfry. The harpoon, too!—toss over the litter there,—d'ye see it?—the forged iron, men, the white

whale's—no, no, no,—blistered fool! this hand did dart it!—
'tis in the fish!—Aloft there! Keep him nailed—Quick!—all
hands to the rigging of the boats—collect the oars—
harpooneers! the irons, the irons!—hoist the royals higher—
a pull on all the sheets!—helm there! steady, steady for your
life! I'll ten times girdle the unmeasured globe; yea and dive
straight through it, but I'll slay him yet!"

"Great God! but for one single instant show thyself," cried
Starbuck; "never, never wilt thou capture him, old man—In
Jesus' name no more of this, that's worse than devil's madness. Two days chased; twice stove to splinters; thy very leg
once more snatched from under thee; thy evil shadow gone—
all good angels mobbing thee with warnings:—what more
wouldst thou have?—Shall we keep chasing this murderous
fish till he swamps the last man? Shall we be dragged by him
to the bottom of the sea? Shall we be towed by him to the
infernal world? Oh, oh,—Impiety and blasphemy to hunt
him more!"

"Starbuck, of late I've felt strangely moved to thee; ever
since that hour we both saw—thou know'st what, in one
another's eyes. But in this matter of the whale, be the front
of thy face to me as the palm of this hand—a lipless, unfea-
tured blank. Ahab is for ever Ahab, man. This whole act's
immutably decreed. 'Twas rehearsed by thee and me a billion
years before this ocean rolled. Fool! I am the Fates' lieutenant; I act under orders. Look thou, underling! that thou
obeyest mine.—Stand round me, men. Ye see an old man cut
down to the stump; leaning on a shivered lance; propped up
on a lonely foot. 'Tis Ahab—his body's part; but Ahab's
soul's a centipede, that moves upon a hundred legs. I feel
strained, half stranded, as ropes that tow dismasted frigates in
a gale; and I may look so. But ere I break, ye'll hear me crack;
and till ye hear *that*, know that Ahab's hawser tows his purpose yet. Believe ye, men, in the things called omens? Then
laugh aloud, and cry encore! For ere they drown, drowning
things will twice rise to the surface; then rise again, to sink
for evermore. So with Moby Dick—two days he's floated—
to-morrow will be the third. Aye, men, he'll rise once
more,—but only to spout his last! D'ye feel brave, men,
brave?"

"As fearless fire," cried Stubb.

"And as mechanical," muttered Ahab. Then as the men went forward, he muttered on:—"The things called omens! And yesterday I talked the same to Starbuck there, concerning my broken boat. Oh! how valiantly I seek to drive out of others' hearts what's clinched so fast in mine!—The Parsee—the Parsee!—gone, gone? and he was to go before:—but still was to be seen again ere I could perish—How's that?—There's a riddle now might baffle all the lawyers backed by the ghosts of the whole line of judges:—like a hawk's beak it pecks my brain. *I'll, I'll* solve it, though!"

When dusk descended, the whale was still in sight to leeward.

So once more the sail was shortened, and everything passed nearly as on the previous night; only, the sound of hammers, and the hum of the grindstone was heard till nearly daylight, as the men toiled by lanterns in the complete and careful rigging of the spare boats and sharpening their fresh weapons for the morrow. Meantime, of the broken keel of Ahab's wrecked craft the carpenter made him another leg; while still as on the night before, slouched Ahab stood fixed within his scuttle; his hid, heliotrope glance anticipatingly gone backward on its dial; set due eastward for the earliest sun.

Chapter 135

The Chase—Third Day

THE MORNING of the third day dawned fair and fresh, and once more the solitary night-man at the fore-mast-head was relieved by crowds of the daylight look-outs, who dotted every mast and almost every spar.

"D'ye see him?" cried Ahab; but the whale was not yet in sight.

"In his infallible wake, though; but follow that wake, that's all. Helm there; steady, as thou goest, and hast been going. What a lovely day again! were it a new-made world, and made for a summer-house to the angels, and this morning the first of its throwing open to them, a fairer day could not dawn upon that world. Here's food for thought, had Ahab time to think; but Ahab never thinks; he only feels, feels, feels; *that's* tingling enough for mortal man! to think's audacity. God only has that right and privilege. Thinking is, or ought to be, a coolness and a calmness; and our poor hearts throb, and our poor brains beat too much for that. And yet, I've sometimes thought my brain was very calm—frozen calm, this old skull cracks so, like a glass in which the contents turn to ice, and shiver it. And still this hair is growing now; this moment growing, and heat must breed it; but no, it's like that sort of common grass that will grow anywhere, between the earthy clefts of Greenland ice or in Vesuvius lava. How the wild winds blow it; they whip it about me as the torn shreds of split sails lash the tossed ship they cling to. A vile wind that has no doubt blown ere this through prison corridors and cells, and wards of hospitals, and ventilated them, and now comes blowing hither as innocent as fleeces. Out upon it!—it's tainted. Were I the wind, I'd blow no more on such a wicked, miserable world. I'd crawl somewhere to a cave, and slink there. And yet, 'tis a noble and heroic thing, the wind! who ever conquered it? In every fight it has the last and bitterest blow. Run tilting at it, and you but run through it. Ha! a coward wind that strikes stark naked men, but will not stand to receive a single blow. Even Ahab is a braver thing—a nobler thing than *that*. Would now the wind but had a body; but all the things that most exasperate and outrage mortal man, all these things are bodiless, but only bodiless as objects, not as agents. There's a most special, a most cunning, oh, a most malicious difference! And yet, I say again, and swear it now, that there's something all glorious and gracious in the wind. These warm Trade Winds, at least, that in the clear heavens blow straight on, in strong and steadfast, vigorous mildness; and veer not from their mark, however the baser currents of the sea may turn and tack, and mightiest Mississippies of the land swift and swerve about, uncertain where to go at last. And by the eternal Poles! these same Trades that so directly blow my good ship on; these Trades, or something like them—something so unchangeable, and full as strong, blow my keeled soul along! To it! Aloft there! What d'ye see?"

"Nothing, sir."

"Nothing! and noon at hand! The doubloon goes a-begging! See the sun! Aye, aye, it must be so. I've oversailed him. How, got the start? Aye, he's chasing *me* now; not I, *him*—that's bad; I might have known it, too. Fool! the lines—the harpoons he's towing. Aye, aye, I have run him by last night. About! about! Come down, all of ye, but the regular look outs! Man the braces!"

Steering as she had done, the wind had been somewhat on the Pequod's quarter, so that now being pointed in the reverse direction, the braced ship sailed hard upon the breeze as she rechurned the cream in her own white wake.

"Against the wind he now steers for the open jaw," murmured Starbuck to himself, as he coiled the new-hauled mainbrace upon the rail. "God keep us, but already my bones feel damp within me, and from the inside wet my flesh. I misdoubt me that I disobey my God in obeying him!"

"Stand by to sway me up!" cried Ahab, advancing to the hempen basket. "We should meet him soon."

"Aye, aye, sir," and straightway Starbuck did Ahab's bidding, and once more Ahab swung on high.

A whole hour now passed; gold-beaten out to ages. Time itself now held long breaths with keen suspense. But at last, some three points off the weather bow, Ahab descried the spout again, and instantly from the three mast-heads three shrieks went up as if the tongues of fire had voiced it.

"Forehead to forehead I meet thee, this third time, Moby Dick! On deck there!—brace sharper up; crowd her into the wind's eye. He's too far off to lower yet, Mr. Starbuck. The sails shake! Stand over that helmsman with a top-maul! So, so; he travels fast, and I must down. But let me have one more good round look aloft here at the sea; there's time for that. An old, old sight, and yet somehow so young; aye, and not changed a wink since I first saw it, a boy, from the sand-hills of Nantucket! The same!—the same!—the same to Noah as to me. There's a soft shower to leeward. Such lovely leewardings! They must lead somewhere—to something else than common land, more palmy than the palms. Leeward! the white whale goes that way; look to windward, then; the better if the bitterer quarter. But good bye, good bye, old mast-head! What's this?— green? aye, tiny mosses in these warped cracks. No such green weather stains on Ahab's head! There's the difference now between man's old age and matter's. But aye, old mast, we both grow old together; sound in our hulls, though, are we not, my ship? Aye, minus a leg, that's all. By heaven this dead wood has the better of my live flesh every way. I can't compare with it; and I've known some ships made of dead trees outlast the lives of men made of the most vital stuff of vital fathers. What's that he said? he should still go before me, my pilot; and yet to be seen again? But where? Will I have eyes at the bottom of the sea, supposing I descend those endless stairs? and all night I've been sailing from him, wherever he did sink to. Aye, aye, like many more thou told'st direful truth as touching thyself, O Parsee; but, Ahab, there thy shot fell short. Good by, mast-head—keep a good eye upon the whale, the while I'm gone. We'll talk to-morrow, nay, to-night, when the white whale lies down there, tied by head and tail."

He gave the word; and still gazing round him, was steadily lowered through the cloven blue air to the deck.

In due time the boats were lowered; but as standing in his

shallop's stern, Ahab just hovered upon the point of the descent, he waved to the mate,—who held one of the tackle-ropes on deck—and bade him pause.

"Starbuck!"

"Sir?"

"For the third time my soul's ship starts upon this voyage, Starbuck."

"Aye, sir, thou wilt have it so."

"Some ships sail from their ports, and ever afterwards are missing, Starbuck!"

"Truth, sir: saddest truth."

"Some men die at ebb tide; some at low water; some at the full of the flood;—and I feel now like a billow that's all one crested comb, Starbuck. I am old;—shake hands with me, man."

Their hands met; their eyes fastened; Starbuck's tears the glue.

"Oh, my captain, my captain!—noble heart—go not—go not!—see, it's a brave man that weeps; how great the agony of the persuasion then!"

"Lower away!"—cried Ahab, tossing the mate's arm from him. "Stand by the crew!"

In an instant the boat was pulling round close under the stern.

"The sharks! the sharks!" cried a voice from the low cabin-window there; "O master, my master, come back!"

But Ahab heard nothing; for his own voice was high-lifted then; and the boat leaped on.

Yet the voice spake true; for scarce had he pushed from the ship, when numbers of sharks, seemingly rising from out the dark waters beneath the hull, maliciously snapped at the blades of the oars, every time they dipped in the water; and in this way accompanied the boat with their bites. It is a thing not uncommonly happening to the whale-boats in those swarming seas; the sharks at times apparently following them in the same prescient way that vultures hover over the banners of marching regiments in the east. But these were the first sharks that had been observed by the Pequod since the White Whale had been first descried; and whether it was that Ahab's crew were all such tiger-yellow barbarians, and therefore their flesh more musky to the senses of the sharks—a matter sometimes well known to affect them,—however it was, they seemed to follow that one boat without molesting the others.

"Heart of wrought steel!" murmured Starbuck gazing over the side, and following with his eyes the receding boat— "canst thou yet ring boldly to that sight?—lowering thy keel among ravening sharks, and followed by them, open-mouthed to the chase; and this the critical third day?—For when three days flow together in one continuous intense pursuit; be sure the first is the morning, the second the noon, and the third the evening and the end of that thing—be that end what it may. Oh! my God! what is this that shoots through me, and leaves me so deadly calm, yet expectant,— fixed at the top of a shudder! Future things swim before me, as in empty outlines and skeletons; all the past is somehow grown dim. Mary, girl! thou fadest in pale glories behind me; boy! I seem to see but thy eyes grown wondrous blue. Strangest problems of life seem clearing; but clouds sweep between—Is my journey's end coming? My legs feel faint; like his who has footed it all day. Feel thy heart,—beats it yet?—Stir thyself, Starbuck!—stave it off—move, move! speak aloud!—Mast-head there! See ye my boy's hand on the hill?—Crazed;—aloft there!—keep thy keenest eye upon the boats:—mark well the whale!—Ho! again!—drive off that hawk! see! he pecks—he tears the vane"—pointing to the red flag flying at the main-truck—"Ha! he soars away with it!— Where's the old man now? sees't thou that sight, oh Ahab!— shudder, shudder!"

The boats had not gone very far, when by a signal from the mast-heads—a downward pointed arm, Ahab knew that the whale had sounded; but intending to be near him at the next rising, he held on his way a little sideways from the vessel; the becharmed crew maintaining the profoundest silence, as the head-beat waves hammered and hammered against the opposing bow.

"Drive, drive in your nails, oh ye waves! to their uttermost heads drive them in! ye but strike a thing without a lid; and no coffin and no hearse can be mine:—and hemp only can kill me! Ha! ha!"

Suddenly the waters around them slowly swelled in broad circles; then quickly upheaved, as if sideways sliding from a submerged berg of ice, swiftly rising to the surface. A low rumbling sound was heard; a subterraneous hum; and then all held their breaths; as bedraggled with trailing ropes, and harpoons, and lances, a vast form shot lengthwise, but obliquely from the sea. Shrouded in a thin drooping veil of mist, it hovered for a moment in the rainbowed air; and then fell swamping back into the deep. Crushed thirty feet upwards, the waters flashed for an instant like heaps of fountains, then brokenly sank in a shower of flakes, leaving the circling surface creamed like new milk round the marble trunk of the whale.

"Give way!" cried Ahab to the oarsmen, and the boats darted forward to the attack; but maddened by yesterday's fresh irons that corroded in him, Moby Dick seemed combinedly possessed by all the angels that fell from heaven. The wide tiers of welded tendons overspreading his broad white forehead, beneath the transparent skin, looked knitted together; as head on, he came churning his tail among the boats; and once more flailed them apart; spilling out the irons and lances from the two mates' boats, and dashing in one side of the upper part of their bows, but leaving Ahab's almost without a scar.

While Daggoo and Tashtego were stopping the strained planks; and as the whale swimming out from them, turned, and showed one entire flank as he shot by them again; at that moment a quick cry went up. Lashed round and round to the fish's back; pinioned in the turns upon turns in which, during the past night, the whale had reeled the involutions of the lines around him, the half torn body of the Parsee was seen; his sable raiment frayed to shreds; his distended eyes turned full upon old Ahab.

The harpoon dropped from his hand.

"Befooled, befooled!"—drawing in a long lean breath—"Aye, Parsee! I see thee again.—Aye, and thou goest before; and this, *this* then is the hearse that thou didst promise. But I hold thee to the last letter of thy word. Where is the second hearse? Away, mates, to the ship! those boats are useless now; repair them if ye can in time, and return to me; if not, Ahab

is enough to die—Down, men! the first thing that but offers
to jump from this boat I stand in, that thing I harpoon. Ye
are not other men, but my arms and my legs; and so obey
me.—Where's the whale? gone down again?"

But he looked too nigh the boat; for as if bent upon escaping with the corpse he bore, and as if the particular place of
the last encounter had been but a stage in his leeward voyage,
Moby Dick was now again steadily swimming forward; and
had almost passed the ship,—which thus far had been sailing
in the contrary direction to him, though for the present her
headway had been stopped. He seemed swimming with his
utmost velocity, and now only intent upon pursuing his own
straight path in the sea.

"Oh! Ahab," cried Starbuck, "not too late is it, even now,
the third day, to desist. See! Moby Dick seeks thee not. It is
thou, thou, that madly seekest him!"

Setting sail to the rising wind, the lonely boat was swiftly
impelled to leeward, by both oars and canvas. And at last
when Ahab was sliding by the vessel, so near as plainly to
distinguish Starbuck's face as he leaned over the rail, he hailed
him to turn the vessel about, and follow him, not too swiftly,
at a judicious interval. Glancing upwards, he saw Tashtego,
Queequeg, and Daggoo, eagerly mounting to the three mast-
heads; while the oarsmen were rocking in the two staved
boats which had but just been hoisted to the side, and were
busily at work in repairing them. One after the other,
through the port-holes, as he sped, he also caught flying
glimpses of Stubb and Flask, busying themselves on deck
among bundles of new irons and lances. As he saw all this; as
he heard the hammers in the broken boats; far other hammers
seemed driving a nail into his heart. But he rallied. And now
marking that the vane or flag was gone from the main-mast-
head, he shouted to Tashtego, who had just gained that
perch, to descend again for another flag, and a hammer and
nails, and so nail it to the mast.

Whether fagged by the three days' running chase, and the
resistance to his swimming in the knotted hamper he bore; or
whether it was some latent deceitfulness and malice in him:
whichever was true, the White Whale's way now began to
abate, as it seemed, from the boat so rapidly nearing him once

more; though indeed the whale's last start had not been so long a one as before. And still as Ahab glided over the waves the unpitying sharks accompanied him; and so pertinaciously stuck to the boat; and so continually bit at the plying oars, that the blades became jagged and crunched, and left small splinters in the sea, at almost every dip.

"Heed them not! those teeth but give new rowlocks to your oars. Pull on! 'tis the better rest, the shark's jaw than the yielding water."

"But at every bite, sir, the thin blades grow smaller and smaller!"

"They will last long enough! pull on!—But who can tell"—he muttered—"whether these sharks swim to feast on the whale or on Ahab?—But pull on! Aye, all alive, now—we near him. The helm! take the helm; let me pass,"—and so saying, two of the oarsmen helped him forward to the bows of the still flying boat.

At length as the craft was cast to one side, and ran ranging along with the White Whale's flank, he seemed strangely oblivious of its advance—as the whale sometimes will—and Ahab was fairly within the smoky mountain mist, which, thrown off from the whale's spout, curled round his great, Monadnock hump; he was even thus close to him; when, with body arched back, and both arms lengthwise high-lifted to the poise, he darted his fierce iron, and his far fiercer curse into the hated whale. As both steel and curse sank to the socket, as if sucked into a morass, Moby Dick sideways writhed; spasmodically rolled his nigh flank against the bow, and, without staving a hole in it, so suddenly canted the boat over, that had it not been for the elevated part of the gunwale to which he then clung, Ahab would once more have been tossed into the sea. As it was, three of the oarsmen—who foreknew not the precise instant of the dart, and were therefore unprepared for its effects—these were flung out; but so fell, that, in an instant two of them clutched the gunwale again, and rising to its level on a combing wave, hurled themselves bodily inboard again; the third man helplessly dropping astern, but still afloat and swimming.

Almost simultaneously, with a mighty volition of ungraduated, instantaneous swiftness, the White Whale darted through the weltering sea. But when Ahab cried out to the steersman to take new turns with the line, and hold it so; and commanded the crew to turn round on their seats, and tow the boat up to the mark; the moment the treacherous line felt that double strain and tug, it snapped in the empty air!

"What breaks in me? Some sinew cracks!—'tis whole again; oars! oars! Burst in upon him!"

Hearing the tremendous rush of the sea-crashing boat, the whale wheeled round to present his blank forehead at bay; but in that evolution, catching sight of the nearing black hull of the ship; seemingly seeing in it the source of all his persecutions; bethinking it—it may be—a larger and nobler foe; of a sudden, he bore down upon its advancing prow, smiting his jaws amid fiery showers of foam.

Ahab staggered; his hand smote his forehead. "I grow blind; hands! stretch out before me that I may yet grope my way. Is't night?"

"The whale! The ship!" cried the cringing oarsmen.

"Oars! oars! Slope downwards to thy depths, O sea, that ere it be for ever too late, Ahab may slide this last, last time upon his mark! I see: the ship! the ship! Dash on, my men! Will ye not save my ship?"

But as the oarsmen violently forced their boat through the sledge-hammering seas, the before whale-smitten bow-ends of two planks burst through, and in an instant almost, the temporarily disabled boat lay nearly level with the waves; its half-wading, splashing crew, trying hard to stop the gap and bale out the pouring water.

Meantime, for that one beholding instant, Tashtego's mast-head hammer remained suspended in his hand; and the red flag, half-wrapping him as with a plaid, then streamed itself straight out from him, as his own forward-flowing heart; while Starbuck and Stubb, standing upon the bowsprit beneath, caught sight of the down-coming monster just as soon as he.

"The whale, the whale! Up helm, up helm! Oh, all ye sweet powers of air, now hug me close! Let not Starbuck die, if die he must, in a woman's fainting fit. Up helm, I say—ye fools, the jaw! the jaw! Is this the end of all my bursting prayers? all my life-long fidelities? Oh, Ahab, Ahab, lo, thy work.

Steady! helmsman, steady. Nay, nay! Up helm again! He turns to meet us! Oh, his unappeasable brow drives on towards one, whose duty tells him he cannot depart. My God, stand by me now!"

"Stand not by me, but stand under me, whoever you are that will now help Stubb; for Stubb, too, sticks here. I grin at thee, thou grinning whale! Who ever helped Stubb, or kept Stubb awake, but Stubb's own unwinking eye? And now poor Stubb goes to bed upon a mattrass that is all too soft; would it were stuffed with brushwood! I grin at thee, thou grinning whale! Look ye, sun, moon, and stars! I call ye assassins of as good a fellow as ever spouted up his ghost. For all that, I would yet ring glasses with ye, would ye but hand the cup! Oh, oh! oh, oh! thou grinning whale, but there 'll be plenty of gulping soon! Why fly ye not, O Ahab! For me, off shoes and jacket to it; let Stubb die in his drawers! A most mouldy and over salted death, though;—cherries! cherries! cherries! oh, Flask, for one red cherry ere we die!"

"Cherries? I only wish that we were where they grow. Oh, Stubb, I hope my poor mother's drawn my part-pay ere this; if not, few coppers will now come to her, for the voyage is up."

From the ship's bows, nearly all the seamen now hung inactive; hammers, bits of plank, lances, and harpoons, mechanically retained in their hands, just as they had darted from their various employments; all their enchanted eyes intent upon the whale, which from side to side strangely vibrating his predestinating head, sent a broad band of overspreading semicircular foam before him as he rushed. Retribution, swift vengeance, eternal malice were in his whole aspect, and spite of all that mortal man could do, the solid white buttress of his forehead smote the ship's starboard bow, till men and timbers reeled. Some fell flat upon their faces. Like dislodged trucks, the heads of the harpooneers aloft shook on their bull-like necks. Through the breach, they heard the waters pour, as mountain torrents down a flume.

"The ship! The hearse!—the second hearse!" cried Ahab from the boat; "its wood could only be American!"

Diving beneath the settling ship, the whale ran quivering

along its keel; but turning under water, swiftly shot to the surface again, far off the other bow, but within a few yards of Ahab's boat, where, for a time, he lay quiescent.

"I turn my body from the sun. What ho, Tashtego! let me hear thy hammer. Oh! ye three unsurrendered spires of mine; thou uncracked keel; and only god-bullied hull; thou firm deck, and haughty helm, and Pole-pointed prow,—death-glorious ship! must ye then perish, and without me? Am I cut off from the last fond pride of meanest shipwrecked captains? Oh, lonely death on lonely life! Oh, now I feel my topmost greatness lies in my topmost grief. Ho, ho! from all your furthest bounds, pour ye now in, ye bold billows of my whole foregone life, and top this one piled comber of my death! Towards thee I roll, thou all-destroying but unconquering whale; to the last I grapple with thee; from hell's heart I stab at thee; for hate's sake I spit my last breath at thee. Sink all coffins and all hearses to one common pool! and since neither can be mine, let me then tow to pieces, while still chasing thee, though tied to thee, thou damned whale! *Thus*, I give up the spear!"

The harpoon was darted; the stricken whale flew forward; with igniting velocity the line ran through the groove;—ran foul. Ahab stooped to clear it; he did clear it; but the flying turn caught him round the neck, and voicelessly as Turkish mutes bowstring their victim, he was shot out of the boat, ere the crew knew he was gone. Next instant, the heavy eye-splice in the rope's final end flew out of the stark-empty tub, knocked down an oarsman, and smiting the sea, disappeared in its depths.

For an instant, the tranced boat's crew stood still; then turned. "The ship? Great God, where is the ship?" Soon they through dim, bewildering mediums saw her sidelong fading phantom, as in the gaseous Fata Morgana; only the uppermost masts out of water; while fixed by infatuation, or fidelity, or fate, to their once lofty perches, the pagan harpooneers still maintained their sinking lookouts on the sea. And now, concentric circles seized the lone boat itself, and all its crew, and each floating oar, and every lance-pole, and spinning, animate and inanimate, all round and round in one vortex, carried the smallest chip of the Pequod out of sight.

But as the last whelmings intermixingly poured themselves over the sunken head of the Indian at the mainmast, leaving a few inches of the erect spar yet visible, together with long streaming yards of the flag, which calmly undulated, with ironical coincidings, over the destroying billows they almost touched;—at that instant, a red arm and a hammer hovered backwardly uplifted in the open air, in the act of nailing the flag faster and yet faster to the subsiding spar. A sky-hawk that tauntingly had followed the main-truck downwards from its natural home among the stars, pecking at the flag, and incommoding Tashtego there; this bird now chanced to intercept its broad fluttering wing between the hammer and the wood; and simultaneously feeling that etherial thrill, the submerged savage beneath, in his death-grasp, kept his hammer frozen there; and so the bird of heaven, with archangelic shrieks, and his imperial beak thrust upwards, and his whole captive form folded in the flag of Ahab, went down with his ship, which, like Satan, would not sink to hell till she had dragged a living part of heaven along with her, and helmeted herself with it.

Now small fowls flew screaming over the yet yawning gulf; a sullen white surf beat against its steep sides; then all collapsed, and the great shroud of the sea rolled on as it rolled five thousand years ago.

Epilogue

"And I only am escaped alone to tell thee."

Job

THE drama's done. Why then here does any one step forth? —
Because one did survive the wreck.

It so chanced, that after the Parsee's disappearance, I was he
whom the Fates ordained to take the place of Ahab's bowsman,
when that bowsman assumed the vacant post; the same, who, when
on the last day the three men were tossed from out the rocking
boat, was dropped astern. So, floating on the margin of the ensu-
ing scene, and in full sight of it, when the half-spent suction of the
sunk ship reached me, I was then, but slowly, drawn towards the
closing vortex. When I reached it, it had subsided to a creamy pool.
Round and round, then, and ever contracting towards the button-
like black bubble at the axis of that slowly wheeling circle, like
another Ixion I did revolve. Till, gaining that vital centre, the
black bubble upward burst; and now, liberated by reason of its
cunning spring, and, owing to its great buoyancy, rising with
great force, the coffin life-buoy shot lengthwise from the sea, fell
over, and floated by my side. Buoyed up by that coffin, for almost
one whole day and night, I floated on a soft and dirge-like main.
The unharming sharks, they glided by as if with padlocks on their
mouths; the savage sea-hawks sailed with sheathed beaks. On the
second day, a sail drew near, nearer, and picked me up at last. It
was the devious-cruising Rachel, that in her retracing search after
her missing children, only found another orphan.

FINIS

Chronology

1819   Herman Melville born August 1, New York City, third child (second son) of Allan Melvill, importer and merchant of Scottish descent, and Maria Gansevoort, daughter of General Peter Gansevoort, a hero of the American Revolution and member of a prominent Albany family.

1825–29   Attends New-York Male High School.

1829–30   Attends Columbia Grammar School, New York, beginning September 1829.

1830   Father fails in business, and family moves to Albany in October.

1830–31   Attends Albany Academy, October 1830 to October 1831.

1832   Father dies, January 28, in debt.

1832–34   Works as clerk at the New York State Bank in Albany.

1834–35   Works on his uncle Thomas's farm near Pittsfield, Mass.

1835–37   Works in Albany as bookkeeper and clerk in his brother's fur business. Attends Albany Classical School in 1835; returns to Albany Academy, September 1, 1836, to March 1, 1837.

1837   Brother's business fails, April. Teaches in Sikes District School near Pittsfield for the fall term. Returns to Albany at the end of the year.

1838   Moves with family to nearby Lansingburgh in the spring. Returns briefly to his uncle's farm in the autumn. Back in Lansingburgh in November, studies surveying at the Lansingburgh Academy.

1839   Two sketches, "Fragments from a Writing Desk," published pseudonymously in *Democratic Press and Lansingburgh Advertiser*, May. Sails from New York to Liverpool and back as crew member on the trading ship *St. Lawrence*, June 5 to October 1.

1839–40   Teaches school in Greenbush, N.Y., and briefly (late May 1840) in Brunswick, N.Y.

1840   Visits his uncle Thomas in Galena, Ill., in the summer, accompanied by his friend, Eli Fly, and probably travels on a Mississippi River steamer during the visit. In autumn searches for a job in New York.

1841–42   Sails from New Bedford harbor, January 3, 1841, on the maiden voyage of the whaling ship *Acushnet*, bound for the South Seas. On July 9, 1842, deserts the *Acushnet* with Richard Tobias Greene at Nuku Hiva in the Marquesas.

1842   After a month in the Taipi valley, sails August 9 on the Australian whaling ship *Lucy Ann*; at Tahiti, is sent ashore with others as mutineer; escapes with John B. Troy in October; the two explore Tahiti and Eimeo and work on a potato farm.

1842–43   Sails on the Nantucket whaling ship *Charles and Henry* from November 7, 1842, through April 27, 1843; is discharged at Lahaina in the Hawaiian Islands, May 2, and takes various jobs in Honolulu.

1843–44   Enlists in the United States Navy in Honolulu; sails August 19, 1843, aboard the frigate *United States*, on which his superior and friend is John J. Chase; arrives in Boston October 3, 1844—having been away nearly four years—and is discharged October 14. Returns to Lansingburgh.

1845   Works on manuscript of a book based on his adventures in the Marquesas; it is rejected by Harper & Brothers in New York but is accepted by John Murray in London, through the efforts of his brother Gansevoort, secretary of the American Legation there.

1846   *Narrative of a Four Months' Residence among the Natives of a Valley of the Marquesas Islands* published by John Murray in London, February 26; published by Wiley & Putnam in New York, under the title *Typee*, about March 20. A "Revised Edition" published in New York in August.

1847   *Omoo* published by Murray in London, March 30, and by Harper & Brothers in New York, about May 1. Marries Elizabeth Shaw, daughter of Chief Justice Lemuel Shaw of the Massachusetts Supreme Court, August 4, and moves to Manhattan.

1847–50   Publishes anonymous reviews (including "Hawthorne and His Mosses," August 1850) and satirical pieces, the former in the *Literary World*, edited by his friend Evert A. Duyckinck, and the latter in *Yankee Doodle*, edited by a member of Duyckinck's circle, Cornelius Mathews.

1849   A son, Malcolm, born, February 16. *Mardi* published by Richard Bentley in London, March 16, and by Harper in New York, April 14. *Redburn* published by Bentley in London, September 29, and by Harper in New York, November 14.

1849–50   Makes a trip to London (to visit publishers) and the continent, October 11, 1849, to February 1, 1850.

1850   *White-Jacket* published by Bentley in London, January 23, and by Harper in New York, March 21. Meets Nathaniel Hawthorne at a picnic near Pittsfield, Mass., August 5, and they become friends. Borrowing money from his father-in-law, Melville purchases a farm (which he names "Arrowhead") near Pittsfield, September 14, and his family is in residence there by early October.

1851   *Moby-Dick* published by Bentley in London, October 18 (under the title *The Whale*), and by Harper in New York, November 14. A second son, Stanwix, born, October 22.

1852   *Pierre* published by Harper in New York, August 6, and by Sampson Low in London in November.

1853   Melville's family and friends, concerned about his health, attempt unsuccessfully during the spring to secure a consulship for him. A daughter, Elizabeth, born, May 22. From about this time, and through the next quarter century, his wife's family worries about her life with Melville, involving financial insecurity and his recurrent depression.

1853–56   Publishes fourteen tales and sketches in *Putnam's Monthly Magazine* and *Harper's New Monthly Magazine*.

1855   *Israel Potter* published by G.P. Putnam in New York in early March (having been serialized in *Putnam's Monthly Magazine*, July 1854–March 1855) and—without authorization—by George Routledge in London in May. A second daughter, Frances, born, March 2.

1856   *The Piazza Tales*, consisting of five of the *Putnam's* pieces and a newly written title piece, published by Dix & Edwards in New York in late May and distributed in England by Sampson Low.

1856–57   Takes a trip (financed by his father-in-law) for his health, sailing for Glasgow October 11, 1856; visits Hawthorne in Liverpool; then tours the Holy Land, Greece, and Italy; returns to Liverpool and, on May 5, 1857, begins the voyage back to New York, arriving May 20.

1857   *The Confidence-Man* published by Dix & Edwards in New York, April 1, and by Longman, Brown, Green, Longmans & Roberts in London in early April.

1857–60   Goes on the lecture circuit for three seasons, lecturing the first season on "Statues in Rome," the second on "The South Seas," and the third on "Traveling."

1860   Embarks May 28 for San Francisco on the clipper ship *Meteor* as a guest of the captain, his brother Thomas; returns via Panama, arriving in New York on November 12.

1861   Travels to Washington in March to attempt to secure a consular appointment. Father-in-law dies. Family spends the winter in New York.

1863   Leaves Pittsfield permanently in October, trading Arrowhead for his brother Allan's New York house at 104 East 26th Street.

1864   Visits his cousin Col. Henry Gansevoort in an army camp on the Virginia front, April.

1866   Publishes some Civil War poems in *Harper's*. A collection of his war poems, *Battle-Pieces and Aspects of the War*, published by Harper, August 23. Appointed a deputy inspector of customs at the port of New York, December 5.

1867   In the spring, Melville's wife's family (some of whom regard him as insane) discuss with her minister the possibility of a legal separation between her and Melville. Their son Malcolm dies by his own pistol, September 11.

1876   The long poem *Clarel* published (at his uncle Peter Gansevoort's expense) by Putnam in early June.

1878   Melville's wife inherits money from the estate of her aunt, Martha Marett.

1885   Resigns position as customs inspector, December 31.

1886   Son Stanwix dies in San Francisco, February 23.

1887   Receives his last royalty statement from the Harper firm, March 4, there having been no printings of his books since 1876; some copies of *Typee*, *Mardi*, *Redburn*, *Pierre*, and *Battle-Pieces* are still in stock, but *Omoo*, *White-Jacket*, and *Moby-Dick* are out of print. (The total sales of these eight books during Melville's lifetime amounted to about 35,000 copies in the United States and 16,000 in Britain; his lifetime earnings from all his books came to about $5900 from the United States and $4500 from Britain.)

1888   *John Marr and Other Sailors* privately printed at the De Vinne Press in an edition of 25 copies.

1891   *Timoleon* privately printed at the Caxton Press in May in an edition of 25 copies. Dies September 28, leaving a number of poems and *Billy Budd, Sailor* in manuscript.

Note on the Texts

The texts of *Redburn*, *White-Jacket*, and *Moby-Dick* presented in this volume are those of the Northwestern-Newberry Edition of *The Writings of Herman Melville*, edited by Harrison Hayford, Hershel Parker, and G. Thomas Tanselle and published by the Northwestern University Press and The Newberry Library (*Redburn* in 1969, *White-Jacket* in 1970, and *Moby-Dick* forthcoming). Those texts were prepared according to the standards established by—and they have received the official approval of—the Center for Editions of American Authors of the Modern Language Association of America. (See its *Statement of Editorial Principles and Procedures*, revised edition, 1972.)

The textual problems with which the Northwestern-Newberry editors have to deal increase in complexity from *Redburn* to *White-Jacket* to *Moby-Dick*, although the publication history of all three is essentially the same. In each case the American edition was set from manuscript and the English edition from proofs of the American. It was the English edition, however, that was actually published first. In the uncertain climate of international copyright in the nineteenth century, many English publishers of American works felt on stronger ground if their editions preceded the American editions. As a result, *Redburn* was published by Richard Bentley in London in early autumn 1849 in two volumes and by Harper & Brothers in New York in mid-November; *White-Jacket* was officially published in Bentley's two-volume London edition in late January 1850 and in the Harper edition in New York in March; and *Moby-Dick* appeared in Bentley's handsome three-volume edition, entitled *The Whale* and with whales on the spines, in mid-October 1851 and in the rather pedestrian Harper edition about a month later. The fact that the English editions came out first does not of course alter the fact that they are one step further removed from the manuscripts than are the American editions. Therefore the basic texts of these three works adopted by the Northwestern-Newberry editors are those of the American editions.

Whenever there is a difference between the American and English texts and both readings seem to be authorial (as opposed to those situations in which one of the readings is clearly erroneous or is almost certainly the work of someone in the printer's or the publisher's office), the question arises as to which reading supersedes the other. Theoretically either could be the later one: Melville could have made alterations on the proofs for England that he had not made on the proofs for America; or he could have continued to read over the proofs for America, and make revisions on them, after furnishing one set of proofs to the English publisher. *Redburn*, however, provides almost no complications, for the relatively few differences between the American and English texts—with perhaps one exception (see the note on 271.10)—do not appear to result from authorial revision. This situation is not surprising, because Melville was occupied with the writing of *White-Jacket* at the time when he had to read the proofs for *Redburn*. The Northwestern-Newberry editors do correct some erroneous readings in the American text, but in most instances there is no reason to depart from it.

In the case of *White-Jacket*, Melville had more time for revisions on the proofs for the English publisher, because he took those proofs with him when he sailed for London on October 11, 1849. He had received proofs at least a month earlier, and any alterations made before he sailed were presumably entered on the proofs for America as well as those for England. But he had three and a half weeks on shipboard to make additional changes for the English edition, as well as six weeks after he arrived in London, since he did not give the proofs to Bentley (according to his journal) until after December 18. The English edition does in fact exhibit a considerable number of differences from the American edition. One cannot automatically accept all of them as Melville's revisions, however, because some are certainly the result of changes made in Bentley's office. Others could be the earlier readings, revised by Melville for the American edition after he returned to the United States on February 1, 1850, roughly six weeks before American publication (though in general the American readings do not seem to be later). Unquestionably Melville's are seven additional passages in the English edition.

They range from one to sixteen sentences and total more than seven hundred words (in this edition: 376.28–35, 377.35–36, 467.29–38, 548.15–16, 650.26–651.29, 750.31, 750.35–41), as well as eight additional phrases, clauses, and single words ("in . . . time", 359.23–24; and . . . elsewhere", 464.39–40; "and . . . offence", 494.39; "or steersmen", 516.5–6; "little", 553.33; "ever", 594.3; "or . . . that", 602.9; "—Mr. Pert,—", 714.30). All these are accepted by the Northwestern-Newberry editors, along with some other alterations that a publisher's reader would be unlikely to make (e.g., see the note on 372.39). The remaining differences, which range from simple oversights and indifferent substitutions to attempted grammatical or stylistic improvements and the softening of vigorous expressions, are not accepted; they are not clearly Melville's and do in fact correspond to the kinds of changes that Bentley's staff is known to have engaged in. (Bentley's use of a reader to expurgate or tone down forceful passages is established for *Moby-Dick* and therefore is a possibility for *White-Jacket*, and even if Melville made some alterations of this kind himself in anticipation of Bentley's reaction they would not represent his true intention; the notes for *White-Jacket* provide the English wording in a dozen or so instances of this kind.)

Moby-Dick presents an editor with still more difficulties. Leaving aside many obvious errors and thousands of differences in punctuation, there are some six hundred differences in wording between the American and English editions. Melville again had considerable time to spend going over the proofs for England, but for different reasons this time. In the summer of 1851 he had the text set in type and plated on his own without waiting for arrangements to be concluded with an American publisher. His proofreading for the American plates was finished in late July, but he did not send a set of proofs to Bentley in England until September 10, two days before a contract with Harper & Brothers was signed for American publication. During those six weeks Melville would have been under no pressure to speed the proofs to England for prior publication there. No American publication was yet scheduled (indeed, the English contract did not arrive until late August or early September), and he had good reason for wanting to linger over the proofs and make further alterations, since at the time of his previous proofreading of the early part of the book he was still writing some of the later part and undoubtedly read those proofs more hurriedly than he would have otherwise. He was of course free to make as extensive alterations as he wished for England, because the text had to be reset there; but alterations made at this point could not be incorporated into the American text, already set and probably plated, without incurring additional expense. Under these circumstances the English text at points of variation is almost certainly later than the American. The problem is to try to distinguish the alterations for which Melville was responsible from those made in Bentley's office or at his direction. Like other Victorian publishers, Bentley employed readers who not only gave advice on submitted manuscripts but also revised accepted ones: Bentley told Melville the next spring, after seeing the manuscript of *Pierre*, that it would require alterations by a "judicious literary friend" in order to be "properly appreciated" in England.

Some of the most striking differences between the two editions are easy enough to classify. The English edition omits thirty-eight passages of a sentence or more, totaling some 2,000 words (in this edition: 798.21–23, 798.36–39, 799.18–22, 803.37–804.4, 804.9–24, 810.9–12, 828.30, 849.15–18, 884.23–37, 886.19–887.13, 904.40–905.1, 913.1–30, 916.25–27, 977.4–5, 981.20–21, 996.39–41, 1014.14–15, 1071.31–33, 1110.21–22, 1110.26–27, 1110.30–35, 1114.3–9, 1116.18–21, 1126.40–1127.2, 1161.17–19, 1162.2, 1175.15, 1198.14–17, 1208.32, 1209.37–39, 1222.1–3, 1245.25–27, 1258.36–39, 1274.31–35, 1369.6–13, 1372.17–22, 1372.28–34, 1408.1–26); and the bulk of these changes, along with many smaller omissions or alterations (such as the omission of "bridegroom", 821.37, "matrimonial", 822.9, "thrown . . . day", 829.3–4, "in . . . honeymoon," 849.35, "and Queequeg . . . we;", 850.4–6, "democratic", 916.37, "to . . . worlds;", 989.9–10, "archangel", 995.26, "so . . . within;", 1001.20–22, "ripening . . . thigh", 1060.29–30, "hermaphroditical", 1195.15, "like . . . concubines", 1213.25–26, "impotent," 1214.1, and "before . . . again", 1297.39–1298.2; and the substitution of "fellow" for "Jonah", 809.1; "who can do this?" for "Jove himself cannot.", 833.15, "an apparently eternal anguish" for "a crucifixion", 925.33, "Hang" or "D—n" for "Blast", 1107.30,

1141.16, "dexterities" for "obstetrics," 1162.1, "and how" for
"and . . . Abednego," 1250.10–11, and "unearthly" for "archangelic", 1407.15), consist of expurgations of comments deal-
ing with religion, sex, and politics. Anything that could
remotely be regarded as sacrilegious, sexually explicit, or anti-
British—including all of chapter 25—was eliminated or revised, thereby considerably altering the tone of the book. Obviously these changes are the work of Bentley's "judicious
literary friend" (whom readers may wish to describe with a
different adjective), and not of Melville. At the other extreme,
it is equally clear that only Melville could have added the 140-
word footnote on the term "galley" (1204.28–41) or inserted
certain other words not required for sense ("out-hanging" in
803.4, "quick" in 932.31, "a doubloon" in 964.35, "embryo" in
1277.5, "sometimes," in 1326.13, and "braced" in 1345.30). In
between these extremes are the great majority of the differences, where the English variants could conceivably be either
Melville's or the English editor's. It seems safe to say, however, that Melville was probably not responsible for the two
hundred or so instances in which the English variant either
produces a distinctly inferior reading (for example, "was" for
"slept", 898.21; "sore" for "scorched", 991.23; "slices" for "slicings", 1118.22; "powerful" for "powerless", 1124.6–7; the omission of "iron", 1311.21; "nameless" for "unnamable", 1323.12;
and "wretched" for "wrenched", 1380.9) or results in hyper-
correct grammar (for example, "on" for "of", 795.29; "that"
for "what", 811.12; "upon" for "on", 864.12; "I" for "me",
974.1; "previously" for "previous", 1010.8; "shall" for "will",
1198.12; and "pointed" for "did point", 1389.16–17). Although
Melville could have made revisions that were not improve-
ments, it is unlikely that he was responsible for the bulk of
such a large number of changes that seem insensitive to the
style of a passage (and are perhaps nothing more than type-
setters' errors); and although he could have decided to "correct" his grammar at certain points, such a concern was not
characteristic of him, whereas it is in line with what a publisher's reader would have been expected to think about. Furthermore, in nearly two hundred more variants the difference
seems so slight that it is hard to see why anyone would have
made the change (such as replacing "so long been" with

"been so long", 817.39, or "our" with "the", 995.40; omitting "most", 1059.34; and adding "he", 1367.37). The conservative approach in such cases, given the doubt about whether Melville was responsible, is not to accept these changes as his. The two dozen additional points at which the English edition makes a statement more cautious or less colorful can generally be regarded as characteristic of Bentley's reader (such as altering "Louis the Devil" to "Louis Napoleon", 957.13, or "hangs for candelabra" to "is preserved", 1077.5), but occasionally a change of this kind occurs that is difficult to attribute to anyone except Melville (see the note on 958.37). The Northwestern-Newberry editors accept the few changes of this sort into the text, along with a final category of about three dozen alterations in which the English reading improves on the American so skillfully and thoughtfully that it is difficult to ascribe them to anyone other than Melville—such changes as "haply" for "happily" (853.6), "direst" for "direct" (949.16), "covertly" for "correctly" (1006.15), "modified" for "directed" (1022.5), "breath" for "life" (1137.25), "considerateness" for "considerations" (1236.16), "laving" for "leaving" (1379.36), and "death-grasp" for "death-gasp" (1407.14), or those commented on in the notes for 922.3, 962.7, 1084.3–4, and 1223.4. Melville by no means noticed all the discrepancies and incorrect words, however, and the Northwestern-Newberry editors correct about three dozen clearly erroneous readings that exist in both the American and English editions (for example, see the notes on 877.24, 1227.1, and 1389.14); but they do not alter certain others that could only be repaired through extensive rewriting (see the notes on 868.7, and 1281.6), and still others no doubt remain undetected. A particular problem is posed by Melville's liberal use of quotations from and paraphrases of other writers—a characteristic practice, noticeable in his previous books, that reaches its culmination here (most conspicuously in the eighty "extracts" prefacing the text, but in many other passages as well). The Northwestern-Newberry edition corrects such quotations or paraphrases by reference to the originals (or the editions Melville used, if known) only when the inaccuracy appears to be inadvertent. Whenever a good case can be made for Melville's intentional distortion of the original, no change is made (see, for instance, the notes on 787.1–3,

790.18, 790.31, 791.17, and 793.1). A much more detailed discussion of the differences between the American and English editions and of other editorial problems in *Moby-Dick* appears in the Northwestern-Newberry edition.

The standards for American English continue to fluctuate and in some ways were conspicuously different in earlier periods from what they are now. In nineteenth-century writings, for example, a word might be spelled in more than one way, even in the same work, and such variations might be carried into print. Commas were sometimes used expressively to suggest the movements of voice, and capitals were sometimes meant to give significances to a word beyond those it might have in its uncapitalized form. Since modernization would remove such effects, this volume preserves the spelling, punctuation, capitalization, and wording of the Northwestern-Newberry edition, which strives to be as faithful to Melville's usage as surviving evidence permits. It also retains the original tables of contents despite their inconsistencies with the chapter headings found in the body of the texts.

The texts in this volume follow exactly the Northwestern-Newberry *Redburn* (3rd printing), *White-Jacket* (1st printing), and *Moby-Dick* (page proofs), with three exceptions: in *White-Jacket* at 526.31–32, "dentifrice" replaces the erroneous "dentrifice"; at 570.10, "Rio is" replaces "Rio in"; and at 752.29, "Landless" corrects "Landlass". (These errors in the Northwestern-Newberry edition will be corrected in future printings.) The present edition is concerned only with representing the *texts* of these editions; it does not attempt to reproduce features of the typographic design—such as the display capitalization of chapter openings. In this volume the reader has the results of the most detailed scholarly effort thus far made to establish the texts of *Redburn*, *White-Jacket*, and *Moby-Dick*. Errors corrected third printing: 1041:16, described (*LOA*). Errors corrected fifth printing: 417.5, pecularly (*LOA*); 875.33, "Lay (*LOA*).

Notes

For more detailed notes, references to other studies, and further biographical background than is provided in the Chronology, see the relevant volumes of the Northwestern-Newberry edition; and, for *Moby-Dick*, see also Luther S. Mansfield and Howard P. Vincent's edition (New York: Hendricks House, 1952) and Harrison Hayford and Hershel Parker's edition (New York: W. W. Norton, 1967). For further information on biography and sources, see William H. Gilman, *Melville's Early Life and Redburn* (New York: New York University Press, 1951), Willard Thorp's essay in the Northwestern-Newberry edition of *White-Jacket*, and Howard P. Vincent, *The Tailoring of Melville's White-Jacket* (Evanston: Northwestern University Press, 1970) and *The Trying Out of Moby-Dick* (Boston: Houghton Mifflin, 1949). In the notes below, the reference numbers denote page and line of the present volume (the line count includes chapter headings). Notes printed at the foot of pages of the text are Melville's own. No note is made for material included in a standard desk-reference book.

REDBURN

8.28   must] Both the American and English editions read "much", a word that violates the grammatical parallelism of the paragraph and that is redundant with "abound". The Northwestern-Newberry edition substitutes "must" as the word Melville apparently intended.

9.5   importer] Melville's own father had been a New York importer who "had several times crossed the Atlantic on business affairs." Some further details suggesting an autobiographical element in the character of Redburn are mentioned in the notes for 12.8–11, 66.3, and 158.10. But the book is not a literal autobiographical account, and the experiences and attitudes of Redburn are not necessarily those of Melville.

12.8–11   great-uncle . . . named.] Melville's own great-uncle Leonard Gansevoort had been a member of the Continental Congress, and Melville's elder brother was named Gansevoort.

43.16   Captain Langsdorff] Georg Heinrich von Langsdorff, whose *Voyages and Travels in Various Parts of the World* (1813–14) is quoted in chapter 45 of *Moby-Dick*.

59.19   lowered] The Northwestern-Newberry edition substitutes the conventional term "lowered" for "loosed", the unidiomatic reading of the

American and English editions (presumably a misreading of Melville's handwriting).

66.3   JACKSON] One of Melville's fellow sailors on board the *St. Lawrence* in 1839 was named Robert Jackson. In creating the fictional Jackson, however, Melville did not limit himself to events that occurred to Robert Jackson. Other figures on board the *Highlander* were also no doubt suggested by persons Melville encountered on the *St. Lawrence*, but it is impossible to draw a precise line between the facts of Melville's experience, as reflected here, and his additions to them for artistic purposes.

81.1   When] It is possible that Melville intended "Then", the word that in fact appears at this spot in the *Literary World* printing of this passage. (The *Literary World*, edited by Melville's friend Evert A. Duyckinck, printed several extracts from *Redburn* in the issues of November 10 and 17, 1849, but it is unlikely that Melville had an opportunity to make revisions in them.) However, the use of "When" (the reading of the American and English editions) to mean "Then" can be found elsewhere in similar constructions in Melville's work.

88.26   Sam Patch] Patch's leap into Niagara Falls, referred to in chapter 24 (128.19), was the subject of an 1836 play by E. H. Thompson.

95.39–40   *"takes . . . Hemp-street."*] This saying appears in virtually identical wording in Nathaniel Ames's *A Mariner's Sketches* (1830), a book mentioned by Richard Henry Dana in the preface to *Two Years before the Mast* and used by Melville in writing *White-Jacket*.

110.18   headway] The Northwestern-Newberry editors substitute this word, which appears frequently in the book, for "heading", the reading of the American and English editions and evidently a misreading of Melville's hand.

155.14–20   *"Voyage . . . Ville;"*] By Louis Marie Prudhomme (1814) and Mariano Vasi (1815), respectively.

156.36–37   "THE . . . LIVERPOOL."] This book, the title page of which is set out below (160.10–25 with "1803" for 1808), is the only printed source thus far known that Melville drew on extensively for *Redburn*. Although Redburn says at the end of the chapter that he will not quote further from it (lest he be "charged with swelling out" his own book "by plagiarizing from a guide-book—the most vulgar and ignominious of thefts!"), some of the descriptions of Liverpool that follow (especially in chapters 31, 32, 36, and 40) incorporate passages from it in slightly altered form. The long list of titles that lead up to this one is of actual books, though Melville occasionally alters the wording for effect.

158.10   Liverpool, March 20th,] Melville's own father had arrived in Liverpool on a March 20th, in 1811.

161.13   Dr. Aiken] John Aikin, who with Anna Letitia Barbauld published *Evenings at Home* (1792–95).

189.36   "*sagoon*,"] The account that follows is drawn from the *Penny Cyclopædia* (1833–43), a work that Melville used more extensively in *White-Jacket* and *Moby-Dick*; the *Penny Magazine* (mentioned in 227.16) also appears to underlie several descriptions.

250.4–5   Guido's . . . Apollo] Guido Reni's *Aurora* (1613).

250.11–12   Portia . . . Jessica] In *The Merchant of Venice*.

271.10   large and womanly.] The only significant difference between the American and English editions occurs at this point. In place of the American wording (followed here), the English edition reads "not an eye like Harry's— quick, small, and glittering." Since Harry's eyes are elsewhere described (in both editions) with the adjectives "large" and "womanly" (237.13), the English reading creates a contradiction. It is impossible to say how the discrepancy came about; among the possibilities is that someone in the English publishing firm, objecting to "womanly", made the change without noticing the other passage, or that the English wording is Melville's original wording, changed in the American proofs (after the set of proofs for England had been sent off) when Melville recognized the problem. In any event, the likelihood seems to be that the American wording is what Melville finally intended.

274.22   morning] The English edition prints "mourning" at this point, perhaps as a result of the preceding word, "pensive". But the correctness of the American reading, "morning", is shown by the contrast of "twilight" and "morning" earlier in the chapter: "the twilight pensiveness of his full morning eyes" (271.7–8).

294.31   their] The English edition substitutes this word for "there" in the American edition; the American reading is clearly wrong, since it makes this clause express the same point as the next one.

WHITE-JACKET

342.3   FULLER'S "Good Sea-Captain."] "The Good Sea-Captain" is a section of Thomas Fuller's *The Holy State and the Profane State* (1642), from which Melville also drew the twenty-fifth of the extracts prefaced to *Moby-Dick*. (785.25–26).

343.1–9   Note] Instead of this brief "Note," dated March 1850, the English edition prints a longer "Preface," dated October 1849. One of the few surviving pieces of manuscript material for Melville's books of this period is an earlier version of this preface (now in the Houghton Library, Harvard University), in a copyist's hand but with revisions by Melville, who evidently made still further alterations to produce the version that was finally printed. The direction of Melville's revision was to make less specific the relation of the book to actual events and particular sources, and this tendency obviously culminated in the brief "Note" to the American edition (though with a shift to the first person). The "Preface" that appeared in the English edition reads as follows:

> *The object of this work is to give some idea of the interior life in a man-of-war. In the year 1843, the author shipped as a common sailor on board of a United States frigate, then lying in a harbour of the Pacific Ocean. After serving on board of this frigate for more than a year, he was discharged, with the rest of the crew, upon the vessel's arrival home. His man-of-war experiences and observations have been incorporated into the present volumes. But these volumes are not presented as a journal of the cruise.*
>
> *As the object of this work is not to portray the particular man-of-war in which the author sailed, and its officers and crew, but, by illustrative scenes, to paint general life in the Navy, the true name of the frigate is not given. Nor is it here asserted that any of the persons introduced in the following chapters are real individuals. Wherever statements are made in any way concerning the established laws and usages of the Navy, facts have been strictly adhered to. Allusion is sometimes made to events or facts in the past history of Navies. In these cases, no statement is presented unless supported by the best authorities. For the hitherto unrecorded by-play of circumstances in one or two well-known naval actions referred to, the writer is indebted to the seamen into whose mouths these things are put.*
>
> *The work opens at the frigate's last harbour in the Pacific, just previous to weighing her anchor for the homeward-bound passage, by the way of Cape Horn.*

352.19   *Me?* Ah me!] These words are not present in the English edition.

359.23–24   in . . . time] This phrase, which appears in the English but not the American edition, is the first of a series of phrases and clauses that Melville added to the English text; these are listed in the Note on the Texts.

360.10   Jack Chase] A 53-year-old British seaman, John J. Chase, was indeed captain of the main-top on the frigate *United States*, on which Melville sailed in 1843–44; it was to him that Melville later dedicated *Billy Budd, Sailor*. Melville departs from the facts about Chase, however, at various points, as in his reference to Chase's desertion in the next chapter. (Chase actually deserted another ship, the *St. Louis*, at Callao and joined the *United States* in May 1842.) Although a number of the characters on board the fictional *Neversink* (see 365.6) and some of the events that take place there are based on Melville's experiences on the *United States* (he did in fact wear a white jacket on the voyage, as he wrote to Richard Henry Dana shortly after the publication of the book), Melville embroidered the facts and drew on other sources as he pleased.

369.31–32   Perhaps . . . afloat.] The English edition reads, "Why was this? Why not be companionable with his officers?"

372.39   The . . . it,] The Northwestern-Newberry editors accept this clause from the English edition as Melville's revision of the reading in the American edition, "I never had a good interior look at it but once; and then".

374.27   perilous]   In the English text, "dignified".

381.23–24   Alceste . . . Medusa]   John McLeod's account of the *Alceste* and J. B. H. Savigny and Alexandre Corréard's of the *Méduse* (both 1817) were abridged together in Dublin in 1831.

403.2   DROUGHT]   Although both the American and the English editions read "DRAUGHT" here, the intended word is probably "Drought", which both editions have in the table of contents. The episode described in this chapter comes from the book that was more important to Melville than any other as a source of material for *White-Jacket*: Henry J. Mercier and William Gallop's *Life in a Man-of-War; or, Scenes in "Old Ironsides"* (1841). In his draft preface (see the note on 343.1–9)—though not in the version actually published in the English edition—Melville says, rather disingenuously, "The writer has to thank the light-hearted author of a book called 'Scenes in old Ironsides', for supplying corroborative hints for some few scenes." At least eight other chapters, including those on the theatricals (23) and on the auction (47), are based on this book.

406.7–8   "For . . . smiled."]   *Paradise Lost*, IV, 164–65 (slightly altered).

409.15   *Banyan Day*]   See 710.22.

428.21   still]   The more cautious English text inserts "almost" after "still".

435.23   was . . . heard of]   In the English edition, "is not a regular thing".

438.28–29   the most]   The English edition characteristically qualifies the statement by inserting "perhaps" before "the most" (and substituting "severe" for "arbitrary").

443.6   *"The Ruffian Boy,"*]   By Thomas Dibdin, after Amelia Opie's novel.

465.23–24   or reverses]   In the English edition these two words are not present.

476.7   the less painful]   This is softened in the English text to "some of the."

483.23-26   acting . . . war.]   Thomas Walker Gilmer, Secretary of the Navy, Abel Parker Upshur, Secretary of State, and Commodore Beverly Kennon were all killed aboard the steamer *Princeton* on February 28, 1844, when a new gun exploded.

489.25–26   in agony]   In the English text, "if scourged".

502.2   FLOGGING NOT NECESSARY]   The title of this chapter in the English edition, "IS FLOGGING NECESSARY?", probably is the earlier version, which Melville revised on the American proofs in order to make it parallel with the title of the preceding chapter. At that time he may also have deleted "But" (present in the English edition) from the beginning of chapter 35. Melville's powerful series of chapters on flogging makes use of several sources, notably (for chapters 34 and 35) William McNally's *Evils and Abuses in the Naval and Merchant Service, Exposed* (1839) and (for chapter 36) Francis Jeffrey's review of Collingwood's correspondence in *Edinburgh Review*, 47 (May 1828), 385–418.

505.12   Edinburgh Review] Melville refers to Thomas Hodgskin's article, "Abolition of Impressment," in *Edinburgh Review*, 41 (October 1824), 154–81, an article that he also drew on for chapter 90.

506.23   The . . . rear.] The English edition does not include this sentence.

511.24–25   in . . . is] This wording is toned down in the English edition to "it is, in some governments,".

541.21–22   almost numberless] The English text more guardedly reads "repeated".

544.38–545.1   Goëthe's . . . Mephistophiles.] In the English edition, "Clanqui's"—with "Zantua" in place of "Margaret" and "Don" for "Mephistophiles".

556.21   Yes:] The substitution of this word in the English edition for the "And" that appeared in the American would seem to be an indication of the care with which Melville examined some passages in reading the American proofs that he took with him to England.

565.6   Northeastern] Perhaps "Northwestern", if the dates of White-Jacket's presence at Callao and Rio are presumed to be those of Melville's. The dispute over the northern boundary of the Oregon territory was accelerating during 1843 and 1844 and figured in the 1844 presidential election campaign, whereas the dispute over the boundary between Maine and New Brunswick had been settled in 1842 by the Webster-Ashburton Treaty.

575.6   despotic] In the English text, "certain".

587.9–10   Similia Similibus Curantur] "Like cures like." Christian Friedrich Samuel Hahnemann was the founder of homeopathy.

603.1–606.6   *Chapter 59*] The episode described in this chapter probably has an autobiographical source. When Melville was in Callao on the *United States* in February 1844, the supply ship *Erie*—on which Melville's cousin Stanwix Gansevoort was an officer of the deck—arrived and transferred supplies to the *United States*.

626.12   Hennen] John Hennen, author of *Principles of Military Surgery* (3rd edition, 1829), is one of the authorities (less well known than Bell, Brodie, and Larrey, mentioned in 621.24) referred to in the article on "Gun-Shot Wounds" in the *Penny Cyclopædia* (1833–43); Melville drew on several of the medical articles in this work, and perhaps directly on some of the *Cyclopædia*'s sources as well, for his description of Surgeon Cuticle and the operation (chapters 60–63).

650.26–651.29   In . . . goose.] These three paragraphs, not in the American edition, constitute the largest of the passages Melville added to the English edition. Such additions are specified in the Note on the Texts.

653.18   invariably] Again the English text is more cautious: "often".

659.24   three men] At the time of the alleged mutiny aboard the *Somers*, Melville's cousin, Guert Gansevoort, was first officer and took part in the decision to hang the men. (See also 669.2–5.) The word "men" in the English edition would appear to be Melville's revision of "sailors" (the reading of the American edition), here and at 659.28 and 659.30; it is both a factual and a stylistic improvement.

677.10–11   *"Spanish Ladies"*] Melville quotes from this traditional sea song at the beginning of chapter 40 of *Moby-Dick*.

678.1   Macedonian] The high point of the previous history of Melville's ship, the *United States*, was its capture of the *Macedonian* in the War of 1812. The account in this chapter comes largely from one of Melville's principal sources, Samuel Leech's *Thirty Years from Home* (1843).

684.29   battle of Navarino] The description that follows is closely based on the anonymous *Life on Board a Man-of-War* (1829), which also includes an account of a fall from a yard-arm, resembling White-Jacket's in chapter 92.

712.31   *"The Professor"*] Henry Hayes Lockwood, who taught mathematics on the *United States* when Melville was on board, was the brother of John A. Lockwood, who wrote a series of anonymous articles on flogging in the Navy for the *United States Magazine and Democratic Review* in 1849. Melville drew on the first of the articles in chapters 71 and 72.

749.24   "John Nicol, Mariner,"] Melville made use of *The Life and Adventures of John Nicol, Mariner* (1822) in other chapters as well, as in some of Jack Chase's stories in chapter 75.

752.24–25   glandular] This word is not present in the English edition.

761.1–764.39   *Chapter 92*] The principal source for the fall described in this chapter is *A Mariner's Sketches* (1830) by Nathaniel Ames, who served on the *United States* from 1824 to 1827. (See also the note on 684.29.) For White-Jacket's sensations under water, Melville drew on Bulwer-Lytton's translation (1844) of Schiller's poem "The Diver."

766.4   *Denique Cælum*] "Heaven at last," the Melville family motto according to Robert Douglas, *The Baronage of Scotland* (1798).

MOBY-DICK

771.1   MOBY-DICK]   The title of the English edition, *The Whale*, was Melville's earlier title for the book. In an undated letter to Bentley, Allan Melville
wrote, "Since sending proofs of my brothers new work,. . . he has determined upon a new title & dedication—Enclosed you have proof of both—
It is thought here that the new title will be a better *selling* title—". Allan's
letter arrived in time for Bentley to include the dedication to Hawthorne;
but presumably it was already too late to change the title, which appears
twice in each of the three volumes and had been used in advertising. In his
letter Allan spells "Moby-Dick" with the hyphen, as it also appears on the
title page and divisional title page of the American edition; but only one of
the many occurrences of the name in the text includes the hyphen. The
Northwestern-Newberry editors retain the hyphen in the title, arguing that
hyphenated titles were conventional in mid-nineteenth-century America. As
a result, the hyphenated form refers to the book, the unhyphenated to the
whale. (The conclusion that the English readings at points of variation are
later than the American, stated above in the Note on the Texts, holds for the
body of the text but, as the difference in title shows, is not necessarily true
for the preliminaries, which could have been added to without affecting the
main text already in plates. Whether the "Etymology" and the "Extracts"
could be late additions is not clear; but for some reason they come in the
English edition at the end rather than the beginning of the book, with the
twenty-fourth extract, from *Paradise Lost*, included on the title pages of
the three volumes.)

773.1–779.14   Contents]   In nineteen instances the wording of chapter titles in this table of contents differs from that at the heads of the corresponding chapters. This list of contents, from the American first edition, is retained
in the Northwestern-Newberry edition on the ground that it appears to be
based on a document that contained Melville's own wording (though
whether that wording is earlier or later than the wording at the heads of the
chapters is not clear).

781.1–25   *Etymology*]   Charles Richardson's entry for "whale" in *A New
Dictionary of the English Language* (1836–37), the named source for the third
quotation, was also Melville's source for the opening quotation from Hakluyt
(spelled "Hackluyt" in Richardson), as well as for the extracts from Pliny
(783.19–21) and Spenser (784.23–27). Some of the words for "whale" in the
list are not the conventional forms but are allowed to stand by the Northwestern-Newberry editors if they correspond to forms present in Melville's
source books or if they seem to be the forms Melville wished to use.

783.1–793.21   *Extracts*]   Precise citations of Melville's sources for these extracts (and for quotations and paraphrases in the body of the text as well)
and much additional information about them are provided in the Northwestern-Newberry edition. The notes below—which take all their facts about
sources from the extensive notes in the Northwestern-Newberry edition—

can do no more than give a few examples of Melville's alteration of quotations to suit his own purposes and comment on a few of his less clear citations. One should keep in mind that other quotations, not annotated here, are not necessarily identical to the original passages and may have been taken from intermediate sources that quote the originals. Melville's most important source books for whaling information—Beale (790.31), Bennett (790.39), Browne (791.15), Cheever (791.37), and Scoresby (790.18)—are all represented among these extracts.

783.28–784.3   "He . . . days."]   Quoted from J. Ross Browne (see 791.15 and 911.14–16).

785.4   *V.E.*]   That is, "Vulgar Errors," the commonly used name for Thomas Browne's *Pseudodoxia Epidemica* (1646); Melville owned a copy of the 1686 edition.

785.12   *Opening*]   This is *an* opening sentence (the fifth), not *the* opening sentence.

785.14   *Holy War.*]   The American edition cites *Pilgrim's Progress* here, but the reference was corrected (probably by Melville) in the English edition to another work of Bunyan's, *The Holy War* (1682). Actually this passage is a paraphrase of Bunyan appearing in Cheever (see 791.37).

785.35   *Purchass*]   Despite this citation, Melville's source is not *Purchas His Pilgrimes* (1625) but the paraphrase in John Harris's *Navigantium atque Itinerantium Bibliotheca* (1705)—the "Harris Collection" from which the next three extracts are also taken. (The voyage to Greenland referred to in 786.9–18 is that of Friedrich Martens.) For other uses of Harris, see 1074.39 and 1282.12–28.

786.37   1729.]   William A. Cowley's voyage took place in 1683–86; the date here shows that Melville's source was the 1729 edition of William Hacke's *A Collection of Voyages* (a part of William Dampier's *A Collection of Voyages*), which was originally published in 1699.

787.1–3   "and . . . brain."]   This passage is apparently Melville's invention, using only the phrase "an insupportable smell" from Antonio de Ulloa's *A Voyage to South-America* (1758), where it does not refer to whales.

787.13–14   "If . . . whales."]   Paraphrased from James Boswell's life of Samuel Johnson.

787.31   "And . . . it?"]   Melville probably quoted this question from Beale (see 790.31) or Browne (see 791.15), not directly from the 1775 pamphlet printing Burke's speech. The next quotation, also attributed to Burke, paraphrases what he is reported to have said in a debate on the French Revolution. (Cf. 911.17–18.)

788.22–23   "Ten . . . velocity."]   This wording is not Hunter's but a paraphrase of Hunter in William Paley's *Natural Theology* (1802), the source of the next extract as well.

789.28   *Twice Told Tales*] This quotation is from "The Village Uncle," the next from "Chippings with a Chisel."

790.3–6   *"Narrative . . . 1821.*] Melville drew on Chase's pamphlet in describing the parallel event at the end of *Moby-Dick*. See also his reference to Chase, with more extensive quotation, in chapter 45 (1012.29–1013.8, 1013.19–44).

790.18   *Scoresby.*] William Scoresby's *An Account of the Arctic Regions with a History and Description of the Northern Whale-Fishery* (1820) was one of Melville's principal source books. (For other uses of it, see the note on 959.13 and the passage at 934.9–14.) This extract illustrates Melville's alteration of his sources to emphasize the magnitude and power of whales: instead of "three or four miles" Scoresby has "two or three miles"; and for "of this one whale" in the earlier sentence Scoresby reads "was singularly great. It".

790.31   *Beale's History*] Beale's *The Natural History of the Sperm Whale* (1839) was Melville's most important source book for whaling information. (For other uses of it, see the notes on 933.16-26 and 985.39-986.1.) In this extract Melville makes clear the reference to sperm whales by substituting "Sperm Whale" for "sea beast" (790.20) and inserting the phrase "(as the Sperm Whale)" (790.26).

791.17   Whale-ship] Melville's substitution of "Whale-ship" for "ship" (in William Lay and Cyrus M. Hussey's original) is another example of his altering a quotation to make its relevance clearer.

792.5–8   "The . . . whale."] This quotation from John Ramsay Mc-Culloch's 1832 work is another of the extracts that Melville probably took from Browne (see 791.15). The extract that follows extends McCulloch's point but appears in neither Browne nor McCulloch; the *"'Something' unpublished"* therefore may be by Melville himself.

792.14   mere] This correction, made in the English edition, of the American reading "near" is an example of the English variants for which Melville must have been responsible. Melville may have taken the passage from Browne (see 791.15) rather than directly from Charles Wilkes's *Narrative of the United States Exploring Expedition* (1844, 1845).

792.22   *Whale*] Melville inserted this word into the title of Robert P. Gillies's book (1826).

792.27   *Newspaper Account*] Probably Melville's invention. The event described did not occur on the Falmouth ship *Hobomok,* but similar occurrences happened on another Falmouth ship, *Awashonks* (the third mate of which later became captain of the *Hobomok*), and on the Fairhaven ship *Sharon.*

792.30   (American)] Melville added this word to his extract from James A. Rhodes's book (1848).

792.34 *Miriam Coffin*] Joseph C. Hart's novel (1834) was also probably the source of an earlier extract (788.9–11).

793.1 Whale] Melville substituted this word for "prize" in the passage from *Ribs and Trucks . . . by W.A.G.* (1842).

793.13 *Wharton . . . Killer.*] Harry Halyard's *Wharton's the Killer!* (1848).

793.14–15 "So . . . whale!"] Quoted from Browne (see 791.15); Melville quotes these lines again (with one difference in wording) in chapter 40 (976.21–22).

793.17–20 "Oh . . . sea."] Quoted from the title page of Cheever (see 791.37).

799.7–8 Pythagorean maxim] "Not to eat beans."

801.4 Cape Horn] This is the first of a number of references to Cape Horn in the first third of the book. Since the *Pequod* actually proceeds by way of the Cape of Good Hope, these references may be vestiges of an earlier draft that Melville neglected to alter; but the Northwestern-Newberry edition does not change them, since they can be read figuratively.

803.26 old writer] The quotation was probably written by Melville himself.

827.10–15 Broadway . . . Wapping.] Streets in New York, Philadelphia, London, Liverpool, and London, respectively.

828.30 Herr Alexander] A German magician appearing in the United States in the 1840s.

837.22 left] This past-tense verb in the English edition is more appropriate than the present-tense "lift" in the American edition, and more in keeping with the passage Melville was adapting, a rhymed rendering of part of Psalm 18 in *The Psalms and Hymns . . . of the Reformed Dutch Church in North America* (1814).

861.27 rests] The Northwestern-Newberry edition substitutes this word for "riots"; it fits the pattern of imagery in the paragraph and could have been misread as "riots" in Melville's hand.

868.7 tiller] Although the tiller is carefully described here and we are told that the *Pequod* scorned "a turnstile wheel", at two later points (1096.12, 1326.6) the ship is said to have a wheel helm with "spokes". There is no way to remove this inconsistency without rewriting the passages, for a simple substitution of terms would not take care of the problem. The reader will notice a number of such inconsistencies in the book, perhaps resulting from Melville's incomplete revision of passages written at widely separate times or with different conceptions in mind.

875.33   *Lay*] Bildad begins here a quotation from Matthew 6:19–21, which he returns to at 875.39 and 876.16–17.

877.24   "Thank ye;"] The American and English editions read "That's he;" which is clearly erroneous and probably results from a misreading of Melville's hand.

895.34   running] This word, from the English edition, may be Melville's correction of the American reading, "hobbling", which is inconsistent with the description of Peleg elsewhere.

902.21   Booble Alley] See *Redburn*, chapter 39.

903.19–22   "Sweet . . . between."] The third stanza of Isaac Watts's "A Prospect of Heaven Makes Death Easy."

913.1–30   *Chapter 25*] This chapter was entirely omitted from the English edition, presumably because it did not treat royalty with sufficient seriousness. For discussion of the expurgations, and other classes of alteration, in the English edition, see the Note on the Texts.

914.26   words] The Northwestern-Newberry editors substitute "words" for "sounds" as the word Melville must have intended.

920.1   presently] This word is substituted by the Northwestern-Newberry editors for "probably".

922.3   did!] The Northwestern-Newberry edition follows the English edition in eliminating the five words that come after "did!" in the American edition: "oh, no! he went before." They probably reflect an earlier conception of Pip's role, and Melville probably noticed his oversight, and rectified it, when going over the proofs to be sent to England.

933.16–26   "No . . . naturalists."] All these quotations come from Beale (see 790.31), the middle paragraph from the body of his work, the first and third from the quotations he uses as epigraphs. In the third of these paragraphs, the first sentence is (according to Beale) from John Hunter, the second and third from René Primevère Lesson, and the fourth (not translated in Beale) from Georges Cuvier—the writers named by Melville (in a different order) at the beginning of the next paragraph.

935.28   "I . . . fish."] Melville takes this quotation, and others in this chapter, from the article on "Whale" in the *Penny Cyclopædia* (cf. note 626.12), although the first two words, "I hereby", are not present there. The Northwestern-Newberry editors emend the date from "1776" (the reading of the American and English editions) to "1766" (the date given in Melville's source); no edition of 1776 has been located.

935.36–38   penem . . . meritoque."] A penis that enters the female, who gives milk from breasts; from the law of nature justly and deservedly.

943.4   Black Letter] Perhaps Hakluyt, whose *Principal Navigations*

(1600) contains an account of Frobisher's voyages—though the quotation that follows is not present in that account.

958.37   coolish] The Northwestern-Newberry editors accept this word from the English edition in place of the American reading "cold"; Melville would have been more likely to use "coolish" than Bentley's reader (who, if he had wanted to change the meaning, would probably have chosen "cool").

959.13   Captain Sleet] This name and the title of the book are obviously fabrications of Melville, but they refer to Scoresby (see 790.18), who tells of his father's invention of the crow's-nest. For other comic uses of Scoresby, see 1112.26–28, 1231.35–36, and 1268.31–1269.20.

961.19   blubber-hunters] In this well-known quotation from Byron's *Childe Harold's Pilgrimage* (1818), Melville substitutes "blubber-hunters" for "fleets".

962.7   Wickliff's] The American edition erroneously reads "Cranmer's", and this correction in the English edition is more likely to have been made by Melville than by Bentley's reader.

972.3   Burkes . . . Bendigoes!] Champion English boxers in the 1830s and 1840s.

975.23–26   We'll . . . meeting.] From Charles Fenno Hoffman's "Sparkling and Bright" (1840), collected in *Love's Calendar* (1847).

976.8   Our captain's commanded—] Melville departs from the usual wording of this traditional song, which reads "For we've received orders."

976.13–22   Our . . . whale!] Despite some minor differences, Melville probably took this version of "Captain Bunker" from Browne (see 791.15 and 793.14–15).

985.39–986.1   "struck . . . death."] These lines—which do not come from Cuvier but from *The Animal Kingdom* by Edward Griffith *et al.* (vol. 4, 1827)—are quoted from Beale (see 790.31).

987.12   Strella] Serra da Estrela.

1011.18   Church] Benjamin Church, in 1676. (The American and English editions erroneously read "Captain Butler": William Butler, whose name is associated with a later Indian, in 1778.)

1014.16   Langsdorff's Voyages] See the note on *Redburn*, 43.16.

1015.14–15   voyage of Lionel Wafer] *A New Voyage and Description of the Isthmus of America* (1699), which is quoted below with slight differences of wording.

1029.21   third mate] Stubb is, of course, the second mate; what Melville means here is that Stubb is the third to be discussed.

1052.2–1072.5   THE TOWN-HO'S STORY]   This chapter was published separately, before the appearance of the book, in *Harper's New Monthly Magazine* for October 1851—the only part of *Moby-Dick* so published. The magazine text, which was probably set from proof sheets for the book, shows about 125 differences (principally in spelling and punctuation) from the book text, differences of a kind for which Melville is not likely to have been responsible. One improvement in wording—"three" for "these" (1065.5)—does seem to be Melville's and is accepted in the Northwestern-Newberry edition.

1054.31   Tartar Emperors]   Not literally, because the empire broke up in the late fifteenth century; but one of the resulting Tartar states, Crimea, lasted for three more centuries.

1060.23   St. Dominic]   The patron saint of the Cathedral of Lima.

1074.15   Prodromus whales]   Melville perhaps means the kind of whales discussed in Robert Sibbald's "prodromus" (i.e., "introduction") of 1684 or illustrated in his 1692 book on whales. (Another work of Sibbald's is the source of one of the extracts, 786.25.)

1074.25–26   old Italian publisher]   Aldus Manutius, who established a printing firm in Venice in 1495.

1074.39   Harris's collection]   From which four of the extracts and one later quotation are also taken; see the note on 785.35.

1075.9   Captain Colnett]   James Colnett; see the extract at 788.32–33.

1084.3–4   —so . . . hills—]   In the American edition this clause was not set off with dashes, and "hills" was followed by a comma and "that"; the neat correction of this awkward syntax in the English edition seems likely to have been by Melville and is adopted in the Northwestern-Newberry edition.

1104.12   Hang-Ho]   Huang Ho is the Yellow River; the name of the canal is Yün Ho.

1142.9   Three Spaniards]   The title of a novel (1800) by George Walker.

1150.30   "hogs' bristles;"]   Melville probably took this phrase from a quotation from Aristotle included in the article on whales in the *Penny Cyclopædia* (1833–43).

1150.30–31   old gentleman]   The gentleman is Thomas Edge; the quotation paraphrases a comment not in Hakluyt but in *Purchas His Pilgrimes* (1625).

1155.12   Sais]   See Schiller's poem on the veiled statue of Isis at Sais.

1175.9–14   "Canst . . . spear!"]   From Job 41:7, 26–29, with some omissions.

1181.4–5   "Thou . . . Ezekiel;]   The quotation, slightly altered, is from the Geneva version of Ezekiel as quoted in the article on whales in the *Penny Cyclopædia* (which points out that the King James version uses "whale").

1185.3   Harris's Voyages] Melville's source was in fact the article on "Jonas" in the 1710 translation of Pierre Bayle's *An Historical and Critical Dictionary*.

1213.12   bed in common.] The English edition substitutes "have very vague ideas of the connubial tie." This is one of the wittier instances of revision in the English edition to make an allusion to sex more circumspect, and it raises the possibility that Melville may have engaged in some changes of this kind. Even so, he cannot have intended the expurgations in general, nor even the others that were made in this same passage; and this one, if he made it, would presumably have been motivated by his knowledge of the concerns of Bentley's office, not by artistic considerations.

1220.3–4   *"De* . . . c. *3*.] The epigraph is a slightly altered quotation from Henry de Bracton, *De Legibus & Consuetudinibus Angliae* (1569).

1222.16   Prynne] The statement that follows paraphrases a passage in Prynne's *Aurum Reginae* (1668).

1223.4   *that*] The American edition reads "not"; the correction to "that" in the English edition suggests that this was one of the alterations made by Melville on the proofs for England. (On "V.E.", see the note on 785.4.)

1227.1   augured] The Northwestern-Newberry editors substitute "augured" for "argued" as the word obviously meant.

1233.1–1237.6   *Chapter 93*] That some of the events aboard the *Pequod* are based on Melville's own experiences on the *Acushnet*—as one might expect— is shown by testimony to the fact that a black boy on the *Acushnet* made at least one leap overboard—an occurrence that provided the source for this chapter. In a copy of the English edition (now in the University of Chicago Library) presented by Melville to his former shipmate Henry F. Hubbard in 1853, Hubbard made a note identifying Pip's "real name" as Backus, adding, "I was in the boat at the time he made the leap overboard."

1248.12–14   "the . . . dead."] Proverbs 21:16.

1257.4–5   nine hundred and sixty] Whether this figure represents an error in arithmetic is not clear, since "dollar" may here mean (as it often did among American seamen) a Spanish-American dollar, the equivalent of a British crown (equal at this time to $1.20).

1258.38–39   Jenny . . . done!"] An approximate quotation of the refrain to the minstrel song "Old King Crow."

1272.31   Icy Glen] Not far from Pittsfield, where Melville was living at this time.

1281.6   Owen] The bones that Richard Owen reported to the Geological

Society of London (in 1839) were from an earlier discovery (in 1832) on Judge Creagh's plantation; Melville here merges that 1832 discovery of fragments with the discovery of an "almost complete vast skeleton" in 1842.

1282.12–28   "Not . . . Temple."]   Melville took this passage from the "Harris Collection" (see the note on 785.35), not from an edition of Leo (Johannes Leo Africanus).

1286.25   New Holland]   Australia.

1299.14   Matsmai]   Not an island, but included in a list of "Islands, and their provinces" in McCulloch's *Universal Gazetteer* (1840). (Cf. 792. 5–8.)

1304.21   Lackaday islands]   Perhaps the Laccadives.

1315.32–33   "Ego . . . diaboli!"]   I do not baptize you in the name of the father, but in the name of the devil.

1318.3–22   "Oh, . . . it."]   The Northwestern-Newberry editors add the quotation marks, thus making the paragraph a speech of Ahab's, as the context clearly demands.

1330.1–15   Oh! . . . oh!]   Melville may have written this song himself, catching the spirit of such shanties as "Do me Johnny Boker" or "Jibber a hokey-pokey."

1350.15   clay!]   The Northwestern-Newberry editors add the exclamation point as a way of making sense of the passage. (The American and English editions read "One hundred pounds of clay reward for Pip".)

1356.32   the play]   *Hamlet*.

1357.26   deaf]   The American and English editions read "dumb", but "deaf" is what Melville must have intended, and the Northwestern-Newberry editors make the substitution.

1363.7–8   Like cures like;]   See *White-Jacket,* 587.9–10, and the note on it.

1375.19   Is Ahab, Ahab?]   The reading of the English edition—"Is it Ahab, Ahab?"—provides a dilemma for an editor, since a plausible argument can obviously be made for both the American and the English readings, and each reading results in a significantly different development of meaning in a key passage. The repetition of "Ahab", however, is more necessary to the American reading than to the English, and the "it" could easily have been inserted by the English typesetter, looking ahead to the next sentence; the Northwestern-Newberry editors decide to retain the reading of the American edition.

1389.14   guiltlessness]   The American and English editions read "guiltiness," which is obviously wrong; the Northwestern-Newberry edition replaces it with "guiltlessness".

CATALOGING INFORMATION

Melville, Herman, 1819–1891.
  Redburn, White-Jacket, Moby-DIck.

  (The Library of America)
  Contents: Redburn: His first voyage—White-Jacket: or The world in a
man-of-war—Moby-Dick: or, The whale.
    I. Tanselle, G. T. (George Thomas), 1934–   . II. Title.
III. White-Jacket, 1983.   IV. Moby-Dick, 1983.   V. Series:
The Library of America.
PS2382.T3 1983   813'.3   82-18677
ISBN   0-940450-09-7

This book is set in 10 point Linotron Galliard, a face designed for photocomposition by Matthew Carter and based on the sixteenth-century face Granjon. The paper is Olin Nyalite and conforms to guidelines adopted by the Committee on Book Longevity of the Council on Library Resources. The binding material is Brillianta, a 100% rayon cloth made by Van Heek-Scholco Textielfabrieken, Holland. Composition by Haddon Craftsmen, Inc. and The Clarinda Company. Printing and binding by R. R. Donnelley & Sons Company. Designed by Bruce Campbell.